PHILIP K. DICK

Philip K. Dick

FIVE NOVELS OF THE 1960s & 70s

Martian Time-Slip
Dr. Bloodmoney
Now Wait for Last Year
Flow My Tears, the Policeman Said
A Scanner Darkly

THE LIBRARY OF AMERICA

The paper used in this publication meets the
minimum requirements of the American National Standard for
Information Sciences—Permanence of Paper for Printed
Library Materials, ANSI Z39.48—1984.

Distributed to the trade in the United States
by Penguin Putnam Inc.
and in Canada by Penguin Books Canada Ltd.

Library of Congress Control Number: 2007942807
ISBN 978–1–59853–025–4

—

First Printing
The Library of America—183

Manufactured in the United States of America

JONATHAN LETHEM
SELECTED THE CONTENTS AND
WROTE THE NOTES FOR THIS VOLUME

Contents

MARTIAN TIME-SLIP

One

F ROM the depths of phenobarbital slumber, Silvia Bohlen heard something that called. Sharp, it broke the layers into which she had sunk, damaging her perfect state of nonself.

"Mom," her son called again, from outdoors.

Sitting up, she took a swallow of water from the glass by the bed; she put her bare feet on the floor and rose with difficulty. Time by the clock: nine-thirty. She found her robe, walked to the window.

I must not take any more of that, she thought. Better to succumb to the schizophrenic process, join the rest of the world. She raised the window shade; the sunlight, with its familiar reddish, dusty tinge, filled her sight and made it impossible to see. She put up her hand, calling, "What is it, David?"

"Mom, the ditch rider's here!"

Then this must be Wednesday. She nodded, turned and walked unsteadily from the bedroom to the kitchen, where she managed to put on the good, solid, Earth-made coffeepot.

What must I do? she asked herself. All's ready for him. David will see, anyhow. She turned on the water at the sink and splashed her face. The water, unpleasant and tainted, made her cough. We should drain the tank, she thought. Scour it, adjust the chlorine flow and see how many of the filters are plugged; perhaps all. Couldn't the ditch rider do that? No, not the UN's business.

"Do you need me?" she asked, opening the back door. The air swirled at her, cold and choked with the fine sand; she averted her head and listened for David's answer. He was trained to say no.

"I guess not," the boy grumbled.

Later, as she sat in her robe at the kitchen table drinking coffee, her plate of toast and applesauce before her, she looked out on the sight of the ditch rider arriving in his little flat-bottom boat which put-putted up the canal in its official way, never hurrying and yet always arriving on schedule. This was 1994, the second week in August. They had waited eleven days, and now they would receive their share of water from the great ditch which passed by their line of houses a mile to the Martian north.

The ditch rider had moored his boat at the sluice gate and was hopping up onto dry land, encumbered with his ringed binder—in which he kept his records—and his tools for switching the gate. He wore a gray uniform spattered with mud, high boots almost brown from the dried silt. German? But he was not; when the man turned his head she saw that his face was flat and Slavic and that in the center of the visor of his cap was a red star. It was the Russians' turn, this time; she had lost track.

And she evidently was not the only one who had lost track of the sequence of rotation by the managing UN authorities. For now she saw that the family from the next house, the Steiners, had appeared on their front porch and were preparing to approach the ditch rider: all six of them, father and heavy-set mother and the four blonde, round, noisy Steiner girls.

It was the Steiners' water which the rider was now turning off.

"Bitte, mein Herr," Norbert Steiner began, but then he, too, saw the red star, and became silent.

To herself, Silvia smiled. Too bad, she thought.

Opening the back door, David hurried into the house. "Mom, you know what? The Steiners' tank sprang a leak last night, and around half their water drained out! So they don't have enough water stored up for their garden, and it'll die, Mr. Steiner says."

She nodded as she ate her last bit of toast. She lit a cigarette.

"Isn't that terrible, Mom?" David said.

Silvia said, "And the Steiners want him to leave their water on just a little longer."

"We can't let their garden die. Remember all the trouble we had with our beets? And Mr. Steiner gave us that chemical from Home that killed the beetles, and we were going to give them some of our beets but we never did; we forgot."

That was true. She recalled with a guilty start; we did promise them . . . and they've never said anything, even though they must remember. And David is always over there playing.

"Please go out and talk to the rider," David begged.

She said, "I guess we could give them some of our water

later on in the month; we could run a hose over to their garden. But I don't believe them about the leak—they always want more than their share."

"I know," David said, hanging his head.

"They don't deserve more, David. No one does."

"They just don't know how to keep their property going right," David said. "Mr. Steiner, he doesn't know anything about tools."

"Then that's their responsibility." She felt irritable, and it occurred to her that she was not fully awake; she needed a Dexamye, or her eyes would never be open, not until it was nightfall once more and time for another phenobarbital. Going to the medicine cabinet in the bathroom, she got down the bottle of small green heart-shaped pills, opened it, and counted; she had only twenty-three left, and soon she would have to board the big tractor-bus and cross the desert to town, to visit the pharmacy for a refill.

From above her head came a noisy, echoing gurgle. The tank on the roof, their huge tin water storage tank, had begun to fill. The ditch rider had finished switching the sluice gate; the pleas of the Steiners had been in vain.

Feeling more and more guilty, she filled a glass with water in order to take her morning pill. If only Jack were home more, she said to herself; it's so empty around here. It's a form of barbarism, this pettiness we're reduced to. What's the point of all this bickering and tension, this terrible concern over each drop of water, that dominates our lives? There should be something more. . . . We were promised so much, in the beginning.

Loudly, from a nearby house, the racket of a radio blared up suddenly; dance music, and then an announcer giving a commercial for some sort of farm machinery.

". . . Depth and angle of the furrow," the voice declared, echoing in the cold bright morning air, "pre-set and self-adjusting so that even the most unskilled owner can—almost the first time—"

Dance music returned; the people had turned to a different station.

The squabble of children rose up. Is it going to be like this all day? she asked herself, wondering if she could face it. And

Jack, away until the weekend at his job—it was almost like not being married, like not having a man. Did I emigrate from Earth for this? She clapped her hands to her ears, trying to shut out the noise of radios and children.

I ought to be back in bed; that's where I belong, she thought as she at last resumed dressing for the day which lay ahead of her.

In his employer's office in downtown Bunchewood Park, Jack Bohlen talked on the radio-telephone to his father in New York City. The contact, made through a system of satellites over millions of miles of space, was none too good, as always; but Leo Bohlen was paying for the call.

"What do you mean, the Franklin D. Roosevelt Mountains?" Jack said loudly. "You must be mistaken, Dad, there's nothing there—it's a total waste area. Anybody in real estate can tell you that."

His father's faint voice came. "No, Jack, I believe it's sound. I want to come out and have a look and discuss it with you. How's Silvia and the boy?"

"Fine," Jack said. "But listen—don't commit yourself, because it's a known fact that any Mars real estate away from the part of the canal network that works—and remember that only about one-tenth of it works—comes close to being an outright fraud." He could not understand how his father, with his years of business experience, especially in investments in unimproved land, could have gotten on to such a bum steer. It frightened him. Maybe his dad, in the years since he had seen him, had gotten old. Letters told very little; his dad dictated them to one of his company stenographers.

Or perhaps time flowed differently on Earth than on Mars; he had read an article in a psychology journal suggesting that. His father would arrive a tottering, white-haired old relic. Was there any way to get out of the visit? David would be glad to see his grandfather, and Silvia liked him, too. In Jack Bohlen's ear the faint, distant voice related news of New York City, none of any interest. It was unreal to Jack. A decade ago he had made a terrific effort to detach himself from his community on Earth, and he had succeeded; he did not want to hear about it.

And yet the link with his father remained, and it would be

shored up in a little while by his father's first trip off Earth; he had always wanted to visit another planet before it was too late—before his death, in other words. Leo was determined. But despite improvements in the big interplan ships, travel was hazardous. That did not bother him. Nothing would deter him; he had already made reservations, in fact.

"Gosh, Dad," Jack said, "it sure is wonderful that you feel able to make such an arduous trip. I hope you're up to it." He felt resigned.

Across from him his employer, Mr. Yee, regarded him and held up a slip of yellow paper on which was written a service call. Skinny, elongated Mr. Yee in his bow tie and single-breasted suit . . . the Chinese style of dress rigorously rooted here on alien soil, as authentic as if Mr. Yee did business in downtown Canton.

Mr. Yee pointed to the slip and then solemnly acted out its meaning: he shivered, poured from left hand to right, then mopped his forehead and tugged at his collar. Then he inspected the wrist watch on his bony wrist. A refrigeration unit on some dairy farm had broken down, Jack Bohlen understood, and it was urgent; the milk would be ruined as the day's heat increased.

"O.K., Dad," he said, "we'll be expecting your wire." He said good-bye and hung up. "Sorry to be on the phone so long," he said to Mr. Yee. He reached for the slip.

"An elderly person should not make the trip here," Mr. Yee said in his placid, implacable voice.

"He's made up his mind to see how we're doing," Jack said.

"And if you are not doing as well as he would wish, can he help you?" Mr. Yee smiled with contempt. "Are you supposed to have struck it rich? Tell him there are no diamonds. The UN got them. As to the call which I gave you: that refrigeration unit, according to the file, was worked on by us two months ago for the same complaint. It is in the power source or conduit. At unpredictable times the motor slows until the safety switch cuts it off to keep it from burning out."

"I'll see what else they have drawing power from their generator," Jack said.

It was hard, working for Mr. Yee, he thought as he went upstairs to the roof where the company's copters were parked.

Everything was conducted on a rational basis. Mr. Yee looked and acted like something put together to calculate. Six years ago, at the age of twenty-two, he had calculated that he could operate a more profitable business on Mars than on Earth. There was a crying need on Mars for service maintenance on all sorts of machinery, on anything with moving parts, since the cost of shipping new units from Earth was so great. An old toaster, thoughtlessly scrapped on Earth, would have to be kept working on Mars. Mr. Yee had liked the idea of salvaging. He did not approve of waste, having been reared in the frugal, puritanical atmosphere of People's China. And being an electrical engineer in Honan Province, he possessed training. So in a very calm and methodical way he had come to a decision which for most people meant a catastrophic emotional wrenching; he had made arrangements to emigrate from Earth, exactly as he would have gone about visiting a dentist for a set of stainless steel dentures. He knew to the last UN dollar how far he could cut his overhead, once he had set up shop on Mars. It was a low-margin operation, but extremely professional. In the six years since 1988 he had expanded until now his repairmen held priority in cases of emergency—and what, in a colony which still had difficulty growing its own radishes and cooling its own tiny yield of milk, was not an emergency?

Shutting the 'copter door, Jack Bohlen started up the engine, and soon was rising above the buildings of Bunchewood Park, into the hazy dull sky of midmorning, on his first service call of the day.

Far to his right, an enormous ship, completing its trip from Earth, was settling down onto the circle of basalt which was the receiving field for living cargoes. Other cargoes had to be delivered a hundred miles to the east. This was a first-class carrier, and shortly it would be visited by remote-operated devices which would fleece the passengers of every virus and bacteria, insect and weed-seed adhering to them; they would emerge as naked as the day they were born, pass through chemical baths, sputter resentfully through eight hours of tests— and then at last be set free to see about their personal survival, the survival of the colony having been assured. Some might even be sent back to Earth; those whose condition implied genetic defects revealed by the stress of the trip. Jack thought of his dad patiently enduring the immigration processing. Has to be done, my boy, his dad would say. Necessary. The old man, smoking his cigar and meditating . . . a philosopher whose total formal education consisted of seven years in the New York public school system, and during its most feral period. Strange, he thought, how character shows itself. The old man was in touch with some level of knowledge which told him how to behave, not in the social sense, but in a deeper, more permanent way. He'll adjust to this world here, Jack decided. In his short visit he'll come to terms better than Silvia and I. About as David has. . . .

They would get along well, his father and his boy. Both shrewd and practical, and yet both haphazardly romantic, as witness his father's impulse to buy land somewhere in the F.D.R. Mountains. It was a last gasp of hope springing eternal in the old man; here was land selling for next to nothing, with no takers, the authentic frontier which the habitable parts of Mars were patently not. Below him, Jack noted the Senator Taft Canal and aligned his flight with it; the canal would lead him to the McAuliff dairy ranch with its thousands of acres of withered grass, its once prize herd of Jerseys, now bent into something resembling their ancestors by the unjust environment. This was habitable Mars, this almost-fertile spiderweb of lines, radiating and crisscrossing but always barely adequate to support life, no more. The Senator Taft, directly below now, showed a sluggish and repellent green; it was water sluiced and filtered in its final stages, but here it showed the accretions of time, the underlying slime and sand and contaminants which made it anything but potable. God knew what alkalines the population had absorbed and built into its bones by now. However, they were alive. The water had not killed them, yellow-brown and full of sediment as it was. While over to the west—the reaches, which were waiting for human science to rare back and pass its miracle.

The archaeological teams which had landed on Mars early in the '70's had eagerly plotted the stages of retreat of the old civilization which human beings had now begun to replace. It had not at any time settled in the desert proper. Evidently, as with the Tigris and Euphrates civilization on Earth, it had clung to what it could irrigate. At its peak, the old Martian culture had occupied a fifth of the planet's surface, leaving the rest as it had found it. Jack Bohlen's house, for instance, near the junction of the William Butler Yeats Canal with the Herodotus; it stood almost at the edge of the network by which fertility had been attained for the past five thousand years. The Bohlens were latecomers, although no one had known, eleven years ago, that emigration would fall off so startlingly.

The radio in the 'copter made static noises, and then a tinny version of Mr. Yee's voice said, "Jack, I have a service call for you to add. The UN Authority says that the Public School is malfunctioning and their own man is unavailable."

Picking up the microphone, Jack said into it, "I'm sorry, Mr. Yee—as I thought I'd told you, I'm not trained to touch those school units. You'd better have Bob or Pete handle that." As I know I told you, he said to himself.

In his logical way, Mr. Yee said, "This repair is vital, and therefore we can't turn it down, Jack. We have never turned down any repair job. Your attitude is not positive. I will have to insist that you tackle the job. As soon as it is possible I will have another repairman out to the school to join you. Thank you, Jack." Mr. Yee rang off.

Thank you, too, Jack Bohlen said acidly to himself.

Below him now he saw the beginnings of a second settlement; this was Lewistown, the main habitation of the plumbers' union colony which had been one of the first to be organized on the planet, and which had its own union members as its repairmen; it did not patronize Mr. Yee. If his job became too unpleasant, Jack Bohlen could always pack up and migrate to Lewistown, join the union, and go to work at perhaps an even better salary. But recent political events in the plumbers' union colony had not been to his liking. Arnie Kott, president of the Water Workers' Local, had been elected only after much peculiar campaigning and some more-than-average balloting irregularities. His regime did not strike Jack as the sort he wanted to live under; from what he had seen of it, the old man's rule had all the elements of early Renaissance tyranny, with a bit of nepotism thrown in. And yet the colony appeared to be prospering economically. It had an advanced public works program, and its fiscal policies had brought into exis-

tence an enormous cash reserve. The colony was not only efficient and prosperous, it was also able to provide decent jobs
for all its inhabitants. With the exception of the Israeli settlement to the north, the union colony was the most viable on
the planet. And the Israeli settlement had the advantage of
possessing die-hard Zionist shock units, encamped on the
desert proper, engaged in reclamation projects of all sorts,
from growing oranges to refining chemical fertilizers. Alone,
New Israel had reclaimed a third of all the desert land now
under cultivation. It was, in fact, the only settlement on Mars
which exported its produce back to Earth in any quantity.

The water workers' union capital city of Lewistown passed
by, and then the monument to Alger Hiss, the first UN mar-
tyr; then open desert followed. Jack sat back and lit a cigarette.
Under Mr. Yee's prodding scrutiny, he had left without remembering to bring his thermos of coffee, and he now felt its
lack. He felt sleepy. They won't get me to work on the Public
School, he said to himself, but with more anger than conviction. I'll quit. But he knew he wouldn't quit. He would go to
the school, tinker with it for an hour or so, giving the impression of being busy repairing, and then Bob or Pete would
show up and do the job; the firm's reputation would be preserved, and they could go back to the office. Everyone would
be satisfied, including Mr. Yee.

Several times he had visited the Public School with his son.
That was different. David was at the top of his class, attending
the most advanced teaching machines along the route. He
stayed late, making the most of the tutorial system of which the
UN was so proud. Looking at his watch, Jack saw that it was
ten o'clock. At this moment, as he recalled from his visits and
from his son's accounts, David was with the Aristotle, learning
the rudiments of science, philosophy, logic, grammar, poetics,
and an archaic physics. Of all the teaching machines, David
seemed to derive the most from the Aristotle, which was a relief; many of the children preferred the more dashing teachers
at the School: Sir Francis Drake (English history, fundamentals
of masculine civility) or Abraham Lincoln (United States history, basics of modern warfare and the contemporary state) or
such grim personages as Julius Caesar and Winston Churchill.
He himself had been born too soon to take advantage of the

tutorial school system, he had gone to classes as a boy where he sat with sixty other children, and later, in high school, he had found himself listening and watching an instructor speaking over closed-circuit TV along with a class of a thousand. If, however, he had been allowed into the new school, he could readily have located his own favorite: on a visit with David, on the first parent-teacher day in fact, he had seen the Thomas Edison Teaching Machine, and that was enough for him. It took David almost an hour to drag his father away.

Below the 'copter, the desert land gave way to sparse, prairie-like grassland. A barbed-wire fence marked the beginning of the McAuliff ranch, and with it the area administered by the State of Texas. McAuliff's father had been a Texas oil million-aire, and had financed his own ships for the emigration to Mars; he had beaten even the plumbers' union people. Jack put out his cigarette and began to lower the 'copter, searching against the glare of the sun for the buildings of the ranch.

A small herd of cows panicked and galloped off at the noise of the 'copter; he watched them scatter, hoping that McAuliff, who was a short, dour-faced Irishman with an obsessive atti-tude toward life, hadn't noticed. McAuliff, for good reasons, had a hypochondriacal view of his cows; he suspected that all manner of Martian *things* were out to get them, to make them lean, sick, and fitful in their milk production.

Turning on his radio transmitter, Jack said into the micro-phone, "This is a Yee Company repairship. Jack Bohlen asking permission to land on the McAuliff strip, in answer to your call."

He waited, and then there came the answer from the huge ranch. "O.K., Bohlen, all clear. No use asking what took you so long." McAuliff's resigned, grumpy voice.

"Be there any minute now," Jack said, with a grimace.

Presently he made out the buildings ahead, white against the sand.

"We've got fifteen thousand gallons of milk here." McAu-liff's voice came from the radio speaker. "And it's all going to spoil unless you get this damned refrigeration unit going soon."

"On the double," Jack said. He put his thumbs in his ears and leered a grotesque, repudiating face at the radio speaker.

Two

THE ex-plumber, Supreme Goodmember Arnie Kott of the Water Workers' Local, Fourth Planet Branch, rose from his bed at ten in the morning and as was his custom strolled directly to the steam bath.

"Hello, Gus."

"Hi there, Arnie."

Everybody called him by his first name, and that was good. Arnie Kott nodded to Bill and Eddy and Tom, and they all greeted him. The air, full of steam, condensed around his feet and drained off across the tiles, to be voided. That was a touch which pleased him: the baths had been constructed so as not to preserve the run-off. The water drained out onto the hot sand and disappeared forever. Who else could do that? He thought, Let's see if those rich Jews up in New Israel have a steam bath that wastes water.

Placing himself under a shower, Arnie Kott said to the fellows around him, "I heard some rumor I want checked on soon as possible. You know that combine from California, those Portugees that originally held title on the F.D.R. Mountain Range, and they tried to extract iron ore there, but it was too low grade, and the cost was way out of line? I heard they sold their holdings."

"Yeah, I heard that too." All the boys nodded. "I wonder how much they lost. Must have taken a terrible beating."

Arnie said, "No, I heard they found a buyer that was willing to put up more than they paid; they made a profit, after all these years. So it paid them to hold out. I wonder who's nuts enough to want that land. I got some mineral rights there, you know. I want you to check into who bought that land and what kind of operation they represent. I want to know what they're doing over there."

"Good to know those things." Again everyone nodded, and one man—Fred, it looked like—detached himself from his shower and padded off to dress. "I'll check into that, Arnie," Fred said over his shoulder. "I'll get to it right away."

Addressing himself to the remaining men, Arnie soaped

himself all over and said, "You know I got to protect my mineral rights; I can't have some smoozer coming in here from Earth and making those mountains into like for instance a national park for picnickers. I tell you what I heard. I know that a bunch of Communist officials from Russia and Hungary, big boys, was over here around a week ago, no doubt looking around. You think because that collective of theirs failed last year they gave up? No. They got the brains of bugs, and like bugs they always come back. Those Reds are aching to establish a successful collective on Mars; it's practically a wet dream of theirs back Home. I wouldn't be surprised if we find out that those Portugees from California sold to Communists, and pretty soon we're seeing the name changed from the F.D.R. Mountains, which is right and proper, to something like the Joe Stalin Mountains."

The men all laughed appreciatively.

"Now, I got a lot of business ahead of me today to conduct," Arnie Kott said, washing the soapsuds from him with furious streams of hot water. "So I can't devote myself to this matter any further; I'm relying on you to dig into it. For example, I have been traveling east where we got that melon experiment in progress, and it seems like we're about to be entirely successful in inducing the New England type of melon into growing here in this environment. I know you all have been wondering about that, because everybody likes a good slice of cantaloupe in the morning for his breakfast, if it's at all possible."

"That's true, Arnie," the boys agreed.

"But," Arnie said, "I got more on my mind than melons. We had one of those UN boys visiting us the other day protesting our regulations concerning the niggers. Or maybe I shouldn't say that; maybe I should talk like the UN boys and say 'indigenous population remnants,' or just Bleekmen. What he had reference to was our licensing the mines owned by our settlement to use Bleekmen at below scale, I mean, below the minimum wage—because even those fairies at the UN don't seriously propose we pay scale to Bleekmen niggers. However, we have this problem that we can't pay any minimum wage to the Bleekmen niggers because their work is so inconsistent that we'd go broke, and we have to use them in mining operations because they're the only ones who can breathe down there, and we can't get oxygen equipment in quantity transported over here at any price less than outrageous. Somebody's making a lot of money back Home on those oxygen tanks and compressors and all that. It's a racket, and we're not going to get gouged, I can tell you."

Everybody nodded somberly.

"Now, we can't allow the UN bureaucrats to dictate to us how we'll run our settlement," Arnie said. "We set up operations here before the UN was anything here but a flag planted in the sand; we had houses built before they had a pot to piss in anywhere on Mars, including all that disputed area in the south between the U.S. and France."

"Right, Arnie," the boys all agreed.

"However," Arnie said, "there's the problem that those UN fruits control the waterways, and we got to have water; we need them for conveyance into and out of the settlement and for source of power and to drink and like now, like we're here bathing. I mean, those buggers can cut off our water any time; they've got us by the short hairs."

He finished his shower and padded across the warm, wet tiles to get a towel from the attendant. Thinking about the UN made his stomach rumble, and his onetime duodenal ulcer began to burn way down in his left side, almost at the groin. Better get some breakfast, he realized.

When he had been dressed by the attendant, in his gray flannel trousers and T-shirt, soft leather boots, and nautical cap, he left the steam bath and crossed the corridor of the Union Hall to his dining room, where Helio, his Bleekman cook, had his breakfast waiting. Shortly, he sat before a stack of hotcakes and bacon, coffee and a glass of orange juice, and the previous week's New York *Times*, the Sunday edition.

"Good morning, Mr. Kott." In answer to his button-pressing, a secretary from the pool had appeared, a girl he had never seen before. Not too good-looking, he decided after a brief glance; he returned to reading the newspaper. And calling him Mr. Kott, too. He sipped his orange juice and read about a ship that had perished in space with all three hundred aboard killed. It was a Japanese merchantman carrying bicycles. That made him laugh. Bicycles in space, and all gone, now; too bad, because on a planet with little mass like Mars, where there was virtually no power source—except the sluggish canal system—and where even kerosene cost a fortune, bicycles were of great economic value. A man could pedal free of cost for hundreds of miles, right over the sand, too. The only people who used kerosene-powered turbine conveyances were vital functionaries, such as the repair and maintenance men, and of course important officials such as himself. There were public transports, of course, such as the tractor-buses which connected one settlement with the next and the outlying residential areas with the world at large . . . but they ran irregularly, being dependent on shipments from Earth for their fuel. And personally speaking the buses gave him a case of claustrophobia, they moved so slow.

Reading the New York *Times* made him feel for a little while as if he were back Home again, in South Pasadena; his family had subscribed to the West Coast edition of the *Times*, and as a boy he remembered bringing it in from the mailbox, in from the street lined with apricot trees, the warm, smoggy little street of neat one-story houses and parked cars and lawns tended from one weekend to the next without fail. It was the lawn, with all its equipment and medicines, that he missed most—the wheelbarrow of fertilizer, the new grass seed, the snippers, the poultry-netting fence in the early spring . . . and always the sprinklers at work throughout the long summer, whenever the law allowed. Water shortage there, too. Once his Uncle Paul had been arrested for washing his car on a water-ration day.

Reading further in the paper he came upon an article about a reception at the White House for a Mrs. Lizner who, as an official of the Birth Control Agency, had performed eight thousand therapeutic abortions and had thereby set an example for American womanhood. Kind of like a nurse, Arnie Kott decided. Noble occupation for females. He turned the page.

There, in big type, was a quarter-page ad which he himself had helped compose, a glowing come-on to get people to emigrate. Arnie sat back in his chair, folded the paper, felt deep pride as he studied the ad; it looked good, he decided. It would surely attract people, if they had any guts at all and a sincere desire for adventure, as the ad said.

The ad listed all the skills in demand on Mars, and it was a long list, excluding only canary raiser and proctologist, if that. It pointed out how hard it was now for a person with only a master's degree to get a job on Earth, and how on Mars there were good-paying jobs for people with only B.A.'s.

That ought to get them, Arnie thought. He himself had emigrated due to his having only a B.A. Every door had been shut to him, and then he had come to Mars as nothing but a union plumber, and within a few short years, look at him. On Earth, a plumber with only a B.A. would be raking up dead locusts in Africa as part of a U.S. foreign aid work gang. In fact, his brother Phil was doing that right now; he had graduated from the University of California and had never had a chance to practice his profession, that of milk tester. In his class, over a hundred milk testers had been graduated, and for what? There were no opportunities on Earth. You have to come to Mars, Arnie said to himself. We can use you here. Look at the pokey cows on those dairy ranches outside of town. They could use some testing.

But the catch in the ad was simply that, once on Mars, the emigrant was guaranteed nothing, not even the certainty of being able to give up and go home; trips back were much more expensive, due to the inadequate field facilities. Certainly, he was guaranteed nothing in the way of employment. The fault lay with the big powers back Home, China and the U.S. and Russia and West Germany. Instead of properly backing the development of the planets, they had turned their attention to further exploration. Their time and brains and money were all committed to the sidereal projects, such as that frigging flight to Centaurus, which had already wasted billions of dollars and man-hours. Arnie Kott could not see the sidereal projects for beans. Who wanted to take a four-year trip to another solar system which maybe wasn't even there?

And yet at the same time Arnie feared a change in the attitude of the great terrestrial powers. Suppose one morning they woke up and took a new look at the colonies on Mars and Venus? Suppose they eyed the ramshackle developments there and decided something should be done about them? In other words, what became of Arnie Kott when the Great Powers came to their senses? It was a thought to ponder.

However, the Great Powers showed no symptoms of rationality. Their obsessive competitiveness still governed them;
right this moment they were locking horns, two light years
away, to Arnie's relief.

Reading further in the paper, he came across a brief article
having to do with a women's organization in Berne, Switzerland, which had met to declare once more its anxiety about
colonization.

COLONIAL SAFETY COMMITTEE ALARMED OVER CONDITIONS OF MARS LANDING FIELDS

The ladies, in a petition presented to the Colonial Department of the UN, had expressed once more their conviction
that the fields on Mars at which ships from Earth landed were
too remote from habitation and from the water system. Passengers in some cases had been required to trek over a hundred miles of wasteland, and these included women and
children and old people. The Colonial Safety Committee
wanted the UN to pass a regulation compelling ships to land at
fields within twenty-five miles of a major (named) canal.

Do-gooders, Arnie Kott thought as he read the article.
Probably not one of them has ever been off Earth; they just
know what somebody wrote home in a letter, some aunt retiring to Mars on a pension, living on free UN land and naturally griping. And of course they also depended on their
member in residence on Mars, a certain Mrs. Anne Esterhazy;
she circulated a mimeographed newsletter to other public-
spirited ladies throughout the settlements. Arnie received and
read her newsletter, *The Auditor Speaks Back*, a title at which
he gagged. He gagged, too, at the one- and two-line squibs
inserted between longer articles:

*   *   *   *   *   *   *

Pray for potable purification! ! Contact colony
charismatic councilors and witness for water filtra-
tion we can be proud of!

*   *   *   *   *   *   *

He could hardly make out the meaning of some of the
Auditor Speaks Back articles, they were phrased in such special
jargon. But evidently the newsletter had attracted an audience

of devoted women who grimly took each item to heart and acted out the deeds asked of them. Right now they were undoubtedly complaining, along with the Colonial Safety Committee back on Earth, about the hazardous distances separating most of the landing fields on Mars from water sources and human habitation. They were doing their part in one of the many great fights, and in this particular case, Arnie Kott had managed to gain control of his nausea. For of the twenty or so landing fields on Mars, only one lay within twenty-five miles of a major canal, and that was Samuel Gompers Field, which served his own settlement. If by some chance the pressure of the Colonial Safety Committee was effective, then all incoming passenger ships from Earth would have to land at Arnie Kott's field, with the revenue received going to his settlement.

It was far from accidental that Mrs. Esterhazy and her newsletter and organization on Earth were advocating a cause which would be of economic value to Arnie. Anne Esterhazy was Arnie's ex-wife. They were still good friends, and still owned jointly a number of economic ventures which they had founded or bought into during their marriage. On a number of levels they still worked together, even though on a strictly personal basis they had no common ground whatsoever. He found her aggressive, domineering, overly masculine, a tall and bony female with a long stride, wearing low-heeled shoes and a tweed coat and dark glasses, a huge leather purse slung from a strap over her shoulder . . . but she was shrewd and intelligent and a natural executive. As long as he did not have to see her outside of the business context, he could get along with her.

The fact that Anne Esterhazy had once been his wife and that they still had financial ties was not well known. When he wanted to get in touch with her he did not dictate a letter to one of the settlement's stenographers; instead he used a little encoding dictation machine which he kept in his desk, sending the reel of tape over to her by special messenger. The messenger dropped off the tape at an art object shop which Anne owned over in the Israeli settlement, and her answer, if any, was deposited the same way at the office of a cement and gravel works on the Bernard Baruch Canal which belonged to Arnie's brother-in-law, Ed Rockingham, his sister's husband.

A year ago, when Ed Rockingham had built a house for himself and Patricia and their three children, he had acquired the unacquirable: his own canal. He had had it built, in open violation of the law, for his private use, and it drew water from the great common network. Even Arnie had been outraged. But there had been no prosecution, and today the canal, modestly named after Rockingham's eldest child, carried water eighty miles out into the desert, so that Pat Rockingham could live in a lovely spot and have a lawn, a swimming pool, and a fully irrigated flower garden. She grew especially large camellia bushes, which were the only ones that had survived the transplanting to Mars. All during the day, sprinklers revolved and sprayed her bushes, keeping them from drying up and dying.

Twelve huge camellia bushes seemed to Arnie Kott an ostentation. He did not get along well with his sister or Ed Rockingham. What had they come to Mars for? he asked himself. To live, at incredible expense and effort, as much as possible as they had back Home on Earth. To him it was absurd. Why not remain on Earth? Mars, for Arnie, was a new place, and it meant a new life, lived with a new style. He and the other settlers, both big and small, had made in their time on Mars countless minute adjustments in a process of adaptation through so many stages that they had in fact evolved; they were new creatures, now. Their children born on Mars started out like this, novel and peculiar, in some respects enigmatic to their parents. Two of his own boys—his and Anne's—now lived in a settlement camp at the outskirts of Lewistown. When he visited them he could not make them out; they looked toward him with bleak eyes, as if waiting for him to go away. As near as he could tell, the boys had no sense of humor. And yet they were sensitive; they could talk forever about animals and plants, the landscape itself. Both boys had pets, Martian critters that struck him as horrid: praying mantis types of bugs, as large as donkeys. The damn things were called *boxers*, because they were often seen propped up erect and squaring off at one another in a ritual battle which generally ended up with one killing and eating the other. Bert and Ned had gotten their pet boxers trained to do manual chores of a low caliber, and not to eat each other. And the things were their companions; children on Mars were lonely, partly because there were still so few of them and partly because . . . Arnie did not know. The children had a large-eyed, haunted look, as if they were starved for something as yet invisible. They tended to become reclusive, if given half a chance, wandering off to poke about in the wastelands. What they brought back was worthless, to themselves and to the settlements, a few bones or relics of the old nigger civilization, perhaps. When he flew by 'copter, Arnie always spotted some isolated children, one here and another there, toiling away out in the desert, scratching at the rock and sand as if trying vaguely to pry up the surface of Mars and get underneath. . . .

Unlocking the bottom drawer of his desk, Arnie got out the little battery-powered encoding dictation machine and set it up for use. Into it he said, "Anne, I'd like to meet with you and talk. That committee has too many women on it, and it's going the wrong way. For example, the last ad in the *Times* worries me because—" He broke off, for the encoding machine had groaned to a stop. He poked at it, and the reels turned slowly and then once more settled back into silence.

Thought it was fixed, Arnie thought angrily. Can't those jerks fix nothing? Maybe he would have to go to the black market and buy, at an enormous price, another. He winced at the thought.

The not-too-good-looking secretary from the pool, who had been sitting quietly across from him waiting, now responded to his nod. She produced her pencil and pad and began as he dictated.

"Usually," Arnie Kott said, "I can understand how hard it is to keep things running, what with no parts hardly, and the way the local weather affects metal and wiring. However, I'm fed up with asking for competent repair service on a vital item like my encoding machine. I just got to have it, that's all. So if you guys can't keep it working, I'm going to disband you and withdraw your franchise to practice the craft of repairing within the settlement, and I'll rely on outside service for our maintenance." He nodded once more, and the girl ceased writing.

"Shall I take the encoder over to the repair department, Mr. Kott?" she asked. "I'd be happy to, sir."

"Naw," Arnie grumbled. "Just run along."

As she departed, Arnie once more picked up his New York

Times and again read. Back home on Earth you could buy a new encoder for almost nothing; in fact, back home you could —hell. Look at the stuff being advertised . . . from old Roman coins to fur coats to camping equipment to diamonds to rocket ships to crabgrass poison. Jeez!

However, his immediate problem was how to contact his ex-wife without the use of his encoder. Maybe I can just drop by and see her, Arnie said to himself. Good excuse to get out of the office.

He picked up the telephone and called for a 'copter to be made ready up above him on the roof of the Union Hall, and then he finished off the remains of his breakfast, wiped his mouth hurriedly, and set off for the elevator.

"Hi, Arnie," the 'copter pilot greeted him, a pleasant-faced young man from the pilot pool.

"Hi, my boy," Arnie said, as the pilot assisted him into the special leather seat which he had had made at the settlement's fabric and upholstery shop. As the pilot got into the seat ahead of him Arnie leaned back comfortably, crossed his legs, and said, "Now you just take off and I'll direct you in flight. And take it easy because I'm in no hurry. It looks like a nice day."

"Real nice day," the pilot said, as the blades of the 'copter began to rotate. "Except for that haze over around the F.D.R. Range."

They had hardly gotten into the air when the 'copter's loud-speaker came on. "Emergency announcement. There is a small party of Bleekmen out on the open desert at gyrocompass point 4.65003 dying from exposure and lack of water. Ships north of Lewistown are instructed to direct their flights to that point with all possible speed and give assistance. United Nations law requires all commercial and private ships to respond." The announcement was repeated in the crisp voice of the UN announcer, speaking from the UN transmitter on the artificial satellite somewhere overhead.

Feeling the 'copter alter its course, Arnie said, "Aw, come on, my boy."

"I have to respond, sir." the pilot said. "It's the law."

Chrissake, Arnie thought with disgust. He made a mental note to have the boy sacked or at least suspended as soon as they got back from their trip.

Now they were above the desert, moving at good speed toward the intersect which the UN announcer had given. Bleekmen niggers, Arnie thought. We have to drop everything we're doing to bail them out, the damn fools—can't they trot across their own desert? Haven't they been doing it without our help for five thousand years?

As Jack Bohlen started to lower his Yee Company repairship toward McAuliff's dairy ranch below, he heard the UN announcer come on with the emergency notification, the like of which Bohlen had heard many times before and which never failed to chill him.

". . . Party of Bleekmen out on the open desert," the matter-of-fact voice declared. ". . . Dying from exposure and lack of water. Ships north of Lewistown—"

I've got it, Jack Bohlen said to himself. He cut his mike on and said, "Yee Company repairship close by gyrocompass point 4.65003, ready to respond at once. Should reach them in two or three minutes." He swung his 'copter south, away from McAuliff's ranch, getting a golden-moment sort of satisfaction at the thought of McAuliff's indignation right now as he saw the 'copter swing away and guessed the reason. No one had less use for the Bleekmen than did the big ranchers; the poverty-stricken, nomadic natives were constantly showing up at the ranches for food, water, medical help, and sometimes just a plain old-fashioned handout, and nothing seemed to madden the prosperous dairymen more than to be used by the creatures whose land they had appropriated.

Another 'copter was responding, now. The pilot was saying, "I am just outside Lewistown at gyrocompass point 4.78995 and will respond as soon as possible. I have rations aboard including fifty gallons of water." He gave his identification and then rang off.

The dairy ranch with its cows fell away to the north, and Jack Bohlen was gazing intently down at the open desert once more, seeking to catch sight of the party of Bleekmen. Sure enough, there they were. Five of them, in the shade cast by a small hill of stone. They were not moving. Possibly they were already dead. The UN satellite, in its swing across the sky, had discovered them, and yet it could not help them. Their mentors were powerless. And we who can help them—what do we care? Jack thought. The Bleekmen were dying out anyhow, the remnants getting more tattered and despairing every year. They were wards of the UN, protected by them. Some protection, Jack thought.

But what could be done for a waning race? Time had run out for the natives of Mars long before the first Soviet ship had appeared in the sky with its television cameras grinding away, back in the '60's. No human group had conspired to exterminate them; it had not been necessary. And anyhow they had been a vast curiosity, at first. Here was a discovery worth the billions spent in the task of reaching Mars. Here was an extraterrestrial race.

He landed the 'copter on the flat sand close by the party of Bleekmen, switched off the blades, opened the door, and stepped out.

The hot morning sun beat down on him as he walked across the sand toward the unmoving Bleekmen. They were alive; they had their eyes open and were watching him.

"Rains are falling from me onto your valuable persons," he called to them, the proper Bleekman greeting in the Bleeky dialect.

Close to them now he saw that the party consisted of one wrinkled old couple, a young male and female, no doubt husband and wife, and their infant. A family, obviously, which had set out across the desert alone on foot, probably seeking water or food; perhaps the oasis at which they had been subsisting had dried up. It was typical of the plight of the Bleekmen, this conclusion to their trek. Here they lay, unable to go on any farther; they had withered away to something resembling heaps of dried vegetable matter and they would have died soon had not the UN satellite spotted them.

Rising to his feet slowly, the young Bleekman male genuflected and said in a wavering, frail voice, "The rains falling from your wonderful presence envigor and restore us, Mister."

Jack Bohlen tossed his canteen to the young Bleekman, who at once knelt down, unscrewed the cap, and gave it to the supine elderly couple. The old lady seized it and drank from it.

The change in her came at once. She seemed to swell back

into life, to change from the muddy gray color of death before his eyes.

"May we fill our eggshells?" the young Bleekman male asked Jack. Lying upright on the sand were several paka eggs, pale hollow shells which Jack saw were completely empty. The Bleekmen transported water in these shells; their technical ability was so slight that they did not even possess clay pots. And yet, he reflected, their ancestors had constructed the great canal system.

"Sure," he said. "There's another ship coming with plenty of water." He went back to his 'copter and got his lunch pail; returning with it, he handed it to the Bleekman male. "Food," he explained. As if they didn't know. Already the elderly couple were on their feet, tottering up with their hands stretched out.

Behind Jack, the roar of a second 'copter grew louder. It was landing, a big two-person 'copter that now coasted up and halted, its blades slowly spinning.

The pilot called down, "Do you need me? If not, I'll go on."

"I don't have much water for them," Jack said.

"O.K.," the pilot said, and switched off his blades. He hopped out, lugging a five-gallon can. "They can have this."

Together, Jack and the pilot stood watching the Bleekmen filling their eggshells from the can of water. Their possessions were not many—a quiver of poisoned arrows, an animal hide for each of them; the two women had their pounding blocks, their sole possessions of value: without the blocks they were not fit women, for on them they prepared either meat or grain, whatever food their hunt might bring. And they had a few cigarettes.

"My passenger," the young pilot said in a low voice in Jack's ear, "isn't too keen about the UN being able to compel us to stop like this. But what he doesn't realize is they've got that satellite up there and they can see if you fail to stop. And it's a hell of a big fine."

Jack turned and looked up into the parked 'copter. He saw seated inside it a heavy-set man with a bald head, a well-fed, self-satisfied-looking man who gazed out sourly, paying no attention to the five Bleekmen.

"You have to comply with the law," the pilot said in a defensive voice. "It'd be me who they'd sock with the fine."

Walking over to the ship, Jack called up to the big bald-headed man seated within, "Doesn't it make you feel good to know you saved the lives of five people?"

The bald-headed man looked down at him and said, "Five niggers, you mean. I don't call that saving five people. Do you?"

"Yeah, I do," Jack said. "And I intend to continue doing so."

"Go ahead, call it that," the bald-headed man said. Flushing, he glanced over at Jack's 'copter, read the markings on it. "See where it gets you."

Coming over beside Jack, the young pilot said hurriedly, "That's Arnie you're talking to. Arnie Kott." He called up, "We can leave now, Arnie." Climbing up, the pilot disappeared inside the 'copter, and once more the blades began to turn.

The 'copter rose into the air, leaving Jack standing alone by the five Bleekmen. They had now finished drinking and were eating from the lunch pail which he had given them. The empty water can lay off to one side. The paka eggshells had been filled and were now stoppered. The Bleekmen did not glance up as the 'copter left. They paid no attention to Jack, either; they murmured among themselves in their dialect.

"What's your destination?" Jack asked them.

The young Bleekman named an oasis very far to the south.

"You think you can make it?" Jack asked. He pointed to the old couple. "Can they?"

"Yes, Mister," the young Bleekman answered. "We can make it now, with the food and water yourself and the other Mister gave us."

I wonder if they can, Jack said to himself. Naturally they'd say it, even if they knew it wasn't possible. Racial pride, I guess.

"Mister," the young Bleekman said, "we have a present for you because you stopped." He held out something to Jack.

Their possessions were so meager that he could not believe they had anything to spare. He held his hand out, however, and the young Bleekman put something small and cold into it, a dark, wrinkled, dried bit of substance that looked to Jack like a section of tree root.

"It is a water witch," the Bleekman said. "Mister, it will bring you water, the source of life, any time you need."

"It didn't help you, did it?" Jack said.

With a sly smile the young Bleekman said, "Mister, it helped; it brought you."

"What'll you do without it?" Jack asked.

"We have another. Mister, we fashion water witches." The young Bleekman pointed to the old couple. "They are authorities."

More carefully examining the water witch, Jack saw that it had a face and vague limbs. It was mummified, once a living creature of some sort; he made out its drawn-up legs, its ears . . . he shivered. The face was oddly human, a wizened, suffering face, as if it had been killed while crying out.

"How does it work?" he asked the young Bleekman.

"Formerly, when one wanted water, one pissed on the water witch, and she came to life. Now we do not do that, Mister; we have learned from you Misters that to piss is wrong. So we spit on her instead, and she hears that, too, almost as well. It wakes her, and she opens her eyes and looks around, and then she opens her mouth and calls the water to her. As she did with you, Mister, and that other Mister, the big one who sat and did not come down, the Mister with no hair on his head."

"That Mister is a powerful Mister," Jack said. "He is monarch of the plumbers' union settlement, and he owns all of Lewistown."

"That may be," the young Bleekman said. "If so, we will not stop at Lewistown, because we could see that the Mister with no hair did not like us. We did not give him a water witch in return for his water, because he did not want to give us water; his heart was not with him in that deed, it came from his hands only."

Jack said goodbye to the Bleekmen and got back into his 'copter. A moment later he was ascending; below him, the Bleekmen waved solemnly.

I'll give the water witch to David, he decided. When I get home at the end of the week. He can piss on it or spit on it, whichever he prefers, to his heart's content.

Three

NORBERT STEINER had a certain freedom to come and go as he pleased, because he was self-employed. In a small iron building outside of Bunchewood Park he manufactured health foods, made entirely from domestic plants and minerals, with no preservatives or chemical sprays or nonorganic attractive fertilizers. A firm at Bunchewood Park packaged his products for him in professional-type boxes, cartons, jars, and envelopes, and then Steiner drove about Mars selling them direct to the consumer.

His profit was fair, because after all he had no competition; his was the sole health food business on Mars.

And then, too, he had a sideline. He imported from Earth various gourmet food items such as truffles, goose-liver paté, caviar, kangaroo tail soup, Danish blue cheese, smoked oysters, quail eggs, rum babas, all of which were illegal on Mars, due to the attempt by the UN to force the colonies to become self-sufficient foodwise. The UN food experts claimed that it was unsafe to transport food across space, due to the chance of harmful radiation contaminating it, but Steiner knew better; the actual reason was their fear of the consequences to the colonies in case of war back Home. Food shipments would cease, and unless the colonies were self-sufficient they probably would starve themselves out of existence within a short time.

While he admired their reasoning, Steiner did not wish to acquiesce in fact. A few cans of French truffles imported on the sly would not cause the dairy ranchers to stop trying to produce milk, nor the hog, steer, and sheep ranchers from keeping on with the struggle to make their farms pay. Apple and peach and apricot trees would still be planted and tended, sprayed and watered, even if glass jars of caviar showed up in the various settlements at twenty dollars each.

At this moment, Steiner was inspecting a shipment of tins of halvah, a Turkish pastry, which had arrived the night before aboard the self-guiding ship which shuttled between Manila and the tiny field in the wastelands of the F.D.R. Mountains which Steiner had constructed, using Bleekmen as laborers. Halvah sold well, especially in New Israel, and Steiner, inspecting the tins for signs of damage, estimated that he could get at least five dollars for each one. And then also old Arnie Kott at Lewistown took almost anything sweet that Steiner could lay his hands on, plus cheeses and canned fish of every kind, not to mention the Canadian smoked bacon which showed up in five-pound tins, the same as Dutch hams. In fact, Arnie Kott was his best single customer.

The storage shed, where Steiner now sat, lay within sight of his small, private, illegal landing field. Upright on the field stood the rocket which had come in last night; Steiner's technician—he himself had no manual ability of any sort—was busy preparing it for its return flight to Manila. The rocket was small, only twenty feet high, but it was Swiss-made and quite stable. Above, the ruddy Martian sun cast elongated shadows from the peaks of the surrounding range, and Steiner had turned on a kerosene heater to warm his storage shed. The technician, seeing Steiner look out through the window of the shed, nodded to indicate that the rocket was ready for its return load, so Steiner put down his tins of halvah temporarily. Taking hold of the hand truck, he began pushing the load of cartons through the doorway of the shed and out onto the rocky ground.

"That looks like over a hundred pounds," his technician said critically, as Steiner came up pushing the hand truck.

"Very light cartons," Steiner said. They contained a dried grass which, back in the Philippines, was processed in such a way that the end result very much resembled hashish. It was smoked in a mixture with ordinary Virginia burley tobacco, and got a terrific price in the United States. Steiner had never tried the stuff himself; to him, physical and moral health were one—he believed in his health foods, and neither smoked nor drank.

Together he and Otto loaded the rocket with its cargo, sealed it, and then Otto set the guidance system's clock. In a few days José Pesquito back Home at Manila would be unloading the cargo, going over the order form included, and assembling Steiner's needs for the return trip.

"Will you fly me back with you?" Otto asked.

"I'm going first to New Israel," Steiner said.

"That's O.K. I've got plenty of time."

On his own, Otto Zitte had once operated a small black-market business; he dealt exclusively in electronic equipment, components of great fragility and small size, which were smuggled in aboard the common carriers operating between Earth and Mars. And at former times he had tried to import such prize black-market items as typewriters, cameras, tape recorders, furs, and whiskey, but there competition had driven him out. Trade in those necessities of life, selling on a mass basis throughout the colonies, had been taken over by the big professional black-market operators who had enormous capital to back them up and their own full-scale transportation system. And, anyhow, Otto's heart was not in it. He wanted to be a repairman; in fact, he had come to Mars for that purpose, not knowing that two or three firms monopolized the repair business, operating like exclusive guilds, such as the Yee Company, for whom Steiner's neighbor, Jack Bohlen, worked. Otto had taken the aptitude tests, but he was not good enough. Therefore, after a year or so on Mars, he had turned to working for Steiner and running his small import operation. It was humiliating for him, but at least he was not doing manual labor on one of the colonies' work gangs, out under the sun reclaiming the desert.

As Otto and Steiner walked back to the storage shed, Steiner said, "I personally can't stand those Israelis, even though I have to deal with them all the time. They're unnatural, the way they live, in those barracks, and always out trying to plant orchards, oranges or lemons, you know. They have the advantage over everybody else because back Home they lived almost like we live here, with desert and hardly any resources."

"True," Otto said. "But you have to hand it to them; they really hustle. They're not lazy."

"And not only that," Steiner said, "they're hypocrites regarding food. Look at how many cans of nonkosher meat they buy from me. None of them keep the dietary laws."

"Well, if you don't approve of them buying smoked oysters from you, don't sell to them," Otto said.

"It's their business, not mine," Steiner said.

He had another reason for visiting New Israel, a reason

which even Otto did not know about. A son of Steiner's lived there, in a special camp for what were called "anomalous children." The term referred to any child who differed from the norm either physically or psychologically to the extent that he could not be educated in the Public School. Steiner's son was autistic, and for three years the instructor at the camp had been working with him, trying to bring him into communication with the human culture into which he had been born.

To have an autistic child was a special shame, because the psychologists believed that the condition came from a defect in the parents, usually a schizoid temperament. Manfred Steiner, age ten, had never spoken a word. He ran about on tiptoe, avoiding people as if they were things, sharp-pointed and dangerous. Physically, he was a large healthy blond-haired boy, and for the first year or so the Steiners had rejoiced in having him. But now—even the instructor at Camp B-G could offer little hope. And the instructor was always optimistic; it was her job.

"I may be in New Israel all day," Steiner said, as he and Otto loaded the cans of halvah into the 'copter. "I have to visit every damn kibbutz in the place, and that takes hours."

"Why don't you want me along?" Otto demanded, with hot anger.

Steiner shuffled his feet, hung his head, and said guiltily, "You misunderstand. I'd love to have company, but—" For an instant he thought of telling Otto the truth. "I'll take you to the tractor-bus terminal and drop you off—O.K.?" He felt weary. When he got to Camp B-G he would find Manfred just the same, never meeting anyone's eye, always darting about on the periphery, more like a taut, wary animal than a child. . . . It was hardly worth going, but still he would go.

In his own mind, Steiner blamed it all on his wife; when Manfred was a baby, she had never talked to him or shown him any affection. Having been trained as a chemist, she had an intellectual, matter-of-fact attitude, inappropriate in a mother. She had bathed and fed the baby as if he were a laboratory animal like a white rat. She kept him clean and healthy but she had never sung to him, laughed with him, had not really used language to or with him. So naturally he had become autistic; what else could he do? Steiner, thinking about it, felt grim. So much for marrying a woman with a master's degree. When he thought of the Bohlen boy next door, yelling and playing— but look at Silvia Bohlen; she was a genuine mother and woman, vital, physically attractive, *alive*. True, she was domineering and selfish . . . she had a highly developed sense of what was hers. But he admired her for that. She was not sentimental; she was strong. For instance, consider the water question, and her attitude. It was not possible to break her down, even by alleging that his own water tank had leaked out their two weeks' supply. Thinking about that, Steiner smiled ruefully. Silvia Bohlen hadn't been taken in, even for a moment.

Otto said, "Drop me off at the bus terminal, then."

With relief, Steiner said, "Good enough. And you won't have to endure those Israelis."

Eying him, Otto said, "I told you, Norbert, I don't mind them."

Together, they entered the 'copter, and Steiner seated himself at the controls and started the engine. He said nothing more to Otto.

As he set his 'copter down at Weizmann Field north of New Israel, Steiner felt guilty that he had talked badly about the Israelis. He had done it only as part of his speech designed to dissuade Otto from coming along with him, but nevertheless it was not right; it went contrary to his authentic feelings. Shame, he realized. That was why he had said it; shame because of his defective son at Camp B-G . . . what a powerful drive it was, it could make a man say anything.

Without the Israelis, his son would be uncared for. No other facilities for anomalous children existed on Mars, although there were dozens of such institutions back Home, as was every other facility one could think of. And the cost of keeping Manfred at the camp was so low as to be a mere formality. As he parked his 'copter and got out, Steiner felt his guilt grow until he wondered how he could face the Israelis. It seemed to him that, God forbid, they might be able to read his mind, might somehow intuit what he had said about them when he was elsewhere.

However, the Israeli field personnel greeted him pleasantly, and his guilt began to fade; evidently it did not show after all.

Lugging his heavy suitcases, he crossed the field to the parking lot where the tractor-bus waited to take passengers into the central business district.

He had already boarded the bus and was making himself comfortable when he remembered that he had not brought any present for his son. Miss Milch, the instructor, had told him always to bring a gift, a durable object by which Manfred could recall his father after he had left. I'll just have to stop somewhere, Steiner said to himself. Buy a toy, a game perhaps. And then he remembered that one of the parents who visited her child at Camp B-G ran a gift shop in New Israel; Mrs. Esterhazy. He could stop there; Mrs. Esterhazy had seen Manfred and understood about the anomalous children in general. She would know what to give him, and there would be no embarrassing questions such as, How old is the boy?

At the stop nearest the gift shop he got off the bus and walked up the sidewalk, enjoying the sight of small, well-kept stores and offices. New Israel in many ways reminded him of Home; it was a true city, more so than Bunchewood Park itself or Lewistown. Many people could be seen, most of them hurrying as if they had business to conduct, and he drank in the atmosphere of commerce and activity.

He came to the gift shop, with its modern sign and sloping glass windows. Except for the Martian shrub growing in the windowbox, it could have been a store in downtown Berlin. He entered, and found Mrs. Esterhazy standing at the counter, smiling as she recognized him. She was an attractive matronly woman in her early forties, with dark hair, and always well-dressed, always looking fresh and intelligent. As everyone knew, Mrs. Esterhazy was terribly active in civic affairs and politics; she put out a newsletter and belonged to one committee after another.

That she had a child in Camp B-G: that was a secret, known only to a few of the other parents and of course the staff at the camp. It was a young child, only three, suffering from one of the formidable physical defects associated with exposure to gamma rays during its intrauterine existence. He had seen it only once. There were many sobering anomalies at Camp B-G, and he had come to accept them, whatever they looked like. At first it had startled him, the Esterhazy child; it was so small and shriveled, with enormous eyes like a lemur's. It had peculiar webbed fingers, as if it had been fashioned for an aquatic world. He had the feeling about it that it was astonishingly acute in its perceptions; it had studied him with deep intensity, seeming to reach some depth in him usually inaccessible, perhaps even to himself. . . . It had seemed to reach out somehow and probe his secrets and then it had withdrawn, accepting him on the basis of what it had picked up.

The child, he had surmised, was a Martian, that is, born on Mars, to Mrs. Esterhazy and some man who was not her husband, since she no longer had a husband. That fact he had picked up from her in conversation; she announced it calmly, making no bones about it. She had been divorced for a number of years. Obviously, then, the child at Camp B-G had been born out of wedlock, but Mrs. Esterhazy, like so many modern women, did not consider that a disgrace. Steiner shared her opinion.

Setting down his heavy suitcases, Steiner said, "What a nice little shop you have here, Mrs. Esterhazy."

"Thank you," she said, coming around from behind the counter. "What can I do for you, Mr. Steiner? Are you here to sell me yogurt and wheat germ?" Her dark eyes twinkled.

"I need a present for Manfred," Steiner said.

A soft, compassionate expression appeared on her face. "I see. Well—" She moved away from him, toward one of the counters. "I saw your son the other day, when I was visiting B-G. Has he shown any interest in music? Often autistic children enjoy music."

"He's fond of drawing. He paints pictures all the time."

She picked up a small wooden flutelike instrument. "This is locally made. And very well made, too." She held it out to him.

"Yes," he said. "I'll take this."

"Miss Milch is utilizing music as a method of reaching the autistic children at B-G," Mrs. Esterhazy said as she went to wrap up the wooden flute. "The dance, in particular." She hesitated, then. "Mr. Steiner, you know that I'm in constant touch with the political scene back Home. I—there's a rumor that the UN is considering—" She lowered her voice, her face pale. "I do so hate to inflict suffering on you, Mr. Steiner, but if there is any truth in this, and there certainly seems to be . . ."

"Go ahead." But he wished now that he had not come in. Yes, Mrs. Esterhazy was in touch with important happenings, and it made him uneasy just to know that, without hearing anything more.

Mrs. Esterhazy said, "There's supposed to be a measure under debate at the UN right now, having to do with anomalous children." Her voice shook. "It would require the closing of Camp B-G."

After a moment he was able to say, "But, why?" He stared at her.

"They're afraid—well, they don't want to see what they call 'defective stock' appearing on the colonial planets. They want to keep the race pure. Can you understand that? I can, and yet I—well, I can't agree. Probably because of my own child. No, I just can't agree. They're not worried about the anomalous children at Home, because they don't have the aspirations for themselves that they do for us. You have to understand the idealism and anxiety which they have about us. . . . Do you remember how you felt before you emigrated here with your family? Back Home they see the existence of anomalous children on Mars as a sign that one of Earth's major problems has been transplanted into the future, because we *are* the future, to them, and—"

Steiner interrupted her. "You're certain about this bill?"

"I feel certain." She faced him, her chin up, her intelligent eyes calm. "We can't be too careful; it would be dreadful if they closed Camp B-G and—" She did not finish. In her eyes he read something unspeakable. The anomalous children, his boy and hers, would be killed in some scientific, painless, instantaneous way. Did she mean that?

"Say it," he said.

Mrs. Esterhazy said, "The children would be put to sleep."

Revolted, he said, "Killed, you mean."

"Oh," she said, "how can you speak it like that, as if you didn't care?" She gazed at him in horror.

"Christ," he said with violent bitterness. "If there's any truth in this—" But he did not believe her. Because, perhaps, he didn't want to? Because it was too ghastly? No, he thought. Because he did not trust her instincts, her sense of reality; she had picked up some garbled hysterical rumor. Perhaps there was a bill directed toward some tangential aspect of this that might affect Camp B-G and its children in some fashion. But they—the parents of anomalous children—had always lived under that cloud. They had read of the mandatory sterilization of both parents and offspring in cases where it was proved that the gonads had been permanently altered, generally in cases of exposure to gamma radiation in unusual mass quantity.

"Who in the UN are authors of this bill?" he asked.

"There are six members of the In-planet Health and Welfare Committee who are supposed to have written the bill." She began writing. "Here are their names. Now, Mr. Steiner, what we'd like you to do is to write to these men, and have anybody you know who—"

He barely listened. He paid for his flute, thanked her, accepted the folded piece of paper, and made his way out of the gift shop.

Goddamn, how he wished he hadn't gone in there! Did she enjoy telling such stories? Wasn't there trouble enough in the world as it was, without old wives' tales being peddled by middle-aged females who should not have had anything to do with public affairs in the first place?

But in him a quiet voice said, She may be right. You have to face it. Gripping his heavy suitcases, he walked on, confused and frightened, hardly aware of the small new shops which he passed as he hurried toward Camp B-G and his waiting son.

When he entered the great glass-domed solarium of Camp Ben-Gurion, there stood young, sandy-haired Miss Milch in her work smock and sandals, with clay and paint splattered on her, a hectic expression knitting her eyebrows. She tossed her head and pushed her tousled hair back from her face as she came toward him. "Hello, Mr. Steiner. What a day we've had. Two new children, and one of them a holy terror."

"Miss Milch," he said, "I was talking to Mrs. Esterhazy at her shop just now—"

"She told you about the supposed bill at the UN?" Miss Milch looked tired. "Yes, there is such a bill. Anne gets every sort of inside piece of news, although how she does it I have no idea. Try to keep from showing any agitation around Manfred, if you possibly can; he's been upset by the new arrivals today." She started off, to lead Mr. Steiner from the solarium down the corridor to the playroom in which his son would be found, but he hurried after her, halting her.

"What can we do about this bill?" he demanded breathlessly. He set down his suitcases, holding now only the paper bag in which Mrs. Esterhazy had put the wooden flute.

"I don't know that we can do anything," Miss Milch said. She went on slowly to the door and opened it. The sound of children's voices came shrill and loud to their ears. "Naturally, the authorities at New Israel and back Home in Israel itself have made furious protests, and so have several other governments. But so much of this is secret; the bill is secret, and it all has to be done sub rosa, so they won't start a panic. It's such a touchy subject. Nobody really knows what public sentiment is, on this, or even if it should be listened to." Her voice, weary and brittle, dragged, as if she were running down. But then she seemed to perk up. She patted him on the shoulder. "I think the worst they would do, once they closed B-G, is deport the anomalous children back Home; I don't think they'd ever go so far as to destroy them."

Steiner said quickly, "To camps back on Earth."

"Let's go and find Manfred," Miss Milch said. "All right? I think he knows this is the day you come; he was standing by the window, but of course he does that a lot."

Suddenly, to his own surprise, he burst out in a choked voice, "I wonder if maybe they might be right. What use is it to have a child that can't talk or live among people?"

Miss Milch glanced at him but said nothing.

"He'll never be able to hold a job," Steiner said. "He'll always be a burden on society, like he is now. Isn't that the truth?"

"Autistic children still baffle us," Miss Milch said. "By what they are, and how they got that way, and by their tendency to begin to evolve mentally, all at once, for no apparent reason, after years of complete failure to respond."

"I think I can't in good conscience oppose this bill," Steiner said. "Not after thinking it over. Now that the first shock is over. It would be fair. I feel it's fair." His voice shook.

"Well," Miss Milch said, "I'm glad you didn't say that to Anne Esterhazy, because she'd never let you go; she'd be after you making speeches at you until you came around to her side." She held open the door to the big playroom. "Manfred is over in the corner."

Seeing his son from a distance, Steiner thought, You would never know to look at him. The large, well-formed head, the curly hair, the handsome features . . . The boy was bent over, absorbed in some object which he held. A genuinely good-looking boy, with eyes that shone sometimes mockingly, sometimes with glee and excitement . . . and such terrific co-ordination. The way he sprinted about, on the tips of his toes, as if dancing to some unheard music, some tune from inside his own mind whose rhythms kept him enthralled.

We are so pedestrian, compared to him, Steiner thought. Leaden. We creep along like snails, while he dances and leaps, as if gravity does not have the same influence on him as it does on us. Could he be made from some new and different kind of atom?

"Hi, Manny," Mr. Steiner said to his son.

The boy did not raise his head or show any sign of awareness; he continued fooling with the object.

I will write to the framers of the bill, Steiner thought, and tell them I have a child in the camp. And that I agree with them.

His thoughts frightened him.

Murder, of Manfred—he recognized it. My hatred of him coming out, released by this news. I see why they're debating it in secret; many people have this hate, I bet. Unrecognized inside.

"No flute for you, Manny," Steiner said. "Why should I give it to you, I wonder? Do you give a damn? No." The boy did not look up or give any indication of hearing. "Nothing," Steiner said. "Emptiness."

While Steiner stood there, tall, slender Dr. Glaub in his white coat, carrying his clipboard, approached. Steiner became suddenly aware of him and started.

"There is a new theory about autism," Dr. Glaub said. "From Berghölzlei, in Switzerland. I wished to discuss it with you, because it seems to offer us a new avenue with your son, here."

"I doubt it," Steiner said.

Dr. Glaub did not seem to hear him, he continued, "It assumes a derangement in the sense of time in the autistic individual, so that the environment around him is so accelerated that he cannot cope with it, in fact, he is unable to perceive it properly, precisely as we would be if we faced a speeded-up television program, so that objects whizzed by so fast as to be invisible, and sound was a gobbledegook—you know? Just extremely high-pitched mishmash. Now, this new theory would place the autistic child in a closed chamber, where he faced a screen on which filmed sequences were projected slowed down—do you see? Both sound and video slowed, at last so slow that you and I would not be able to perceive motion or comprehend the sounds as human speech."

Wearily, Steiner said, "Fascinating. There's always something new, isn't there, in psychotherapy?"

"Yes," Dr. Glaub said, nodding. "Especially from the Swiss; they're ingenious in comprehending the world-views of disturbed persons, of encapsulated individuals cut off from ordinary means of communication, isolated—you know?"

"I know," Steiner said.

Dr. Glaub, still nodding, had moved on, to stop by another parent, a woman, who was seated with her small girl, both of them examining a cloth picture book.

Hope before the deluge, Steiner thought. Does Dr. Glaub know that any day the authorities back on Earth may close Camp B-G? The good doctor labors on in idiotic innocence . . . happy in his schemes.

Walking after Dr. Glaub, Steiner waited until there was a pause in the conversation and then he said, "Doctor, I'd like to discuss this new theory a little further."

"Yes, yes," Dr. Glaub said, excusing himself from the woman and her child; he led Steiner over to one side, where they could talk privately. "This concept of time-rates may open a doorway to minds so fatigued by the impossible task of communicating in a world where everything happens with such rapidity that—"

Steiner interrupted, "Suppose your theory works out. How can you help such an individual function? Did you intend for him to stay in the closed chamber with the slowed-down picture screen the rest of his life? I think, Doctor, that you're all playing games, here. You're not facing reality. All of you at Camp B-G; you're so virtuous. So without guile. But the outside world—it's not like that. This is a noble, idealistic place, in here, but you're fooling yourselves. So in my opinion you're also fooling the patients; excuse me for saying it. This sloweddown closed chamber, it epitomizes you all, here, your attitude."

Dr. Glaub listened, nodding, with an intent expression on his face. "We have practical equipment promised," he said, when Steiner had finished. "From Westinghouse, back on Earth. Rapport with others in society is achieved primarily through sound, and Westinghouse has designed for us an audio recorder which picks up the message directed at the psychotic individual—for example, your boy Manfred—then, having recorded this message on iron-oxide tape, replays it almost instantly for him at lower speed, then erases itself and records the next message and so on, with the result that a permanent contact with the outside world, at his own rate of time, is maintained. And later we hope to have in our hands here a video recorder which will present a constant but sloweddown record to him of the visual portion of reality, synchronized with the audio portion. Admittedly, he will be one step removed from contact with reality, and the problem of touch presents difficulties—but I disagree when you say this is too idealistic to be of use. Look at the widespread chemical therapy that was tried not so long ago. Stimulants speeded up the psychotic's interior time-sense so that he could comprehend the stimuli pouring in on him, but as soon as the stimulant wore off, the psychotic's cognition slowed down as his faulty metabolism reestablished itself—you know? Yet we learned a good deal from that; we learned that psychosis has a chemical basis, not a psychological basis. Sixty years of erroneous notions were upset in a single experiment, using sodium amytal—"

"Dreams," Steiner interrupted. "You will never make contact with my boy." Turning, he walked away from Dr. Glaub.

From Camp B-G he went by bus to a swanky restaurant, the Red Fox, which always bought a good deal of his wares. After he had finished his business with the owner he sat for a time at the bar, drinking a beer.

The way Dr. Glaub had babbled on—that was the kind of idiocy that had brought them to Mars in the first place. To a planet where a glass of beer cost twice what a shot of Scotch cost, because it had so much more water in it.

The owner of the Red Fox, a small, bald, portly man wearing glasses, seated himself next to Steiner and said, "Why you looking so glum, Norb?"

Steiner said, "They're going to close down Camp B-G."

"Good," the owner of the Red Fox said. "We don't need those freaks here on Mars; it's bad advertising."

"I agree," Steiner said, "at least to a certain extent."

"It's like those babies with seal flippers back in the '60's, from them using that German drug. They should have destroyed all of them; there's plenty of healthy normal children born, why spare those others? If you had a kid with extra arms or no arms, deformed in some way, you wouldn't want it kept alive, would you?"

"No," Steiner said. He did not say that his wife's brother back on Earth was a phocomelus; he had been born without arms and made use of superb artificial ones designed for him by a Canadian firm which specialized in such equipment.

In fact he said nothing to the little portly man; he drank his beer and stared at the bottles behind the bar. He did not like the man at all, and he had never told him about Manfred. He knew the man's deepseated prejudice. Nor was he unusual. Steiner could summon up no resentment toward him; he merely felt weary, and did not want to discuss it.

"That was the beginning," the owner said. "Those babies born in the early '60's—are there any of them at Camp B-G— I've never set foot inside there and I never will."

Steiner said, "How could they be at B-G? They're hardly anomalous; anomalous means one of a kind."

"Oh, yeah," the man admitted. "I see what you mean. Anyhow, if they'd destroyed them years ago we wouldn't have such places as B-G, because in my mind there's a direct link between the monsters born in the '60's and all the freaks supposedly born due to radiation ever since; I mean, it's all due to substandard genes, isn't it? Now, I think that's where the Nazis were right. They saw the need of weeding out the inferior genetic strains as long ago as 1930; they saw—"

"My son," Steiner began, and then stopped. He realized what he had said. The portly man stared at him. "My son is there," Steiner at last went on, "means as much to me as your son does to you. I know that someday he will emerge into the world once more."

"Let me buy you a drink, Norbert," the portly man said, "to show you how sorry I am; I mean, about the way I talked."

Steiner said, "If they close B-G it will be a calamity too great for us to bear, we who have children in there. I can't face it."

"I see what you mean," the portly man said. "I understand your feeling."

"You are superior to me if you understand how I feel," Steiner said, "because I can make no sense out of it." He set down his empty beer glass and stepped off the stool. "I don't want another drink," he said. "Excuse me; I have to leave." He picked up his heavy suitcases.

"You've been coming in here all this time," the owner said, "and we talked about that camp a lot, and you never told me you had a son in there. That wasn't right." He looked angry, now.

"Why wasn't it right?"

"Hell, if I had known I wouldn't have said what I said; you're responsible, Norbert—you could have told me, but you deliberately didn't. I don't like that one bit." His face was red with indignation.

Carrying his suitcases, Steiner left the bar.

"This is not my day," he said aloud. Argued with everybody; I'll have to spend the next visit here making apologies . . . if I come back at all. But I have to come back; my business depends on it. And I have to stop at Camp B-G; there is no other way.

Suddenly it came to him that he should kill himself. The idea appeared in his mind full blown, as if it had always been there, always a part of him. Easy to do it, just crash the 'copter. He thought, I am goddamn tired of being Norbert Steiner; I didn't ask to be Norbert Steiner or sell black-market food or anything else. What is my reason for staying alive? I'm not good with my hands, I can't fix or make anything; I can't use my mind, either, I'm just a salesman. I'm tired of my wife's scorn because I can't keep our water machinery going—I'm tired of Otto who I had to hire because I'm helpless even in my own business.

In fact, he thought, why wait until I can get back to the 'copter? Along the street came a huge, rumbling tractor-bus, its sides dull with sand; it had crossed the desert just now, was coming to New Israel from some other settlement. Steiner set down his suitcases and ran out into the street, directly at the tractor-bus.

The bus honked; its airbrakes screeched. Other traffic halted as Steiner ran forward with his head down, his eyes shut. Only at the last moment, with the sound of the air horn so loud in his ears that it became unbearably painful, did he open his eyes; he saw the driver of the bus gaping down at him, saw the steering wheel and the number on the driver's cap. And then—

In the solarium at Camp Ben-Gurion, Miss Milch heard the sounds of sirens, and she paused in the middle of the Dance of the Sugar Plum Fairy from Tchaikovsky's *Nutcracker Suite*, which she was playing on the piano for the children to dance to.

"Fire!" one of the little boys said, going to the window. The other children followed.

"No, it's an ambulance, Miss Milch," another boy said, at the window, "going downtown."

Miss Milch resumed playing, and the children, at the sound of the rhythms coming from the piano, straggled back to their places. They were bears at the zoo, cavorting for peanuts; that was what the music suggested to them, Miss Milch told them to go ahead and act it out.

Off to one side, Manfred stood heedless of the music, his head down, a thoughtful expression on his face. As the sirens wailed up loudly for a moment, Manfred lifted his head. Noticing that, Miss Milch gasped and breathed a prayer. The boy had heard! She thumped away at the Tchaikovsky music even more loudly than before, feeling exultation: she and the doctors had been right, for through sound there had come about a contact with the boy. Now Manfred went slowly to the window to look out; all alone he gazed down at the buildings and streets below, searching for the origin of the noise which had aroused him, attracted his attention.

Things are not so hopeless after all, Miss Milch said to herself. Wait until his father hears; it shows we must never talk of giving up.

She played on, loudly and happily.

Four

D AVID BOHLEN, building a dam of wet soil at the end of his family's vegetable garden under the hot midafternoon Martian sun, saw the UN police 'copter settle down and land before the Steiners' house, and he knew instantly that something was going on.

A UN policeman in his blue uniform and shiny helmet stepped from the 'copter and walked up the path to the Steiners' front door, and when two of the little girls appeared the policeman greeted them. He then spoke to Mrs. Steiner and then he disappeared on inside, and the door shut after him.

David got to his feet and hurried from the garden, across the stretch of sand to the ditch; he leaped the ditch and crossed the patch of flat soil where Mrs. Steiner had tried unsuccessfully to raise pansies, and at the corner of the house he suddenly came upon one of the Steiner girls; she was standing inertly, picking apart a stalk of wur-weed, her face white. She looked as if she were going to be sick.

"Hey, what's wrong?" he asked her. "Why's the policeman talking to your mom?"

The Steiner girl glanced at him and then bolted off, leaving him.

I'll bet I know what it is, David thought. Mr. Steiner has been arrested because he did something illegal. He felt excited and he jumped up and down. I wonder what he did. Turning, he ran back the way he had come, hopped once more across the ditch of water, and at last threw open the door to his own house.

"Mom!" he shouted, running from room to room. "Hey, you know how you and Dad always are talking about Mr. Steiner being outside the law, I mean in his work? Well, you know what?"

His mother was nowhere to be found; she must have gone visiting, he realized. For instance, Mrs. Henessy who lived within walking distance north along the ditch; often his mom was gone most of the day visiting other ladies, drinking coffee with them and exchanging gossip. Well, they're really missing out, David declared to himself. He ran to the window and looked out, to be sure of not missing anything.

The policeman and Mrs. Steiner had gone outside, now, and both were walking slowly to the police 'copter. Mrs. Steiner held a big handkerchief to her face, and the policeman had hold of her shoulder, as if he was a relative or something. Fascinated, David watched the two of them get into the 'copter. The Steiner girls stood together in a small group, their faces peculiar. The policeman went over and spoke to them, and then he returned to the 'copter—and then he noticed David. He beckoned to him to come outdoors, and David, feeling fright, did so; he emerged from the house, blinking in the sunlight, and step by step approached the policeman with his shining helmet and his armband and the gun at his waist.

"What's your name, son?" the policeman asked, with an accent.

"David Bohlen." His knees shook.

"Is Mother or Father home, David?"

"No," he said, "just me."

"When your parents return, you tell them to keep watch on the Steiner children until Mrs. Steiner is back." The policeman started up the motor of the 'copter, and the blades began to turn. "You do that, David? Do you understand?"

"Yes, sir," David said, noticing that the policeman had on the blue stripe which meant he was Swedish. The boy knew all the identifying marks which the different UN units wore. He wondered how fast the police 'copter could go; it looked like a special fast job, and he wished he could ride in it: he was no longer frightened of the policeman and he wished they could talk more. But the policeman was leaving; the 'copter rose from the ground, and torrents of wind and sand blew around David, forcing him to turn away and put his arm across his face.

The four Steiner girls still stood gathered together, none of them speaking. One, the oldest, was crying; tears ran down her cheeks but she made no sound. The smallest, who was only three, smiled shyly at David.

"You want to help me with my dam?" David called to them. "You can come over; the policeman told me it was O.K."

After a moment the youngest Steiner girl came toward him, and then the others followed.

"What did your dad do?" David asked the oldest girl. She was twelve, older than he. "The policeman said you could say," he added.

There was no answer; the girl merely stared at him.

"If you tell me," David said, "I won't tell anyone. I promise to keep it a secret."

Sunbathing out on June Henessy's fenced, envined patio, sipping iced tea and drowsily conversing, Silvia Bohlen heard the radio from within the Henessy house give the late afternoon news.

Beside her, June raised herself up and said, "Say, isn't he the man who lives next door to you?"

"Shh," Silvia said, intently listening to the announcer. But there was no more, only the brief mention: Norbert Steiner, a dealer in health foods, had committed suicide on a downtown New Israel street by throwing himself in the path of a bus. It was the same Steiner, all right; it was their neighbor, she knew it at once.

"How dreadful," June said, sitting up and fastening the straps of her polka-dot cotton halter. "I only saw him a couple of times, but—"

"He was a dreadful little man," Silvia said. "I'm not surprised he did it." And yet she felt horrified. She could not believe it. She got to her feet, saying, "With four children—he left her to take care of four children! Isn't that dreadful? What's going to happen to them? They're so helpless anyhow."

"I heard," June said, "that he deals on the black market. Had you heard that? Maybe they were closing in on him."

Silvia said, "I better go right home and see if there's anything I can do for Mrs. Steiner. Maybe I can take the children for a while." Could it have been my fault? she asked herself. Could he have done it because I refused them that water, this morning? It could be, because he was there; he had not gone to work yet.

So maybe it is our fault, she thought. The way we treated them—which of us has ever been really nice to them and accepted them? But they are such dreadful whining people, always asking for help, begging and borrowing . . . who could respect them?

Going into the house she changed, in the bedroom, to her slacks and t-shirt. June Henessy followed along with her.

"Yes," June said, "you're right—we all have to pitch in and help where we can. I wonder if she'll stay on or if she'll go back to Earth. I'd go back—I'm practically ready to go back anyhow, it's so dull here."

Getting her purse and cigarettes, Silvia said goodbye to June and set out on the walk back down the ditch to her own home. Breathless, she arrived in time to see the police 'copter disappearing into the sky. That was them notifying her, she decided. In the backyard she found David with the four Steiner girls; they were busy playing.

"Did they take Mrs. Steiner with them?" she called to David.

The boy scrambled at once to his feet and came up to her excitedly. "Mom, she went along with him. I'm taking care of the girls."

That's what I was afraid of, Silvia thought. The four girls still sat at the dam, playing a slow-motion, apathetic game with the mud and water, none of them looking up or greeting her; they seemed inert, no doubt from the shock of learning about their father's death. Only the smallest one showed any signs of reviving, and she probably had not comprehended the news in the first place. Already, Silvia thought, that little man's death has reached out and touched others, and the coldness is spreading. She felt the chill in her own heart. And I did not even like him, she thought.

The sight of the four Steiner girls made her quake. Am I going to have to take on these pudding-y, plump, vapid, low-class children? she asked herself. The answering thought thrust its way up, tossing every other consideration aside: *I don't want to!* She felt panic, because it was obvious that she had no choice; even now they were playing on her land, in her garden —she had them already.

Hopefully, the smallest girl asked, "Miz Bohlen, could we have some more water for our dam?"

Water, always wanting water, Silvia thought. Always leeching on us, as if it was a trait born into them. She ignored the child and said instead to her son, "Come into the house—I want to talk to you."

Together, they went indoors, where the girls could not overhear.

"David," she said, "their father is dead, it came over the radio. That's why the police came and took her. We'll have to help out for a while." She tried to smile, but it was impossible. "However much we may dislike the Steiners—"

David burst out—"I don't dislike them, Mom. How come he died? Did he have a heart attack? Was he set on by wild Bleekmen, could that be?"

"It doesn't matter how he happened to die; what we have to think of now is what we can do for those girls." Her mind was empty; she could think of nothing. All she knew was that she did not want to have the girls near her. "What should we do?" she asked David.

"Maybe fix them lunch. They told me they didn't have any; she was just about to fix it."

Silvia went out from the house and down the path. "I'm going to fix lunch, girls, for any of you who want it. Over at your house." She waited a moment and then started toward the Steiner house. When she looked back she saw that only the smallest child was following.

The oldest girl said in a tear-choked voice, "No, thank you."

"You'd better eat," Silvia said, but she was relieved. "Come along," she said to the little girl. "What's your name?"

"Betty," the little girl said shyly. "Could I have a egg sandwich? And cocoa?"

"We'll see what there is," Silvia said.

Later, while the child ate her egg sandwich and drank her cocoa, Silvia took the opportunity to explore the Steiner house. In the bedroom she came upon something which interested her: a picture of a small boy with dark, enormous, luminous eyes and curly hair; he looked, Silvia thought, like a despairing creature from some other world, some divine and yet dreadful place beyond their own.

Carrying the picture into the kitchen she asked little Betty who the boy was.

"That's my brother Manfred," Betty answered, her mouth full of egg and bread. Then she began to giggle. Between the giggles a few hesitant words emerged, and Silvia caught the fact that the girls were not supposed to mention their brother to anyone.

"Why doesn't he live with you?" Silvia asked, full of curiosity.

"He's at camp," Betty said. "Because he can't talk."

"What a shame," Silvia said, and she thought, At that camp in New Israel, no doubt. No wonder the girls aren't supposed to mention him; he's one of those anomalous children you hear of but never see. The thought made her sad. Unglimpsed tragedy in the Steiner household; she had never guessed. And it was in New Israel that Mr. Steiner had taken his life. Undoubtedly he had been visiting his son.

Then it has nothing to do with us, she decided as she returned the picture to its place in the bedroom. Mr. Steiner's decision was based on a personal matter. So she felt relieved.

Strange, she thought, how one has the immediate reaction of guilt and responsibility when one hears of a suicide. If only I hadn't done this, or had done that . . . I could have averted it. I'm at fault. And it was not so in this situation, not at all; she was a total outsider to the Steiners, sharing no part of their actual life, only imagining, in a fit of neurotic guilt, that she did so.

"Do you ever see your brother?" she asked Betty.

"I think I saw him last year," Betty said hesitantly. "He was playing tag, and there were a lot of other boys bigger than me."

Now, silently, the three older Steiner girls filed into the kitchen and stood by the table. At last the eldest burst out, "We changed our mind, we would like lunch."

"All right," Silvia said. "You can help me crack the eggs and peel them. Why don't you go and get David, and I'll feed him at the same time? Wouldn't that be fun, to all eat together?"

They nodded mutely.

Walking up the main street of New Israel, Arnie Kott saw a crowd ahead and cars pulled to a halt at the curb, and he paused momentarily before turning in the direction of Anne Esterhazy's Contemporary Arts Gift Shop. Something up, he said to himself. Robbery? Street brawl?

However, he did not have time to investigate. He continued on his way and arrived presently at the small modern shop

which his ex-wife ran; hands in his trouser pockets, he sauntered in.

"Anybody home?" he called jovially.

No one there. She must have taken off to see the excitement,
Arnie said to himself. Some business sense; didn't even lock up
the store.

A moment later Anne came hurrying breathlessly back into
the store. "Arnie," she said in surprise, seeing him. "Oh my
God, do you know what happened? I was just talking to
him, just talking, not more than an hour ago. And now he's
dead." Tears filled her eyes. She collapsed onto a chair, found
a Kleenex, and blew her nose. "It's just terrible," she said in
a muffled voice. "And it wasn't an accident; he did it deliberately."

"Oh, so that's what's going on," Arnie said, wishing now
that he had gone on and taken a look. "Who do you mean?"

"You wouldn't know him. He has a child at the camp; that's
how I met him." She rubbed her eyes and sat for a time, while
Arnie meandered about the store. "Well," she said at last,
"what can I do for you? It's nice to see you."

"My goddamn encoder broke down," Arnie said. "You know
how hard it is to get decent repair service. What could I do but
come by? What do you say to having lunch with me? Lock up
the store a little while."

"Of course," she said distractedly. "Just let me go wash my
face. I feel as if it was me. I saw him, Arnie. The bus rolled
right over him; they have such mass, they just can't stop. I
would like some lunch—I want to get out of here." She hurried into the washroom—and closed the door.

Soon afterwards the two of them were walking up the sidewalk together.

"Why do people take their own lives?" Anne asked. "I keep
thinking I could have prevented it. I sold him a flute for his
boy. He still had the flute; I saw it with his suitcases on the
curb—he never gave it to his son. Is that the reason, something to do with the flute? I debated between the flute and—"

"Cut it out," Arnie said. "It's not your fault. Listen, if a man
is going to take his life nothing can stop him. And you can't
cause a person to do it; it's in his bloodstream, it's his destiny.

They work themselves up to doing it years in advance, and then it's just like a sudden inspiration; all of a sudden—wham. They do it, see?" He wrapped his arm around her and patted her.

She nodded.

"Now, I mean, *we've* got a kid there at Camp B-G, but it doesn't get us down," Arnie went on. "It's not the end of the world, right? We go on. Where do you want to eat? How's that place across the street, that Red Fox? Any good? I'd like some fried prawns, but hell, it's been almost a year since I saw them. This transportation problem has got to be licked or nobody is emigrating."

"Not the Red Fox," Anne said. "I loathe the man who runs it. Let's try that place on the corner; it's new, I haven't ever eaten in there. I hear it's supposed to be good."

As they sat at a table in the restaurant, waiting for their food to come, Arnie went on and developed his point. "One thing, when you hear about a suicide, you can be sure the guy knows this: he knows he's not a useful member of society. That's the real truth he's facing about himself, that's what does it, knowing you're not important to anybody. If there's one thing I'm sure of it's that. It's nature's way—the expendable are re-moved, by their own hand, too. So I don't lose any sleep when I hear of a suicide, and you'd be surprised how many so-called natural deaths here on Mars are actually suicides; I mean, this is a harsh environment. This place weeds out the fit from the unfit."

Anne Esterhazy nodded but did not seem cheered up.

"Now this guy—" Arnie continued.

"Steiner," Anne said.

"Steiner!" He stared at her. "Norbert Steiner, the black-market operator?" His voice rose.

"He sold health foods."

"That's the guy!" He was flabbergasted. "Oh, no, not Steiner." Good grief, he got all his goodies from Steiner; he was utterly dependent on the man.

The waiter appeared with their food.

"This is awful," Arnie said, "I mean, really awful. What am I going to do?" Every party he threw, every time he had a cozy two-person dinner arranged for himself and some girl, for instance Marty or especially of late Doreen . . . It was just too goddamn much in one day, this and his encoder, both together.

"Don't you think," Anne said, "it might have something to do with him being German? There's been so much sorrow in Germans since that drug plague, those children born with flippers. I've talked to some who've said openly they thought it was God's punishment on them for what was done during the Nazi period. And these weren't religious men, these were businessmen, one here on Mars, the other at Home."

"That damn stupid Steiner," Arnie said. "That cabbage head."

"Eat your food, Arnie." She began to unfold her napkin. "The soup looks good."

"I can't eat," he said. "I don't want this slop." He pushed his soup bowl away.

"You're still just like a big baby," Anne said. "Still having your tantrums." Her voice was soft and compassionate.

"Hell," he said, "sometimes I feel like I've got the weight of the entire planet on me, and you call me a baby!" He glared at her in baffled outrage.

"I didn't know that Norbert Steiner was involved in the black market," Anne said.

"Naturally you wouldn't, you and your lady-committees. What do you know about the world around you? That's why I'm here—I read that last ad you had in the *Times* and it stank. You have to stop giving out that crap like you do; it repels intelligent people—it's just for other cranks like yourself."

"Please," Anne said. "Eat your food. Calm down."

"I'm going to assign a man from my Hall to look over your material before you distribute it. A professional."

"Are you?" she said mildly.

"We've got a real problem—we're not getting the skilled people to come over from Earth any more, the people we need. We're rotting—everybody knows that. We're falling apart."

Smiling, Anne said, "Somebody will take Mr. Steiner's place; there must be other black-market operators."

Arnie said, "You're deliberately misunderstanding me so as to make me look greedy and small, whereas actually I'm one of the most responsible members of the entire colonization attempt here on Mars, and that's why our marriage broke down, because of your belittling me out of jealousy and competitiveness. I don't know why I came over here today—it's impossible for you to work things out on a rational basis, you have to inflict personalities into everything."

"Did you know there's a bill before the UN to shut Camp B-G?" Anne said calmly.

"No," Arnie said.

"Does it distress you to think of B-G being closed?"

"Hell, we'll give Sam private individual care."

"What about the other children there?"

"You changed the subject," Arnie said. "Listen, Anne, you have to knuckle down to what you call masculine domination and let my people edit what you write. Honest to God, it does more harm than good—I hate to say this to your face but it's the truth. You're a worse friend than you would be an enemy, the way you go about things. You're a dabbler! Like most women. You're—irresponsible." He wheezed with wrath. Her face showed no reaction; what he said had no effect on her.

"Can you bring any pressure to bear to help keep B-G open?" she asked. "Maybe we can make a deal. I want to see it kept open."

"A *cause*," Arnie said ferociously.

"Yes."

"You want my blunt answer?"

She nodded, facing him coolly.

"I've been sorry ever since those Jews opened that camp."

Anne said, "Bless you, honest blunt Arnie Kott, mankind's friend."

"It tells the entire world we've got nuts here on Mars, that if you travel across space to get here you're apt to damage your sexual organs and give birth to a monster that would make those German flipper-people look like your next-door neighbor."

"You and the gentleman who runs the Red Fox."

"I'm just being hard-headedly realistic. We're in a struggle for our life; we've got to keep people emigrating here or we're dead on the vine, Anne. You know that. If we didn't have Camp B-G we could advertise that away from Earth's H-bomb-testing, contaminated atmosphere there are no abnormal births. I hoped to see that, but B-G spoils it."

"Not B-G. The births themselves."

"No one would be able to check up and show our abnormal births," Arnie said, "without B-G."

"You'd say it, knowing it's not true, if you could get away with it, telling them back Home that they're safer here—"

"Sure." He nodded.

"That's—immoral."

"No. Listen. You're the immoral one, you and those other ladies. By keeping Camp B-G open you're—"

"Let's not argue, we'll never agree. Let's eat, and then you go on back to Lewistown. I can't take any more."

They ate their meal in silence.

Dr. Milton Glaub, member of the psychiatric pool at Camp B-G, on loan from the Interplan Truckers' Union settlement, sat by himself in his own office once more, back from B-G, his stint there over for today. In his hands he held a bill for roof repairs done on his home the month before. He had put off the work—it involved the use of the scraper which kept the sand from piling up—but finally the settlement building inspector had mailed him a thirty-day condemnation notice. So he had contacted the Roofing Maintenance workers, knowing that he could not pay, but seeing no alternative. He was broke. This had been the worst month so far.

If only Jean, his wife, could spend less. But the solution did not lie there, anyhow; the solution was to acquire more patients. The ITU paid him a monthly salary, but for every patient he received an additional fifty-dollar bonus: incentive, it was called. In actuality it meant the difference between debt and solvency. Nobody with a wife and children could possibly live on the salary offered to psychiatrists, and the ITU, as everyone knew, was especially parsimonious.

And yet, Dr. Glaub continued to live in the ITU settlement; it was an orderly community, in some respects much like Earth. New Israel, like the other national settlements, had a charged, explosive quality.

As a matter of fact, Dr. Glaub had once lived in another

national colony, the United Arab Republic one, a particularly opulent region in which much vegetation, imported from Home, had been induced to grow. But, to him, the settlers' constant animosity toward neighboring colonies had been first irritating and then appalling. Men, at their daily jobs, brooded over wrongs committed. The most charming individuals blew up when certain topics were mentioned. And at night the hostility took practical shape; the national colonies lived for the night. Then, the research labs, which were scenes of scientific experimentation and development during the day, were thrown open to the public, and infernal machines were turned out—it was all done with much excitement and glee, and of course national pride.

The hell with them, Dr. Glaub thought. Their lives were wasted; they had simply carried over the old quarrels from Earth—and the purpose of colonization had been forgotten. For instance, in the UN newspaper that morning he had read about a fracas in the streets of the electrical workers' settlement; the newspaper account implied that the nearby Italian colony was responsible, since several of the aggressors had been wearing the long waxed mustaches popular in the Italian colony. . . .

A knock at his office door broke his line of thought. "Yes," he said, putting the roofing bill away in a desk drawer.

"Are you ready for Goodmember Purdy?" his wife asked, opening the door in the professional manner that he had taught her.

"Send Goodmember Purdy in," Dr. Glaub said. "Wait a couple of minutes, though, so I can read over his case history."

"Did you eat lunch?" Jean asked.

"Of course. Everybody eats lunch."

"You look wan," she said.

That's bad, Dr. Glaub thought. He went from his office into the bathroom, where he carefully darkened his face with the caramel-colored powder currently in fashion. It did improve his looks, although not his state of mind. The theory behind the powder was that the ruling circles in the ITU were of Spanish and Puerto Rican ancestry, and they were apt to feel intimidated if a hired person had skin lighter than their own.

Of course the ads did not put it like that; the ads merely pointed out to hired men in the settlement that "the Martian climate tends to allow natural skin tone to fade to unsightly white."

It was now time to see his patient.

"Good afternoon, Goodmember Purdy."

"Afternoon, Doc."

"I see from your file that you're a baker."

"Yeah, that's right."

A pause. "What did you wish to consult with me about?"

Goodmember Purdy, staring at the floor and fooling with his cap, said, "I never been to a psychiatrist before."

"No, I can see here that you haven't."

"There's this party my brother-in-law's giving . . . I'm not much on going to parties."

"Are you compelled to attend?" Dr. Glaub had quietly set the clock on his desk; it ticked away the goodmember's half-hour.

"They're sort of throwing it for me. They, uh, want me to take on my nephew as an apprentice so he'll be in the union eventually." Purdy droned on. ". . . And I been lying awake at night trying to figure out how to get out of it—I mean, these are my relatives, and I can't hardly come out and tell them no. But I just can't go, I don't feel good enough to. So that's why I'm here."

"I see," Dr. Glaub said. "Well, you'd better give me the particulars on this party, when and where it is, the names of the persons involved, so I can do a right bang-up job while I'm there."

With relief, Purdy dug into his coat pocket and brought out a neatly typed document. "I sure appreciate your going in my place, Doc. You psychiatrists really take a load off a man's back; I'm not joking when I say I been losing sleep over this." He gazed with grateful awe at the man before him, skilled in the social graces, capable of treading the narrow, hazardous path of complex interpersonal realtions which had defeated so many union members over the years.

"Don't worry any further about it," Dr. Glaub said. For after all, he thought, what's a little schizophrenia? That is, you know, what you're suffering from. I'll take the social pressure from you, and you can continue in your chronic maladaptive state, at least for another few months. Until the next overpowering social demand is made on your limited capabilities. . . .

As Goodmember Purdy left the office, Dr. Glaub reflected that this certainly was a practical form of psychotherapy which had evolved here on Mars. Instead of curing the patient of his phobias, one became in the manner of a lawyer the actual advocate in the man's place at—

Jean called into the office, "Milt, there's a call for you from New Israel. It's Bosley Touvim."

Oh, God, Dr. Glaub thought. Touvim was the President of New Israel; something was wrong. Hurriedly he picked up the phone on his desk. "Dr. Glaub here."

"Doctor," sounded the dark, stern, powerful voice, "this is Touvim. We have a death here, a patient of yours, I understand. Will you kindly fly back here and attend to this? Allow me to give you a few token details . . . Norbert Steiner, a West German—"

"He's not my patient, sir," Dr. Claub interrupted. "However, his son is—a little autistic child at Camp B-G. What do you mean, Steiner is dead? For heaven's sake, I was just talking to him this morning—are you sure it's the same Steiner? If it is, I do have a file on him, on the entire family, because of the nature of the boy's illness. In child autism we feel that the family situation must be understood before therapy can begin. Yes, I'll be right over."

Touvim said, "This is evidently a suicide."

"I can't believe it," Dr. Glaub said.

"For the past half-hour I have been discussing this with the staff at Camp B-G; they tell me you had a long conversation with Steiner shortly before he left the camp. At the inquest our police will want to know what indications if any Steiner gave of a depressed or morbidly introspective mood, what he said that might have given you the opportunity to dissuade him or, barring that, compel him to undergo therapy. I take it the man said nothing that would alert you to his intentions."

"Absolutely nothing," Dr. Glaub said.

"Then if I were you I wouldn't worry," Touvim said. "Merely

be prepared to give the clinical background of the man . . .
discuss possible motives which might have led him to take his
life. You understand."

"Thank you, Mr. Touvim," Dr. Glaub said weakly. "I suppose it is possible he was depressed about his son, but I outlined a new therapy to him; we have very high hopes for it.
However, he did seem cynical and shut in, he did not respond
as I would have expected. But suicide!"

What if I lose the B-G assignment? Doctor Glaub was asking
himself. I just can't. Working there once a week added enough
to his income so that he could imagine—although not attain—
financial security. The B-G check at least made the goal
plausible.

Didn't it occur to that idiot Steiner what effect his death
might have on others? Yes, it must have; he did it to get
vengeance on us. Paying us back—but for what? For trying to
heal his child?

This is a very serious matter, he realized. A suicide, so close
on the heels of a doctor-patient interview. Thank God Mr.
Touvim warned me. Even so, the newspapers will pick it up,
and all those who want to see Camp B-G closed will benefit
from this.

Having repaired the refrigeration equipment at McAuliff's
dairy ranch, Jack Bohlen returned to his 'copter, put his tool
box behind the seat, and contacted his employer, Mr. Yee.

"The school," Mr. Yee said. "You must go there, Jack; I still
have no one else to take that assignment."

"O.K., Mr. Yee." He started up the motor of the 'copter,
feeling resigned to it.

"A message from your wife, Jack."

"Oh?" He was surprised; his employer frowned on wives of
his employees phoning in, and Silvia knew that. Maybe something had happened to David. "Can you tell me what she said?"
he asked.

Mr. Yee said, "Mrs. Bohlen asked our switchboard girl to inform you that a neighbor of yours, a Mr. Steiner, has taken his
own life. Mrs. Bohlen is caring for the Steiner children, she
wants you to know. She also asked if it was possible for you to

come home tonight, but I told her that although we regretted it we could not spare you. You must stay available on call until the end of the week, Jack."

Steiner dead, Jack said to himself. The poor ineffectual sap. Well, maybe he's better off.

"Thank you, Mr. Yee," he said into the microphone.

As the 'copter lifted from the sparse grass of the pasture, Jack thought, This is going to affect all of us, and deeply. It was a strong and acute feeling, an intuition. I don't believe I ever exchanged more than a dozen words with Steiner at any one time, and yet—there is something enormous about the dead. Death itself has such authority. A transformation as awesome as life itself, and so much harder for us to understand.

He turned the 'copter in the direction of the UN headquarters on Mars, on his way to the great self-winding entity of their lives, the unique artificial organism which was their Public School, a place he feared more than any other in his experience away from Home.

Five

WHY was it that the Public School unnerved him? Scrutinizing it from above, he saw the duck-egg-shaped building, white against the dark, blurred surface of the planet, apparently dropped there in haste; it did not fit into its surroundings.

As he parked in the paved lot at the entrance he discovered that the tips of his fingers had whitened and lost feeling, a sign, familiar to him, that he was under tension. And yet this place did not bother David, who was picked up and flown here three days a week, along with other children of his achievement group. Evidently it was some factor in his own personal make-up; perhaps, because his knowledge of machines was so great, he could not accept the illusion of the school, could not play the game. For him, the artifacts of the school were neither inert nor alive; they were in some way both.

Soon he sat in a waiting room, his tool box beside him.

From a magazine rack he took a copy of *Motor World*, and heard, with his trained ears, a switch click. The school had noted his presence. It noted which magazine he selected, how long he sat reading, and what he next took. It measured him.

A door opened, and a middle-aged woman wearing a tweed suit, smiling at him, said, "You must be Mr. Yee's repairman."

"Yes," he said, standing.

"So glad to see you." She beckoned him to follow her. "There's been so much fuss about this one Teacher, but it is at the output stage." Striding down a corridor, she held a door open for him as he caught up. "The Angry Janitor," she said, pointing.

He recognized it from his son's description.

"It broke down suddenly," the woman was saying in his ear. "See? Right in the middle of its cycle—it had gone down the street and shouted and then it was just about to wave its fist."

"Doesn't the master circuit know—"

"I am the master circuit," the middle-aged woman said, smiling at him cheerfully, her steel-rimmed glasses bright with the sparkle in her eyes.

"Of course," he said, chagrined.

"We think it might be this," the woman—or rather this peripatetic extension of the school—said, holding out a folded paper.

Unwadding it, he found a diagrammed congeries of self-regulating feedback valves.

"This is an authority figure, isn't it?" he said. "Teaches the child to respect property. Very righteous type, as the Teachers go."

"Yes," the woman said.

Manually, he reset the Angry Janitor and restarted it. After clicking for a few moments, it turned red in the face, raised its arm and shouted, "You boys keep out of here, you understand?" Watching the whiskery jowls tremble with indignation, the mouth open and shut, Jack Bohlen could imagine the powerful effect it would have on a child. His own reaction was one of dislike. However, this construct was the essence of the successful teaching machine; it did a good job, in conjunction with two dozen other constructs placed, like booths in an amusement park, here and there along the corridors which made up the school. He could see the next teaching machine, just around the corner; several children stood respectfully in front of it as it delivered its harangue.

". . . And then I thought," it was telling them in an affable, informal voice, "my gosh—what is it we folks can learn from an experience like that? Do any of you know? You, Sally."

A small girl's voice: "Um, well, maybe we can learn that there is some good in everybody, no matter how bad they act."

"What do you say, Victor?" the teaching machine bumbled on. "Let's hear from Victor Plank."

A boy stammered, "I'd say about what Sally said, that most people are really good underneath if you take the trouble to really look. Is that right, Mr. Whitlock?"

So Jack was overhearing the Whitlock Teaching Machine. His son had spoken of it many times; it was a favorite of his. As he got out his tools, Jack listened to it. The Whitlock was an elderly, white-haired gentleman, with a regional accent, perhaps that of Kansas. . . . He was kindly, and he let others express themselves; he was a permissive variety of teaching machine, with none of the gruffness and authoritarian manner of the Angry Janitor; he was, in fact, as near as Jack could tell, a combination of Socrates and Dwight D. Eisenhower.

"Sheep are funny," the Whitlock said. "Now, you look at how they behave when you throw some grub over the fence to them, such as corn stalks. Why, they'll spot that from a mile away." The Whitlock chuckled. "They're smart when it comes to what concerns them. And maybe that helps us see what true smartness is; it isn't having read a lot of big books, or knowing long words . . . it's being able to spot what's to our advantage. It's got to be useful to be real smartness."

Kneeling down, Jack began unscrewing the back from the Angry Janitor. The master circuit of the school stood watching.

This machine, he knew, went through its song-and-dance in response to a reel of instruction tape, but its performance was open to modification at each stage, depending on the behavior of its audience. It was not a closed system; it compared the children's answers with its own tape, then matched, classified, and at last responded. There was no room for a unique answer because the Teaching Machine could recognize only a limited number of categories. And yet, it gave a convincing illusion of being alive and viable; it was a triumph of engineering.

Its advantage over a human teacher lay in its capacity to deal with each child individually. It tutored, rather than merely teaching. A teaching machine could handle up to a thousand pupils and yet never confuse one with the next; with each child its responses altered so that it became a subtly different entity. Mechanical, yes—but almost infinitely complex. The teaching machines demonstrated a fact that Jack Bohlen was well aware of: there was an astonishing depth to the so-called "artificial."

And yet he felt repelled by the teaching machines. For the entire Public School was geared to a task which went contrary to his grain: the school was there not to inform or educate, but to mold, and along severely limited lines. It was the link to their inherited culture, and it peddled that culture, in its entirety, to the young. It bent its pupils to it; perpetuation of the culture was the goal, and any special quirks in the children which might lead them in another direction had to be ironed out.

It was a battle, Jack realized, between the composite psyche of the school and the individual psyches of the children, and the former held all the key cards. A child who did not properly respond was assumed to be autistic—that is, oriented according to a subjective factor that took precedence over his sense of objective reality. And that child wound up by being expelled from the school; he went, after that, to another sort of school entirely, one designed to rehabilitate him: he went to Camp Ben-Gurion. He could not be taught; he could only be dealt with as *ill*.

Autism, Jack reflected, as he unscrewed the back of the Angry Janitor, had become a self-serving concept for the authorities who governed Mars. It replaced the older term "psychopath," which in its time had replaced "moral imbecile," which had replaced "criminally insane." And at Camp B-G, the child had a human teacher, or rather *therapist*.

Ever since his own son David had entered the Public School, Jack had waited to hear the bad news, that the boy could not be graded along the scale of achievement by which the teaching machines classified their pupils. However, David had responded heartily to the teaching machines, had in fact scored very high. The boy liked most of his Teachers and came home raving about them; he got along fine with even the most severe of them, and by now it was obvious that he had no problems—he was not autistic, and he would never see the inside of Camp B-G. But this had not made Jack feel better. Nothing, Silvia had pointed out, would make him feel better. Only the two possibilities lay open, the Public School and Camp B-G, and Jack distrusted both. And why was that? He did not know.

Perhaps, he had once conjectured, it was because there really was such a condition as autism. It was a childhood form of schizophrenia, which a lot of people had; schizophrenia was a major illness which touched sooner or later almost every family. It meant, simply, a person who could not live out the drives implanted in him by his society. The reality which the schizophrenic fell away from—or never incorporated in the first place—was the reality of interpersonal living, of life in a given culture with given values; it was not biological life, or any form of inherited life, but *life which was learned*. It had to be picked up bit by bit from those around one, parents and teachers, authority figures in general . . . from everyone a person came in contact with during his formative years.

The Public School, then, was right to eject a child who did not learn. Because what the child was learning was not merely facts or the basis of a money-making or even useful career. It went much deeper. The child learned that certain things in the culture around him were worth preserving at any cost. His values were fused with some objective human enterprise. And so he himself became a part of the tradition handed down to him; he maintained his heritage during his lifetime and even improved on it. He cared. True autism, Jack had decided, was in the last analysis an apathy toward public endeavor; it was a private existence carried on as if the individual person were the creator of all value, rather than merely the repository of inherited values. And Jack Bohlen, for the life of him, could not accept the Public School with its teaching machines as the sole arbiter of what was and what wasn't of value. For the values of a society were in ceaseless flux, and the Public School was an attempt to stabilize those values, to jell them at a fixed point— to embalm them.

The Public School, he had long ago decided, was neurotic. It wanted a world in which nothing new came about, in which there were no surprises. And that was the world of the compulsive-obsessive neurotic; it was not a healthy world at all.

Once, a couple of years ago, he had told his wife his theory. Silvia had listened with a reasonable amount of attention and then she had said, "But you don't see the point, Jack. Try to understand. There are things so much worse than neurosis." Her voice had been low and firm, and he had listened. "We're just beginning to find them out. You know what they are. *You've gone through them.*"

And he had nodded, because he did know what she meant. He himself had had a psychotic interlude, in his early twenties. It was common. It was natural. And, he had to admit, it was horrible. It made the fixed, rigid, compulsive-neurotic Public School seem a reference point by which one could gratefully steer one's course back to mankind and shared reality. It made him comprehend why a neurosis was a deliberate artifact, deliberately constructed by the ailing individual or by a society in crisis. It was an invention arising from necessity.

"Don't knock neurosis," Silvia had said to him and he understood. Neurosis was a deliberate stopping, a freezing somewhere along the path of life. Because beyond lay—

Every schizophrenic knew what lay there. And every ex-schizophrenic, Jack thought, as he remembered his own episode.

The two men across the room from him gazed at him queerly. What had he said? *Herbert Hoover was a much better head of the FBI than Carrington will ever be.* "I know I'm right," he added. "I'll lay you odds." His mind seemed fuzzy, and he sipped at his beer. Everything had become heavy, his arm, and the glass itself; it was easier to look down rather than up. . . . He studied the match folder on the coffee table.

"You don't mean Herbert Hoover," Lou Notting said. "You mean J. Edgar—"

Christ! Jack thought in dismay. Yes, he had said Herbert Hoover, and until they had pointed it out it seemed O.K. What's the matter with me? he wondered. I feel like I'm half asleep. And yet he had gone to bed at ten the night before, had slept almost twelve hours. "Excuse me," he said. "Of course I mean . . ." He felt his tongue stumble. With care he said, "J. Edgar Hoover." But his voice sounded blurred and slowed down, like a turntable losing its momentum. And now it was almost impossible for him to raise his head; he was falling asleep where he sat, there in Notting's living room, and yet his eyes weren't closing—he found when he tried that he couldn't close them. His attention had become riveted on the match folder. Close cover before striking, he read. Can you draw this horse? First art lesson free, no obligation. Turn over for free enrollment blank. Unblinking, he stared on and on, while Lou Notting and Fred Clarke argued about abstract ideas such as the curtailment of liberties, the democratic process . . . he heard all the words perfectly clearly, and he did not mind listening. But he felt no desire to argue, even though he knew they both were wrong. He let them argue on; it was easier. It simply happened. And he let it happen.

"Jack's not with us tonight," Clarke was saying. With a start, Jack Bohlen realized they had turned their attention on him; he had to do or say something, now.

"Sure I am," he said, and it cost him terrific effort; it was like rising up out of the sea. "Go on, I'm listening."

"God, you're like a dummy," Notting said. "Go home and go to bed, for chrissakes."

Entering the living room, Lou's wife Phyllis said, "You'll never get to Mars in the state you're in now, Jack." She turned up the hi-fi; it was a progressive jazz group, vibes and double bass, or perhaps it was an electronic instrument playing. Blonde, pert Phyllis seated herself on the couch near him and studied him. "Jack, are you sore at us? I mean, you're so withdrawn."

"It's just one of his moods," Notting said. "When we were in the service he used to get them, especially on Saturday night. Morose and silent, brooding. What are you brooding about right now, Jack?"

The question seemed odd to him; he was not brooding about anything, his mind was empty. The match folder still filled up his range of perception. Nevertheless, it was necessary that he give them an account of what he was brooding over; they all expected it, so, dutifully, he made up a topic. "The air," he said. "On Mars. How long will it take me to adjust? Varies, among different people." A yawn, which never came out, had lodged in his chest, diffusing throughout his lungs and windpipe. It left his mouth hanging partly open; with an effort he managed to close his jaws. "Guess I better go on," he said. "Hit the sack." With the use of all his strength he managed to get to his feet.

"At nine o'clock?" Fred Clarke yelled.

Later, as he walked home to his own apartment, along the cool dark streets of Oakland, he felt fine. He wondered what had been wrong back there at Notting's. Maybe bad air or the ventilation.

But something was wrong.

Mars, he thought. He had cut the ties, in particular his job, had sold his Plymouth, given notice to the official who was his landlord. And it had taken him a year to get the apartment; the building was owned by the nonprofit West Coast Co-op, an enormous structure partly underground, with thousands of units, its own supermarket, laundries, child-care center, clinic, even its own psychiatrist, down below in the arcade of shops beneath the street level. There was an FM radio station on the top floor which broadcast classical music chosen by the building residents, and in the center of the building could be found a theater and meeting hall. This was the newest of the huge cooperative apartment buildings—and he had given it all up, suddenly. One day he had been in the building's bookstore, waiting in line to buy a book, and the idea came to him.

After he had given notice he had wandered along the corridors of the co-op arcade. When he came to the bulletin board with its tacked-up notices, he had halted automatically to read them. Children scampered past him, on their way to the playground behind the building. One notice, large and printed, attracted his attention.

> HELP SPREAD THE CO-OP MOVEMENT TO NEWLY
> COLONIZED AREAS. EMIGRATION PREPARED BY
> THE CO-OP BOARD IN SACRAMENTO IN ANSWER TO
> BIG BUSINESS AND BIG LABOR UNION EXPLOITATION
> OF MINERAL-RICH AREAS OF MARS. SIGN UP NOW!

It read much like all the co-op notices, and yet—why not? A lot of young people were going. And what was left for him on Earth? He had given up his co-op apartment, but he was still a member; he still had his share of stock and his number.

Later on, when he had signed up and was in the process of being given his physical and his shots, the sequence had blurred in his mind; he remembered the decision to go to Mars *as coming first*, and then the giving up of his job and apartment. It seemed more rational that way, and he told that story to his friends. But it simply wasn't true. What was true? For almost two months he had wandered about, confused and despairing, not certain of anything except that on November 14, his group, two hundred co-op members, would leave for Mars, and then everything would be changed; the confusion would lift and he would see clearly, as he had once at some vague period in the past. He knew that: once, he had been able to establish the order of things in space and time; now, for reasons unknown to him, both space and time had shifted so that he could not find his bearings in either one.

His life had no purpose. For fourteen months he had lived with one massive goal: to acquire an apartment in the huge new co-op building, and then, when he had gotten it, there was nothing. The future had ceased to exist. He listened to the Bach suites which he requested; he bought food at the supermarket and browsed in the building bookstore . . . but what for? he asked himself. Who am I? And at his job, his ability faded away. That was the first indication, and in some ways the most ominous of all; that was what had first frightened him.

It began with a weird incident which he was never able fully to account for. Apparently, part of it had been pure hallucination. But which part? It had been dreamlike, and he had had a moment of overwhelming panic, the desire to run, to get out at any cost.

His job was with an electronics firm in Redwood City, south of San Francisco; he operated a machine which maintained quality control along the assembly line. It was his responsibility to see that his machine did not deviate from its concept of acceptable tolerances in a single component: a liquid-helium battery no larger than a match-head. One day he was summoned to the personnel manager's office, unexpectedly; he did not know why they wanted him, and as he took the elevator up he was quite nervous. Later, he remembered that; he was unusually nervous.

"Come in, Mr. Bohlen." The personnel manager, a fine-looking man with curly gray hair—perhaps a fashion wig—welcomed him into his office. "This won't take but a moment." He eyed Jack keenly. "Mr. Bohlen, why aren't you cashing your paychecks?"

There was silence.

"Aren't I?" Jack said. His heart thudded ponderously, making his body shake. He felt unsteady and tired. I thought I was, he said to himself.

"You could stand a new suit," the personnel manager said, "and you need a haircut. Of course, it's your business."

Putting his hand to his scalp, Jack felt about, puzzled; did he need a haircut? Hadn't he just had one last week? Or maybe it was longer ago than that. He said, "Thanks." He nodded. "O.K., I will. What you just said."

And then the hallucination, if it was that, happened. He saw the personnel manager in a new light. The man was dead.

He saw, through the man's skin, his skeleton. It had been

wired together, the bones connected with fine copper wire. The organs, which had withered away, were replaced by artificial components, kidney, heart, lungs—everything was made of plastic and stainless steel, all working in unison but entirely without authentic life. The man's voice issued from a tape, through an amplifier and speaker system.

Possibly at some time in the past the man had been real and alive, but that was over, and the stealthy replacement had taken place, inch by inch, progressing insidiously from one organ to the next, and the entire structure was there to deceive others. To deceive him, Jack Bohlen, in fact. He was alone in this office; there was no personnel manager. No one spoke to him, and when he himself talked, no one heard; it was entirely a lifeless, mechanical room in which he stood.

He was not sure what to do; he tried not to stare too hard at the manlike structure before him. He tried to talk calmly, naturally, about his job and even his personal problems. The structure was probing; it wanted to learn something from him. Naturally, he told it as little as possible. And all the time, as he gazed down at the carpet, he saw its pipes and valves and working parts functioning away; he could not keep from seeing.

All he wanted to do was get away as soon as possible. He began to sweat; he was dripping with sweat and trembling, and his heart pounded louder and louder.

"Bohlen," the structure said, "are you sick?"

"Yes," he said. "Can I go back down to my bench now?" He turned and started toward the door.

"Just a moment," the structure said from behind him.

That was when panic overtook him, and he ran; he pulled the door open and ran out into the hall.

An hour or so later he found himself wandering along an unfamiliar street in Burlingame. He did not remember the intervening time and he did not know how he had gotten where he was. His legs ached. Evidently he had walked, mile after mile.

His head was much clearer. I'm schizophrenic, he said to himself. I know it. Everyone knows the symptoms; it's catatonic excitement with paranoid coloring: the mental health people drill it into us, even into the school kids. I'm another one of those. That was what the personnel manager was probing.

I need medical help.

*

As Jack removed the power supply of the Angry Janitor and laid it on the floor, the master circuit of the school said, "You are very skillful."

Jack glanced up at the middle-aged female figure and thought to himself, It's obvious why this place unnerves me. It's like my psychotic experience of years ago. *Did I, at that time, look into the future?*

There had been no schools of this kind, then. Or if there had, he had not seen them or known about them.

"Thank you," he said.

What had tormented him ever since the psychotic episode with the personnel manager at Corona Corporation was this: suppose it was not a hallucination? Suppose the so-called personnel manager was as he had seen him, an artificial construct, a machine like these teaching machines?

If that had been the case, *then there was no psychosis.*

Instead of a psychosis, he had thought again and again, it was more on the order of a vision, a glimpse of absolute reality, with the façade stripped away. And it was so crushing, so radical an idea, that it could not be meshed with his ordinary views. And the mental disturbance had come out of that.

Reaching into the exposed wiring of the Angry Janitor, Jack felt expertly with his long fingers until at last he touched what he knew to be there: a broken lead. "I think I've got hold of it," he said to the master circuit of the school. Thank God, he thought, these aren't the old-fashioned printed circuits; were that the case, he would have to replace the unit. Repair would be impossible.

"My understanding," the master circuit said, "is that much effort went into the designing of the Teachers re problems of repair. We have been fortunate so far; no prolonged interruption of service has taken place. However, I believe that preventive maintenance is indicated wherever possible; therefore I would like you to inspect one additional Teacher which has as yet shown no signs of a breakdown. It is uniquely vital to the total functioning of the school." The master circuit paused politely as Jack struggled to get the long tip of the soldering gun past the layers of wiring. "It is Kindly Dad which I want you to inspect."

Jack said, "Kindly Dad." And he thought acidly, I wonder if there's an Aunt Mom in here somewhere. Aunt Mom's delicious home-baked tall tales for little tots to imbibe. He felt nauseated.

"You are familiar with that Teacher?"

As a matter of fact he was not; David hadn't mentioned it.

From farther down the corridor he could hear the children still discussing life with the Whitlock; their voices reached him as he lay on his back, holding the soldering gun above his head and reaching into the works of the Angry Janitor to keep the tip in place.

"Yes," the Whitlock was saying in its never-ruffled, absolutely placid voice, "the raccoon is an amazing fellow, ol' Jimmy Raccoon is. Many times I've seen him. And he's quite a large fellow, by the way, with powerful, long arms which are really quite agile."

"I saw a raccoon once," a child piped excitedly. "Mr. Whitlock, I saw one, and he was this close to me!"

Jack thought, You saw a raccoon on Mars?

The Whitlock chuckled. "No, Don, I'm afraid not. There aren't any raccoons around here. You'd have to go all the way across over to old mother Earth to see one of those amazing fellows. But the point I'd like to make is this, boys and girls. You know how ol' Jimmy Raccoon takes his food, and carries it oh so stealthily to the water, and washes it? And how we laughed at ol' Jimmy when the lump of sugar dissolved and he had nothing at all left to eat? Well, boys and girls, do you know that we've got Jimmy Raccoons right here in this very—"

"I think I'm finished," Jack said, withdrawing the gun. "Do you want to help me put this back together?"

The master circuit said, "Are you in a rush?"

"I don't like that thing talking away in there," Jack said. It made him tense and shaky, so much so that he could hardly do his work.

A door rolled shut, down the corridor from them; the sound of the Whitlock's voice ceased. "Is that better?" the master circuit asked.

"Thanks," Jack said. But his hands were still shaking. The master circuit noted that; he was aware of her precise scrutiny. He wondered what she made of it.

*

The chamber in which Kindly Dad sat consisted of one end of a living room with fireplace, couch, coffee table, curtained picture window, and an easy chair in which Kindly Dad himself sat, a newspaper open on his lap. Several children sat attentively on the couch as Jack Bohlen and the master circuit entered; they were listening to the expostulations of the teaching machine and did not seem aware that anyone had come in. The master circuit dismissed the children, and then she started to leave, too.

"I'm not sure what you want me to do," Jack said.

"Put it through its cycle. It seems to me that it repeats portions of the cycle or stays stuck; in any case, too much time is consumed. It should return to its starting stage in about three hours." A door opened for the master circuit, and she was gone; he was alone with Kindly Dad and he was not glad of it.

"Hi, Kindly Dad," he said without enthusiasm. Setting down his tool case he began unscrewing the back plate of the Teacher.

Kindly Dad said in a warm, sympathetic voice, "What's your name, young fellow?"

"My name," Jack said, as he unfastened the plate and laid it down beside him, "is Jack Bohlen, and I'm a kindly dad, too, just like you, Kindly Dad. My boy is ten years old, Kindly Dad. So don't call me young fellow, O.K.?" Again he was trembling hard, and sweating.

"Ohh," Kindly Dad said. "I see!"

"What do you see?" Jack said, and discovered that he was almost shouting. "Look," he said. "Go through your goddamn cycle, O.K.? If it makes it easier for you, go ahead and pretend I'm a little boy." I just want to get this done and get out of here, he said to himself, with as little trouble as possible. He could feel the swelling, complicated emotions inside him. Three hours! he thought dismally.

Kindly Dad said, "Little Jackie, it seems to me you've got a mighty heavy weight on your chest today. Am I right?"

"Today and every day." Jack clicked on his trouble-light and shone it up into the works of the Teacher. The mechanism seemed to be moving along its cycle properly so far.

"Maybe I can help you," Kindly Dad said. "Often it helps if

an older, more experienced person can sort of listen in on your troubles, can sort of share them and make them lighter."

"O.K.," Jack agreed, sitting back on his haunches. "I'll play along; I'm stuck here for three hours anyhow. You want me to go all the way back to the beginning? To the episode back on Earth when I worked for Corona Corporation and had the occlusion?"

"Start wherever you like," Kindly Dad said graciously.

"Do you know what schizophrenia is, Kindly Dad?"

"I believe I've got a pretty good idea, Jackie," Kindly Dad said.

"Well, Kindly Dad, it's the most mysterious malady in all medicine, that's what it is. And it shows up in one out of every six people, which is a lot of people."

"Yes, that certainly is," Kindly Dad said.

"At one time," Jack said, as he watched the machinery moving, "I had what they call situational polymorphous schizophrenia simplex. And, Kindly Dad, it was rough."

"I just bet it was," Kindly Dad said.

"Now, I know what you're supposed to be for," Jack said, "I know your purpose, Kindly Dad. We're a long way from Home. Millions of miles away. Our connection with our civilization back Home is tenuous. And a lot of folks are mighty scared, Kindly Dad, because with each passing year that link gets weaker. So this Public School was set up to present a fixed milieu to the children born here, an Earthlike environment. For instance, this fireplace. We don't have fireplaces here on Mars; we heat by small atomic furnaces. That picture window with all that glass—sandstorms would make it opaque. In fact there's not one thing about you that's derived from our actual world here. Do you know what a Bleekman is, Kindly Dad?"

"Can't say that I do, Little Jackie. What is a Bleekman?"

"It's one of the indigenous races of Mars. You do know you're on Mars, don't you?"

Kindly Dad nodded.

"Schizophrenia," Jack said, "is one of the most pressing problems human civilization has ever faced. Frankly, Kindly Dad, I emigrated to Mars because of my schizophrenic episode when I was twenty-two and worked for Corona Corporation. I was cracking up. I had to move out of a complex urban environment and into a simpler one, a primitive frontier environment with more freedom. The pressure was too great for me; it was emigrate or go mad. That co-op building; can you imagine a thing going down level after level and up like a skyscraper, with enough people living there for them to have their own supermarket? I went mad standing in line at the bookstore. Everybody else, Kindly Dad, every single person in that bookstore and in that supermarket—all of them lived in the same building I did. It was a society, Kindly Dad, that one building. And today it's small by comparison with some that have been built. What do you say to that?"

"My, my," Kindly Dad said, shaking his head.

"Now here's what I think," Jack said. "I think this Public School and you teaching machines are going to rear another generation of schizophrenics, the descendents of people like me who are making a fine adaptation to this new planet. You're going to split the psyches of these children because you're teaching them to expect an environment which doesn't exist for them. It doesn't even exist back on Earth, now; it's obsolete. Ask that Whitlock Teacher if intelligence doesn't have to be practical to be true intelligence. I heard it say so, it has to be a tool for adaptation. Right, Kindly Dad?"

"Yes, Little Jackie, it has to be."

"What you ought to be teaching," Jack said, "is, how do we—"

"Yes, Little Jackie," Kindly Dad interrupted him, "it has to be." And as it said this, a gear-tooth slipped in the glare of Jack's trouble-light, and a phase of the cycle repeated itself.

"You're stuck," Jack said. "Kindly Dad, you've got a worn gear-tooth."

"Yes, Little Jackie," Kindly Dad said, "it has to be."

"You're right," Jack said. "It does have to be. Everything wears out eventually; nothing is permanent. Change is the one constant of life. Right, Kindly Dad?"

"Yes, Little Jackie," Kindly Dad said, "it has to be."

Shutting off the teaching machine at its power supply, Jack began to disassemble its main-shaft, preparatory to removing the worn gear.

"So you found it," the master circuit said, when Jack emerged a half hour later, wiping his face with his sleeve.

"Yes," he said. He was exhausted. His wrist watch told him that it was only four o'clock; an hour more of work lay ahead of him.

The master circuit accompanied him to the parking lot. "I am quite pleased with the promptness with which you attended to our needs," she said. "I will telephone Mr. Yee and thank him."

He nodded and climbed into his 'copter, too worn out even to say goodbye. Soon he was ascending; the duck egg which was the UN-operated Public School became small and far away below him. Its stifling presence vanished, and he could breathe again.

Flipping on his transmitter he said, "Mr. Yee. This is Jack; I'm done at the school. What next?"

After a pause Mr. Yee's pragmatic voice answered. "Jack, Mr. Arnie Kott at Lewistown called us. He requested that we service an encoding dictation machine in which he places great trust. Since all others of our crew are tied up, I am sending you."

Six

ARNIE KOTT owned the only harpsichord on Mars. However, it was out of tune, and he could find no one to service it. No matter which way you cut it, there were no harpsichord tuners on Mars.

For a month now he had been training his tame Bleekman to tackle this task; Bleekmen had a fine ear for music, and his particular one seemed to understand what Arnie wanted. Heliogabalus had been provided with a translation into the Bleeky dialect of a manual on keyboard instrument maintenance, and Arnie expected results any day now. But meanwhile the harpsichord was virtually unplayable.

Back in Lewistown from his visit to Anne Esterhazy, Arnie Kott felt glum. The death of the black-market goodies man, Norbert Steiner, was a solid blow below the belt, and Arnie knew that he would have to make a move, probably a drastic and unprecedented one, to compensate for it. It was now three o'clock in the afternoon. What had he gotten out of his trip to New Israel? Only a piece of bad news. Anne, as usual, could not be talked into anything; she intended to go right on with her amateurish campaigns and causes, and if she were the laughingstock of Mars it did not matter to her.

"Goddamn you, Heliogabalus," Arnie said with fury, "you get that goddamn instrument playing right or I'm kicking you out of Lewistown. You can go back to eating beetles and roots in the desert with the rest of your kind."

Seated on the floor beside the harpsichord, the Bleekman winced, glanced up acutely at Arnie Kott, then lowered his eyes to the manual once more.

"Nothing ever gets fixed around here," Arnie grumbled.

All Mars, he decided, was a sort of Humpty Dumpty; the original state had been one of perfection, and they and their property had all fallen from that state into rusty bits and useless debris. He felt sometimes as if he presided over an enormous junkyard. And then, once more, he thought about the Yee Company repair 'copter which he had run into in the desert, and the zwepp piloting it. Independent bastards, Arnie said to himself. Ought to be taken down a peg or two. But they knew their worth. Vital to the economy of the planet; it was written on their faces. We bow to no man, etcetera. Arnie paced about the big front room of the Lewistown house which he maintained in addition to his apartment at Union Hall, hands in his pockets, scowling.

Imagine: that guy talked back to me just like that, Arnie reflected. He must be a hell of a good repairman to be so confident.

And Arnie also thought, I'm going to get that guy if it's the last thing I do. Nobody talks to me like that and gets away with it.

But of the two thoughts about the Yee Company uppity repairman, the former slowly began to dominate his mind, because he was a practical man and he knew that things had to be kept running. Codes of conduct had to come second. We're not running a medieval society here, Arnie said to himself. If the guy's really good he can say what he wants to me; all I care about is results.

With that in mind, he telephoned the Yee Company at Bunchewood Park, and soon had Mr. Yee himself on the line.

"Listen," Arnie said, "I got a sick encoder over here, and if you fellows can get it working maybe I can use you on a permanent contract basis; you follow me?"

There was no doubt of it; Mr. Yee followed him, all right. He saw the entire picture. "Our best man, sir. Right away. And I know we'll give absolute satisfaction, any hour of the day or night."

"I want one particular man," Arnie said, and he thereupon described the repairman he had met in the desert.

"Young, dark-haired, slender," Mr. Yee repeated. "Glasses, and with a nervous manner. That would be Mr. Jack Bohlen. Our finest."

"Let me tell you," Arnie said, "that this Bohlen guy talked to me in a way I don't let nobody talk to me, but after I thought it over I realized he was in the right, and when I see him I'm going to tell him that to his face." However, in actuality Arnie Kott no longer could recall what the issue had been. "That guy Bohlen seems to have a good head on him," he wound up. "Can he get over here today?"

Without hesitation Mr. Yee promised service by five o'clock.

"I appreciate that," Arnie said. "And be sure and tell him that Arnie holds no grudges. Sure, I was taken aback at the time; but that's all over. Tell him—" He pondered. "Tell Bohlen he's got absolutely nothing to worry about regarding me." He rang off, then, and sat back with a feeling of grim, honest accomplishment.

So the day after all wasn't a total waste. And, too, he had gotten an interesting bit of information from Anne, while over at New Israel. He had brought up the topic of the rumored goings-on in the F.D.R. Mountains, and as usual Anne knew a few inside yarns emanating from Home, accounts no doubt garbled in the chain of oral tellings . . . yet the nugget of veracity was there. The UN back Home was in the process of staging one of its periodic coups. It was going to descend on the F.D.R. Mountains in another couple of weeks and lay claim to them as public domain land belonging to no one—which was palpably true. But why was it that the UN wanted a big hunk of worthless real estate? There, Anne's tale got perplexing. One story noised about back at Geneva was that the UN intended to build an enormous supernational park, a sort of Garden of Eden, to lure emigrants out of Earth. Another had it that the UN engineers were going to make a vast final attack on the problem of beefing up the power sources on Mars; they were going to set up a huge hydrogen atomic energy power plant, unique in both size and scope. The water system would be revitalized. And, with adequate sources of power, heavy industry could at last move over to Mars, taking advantage of free land, light gravity, low taxation.

And then another rumor had it that the UN was going to set up a military base in the F.D.R. Mountains to offset United States and Soviet plans along the same general lines.

Whichever rumor was true, one fact stuck out: certain parcels of land in the F.D.R. range were going to be acutely valuable, pretty soon. The entire range was up for sale right now, in pieces varying from half an acre to a hundred thousand acres, and at a staggeringly low price. Once speculators got wind of the UN's plans, this would change . . . no doubt the speculators were already beginning to act. To claim land on Mars they had to be on the spot; it could not be done from

Home—that was the law. So one could expect the speculators to start coming over any time now, if Anne's rumors were correct. It would be like the first year of colonization, when speculators were active everywhere.

Seating himself at his out-of-tune harpsichord, Arnie opened a book of Scarlatti sonatas and began to bang away at one of his favorites, a cross-hand one on which he had been practicing for months. It was strong, rhythmic, vigorous music, and he pounded the keys with delight, ignoring the distorted sound itself. Heliogabalus moved further off to study his manual; the sound hurt his ears.

"I've got a long-playing record of this," he said to Heliogabalus as he played. "So goddamn old and valuable that I don't dare play it."

"What is a long-playing record?" the Bleekman asked.

"You wouldn't understand if I told you. Glenn Gould playing. It's forty years old; my family passed it down to me. It was my mother's. That guy could really hammer these cross-hand sonatas out." His own playing discouraged him, and he gave up. I could never be any good, he decided, even if this instrument were in peak condition like it was before I had it shipped here from Home.

Seated on the bench but not playing, Arnie ruminated once more on the golden opportunities involved in the F.D.R. Mountains land. I could buy in any time, he thought, with Union funds. But *where*? It's a big range; I can't buy it *all*.

Who knows that range? he asked himself. That Steiner probably did, because as I understand it his base of operations is—or rather was—someplace near there. And there are prospectors coming and going. And Bleekmen live there, too.

"Helio," he said, "do you know the F.D.R. range?"

"Mister, I do know them," the Bleekman said. "I shun them. They are cold and empty and have no life."

"Is it true," Arnie said, "that you Bleekmen have an oracular rock that you go to when you want to know the future?"

"Yes, Mister. The uncivilized Bleekmen have that. But it is vain superstition. Dirty Knobby, the rock is called."

"You never consult it, yourself."

"No, Mister."

"Could you find that rock, if necessary?"

"Yes, Mister."

"I'll give you a dollar," Arnie said, "if you take a question to your goddamn Dirty Knobby rock for me."

"Thank you, Mister, but I cannot do it."

"Why not, Helio?"

"It would proclaim my ignorance, to consult with such fraudulency."

"Christ," Arnie said, disgusted. "Just as a game—can't you do that? For a joke."

The Bleekman said nothing, but his dark face was tight with resentment. He pretended to resume his reading of the manual.

"You fellows were stupid to give up your native religion," Arnie said. "You showed how weak you are. I wouldn't have. Tell me how to find Dirty Knobby and I'll ask it myself. I know goddamn well that your religion teaches that you can foretell the future, and what's so peculiar about that? We've got extrasensory individuals back Home, and some of them have precognition, can read the future. Of course we have to lock them up with the other nuts, because that's a symptom of schizophrenia, if you happen to know what that means."

"Yes, Mister," Heliogabalus said. "I know schizophrenia; it is the savage within the man."

"Sure, it's the reversion to primitive ways of thought, but so what, if you can read the future? In those mental health camps back Home there must be hundreds of precogs—" And then a thought struck Arnie Kott. Maybe there're a couple here on Mars, at Camp B-G.

The hell with Dirty Knobby rock, then, Arnie thought. I'll drop by B-G one day before they close it and get me a precog nut; I'll bail him out of the camp and put him on the payroll, right here in Lewistown.

Going to his telephone, he called the Union steward, Edward L. Goggins. "Eddy," he said, when he had hold of the steward, "you trot over to our psychiatric clinic and collar those doctors, and you bring back a description of what a precog nut is like, I mean, what symptoms, and if they know one at Camp B-G we could nab."

"O.K., Arnie. Will do."

"Who's the best psychiatrist on Mars, Eddy?"

"Gosh, Arnie, I'd have to check into it. The Truckers have a good one, Milton Glaub. Reason I know that is, my wife's brother is a Trucker and got analysis from Glaub last year, plus naturally effective representation."

"I suppose this Glaub knows B-G pretty good."

"Oh, yeah, Arnie; he's over there once a week, they all take turns. The Jews pay pretty good, they've got so much dough to spend. They get the dough from Israel back on Earth, you know."

"Well, get hold of this Glaub and tell him to rustle up a pre-cog schizophrenic for me as soon as possible. Put Glaub on the payroll, but only if you have to; most of those psychiatrists are aching for regular money, they see so little of it. Understand, Eddy?"

"Right, Arnie." The steward rang off.

"You ever been psychoanalyzed, Helio?" Arnie said to him, feeling cheerful, now.

"No, Mister. Entire psychoanalysis is a vainglorious foolishness."

"How zat, Helio?"

"Question they never deal with is, what to remold sick person like. There is no what, Mister."

"I don't get you, Helio."

"Purpose of life is unknown, and hence way to be is hidden from the eyes of living critters. Who can say if perhaps the schizophrenics are not correct? Mister, they take a brave journey. They turn away from mere things, which one may handle and turn to practical use; they turn inward to *meaning*. There, the black-night-without-bottom lies, the pit. Who can say if they will return? And if so, what will they be like, having glimpsed meaning? I admire them."

"Kee-rist," Arnie said, with derision, "you half-educated freak— I'll bet if human civilization disappeared from Mars you'd be right back there among those savages in ten seconds flat, worshipping idols and all the rest of it. Why do you pretend you want to be like us? Why are you reading that manual?"

Heliogabalus said, "Human civilization will never leave Mars, Mister; that is why I study this book."

"Out of that book," Arnie said, "you better be able to tune

up my goddamn harpsichord, or you will be back in the desert, whether human civilization stays on Mars or not."

"Yes sir," his tame Bleekman said.

Ever since he had lost his union card and could not then legally perform his job, Otto Zitte's life had been a continual mess. With a card he would be by now a first-class repairman. It was his secret that he had once held such a card and had managed to lose it; even his employer, Norb Steiner, did not know it. For reasons he himself did not understand, Otto preferred others to believe he had simply failed the aptitude tests. Perhaps it was easier to think of himself as a failure; after all, the repair business was almost impossible to get into . . . and after having gotten into it, to be booted out—

It was his own fault. There he had been, three years ago, a paid-up member of the union in good standing, in other words a bona fide Goodmember. The future was wide open for him; he was young, he had a girl friend and his own 'copter —the latter, leased; the former, although he had not known it at the time, shared—and what could hold him back? What, except possibly his own stupidity.

He had broken a union ruling which was a basic law. In his opinion it was a foolish ruling, but nonetheless . . . vengeance is mine, sayeth the Extraterrestrial Repairmen's Union, Martian Branch. Wow, how he hated the bastards; his hatred had warped his life and he recognized that—and he did nothing about it: he wanted it to warp him. He wanted to keep on hating them, the vast monolithic structure, wherever it existed.

They had caught him for giving socialized repair.

And the hell of it was that it wasn't actually socialized, because he expected to get back a profit. It was just a new way of charging his customers, and in a sense not so new, anyhow. It was actually the oldest way in the world, a barter system. But his revenue could not be divvied up so that the union got its cut. His trade had been with certain housewives living out in remote tracts, very lonely women whose husbands stayed in the city five days a week, coming home only on weekends. Otto, who was good-looking, slender, with long, combed-back black hair (in his account of himself, anyhow), had made time with one woman after another; and an outraged husband, on finding out, had, instead of shooting Otto to death, gone instead to the Union Hiring Hall and lodged a formal charge: repairs without compensation at scale.

Well, it certainly was not scale; he admitted that.

And so now this job with Norb Steiner, which meant that he had practically to live in the wastelands of the F.D.R. Mountains, alienated from society for weeks on end, growing more and more lonely, more embittered all the time. It had been his need for intimate personal contact that had gotten him into trouble in the first place, and now look at him. As he sat in the storage shed waiting for the next rocket to show up, he looked back on his life and reflected that even the Bleekmen wouldn't be willing or able to live as he lived, cut off from everyone like this. If only his own black-market operations had succeeded! He, like Norb Steiner, had been able to swing around the planet daily, visiting one person after another. Was it his fault that the items he chose to import were hot enough to interest the big boys? His judgment had been too good; his line had sold too well.

He hated the big racketeers, too, same as he hated the big unions. He hated bigness per se; bigness had destroyed the American system of free enterprise, the small businessman had been ruined—in fact, he himself had been perhaps the last authentic small businessman in the solar system. That was his real crime; he had tried to live the American way of life, instead of just talking about it.

"Screw them," he said to himself, seated on a crate, surrounded by boxes and cartons and packages and the workings of several dismantled rocketships which he had been revamping. Outside the shed window . . . silent, desolate rock hills, with only a few shrubs, dried up and dying, as far as the eye could see.

And where was Norb Steiner right now? No doubt ensconced in some bar or restaurant or some woman's cheery living room, prattling his line, handing over tins of smoked salmon and getting in return—

"Screw them all," Otto mumbled, getting up to pace back

and forth. "If that's what they want, let 'em have it. Bunch of animals."

Those Israeli girls . . . that's where Steiner was, with a kibbutzful of them, those hot, black-eyed, heavy-lipped, big-breasted, sexy ones who got tanned working out in the fields in shorts and cotton shirts clinging to them, no bras, just those big solid breasts—you could actually see their nipples, because the damp fabric stuck to them.

That's why he wouldn't let me go with him, Otto decided.

The only women he ever saw out here in the F.D.R. range were those stunted, black, dried-out Bleekman women, not even human, at least not to him. He wasn't taken in by those anthropologists saying that the Bleekmen were from the same stock as homo sapiens, that probably both planets were colonized a million years ago from one interplanetary race. Those toads, human? Sleep with one of those? Christ, better to chop it off, first.

As a matter of fact, here came a party of Bleekmen right now, stepping gingerly with bare feet down the irregular rock surface of a northern hill. On their way here, Otto observed. As usual.

He opened the door of the shed, waiting until they had reached him. Four bucks, two of them elderly, one elderly woman, several skinny kids, carrying their bows, their pounding blocks, their paka eggshells.

Halting, they regarded him silently, and then one of the bucks said, "Rains are falling from me onto your valuable person."

"Likewise," Otto said, leaning against the shed and feeling dull, weighed down with hopelessness. "What do you want?"

The Bleekman buck held out a small bit of paper, and Otto, taking it, saw that it was a label from a can of turtle soup. The Bleekmen had eaten the soup, retaining the label for this purpose; they could not tell him what they wanted because they did not know what it was called.

"O.K.," he said. "How many?" He held up fingers. At five they nodded. Five cans. "Whatcha got?" Otto demanded, not stirring.

One of the young Bleekman women stepped forward and

pointed to that part of herself which had been so much in Otto's thoughts for so long.

"Oh Christ," Otto said in despair. "No, go on. Beat it. Not any more; I don't want any more." He turned his back on them, made his way into the storage shed and slammed the door so hard that the shed walls trembled; he threw himself down on a packing crate, his head in his hands. "I'm going crazy," he said to himself, his jaw stiff, his tongue swelling up so that he could hardly talk. His chest ached. And then, to his amazement, he began to cry. Jesus, he thought in fright, I really am going crazy; I'm breaking down. Why? Tears rolled down his cheeks. He hadn't cried in years. What's this all about? he wondered. His mind had no concept in it; it was only his body bawling away, and he was a spectator to it.

But it brought him relief. With his handkerchief he wiped his eyes, his face, and cursed as he saw that his hands were clawlike with rigidity, the fingers writhing.

Outside the window of the shed the Bleekmen remained, perhaps seeing him; he could not tell. Their faces showed no expression, but he felt sure they must have seen, and probably were as perplexed as he. It sure is a mystery, he thought. I agree with you.

The Bleekmen gathered together in a huddle and conferred, and then one of them detached himself from the group and approached the shed. Otto heard a rap on the door. Going over to it and opening it, he found the young Bleekman standing there holding out something.

"This, then," the young Bleekman said.

Otto took it, but for the life of him he could not make out what it was. It had glass and metal to it, and calibrations. And then he realized that it was an instrument used in surveying. On its side was stamped: UN PROPERTY.

"I don't want it," he said irritably, turning it over and over. The Bleekmen must have stolen it, he realized. He handed it back; the young buck accepted it stoically and returned to his group. Otto shut the door.

This time they went off; he watched them through the window as they trailed away up the side of the hill. Steal you blind, he said to himself. Anyhow, what was a UN survey company doing in the F.D.R. range?

To cheer himself up he rummaged around until he found a can of smoked frogs' legs; opening it, he sat eating morosely, not getting from the dainty anything at all, and yet methodically finishing the can.

Into the microphone Jack Bohlen said, "Don't send me, Mr. Yee—I already ran into Kott today and offended him." Weariness settled over him. Naturally I ran into Kott, for the first time in my life, and naturally I insulted him, he thought to himself. And just as naturally, because that's how my life works, it's the same day that Arnie Kott decides to call up Yee Company and ask for service. It's typical of the little game I play with the powerful, inanimate forces of life.

"Mr. Kott mentioned meeting you on the desert," Mr. Yee said. "In fact, his decision to call us was based on that meeting."

"The hell you say." He was dumbfounded.

"I do not know what the issue was, Jack, but no harm has been done. Direct your ship to Lewistown. If you run over beyond five o'clock you will be paid time and a half. And Mr. Kott, who is known as a generous man, is so anxious to have his encoder working that he promises to see that you receive a bountiful meal."

"All right," Jack said. It was too much for him to dope out. After all, he knew nothing of what went on in Arnie Kott's mind.

Not long thereafter, he was lowering his 'copter to the roof parking lot of the Water Workers' Union Hall at Lewistown.

A slavey sauntered out and regarded him suspiciously.

"Yee Company repairman," Jack said. "Call put in by Arnie Kott."

"O.K., buddy," the slavey said, and led him to the elevator.

He found Arnie Kott in a well-furnished, Earth-type living room; the big, bald-headed man was on the telephone, and he nodded his head at Jack's appearance. The nod indicated the desk, on which a portable encoding dictation machine sat. Jack walked over to it, removed the lid, turned it on. Meanwhile, Arnie Kott continued his phone conversation.

"Sure I know it's a tricky talent. Sure, there's a good reason why nobody's been able to make use of it—but what am I supposed to do, give up and pretend it don't exist just because people have been too damn dumb for fifty thousand years to take it seriously? I still want to try it." A long pause. "O.K., Doctor. Thanks." Arnie hung up. To Jack he said, "You ever been to Camp B-G?"

"No," Jack said. He was busy opening up the encoder.

Arnie strolled over and stood beside him. As he worked, Jack could feel the astute gaze fixed on him; it made him nervous, but there was nothing he could do except try to ignore the man and go on. A little like the master circuit, he thought to himself. And then he wondered, as he often did, if he was going to have another one of his spells; true, it had been a long time, but here was a powerful figure looming close to him, scrutinizing him, and it did feel somewhat like that old interview with Corona's personnel manager.

"That was Glaub on the phone," Arnie Kott said. "The psychiatrist. You ever heard of him?"

"No," Jack said.

"What do you do, live your life entirely with your head stuck in the back of machines?"

Jack looked up, met the man's gaze. "I've got a wife and son. That's my life. What I'm doing right now is a means of keeping my family going." He spoke calmly. Arnie did not seem to take offense; he even smiled.

"Something to drink?" Arnie asked.

"Coffee, if you have it."

"I've got authentic Home coffee," Arnie said. "Black?"

"Black."

"Yeah, you look like a black coffee man. You think you can fix that machine right here and now, or are you going to have to take it with you?"

"I can fix it here."

Arnie beamed. "That's swell! I really depend on that machine."

"Where's the coffee?"

Turning, Arnie went off dutifully; he rustled about in another room and then returned with a ceramic coffee mug, which he set down on the desk near Jack. "Listen, Bohlen. I have a person coming here any minute now. A girl. It won't interfere with your work, will it?"

Jack glanced up, supposing the man was being sarcastic. But

evidently not; Arnie was eyeing him and then the partly disassembled machine, obviously concerned with how the repair was progressing. He certainly is dependent on this, Jack decided. Strange, how people cling to their possessions, as if they're extensions of their bodies, a sort of hypochondria of the machine. You'd think a man like Arnie Kott could scrap this encoder and shell out the money for a new one.

There sounded a knock on the door, and Arnie hurried to open it. "Oh, hi." His voice came to Jack. "Come on in. Hey, I'm getting my doodad fixed."

A girl's voice said, "Arnie, you'll never get your doodad fixed."

Arnie laughed nervously. "Hey, meet my new repairman, Jack Bohlen. Bohlen, this is Doreen Anderton, our Union treasurer."

"Hi," Jack said. Out of the corner of his eye—he did not stop working—he could see that she had red hair and extremely white skin and large, wonderful eyes. Everybody's on the payroll, he thought tartly. What a great world. What a great union you've got going here for yourself, Arnie.

"Busy, isn't he?" the girl said.

"Oh, yeah," Arnie agreed, "these repair guys are bugs on getting the job done right, I mean these outside guys, not our own—ours are a bunch of slobs that sit around playing with themselves at our expense. I'm through with them, Dor. I mean, this guy Bohlen is a whiz; he's going to have the encoder working any minute now, aren't you, Jack?"

"Yeah," Jack said.

The girl said, "Don't you say hello, Jack?"

Halting his work he turned his attention on her; he faced her levelly. Her expression was cool and intelligent, with a faintly mocking quality which was peculiarly rewarding and annoying. "Hello," Jack said.

"I saw your 'copter on the roof," the girl said.

"Let him work," Arnie said peevishly. "Gimme your coat." He stood behind her, helping her out of her coat. The girl wore a dark wool suit, obviously an import from Earth and therefore expensive to an appalling degree. I'll bet that set the Union pension fund back plenty, Jack decided.

Observing the girl, he saw in her a vindication of a piece of old wisdom. Nice eyes, hair, and skin produced a pretty woman, but a truly excellent nose created a beautiful woman. This girl had such a nose: strong, straight, dominating her features, forming a basis for her other features. Mediterranean women reach the level of beauty much more easily than, say, Irish or English women, he realized, because genetically speaking the Mediterranean nose, whether Spanish or Hebrew or Turkish or Italian, played a naturally greater part in physiognomic organization. His own wife Silvia had a gay, turned-up Irish nose; she was pretty enough by any standard. But—there was a difference.

He guessed that Doreen was in her early thirties. And yet she possessed a freshness that gave her a stable quality. He had seen such clear coloration in high-school girls approaching nubility, and once in a long while one saw it in fifty-year-old women who had perfect gray hair and wide, lovely eyes. This girl would still be attractive twenty years from now, and probably had always been so; he could not imagine her any other way. Arnie, by investing in her, had perhaps done well with the funds entrusted to him; she would not wear out. Even now he saw maturity in her face, and that among women was rare.

Arnie said to him, "We're going out and have a drink. If you get that machine fixed in time—"

"It's fixed now." He had found the broken belt and had replaced it with one from his tool kit.

"Good deal," Arnie said, grinning like a happy child. "Then come on along with us." To the girl he explained, "We're meeting Milton Glaub, the famous psychiatrist; you probably heard of him. He promised to have a drink with me. I was talking to him on the phone just now, and he sounds like a topnotch sort of guy." He whacked Jack loudly on the shoulder. "I bet when you landed your 'copter on the roof you didn't think you'd be having a drink with one of the solar system's best-known psychoanalysts, did you?"

I wonder if I should go along, Jack thought. But why not? He said, "O.K., Arnie."

Arnie said, "Doc Glaub is going to scare up a schizophrenic for me; I need one, I need its professional services." He laughed, eyes twinkling, finding his own utterance outstandingly funny.

"Do you?" Jack said. "I'm a schizophrenic."

Arnie stopped laughing. "No kidding. I never would have guessed; what I mean is, you look all right."

Finishing up the task of putting the encoder back together, Jack said, "I am all right. I'm cured."

Doreen said, "No one is ever cured of schizophrenia." Her tone was dispassionate; she was simply stating a fact.

"They can be," Jack said, "if it's what is called situational schizophrenia."

Arnie eyed him with great interest, even suspicion. "You're pulling my leg. You're just trying to worm your way into my confidence."

Jack shrugged, feeling himself flush. He turned his attention back, completely, to his work.

"No offense," Arnie said. "You really are, no kidding? Listen, Jack, let me ask you; do you have any sort of ability or power to read the future?"

After a long pause, Jack said, "No."

"You sure?" Arnie said, with suspicion.

"I'm sure." He wished now that he had turned down flat that invitation to accompany them. The intent questioning made him feel exposed; Arnie was nudging too close, encroaching on him—it was difficult to breathe, and Jack moved around to the far side of the desk, to put more distance between himself and the plumber.

"Whatzamatter?" Arnie asked acutely.

"Nothing." Jack continued working, not looking at either Arnie or the girl. Both of them were watching him, and his hands shook.

Presently Arnie said, "Jack, let me tell you how I got where I am. One talent got me up here. I can judge people and tell what they're like down inside, what they really are, not just what they do and say. I don't believe you; I bet you're lying to me about your precognition. Isn't that right? You don't even have to answer." Turning to the girl, Arnie said, "Let's get balling; I want that drink." He beckoned to Jack to follow.

Laying down his tools, Jack reluctantly did so.

Seven

O N his journey by 'copter to Lewistown to meet Arnie
Kott and have a drink with him, Dr. Milton Glaub asked
himself if his good luck were true. I can't believe it, he
thought, a turning point in my life like this.

He was not certain what Arnie wanted; the phone call had
been so unexpected and Arnie had talked so fast that Dr.
Glaub had wound up perplexed, knowing only that it had to
do with parapsychological aspects of the mentally ill. Well, he
could tell Arnie practically all there was to know on that topic.
And yet Glaub sensed that there was something deeper in the
inquiry.

Generally, a concern with schizophrenia was a symptom of
the person's own inner struggle in that area. Now, it was a fact
that often the first signs of the insidious growth of the schizophrenic process in a person was an inability to eat in public.
Arnie had noisily gabbed on about his desire to meet Glaub—
not in his own home or in the doctor's office—but at a well-
known bar and restaurant in Lewistown, the Willows. Was this
perhaps a reaction-formation? Mysteriously made tense by
public situations, and especially by those involving the nutri-
tive function, Arnie Kott was leaning over backward to regain
the normalcy which was beginning to abandon him.

Piloting his 'copter, Glaub thought about this, but then, by
slow and stealthy stages, his thinking returned to the topic of
his own problems.

Arnie Kott, a man controlling a multimillion-dollar union
fund; a prominent person in the colonial world, although virtually unknown back Home. A feudal baron, virtually. If Kott
were to put me on his staff, Glaub speculated, I could pay off
all the debts we've piled up, those hideous charge-account bills
at twenty per cent interest that just seem to loom there always,
never getting smaller or going away. And then we could start
over, not go into debt, live within our means . . . and a
highly expanded means, at that.

Then, too, old Arnie was a Swede or a Dane, something like

that and so it wouldn't be necessary for Glaub to season his skin-color before receiving each patient. Plus the fact that Arnie had a reputation for informality. Milt and Arnie, it would be. Dr. Glaub smiled.

What he had to be sure to do in this initial interview was to ratify Arnie's concepts, sort of play along and not dash cold water on things, even if, say, old Arnie's notions were way out of line. A hell of a thing it would be to discourage the man! That wasn't right.

I see your point, Arnie, Dr. Glaub said to himself, practicing away as he piloted his 'copter closer and closer to Lewistown. Yes, there is a good deal to be said for that world-view.

He had handled so many types of social situations for his patients, appearing in public for them, representing those timid, shut-in schizoid personalities who shrank from interpersonal exposure, that this would undoubtedly be a snap. And—if the schizophrenic process in Arnie were beginning to bring up its heavy artillery—Arnie might need to lean on him for his very survival.

Hot dog, Dr. Glaub said to himself, and increased the velocity of the 'copter to its maximum.

Around the Willows ran a moat of cold blue water. Fountains sprayed water into the air, and bougainvillaea, purple and amber and rusty-red, grew to great heights, encircling the single-story glass structure. As he descended the black wrought-iron staircase from the parking lot, Dr. Glaub perceived his party within: Arnie Kott seated with a stunning redhead and nondescript male companion wearing repairman's overalls and canvas shirt.

True classless society, here, Dr. Glaub reflected.

A rainbow-style bridge assisted him in his crossing of the moat. Doors opened before him; he entered the lounge, passed by the bar, halted to sniff in the sight of the jazz combo composing meditatively, and then hailed Arnie. "Hi, Arnie!"

"Hi, Doc." Arnie rose to introduce him. "Dor, this is Doc Glaub. Doreen Anderton. This is my repairman, Jack Bohlen, a real fireballer. Jack, this is the foremost living psychiatrist, Milt Glaub."

They all nodded and shook hands.

"Hardly foremost," Glaub murmured, as they sat down. "It's still the Swiss at Berghölzlei, the existential psychiatrists, who dominate the field." But he was deeply gratified, untrue as Arnie's announcement had been. He could feel his face flushing with pleasure. "Sorry it took me so long to get here— I had to dash over to New Israel. Bo—Bosley Touvim—needed my advice on a medical matter which he considered pressing."

"Quite a guy, that Bos," Arnie said. He had lit a cigar, a genuine Earth-rolled Optimo Admiral. "A real go-getter. But let's get down to business. Wait, I'll get you a drink." He looked inquiringly at Glaub, while waving the cocktail waitress over.

"Scotch, if you have it," Glaub said.

"Cutty Sark, sir," the waitress said.

"Oh, fine. No ice, please."

"O.K.," Arnie said impatiently. "Now look, Doc. You got the name of a really advanced schizo for me, or not?" He scrutinized Glaub.

"Uh," said Glaub, and then he recalled his visit to New Israel not more than a short while ago. "Manfred Steiner," he said.

"Any relation to Norbert Steiner?"

"As a matter of fact, his boy. At Camp B-G—I imagine there's no breach of confidence in telling you. Totally autistic, from birth. Mother, the cold, intellectual schizoid personality, doing it by the rulebook. Father—"

"Father dead," Arnie said shortly.

"Right. Very regrettable. Nice chap, but depressive. It was suicide, you know. Typical impulse during his low-swing. A wonder he didn't do it years ago."

Arnie said, "You told me on the phone you've got a theory about the schizophrenic being out of phase in time."

"Yes, it's a derangement in the interior time-sense." Dr. Glaub had all three of them listening, and he warmed to his topic; it was his favorite. "We have yet to get total experimental verification, but that will come." And then, without hesitation or shame, he passed off the Berghölzlei theory as his own.

Evidently much impressed, Arnie said, "Very interesting." To the repairman, Jack Bohlen, he said, "Could such slow-motion chambers be built?"

"No doubt," Jack murmured.

"And sensors," Glaub said. "To get the patient out of the chamber and into the real world. Sight, hearing—"

"It could be done," Bohlen said.

"How about this," Arnie said impatiently and enthusiastically. "Could the schizophrenic be running so fast, compared to us, in time, that he's actually in what to us is the future? Would that account for his precognition?" His light-colored eyes glittered excitedly.

Glaub shrugged in a manner indicating agreement.

Turning to Bohlen, Arnie stuttered, "Hey, Jack, that's it! Goddamn it, I ought to be a psychiatrist. Slow him down, hell. Speed him up, I say. Let him live out of phase in time, if he wants to. But let's get him to share his perceptions with us—right, Bohlen?"

Glaub said, "Now, there is the rub. In autism, especially, the faculty of interpersonal communication is drastically impaired."

"I see," Arnie said, but he was not daunted. "Hell, I know enough about that to see a way out. Didn't that early guy, Carl Jung—didn't he manage to decode the schizophrenic's language years ago?"

"Yes," Glaub said, "decades ago Jung cracked the private language of the schizophrenic. But in child autism, as with Manfred, there is no language at all, at least no spoken language. Possibly totally personal private thoughts . . . but no words."

"Shit," Arnie said.

The girl glanced at him admonishingly.

"This is a serious matter," Arnie said to her. "We've got to get these unfortunates, these autistic kids, to talk to us and tell us what they knew; isn't that right, Doc?"

"Yes," Glaub said.

"That kid's an orphan now," Arnie said, "that Manfred."

"Well, he has the mother, still," Glaub said.

Waving his hand excitedly, Arnie said, "But they don't care enough about the kid to have him at home; they junked him in that camp. Hell, I'll spring him and bring him here. And, Jack, you get on this and engineer a machine to make contact with him—you see the picture?"

After a moment Bohlen said, "I don't know what to say." He laughed briefly.

"Sure you know what to say—hell, it ought to be easy for you, you're a schizophrenic yourself, like you said."

Glaub, interested, said to Bohlen, "Is that the case?" He had already noted, automatically, the repairman's skeletal tension as he sat sipping his drink, and the rigid musculature, not to mention the asthenic build. "But you appear to have made enormous strides toward recovery."

Raising his head, Bohlen met his glance, saying, "I'm totally recovered. For many years, now." His face was affect-laden.

No one makes a total recovery, Glaub thought. But he did not say it; instead he said, "Perhaps Arnie is right. You could empathize with the autistic, whereas that is our basic problem; the autistic can't take our roles, see the world as we do, and we can't take his role either. So a gulf separates us."

"Bridge that gulf, Jack!" Arnie cried. He whacked Bohlen on the back. "That's your job; I'm putting you on the payroll."

Envy filled Dr. Glaub. He glared down at his drink, hiding his reaction. The girl, however, saw it and smiled at him. He did not smile back.

Contemplating Dr. Glaub sitting opposite him, Jack Bohlen felt the gradual diffusion of his perception which he so dreaded, the change in his awareness which had attacked him this way years ago in the personnel manager's office at Corona Corporation, and which always seemed still with him, just on the edge.

He saw the psychiatrist under the aspect of absolute reality: a thing composed of cold wires and switches, not a human at all, not made of flesh. The fleshy trappings melted and became transparent, and Jack Bohlen saw the mechanical device beyond. Yet he did not let his terrible state of awareness show; he continued to nurse his drink; he went on listening to the conversation and nodding occasionally. Neither Dr. Glaub nor Arnie Kott noticed.

But the girl did. She leaned over and said softly in Jack's ear, "Aren't you feeling well?"

He shook his head. No, he was saying, I'm not feeling well.

"Let's get away from them," the girl whispered. "I can't stand it either." Aloud, to Arnie, she said, "Jack and I are going to leave you two alone. Come on." She tapped Jack on the arm and rose to her feet; he felt her light, strong fingers, and he, too, rose.

Arnie said, "Don't be gone long," and resumed his earnest conversation with Dr. Glaub.

"Thanks," Jack said, as they walked up the aisle, between tables.

Doreen said, "Did you see how jealous he was, when Arnie said he was putting you on the payroll?"

"No. Glaub?" But he was not surprised. "I get this way," he said to the girl, by way of apology. "Something to do with my eyes; it may be astigmatism. Due to tension."

The girl said, "Do you want to sit at the bar? Or go outside?"

"Outside," Jack said.

Presently they stood on the rainbow bridge, over the water. In the water fish slid about, luminous and vague, half-real beings, as rare on Mars as any form of matter conceivable. They were a miracle in this world, and Jack and the girl, gazing down, both felt it. And both knew they felt this same thought without having to speak it aloud.

"It's nice out here," Doreen said finally.

"Yeah." He did not want to talk.

"Everybody," Doreen said. "Has at one time or another known a schizophrenic . . . if they're not one themselves. It was my brother, back Home, my younger brother."

"I'll be O.K.," Jack said. "I'm O.K. now."

"But you're not," Doreen said.

"No," he admitted, "but what the hell can I do? You said it yourself. Once a schizophrenic, always a schizophrenic." He was silent, then, concentrating on the gliding, pale fish.

"Arnie thinks a lot of you," the girl said. "When he says his talent is judging the value of people he's telling the truth. He can see already that that Glaub is desperately eager to sell himself and get on the staff, here in Lewistown. I guess psychiatry doesn't pay any more, as it did once; too many in the business. There are twenty of them here in this settlement already, and none do a genuinely good traffic. Didn't your—condition cause you trouble when you applied for permission to emigrate?"

He said, "I don't want to talk about it. Please."

"Let's walk," the girl said.

They walked along the street, past the shops, most of which had closed for the day.

"What was it you saw," the girl said, "when you looked at Dr. Glaub, there at the table?"

Jack said, "Nothing."

"You'd rather not say about that, either."

"That's right."

"Do you think if you tell me things will get worse?"

"It's not things; it's me."

"Maybe it is the things," Doreen said. "Maybe there is something in your vision, however distorted and garbled it's become. I don't know. I used to try like hell to comprehend what it was Clay—my brother—saw and heard. He couldn't say. I know that his world was absolutely different from the rest of ours in the family. He killed himself, like Steiner did." She had paused at a newsstand, to look over the item, on page one, about Norbert Steiner. "The existential psychiatrists often say to let them go ahead and take their lives; it's the only way, for some of them . . . the vision becomes too awful to bear."

Jack said nothing.

"Is it awful?" Doreen asked.

"No. Just—disconcerting." He struggled to explain. "There's no way you can work it in with what you're supposed to see and know; it makes it impossible to go on, in the accustomed way."

"Don't you very often try to pretend, and sort of—go along with it, by acting? Like an actor?" When he did not answer, she said, "You tried to do that in there, just now."

"I'd love to fool everybody," he conceded. "I'd give anything if I could go on acting it out, playing a role. But that's a real split—there's no split up until then; they're wrong when they say it's a split in the mind. If I wanted to keep going entire, without a split, I'd have to lean over and say to Dr. Glaub—" He broke off.

"Tell me," the girl said.

"Well," he said, taking a deep breath, "I'd say, Doc, I can see you under the aspect of eternity and you're dead. That's the substance of the sick, morbid vision. I don't want it; I didn't ask for it."

The girl put her arm within his.

"I never told anybody before," Jack said, "not even Silvia, my wife, or my son David. You know, I watch him; I look every day to be sure it isn't showing up in him too. It's so easy for this stuff to get passed along as with the Steiners. I didn't know they had a boy at B-G until Glaub said so. And they're neighbors of ours for years back. Steiner never let it out."

Doreen said, "We're supposed to go back to the Willows for dinner. Do you want to? I think it would be a good idea. You know, you don't have to join Arnie's staff; you can stay with Mr. Yee. That's a nice 'copter you have. You don't have to give all that up just because Arnie decides he can use you; maybe you can't use him."

Shrugging, he said, "It's an interesting challenge, building a conduit for communication between an autistic child and our world. I think there's a lot in what Arnie says. I could be the intermediary—I could do a useful job there." It doesn't really matter why Arnie wants to bring out the Steiner boy, he realized. Probably he's got some solid selfish motive, something that will bring him a profit in cold hard cash. I certainly couldn't care less.

In fact I can have it both ways, he realized. Mr. Yee can lease me to the Water Workers' Union; I'd be paid by Mr. Yee and he'd be paid by Arnie. Everyone would be happy, and why not? Tinkering with the broken, malfunctioning mind of a child certainly has more to recommend it than tinkering with refrigerators and encoders; if the child is suffering some of the visions that I know—

He knew of the time-theory which Glaub had trotted out as his own. He had read about it in *Scientific American*; naturally, he read anything on schizophrenia that he could get his hands on. He knew that it had orginated with the Swiss, that Glaub hadn't invented it. What an odd theory it is, he thought to himself. And yet, it rings true.

"Let's go back to the Willows," he said. He was very hungry, and it would no doubt be a bang-up meal.

Doreen said, "You're a brave person, Jack Bohlen."

"Why?" he asked.

"Because you're going back to the place that troubled you, to the people that brought on your vision of, as you said, eternity. I wouldn't do that, I'd flee."

"But," he said, "that's the whole point; it's designed to make you flee—the vision's for that purpose, to nullify your relations with other people, to isolate you. If it's successful, your life with human beings is over. That's what they mean when they say the term schizophrenia isn't a diagnosis; it's a prognosis—it doesn't say anything about what you have, only about how you'll wind up." *And I'm not going to wind up like that*, he said to himself. Like Manfred Steiner, mute and in an institution; I intend to keep my job, my wife and son, my friendships—he glanced at the girl holding on to his arm. Yes, and even love affairs, if such there be.

I intend to keep trying.

Putting his hands in his pockets as he walked along, he touched something small, cold and hard; lifting it out in surprise, he saw it was a wrinkled little object like a tree root.

"What in the world's that?" Doreen asked him.

It was the water witch which the Bleekmen had given him that morning, out in the desert; he had forgotten all about it.

"A good luck charm," Jack said to the girl.

Shivering, she said, "It's awfully ugly."

"Yes," he agreed, "but it's friendly. And we do have this problem, we schizophrenics; we do pick up other people's unconscious hostility."

"I know. The telepathic factor. Clay had it worse and worse until—" She glanced at him. "The paranoid outcome."

"It's the worst thing about our condition, this awareness of the buried, repressed sadism and aggression in others around us, even strangers. I wish to hell we didn't have it; we even pick it up from people in restaurants—" He thought of Glaub. "In buses, in a theater. Crowds."

Doreen said, "Do you have any idea what Arnie wants to learn from the Steiner boy?"

"Well, this theory about precognition—"

"But what does Arnie want to know about the future? You have no idea, do you? And it would never occur to you to try to find out."

That was so. He had not even been curious.

"You're content," she said slowly, scrutinizing him, "merely to do your technical task of rigging up the essential machinery. That's not right, Jack Bohlen; that's not a good sign at all."

"Oh," he said. He nodded. "It's very schizophrenic, I guess . . . to be content with a purely technical relationship."

"Will you ask Arnie?"

He felt uncomfortable. "It's his business, not mine. It's an interesting job, and I like Arnie, I prefer him to Mr. Yee. I just—haven't got it in me to pry. That's the way I am."

"I think you're afraid. But I don't see why—you're brave, and yet in some deep way you're terribly, terribly frightened."

"Maybe so," he said, feeling sad.

Together, they walked on back to the Willows.

That night, after everyone had gone, including Doreen Anderton, Arnie Kott sat alone in his living room gloating. What a day it had been.

He had snared a good repairman who had already repaired his invaluable encoder and who was going to build an electronic wing-ding to tap the precog faculties of an autistic child.

He had milked, for nothing, the information he needed from a psychiatrist, and then managed to get rid of the psychiatrist.

So all in all it had been an exceptional day. It left only two problems: his harpsichord was still untuned and—what the hell else? It had slipped his mind. He pondered as he sat before his TV set, watching the fights from America the Beautiful, the U.S.A. colony on Mars.

Then he remembered. Norb Steiner's death. There was no source of goodies any more.

"I'll fix that," Arnie said aloud. He shut off the TV and got his encoder out; seated before it, mike in hand, he delivered a message. It was to Scott Temple, with whom he had worked on countless important business ventures; Temple was a cousin of Ed Rockingham, and a good egg to know—he had managed, through a charter arrangement with the UN, to gain control of most of the medical supplies entering Mars, and what a top-notch monopoly that amounted to.

The drums of the encoder turned encouragingly.

"Scott!" Arnie said, "how are you. Hey, you know that poor guy Norb Steiner? Too bad, I mean, his dying and all. I understand he was mentally you-know-what. Like the rest of us." Arnie laughed at that long and hard. "So anyhow, it leaves us with a little problem—I mean, one of procurement. Right? So listen, Scott, old man. I'd like to talk it over with you. I'm in. You get me? Stop by here in around a day or two, so we can work out the exact arrangements. I think we should forget the gear that Steiner was using; we'll start out fresh, get our own little bitty field in an out-of-the-way place, our own slave rockets, whatever else we need. Keep those smoked oysters rolling in, like they ought to." He shut the machine off and tried to think if there was more. No, he had said it all; between him and a man like Scott Temple, no more had to be said; it was a deal then and there. "O.K., Scott, boy," he said. "I'll expect to see you."

After he had removed the spool it occurred to him to play it back just to be sure it had gone into code. God, what a calamity if by some freak chance it came out in clear!

But it was in code, all right, and his dearest: the machine had put the semantic units into a catfight-like parody of contemporary electronic music. Arnie, hearing the whistles, growls, beeps, hoots, hums, laughed until tears ran down his cheeks; he had to go off to the bathroom and slap cold water on his face to stop himself.

Then, back at the encoder, he carefully marked the box into which the spool went:

Song of the Wind Spirit, A Cantata by Karl William Dittershand

That composer, Karl William Dittershand, was the current favorite back on Earth among the intellectuals, and Arnie detested the man's electronic so-called music; he was a purist, himself: his tastes stopped firmly at Brahms. Arnie had a good laugh at that—marking his encoded message proposing his and Scott's going into the black-market importation of foodstuffs as a cantata by Dittershand—and then rang up a union Goodmember to convey the spool up north to Nova Britannica, the U.K. colony on Mars.

That, at eight-thirty in the evening, wound up the business of the day, and Arnie returned to his TV set to see the finish of the fights. He lit himself another Optimo extra-mild Admiral, leaned back, broke wind, relaxed.

I wish all days could be like this, he said to himself. I could live forever, if they were; days like this made him younger, not older. He felt as if he could see forty come by again.

Imagine me going into the black market, he said to himself. And for little stuff, little tins of wild blackberry jelly and slices of pickled eel and lox. But that was vital, too; for him especially. Nobody is going to rob me of my treats, he thought grimly. If that Steiner thought by killing himself he could cut me off where it hurts—

"Come on," he urged the colored boy taking a licking on the TV screen. "Gut up, you bugger, and give it to him."

As if he had heard, the Negro fighter scrambled back up, and Arnie Kott chuckled with deep, keen pleasure.

In the small hotel room, where he traditionally stayed weekend nights in Bunchewood Park when on call, Jack Bohlen sat by the window smoking a cigarette and pondering.

It had returned, after all these years, that which he dreaded; he had to face it. Now it was not anguished anticipation, it was actuality. Christ, he thought miserably, they're right—once you have it you've got it for keeps. The visit to the Public School had set him up for it, and at the Willows it had appeared and smitten him, as intact and full as if he were in his twenties again, back on Earth, working for Corona Corporation down in Redwood City.

And I know, he thought, that Norbert Steiner's death figured into it. Death upsets everyone, makes them do peculiar things; it sets a radiating process of action and emotion going that works its way out, farther and farther, to embrace more people and things.

Better call Silvia, he thought, and see how she's making out with Frau Steiner and the children.

But he shrank from it. There's nothing I can do to help anyhow, he decided. I have to be on twenty-four-hour call here in town, where Mr. Yee's switchboard can get hold of me. And now, too, he had to be available to Arnie Kott at Lewistown.

There had been, however, compensation. A fine, deep, subtle, highly envigorating compensation. In his wallet he had Doreen Anderton's address and phone number.

Should he call her tonight? Imagine, he thought, finding someone, a woman, too, with whom he could talk freely, who understood about his situation, who genuinely wanted to hear and was not frightened.

It helped a lot.

His wife was the last person in the world he could talk to about his schizophrenia; on the few occasions he had tried she had simply collapsed with fear. Like everybody else, Silvia was terrified at the idea of it entering her life; she herself warded it off with the magic charms of drugs . . . as if phenobarbital could halt the most pervasive, ominous psychic process known to man. God knew how many pills he himself had swallowed during the last decade, enough to pave a road from his home to this hotel and possibly back.

He decided after some reflection not to call Doreen. Better to leave it as a way out when the going got exceptionally rough. Right now he felt fairly placid. There would be plenty of time in the future, and plenty of need, to seek out Doreen Anderton.

Of course, he would have to be incredibly careful; obviously Doreen was Arnie Kott's mistress. But she seemed to know what she was doing, and certainly she knew Arnie; she must have taken him into account when she gave out her phone number and address, and, for that matter, when she got up and left the restaurant.

I trust her, Jack said to himself. And for someone with a streak of schizophrenia, that is something.

Pondering that, Jack Bohlen put out his cigarette, went and got his pajamas, and prepared to go to bed.

He was just getting under the covers when the phone in his room rang. A service call, he thought, leaping up automatically to get it.

But it was not. A woman's voice said softly in his ear, "Jack?"

"Yes," he said.

"This is Doreen. I just wondered—if you were O.K."

"I'm fine," he said, seating himself on the edge of the bed.

"Do you think you'd want to come over tonight? To my place?"

He hesitated. "Umm," he said.

"We could play records and talk. Arnie lent me a lot of rare old stereophonic LP records from his collection . . . some of them are awfully scratchy, but some are terrific. He's quite a collector, you know; he has the largest collection of Bach on Mars. And you saw his harpsichord."

So that's what that had been, there in Arnie's living room.

"Is it safe?" he asked.

"Yes. Don't worry about Arnie; he's not possessive, if you know what I mean."

Jack said, "O.K. I'll be over." And then he realized that he couldn't, because he had to be available for service calls. Unless he could switch it through her phone.

"That's no problem," she said, when he explained it to her. "I'll call Arnie and tell him."

Dumbfounded, he said, "But—"

"Jack, you're out of your mind if you think we can do it any other way—Arnie knows everything that goes on in the settlement. Leave it to me, dear. I'll call him right now. And you come right on over here. If any calls come through while you're on your way I'll write them down, but I don't think there will be any; Arnie doesn't want you out fixing people's toasters, he wants you for his own jobs, for making that machine for talking to the Steiner boy."

"O.K.," he said, "I'll be over. Goodbye." He hung up the phone.

Ten minutes later he was on his way, flying the bright and shiny Yee Company repairship through the night sky of Mars, to Lewistown and Arnie Kott's mistress.

Eight

DAVID BOHLEN knew that his grandfather Leo had a lot of money and didn't mind spending it. For instance, before they had even left the rocket terminal building, the old man in his stiff suit with his vest and gold cuff links—it was the suit that the boy had watched to catch sight of, along the ramp from where the passengers appeared—stopped at the flower counter and bought the boy's mother a bunch of large blue Earth flowers. And he wanted to buy something for David, too, but they didn't have any toys, only candy, which Grandfather Leo bought: a two-pound box.

Under his arm Grandfather Leo had a white carton tied with string: he hadn't let the rocketship officials take it and put it with the luggage. When they had left the terminal building and were in his dad's 'copter, Grandfather Leo opened the package. It was full of Jewish bread and pickles and thin-sliced corned beef wrapped in protective plastic, three pounds of corned beef in all.

"My gosh," Jack exclaimed in delight. "All the way from New York. You can't get that out here in the colonies, Dad."

"I know that, Jack," Grandfather Leo said. "A Jewish fella told me where to get it, and I like it so much I knew you'd like it, you and I have the same tastes." He chuckled, pleased to see how happy he had made them. "I'm gonna make you a sandwich when we get to the house. First thing we get there."

The 'copter rose now above the rocketship terminal and passed on over the dark desert.

"How's the weather you been having here?" Grandfather Leo asked.

"Lots of storms," Jack said. "Practically buried us, a week or so ago. We had to rent power equipment to dig out."

"Bad," Grandfather Leo said. "You ought to get that cement wall up you were talking about in your letters."

"It costs a fortune to have construction work done out here," Silvia said, "it's not like back on Earth."

"I know that," Grandfather Leo said, "but you got to protect your investment—that house is worth a lot, and the land, you have water nearby; don't forget that."

"How could we forget that?" Silvia said. "Good Lord, without the ditch we'd die."

"That canal any wider this year?" Grandfather Leo asked.

"Just the same," Jack said.

David spoke up. "They dredged it, Grandfather Leo. I watched them; the UN men, they used a big machine that sucked up the sand from the bottom, and the water's a lot cleaner. So my dad shut off the filter system, and now when the rider comes and opens the gate our way, we can pump it so fast that my dad let me put in a whole new vegetable garden I can water with overflow, and I have corn and squash and a couple of carrots, but something ate all the beets. We had corn last night from it. We put up a fence to keep those little animals from getting in—what are they called, Dad?"

"Sand rats, Leo," Jack said. "As soon as David's garden started to bear, the sand rats moved in. They're yay long." He held up his hands to show. "Harmless, except that they can eat their weight in ten minutes. The older settlers warned us, but we had to try."

"Good to grow your own produce," Grandfather Leo said. "Yeah, you wrote me about the garden, David: I'd like to see it tomorrow. Tonight I'm tired; that's a long trip I took, even with the new ships they got, what do they call it? Fast as light, but it really isn't; still a lot of time taking off and landing and a lot of concussion. I had a woman next to me, she was terrified, thought we'd burn up, it got so hot inside there, even with the air conditioning. I don't know why they let it get so hot, they certainly charge enough. But it's a big improvement over—remember the ship you took when you emigrated years ago? Two months!"

Jack said, "Leo, you brought your oxygen mask, I hope. Ours is too old now, unreliable."

"Sure, I got it in my brown suitcase. Don't worry about me, I can take this atmosphere—I got a different heart pill, really improved. Everything's improving back Home. Of course, it's overcrowded. But more and more people going to be emigrating over here—take my word for that. Smog's so bad back home it nearly kills you."

David spoke up, "Grandfather Leo, the man next door, Mr. Steiner, he took his own life, and now his son Manfred is home from the camp for anomalous children, and my dad is building a mechanism so he can talk to us."

"Well," Grandfather Leo said, in a kindly way. He beamed at the boy. "That's interesting, David. How old is this boy?"

"Ten," David said, "but he can't talk at all to us, yet. But my dad is going to fix that up with his mechanism, and you know who my dad is working for right now? Mr. Kott, who runs the Water Workers' Union and their settlement; he's really a big important man."

"I believe I heard about him," Grandfather Leo said, with a wink at Jack which the boy caught.

Jack said to his father, "Dad, are you still going ahead with this business of buying land in the F.D.R. range?"

"Oh, certainly," Grandfather Leo said. "You bet your life, Jack. Naturally, I came out on this trip sociably, to see you all, but I couldn't have taken off so much time as this unless it was business, too."

"I hoped you'd given that up," Jack said.

"Now Jack," Grandfather Leo said, "don't you worry; you let me worry if I'm doing the right thing; I been in land investment for many years now. Listen. You going to pilot me out there to that mountain range so I can take a first-hand look? I got a lot of maps; I want to see with my own eyes, though."

"You're going to be disappointed when you see it," Silvia said. "It's so desolate there, no water, scarcely anything living."

"Let's not worry about it right now," Grandfather Leo said, with a smile at David. He nudged the boy in the ribs. "Good to see a young man straight and healthy and out here away from the polluted air we have back Home."

"Well, Mars has its drawbacks," Silvia said. "Try living with bad water or no water at all for a while and you'll see."

"I know," Grandfather Leo said soberly. "You people sure have guts to live out here. But it's healthy; don't forget that."

Below them now, the lights of Bunchewood Park glittered. Jack turned the 'copter toward the north and their home.

*

As he piloted the Yee Company 'copter, Jack Bohlen glanced at his father and marveled at how little he had aged, how vigorous and well knit Leo looked, for a man in his late seventies. And still at his job, fulltime, getting as much enjoyment out of speculating as ever.

And yet, although it did not show, he was certain that the long trip from Earth had tired Leo out more than he admitted. In any case, they were almost at the house, now. The gyrocompass reading was point 7.08054; they were only minutes away.

When they had parked on the roof of the house, and had gone downstairs, Leo at once fulfilled his promise; in the kitchen he set to work, joyfully making each of them a kosher corned-beef sandwich on Jewish bread. Soon they were all seated in the living room, eating. Everyone was peaceful and relaxed.

"You just don't know how we're starved for food of this sort," Silvia said finally. "Even on the black market—" She glanced at Jack.

"Sometimes you can pick up delicatessen foods on the black market," Jack said, "although lately it's gotten harder. We don't, personally. No moral reason: it's just too expensive."

They talked for a while, finding out about Leo's trip and about conditions back Home. David was sent to bed at ten-thirty, and then, at eleven, Silvia excused herself and went to bed, too. Leo and Jack were left in the living room, still sitting, just the two of them.

Leo said, "Can we step outside and take a glance at the boy's garden? You got a big flashlight?"

Finding his trouble-lantern, Jack led the way out of the house and into the cold night air.

As they stood at the edge of the patch of corn, Leo said to him in a low voice, "How are you and Silvia getting along these days?"

"Fine," Jack said, a little taken aback by the question.

"Seems to me there's a coolness between the two of you," Leo said. "It sure would be terrible, Jack, if you grew apart. That's a fine woman you got, there—one in a million."

"I recognize that," Jack said uncomfortably.

"Back Home," Leo said, "when you were a young fellow, you always played around a lot. But I know you're settled down, now."

"I am," Jack said. "And I think you're imagining things."

"You do seem withdrawn, Jack," his father said. "I hope that old trouble of yours, you know what I mean, isn't bothering you. I'm talking about—"

"I know what you're talking about."

Relentlessly, Leo went on, "When I was a boy there was no mental illness like there is now. It's a sign of the times; too many people, too much overcrowding. I remember when you first got sick, and a long time before that, say from when you were seventeen on, you were cold toward other people, uninterested in them. Moody, too. Seems to me you're like that, now."

Jack glared at his father. This was the trouble with having one's folks visit; they could never resist the temptation to resume their old roles as the All-wise, the All-knowing. To Leo, Jack was not a grown man with a wife and child; he was simply his son Jack.

"Look, Leo," Jack said. "Out here there are very few people; this is a sparsely settled planet, as yet. Naturally, people here are less gregarious; they have to be more inner-directed than back Home where it's like you said, just a mob-scene day after day."

Leo nodded. "Hmm. But that should make you more glad to see fellow humans."

"If you're referring to yourself, I'm very glad to see you."

"Sure, Jack," Leo said, "I know. Maybe I'm just tired. But you don't seem to say much; you're preoccupied."

"My work," Jack said. "This boy Manfred, this autistic child —I have that on my mind all the time."

But, as in the old days, his father could see through his pretexts effortlessly, with true parental instinct. "Come on, boy," Leo said. "You got a lot on your mind, but I know how you work; your job is with your hands, and I'm talking about your mind, it's your mind that's turned inward. Can you get that psychotherapy business here on Mars? Don't tell me no, because I know better."

"I'm not going to tell you no," Jack said, "but I will tell you that it's none of your goddamn business."

Beside him in the darkness his father seemed to shrink, to settle. "O.K., boy," he murmured. "Sorry I butted in."

They were both uncomfortably silent.

"Hell," Jack said, "let's not quarrel, Dad. Let's go back inside and have a drink or something and then turn in. Silvia fixed up a good soft bed for you in the other bedroom; I know you'll have a good rest."

"Silvia's very attentive to a person's needs," Leo said, with a faint note of accusation toward his son. Then his voice softened as he said, "Jack, I always worry about you. Maybe I'm old-fashioned and don't understand about this—mental illness business; everybody seems to have it nowadays; it's common, like flu and polio used to be, like when we were kids and almost everybody caught measles. Now you have this. One out of every three, I heard on TV, one time. Skizo—whatever. I mean, Jack, with so much to live for, why would anyone turn his back on life, like these skizo people do. It doesn't make sense. You got a whole planet to conquer, here. Tomorrow, for instance, I'm going with you to the F.D.R. Mountains, and you can show me around all over, and then I've got all the details on legal procedure here; I'm going to be buying. Listen: You buy in, too, you hear me? I'll advance you the money." He grinned hopefully at Jack, showing his stainless-steel teeth.

"It's not my cup of tea," Jack said. "But thanks."

"I'll pick out the parcel for you," Leo offered.

"No. I'm just not interested."

"You—enjoying your job, now, Jack? Making this machine to talk to the little boy who can't speak? Sounds like a worthy occupation; I'm proud to hear about it. David is a swell kid, and boy, is he proud of his dad."

"I know he is," Jack said.

"David doesn't show any signs of that skizo thing, does he?"

"No," Jack said.

Leo said, "I don't know where you got yours, certainly not from me—I love people."

"I do, too," Jack said. He wondered how his father would act if he knew about Doreen. Probably Leo would be grief-stricken;

he came from a strait-laced generation—born in 1924, a long, long time ago. It was a different world, then. Amazing, how his father had adapted to this world, now; a miracle. Leo, born in the boom period following World War One, and now standing here on the edge of the Martian desert . . . but he still would not understand about Doreen, about how vital it was for him to maintain an intimate contact of this sort, at any cost; or rather, almost any cost.

"What's her name?" Leo said.

"W-what?" Jack stammered.

"I got a little of that telepathic sense," Leo said in a toneless voice. "Don't I?"

After a pause, Jack said, "Evidently."

"Does Silvia know?"

"No."

"I could tell because you didn't look me in the eye."

"Balls," Jack said fiercely.

"Is she married, too? She got kids, too, this other woman you're mixed up with?"

Jack said in as level a voice as possible, "Why don't you use your telepathic sense and find out?"

"I just don't want to see Silvia hurt," Leo said.

"She won't be," Jack said.

"Too bad," Leo said, "to come all this way and find out something like this. Well—" He sighed. "I got my business, anyhow. Tomorrow you and I'll get up good and early and get started."

Jack said, "Don't be too harsh a judge, Dad."

"All right," Leo agreed. "I know, it's modern times. You think by this playing around you keep yourself well—right? Maybe so. Maybe it's a way to sanity. I don't mean you're not sane—"

"Just tainted," Jack said, with violent bitterness. Christ, your own father, he thought. What an ordeal. What a miserable tragedy.

"I know you'll come out O.K.," Leo said. "I can see now that you're struggling; it's not just playing around. I can tell by your voice—you got troubles. Same ones you always had, only as you get older you wear out, and it's harder—right? Yeah, I see that. This planet is lonely. It's a wonder all you emigrants didn't go crazy right off the bat. I can see why you would value love anywhere you can find it. What you need is something like what I've got, this land thing of mine; maybe you can find it in building your machine for that poor mute kid. I'd like to see him."

"You will," Jack said. "Possibly tomorrow."

They stood for a moment longer, and then they walked back into the house. "Does Silvia still take dope?" Leo asked.

"Dope!" He laughed. "Phenobarbital. Yes, she does."

"Such a nice girl," Leo said. "Too bad she's so tense and worries so much. And helping that unfortunate widow next door, like you were telling me." In the living room, Leo seated himself in Jack's easy chair, crossed his legs and leaned back, sighing, making himself comfortable so that he could continue talking . . . he definitely had much more to say, on a variety of subjects, and he intended to say it.

In bed, Silvia lay almost lost in sleep, her faculties doused by the 100 milligram tablet of phenobarbital which she had taken, as usual, upon retiring. Vaguely, she had heard the murmur of her husband's and her father-in-law's voices from the yard; once, their tone became sharp and she had sat up, alarmed.

Are they going to bicker? she asked herself. God, I hope not; I hope Leo's stay isn't going to disrupt things. However, their voices had sunk back down, and now she rested easily once more.

He certainly is a fine old man, she thought. Much like Jack, only more set in his ways.

Lately, since he had started working for Arnie Kott, her husband had changed. No doubt it was the eerie job which he had been given; the mute, autistic Steiner boy upset her, and she had been sorry from the first to see him appear. Life was complicated enough already. The boy flitted in and out of the house, always running on his toes, his eyes always darting as if he saw objects not present, heard sounds beyond the normal range. If only time could be turned back and Norbert Steiner could be somehow restored to life! If only . . .

In her drugged mind she saw, in a flash, that ineffectual little man setting out in the morning with his suitcases of wares, salesman off on his rounds, yogurt and blackstrap molasses.

Is he still alive somewhere? Perhaps Manfred saw him, lost as the boy was—according to Jack—in disfigured time. What a surprise is in store for them when they make contact with the boy and find they have rekindled that sad little specter . . . but more likely their theory is right, and it is the next, he sees the next. They will have what they want. Why is it Jack? What do you want it for, Jack? Affinity between you and that ill child. That it? Oh . . . Her thoughts gave way to darkness.

And then what? Will you care about me again?

No affinity between the sick and the sound. You are different; it weighs me down. Leo knows it, I know it. Do you? Care?

She slept.

High in the sky circled meat-eating birds. At the base of the windowed building lay their excrement. He picked up the wads until he held several. They twisted and swelled like dough, and he knew there were living creatures within; he carried them carefully into the empty corridor of the building. One wad opened, parted with a split in its woven, hairlike side; it became too large to hold, and he saw it now in the wall. A compartment where it lay on its side, the rent so wide that he perceived the creature within.

Gubbish! A worm, coiled up, made of wet, bony-white pleats, the inside gubbish worm, from a person's body. If only the high-flying birds could find it and eat it down, like that. He ran down the steps, which gave beneath his feet. Boards missing. He saw down through the sieve of wood to the soil beneath, the cavity, dark, cold, full of wood so rotten that it lay in damp powder, destroyed by gubbish-rot.

Arms lifted up, tossed him to the circling birds; he floated up, falling at the same time. They ate his head off. And then he stood on a bridge over the sea. Sharks showed in the water, their sharp, cutting fins. He caught one on his line and it came sliding up from the water, mouth open, to swallow him. He stepped back, but the bridge caved in and sagged so that the water reached his middle.

It rained gubbish, now; all was gubbish, wherever he looked. A group of those who didn't like him appeared at the end of the bridge and held up a loop of shark teeth. He was emperor. They crowned him with the loop, and he tried to thank them. But they forced the loop down past his head to his neck, and they began to strangle him. They knotted the loop and the shark teeth cut his head off. Once more he sat in the dark, damp basement with the powdery rot around him, listening to the tidal water lap-lapping everywhere. A world where gubbish ruled, and he had no voice; the shark teeth had cut his voice out.

I am Manfred, he said.

"I tell you," Arnie Kott said to the girl beside him in the wide bed, "you're really going to be delighted when we make contact with him—I mean, we got an inside track, there: we got the future, and where else do you think things happen except in the future?"

Stirring, Doreen Anderton murmured.

"Don't go to sleep," Arnie said, leaning over to light another cigarette. "Listen, guess what—a big-time land speculator came over from Earth, today; we had a union guy at the rocket terminal, and he recognized him, although naturally the speculator registered under an assumed name. We checked with the carrier, and he got right out of there, eluding our guy. I predicted they'd be showing up! Listen, when we hear from that Steiner kid, it'll blow the lid off this whole thing. Right?" He shook the sleeping girl. "If you don't wake up," Arnie said, "I'm gonna shove you right out of bed on your ass, and you can walk home to your apartment."

Doreen groaned, turned over, sat up. In the dim light of Arnie Kott's master bedroom, she sat palely translucent, tucking her hair back from her eyes and yawning. One strap of her nightgown slipped down her arm, and Arnie saw with appreciation her high, hard left breast with its gem of a nipple set dead-center.

Gosh, I really got a gal, Arnie said to himself. She's really something. And she's done a terrific job in keeping that Bohlen from shucking it all and wandering off, the way those hebephrenic schizophrenics do—I mean, it's almost impossible to keep them at the grindstone, they're so moody and irresponsible. That guy Bohlen; he's an idiot savant, an idiot who can fix things, and we have to cater to his idiocy, we have to yield. You can't force a guy like that; he don't force. Arnie took hold of the covers and tossed them aside, off Doreen; he smiled at her bare legs, smiled to see her draw her nightgown down to her knees.

"How can you be tired?" he asked her. "You ain't done nothin' but lie. Isn't that so? Is lying there so hard?"

She eyed him narrowly. "No more," she said.

"What?" he said. "You kidding? We just begun. Take off that nightgown." Catching it by the hem he whisked it back up once more; he put his arm beneath her, lifted her up, and in an instant had it off over her head. He deposited it on the chair by the bed.

"I'm going to sleep," Doreen said, closing her eyes. "If you don't mind."

"Why should I mind?" Arnie said. "You're still there, aren't you? Awake or asleep—you're plenty there in the flesh, and how."

"Ouch," she protested.

"Sorry." He kissed her on the mouth. "Didn't mean to hurt you."

Her head lolled; she actually was going to sleep. Arnie felt offended. But what the hell—she never did much anyhow.

"Put my nightgown back on me," Doreen murmured, "when you're through."

"Yeah, well I'm not through." I'm good for an hour more, Arnie said to himself. Maybe even two. I sort of like it this way, too. A woman asleep don't talk. That's what spoils it, when they start to talk. Or make those moans. He could never stand the moans.

He thought, I'm dying to get results on that project of Bohlen's. I can't wait; I know we're going to hear something really downright wonderful when we do start hearing. The closed-up mind of that kid; think of all the treasures it contains. Must be like fairyland, in there, all beautiful and pure and real innocent.

In her half-sleep Doreen moaned.

Nine

INTO Leo Bohlen's hand his son Jack put a large green seed. Leo examined it, handed it back.

"What did you see?" Jack asked.

"I saw it, the seed."

"Did anything happen?"

Leo pondered, but he could not think of anything he had seen happen, so at last he said, "No."

Seated at the movie projector, Jack said, "Now watch." He snapped off the lights in the room, and then, on the screen, an image appeared as the projector whirred. It was a seed, embedded in soil. As Leo watched, the seed split open. Two probing feelers appeared; one started upward, the other divided into fine hairs and groped down. Meanwhile, the seed revolved in the soil. Enormous projections unfolded from the upward moving feeler, and Leo gasped.

"Say, Jack," he said, "some seeds you got here on Mars; look at it go. My gosh, it's working away like mad."

Jack said, "That's a plain ordinary lima bean, the same as I gave you just now. This film is speeded up, five days compressed into seconds. We can now see the motion that goes on in a germinating seed; normally, the process takes place too slowly for us to see any motion at all."

"Say, Jack," Leo said, "that's really something. So this kid's time-rate is like this seed. I understand. Things that we can see move would whiz around him so darn fast they'd be practically invisible, and I bet he sees slow processes like this seed here; I bet he can go out in the yard and sit down and watch the plants growing, and five days for him is like say ten minutes for us."

Jack said, "That's the theory, anyhow." He went on, then, to explain to Leo how the chamber worked. The explanation was filled with technical terms, however, which Leo did not understand, and he felt a little irritable as Jack droned on. The time was eleven A.M., and still Jack showed no sign of taking him on his trip over the F.D.R. Mountains; he seemed completely immersed in this.

"Very interesting," Leo murmured, at one point.

"We take a tape recording, done at fifteen inches per second, and run it off for Manfred at three and three-fourths inches per second. A single word, such as 'tree.' And at the same time we flash up a picture of a tree and the word beneath it, a still, which we keep in sight for fifteen or twenty minutes. Then what Manfred says is recorded at three and three-fourths inches per second, and for our own listening we speed it up and replay at fifteen."

Leo said, "Listen, Jack, we just gotta get going on that trip."

"Christ," Jack said, "this is my job." He gestured angrily. "I thought you wanted to meet him—he'll be over here any time now. She sends him over—"

Breaking in, Leo said, "Look, son, I came millions of miles to have a look at that land. Now are we going to fly there or not?"

Jack said, "We'll wait until the boy comes, and we'll take him with us."

"O.K.," Leo said. He wanted to avoid friction; he was willing to compromise, at least as much as was humanly possible.

"My God, here you are for the first time in your life on the surface of another planet. I should think you'd want to walk around, take a look at the canal, the ditch." Jack gestured over toward the right. "You haven't even glanced at it, and people have been wanting to see the canals—they've argued about their existence—for centuries!"

Feeling chagrined, Leo nodded dutifully. "Show me, then." He followed Jack from the workshop, outdoors into the dull ruddy sunlight. "Cold," Leo observed, sniffing the air. "Say, it's sure easy to walk around; I noticed that last night I felt like I weighed only fifty or sixty pounds. Must be because Mars is so small—right? Must be good for people with cardiac conditions, except the air's so thin. I thought last night it was the corned beef that made me—"

"Leo," his son said, "be quiet and look around, will you?"

Leo looked around. He saw a flat desert with meager mountains in the far distance. He saw a deep ditch of sluggish brown water, and, beside the ditch, a mosslike vegetation, green.

That was all, except for Jack's house and the Steiner house a little farther on. He saw the garden, but he had seen that last night.

"Well?" Jack said.

Being obliging, Leo said, "Very impressive, Jack. You've got a nice place here; a nice little modern place. A little more planting, landscaping, and I'd say it was perfect."

Grinning at him crookedly, Jack said, "This is the dream of a million years, to stand here and see this."

"I know that, son, and I'm exceptionally proud of what you've accomplished, you and that fine woman." Leo nodded solemnly. "Now can we get started? Maybe you could go over to that other house where that boy is and get him, or did David go over? Maybe David's getting him; I don't see him around."

"David's at school. He was picked up while you were sleeping."

Leo said, "I don't mind going over and getting that boy, Manfred or whatever his name is, if it's OK. with you."

"Go ahead," Jack said. "I'll come along."

They walked past a small ditch of water, crossed an open field of sand and sparse fernlike plants, and arrived at the other house. Leo heard from within the sound of small girls' voices. Without hesitation he ascended the steps to the porch and rang the bell.

The door opened and there stood a big, blond-haired woman with tired, pain-filled eyes. "Good morning," Leo said, "I'm Jack Bohlen's dad; I guess you're the lady of the house. Say, we'll take your boy with us on a trip and bring him back safe and sound."

The big blonde woman looked past him to Jack, who had come up on the porch; she said nothing, but turned and went off back into the interior of her house. When she returned she had a small boy with her. So this is the skizo little fellow, Leo thought. Nice-looking, you'd never know in a million years.

"We're going on a ride, young man," Leo said to him. "How does that sound?" Then, remembering what Jack had said about the boy's timesense, he repeated what he had said very slowly, dragging each word out.

The boy darted past him and shot down the steps and off toward the canal; he moved in a blur of speed and disappeared from sight behind the Bohlen house.

"Mrs. Steiner," Jack said, "I want you to meet my father."

The big blonde woman put out her hand vaguely; she did not seem to be all there herself, Leo observed. However, he shook hands with her. "Glad to meet you," he said politely. "Sorry to hear about the loss of your husband; it's a terrible thing, something striking like that, without any warning. I knew a fella back in Detroit, good friend of mine, did the same thing one weekend; went out of the shop and said goodbye and that was the last anybody saw of him."

Mrs. Steiner said, "How do you do, Mr. Bohlen."

"We'll go round up Manfred," Jack said to her. "We should be home late this afternoon."

As Leo and his son walked back, the woman remained where she was on the porch, looking after them.

"Pretty odd herself," Leo murmured. Jack said nothing.

They located the boy, standing off by himself in David's overflow garden, and presently the three of them were in the Yee Company 'copter, flying above the desert in the direction of the line of mountains to the north. Leo unfolded a great map which he had brought with him and began to make marks on it.

"I guess we can talk freely," he said to Jack, nodding his head toward the boy. "He won't—" He hesitated. "You know."

"If he understands us," Jack said drily, "it'll be—"

"O.K., O.K.," Leo said, "I just wanted to be sure." He carefully refrained from marking the place on the map that he had heard would be the UN site. But he did mark their route, using the gyrocompass reading visible on the dashboard of the 'copter. "What rumors have you heard, son?" he asked. "About UN interest in the F.D.R. range?"

Jack said, "Something about a park or a power station."

"Want to know exactly what it is?"

"Sure."

Leo reached into his inside coat pocket and brought out an envelope. From it he took a photograph, which he handed to Jack. "Does this remind you of anything?"

Glancing at it, Jack saw that it was a picture of a long, thin building. He stared at it a long time.

"The UN," Leo said, "is going to build these. Multiple-unit dwellings. Whole tracts of them, mile after mile, with shopping centers, complete—supermarkets, hardware stores, drugstores, laundries, ice cream parlors. All built by slave equipment, those construction automatons that feed themselves their own instructions."

Presently, Jack said, "It looks like the co-op apartment house I lived in years ago when I had my breakdown."

"Exactly. The co-op movement will be in with the UN on this. These F.D.R. Mountains were once fertile, as everybody knows; there was plenty of water here. The UN hydraulic engineers believe they can bring enormous quantities of water up to the surface from the table below. The water table is closer to the surface in these mountains than anywhere else on Mars; this is the original water source for the canal network, the UN engineers believe."

"The co-op," Jack said in a strange voice, "here on Mars."

"They'll be fine modern structures," Leo said. "It's quite an ambitious project. The UN will be transporting people here free, providing their passage right to their new homes, and the cost of buying each unit will be small. It will take quite a big slice of these mountains, as you might guess, and as I heard it, they expect it to be ten to fifteen years before the project is completed."

Jack said nothing.

"Mass emigration," Leo said. "This will ensure it."

"I guess so," Jack said.

"The appropriations for this are fantastic," Leo said. "The co-op alone is putting up almost a trillion dollars. It has huge reserves of cash, you know; it's one of the richest groups on Earth—it has greater assets than the insurance group or any of the big banking systems. There's not a chance in the world that with them in on it the thing could fail." He added, "The UN has been negotiating with them for six years on this matter."

Finally, Jack said, "What a change it will mean for Mars. Just to have the F.D.R. range fertile—that alone."

"And densely populated," Leo reminded him.

"It's hard to believe," Jack said.

"Yeah, I know, boy, but there's no doubt of it; within another few weeks it'll be generally known. I knew it a month ago. I've been getting investors I know to put up risk capital . . . I represent them, Jack. Alone, I just don't have the money."

Jack said, "You mean, your whole idea is to get here before the UN actually takes the land. You're going to buy it for very little and then resell it to the UN for much more."

"We're going to buy it in great pieces," Leo said, "and then at once subdivide. Cut it up into lots, say, one hundred feet by eighty. Title will be in the hands of a fairly large number of individuals: wives, cousins, employees, friends of the members of my group."

"Of your syndicate," Jack said.

"Yes, that's what it is," Leo said, pleased. "A syndicate."

After a time Jack said in a hoarse voice, "And you don't feel there's anything wrong with doing this?"

"Wrong in what sense? I don't get you, son."

"Christ," Jack said. "It's obvious."

"Not to me. Explain."

"You're gypping the entire population of Earth—they're the ones who'll have to put up all the money. You're increasing the costs of this project in order to make a killing."

"But Jack, that's what's meant by land speculation." Leo was puzzled. "What did you think land speculation was? It's been going on for centuries; you buy land cheap when nobody wants it because you believe for one reason or another that one day it will be worth a lot more. And it's inside tips that you go on. That's about all there is to go on, when you get down to it. Every land speculator in the world will be trying to buy in, when they get word; in fact they're doing that right now. I beat them here by a matter of days. It's this regulation that you have to actually be on Mars that gets them; they're not prepared at the drop of a hat to come here. So—they've missed out. Because by nightfall I expect to have put our deposit down on the land we want." He pointed ahead of them. "It's in there. I've got all sorts of maps; I won't have any trouble locating it. The location of the piece is in a vast canyon area called the Henry Wallace. To comply with the law, I have to actually set foot on the piece I intend to buy, and place some permanent marker, fully identifiable, in an exposed spot. I have such a marker with me, a regulation steel stake which bears my name. We'll land in the Henry Wallace and you can help me drive the stake in. It's just a formality; it won't take more than a few minutes." He smiled at his son.

Looking at his father, Jack thought, *He's insane.* But Leo smiled calmly at him, and Jack knew that his father was not insane, that it was exactly as he said: land speculators did this, it was their way of going about their business, and there really was such a mammoth UN–co-op project about to start. As shrewd and experienced a businessman as his father could not be wrong. Leo Bohlen, and the men with him, did not act on the basis of a rumor. They had top connections. There had been a leak, either at the co-op or the UN or both, and Leo was putting all his resources to work to take advantage of it.

"It's—the biggest news so far," Jack said, "regarding the development of Mars." He could still hardly believe it.

"Long overdue," Leo said. "Should have taken place right from the start. But they expected private capital to be put up; they waited for the other fella to do it."

"This will change the lives of everybody who lives on Mars," Jack said. It would alter the balance of power, create a totally new ruling class: Arnie Kott, Bosley Touvim—the union settlements and the national settlements—would be small fry, once the co-op, in conjunction with the UN, had moved in.

Poor Arnie, he thought. He won't survive this. Time, progress, and civilization, all will have passed him by, Arnie and his steam baths that waste water, his tiny symbol of pomp.

"Now listen, Jack," his father said, "don't spread this information around, because it's confidential. What we want to watch is crooked business at the abstract company—that's the outfit that records your title. I mean, we put up our deposit, and then other speculators, especially local ones here, get tipped off and then have pull at the abstract company, so it turns out—"

"I see," Jack said. The abstract company would predate the

deposit of a local speculator, giving him seeming priority over Leo. There must be many tricks that can be played in a game like this, Jack said to himself; no wonder Leo works carefully.

"We've investigated the abstract company here, and it appears to be honest. But you never know, when there's so much involved."

Suddenly Manfred Steiner gave a hoarse grunt.

Both Jack and Leo glanced up, startled. They had both forgotten about him; he was at the rear of the cab of the 'copter, his face pressed to the glass, staring down. He pointed excitedly.

Far below, Jack saw a party of Bleekmen threading its way along a mountain trail. "That's right," Jack said to the boy, "people down there, probably hunting." It occurred to him that very possibly Manfred had never seen a Bleekman. I wonder what his reaction would be, Jack mused, if he found himself facing them, all at once. How easy it would be to arrange it; all he had to do, really, was land the 'copter ahead of this particular party.

"What are those?" Leo asked, looking down. "Martians?"

"That's what they are," Jack said.

"I'll be darned." Leo laughed. "So those are Martians . . . they look more like aboriginal Negroes, like the African Bushmen."

"They're closely related to them," Jack said.

Manfred had become quite excited; his eyes shone and he ran back and forth from window to window, peering down and muttering.

What would happen if Manfred lived with a family of Bleekmen for a time? Jack wondered. They move slower then we do; their lives are less complex and hectic. Possibly their sense of time is close to his . . . to the Bleekmen, we Earthmen may very well be hypomanic types, whizzing about at enormous velocity, expending huge amounts of energy over nothing at all.

But it would not bring Manfred into his own society, to put him with the Bleekmen. In fact, he realized, it might draw him so far away from us that there would be no chance of our ever communicating with him.

Thinking that, he decided not to land the 'copter.

"Do those fellas do any work?" Leo asked. "Those Martians?"

"A few have been tamed," Jack said, "as the phrase goes. But most of them continue to exist as they always have, as hunters and fruit-gatherers. They haven't reached the farming stage yet."

When they reached the Henry Wallace, Jack set the 'copter down, and he and his father and Manfred stepped out onto the parched, rocky soil. Manfred was given paper and crayons to amuse himself, and then the two men set out to search for a suitable spot at which to drive the stake.

The spot, a low plateau, was found, and the stake was driven, mostly by Jack; his father wandered about, inspecting rock formations and plants, with a clearly irritated and impatient frown. He did not seem to enjoy it here in this uninhabited region—however, he said nothing; he politely took note of a fossil formation which Jack pointed out to him.

They took photographs of the stake and the surrounding area, and then, their business done, they returned to the 'copter. There sat Manfred, on the ground, busily drawing with the crayons. The desolation of the area did not seem to bother him, Jack decided. The boy, wrapped up in his inner world, drew and ignored them; he glanced up now and then, but not at the two men. His eyes were blank.

What's he drawing? Jack wondered, and walked around behind the boy to see.

Manfred, glancing up now and then to peer sightlessly at the landscape around him, had drawn great, flat apartment buildings.

"Look at this, Dad," Jack said, and he managed to keep his voice calm and steady.

Together, the two of them stood behind the boy, watching him draw, watching the buildings become more and more distinct on the paper.

Well, there's no mistaking it, Jack thought. The boy is drawing the buildings that will be here. He is drawing the landscape which will come, not the landscape visible to our eyes.

"I wonder if he saw the photo I showed you," Leo said. "That one of the models."

"Maybe so," Jack said. It would provide an explanation; the boy had understood their conversation, seen the papers, gotten his inspiration from that. But the photo had shown the buildings from above; it was a different perspective from this. The boy had sketched the buildings as they would appear to an observer on the ground. As they would appear, Jack realized, to someone seated where we are right now.

"I wouldn't be surprised if you've got something in this time theory," Leo said. He glanced at his wrist watch. "Now, speaking of time, I'd say—"

"Yes," Jack agreed thoughtfully, "we'll get started back."

There was something more in the child's drawing which he had noticed. He wondered if his father had seen it. The buildings, the enormous co-op apartments, which the boy was sketching, were developing in an ominous direction before their eyes. As they watched, they saw some final details which made Leo glare; he snorted and glanced at his son.

The buildings were old, sagging with age. Their foundations showed great cracks radiating upward. Windows were broken. And what looked like stiff tall weeds grew in the land around. It was a scene of ruin and despair, and of a ponderous, timeless, inertial heaviness.

"Jack, he's drawing a slum!" Leo exclaimed.

That was it, a decaying slum. Buildings that had stood for years, perhaps even decades, which had passed their prime and dwindled into their twilight, into senility and partial abandonment.

Pointing at a yawning crack which he had just drawn, Manfred said, "Gubbish." His hand traced the weeds, the broken windows. Again he said, "Gubbish." He glanced at them, smiling in a frightened way.

"What does that mean, Manfred?" Jack asked.

There was no answer. The boy continued to sketch. And as he sketched, the buildings, before their eyes, grew older and older, more in ruins with each passing moment.

"Let's go," Leo said hoarsely.

Jack took the boy's paper and crayons and got him on his feet. The three of them re-entered the 'copter.

"Look, Jack," Leo said. He was intently examining the

boy's drawing. "What he's written over the entrance of the building."

In twisted, wavering letters Manfred had written:

AM-WEB

"Must be the name of the building." Leo said.

"It is," Jack said, recognizing the word; it was a contraction of a co-op slogan "Alle Menschen werden Brüder." "All men become brothers," he said under his breath. "It's on co-op stationery." He remembered it well.

Now, taking his crayons once more, Manfred resumed his work. As the two men watched, the boy began to draw something at the top of the picture. Dark birds, Jack saw. Enormous, dusky, vulture-like birds.

At a broken window of the building, Manfred drew a round face with eyes, nose, a turned-down, despairing mouth. Someone within the building, gazing out silently and hopelessly, as if trapped within.

"Well," Leo said. "Interesting." His expression was one of grim outrage. "Now, why would he want to draw that? I don't think that's a very wholesome or positive attitude; why can't he draw it like it's going to be, new and immaculate, with children playing and pets and contented people?"

Jack said, "Maybe he draws what he sees."

"Well, if he sees that, he's ill," Leo said. "There are so many bright, wonderful things he could see instead; why would he want to see that?"

"Perhaps he has no choice," Jack said. *Gubbish*, he thought. I wonder; could *gubbish* mean time? The force that to the boy means decay, deterioration, destruction, and, at last, death? The force at work everywhere, on everything in the universe.

And is that all he sees?

If so, Jack thought, no wonder he's autistic; no wonder he can't communicate with us. A view of the universe that partial —it isn't even a complete view of time. Because time also brings new things into existence; it's also the process of maturation and growth. And evidently Manfred does not perceive time in that aspect.

Is he sick because he sees this? Or does he see this because he is sick? A meaningless question, perhaps, or anyhow one that can't be answered. This is Manfred's view of reality, and according to us, he is desperately ill; he does not perceive the rest of reality, which we do. And it is a dreadful section which he does see: reality in its most repellent aspect.

Jack thought, *And people talk about mental illness as an escape!* He shuddered. It was no escape; it was a narrowing, a contracting of life into, at last, a moldering, dank tomb, a place where nothing came or went; a place of total death.

The poor damned kid, he thought. How can he live from one day to the next, having to face the reality he does?

Somberly, Jack returned to the job of piloting the 'copter. Leo looked out the window, contemplating the desert below. Manfred, with the taut, frightened expression on his face, continued to draw.

They gubbled and gubbled. He put his hands to his ears, but the product crept up through his nose. Then he saw the place. It was where he wore out. They threw him away there, and gubbish lay in heaps up to his waist; gubbish filled the air.

"What is your name?"

"Steiner, Manfred."

"Age."

"Eighty-three."

"Vaccinated against small pox?"

"Yes."

"Any venereal diseases?"

"Well, a little clap, that's all."

"V.D. clinic for this man."

"Sir, my teeth. They're in the bag, along with my eyes."

"Your eyes, oh yes. Give this man his teeth and eyes before you take him to the V.D. clinic. How about your ears, Steiner?"

"Got 'em on, sir. Thank you, sir."

They tied his hands with gauze to the sides of the bed because he tried to pull out the catheter. He lay facing the window, seeing through the dusty, cracked glass.

Outside, a bug on tall legs picked through the heaps. It ate, and then something squashed it and went on, leaving it squashed with its dead teeth sunk into what it had wanted to eat. Finally its dead teeth got up and crawled out of its mouth in different directions.

He lay there for a hundred and twenty-three years and then his artificial liver gave out and he fainted and died. By that time they had removed both his arms and legs up to the pelvis because those parts of him had decayed.

He didn't use them anyhow. And without arms he didn't try to pull the catheter out, and that pleased them.

I been at AM-WEB for a long time, he said. Maybe you can get me a transistor radio so I can tune in Friendly Fred's Breakfast Club; I like to hear the tunes, they play a lot of the old-time favorites.

Something outside gives me hayfever. Must be those yellow flowering weeds, why do they let them get so tall?

I once saw a ballgame.

For two days he lay on the floor, in a big puddle, and then the landlady found him and called for the truck to bring him here. He snored all the way, it woke him up. When they tried to give him grapefruit juice he could only work one arm, the other never worked again ever. He wished he could still make those leather belts, they were fun and took lots of time. Sometimes he sold them to people who came by on the week-end.

"Do you know who I am, Manfred?"

"No."

"I'm Arnie Kott. Why don't you laugh or smile sometimes, Manfred? Don't you like to run around and play?"

As he spoke Mr. Kott gubbled from both his eyes.

"Obviously he doesn't, Arnie, but that's not what concerns us here anyhow."

"What do you see, Manfred? Let us in on what you see. All those people, are they going to live there, is that it? Is that right, Manfred? Can you see lots of people living there?"

He put his hands over his face, and the gubble stopped.

"I don't see why this kid never laughs."

Gubble, gubble.

Ten

INSIDE Mr. Kott's skin were dead bones, shiny and wet. Mr. Kott was a sack of bones, dirty and yet shiny-wet. His head was a skull that took in greens and bit them; inside him the greens became rotten things as something ate them to make them dead.

He could see everything that went on inside Mr. Kott, the teeming gubbish life. Meanwhile, the outside said, "I love Mozart. I'll put this tape on." The box read: "Symphony 40 in G mol., K. 550." Mr. Kott fiddled with the knobs of the amplifier. "Bruno Walter conducting," Mr. Kott told his guests. "A great rarity from the golden age of recordings."

A hideous racket of screeches and shrieks issued from the speakers, like the convulsions of corpses. Mr. Kott shut off the tape transport.

"Sorry," he muttered. It was an old coded message, from Rockingham or Scott Temple or Anne, from someone, anyhow; Mr. Kott, he knew that. He knew that by accident it had found its way into his library of music.

Sipping her drink, Doreen Anderton said, "What a shock. You should spare us, Arnie. Your sense of humor—"

"An accident," Arnie Kott said angrily. He rummaged for another tape. Aw, the hell with it, he thought. "Listen, Jack," he said, turning. "I'm sorry to make you come here when I know your dad's visiting, but I'm running out of time; show me your progress with the Steiner boy, O.K.?" His anticipation and concern made him stutter. He looked at Jack expectantly.

But Jack Bohlen hadn't heard him; he was saying something to Doreen there on the couch where the two of them sat together.

"We're out of booze," Jack said, setting down his empty glass.

"God sake," Arnie said, "I got to hear how you've done, Jack. Can't you give me anything? Are you two just going to sit there necking and whispering? I don't feel good." He went unsteadily into the kitchen, where Heliogabalus sat on a tall stool, like a dunce, reading a magazine. "Fix me a glass of warm water and baking soda," Arnie said.

"Yes, Mister." Heliogabalus closed his magazine and stepped down from the stool. "I overheard. Why don't you send them out? They are no good, no good at all, Mister." From the cabinet over the sink he took the package of bicarbonate of soda; he spooned out a teaspoonful.

"Who cares about your opinion?" Arnie said.

Doreen entered the kitchen, her face drawn and tired. "Arnie, I think I'll go home. I really can't take much of Manfred; he never stops moving around, never sits still. I can't stand it." Going up to Arnie she kissed him on the ear. "Goodnight, dear."

"I read about a kid who thought he was a machine," Arnie said. "He had to be plugged in, he said, to work. I mean, you have to be able to stand these fruits. Don't go. Stay for my sake. Manfred's a lot quieter when a woman's around, I don't know why. I have the feeling that Bohlen's accomplished nothing; I'm going out there and tell him to his face." A glass of warm water and baking soda was put into his right hand by his tame Bleekman. "Thanks." He drank it gratefully.

"Jack Bohlen," Doreen said, "has done a fine job under difficult conditions. I don't want to hear anything said against him." She swayed slightly, smiling. "I'm a little drunk."

"Who isn't?" Arnie said. He put his arm around her waist and hugged her. "I'm so drunk I'm sick. O.K., that kid gets me, too. Look, I put on that old coded tape; I must be nuts." Setting down his glass he unbuttoned the top buttons of her blouse. "Look away, Helio. Read your book." The Bleekman looked away. Holding Doreen against him, Arnie unbuttoned all the buttons of her blouse and began on her skirt. "I know they're ahead of me, those Earth bastards coming in everywhere you look. My man at the terminal can't even count them any more; they been coming in all day long. Let's go to bed." He kissed her on the collar bone, nuzzled lower and lower until she raised his head with the strength of her hands.

In the living room, his hotshot repairman hired away from Mr. Yee fiddled with the tape recorder, clumsily putting on a fresh reel. He had knocked over his empty glass.

What happens if they get there before me? Arnie Kott asked himself as he clung to Doreen, wheeling slowly about the kitchen with her as Heliogabalus read to himself. What if I can't buy in at all? Might as well be dead. He bent Doreen backwards, but all the time thinking, There has to be a place for me. I love this planet.

Music blared; Jack Bohlen had gotten the tape going.

Doreen pinched him savagely, and he let go of her; he walked from the kitchen, back into the living room, turned down the volume, and said, "Jack, let's get down to business."

"Right," Jack Bohlen agreed.

Coming from the kitchen after him, buttoning her blouse, Doreen made a wide circuit to avoid Manfred, who was down on his hands and knees; the boy had spread out a length of butcher paper and was pasting bits cut from magazines onto it with library paste. Patches of white showed on the rug where he had slopped.

Going up to the boy, Arnie bent down close to him and said, "Do you know who I am, Manfred?"

There was no answer from the boy, nothing to show he had even heard.

"I'm Arnie Kott," Arnie said. "Why don't you laugh or smile sometimes, Manfred? Don't you like to run around and play?" He felt sorry for the boy, sorry and distressed.

Jack Bohlen said in an unsteady, thick voice, "Obviously he doesn't, Arnie, but that's not what concerns us here, anyhow." His gaze was befuddled; the hand that held the glass shook.

But Arnie continued. "What do you see, Manfred? Let us in on what you see." He waited, but there was only silence. The boy concentrated on his pasting. He had created a collage on the paper: a jagged strip of green, then a perpendicular rise, gray and dense, forbidding.

"What's it mean?" Arnie said.

"It's a place," Jack said. "A building. I brought it along." He went off, returning with a manila envelope; from it he brought a large crumpled child's crayon drawing, which he held up for Arnie to examine. "There," Jack said. "That's it. You wanted me to establish communication with him; well, I established it." He had some trouble with the two long words; his tongue seemed to catch.

Arnie, however, did not care how drunk his repairman was. He was accustomed to having his guests tank up; hard liquor was rare on Mars, and when people came upon it, as they did at Arnie's place, they generally reacted as Jack Bohlen had. What mattered was the task which Jack had been given. Arnie picked up the picture and studied it.

"This it?" he asked Jack. "What else?"

"Nothing else."

"What about that chamber that slows things down?"

"Nothing," Jack said.

"Can the boy read the future?"

"Absolutely," Jack said. "There's no doubt of it. That picture is proof right there, unless he heard us talking." Turning to Doreen he said, in a slow, thick voice, "Did he hear us, do you think? No, you weren't there. It was my dad. I don't think he heard. Listen, Arnie. You aren't supposed to see this, but I guess it's O.K. It's too late now. This is a picture nobody is supposed to see; this is the way it's going to be a century from now, when it's in ruins."

"What the hell is it?" Arnie said. "I can't read a kid's nutty drawing; explain it to me."

"This is AM-WEB," Jack said. "A big, big housing tract. Thousands of people living there. Biggest on Mars. Only, it's crumbling into rubble, according to the picture."

There was silence. Arnie was baffled.

"Maybe you're not interested," Jack said.

"Sure I am," Arnie said angrily. He appealed to Doreen, who stood off to one side, looking pensive. "Do you understand this?"

"No, dear," she said.

"Jack," Arnie said, "I called you here for your report. And all I get is this dim-witted drawing. Where is this big housing tract?"

"In the F.D.R. Mountains," Jack said.

Arnie felt his pulse slow, then with difficulty labor on. "Oh, yeah, I see," he said. "I understand."

Grinning, Jack said, "I thought you would. You're interested in that. You know, Arnie, you think I'm a schizophrenic, and Doreen thinks so, and my father thinks so . . . but I *do* care what your motives are. I can get you plenty of information about the UN project in the F.D.R. Mountains. What else do you want to know about it? It's not a power station and it's not a park. It's in conjunction with the co-op. It's a multiple-unit, infinitely large structure with supermarkets and bakeries, dead center in the Henry Wallace."

"You got all this from this kid?"

"No," Jack said. "From my dad."

They looked at each other a long time.

"Your dad is a speculator?" Arnie said.

"Yes," Jack said.

"He just arrived from Earth the other day?"

"Yes," Jack said.

"Jesus," Arnie said to Doreen. "Jesus, it's this guy's father. And he's already bought in."

"Yes," Jack said.

"Is there anything left?" Arnie said.

Jack shook his head.

"Oh, Jesus Christ," Arnie said. "And he's on my payroll. I never had such bad luck."

Jack said, "I didn't know until just now that this was what you wanted to find out, Arnie."

"Yeah, that's true," Arnie said. Speaking to Doreen, he said, "I never told him, so it's not his fault." He aimlessly picked up the boy's drawing. "And this is what it'll look like."

"Eventually," Jack said. "Not at first."

To Manfred, Arnie said, "You did have the information, but we got it from you too late."

"Too late," Jack echoed. He seemed to understand; he looked stricken. "Sorry, Arnie. I really am sorry. You should have told me."

"I don't blame you," Arnie said. "We're still friends, Bohlen. It's just a case of bad luck. You've been completely honest with me; I can see that. Goddamn, it sure is too bad. He's already filed his claim, your dad? Well, that's the way it goes."

"He represents a group of investors," Jack said hoarsely.

"Naturally," Arnie said. "With unlimited capital. What could I do anyhow? I can't compete. I'm just one guy." To Manfred he said, "All these people—" He pointed to the drawing. "Are they going to live there, is that it? Is that right,

Manfred? Can you see lots of people living there?" His voice
rose, out of control.

"Please, Arnie," Doreen said. "Calm down; I can see how
upset you are, and you shouldn't be."

Raising his head, Arnie said to her in a low voice, "I don't
see why this kid never laughs."

The boy suddenly said, "Gubble, gubble."

"Yeah," Arnie said, with bitterness. "That's right. That's
real good communication, kid. Gubble, gubble." To Jack he
said, "You have a fine communication established; I can see
that."

Jack said nothing. Now he looked grim and uneasy.

"I can see it's going to take a long time more," Arnie said,
"to bring this kid out so we can talk to him. Right? Too bad
we can't continue. I'm not going any further with it."

"No reason why you should," Jack said in a leaden voice.

"Right," Arnie said. "So that's it. The end of your job."

Doreen said, "But you can still use him for—"

"Oh, of course," Arnie said. "I need a skilled repairman anyhow, for stuff like that encoder; I got a thousand items busting
down every goddamn day. I just mean this one particular job,
here. Send him back to B-G, this kid. AM-WEB. Yeah, the
co-op buildings get funny names like that. The co-op coming
over to Mars! That's a big outfit, that co-op. They'll pay high
for their land; they've got the loot. Tell your dad from me that
he's a shrewd businessman."

"Can we shake hands, Arnie?" Jack asked.

"Sure, Jack." Arnie stuck out his hand and the two of them
shook, hard and long, looking each other in the eye. "I expect
to see a lot of you, Jack. This isn't the end between you and
me; it's just the beginning." He let go of Jack Bohlen's hand,
walked back into the kitchen, and stood by himself, thinking.

Presently Doreen joined him. "That was dreadful news for
you, wasn't it?" she said, putting her arm around him.

"Very bad," Arnie said. "Worst I had in a long time. But I'll
be O.K.; I'm not scared of the co-op movement. Lewistown
and the Water Workers were here first, and they'll be here a lot
longer. If I had gotten this project with the Steiner boy started
sooner, it would have worked out differently, and I sure don't

blame Jack for that." But inside him, in his heart, he thought, You were working against me, Jack. All the time. You were working with your father. From the start, too; from the day I hired you.

He returned to the living room. At the tape transport, Jack stood morose and silent, fooling with the knobs.

"Don't take it hard," Arnie said to him.

"Thanks, Arnie," Jack said. His eyes were dull. "I feel I've let you down."

"Not me," Arnie assured him. "You haven't let me down, Jack. Because nobody lets me down."

On the floor, Manfred Steiner pasted away, ignoring them all.

As he flew his father back to the house, leaving the F.D.R. range behind them, Jack thought, Should I show the boy's picture to Arnie? Should I take it to Lewistown and hand it over to him? It's so little . . . it just doesn't look like what I ought to have produced, by now.

He knew that tonight he would have to see Arnie, in any case.

"Very desolate down there," his dad said, nodding toward the desert below. "Amazing you people have done so much reclamation work; you should all be proud." But his attention was actually on his maps. He spoke in a perfunctory manner; it was a formality.

Jack snapped on his radio transmitter and called Arnie, at Lewistown. "Excuse me, dad; I have to talk to my boss."

The radio made a series of noises, which attracted Manfred momentarily; he ceased poring over his drawing and raised his head.

"I'll take you along," Jack said to the boy.

Presently he had Arnie. "Hi, Jack." Arnie's voice came boomingly. "I been trying to get hold of you. Can you—"

"I'll be over to see you tonight," Jack said.

"Not before? How about this afternoon?"

"Afraid tonight is as soon as I can make it," Jack said. "There—" He hesitated. "Nothing to show you until tonight." If I get near him, he thought, I'll tell him about the UN–co-op project; he'll get everything out of me. I'll wait until after my dad's claim has been filed, and then it won't matter.

"Tonight, then," Arnie agreed. "And I'll be on pins, Jack. Sitting on pins. I know you're going to come up with something; I got a lot of confidence in you."

Jack thanked him, said goodbye, and rang off.

"Your boss sounds like a gentleman," his dad said, after the connection had been broken. "And he certainly looks up to you. I expect you're of priceless value to his organization, a man with your ability."

Jack said nothing. Already he felt guilty.

"Draw me a picture," he said to Manfred, "of how it's going to go tonight, between me and Mr. Kott." He took away the paper on which the boy was drawing and handed him a blank piece. "Will you, Manfred? You can see ahead to tonight. You, me, Mr. Kott, at Mr. Kott's place."

The boy took a blue crayon and began to draw. As he piloted the 'copter, Jack watched.

With great care, Manfred drew. At first Jack could not make it out. Then he grasped what the scene showed. Two men. One was hitting the other in the eye.

Manfred laughed, a long, high-pitched, nervous laugh, and suddenly hugged the picture against himself.

Feeling cold, Jack turned his attention back to the controls before him. He felt himself perspire, the damp sweat of anxiety. Is that how it's going to be? he asked, silently, within himself. A fight between me and Arnie? And you will witness it, perhaps . . . or at least know of it, one day.

"Jack," Leo was saying, "you'll take me to the abstract company, won't you? And let me off there? I want to get my papers filed. Can we go right there, instead of back to the house? I have to admit I'm uneasy. There must be local operators who're watching all this, and I can't be too careful."

Jack said, "I can only repeat: it's immoral, what you're doing."

"Just let me handle it," his father said. "It's my way of doing business, Jack. I don't intend to change."

"Profiteering," Jack said.

"I won't argue it with you," his father said. "It's none of your concern. If you don't feel like assisting me, after I've come millions of miles from Earth, I guess I can manage to round up public transportation." His tone was mild, but he had turned red.

"I'll take you there," Jack said.

"I can't stand to be moralized at," his father said.

Jack said nothing. He turned the 'copter south, toward the UN buildings at Pax Grove.

Drawing away with his blue crayon, Manfred made one of the two men in his picture, the one who had been hit in the eye, fall down and become dead. Jack saw that, saw the figure become supine and then still. Is that me? he wondered. Or is it Arnie?

Someday—perhaps soon—I will know.

Inside Mr. Kott's skin were dead bones, shiny and wet. Mr. Kott was a sack of bones, dirty and yet shiny-wet. His head was a skull that took in greens and bit them; inside him the greens became rotten things as something ate them to make them dead.

Jack Bohlen, too, was a dead sack, teeming with gubbish. The outside that fooled almost everyone, it was painted pretty and smelled good, bent down over Miss Anderton, and he saw that; he saw it wanting her in an awful fashion. It poured its wet, sticky self nearer to her and the dead bug words popped from its mouth.

"I love Mozart," Mr. Kott was saying. "I'll put this tape on." He fiddled with the knobs of the amplifier. "Bruno Walter conducting. A great rarity from the golden age of recordings."

A hideous racket of screeches and shrieks issued from the speakers, like the convulsions of corpses. He shut off the tape transport.

"Sorry," Arnie Kott muttered.

Wincing at the sound, Jack Bohlen sniffed the woman's body beside him, saw shiny perspiration on her upper lip where a faint smear of her lipstick made her mouth look cut. He wanted to bite her lips, he wanted to make blood, there. His thumbs wanted to dig into her armpits and make an upward circle so that he worked her breasts, then he would feel they belonged to him to do with what he wanted. He had made them move already; it was fun.

"What a shock," she said. "You should spare us, Arnie. Your sense of humor—"

"An accident," Arnie said. He rummaged for another tape.

Reaching out his hand Jack Bohlen touched the woman's lap. There was no underwear there beneath her skirt. He rubbed her legs and she drew her legs up and turned toward him so that her knees pressed into him; she sat like an animal, crouching in expectation. I can't wait to get you and me out of here and where we can be alone, Jack thought. God, how I want to feel you, and not through clothing. He closed his fingers around her bare ankle and she yapped with pain, smiling at him.

"Listen, Jack," Arnie Kott said, turning toward him. "I'm sorry—" His words were cut off. Jack did not hear the rest. The woman beside him was telling him something. Hurry, she was saying. I can't wait either. Her breath came in short, brisk hisses from her mouth, and she gazed at him fixedly, her face close to his, her eyes huge, as if she were impaled. Neither of them heard Arnie. The room, now, was silent.

Had he missed something Arnie had said? Jack reached out and took hold of his glass, but there was nothing in it. "We're out of booze," he said, setting it back down on the coffee table.

"God sake," Arnie said. "I got to hear how you've done, Jack. Can't you give me anything?" Talking still, he moved away, from the living room into the kitchen; his voice dimmed. Beside Jack the woman still stared up at him, her mouth weak, as if he were holding her tightly to him, as if she could hardly breathe. We have to get out of this place and be by ourselves, Jack realized. Then, looking around, he saw that they were alone; Arnie had gone out of the room and could no longer see them. In the kitchen he was conversing with his tame Bleekman. And so he was already alone with her.

"Not here," Doreen said. But her body fluttered, it did not resist him as he squeezed her about the waist; she did not mind being squashed because she wanted to, too. She could not hold back either. "Yes," she said. "But hurry." Her nails dug into his shoulders and she shut her eyes tight, moaning and shuddering. "At the side," she said. "It unbuttons, my skirt."

Bending over her he saw her lanquid, almost rotting beauty fall away. Yellow cracks spread through her teeth, and the teeth split and sank into her gums, which in turn became green and dry like leather, and then she coughed and spat up into his face quantities of dust. The Gubbler had gotten her, he realized, before he had been able to. So he let her go. She settled backward, her breaking bones making little sharp splintering sounds.

Her eyes fused over, opaque, and from behind one eye the lashes became the furry, probing feet of a thick-haired insect stuck back there wanting to get out. Its tiny pin-head red eye peeped past the loose rim of her unseeing eye, and then withdrew; after that the insect squirmed, making the dead eye of the woman bulge, and then, for an instant, the insect peered through the lens of her eye, looked this way and that, saw him but was unable to make out who or what he was; it could not fully make use of the decayed mechanism behind which it lived.

Like over ripe puffballs, her boobies wheezed as they deflated into flatness, and from their dry interiors, through the web of cracks spreading across them, a cloud of spores arose and drifted up into his face, the smell of mold and age of the Gubbler, who had come and inhabited the inside long ago and was now working his way out to the surface.

The dead mouth twitched and then from deep inside at the bottom of the pipe which was the throat a voice muttered, "You weren't fast enough." And then the head fell off entirely, leaving the white pointed stick-like end of the neck projecting.

Jack released her and she folded up into a little dried-up heap of flat, almost transparent plates, like the discarded skin of a snake, almost without weight; he brushed them away from him with his hand. And at the same time, to his surprise, he heard her voice from the kitchen.

"Arnie, I think I'll go home. I really can't take much of Manfred; he never stops moving around, never sits still." Turning his head he saw her in there, with Arnie, standing very close to him. She kissed him on the ear. "Good night, dear," she said.

"I read about a kid who thought he was a machine," Arnie

said, and then the kitchen door shut; Jack could neither hear nor see them.

Rubbing his forehead he thought, I really am drunk. *What's wrong with me?* My mind, splitting . . . he blinked, tried to gather his faculties. On the rug, not far from the couch, Manfred Steiner cut out a picture from a magazine with blunt scissors, smiling to himself; the paper rustled as he cut it, a sound that distracted Jack and made it even more difficult for him to put in focus his wandering attention.

From beyond the kitchen door he heard heavy breathing and then labored, prolonged grunts. What are they doing? he asked himself. The three of them, she and Arnie and the tame Bleekman, together . . . the grunts became slower and then ceased. There was no sound at all.

I wish I was home, Jack said to himself with desperate, utter confusion. I want to get out of here, but how? He felt weak and terribly sick and he remained on the couch, where he was, unable to break away, to move or think.

A voice in his mind said, Gubble gubble gubble, I am gubble gubble gubble gubble.

Stop, he said to it.

Gubble, gubble, gubble, gubble, it answered.

Dust fell on him from the walls. The room creaked with age and dust, rotting around him. Gubble, gubble gubble, the room said. The Gubbler is here to gubble gubble you and make you into gubbish.

Getting unsteadily to his feet he managed to walk, step by step, over to Arnie's amplifier and tape recorder. He picked up a reel of tape and got the box open. After several faulty, feeble efforts he succeeded in putting it on the spindle of the transport.

The door to the kitchen opened a crack, and an eye watched him; he could not tell whose it was.

I have to get out of here, Jack Bohlen said to himself. Or fight it off; I have to break this, throw it away from me or be eaten.

It is eating me up.

He twisted the volume control convulsively so that the music blared up and deafened him, roared through the room, spilling over the walls, the furniture, lashing at the ajar kitchen door, attacking everyone and everything in sight.

The kitchen door fell forward, its hinges breaking; it crashed over and a thing came hurriedly sideways from the kitchen, dislodged into belated activity by the roar of the music. The thing scrabbled up to him and past him, feeling for the volume control knob. The music ebbed.

But he felt better. He felt sane, once more, thank God.

Jack Bohlen dropped his father off at the abstract office and then, with Manfred, flew on to Lewistown, to Doreen Anderton's apartment.

When she opened the door and saw him she said, "What is it, Jack?" She quickly held the door open and he and Manfred went on inside.

"It's going to be very bad tonight," he told her.

"Are you sure?" She seated herself across from him. "Do you have to go at all? Yes, I suppose so. But maybe you're wrong."

Jack said, "Manfred has already told me. He's already seen it."

"Don't be scared," Doreen said softly.

"But I am," he said.

"*Why* will it be bad?"

"I don't know. Manfred couldn't tell me that."

"But—" She gestured. "You've made contact with him; that's wonderful. That's what Arnie wants."

"I hope you'll be there," Jack said.

"Yes, I'll be there. But—there's not much I can do. Is my opinion worth anything? Because I'm positive that Arnie will be pleased; I think you're having an anxiety attack for no reason."

"It's the end," Jack said, "between me and Arnie—tonight. I know it, and I don't know why." He felt sick to his stomach. "It almost seems to me that Manfred does more than know the future; in some way he *controls* it, he can make it come out the worst possible way because that's what seems natural to him, that's how he sees reality. It's as if by being around him we're sinking into his reality. It's starting to seep over us and replace our own way of viewing things, and the kind of events we're accustomed to see come about now somehow *don't* come about. It's not natural for me to feel this way; I've never had this feeling about the future before."

He was silent, then.

"You've been around him too much," Doreen said. "Tendencies in you that are—" She hesitated. "Unstable tendencies, Jack. Allied to his; you were supposed to draw him into our world, the shared reality of our society . . . instead, hasn't he drawn you into his own? I don't think there's any precognition; I think it's been a mistake from the start. It would be better if you got out of it, if you left that boy—" She glanced toward Manfred, who had gone to the window of her apartment to stare out at the street below. "If you didn't have anything more to do with him."

"It's too late for that," Jack said.

"You're not a psychotherapist or a doctor," Doreen said. "It's one thing for Milton Glaub to be in close contact day after day with autistic and schizophrenic persons, but you— you're a repairman who blundered into this because of a crazy impulse on Arnie's part; you just happened to be there in the same room with him fixing his encoder and so you wound up with this. You shouldn't be so passive, Jack. You're letting your life be shaped by chance, and for God's sake—don't you recognize that passivity for what it is?"

After a pause he said, "I suppose I do."

"Say it."

He said, "There's a tendency for a schizophrenic individual to be passive; I know that."

"Be decisive; don't go any further with this. Call Arnie and tell him you're simply not competent to handle Manfred. He should be back at Camp B-G where Milton Glaub can work with him. They can build that slowed-down chamber there; they were starting to, weren't they?"

"They'll never get around to it. They're talking about importing the equipment from Home; you know what that means."

"And you'll never get around to it," Doreen said, "because, long before you do, you'll have cracked up mentally. I can look into the future too; you know what I see? I see you having a much more serious collapse than ever before; I see—total psychological collapse for you, Jack, if you keep working on this. Already you're being mauled by acute schizophrenic anxiety, by *panic*—isn't that so? Isn't it?"

He nodded.

"I saw that in my brother," Doreen said. "Schizophrenic panic, and once you see it break out in a person, you can never forget it. The collapse of their reality around them . . . the collapse of their perceptions of time and space, cause and effect . . . and isn't that what's happening to you? You're talking as if this meeting with Arnie can't be altered by anything you do—and that's a deep regression on your part from adult responsibility and maturity; that's not like you at all." Breathing deeply, her chest rising and falling painfully, she went on, "I'll call Arnie and tell him you're pulling out, and he'll have to get someone else to finish with Manfred. And I'll tell him that you've made no progress, that it's pointless for you and for him to continue with this. I've seen Arnie get these whims before; he keeps them percolating for a few days or weeks, and then he forgets them. He can forget this."

Jack said, "He won't forget this one."

"Try," she said.

"No," he said. "I have to go there tonight and give him my progress report. I said I would; I owe it to him."

"You're a damn fool," Doreen said.

"I know it," Jack said. "But not for the reason you think. I'm a fool because I took on a job without looking ahead to its consequences. I—" He broke off. "Maybe it is what you said. I'm not competent to work with Manfred. That's it, period."

"But you're still going ahead. What do you have to show Arnie tonight? Show it to me, right now."

Getting out a manila envelope, Jack reached into it and drew out the picture of the buildings which Manfred had drawn. For a long time Doreen studied it. And then she handed it back to him.

"That's an evil and sick drawing," she said in a voice almost inaudible. "I know what it is. It's the Tomb World, isn't it? That's what he's drawn. The world after death. And that's what he sees, and through him, that's what you're beginning to see. You want to take that to Arnie? You have lost your grip on reality; do you think Arnie wants to see an abomination like that? Burn it."

"It's not that bad," he said, deeply perturbed by her reaction.

"Yes, it is," Doreen said. "And it's a dreadful sign that it doesn't strike you that way. Did it at first?"

He had to nod yes.

"Then you know I'm right," she said.

"I have to go on," he said. "I'll see you at his place tonight." Going over to the window, he tapped Manfred on the shoulder. "We have to go, now. We'll see this lady tonight, and Mr. Kott, too."

"Goodbye, Jack," Doreen said, accompanying him to the door. Her large dark eyes were heavy with despair. "There's nothing I can say to stop you; I can see that. You've changed. You're so less—alive—now than you were just a day or so ago . . . do you know that?"

"No," he said. "I didn't realize that." But he was not surprised to hear it; he could feel it, hanging heavy over his limbs, choking his heart. Leaning toward her, he kissed her on her full, good-tasting lips. "I'll see you tonight."

She stood at the doorway, silently watching him and the boy go.

In the time remaining before evening, Jack Bohlen decided to drop by the Public School and pick up his son. There, in that place which he dreaded before any other, he would find out if Doreen were right; he would learn if his morale and ability to distinguish reality from the projections of his own unconscious had been impaired or not. For him, the Public School was the crucial location. And, as he directed his Yee Company 'copter toward it, he felt deep within himself that he would be capable of handling a second visit there.

He was violently curious, too, to see Manfred's reaction to the place, and to its simulacra, the teaching machines. For some time now he had had an abiding hunch that Manfred, confronted by the School's Teachers, would show a significant response, perhaps similar to his own, perhaps totally opposite. In any case the reaction would be there; he was positive of that.

But then he thought resignedly, Isn't it too late? Isn't the job over, hasn't Arnie cancelled it because it doesn't matter?

Haven't I already been to his place tonight? What time is it? He thought in fright, I've lost all sense of time.

"We're going to the Public School," he murmured to Manfred. "Do you like that idea? See the school where David goes."

The boy's eyes gleamed with anticipation. Yes, he seemed to be saying. I'd like that. Let's go.

"O.K.," Jack said, only with great difficulty managing to operate the controls of the 'copter; he felt as if he were at the bottom of a great stagnant sea, struggling merely to breathe, almost unable to move. But why?

He did not know. He went on, as best he could.

Eleven

INSIDE Mr. Kott's skin were dead bones, shiny and wet. Mr. Kott was a sack of bones, dirty and yet shiny-wet. His head was a skull that took in greens and bit them; inside him the greens became rotten things as something ate them to make them dead. Jack Bohlen, too, was a dead sack, teeming with gubbish. The outside that fooled almost everyone, it was painted pretty and smelled good, bent down over Miss Anderton, and he saw that; he saw it wanting her in a filthy fashion. It poured its wet, sticky self nearer and nearer to her, and the dead bug words popped from its mouth and fell on her. The dead bug words scampered off into the folds of her clothing, and some squeezed into her skin and entered her body.

"I love Mozart," Mr. Kott said. "I'll put this tape on."

Her clothing itched her, it was full of hair and dust and the droppings of the bug words. She scratched at it and the clothing tore in strips. Digging her teeth into the strips, she chewed them away.

Fiddling with the knobs of the amplifier, Mr. Kott said, "Bruno Walter conducting. A great rarity from the golden age of recordings."

A hideous racket of screeches and shrieks issued from somewhere in the room, and after a time she realized that it was her; she was convulsed from within, all the corpse-things in her were heaving and crawling, struggling out into the light of the room. God, how could she stop them? They emerged from her pores and scuttled off, dropping from strands of gummy web to the floor, to disappear into the cracks between the boards.

"Sorry," Arnie Kott muttered.

"What a shock," she said. "You should spare us, Arnie." Getting up from the couch she pushed away the dark, bad-smelling object that clung to her. "Your sense of humor—" she said.

He turned and saw her as she stripped herself of the last of her clothing. He had put down the reel of tape, and now he came toward her, reaching out.

"Do it," she said, and then they were both on the floor, together; he used his feet to remove his own clothing, hooking his toes into the fabric and tearing until it was away. Arms locked around each other, they rolled into the darkness beneath the stove and lay there, sweating and thumping, gulping in the dust and the heat and the damp of their own bodies. "Do it more," she said, digging her knees into his sides to hurt him.

"An accident," he said, squashing her against the floor, breathing into her face.

Eyes appeared beyond the edge of the stove; something peeped in at them as they lay together in the darkness— something watched. It had put away its paste and scissors and magazines, dropped all that to watch this and gloat and savor each thump they made.

"Go away," she gasped at it. But it did not go away. "More," she said, then, and it laughed at her. It laughed and laughed, as she and the weight squashing her kept on. They could not stop.

Gubble me more, she said. Gubble gubble gubble me, put your gubbish into me, into my gubbish, you Gubbler. Gubble gubble, I like gubble! Don't stop. Gubble, gubble gubble gubble, *gubble!*

As Jack Bohlen lowered the Yee Company 'copter toward the landing field of the Public School directly below, he glanced at Manfred and wondered what the boy was thinking. Wrapped up in his thoughts, Manfred Steiner stared sightlessly out, his features twisted into a grimace that repelled Jack and made him instantly look away.

Why did he have anything to do with this boy? Jack wondered. Doreen was right; he was in over his head, and the unstable, schizophrenic aspects of his own personality were being stirred into life by the presence beside him. And yet he did not know how to get out; somehow it was too late, as if time had collapsed and left him here, for eternity, caught in a symbiosis with this unfortunate, mute creature who did nothing but rake over and inspect his own private world, again and again.

He had imbibed, on some level, of Manfred's world-view, and it was obviously bringing about the stealthy disintegration of his own.

Tonight, he thought. I have to keep going until tonight: somehow I must hold out until I can see Arnie Kott. Then I can jettison all this and return to my own space, my own world; I will never have to look at Manfred Steiner again.

Arnie, for Christ's sake, save me, he thought.

"We're here," he said as the 'copter bumped to a halt on the roof field. He switched off the motor.

At once Manfred moved to the door, eager to get out.

So you want to see this place, Jack thought. I wonder why. He got to his feet and went to unlock the door of the 'copter; at once Manfred hopped out onto the roof and scampered toward the descent ramp, almost as if he knew the way by heart.

As Jack stepped from the ship the boy disappeared from sight. On his own he had hurried down the ramp and plunged into the school.

Doreen Anderton and Arnie Kott, Jack said to himself. The two people who mean the most to me, the friends with whom my contacts, my intimacy with life itself, is the strongest. And yet it's right there that the boy has managed to infiltrate; he has unfastened me from my relationships where they are the strongest.

What's left? he asked himself. Once I have been isolated there, the rest—my son, my wife, my father, Mr. Yee—all follow almost automatically, without a fight.

I can see what lies ahead for me if I continue to lose, step by step, to this completely psychotic boy. Now I can see what psychosis is: the utter alienation of perception from the objects of the outside world, especially the objects which matter: the warmhearted people there. And what takes their place? A dreadful preoccupation with—the endless ebb and flow of one's own self. The changes emanating from within which affect only the inside world. It is a splitting apart of the two worlds, inner and outer, so that neither registers on the other. Both still exist, but each goes its own way.

It is the stopping of time. The end of experience, of anything new. Once the person becomes psychotic, nothing ever happens to him again.

And, he realized, I stand on the threshold of that. Perhaps I always did; it was implicit in me from the start. But this boy has led me a long way. Or, rather, because of him I have gone a long way.

A coagulated self, fixed and immense, which effaces everything else and occupies the entire field. Then the most minute change is examined with the greatest attention. That is Manfred's state now; has been, from the beginning. The ultimate stage of the schizophrenic process.

"Manfred, wait," he called, and followed slowly after the boy, down the ramp and into the Public School building.

Seated in June Henessy's kitchen, sipping coffee, Silvia Bohlen discoursed on her problems of late.

"What's so awful about them," she said, meaning Erna Steiner and the Steiner children, "is that, let's face it, they're vulgar. We're not supposed to talk in terms like that, but I've been forced to see so much of them that I can't ignore it; my face has been rubbed in it every day."

June Henessy, wearing white shorts and a skimpy halter, padded barefoot here and there in the house, watering from a glass pitcher her various indoor plants. "That's really a weird boy. He's the worst of all, isn't he?"

Shuddering, Silvia said, "And he's over all day long. Jack is working with him, you know, trying to make him part of the human race. I think myself they ought to just wipe out freaks and sports like that; it's terribly destructive in the long run to let them live; it's a false mercy to them and to us. That boy will have to be cared for for the rest of his life; he'll never be out of an institution."

Returning to the kitchen with the empty pitcher, June said, "I want to tell you what Tony did the other day." Tony was her current lover; she had been having an affair with him for six months now, and she kept the other ladies, especially Silvia, up to date. "We had lunch together over at Geneva II, at a French restaurant he knows; we had escargots—you know, snails. They serve them to you in the shells and you get them out with a horrible-looking fork that has tines a foot long. Of course, that's all black-market food; did you know that? That there're restaurants serving exclusively black-market delicacies? I didn't until Tony took me there. I can't tell you the name of it, of course."

"Snails," Silvia said with aversion, thinking of all the wonderful dishes she herself would have ordered, if she had a lover and he had taken her out.

How would it be to have an affair? Difficult, but surely worth it, if she could keep it from her husband. The problem, of course, was David. And now Jack worked a good deal of the time at home, and her father-in-law was visiting as well. And she could never have him, her lover, at the house, because of Erna Steiner next door; the big baggy hausfrau would see, comprehend, and probably at once, out of a Prussian sense of duty, inform Jack. But then, wasn't the risk part of it? Didn't it help add that—flavor?

"What would your husband do if he found out?" she asked June. "Cut you to bits? Jack would."

June said, "Mike has had several affairs of his own since we've been married. He'd be sore and possibly he'd give me a black eye and go off for a week or so with one of his girl friends, leaving me stuck with the kids, of course. But he'd get over it."

To herself, Silvia wondered if Jack had ever had an affair. It did not seem probable. She wondered how she would feel if he had and she found out—would it end the marriage? Yes, she thought. I'd get a lawyer right away. Or would I? There's no way to tell in advance. . . .

"How are you and your father-in-law getting along?" June asked.

"Oh, not badly. He and Jack and the Steiner boy are off somewhere today, taking a business trip. I don't see much of Leo, actually; he came mainly on business—June, how many affairs have you had?"

"Six," June Henessy said.

"Gee," Silvia said. "And I haven't had any."

"Some women aren't built for it."

That sounded to Silvia like a rather personal, if not outright anatomical, insult. "What do you mean?"

"Aren't constituted psychologically," June explained glibly. "It takes a certain type of woman who can create and sustain a complex fiction, day after day. I enjoy it, what I make up to tell

Mike. You're different. You have a simple, direct sort of mind; deception isn't your cup of tea. Anyhow, you have a nice husband." She emphasized the authority of her judgement by a lifting of her eyebrows.

"Jack used to be gone all week long," Silvia said. "I should have had one then. Now it would be so much harder." She wished, fervently, that she had something creative or useful or exciting to do that would fill up the long empty afternoons; she was bored to death with sitting in some other woman's kitchen drinking coffee hour after hour. No wonder so many women had affairs. It was that or madness.

"If you're limited to your husband for emotional experience," June Henessy said, "you have no basis of judgment; you're more or less stuck with what he has to offer, but if you've gone to bed with other men you can tell better what your husband's deficiencies are, and it's much more possible for you to be objective about him. And what needs to be changed in him, you can insist that he change. And for your own part, you can see where you've been ineffective and with these other men you can learn how to improve yourself, so that you give your husband more satisfaction. I fail to see who loses by that."

Put that way, it certainly sounded like a good healthy idea for all concerned. Even the husband benefited.

While she sat sipping her coffee and meditating about that, Silvia looked out the window and saw to her surprise a 'copter landing. "Who's that?" she asked June.

"Heaven's sake, I don't know," June said, glancing out.

The 'copter rolled to a halt near the house; the door opened and a dark-haired, good-looking man wearing a bright nylon shirt and necktie, slacks, and stylish European loafers stepped out. Behind him came a Bleekman who lugged two heavy suitcases.

Inside her, Silvia Bohlen felt her heart quiver as she watched the dark-haired man stroll toward the house, the Bleekman following with the suitcases. This was the way she imagined June's Tony to look.

"Gosh," June said. "I wonder who he is. A salesman?" A rap sounded at the front door and she went to open it. Silvia set down her cup and followed along. At the door June halted. "I feel sort of—undressed." She put her hand nervously to her shorts. "You talk to him while I run into the bedroom and change. I wasn't expecting anybody strange to drop by; you know, we have to be careful, we're so isolated and our husbands are away—" She darted off to the bedroom, her hair flying.

Silvia opened the door.

"Good day," the good-looking man said, with a smile revealing perfect white Mediterranean teeth. He had a faint accent. "Are you the lady of the house?"

"I guess so," Silvia said, feeling timid and ill at ease; she glanced down at her own self, wondering if she were dressed modestly enough to be standing out here talking to this man.

"I wish to introduce a very fine line of health foods which you may be familiar with," the man said. He kept his eyes on her face, and yet Silvia had the distinct impression that somehow he managed at the same time to examine the rest of her detail by detail. Her self-consciousness grew, but she did not feel resentful; the man had a charming manner, simultaneously shy and yet oddly forthright.

"Health food," she murmured. "Well, I—"

The man gave a nod, and his Bleekman stepped up, laid down one of the suitcases, and opened it. Baskets, bottles, packages . . . she was very much interested.

"Unhomogenized peanut butter," the man declared. "Also dietetic sweets without calories, to keep your lovely slimness. Wheat germ. Yeast. Vitamin E; that is the vitamin of *vitality* . . . but of course for a young woman like yourself, not yet appropriate." His voice purred along as he indicated one item after another; she found herself bending down beside him, so close to him that their shoulders touched. Quickly she drew away, startled into apprehension.

At the door, June put in a momentary appearance, now wearing a skirt and a wool sweater; she hung about for a moment and then drew back inside and shut the door. The man failed to notice her.

"Also," he was saying, "there is much in the gourmet line that Miss might be interested in—these." He held up a jar. Her breath left her: it was caviar.

"Good grief," she said, magnetized. "Where did you get that?"

"Expensive, but well worth it." The man's dark eyes bored into hers. "Don't you agree? Reminder of days at Home, soft candlelight and dance music by an orchestra . . . days of romance in a whirl of places delightful to the ear and eye." He smiled long and openly at her.

Black market, she realized.

Her pulse hammered in her throat as she said, "Look, this isn't my house. I live about a mile down along the canal." She pointed. "I—am very much interested."

The man's smile seared her.

"You've never been by before, have you?" she said, now rattled and stammering. "I've never seen you. What's your name? Your firm name."

"I am Otto Zitte." He handed her a card, which she scarcely glanced at; she could not take her eyes from his face. "My business is long established but has just recently—due to an unforeseen circumstance—been completely reorganized, so that now I am in a position to greet new customers direct. Such as yourself."

"You'll be by?"

"Yes, slightly later in the afternoon . . . and we can at leisure pore over a dazzling assortment of imported dainties of which I have exclusive distribution. Good afternoon." He rose catlike to his feet.

June Henessy had reappeared. "Hello," she said in a low, cautious, interested voice.

"My card." Otto Zitte held the embossed white square out to her. Now both ladies had his card; each read hers intently.

Smiling his astute, insinuating, brilliant smile, Otto Zitte beckoned to his tame Bleekman to lay out and open the other suitcase.

As he sat in his office at Camp Ben-Gurion, Dr. Milton Glaub heard a woman's voice in the corridor, husky and full of authority but still unmistakably feminine. Listening, he heard the nurse defer to her, and he knew that it was Anne Esterhazy, come to visit her son Sam.

Opening the file he turned to *E,* and presently he had the folio *Esterhazy, Samuel* spread out before him on his desk.

It was interesting. The little boy had been born out of wedlock, a year or more after Mrs. Esterhazy had divorced Arnie Kott. And he had entered Camp B-G under her name, too. However it was undoubtedly Arnie Kott's progeny; the folio contained a great packet of information on Arnie, for the examining doctors had taken that blood relationship for granted throughout.

Evidently, even though their marriage had long been over, Arnie and Anne Esterhazy still saw one another, enough in fact to produce a child. Their relationship therefore was not merely a business one.

For a time Dr. Glaub ruminated as to the possible uses that this information could be put to. Did Arnie have enemies? None that he knew of; everybody liked Arnie—that is, everyone but Dr. Milton Glaub. Evidently Dr. Glaub was the sole person on Mars to have suffered at Arnie's hands, a realization that did not make Dr. Glaub feel any happier about it.

That man treated me in the most inhumane and cavalier fashion, he said to himself for the millionth time. But what could be done about it? He could still bill Arnie . . . hope to collect some trifle for his services. That, however, would not help. He wanted—was entitled to—much more. Again Dr. Glaub studied the folio. An odd sport, Samuel Esterhazy; he knew of no other case precisely like it. The boy seemed to be a throwback to some ancient line of near-man, or to some variant which had not survived: one which had lived partly in the water. It recalled to Glaub the theory being advanced by a number of anthropologists that man had descended from aquatic apes who had lived in the surf and shallows.

Sam's IQ., he noted, was only 73. A shame.

—Especially so, he thought suddenly, in that Sam could beyond doubt be classified as mentally retarded rather than anomalous. Camp B-G had not been intended as an institution for the purely retarded, and its director, Susan Haynes, had sent back to their parents several pseudoautistic children who had turned out to be nothing more than standard imbeciles. The diagnostic problem had hampered their screening, of course. In the case of the Esterhazy boy, there was also the physical stigmata. . . .

No doubt of it, Dr. Glaub decided. I have the basis for it: I can send the Esterhazy child home. The Public School could teach him without trouble, could gear down to his level. It is only in the physical area that he could be called "anomalous," and it is not our task here to care for the physically disabled.

But what is my motive? he asked himself.

Possibly I am doing it to get back at Arnie Kott for treating me in a cruel manner.

No, he decided, that does not seem probable; I am not the psychological type who would seek revenge—that would be more the anal-expulsive or perhaps the oral-biting type. And long ago he had classified himself as the late genital type, devoted to the mature genital strivings.

On the other hand, his altercation with Arnie Kott had admittedly caused him to probe into the Esterhazy child's folio . . . so there was a small but finite causal connective.

Reading the folio through, he was struck once more by the bizarre relationship which it implied. Here they were, carrying on a sexual union years after their marriage had terminated. Why had they gotten divorced? Perhaps there had been a serious power-clash between them; Anne Esterhazy was clearly a domineering type of female with strong masculine components, what Jung called the "animus-ridden" woman. In successfully dealing with such a type, one had to play a definite role; one had to capture the position of authority right off the bat and never relinquish it. One had to be the ancestral, or else be quickly defeated.

Dr. Glaub put the folio away and then sauntered down the corridor to the playroom. He located Mrs. Esterhazy; she was playing beanbag with her boy. Walking over, he stood observing them until she became aware of him and paused.

"Hello, Dr. Glaub," she said cheerfully.

"Good afternoon, Mrs. Esterhazy. Um, when you're finished visiting, may I see you in my office?"

It was rewarding to see the woman's competent, self-satisfied expression wilt with concern. "Of course, Dr. Glaub."

Twenty minutes later he sat facing her across his desk.

"Mrs. Esterhazy, when your boy first came to Camp B-G, there was a good deal of doubt as to the nature of his problem.

It was believed for some time that it lay in the realm of mental disturbance, possibly a traumatic neurosis or—"

The woman broke in, firmly. "Doctor, you're going to tell me that since Sam has no problems except his defective learning ability, he is not to remain here; is that correct?"

"And the physical problem," Dr. Glaub said.

"But that is not your concern."

He made a gesture of resignation and agreement.

"When do I have to take him home?" She was white-faced and trembling; her hands gripped her purse, clutched at it.

"Oh, three or four days. A week."

Chewing her knuckle, Mrs. Esterhazy stared blindly down at the carpet of the office. Time passed. Then in a quavering voice she said, "Doctor, as you perhaps know, I have been active for some time in fighting a bill now before the UN which would close Camp B-G." Her voice gained strength. "If I am forced to remove Sam, I will withdraw my assistance in this matter, and you can be certain that the bill will be passed. And I will inform Susan Haynes as to the reason why I am withdrawing my assistance."

A slow cold wave of shock passed over Dr. Milton Glaub's mind. He could think of nothing to say.

"You understand, Doctor?" Mrs. Esterhazy said.

He managed to nod.

Rising to her feet, Mrs. Esterhazy said, "Doctor, I have been in politics a long time. Arnie Kott considers me a do-gooder, an amateur, but I am not. Believe me, in certain areas I am quite shrewd politically."

"Yes," Dr. Glaub said, "I see that you are." Automatically he too rose; he escorted her to the door of the office.

"Please don't ever bring up this issue about Sam again," the woman said, as she opened the door. "I find it too painful. It is much easier for me to regard him as anomalous." She faced him squarely. "It is not within my capacity to think of him as retarded." Turning, she walked swiftly off.

That did not work out too well, Dr. Glaub said to himself as he shakily closed his office door. The woman is obviously sadistic—strong hostility drives coupled with out-and-out aggression.

Seating himself at his desk he lit a cigarette and puffed at it despondently as he struggled to collect his aplomb.

When Jack Bohlen reached the bottom of the descent ramp he saw no sign of Manfred. Several children trotted by, no doubt on their way to their Teachers. He began to roam about, wondering where the boy had gone. And why so quickly? It was not good.

Ahead, a group of children had collected around a Teacher, a tall, white-haired, bushy-browed gentleman whom Jack recognized as Mark Twain. Manfred, however, was not among them.

As Jack started to walk past the Mark Twain it broke off its monolog to the children, puffed several times at its cigar, and called after Jack, "My friend, can I be of any assistance to you?"

Pausing, Jack said, "I'm looking for a little boy I brought here with me."

"I know all the young fellows," the Mark Twain Teaching Machine answered. "What is his name?"

"Manfred Steiner." He described the boy as the teaching machine listened alertly.

"Hmm," it said, when he had finished. It smoked for a moment and then once more lowered its cigar. "I believe you will find that young man over colloquizing with the Roman emperor Tiberius. Or at least so I am informed by the authorities in whose care this organization has been entrusted; I speak of the master circuit, sir."

Tiberius. He had not realized that such figures were represented here at the Public School: the base and deranged personages of history. Evidently from his expression the Mark Twain understood his thoughts.

"Here in the school," it informed him, "as examples not to be emulated but to be avoided with the most scrupulous zeal, you will find, sir, as you make your peregrinations about these halls, that many rascals, pirates, and scamps are on display, sermonizing in dolorous and lamentable tones their edifying histories for the enlightenment of the young." The Mark Twain, again puffing on its cigar, winked at him. Disconcerted, Jack hurried on.

At the Immanuel Kant he halted to ask directions. Several pupils, in their teens, stood aside for him.

"The Tiberius," it told him in heavily accented English, "can be found down that way." It pointed with absolute authority; it did not have any doubts, and Jack hurried at once down that particular hall.

A moment later he found himself approaching the slight, white-haired, fragile-looking figure of the Roman emperor. It seemed to be musing as he came up to it, but before he could speak it turned its head in his direction.

"The boy whom you are searching for has passed on. He was yours, was he? An exceeding attractive youth." Then it was silent, as if communing within itself. Actually, Jack knew, it was reconnecting itself with the master circuit of the school, which was now utilizing all the teaching machines in an attempt to locate Manfred for him. "He is talking to no one at this moment," the Tiberius said presently.

Jack went on, then. A sightless, middle-aged female figure smiled past him; he did not know who it was, and no children were conversing with it. But all at once it said, "The boy you want is with Philip Second of Spain." It pointed to the corridor to the right, and then it said in a peculiar voice, "Kindly hurry; we would appreciate it if you would remove him from the school as soon as possible. Thank you very much." It snapped off into silence. Jack hurried down the hall which it had pointed out.

Almost at once he turned a corridor and found himself before the bearded, ascetic figure of Philip the Second. Manfred was not there, but some intangible quality of his essence seemed still to hover in this area.

"He has only now departed, dear sir," the teaching machine said. Its voice held the same note of peculiar urgency as had the female figure's, a moment ago. "Kindly find him and remove him; it would be appreciated."

Without waiting any longer, Jack plunged down the corridor, a chill fear biting at him as he ran.

". . . Much appreciated," a seated, white-robed figure said, as he passed it. And then, as he passed a gray-haired man in a frock coat, it, too, took up the school's urgent litany. ". . . Soon as possible."

He turned the corner. And there was Manfred.

The boy was alone, seated on the floor, resting against the wall, his head down, apparently deep in thought.

Bending down, Jack said, "Why did you run off?"

The boy gave no response. Jack touched him, but still there was no reaction.

"Are you all right?" Jack asked him.

All at once the boy stirred, rose to his feet, and stood facing Jack.

"What is it?" Jack demanded.

There was no answer. But the boy's face was clouded with a blurred, distorted emotion that found no outlet; he gazed at Jack as if not seeing him. Totally absorbed in himself, unable to break out into the outside world.

"What happened?" Jack said. But he knew that he would never find out; no way existed for the creature before him to express itself. There was only silence, the total absence of communication between the two of them, the emptiness that could not be filled.

The boy looked away, then, and settled back down into a heap on the floor.

"You stay here," Jack said to him. "I'll have them go get David for me." Warily, he moved away from the boy, but Manfred did not stir. When he reached a teaching machine, Jack said to it, "I would like to have David Bohlen, please; I'm his father. I'll take him home."

It was the Thomas Edison Teaching Machine, an elderly man who glanced up, startled, and cupped his ear. Jack repeated what he had said.

Nodding, it said, "Gubble gubble."

Jack stared at it. And then he turned to look back at Manfred. The boy still sat slumped down, his back against the wall.

Again the Thomas Edison Teaching Machine opened its mouth and said to Jack, "Gubble gubble." There was nothing more; it became silent.

Is it me? Jack asked himself. Is this the final psychotic breakdown for me? Or—

He could not believe the alternative; it simply was not possible.

Down the hall, another teaching machine was addressing a

group of children; its voice came from a distance, echoing and metallic. Jack strained to listen.

"Gubble gubble," it was saying to the children.

He closed his eyes. He knew in a moment of perfect aware-ness that his own psyche, his own perceptions, had not misin-formed him; it was happening, what he heard and saw.

Manfred Steiner's presence had invaded the structure of the Public School, penetrated its deepest being.

Twelve

STILL at his desk in his office at Camp B-G, brooding over the behavior of Anne Esterhazy, Dr. Milton Glaub received an emergency call. It was from the master circuit of the UN's Public School.

"Doctor," its flat voice declared, "I am sorry to disturb you but we require assistance. There is a male citizen wandering about our premises in an evident state of mental confusion. We would like you to come and remove him."

"Certainly," Dr. Glaub murmured. "I'll come straight there."

Soon he was in the air, piloting his 'copter across the desert from New Israel toward the Public School.

When he arrived, the master circuit met him and escorted him at a brisk pace through the building until they reached a closed-off corridor. "We felt we should keep the children away from him," the master circuit explained as she caused the wall to roll back, exposing the corridor.

There, with a dazed expression on his face, stood a man familiar to Dr. Glaub. The doctor had an immediate reaction of satisfaction, in spite of himself. So Jack Bohlen's schizophrenia had caught up with him. Bohlen's eyes were without focus; obviously he was in a state of catatonic stupor, probably alternating with excitement—he looked exhausted. And with him was another person whom Dr. Glaub recognized. Manfred Steiner sat curled up on the floor, bent forward, likewise in an advanced state of withdrawal.

Your association did not cause either of you to prosper, Dr. Glaub observed to himself.

With the help of the master circuit he got both Bohlen and the Steiner boy into his 'copter, and presently he was flying back to New Israel and Camp B-G.

Hunched over, his hands clenched, Bohlen said, "Let me tell you what happened."

"Please do," Dr. Glaub said, feeling—at last—in control.

Jack Bohlen said in an uneven voice, "I went to the school to pick up my son. I took Manfred." He twisted in his seat to

162

look at the Steiner boy, who had not come out of his catalepsy; the boy lay rolled up on the floor of the 'copter, as inert as a carving. "Manfred got away from me. And then—communication between me and the school broke down. All I could hear was—" He broke off.

"Folie à deux," Glaub murmured. Madness of two.

Bohlen said, "Instead of the school, I heard *him*. I heard his words coming from the Teachers." He was silent, then.

"Manfred has a powerful personality," Dr. Glaub said. "It is a drain on one's resources to be around him for long. I think it would be well for you, for your own health, to abandon this project. I think you risk too much."

"I have to see Arnie tonight," Bohlen said in a ragged, harsh whisper.

"What about yourself? What's going to become of you?"

Bohlen said nothing.

"I can treat you," Dr. Glaub said, "at this stage of your difficulty. Later on—I'm not so sure."

"In there, in that damn school," Bohlen said, "I got completely confused; I didn't know what to do. I kept going on, looking for someone who I could still talk to. Who wasn't like—him." He gestured toward the boy.

"It is a massive problem for the schizophrenic to relate to the school," Glaub said. "The schizophrenic, such as yourself, very often deals with people through their unconscious. The teaching machines, of course, have no shadow personalities; what they are is all on the surface. Since the schizophrenic is accustomed constantly to ignore the surface and look beneath —he draws a blank. He is simply unable to understand them."

Bohlen said, "I couldn't understand anything they said; it was all just that—meaningless talk Manfred uses. That private language."

"You're fortunate you could come out of it," Dr. Glaub said.

"I know."

"So now what will it be for you, Bohlen? Rest and recovery? Or more of this dangerous contact with a child so unstable that—"

"I have no choice," Jack Bohlen said.

"That's right. You have no choice; you must withdraw."

Bohlen said, "But I learned something. I learned how great the stakes are for me personally, in all this. Now I know what it would be like to be cut off from the world, isolated, the way Manfred is. I'd do anything to avoid that. I have no intention of giving up now." With shaking hands he got a cigarette from his pocket and lit up.

"The prognosis for you is not good," Dr. Glaub said.

Jack Bohlen nodded.

"There's been a remission of your difficulty, due no doubt to your being removed from the environment of the school. Shall I be blunt? There's no telling how long you'll be able to function; perhaps another ten minutes, another hour—possibly until tonight, and then you may well find yourself enduring a worse collapse. The nocturnal hours are especially bad, are they not?"

"Yes," Bohlen said.

"I can do two things for you. I can take Manfred back to Camp B-G and I can represent you at Arnie's tonight, be there as your official psychiatrist. I do that all the time; it's my business. Give me a retainer and I'll drop you off at your home."

"Maybe after tonight," Bohlen said. "Maybe you can represent me later on, if this gets worse. But tonight I'm taking Manfred with me to see Arnie Kott."

Dr. Glaub shrugged. Impervious to suggestion, he realized. A sign of autism. Jack Bohlen could not be persuaded; he was too cut off already to hear and understand. Language for him had become a hollow ritual, signifying nothing.

"My boy David," Bohlen said all at once. "I have to go back there to the school and pick him up. And my Yee Company 'copter; it's there, too." His eyes had become clearer, now, as if he were emerging from his state.

"Don't go back there," Dr. Glaub urged him.

"Take me back."

"Then don't go down into the school; stay up on the field. I'll have them send up your son—you can sit in your 'copter until he's up. That would be safe for you, perhaps. I'll deal with the master circuit for you." Dr. Glaub felt a rush of sympathy for this man, for his dogged instincts to go on in his own manner.

"Thanks," Bohlen said. "I'd appreciate that." He shot a smile at the doctor, and Glaub smiled back.

Arnie Kott said plaintively, "Where's Jack Bohlen?" It was six o'clock in the evening, and Arnie sat by himself in his living room, drinking a slightly too sweet Old Fashioned which Helio had fixed.

At this moment his tame Bleekman was in the kitchen preparing a dinner entirely of black-market goodies, all from Arnie's new stock. Reflecting that he now obtained his spread at wholesale prices, Arnie felt good. What an improvement on the old system, where Norbert Steiner made all the profit! Arnie sipped his drink and waited for his guests to arrive. In the corner, music emerged from the speakers, subtle and yet pervasive; it filled the room and lulled Goodmember Kott.

He was still in that trancelike mood when the noise of the telephone startled him awake.

"Arnie, this is Scott."

"Oh?" Arnie said, not pleased; he preferred to deal through his cunning code system. "Look, I've got a vital business meeting tonight here, and unless you've got something—"

"This is important, all right," Scott said. "There's some-body else hoeing away at our row."

Puzzled, Arnie said, "What?" And then he understood what Scott Temple meant. "You mean the goodies?"

"Yes," Scott said. "And he's all set up. He's got his field, his incoming rockets, his route—he must have taken over Stein—"

"Don't talk any further," Arnie interrupted. "Come on over here right away."

"Will do." The phone clicked as Scott rang off.

How do you like that, Arnie said to himself. Just as I'm get-ting good and started, some bugger horns in. And I mean, I didn't even want to get into this black-market business in the first place—why didn't this guy tell me he wanted to take over where Steiner left off? But it's too late now; I'm in it, and no-body's going to force me out.

Half an hour later Scott appeared at the door, agitated; he paced about Arnie Kott's living room, eating hors d'oeuvres and talking away at a great rate. "He's a real pro, this guy;

must have been in the business before sometime—he's already gone all over Mars, to practically everybody, including isolated houses way out in the goddam fringes, to those housewives out there who only buy maybe one jar of something; so he's leaving no stone unturned. There won't be any room for us, and we're just barely beginning to get our operation moving. This guy, let's face it, is running rings around us."

"I see," Arnie said, rubbing the bald part of his scalp.

"We've got to do something, Arnie."

"Do you know where his base of operations is?"

"No, but it's probably in the F.D.R. Mountains; that's where Norb Steiner had his field. We'll look there first." In his memo book, Scott made a note of that.

"Find his field," Arnie said, "and let me know. And I'll have a Lewistown police ship out there."

"Then he'll know who's against him."

"That's correct. I want him to know it's Arnie Kott he's got to contend with and not no ordinary opposition. I'll have the police ship drop a tactical A-bomb or some other minor demolition type of weapon and put an end to his field. So the bugger will see we're genuinely sore at him for his effrontery. And that's what it is, him coming in and competing against me, when I didn't even want to get into this business! It's bad enough without him making it harder."

In his memo book, Scott made notes of all that: *him making it even harder, etc.*

"You get me the location," Arnie concluded, "and I'll see that he's taken care of. I won't have the police get him, just his equipment; we don't want to find ourselves in trouble with the UN. I'm sure this'll blow over right away. Just one guy, do you think? It's not for instance a big outfit from Home?"

"The story I get is it's definitely one guy."

"Fine," Arnie said, and sent Scott off. The door shut after him and once more Arnie Kott was alone in his living room, while his tame Bleekman puttered in the kitchen.

"How's the bouillabaisse coming?" Arnie called into him.

"Fine, Mister," Heliogabalus said. "May I inquire who is to come this evening to eat all this?" At the stove he toiled surrounded by several kinds of fish, plus many herbs and spices.

Arnie said, "It'll be Jack Bohlen, Doreen Anderton and

some autistic child Jack's working with that Dr. Glaub recommended . . . Norb Steiner's son."

"Low types all," Heliogabalus murmured.

Well, same to you, Arnie thought. "Just fix the food right," he said with irritation; he shut the kitchen door and returned to the living room. You black bastard, you got me into this, he thought to himself; it was you and your prognosticating stone that gave me the idea. And it better have worked out, because I got everything riding on it. And in addition—

The door chimes sounded over the music from the speakers.

Opening the front door, Arnie found himself facing Doreen; she smiled warmly at him as she entered the living room on high heels, a fur around her shoulders. "Hi. What smells so good?"

"Some darn fish thing." Arnie took her wrap; removed, it left her shoulders smooth, tanned and faintly freckled, bare. "No," he said at once, "this isn't that kind of evening; this is business. You go in and put on a decent blouse." He steered her to the bedroom. "Next time."

As he stood in the bedroom doorway watching her change he thought, What a terrific high-type looking woman I got, here. As she carefully laid her strapless gown out on the bed he thought, I gave her that. He recalled the model at the department store appearing wearing it. But Doreen looked a lot better; she had all that flaming red hair that plunged down the back of her neck like a drizzle of fire.

"Arnie," she said, turning to face him as she buttoned her blouse up, "you go easy on Jack Bohlen tonight."

"Aw hell," he protested, "whadya mean? All I want from good old Jack is results; I mean, he's had long enough—time's run out!"

Doreen repeated, "Go easy, Arnie. Or I'll never forgive you."

Grumbling, he walked away, to the sideboard in the living room, and began fixing her a drink. "What'll you have? I got a bottle of this ten-year-old Irish whisky; it's O.K."

"I'll have that, then," Doreen said, emerging from the bedroom. She seated herself on the couch and smoothed her skirt over her crossed knees.

"You look good in anything," Arnie said.

"Thank you."

"Listen, what you're doing with Bohlen has my sanction, of course, as you know. But it's all on the surface, what you're doing; right? Deep inside you're saving yourself for me."

Quizzically, Doreen said, "What do you refer to by 'deep inside'?" She eyed him until he laughed. "Watch it," she said. "Yes, of course I'm yours, Arnie. Everything here in Lewistown is yours, even the bricks and straw. Every time I pour a little water down the kitchen drain I think of you."

"Why me?"

"Because you're the totem god of wasted water." She smiled at him. "It's a little joke, that's all; I was thinking about your steam bath with all its run-off."

"Yeah," Arnie said. "Remember that time you and I went there late at night, and I unlocked it with my key, and we went in, like a couple of bad kids . . . sneaked in, turned on the hot water showers until the whole place was nothing but steam. And then we took off our clothes—we really must have been drinking—and we ran all around naked in the steam, hiding from each other. . . ." He grinned. "And I caught you, too, right there where that bench is where the masseuse pounds on you to flatten your ass out. And we sure had fun there on that bench."

"Very primordial," Doreen said, recalling.

"I felt like I was nineteen again that night," Arnie said. "I really am young, for an old guy—I mean, I got a lot left to me, if you know what I mean." He paced about the room. "When is that Bohlen going to get here, for chrissakes?"

The telephone rang.

"Mister," Heliogabalus called from the kitchen. "I am unable to attend to that; I must ask you to get it."

To Doreen, Arnie said, "If it's Bohlen calling to say he can't make it—" He made a dour, throat-cutting motion and picked up the receiver.

"Arnie," a man's voice came. "Sorry to bother you; this is Dr. Glaub."

Relieved, Arnie said, "Hi, Doc Glaub." To Doreen he said, "It's not Bohlen."

Dr. Glaub said, "Arnie, I know you're expecting Jack Bohlen tonight—he's not there yet, is he?"

"Naw."

Hesitating, Glaub said, "Arnie, I happen to have spent some time with Jack today, and although—"

"What's the matter, has he had a schizophrenic seizure?" With acute intuition, Arnie knew it was so; that was the point of the doctor's call. "O.K." Arnie said, "he's under a strain, under the pressure of time; granted. But so are we all. I gotta disappoint you if you want me to excuse him like some kid who's too sick to go to school. I can't do that. Bohlen knew what he was getting into. If he doesn't have any results to show me tonight, I'll fix him so he never repairs another toaster on Mars the rest of his life."

Dr. Glaub was silent and then he said, "It's people like you with your harsh driving demands that create schizophrenics."

"So what? I've got standards; he's got to meet them; that's all. Very high standards, I know that."

"So does he have high standards."

Arnie said, "Not as high as mine. Well, you got anything else to say, Doc Glaub?"

"No," Glaub said. "Except that—" His voice shook. "Nothing else. Thanks for your time."

"Thanks for calling." Arnie hung up. "That gutless wonder; he's too cowardly to say what he was thinking." Disgustedly, he walked away from the phone. "Afraid to stick up for what he believes in; I got nothing but contempt for him. Why'd he call if he's got no guts?"

Doreen said, "I'm amazed he called. Sticking his neck out. What did he say about Jack?" Her eyes were darkened by concern; she rose and approached Arnie, putting her hand on his arm to stop his pacing. "Tell me."

"Aw, he just said he was with Bohlen today for a while; I suppose Bohlen had some sort of fit, his ailment, you know."

"Is he coming?"

"Christ, I don't know. Why does everything have to be so complicated? Doctors calling, you pawing at me like a whipped dog or something." With resentment and aversion he loosened her fingers from his arm and pushed her aside. "And that nutty nigger in the kitchen; Christ! Is he baking some witchdoctor brew in there? He's been going for hours!"

In a faint but controlled voice Doreen said, "Arnie, listen. If you push Jack too far and injure him, I'll never go to bed with you again. I promise."

"Everybody's protecting him, no wonder he's sick."

"He's a good person."

"He better be a good technician, too; he better have that kid's mind spread out like a road map for me to read."

They faced each other.

Shaking her head, Doreen turned away, picking up her drink, and moved off, her back to Arnie. "O.K. I can't tell you what to do. You can pick up a dozen women as good in bed as me; what am I to big Arnie Kott?" Her voice was bleak and envenomed.

He followed after her awkwardly. "Hell, Dor, you're unique, I swear, you're incredible, like what a swell smooth back you got, that dress you wore here, it showed it." He stroked her neck. "A knockout, even by Home standards."

The door chimes sounded.

"That's him," Arnie said, moving at once toward the door.

He opened the door, and there stood Jack Bohlen, looking tired. With him was a boy who danced unceasingly about on tiptoe, from one side of Jack to the other, his eyes shining, taking in everything and yet not focusing on any one thing. The boy at once slithered past Arnie and into the living room, where Arnie lost sight of him.

Disconcerted, Arnie said to Jack Bohlen, "Enter."

"Thanks, Arnie," Jack said, coming in. Arnie shut the door, and the two of them looked around for Manfred.

"He went in the kitchen," Doreen said.

Sure enough, when Arnie opened the kitchen door, there stood the boy, raptly observing Heliogabalus. "What's the matter?" Arnie said to the boy. "You never saw a Bleekman before?"

The boy said nothing.

"What's that dessert you're making, Helio?" Arnie said.

"Flan," Heliogabalus said. "A filipino dish, a custard with a caramel sauce. From Mrs. Rombauer's cookbook."

"Manfred," Arnie said, "this here is Heliogabalus."

Standing at the kitchen doorway, Doreen and Jack watched, too. The boy seemed deeply affected by the Bleekman, Arnie noticed. As if under a spell, he followed with his eyes every move Helio made. With painstaking care, Helio was pouring the flan into molds which he carried to the freezing compartment of the refrigerator.

Almost shyly, Manfred said, "Hello."

"Hey," Arnie said. "He said an actual word."

Helio said in a cross voice, "I must ask all of you to leave the kitchen. Your presence makes me self-conscious so that I cannot work." He glared at them until, one by one, they left the kitchen. The door, shut from within, swung closed after them, cutting off the sight of Helio at his job.

"He's sort of odd," Arnie apologized. "But he sure can cook."

Jack said to Doreen, "That's the first time I've heard Manfred do that." He seemed impressed, and he walked off by himself, ignoring the rest of them, to stand at the window.

Joining him, Arnie said, "What do you want to drink?"

"Bourbon and water."

"I'll fix it," Arnie said. "I can't bother Helio with trivia like this." He laughed, but Jack did not.

The three of them sat with their drinks, for a time. Manfred, given some old magazines to read, stretched out on the carpet, once more oblivious to their presence.

"Wait'll you taste this meal," Arnie said.

"Smells wonderful," Doreen said.

"All black market," Arnie said.

Both Doreen and Jack, together on the couch, nodded.

"This is a big night," Arnie said.

Again they nodded.

Raising his drink, Arnie said, "Here's to communication, Without which there wouldn't be a goddamn nothin'."

Somberly, Jack said, "I'll drink to that, Arnie." However, he had already finished his drink; he gazed at the empty glass, evidently at a loss.

"I'll get you another," Arnie said, taking it from him.

At the sideboard, as he fixed a fresh drink for Jack, he saw that Manfred had grown bored with the magazines; once more the boy was on his feet, roaming around the room. Maybe he'd like to cut out and paste, Arnie decided. He gave Jack his fresh drink and then went into the kitchen.

"Helio, get some glue and scissors for the kid, and some paper for him to paste things on."

Helio had finished with the flan; his work evidently was done, and he had seated himself with a copy of *Life*. With reluctance he got up and went in search of glue, scissors, and paper.

"Funny kid, isn't he?" Arnie said to Helio, when the Bleekman returned. "What's your opinion about him, is it the same as mine?"

"Children are all alike," Helio said, and went out of the kitchen, leaving Arnie alone.

Arnie followed. "We'll eat pretty soon," he announced. "Everybody had some of these Danish blue cheese hors d'oeuvres? Anybody need anything at all?"

The phone rang. Doreen, who was closest, answered it. She handed it to Arnie. "For you. A man."

It was Dr. Glaub again. "Mr. Kott," Dr. Glaub said in a thin, unnatural voice, "it is essential to my integrity to protect my patients. Two can play at this bullying game. As you know, your out-of-wedlock child Sam Esterhazy is at Camp B-G, where I am in attendance."

Arnie groaned.

"If you do not treat Jack Bohlen fairly," Glaub continued, "if you apply your inhumane, cruel, aggressive, domineering tactics on him, I will retaliate by discharging Sam Esterhazy from Camp B-G on the grounds that he is mentally retarded. Is that comprehended?"

"Oh, Christ, anything you say," Arnie groaned. "I'll talk to you about it tomorrow. Go to bed or something. Take a pill. Just get off me." He slammed down the phone.

The tape on the tape transport had reached its end; the music had ceased a long time ago. Arnie stalked over to his tape library and snatched up a box at random. That doctor, he said to himself. I'll get him, but not now. No time now. There must be something the matter with him; he must have some wild hair up his bung.

Examining the box he read:

W.A. Mozart, Symphony 40 in G mol., K. 550

"I love Mozart," he said to Doreen, Jack Bohlen, and the

Steiner boy. "I'll put this on." He removed the reel of tape from the box and put it on the transport; he fiddled with the knobs of the amplifier until he could hear the hiss of the tape as it passed through the head. "Bruno Walter conducting," he told his guests. "A great rarity from the golden age of recordings."

A hideous racket of screeches and shrieks issued from the speakers. Noises like the convulsions of the dead, Arnie thought in horror. He ran to shut off the tape transport.

Seated on the carpet, snipping pictures from the magazines with his scissors and pasting them into new configurations, Manfred Steiner heard the noise and glanced up. He saw Mr. Kott hurry to the tape machine to shut it off. How blurred Mr. Kott became, Manfred noticed. It was hard to see him when he moved so swiftly; it was as if in some way he had managed to disappear from the room and then reappear in another spot. The boy felt frightened.

The noise, too, frightened him. He looked to the couch where Mr. Bohlen sat, to see if he were upset. But Mr. Bohlen remained where he was with Doreen Anderton, interlinked with her in a fashion that made the boy cringe with concern. How could two people stand being so close? It was, to Manfred, as if their separate identities had flowed together, and the idea that such a muddling could be terrified him. He pretended not to see; he saw past them, at the safe, unblended wall.

The voice of Mr. Kott broke over the boy, harsh and jagged tones that he did not understand. Then Doreen Anderton spoke, and then Jack Bohlen; they were all chattering in a chaos, now, and the boy clapped his hands to his ears. All at once, without warning of any kind, Mr. Kott shot across the room and vanished entirely.

Where had he gone? No matter where he looked the boy could not find him. He began to tremble, wondering what was going to happen. And then he saw, to his bewilderment, that Mr. Kott had reappeared in the room where the food was; he was chattering to the dark figure there.

The dark figure, with rhythmic grace, ebbed from his spot on top of the high stool, flowed step by step across the room

and got a glass from the cabinet. Awed by the movement of
the man, Manfred looked directly at him, and at that moment
the dark man looked back, meeting his gaze.

"You must die," the dark man said to him in a far-off voice.
"Then you will be reborn. Do you see, child? There is nothing
for you as you are now, because something went wrong and
you cannot see or hear or feel. No one can help you. Do you
see, child?"

"Yes," Manfred said.

The dark figure glided to the sink, put some powder and
water into the glass, presented it to Mr. Kott, who drank down
the contents, chattering all the while. How beautiful the dark
figure was. Why can't I be like that? Manfred thought. No one
else looked like that.

His glimpse, his contact with the shadow-like man, was cut
off. Doreen Anderton had passed between them as she ran
into the kitchen and began talking in high-pitched tones.
Once more Manfred put his hands to his ears, but he could
not shut out the noise.

He looked ahead, to escape. He got away from the sound
and the harsh, blurred comings and goings.

Ahead of him a mountain path stretched out. The sky overhead was heavy and red, and then he saw dots: hundreds of gigantic specks that grew and came closer. Things rained down
from them, men with unnatural thoughts. The men struck the
ground and dashed about in circles. They drew lines, and then
great things like slugs landed, one after another, without
thoughts of any sort, and began digging.

He saw a hole as large as a world; the earth disappeared and
became black, empty, and nothing. . . . Into the hole the
men jumped one by one, until none of them were left. He was
alone, with the silent world-hole.

At the rim of the hole he peeped down. At the bottom, in
the nothing, a twisted creature unwound as if released. It
snaked up, became wide, contained square space, and grew
color.

I am in you, Manfred thought. Once again.

A voice said, "He has been here at AM-WEB longer than anyone else. He was here when the rest of us came. He is extremely old."

"Does he like it?"

"Who knows? He can't walk or feed himself. The records were lost in that fire. Possibly he's two hundred years old. They amputated his limbs and of course most of his internal organs were taken out on entry. Mostly he complains about hayfever."

No, Manfred thought. I can't stand it; my nose burns. I can't breathe. Is this the start of life, what the dark shadow-figure promised? A new begininng where I will be different and someone can help me?

Please help me, he said. I need someone, anyone. I can't wait here forever; it must be done soon or not at all. If it is not done I will grow and become the world-hole, and the hole will eat up everything.

The hole, beneath AM-WEB, waited to be all those who walked above, or had ever walked above; it waited to be everyone and everything. And only Manfred Steiner held it back.

Setting down his empty glass, Jack Bohlen felt the coming apart of every piece of his body. "We're out of booze," he managed to say to the girl beside him.

To him, Doreen said in a rapid whisper, "Jack, you must remember, you've got friends. I'm your friend, Dr. Glaub called —he's your friend." She looked into his face anxiously. "Will you be O.K.?"

"God sake," Arnie yelled. "I got to hear how you've done, Jack. Can't you give me anything?" With envy he faced the two of them; Doreen drew away from Jack imperceptibly. "Are you two just going to sit there necking and whispering? I don't feel good." He left them, then, going into the kitchen.

Leaning toward Jack until her lips almost touched his, Doreen whispered, "I love you."

He tried to smile at her. But his face had become stiff; it would not yield. "Thanks," he said, wanting her to know how much it meant to him. He kissed her on the mouth. Her lips were warm, soft with love; they gave what they had to him, holding nothing back.

Her eyes full of tears, she said, "I feel you sliding away farther and farther into yourself again."

"No," he said. "I'm O.K." But it was not so; he knew it.

"Gubble gubble," the girl said.

Jack closed his eyes. I can't get away, he thought. It has closed over me completely.

When he opened his eyes he found that Doreen had gotten up from the couch and was going into the kitchen. Voices, hers and Arnie's, drifted to him where he sat.

"Gubble gubble gubble."

"Gubble."

Turning toward the boy who sat snipping at his magazines on the rug, Jack said to him, "Can you hear me? Can you understand me?"

Manfred glanced up and smiled.

"Talk to me," Jack said. "Help me."

There was no response.

Getting to his feet, Jack made his way to the tape recorder; he began inspecting it, his back to the room. Would I be alive now, he asked himself, if I had listened to Dr. Glaub? If I hadn't come here, had let him represent me? Probably not. Like the earlier attack: it would have happened anyhow. It is a process which must unfold; it must work itself out to its conclusion.

The next he knew he was standing on a black, empty sidewalk. The room, the people around him, were gone; he was alone.

Buildings, gray, upright surfaces on both sides. Was this AM-WEB? He looked about frantically. Lights, here and there; he was in a town, and now he recognized it as Lewistown. He began to walk.

"Wait," a voice, a woman's voice, called.

From the entrance of a building a woman in a fur wrap hurried, her high heels striking the pavement and setting up echoes. Jack stopped.

"It didn't go so bad after all," she said, catching up with him, out of breath. "Thank God it's over; you were so tense— I felt it all evening. Arnie is dreadfully upset by the news about the co-op; they're so rich and powerful, they make him feel so little."

Together, they walked in no particular direction, the girl holding on to his arm.

"And he did say," she said, "that he's going to keep you on

as his repairman; I'm positive he means it. He's sore, though, Jack. All the way through him. I know; I can tell."

He tried to remember, but he could not.

"Say something," Doreen begged.

After a bit he said, "He—would make a bad enemy."

"I'm afraid that's so." She glanced up into his face. "Shall we go to my place? Or do you want to stop somewhere and get a drink?"

"Let's just walk," Jack Bohlen said.

"Do you still love me?"

"Of course," he said.

"Are you afraid of Arnie? He may try to get revenge on you, for—he doesn't understand about your father; he thinks that on some level you must have—" She shook her head. "Jack, he will try to get back at you; he does blame you. He's so god-damn primitive."

"Yes," Jack said.

"*Say* something," Doreen said. "You're just like wood, like you're not alive. Was it so terrible? It wasn't, was it? You seemed to pull yourself together."

With effort he said, "I'm—not afraid of what he'll do."

"Would you leave your wife for me. Jack? You said you loved me. Maybe we could emigrate back to Earth, or something."

Together, they wandered on.

Thirteen

FOR Otto Zitte it was as if life had once more opened up; since Norb Steiner's death he moved about Mars as in the old days, making his deliveries, selling, meeting people face to face and gabbing with them.

And, most particularly, he had already encountered several good-looking women, lonely housewives stranded out in the desert in their homes day after day, yearning for companionship . . . so to speak.

So far he had not been able to call at Mrs. Silvia Bohlen's house. But he knew exactly where it was; he had marked it on his map.

Today he intended to go there.

For the occasion he put on his best suit: a single-breasted gray English sharkskin suit he had not worn for years. The shoes, regrettably, were local, and so was the shirt. But the tie: ah. It had just arrived from New York, the latest in bright, cheerful colors; it divided at the bottom into a wild fork shape. Holding it up before him he admired it. Then he put it on and admired it there, too.

His long dark hair shone. He felt happy and confident. This day begins it all afresh for me, with a woman like Silvia, he said to himself as he put on his wool topcoat, picked up his suitcases, and marched from the storage shed—now made over into truly comfortable living quarters—to the 'copter.

In a great soaring arc he lifted the 'copter into the sky and turned it east. The bleak F.D.R. Mountains fell away behind him; he passed over the desert, saw at last the George Washington Canal by which he oriented himself. Following it, he approached the smaller canal system which branched from it, and soon he was above the junction of the William Butler Yeats and the Herodotus, near which the Bohlens lived.

Both those women, he ruminated, are attractive, that June Henessy and Silvia Bohlen, but of the two of them, Silvia's more to my liking; she has that sleepy, sultry quality that a deeply emotional woman always has. June is too pert and frisky; that kind talks on and on, sort of wiseguy-like. I want a woman who's a good listener.

He recalled the trouble he had gotten into before. Wonder what her husband's like, he wondered. Must inquire. A lot of these men take the pioneer life seriously, especially the ones living far out from town; keep guns in their houses and so forth.

However, that was the risk one ran, and it was worth it.

Just in case trouble did occur, Otto Zitte had a gun of his own, a small pistol, .22 caliber, which he kept in a hidden side-pocket of one of his suitcases. It was there now, and fully loaded.

Nobody messes around with me, he said to himself. If they want trouble—they'll soon find it.

Cheered by that thought, he dipped his 'copter, scouted out the land below—there was no 'copter parked at the Bohlen house—and prepared to land.

It was innate caution which caused him to park the 'copter over a mile from the Bohlen house, at the entrance of a service canal. From there he hiked on foot, willing to endure the weight of the suitcase; there was no alternative. A number of houses stood between him and the Bohlen place, but he did not pause to knock at any door; he went directly along the canal without halting.

When he neared the Bohlen place he slowed, regaining his wind. He eyed the nearby houses carefully . . . from the one right next door there came the racket of small children. People home, there. So he approached the Bohlen place from the opposite side, walking silently and in a line which kept him entirely hidden from the house where he heard the children's voices.

He arrived, stepped up on the porch, rang the bell.

Someone peeped out at him from behind the red drapes of the living-room window. Otto maintained a formal, correct smile on his face, one that would do in any eventuality.

The front door opened; there stood Silvia Bohlen, with her hair expertly done, lipstick, wearing a jersey sweater and tight pink capri pants, sandals on her feet. Her toenails were painted a bright scarlet; he noticed that from the corner of his eye.

Obviously, she had fixed herself up in expectation of his visit. However, she of course assumed a bland, detached pose; she regarded him in aloof silence, holding on to the door knob.

"Mrs. Bohlen," he said in his most intimate tone of voice. Bowing, he said, "Passage across barren miles of desert wastelands finds its just reward in seeing you once more at last. Would you be interested in seeing our special in kangaroo-tail soup? It is incredible and delightful, a food never before available on Mars at any price. I have come straight here to you with it, seeing that you are qualified in judging fine foods and can discriminate the worthy without consulting the expense." And all this time, as he reeled off his set speech, he edged himself and his wares toward the open door.

A trifle stiffly and hesitantly, Silvia said, "Uh, come in." She let the door swing freely open, and he at once passed on inside and laid his suitcases on the floor by the low table in the living room.

A boy's bow and quiver of arrows caught his eye. "Is your young son about?" he inquired.

"No," Silvia said, moving edgily about the room with her arms folded before her. "He's at the school today." She tried to smile. "And my father-in-law went into town; he won't be home until very late."

Well, Otto thought; I see.

"Please be seated," he urged her. "So that I may display to you properly, don't you agree?" In one motion, he moved a chair, and Silvia perched on the edge of it, her arms still hugged about her, lips pressed together. How tense she is, he observed. It was a good sign because it meant that she was fully aware of the meaning of all that went on, his visit here, the absence of her son, the fact that she had carefully closed the front door; the living-room drapes still shut, he noticed.

Silvia blusted out, "Would you like coffee?" She bolted from her chair and dived into the kitchen. A moment later she reappeared with a tray on which was a pot of coffee, sugar, cream, two china cups.

"Thank you," he purred. During her absence he had drawn another chair up beside hers.

They drank coffee.

"Are you not frightened to live out here alone so much of the time?" he asked. "In this desolate region?"

She glanced at him sideways. "Golly, I guess I'm used to it."

"What part of Earth are you from originally?"

"St. Louis."

"It is much different here. A new, freer life. Where one can cast off the shackles and be oneself; do you agree? The old mores and customs, an antiquated Old World, best forgotten in its own dust. Here—" He glanced about the living room, with its commonplace furnishings; he had seen such chairs, carpeting, bric-a-brac hundreds of times, in similar homes. "Here we see the clash of the extraordinary, the pulse, Mrs. Bohlen, of opportunity which strikes the brave person only once—once—in his lifetime."

"What else do you have beside kangaroo-tail soup?"

"Well," he said, frowning inwardly, "quail eggs; very good. Real cow butter. Sour cream. Smoked oysters. Here—you please bring forth ordinary soda crackers and I will supply the butter and caviar, as a treat." He smiled at her, and was rewarded by a spontaneous, beaming smile in return; her eyes sparkled with anticipation and she hopped impulsively to her feet to go scampering, like a little child, to the kitchen.

Presently they sat together, huddled over the table, scraping the black, oily fish eggs from the tiny jar onto crackers.

"There's nothing like genuine caviar," Silvia said, sighing. "I only had it once before in my life, at a restaurant in San Francisco."

"Observe what else I have." From his suitcase he produced a bottle. "Green Hungarian, from the Buena Vista winery in California; the oldest winery in that state!"

They sipped wine from long-stemmed glasses. (He had brought the glasses, too.) Silvia lay back against the couch, her eyes half-closed. "Oh, dear. This is like a fantasy. It can't really be happening."

"But it is." Otto set his glass down and leaned over her. She breathed slowly, regularly, as if asleep; but she was watching him fixedly. She knew exactly what was going on. And as he bent nearer and nearer she did not stir; she did not try to slide away.

The food and wine, he reckoned as he took hold of her, had set him back—in retail value—almost a hundred UN dollars. It was well worth it, to him, at least.

His old story, repeating itself. Again, it was not union scale. It was much more, Otto thought a little later on, when they had moved from the living room to the bedroom with its window shades pulled down, the room in unstirring gloom, silent and receptive to them, made, as he well knew, for just such happenings as this.

"Nothing like this," Silvia murmured, "has ever happened before in my entire life." Her voice was full of contentment and acquiescence, as if emerging from far away. "Am I drunk, is that it? Oh, my Lord."

For a long time, then, she was silent.

"Am I out of my mind?" she murmured, later on. "I must be insane. I just can't believe it, I know it isn't real. So how can it matter, how can what you do in a dream be wrong?"

After that, she said nothing at all.

She was exactly the kind he liked: the kind that didn't talk a lot.

What is insanity? Jack Bohlen thought. It was, for him, the fact that somewhere he had lost Manfred Steiner and did not remember how or when. He remembered almost nothing of the night before, at Arnie Kott's place; piece by piece, from what Doreen told him, he had managed to patch together an image of what had taken place. Insanity—to have to construct a picture of one's life, by making inquiries of others.

But the lapse in memory was a symptom of a deeper disturbance. It indicated that his psyche had taken an abrupt leap ahead in time. And this had taken place after a period in which he had lived through, several times, on some unconscious level, that very section which was now missing.

He had sat, he realized, in Arnie Kott's living room again and again, experiencing that evening before it arrived; and then, when at last it had taken place in actuality, he had bypassed it. The fundamental disturbance in time-sense, which Dr. Glaub believed was the basis of schizophrenia, was now harassing him.

That evening at Arnie's had taken place, and had existed for him . . . but out of sequence.

In any case, there was no way that it could be restored. For it now lay in the past. And a disturbance of the sense of past time was not symptomatic of schizophrenia but of compulsive-obessive neurosis. His problem—as a schizophrenic—lay entirely with the future.

And his future, as he now saw it, consisted mostly of Arnie Kott and Arnie's instinctive drive for revenge.

What chance do we have against Arnie? he asked himself.

Almost none.

Turning from the window of Doreen's living room, he walked slowly into the bedroom and gazed down at her as she lay, still asleep, in the big, rumpled double bed.

While he stood there looking at her, she woke, saw him, smiled up at him. "I was having the strangest dream," she said. "In the dream I was conducting the Bach B minor Mass, the Kyrie part. It was in four-four time. But when I was right in the middle, someone came along and took away my baton and said it wasn't in four-four time." She frowned. "But it really is. Why would I be conducting that? I don't even like the Bach B minor Mass. Arnie has a tape of it; he plays it all the time, very late in the evening."

He thought of the dreams he had been having of late, vague forms that shifted, flitted away; something to do with a tall building of many rooms; hawks or vultures circling endlessly overhead. And some dreadful thing in a cupboard . . . he had not seen it, had only felt its presence there.

"Dreams usually relate to the future," Doreen said. "They have to do with the potential in a person. Arnie wants to start a symphony orchestra at Lewistown; he's been talking to Bosley Touvim at New Israel. Maybe I'll be the conductor; maybe that's what my dream means." She slid from the bed and stood up, naked and slim and smooth.

"Doreen," he said steadily, "I don't remember last night. What became of Manfred?"

"He stayed with Arnie. Because he has to go back to Camp B-G, now, and Arnie said he'd take him. He goes to New Israel all the time to visit his own boy there, Sam Esterhazy. He's going there today, he told you." After a pause she said, "Jack . . . have you ever had amnesia before?"

"No," he said.

"It's probably due to the shock of quarreling with Arnie; it's awfully hard on a person to tangle with Arnie, I've noticed."

"Maybe that's it," he said.

"What about breakfast?" Now she began getting fresh clothes from her dresser drawers, a blouse, underwear. "I'll cook bacon and eggs—delicious canned Danish bacon." She hesitated and then she said, "More of Arnie's black-market goodies. But they really are good."

"It's fine with me," he said.

"After we went to bed last night I lay awake for hours wondering what Arnie will do. To us, I mean. I think it'll be your job, Jack; I think he'll put pressure on Mr. Yee to let you go. You must be prepared for that. We both must be. And of course, he'll just dump me; that's obvious. But I don't mind—I have you."

"Yes that's so, you do have me," he said, as by reflex.

"The vengeance of Arnie Kott," Doreen said, as she washed her face in the bathroom. "But he's so human; it's not so scary. I prefer him to that Manfred; I really couldn't stand that child. Last night was a nightmare—I kept feeling awful cold squishy tendrils drifting around the room and in my mind . . . intimations of filth and evil that didn't seem to be either in me or outside of me—just nearby. I know where they came from." After a moment she finished, "It was that child. It was his thoughts."

Presently she was frying the bacon and heating coffee; he set the table, and then they sat down to eat. The food smelled good, and he felt much better, tasting it and seeing it and smelling it, and being aware of the girl across from him, with her red hair, long and heavy and sleek, tied back with a gay ribbon.

"Is your son at all like Manfred?" she asked.

"Oh, hell, no."

"Does he take after you or—"

"Silvia," he said. "He takes after his mother."

"She's pretty, isn't she?"

"I would say so."

"You know, Jack, last night when I was lying there awake and thinking . . . I thought, Maybe Arnie won't turn Manfred over to Camp B-G. What would he do with him, with a creature like that? Arnie's very imaginative. Now this scheme to buy into the F.D.R. land is over . . . maybe he'll find an entirely new use for Manfred's precognition. It occurred to me—you'll laugh. Maybe he'll be able to contact Manfred through Heliogabalus, that tame Bleekman of his." She was quiet, then, eating breakfast and staring down at the plate.

Jack said, "You could be right." He felt bad, just to hear her say it. It rang so true; it was so plausible.

"You never talked to Helio," Doreen said. "He's the most cynical, bitter person I ever met. He's even sardonic with Arnie; he hates everybody. I mean, he's really twisted inside."

"Did I ask Arnie to take the boy? Or was it his idea?"

"Arnie suggested it. At first you wouldn't agree. But you had become so—inert and withdrawn. It was late and we all had drunk a lot—do you remember that?"

He nodded.

"Arnie serves that Black Label Jack Daniels. I must have drunk a whole fifth of it alone." She shook her head mournfully. "Nobody else on Mars has the liquor Arnie has; I'll miss it."

"There isn't much I can do along that line," Jack said.

"I know. That's O.K. I don't expect you to; I don't expect anything, in fact. It all happened so fast last night; one minute we were all working together, you and I and Arnie—then, it seemed like all of a sudden, it was obvious that we were on opposite sides, that we'd never be together again, not as friends, anyhow. It's sad." She put up the side of her hand and rubbed at her eye. A tear slid down her cheek. "Jesus. I'm crying," she said with anger.

"If we could go back and relive last night—"

"I wouldn't change it," she said. "I don't regret anything. And you shouldn't either."

"Thanks," he said. He took hold of her hand. "I'll do the best I can by you. As the guy said, I'm not much but I'm all I have."

She smiled, and, after a moment, resumed eating her breakfast.

*

At the front counter of her shop, Anne Esterhazy wrapped a package for mailing. As she began addressing the label, a man strode into the store; she glanced up, saw him, a tall, thin man wearing glasses much too large for him. Memory brought distaste as she recognized Dr. Glaub.

"Mrs. Esterhazy," Dr. Glaub said, "I want to talk to you, if I may. I regret our altercation; I behaved in a regressive, oral-sucking fashion, and I'd like to apologize."

She said coolly, "What do you want, Doctor? I'm busy."

Lowering his voice, he said in a rapid monotone, "Mrs. Esterhazy, this has to do with Arnie Kott and a project he has with an anomalous boy whom he took from the camp. I want you to use your influence over Mr. Kott and your great zeal for humanitarian causes to see that a severe cruelty is not done to an innocent, introverted schizoid individual who was drawn into Mr. Kott's scheme due to his line of work. This man—"

"Wait," she interrupted. "I can't follow." She beckoned him to accompany her to the rear of the store, where no one entering would overhear.

"This man, Jack Bohlen," Dr. Glaub said, even more rapidly than before, "could become permanently psychotic as a result of Kott's desire for revenge, and I ask you, Mrs. Esterhazy—" He pleaded on and on.

Oh, good grief, she thought. Another cause that somebody wants to enlist me in—don't I have enough already?

But she listened; she had no choice. And it was her nature.

On and on mumbled Dr. Glaub, and gradually she began to build up an idea of the situation which he was trying to describe. It was clear that he held a grudge against Arnie. And yet—there was more. Dr. Glaub was a curious mixture of the idealistic and the childishly envious, a queer sort of person, Anne Esterhazy thought as she listened.

"Yes," she said at one point, "that does sound like Arnie."

"I thought of going to the police." Dr. Glaub rambled on. "Or to the UN authorities, and then I thought of you, so I came here." He peered at her, disingenuously but with determination.

At ten o'clock that morning Arnie Kott entered the front office of the Yee Company at Bunchewood Park. An elongated, intelligent-looking Chinese in his late thirties approached him and asked what he wished.

"I am Mr. Yee." They shook hands.

"This guy Bohlen that I'm leasing from you."

"Oh, yes. Isn't he a top-drawer repairman? Naturally, he is." Mr. Yee regarded him with shrewd caution.

Arnie said, "I like him so much I want to buy his contract from you." He got out his checkbook. "Give me the price."

"Oh, we must keep Mr. Bohlen," Mr. Yee protested, throwing up his hands. "No, sir, we can only lease him, not ever part with him."

"Name me the price." You skinny, smart cookie, Arnie thought.

"To part with Mr. Bohlen—we couldn't replace him!"

Arnie waited.

Considering, Mr. Yee said, "I suppose I could go over our records. But it would take hours to determine Mr. Bohlen's even approximate value."

Arnie waited, checkbook in hand.

After he had purchased Jack Bohlen's work contract from the Yee Company, Arnie Kott flew back home to Lewistown. He found Helio with Manfred, in the living room together; Helio was reading aloud to the boy from a book. "What's all this mumbo-jumbo?" Arnie demanded.

Helio, lowering his book, said, "This child has a speech impediment which I am overcoming."

"Bull," Arnie said, "you'll never overcome it." He took off his coat and held it out to Helio. After a pause the Bleekman reluctantly laid down the book and accepted the coat; he moved off to hang it in the hall closet.

From the corner of his eye Manfred seemed to be looking at Arnie.

"How you doin', kid," Arnie said in a friendly voice. He whacked the boy on the back. "Listen, you want to go back to that nuthouse, that no-good Camp B-G? Or do you want to stay with me? I'll give you ten minutes to decide."

To himself, Arnie thought, You're staying with me, no matter what you decide. You crazy fruity dumb kid, you and your dancing around on your toes and not talking and not noticing anybody. And your future-reading talent, which I know you got down there in that fruity brain of yours, which last night proved there's no doubt of.

Returning, Helio said, "He wants to stay with you, Mister."

"Sure he does," Arnie said, pleased.

"His thoughts," Helio said, "are as clear as plastic to me, and mine likewise to him. We are both prisoners, Mister, in a hostile land."

At that Arnie laughed loud and long.

"Truth always amuses the ignorant," Helio said.

"O.K.," Arnie said, "so I'm ignorant. I just get a kick out of you liking this warped kid, that's all. No offense. So you got something in common, you two? I'm not surprised." He swept up the book which Helio had been reading. "Pascal," he read. "*Provincial Letters.* Christ on the cross, what's the point of this? Is there a point?"

"The rhythms," Helio said, with patience. "Great prose establishes a cadence which attracts and holds the boy's wandering attention."

"Why does it wander?"

"From dread."

"Dread of what?"

"Of death," Helio said.

Sobered, Arnie said, "Oh. Well. His death? Or just death in general?"

"This boy experiences his own old age, his lying in a dilapidated state, decades from now, in an old persons' home which is yet to be built here on Mars, a place of decay which he loathes beyond expression. In this future place he passes empty, weary years, bedridden—an object, not a person, kept alive through stupid legalities. When he tries to fix his eyes on the present, he almost at once is smitten by that dread vision of himself once again."

"Tell me about this old persons' home," Arnie said.

"It is to be built soon," Helio said. "Not for that purpose, but as a vast dormitory for immigrants to Mars."

"Yeah," Arnie said, recognizing it. "In the F.D.R. range."

"The people arrive," Helio said, "and settle, and live, and drive the wild Bleekmen from their last refuge. In turn, the Bleekmen put a curse on the land, sterile as it is. The Earth settlers fail; their buildings deteriorate year after year. Settlers return to Earth faster than they come here. At last this other use is made of the building: it becomes a home for the aged, for the poor, the senile and infirm."

"Why doesn't he talk? Explain that."

"To escape from his dread vision he retreats back to happier days, days inside his mother's body where there is no one else, no change, no time, no suffering. The womb life. He directs himself there, to the only happiness he has ever known. Mister, he refuses to leave that dear spot."

"I see," Arnie said, only half-believing the Bleekman.

"His suffering is like our own, like all other persons'. But in him it is worse, for he has his preknowledge, which we lack. It is a terrible knowledge to have. No wonder he has become—dark within."

"Yeah, he's as dark as you are," Arnie said, "and not outside, either, but like you said—inside. How can you stand him?"

"I stand everything," the Bleekman said.

"You know what I think?" Arnie said. "I think he does more than just see into time. I think he controls time."

The Bleekman's eyes became opaque. He shrugged.

"Doesn't he?" Arnie persisted. "Listen, Heliogabalus, you black bastard; this kid fooled around with last night. I know it. He saw it in advance and he tried to tamper with it. Was he trying to make it not happen? He was trying to halt time."

"Perhaps," Helio said.

"That's quite a talent," Arnie said. "Maybe he could go back into the past, like he wants to, and maybe alter the present. You keep working with him, keep after this. Listen, has that Doreen Anderton called or stopped by this morning? I want to talk to her."

"No."

"You think I'm nuts? As to what I imagine about this kid and his possible abilities?"

"You are driven by rage, Mister," the Bleekman said. "A man driven by rage may stumble, in his passion, onto truth."

"What crap," Arnie said, disgusted. "Can't you just say yes or no? Do you have to babble like you do?"

Helio said, "Mister, I will tell you something about Mr. Bohlen, whom you wish to injure. He is very venerable—"

"Vulnerable," Arnie corrected.

"Thank you. He is frail, easily hurt. It should be easy for you to put an end to him. However, he has with him a charm, given to him by someone who loves him or perhaps by several who love him. A Bleekman water witch charm. It may guarantee him in safety."

After an interval, Arnie said, "We'll see."

"Yes," Helio said in a voice which Arnie had never heard him use before. "We will have to wait and see what strength still lives in such ancient items."

"The living proof that such junk is just so much worthless crap is you yourself. That you'd rather be here, taking orders from me, serving me my food and sweeping the floor and hanging up my coat, than roaming around out on that Martian desert like you were when I found you. Out there like a dying beast, begging for water."

"Hmm," the Bleekman murmured. "Possibly so."

"And keep that in mind," Arnie said. Or you might find yourself back out there again, with your paka eggs and your arrows, stumbling along going nowhere, nowhere at all, he thought to himself. I'm doing you a big favor, letting you live here like a human.

In the early afternoon Arnie Kott received a message from Scott Temple. He placed it on the spindle of his decoding equipment, and soon he was listening to the message.

"We located this character's field, Arnie, out in the F.D.R. range, all right. He wasn't there, but a slave rocket had just landed; in fact, that's how we found it right off—we followed the trail of the rocket in. Anyhow, the guy had a large storage shed full of goodies; we took all the goodies, and they're in our warehouse now. Then we planted a seed-type A-weapon and blew up the field and the shed and all the equipment lying around."

Good deal, Arnie thought.

"And, like you said, so he'd realize who he's up against, we left a message. We stuck a note up on the remains of the landing field guidance tower that said, *Arnie Kott doesn't like what you stand for.* How does that strike you, Arnie?"

"That strikes me fine," Arnie said aloud, although it did seem a little—what was the word? Corny.

The message continued, "And he'll discover it when he gets back. And I thought—this is my idea, subject to your correction—that we'd take a trip out there later in the week, just to be sure he's not rebuilding. Some of these independent operators are sort of screwy, like those guys last year that tried to set up their own telephone system. Anyhow, I believe that takes care of it. And by the way—he was using Norb Steiner's old gear; we found records around with Steiner's name on them. So you were right. It's a good thing we moved right onto this guy, because he could have been trouble."

The message ended. Arnie put the reel on his encoder, seated himself at the mike, and answered.

"Scott, you did good. Thanks. I trust we've heard the last from that guy, and I approve your confiscating his stock; we can use it all. Drop by some evening and have a drink." He stopped the mechanism, then, and rewound the reel.

From the kitchen came the insistent, muffled sound of Heliogabalus reading aloud to Manfred Steiner. Hearing it, Arnie felt irritation, and then his resentment toward the Bleekman surged up. Why'd you let me get mixed up with Jack Bohlen when you could read the kid's mind? he demanded. Why didn't you speak up?

He felt outright hatred for Heliogabalus. You betrayed me, too, he said to himself. Like the rest of them, Anne and Jack and Doreen; all of them.

Going to the kitchen door he yelled in, "You getting results, or aren't you?"

Heliogabalus lowered his book and said, "Mister, this requires time and effort."

"Time!" Arnie said. "Hell, that's the whole problem. Send him back into the past, say two years ago, and have him buy the Henry Wallace in my name—can you do that?"

There was no answer. The question, to Heliogabalus, was too absurd even to consider. Flushing, Arnie slammed the kitchen door shut and stalked back into the living room.

Then have him send me back into the past, Arnie said to himself. This time-travel ability must be worth something;

why can't I get the kind of results I want? What's the matter with everyone?

They're making me wait just to annoy me, he said to himself.

And, he decided, I'm not going to wait much longer.

By one o'clock in the afternoon still no service calls had come in from the Yee Company. Jack Bohlen, waiting by the phone in Doreen Anderton's apartment, knew that something was wrong.

At one-thirty he phoned Mr. Yee.

"I assumed that Mr. Kott would inform you, Jack," Mr. Yee said in his prosaic manner. "You are no longer my employee, Jack; you are his. Thank you for your fine service record."

Demoralized by the news, Jack said, "Kott bought my contract?"

"That is the case, Jack."

Jack hung up the phone.

"What did he say?" Doreen asked, watching him wide-eyed.

"I'm Arnie's."

"What's he going to do?"

"I don't know," he said. "I guess I better call him and find out. It doesn't look as if he's going to call me." Playing with me, he thought. Sadistic games . . . enjoying himself, perhaps.

"There's no use telephoning him," Doreen said. "He never says anything on the phone. We'll have to go over to his place. I want to go along; please let me."

"O.K.," he said, going to the closet to get his coat. "Let's go," he said to her.

Fourteen

A<small>T</small> two o'clock in the afternoon Otto Zitte poked his head out the side door of the Bohlen house and ascertained that no one was watching. He could leave safely, Silvia Bohlen realized, as she saw what he was doing.

What have I done? she asked herself as she stood in the middle of the bedroom clumsily buttoning her blouse. How can I expect to keep it secret? Even if Mrs. Steiner doesn't see him, he'll surely tell that June Henessy, and she'll blab it to everybody along the William Butler Yeats; she loves gossip. I know Jack will find out. And Leo might have come home early—

But it was too late now. Over and done with. Otto was gathering up his suitcases, preparing to depart.

I wish I was dead, she said to herself.

"Goodbye, Silvia," Otto said hurriedly as he started toward the front door, "I will call you."

She did not answer; she concentrated on putting on her shoes.

"Aren't you going to say goodbye?" he asked, pausing at the bedroom door.

Shooting a glance at him she said, "No. And get out of here. Don't ever come back— I hate you, I really do."

He shrugged. "Why?"

"Because," she said, with perfect logic, "you're a horrible person. I never had anything to do with a person like you before. I must be out of my mind, it must be the loneliness."

He seemed genuinely hurt. Flushed red, he hung around at the doorway of the bedroom. "It was as much your idea as mine," he mumbled finally, glaring at her.

"Go away," she said, turning her back to him.

At last the front door opened and shut. He had gone.

Never, never again, Silvia said to herself. She went to the medicine cabinet in the bathroom and got down her bottle of phenobarbital; hastily pouring herself a glass of water, she took 150 milligrams, gulping them down and gasping.

I shouldn't have been so mean to him, she realized in a flash of conscience. It wasn't fair; it wasn't really his fault, it was mine. If I'm no good, why blame him? If it hadn't been him it would have been someone else, sooner or later.

She thought, *Will he ever come back?* Or have I driven him off forever? Already she felt lonely, unhappy and completely at a loss once more, as if she were doomed to drift in a hopeless vacuum for ever and ever.

He was actually very nice, she decided. Gentle and considerate. I could have done a lot worse.

Going into the kitchen, she seated herself at the table, picked up the telephone, and dialed June Henessy's number.

Presently June's voice sounded in her ear. "Hello?"

Silvia said, "Guess what."

"Tell me."

"Wait'll I light a cigarette." Silvia Bohlen lit a cigarette, got an ashtray, moved her chair so that she was comfortable, and then, with an infinitude of detail, plus a little essential invention at critical points, she told her.

To her surprise she found the telling to be as enjoyable as the experience itself.

Perhaps even a bit more so.

Flying back across the desert to his base in the F.D.R. Mountains, Otto Zitte ruminated on his assignation with Mrs. Bohlen and congratulated himself; he was in a good mood, despite Silvia's not unnatural fit of remorse and accusation just as he was leaving.

You have to expect that, he advised himself.

It had happened before; true, it always upset him, but that was one of the odd little tricks typical of a woman's mind: there always came a point when they had to sidestep reality and start casting blame in all directions, toward anyone and anything handy.

He did not much care; nothing could rob him of the memory of the happy time which the two of them had engaged in.

So now what? Back to the field to have lunch, rest up, shave, shower and change his clothes. . . . There would still be time enough to start out once more on an authentic selling trip with nothing else in mind this time but pure business itself.

Already, he could see the ragged peaks of the mountains ahead; he would soon be there.

It seemed to him that he saw a plume of ugly gray smoke drifting up from the mountains directly ahead.

Frightened, he stepped up the velocity of the 'copter. No doubt of it; the smoke rose at or near his field. They found me! he said to himself with a sob. The UN—they wiped me out and they're waiting for me. But he went on anyhow; he had to know for sure.

Below lay the remains of his field. A smoking, rubble-strewn ruin. He circled aimlessly, crying openly, tears spilling down his cheeks. There was no sign of the UN, however, no military vehicles or soldiers.

Could an incoming rocket have exploded?

Quickly, Otto landed the 'copter; on foot he ran across the hot ground, toward the debris that had been his storage shed.

As he reached the signal tower of the field he saw, pinned to it, a square of cardboard.

ARNIE KOTT DOESN'T LIKE WHAT YOU STAND FOR

Again and again he read it, trying to understand it. Arnie Kott—he was just getting ready to call on him—Arnie had been Norb's best customer. What did this mean? Had he already provided poor service to Arnie, or how else had he made Arnie mad? It didn't make sense—what had he done to Arnie Kott to deserve this?

Why? Otto asked. What did I do to you? Why have you destroyed me?

Presently he made his way over to the shed, hoping beyond hope that some of the stocks could be salvaged, hoping to find something among the remains. . . .

There were no remains. The stock had been taken; he saw no single can, glass jar, package, or bag. The litter of the building itself, yes, but only that. Then they—those who had dropped the bomb—had come in first and pilfered the stock.

You bombed me, Arnie Kott, and you stole my goods, Otto said, as he wandered in a circle, clenching and unclenching his fists and darting glances of rage and frenzy up at the sky.

And still he did not understand why.

There has to be a reason, he said to himself. And I will find it out; I will not rest, goddamn you, Arnie Kott, until I know. And when I find out I will get you. I will pay you back for what you did.

He blew his nose, snuffled, dragged himself back to his 'copter with slow steps, seated himself inside, and stared ahead for a long, long time.

At last he opened one of the suitcases. From it he took the .22-caliber pistol; he sat holding it on his lap, thinking about Arnie Kott.

To Arnie Kott, Heliogabalus said, "Mister, excuse me for disturbing you. But if you are ready I will explain to you what you must do."

Delighted, Arnie stopped at his desk. "Fire away."

With a sad and haughty expression on his face, Helio said, "You must take Manfred out into the desert and cross, on foot, to the Franklin Delano Roosevelt Mountains. There your pilgrimage must end when you bring the boy to Dirty Knobby, the Rock which is sacred to the Bleekmen. Your answer lies there, when you have introduced the boy to Dirty Knobby."

Wagging his finger at the tame Bleekman, Arnie said slyly, "And you told me it was a fraud." He had felt all the time that there was something to the Bleekman religion. Helio had tried to deceive him.

"At the sanctuary of the rock you must commune. The spirit which animates Dirty Knobby will receive your collective psyches and perhaps if it is merciful, it will grant what you request." Helio added, "It is in actuality the capacity within the boy which you must depend on. The rock alone is powerless. However, it is as follows: time is weakest at that spot where Dirty Knobby lies. Upon that fact the Bleekman has prevailed for centuries."

"I see," Arnie said. "A sort of puncture in time. And you guys get at the future through it. Well, it's the past I'm interested in, now, and frankly this all sounds fishy to me. But I'll try it. You've told me so many different yarns about that rock—"

Helio said, "What I said before is true. Alone, Dirty Knobby could have done nothing for you." He did not cringe; he met Arnie's gaze.

"You think Manfred will cooperate?"

"I have told him of the rock and he is excited at the idea of seeing it. I said that, in that place, one might escape backward into the past. That idea enthralls him. However—" Helio paused. "You must repay the boy for his effort."

"You can offer him something of priceless value. . . . Mister, you can banish the specter of AM-WEB from his life forever. Promise him that you will send him back to Earth. Then no matter what becomes of him, he will never see the interior of that abominable building. If you do that for him, he will turn all his mental powers in your behalf."

"It sounds fine to me," Arnie said.

"And you will not fail the boy."

"Oh, heck, no," Arnie promised. "I'll make all the arrangements with the UN right away—it's complicated, but I got lawyers who can handle stuff like that without even half trying."

"Good," Helio said, nodding. "It would be foul to let the boy down. If you could for a moment experience his terrible anxiety about his future life in that place—"

"Yeah, it sounds awful," Arnie agreed.

"What a shame it would be," Helio said, eying him, "if you yourself did ever have to endure that."

"Where is Manfred right now?"

"He is walking about the streets of Lewistown," Helio said. "Taking in the sights."

"Cripes, is it safe?"

"I think so," Helio said. "He is much excited by the people and stores and activity; it is all new to him."

"You sure have helped that kid," Arnie said.

The door chimes sounded, and Helio went to answer. When Arnie looked up, there stood Jack Bohlen and Doreen Anderton, both of them with fixed, high-strung expressions.

"Oh, hi," Arnie said, preoccupied. "Come on in; I was about to call you, Jack. Listen, I got a job for you."

Jack Bohlen said, "Why did you buy my contract from Mr. Yee?"

"Because I need you," Arnie said. "I'll tell you why right

now. I'm going on a pilgrimage with Manfred and I want somebody to circle around overhead so we don't get lost and die of thirst. We got to walk across the desert to the F.D.R. Mountains; isn't that right, Helio?"

"Yes, Mister," Helio said.

"I want to get started right away," Arnie explained. "I figure it's about a five-day hike. We'll take a portable communications rig with us so we can notify you when we need something like food or water. At night you can land the 'copter and pitch a tent for us to sleep in. Make sure you get medical supplies on board in case either Manfred or I get bit by a desert animal; I hear there's Martian snakes and rats running around wild out there." He examined his watch. "It's three now; I'd like to get started by four and get in maybe five hours tonight."

"What's the purpose of this—pilgrimage?" Doreen asked presently.

"I got business out there to attend to," Arnie said. "Out among those desert Bleekman. Private business. Are you coming along in the 'copter? If so you better put on something different, maybe boots and heavy pants, because it's always possible you fellas might get forced down. That's a long time, five days, to keep circling. Make sure in particular about the water."

Doreen and Jack looked at each other.

"I'm serious," Arnie said. "So let's not stop to mess around. O.K.?"

"As far as I can tell," Jack said to Doreen, "I have no choice. I have to do what he tells me."

"That's the truth, buddy," Arnie agreed. "So start rounding up the equipment we'll need. Portable stove to cook on, portable light, portable bathroom, food and soap and towels, a gun of some sort. You know what we'll need; you've been living on the edge of the desert."

Jack nodded slowly.

"What is this business?" Doreen said. "And why do you have to walk? If you have to go there, why can't you fly as you usually do?"

"I just have to walk," Arnie said with irritation. "That's the way it is; it wasn't my idea." To Helio he said, "I can fly back, can't I?"

"Yes, Mister," Helio said. "You may return any way you prefer."

"It's a good thing I'm in top-notch physical shape." Arnie said, "or this would be out of the question. I hope Manfred can make it."

"He is quite strong, Mister," Helio said.

"You're taking the boy," Jack murmured.

"That's right," Arnie said. "Any objections?"

Jack Bohlen did not answer, but he looked more grim than ever. Suddenly he burst out, "You can't make the boy walk for five days across the desert—it'll kill him."

"Why can't you go in some surface vehicle?" Doreen asked. "One of those little tractor-jitneys that the UN post office people use to deliver the mail. It would still take a long time; it would still be a pilgrimage."

"What about that?" Arnie said to Helio.

After some reflection, the Bleekman said, "I suppose that little cart of which you speak would do."

"Fine," Arnie said, deciding then and there. "I'll phone a couple of guys I know and pick up one of those PO jitneys. That's a good idea you gave me, Doreen; I appreciate it. Of course, you two still have to be there overhead to make sure we don't break down."

Both Jack and Doreen nodded.

"Maybe when I get there, where I'm going," Arnie said, "you'll maybe find out what I'm up to." In fact you darn well are going to, he said to himself; there's no doubt about that.

"This is all very strange," Doreen said; she stood close to Jack Bohlen, holding on to his arm.

"Don't blame me," Arnie said. "Blame Helio." He grinned.

"That is true," Helio said. "It was my idea."

But their expressions remained.

"Talked to your dad yet today?" Arnie asked Jack.

"Yes. Briefly, on the phone."

"His claim filed now, all recorded? No hitches?"

Jack said, "He says it was processed properly. He's preparing to return to Earth."

"Efficient operation," Arnie said. "I admire that. Shows up here on Mars, stakes out his claim, goes to the abstract office and records it, then flies back. Not bad."

"What are you up to, Arnie?" Jack said in a quiet voice.

Arnie shrugged. "I got this holy pilgrimage to make, along with Manfred. That's all." He was, however, still grinning; he could not help it. He could not stop, and he did not bother to try.

Use of the UN post office jitney cut the proposed pilgrimage from Lewistown to Dirty Knobby from five days to a mere eight hours; or so Arnie calculated. Nothing to do now but go, he said to himself as he paced about his living room.

Outside the building, at the curb, Helio sat in the parked jitney with Manfred. Through the window Arnie could see them, far below. He got his gun from his desk drawer, strapped it on inside his coat, locked up the desk, and hurried out into the hall.

A moment later he emerged on the sidewalk and made for the jitney.

"Here we go," he said to Manfred. Helio stepped from the jitney, and Arnie seated himself behind the tiller. He revved up the tiny turbine engine; it made a noise like a bumblebee in a bottle. "Sounds good," he said heartily. "So long, Helio. If this goes off O.K., there's a reward for you—remember that."

"I expect no reward," Helio said. "I am only doing my duty by you, Mister; I would do it for anyone."

Releasing the parking brake, Arnie pulled out into downtown Lewistown late-afternoon traffic. They were on their way. Overhead, Jack Bohlen and Doreen were no doubt cruising in the 'copter; Arnie did not bother to search for sign of them, taking it for granted that they were there. He waved goodbye to Helio, and then a huge tractor-bus filled in all the space behind the jitney; Helio was cut off from view.

"How about this, Manfred?" Arnie said, as he guided the jitney toward the perimeter of Lewistown and the desert beyond. "Isn't this something? It makes almost fifty miles an hour, and that isn't hay."

The boy did not respond, but his body trembled with excitement.

"This is the nuts," Arnie declared, in answer to his own query.

They had almost left Lewistown when Arnie became aware of a car which had pulled up beside them and was proceeding at the same speed as theirs. He saw, within the car, two figures, a man and a woman; at first he thought it was Jack and Doreen, and then he discovered that the woman was his ex-wife Anne Esterhazy and the man was Dr. Milton Glaub.

What the hell do they want? Arnie wondered. Can't they see I'm busy, I can't be bothered, whatever it is?

"Kott," Dr. Glaub yelled, "pull over to the curb so we can talk to you! This is vital!"

"The hell," Arnie said, increasing the speed of the jitney. He felt with his left hand for his gun. "I got nothing to say, and what are you two doing in cahoots?" He didn't like the look of it one bit. Just like them to gang up, he said to himself. I should have expected it. Snapping on the portable communications rig, he put in a call to his steward, Eddy Goggins at Union Hall. "This is Arnie. My gyrocompass point is 8.45702, right at the edge of town. Get over here quick—I got a party that has to be took care of. Make it fast, they're gaining on me." They had, in fact, never fallen behind; it was easy for them to match the speed of the little jitney, and even to exceed it.

"Will do, Arnie," Eddy Goggins said. "I'll send some of the boys on the double; don't worry."

Now the car edged ahead and drew toward the curb. Arnie reluctantly slowed the jitney to a stop. The car placed itself in a position to block escape, and then Glaub jumped from it and scuttled up crablike to the jitney, waving his arms.

"This ends your career of bullying and domineering," he shouted at Arnie.

Kee-rist, Arnie thought. At a time like this. "What do you want?" he said. "Make it snappy; I got business."

"Leave Jack Bohlen alone," Dr. Glaub panted. "I represent him, and he needs rest and quiet. You'll have to deal with me."

From the car Anne Esterhazy emerged; she approached the jitney and confronted Arnie. "As I understand the situation—" she began.

"You understand nothin'," Arnie said, with venom. "Let me by, or I'll take care of both of you."

Overhead, a 'copter with the Water Workers' Union marking on it appeared and began to descend; it was Jack and Doreen, Arnie guessed. And behind it came a second 'copter at tremendous speed; that no doubt was Eddy and the Goodmembers. Both 'copters prepared to land close by.

Anne Esterhazy said, "Arnie, I know that something bad is going to happen to you if you don't stop what you're doing."

"To me?" he said, amused and incredulous.

"I feel it. Please, Arnie. Whatever it is you're up to—think twice. There's so much good in the world; must you have your revenge?"

"Go back to New Israel and tend your goddamn store." He fast-idled the motor of the jitney.

"That boy," Anne said. "That's Manfred Steiner, isn't it? Let Milton take him back to Camp B-G; it's better for everyone, better for him and for you."

One of the 'copters had landed. From it hopped three or four WWU men; they came running up the street, and Dr. Glaub, seeing them, plucked dolefully at Anne's sleeve.

"I see them." She remained unruffled. "Please, Arnie. You and I have worked together so often, on so many worthwhile things . . . for my sake, for Sam's sake—if you go ahead with this, I know you and I will never be together again in any way whatever. Can't you feel that? Is this so important as all that, to lose so much?"

Arnie said nothing.

Puffing, Eddy Goggins appeared beside the jitney. The union men fanned out toward Anne Esterhazy and Dr. Glaub. Now the other 'copter had landed, and from it stepped Jack Bohlen.

"Ask him," Arnie said. "He's coming of his own free will; he's a grown man, he knows what he's doing. Ask him if he isn't voluntarily coming along on this pilgrimage."

As Glaub and Anne Esterhazy turned toward Jack, Arnie Kott backed up the jitney; he shifted into forward and shot around the side of the parked car. A scuffle broke out, as Glaub tried to get back into the car; two Goodmembers grabbed him and they wrestled. Arnie steered the jitney straight ahead, and the car and the people fell behind.

"Here we go," he said to Manfred.

Ahead, the street became a vague level strip passing from the city out onto the desert, in the direction of the hills far beyond. The jitney bumped along at near top speed, and Arnie smiled. Beside him the boy's face shone with excitement.

Nobody can stop me, Arnie said to himself.

The sounds of the squabble faded from his ears; he heard now only the buzz of the tiny turbine of the jitney. He settled back.

Dirty Knobby, get ready, he said to himself. And then he thought of Jack Bohlen's magic charm, the water witch which Helio said the man had on him, and Arnie frowned. But the frown was momentary. He did not slow down.

Beside him Manfred crowed excitedly, "Gubble gubble!"

"What's that mean, gubble gubble?" Arnie asked.

There was no answer, as the two of them bounced along in the UN post office jitney toward the F.D.R. Mountains directly ahead.

Maybe I'll find out what it means when we get there, Arnie said to himself. I'd like to know. For some reason the sounds which the boy made, the unintelligible words, made him nervous, more so than anything else. He wished suddenly that Helio was along.

"Gubble gubble!" Manfred cried as they sped along.

Fifteen

THE black, lopsided projection of sandstone and volcanic glass which was Dirty Knobby poked up huge and gaunt ahead of them in the glow of early morning. They had spent the night on the desert, in a tent, the 'copter parked close by. Jack Bohlen and Doreen Anderton had exchanged no words with them; at dawn the 'copter had taken off to circle overhead. Arnie and the boy Manfred Steiner had eaten a good breakfast and then packed up and resumed their trip.

Now the trip, the pilgrimage to the sacred rock of the Bleekmen, was over.

Seeing Dirty Knobby close up like this, Arnie thought, There's the place that'll cure us all of whatever ails us. Letting Manfred take the tiller of the jitney, he consulted the map which Heliogabalus had drawn. It showed the path up into the range to the rock. There was, Helio had told him, a hollowed-out chamber on the north side of the rock, where a Bleekman priest could generally be found. Unless, Arnie said to himself, he's off somewhere sleeping off a binge. He knew the Bleekmen priests; they were old winos, for the most part. Even the Bleekmen had contempt for them.

At the base of the first hill, in the shadows, he parked the jitney and shut off its engine. "From here we climb on foot," he said to Manfred. "We'll carry as much gear as we can, food and water naturally, and the communications rig, and I guess if we need to cook we can come back for the stove. It's only supposed to be a few more miles."

The boy hopped from the jitney. He and Arnie unloaded the gear, and soon they were trudging up a rocky trail, into the F.D.R. range.

Glancing about with apprehension, Manfred huddled and shivered. Perhaps the boy was experiencing AM-WEB once more, Arnie conjectured. The Henry Wallace was only a hundred miles from here. The boy might well have picked up the emanations of the structure to come, close as they were, now. In fact he could almost feel them himself.

Or was it the rock of the Bleekmen which he felt?

He did not like the sight of it. Why make a shrine out of this? he asked himself. Perverse—this arid place. But maybe a long time ago this region had been fertile. Evidence of one-time Bleekmen camps could be made out along the path. Maybe the Martians had originated here; the land certainly had an old, used appearance. As if, he thought, a million gray-black creatures had handled all this throughout the ages. And now what was it? A last remains for a dying race. A relic for those who were not going to be around much longer.

Wheezing from the exertion of climbing with a heavy load, Arnie halted. Manfred toiled up the steep acclivity after him, still casting anxiety-stricken looks around.

"Don't worry," Arnie said encouragingly. "There's nothing here to be scared of." Was the boy's talent already blending with that of the rock? And, he wondered, had the rock itself become apprehensive, too? Was it capable of that?

The trail leveled out and became wider. And all was in shadow; cold and damp hung over everything, as if they were treading within a great tomb. The vegetation that grew thin and noxious along the surface of rocks had a dead quality to it, as if something had poisoned it in its act of growing. Ahead lay a dead bird on the path, a rotten corpse that might have been there for weeks; he could not tell. It had a mummified appearance.

I sure don't enjoy this place, Arnie said to himself.

Halting at the bird, Manfred bent down and said, "Gubbish."

"Yeah," Arnie murmured. "Come on, let's go."

They arrived all at once at the base of the rock.

Wind rustled the leaves of vegetation, the shrubs which looked as if they had been skinned down to their elements: bare and picked over, like bones stuck upright in the soil. The wind emerged from a crack in Dirty Knobby and it smelled, he thought, as if some sort of animal lived there. Maybe the priest himself; he saw with no real surprise an empty wine bottle lying off to one side, with other bits of debris caught on the sharp foliage nearby.

"Anybody around?" Arnie called.

After a long time an old man, a Bleekman, gray as if wrapped in webs, edged out of the chamber within the rock.

The wind seemed to blow him along, so that he crept side-ways, pausing against the side of the cavity and then stirring forward once more. His eyes were red-rimmed.

"You old drunk," Arnie said in a low voice. And then from a piece of paper Helio had given him he greeted the old man in Bleeky.

The priest mumbled a toothless, mechanical response.

"Here." Arnie held out a carton of cigarettes. The priest, mumbling, sidled forward and took the carton in his claws; he tucked the carton beneath his gray-webbed robes. "You like that, huh?" Arnie said. "I thought you would."

From the piece of paper he read, in Bleeky, the purpose of his visit and what he wanted the priest to do. He wanted the priest to leave him and Manfred in peace for an hour or so, at the chamber, so that they could summon the spirit of the rock.

Still mumbling, the priest backed away, fussed with the hem of his robes, then turned and shambled off. He disappeared down a side trail without a backward look at Arnie and Manfred.

Arnie turned the paper over and read the instructions that Helio had written out.

(1) Enter chamber.

Taking Manfred by the arm, he led him step by step into the dark cleft of the rock; flashing on his light, he led the boy along until the chamber became large. It still smelled bad, he thought, as if it had been kept closed up for centuries. Like an old box full of decayed rags, a vegetable rather than animal scent.

Now what? Again he consulted Helio's paper.

(2) Light fire.

An uneven ring of boulders surrounded a blackened pit in which lay fragments of wood and what appeared to be bones. . . . It looked as if the old wino fixed his meals here.

In his pack Arnie had kindling; he got it out now, laying the pack on the floor of the cavern and fumbling stiff-fingered with the straps. "Don't get lost, kid," he said to Manfred. I wonder if we're ever coming out of here again? he asked himself.

Both of them felt better, however, when the fire had been lit. The cavern became warmer, but not dry; the smell of mold persisted and even seemed to become stronger, as if the fire were attracting it, whatever it was.

The next instruction bewildered him; it did not seem to fit in, but nonetheless he complied.

(3) Turn on portable radio to 574 kc.

Arnie got out the little Japanese-made transistor portable and turned it on. At 574 kc. nothing but static issued forth. It seemed, though, to obtain a response from the rock around them; the rock seemed to change and become more alert, as if the noise from the radio had awakened it to their presence. The next instruction was equally annoying.

(4) Take Nembutal (boy not take).

Using the canteen, Arnie swallowed the Nembutal down, wondering if its purpose was to blur his senses and make him credulous. Or was it to stifle his anxiety?

Only one instruction remained.

(5) Throw enclosed packet on fire.

Helio had put into Arnie's pack a small paper, a wadded-up page from the New York Times, with some kind of grass within it. Kneeling by the fire, Arnie carefully unwrapped the packet and dumped the dark, dry strands into the flames. A nauseating smell arose and the flames died down. Smoke billowed out, filling the chamber; he heard Manfred cough. Goddamn, Arnie thought, it'll kill us yet if we keep on.

The smoke disappeared almost at once. The cavern seemed now dark and empty and much larger than before, as if the rock around them had receded. He felt, all at once, as if he were going to fall; he seemed no longer to be standing precisely upright. Sense of balance gone, he realized. Nothing to use as bearing.

"Manfred," he said, "now listen. On account of me you don't have to worry about that AM-WEB any more, like Helio explained. You got that? O.K. Now regress back around three weeks. Can you do that? Really put your back into it, try hard as you can."

In the gloom the boy peeped at him, eyes wide with fear.

"Back to before I knew Jack Bohlen," Arnie said. "Before I met him out on the desert that day those Bleekmen were dying of thirst. You get it?" He walked toward the boy—

He fell flat on his face.

The Nembutal, he thought. Better get back up before I pass out entirely. He struggled up, groping for something to catch on to. Light flared, searing him; he put his hands . . . and then he was in water. Warm water poured over him, over his face; he spluttered, choked, saw around him billowing steam, felt beneath his feet familiar tile.

He was in his steam bath.

Voices of men conversing. Eddy's voice, saying, "Right, Arnie." Then the outline of shapes around him, other men taking showers.

Down inside him, near his groin, his duodenal ulcer began to burn and he realized that he was terribly hungry. He stepped from the shower and with weak, unwilling legs padded across the warm, wet tiles, searching for the attendant so that he could get his great terrycloth bathtowel.

I been here before, he thought. I've done all this, said what I'm going to say; it's uncanny. What do they call it? French word . . .

Better get some breakfast. His stomach rumbled and the ulcer pain increased.

"Hey, Tom," he called to the attendant. "Dry me off and get me dressed so I can go eat; my ulcer's killing me." He had never felt such pain from it before.

"Right, Arnie," the attendant said, stepping toward him, holding out the huge soft white towel.

When he had been dressed by the attendant, in his gray flannel trousers and T-shirt, soft leather boots, and nautical cap, Goodmember Arnie Kott left the steam bath and crossed the corridor of the Union Hall to his dining room, where Heliogabalus had his breakfast waiting.

At last he sat before a stack of hotcakes and bacon, genuine Home coffee, a glass of orange juice from New Israel oranges, and the previous week's New York Times, the Sunday edition.

He trembled with consternation as he reached to pick up

the glass of chilled, strained, sweet orange juice; the glass was slippery and smooth to the touch and almost eluded him in mid-trip. . . . He thought, I have to be careful, slow down and take it easy. *It's really so; I'm back here where I was, several weeks ago. Manfred and the rock of the Bleekmen did it together.* Wow, he thought, his mind a hubbub of anticipation. This is something! He sipped at the orange juice, enjoying each swallow of it until the glass had been emptied.

I got what I wanted, he said to himself.

Now, I have to be careful, he told himself; there are some things I sure don't want to change. I want to be sure I don't foul up my black-market business by doing the natural thing and interfering so that old Norb Steiner doesn't take his own life. I mean, it's sad about him, but I don't intend to get out of the business; so that stays as it is. As it's going to be, he corrected himself.

Mainly I got two things to do. First, I see that I get a legal deed to land in the F.D.R. range all around the Henry Wallace area, and that deed'll predate old man Bohlen's deed by several weeks. So the hell with the old speculator, flying out here from Earth. When he does come, weeks from now, he'll discover the land's been bought. Trip all the way here and back for nothing. Maybe he'll have a heart attack. Arnie chuckled, thinking about that. Too bad.

And then the other thing. Jack Bohlen himself.

I'm going to fix him, he said to himself, a guy I haven't met yet, that doesn't know me, although I know him.

What I am to Jack Bohlen now is fate.

"Good morning, Mr. Kott."

Annoyed at having his meditation interrupted, he glanced up and saw that a girl had entered the room and was standing by his desk expectantly. He did not recognize her. A girl from the secretary pool, he realized, come to take the morning's dictation.

"Call me Arnie," he muttered. "Everybody's supposed to call me that. How come you didn't know, you new around here?"

The girl, he thought, was not too good-looking, and he returned to his newspaper. But on the other hand, she had a heavy, full figure. The black silk dress she wore: there isn't much on under that, he said to himself as he observed her around the side of the newspaper. Not married; he saw no wedding ring on her finger.

"Come over here," he said. "You scared of me because I'm the famous great Arnie Kott, in charge of this whole place?"

The girl approached in a luxuriant sidling motion that surprised him; she seemed to creep sideways over to the desk. And in an insinuating, hoarse voice, she said, "No, Arnie, I'm not scared of you." Her blunt stare did not seem to be one of innocence; on the contrary, its implied knowledge jolted him. It seemed to him as if she were conscious of every whim and urge in him, especially those that applied to her.

"You been working here long?" he asked.

"No, Arnie." She moved closer, now, and rested against the edge of the desk so that one leg—he could hardly believe it—gradually came in to contact with his own.

Methodically, her leg undulated against his own in a simple, reflexive, rhythmic way that made him recoil and say weakly, "Hey."

"What's the matter, Arnie?" the girl said, and smiled. It was a smile like nothing he had ever seen in his life before, cold and yet full of intimation; utterly without warmth, as if a machine had stamped it there, constructed it by pattern out of lips, teeth, tongue . . . and yet it swamped him with its sensuality. It poured forth a saturated, sopping heat that made him sit rigid in his chair, unable to look away. Mostly it was the tongue, he thought. It vibrated. The end, he noticed, had a pointed quality, as if it was good at cutting; a tongue that could hurt, that enjoyed slitting into something alive, tormenting it, and making it beg for mercy. That was the part it liked most: to hear the pleas. The teeth, too, white and sharp . . . made for rending.

He shivered.

"Do I bother you, Arnie?" the girl murmured. She had, by degrees, slid her body along the desk so that now—he could not understand how it had been accomplished—she rested almost entirely against him. My God, he thought, she's—it was impossible.

"Listen," he said, swallowing and finding his throat dry; he could hardly croak out the words. "Get going and let me read my newspaper." Grabbing up the paper he held it between himself and her. "Go on," he said gratingly.

The shape ebbed a little. "What's the matter, Arnie?" her voice purred, like metal wheels rubbing, an automatic sound coming forth from her, like on a recording, he thought.

He said nothing; he gripped his paper and read.

When he next looked up the girl had gone. He was alone.

I don't remember that, he said to himself, quaking inside, down deep within his stomach. What kind of a creature was that? I don't get it—what was happening, just then?

He began automatically to read an item in the paper about a ship which had been lost in deep space, a freighter from Japan carrying a cargo of bicycles. He felt amused, even though three hundred people aboard had perished; it was just too goddamn funny, the idea of all those thousands of little light Jap bikes floating as debris, circling the sun forever. . . . Not that they weren't needed on Mars, with its virtual lack of power sources . . . a man could pedal free of cost for hundreds of miles in the planet's slight gravity.

Reading further, he came across an item about a reception at the White House for—he squinted. The words seemed to run together; he could hardly read them. Printing error of some kind? What did it say? He held the newspaper closer. . . .

Gubble gubble, it said. The article became meaningless, nothing but the gubble-gubble words one after another. Good grief! He stared at it in disgust, his stomach reacting; his duodenal ulcer hurt worse than ever now. He had become tense and angry, the worst possible combination for an ulcer patient, especially at meal time. Darn those gubble-gubble words, he said to himself. That's what that kid says! They sure spoil the article in the paper.

Glancing through the paper he saw that almost all the articles devolved into nonsense, became blurred after a line or so. His irritation grew, and he tossed the paper away. What the hell good is it like that he asked himself.

That's that schizophrenia talk, he realized. Private language. I don't like that here at all! It's O.K. if he wants to talk like that himself, but it doesn't belong here! He's got no right to push that stuff into my world. And then Arnie thought, Of course, he did bring me back here, so maybe he thinks that does give him the right. Maybe the boy thinks of this as his world.

That thought did not please Arnie; he wished it had never come to him.

Getting up from his desk he went over to the window and looked down at the street of Lewistown far below. People hurrying along; how fast they went. And the cars, too; why so fast? There was an unpleasant kinetic quality to their movements, a jerkiness, they seemed either to bang into one another or to be about to. Colliding objects like billiard balls, hard and dangerous . . . the buildings, he noticed, seemed to bristle with sharp corners. And yet, when he tried to pinpoint the change —and it was a change, no doubt of that—he could not. This was the familiar scene he saw every day. And yet—

Were they moving too fast? Was that it? No, it was deeper than that. There was an omnipresent *hostility* in everything; things did not merely collide—they struck one another, as if doing it deliberately.

And then he saw something else, something which made him gasp. The people on the street below, hurrying back and forth, had almost no faces, just fragments or remnants of faces . . . as if they had never formed.

Aw, this will never do, Arnie said to himself. He felt fear now, deeply and intensely. What's going on? What are they handing me?

He returned, shaken, to his desk and sat down again. Picking up his cup of coffee, he drank, trying to forget the scene below, trying to resume his routine of the morning.

The coffee had a bitter, acrid, foreign taste to it, and he had to set the cup back down at once. I suppose the kid imagines all the time he's being poisoned, Arnie thought in desperation. Is that it? I got to find myself eating awful-tasting food because of his delusions? God, he thought; that's terrible.

Best thing for me, he decided, is to get my task here done as fast as possible and then get back to the present.

Unlocking the bottom drawer of his desk, Arnie got out the little battery-powered encoding dictation machine and set it up for use. Into it he said, "Scott, I got a terribly important item here to transmit to you. I insist you act on this at once. What I want to do is buy into the F.D.R. Mountains because the UN is going to establish a gigantic housing tract area there, specifically around the Henry Wallace Canyon. Now you transfer enough Union funds, in my name of course, to insure that I get title to all that, because in about two weeks speculators from—"

He broke off, for the encoding machine had groaned to a stop. He poked at it, and the reels turned slowly and then once more settled back into silence.

Thought it was fixed, Arnie thought angrily. Didn't that Jack Bohlen work on it? And then he remembered that this was back in the past before Jack Bohlen had been called in; of course it didn't work.

I've got to dictate it to the secretary-creature, he realized. He started to press the button on his desk that would summon her, but drew back. How can I let that back in here? he asked himself. But there was no alternative. He pressed the button.

The door opened and she came in. "I knew you would want me, Arnie," she said, hurrying toward him, strutting and urgent.

"Listen," he said, with authority in his voice. "Don't get too close to me, I can't stand it when people get too close." But even as he spoke he recognized his fears for what they were; it was a basic fear of the schizophrenic that people might get too close to him, might encroach into his space. Nearness fear, it was called; it was due to the schizophrenic's sensing hostility in everyone around him. That's what I'm doing, Arnie thought. And yet, even knowing this, he could not endure having the girl come close to him; he got abruptly to his feet and walked away, back once more to the window.

"Anything you say, Arnie," the girl said, in a tone that was insatiable, and despite what she said she crept toward him until, as before, she was almost touching him. He found himself hearing the noises of her breathing, smelling her, the sour body scent, her breath, which was thick and unpleasant. . . . He felt choked, unable to get enough air into his lungs.

"I'm going to dictate to you now," he said, walking away from her, keeping distance between the two of them. "This is to Scott Temple, and should go in code so they can't read it." They, he thought. Well, that had always been his fear; he couldn't blame that on the boy. "I got a terribly important item here," he dictated. "Act on it at once; it means plenty, it's a real inside tip. The UN's going to buy a huge hunk of land in the F.D.R. Mountains—"

On and on he dictated, and even as he talked a fear assailed him, an obsessive fear that grew each moment. Suppose she was just writing down those gubble-gubble words? I just got to look, he told himself; I got to walk over close to her and see. But he shrank from it, the closeness.

"Listen, miss," he said, interrupting himself. "Give me that pad of yours; I want to see what you're writing."

"Arnie," she said in her rough, dragging voice, "you can't tell anything by looking at it."

"W-what?" he demanded in fright.

"It's in shorthand." She smiled at him, coldly, with what seemed to him palpable malevolence.

"O.K.," he said, giving up. He went on and completed his dictation, then told her to get it into code and off to Scott at once.

"And what then?" she said.

"What do you mean?"

"You know, Arnie," she said, and the tone in which she said it made him cringe with dismay and pure physical disgust.

"Nothing after that," he said. "Just get out; don't come back." Following after her, he slammed the door shut behind her.

I guess, he decided, I'll have to contact Scott direct; I can't trust her. Seating himself at the desk he picked up the telephone and dialed.

Presently the line was ringing. But it rang in vain; there was no response. Why? he wondered. Has he run out on me? Is he against me? Working with them? I can't trust him; I can't trust anybody. And then, all at once, a voice said, "Hello. Scott Temple speaking." And he realized that only a few seconds and a few rings had actually gone by; all those thoughts of betrayal, of doom, had flitted through his mind in an instant.

"This is Arnie."

"Hi, Arnie. What's up? I can tell by your tone something's cooking. Spill it."

My sense of time is fouled up, Arnie realized. It seemed to me the phone rang for half an hour, but it wasn't at all.

"Arnie," Scott was saying. "Speak up. Arnie, you there?"

It's the schizophrenic confusion, Arnie realized. It's basically a breakdown in time-sense. Now I'm getting it because that kid has it.

"Chrissake!" Scott said, outraged.

With difficulty, Arnie broke his chain of thought and said, "Uh, Scott. Listen. I got an inside scoop; we have to act on this right now, you understand?" In detail, he told Scott about the UN and the F.D.R. Mountains. "So you can see," he wound up, "it's worth it to us to buy in with all we got, and pronto. You agree?"

"You're sure of this scoop?" Scott said.

"Yes, I am! I am!"

"How come? Frankly, Arnie, I like you, but I know you get crazy schemes, you're always flying off at a tangent. I'd hate to get stuck with that dog's breakfast F.D.R. land."

Arnie said, "Take my word for it."

"I can't."

He could not believe his ears. "We been working together for years, and it's always been on a word-of-mouth confidence basis," he choked. "What's going on, Scott?"

"That's what I'm asking you," Scott said calmly. "How come a man of your business experience could bite on this phony nothing so-called scoop? The scoop is that the F.D.R. range is worthless, and you know it; I know you know it. Everybody knows it. So what are you up to?"

"You don't *trust* me?"

"Why should I *trust* you? *Prove* you got real inside scoop stuff here, and not just your usual hot air."

With difficulty, Arnie said, "Hell, man, if I could prove it, you wouldn't have to trust me; it wouldn't involve trust. O.K. I'll go into this alone, and when you find out what you missed, blame yourself, not me." He slammed down the phone, shaking with rage and despair. What a thing to happen! He couldn't believe it; Scott Temple, the one person in the world he could do business with over the phone. The rest of them you could throw in the ocean, they were such crooks. . . .

It's a misunderstanding, he told himself. But based on a deep, fundamental, insidious distrust. A schizophrenic distrust.

A collapse, he realized, of the ability to communicate.

Standing up, he said aloud, "I guess I got to go to Pax Grove myself and see the abstract people. Put in my claim." And then he remembered. He would have to first stake his claim, actually go to the site, in the F.D.R. Mountains. And everything in him shrieked out in rebellion at that. At that hideous place, where the building would one day appear.

Well, there was no way out. First have a stake made for him in one of the Union shops, then take a 'copter and head for the Henry Wallace.

It seemed, thinking about it, an agonizingly difficult series of actions to accomplish. How could he do all that? First he would have to find some Union metal worker who could engrave his name for him on the stake; that might take days. Who did he know in the shops here in Lewistown who could do it for him? And if he didn't know the guy, how could he trust him?

At last, as if swimming against an intolerable current, he managed to lift the receiver from the hook and place the call to the shop.

I'm so tired I can hardly move, he realized. Why? What have I done so far today? His body felt crushed flat with fatigue. *If only I could get some rest,* he thought to himself. *If only I could sleep.*

It was late in the afternoon before Arnie Kott was able to procure the metal stake with his name engraved on it from the Union shop and make arrangements for a WWU 'copter to fly him to the F.D.R. Mountains.

"Hi, Arnie," the pilot greeted him, a pleasant-faced young man from the Union's pilot pool.

"Hi, my boy," Arnie murmured, as the pilot assisted him into the comfortable, special leather seat which had been built for him at the settlement's fabric and upholstery shop. As the pilot got into the seat ahead of him, Arnie said, "Now let's hurry because I'm late; I got to get all the way there and then to the abstract office at Pax Grove."

And I know we won't make it, he said to himself. There just *isn't enough time.*

Sixteen

THE Water Workers' Union 'copter with Goodmember Arnie Kott in it had hardly gotten into the air when the loudspeaker came on.

"Emergency announcement. There is a small party of Bleekmen out on the open desert at gyrocompass point 4.65003 dying from exposure and lack of water. Ships north of Lewistown are instructed to direct their flights to that point with all possible speed and give assistance. United Nations law requires all commercial and private ships to respond."

The announcement was repeated in the crisp voice of the UN announcer, speaking from the UN transmitter on the artificial satellite somewhere overhead.

Feeling the 'copter alter course, Arnie said, "Aw, come on, my boy." It was the last straw. They would never get to the F.D.R. range, let alone to Pax Grove and the abstract office.

"I have to respond, Sir," the pilot said. "It's the law."

Now they were above the desert, moving at good speed toward the intersect which the UN announcer had given. Niggers, Arnie thought. We have to drop everything we're doing to bail them out, the damn fools—and the worst part of it is that now I will meet Jack Bohlen. It can't be avoided. I forgot about it: now it is too late.

Patting his coat pocket he found the gun still there. That made him a little more cheerful; he kept his hand on it as the 'copter lowered for its landing. Hope we can beat him here, he thought. But to his dismay he saw that the Yee Company 'copter had landed ahead of him, and Jack Bohlen was already busy giving water to the five Bleekmen. Damm it, he thought.

"Do you need me?" Arnie's pilot called down from his seat, "If not I'll go on."

In answer Jack Bohlen called back, "I don't have much water for them." He mopped his face with his handkerchief, sweating in the hot sun.

"O.K.," the pilot said, and switched off his blades.

To his pilot, Arnie said, "Tell him to step over here."

Hopping out with a five-gallon water can, the pilot strode

over to Jack, and after a moment Jack ceased attending to the Bleekmen and walked toward Arnie Kott.

"You wanted me?" Jack said, standing there looking up at Arnie.

"Yes," Arnie said. "I'm going to kill you." He brought out his pistol and aimed it at Jack Bohlen.

The Bleekmen had been filling their paka eggshells with water; now they stopped. A young male, dark and skinny, almost naked under the ruddy Martian sun, reached backward, behind him, to his quiver of poisoned arrows; he drew an arrow forward, fitting it onto his bow, and in a single motion he fired the arrow. Arnie Kott saw nothing; he felt a sharp pain, and looked down to see the arrow protruding from his chest, slightly below the breast bone.

They read minds, Arnie thought. Intentions. He tried to pull the arrow out, but it would not budge. And then he realized that he was already dying. It was poisoned, and he felt it entering his limbs, stopping his circulation, rising upward to invest his brain and mind.

Jack Bohlen, standing below him, said, "Why would you want to kill me? You don't even know who I am."

"Sure I do," Arnie managed to grunt. "You're going to fix my encoder, and take Doreen away from me, and your father will steal all I've got, all that matters to me, the F.D.R. range and what's coming." He shut his eyes and rested.

"You must be crazy," Jack Bohlen said.

"Naw," Arnie said. "I know the future."

"Let me get you to a doctor," Jack Bohlen said, leaping up into the 'copter, pushing aside the dazed young pilot to inspect the protruding arrow. "They can give you an antidote if they get you in time." He clicked on the motor; the blades of the 'copter began to turn slowly and then more quickly.

"Take me to the Henry Wallace," Arnie muttered. "So I can drive my claim stake."

Jack Bohlen eyed him. "You're Arnie Kott, aren't you?" Getting the pilot out of the way, he seated himself at the controls, and at once the 'copter began to rise into the air. "I'll take you to Lewistown; it's closest and they know you there."

Saying nothing, Arnie lay back, his eyes still shut. It had all gone wrong. He had not staked his claim and he had not done anything to Jack Bohlen. And now it was over.

Those Bleekmen, Arnie thought as he felt Bohlen lifting him from the 'copter. This was Lewistown; he saw, through pain-darkened eyes, buildings and people. It's those Bleekmen's fault, from the start; if it wasn't for them I never would have met Jack Bohlen. I blame them for the whole thing.

Why wasn't he dead yet? he wondered as Bohlen carried him across the hospital's roof field to the emergency descent ramp. A lot of time had passed; the poison surely had gone all through him. And yet he still felt, thought, understood . . . perhaps I can't die back here in the past, he said to himself; maybe I got to linger on, unable to die and unable to return to my own time.

How did that young Bleekman catch on so fast? They don't ordinarily use their arrows on Earth people; it's a capital crime. It means the end of them.

Maybe, he thought, they were expecting me. They conspired to save Bohlen because he gave them food and water. Arnie thought, I bet they're the ones who gave him the water witch. Of course. *And when they gave it to him they knew. They knew about all this, even back then, at the very beginning.*

I'm helpless in this terrible damn schizophrenic past of Manfred Steiner's. Let me back to my own world, my own time; I just want to get out of here, I don't want to stake my claim or harm anybody. I just want to be back at Dirty Knobby, in the cavern with that goddamn boy. Like I was. Please, Arnie thought. Manfred!

They—someone—was wheeling him up a dark hall on a cart of some kind. Voices. Door opening, gleaming metal: surgical instruments. He saw masked faces, felt them lay him on a table . . . help me, Manfred, he shouted down deep inside himself. They're going to kill me! You have to take me back. Do it now or forget it, because—

A mask of emptiness and total darkness appeared above him and was lowered. No, Arnie cried out. It's not over; it can't be the end of me. Manfred, for God's sake, before this goes further and it's too late, too late.

I must see the bright normal reality once more, where there

is not this schizophrenic killing and alienation and bestial lust and death.

Help me get away from death, back where I belong once more

Help, Manfred

Help me

A voice said, "Get up, Mister, your time has expired."

He opened his eyes.

"More cigarettes, Mister." The dirty, ancient Bleekman priest, in his gray, cobweb-like robes, bent over him, pawing at him, whining his litany again and again against his ear. "If you want to stay, Mister, you have to pay me." He scratched at Arnie's coat, searching.

Sitting up, Arnie looked for Manfred. The boy was gone.

"Get away from me," Arnie said, rising to his feet; he put his hands to his chest and felt nothing, no arrow there.

He went unsteadily to the mouth of the cavern and squeezed out through the crack, into the cold midmorning sunlight of Mars.

"Manfred!" he yelled. No sign of the boy. Well, he thought, anyhow, I am back in the real world. That's what matters.

And he had lost his desire to get Jack Bohlen. He had lost his desire, too, to buy into the land development of these mountains. And he can have Doreen Anderton, for all I care, Arnie said to himself as he started toward the trail up which they had previously come. But I'll keep my word to Manfred; I'll mail him to Earth first chance I get, and maybe the change'll cure him, or maybe they have better psychiatrists back Home by now. Anyhow, he won't wind up at that AM-WEB.

As he made his way down the trail, still searching for Manfred, he saw a 'copter flying low overhead and circling. Maybe they saw where the boy went, he said to himself. Both of them, Jack and Doreen, must have been watching all this time. Halting, he waved his arms at the 'copter, indicating that he wanted it to land.

The 'copter dropped cautiously until it rested up the trail from him; in the wide place before the entrance to Dirty Knobby. The door slid aside, and a man stepped out.

"I'm looking for that kid," Arnie began. And then he saw

that it was not Jack Bohlen. It was a man he had never seen before. Good-looking, dark-haired, with wild, emotional eyes, a man who came toward him on a dead run, at the same time waving something that glinted in the sunlight.

"You're Arnie Kott," the man called to him in a shrill voice.

"Yeah, so what?" Arnie said.

"You destroyed my field," the man shrieked at him, and, raising the gun, fired.

The first bullet missed Arnie. Who are you and why are you shooting at me? Arnie Kott wondered, as he groped in his coat for his own gun. He found it, brought it out, fired back at the running man. Then it came to him who this was; this was the feeble little black-market operator who had been trying to horn in. The one we gave that lesson to, Arnie said to himself.

The running man dodged, fell, rolled over, and fired from where he lay. Arnie's shot had missed him, too. The shot whistled so close to Arnie this time that for a moment he thought he was hit; he put his hand instinctively to his chest. No, he realized, you didn't get me, you bastard. Raising his pistol, Arnie aimed and prepared to fire once more at the figure.

The world blew up around him. The sun fell from the sky; it dropped into darkness, and with it went Arnie Kott.

After a long time the prone figure stirred. The wild-eyed man crept to his feet cautiously, stood studying Arnie, and then started toward him. As he walked he held his pistol with both hands and aimed it.

A buzzing from above made him peer up. A shadow had swept over him and now a second 'copter bumped to a landing between him and Arnie. The 'copter cut the two men off from one another and Arnie Kott could no longer see the miserable little black-market operator. Out of the 'copter leaped Jack Bohlen. He ran over to Arnie and bent down.

"Get that guy," Arnie whispered.

"Can't," Jack said, and pointed. The black-market operator had taken off; his 'copter rose above Dirty Knobby, floundered, then lurched forward, cleared the peak, and was gone. "Forget about him. You're badly shot—think about yourself."

Arnie whispered, "Don't worry about it, Jack. Listen to me." He caught hold of Jack's shirt and dragged him down so that Jack's ear was close by. "I'll tell you a secret," Arnie said.

"Something I've discovered. This is another of those schizo-phrenic worlds. All this goddamn schizophrenic hate and lust and death, it already happened to me once and it couldn't kill me. First time, it was one of those poisoned arrows in the chest; now this. I'm not worried." He shut his eyes, struggling to keep himself conscious. "Just dig up that kid, he's around somewhere. Ask him and he'll tell you."

"You're wrong, Arnie," Jack said, bending down beside him.

"Wrong how?" He could barely see Bohlen, now; the scene had sunk into twilight, and Jack's shape was dim and wraith-like.

You can't fool me, Arnie thought. I know I'm still in Man-fred's mind; pretty soon I'll wake up and I won't be shot, I'll be O.K. again, and I'll find my way back to my own world where things like this don't happen. Isn't that right? He tried to speak but was unable to.

Appearing beside Jack, Doreen Anderton said, "He's going to die, isn't he?"

Jack said nothing. He was trying to get Arnie Kott over his shoulder so that he could lug him to the 'copter.

Just another of those gubble-gubble worlds, Arnie said to himself as he felt Jack lift him. It sure taught me a lesson, too. I won't do a nutty thing like this again. He tried to explain that, as Jack carried him to the 'copter. You just did this, he wanted to say. Took me to the hospital at Lewistown to get the arrow out. Don't you remember?

"There's no chance," Jack said to Doreen as he set Arnie in-side the 'copter, "of saving him." He panted for breath as he seated himself at the controls.

Sure there is, Arnie thought with indignation. What's the matter with you, aren't you trying? Better try, goddamn you. He made an attempt to speak, to tell Jack that, but he could not; he could say nothing.

The 'copter began to rise from the ground, laboring under the weight of the three people.

During the flight back to Lewistown, Arnie Kott died.

Jack Bohlen had Doreen take the controls, and he sat beside the dead man, thinking to himself that Arnie had died still believing he was lost in the dark currents of the Steiner boy's mind. Maybe it's for the best, Jack thought. Maybe it made it easier for him, at the last.

The realization that Arnie Kott was dead filled him, to his incredulity, with grief. It doesn't seem right, he said to himself as he sat by the dead man. It's too harsh; Arnie didn't deserve it, for what he did—the things he did were bad but not that bad.

"What was it he was saying to you?" Doreen asked. She seemed to be quite calm, to have taken Arnie's death in her stride; she piloted the 'copter with matter-of-fact skill.

Jack said, "He imagined this wasn't real. That he was blundering about in a schizophrenic fantasy."

"Poor Arnie," she said.

"Do you know who that man was who shot him?"

"Some enemy he must have made along the way somewhere."

They were both silent for a while.

"We should look for Manfred," Doreen said.

"Yes," Jack said. But I know where the boy is right now, he said to himself. He's found some wild Bleekmen there in the mountains, and he's with them; it's obvious and certain, and it would have happened sooner or later in any case. He was not worried—he did not care—about Manfred. Perhaps, for the first time in his life, the boy was in a situation to which he might make an adjustment; he might, with the wild Bleekmen, discern a style of living which was genuinely his and not a pallid, tormented reflection of the lives of those around him, beings who were innately different from him and whom he could never resemble, no matter how hard he tried.

Doreen said, "Could Arnie have been right?"

For a moment he did not understand her. And then, when he had made out her meaning, he shook his head. "No."

"Why was he so sure of it, then?"

Jack said, "I don't know." But it had to do with Manfred; Arnie had said so, just before he died.

"In many ways," Doreen said, "Arnie was shrewd. If he thought that, there must have been some very good reason."

"He was shrewd," Jack pointed out, "but he always believed what he wanted to believe." And, he realized, did whatever he wanted to. And so, at last, had brought about his own death; engineered it somewhere along the pathway of his life.

"What's going to become of us now?" Doreen said. "Without him? It's hard for me to imagine it without Arnie . . . do you know what I mean? I think you do. I wish, when we first saw that 'copter land, we had understood what was going to happen; if only we had gotten down there a few minutes earlier—" She broke off. "No use saying that now."

"No use at all," Jack said briefly.

"You know what I think is going to happen to us now?" Doreen said. "We're going to drift away from each other, you and I. Maybe not right away, maybe not for months or possibly even years. But sooner or later we will, without him."

He said nothng; he did not try to argue. Perhaps it was so. He was tired of struggling to see ahead to what lay before them all.

"Do you love me still?" Doreen asked. "After what's happened to us?" She turned toward him to see his face as he answered.

"Yes, naturally I do," he said.

"So do I," she said in a low, wan voice. "But I don't think it's enough. You have your wife and your son—that's so much, in the long run. Anyhow, it was worth it; to me, at least. I'll never be sorry. We're not responsible for Arnie's death; we mustn't feel guilty. He brought it on himself, by what he was up to, there at the end. And we'll never know exactly what that was. But I know it was something to hurt us."

He nodded.

Silently, they continued on back to Lewistown, carrying with them the body of Arnie Kott; carrying Arnie home to his settlement, where he was—and probably always would be— Supreme Goodmember of his Water Workers' Union, Fourth Planet Branch.

Ascending an ill-marked path in the arid rocks of the F.D.R. Mountains, Manfred Steiner halted as he saw ahead of him a party of six dark, shadowy men. They carried with them paka eggs filled with water, quivers of poisoned arrows, and each woman had her pounding block. All smoked cigarettes as they toiled, single file, along the trail.

Seeing him, they halted.

One of them, a gaunt young male, said politely, "The rains falling from your wonderful presence envigor and restore us, Mister."

Manfred did not understand the words, but he got their thoughts: cautious and friendly, with no undertones of hate. He sensed inside them no desire to hurt him, and that was pleasant; he forgot his fear of them and turned his attention on the animal skins which each wore. What sort of animal is that? he wondered.

The Bleekmen were curious about him, too. They advanced until they stood around him on all sides.

"There are monster ships," one of them thought in his direction, "landing in these mountains, with no one aboard. They have excited wonder and speculation, for they appear to be a portent. Already they have begun to assemble themselves on the land to work changes. Are you from them, by any chance?"

"No," Manfred answered, inside his mind, in a way for them to hear and understand.

The Bleekmen pointed, and he saw, toward the center of the mountain range, a fleet of UN slave rocket vehicles hovering in the air. They had arrived from Earth, he realized. They were here to break ground; the building of the tracts of houses had begun. AM-WEB and the other structures like it would soon be appearing on the face of the fourth planet.

"We are leaving the mountains because of that," one of the older Bleekman males thought to Manfred. "There is no manner by which we can live here, now that this has started. Through our rock, we saw this long ago, but now it is here in actuality."

Within himself, Manfred said, "Can I go with you?"

Surprised, the Bleekmen withdrew to discuss his request. They did not know what to make of him and what he wanted; they had never run across it in an immigrant before.

"We are going out into the desert," the young male told him at last. "It is doubtful if we can survive there; we can only try. Are you certain you want that for yourself?"

"Yes," Manfred said.

"Come along, then," the Bleekmen decided.

They resumed their trek. They were tired, but they swung almost at once into a good pace. Manfred thought at first that he would be left behind, but the Bleekmen hung back for him and he was able to keep up.

The desert lay ahead, for them and for him. But none of them had any regrets; it was impossible for them to turn back anyhow, because they could not live under the new conditions.

I will not have to live in AM-WEB, Manfred said to himself as he kept up with the Bleekmen. Through these dark shadows I will escape.

He felt very good, better than he could remember ever having felt before in his life.

One of the Bleekman females shyly offered him a cigarette from those she carried. Thanking her, he accepted it. They continued on.

And as they moved along, Manfred Steiner felt something strange happening inside him. He was changing.

At dusk, as she was fixing dinner for herself and David and her father-in-law, Silvia Bohlen saw a figure on foot, a figure that walked along the edge of the canal. A man, she said to herself; frightened, she went to the front door, opened it, and peered out to see who it was. God, it wasn't that so-called health food salesman, that Otto whatever his name was again—

"It's me, Silvia," Jack Bohlen said.

Running out of the house and up to his father excitedly, David shouted, "Hey, how come you didn't bring your 'copter? Did you come on the tractor-bus? I bet you did. What happened to your 'copter, Dad? Did it break down and strand you out in the desert?"

"No more 'copter," Jack said. He looked tired.

"I heard on the radio," Silvia said.

"About Arnie Kott?" He nodded. "Yeah, it's true." Entering the house he took off his coat; Silvia hung it in the closet for him.

"That affects you a lot, doesn't it?" she said.

Jack said, "No job. Arnie had bought my contract." He looked around. "Where's Leo?"

"Taking his nap. He's been gone most of the day, on business. I'm glad you got home before he goes; he's leaving for

Earth tomorrow, he said. Did you know that the UN has started taking the land in the F.D.R. range already? I heard that on the radio, too."

"I didn't know," Jack said, going into the kitchen and seating himself at the table. "How about some iced tea?"

As she fixed the iced tea for him she said, "I guess I shouldn't ask you how serious this job business is."

Jack said, "I can get on with almost any repair outfit. Mr. Yee would take me back, as a matter of fact. I'm sure he didn't want to part with my contract in the first place."

"Then why are you so despondent?" she said, and then she remembered about Arnie.

"It's a mile and a half from where that tractor-bus let me off," he said. "I'm just tired."

"I didn't expect you home." She felt on edge, and it was difficult for her to return to preparing dinner. "We're only having liver and bacon and grated carrots with synthetic butter and a salad. And Leo said he'd like a cake of some sort for dessert; David and I were going to make that later on as a treat for him, because after all he is going, and we may not see him ever again; we have to face that."

"That's fine about the cake," Jack murmured.

Silvia burst out, "I wish you would tell me what's the matter —I've never seen you like this. You're not just tired; it must be that man's death."

Presently, he said, "I was thinking of something Arnie said before he died. I was there with him. Arnie said he wasn't in a real world; he was in the fantasy of a schizophrenic, and that's been preying on my mind. It never occurred to me before how much our world is like Manfred's—I thought they were absolutely distinct. Now I see that it's more a question of degree."

"You don't want to tell me about Mr. Kott's death, do you? The radio just said he was killed in a 'copter accident in the rugged terrain of the F.D.R. Mountains."

"It was no accident. Arnie was murdered by an individual who had it in for him, no doubt because he was mistreated and had a legitimate grudge. The police are looking for him now, naturally. Arnie died thinking it was senseless, psychotic hate that was directed at him, but actually it was probably very rational hate with no psychotic elements in it at all."

With overwhelming guilt, Silvia thought, The kind of hate you'd feel for me if you knew what awful thing I plunged into today. "Jack—" she said clumsily, not sure how to put it, but feeling she had to ask. "Do you think our marriage is finished?"

He stared at her a long, long time. "Why do you say that?"

"I just want to hear you say it isn't."

"It isn't," he said, still staring at her; she felt exposed, as if he could read her mind, as if he knew somehow exactly what she had done. "Is there any reason to think it is? Why do you imagine I came home? If we had no marriage, would I have shown up here today after—" He was silent, then. "I'd like my iced tea," he murmured.

"After what?" she asked.

He said, "After Arnie's death."

"Where else would you go?"

"A person can always find two places to choose from. Home, and the rest of the world with all the other people in it."

Silvia said, "What's she like?"

"Who?"

"The girl. You almost said it, just now."

He did not answer for such a long time that she did not think he was going to. And then he said, "She has red hair. I almost stayed with her. But I didn't. Isn't that enough for you to know?"

"There's a choice for me, too," Silvia said.

"I didn't know that," he said woodenly. "I didn't realize." He shrugged. "Well, it's good to realize; it's sobering. You're not speaking about theory, now, are you? You're speaking about concrete reality."

"That's correct," Silvia said.

David came running into the kitchen. "Grandfather Leo's awake," he shouted. "I told him you were home, Dad, and he's real glad and he wants to find out how things are going with you."

"They're going swell," Jack said.

Silvia said to him, "Jack, I'd like for us to go on. If you want to."

"Sure," he said. "You know that, I'm back here again." He smiled at her so forlornly that it almost broke her heart. "I came a long way, first on that no-good damn tractor-bus, which I hate, and then on foot."

"There won't be any more," Silvia said, "of—other choices, will there, Jack? It really has to be that way."

"No more," he said, nodding emphatically.

She went over to the table, then, and bending, kissed him on the forehead.

"Thanks," he said, taking hold of her by the wrist. "That feels good." She could feel his fatigue; it traveled from him into her.

"You need a good meal," she said. "I've never seen you so—crushed." It occurred to her, then, that he might have had a new bout with his mental illness from the past, his schizophrenia; that would go far in explaining things. But she did not want to press him on the subject; instead, she said, "We'll go to bed early tonight, O.K.?"

He nodded in a vague fashion, sipping his iced tea.

"Are you glad now?" she asked. "That you came back here?" Or have you changed your mind? she wondered.

"I'm glad," he said, and his tone was strong and firm. Obviously he meant it.

"You get to see Grandfather Leo before he goes—" she began.

A scream made her jump, turn to face Jack.

He was on his feet. "Next door. The Steiner house." He pushed past her; they both ran outside.

At the front door of the Steiner house one of the Steiner girls met them. "My brother—"

She and Jack pushed past the child, and into the house. Silvia did not understand what she saw, but Jack seemed to; he took hold of her hand, stopped her from going any farther.

The living room was filled with Bleekmen. And in their midst she saw part of a living creature, an old man only from the chest on up; the rest of him became a tangle of pumps and hoses and dials, machinery that clicked away, unceasingly active. It kept the old man alive; she realized that in an instant. The missing portion of him had been replaced by it. Oh, God, she thought. Who or what was it, sitting there with a smile on its withered face? Now it spoke to them.

"Jack Bohlen," it rasped, and its voice issued from a mechanical speaker, out of the machinery: not from its mouth. "I am here to say goodbye to my mother." It paused, and she heard the machinery speed up, as if it were laboring. "Now I can thank you," the old man said.

Jack, standing by her, holding her hand, said, "For what? I didn't do anything for you."

"Yes, I think so." The thing seated there nodded to the Bleekmen, and they pushed it and its machinery closer to Jack and straightened it so that it faced him directly. "In my opinion . . ." It lapsed into silence and then it resumed, more loudly, now. "You tried to communicate with me, many years ago. I appreciate that."

"It wasn't long ago," Jack said. "Have you forgotten? You came back to us; it was just today. This is your distant past, when you were a boy."

She said to her husband, "*Who is it?*"

"Manfred."

Putting her hands to her face she covered her eyes; she could not bear to look any longer.

"Did you escape AM-WEB?" Jack asked it.

"Yesss," it hissed, with a gleeful tremor. "I am with my friends." It pointed to the Bleekmen who surrounded it.

"Jack," Silvia said, "take me out of here—please, I can't stand it." She clung to him, and he then led her from the Steiner house, out once more into the evening darkness.

Both Leo and David met them, agitated and frightened. "Say, son," Leo said, "what happened? What was that woman screaming about?"

Jack said, "It's all over. Everything's O.K." To Silvia he said, "She must have run outside. She didn't understand, at first."

Shivering, Silvia said, "I don't understand either and I don't want to; don't try to explain it to me." She returned to the stove, turning down the burners, looking into pots to see what had burned.

"Don't worry," Jack said, patting her.

She tried to smile.

"It probably won't happen again," Jack said. "But even if it does—"

"Thanks," she said. "I thought when I first saw him that it was his father, Norbert Steiner; that's what frightened me so."

"We'll have to get a flashlight and hunt around for Erna Steiner," Jack said. "We want to be sure she's all right."

"Yes," she said. "You and Leo go and do that while I finish here; I have to stay with the dinner or it'll be spoiled."

The two men, with a flashlight, left the house. David stayed with her, helping her set the table. Where will you be? she wondered as she watched her son. When you're old like that, all hacked away and replaced by machinery. . . . Will you be like that, too?

We are better off not being able to look ahead, she said to herself. Thank God we can't see.

"I wish I could have gone out," David was complaining. "Why can't you tell me what it was that made Mrs. Steiner yell like that?"

Silvia said, "Maybe someday."

But not now, she said to herself. It is too soon, for any of us.

Dinner was ready now, and she went out automatically onto the porch to call Jack and Leo, knowing even as she did so that they would not come; they were far too busy, they had too much to do. But she called them anyhow, because it was her job.

In the darkness of the Martian night her husband and father-in-law searched for Erna Steiner; their light flashed here and there, and their voices could be heard, business-like and competent and patient.

DR. BLOODMONEY

Or How We Got Along After the Bomb

I

EARLY in the bright sun-yellowed morning, Stuart McConchie swept the sidewalk before Modern TV Sales & Service, hearing the cars along Shattuck Avenue and the secretaries hurrying on high heels to their offices, all the stirrings and fine smells of a new week, a new time in which a good salesman could accomplish things. He thought about a hot roll and coffee for his second breakfast, along about ten. He thought of customers whom he had talked to returning to buy, all of them perhaps today, his book of sales running over, like that cup in the Bible. As he swept he sang a song from a new Buddy Greco album and he thought too how it might feel to be famous, a world-famous great singer that everyone paid to see at such places as Harrah's in Reno or the fancy expensive clubs in Las Vegas which he had never seen but heard so much about.

He was twenty-six years old and he had driven, late on certain Friday nights, from Berkeley along the great ten-lane highway to Sacramento and across the Sierras to Reno, where one could gamble and find girls; he worked for Jim Fergesson, the owner of Modern TV, on a salary and commission basis, and being a good salesman he made plenty. And anyhow this was 1981 and business was not bad. Another good year, booming from the start, where America got bigger and stronger and everybody took more home.

"Morning, Stuart." Nodding, the middle-aged jeweler from across Shattuck Avenue passed by. Mr. Crody, on his way to his own little store.

All the stores, the offices, opening, now; it was after nine and even Doctor Stockstill, the psychiatrist and specialist in psychosomatic disorders, appeared, key in hand, to start up his high-paying enterprise in the glass-sided office building which the insurance company had built with a bit of its surplus money. Doctor Stockstill had parked his foreign car in the lot; he could afford to pay five dollars a day. And now came the tall, long-legged pretty secretary of Doctor Stockstill's, a head taller than he. And, sure enough as Stuart watched, leaning on his broom, the furtive first nut of the day sidled guiltily toward the psychiatrist's office.

It's a world of nuts, Stuart thought, watching. Psychiatrists make a lot. If I had to go to a psychiatrist I'd come and go by the back door. Nobody'd see me and jeer. He thought, Maybe some of them do; maybe Stockstill has a back door. For the sicker ones, or rather (he corrected his thought) the ones who don't want to make a spectacle out of themselves; I mean the ones who simply have a problem, for instance worry about the Police Action in Cuba, and who aren't nuts at all, just—concerned.

And he was concerned, because there was still a good chance that he might be called up for the Cuban War, which had now become bogged down in the mountains once more, despite the new little anti-personnel bombs that picked out the greasy gooks no matter how well dug in. He himself did not blame the president—it wasn't the president's fault that the Chinese had decided to honor their pact. It was just that hardly anyone came home from fighting the greasy gooks free of virus bone infections. A thirty-year-old combat veteran re-turned looking like some dried mummy left out of doors to hang for a century . . . and it was hard for Stuart McConchie to imagine himself picking up once more after that, selling stereo TV again, resuming his career in retail selling.

"Morning, Stu," a girl's voice came, startling him. The small, dark-eyed waitress from Edy's candy store. "Day dreaming so early?" She smiled as she passed on by along the sidewalk.

"Heck no," he said, again sweeping vigorously.

Across the street the furtive patient of Doctor Stockstill's, a man black in color, black hair and eyes, light skin, wrapped tightly in a big overcoat itself the color of deep night, paused to light a cigarette and glance about. Stuart saw the man's hollow face, the staring eyes and the mouth, especially the mouth. It was drawn tight and yet the flesh hung slack, as if the pressure, the tension there, had long ago ground the teeth and the jaw away; the tension remained there in that unhappy face, and Stuart looked away.

Is that how it is? he wondered. To be crazy? Corroded away like that, as if devoured by . . . he did not know what by.

Time or perhaps water; something slow but which never stopped. He had seen such deterioration before, in watching the psychiatrist's patients come and go, but never this bad, never this complete.

The phone rang from inside Modern TV, and Stuart turned to hurry toward it. When next he looked out onto the street the black-wrapped man had gone, and once more the day was regaining its brightness, its promise and smell of beauty. Stuart shivered, picked up his broom.

I know that man, he said to himself. I've seen his picture or he's come into the store. He's either a customer—an old one, maybe even a friend of Fergesson's—or he's an important celebrity.

Thoughtfully, he swept on.

To his new patient, Doctor Stockstill said, "Cup of coffee? Or tea or Coke?" He read the little card which Miss Purcell had placed on his desk. "Mr. Tree," he said aloud. "Any relation to the famous English literary family? Iris Tree, Max Beerbohm . . ."

In a heavily-accented voice Mr. Tree said, "That is not actually my name, you know." He sounded irritable and impatient. "It occurred to me as I talked to your girl."

Doctor Stockstill glanced questioningly at his patient.

"I am world-famous," Mr. Tree said. "I'm surprised you don't recognize me; you must be a recluse or worse." He ran a hand shakily through his long black hair. "There are thousands, even millions of people in the world, who hate me and would like to destroy me. So naturally I have to take steps; I have to give you a made-up name." He cleared his throat and smoked rapidly at his cigarette; he held the cigarette European style, the burning end within, almost touching his palm.

Oh my god, Doctor Stockstill thought. This man, I do recognize him. This is Bruno Bluthgeld, the physicist. And he is right; a lot of people both here and in the East would like to get their hands on him because of his miscalculation back in 1972. Because of the terrible fall-out from the high-altitude blast which wasn't supposed to hurt anyone; Bluthgeld's figures *proved* it in advance.

"Do you want me to know who you are?" Doctor Stockstill asked. "Or shall we accept you simply as 'Mr. Tree'? It's up to you; either way is satisfactory to me."

"Let's simply get on," Mr. Tree grated.

"All right." Doctor Stockstill made himself comfortable, scratched with his pen against the paper on his clipboard. "Go ahead."

"Does an inability to board an ordinary bus—you know, with perhaps a dozen persons unfamiliar to you—signify anything?" Mr. Tree watched him intently.

"It might," Stockstill said.

"I feel they're staring at me."

"For any particular reason?"

"Because," Mr. Tree said, "of the disfiguration of my face."

Without an overt motion, Doctor Stockstill managed to glance up and scrutinize his patient. He saw this middle-aged man, heavy-set, with black hair, the stubble of a beard dark against his unusually white skin. He saw circles of fatigue and tension beneath the man's eyes, and the expression in the eyes, the despair. The physicist had bad skin and he needed a haircut, and his entire face was marred by the worry within him . . . but there was no "disfiguration." Except for the strain visible there, it was an ordinary face; it would not have attracted notice in a group.

"Do you see the blotches?" Mr. Tree said hoarsely. He pointed at his cheeks, his jaw. "The ugly marks that set me apart from everybody?"

"No," Stockstill said, taking a chance and speaking directly.

"They're there," Mr. Tree said. "They're on the inside of the skin, of course. But people notice them anyhow and stare. I can't ride on a bus or go into a restaurant or a theater; I can't go to the San Francisco opera or the ballet or the symphony orchestra or even a nightclub to watch one of those folk singers; if I do succeed in getting inside I have to leave almost at once because of the staring. And the remarks."

"Tell me what they say."

Mr. Tree was silent.

"As you said yourself," Stockstill said, "you are world-famous—and isn't it natural for people to murmur when a world-famous personage comes in and seats himself among them? Hasn't this been true for years? And there is controversy about your work, as you pointed out . . . hostility and perhaps one hears disparaging remarks. But everyone in the public eye—"

"Not that," Mr. Tree broke in. "I expect that; I write articles and appear on the TV, and I expect that; I know that. This—has to do with my private life. My most innermost thoughts." He gazed at Stockstill and said, "They read my thoughts and they tell me about my private personal life, in every detail. They have access to my brain."

Paranoia sensitiva, Stockstill thought, although of course there have to be tests . . . the Rorschach in particular. It could be advanced insidious schizophrenia; these could be the final stages of a life-long illness process. Or—

"Some people can see the blotches on my face and read my personal thoughts more accurately than others," Mr. Tree said. "I've noted quite a spectrum in ability—some are barely aware, others seem to make an instantaneous Gestalt of my differences, my stigmata. For example, as I came up the sidewalk to your office, there was a Negro sweeping on the other side . . . he stopped work and concentrated on me, although of course he was too far away to jeer at me. Nevertheless, he saw. It's typical of lower class people, I've noticed. More so than educated or cultured people."

"I wonder why that is," Stockstill said, making notes.

"Presumably, you would know, if you're competent at all. The woman who recommended you said you were exceptionally able." Mr. Tree eyed him, as if seeing no sign of ability as yet.

"I think I had better get a background history from you," Stockstill said. "I see that Bonny Keller recommended me. How is Bonny? I haven't seen her since last April or so . . . did her husband give up his job with that rural grammar school as he was talking about?"

"I did not come here to discuss George and Bonny Keller," Mr. Tree said. "I am desperately pressed, Doctor. They may decide to complete their destruction of me any time now; this harassment has gone on for so long now that—" He broke off.

"Bonny thinks I'm ill, and I have great respect for her." His tone was low, almost inaudible. "So I said I'd come here, at least once."

"Are the Kellers still living up in West Marin?"

Mr. Tree nodded.

"I have a summer place up there," Stockstill said. "I'm a sailing buff; I like to get out on Tomales Bay every chance I get. Have you ever tried sailing?"

"No."

"Tell me when you were born and where."

Mr. Tree said, "In Budapest, in 1934."

Doctor Stockstill, skillfully questioning, began to obtain in detail the life-history of his patient, fact by fact. It was essential for what he had to do: first diagnose and then, if possible, heal. Analysis and then therapy. A man known all over the world who had delusions that strangers were staring at him—how in this case could reality be sorted out from fantasy? What was the frame of reference which would distinguish them one from the other?

It would be so easy, Stockstill realized, to find pathology here. So easy—and so tempting. A man this hated . . . I share their opinion, he said to himself, the *they* that Bluthgeld—or rather Tree—talks about. After all, I'm part of society, too, part of the civilization menaced by the grandiose, extravagant miscalculations of this man. It could have been—could some-day be—my children blighted because this man had the arrogance to assume that he could not err.

But there was more to it than that. At the time, Stockstill had felt a twisted quality about the man; he had watched him being interviewed on TV, listened to him speak, read his fantastic anti-communist speeches—and come to the tentative conclusion that Bluthgeld had a profound hatred for *people*, deep and pervasive enough to make him want, on some unconscious level, to err, to make him want to jeopardize the lives of millions.

No wonder that the Director of the FBI, Richard Nixon, had spoken out so vigorously against "militant amateur anti-communists in high scientific circles." Nixon had been alarmed, too, long before the tragic error of 1972. The elements of paranoia, with the delusions not only of reference but of grandeur, had been palpable; Nixon, a shrewd judge of men, had observed them, and so had many others.

And evidently they had been correct.

"I came to America," Mr. Tree was saying, "in order to escape the Communist agents who wanted to murder me. They were after me even then . . . so of course were the Nazis. They were all after me."

"I see," Stockstill said, writing.

"They still are, but ultimately they will fail," Mr. Tree said hoarsely, lighting a new cigarette. "For I have God on my side; He sees my need and often He has spoken to me, giving me the wisdom I need to survive my pursuers. I am at present at work on a new project, out at Livermore; the results of this will be definitive as regards our enemy."

Our enemy, Stockstill thought. Who is our enemy . . . isn't it you, Mr. Tree? Isn't it you sitting here rattling off your paranoid delusions? How did you ever get the high post that you hold? Who is responsible for giving you power over the lives of others—and letting you keep that power even after the fiasco of 1972? You—and they—are surely our enemies.

All our fears about you are confirmed; you are deranged— your presence here proves it. Or does it? Stockstill thought, No, it doesn't, and perhaps I should disqualify myself; perhaps it is unethical for me to try to deal with you. Considering the way I feel . . . I can't take a detached, disinterested position regarding you; I can't be genuinely scientific, and hence my analysis, my diagnosis, may well prove faulty.

"Why are you looking at me like this?" Mr. Tree was saying.

"Beg pardon?" Stockstill murmured.

"Are you repelled by my disfigurations?" Mr. Tree said.

"No-no," Stockstill said. "It isn't that."

"My thoughts, then? You were reading them and their disgusting character causes you to wish I had not consulted you?" Rising to his feet, Mr. Tree moved abruptly toward the office door. "Good day."

"Wait." Stockstill came after him. "Let's get the biographical material concluded, at least; we've barely begun."

Mr. Tree, eying him, said presently, "I have confidence in Bonny Keller; I know her political opinions . . . she is not a part of the international Communist conspiracy seeking to kill me at any opportunity." He reseated himself, more composed, now. But his posture was one of wariness; he would not permit himself to relax a moment in Stockstill's presence, the psychiatrist knew. He would not open up, reveal himself candidly. He would continue to be suspicious—and perhaps rightly, Stockstill thought.

As he parked his car Jim Fergesson, the owner of Modern TV, saw his salesman Stuart McConchie leaning on his broom before the shop, not sweeping but merely daydreaming or whatever it was he did. Following McConchie's gaze he saw that the salesman was enjoying not the sight of some girl passing by or some unusual car—Stu liked girls and cars, and that was normal—but was instead looking in the direction of patients entering the office of the doctor across the street. That wasn't normal. And what business of McConchie's was it anyhow?

"Look," Fergesson called as he walked rapidly toward the entrance of his shop. "You cut it out; someday maybe you'll be sick, and how'll you like some goof gawking at you when you try to seek medical help?"

"Hey," Stuart answered, turning his head, "I just saw some important guy go in there but I can't recall who."

"Only a neurotic watches other neurotics," Fergesson said, and passed on into the store, to the register, which he opened and began to fill with change and bills for the day ahead.

Anyhow, Fergesson thought, wait'll you see what I hired for a TV repairman; you'll really have something to stare at.

"Listen, McConchie," Fergesson said. "You know that kid with no arms and legs that comes by on that cart? That phocomelus with just those dinky flippers whose mother took that drug back in the early '60s? The one that always hangs around because he wants to be a TV repairman?"

Stuart, standing with his broom, said, "You hired him."

"Yeah, yesterday while you were out selling."

Presently McConchie said, "It's bad for business."

"Why? Nobody'll see him; he'll be downstairs in the repair department. Anyhow you have to give those people jobs; it isn't their fault they have no arms or legs, it's those Germans' fault."

After a pause Stuart McConchie said, "First you hire me, a Negro, and now a phoce. Well, I have to hand it to you, Fergesson; you're trying to do right."

Feeling anger, Fergesson said, "I not only try, I do; I'm not just daydreaming, like you. I'm a man who makes up his mind and acts." He went to open the store safe. "His name is Hoppy. He'll be in this morning. You ought to see him move stuff with his electronic hands; it's a marvel of modern science."

"I've seen," Stuart said.

"And it pains you."

Gesturing, Stuart said, "It's—unnatural."

Fergesson glared at him. "Listen, don't say anything along the lines of razzing to the kid; if I catch you or any of the other salesmen or anybody who works for me—"

"Okay," Stuart muttered.

"You're bored," Fergesson said, "and boredom is bad because it means you're not exerting yourself fully; you're slacking off, and on my time. If you worked hard, you wouldn't have time to lean on that broom and poke fun at poor sick people going to the doctor. I forbid you to stand outside on the sidewalk ever again; if I catch you you're fired."

"Oh Christ, how am I supposed to come and go and go eat? How do I get into the store in the first place? Through the wall?"

"You can come and go," Fergesson decided, "but you can't loiter."

Glaring after him dolefully, Stuart McConchie protested, "Aw cripes!"

Fergesson however paid no attention to his TV salesman; he began turning on displays and signs, preparing for the day ahead.

II

THE phocomelus Hoppy Harrington generally wheeled up to Modern TV Sales & Service about eleven each morning. He generally glided into the shop, stopping his cart by the counter, and if Jim Fergesson was around he asked to be allowed to go downstairs to watch the two TV repairmen at work. However, if Fergesson was not around, Hoppy gave up and after a while wheeled off, because he knew that the salesmen would not let him go downstairs; they merely ribbed him, gave him the run-around. He did not mind. Or at least as far as Stuart McConchie could tell, he did not mind.

But actually, Stuart realized, he did not understand Hoppy, who had a sharp face with bright eyes and a quick, nervous manner of speech which often became jumbled into a stammer. He did not understand him *psychologically*. Why did Hoppy want to repair TV sets? What was so great about that? The way the phoce hung around, one would think it was the most exalted calling of all. Actually, repairwork was hard, dirty, and did not pay too well. But Hoppy was passionately determined to become a TV repairman, and now he had succeeded, because Fergesson was determined to do right by all the minority groups in the world. Fergesson was a member of the American Civil Liberties Union and the NAACP and the Help for the Handicapped League—the latter being, as far as Stuart could tell, nothing but a lobby group on an international scale, set up to promote soft berths for all the victims of modern medicine and science, such as the multitude from the Bluthgeld Catastrophe of 1972.

And what does that make me? Stuart asked himself as he sat upstairs in the store's office, going over his sales book. I mean, he thought, with a phoce working here . . . that practically makes me a radiation freak, too, as if being colored was a sort of early form of radiation burn. He felt gloomy thinking about it.

Once upon a time, he thought, all the people on Earth were white, and then some horse's ass set off a high-altitude bomb back say around ten thousand years ago, and some of us got seared and it was permanent; it affected our genes. So here we are today.

Another salesman, Jack Lightheiser, came and sat down at the desk across from him and lit a Corina cigar. "I hear Jim's hired that kid on the cart," Lightheiser said. "You know why he did it, don't you? For publicity. The S.F. newspapers'll write it up. Jim loves getting his name in the paper. It's a smart move, when you get down to it. The first retail dealer in the East Bay to hire a phoce."

Stuart grunted.

"Jim's got an idealized image of himself," Lightheiser said. "He isn't just a merchant; he's a modern Roman, he's civic-minded. After all, he's an educated man—he's got a master's degree from Stanford."

"That doesn't mean anything any more," Stuart said. He himself had gotten a master's degree from Cal, back in 1975, and look where it had got him.

"It did when he got it," Lightheiser said. "After all, he graduated back in 1947; he was on that GI Bill they had."

Below them, at the front door of Modern TV, a cart appeared, in the center of which, at a bank of controls, sat a slender figure. Stuart groaned and Lightheiser glanced at him.

"He's a pest," Stuart said.

"He won't be when he gets started working," Lightheiser said. "The kid is all brain, no body at all, hardly. That's a powerful mind he's got, and he also has ambition. God, he's only seventeen years old and what he wants to do is work, get out of school and work. That's admirable."

The two of them watched Hoppy on his cart; Hoppy was wheeling toward the stairs which descended to the TV repair department.

"Do the guys downstairs know, yet?" Stuart asked.

"Oh sure, Jim told them last night. They're philosophical; you know how TV repairmen are—they griped about it but it doesn't mean anything; they gripe all the time anyhow."

Hearing the salesman's voice, Hoppy glanced sharply up. His thin, bleak face confronted them; his eyes blazed and he said stammeringly, "Hey, is Mr. Fergesson in right now?"

"Naw," Stuart said.

"Mr. Fergesson hired me," the phoce said.

"Yeah," Stuart said. Neither he nor Lightheiser moved; they remained seated at the desk, gazing down at the phoce.

"Can I go downstairs?" Hoppy asked.

Lightheiser shrugged.

"I'm going out for a cup of coffee," Stuart said, rising to his feet. "I'll be back in ten minutes; watch the floor for me, okay?"

"Sure," Lightheiser said, nodding as he smoked his cigar.

When Stuart reached the main floor he found the phoce still there; he had not begun the difficult descent down to the basement.

"Spirit of 1972," Stuart said as he passed the cart.

The phoce flushed and stammered, "I was born in 1964; it had nothing to do with that blast." As Stuart went out the door onto the sidewalk the phoce called after him anxiously, "It was that drug, that thalidomide. Everybody knows that."

Stuart said nothing; he continued on toward the coffee shop.

It was difficult for the phocomelus to maneuver his cart down the stairs to the basement where the TV repairmen worked at their benches, but after a time he managed to do so, gripping the handrail with the manual extensors which the U.S. Government had thoughtfully provided. The extensors were really not much good; they had been fitted years ago, and were not only partly worn out but were—as he knew from reading the current literature on the topic—obsolete. In theory, the Government was bound to replace his equipment with the more recent models; the Remington Act specified that, and he had written the senior California senator, Alf M. Partland, about it. As yet, however, he had received no answer. But he was patient. Many times he had written letters to U.S. Congressmen, on a variety of topics, and often the answers were tardy or merely mimeographed and sometimes there was no answer at all.

In this case, however, Hoppy Harrington had the law on his side, and it was only a matter of time before he compelled someone in authority to give him that which he was entitled to. He felt grim about it, patient and grim. They *had* to help him, whether they wanted to or not. His father, a sheep rancher in the Sonoma Valley, had taught him that: taught him always to demand what he was entitled to.

Sound blared. The repairmen at work; Hoppy paused, opened the door and faced the two men at the long, littered bench with its instruments and meters, its dials and tools and television sets in all stages of decomposition. Neither repairman noticed him.

"Listen," one of the repairmen said all at once, startling him. "Manual jobs are looked down on. Why don't you go into something mental, why don't you go back to school and get a degree?" The repairman turned to stare at him questioningly.

No, Hoppy thought. I want to work with—my hands.

"You could be a scientist," the other repairman said, not ceasing his work; he was tracing a circuit, studying his voltmeter.

"Like Bluthgeld," Hoppy said.

The repairman laughed at that, with sympathetic understanding.

"Mr. Fergesson said you'd give me something to work on," Hoppy said. "Some easy set to fix, to start with. Okay?" He waited, afraid that they were not going to respond, and then one of them pointed to a record changer. "What's the matter with it?" Hoppy said, examining the repair tag. "I know I can fix it."

"Broken spring," one of the repairmen said. "It won't shut off after the last record."

"I see," Hoppy said. He picked up the record changer with his two manual extensors and rolled to the far end of the bench, where there was a cleared space. "I'll work here." The repairmen did not protest, so he picked up pliers. This is easy, he thought to himself. I've practiced at home; he concentrated on the record changer but also watching the two repairmen out of the corner of his eye. I've practiced many times; it nearly always works, and all the time it's better, more accurate. More predictable. A spring is a little object, he thought, as little as they come. So light it almost blows away. I see the break in you, he thought. Molecules of metal not touching, like before. He concentrated on that spot, holding the pliers so that the repairman nearest him could not see; he pretended to tug at the spring, as if trying to remove it.

As he finished the job he realized that someone was standing behind him, had come up to watch; he turned, and it was Jim Fergesson, his employer, saying nothing but just standing there with a peculiar expression on his face, his hands stuck in his pockets.

"All done," Hoppy said nervously.

Fergesson said, "Let's see." He took hold of the changer, lifted it up into the overhead fluorescent light's glare.

Did he see me? Hoppy wondered. Did he understand, and if so, what does he think? Does he mind, does he really care? Is he—horrified?

There was silence as Fergesson inspected the changer.

"Where'd you get the new spring?" he asked suddenly.

"I found it lying around," Hoppy said, at once.

It was okay. Fergesson, if he had seen, had not understood. The phocomelus relaxed and felt glee, felt a superior pleasure take the place of his anxiety; he grinned at the two repairmen, looked about for the next job expected of him.

Fergesson said, "Does it make you nervous to have people watch you?"

"No," Hoppy said. "People can stare at me all they want; I know I'm different. I've been stared at since I was born."

"I mean when you work."

"No," he said, and his voice sounded loud—perhaps too loud—in his ears. "Before I had a cart," he said, "before the Government provided me anything, my dad used to carry me around on his back, in a sort of knapsack. Like a papoose." He laughed uncertainly.

"I see," Fergesson said.

"That was up around Sonoma," Hoppy said. "Where I grew up. We had sheep. One time a ram butted me and I flew through the air. Like a ball." Again he laughed; the two repairmen regarded him silently, both of them pausing in their work.

"I'll bet," one of them said after a moment, "that you rolled when you hit the ground."

"Yes," Hoppy said, laughing. They all laughed, now, himself and Fergesson and the two repairmen; they imagined how it looked, Hoppy Harrington, seven years old, with no arms or legs, only a torso and head, rolling over the ground, howling with fright and pain—but it was funny; he knew it. He told it so it would be funny; he made it become that way.

"You're a lot better set up now, with your cart," Fergesson said.

"Oh yes," he said. "And I'm designing a new one, my own design; all electronic—I read an article on brain-wiring, they're using it in Switzerland and Germany. You're wired directly to the motor centers of the brain so there's no lag; you can move even quicker than—a regular physiological structure." He started to say, *than a human.* "I'll have it perfected in a couple of years," he said, "and it'll be an improvement even on the Swiss models. And then I can throw away this Government junk."

Fergesson said in a solemn, formal voice, "I admire your spirit."

Laughing, Hoppy said with a stammer, "Th-thanks, Mr. Fergesson."

One of the repairmen handed him a multiplex FM tuner. "It drifts. See what you can do for the alignment."

"Okay," Hoppy said, taking it in his metal extensors. "I sure will. I've done a lot of aligning, at home; I'm experienced with that." He had found such work easiest of all: he barely had to concentrate on the set. It was as if the task were made to order for him and his abilities.

Reading the calendar on her kitchen wall, Bonny Keller saw that this was the day her friend Bruno Bluthgeld saw her psychiatrist Doctor Stockstill at his office in Berkeley. In fact, he had already seen Stockstill, had had his first hour of therapy and had left. Now he no doubt was driving back to Livermore and his own office at the Radiation Lab, the lab at which she had worked years ago before she had gotten pregnant: she had met Doctor Bluthgeld, there, back in 1975. Now she was thirty-one years old and living in West Marin; her husband George was now vice-principal of the local grammar school, and she was very happy.

Well, not *very* happy. Just moderately—tolerably—happy. She still took analysis herself—once a week now instead of three times—and in many respects she understood herself, her unconscious drives and paratactic systematic distortions of the reality situation. Analysis, six years of it, had done a great deal for her, but she was not cured. There was really no such thing as being cured; the "illness" was life itself, and a constant growth (or rather a viable growing adaptation) had to continue, or psychic stagnation would result.

She was determined not to become stagnant. Right now she was in the process of reading *The Decline of the West* in the original German; she had gotten fifty pages read, and it was well worth it. And who else that she knew had read it, even in the English?

Her interest in German culture, in its literary and philosophical works, had begun years ago through her contact with Doctor Bluthgeld. Although she had taken three years of German in college, she had not seen it as a vital part of her adult life; like so much that she had carefully learned, it had fallen into the unconscious, once she had graduated and gotten a job. Bluthgeld's magnetic presence had reactivated and enlarged many of her academic interests, her love of music and art . . . she owed a great deal to Bluthgeld, and she was grateful.

Now, of course, Bluthgeld was sick, as almost everyone at Livermore knew. The man had profound conscience, and he had never ceased to suffer since the error of 1972—which, as they all knew, all those who had been a part of Livermore in those days, was not specifically his fault; it was not his personal burden, but he had chosen to make it so, and because of that he had become ill, and more ill with each passing year.

Many trained people, and the finest apparati, the foremost computers of the day, had been involved in the faulty calculation—not faulty in terms of the body of knowledge available in 1972 but faulty in relationship to the reality situation. The enormous masses of radioactive clouds had not drifted off but had been attracted by the Earth's gravitational field, and had returned to the atmosphere; no one had been more surprised than the staff at Livermore. Now, of course, the Jamison-French Layer was more completely understood; even the popular magazines such as *Time* and *US News* could lucidly explain what had gone wrong and why. But this was nine years later.

Thinking of the Jamison-French Layer, Bonny remembered the event of the day, which she was missing. She went at once to the TV set in the living room and switched it on. Has it been fired off yet? she wondered, examining her watch. No, not for another half hour. The screen lighted, and sure enough, there was the rocket and its tower, the personnel, trucks, gear; it was decidedly still on the ground, and probably Walter Dangerfield and Mrs. Dangerfield had not even boarded it yet.

The first couple to emigrate to Mars, she said to herself archly, wondering how Lydia Dangerfield felt at this moment . . . the tall blond woman, knowing that their chances of getting to Mars were computed at only about sixty per cent. Great equipment, vast diggings and constructions, awaited them, but so what if they were incinerated along the way? Anyhow, it would impress the Soviet bloc, which had failed to establish its colony on Luna; the Russians had cheerfully suffocated or starved—no one knew exactly for sure. In any case, the colony was gone. It had passed out of history as it had come in, mysteriously.

The idea of NASA sending just a couple, one man and his wife, instead of a group, appalled her; she felt instinctively that they were courting failure by not randomizing their bets. It should be a few people leaving New York, a few leaving California, she thought as she watched on the TV screen the technicians giving the rocket last-minute inspections. What do they call that? Hedging your bets? Anyhow, not all the eggs should be in this one basket . . . and yet this was how NASA had always done it: one astronaut at a time from the beginning, and plenty of publicity. When Henry Chancellor, back in 1967, had burned to particles in his space platform, the entire world had watched on TV—grief-stricken, to be sure, but nonetheless they had been permitted to watch. And the public reaction had set back space exploration in the West five years.

"As you can see now," the NBC announcer said in a soft but urgent voice, "final preparations are being made. The arrival of Mr. and Mrs. Dangerfield is expected momentarily. Let us review just for the sake of the record the enormous preparations made to insure—"

Blah, Bonny Keller said to herself, and, with a shudder, shut off the TV. I can't watch, she said to herself.

On the other hand, what was there to do? Merely sit biting her nails for the next six hours—for the next two weeks, in fact? The only answer would have been *not* to remember that this was the day the First Couple was being fired off. However, it was too late now not to remember.

She liked to think of them as that, the *first couple* . . . like something out of a sentimental, old-time, science-fiction story. Adam and Eve, once over again, except that in actuality Walt Dangerfield was no Adam; he had more the quality of the last, not the first man, with his wry, mordant wit, his halting, almost cynical manner of speech as he faced the reporters. Bonny admired him; Dangerfield was no punk, no crewcut-haired young blond automaton, hacking away at the Air Force's newest task. Walt was a real person, and no doubt that was why NASA had selected him. His genes—they were probably stuffed to overflowing with four thousand years of culture, the heritage of mankind built right in. Walt and Lydia would found a Nova Terra . . . there would be lots of so-phisticated little Dangerfields strolling about Mars, declaiming intellectually and yet with that amusing trace of sheer jazziness that Dangerfield had.

"Think of it as a long freeway," Dangerfield had once said in an interview, answering a reporter's query about the hazards of the trip. "A million miles of ten lanes . . . with no oncoming traffic, no slow trucks. Think of it as being four o'clock in the morning . . . just your vehicle, no others. So like the guys says, what's to worry?" And then his good smile.

Bending, Bonny turned the TV set back on.

And there, on the screen, was the round, bespectacled face of Walt Dangerfield; he wore his space suit—all but the helmet —and beside him stood Lydia, silent, as Walt answered questions.

"I hear," Walt was drawling, with a chewing-movement of his jaw as if he were masticating the question before an-swering, "that there's a LOL in Boise, Idaho who's worried about me." He glanced up, as someone in the rear of the room asked something. "A LOL?" Walt said, "Well,—that was the great now-departed Herb Caen's term for Little Old Ladies . . . there's always one of them, everywhere. Probably there's one on Mars already, and we'll be living down the street from her. Anyhow, this one in Boise, or so I understand, is a little nervous about Lydia and myself, afraid something might happen to us. So she's sent us a good luck charm." He displayed it, holding it clumsily with the big gloved fingers of his suit. The reporters all murmured with amusement. "Nice, isn't it?" Dangerfield said. "I'll tell you what it does; it's good for rheumatism." The reporters laughed. "In case we get rheumatism while we're on Mars. Or is it gout? I think it's gout, she said in her letter." He glanced at his wife. "Gout, was it?"

I guess, Bonny thought, they don't make charms to ward off meteors or radiation. She felt sad, as if a premonition had come over her. Or was it just because this was Bruno Bluth-geld's day at the psychiatrist's? Sorrowful thoughts emanating from that fact, thoughts about death and radiation and miscal-culation and terrible, unending illness.

I don't believe Bruno has become a paranoid schizophrenic, she said to herself. This is only a situation deterioration, and with the proper psychiatric help—a few pills here and there—he'll be okay. It's an endocrine disturbance manifesting itself psychically, and they can do wonders with that; it's not a char-acter defect, a psychotic constitution, unfolding itself in the face of stress.

But what do I know, she thought gloomily. Bruno had to practically sit there and tell us "they" were poisoning his drinking water before either George or I grasped how ill he was . . . he merely seemed depressed.

Right this moment she could imagine Bruno with a pre-scription for some pill which stimulated the cortex or sup-pressed the diencephalon; in any case the modern Western equivalent for contemporary Chinese herbal medicine would be in action, altering the metabolism of Bruno's brain, clearing away the delusions like so many cobwebs. And all would be well again; she and George and Bruno would be together again with their West Marin Baroque Recorder Consort, playing Bach and Handel in the evenings . . . it would be like old times. Two wooden Black Forest (genuine) recorders and then herself at the piano. The house full of baroque music and the smell of home-baked bread, and a bottle of Buena Vista wine from the oldest winery in California . . .

On the television screen Walt Dangerfield was wise-cracking in his adult way, a sort of Voltaire and Will Rogers combined. "Oh yeah," he was saying to a lady reporter who wore a funny large hat. "We expect to uncover a lot of strange life forms on Mars." And he eyed her hat, as if saying, "There's one now, I think." And again, the reporters all laughed. "I think it moved," Dangerfield said, indicating the hat to his quiet, cool-eyed wife. "It's coming for us, honey."

He really loves her, Bonny realized, watching the two of them. I wonder if George ever felt toward me the way Walt Dangerfield feels toward his wife; I doubt it, frankly. If he did, he never would have allowed me to have those two therapeutic abortions. She felt even more sad, now, and she got up and walked away from the TV set, her back to it.

They ought to send George to Mars, she thought with bitterness. Or better yet, send us all, George and me and the Dangerfields; George can have an affair with Lydia Dangerfield—if he's able—and I can bed down with Walt; I'd be a fair to adequate partner in the great adventure. Why not?

I wish something would happen, she said to herself. I wish Bruno would call and say Doctor Stockstill had cured him, or I wish Dangerfield would suddenly back out of going, or the Chinese would start World War Three, or George would really hand the school board back that awful contract as he's been saying he's going to. Something, anyhow. Maybe, she thought, I ought to get out my potter's wheel and pot; back to so-called creativity, or anal play or whatever it is. I could make a lewd pot. Design it, fire it in Violet Clatt's kiln, sell it down in San Anselmo at Creative Artworks, Inc., that society ladies' place that rejected my welded jewelry last year. I know they'd accept a lewd pot if it was a *good* lewd pot.

At Modern TV, a small crowd had collected in the front of the store to watch the large stereo color TV set, the Danger-fields' flight being shown to all Americans everywhere, in their homes and at their places of work. Stuart McConchie stood with his arms folded, back of the crowd, also watching.

"The ghost of John L. Lewis," Walt Dangerfield was saying in his dry way, "would appreciate the true meaning of portal to portal pay . . . if it hadn't been for him, they'd probably be paying me about five dollars to make this trip, on the grounds that my job doesn't actually begin until I get there." He had a sobered expression, now; it was almost time for him and Lydia to enter the cubicle of the ship. "Just remember this . . . if something happens to us, if we get lost, don't come out looking for us. Stay home and I'm sure Lydia and I will turn up somewhere."

"Good luck," the reporters were murmuring, as officials and technicians of NASA appeared and began bundling the Dangerfields off, out of view of the TV cameras.

"Won't be long," Stuart said to Lightheiser, who now stood beside him, also watching.

"He's a sap to go," Lightheiser said, chewing on a toothpick. "He'll never come back; they make no bones about that."

"Why should he want to come back?" Stuart said. "What's so great about it here?" He felt envious of Walt Dangerfield; he wished it was he, Stuart McConchie, up there before the TV cameras, in the eyes of the entire world.

Up the stairs from the basement came Hoppy Harrington on his cart, wheeling eagerly forward. "Have they shot him off?" he asked Stuart in a nervous, quick voice, peering at the screen. "He'll be burned up; it'll be like that time in '65; I don't remember it, naturally, but—"

"Shut up, will you," Lightheiser said softly, and the phocomelus, flushing, became silent. They all watched, then, each with his own private thoughts and reactions as on the TV screen the last inspection team was lifted by an overhead boom from the nose cone of the rocket. The countdown would soon begin; the rocket was fueled, checked over, and now the two people were entering it. The small group around the TV set stirred and murmured.

Sometime later today, sometime in the afternoon, their waiting would be rewarded, because Dutchman IV would take off; it would orbit the Earth for an hour or so, and the people would stand at the TV screen watching that, seeing the rocket go around and around, and then finally the decision would be made and someone below in the blockhouse would fire off the final stage and the orbiting rocket would change trajectory and leave the world. They had seen it before; it was much like this every time, but this was new because the people in this one this time would never be returning. It was well worth spending a day in front of the set; the crowd of people was ready for the wait.

Stuart McConchie thought about lunch and then after that he would come back here and watch again; he would station himself here once more, with the others. He would get little or no work done today, would sell no TV sets to anybody. But this was more important. He could not miss this. That might be me up there someday, he said to himself; maybe I'll emigrate later on when I'm earning enough to get married, take my wife and kids and start a new life up there on Mars, when they get a really good colony going, not just machines.

He thought of himself in the nose cone, like Walt Dangerfield, strapped next to a woman of great physical attractiveness. Pioneers, he and her, founding a new civilization on a new planet. But then his stomach rumbled and he realized how hungry he was; he could not postpone lunch much longer.

Even as he stood watching the great upright rocket on the TV screen, his thoughts turned toward soup and rolls and beef stew and apple pie with ice cream on it, up at Fred's Fine Foods.

III

ALMOST every day Stuart McConchie ate lunch at the coffee shop up the street from Modern TV. Today, as he entered Fred's Fine Foods, he saw to his irritation that Hoppy Harrington's cart was parked in the back, and there was Hoppy eating his lunch in a perfectly natural and easy-going manner, as if he were used to coming here. Goddam, Stuart thought. He's taking over; the phoces are taking over. And I didn't even see him leave the store.

However, Stuart seated himself in a booth and picked up the menu. He can't drive me off, he said to himself as he looked to see what the special of the day was, and how much it cost. The end of the month had arrived, and Stuart was nearly broke. He looked ahead constantly to his twice-monthly paycheck; it would be handed out personally by Fergesson at the end of the week.

The shrill sound of the phoce's voice reached Stuart as he sipped his soup; Hoppy was telling a yarn of some sort, but to whom? To Connie, the waitress? Stuart turned his head and saw that both the waitress and Tony the frycook were standing near Hoppy's cart, listening, and neither of them showed any revulsion toward the phoce.

Now Hoppy saw and recognized Stuart. "Hi!" he called.

Stuart nodded and turned away, concentrating on his soup.

The phoce was telling them all about an invention of his, some kind of electronic contraption he had either built or intended to build—Stuart could not tell which, and he certainly did not care. It did not matter to him what Hoppy built, what crazy ideas emanated from the little man's brain. No doubt it's something sick, Stuart said to himself. Some crank gadget, like a perpetual motion machine . . . maybe a perpetual motion cart for him to ride on. He laughed at that idea, pleased with it. I have to tell that to Lightheiser, he decided. Hoppy's perpetual motion—and then he thought, His phocomobile. At that, Stuart laughed aloud.

Hoppy heard him laugh, and evidently thought he was laughing at something which he himself was saying. "Hey,

Stuart," he called, "come on over and join me and I'll buy you a beer."

The moron, Stuart thought. Doesn't he know Fergesson would never let us have a beer on our lunch hour? It's a rule; if we have a beer we're supposed to never come back to the store and he'll mail us our check.

"Listen," he said to the phoce, turning around in his seat, "when you've worked for Fergesson a little longer you'll know better than to say something stupid like that."

Flushing, the phoce murmured, "What do you mean?"

The frycook said, "Fergesson don't allow his employees to drink; it's against his religion, isn't it, Stuart?"

"That's right," Stuart said. "And you better learn that."

"I wasn't aware of that," the phoce said, "and anyhow I wasn't going to have a beer myself. But I don't see what right an employer has to tell his employees what they can't have on their own time. It's their lunch hour and they should have a beer if they want it." His voice was sharp, full of grim indignation. He was no longer kidding.

Stuart said, "He doesn't want his salesmen coming in smelling like a brewery; I think that's his right. It'd offend some old lady customer."

"I can see that for the salesmen like you," Hoppy said, "but I'm not a salesman; I'm a repairman, and I'd have a beer if I wanted it."

The frycook looked uneasy. "Now look, Hoppy—" he began.

"You're too young to have a beer," Stuart said. Now everyone in the place was listening and watching.

The phoce had flushed a deep red. "I'm of age," he said in a quiet, taut voice.

"Don't serve him any beer," Connie, the waitress, said to the frycook. "He's just a kid."

Reaching into his pocket with his extensor, Hoppy brought out his wallet; he laid it open on the counter. "I'm twenty-one," he said.

Stuart laughed. "Bull." He must have some phony identification in there, he realized. The nut printed it himself or forged it or something. He has to be exactly like everyone; he's got an obsession about it.

Examining the identification in the wallet, the frycook said,

"Yeah, it says he's of age. But Hoppy, remember that other time you were in here and I served you a beer; remember—"

"You have to serve me," the phoce said.

Grunting, the frycook went and got a bottle of Hamm's beer, which he placed, unopened, before Hoppy.

"An opener," the phoce said.

The frycook went and got an opener; he tossed it on the counter, and Hoppy pried open the bottle.

Taking a deep breath, the phoce drank the beer.

What's going on? Stuart wondered, noticing the way that the frycook and Connie—and even a couple of the patrons— were watching Hoppy. Does he pass out or something? Goes berserk, maybe? He felt repelled and at the same time deeply uneasy. I wish I was through with my food, he thought; I wish I was out of here. Whatever it is, I don't want to be a witness to it. I'm going back to the shop and watch the rocket again, he decided. I'm going to watch Dangerfield's flight, something vital to America, not this freak; I don't have time to waste on this.

But he stayed where he was, because something was happening, some peculiar thing involving Hoppy Harrington; he could not draw his attention away from it, try as he might.

In the center of his cart the phocomelus had sunk down, as if he were going to sleep. He lay with his head resting on the tiller which steered the cart, and his eyes became almost shut; his eyes had a glazed look.

"Jeez," the frycook said. "He's doing it again." He appealed around to the rest of them, as if asking them to do something, but no one stirred; they all stood or sat where they were.

"I knew he would," Connie said in a bitter, accusing voice.

The phoce's lips trembled and in a mumble he said, "Ask me. Now somebody ask me."

"Ask you what?" the frycook said angrily. He made a gesture of disgust, turned and walked away, back to his grill.

"Ask me," Happy repeated, in a dull, far-off voice, as if he were speaking in a kind of fit. Watching, Stuart realized that it was a fit, a kind of epilepsy. He yearned to be out of the place and away, but still he could not stir; he still, like the others, had to go on watching.

Connie said to Stuart, "Can't you push him back to the store? Just start pushing!" She glowered at him, but it wasn't his fault; Stuart shrank away and gestured to show his helplessness.

Mumbling, the phoce flopped about on his cart, his plastic and metal manual extensors twitching. "Ask me about it," he was saying. "Come on, before it's too late; I can tell you now, I can see."

At his grill the frycook said loudly, "I wish one of you guys would ask him. I wish you'd get it over with; I know somebody's going to ask him and if you don't I will—I got a couple of questions." He threw down his spatula and made his way back to the phoce. "Hoppy," he said loudly, "you said last time it was all dark. Is that right? No light at all?"

The phoce's lips twitched. "Some light. Dim light. Yellow, like it's about burned out."

Beside Stuart appeared the middle-aged jeweler from across the street. "I was here last time," he whispered to Stuart. "Want to know what it is he sees? I can tell you; listen, Stu, he sees *beyond*."

"Beyond what?" Stuart said, standing up so that he could watch and hear better; everyone had moved closer, now, so as not to miss anything.

"You know," Mr. Crody said. "Beyond the grave. The after life. You can laugh, Stuart, but it's true; when he has a beer he goes into this trance, like you see him in now, and he has occult vision or something. You ask Tony or Connie and some of these other people; they were here, too."

Now Connie was leaning over the slumped, twitching figure in the center of the cart. "Hoppy, what's the light from? Is it God?" She laughed nervously. "You know, like in the Bible. I mean, is it true?"

Hoppy said mumblingly, "Gray darkness. Like ashes. Then a great flatness. Nothing but fires burning, light is from the burning fires. They burn forever. Nothing alive."

"And where are you?" Connie asked.

"I'm—floating," Hoppy said. "Floating near the ground . . . no, now I'm very high. I'm weightless, I don't have a body any more so I'm high up, as high as I want to be. I can hang here, if I want; I don't have to go back down. I like it up here and I can go around the Earth forever. There it is down below me and I can just keep going around and around."

Going up beside the cart, Mr. Crody the jeweler said, "Uh, Hoppy, isn't there anybody else? Are each of us doomed to isolation?"

Hoppy mumbled, "I—see others, now. I'm drifting back down, I'm landing among the grayness. I'm walking about."

Walking, Stuart thought. On what? Legs but no body; what an after life. He laughed to himself. What a performance, he thought. What crap. But he, too, came up beside the cart, now, squeezing in to be able to see.

"Is it that you're born into another life, like they teach in the East?" an elderly lady customer in a cloth coat asked.

"Yes," Hoppy said, surprisingly. "A new life. I have a different body; I can do all kinds of things."

"A step up," Stuart said.

"Yes," Hoppy mumbled. "A step up. I'm like everybody else; in fact I'm better than anybody else. I can do anything they can do and a lot more. I can go wherever I want, and they can't. They can't move."

"Why can't they move?" the frycook demanded.

"Just can't," Hoppy said. "They can't go into the air or on roads or ships; they just stay. It's all different from this. I can see each of them, like they're dead, like they're pinned down and dead. Like corpses."

"Can they talk?" Connie asked.

"Yes," the phoce said, "they can converse with each other. But—they have to—" He was silent, and then he smiled; his thin, twisted face showed joy. "They can only talk through me."

I wonder what that means, Stuart thought. It sounds like a megalomaniacal daydream, where he rules the world. Compensation because he's defective . . . just what you'd expect a phoce to imagine.

It did not seem so interesting to Stuart, now that he had realized that. He moved away, back toward his booth, where his lunch waited.

The frycook was saying, "Is it a good world, there? Tell me if it's better than this or worse."

"Worse," Hoppy said. And then he said, "Worse for you. It's what everybody deserves; it's justice."

"Better for you, then," Connie said, in a questioning way.

"Yes," the phoce said.

"Listen," Stuart said to the waitress from where he sat, "can't you see it's just psychological compensation because he's defective? It's how he keeps going, imagining that. I don't see how you can take it seriously."

"I don't take it seriously," Connie said. "But it's interesting; I've read about mediums, like they're called. They go into trances and can commune with the next world, like he's doing. Haven't you ever heard of that? It's a scientific fact, I think. Isn't it, Tony?" She turned to the frycook for support.

"I don't know," Tony said moodily, walking slowly back to his grill to pick up his spatula.

The phoce, now, seemed to have fallen deeper into his beer-induced trance; he seemed asleep, in fact, no longer seeing anything or at least no longer conscious of the people around him or attempting to communicate his vision—or whatever it was—to them. The séance was over.

Well, you never know, Stuart said to himself. I wonder what Fergesson would say to this; I wonder if he'd want somebody who's not only physically crippled but an epileptic or whatever working for him. I wonder if I should or shouldn't mention this to him when I get back to the store. If he hears he'll probably fire Hoppy right on the spot; I wouldn't blame him. So maybe I better not say anything, he decided.

The phoce's eyes opened. In a weak voice he said, "Stuart."

"What do you want?" Stuart answered.

"I—" The phoce sounded frail, almost ill, as if the experience had been too much for his weak body. "Listen, I wonder . . ." He drew himself up, then rolled his cart slowly over to Stuart's booth. In a low voice he said, "I wonder, could you push me back to the store? Not right now but when you're through eating. I'd really appreciate it."

"Why?" Stuart said. "Can't you do it?"

"I don't feel good," the phoce said.

Stuart nodded. "Okay. When I'm finished eating."

"Thanks," the phoce said.

Ignoring him stonily, Stuart continued eating. *I wish it wasn't obvious I know him,* he thought to himself. *I wish he'd wheel off and wait somewhere else.* But the phoce had sat down, rubbing his forehead with the left extensor, looking too spent to move away again, even to his place at the other end of the coffee shop.

Later, as Stuart pushed the phoce in his cart back up the sidewalk toward Modern TV, the phoce said in a low voice, "It's a big responsibility, to see beyond."

"Yeah," Stuart murmured, maintaining his remoteness, doing his duty only, no more; he pushed the cart and that was all. *Just because I'm pushing you,* he thought, *doesn't mean I have to converse with you.*

"The first time it happened," the phoce went on, but Stuart cut him off.

"I'm not interested." He added, "I just want to get back and see if they fired off the rocket yet. It's probably in orbit by now."

"I guess so," the phoce said.

At the intersection they waited for the light to change.

"The first time it happened," the phoce said, "it scared me." As Stuart pushed him across the street he went on, "I knew right away what it was I was seeing. The smoke and the fires . . . everything all smudged. Like a mining pit or a place where they process slag. Awful." He shuddered. "But is this so terrific the way it is now? Not for me."

"I like it," Stuart said shortly.

"Naturally," the phoce said. "You're not a biological sport."

Stuart grunted.

"You know what my earliest memory from childhood is?" the phoce said in a quiet voice. "Being carried to church in a blanket. Laid out on a pew like a—" His voice broke. "Carried in and out in that blanket, inside it, so no one could see me. That was my mother's idea. She couldn't stand my father carrying me on his back, where people could see."

Stuart grunted.

"This is a terrible world," the phoce said. "Once you Negroes had to suffer; if you lived in the South you'd be suffering now. You forget all about that because they let you forget, but me—they don't let me forget. Anyhow, I don't want to forget, about myself I mean. In the next world it all will be different. You'll find out because you'll be there, too."

"No," Stuart said. "When I die I'm dead; I don't have a soul."

"You, too," the phoce said, and he seemed to be gloating; his voice had a malicious, cruel tinge of relish. "I know."

"How do you know?"

"Because," the phoce said, "one time I saw you."

Frightened in spite of himself, Stuart said, "Aw—"

"One time," the phoce insisted, more firmly now. "It was you; no doubt about it. Want to know what you were doing?"

"Naw."

"You were eating a dead rat raw."

Stuart said nothing, but he pushed the cart faster and faster, down the sidewalk as fast as he could go, back to the store.

When they got back to the store they found the crowd of people still in front of the TV set. And the rocket had been fired off; it had just left the ground, and it was not known yet if the stages had performed properly.

Hoppy wheeled himself back downstairs to the repair department and Stuart remained upstairs before the set. But the phoce's words had upset him so much that he could not concentrate on the TV screen; he wandered off, and then, seeing Fergesson in the upstairs office, walked that way.

At the office desk, Fergesson sat going over a pile of contracts and charge tags. Stuart approached him. "Listen. That goddam Hoppy—"

Fergesson glanced up from his tags.

"Forget it," Stuart said, feeling discouraged.

"I watched him work," Fergesson said. "I went downstairs and watched him when he didn't know I was. I agree there's something unsavory about it. But he's competent; I looked at what he'd done, and it was done right, and that's all that counts." He scowled at Stuart.

"I said forget it," Stuart said.

"Did they fire the rocket off?"

"Just now."

"We haven't moved a single item today, because of that circus," Fergesson said.

"Circus!" He seated himself in the chair opposite Fergesson, in such a manner that he could watch the floor below them. "It's history!"

"It's a way of you guys standing around doing nothing." Once more Fergesson sorted through the tags.

"Listen, I'll tell you what Hoppy did." Stuart leaned toward him. "Up at the café, at Fred's Fine Foods."

Fergesson eyed him, pausing in his work.

"He had a fit," Stuart said. "He went nuts."

"No kidding." Fergesson looked displeased.

"He passed out because—he had a beer. And he saw beyond the grave. He saw me eating a dead rat. And it was raw. So he said."

Fergesson laughed.

"It's not funny."

"Sure it is. He's razzing you back for all the razzing you dish out and you're so dumb you get taken in."

"He really saw it," Stuart said stubbornly.

"Did he see me?"

"He didn't say. He does that up there all the time; they give him beers and he goes into his trance and they ask questions. About what it's like. I just happened to be there, eating lunch. I didn't even see him leave the store; I didn't know he would be there."

For a moment Fergesson sat frowning and pondering, and then he reached out and pressed the button of the intercom which connected the office with the repair department. "Hoppy, wheel up here to the office; I want to talk to you."

"It wasn't my intention to get him into trouble," Stuart said.

"Sure it was," Fergesson said. "But I still ought to know; I've got a right to know what my employees are doing when they're in a public place acting in a fashion that might throw discredit on the store."

They waited, and after a time they heard the labored sound of the cart rolling up the stairs to the office.

As soon as he appeared, Hoppy said, "What I do on my lunch hour is my own business, Mr. Fergesson. That's how I feel."

"You're wrong," Fergesson said. "It's my business, too. Did you see me beyond the grave, like you did Stuart? What was I doing? I want to know, and you better give me a good answer or you're through here, the same day you were hired."

The phoce, in a low, steady voice, said, "I didn't see you, Mr. Fergesson, because your soul perished and won't be reborn."

For a while Fergesson studied the phoce. "Why is that?" he asked finally.

"It's your fate," Hoppy said.

"I haven't done anything criminal or immoral."

The phoce said, "It's the cosmic process, Mr. Fergesson. Don't blame me." He became silent, then.

Turning to Stuart, Fergesson said, "Christ. Well, ask a stupid question, get a stupid answer." Returning to the phoce he said, "Did you see anybody else I know, like my wife? No, you never met my wife. What about Lightheiser? What's going to become of him?"

"I didn't see him," the phoce said.

Fergesson said, "How did you fix that changer? How did you *really* do that? It looked like—you healed it. It looked like instead of replacing that broken spring you made the spring whole again. How did you do that? Is that one of those extrasensory powers or whatever they are?"

"I repaired it," the phoce said in a stony voice.

To Stuart, Fergesson said, "He won't say. But I saw him. He was concentrating on it in some peculiar way. Maybe you were right, McConchie; maybe it was a mistake to hire him. Still, it's the results that count. Listen, Hoppy, I don't want you messing around with trances out in public anywhere along this street now that you're working for me; that was okay before, but not now. Have your trances in the privacy of your own home, is that clear?" He once more picked up his stack of tags. "That's all. Both you guys, go down and do some work instead of standing around."

The phoce at once spun his cart around and wheeled off,

toward the stairs. Stuart, his hands in his pockets, slowly followed.

When he got downstairs and back to the TV set and the
people standing around it he heard the announcer say excitedly that the first three stages of the rocket appeared to have
fired successfully.

That's good news, Stuart thought. A bright chapter in the
history of the human race. He felt a little better, now, and he
parked himself by the counter, where he could obtain a good
view of the screen.

Why would I eat a dead rat? he asked himself. It must be a
terrible world, the next reincarnation, to live like that. Not
even to cook it but just to snatch it up and gobble it down.
Maybe, he thought, even fur and all; fur and tail, everything.
He shuddered.

How can I watch history being made? he wondered angrily.
When I have to think about things like dead rats—I want to
fully meditate on this great spectacle unfolding before my very
eyes, and instead—I have to have garbage like that put into my
mind by that sadistic, that radiation-drug freak that Fergesson
had to go and hire. Sheoot!

He thought of Hoppy, then, no longer bound to his cart,
no longer an armless, legless cripple, but somehow floating.
Somehow master of them all, of—as Hoppy had said—the
world. And that thought was even worse than the one about
the rat.

I'll bet there's plenty he saw, Stuart said to himself, that he
isn't going to say, that he's deliberately keeping back. He just
tells us enough to make us squirm and then he shuts up. If he
can go into a trance and see the next reincarnation then he can
see *everything* because what else is there? But I don't believe in
that Eastern stuff anyhow, he said to himself. I mean, that isn't
Christian.

But he believed what Hoppy had said; he believed because
he had seen with his own eyes. There really was a trance. That
much was true.

Hoppy had seen *something*. And it was a dreadful something; there was no doubt of that.

What else does he see? Stuart wondered. I wish I could

make the little bastard say. What else has that warped, wicked mind perceived about me and about the rest of us, all of us?

I wish, he thought, I could look, too. Because it seemed to Stuart very important, and he ceased looking at the TV screen. He forgot about Walter and Lydia Dangerfield and history in the making; he thought only about Hoppy and the incident at the café. He wished he could stop thinking about it but he could not.

He thought on and on.

IV

THE far-off popping noise made Mr. Austurias turn his head to see what was coming along the road. Standing on the hillside at the edge of the grove of live oaks, he shielded his eyes and saw on the road below the small phocomobile of Hoppy Harrington; in the center of his cart the phocomelus guided himself along, picking a way past the potholes. But the popping noise had not been made by the phocomobile, which ran from an electric battery.

A truck, Mr. Austurias realized. One of Orion Stroud's converted old wood-burners; he saw it now, and it moved at great speed, bearing down on Hoppy's phocomobile. The phocomelus did not seem to hear the big vehicle behind him.

The road belonged to Orion Stroud; he had purchased it from the county the year before, and it was up to him to maintain it and also to allow traffic to move along it other than his own trucks. He was not permitted to charge a toll. And yet, despite the agreement, the wood-burning truck clearly meant to sweep the phocomobile from its path; it headed straight without slowing.

God, Mr. Austurias thought. He involuntarily raised his hand, as if warding off the truck. Now it was almost upon the cart, and still Hoppy paid no heed.

"Hoppy!" Mr. Austurias yelled, and his voice echoed in the afternoon quiet of the woods, his voice and the pop-popping of the truck's engine.

The phocomelus glanced up, did not see him, continued on with the truck now so close that—Mr. Austurias shut his eyes. When he opened them again he saw the phocomobile off onto the shoulder of the road; the truck roared on, and Hoppy was safe: he had gotten out of the way at the last moment.

Grinning after the truck, Hoppy waved an extensor. It had not bothered him, not frightened him in the least, although he must have known that the truck intended to grind him flat. Hoppy turned, waved at Mr. Austurias, who he could not see but who he knew to be there.

His hands trembled, the hands of the grade school teacher;

he bent, picked up his empty basket, stepped up the hillside toward the first old oak tree with its damp shadows beneath. Mr. Austurias was out picking mushrooms. He turned his back on the road and went up, into the gloom, knowing that Hoppy was safe, and so he could forget him and what he had just now seen; his attention returned swiftly to the image of great orange *Cantharellus cibarius*, the chanterelle mushrooms.

Yes, the color glowed, a circle in the midst of the black humus, the pulpy, spirited flower very low, almost buried in the rotting leaves. Mr. Austurias could taste it already; it was big and fresh, this chanterelle; the recent rains had called it out. Bending, he broke its stalk far down, so as to get all there was for his basket. One more and he had his evening meal. Crouching, he looked in every direction, not moving.

Another, less bright, perhaps older . . . he rose, started softly toward it, as if it might escape or he might somehow lose it. Nothing tasted as good as the chanterelle to him, not even the fine shaggy manes. He knew the locations of many stands of chanterelles here and there in West Marin County, on the oak-covered hillsides, in the woods. In all, he gathered eight varieties of forest and pasture mushrooms; he had been almost that many years learning where to expect them, and it was well worth it. Most people feared mushrooms, especially since the Emergency; they feared the new, mutant ones above all, because there the books could not help them.

For instance, Mr. Austurias thought, the one he now broke . . . wasn't the color a little off? Turning it over he inspected the veins. Perhaps a pseudo-chanterelle, not seen before in this region, toxic or even fatal, a mutation. He sniffed it, catching the scent of mould.

Should I be afraid to eat this fellow? he asked himself. If the phocomelus can calmly face his danger, I should be able to face mine.

He put the chanterelle in his basket and walked on.

From below, from the road, he heard a strange sound, a grating, rough noise; pausing, he listened. The noise came again, and Mr. Austurias strode quickly back the way he had come until he emerged from the oaks and once more stood above the road.

The phocomobile was still pulled off onto the shoulder; it

had not gone on, and in it sat the armless, legless handyman, bent over. What was he doing? A convulsion jerked Hoppy about, lifting his head, and Mr. Austurias saw to his amazement that the phocomelus was crying.

Fear, Mr. Austurias realized. The phocomelus had been terrified by the truck but had not shown it, had by enormous effort hidden it until the truck was out of sight—until, the phocomelus had imagined, everyone was out of sight and he was alone, free to express his emotions.

If you're that frightened, Mr. Austurias thought, then why did you wait so long to pull out of the truck's way?

Below him, the phocomelus' thin body shook, swayed back and forth; the bony, hawk-like features bulged with grief. I wonder what Doctor Stockstill, our local medical man, would make of this, Mr. Austurias thought. After all, he used to be a psychiatrist, before the Emergency. He always has all sorts of theories about Hoppy, about what makes him plunk along.

Touching the two mushrooms in his basket, Mr. Austurias thought, We're very close, all the time, to death. But then was it so much better before? Cancer-producing insecticides, smog that poisoned whole cities, freeways and airline crashes . . . it hadn't been so safe then; it hadn't been any easy life. One had to hop aside both then and now.

We must make the best of things, enjoy ourselves if possible, he said to himself. Again he thought of the savory frying pan of chanterelles, flavored with actual butter and garlic and ginger and his home-made beef broth . . . what a dinner it would be; who could he invite to share it with him? Someone he liked a lot, or someone important. If he could only find one more growing—I could invite George Keller, he thought. George, the school superintendent, my boss. Or even one of the school board members; even Orion Stroud, that big, round fat man, himself.

And then, too, he could invite George's wife, Bonny Keller, the prettiest woman in West Marin; perhaps the prettiest woman in the county. There, he thought, is a person who has managed to survive in this present society of . . . both of the Kellers, in fact, had done well since E Day. If anything, they were better off than before.

Glancing up at the sun, Mr. Austurias computed the time.

Possibly it was getting close to four o'clock; time for him to hurry back to town to listen to the satellite as it passed over. Must not miss that, he told himself as he began to walk. Not for a million silver dollars, as the expression used to go. *Of Human Bondage*—forty parts had been read already, and it was getting really interesting. Everyone was attending this particular reading; no doubt of it: the man in the satellite had picked a terrific one this time to read. I wonder if he knows? Mr. Austurias asked himself. No way for me to tell him; just listen, can't reply from down here in West Marin. Too bad. It might mean a lot to him, to know.

Walt Dangerfield must be terribly lonely up there alone in the satellite, Mr. Austurias said to himself. Circling the Earth, day after day. Awful damn tragedy when his wife died; you can tell the difference—he's never been the same again. If only we could pull him down . . . but then, if we did, we wouldn't have him up there talking to us. No, Mr. Austurias concluded. It wouldn't be a good idea to reach him, because that way he'd be sure never to go back up; he must be half-crazy to get out of the thing by now, after all these years.

Gripping his basket of mushrooms, he hurried in the direction of Point Reyes Station, where the one radio could be found, their one contact with Walt Dangerfield in the satellite, and through him the outside world.

"The compulsive," Doctor Stockstill said, "lives in a world in which everything is decaying. This is a great insight. Imagine it."

"Then we must all be compulsives," Bonny Keller said, "because that's what's going on around us . . . isn't it?" She smiled at him, and he could not help returning it.

"You can laugh," he said, "but there's need for psychiatry, maybe more so even than before."

"There's no need for it at all," Bonny contradicted flatly. "I'm not so sure there was any need for it even then, but at the time I certainly thought so. I was devoted to it, as you well know."

At the front of the large room, tinkering with the radio, June Raub said, "Quiet please. We're about to receive him."

Our authority-figure speaks, Doctor Stockstill thought to

himself, and we do what it tells us. And to think that before the Emergency she was nothing more than a typist at the local Bank of America.

Frowning, Bonny started to answer Mrs. Raub, and then she abruptly leaned close to Doctor Stockstill and said, "Let's go outside; George is coming with Edie. Come on." She took hold of his arm and propelled him past the chairs of seated people, toward the door. Doctor Stockstill found himself being led outdoors, onto the front porch.

"That June Raub," Bonny said. "She's so goddam bossy." She peered up and down the road which led past the Foresters' Hall. "I don't see my husband and daughter; I don't even see our good teacher. Austurias, of course, is out in the woods gathering poisonous toadstools to do us all in, and god knows what Hoppy is up to at the moment. Some peculiar puttering-about." She pondered, standing there in the dim late-afternoon twilight, looking especially attractive to Doctor Stockstill; she wore a wool sweater and a long, heavy, hand-made skirt, and her hair was tied back in a fierce knot of red. What a fine woman, he said to himself. Too bad she's spoken for. And then he thought, with a trace of involuntary maliciousness, spoken for a number of times over.

"Here comes my dear husband," Bonny said. "He's managed to break himself off from his school business. And here's Edie."

Along the road walked the tall, slender figure of the grammar school principal; beside him, holding his hand, came the diminutive edition of Bonny, the little red-haired child with the bright, intelligent, oddly dark eyes. They approached, and George smiled in greeting.

"Has it started?" he called.

"Not yet," Bonny said.

The child, Edie, said, "That's good because Bill hates to miss it. He gets very upset."

"Who's 'Bill'?" Doctor Stockstill asked her.

"My brother," Edie said calmly, with the total poise of a seven-year-old.

I didn't realize that the Kellers had two children, Stockstill thought to himself, puzzled. And anyhow he did not see another child; he saw only Edie. "Where is Bill?" he asked her.

"With me," Edie said. "Like he always is. Don't you know Bill?"

Bonny said, "Imaginary playmate." She sighed wearily.

"No he is not imaginary," her daughter said.

"Okay," Bonny said irritably. "He's real. Meet Bill," she said to Doctor Stockstill. "My daughter's brother."

After a pause, her face set with concentration, Edie said, "Bill is glad to meet you at last, Doctor Stockstill. He says hello."

Stockstill laughed. "Tell him I'm glad to meet him, too."

"Here comes Austurias," George Keller said, pointing.

"With his dinner," Bonny said in a grouchy voice. "Why doesn't he teach us to find them? Isn't he our teacher? What's a teacher for? I must say, George, sometimes I wonder about a man who—"

"If he taught us," Stockstill said, "we'd eat all the mushrooms up." He knew her question was merely rhetorical anyhow; although they did not like it, they all respected Mr. Austurias' retention of secret lore—it was his right to keep his mycological wisdom to himself. Each of them had some sort of equivalent fund to draw from. Otherwise, he reflected, they would not now be alive: they would have joined the great majority, the silent dead beneath their feet, the millions who could either be considered the lucky ones or the unlucky ones, depending on one's point of view. Sometimes it seemed to him that pessimism was called for, and on those days he thought of the dead as lucky. But for him pessimism was a passing mood; he certainly did not feel it now, as he stood in the shadows with Bonny Keller, only a foot or so from her, near enough to reach out easily and touch her . . . but that would not do. She would pop him one on the nose, he realized. A good hard blow—and then George would hear, too, as if being hit by Bonny was not enough.

Aloud, he chuckled. Bonny eyed him with suspicion.

"Sorry," he said. "I was just wool-gathering."

Mr. Austurias came striding up to them, his face flushed with exertion. "Let's get inside," he puffed. "So we don't miss Dangerfield's reading."

"You know how it comes out," Stockstill said. "You know Mildred comes back and reënters his life again and makes him miserable; you know the book as well as I do—we all do." He was amused by the teacher's concern.

"I'm not going to listen tonight," Bonny said. "I can't stand to be shushed by June Raub."

With a glance at her, Stockstill said, "Well, you can be community leader next month."

"I think June needs a little psychoanalysis," Bonny said to him. "She's so aggressive, so masculine; it's not natural. Why don't you draw her aside and give her a couple of hours' worth?"

Stockstill said, "Sending another patient to me, Bonny? I still recall the last one." It was not hard to recall, because it had been the day the bomb had been dropped on the Bay Area. Years ago, he thought to himself. In another incarnation, as Hoppy would put it.

"You would have done him good," Bonny said, "if you had been able to treat him, but you just didn't have the time."

"Thanks for sticking up for me," he said, with a smile.

Mr. Austurias said, "By the way, Doctor, I observed some odd behavior on the part of our little phocomelus, today. I wanted to ask your opinion about him, when there's the opportunity. He perplexes me, I must admit . . . and I'm curious about him. The ability to survive against all odds—Hoppy certainly has that. It's encouraging, if you see what I mean, for the rest of us. If he can make it—" The school teacher broke off. "But we must get inside."

To Bonny, Stockstill said, "Someone told me that Dangerfield mentioned your old buddy the other day."

"Mentioned Bruno?" Bonny at once became alert. "Is he still alive, is that it? I was sure he was."

"No, that's not what Dangerfield said. He said something caustic about the first great accident. You recall. 1972."

"Yes," she said tightly. "I recall."

"Dangerfield, according to whoever told me—" Actually, he recalled perfectly well who had told him Dangerfield's *bon mot*; it had been June Raub, but he did not wish to antagonize Bonny any further. "What he said was this. We're *all* living in Bruno's accident, now. We're all the spirit of '72. Of course, that's not so original; we've heard that said before. No doubt I've failed to capture the way Dangerfield said it . . . it's his style, of course, how he says things. No one can give things the twist he gives them."

At the door of the Foresters' Hall, Mr. Austurias had halted, had turned and was listening to them. Now he returned. "Bonny," he said, "did you know Bruno Bluthgeld before the Emergency?"

"Yes," she said. "I worked at Livermore for a while."

"He's dead now, of course," Mr. Austurias said.

"I've always thought he was alive somewhere," Bonny said remotely. "He was or is a great man, and the accident in '72 was not his fault; people who know nothing about it hold him responsible."

Without a word, Mr. Austurias turned his back on her, walked off up the steps of the Hall and disappeared inside.

"One thing about you," Stockstill said to her, "you can't be accused of concealing your opinions."

"Someone has to tell people where to head in," Bonny said. "He's read in the newspapers all about Bruno. The newspapers. That's one thing that's better off, now; the newspapers are gone, unless you count that dumb little *News & Views,* which I don't. I will say this about Dangerfield: he isn't a liar."

Together, she and Stockstill followed after Mr. Austurias, with George and Edie following, into the mostly-filled Foresters' Hall, to listen to Dangerfield broadcasting down to them from the satellite.

As he sat listening to the static and the familiar voice, Mr. Austurias thought to himself about Bruno Bluthgeld and how the physicist was possibly alive. Perhaps Bonny was right. She had known the man, and, from what he had overheard of her conversation with Stockstill (a risky act, these days, over-hearing, but he could not resist it) she had sent Bluthgeld to the psychiatrist for treatment . . . which bore out one of his own very deeply held convictions: that Doctor Bruno Bluthgeld had been mentally disturbed during his last few years before the Emergency—had been palpably, dangerously in-sane, both in his private life and, what was more important, in his public life.

But there had really been no question of that. The public, in its own fashion, had been conscious that something fundamental was wrong with the man; in his public statements there had been an obsessiveness, a morbidity, a tormented expression that had drenched his face, convoluted his manner of speech. And Bluthgeld had talked about the enemy, with its infiltrating tactics, its systematic contamination of institutions at home, of schools and organizations—of the domestic life itself. Bluthgeld had seen the enemy everywhere, in books and in movies, in people, in political organizations that urged views contrary to his own. Of course, he had done it, put forth his views, in a learned way; he was not an ignorant man spouting and ranting in a backward Southern town. No, Bluthgeld had done it in a lofty, scholarly, educated, deeply-worked-out manner. And yet in the final analysis it was no more sane, no more rational or sober, than had been the drunken ramblings of the boozer and woman-chaser, Joe McCarthy, or of any of the others of them.

As a matter of fact, in his student days Mr. Austurias had once met Joe McCarthy, and had found him likeable. But there had been nothing likeable about Bruno Bluthgeld, and Mr. Austurias had met him too—had more than met him. He and Bluthgeld had both been at the University of California at the same time; both had been on the staff, although of course Bluthgeld had been a full professor, chairman of his department, and Austurias had been only an instructor. But they had met and argued, had clashed both in private—in the corridors after class—and in public. And, in the end, Bluthgeld had engineered Mr. Austurias' dismissal.

It had not been difficult, because Mr. Austurias had sponsored all manner of little radical student groups devoted to peace with the Soviet Union and China, and such like causes, and in addition he had spoken out against bomb testing, which Doctor Bluthgeld advocated even after the catastrophe of 1972. He had in fact denounced the test of '72 and called it an example of psychotic thinking at top levels . . . a remark directed at Bluthgeld and no doubt so interpreted by him.

He who pokes at the serpent, Mr. Austurias thought to himself, runs the risk of being bitten . . . his dismissal had not surprised him but it had confirmed him more deeply in his views. And probably, if he thought of it at all, Doctor Bluthgeld had become more entrenched, too. But most likely

Bluthgeld had never thought of the incident again; Austurias had been an obscure young instructor, and the University had not missed him—it had gone on as before, as no doubt had Bluthgeld.

I must talk to Bonny Keller about the man, he said to himself. I must find out all she knows, and it is never hard to get her to talk, so there will be no problem. And I wonder what Stockstill has to offer on the topic, he wondered. Surely if he saw Bluthgeld even once he would be in a position to confirm my own diagnosis, that of paranoid schizophrenia.

From the radio speaker, Walt Dangerfield's voice droned on in the reading from *Of Human Bondage*, and Mr. Austurias began to pay attention, drawn, as always, by the powerful narrative. The problems which seemed vital to us, he thought, back in the old days . . . inability to escape from an unhappy human relationship. Now we prize *any* human relationship. We have learned a great deal.

Seated not far from the school teacher, Bonny Keller thought to herself, Another one looking for Bruno. Another one blaming him, making him the scapegoat for all that's happened. As if *one man* could bring about a world war and the deaths of millions, even if he wanted to.

You won't find him through me, she said to herself. I could help you a lot, but I won't, Mr. Austurias. So go back to your little pile of coverless books; go back to your hunting mushrooms. Forget about Bruno Bluthgeld, or rather Mr. Tree, as he calls himself now. As he has called himself since the day, seven years ago, when the bombs began to fall on things and he found himself walking around the streets of Berkeley in the midst of the debris, unable to understand—just as the rest of us could not understand—what was taking place.

V

OVERCOAT over his arm, Bruno Bluthgeld walked up Oxford Street, through the campus of the University of California, bent over and not looking about him; he knew the route well and he did not care to see the students, the young people. He was not interested in the passing cars, or in the buildings, so many of them new. He did not see the city of Berkeley because he was not interested in it. He was thinking, and it seemed to him very clearly now that he understood what it was that was making him sick. He did not doubt that he was sick; he felt deeply sick—it was only a question of locating the source of contamination.

It was, he thought, coming to him from the outside, this illness, the terrible infection that had sent him at last to Doctor Stockstill. Had the psychiatrist, on the basis of today's first visit, any valid theory? Bruno Bluthgeld doubted it.

And then, as he walked, he noticed that all the cross streets to the left leaned, as if the city was sinking on that side, as if gradually it was keeling over. Bluthgeld felt amused, because he recognized the distortion; it was his astigmatism, which became acute when he was under stress. Yes, he felt as if he were walking along a tilted sidewalk, raised on one side so that everything had a tendency to slide; he felt himself sliding very gradually, and he had trouble placing one foot before the other. He had a tendency to veer, to totter to the left, too, along with the other things.

Sense-data so vital, he thought. Not merely what you perceive but how. He chuckled as he walked. Easy to lose your balance when you have an acute astigmatic condition, he said to himself. How pervasively the sense of balance enters into our awareness of the universe around us . . . hearing is derived from the sense of balance; it's an unrecognized basic sense underlying the others. Perhaps I have picked up a mild labyrinthitis, a virus infection of the middle ear. Should have it looked into.

And yes, now it—the distortion in his sense of balance—had begun affecting his hearing, as he had anticipated. It was fascinating, how the eye and the ear joined to produce a Gestalt; first his eyesight, then his balance, now he heard things askew.

He heard, as he walked, a dull, deep echo which rose from his own footsteps, from his shoes striking the pavement; not the sharp brisk noise that a woman's shoe might make, but a shadowy, low sound, a rumble, almost as if it rose from a pit or cave.

It was not a pleasant sound; it hurt his head, sending up reverberations that were acutely painful. He slowed, altered his pace, watched his shoes strike the pavement so as to anticipate the sound.

I know what this is due to, he said to himself. He had experienced it in the past, this echoing of normal noises in the labyrinths of his ear-passages. Like the distortion in vision it had a simple physiological basis, although for years it had puzzled and frightened him. It was due—simply—to tense posture, skeletal tension, specifically at the base of the neck. In fact, by turning his head from side to side, he could test his theory out; he heard the neck-vertebrae give a little crack, a short, sharp sound that set up immediately the most immensely painful reverberations in his ear-channels.

I must be dreadfully worried today, Bruno Bluthgeld said to himself. For now an even graver alteration in his sense-perceptions was setting in, and one unfamiliar to him. A dull, smoky cast was beginning to settle over all the environment around him, making the buildings and cars seem like inert, gloomy mounds, without color or motion.

And where were the people? He seemed to be plodding along totally by himself in his listing, difficult journey up Oxford Street to where he had parked his Cadillac. Had they (odd thought) all gone indoors? As if, he thought, to get out of the rain . . . this rain of fine, sooty particles that seemed to fill the air, to impede his breathing, his sight, his progress.

He stopped. And, standing there at the intersection, seeing down the side street where it descended into a kind of darkness, and then off to the right where it rose and snapped off, as if twisted and broken, he saw to his amazement—and this he could not explain immediately in terms of some specific physiological impairment of function—that cracks had opened up.

The buildings to his left had split. Jagged breaks in them, as if the hardest of substances, the cement itself which underlay the city, making up the streets and buildings, the very foundations around him, were coming apart.

Good Christ, he thought. What is it? He peered into the sooty fog; now the sky was gone, obscured entirely by the rain of dark.

And then he saw, picking about in the gloom, among the split sections of concrete, in the debris, little shriveled shapes: people, the pedestrians who had been there before and then vanished—they were back now, but all of them dwarfed, and gaping at him sightlessly, not speaking but simply poking about in an aimless manner.

What is it? he asked himself again, this time speaking aloud; he heard his voice dully rebounding. It's all broken; the town is broken up into pieces. What has hit it? What has happened to it? He began to walk from the pavement, finding his way among the strewn, severed parts of Berkeley. It isn't me, he realized; some great terrible catastrophe has happened. The noise, now, boomed in his ears, and the soot stirred, moved by the noise. A car horn sounded stuck on, but very far off and faint.

Standing in the front of Modern TV, watching the television coverage of Walter and Mrs. Dangerfield's flight, Stuart McConchie saw to his surprise the screen go blank.

"Lost their picture," Lightheiser said, disgustedly. The group of people stirred with indignation. Lightheiser chewed on his toothpick.

"It'll come back on," Stuart said, bending to switch to another channel; it was, after all, being covered by all networks.

All channels were blank. And there was no sound, either. He switched it once more. Still nothing.

Up from the basement came one of the repairmen, running toward the front of the store and yelling, "Red alert!"

"What's that?" Lightheiser said wonderingly, and his face became old and unhealthy-looking; seeing it, Stuart McConchie knew without the words or the thoughts ever occurring in his mind. He did not have to think; he knew, and he ran out of the store onto the street, he ran onto the empty sidewalk and stood, and the group of people at the TV set, seeing him and the repairman running, began to run, too, in different directions, some of them across the street, out into traffic, some of them in circles, some of them away in a straight line, as if each of them saw something different, as if it was not the same thing happening to any two of them.

Stuart and Lightheiser ran up the sidewalk to where the gray-green metal sidewalk doors were which opened onto the underground storage basement that once, a long time ago, a drugstore had used for its stock but which now was empty. Stuart tore at the metal doors, and so did Lightheiser, and both of them yelled that it wouldn't open; there was no way to open it except from below. At the entrance of the men's clothing store a clerk appeared, saw them; Lightheiser shouted at him, yelled for him to run downstairs and open up the sidewalk. "Open the sidewalk!" Lightheiser yelled, and so did Stuart, and now so did several people all standing or squatting at the sidewalk doors, waiting for the sidewalk to open. So the clerk turned and ran back into the clothing store. A moment later a clanking noise sounded under Stuart's feet.

"Get back," a heavy-set elderly man said. "Get off the doors." The people saw down into cold gloom, a cave under the sidewalk, an empty cavity. They all jumped down into it, falling to the bottom; they lay pressed against damp concrete, rolling themselves up into balls or flattening themselves out— they squirmed and pressed down into crumbly soil with the dead sowbugs and the smell of decay.

"Close it from above," a man was saying. There did not seem to be any women, or if there were they were silent; his head pressed into a corner of the concrete, Stuart listened but heard only men, heard them as they grabbed at the doors above, trying to shut them. More people came down now, falling and tumbling and yelling, as if dumped from above.

"How long, oh Lord?" a man was saying.

Stuart said, "Now." He knew it was now; he knew that the bombs were going off—he felt them. It seemed to occur inside him. Blam, blam, blam, blam, went the bombs, or perhaps it was things sent up by the Army to help, to stop the bombs; perhaps it was defense. Let me down, Stuart thought. Low as

I can be. Let me into the ground. He pressed down, rolled his body to make a depression. People lay now on top of him, choking coats and sleeves, and he was glad; he did not mind—he did not want emptiness around him: he wanted solidness on every side. He did not need to breathe. His eyes were shut; they, and the other openings of his body, his mouth and ears and nose, all had shut; he had walled himself in, waiting.

Blam, blam, blam.

The ground jumped.

We'll get by, Stuart said. Down here, safe in the earth. Safe inside where it's safe; it'll pass by overhead. The wind.

The wind, above on the surface, passed by at huge speed; he knew it moved up there, the air itself, driven along altogether, as a body.

In the nose cone of Dutchman IV, Walt Dangerfield, while still experiencing the pressure of many gravities on his body, heard in his earphones the voices from below, from the control bunker.

"Third stage successful, Walt. You're in orbit. We'll fire off the final stage at 15:45 instead of 15:44, they tell me."

Orbital velocity, Dangerfield said to himself, straining to see his wife. She had lost consciousness; he looked away from her at once, concentrating on his oxygen supply, knowing she was all right but not wanting to witness her suffering. Okay, he thought, we're both okay. In orbit, waiting for the final thrust. It wasn't so bad.

The voice in his earphones said, "A perfect sequence so far, Walt. The President is standing by. You have eight minutes six seconds before the initial corrections for the fourth-stage firing. If in correcting minor—"

Static erased the voice; he no longer heard it.

If in correcting minor but vital errors in attitude, Walter Dangerfield said to himself, there is a lack of complete success, we will be brought back down, as they did before in the robot-runs. And later on we will try it again. There is no danger; reëntry is an old story. He waited.

The voice in his earphones came on again. "*Walter, we are under attack down here.*"

What? he said. What did you say?

"God save us," the voice said. It was a man already dead; the voice had no feeling, it was empty and then it was silent. Gone.

"From whom?" Walt Dangerfield said into his microphone. He thought of pickets and rioters, he thought of bricks, angry mobs. Attacked by nuts or something, is that it?

He struggled up, disconnected himself from the straps, saw through the port the world below. Clouds, and the ocean, the globe itself. Here and there on it matches were lit; he saw the puffs, the flares. Fright overcame him, as he sailed silently through space, looking down at the pinches of burning scattered about; he knew what they were.

It's death, he thought. Death lighting up spots, burning up the world's life, second by second.

He continued to watch.

There was, Doctor Stockstill knew, a community shelter under one of the big banks, but he could not remember which one. Taking his secretary by the hand he ran from the building and across Center Street, searching for the black and white sign that he had noticed a thousand times, that had become part of the perpetual background of his daily, business existence on the public street. The sign had merged into the unchanging, and now he needed it; he wanted it to step forward so that he could notice it as he had at the beginning: as a real sign, meaning something vital, something by which to preserve his life.

It was his secretary, tugging at his arm, who pointed the way to him; she yelled in his ear over and over again and he saw— he turned in that direction and together they crossed the street, running out into the dead, stalled traffic and among the pedestrians, and then they were struggling and fighting to get into the shelter, which was the basement of the building.

As he burrowed down, lower and lower, into the basement shelter and the mass of people pressed together in it, he thought about the patient whom he had just seen; he thought about Mr. Tree and in his mind a voice said with clarity, You did this. See what you did, you've killed us all.

His secretary had become separated from him and he was

alone with people he did not know, breathing into their faces
and being breathed on. And all the time he heard a wailing,
the noise of women and probably their small children, shop-
pers who had come in here from the department stores, midday mothers. Are the doors shut? he wondered. Has it begun?
It has; the moment has. He closed his eyes and began to pray
out loud, noisily, trying to hear the sound. But the sound was
lost.

"Stop that racket," someone, a woman, said in his ear,
so close that his ear hurt. He opened his eyes; the woman,
middle-aged, glared at him, as if this was all that mattered, as if
nothing was happening except his noisy praying. Her attention
was directed on stopping him, and in surprise he stopped.

Is that what you care about? he wondered, awed by her, by
the narrowness of her attention, by its mad constrictedness.
"Sure," he said to her. "You damn fool," he said, but she did
not hear him. "Was I bothering you?" he went on, unheeded;
she was now glaring at someone else who had bumped or
shoved her. "Sorry," he said. "Sorry, you stupid old crow,
you—" He cursed at the woman, cursing instead of praying
and feeling more relief by that; he got more out of that.

And then, in the middle of his cursing, he had a weird, vivid
notion. The war had begun and they were being bombed and
would probably die, but it was Washington that was dropping
the bombs on them, not the Chinese or the Russians; something had gone wrong with an automatic defense system out
in space, and it was acting out its cycle this way—and no one
could halt it, either. It was war and death, yes, but it was error;
it lacked intent. He did not feel any hostility from the forces
overhead. They were not vengeful or motivated; they were
empty, hollow, completely cold. It was as if his car had run
over him: it was real but meaningless. It was not policy, it was
breakdown and failure, chance.

So at this moment, he felt himself devoid of retaliatory
hatred for the enemy because he could not imagine—did not
actually believe in or even understand—the concept. It was as
if the previous patient, Mr. Tree or Doctor Bluthgeld or whoever he had been, had taken in, absorbed all that, left none of
it for anyone else. Bluthgeld had made Stockstill over into a

different person, one who could not think that way even now. Bluthgeld, by being insane, had made the concept of *the enemy* unbelievable.

"We'll fight back, we'll fight back, we'll fight back," a man near Doctor Stockstill was chanting. Stockstill looked at him in astonishment, wondering who he would fight back against. Things were falling on them; did the man intend to fall back upward into the sky in some kind of revenge? Would he reverse the natural forces at work, as if rolling a film-sequence backward? It was a peculiar, nonsensical idea. It was as if the man had been gripped by his unconscious. He was no longer living a rational, ego-directed existence; he had surrended to some archetype.

The impersonal, Doctor Stockstill thought, has attacked us. That is what it is; attacked us from inside and out. The end of the co-operation, where we applied ourselves together. Now it's atoms only. Discrete, without any windows. Colliding but not making any sound, just a general hum.

He put his fingers in his ears, trying not to hear the noises from around him. The noises appeared—absurdly—to be below him, rising instead of descending. He wanted to laugh.

Jim Fergesson, when the attack began, had just gone downstairs into the repair department of Modern TV. Facing Hoppy Harrington he saw the expression on the phocomelus' face when the red alert was announced over the FM radio and the conalrad system went at once into effect. He saw on the lean, bony face a grin like that of greed, as if in hearing and understanding, Hoppy was filled with joy, the joy of life itself. He had become lit up for an instant, had thrown off everything that inhibited him or held him to the surface of the earth, every force that made him slow. His eyes burst into light and his lips twitched; he seemed to be sticking out his tongue, as if mocking Fergesson.

To him Fergesson said, "You dirty little freak."

The phoce yelled, "It's the end!" The look on his face was already gone. Perhaps he had not even heard what Fergesson had said; he seemed to be in a state of self-absorption. He shivered, and the artificial manual extensors emanating from his cart danced and flicked like whips.

"Now listen," Fergesson said. "We're below street-level." He caught hold of the repairman, Bob Rubenstein. "You moronic jackass, stay where you are. I'll go upstairs and get those people down here. You clear as much space as you can; make space for them." He let go of the repairman and ran to the stairs.

As he started up the steps two at a time, clutching the handrail and using it as a fulcrum, something happened to his legs. The bottom part of him fell off and he pitched backward, rolled back and down, and onto him rained tons of white plaster. His head hit the concrete floor and he knew that the building had been hit, taken away, and the people were gone. He was hurt, too, cut into two pieces, and only Hoppy and Bob Rubenstein would survive and maybe not even they.

He tried to speak but could not.

Still at the repairbench Hoppy felt the concussion and saw the doorway fill up with pieces of the ceiling and the wood of the steps turned into flying fragments and among the fragments of wood something soft, bits of flesh; it, the pieces, were Fergesson—he was dead. The building shook and boomed, as if doors were shutting. We're shut in, Hoppy realized. The overhead light popped, and now he saw nothing. Blackness. Bob Rubenstein was screeching.

The phoce wheeled his cart backward, into the black cavity of the basement, going by the touch of his extensors. He felt his way among the stock inventory, the big television sets in their cardboard cartons; he got as deep as possible, slowly and carefully burrowed in all the way to the back as far from the entrance as he could. Nothing fell on him. Fergesson had been right. This was safe, here, below the street level. Upstairs they were all rags of flesh mixed with the white, dry powder that had been the building, but here it was different.

Just not time, he thought. They told us and then it began; it's still going on. He could feel the wind moving over the surface upstairs; it moved unimpeded, because everything which had stood was now down. We must not go up even later, because of radiation, he realized. That was the mistake those Japs made; they came right up and smiled.

How long will I live down here? he wondered. A month?

No water, unless a pipe breaks. No air after a while, unless molecules filtering through the debris. Still, better than trying to come out. I will not come out, he reiterated. I know better; I'm not dumb like the others.

Now he heard nothing. No concussion, no rain of falling pieces in the darkness around him: small objects jarred loose from stacks and from shelves. Just silence. He did not hear Bob Rubenstein. Matches. From his pocket he got matches, lit one; he saw that TV cartons had toppled to enclose him. He was alone, in a space of his own.

Oh boy, he said to himself with exultation. Am I lucky; this space was just made for me. I'll stay and stay; I can go days and then be alive, I know I was *intended* to be alive. Fergesson was intended to die right off the bat. It's God's will. God knows what to do; He watches out, there is no chance about this. All this, a great cleansing of the world. Room must be made, new space for people, for instance myself.

He put out the match and the darkness returned; he did not mind it. Waiting, in the middle of his cart, he thought, This is my chance, it was made for me deliberately. It'll be different when I emerge. Destiny at work from the start, back before I was born. Now I understand it all, my being so different from the others; I see the reason.

How much time has passed? he wondered presently. He had begun to become impatient. An hour? I can't stand to wait, he realized. I mean, I have to wait, but I wish it would hurry up. He listened for the possible sound of people overhead, rescue teams from the Army beginning to dig people out, but not yet; nothing so far.

I hope it isn't too long, he said to himself. There's lots to do; I have work ahead of me.

When I get out of here I have to get started and organize, because that's what will be needed: organization and direction; everyone will be milling around. Maybe I can plan now.

In the darkness he planned. All manner of inspirations came to him; he was not wasting his time, not being idle just because he had to be stationary. His head wildly rang with original notions; he could hardly wait, thinking about them and how they would work when tried out. Most of them had to do with ways of survival. No one would be dependent on

big society; it would all be small towns and individuality, like
Ayn Rand talked about in her books. It would be the end of
conformity and the mass mind and junk; no more factory-
produced junk, like the cartons of color 3-D television sets
which had fallen on all sides of him.

His heart pounded with excitement and impatience; he
could hardly stand waiting—it was like a million years already.
And still they hadn't found him yet, even though they were
busy looking. He knew that; he could feel them at work, getting nearer.

"Hurry!" he exclaimed aloud, lashing his manual extensors;
the tips scratched against the TV cartons, making a dull sound.
In his impatience he began to beat on the cartons. The drumming filled the darkness, as if there were many living things
imprisoned, an entire nest of people, not just Hoppy Harrington alone.

In her hillside home in West Marin County, Bonny Keller
realized that the classical music on the stereo set in the living
room had gone off. She emerged from the bedroom, wiping
the water color paint from her hands and wondering if the
same tube as before had—as George put it—cut out.

And then through the window she saw against the sky to the
south a stout trunk of smoke, as dense and brown as a living
stump. She gaped at it, and then the window burst; it pulverized and she crashed back and slid across the floor along with
the powdery fragments of it. Every object in the house tumbled, fell and shattered and then skidded with her, as if the
house had tilted on end.

The San Andreas Fault, she knew. Terrible earthquake, like
back ago eighty years; all we've built . . . all ruined. Spinning, she banged into the far wall of the house, only now it
was level and the floor had raised up; she saw lamps and tables
and chairs raining down and smashing, and it was amazing to
her how flimsy everything was. She could not understand how
things she had owned for years could break so easily; only the
wall itself, now beneath her, remained as something hard.

My house, she thought. Gone. Everything that's mine, that
means something to me. Oh, it isn't fair.

Her head ached as she lay panting; she smoothed herself,

saw her hands white and covered with fine powder and trembling—blood streaked her wrist, from some cut she could not make out. On my head, she thought. She rubbed her forehead, and bits of material fell from her hair. Now—she could not understand it—the floor was flat again, the wall was upright as it had always been. Back to normal. But the objects; they were all broken. That remained. The garbage house, she thought. It'll take weeks, months. We'll never build back. It's the end of our life, our happiness.

Standing, she walked about; she kicked the pieces of a chair aside. She kicked through the trash, toward the door. The air swirled with particles and she inhaled them; she choked on them, hating them. Glass everywhere, all her lovely plateglass windows gone. Empty square holes with a few shards which still broke loose and dropped even as she watched. She found a door—it had been bent open. Shoving it, putting her weight against it, she made it move aside so that she could go unsteadily out of the house to stand a few yards away, surveying what had happened.

Her headache had become worse. Am I blinded? she wondered; it was hard to keep her eyes open. Did I see a light? She had a memory of one click of light, like a camera shutter opening so suddenly, so swiftly, that her optic nerves had not responded—she had not really *seen* it. And yet, her eyes were hurt; she felt the injury there. Her body, all of her, seemed damaged, and no wonder. But the ground. She did not see any fissure. And the house stood; only the windows and the household goods had been destroyed. The structure, the empty container, remained with nothing left in it.

Walking slowly along, she thought, I better go get help. I need medical help. And then, as she stumbled and half fell, she looked around her, up into the air, and saw once again the column of brown smoke from the south. Did San Francisco catch fire already? she asked herself.

It's burning, she decided. It's a calamity. The city got it, not just West Marin, here. Not just a few rural people up here, but all the city people; there must be thousands dead. They'll have to declare a national emergency and get the Red Cross and Army; we'll remember this to the day we die. Walking, she began to cry, holding her hands to her face, not seeing where she was going, not caring. She did not cry for herself or her ruined house, now; she cried for the city to the south. She cried for all the people and things in it and what had happened to them.

I'll never see it again, she knew. There is no more San Francisco; it is over. The end had come about, today. Crying, she wandered on in the general direction of town; already she could hear people's voices, rising up from the flatland below. Going by the sound she moved that way.

A car drew up beside her. The door opened; a man reached out for her. She did not know him; she did not even know if he lived around here or if he was passing through. Anyhow, she hugged him.

"All right," the man said, squeezing her around the waist.

Sobbing, she struggled closer to him, pressing herself against the car seat and drawing him over her.

Later, she once more found herself walking, this time down a narrow road with oak trees, the gnarled old live oaks which she loved so much, on both sides of her. The sky overhead was bleak and gray, swept by heavy clouds which drifted in monotonous procession toward the north. This must be Bear Valley Ranch Road, she said to herself. Her feet hurt and when she stopped she discovered that she was barefoot; somewhere along the way she had lost her shoes.

She still wore the paint-splattered jeans which she had had on when the quake had happened, when the radio had gone off. Or had it really been a quake after all? The man in the car, frightened and babbling like a baby, had said something else, but it had been too garbled, too full of panic, for her to understand.

I want to go home, she said to herself. I want to be back in my own home and I want my shoes. I'll bet that man took them; I'll bet they're back in his car. And I'll never see them again.

She plodded on, wincing at the pain, wishing she could find somebody, wondering about the sky overhead and becoming more lonely with each passing moment.

VI

DRIVING his Volkswagen bus away, Andrew Gill caught one last sight of the woman in the paint-spattered jeans and sweater whom he had just let off; he watched her as she trudged barefoot along the road and then he lost her as his bus passed a bend. He did not know her name but it seemed to him that she was about the prettiest woman he had ever seen, with her red hair and small, delicately-formed feet. And, the thought to himself in a daze, he and she had just now made love, in the back of his VW bus.

It was, to him, a pageant of figments, the woman and the great explosions from the south that had torn up the country-side and raised the sky of gray overhead. He knew that it was war of some sort or at least a bad event of some modern kind entirely new to the world and to his experience.

He had, that morning, driven from his shop in Petaluma to West Marin to deliver to the pharmacy at Point Reyes Station a load of imported English briar pipes. His business was fine liquors—especially wines—and tobaccos, everything for the serious smoker including little nickel-plated devices for cleaning pipes and tamping the tobacco down. Now as he drove he wondered how his shop was; had the event encompassed the Petaluma area?

I had better get the hell back there and see how it is, he said to himself, and then he thought once again of the small red-haired woman in the jeans who had hopped into his bus—or allowed him to draw her into it; he no longer was certain which had happened—and it seemed to him that he ought to drive after her and make sure she was all right. Does she live around here? he asked himself. And how do I find her again? Already he wanted to find her again; he had never met or seen anyone like her. And did she do it because of shock? he wondered. Was she in her right mind at the time? Had she ever done such a thing before . . . and, more important, would she ever do it again?

However, he kept on going, not turning back; his hands felt

numb, as if they were lifeless. He was exhausted. I know
there're going to be other bombs or explosions, he said to
himself. They landed one on the Bay Area and they'll keep
shooting them off at us. In the sky overhead he saw now
flashes of light in quick succession and then after a time a distant rumble seized his bus and made it buck and quake. Bombs
going off up there, he decided. Maybe our defenses. But there
will be more getting through.

Then, too, there was the radiation.

Drifting overhead, now, the clouds of what he knew to be
deadly radiation passed on north, and did not seem to be low
enough yet to affect life on the surface, his life and that of the
bushes and trees along the road. Maybe we'll wither and die in
another few days, he thought. Maybe it's only a question of
time. Is it worth hiding? Should I head north, try to escape?
But the clouds were moving north. I better stay here, he said
to himself, and try to find some local shelter. I think I read
somewhere once that this is a protected spot; the winds blow
on past West Marin and go inland, toward Sacramento.

And still he saw no one. Only the girl—the only person he
had seen since the first great bomb and the realization of what
it meant. No cars. No people on foot. They'll be showing up
from down below pretty soon, he reasoned. By the thousands.
And dying as they go. Refugees. Maybe I should get ready to
help. But all he had in his VW truck were pipes and cans of
tobacco and bottles of California wine from small vintners; he
had no medical supplies and no know-how. And anyhow he was
over fifty years old and he had a chronic heart problem called
paroxysmal tachycardia. It was a wonder, in fact, that he had
not had an attack of it back there when he was making love
with the girl.

My wife and the two kids, he thought. Maybe they're dead.
I just have to get back to Petaluma. A phone call? Absurd. The
phones are certainly out. And still he drove on, pointlessly, not
knowing where to go or what to do. Not knowing how much
danger he was in, if the attack by the enemy was over or if this
was just the start. I could be wiped out any second, he realized.

But he felt safe in the familiar VW bus, which he had owned
for six years now. It had not been changed by what had

happened; it was sturdy and reliable, whereas—he felt—the world, the rest of things, all had undergone a permanent, dreadful metamorphosis.

He did not wish to look.

What if Barbara and the boys are dead? he asked himself. Oddly, the idea carried with it the breath of release. A new life, as witness me meeting that girl. The old is all over; won't tobacco and wines be very valuable now? Don't I in actual fact have a fortune here in this bus? I don't have to go back to Petaluma ever; I can disappear, and Barbara will never be able to find me. He felt buoyed up, cheerful, now.

But that would mean—God forbid—he would have to abandon his shop, and that was a horrible notion, overlain with the sense of peril and isolation. I can't give that up, he decided. That represents twenty years of gradually building up a good customer-relationship, of genuinely finding out people's wants and serving them.

However, he thought, those people are possibly dead now, along with my family. I have to face it: *everything* has changed, not merely the things I don't care for.

Driving slowly along, he tried to cogitate over each possibility, but the more he cogitated the more confused and uneasy he became. I don't think any of us will survive, he decided. We probably all have radiation exposure; my relationship with that girl is the last notable event in my life, and the same for her— she is no doubt doomed too.

Christ, he thought bitterly. Some numbskull in the Pentagon is responsible for this; we should have had two or three hours warning, and instead we got—five minutes. At the most!

He felt no animosity toward the enemy, now; he felt only a sense of shame, a sense of betrayal. Those military saps in Washington are probably safe and sound down in their concrete bunkers, like Adolf Hitler at the end, he decided. And we're left up here to die. It embarrassed him; it was awful.

Suddenly he noticed that on the seat beside him lay two empty shoes, two worn slippers. The girl's. He sighed, feeling weary. Some memento, he thought with gloom.

And then he thought in excitement, it's not a memento; it's a sign—for me to stay here in West Marin, to begin all over again here. If I stay here I'll run into her again; I know I will.

It's just a question of being patient. That's why she left her shoes; she already knew it, that I'm just beginning my life here, that after what's happened I won't—can't—leave. The hell with my shop, with my wife and children, in Petaluma.

As he drove along he began to whistle with relief and glee.

There was no doubt in the mind of Bruno Bluthgeld now; he saw the unceasing stream of cars all going one way, going north toward the highway that emptied into the countryside. Berkeley had become a sieve, out of which at every hole leaked the people pressing upward from beneath, the people from Oakland and San Leandro and San Jose; they were all passing through along the streets that had become one-way streets, now. It's not me, Doctor Bluthgeld said to himself as he stood on the sidewalk, unable to cross the street to get to his own car. And yet, he realized, even though it is real, even though it is the end of everything, the destruction of the cities and the people on every side, I am responsible.

He thought, In some way I made it happen.

I must make amends, he told himself. He clasped his hands together, tense with concern. It must unhappen, he realized. I must shut it back off.

What has happened is this, he decided. They were developing their arrangements to injure me but they hadn't counted on my ability, which in me seems to lie partly in the subconscious. I have only a dubious control over it; it emanates from supra-personal levels, what Jung would call the collective unconscious. They didn't take into account the almost limitless potency of my reactive psychic energy, and now it's flowed back out at them in response to their arrangements. I didn't will it to; it simply followed a psychic law of stimulus and response, but I must take moral responsibility for it anyhow, because it is I, the greater I, the Self which transcends the conscious ego. I must wrestle with it, now that it's done its work contra the others. Surely it has done enough; isn't, in fact, the damage too great?

But no, it was not too great, in the pure physical sense, the pure realm of action and reaction. A law of conservation of energy, a parity, was involved; his collective unconscious had responded commensurate to the harm intended by the others.

Now, however, it was time to atone for it; that was, logically, the next step. It had expended itself . . . or had it? He felt doubt and a deep confusion; had the reactive process, his meta-biological defense system, completed its cycle of response, *or was there more?*

He sniffed the atmosphere, trying to anticipate. The sky, an admixture of particles: debris light enough to be carried. What lay behind it, concealed as in a womb? The womb, he thought, of pure essence within me, as I stand here debating. I wonder if these people driving by in these cars, these men and women with their blank faces—I wonder if they know *who I am*. Are they aware that I am the omphalos, the center, of all this cataclysmic disruption? He watched the passing people, and presently he knew the answer; they were quite aware of him, that he was the source of this all, but they were afraid to attempt any injury in his direction. They had learned their lesson.

Raising his hand toward them he called, "Don't worry; there won't be any more. I promise."

Did they understand and believe him? He felt their thoughts directed at him, their panic, their pain, and also their hatred toward him now held in abeyance by the tremendous demonstration of what he could accomplish. I know how you feel, he thought back, or perhaps said aloud—he could not tell which. You have learned a hard, bitter lesson. And so have I. I must watch myself more carefully; in the future I must guard my powers with a greater awe, a greater reverence at the trust placed in my hands.

Where should I go now? he questioned himself. Away from here, so that this will gradually die down, of its own accord? For their sakes; it would be a good idea, a kind, humane, equitable solution.

Can I leave? he asked himself. Of course. Because the forces at work were to at least some extent disposable; he could summon them, once he was aware of them, as he was now. What had been wrong before had simply been his ignorance of them. Perhaps, through intense psychoanalysis, he would have gotten to them in time, and this great disturbance might have been avoided. But too late to worry about that now. He began to walk back the way he had come. I can pass over this traffic and absent myself from this region, he assured himself. To prove it, he stepped from the curb, out into the solid stream of cars; other people were doing so, too, other individuals on foot, many of them carrying household goods, books, lamps, even a bird in a cage or a cat. He joined them, waving to them to indicate that they should cross with him, follow him because he could pass on through at will.

The traffic had almost halted. It appeared to be due to cars forcing their way in from a side street ahead, but he knew better; that was only the apparent cause—the genuine cause was his desire to cross. An opening between two cars lay directly ahead, and Doctor Bluthgeld led the group of people on foot across to the far side.

Where do I want to go? he asked himself, ignoring the thanks of the people around him; they were all trying to tell him how much they owed him. Out into the country, away from the city? I am dangerous to the city, he realized. I should go fifty or sixty miles to the east, perhaps all the way to the Sierras, to some remote spot. West Marin; I could go back up there. Bonny is up there. I could stay with her and George. I think that would be far enough away, but if it is not I will continue on—I must absent myself from these people, who do not deserve to be punished any further. If necessary, I will continue on forever; I will never stop in one place.

Of course, he realized, I can't get to West Marin by car; none of these cars are moving or are ever going to move again. The congestion is too great. And the Richardson Bridge is certainly gone. I will have to walk; it will take days, but eventually I will make it there. I will go up to the Black Point Road, up toward Vallejo, and follow the route across the sloughs. The land is flat; I can cut directly across the fields if necessary.

In any case it's a penance for what I've done. This will be a voluntary pilgrimage, a way of healing the soul.

He walked, and as he did so he concentrated on the damage about him; he viewed it with the idea of healing it, of restoring the city, if at all possible, to its pure state. When he came to a building that had collapsed he paused and said, *Let this building be restored.* When he saw injured people he said, *Let these people be adjudged innocent and so forgiven.* Each time, he made a motion with his hand which he had devised; it indicated his determination to see that things such as this did not reoccur. Perhaps they have learned a permanent lesson, he thought. They may leave me alone, now.

But, it occurred to him, perhaps they would go in the opposite direction; they would, after they had dragged themselves from the ruins of their houses, develop an even greater determination to destroy him. This might in the long run increase, rather than dispel, their animosity.

He felt frightened, thinking about their vengeance. Maybe I should go into hiding, he thought. Keep the name "Mr. Tree," or use some other fictive name for purposes of concealment. Right now they are wary of me . . . but I'm afraid it will not last.

And yet, even knowing that, he still continued to make his special sign to them as he walked along. He still bent his efforts to achieving a restoration for them. His own emotions contained no hostility; he was free of that. It was only they who harbored any hate.

At the edge of the Bay, Doctor Bluthgeld emerged from the traffic to see the white, shattered, glass-like city of San Francisco lying everywhere on the far side of the water. Nothing stood. Overhead, smoke and yellow fire manifested themselves in a way that he could not believe. It was as if the city had become a stick of stove wood, incinerated without leaving a trace. And yet there were people coming out of it. He saw, on the water, bobbing chunks; the people had floated every kind of object out, and were clinging to them, trying to push across to Marin County.

Doctor Bluthgeld stood there, unable to go on, his pilgrimage forgotten. First he had to cure them, and then if possible cure the city itself. He forgot his own needs. He concentrated on the city, using both hands, making new gestures which he had never hit on before; he tried everything, and after a long time he saw the smoke begin to clear. That gave him hope. But the people bobbing across, escaping, began to diminish in number; he saw fewer and fewer until the bay was empty of them, and only naked debris remained.

So he concentrated then on saving the people themselves; he thought of the escape routes north, where the people should go and what they would need to find. Water, first of all,

and then rations. He thought of the Army bringing in supplies, and the Red Cross; he thought of small towns in the
country making their possessions available. Finally, what he
willed began reluctantly to come to pass, and he remained
where he was a long time, getting it to be. Things improved.
The people found treatment for burns; he saw to that. He saw,
too, to the healing of their great fear; that was important. He
saw to the first glimmerings of their getting themselves established once more, in at least a rudimentary way.

But curiously, at the same time that he devoted himself to
improving their condition, he noticed to his surprise and
shock that his own had deteriorated. He had lost everything in
the service of the general welfare, because now his clothes
were in rags, like sacks. His toes poked through his shoes. On
his face a ragged beard hung down; a mustache had grown
over his mouth, and his hair fell all the way over his ears and
brushed his torn collar, and his teeth—even his teeth—were
gone. He felt old and sick and empty, but nonetheless it was
worth it. How long had he stood here, doing this job? The
streams of cars had long since ceased. Only damaged, abandoned wrecks of autos lay along the freeway to his right. Had
it been weeks? Possibly months. He felt hungry, and his legs
trembled with the cold. So once more he began to walk.

I gave them everything I had, he told himself, and thinking
that he felt a little resentment, more than a trace of anger.
What did I get back? I need a haircut and a meal and medical
attention; I need a few things myself. Where can I get them?
Now, he thought, I'm too tired to walk to Marin County; I'll
have to stay here, on this side of the Bay, for a while, until I can
rest up and get my strength back. His resentment grew as he
walked slowly along.

But anyhow he had done his job. He saw, not far ahead, a
first aid station with rows of dingy tents; he saw women with
armbands and knew they were nurses. He saw men with metal
helmets carrying guns. Law and order, he realized. Because of
my efforts it's being reëstablished, here and there. They owe
me a lot, but of course they don't acknowledge it. I'll let it
pass, he decided.

When he reached the first dingy tent, one of the men
with guns stopped him. Another man, carrying a clipboard,

approached. "Where are you from?" the man with the clipboard asked.

"From Berkeley," he answered.

"Name."

"Mr. Jack Tree."

They wrote that down, then tore off a card and handed it to him. It had a number on it, and the two men explained that he should keep the number because without it he could not obtain food rations. Then he was told that if he tried—or had tried—to collect rations at another relief station he would be shot. The two men then walked off, leaving him standing there with his numbered card in his hand.

Should I tell them that I did all this? he wondered. That I'm solely responsible, and eternally damned for my dreadful sin in bringing this about? No, he decided, because if I do they'll take my card back; I won't get any food ration. And he was terribly, terribly hungry.

Now one of the nurses approached him and in a matter of fact voice said, "Any vomiting, dizziness, change of color of the stool?"

"No," he said.

"Any superficial burns which have failed to heal?"

He shook his head no.

"Go over there," the nurse said, pointing, "and get rid of your clothing. They'll delouse you and shave your head, and you can get your shots there. We're out of the typhoid serum so don't ask for that."

To his bewilderment he saw a man with an electric razor powered by a gasoline generator shaving the heads of men and women both; the people waited patiently in line. A sanitary measure? he wondered.

I thought I had fixed that, he thought. Or did I forget about disease. Evidently I did. He began to walk in that direction, bewildered by his failure to have taken everything into account. I must have left out a variety of vital things, he realized as he joined the line of people waiting to have their heads shaved.

In the ruins of a cement basement of a house on Cedar Street in the Berkeley hills, Stuart McConchie spied something fat and gray that hopped from one split block and behind the next. He picked up his broom handle—one end came to a cracked, elongated point—and wriggled forward.

The man with him in the basement, a sallow, lean man named Ken, who was dying of radiation exposure, said, "You're not going to eat that."

"Sure I am," Stuart said, wriggling through the dust which had settled into the open, exposed basement until he lay against the split block of cement. The rat, aware of him, squeaked with fear. It had come up from the Berkeley sewer and now it wanted to get back. But he was between it and the sewer; or rather, he thought, between her and the sewer. It was no doubt a big female. The males were skinnier.

The rat scurried in fright, and Stuart drove the sharp end of the stick into it. Again it squeaked, long and sufferingly. On the end of the stick it was still alive; it kept on squeaking. So he held it against the ground, held the stick down, and crushed its head with his foot.

"At least," the dying man with him said, "you can cook it."

"No," Stuart said, and, seating himself, got out the pocket knife which he had found—it had been in the pants pocket of a dead school boy—and began skinning the rat. While the dying man watched with disapproval, Stuart ate the dead, raw rat.

"I'm surprised you don't eat me," the man said, afterward.

"It's no worse than eating raw shrimp," Stuart said. He felt much better now; it was his first food in days.

"Why don't you go looking for one of those relief stations that helicopter was talking about when it flew by yesterday?" the dying man said. "It said—or I understood it to say—that there's a station over near the Hillside Grammar School. That's only a few blocks from here; you could get that far."

"No," Stuart said.

"Why not?"

The answer, although he did not want to say it, was simply that he was afraid to venture out of the basement onto the street. He did not know why, except that there were things moving in the settling ash which he could not identify; he believed they were Americans but possibly they were Chinese or Russians. Their voices sounded strange and echoey, even in daytime. And the helicopter, too; he was not certain about that. It could have been an enemy trick to induce people to come out and be shot. In any case he still heard gunfire from the flat part of the city; the dim sounds started before the sun rose and occurred intermittently until nightfall.

"You can't stay here forever," Ken said. "It isn't rational." He lay wrapped up in the blankets which had belonged to one of the beds in the house; the bed had been hurled from the house as the house disintegrated, and Stuart and the dying man had found it in the backyard. Its neatly tucked in covers had been still on it, all in place including its two duck-feather pillows.

What Stuart was thinking was that in five days he had collected thousands of dollars in money from the pockets of dead people he had found in the ruins of houses along Cedar Street—from their pockets and from the houses themselves. Other scavengers had been after food and different objects such as knives and guns, and it made him uneasy that he alone wanted money. He felt, now, that if he stirred forth, if he reached a relief station, he would discover the truth: the money was worthless. And if it was, he was a horse's ass for collecting it, and when he showed up at the relief station carrying a pillowcase full of it, everyone would jeer at him and rightly so, because a horse's ass deserved to be jeered at.

And also, no one else seemed to be eating rats. Perhaps there was a superior food available of which he knew nothing; it sounded like him, down here eating something everyone else had discarded. Maybe there were cans of emergency rations being dropped from the air; maybe the cans came down early in the morning while he was still asleep and got all picked up before he had a chance to see them. He had had for several days now a deep and growing dread that he was missing out, that something free was being dispensed—perhaps in broad daylight—to everyone but him. Just my luck, he said to himself, and he felt glum and bitter, and the rat, which he had just eaten, no longer seemed a surfeit, as before.

Hiding, these last few days, down in the ruined cement basement of the house on Cedar Street, Stuart had had a good deal of time to think about himself, and he had realized that it had always been hard for him to make out what other people were doing; it had only been by the greatest effort that he had managed to act as they acted, appear like them. It had nothing to do, either, with his being a Negro because he had the same problem with black people as with white. It was not a social difficulty in the usual sense; it went deeper than that. For instance, Ken, the dying man lying opposite him. Stuart could not understand him; he felt cut off from him. Maybe that was because Ken was dying and he was not. Maybe that set up a barrier; the world was clearly divided into two new camps now: people who were getting weaker with each passing moment, who were perishing, and people like himself, who were going to make it. There was no possibility of communication between them because their worlds were too different.

And yet that was not it only, between himself and Ken; there was still more, the same old problem that the bomb attack had not created but merely brought to the surface. Now the gulf was wider; it was obvious that he did not actually comprehend the meaning of most activities conducted around him . . . he had been brooding, for instance, about the yearly trip to the Department of Motor Vehicles for his auto license renewal. As he lay in the basement it seemed to him more clearly each moment that the other people had gone to the Department of Motor Vehicles office over on Sacramento Street for a *good reason*, but he had gone because they had gone; he had, like a little kid, merely tagged along. And now there was no one present to tag after; now he was alone. And therefore he could not think up any action to follow, he could not make any decision or follow any plan for the life of him.

So he simply waited, and as he waited, wondered about the 'copter which flew overhead now and then and about the vague shapes in the street, and more than anything else if he was a horse's ass or not.

And then, all at once, he thought of something; he remembered what Hoppy Harrington had seen in his vision at Fred's Fine Foods. Hoppy had seen him, Stuart McConchie, eating rats, but in the excitement and fear of all that had happened since, Stuart had forgotten. This now was what the phoce had seen; this was the vision—not the afterlife at all!

God damn that little crippled freak, Stuart thought to himself as he lay picking his teeth with a piece of wire. He was a fraud; he put something over on us.

Amazing how gullible people are, he said to himself. We believed him, maybe because he's so peculiarly built anyhow . . . it seemed more credible with him being like he is—or was. He's probably dead now, buried down in the service department. Well, that's one good thing this war has done: wiped out all the freaks. But then, he realized, it's also brewed up a whole new batch of them; there'll be freaks strutting around for the next million years. It'll be Bluthgeld's paradise; in fact he's probably quite happy right now—because this was really bomb testing.

Ken stirred and murmured, "Could you be induced to crawl across the street? There's that corpse there and it might have cigarettes on it."

Cigarettes, hell, Stuart thought. It probably has a walletful of money. He followed the dying man's gaze and saw, sure enough, the corpse of a woman lying among the rubble on the far side. His pulse raced, because he could see a bulging handbag still clutched.

In a weary voice Ken said, "Leave the money, Stuart. It's an obsession with you, a symbol of God knows what." As Stuart crawled out from the basement Ken raised his voice to call, "A symbol of the opulent society." He coughed, retched. "And that's gone now," he managed to add.

Up yours, Stuart thought as he crawled on across the street to the purse lying there. Sure enough, when he opened it he found a wad of bills, ones and fives and even a twenty. There was also a U-No candy bar in the purse, and he got that, too. But as he crawled back to the basement it occurred to him that the candy bar might be radioactive, so he tossed it away.

"The cigarettes?" Ken asked, when he returned.

"None." Stuart opened the pillow case, which was buried up to its throat in the dry ash which had filled the basement; he stuffed the bills in with the others and tied the pillow case shut again.

"How about a game of chess?" Ken propped himself up weakly, opened the wooden box of chessmen which he and Stuart had found in the wreckage of the house. Already, he had managed to teach Stuart the rudiments of the game; before the war Stuart had never played.

"Naw," Stuart said. He was watching, far off in the gray sky, the moving shape of some plane or rocket ship, a cylinder. God, he thought, could it be a bomb? Dismally, he watched it sink lower and lower; he did not even lie down, did not seek to hide as he had done that first time, in the initial few minutes on which so much—their being alive now—had depended. "What's that?" he asked.

The dying man scrutinized it. "It's a balloon."

Not believing him, Stuart said, "It's the Chinese!"

"It really is a balloon, a little one. What they used to call a blimp, I think. I haven't seen one since I was a boy."

"Could the Chinese float across the Pacific in balloons?" Stuart said, imagining thousands of such small gray cigar-shaped balloons, each with a platoon of Mongolian-type Chinese peasant soldiers, armed with Czech automatic rifles, clutching handholds, clinging to every fold. "It's just what you'd expect them to think up from the beginning; they reduce the world to their level, back a couple centuries. Instead of catching up with us—" He broke off, because now he saw that the balloon had on its side a sign in English:

HAMILTON AIR FORCE BASE

The dying man said drily, "It's one of ours."

"I wonder where they got it," Stuart said.

"Ingenious," the dying man said, "isn't it? I suppose all the gasoline and kerosene are gone by now. Used right up. We'll be seeing a lot of strange transportation from now on. Or rather, you will."

"Stop feeling sorry for yourself," Stuart said.

"I don't feel sorry for myself or anyone," the dying man said as he carefully laid out the chess pieces. "This is a nice set," he said. "Made in Mexico, I notice. Hand-carved, no doubt . . . but very fragile."

"Explain to me again how the bishop moves," Stuart said.

Overhead, the Hamilton Air Force Base balloon loomed larger as it drifted closer. The two men in the basement bent over their chess board, paying no attention to it. Possibly it was taking pictures. Or possibly it was on a strategic mission; it might have a walkie-talkie aboard and was in contact with the Sixth Army units south of San Francisco. Who knew? Who cared? The balloon drifted by as the dying man advanced his king's pawn two spaces to open the game.

"The game begins," the dying man said. And then he added in a low voice, "For you, anyhow, Stuart. A strange, unfamiliar, new game ahead . . . you can even bet your pillow case of money, if you want."

Grunting, Stuart pondered his own men and decided to move a rook's pawn as his opening gambit—and knew, as soon as he had touched it, that it was an idiotic move.

"Can I take it back?" he asked hopefully.

"When you touch a piece you must move it," Ken said, bringing out one of his knights.

"I don't think that's fair; I mean, I'm just learning," Stuart said. He glared at the dying man, but the sallow face was adamant. "Okay," he said resignedly, this time moving his king's pawn, as Ken had done. I'll watch his moves and do what he does, he decided. That way I'll be safer.

From the balloon, now directly overhead, bits of white paper scattered, drifted and fluttered down. Stuart and the dying man paused in their game. One of the bits of paper fell near them in the basement and Ken reached out and picked it up. He read it, passed it to Stuart.

"Burlingame!" Stuart said, reading it. It was an appeal for volunteers, for the Army. "They want us to hike from here to *Burlingame* and be inducted? That's fifty or sixty miles, all the way down this side of the Bay and around. They're nuts!"

"They are," Ken said. "They won't get a soul."

"Why hell, I can't even make it down to LeConte Street to the relief station," Stuart said. He felt indignant and he glared at the Hamilton Field balloon as it drifted on. They're not going to get me to join up, he said to himself. Fork that.

"It says," Ken said, reading the back of the proclamation, "that if you reach Burlingame they guarantee you water, food, cigarettes, anti-plague shots, treatment for radiation burns. How about that? But no girls."

"Can you get interested in sex?" He was amazed. "Christ, I haven't felt the slightest urge since the first bomb fell; it's like the thing dropped off in fear, fell right off."

"That's because the diencephalic center of the brain suppresses the sex instinct in the face of danger," Ken said. "But it'll return."

"No," Stuart said, "because any child born would be a freak; there shouldn't be any intercourse for say around ten years. They ought to make it a law. I can't stand the idea of the world populated by freaks because I have had personal experience; one worked at Modern TV Sales with me, or rather in the service department. One was enough. I mean, they ought to hang that Bluthgeld up by his balls for what he did."

"What Bluthgeld did in the '70s," Ken said, "is insignificant when compared to this." He indicated the ruins of the basement around them.

"I'll grant you that," Stuart said, "but it was the start."

Overhead, now, the balloon was drifting back the way it had come. Perhaps it had run out of little messages and was returning to Hamilton Field, over on the other side of the Bay or wherever it was.

Gazing up at it, Stuart said, "Talk to us some more."

"It can't," Ken said. "That's all it had to say; it's a very simple creature. Are you going to play, or should I move your pieces? Either is satisfactory to me."

With great caution, Stuart moved a bishop—and again knew at once that it had been the wrong move; he could tell by the dying man's face.

In the corner of the basement, among the cement blocks, something agile and frightened plopped to safety, scurried and twittered with anxiety as it spied them. Stuart's attention wandered from the board to the rat, and he looked about for his broom handle.

"Play!" Ken said angrily.

"Okay, okay," Stuart said, feeling grumpy about it. He made a random move, his attention still on the rat.

VII

IN front of the pharmacy in Point Reyes Station, at nine in the morning, Eldon Blaine waited. Under his arm he held tightly his worn briefcase tied together with string. Meanwhile, inside the building, the pharmacist removed chains and struggled with the metal doors; Eldon listened to the sound and felt impatience.

"Just a minute," the pharmacist called, his voice muffled. As he at last got the doors open he apologized, "This was formerly the back end of a truck. You have to use both your hands and feet to make it work. Come on in, mister." He held the high door aside, and Eldon saw into the dark interior of the pharmacy, with its unlit electric light bulb which hung from the ceiling by an ancient cord.

"What I'm here for," Eldon said rapidly, "is a wide-spectrum antibiotic, the kind used in clearing up a respiratory infection." He made his need sound casual; he did not tell the pharmacist how many towns in Northern California he had visited in the last few days, walking and hitching rides, nor did he mention how sick his daughter was. It would only jack up the price asked, he knew. And anyhow he did not see much actual stock, here. Probably the man did not have it.

Eying him, the pharmacist said, "I don't see anything with you; what do you have in exchange, assuming I have what you're after?" In a nervous manner he smoothed his thinning gray hair back; he was an elderly, small man, and it was obvious that he suspected Eldon of being a napper. Probably he suspected everyone.

Eldon said, "Where I come from I'm known as the glasses man." Unzipping his briefcase, he showed the pharmacist the rows of intact and nearly-intact lenses, frames, and lenses in frames, scavenged from all over the Bay Area, especially from the great deposits near Oakland. "I can compensate almost any eye defect," he said. "I've got a fine variety, here. What are you, near- or far-sighted or astigmatic? I can fix you up in ten minutes, by changing around a lens or two."

"Far-sighted," the pharmacist said slowly, "but I don't think

I have what *you* want." He looked at the rows of glasses longingly.

With anger, Eldon said, "Then why didn't you say so right off, so I can go on? I want to make Petaluma today; there's a lot of drugstores there—all I have to do is find a hay truck going that way."

"Couldn't you trade me a pair of glasses for something else?" the pharmacist asked plaintively, following after him as he started away. "I got a valuable heart medicine, quinidine gluconate; you could most likely trade it for what you want. Nobody else in Marin County has quinidine gluconate but me."

"Is there a doctor around here?" Eldon said, pausing at the edge of the weed-infested county road with its several stores and houses.

"Yes," the pharmacist said, with a nod of pride. "Doctor Stockstill; he migrated here several years ago. But he doesn't have any drugs. Just me."

Briefcase under his arm, Eldon Blaine walked on along the county road, listening hopefully for the pop-popping noise of the wood-burning truck motor rising out of the stillness of the early-morning California countryside. But the sound faded. The truck, alas, was going the other way.

This region, directly north of San Francisco, had once been owned by a few wealthy dairy ranchers; cows had cropped in these fields, but that was gone now, along with the meat-animals, the steer and sheep. As everyone knew, an acre of land could function better as a source of grains or vegetables. Around him now he saw closely-planted rows of corn, an early-ripening hybrid, and between the rows, great hairy squash plants on which odd yellow squash like bowling balls grew. This was an unusual eastern squash which could be eaten skin and seeds and all; once it had been disdained in California valleys . . . but that was changed, now.

Ahead, a little group of children ran across the little-used road on their way to school; Eldon Blaine saw their tattered books and lunch pails, heard their voices, thought to himself how calming this was, other children well and busy, unlike his own child. If Gwen died, others would replace her. He accepted that unemotionally. One learned how. One had to.

The school, off to the right in the saddle of two hills: most of it the remains of a single-story modern building, put up no doubt just before the war by ambitious, public-spirited citizens who had bonded themselves into a decade of indebtedness without guessing that they would not live to make payment. Thus they had, without intending it, gotten their grammar school free.

Its windows made him laugh. Salvaged from every variety of old rural building, the windows were first tiny, then huge, with ornate boards holding them in place. Of course the original windows had been blown instantly out. Glass, he thought. So rare these days . . . if you own glass in any form you are rich. He gripped his briefcase tighter as he walked.

Several of the children, seeing a strange man, stopped to peer at him with anxiety augmented by curiosity. He grinned at them, wondering to himself what they were studying and what teachers they had. An ancient senile old lady, drawn out of retirement, to sit once more behind a desk? A local man who happened to hold a college degree? Or most likely some of the mothers themselves, banded together, using a precious armload of books from the local library.

A voice from behind him called; it was a woman, and as he turned he heard the squeak-squeak of a bicycle. "Are you the glasses man?" she called again, severe and yet attractive, with dark hair, wearing a man's cotton shirt and jeans, pedaling along the road after him, bouncing up and down with each rut. "Please stop. I was talking to Fred Quinn our druggist just now and he said you were by." She reached him, stopped her bicycle, panting for breath. "There hasn't been a glasses man by here in months; why don't you come oftener?"

Eldon Blaine said, "I'm not here selling; I'm here trying to pick up some antibiotics." He felt irritated. "I have to get to Petaluma," he said, and then he realized that he was gazing at her bike with envy; he knew it showed on his face.

"We can get them for you," the woman said. She was older than he had first thought; her face was lined and a little dark, and he guessed that she was almost forty. "I'm on the Planning Committee for everyone, here in West Marin; I know we can scare up what you need, if you'll just come back with me

and wait. Give us two hours. We need several pairs . . . I'm
not going to let you go." Her voice was firm, not coaxing.

"You're not Mrs. Raub, are you?" Eldon Blaine asked.

"Yes," she said. "You recognized me—how?"

He said, "I'm from the Bolinas area; we know all about
what you're doing up here. I wish we had someone like you on
our Committee." He felt a little afraid of her. Mrs. Raub
always got her own way, he had heard. She and Larry Raub
had organized West Marin after the Cooling-off; before, in the
old days, she had not amounted to anything and the Emergency had given her her chance, as it had many people, to
show what she was really made of.

As they walked back together, Mrs. Raub said, "Who are
the antibiotics for? Not yourself; you look perfectly healthy
to me."

"My little girl is dying," he said.

She did not waste sympathetic words; there were none left
in the world, any more—she merely nodded. "Infectious hepatitis?" she asked. "How's your water supply? Do you have a
chlorinator? If not—"

"No, it's like strep throat," he said.

"We heard from the satellite last night that some German
drug firms are in operation again, and so if we're lucky we'll be
seeing German drugs back on the market, at least on the East
Coast."

"You get the satellite?" Excitedly, he said, "Our radio went
dead, and our handy is down somewhere near South San Francisco, scavenging for refrigeration parts and won't be back
probably for another month. Tell me; what's he reading now?
The last time we picked him up, it was so darn long ago—he
was on Pascal's *Provincial Letters.*"

Mrs. Raub said, "Dangerfield is now reading *Of Human
Bondage.*"

"Isn't that about that fellow who couldn't shake off that girl
he met?" Eldon said. "I think I remember it from the previous
time he read it, several years ago. She kept coming back into
his life. Didn't she finally ruin his life, in the end?"

"I don't know; I'm afraid we didn't pick it up the previous
time."

"That Dangerfield is really a great disc jockey," Eldon said, "the best I've ever heard even *before* the Emergency. I mean, we never miss him; we generally get a turnout of two hundred people every night at our fire station. I think one of us could fix that damn radio, but our Committee ruled that we had to let it alone and wait until the handy's back. If he ever is . . . the last one disappeared on a scavenging trip."

Mrs. Raub said, "Now perhaps your community understands the need of standby equipment, which I've always said is essential."

"Could—we send a representative up to listen with your group and report back to us?"

"Of course," Mrs. Raub said. "But—"

"It wouldn't be the same," he agreed. "It's not—" He gestured. What was it about Dangerfield, stitting up there above them in the satellite as it passed over them each day? Contact with the world . . . Dangerfield looked down and saw everything, the rebuilding, all the changes both good and bad; he monitored every broadcast, recording and preserving and then playing back, so that through him they were joined.

In his mind, the familiar voice now gone so long from their community—he could summon it still, hear the rich low chuckle, the earnest tones, the intimacy, and never anything phony. No slogans, no Fourth-of-July expostulations, none of the stuff that had gotten them all where they were now.

Once he had heard Dangerfield say, "Want to know the real reason I wasn't in the war? Why they carefully shot me off into space a little bit in advance? They knew better than to give me a gun . . . I would have shot an officer." And he had chuckled, making it a joke; but it was true, what he said, everything he told them was true, even when it was made funny. Dangerfield hadn't been politically reliable, and yet now he sat up above them passing over their heads year in, year out. And he was a man they believed.

Set on the side of a ridge, the Raub house overlooked West Marin County, with its vegetable fields and irrigation ditches, an occasional goat staked out, and of course the horses; standing at the living room window, Eldon Blaine saw below him, near a farmhouse, a great Percheron which no doubt pulled a plow . . . pulled, too, an engineless automobile along the road to Sonoma County when it was time to pick up supplies.

He saw now a horse-car moving along the county road; it would have picked him up if Mrs. Raub hadn't found him first, and he would have soon reached Petaluma.

Down the hillside below him pedaled Mrs. Raub on her way to find him his antibiotics; to his amazement she had left him alone in her house, free to nap everything in sight, and now he turned to see what there was. Chairs, books, in the kitchen, food and even a bottle of wine, clothes in all the closets—he roamed about the house, savoring everything; it was almost like before the war, except that of course the useless electrical appliances had been thrown out long ago.

Through the back windows of the house he saw the green wooden side of a large water-storage tank. The Raubs, he realized, had their own supply of water. Going outside he saw a clear, untainted stream.

At the stream a kind of contraption lurked, like a cart on wheels. He stared at it; extensions from it were busily filling buckets with water. In the center of it sat a man with no arms or legs. The man nodded his head as if conducting music, and the machinery around him responded. It was a phocomelus, Eldon realized, mounted on his phocomobile, his combination cart and manual grippers which served as mechanical substitutes for his missing limbs. What was he doing, stealing the Raubs' water?

"Hey," Eldon said.

At once the phocomelus turned his head; his eyes blazed at Eldon in alarm, and then something whacked into Eldon's middle—he was thrown back, and as he wobbled and struggled to regain his balance he discovered that his arms were pinned at his sides. A wire mesh had whipped out at him from the phocomobile, had fastened in place. The phocomelus' means of defense.

"Who are you?" the phocomelus said, stammering in his wary eagerness to know. "You don't live around here; I don't know you."

"I'm from Bolinas," Eldon said. The metal mesh crushed in until he gasped. "I'm the glasses man. Mrs. Raub, she told me to wait here."

Now the mesh seemed to ease. "I can't take chances," the phocomelus said. "I won't let you go until June Raub comes back." The buckets once more began dipping in the water; they filled methodically until the tank lashed to the phocomobile was slopping over.

"Are you supposed to be doing that?" Eldon asked. "Taking water from the Raubs' stream?"

"I've got a right," the phocomelus said. "I give back more than I take, to everybody around here."

"Let me go," Eldon said. "I'm just trying to get medicine for my kid; she's dying."

" 'My kid, she's dying,' " the phocomelus mimicked, picking up the quality of his voice with startling accuracy. He rolled away from the stream, now, closer to Eldon. The 'mobile gleamed; all its parts were new-looking and shiny. It was one of the best-made mechanical constructions that Eldon Blaine had ever seen.

"Let me go," Eldon said, "and I'll give you a pair of glasses free. Any pair I have."

"My eyes are perfect," the phocomelus said. "Everything about me is perfect. Parts are missing, but I don't need them; I can do better without them. I can get down this hill faster than you, for instance."

"Who built your 'mobile?" Eldon asked. Surely in seven years it would have become tarnished and partly broken, like everything else.

"I built it," the phocomelus said.

"How can you build your own 'mobile? That's a contradiction."

"I used to be body-wired. Now I'm brain-wired; I did that myself, too. I'm the handy, up here. Those old extensors the Government built before the war—they weren't even as good as the flesh things, like you have." The phocomelus grimaced. He had a thin, flexible face, with a sharp nose and extremely white teeth, a face ideal for the emotion which he now showed Eldon Blaine.

"Dangerfield says that the handies are the most valuable

people in the world," Eldon said. "He declared Worldwide Handyman Week, one time we were listening, and he named different handies who were especially well-known. What's your name? Maybe he mentioned you."

"Hoppy Harrington," the phocomelus said. "But I know he didn't mention me because I keep myself in the background, still; it isn't time for me to make my name in the world, as I'm going to be doing. I let the local people see a little of what I can do, but they're supposed to be quiet about it."

"Sure they'd be quiet," Eldon said. "They don't want to lose you. We're missing our handy, right now, and we really feel it. Could you take on the Bolinas area for a little while, do you think? We've got plenty to trade you. In the Emergency hardly anybody got over the mountain to invade us, so we're relatively untouched."

"I've been down there to Bolinas," Hoppy Harrington said. "In fact I've traveled all around, even as far inland as Sacramento. Nobody has seen what I've seen; I can cover *fifty miles a day* in my 'mobile." His lean face twitched and then he stammered, "I wouldn't go back to Bolinas because there are sea monsters in the ocean, there."

"Who says so?" Eldon demanded. "That's just superstition —tell me who said that about our community."

"I think it was Dangerfield."

"No, he couldn't," Eldon said. "He can be relied on, he wouldn't peddle such trash as that. I never once heard him tell a superstition on any of his programs. Maybe he was kidding; I bet he was kidding and you took him seriously."

"The hydrogen bombs woke up the sea monsters," Hoppy said, "From their slumber in the depths." He nodded earnestly.

"You come and see our community," Eldon said. 'We're orderly and advanced, a lot more so than any city. We even have streetlights going again, four of them for an hour in the evening. I'm surprised a handy would believe such superstition."

The phocomelus looked chagrined. "You never can be sure," he murmured. "I guess maybe it wasn't Dangerfield I heard it from."

Below them, on the ascending road, a horse moved; the sound of its hoofs reached them and they both turned. A big fleshy man with a red face came riding up and up, toward them, peering at them. As he rode he called, "Glasses man! Is that you?"

"Yes," Eldon said, as the horse veered into the grass-extinguished driveway of the Raub house. "You have the antibiotics, mister?"

"June Raub will bring them," the big florid man said, reining his horse to a stop. "Glasses man, let's see what you have. I'm near-sighted but I also have an acute astigmatism in my left eye; can you help me?" He approached on foot, still peering.

"I can't fit you," Eldon said, "because Hoppy Harrington has me tied up."

"For God's sake, Hoppy," the big florid man said with agitation. "Let the glasses man go so he can fit me; I've been waiting months and I don't mean to wait any longer."

"Okay, Leroy," Hoppy Harrington said sullenly. And, from around Eldon, the metal mesh uncoiled and then slithered back across the ground to the waiting phocomelus in the center of his shiny, intricate 'mobile.

As the satellite passed over the Chicago area its wing-like extended sensors picked up a flea signal, and in his earphones Walter Dangerfield heard the faint, distant, hollowed-out voice from below.

". . . and please play 'Waltzing Matilda,' a lot of us like that. And play 'The Woodpecker Song.' And—" The flea signal faded out, and he heard only static. It had definitely not been a laser beam, he thought to himself archly.

Into his microphone, Dangerfield said, "Well, friends, we have a request here for 'Waltzing Matilda.'" He reached to snap a switch at the controls of a tape transport. "The great bass-baritone Peter Dawson—which is also the name of a very good brand of Scotch—in 'Waltzing Matilda.'" From well-worn memory he selected the correct reel of tape, and in a moment it was on the transport, turning.

As the music played, Walt Dangerfield tuned his receiving equipment, hoping once more to pick up the same flea signal. However, instead he found himself party to a two-way transmission between military units involved in police action somewhere in upstate Illinois. Their brisk chatter interested him, and he listened until the end of the music.

"Lots of luck to you boys in uniform," he said into the microphone, then. "Catch those boodle-burners and bless you all." He chuckled, because if ever a human being had immunity from retaliation, it was he. No one on Earth could reach him—it had been attempted six times since the Emergency, with no success. "Catch those bad guys . . . or should I say catch those *good* guys. Say, who are the good guys, these days?" His receiving equipment had picked up, in the last few weeks, a number of complaints about Army brutality. "Now let me tell you something, boys," he said smoothly. "Watch out for those squirrel rifles; that's all." He began hunting through the satellite's tape library for the recording of "The Woodpecker Song." "That's all, brother," he said, and put on the tape.

Below him the world was in darkness, its night side turned his way; yet already he could see the rim of day appearing on the edge, and soon he would be passing into that once more. Lights here and there glowed like holes poked in the surface of the planet which he had left seven years ago—left for another purpose, another goal entirely. A much more noble one.

His was not the sole satellite still circling Earth, but it was the sole one with life aboard. Everyone else had long since perished. But they had not been outfitted as he and Lydia had been, for a decade of life on another world. He was lucky: besides food and water and air he had a million miles of video and audio tape to keep him amused. And now, with it, he kept *them* amused, the remnants of the civilization which had shot him up here in the first place. They had botched the job of getting him to Mars—fortunately for them. Their failure had paid them vital dividends ever since.

"Hoode hoode hoo," Walt Dangerfield chanted into his microphone, using the transmitter which should have carried his voice back from millions of miles, not merely a couple hundred. "Things you can do with the timer out of an old R.C.A. washer-dryer combination. This item arrives from a handy in the Geneva area; thanks to you, Georg Schilper—I know everyone will be pleased to hear you give this timely tip in your own words." He played into his transmitter the tape recording

of the handyman himself speaking; the entire Great Lakes region of the United States would now know Georg Schilper's
bit of lore, and would no doubt wisely apply it at once. The
world hungered for the knowledge tucked away in pockets
here and there, knowledge which—without Dangerfield—
would be confined to its point of origin, perhaps forever.

After the tape of Georg Schilper he put on his canned
reading from *Of Human Bondage* and rose stiffly from his seat.

There was a pain in his chest which worried him; it had appeared one day, located beneath his breastbone, and now for
the hundredth time he got down one of the microfilms of
medical information and began scanning the section dealing
with the heart. Does it feel like the heel of a hand squeezing
my breath out of me? he asked himself. Someone pushing down
with all his weight? It was difficult to recall what "weight" felt
like in the first place. Or does it merely burn . . . and if so,
when? Before meals or after?

Last week he had made contact with a hospital in Tokyo,
had described his symptoms. The doctors were not sure what
to tell him. What you need, they had said, is an electrocardiogram, but how could he give himself a test like that up here?
How could anyone, any more? The Japanese doctors were
living in the past, or else there had been more of a revival in
Japan than he realized; than anyone realized.

Amazing, he thought suddenly, that I've survived so long.
It did not seem long, though, because his time-sense had
become faulty. And he was a busy man; at this moment, six of
his tape recorders monitored six much-used frequencies, and
before the reading from the Maugham book had ended he
would be obliged to play them back. They might contain
nothing or they might contain hours of meaningful talk. One
never knew. If only, he thought, I had been able to make use
of the high-speed transmission . . . but the proper decoders
were no longer in existence, below. Hours could have been
compressed into seconds, and he could have given each area
in turn a complete account. As it was, he had to dole it out
in small clusters, with much repetition. Sometimes it took
months to read through a single novel, this way.

But at least he had been able to lower the frequency on

which the satellite's transmitter broadcast to a band which the people below could receive on a common AM radio. That had been his one big achievement; that, by itself, had made him into what he was.

The reading of the Maugham book ended, then automatically restarted itself; it droned from the start once more for the next area below. Walt Dangerfield ignored it and continued to consult his medical reference microfilms. I think it's only spasms of the pyloric valve, he decided. If I had phenobarbital here . . . but it had been used up several years ago; his wife, in her last great suicidal depression, had consumed it all —consumed it and then taken her life anyhow. It had been the abrupt silence of the Soviet space station, oddly enough, that had started her depression; up until then she had believed that they would all be reached and brought safely back down to the surface. The Russians have starved to death, all ten of them, but no one had foreseen it because they had kept up their duty-oriented line of scientific patter right into the last few hours.

"Hoode hoode hoo," Dangerfield said to himself as he read about the pyloric valve and its spasms. "Folks," he murmured. "I have this funny pain brought on by over-indulgence . . . what I need is four-way relief, don't you agree?" He snapped on his microphone, cutting out the tape-in-progress. "Remember those old ads?" he asked his darkened, unseen audience below. "Before the war—let's see, how did they go? Are you building more H-bombs but enjoying it less?" He chuckled. "Has thermonuclear war got you down? New York, can you pick me up, yet? I want every one of you within the reach of my voice, all sixty-five of you, to quick light up a match so I'll know you're there."

In his earphones a loud signal came in. "Dangerfield, this is the New York Port Authority; can you give us any idea of the weather?"

"Oh," Dangerfield said, "we've got *fine* weather coming. You can put out to sea in those little boats and catch those little radioactive fish; nothing to worry about."

Another voice, fainter, came in now. "Mr. Dangerfield, could you possibly please play some of those opera arias you have? We'd especially appreciate 'Thy Tiny Hand is Frozen' from *La Bohème*."

"Heck, I can *sing* that," Dangerfield said, reaching for the tape as he hummed tenorishly into the microphone.

Returning to Bolinas that night, Eldon Blaine fed the first of the antibiotics to his child and then quickly drew his wife aside. "Listen, they have a top-notch handy up in West Marin which they've been keeping quiet about, and only twenty miles from here. I think we should send a delegation up there to nap him and bring him down here." He added, "He's a phoce and you should see the 'mobile he built for himself; none of the handies we've had could do anything half that good." Putting his wool jacket back on he went to the door of their room. "I'm going to ask the Committee to vote on it."

"But our ordinance against funny people," Patricia protested. "And Mrs. Wallace is Chairman of the Committee this month; you know how she feels, she'd never let any more phoces come here and settle. I mean, we have four as it is and she's always complaining about them."

"That ordinance refers only to funny people who could become a financial burden to the community," Eldon said. "I ought to know; I helped draft it. Hoppy Harrington is no burden; he's an asset—the ordinance doesn't cover him, and I'm going to stand up to Mrs. Wallace and fight it out. I know I can get official permission; I've got it all worked out how we'll do the napping. They invited us to come up to their area and listen to the satellite, and we'll do that; we'll show up but not just to listen to Dangerfield. While they're involved in that we'll nap Hoppy; we'll put his phocomobile out of action and haul him down here, and they'll never know what happened. Finders keepers, losers weepers. And our police force will protect us."

Patricia said, "I'm scared of phoces. They have peculiar powers, not natural ones; everybody knows it. He probably built his 'mobile by means of magic."

Laughing with derision, Eldon Blaine said, "So much the better. Maybe that's what we need: magic spells, a community magician. I'm all for it."

"I'm going to see how Gwen is," Patricia said, starting

toward the screened-off portion of the room where their child lay on her cot. "I won't have any part of this; I think it's dreadful, what you're doing."

Eldon Blaine stepped from the room, out into the night darkness. In a moment he was striding down the path toward the Wallaces' house.

As the citizens of West Marin County one by one entered the Foresters' Hall and seated themselves, June Raub adjusted the variable condenser of the twelve-volt car radio and noticed that once again Hoppy Harrington had not shown up to hear the satellite. What was it he had said? "*I don't like to listen to sick people.*" A strange thing to say, she thought to herself.

From the speaker of the radio static issued and then first faint beepings from the satellite. In a few more minutes they would be picking it up clearly . . . unless the wet-cell battery powering the radio chose to give out again, as it had briefly the other day.

The rows of seated people listened attentively as the initial words from Dangerfield began to emerge from the static. ". . . lice-type typhus is said to be breaking out in Washington up to the Canadian border," Dangerfield was saying. "So stay away from there, my friends. If this report is true it's a very bad sign indeed. Also, a report from Portland, Oregon, more on the cheerful side. Two ships have arrived from the Orient. That's welcome news, isn't it? Two big freighters, just plain packed with manufactured articles from little factories in Japan and China, according to what I hear."

The listening roomful of people stirred with excitement.

"And here's a household tip from a food consultant in Hawaii," Dangerfield said, but now his voice faded out; once more the listening people heard only static. June Raub turned up the volume, but it did no good. Disappointment showed clearly on all the faces in the room.

If Hoppy were here, she thought, he could tune it so much better than I can. Feeling nervous, she looked to her husband for support.

"Weather conditions," he said, from where he sat in the first row of chairs. "We just have to be patient."

But several people were glaring at her with hostility, as if it was her fault that the satellite had faded out. She made a gesture of helplessness.

The door of the Foresters' Hall opened and three men awkwardly entered. Two were strangers to her and the third was the glasses man. Ill-at-ease, they searched for seats, while everyone in the room turned to watch.

"Who are you fellows?" Mr. Spaulding, who operated the feed barn, said to them. "Did anyone say you could come in here?"

June Raub said, "I invited this delegation from Bolinas to make the trip up here and listen with us; their radio set is not working."

"Shhh," several people said, because once again the voice from the satellite could be heard.

". . . anyhow," Dangerfield was saying, "I get the pain mostly when I've been asleep and before I eat. It seems to go away when I eat, and that makes me suspect it's an ulcer, not my heart. So if any doctors are listening and they have access to a transmitter, maybe they can give me a buzz and let me know their opinion. I can give them more information, if it'll help them."

Astonished, June Raub listened as the man in the satellite went on to describe in greater and greater detail his medical complaint. Was this what Hoppy meant? she asked herself. Dangerfield had turned into a hypochondriac and no one had noticed the transition, except for Hoppy whose senses were extra acute. She shivered. That poor man up there, doomed to go around and around the Earth until at last, as with the Russians, his food or air gave out and he died.

And what will we do then? she asked herself. Without Dangerfield . . . how can we keep going?

VIII

ORION STROUD, Chairman of the West Marin school board, turned up the Coleman gasoline lantern so that the utility school room in the white glare became clearly lit, and all four members of the board could make out the new teacher.

"I'll put a few questions to him," Stroud said to the others. "First, this is Mr. Barnes and he comes from Oregon. He tells me he's a specialist in science and natural edibles. Right, Mr. Barnes?"

The new teacher, a short, young-looking man wearing a khaki shirt and work pants, nervously cleared his throat and said, "Yes, I am familiar with chemicals and plants and animal-life, especially whatever is found out in the woods such as berries and mushrooms."

"We've recently had bad luck with mushrooms," Mrs. Tallman said, the elderly lady who had been a member of the board even in the old days before the Emergency. "It's been our tendency to leave them alone; we've lost several people either because they were greedy or careless or just plain ignorant."

Stroud said, "But Mr. Barnes here isn't ignorant. He went to the University at Davis, and they taught him how to tell a good mushroom from the poisonous ones. He doesn't guess or pretend; right, Mr. Barnes?" He looked to the new teacher for confirmation.

"There are species which are nutritious and about which you can't go wrong," Mr. Barnes said, nodding. "I've looked through the pastures and woods in your area, and I've seen some fine examples; you can supplement your diet without taking any chances. I even know the Latin names."

The board stirred and murmured. That had impressed them, Stroud realized, that about the Latin names.

"Why did you leave Oregon?" George Keller, the principal, asked bluntly.

The new teacher faced him and said, "Politics."

"Yours or theirs?"

"Theirs," Barnes said. "I have no politics. I teach children how to make ink and soap and how to cut the tails from lambs even if the lambs are almost grown. And I've got my own books." He picked up a book from the small stack beside him, showing the board in what good shape they were. "I'll tell you something else: you have the means here in this part of California to make paper. Did you know that?"

Mrs. Tallman said, "We knew it, Mr. Barnes, but we don't know quite how. It has to do with bark of trees, doesn't it?"

On the new teacher's face appeared a mysterious expression, one of concealment. Stroud knew that Mrs. Tallman was correct, but the teacher did not want to let her know; he wanted to keep the knowledge to himself because the West Marin trustees had not yet hired him. His knowledge was not yet available—he gave nothing free. And that of course was proper: Stroud recognized that, respected Barnes for it. Only a fool gave something away for nothing.

For the first time the newest member of the board, Miss Costigan, spoke up. "I—know a little about mushrooms myself, Mr. Barnes. What's the first thing you look for to be sure it isn't the deadly amanita?" She eyed the new teacher intently, obviously determined to pin the man down to concrete facts.

"The death cup," Mr. Barnes answered. "At the base of the stipe; the volva. The amanitas have it, most other kinds don't. And the universal veil. And generally the deadly amanita has white spores . . . and of course white gills." He smiled at Miss Costigan, who smiled back.

Mrs. Tallman was scrutinizing the new teacher's stack of books. "I see you have Carl Jung's *Psychological Types.* Is one of your sciences psychology? How nice, to acquire a teacher for our school who can tell edible mushrooms and also is an authority on Freud and Jung."

"There's no value in such stuff," Stroud said, with irritation. "We need useful science, not academic hot air." He felt personally let down; Mr. Barnes had not told him about that, about his interest in mere theory. "Psychology doesn't dig any septic tanks."

"I think we're ready to vote on Mr. Barnes," Miss Costigan said. "I for one am in favor of accepting him, at least on a provisional basis. Does anyone feel otherwise?"

Mrs. Tallman said to Mr. Barnes, "We killed our last teacher, you know. That's why we need another. That's why we sent Mr. Stroud out looking up and down the Coast until he found you."

With a wooden expression, Mr. Barnes nodded. "I know. That does not deter me."

"His name was Mr. Austurias and he was very good with mushrooms, too," Mrs. Tallman said, "although actually he gathered them for his own use alone. He did not teach us anything about them, and we appreciated his reasons; it was not for that that we decided to kill him. We killed him because he lied to us. You see, his real reason for coming here had nothing to do with teaching. He was looking for some man named Jack Tree, who, it turned out, lived in this area. Our Mrs. Keller, a respected member of this community and the wife of George Keller, here, our principal, is a dear friend of Mr. Tree, and she brought the news of the situation to us and of course we acted legally and officially, through our chief of police, Mr. Earl Colvig."

"I see," Mr. Barnes said stonily, listening without interrupting.

Speaking up, Orion Stroud said, "The jury which sentenced and executed him was composed of myself, Cas Stone, who's the largest land-owner in West Marin, Mrs. Tallman and Mrs. June Raub. I say 'executed,' but you understand that the act—when he was shot, the shooting itself—was done by Earl. That's Earl's job, after the West Marin Official Jury has made its decision." He eyed the new teacher.

"It sounds," Mr. Barnes said, "very formal and law-abiding to me. Just what I'd be interested in. And—" He smiled at them all. "I'll share *my* knowledge of mushrooms with you; I won't keep it to myself, as your late Mr. Austurias did."

They all nodded; they appreciated that. The tension in the room relaxed, the people murmured. A cigarette—one of Andrew Gill's special deluxe Gold Labels—was lit up; its good, rich smell wafted to them all, cheering them and making them feel more friendly to the new teacher and to one another.

Seeing the cigarette, Mr. Barnes got a strange expression on his face and he said in a husky voice, "You've got *tobacco* up here? After seven years?" He clearly could not believe it.

Smiling in amusement, Mrs. Tallman said, "We don't have any tobacco, Mr. Barnes, because of course no one does. But we do have a tobacco expert. He fashions these special deluxe Gold Labels for us out of choice, aged vegetable and herbal materials the nature of which remain—and justly so—his individual secret."

"How much do they cost?" Mr. Barnes asked.

"In terms of State of California boodle money," Orion Stroud said, "about a hundred dollars apiece. In terms of pre-war silver, a nickel apiece."

"I have a nickel," Mr. Barnes said, reaching shakily into his coat pocket; he fished about, brought up a nickel and held it toward the smoker, who was George Keller, leaning back in his chair with his legs crossed to make himself comfortable.

"Sorry," George said, "I don't want to sell. You better go directly to Mr. Gill; you can find him during the day at his shop. It's here in Point Reyes Station but of course he gets all around; he has a horse-drawn VW minibus."

"I'll make a note of that," Mr. Barnes said. He put his nickel away, very carefully.

"Do you intend to board the ferry?" the Oakland official asked. "If not, I wish you'd move your car, because it's blocking the gate."

"Sure," Stuart McConchie said. He got back into his car, flicked the reins that made Edward Prince of Wales, his horse, begin pulling. Edward pulled, and the engineless 1975 Pontiac passed back through the gate and out onto the pier.

The Bay, choppy and blue, lay on both sides, and Stuart watched through the windshield as a gull swooped to seize some edible from the pilings. Fishing lines, too . . . men catching their evening meals. Several of the men wore the remains of Army uniforms. Veterans who perhaps lived beneath the pier. Stuart drove on.

If only he could afford to telephone San Francisco. But the underwater cable was out again, and the lines had to go all the way down to San Jose and up the other side, along the peninsula, and by the time the call reached San Francisco it would cost him five dollars in silver money. So, except for a rich person, that was out of the question; he had to wait the two hours until the ferry left . . . but could he stand to wait that long?

He was after something important.

He had heard a rumor that a huge Soviet guided missile had been found, one which had failed to go off; it lay buried in the ground near Belmont, and a farmer had discovered it while plowing. The farmer was selling it off in the form of individual parts, of which there were thousands in the guidance system alone. The farmer wanted a penny a part, your choice. And Stuart, in his line of work, needed many such parts. But so did lots of other people. So it was first come, first serve; unless he got across the Bay to Belmont fairly soon, it would be too late—there would be no electronic parts left for him and his business.

He sold (another man made them) small electronic traps. Vermin had mutated and now could avoid or repel the ordinary passive trap, no matter how complicated. The cats in particular had become different, and Mr. Hardy built a superior cat trap, even better than his rat and dog traps.

It was theorized by some that in the years since the war cats had developed a language. At night people heard them mewing to one another in the darkness, a stilted, brisk series of gruff sounds unlike any of the old noises. And the cats ganged together in little packs and—this much at least was certain—collected food for the times ahead. It was these caches of food, cleverly stored and hidden, which had first alarmed people, much more so than the new noises. But in any case the cats, as well as the rats and dogs, were dangerous. They killed and ate small children almost at will—or at least so one heard. And of course wherever possible, they themselves were caught and eaten in return. Dogs, in particular, if stuffed with rice, were considered delicious; the little local Berkeley newspaper which came out once a week, the Berkeley *Tribune*, had recipes for dog soup, dog stew, even dog pudding.

Meditating about dog pudding made Stuart realize how hungry he was. It seemed to him that he had not stopped being hungry since the first bomb fell; his last really adequate meal had been the lunch at Fred's Fine Foods that day he had run into the phoce doing his phony vision-act. And where, he

wondered suddenly, was that little phoce now? He hadn't
thought of him in years.

Now, of course, one saw many phoces, and almost all of
them on their 'mobiles, exactly as Hoppy had been, placed
dead center each in his own little universe, like an armless, legless god. The sight still repelled Stuart, but there were so many
repellent sights these days . . . it was one of many and certainly not the worst. What he objected to the most, he had decided, was the sight of symbiotics ambling along the street:
several people fused together at some part of their anatomy,
sharing common organs. It was a sort of Bluthgeld elaboration
of the old Siamese twins . . . but these were not limited to
two. He had seen as many as six joined. And the fusions had
occurred—not in the womb—but shortly afterward. It saved
the lives of imperfects, those born lacking vital organs, requiring a symbiotic relationship in order to survive. One pan-
creas now served several people . . . it was a biological
triumph. But in Stuart's view, the imperfects should simply
have been allowed to die.

On the surface of the Bay to his right a legless veteran propelled himself out onto the water aboard a raft, rowing himself
toward a pile of debris that was undoubtedly a sunken ship.
On the hulk a number of fishing lines could be seen; they
belonged to the veteran and he was in the process of checking
them. Watching the raft go, Stuart wondered if it could reach
the San Francisco side. He could offer the man fifty cents for a
one-way trip; why not? Stuart got out of his car and walked to
the edge of the water.

"Hey," he yelled. "Come here." From his pocket he got a
penny; he tossed it down onto the pier and the veteran saw it,
heard it. At once he spun the raft about and came paddling
rapidly back, straining to make speed, his face streaked with
perspiration. He grinned up at Stuart, cupping his ear.

"Fish?" he called. "I don't have one yet today, but maybe
later. Or how about a small shark? Guaranteed safe." He held
up the battered Geiger counter which he had connected to his
waist by a length of rope—in case it fell from the raft or someone tried to steal it, Stuart realized.

"No," Stuart said, squatting down at the edge of the pier.

"I want to get over to San Francisco; I'll pay you a quarter for one way."

"But I got to leave my lines to do that," the veteran said, his smile fading. "I got to collect them all or somebody'd steal them while I was gone."

"Thirty-five cents," Stuart said.

In the end they agreed, at a price of forty cents. Stuart locked the legs of Edward Prince of Wales together so no one could steal him, and presently he was out on the Bay, bobbing up and down aboard the veteran's raft, being rowed to San Francisco.

"What field are you in?" the veteran asked him. "You're not a tax collector, are you?" He eyed him calmly.

"Naw," Stuart said. "I'm a small trap man."

"Listen, my friend," the veteran said, "I got a pet rat lives under the pilings with me? He's smart; he can play the flute. I'm not putting you under an illusion, it's true. I made a little wooden flute and he plays it, through his nose . . . it's practically an Asiatic nose-flute like they have in India. Well, I did have him, but the other day he got run over. I saw the whole thing happen; I couldn't go get him or nothing. He ran across the pier to get something, maybe a piece of cloth . . . he has this bed I made for him but he gets—I mean he got—cold all the time because when they mutated, this particular line, they lost their hair."

"I've seen those," Stuart said, thinking how well the hairless brown rat evaded even Mr. Hardy's electronic vermin trap. "Actually I believe what you said," he said. "I know rats pretty well. But they're nothing compared to those little striped gray-brown tabby cats . . . I'll bet you had to make the flute, he couldn't construct it himself."

"True," the veteran said. "But he was an artist. You ought to have heard him play; I used to get a crowd at night, after we were finished with the fishing. I tried to teach him the Bach Chaconne in D."

"I caught one of those tabby cats once," Stuart said, "that I kept for a month until it escaped. It could make little sharp-pointed things out of tin can lids. It bent them or something; I never did see how it did it, but they were wicked."

The veteran, rowing, said, "What's it like south of San Francisco these days? I can't come up on land." He indicated the lower part of his body. "I stay on the raft. There's a little trap door, when I have to go to the bathroom. What I need is to find a dead phoce sometime and get his cart. They call them phocomobiles."

"I knew the first phoce," Stuart said, "before the war. He was brilliant; he could repair anything." He lit up an imitation-tobacco cigarette; the veteran gaped at it longingly. "South of San Francisco it's, as you know, all flat. So it got hit bad and it's just farmland now. Nobody ever rebuilt there, and it was mostly those little tract houses so they left hardly any decent basements. They grow peas and corn and beans down there. What I'm going to see is a big rocket a farmer just found; I need relays and tubes and other electronic gear for Mr. Hardy's traps." He paused. "You ought to have a Hardy trap."

"Why? I live on fish, and why should I hate rats? I like them."

"I like them, too," Stuart said, "but you have to be practical; you have to look to the future. Someday America may be taken over by rats if we aren't vigilant. We owe it to our country to catch and kill rats, especially the wiser ones that would be natural leaders."

The veteran glared at him. "Sales talk, that's all."

"I'm sincere."

"That's what I have against salesmen; they believe their own lies. You know that the best rats can *ever* do, in a million years of evolution, is maybe be useful as servants to us human beings. They could carry messages maybe and do a little manual work. But dangerous—" He shook his head. "How much does one of your traps sell for?"

"Ten dollars silver. No State boodle accepted; Mr. Hardy is an old man and you know how old people are, he doesn't consider boodle to be real money." Stuart laughed.

"Let me tell you about a rat I once saw that did a heroic deed," the veteran began, but Stuart cut him off.

"I have my own opinions," Stuart said. "There's no use arguing about it."

They were both silent, then. Stuart enjoyed the sight of the

Bay on all sides; the veteran rowed. It was a nice day, and as they bobbed along toward San Francisco, Stuart thought of the electronic parts he might be bringing back to Mr. Hardy and the factory on San Pablo Avenue, near the ruins of what had once been the west end of the University of California.

"What kind of cigarette is that?" the veteran asked presently.

"This?" Stuart examined the butt; he was almost ready to put it out and stick it away in the metal box in his pocket. The box was full of butts, which would be opened and made into new cigarettes by Tom Frandi, the local cigarette man in South Berkeley. "This," he said, "is imported. From Marin County. It's a special deluxe Gold Label made by—" He paused for effect. "I guess I don't have to tell you."

"By Andrew Gill," the veteran said. "Say, I'd like to buy a whole one from you; I'll pay you a dime."

"They're worth fifteen cents apiece," Stuart said. "They have to come all the way around Black Point and Sear's Point and along the Lucas Valley Road, from beyond Nicasio somewhere."

"I had one of those Andrew Gill special deluxe Gold Labels one time," the veteran said. "It fell out of the pocket of some man who was getting on the ferry; I fished it out of the water and dried it."

All of a sudden Stuart handed him the butt.

"For God's sake," the veteran said, not looking directly at him. He rowed more rapidly, his lips moving, his eyelids blinking.

"I got more," Stuart said.

The veteran said, "I'll tell you what else you got; you got real humanity, mister, and that's rare today. Very rare."

Stuart nodded. He felt the truth of the veteran's words.

Knocking at the door of the small wooden cabin, Bonny said, "Jack? Are you in there?" She tried the door, found it unlocked. To Mr. Barnes she said, "He's probably out with his flock somewhere. This is lambing season and he's been having trouble; there're so many sports born and a lot of them won't pass through the birth canal without help."

"How many sheep does he have?" Barnes asked.

"Three hundred. They're out in the canyons around here, wild, so an accurate count is impossible. You're not afraid of rams, are you?"

"No," Barnes said.

"We'll walk, then," Bonny said.

"And he's the man the former teacher tried to kill," Barnes murmured, as they crossed a sheep-nibbled field toward a low ridge overgrown with fir and shrubbery. Many of the shrubs, he noticed, had been nibbled; bare branches showed, indicating that a good number of Mr. Tree's sheep were in the vicinity.

"Yes," the woman said, striding along, hands in her pockets. She added quickly, "But I have no idea why. Jack is—just a sheep rancher. I know it's illegal to raise sheep on ground that could be plowed . . . but as you can see, very little of his land could be plowed; most of it is canyon. Maybe Mr. Austurias was jealous."

Mr. Barnes thought to himself, I don't believe her. However, he was not particularly interested. He meant to avoid his predecessor's mistake, in any case, whoever or whatever Mr. Tree was; he sounded, to Barnes, like something that had become part of the environment, no longer fully peripatetic and human. His notion of Mr. Tree made him uncomfortable; it was not a reassuring image that he held in his mind.

"I'm sorry Mr. Gill couldn't come with us," Barnes said. He still had not met the famous tobacco expert, of whom he had heard even before coming to West Marin. "Did you tell me you have a music group? You play some sort of instruments?" It had sounded interesting, because he, at one time, had played the cello.

"We play recorders," Bonny said. "Andrew Gill and Jack Tree. And I play the piano; we play early composers, such as Henry Purcell and Johann Pachelbel. Doctor Stockstill now and then joins us, but—" She paused, frowning. "He's so busy; he has so many towns to visit. He's just too exhausted, in the evenings."

"Can anyone join your group?" Barnes inquired hopefully.

"What do you play? I warn you: we're severely classical. It's not just an amateur get-together; George and Jack and I played in the old days, before the Emergency. We began—nine

years ago. Gill joined us after the Emergency." She smiled, and
Barnes saw what lovely teeth she had. So many people, suffering from vitamin deficiencies and radiation sickness in recent times . . . they had lost teeth, developed soft gums. He
hid his own teeth as best he could; they were no longer good.

"I once played the cello," he said, knowing that it was
worthless as a former skill because there were—very simply—
no cellos anywhere around now. Had he played a metal instrument . . .

"What a shame," Bonny said.

"There are no stringed instruments in this area?" He
believed that if necessary he could learn, say, the viola; he
would be glad to, he thought, if by doing so he could join
their group.

"None," Bonny said.

Ahead, a sheep appeared, a black-faced Suffolk; it regarded
them, then bucked, turned and fled. A ewe, Barnes saw, a big
handsome one, with much meat on it and superb wool. He
wondered if it had ever been sheared.

His mouth watered. He had not tasted lamb in years.

To Bonny he said, "Does he slaughter, or is it for wool only?"

"For wool," she answered. "He has a phobia about slaugh-
tering; he won't do it no matter what he's offered. People
sneak up and steal from his flock, of course . . . if you want
lamb that's the only way you'll get it, so I advise you now: his
flock is well-protected." She pointed, and Barnes saw on a hill-
top a dog standing watching them. At once he recognized it as
an extreme mutation, a useful one; its face was intelligent, in a
new way.

"I won't go near his sheep," Barnes said. "It won't bother
us now, will it? It recognizes you?"

Bonny said, "That's why I came with you, because of the
dog. Jack has only the one. But it's sufficient."

Now the dog trotted toward them.

Once, Barnes conjectured, its folk had been the familiar gray
or black German shepherd; he identified the ears, the muzzle.
But now—he waited rigidly as it approached. In his pocket he
of course carried a knife; it had protected him many times, but
surely this—it would not have done the job, here. He stayed
close to the woman, who walked on unconcernedly.

"Hi," she said to the dog.

Halting before them, the dog opened its mouth and groaned. It was a hideous sound, and Barnes shivered; it sounded like a human spastic, a damaged person trying to work a vocal apparatus which had failed. Out of the groaning he detected—or thought he detected—a word or so, but he could not be sure. Bonny, however, seemed to understand.

"Nice Terry," she said to the dog. "Thank you, nice Terry." The dog wagged its tail. To Barnes she said, "We'll find him a quarter mile along the trail." She strode on.

"What did the dog say?" he asked, when they were out of earshot of the animal.

Bonny laughed. It irritated him, and he scowled. "Oh," she said, "my God, it evolves a million years up the ladder—one of the greatest miracles in the evolution of life—and you can't understand what it said." She wiped her eyes. "I'm sorry, but it's too damn funny. I'm glad you didn't ask me where it could hear."

"I'm not impressed," he said, defensively. "I'm just not very much impressed. You've been stuck here in this small rural area and it seems like a lot to you, but I've been up and down the Coast and I've seen things that would make you—" He broke off. "That's nothing, that dog. Nothing by comparison, although intrinsically I suppose it's a major feat."

Bonny took hold of his arm, still laughing. "Yes, you're from the great outside. You've seen all there is; you're right. What have you seen, Barnes? You know, my husband is your boss, and Orion Stroud is his boss. Why did you come here? Is this so remote? So rustic? I think this is a fine place to live; we have a stable community here. But as you say, we have few wonders. We don't have the miracles and freaks, as you have in the big cities where the radiation was stronger. Of course, we have Hoppy."

"Hell," Barnes said, "phoces are a dime a dozen; you see them everywhere, now."

"But you took a job here," Bonny said, eying him.

"I told you. I got into political trouble with little two-bit local authorities who considered themselves kings in their own little kingdom."

Thoughtfully, Bonny said, "Mr. Austurias was interested in

political matters. And in psychology, as you are." She continued to survey him, as they walked along. "He was not good-looking, and you are. He had a little round head like an apple. And his legs wobbled when he ran; he never should have run." She became sober, now. "He did cook a delightful mushroom stew, shaggy manes and chanterelles—he knew them all. Will you invite me over for a mushroom dinner? It's been too long . . . we did try hunting on our own, but as Mrs. Tallman said, it didn't work out; we got promptly sick."

"You're invited," he said.

"Do you find me attractive?" she asked him.

Startled, he mumbled, "Sure, I certainly do." He held onto her arm tightly, as if she were leading him. "Why do you ask?" he said, with caution and a growing deeper emotion whose nature he could not fathom; it was new to him. It resembled excitement and yet it had a cold, rational quality to it, so perhaps it was not an emotion at all; perhaps it was an awareness, a form of acute intuition, about himself and the landscape, about all things visible about him—it seemed to take in every aspect of reality, and most especially it had to do with her.

In a split second he grasped the fact—without having any data to go on—that Bonny Keller had been having an affair with someone, possibly Gill the tobacco man or even this Mr. Tree or Orion Stroud; in any case the affair was over or leastwise nearly over and she was searching for another to replace it. She searched in an instinctive, practical way, rather than in some starry-eyed romantic school-girl fashion. So no doubt she had had a good many affairs; she seemed expert in this, in the sounding people out to see how they would fit.

And me, he thought; I wonder if I would fit. Isn't it dangerous? My God, her husband, as she said, is my boss, the school principal.

But then perhaps he was imagining it, because it really did not appear very likely that this attractive woman who was a leader in the community and who scarcely knew him would select him like this . . . but she had not selected him; she was merely in the process of exploring. He was being tried, but as yet he had not succeeded. His pride began to swim up as an authentic emotion coloring the cold rational insight of a moment before. Its distorting power made itself felt instantly; all at once he wanted to be successful, to be selected, whatever the risk. And he did not have any love or sexual desire toward her; it was far too early for that. All that was involved was his pride, his desire not to be passed over.

It's weird, he thought to himself; he was amazed at himself, at how simple he was. His mind worked like some low order of life, something on the order of a starfish; it had one or two responses and that was all.

"Listen," he said, "where is this man Tree?" He walked on ahead of her, now, peering to see, concentrating on the ridge ahead with its trees and flowers. He saw a mushroom in a dark hollow and at once started toward it. "Look," he said. "Chicken-of-the-forest, they call it. Very delectable. You don't see it very often, either."

Coming over to see, Bonny Keller bent down. He caught a glimpse of her bare, pale knees as she seated herself on the grass by the mushroom. "Are you going to pick it?" she asked. "And carry it off like a trophy?"

"I'll carry it off," he said, "but not like a trophy. More like a thing to pop into the frying pan with a bit of beef fat."

Her dark, attractive eyes fixed themselves on him somberly; she sat brushing her hair back, looking as if she were going to speak. But she did not. At last he became uncomfortable; apparently she was waiting for him, and it occurred to him—chillingly—that he was not merely supposed to say something; he was supposed to *do* something.

They stared at each other, and Bonny, too, now looked frightened, as if she felt as he did. Neither of them did anything, however; each sat waiting for the other to make a move. He had the sudden hunch that if he reached toward her she would either slap him or run off . . . and there would be unsavory consequences. She might—good lord; they had killed their last teacher. The thought came to him now with enormous force: *could it have been this?* Could she have been having a love affair with him and he started to tell her husband or some damn thing? Is this as dangerous as that? Because if it is, my pride can go to hell; I want to get away.

Bonny said, "Here's Jack Tree."

Over the ridge came the dog, the mutation with the alleged

ability to speak, and slightly behind it came a haggard-faced man, bent, with round, stooped shoulders. He wore a seedy coat, a city man's coat, and dirty blue-gray trousers. In no way did he look like a farmer; he looked, Mr. Barnes thought, like a middle-aged insurance clerk who had been lost in the forest for a month or so. The man had a black-smeared chin which contrasted in an unpleasant manner with his unnaturally white skin. Immediately Mr. Barnes experienced dislike. But, was it because of Mr. Tree's physical appearance? God knew he had seen maimed, burned, damaged and blighted humans and creatures in profusion, during the last years . . . no, his reaction to Mr. Tree was based on the man's peculiar shambling walk. It was the walk—not of a well man—but of a violently sick man. A man sick in a sense that Barnes had never experienced before.

"Hi," Bonny said, rising to her feet.

The dog frisked up, acting in a most natural manner now.

"I'm Barnes, the new school teacher," Barnes said, rising, too, and extending his hand.

"I'm Tree," the sick man said, also extending his hand. When Barnes took it he found it unaccountably moist; it was difficult if not impossible for him to hold onto it—he let it drop at once.

Bonny said, "Jack, Mr. Barnes here is an authority on removing lambs' tails after they're grown and the danger of tetanus is so great."

"I see," Tree nodded. But he seemed only to be going through the motions; he did not seem really to care or even to understand. Reaching down he thumped the dog. "Barnes," he said to the dog distinctly, as if he were teaching the dog the name.

The dog groaned. ". . . brnnnnz . . ." It barked, eying its master with gleaming hopefulness.

"Right," Mr. Tree said, smiling. He displayed almost no teeth at all, just empty gums. Worse even than me, Barnes thought. The man must have been down below, near San Francisco, when the big bomb fell; that's one possibility, or it could simply be diet, as in my case. Anyhow, he avoided looking; he walked away, hands in his pockets.

"You've got a lot of land here," he said over his shoulder. "Through what legal agency did you acquire title? The County of Marin?"

"There's no title," Mr. Tree said. "I just have use. The West Marin Citizens' Council and the Planning Committee allow me, through Bonny's good offices."

"That dog fascinates me," Barnes said, turning. "It really talks; it said my name clearly."

"Say 'good day' to Mr. Barnes," Mr. Tree said to the dog.

The dog woofed, then groaned, "Gddday, Mrbarnzzzzz." It woofed again, this time eying him for his reaction.

To himself, Barnes sighed. "Really terrific," he said to the dog. It whined and skipped about with joy.

At that, Mr. Barnes felt some sympathy for it. Yes, it was a remarkable feat. Yet—the dog repelled him as did Tree himself; both of them had an isolated, warped quality, as if by being out here in the forest alone they had been cut off from normal reality. They had not gone wild; they had not reverted to anything resembling barbarism. They were just plain unnatural. He simply did not like them.

But he did like Bonny and he wondered how the hell she had gotten mixed up with a freak like Mr. Tree. Did owning a lot of sheep make the man a great power in this small community; was it that? Or—was there something more, something which might explain the former—dead—teacher's action in trying to kill Mr. Tree?

His curiosity was aroused; it was the same instinct, perhaps, that came into play when he spotted a new variety of mushroom and felt the intense need to catalogue it, to learn exactly which species it was. Not very flattering to Mr. Tree, he thought caustically, comparing him to a fungus. But it was true; he did feel that way, about both him and his weird dog.

Mr. Tree said to Bonny, "Your little girl isn't along, today."

"No," Bonny said. "Edie isn't well."

"Anything serious?" Mr. Tree said in his hoarse voice. He looked concerned.

"A pain in her stomach, that's all. She gets it every now and then; has as far back as I can remember. It's swollen and hard. Possibly it's appendicitis, but surgery is so dangerous, these days—" Bonny broke off, then turned to Barnes. "My little girl, you haven't met her . . . she loves this dog, Terry. They're good friends, they talk back and forth by the hour when we're out here."

Mr. Tree said, "She and her brother."

"Listen," Bonny said, "I've gotten sick and tired of that. I told Edie to quit that. In fact, that's why I like her to come out here and play with Terry; she should have actual playmates and not become so introverted and delusional. Don't you agree, Mr. Barnes; you're a teacher—a child should relate to actuality, not fantasy, isn't that right?"

"These days," Barnes said thoughtfully, "I can understand a child withdrawing into fantasy . . . it's hard to blame him. Perhaps we all ought to be doing that." He smiled, but Bonny did not smile back, nor did Mr. Tree.

Not for a moment had Bruno Bluthgeld taken his eyes off the new young teacher—if this actually was the truth; if this short young man dressed in khaki trousers and workshirt really was a teacher, as Bonny had said.

Is he after me, too? Bluthgeld asked himself. Like the last one? I suppose so. And Bonny brought him here . . . does that mean that even she, after all, is on their side? Against me?

He could not believe that. Not after all these years. And it had been Bonny who had discovered Mr. Austurias' actual purpose in coming to West Marin. Bonny had saved him from Mr. Austurias and he was grateful; he would not now be alive except for her, and he could never forget that, so perhaps this Mr. Barnes was exactly what he claimed to be and there was nothing to worry about. Bluthgeld breathed a little more relaxedly now; he calmed himself and looked forward to showing Barnes his new-born Suffolk lambs.

But sooner or later, he said to himself, someone will track me here and kill me. It's only a matter of time; they all detest me and they will never give up. The world is still seeking the man responsible for all that happened and I can't blame them. They are right in doing so. After all, I carry on my shoulders the responsibility for the death of millions, the loss of three-fourths of the world, and neither they nor I can forget that. Only God has the power to forgive and forget such a monstrous crime against humanity.

He thought, I would not have killed Mr. Austurias; I would have let him destroy me. But Bonny and the others—the decision was theirs. It was not mine, because I can no longer make decisions. I am no longer allowed to by God; it would not be proper. My job is to wait here, tending my sheep, wait for *him who is to come*, the man appointed to deal out final justice. The world's avenger.

When will he come? Bluthgeld asked himself. Soon? I've waited years now. I'm tired . . . I hope it won't be too much longer.

Mr. Barnes was saying, "What did you do, Mr. Tree, before you became a sheep rancher?"

"I was an atomic scientist," Bluthgeld said.

Hurriedly, Bonny said, "Jack was a teacher; he taught physics. High school physics. That wasn't around here, of course."

"A teacher," Mr. Barnes said. "Then we have something in common." He smiled at Doctor Bluthgeld and automatically Bluthgeld smiled back. With nervousness Bonny watched the two of them, her hands clasped together, as if she were afraid that something was going to happen, something dreadful.

"We must see more of each other," Bluthgeld said, somberly nodding. "We must talk."

IX

WHEN Stuart McConchie returned to the East Bay from his trip to the peninsula south of San Francisco he found that someone—no doubt a group of veterans living under the pier—had killed and eaten his horse, Edward Prince of Wales. All that remained was the skeleton, legs and head, a heap worthless to him or to anyone else. He stood by it, pondering. Well, it had been a costly trip. And he had arrived too late anyhow; the farmer, at a penny apiece, had already disposed of the electronic parts of his Soviet missile.

Mr. Hardy would supply another horse, no doubt, but he had been fond of Edward Prince of Wales. And it was wrong to kill a horse for food because they were so vitally needed for other purposes; they were the mainstay of transportation, now that most of the wood had been consumed by the wood-burning cars and by people in cellars using it in the winter to keep warm, and horses were needed in the job of reconstruction—they were the main source of power, in the absence of electricity. The stupidity of killing Edward maddened him; it was, he thought, like barbarism, the thing they all feared. It was anarchy, and right in the middle of the city; right in downtown Oakland, in broad day. It was what he would expect the Red Chinese to do.

Now, on foot, he walked slowly toward San Pablo Avenue. The sun had begun to sink into the lavish, extensive sunset which they had become accustomed to seeing in the years since the Emergency. He scarcely noticed it. Maybe I ought to go into some other business, he said to himself. Small animal traps—it's a living, but there's no advancement possible in it. I mean, where can you rise to in a business like that?

The loss of his horse had depressed him; he gazed down at the broken, grass-infested sidewalk as he picked his way along, past the rubble which once had been factories. From a burrow in a vacant lot something with eager eyes noted his passing; something, he surmised gloomily, that ought to be hanging by its hind legs minus its skin.

This, he thought, explains why Hoppy might legitimately

have imagined he was seeing the afterlife. These ruins, the smoky, flickering pallor of the sky . . . the eager eyes still following him as the creature calculated whether it could safely attack him. Bending, he picked up a sharp hunk of concrete and chucked it at the burrow—a dense layer of organic and inorganic material packed tightly, glued in place by some sort of white slime. The creature had emulsified some of the debris lying around, had reformed it into a usable paste. Must be a brilliant animal, he thought. But he did not care. The world could do without the brilliant and deranged life forms exposed to the light of day in the past years.

I've evolved, too, he said, turning one last time to face the creature, in case it might scuttle after him from behind. My wits are much clearer than they formerly were; I'm a match for you any time, so give up.

Evidently the creature agreed; it did not even come forth from its burrow.

I'm evolved, he thought, but sentimental. For he genuinely missed the horse. Damn those criminal veterans, he said to himself. They probably swarmed all over Edward the moment we pushed off in the raft. I wish I could get out of town; I wish I could emigrate to the open country where there's none of this brutal cruelty and hoodlumism. That's what that psychiatrist did, after the Emergency. Stockstill got right out of the East Bay; I saw him go. He was smart. He did not try to return to his old rut, he did not merely pick up where he left off, as I did.

I mean, he thought, I'm no better off now than I was before the goddam Emergency; I sold TV sets then and now I sell electronic vermin traps. What is the difference? One's as bad as the other. I'm going downhill, in fact.

To cheer himself he got out one of his remaining special deluxe Gold Label Andrew Gill cigarettes and lit up.

A whole day wasted, he realized, on this wild goose chase to the far side of the Bay. In two hours it would be dark and he would be going to sleep, down in the cat pelt-lined basement room which Mr. Hardy rented him for a dollar in silver a month. Of course, he could light his fat lamp; he could burn it for a little while, read a book or part of a book—most of his library consisted of merely sections of books, the remaining

portions having been destroyed or lost. Or he could visit old
Mr. and Mrs. Hardy and sit in on the evening transmission
from the satellite.

After all, he had personally radioed a request to Dangerfield
just the other day, from the transmitter out on the mudflats in
West Richmond. He had asked for "Good Rockin' Tonight,"
an old-fashioned favorite which he remembered from his
childhood. It was not known if Dangerfield had that tune on
his miles of tapes, however, so perhaps he was waiting in vain.

As he walked along he sang to himself,

> Oh I heard the news:
> There's good rockin' tonight.
> Oh I heard the *news*!
> There's good rockin' tonight!
> Tonight I'll be a mighty fine man,
> I'll hold my baby as tight as I can

It brought tears to his eyes to remember one of the old
songs, from the world the way it was. All gone now, he said to
himself. Bluthgelded out of existence, as they say . . . and
what do we have instead, a rat that can play the noseflute, and
not even that because the rat got run over.

There was another old favorite, the tune about the man who
had the knife; he tried to recall how it had gone. Something
about the shark having teeth or pretty teeth. It was too vague;
he could not recollect it. His mother had played a record of it
for him; a man, with a gravelly voice, had sung it and it was
beautiful.

I'll bet the rat couldn't play that, he said to himself. Not in
a million years. I mean, that's practically sacred music. Out of
our past, our sacred past that no brilliant animal and no funny
person can share. The past belongs only to us genuine human
beings. I wish (the idea stirred him) that I could do like
Hoppy used to do; I wish I could go into a trance, but not see
ahead like he did—I want to go *back*.

If Hoppy's alive now, can he do that? Has he tried it? I wonder where he is, that preview; that's what he was, a preview.
The first phoce. I'll bet he did escape with his life. He probably
went over to the Chinese when they made that landing up
north.

I'd go back, he decided, to that first time I met Jim Fergesson, when I was looking for a job and it was still tough for a Negro to find a job in which he met the public. That was the thing about Fergesson; he didn't have any prejudice. I remember that day; I had a job selling aluminum pans door to door and then I got the job with the Britannica people but that was also door to door. My god, Stuart realized; my first genuine job was with Jim Fergesson, because you can't count that door to door stuff.

While he was thinking about Jim Fergesson—who was now dead and gone all these years since the bomb fell—he arrived on San Pablo Avenue with its little shops open here and there, little shacks which sold everything from coat hangers to hay. One of them, not far off, was HARDY'S HOMEOSTATIC VERMIN TRAPS, and he headed in that direction.

As he entered, Mr. Hardy glanced up from his assembly table in the rear; he worked under the white light of an arc lamp, and all around him lay heaps of electronic parts which he had scavenged from every corner of Northern California. Many had come from the ruins out in Livermore; Mr. Hardy had connections with State officials and they had permitted him to dig there in the restricted deposits.

In former times Dean Hardy had been an engineer for an AM radio station in downtown Oakland; he was a slender, quiet-spoken, elderly man who wore a green sweater and a necktie even now—and a tie was unique, in these times. His hair was gray and curly, and he reminded Stuart of a beardless Santa Claus: he had a droll, dour expression and a roguish sense of humor. Physically, he was small; he weighed only a hundred and twenty pounds. But he had a near-violent temper and Stuart respected him. Hardy was nearly sixty, and in many respects he had become a father-figure to Stuart. Stuart's actual father, dead since the '70s, had been an insurance underwriter, also a quiet man who wore a tie and sweater, but he had not had Hardy's ferocity, his outbursts; or if he had, Stuart had never witnessed them or had repressed the memory of them.

And, too, Dean Hardy resembled Jim Fergesson.

That more than any other factor had drawn Stuart to him,

three years ago. He was conscious of it; he did not deny it or want to deny it. He missed Jim Fergesson and he was drawn to anyone who resembled him.

To Mr. Hardy he said, "They ate my horse." He seated himself on a chair at the front of the shop.

At once Ella Hardy, his employer's wife, appeared from the living quarters in the rear; she had been fixing dinner. "You *left* him?"

"Yes," he admitted. She, a formidable woman, glared at him with accusing indignation. "I thought he was safe out on the City of Oakland public ferry pier; there's an official there who—"

"It happens all the time," Hardy said wearily. "The bastards. It must have been those war vets who hole up down there. Somebody ought to drop a cyanide bomb under that pier; they're down there by the hundreds. What about the car? You had to leave it, I guess."

"I'm sorry," Stuart said.

Mrs. Hardy said caustically, "Edward was worth eighty-five silver U.S. dollars. That's a week's profit gone."

"I'll pay it back," Stuart said, rigidly.

"Forget it," Hardy said. "We have more horses at our store out in Orinda. What about the parts from the rocket?"

"No luck," Stuart said. "All gone when I got there. Except for this." He held up a handful of transistors. "The farmer didn't notice these; I picked them up for nothing. I don't know if they're any good, though." Carrying them over to the assembly table he laid them down. "Not much for an all-day trip." He felt more glum than ever.

Without a word, Ella Hardy returned to the kitchen; the curtain closed after her.

"You want to have some dinner with us?" Hardy said, shutting off his light and removing his glasses.

"I dunno," Stuart said. "I feel strange. It upset me to come back and find Edward eaten." He roamed about the shop. Our relationship, he thought, is different with animals now. It's much closer; there isn't the great gap between us and them that there was. "Over on the other side of the Bay I saw something I've never seen before," he said. "A flying animal like a bat but not a bat. More like a weasel, very skinny and long, with a big head. They call them *tommies* because they're always gliding up against windows and looking in, like peeping toms."

Hardy said, "It's a squirrel. I've seen them." He leaned back in his chair, loosened his necktie. "They evolved from the squirrels in Golden Gate Park." He yawned. "I once had a scheme for them . . . they could be useful—in theory, at least—as message carriers. They can glide or fly or whatever they do for amounts up to a mile. But they're too feral. I gave it up after catching one." He held up his right hand. "Look at the scar, there on my thumb. That's from a tom."

"This man I talked to said they taste good. Like old-time chicken. They sell them at stalls in downtown San Francisco; you see old ladies selling them cooked for a quarter apiece, still hot, very fresh."

"Don't try one," Hardy said. "Many of them are toxic. It has to do with their diet."

"Hardy," Stuart said suddenly, "I want to get out of the city and out into the country."

His employer regarded him.

"It's too brutal here," Stuart said.

"It's brutal everywhere."

"Not so much if you get away from town, really far away, say fifty to a hundred miles."

"But then it's hard to make a living."

"Do you sell any traps in the country?" Stuart asked.

"No," Hardy said.

"Why not?"

"Vermin live in towns, where there's ruins. You know that. Stuart, you're a woolgatherer. The country is sterile; you'd miss the flow of ideas that you have here in the city. Nothing happens; they just farm and listen to the satellite. Anyhow, you're apt to run into the old race prejudice against Negroes, out in the country; they've reverted to the old patterns." Once more he put on his glasses, turned his arc light back on and resumed the assembling of the trap before him. "It's one of the greatest myths that ever existed, the superiority of the country. I know you'd be back here in a week."

"I'd like to take a line of traps say out around Napa," Stuart persisted. "Maybe up to the St. Helena Valley. Maybe I could trade them for wine; they grow grapes up there, I understand, like they used to."

"But it doesn't taste the same," Hardy said. "The ground is altered. The wine is—" He gestured. "You'd have to taste it, I can't tell you, but it's really awful. Foul."

They were both silent, then.

"They drink it, though," Stuart said. "I've seen it here in town, brought in on those old wood-burning trucks."

"Of course, because people will drink anything they can get their hands on now. So do you, so do I." Mr. Hardy raised his head and regarded Stuart. "You know who has liquor? I mean the genuine thing; you can't tell if it's pre-war that he's dug up or new that he's made."

"Nobody in the Bay Area."

Hardy said, "Andrew Gill, the tobacco expert."

"I don't believe it." He sucked in his breath, fully alert, now.

"Oh, he doesn't produce much of it. I've only seen one bottle, a fifth of brandy. I had one single drink from it." Hardy smiled at him crookedly, his lips twitching. "You would have liked it."

"How much does he want for it?" He tried to sound casual.

"More than you have to pay."

"And—it tastes like the real thing? The *pre-war*?"

Hardy laughed and returned to his trap-assembling. "That's right."

I wonder what sort of a man Andrew Gill is, Stuart said to himself. Big, maybe, with a beard, a vest . . . walking with a silver-headed cane; a giant of a man with wavy, snow-white hair, imported monocle—I can picture him. He probably drives a Jaguar, converted of course now to wood, but still a great, powerful Mark XVI Saloon.

Seeing the expression on Stuart's face, Hardy leaned toward him. "I can tell you what else he sells."

"English brier pipes?"

"Yes, that, too." Hardy lowered his voice. "Girly photos. In artistic poses—you know."

"Aw, Christ," Stuart said, his imagination boggling; it was too much. "I don't believe it."

"God's truth. Genuine pre-war girly calendars, from as far back as 1950. They're worth a fortune, of course. I've heard of a thousand silver dollars changing hands over a 1962 *Playboy* calendar; that's supposed to have happened somewhere back East, in Nevada, somewhere like that." Now Hardy had become pensive; he gazed off into space, his vermin trap forgotten.

"Where I worked when the bomb fell," Stuart said, "at Modern TV, we had a lot of girly calendars downstairs in the service department. They were all incinerated, naturally." At least so he had always assumed.

Hardy nodded in a resigned way.

"Suppose a person were poking around in the ruins somewhere," Stuart said. "And he came onto an entire warehouse full of girly calendars. Can you imagine that?" His mind raced. "How much could he get? Millions? He could trade them for real estate; he could acquire a whole county!"

"Right," Hardy said, nodding.

"I mean, he'd be rich forever. They make a few in the Orient, in Japan, but they're no good."

"I've seen them," Hardy agreed. "They're crude. The knowledge of how to do it has declined, passed into oblivion; it's an art that has died out. Maybe forever."

"Don't you think it's partly because there aren't the girls any more who look like that?" Stuart said. "Everybody's scrawny now and have no teeth; the girls most of them now have burn-scars from radiation, and with no teeth what kind of a girly calendar does that make?"

Shrewdly, Hardy said, "I think the girls exist. I don't know where; maybe in Sweden or Norway, maybe in out-of-the-way places like the Solomon Islands. I'm convinced of it from what people coming in by ship say. Not in the U.S. or Europe or Russia or China, any of the places that were hit—I agree with you there."

"Could we find them?" Stuart said. "And go into the business?"

After considering for a little while Hardy said, "There's no film. There're no chemicals to process it. Most good cameras have been destroyed or have disappeared. There's no way you could get your calendars printed in quantity. If you did print them—"

"But if someone could find a girl with no burns and good teeth, the way they had before the war—"

"I'll tell you," Hardy said, "what would be a good business. I've thought about it many times." He faced Stuart meditatively. "Sewing machine needles. You could name your own price; you could have anything."

Gesturing, Stuart got up and paced about the shop. "Listen, I've got my eye on the big time; I don't want to mess around with selling any more—I'm fed up with it. I sold aluminum pots and pans and encyclopedias and TV sets and now these vermin traps. They're good traps and people want them, but I just feel there must be something else for me."

Hardy grunted, frowning.

"I don't mean to insult you," Stuart said, "but I want to grow. I *have* to; you either grow or you go stale, you die on the vine. The war set me back years, it set us all back. I'm just where I was ten years ago, and that's not good enough."

Scratching his nose, Hardy said, "What did you have in mind?"

"Maybe I could find a mutant potato that would feed everybody in the world."

"Just one potato?"

"I mean a type of potato. Maybe I could become a plant breeder, like Luther Burbank. There must be millions of freak plants growing around out in the country, like there're all those freak animals and funny people here in the city."

Hardy said, "Maybe you could locate an intelligent bean."

"I'm not joking about this," Stuart said quietly.

They faced each other, neither speaking.

"It's a service to humanity," Hardy said at last, "to make homeostatic vermin traps that destroy mutated cats and dogs and rats and squirrels. I think you're acting infantile. Maybe your horse being eaten while you were over in South San Francisco—"

Entering the room, Ella Hardy said, "Dinner is ready, and I'd like to serve it while it's hot. It's baked cod-head and rice and it took me three hours standing in line down at Eastshore Freeway to get the cod-head."

The two men rose to their feet. "You'll eat with us?" Hardy asked Stuart.

At the thought of the baked fish head, Stuart's mouth watered. He could not say no and he nodded, following after

Mrs. Hardy toward the little combination living room and kitchen in the rear of the building. It had been a month since he had tasted fish; there were almost none left in the Bay any longer—most of the schools had been wiped out and had never returned. And those that were caught were often radio-active. But it did not matter; people had become able to eat them anyhow. People could eat almost anything; their lives depended on it.

The little Keller girl sat shivering on the examination table, and Doctor Stockstill, surveying her thin, pale body, thought of a joke which he had seen on television years ago, long before the war. A Spanish ventriloquist, speaking through a chicken . . . the chicken had produced an egg.

"My son," the chicken said, meaning the egg.

"Are you sure?" the ventriloquist asked. "It's not your daughter?"

And the chicken, with dignity, answered, "I know my business."

This child was Bonny Keller's daughter, but, Doctor Stockstill thought, it isn't George Keller's daughter; I am certain of that . . . I know my business. Who had Bonny been having an affair with, seven years ago? The child must have been conceived very close to the day the war began. But she had not been conceived before the bomb fell; that was clear. Perhaps it was on that very day, he ruminated. Just like Bonny, to rush out while the bomb was falling, while the world was coming to an end, to have a brief, frenzied spasm of love with someone, perhaps some man she did not even know, the first man she happened onto . . . and now this.

The child smiled at him and he smiled back. Superficially, Edie Keller appeared normal; she did not seem to be a funny child. How he wished, God damn it, that he had an x-ray machine. Because—

He said aloud, "Tell me more about your brother."

"Well," Edie Keller said in her frail, soft voice, "I talk to my brother all the time and sometimes he answers but more often he's asleep. He sleeps almost all the time."

"Is he asleep now?"

For a moment the child was silent. "No, he's awake."

Rising to his feet and coming over to her, Doctor Stockstill said, "I want you to show me exactly where he is."

The child pointed to her left side, low down; near, he thought, the appendix. The pain was there. That had brought the child in; Bonny and George had become worried. They knew about the brother, but they assumed him to be imaginary, a pretend playmate which kept their little daughter company. He himself had assumed so at first; the chart did not mention a brother, and yet Edie talked about him. Bill was exactly the same age as she. Born, Edie had informed the doctor, at the same time as she, of course.

"Why of course?" he had asked, as he began examining her—he had sent the parents into the other room because the child seemed reticent in front of them.

Edie had answered in her calm, solemn way, "Because he's my twin brother. How else could he be inside me?" And, like the Spanish ventriloquist's chicken, she spoke with authority, with confidence; she, too, knew her business.

In the years since the war Doctor Stockstill had examined many hundreds of funny people, many strange and exotic variants on the human life form which flourished now under a much more tolerant—although smokily veiled—sky. He could not be shocked. And yet, this—a child whose brother lived inside her body, down in the inguinal region. For seven years Bill Keller had dwelt inside there, and Doctor Stockstill, listening to the girl, believed her; he knew that it was possible. It was not the first case of this kind. If he had his x-ray machine he would be able to see the tiny, wizened shape, probably no larger than a baby rabbit. In fact, with his hands he could feel the outline . . . he touched her side, carefully noting the firm cyst-like sack within. The head in a normal position, the body entirely within the abdominal cavity, limbs and all. Someday the girl would die and they would open her body, perform an autopsy; they would find a little wrinkled male figure, perhaps with a snowy white beard and blind eyes . . . her brother, still no larger than a baby rabbit.

Meanwhile, Bill slept mostly, but now and then he and his sister talked. What did Bill have to say? What possibly could he know?

To the question, Edie had an answer. "Well, he doesn't

know very much. He doesn't see anything but he thinks. And I tell him what's going on so he doesn't miss out."

"What are his interests?" Stockstill asked. He had completed his examination; with the meager instruments and tests available to him he could do no more. He had verified the child's account and that was something, but he could not see the embryo or consider removing it; the latter was out of the question, desirable as it was.

Edie considered and said, "Well, he uh, likes to hear about food."

"Food!" Stockstill said, fascinated.

"Yes. He doesn't eat, you know. He likes me to tell him over and over again what I had for dinner, because he does get it after a while . . . I think he does anyhow. Wouldn't he have to, to live?"

"Yes," Stockstill agreed.

"He gets it from me," Edie said as she put her blouse back on, buttoning it slowly. "And he wants to know what's in it. He especially likes it if I have apples or oranges. And—he likes to hear stories. He always wants to hear about places. Faraway, especially, like New York. My mother tells me about New York so I told him; he wants to go there someday and see what it's like."

"But he can't see."

"I can, though," Edie pointed out. "It's almost as good."

"You take good care of him, don't you?" Stockstill said, deeply touched. To the girl, it was normal; she had lived like this all her life—she did not know of any other existence. There is nothing, he realized once more, which is "outside" nature; that is a logical impossibility. In a way there are no freaks, no abnormalities, except in the statistical sense. This is an unusual situation, but it's not something to horrify us; actually it ought to make us happy. Life per se is good, and this is one form which life takes. There's no special pain here, no cruelty or suffering. In fact there is solicitude and tenderness.

"I'm afraid," the girl said suddenly, "that he might die someday."

"I don't think he will," Stockstill said. "What's more likely to happen is that he'll get larger. And that might pose a problem; it might be hard for your body to accommodate him."

"What would happen, then?" Edie regarded him with large, dark eyes. "Would he get born, then?"

"No," Stockstill said. "He's not located that way; he would have to be removed surgically. But—he wouldn't live. The only way he can live is as he's living now, inside you." Parasitically, he thought, not saying the word aloud. "We'll worry about that when the time comes," he said, patting the child on the head. "If it ever does."

"My mother and father don't know," Edie said.

"I realize that," Stockstill said.

"I told them about him," Edie said. "But—" She laughed.

"Don't worry. Just go on and do what you'd ordinarily do. It'll all take care of itself."

Edie said, "I'm glad I have a brother; he keeps me from being lonely. Even when he's asleep I can feel him there, I know he's there. It's like having a baby inside me; I can't wheel him around in a baby carriage or anything like that, or dress him, but talking to him is a lot of fun. For instance, I get to tell him about Mildred."

"Mildred!" He was puzzled.

"You know." The child smiled at his ignorance. "The girl that keeps coming back to Philip. And spoils his life. We listen every night. The satellite."

"Of course." It was Dangerfield's reading of the Maugham book. Eerie, Doctor Stockstill thought, this parasite swelling within her body, in unchanging moisture and darkness, fed by her blood, hearing from her in some unfathomable fashion a second-hand account of a famous novel . . . it makes Bill Keller part of our culture. He leads his grotesque social existence, too. God knows what he makes of the story. Does he have fantasies about it, about our life? Does he *dream* about us?

Bending, Doctor Stockstill kissed the girl on her forehead. "Okay," he said, leading her toward the door. "You can go, now. I'll talk to your mother and father for a minute; there're some very old genuine pre-war magazines out in the waiting room that you can read, if you're careful with them."

"And then we can go home and have dinner," Edie said happily, opening the door to the waiting room. George and Bonny rose to their feet, their faces taut with anxiety.

"Come in," Stockstill said to them. He shut the door after them. "No cancer," he said, speaking to Bonny in particular, whom he knew so well. "It's a growth, of course; no doubt of that. How large it may get I can't say. But I'd say, don't worry about it. Perhaps by the time it's large enough to cause trouble our surgery will be advanced enough to deal with it."

The Kellers sighed with relief; they trembled visibly.

"You could take her to the U.C. Hospital in San Francisco," Stockstill said. "They are performing minor surgery there . . . but frankly, if I were you I'd let it drop." Much better for you not to know, he realized. It would be hard on you to have to face it . . . especially you, Bonny. Because of the circumstances involving the conception; it would be so easy to start feeling guilt. "She's a healthy child and enjoys life," he said. "Leave it at that. She's had it since birth."

"Has she?" Bonny said. "I didn't realize. I guess I'm not a good mother; I'm so wrapped up in community activities—"

"Doctor Stockstill," George Keller broke in, "let me ask you this. Is Edie a—special child?"

" 'Special'?" Stockstill regarded him cautiously.

"I think you know what I mean."

"You mean, is she a funny person?"

George blanched, but his intense, grim expression remained; he waited for an answer. Stockstill could see that; the man would not be put off by a few phrases.

Stockstill said, "I presume that's what you mean. Why do you ask? Does she seem to be funny in some fashion? Does she look funny?"

"She doesn't look funny," Bonny said, in a flurry of concern; she held tightly onto her husband's arm, clinging to him. "Christ, that's obvious; she's perfectly normal-looking. Go to hell, George. What's the matter with you? How can you be morbid about your own child; are you bored or something, is that it?"

"There are funny people who don't show it," George Keller said. "After all, I see many children; I see all our children. I've developed an ability to tell. A hunch, which usually is proved correct. We're required, we in the schools, as you know, to turn any funny children over to the State of California for special training. Now—"

"I'm going home," Bonny said. She turned and walked to the door of the waiting room. "Good-bye, Doctor."

Stockstill said, "Wait, Bonny."

"I don't like this conversation," Bonny said. "It's ill. You're both ill. Doctor, if you intimate in any fashion that she's funny I won't ever speak to you again. Or you either, George. I mean it."

After a pause, Stockstill said, "You're wasting your words, Bonny. I am not intimating, because there's nothing to intimate. She has a benign tumor in the abdominal cavity; that's all." He felt angry. He felt, in fact, the desire to confront her with the truth. She deserved it.

But, he thought, after she has felt guilt, after she's blamed herself for going out and having an affair with some man and producing an abnormal birth, then she will turn her attention to Edie; she will hate her. She will take it out on the child. It always goes like that. The child is a reproach to the parents, in some dim fashion, for what they did back in the old days or in the first moments of the war when everyone ran his own crazy way, did his private, personal harm as he realized what was happening. Some of us killed to stay alive, some of us just fled, some of us made fools out of ourselves . . . Bonny went wild, no doubt; she let herself go. And she's that same person now; she would do it again, perhaps has done it again. And she is perfectly aware of that.

Again he wondered who the father was.

Someday I am going to ask her point blank, he decided. Perhaps she doesn't even know; it is all a blur to her, that time in our lives. Those horrible days. Or was it horrible for her? Maybe it was lovely; she could kick the traces, do what she wanted without fear because she believed, we all did, *that none of us would survive.*

Bonny made the most of it, he realized, as she always does; she makes the most out of life in every contingency. I wish I were the same . . . he felt envious, as he watched her move from the room toward her child. The pretty, trim woman; she was as attractive now as she had been ten years ago—the damage, the impersonal change that had descended on them and their lives, did not seem to have touched her.

The grasshopper who fiddled. That was Bonny. In the

darkness of the war, with its destruction, its infinite sporting of life forms, Bonny fiddled on, scraping out her tune of joy and enthusiasm and lack of care; she could not be persuaded, even by reality, to become reasonable. The lucky ones: people like Bonny, who are stronger than the forces of change and decay. That's what she has eluded—the forces of decay which have set in. The roof fell on us, but not on Bonny.

He remembered a cartoon in *Punch*—

Interrupting his thoughts, Bonny said, "Doctor, have you met the new teacher, Hal Barnes?"

"No," he said. "Not yet. I saw him at a distance only."

"You'd like him. He wants to play the cello, except of course he has no cello." She laughed merrily, her eyes dancing with pure life. "Isn't that pathetic?"

"Very," he agreed.

"Isn't that all of us?" she said. "Our cellos are gone. And what does that leave? You tell me."

"Christ," Stockstill said, "I don't know; I haven't the foggiest idea."

Bonny, laughing, said, "Oh, you're so earnest."

"She says that to me, too," George Keller said, with a faint smile. "My wife sees mankind as a race of dungbeetles laboring away. Naturally, she does not include herself."

"She shouldn't," Stockstill said. "I hope she never does."

George glanced at him sourly, then shrugged.

She might change, Stockstill thought, if she understood about her daughter. That might do it. It would take something like that, some odd blow unprecedented and unanticipated. She might even kill herself; the joy, the vitality, might switch to its utter opposite.

"Kellers," he said aloud, "introduce me to the new teacher one day soon. I'd like to meet an ex-cello player. Maybe we can make him something out of a washtub strung with baling wire. He could play it with—"

"With horsetail," Bonny said practically. "The bow we can make; that part is easy. What we need is a big resonating chamber, to produce the low notes. I wonder if we can find an old cedar chest. That might do. It would have to be wood, certainly."

George said, "A barrel, cut in half."

They laughed at that; Edie Keller, joining them, laughed, too, although she had not heard what her father—or rather, Stockstill thought, her mother's husband—had said.

"Maybe we can find something washed up on the beach," George said. "I notice that a lot of wooden debris shows up, especially after storms. Wrecks of old Chinese ships, no doubt, from years ago."

Cheerfully, they departed from Doctor Stockstill's office; he stood watching them go, the little girl between them. The three of them, he thought. Or rather, the four, if the invisible but real presence within the girl was counted.

Deep in thought, he shut the door.

It could be my child, he thought. But it isn't, because seven years ago Bonny was up in West Marin here and I was at my office in Berkeley. But if I had been near her that day—

Who was up here then? he asked himself. When the bombs fell . . . who of us could have been with her that day? He felt a peculiar feeling toward the man, whoever he was. I wonder how he would feel, Stockstill thought, if he knew about his child . . . about his *children*. Maybe someday I'll run into him. I can't bring myself to tell Bonny, but perhaps I will tell him.

X

AT the Foresters' Hall, the people of West Marin sat discussing the illness of the man in the satellite. Agitated, they interrupted one another in their eagerness to speak. The reading from *Of Human Bondage* had begun, but no one in the room wanted to listen; they were all murmuring grim-faced, all of them alarmed, as June Raub was, to realize what would happen to them if the disc jockey were to die.

"He can't really be that sick," Cas Stone, the largest land-owner in West Marin, exclaimed. "I never told anybody this, but listen; I've got a really good doctor, a specialist in heart diseases, down in San Rafael. I'll get him to a transmitter somewhere and he can tell Dangerfield what's the matter with him. And he can cure him."

"But he's got no medicines up there," old Mrs. Lully, the most ancient person in the community, said. "I heard him say once that his departed wife used them all up."

"I've got quinidine," the pharmacist spoke up. "That's probably exactly what he needs. But there's no way to get it up to him."

Earl Colvig, who headed the West Marin Police, said, "I understand that the Army people at Cheyenne are going to make another try to reach him later this year."

"Take your quinidine to Cheyenne," Cas Stone said to the pharmacist.

"To Cheyenne?" the pharmacist quavered. "There aren't any through roads over the Sierras any more. I'd never get there."

In as calm a voice as possible, June Raub said, "Perhaps he isn't actually ill; perhaps it's only hypochondria, from being isolated and alone up there all these years. Something about the way he detailed each symptom made me suspect that." However, hardly anyone heard her. The three representatives from Bolinas, she noticed, had gone quietly over beside the radio and were stooping down to listen to the reading. "Maybe he won't die," she said, half to herself.

At that, the glasses man glanced up at her. She saw on his

face an expression of shock and numbness, as if the realization that the man in the satellite might be sick and would die was too much for him. The illness of his own daughter, she thought, had not affected him so.

A silence fell over the people in the furthest part of the Hall, and June Raub looked to see what had happened.

At the door, a gleaming platform of machinery had rolled into sight. Hoppy Harrington had arrived.

"Hoppy, you know what?" Cas Stone called. "Dangerfield said he's got something wrong with him, maybe his heart."

They all became silent, waiting for the phocomelus to speak.

Hoppy rolled past them and up to the radio, he halted his 'mobile, sent one of his manual extensions over to delicately diddle at the tuning knob. The three representatives from Bolinas respectfully stood aside. Static rose, then faded, and the voice of Walt Dangerfield came in clear and strong. The reading was still in progress, and Hoppy, in the center of his machinery, listened intently. He, and the others in the room, continued to listen without speaking until at last the sound faded out as the satellite passed beyond the range of reception. Then, once again, there was only the static.

All of a sudden, in a voice exactly like Dangerfield's, the phocomelus said, "Well, my dear friends, what'll we have next to entertain us?"

This time the imitation was so perfect that several people in the room gasped. Others clapped, and Hoppy smiled. "How about some more of that juggling?" the pharmacist called. "I like that."

"'Juggling,'" the phocomelus said, this time exactly in the pharmacist's quavering, prissy voice. "'I like that.'"

"No," Cas Stone said, "I want to hear him do Dangerfield; do some more of that, Hoppy. Come on."

The phocomelus spun his 'mobile around so that he faced the audience. "Hoode hoode hoo," he chuckled in the low, easy-going tones which they all knew so well. June Raub caught her breath; it was eerie, the phoce's ability to mimic. It always disconcerted her . . . if she shut her eyes she could imagine that it actually was Dangerfield still talking, still in contact with them. She did so, deliberately pretending to herself. He's not sick, he's not dying, she told herself; listen to him. As if in answer to her own thoughts, the friendly voice was murmuring, "I've got a little pain here in my chest, but it doesn't amount to a thing; don't worry about it, friends. Upset stomach, most likely. Over-indulgence. And what do we take for that? Does anybody out there remember?"

A man in the audience shouted, "I remember: alkalize with Alka Seltzer!"

"Hoode hoode hoo," the warm voice chuckled. "That's right. Good for you. Now let me give you a tip on how to store gladiola bulbs all through the winter without fear of annoying pests. Simply wrap them in aluminum foil."

People in the room clapped, and June Raub heard someone close by her say, "That's exactly what Dangerfield would have said." It was the glasses man from Bolinas. She opened her eyes and saw the expression on his face. I must have looked like that, she realized, that night when I first heard Hoppy imitating him.

"And now," Hoppy continued, still in Dangerfield's voice, "I'll perform a few feats of skill that I've been working on. I think you'll all get a bang out of this, dear friends. Just watch."

Eldon Blaine, the glasses man from Bolinas, saw the phocomelus place a coin on the floor several feet from his 'mobile. The extensions withdrew, and Hoppy, still murmuring in Dangerfield's voice, concentrated on the coin until all at once, with a clatter, it slid across the floor toward him. The people in the Hall clapped. Flushing with pleasure, the phocomelus nodded to them and then once more set the coin down away from him, this time farther than before.

Magic, Eldon thought. What Pat said; the phoces can do that in compensation for not having been born with arms or legs, it's nature's way of helping them survive. Again the coin slid toward the 'mobile and again the people in the Foresters' Hall applauded.

To Mrs. Raub, Eldon said, "He does this every night?"

"No," she answered. "He does various tricks; I've never seen this one before, but of course I'm not always here—I have so much to do, helping to keep our community functioning. It's remarkable, isn't it?"

Action at a distance, Eldon realized. Yes, it is remarkable.

And we must have him, he said to himself. No doubt of it now. For when Walt Dangerfield dies—and it is becoming obvious that he will, soon—we would have this memory of him, this reconstruction, embodied in this phoce. Like a phonograph record, to be played back forever.

"Does he frighten you?" June Raub asked.

"No," Eldon said. "Should he?"

"I don't know," she said in a thoughtful voice.

"Has he ever transmitted to the satellite?" Eldon asked. "A lot of other handies have. Odd he hasn't, with his ability."

June Raub said, "He intended to. Last year he started building a transmitter; he's been working on it off and on, but evidently nothing came of it. He tries all sorts of projects . . . he's always busy. You can see the tower. Come outside a minute and I'll show you."

He followed her to the door of the Foresters' Hall. Together, they stood outside in the darkness until they were able to see. Yes, there it was, a peculiar, crooked mast, rising up into the night sky but then breaking off abruptly.

"That's his house," June Raub said. "It's on his roof. And he did it without any help from us; he can amplify the impulses from his brain into what he calls his servo-assists, and that way he's quite strong, much more so than any unfunny man." She was silent a moment. "We all admire him. He's done a lot for us."

"Yes," Eldon said.

"You came here to nap him away from us," June Raub said quietly. "Didn't you?"

Startled, he protested, "No, Mrs. Raub—honest, we came to listen to the satellite; you know that."

"It's been tried before," Mrs. Raub said. "You can't nap him because he won't let you. He doesn't like your community down there; he knows about your ordinance. We have no such discrimination up here and he's grateful for that. He's very sensitive about himself."

Disconcerted, Eldon Blaine moved away from the woman, back toward the door of the Hall.

"Wait," Mrs. Raub said. "You don't have to worry: I won't say anything to anyone. I don't blame you for seeing him and wanting him for your own community. You know, he wasn't

born here in West Marin. One day, about three years ago, he
came rolling into town on his 'mobile, not this one but the
older one the Government built before the Emergency. He had
rolled all the way up from San Francisco, he told us. He
wanted to find a place where he could settle down, and no one
had given him that, up until us."

"Okay," Eldon murmured. "I understand."

"Everything nowadays can be napped," Mrs. Raub said.
"All it takes is sufficient force. I saw your police-cart parked
down the road, and I know that the two men with you are on
your police force. But Hoppy does what he wants. I think if
you tried to coerce him he'd kill you; it wouldn't be much
trouble for him and he wouldn't mind."

After a pause Eldon said, "I—appreciate your candor."

Together, silently, they re-entered the Foresters' Hall.

All eyes were on Hoppy Harrington, who was still immersed
in his imitation of Dangerfield. ". . . it seems to go away
when I eat," the phocomelus was saying. "And that makes me
think it's an ulcer, not my heart. So if any doctors are listening
and they have access to a transmitter—"

A man in the audience interrupted, "I'm going to get hold
of my doctor in San Rafael; I'm not kidding when I say that.
We can't have another dead man circling around and around
the Earth." It was the same man who had spoken before; he
sounded even more earnest now. "Or if as Mrs. Raub says it's
just in his mind, couldn't we get Doc Stockstill to help him?"

Eldon Blaine thought, But Hoppy was not here in the Hall
when Dangerfield said those words. How can he mimic something he did not hear?

And then he understood. It was obvious. The phocomelus
had a radio receiver at his house; before coming to the
Foresters' Hall he had sat by himself in his house, listening to
the satellite. That meant there were *two* functioning radios in
West Marin, compared to none at all in Bolinas. Eldon felt
rage and despair. We have nothing, he realized. And these
people here have everything, even an extra, private radio set,
for just one person alone.

It's like before the war, he thought blindly. They're living as
good as then. *It isn't fair.*

Turning, he plunged back out of the Hall, into the night

darkness. No one noticed him; they did not care. They were far too busy arguing about Dangerfield and his health to pay attention to anything else.

Coming up the road, carrying a kerosene lantern, three figures confronted him: a tall, skinny man, a young woman with dark red hair, and between them a small girl.

"Is the reading over?" the woman asked. "Are we too late?"

"I don't know," Eldon said, and continued on past them.

"Oh, we missed it," the little girl was clamoring. "I told you we should have hurried!"

"Well, we'll go on inside anyhow," the man told her, and then their voices faded away as Eldon Blaine, despairing, continued on into the darkness, away from the sounds and presence of other people, of the wealthy West Mariners who had so much.

Hoppy Harrington, doing his imitation of Dangerfield, glanced up to see the Kellers, with their little girl, enter the room and take seats in the rear. About time, he said to himself, glad of a greater audience. But then he felt nervous, because the little girl was scrutinizing him. There was something in the way she looked at him that upset him; it had always been so, about Edie. He did not like it, and he ceased suddenly.

"Go ahead, Hoppy," Cas Stone called.

"Go on," other voices chimed in.

"Do that one about Kool Aid," a woman called. "Sing that, the little tune the Kool Aid twins sing; you know."

"'Kool Aid, Kool Aid, can't wait,'" Hoppy sang, but once more he stopped. "I guess that's enough for tonight," he said.

The room became silent.

"My brother," the little Keller girl spoke up, "he says that Mr. Dangerfield is somewhere in this room."

Hoppy laughed. "That's right," he said excitedly.

"Has he done the reading?" Edie Keller asked.

"Oh yeah, the reading's over," Earl Colvig said, "but we weren't listening to that; we're listening to Hoppy and watching what he does. He did a lot of funny things tonight, didn't you, Hoppy?"

"Show the little girl that with the coin," June Raub said. "I think she'd enjoy that."

"Yes, do that again," the pharmacist called from his seat. "That was good; we'd all like to see that again, I'm sure." In his eagerness to watch he rose to his feet, forgetting the people behind him.

"My brother," Edie said quietly, "wants to hear the reading. That's what he came for. He doesn't care about anything with a coin."

"Be still," Bonny said to her.

Brother, Hoppy thought. She doesn't have any brother. He laughed out loud at that, and several people in the audience automatically smiled. "Your brother?" he said, wheeling his 'mobile toward the child. "Your *brother*?" He halted the 'mobile directly before her, still laughing. "I can do the reading," he said. "I can be Philip and Mildred and everybody in the book; I can be Dangerfield—sometimes I actually am. I was tonight and that's why your brother thinks Dangerfield's in the room. What it is, it's me." He looked around at the people. "Isn't that right, folks? Isn't it actually Hoppy?"

"That's right, Hoppy," Cas Stone agreed, nodding. The others nodded, too, all of them, or at least most of them.

"Christ sake, Hoppy," Bonny Keller said severely. "Calm down or you'll shake yourself right off your cart." She eyed him in her stern domineering way and he felt himself recede; he drew back in spite of himself. "What's been going on here?" Bonny demanded.

Fred Quinn, the pharmacist, said, "Why, Hoppy's been imitating Walt Dangerfield so well you'd think it was him!"

The others nodded, chiming in with their agreement.

"You have no brother, Edie," Hoppy said to the little girl. "Why do you say your brother wants to hear the reading when you have no brother?" He laughed and laughed. The girl remained silent. "Can I see him?" he asked. "Can I talk to him? Let me hear him talk and—I'll do an imitation of him." Now he was laughing so hard that he could barely see; tears filled his eyes and he had to wipe them away with an extensor.

"That'll be quite an imitation," Cas Stone said.

"Like to hear that," Earl Colvig said. "Do that, Hoppy."

"I'll do it," Hoppy said, "as soon as he says something to me." He sat in the center of his 'mobile, waiting. "I'm waiting," he said.

"That's enough," Bonny Keller said. "Leave my child alone." Her cheeks were red with anger.

To Edie, ignoring the child's mother, Hoppy said, "Where is he? Tell me where—is he nearby?"

"Lean down," Edie said. "Toward me. And he'll speak to you." Her face, like her mother's, was grim.

Hoppy leaned toward her, cocking his head on one side, in a mock-serious gesture of attention.

A voice, speaking from inside him, as if it were a part of the interior world, said, "How did you fix that record changer? How did you *really* do that?"

Hoppy screamed.

Everyone was staring at him, white-faced; they were on their feet, now, all of them rigid.

"I heard Jim Fergesson," Hoppy said.

The girl regarded him calmly. "Do you want to hear my brother say more, Mr. Harrington? Say some more words to him, Bill; he wants you to say more."

And, in Hoppy's interior world, the voice said, "It looked like you healed it. It looked like instead of replacing that broken spring—"

Hoppy wheeled his cart wildly, spun up the aisle to the far end of the room, wheeled again and sat panting, a long way from the Keller girl; his heart pounded and he stared at her. She returned his stare silently, but now with the faint trace of a smile on her lips.

"You heard my brother, didn't you?" she said.

"Yes," Hoppy said. "Yes I did."

"And you know where he is."

"Yes." He nodded. "Don't do it again. Please. I won't do any more imitations if you don't want me to; okay?" He looked pleadingly at her, but there was no response there, no promise. "I'm sorry," he said to her. "I believe you now."

"Good lord," Bonny said softly. She turned toward her husband, as if questioning him. George shook his head but did not answer.

Slowly and steadily the child said, "You can see him too, if you want, Mr. Harrington. Would you like to see what he looks like?"

"No," he said. "I don't want to."

"Did he scare you?" Now the child was openly smiling at him, but her smile was empty and cold. "He paid you back because you were picking on me. It made him angry, so he did that."

Coming up beside Hoppy, George Keller said, "What happened, Hop?"

"Nothing," he said shortly.

Scared me, he thought. Fooled me, by imitating Jim Fergesson; he took me completely in, I really thought it was Jim again. Edie was conceived the day Jim Fergesson died; I know because Bonny told me once, and I think her brother was conceived simultaneously. But—it's not true; it wasn't Jim. It was —an *imitation*.

"You see," the child said, "Bill does imitations, too."

"Yes." He nodded, trembling. "Yes, he does."

"They're good." Edie's dark eyes sparkled.

"Yes, very good," Hoppy said. As good as mine, he thought. Maybe better than mine. I better be careful of him, he thought, of her brother Bill; I better stay away. I really learned my lesson.

It could have been Fergesson, he realized, in there. Reborn, what they call reincarnation; the bomb might have done it somehow in a way I don't understand. Then it's not an imitation and I was right the first time, but how'll I know? He won't tell me; he hates me, I guess because I made fun of his sister Edie. That was a mistake; I shouldn't have done that.

"Hoode hoode hoo," he said, and a few people turned his way; he got some attention, here and there in the room. "Well, this is your old pal," he said. But his heart wasn't in it; his voice shook. He grinned at them, but no one grinned back. "Maybe we can pick up the reading a little while more," he said. "Edie's brother wants to listen to it." Sending out an extensor, he turned up the volume of the radio, tuned the dial.

You can have what you want, he thought to himself. The reading or anything else. How long have you been in there? Only seven years? It seems more like forever. As if—you've always existed. It had been a terribly old, wizened, white thing that had spoken to him. Something hard and small, floating. Lips overgrown with downy hair that hung trailing, streamers of it, wispy and dry. I bet it was Fergesson, he said to himself; it *felt* like him. He's in there, inside that child.

I wonder. Can he get out?

Edie Keller said to her brother, "What did you do to scare him like you did? He was really scared."

From within her the familiar voice said, "I was someone he used to know, a long time ago. Someone dead."

"Oh," she said, "so that's it. I thought it was something like that." She was amused. "Are you going to do any more to him?"

"If I don't like him," Bill said, "I may do more to him, a lot of different things, maybe."

"How did you know about the dead person?"

"Oh," Bill said, "because—you know why. Because I'm dead, too." He chuckled, deep down inside her stomach; she felt him quiver.

"No you're not," she said. "You're as alive as I am, so don't say that; it isn't right." It frightened her.

Bill said, "I was just pretending; I'm sorry. I wish I could have seen his face. How did it look?"

"Awful," Edie said, "when you said that. It turned all inward, like a frog's. But you wouldn't know what a frog looks like either; you don't know what anything looks like, so there's no use trying to tell you."

"I wish I could come out," Bill said plaintively. "I wish I could be born like everybody else. Can't I be born later on?"

"Doctor Stockstill said you couldn't."

"Then can't he make it so I could be? I thought you said—"

"I was wrong," Edie said. "I thought he could cut a little round hole and that would do it, but he said no."

Her brother, deep within her, was silent, then.

"Don't feel bad," Edie said. "I'll keep on telling you how things are." She wanted to console him; she said, "I'll never do again like I did that time when I was mad at you, when I stopped telling you about what's outside; I promise."

"Maybe I could *make* Doctor Stockstill let me out," Bill said.

"Can you do that? You can't."

"I can if I want."

"No," she said. "You're lying; you can't do anything but sleep and talk to the dead and maybe do imitations like you did. That isn't much; I can practically do that myself, and a lot more."

There was no response from within.

"Bill," she said, "you know what? Well, now two people know about you—Hoppy Harrington does and Doctor Stockstill does. And you used to say nobody would ever find out about you, so you're not so smart. I don't think you're very smart."

Within her, Bill slept.

"If you did anything bad," she said, "I could swallow something that would poison you. Isn't that so? So you better behave."

She felt more and more afraid of him; she was talking to herself, trying to bolster her confidence. Maybe it would be a good thing if you did die, she thought. Only then I'd have to carry you around still, and it—wouldn't be pleasant; I wouldn't like that.

She shuddered.

"Don't worry about me," Bill said suddenly. He had become awake again or maybe he had never been asleep at all; maybe he had just been pretending. "I know a lot of things; I can take care of myself. I'll protect you, too. You better be glad about me because I can—well, you wouldn't understand. You know I can look at everyone who's dead, like the man I imitated. Well, there're a whole lot of them, trillions and trillions of them and they're all different. When I'm asleep I hear them muttering. They're still all around."

"Around where?" she asked.

"Underneath us," Bill said. "Down in the ground."

"Brrr," she said.

Bill laughed. "It's true. And we're going to be there, too. And so is Mommy and Daddy and everybody else. Everybody and everything's there, including animals. That dog's almost there, that one that talks. Not there yet, maybe; but it's the same. You'll see."

"I don't want to see," she said. "I want to listen to the

reading; you be quiet so I can listen. Don't you want to listen, too? You always say you like it."

"He'll be there soon, too," Bill said. "The man who does the reading up in the satellite."

"No," she said. "I don't believe that; are you sure?"

"Yes," her brother said. "Pretty sure. And even before him—do you know who the 'glasses man' is? You don't, but he'll be there very soon, in just a few minutes. And then later on—" He broke off. "I won't say."

"No," she agreed. "Don't say, please. I don't want to hear."

Guided by the tall, crooked mast of Hoppy's transmitter, Eldon Blaine made his way toward the phocomelus' house. It's now or never, he realized. I have only a little time. No one stopped him; they were all at the Hall, including the phocomelus himself. I'll get that radio and nap it, Eldon said to himself. If I can't get him at least I can return to Bolinas with something. The transmitter was now close ahead; he felt the presence of Hoppy's construction—and then all at once he was stumbling over something. He fell, floundered with his arms out. The remains of a fence, low to the ground.

Now he saw the house itself, or what remained of it. Foundations and one wall, and in the center a patched-together cube, a room made out of debris, protected from rain by tar paper. The mast, secured by heavy guy wires, rose directly behind a little metal chimney.

The transmitter was on.

He heard the hum even before he saw the gaseous blue light of its tubes. And from the crack under the door of the tar-paper cube more light streamed out. He found the knob, paused, and then quickly turned it; the door swung open with no resistance, almost as if something inside were expecting him.

A friendly, intimate voice murmured, and Eldon Blaine glanced around, chilled, expecting to see—incredibly—the phocomelus. But the voice came from a radio mounted on a work bench on which lay tools and meters and repair parts in utter disorder. Dangerfield, still speaking, even though the satellite surely had passed on. Contact with the satellite such as no one else had achieved, he realized. They even have that, up here in West Marin. But why was the big transmitter on? What was it doing? He began to look hastily around. . . .

From the radio the low, intimate voice suddenly changed; it became harsher, sharper. "Glasses man," it said, "what are you doing in my house?" It was the voice of Hoppy Harrington, and Eldon stood bewildered, rubbing his head numbly, trying to understand and knowing on a deep, instinctive level that he did not—and never really would.

"Hoppy," he managed to say. "Where are you?"

"I'm here," the voice from the radio said. "I'm coming closer. Wait where you are, glasses man." The door of the room opened and Hoppy Harrington, aboard his phocomobile, his eyes sharp and blazing, confronted Eldon. "Welcome to my home," Hoppy said caustically, and his voice now issued from him and from the speaker of the radio both. "Did you think you had the satellite, there on that set?" One of his manual extensions reached out, and the radio was shut off. "Maybe you did, or maybe you will, someday. Well, glasses man, speak up. What do you want here?"

Eldon said, "Let me go. I don't want anything; I was just looking around."

"Do you want the radio, is that it?" Hoppy said in an expressionless voice. He seemed resigned, not surprised in the least.

Eldon said, "Why is your transmitter on?"

"Because I'm transmitting to the satellite."

"If you'll let me go," Eldon said, "I'll give you all the glasses I have. And they represent months of scavenging all over Northern California."

"You don't have any glasses this time," the phocomelus said. "I don't see your briefcase, anyhow. But you can go, though, as far as I'm concerned; you haven't done anything wrong, here. I didn't give you the chance." He laughed in his brisk, stammering way.

Eldon said, "Are you going to try to bring down the satellite?"

The phocomelus stared at him.

"You are," Eldon said. "With that transmitter you're going to set off that final stage that never fired; you'll make it act as a retro-rocket and then it'll fall back into the atmosphere and eventually come down."

"I couldn't do that," Hoppy said, finally. "Even if I wanted to."

"You can affect things at a distance."

"I'll tell you what I'm doing, glasses man." Wheeling his 'mobile past Eldon, the phocomelus sent an extension thrusting out to pick up an object from his work bench. "Do you recognize this? It's a reel of recording tape. It will be transmitted to the satellite at tremendously high speed, so that hours of information are conveyed in a few moments. And at the same time, all the messages which the satellite has been re-ceiving during its transit will be broadcast down to me the same way, at ultra high speed. This is how it was designed to work originally, glasses man. Before the Emergency, before the monitoring equipment down here was lost."

Eldon Blaine looked at the radio on the work bench and then he stole a glance at the door. The phocomobile had moved so that the door was no longer blocked. He wondered if he could do it, if he had a chance.

"I can transmit to a distance of three hundred miles," Hoppy was saying. "I could reach receivers up and down Northern California, but that's all, by transmitting direct. But by sending my messages to the satellite to be recorded and then played back again and again as it moves on—"

"You can reach the entire world," Eldon said.

"That's right," Hoppy said. "There's the necessary ma-chinery aboard; it'll obey all sorts of instructions from the ground."

"And then you'll be Dangerfield," Eldon said.

The phocomelus smiled and stammered, "And no one will know the difference. I can pull it off; I've got everything worked out. What's the alternative. Silence. The satellite will fall silent any day, now. And then the one voice that unifies the world will be gone and the world will decay. I'm ready to cut Dangerfield off any moment, now. As soon as I'm positive that he's really going to cease."

"Does he know about you?"

"No," Hoppy said.

"I'll tell you what I think," Eldon said. "I think Dangerfield's been dead for a long time, and it's actually been you we've been listening to." As he spoke he moved closer to the radio on the work bench.

"That's not so," the phocomelus said, in a steady voice. He went on, then, "But it won't be long, now. It's amazing he's survived such conditions; the military people did a good job in selecting him."

Eldon Blaine swept up the radio in his arms and ran toward the door.

Astonished, the phocomelus gaped at him; Eldon saw the expression on Hoppy's face and then he was outside, running through the darkness toward the parked police cart. I distracted him, Eldon said to himself. The poor damn phoce had no idea what I was going to do. All that talk—what did it mean? Nothing. Delusions of grandeur; he wants to sit down here and talk to the entire world, receive the entire world, make it his audience . . . but no one can do that except Dangerfield; no one can work the machinery in the satellite from down here. The phoce would have to be inside it, up there, and it's impossible to—

Something caught him by the back of the neck.

How? Eldon Blaine asked himself as he pitched face-forward, still clutching the radio. He's back there in the house and I'm out here. Action at a distance . . . he has hold of me. Was I wrong? Can he really reach out so far?

The thing that had hold of him by the neck squeezed.

XI

Picking up the first mimeographed sheet of the West Marin *News & Views*, the little twice-monthly newspaper which he put out, Paul Dietz scrutinized critically the lead item, which he had written himself.

BOLINAS MAN DIES OF BROKEN NECK
Four days ago Eldon Blaine, a glasses man from Bolinas, California, visiting this part of the country on business, was found by the side of the road with his neck broken and marks indicating violence by someone unknown. Earl Colvig, Chief of the West Marin Police, has begun an extensive investigation and is talking to various people who saw Blaine that night.

Such was the item in its entirety, and Dietz, reading it, felt deep satisfaction; he had a good lead for this edition of his paper—a lot of people would be interested, and maybe for the next edition he could get a few more ads. His main source of income came from Andy Gill, who always advertised his tobacco and liquor, and from Fred Quinn, the pharmacist, and of course he had several classifieds. But it was not like the old days.

Of course the thing he had left out of his item was the fact that the Bolinas glasses man was in West Marin for no good purpose; everyone knew that. There had even been speculation that he had come to nap their handy. But since that was mere conjecture, it could not be printed.

He turned to the next item in terms of importance.

DANGERFIELD SAID TO BE AILING
Persons attending the nightly broadcasts from the satellite report that Walt Dangerfield declared the other day that he "was sick, possibly with an ulcerous or coronary condition," and needed medical attention. Much concern was exhibited by the persons at the Foresters' Hall, it was further reported. Mr. Cas Stone, who informed the *News & Views* of this, stated that as a last resort his

personal specialist in San Rafael would be consulted, and it was discussed without a decision being reached that Fred Quinn, owner of the Point Reyes Pharmacy, might journey to Army Headquarters at Cheyenne to offer drugs for Dangerfield's use.

The rest of the paper consisted of local items of lesser interest; who had dined with whom, who had visited what nearby town . . . he glanced briefly at them, made sure that the ads were printed perfectly, and then began to run off further sheets.

And then, of course, there were items missing from the paper, items which could never be put into print. Hoppy Harrington terrified by seven-year-old child, for instance. Dietz chuckled, thinking of the reports he had received about the phoce's fright, his fit right out in public. Mrs. Bonny Keller having another affair, this time with the new school teacher, Hal Barnes . . . that would have made a swell item. Jack Tree, local sheep rancher, accuses unnamed persons (for the millionth time) of stealing his sheep. What else? Let's see, he thought. Famous tobacco expert, Andrew Gill, visited by unknown city person, probably having to do with a merger of Gill's tobacco and liquor business and some huge city syndicate as yet unknown. At that, he frowned. If Gill moved from the area, the *News & Views* would lose its most constant ad; that was not good at all.

Maybe I ought to print that, he thought. Stir up local feeling against Gill for whatever it is he's doing. Foreign influences felt in local tobacco business . . . I could phrase it that way. Outside persons of questionable origin seen in area. That sort of talk. It might dissuade Gill; after all, he's a newcomer—he's sensitive. He's only been here since the Emergency. He's not really one of us.

Who was this sinister figure seen talking to Gill? Everyone in town was curious. No one liked it. Some said he was a Negro; some thought it was radiation burns—a war-darky, as they were called.

Maybe what happened to that Bolinas glasses man will happen to him, Dietz conjectured. Because there's too many people here who don't like outside foreign influences; it's dangerous to come around here and meddle.

The Eldon Blaine killing reminded him, naturally, of the Austurias one . . . although the latter had been done legally, out in the open, by the Citizens' Council and Jury. Still, there was in essence little difference; both were legitimate expressions of the town's sentiments. As would be the sudden disappearance from this world of the Negro or war-darky or whatever he was who now hung around Gill—and it was always possible that some retaliation might be taken out on Gill as well.

But Gill had powerful friends; for instance, the Kellers. And many people were dependent on his cigarettes and liquor; both Orion Stroud and Cas Stone bought from him in huge quantity. So probably Gill was safe.

But not the darky, Dietz realized. I wouldn't like to be in his shoes. He's from the city and he doesn't realize the depth of feeling in a small community. We have integrity, here, and we don't intend to see it violated.

Maybe he'll have to learn the hard way. Maybe we'll have to see one more killing. A darky-killing. And in some ways that's the best kind.

Gliding down the center street of Point Reyes, Hoppy Harrington sat bolt-upright in the center of his 'mobile as he saw a dark man familiar to him. It was a man he had known years ago, worked with at Modern TV Sales & Service; it looked like Stuart McConchie.

But then the phoce realized that it was another of Bill's imitations.

He felt terror, to think of the power of the creature inside Edie Keller; it could do this, in broad daylight, and what did he himself have to counter it? As with the voice of Jim Fergesson the other night he had been taken in; it had fooled him, despite his own enormous abilities. I don't know what to do, he said to himself frantically; he kept gliding on, toward the dark figure. It did not vanish.

Maybe, he thought, Bill knows I did that to the glasses man. Maybe he's paying me back. Children do things like that.

Turning his cart down a side street he picked up speed, escaping from the vicinity of the imitation of Stuart McConchie.

"Hey," a voice said warningly.

Glancing about, Hoppy discovered that he had almost run over Doctor Stockstill. Chagrined, he slowed his 'mobile to a halt. "Sorry." He eyed the doctor narrowly, then, thinking that here was a man he had known in the old days, before the Emergency; Stockstill had been a psychiatrist with an office in Berkeley, and Hoppy had seen him now and then along Shattuck Avenue. Why was he here? How had he happened to decide on West Marin, as Hoppy had? Was it only coincidence?

And then the phocomelus thought, Maybe Stockstill is a perpetual imitation, brought into existence the day the first bomb fell on the Bay Area; that was the day Bill was conceived, wasn't it?

That Bonny Keller, he thought; it all emanates from her. All the trouble in the community . . . the Austurias situation, which almost wrecked us, divided us into two hostile camps. She saw to it that Austurias was killed, and actually it should have been that degenerate, that Jack Tree up there with his sheep; he's the one who should have been shot, not the former school teacher.

That was a good man, a kindly person, the phoce thought, thinking of Mr. Austurias. And hardly anyone—except me—supported him openly at his so-called trial.

To the phoce, Doctor Stockstill said tartly, "Be more careful with that 'mobile of yours, Hoppy. As a personal favor to me."

"I said I was sorry," Hoppy answered.

"What are you afraid of?" the doctor said.

"Nothing," Hoppy said. "I'm afraid of nothing in the entire world." And then he remembered the incident at the Foresters' Hall, how he had behaved. And it was all over town; Doctor Stockstill knew about it even though he had not been present. "I have a phobia," he admitted, on impulse. "Is that in your line, or have you given that up? It has to do with being trapped. I was trapped once in a basement, the day the first bomb fell. It saved my life, but—" He shrugged.

Stockstill said, "I see."

"Have you ever examined the little Keller girl?" Hoppy said.

"Yes," Stockstill said.

With acuity, Hoppy said, "Then you know. There's not just one child but two. They're combined somehow; you probably know exactly how, but I don't—and I don't care. That's a funny person, that child, or rather she and her brother; isn't that so?" His bitterness spilled out. "They don't look funny. So they get by. People just go on externals, don't they? Haven't you discovered that in your practice?"

Stockstill said, "By and large, yes."

"I heard," Hoppy said, "that according to State law, all funny minors, all children who are in any way funny, either feral or not, have to be turned over to Sacramento, to the authorities."

There was no response from the doctor; Stockstill eyed him silently.

"You're aiding the Kellers in breaking the law," Hoppy said.

After a pause, Stockstill said, "What do you want, Hoppy?" His voice was low and steady.

"N-nothing," Hoppy stammered. "Just justice, I mean; I want to see the law obeyed. Is that wrong? I keep the law. I'm registered with the U.S. Eugenics Service as a—" He choked on the word. "As a biological sport. That's a dreadful thing to do, but I do it; I comply."

"Hoppy," the doctor said quietly, "what did you do to the glasses man from Bolinas?"

Spinning his 'mobile, Hoppy glided swiftly off, leaving the doctor standing there.

What did I do to him, Hoppy thought. I killed him; you know that. Why do you ask? What do you care? The man was from outside this area; he didn't count, and we all know that. And June Raub says he wanted to nap me, and that's good enough for most people—it's good enough for Earl Colvig and Orion Stroud and Cas Stone, and they run this community, along with Mrs. Tallman and the Kellers and June Raub.

He knows I killed Blaine, he realized. He knows a lot about me, even though I've never let him examine me physically; he knows I can perform action at a distance . . . but everyone knows that. Yet, perhaps he's the only one who understands what it signifies. He's an educated man.

If I see that imitation of Stuart McConchie, he thought suddenly, I will reach out and squeeze it to death. I have to.

But I hope I don't see it again, he thought. I can't stand the dead; my phobia is about that, the *grave*: I was buried down in the grave with the part of Fergesson that was not disintegrated, and it was awful. For two weeks, with half of a man who had consideration for me, more so than anyone else I ever knew. What would you say, Stockstill, if you had me on your analyst's couch? Would that sort of traumatic incident interest you, or have there been too many like it in the last seven years?

That Bill-thing with Edie Keller lives somehow with the dead, Hoppy said to himself. Half in our world, half in the other. He laughed bitterly, thinking of the time he had imagined that he himself could contact the other world . . . it was quite a joke on me, he thought. I fooled myself more than anybody else. And they never knew. Stuart McConchie and the rat, Stuart sitting there munching with relish . . .

And then he understood. That meant that Stuart survived; he had not been killed in the Emergency, at least not at first, as Fergesson had. So this perhaps was not an imitation that he had seen just now.

Trembling, he halted his 'mobile and sat rapidly thinking.

Does he know anything about me? he asked himself. Can he get me into any trouble? No, he decided, because in those days —what was I? Just a helpless creature on a Government-built cart who was glad of any job he could find, any scrap tossed to him. A lot has changed. Now I am vital to the entire West Marin area, he told himself; I am a top-notch handy.

Rolling back the way he had come he emerged once more on the main street and searched about for Stuart McConchie. Sure enough, there he was, heading in the direction of Andrew Gill's tobacco and liquor factory. The phoce started to wheel after him, and then an idea came to him.

He caused McConchie to stumble.

Seated within his 'mobile he grinned to himself as he saw the Negro trip, half-fall, then regain his footing. McConchie peered down at the pavement, scowling. Then he continued on, more slowly now, picking his way over the broken cement and around the tufts of weeds with care.

The phoce wheeled after him and when he was a pace or so behind he said, "Stuart McConchie, the TV salesman who eats raw rats."

As if struck the Negro tottered. He did not turn; he simply stood, his arms extended, fingers apart.

"How are you enjoying the afterlife?" Hoppy said.

After a moment the Negro said in a hoarse voice, "Fine." He turned, now. "So you got by." He looked the phoce and his 'mobile up and down.

"Yes," the phoce said, "I did. And not by eating rats."

"I suppose you're the handy here," Stuart said.

"Yes," Hoppy said. "No-hands Handy Hoppy; that's me. What are you doing?"

"I'm—in the homeostatic vermin trap business," Stuart said.

The phoce giggled.

"Is that so goddam funny?" Stuart said.

"No," the phoce said. "Sorry. I'm glad you survived. Who else did? That psychiatrist across from Modern—he's here. Stockstill. Fergesson was killed."

They both were silent then.

"Lightheiser was killed," Stuart said. "So was Bob Rubenstein. So were Connie the waitress and Tony; you remember them."

"Yes," the phoce said, nodding.

"Did you know Mr. Crody, the jeweler?"

"No," the phoce said, "afraid not."

"He was maimed. Lost both arms and was blinded. But he's alive in a Government hospital in Hayward."

"Why are you up here?" the phoce said.

"On business."

"Did you come to steal Andrew Gill's formula for his special deluxe Gold Label cigarette?" Again the phoce giggled, but he thought, It's true. Everyone who comes sneaking up here from outside has a plan to murder or steal; look at Eldon Blaine the glasses man, and he came from Bolinas, a much closer place.

Stuart said woodenly, "My business compels me to travel; I get all around Northern California." After a pause he added. "That was especially true when I had Edward Prince of Wales. Now I have a second-rate horse to pull my car, and it takes a lot longer to get somewhere."

"Listen," Hoppy said, "don't tell anyone you know me from before, because if you do I'll get very upset; do you understand? I've been a vital part of this community for many years and I don't want anything to come along and change it. Maybe I can help you with your business and then you can leave. How about that?"

"Okay," Stuart said. "I'll leave as soon as I can." He studied the phoce with such intensity that Hoppy felt himself squirm with self-consciousness. "So you found a place for yourself." Stuart said. "Good for you."

Hoppy said, "I'll introduce you to Gill; that's what I'll do for you. I'm a good friend of his, naturally."

Nodding, Stuart said, "Fine. I'd appreciate that."

"And don't you do anything, you hear?" The phoce heard his voice rise shrilly; he could not control it. "Don't you nap or do any other crime, or terrible things will happen to you—understand?"

The Negro nodded somberly. But he did not appear to be frightened; he did not cringe, and the phoce felt more and more apprehensive. I wish you would go, the phoce thought to himself. Get out of here; don't make trouble for me. I wish I didn't know you; I wish I didn't know anyone from outside, from before the Emergency. I don't want even to think about that.

"I hid in the sidewalk," Stuart said suddenly. "When the first big bomb fell. I got down through the grating; it was a real good shelter."

"Why do you bring up that?" the phoce squealed.

"I don't know. I thought you'd be interested."

"I'm not," the phoce squealed; he clapped his manual extensors over his ears. "I don't want to hear or think any more about those times."

"Well," Stuart said, plucking meditatively at his lower lip, "then let's go see this Andrew Gill."

"If you knew what I could do to you," the phoce said, "you'd be afraid. I can do—" He broke off; he had been about to mention Eldon Blaine the glasses man. "I can move things," he said. "From a long way off. It's a form of magic; I'm a magician!"

Stuart said, "That's not magic." He voice was toneless. "We call that *freak-tapping*." He smiled.

"N-no," Hoppy stammered. "What's that mean? 'Freak-tapping,' I never heard that word. Like table-tapping?"

"Yes, but with freaks. With funny people."

He's not afraid of me, Hoppy realized. It's because he knew me in the old days when I wasn't anything. It was hopeless; the Negro was too stupid to understand that everything had changed—he was almost as he had been before, seven years ago, when Hoppy had last seen him. He was inert, like a rock.

Hoppy thought of the satellite, then. "You wait," he said breathlessly to Stuart. "Pretty soon even you city people will know about me; everyone in the world will, just like they do around here. It won't be long now; I'm almost ready!"

Grinning tolerantly, Stuart said, "First impress me by introducing me to the tobacco man."

"You know what I could do?" Hoppy said. "I could whisk Andrew Gill's formula right out of his safe or wherever he keeps it and plunk it down in your hands. What do you say to that?" He laughed.

"Just let me meet him," Stuart repeated. "That's all I want; I'm not interested in his tobacco-formula." He looked weary.

Trembling with anxiety and rage, the phoce turned his 'mobile in the direction of Andrew Gill's little factory and led the way.

Andrew Gill glanced up from his task of rolling cigarettes to see Hoppy Harrington—whom he did not like—entering the factory with a Negro—whom he did not know. At once Gill felt uneasy. He set down his tobacco paper and rose to his feet. Beside him at the long bench the other rollers, his employees, continued at their work.

He employed, in all, eight men, and this was in the tobacco division alone. The distillery, which produced brandy, employed another twelve men, but they were north, in Sonoma County. They were not local people. His was the largest commercial enterprise in West Marin, not counting the farming interests such as Orion Stroud or Jack Tree's sheep ranch, and he sold his products all over Northern California; his cigarettes traveled, in slow stages, from one town to another and a few, he understood, had even gotten back to the East Coast and were known there.

"Yes?" he said to Hoppy. He placed himself in front of the phoce's cart, halting him at a distance from the work-area. Once, this had been the town's bakery; being made of cement, it had survived the bomb blasts and made an ideal place for him. And of course he paid his employees almost nothing; they were glad to have jobs at any salary.

Hoppy stammered, "This m-man came up from Berkeley to see you, Mr. Gill; he's an important businessman, he says. Isn't that right?" The phoce turned toward the Negro. "That's what you said to me, isn't it?"

Holding out his hand, the Negro said to Gill, "I represent the Hardy Homeostatic Vermin Trap Corporation of Berkeley, California. I'm here to acquaint you with an amazing proposition that could well mean tripling your profits within six months." His dark eyes blazed.

There was silence.

Gill repressed the impulse to laugh aloud. "I see," he said, nodding and putting his hands in his pockets; he assumed a serious stance. "Very interesting, Mr.—" He glanced questioningly at the Negro.

"Stuart McConchie," the Negro said.

They shook hands.

"My employer, Mr. Hardy," Stuart said, "has empowered me to describe to you in detail the design of a fully automated cigarette-making machine. We at Hardy Homeostatic are well aware that your cigarettes are rolled entirely in the old-fashioned way, by hand." He pointed toward the employees working in the rear of the factory. "Such a method is a hundred years out of date, Mr. Gill. You've achieved superb quality in your special deluxe Gold Label cigarettes—"

"Which I intend to maintain," Gill said quietly.

Mr. McConchie said, "Our automated electronic equipment will in no way sacrifice quality for quantity. In fact—"

"Wait," Gill said. "I don't want to discuss this now." He glanced toward the phoce, who was parked close by, listening. The phoce flushed and at once spun his 'mobile away.

"I'm going," Hoppy said. "This doesn't interest me; good-bye." He wheeled through the open door of the factory, out onto the street. The two of them watched him go until he disappeared.

"Our handy," Gill said.

McConchie started to speak, then changed his mind, cleared his throat and strolled a few steps away, surveying the factory and the men at their work. "Nice place you have here, Gill. I want to state right now how much I admire your product; it's first in its field, no doubt of that."

I haven't heard talk like that, Gill realized, in seven years. It was difficult to believe that it still existed in the world; so much had changed and yet here, in this man McConchie, it remained intact. Gill felt a glow of pleasure. It reminded him of happier times, this salesman's line of chatter. He felt amiably inclined toward the man.

"Thank you," he said, and meant it. Perhaps the world, at last, was really beginning to regain some of its old forms, its civilities and customs and preoccupations, all that had gone into it to make it what it was. This, he thought, this talk by McConchie; it's authentic. It's a survival, not a simulation; this man has somehow managed to preserve his viewpoint, his enthusiasm, through all that has happened—he is still planning, cogitating, bullshitting . . . nothing can or will stop him.

He is, Gill realized, simply a good salesman. He has not let even a hydrogen war and the collapse of society dissuade him.

"How about a cup of coffee?" Gill said. "I'll take a break for ten or fifteen minutes and you can tell me more about this automated machine or whatever it is."

"Real coffee?" McConchie said, and the pleasant, optimistic mask slid for an instant from his face; he gaped at Gill with naked, eager hunger.

"Sorry," Gill said. "It's a substitute, but not bad; I think you'll like it. Better than what's sold in the city at those so-called 'coffee' stands." He went to get the pot of water.

"Quite a place you have here," McConchie said, as they waited for the coffee to heat. "Very impressive and industrious."

"Thank you," Gill said.

"Coming here is a long-time dream fulfilled," McConchie went on. "It took me a week to make the trip and I'd been thinking about it ever since I smoked my first special deluxe

Gold Label. It's—" He groped for words to express his thought. "An island of civilization in these barbaric times."

Gill said, "What do you think of the country, as such? A small town like this, compared to life in the city . . . it's very different."

"I just got here," McConchie said. "I came straight to you; I didn't take time to explore. My horse needed a new right front shoe and I left him at the first stable as you cross the little metal bridge."

"Oh yes," Gill said. "That belongs to Stroud; I know where you mean. His blacksmith'll do a good job."

McConchie said, "Life seems much more peaceful here. In the city if you leave your horse—well, a while ago I left my horse to go across the Bay and when I got back someone had eaten it, and it's things like that that make you disgusted with the city and want to move on."

"I know," Gill said, nodding in agreement. "It's brutal in the city because there're still so many homeless and destitute people."

"I really loved that horse," McConchie said, looking doleful.

'Well," Gill said, "in the country you're faced constantly with the death of animals; that's always been one of the basic unpleasant verities of rural life. When the bombs fell, thousands of animals up here were horribly injured; sheep and cattle . . . but that can't compare of course to the injury to human life down where you come from. You must have seen a good deal of human misery, since E Day."

The Negro nodded. "That and the sporting. The freaks both as regards animals and people. Now Hoppy—"

"Hoppy isn't originally from this area," Gill said. "He showed up here after the war in response to our advertising for a handyman. I'm not from here, either; I was traveling through the day the bomb fell, and I elected to remain."

The coffee being ready, the two of them began to drink. Neither man spoke for a time.

"What sort of vermin trap does your company make?" Gill asked, presently.

"It's not a passive type," McConchie said. "Being homeostatic, that is, self-instructing, it follows for instance a rat—or a cat or dog—down into the network of burrows such as now underlie Berkeley . . . it pursues one rat after another, killing one and going on to the next—until it runs out of fuel or by chance a rat manages to destroy it. There are a few brilliant rats—you know, mutations that are higher on the evolutionary scale—that know how to lame a Hardy Homeostatic Vermin Trap. But not many can."

"Impressive," Gill murmured.

"Now, our proposed cigarette-rolling machine—"

"My friend," Gill said, "I like you but—here's the problem. I don't have any money to buy your machine and I don't have anything to trade you. And I don't intend to let anyone enter my business as a partner. So what does that leave?" He smiled. "I have to continue as I am."

"Wait," McConchie said instantly. "There must be a solution. Maybe we could lease you a Hardy cigarette-rolling machine in exchange for x-number of cigarettes, your special deluxe Gold Label variety, of course, delivered each week for x-number of weeks." His face glowed with animation. "The Hardy Corporation for instance could become sole licensed distributors of your cigarette; we could represent you everywhere, develop a systematic network of outlets up and down Northern California instead of the haphazard system you now appear to employ. What do you say to that?"

"Hmmmm," Gill said. "I must admit it does sound interesting. I admit that distribution has not been my cup of tea . . . I've thought off and on for several years about the need of getting an organization going, especially with my factory being located in a rural spot, as it is. I've even thought about moving into the city, but the napping and vandalism is too great there. And I don't want to move back to the city; this is my home, here."

He did not say anything about Bonny Keller. That was his real reason for remaining in West Marin; his affair with her had ended years ago but he was more in love with her now than ever. He had watched her go from man to man, becoming more dissatisfied with each of them, and Gill believed in his own heart that someday he would get her back. And Bonny was the mother of his daughter; he was well aware that Edie Keller was his child.

"You're sure," he said suddenly, "that you didn't come up here to steal the formula for my cigarettes?"

McConchie laughed.

"You laugh," Gill said, "but you don't answer."

"No, that's not why I'm here," the Negro said. "We're in the business of making electronic machines, not cigarettes." But, it seemed to Gill, he had an evasive look on his face, and his voice was too full of confidence, too nonchalant. All at once Gill felt uneasy.

Or is it the rural mentality? he asked himself. The isolation getting the better of me; suspicion of all newcomers . . . of anything strange.

I had better be careful, though, he decided. I must not get carried away just because this man recalls for me the good old pre-war days. I must inspect this machine with great suspicion. After all, I could have gotten Hoppy to design and build such a machine; he seems quite capable in that direction. I could have done all these things proposed to me *entirely by myself.*

Perhaps I am lonely, he thought. That might be it; I am lonely for city people and their manner of thought. The country gets me down—Point Reyes with its *News & Views* filled up with mediocre gossip, and mimeographed!

"Since you're just up from the city," he said aloud, "I might as well ask you—is there any interesting national or international news, of late, that I might not have heard? We do get the satellite, but I'm frankly tired of disc jockey talk and music. And those endless readings."

They both laughed. "I know what you mean," McConchie said, sipping his coffee and nodding. "Well, let's see. I understand that an attempt is being made to produce an automobile again, somewhere around the ruins of Detroit. It's mostly made of plywood but it does run on kerosene."

"I don't know where they're going to get the kerosene," Gill said. "Before they build a car they better get a few refineries operating again. And repair a few major roads."

"Oh, something else. The Government plans to reopen one of the routes across the Rockies sometime this year. For the first time since the war."

"That's great news," Gill said, pleased. "I didn't know that."

"And the telephone companies—"

"Wait," Gill said, rising. "How about a little brandy in your coffee? How long has it been since you've had a coffee royal?"

"Years," Stuart McConchie said.

"This is Gill's Five Star. My own. From the Sonoma Valley." He poured from the squat bottle into McConchie's cup.

"Here's something else that might interest you." McConchie reached into his coat pocket and brought out something flat and folded. He opened it up, spread it out, and Gill saw an envelope.

"What is it?" Picking it up, Gill examined it without seeing anything unusual. An ordinary envelope with an address, a cancelled stamp . . . and then he understood, and he could scarcely credit his senses. *Mail service*. A letter from New York.

"That's right," McConchie said. "Delivered to my boss, Mr. Hardy. All the way from the East Coast; it only took four weeks. The Government in Cheyenne, the military people; they're responsible. It's done partly by blimp, partly by truck, partly by horse. The last stage is on foot."

"Good lord," Gill said. And he poured some Gill's Five Star into *his* coffee, too.

XII

"IT was Hoppy who killed the glasses man from Bolinas," Bill said to his sister. "And he plans to kill someone later on, too, and then I can't tell but after that it's something more like that, again."

His sister had been playing Rock, Scissors, Paper with three other children; now she stopped, jumped to her feet and quickly ran to the edge of the school grounds, where she would be alone and could talk to Bill. "How do you know that?" she asked, excited.

"Because I talked to Mr. Blaine," Bill said. "He's down below now, and there's others coming. I'd like to come out and hurt Hoppy; Mr. Blaine says I should. Ask Doctor Stockstill again if I can't be born." Her brother's voice was plaintive. "If I could be born even for just a little while—"

"Maybe I could hurt him," Edie said thoughtfully. "Ask Mr. Blaine what I ought to do. I'm sort of afraid of Hoppy."

"I could do imitations that would kill him," Bill said, "if I only could get out. I have some swell ones. You should hear Hoppy's father; I do that real good. Want to hear?" In a low, grown-up man's voice he said, "I see where Kennedy proposes another one of those tax cuts of his. If he thinks he can fix up the economy that way he's crazier than I think he is, and that's damn crazy."

"Do me," Edie said. "Imitate me."

"How can I?" Bill said. "You're not dead yet."

Edie said, "What's it like to be dead? I'm going to be some-day so I want to know."

"It's funny. You're down in a hole looking up. And you're all flat like—well, like you're empty. And, you know what? Then after a while you come back. You blow away and where you get blown away to is back again! Did you know that? I mean, back where you are right now. All fat and alive."

"No," Edie said. "I didn't know that." She felt bored; she wanted to hear more about how Hoppy had killed Mr. Blaine. After a point the dead people down below weren't very inter-esting because they never did anything, they just waited around. Some of them, like Mr. Blaine, thought all the time about killing and others just mooned like vegetables—Bill had told her many times because he was so interested. He thought it mattered.

Bill said, "Listen, Edie, let's try the animal experiment again; okay? You catch some little animal and hold it against your belly and I'll try again and see if I can get outside and in it. Okay?"

"We tried it," she said practically.

"Let's try again! Get something real small. What are those things that—you know. Have shells and make slime."

"Slugs."

"No."

"Snails."

"Yes, that's it. Get a snail and put it as close to me as you can. Get it right up to my head where it can hear me and I can hear it back. Will you do that?" Ominously, Bill said, "If you don't, I'm going to go to sleep for a whole year." He was silent, then.

"Go to sleep, then," Edie said. "I don't care. I have a lot of other people to talk to and you don't."

"I'll die, then, and you won't be able to stand that, because then you'll have to carry a dead thing around forever inside you, or—I tell you what I'll do; I know what I'll do. If you don't get an animal and hold it up near me I'll grow big and pretty soon I'll be so big that you'll pop like an old—you know."

"Bag," Edie said.

"Yes. And that way I'll get out."

"You'll get out," she agreed, "but you'll just roll around and die yourself; you won't be able to live."

"I hate you," Bill said.

"I hate you more," Edie said. "I hated you first, a long time ago when I first found out about you."

"All right for you," Bill said morosely. "See if I care. I'm rubber and you're glue."

Edie said nothing; she walked back to the girls and entered once more the game of Rock, Scissors, Paper. It was much more interesting than anything her brother had to say; he knew so little, did nothing, saw nothing, down there inside her.

But it was interesting, that part about Hoppy squeezing

Mr. Blaine's neck. She wondered who Hoppy was going to squeeze next, and if she should tell her mother or the policeman Mr. Colvig.

Bill spoke up suddenly. "Can I play, too?"

Glancing about, Edie made sure that none of the other girls had heard him. "Can my brother play?" she asked.

"You don't have any brother," Wilma Stone said, with contempt.

"He's made-up," Rose Quinn reminded her. "So it's okay if he plays." To Edie she said, "He can play."

"One, two, three," the girls said, each extending then one hand with all fingers, none or two displayed.

"Bill goes scissors," Edie said. "So he beats you, Wilma, because scissors cuts paper, and you get to hit him, Rose, because rock crushes scissors, and he's tied with me."

"How do I hit him?" Rose said.

Pondering, Edie said, "Hit me very lightly here." She indicated her side, just above the belt of her skirt. "Just with the side of your hand, and be careful because he's delicate."

Rose, with care, rapped her there. Within her Bill said, "Okay, I'll get her back the next time."

Across the playground came Edie's father, the principal of the school, and with him walked Mr. Barnes, the new teacher. They paused briefly by the three girls, smiling.

"Bill's playing, too," Edie said to her father. "He just got hit."

George Keller laughed. To Mr. Barnes he said, "That's what comes of being imaginary; you always get hit."

"How's Bill going to hit me?" Wilma said apprehensively; she drew away and glanced up at the principal and teacher. "He's going to hit me," she explained. "Don't do it hard," she said, speaking in the general direction of Edie. "Okay?"

"He can't hit hard," Edie said, "even when he wants to." Across from her Wilma gave a little jump. "See?" Edie said. "That's all he can do, even when he tries as hard as he can."

"He didn't hit me," Wilma said. "He just scared me. He doesn't have very good aim."

"That's because he can't see," Edie said. "Maybe I better hit you for him; that's more fair." She leaned forward and swiftly rapped Wilma on the wrist. "Now let's do it again. One, two, three."

"Why can't he see, Edie?" Mr. Barnes asked.

"Because," she said, "he has no eyes."

To her father, Mr. Barnes said, "Well, it's a reasonable-enough answer." They both laughed and then strolled on.

Inside Edie her brother said, "If you got a snail I could be it for a while and I could maybe crawl around and see. Snails can see, can't they? You told me once they have eyes on sticks."

"Stalks," Edie corrected.

"Please," Bill said.

She thought, I know what I'll do; I'll hold a worm against me, and when he gets into it he'll be just like he is—a worm can't see or do anything but dig, and won't he be surprised.

"All right," she said, again springing up. "I'll get an animal and do that. Wait a minute until I find one; I have to find it first so be patient."

"Gee, thanks a lot," Bill said, in a voice laden with nervousness and yearning. "I'll do something back for you; on my word of honor."

"What can you do for me?" Edie said, searching about in the grass at the edge of the school yard for a worm; she had seen many of them, since the rains of the previous night. "What can a thing like you do for anybody?" She searched avidly, stirring the grass with eager, swift fingers.

Her brother did not answer; she felt his mute sorrow and to herself she snickered.

"Looking for something you lost?" a man's voice said from above her. She peeped up; it was Mr. Barnes, standing there smiling down.

"I'm looking for a worm," she said shyly.

"What an unsqueamish girl," he said.

"Who are you talking to?" Bill said, in confusion. "Who's that?"

"Mr. Barnes," she said, explaining.

"Yes?" Mr. Barnes said.

"I was talking to my brother, not you," Edie said. "He asked who it was. He's the new teacher," she explained to Bill.

Bill said, "I see; I understand him, he's close so I can get him. He knows Mama."

"Our Mama?" Edie said, surprised.

"Yes," Bill said, in a puzzled voice. "I don't understand but he knows her and he sees her, all the time, when nobody is looking. He and she—" He broke off. "It's awful and bad. It's—" He choked. "I can't say it."

Edie stared at her teacher open-mouthed.

"There," Bill said hopefully. "Didn't I do something back for you? I told you something secret you never would have known. Isn't that something?"

"Yes," Edie said slowly, nodding in a daze. "I guess so."

To Bonny, Hal Barnes said, "I saw your daughter today. And I got the distinct impression that she knows about us."

"Oh Christ, how could she?" Bonny said. "It's impossible." She reached out and turned up the fat-lamp. The living room assumed a much more substantial quality as the chairs and a table and pictures became visible. "And anyhow it doesn't matter; she wouldn't care."

To himself, Barnes thought, But she could tell George.

Thinking about Bonny's husband made him peer past the window shade and out onto the moonlit road. No one stirred; the road was deserted and only foliage, rolling hillsides and the flat farm land below, were to be seen. A peaceful, pastoral sight, he thought. George, being the principal of the school, was at the PTA meeting and would not be home for several hours. Edie, of course, was in bed; it was eight o'clock.

And Bill, he thought. Where is Bill, as Edie calls him? Roaming about the house, somewhere, spying on us? He felt uncomfortable and he moved away from the woman beside him on the couch.

"What's the matter?" Bonny said alertly. "Hear something?"

"No. But—" He gestured.

Bonny reached out, took hold of him and drew him down to her. "My god, you're cowardly. Didn't the war teach you anything about life?"

"It taught me," he said, "to value my existence and not to throw it away; it taught me to play it safe."

Groaning, Bonny sat up; she rearranged her clothes, buttoned her blouse back up. What a contrast this man was to Andrew Gill, who always made love to her right out in the open, in broad daylight, along the oaklined roads of West Marin, where anyone and anything might go past. He had seized her each time as he had the first time—yanking her into it, not gabbling or quaking or mumbling . . . maybe I ought to go back to him, she thought.

Maybe, she thought, I ought to leave them all, Barnes and George and that nutty daughter of mine; I ought to go live with Gill openly, defy the community and be happy for a change.

"Well, if we're not going to make love," she said, "then let's go down to the Foresters' Hall and listen to the satellite."

"Are you serious?" Barnes said.

"Of course." She went to the closet to get her coat.

"Then all you want," he said slowly, "is to make love; that's all you care about in a relationship."

"What do you care about? *Talking?*"

He looked at her in a melancholy way, but he did not answer.

"You fruit," she said, shaking her head. "You poor fruit. Why did you come to West Marin in the first place? Just to teach little kids and stroll around picking mushrooms?" She was overcome with disgust.

"My experience today on the playground—" Barnes began.

"You had no experience," she interrupted. "It was just your goddam guilty conscience catching up with you. Let's go; I want to hear Dangerfield. At least when he talks it's fun to listen." She put on her coat, walked quickly to the front door and opened it.

"Will Edie be all right?" Barnes asked as they started down the path.

"Sure," she said, unable at the moment to care. Let her burn up, she said to herself. Gloomily, she plodded down the road, hands thrust deep in her coat pockets; Barnes trailed along behind her, trying to keep up with her strides.

Ahead of them two figures appeared, turning the corner and emerging into sight; she stopped, stricken, thinking one of them was George. And then she saw that the shorter, heavier man was Jack Tree and the other—she strained to see, still walking as if nothing were wrong. It was Doctor Stockstill.

"Come on," she said over her shoulder, calmly, to Barnes. He came, then, hesitantly, wanting to turn back, to run. "Hi," she called to Stockstill and Bluthgeld; or rather Jack Tree— she had to remember to keep calling him that. "What's this, psychoanalysis out in the dark at night? Does that make it more effective? I'm not surprised to learn it."

Gasping, Tree said in his hoarse, grating voice, "Bonny, *I saw him again*. It's the Negro who understood about me that day when the war began, when I was going into Stockstill's office. Remember, you sent me?"

Jokingly, Stockstill said, "They all look alike, as the saying goes. And anyhow—"

"No, it's the same man," Tree said. "He's followed me here. Do you know what this means?" He looked from Bonny to Stockstill to Barnes, his eyes rubbery and enlarged, terror-stricken. "This means that it's going to start again."

"What's going to start again?" Bonny said.

"The war," Tree said to her. "Because that's why it began last time; the Negro saw me and understood what I had done, he knew who I was and he still does. As soon as he sees me—" He broke off, wheezing and coughing in his agony. "Pardon me," he murmured.

To Stockstill, Bonny said, "There's a Negro here; he's right. I saw him. Evidently he came to talk to Gill about selling his cigarettes."

"It couldn't be the same person," Stockstill said. He and she went off to one side slightly, talking now between themselves.

"Certainly it could," Bonny said. "But that doesn't matter because that's one of his delusions. I've heard him gabble about it countless times. Some Negro was sweeping the sidewalk and saw him go into your office, and that day the war began so he's got them connected in his mind. And now he'll probably completely deteriorate, don't you think?" She felt resigned; she had been expecting this to happen, eventually. "And so the period," she said, "of stable maladjustment is drawing to a close." Perhaps, she thought, for us all. Just plain all of us. We could not have gone on like this forever, Bluthgeld with his sheep, me with George . . . she sighed. "What do you think?"

Stockstill said, "I wish I had some Stelazine, but Stelazine ceased to exist on E Day. That would help him. I can't. I've given that up; you know that, Bonny." He sounded resigned, too.

"He'll tell everyone," she said, watching Bluthgeld, who

stood repeating to Barnes what he had just told her and Stockstill. "They'll know who he is, and they will kill him, as he
fears; he's right."

"I can't stop him," Stockstill said mildly.

"You don't particularly care," she said.

He shrugged.

Going back to Bluthgeld, Bonny said, "Listen, Jack, let's all
go to Gill's and see this Negro and I'll bet he didn't notice you
that day. Do you want to bet? I'll bet you twenty-five silver
cents."

"Why do you say you caused the war?" Barnes was saying to
Bluthgeld. He turned to Bonny with a puzzled expression.
"What is this, a war psychosis? And he says the war's coming
back." Once more to Bluthgeld he said, "It isn't possible for
it to happen again; I can give you fifty reasons. First of all,
there're no hydrogen weapons left. Second—"

Putting her hand on Barnes' shoulder, Bonny said, "Be
quiet." She said to Bruno Bluthgeld, "Let's go down, all of us,
together, and listen to the satellite. Okay?"

Bluthgeld muttered, "What is the satellite?"

"Good lord," Barnes said. "He doesn't know what you're
talking about. He's mentally ill." To Stockstill he said, "Listen,
Doctor, isn't schizophrenia where a person loses track of their
culture and its values? Well, this man has lost track; listen to
him."

"I hear him," Stockstill said in a remote voice.

Bonny said to him, "Doctor, Jack Tree is very dear to me.
He has been in the past very much like a father to me. For
God's sake, do something for him. I can't stand to see him like
this; I just can't stand it."

Spreading his hands helplessly, Stockstill said, "Bonny, you
think like a child. You think anything can be obtained if you
just want it badly enough. That's magical thinking. I can't
help—Jack Tree." He turned away and walked off a few steps,
toward town. "Come on," he said to them over his shoulder.
"We'll do as Mrs. Keller suggests; we'll go sit in the Hall and
listen for twenty minutes to the satellite and then we'll all feel
a good deal better."

Once more Barnes was talking with great earnestness to Jack
Tree. "Let me point out where the error in your logic lies. You

saw a particular man, a Negro, on Emergency Day. Okay. Now, seven years later—"

"Shut up," Bonny said to him, digging her fingers into his arm. "For God's sake—" She walked on, then, catching up with Doctor Stockstill. "I can't stand it," she said. "I know this is the last of him; he won't survive past this, seeing that Negro again."

Tears filled her eyes; she felt tears dropping, escaping her. "Goddam," she said bitterly, walking as fast as possible, ahead of the others, in the direction of town and the Foresters' Hall. Not even to know about the satellite. To be that cut off, that deteriorated . . . I didn't realize. How can I stand it? How can a thing like this be? And once he was brilliant. A man who talked over TV and wrote articles, taught and debated . . .

Behind her, Bluthgeld was mumbling, "I know it's the same man, Stockstill, because when I ran into him on the street—I was buying feed at the feed store—he gave me that same queer look, as if he was about to jeer at me, but then he knew if he jeered I'd make it all happen again, and this time he was afraid. He saw it once before and he knows. Isn't that a *fact*, Stockstill? He would know now. Am I correct?"

"I doubt if he knows you're alive," Stockstill said.

"But I'd have to be alive," Bluthgeld answered. "Or the world—" His voice became a blur and Bonny missed the rest; she heard only the sound of her own heels striking the weedy remains of pavement beneath her feet.

And the rest of us, we're all just as insane, she said to herself. My kid with her imaginary brother, Hoppy moving pennies at a distance and doing imitations of Dangerfield, Andrew Gill rolling one cigarette after another by hand, year after year . . . only death can get us out of this and maybe not even death. Maybe it's too late; we'll carry this deterioration with us to the next life.

We'd have been better off, she thought, if we'd all died on E Day; we wouldn't have lived to see the freaks and the funnies and the radiation-darkies and the brilliant animals—the people who began the war weren't thorough enough. I'm tired and I want to rest; I want to get out of this and go lie down somewhere, off where it's dark and no one speaks. Forever.

And then she thought, more practically, Maybe what's the

matter with me is simply that I haven't found the right man yet. And it isn't too late; I'm still young and I'm not fat, and as everyone says, I've got perfect teeth. It could still happen, and I must keep watching.

Ahead lay the Foresters' Hall, the old-fashioned white wooden building with its windows boarded up—the glass had never been replaced and never would be. Maybe Dangerfield, if he hasn't died of a bleeding ulcer yet, could run a classified ad for me, she conjectured. How would that go over with this community, I wonder? Or I could advertise in *News & Views*, let the worn-out drunk Paul Dietz run a little notice on my behalf for the next six months or so.

Opening the door of the Foresters' Hall she heard the friendly, familiar voice of Walt Dangerfield in his recorded reading; she saw the rows of faces, the people listening, some with anxiety, some with relaxed pleasure . . . she saw, seated inconspicuously in the corner, two men, Andrew Gill and with him a slender, good-looking young Negro. It was the man who had caved in the roof of Bruno Bluthgeld's fragile structure of maladaptation, and Bonny stood there in the doorway not knowing what to do.

Behind her came Barnes and Stockstill and with them Bruno; the three men started past her, Stockstill and Barnes automatically searching for empty seats in the crowded hall. Bruno, who had never shown up before to hear the satellite, stood in confusion, as if he did not comprehend what the people were doing, as if he could make nothing out of the words emanating from the small battery-powered radio.

Puzzled, Bruno stood beside Bonny, rubbing his forehead and surveying the people in the room; he glanced at her questioningly, with a numbed look, and then he started to follow Barnes and Stockstill. And then he saw the Negro. He stopped. He turned back toward her, and now the expression on his face had changed; she saw there the eroding, dreadful suspicion—the conviction that he understood the meaning of all that he saw.

"Bonny," he mumbled, "you have to get him out of here."

"I can't," she said, simply.

"If you don't get him out of here," Bruno said, "I'll make the bombs fall again."

She stared at him and then she heard herself say in a brittle, dry voice, "Will you? Is that what you want to do, Bruno?"

"I have to," he mumbled in his toneless way, staring at her sightlessly; he was completely preoccupied with his own thoughts, the various changes taking place within him. "I'm sorry, but first I'll make the high-altitude test bombs go off again; that's how I started before, and if that doesn't do it then I'll bring them down here, they'll fall on everyone. Please forgive me, Bonny, but my God, I have to protect myself." He tried to smile, but his toothless mouth did not respond beyond a distorted quiver.

Bonny said, "Can you *really* do that, Bruno? Are you sure?"

"Yes," he said, nodding. And he was sure; he had always been sure of his power. He had brought the war once and he could do it again if they pushed him too far: in his eyes she saw no doubt, no hesitation.

"That's an awful lot of power for one man to have," she said to him. "Isn't that strange, that one man would have so much?"

"Yes," he said, "it's all the power in the world rolled together; I am the center. God willed it to be that way."

"What a mistake God made," she said.

Bruno gazed at her bleakly. "You, too," he said. "I thought you never would turn against me, Bonny."

She said nothing; she went to an empty chair and seated herself. She paid no more attention to Bruno. She could not; she had worn herself out, over the years, and now she had nothing left to give him.

Stockstill, seated not far away, leaned toward her and said, "The Negro is here in the room, you know."

"Yes." She nodded. "I know." Seated bolt-upright, she concentrated on the words coming from the radio; she listened to Dangerfield and tried to forget everyone and everything around her.

It's out of my hands now, she said to herself. Whatever he does, whatever becomes of him, it's not my fault. Whatever happens—to all of us. I can't take any more responsibility; it's gone on too long, as it is, and I am glad, at last, to get out from under it.

What a relief, she thought. Thank God.

*

Now it must begin again, Bruno Bluthgeld thought to himself. The war. Because there is no choice; it is forced on me. I
am sorry for the people. All of them will have to suffer, but
perhaps out of it they will be redeemed. Perhaps in the long
run it is a good thing.

He seated himself, folded his hands, shut his eyes and concentrated on the task of assembling his powers. Grow, he said
to them, the forces at his command everywhere in the world.
Join and become potent, as you were in former times. There is
need for you again, all ye agencies.

The voice issuing from the loudspeaker of the radio, however, disturbed him and made it difficult for him to concentrate. Breaking off, he thought, I must not be distracted; that
is contrary to the Plan. Who is this that's talking? They are all
listening . . . are they getting their instructions from him, is
that it?

To the man seated beside him he said, "Who is this we're listening to?"

The man, elderly, turned irritably to regard him. "Why, it's
Walt Dangerfield," he said, in tones of utter disbelief.

"I have never heard of him," Bruno said. Because he had
not wanted to hear of him. "Where is he talking from?"

"The satellite," the elderly man said witheringly, and resumed his listening.

I remember now, Bruno said to himself. That's why we
came here; to listen to the satellite. To the man speaking from
overhead.

Be destroyed, he thought in the direction of the sky above.
Cease, because you are deliberately tormenting me, impeding
my work. Bruno waited, but the voice went on.

"Why doesn't he stop?" he asked the man on the other side
of him. "How can he continue?"

The man, a little taken aback, said, "You mean his illness?
He recorded this a long time ago, before he was sick."

"Sick," Bruno echoed. "I see." He had made the man in the
satellite sick, and that was something, but not enough. It was a
beginning. Be dead, he thought toward the sky and the satellite above. The voice, however, continued uninterrupted.

Do you have a screen of defense erected against me? Bruno

wondered. Have they provided you with it? I will crush it; obviously you have been long prepared to withstand attack, but it will do you no real good.

Let there be a hydrogen instrument, he said to himself. Let it explode near enough to this man's satellite to demolish his ability to resist. Then have him die in complete awareness of who it is that he is up against. Bruno Bluthgeld concentrated, gripping his hands together, squeezing out the power from deep inside his mind.

And yet the reading continued.

You are very strong, Bruno acknowledged. He had to admire the man. In fact, he smiled a little, thinking about it. Let a whole series of hydrogen instruments explode now, he willed. Let his satellite be bounced around; let him discover the truth.

The voice from the loudspeaker ceased.

Well, it is high time, Bruno said to himself. And he let up on his concentration of powers; be sighed, crossed his legs, smoothed his hair, glanced at the man to his left.

"It's over," Bruno observed.

"Yeah," the man said. "Well, now he'll give the news—if he feels well enough."

Astonished, Bruno said, "But he's dead now."

The man, startled, protested, "He can't be dead; I don't believe it. Go on—you're nuts."

"It's true," Bruno said. "His satellite has been totally destroyed and there is nothing remaining." Didn't the man know that? Hadn't it penetrated to the world, yet?

"Doggone it," the man said, "I don't know who you are or why you say something like that, but you sure are a gloomy gus. Wait a second and you'll hear him; I'll even bet you five U.S. Government metal cents."

The radio was silent. In the room, people stirred, murmured with concern and apprehension.

Yes, it has begun, Bruno said to himself. First, high-altitude detonations, as before. And, soon—for all of you here. The world itself wiped out, as before, to halt the steady advance of cruelty and revenge; it must be halted before too late. He glanced in the direction of the Negro and smiled. The Negro pretended not to see him; he pretended to be involved in discussion with the man beside him.

You are aware, Bruno thought. I can tell; you can't fool me. You, more than anyone else, know what is beginning to happen.

Something is wrong, Doctor Stockstill thought. Why doesn't Walt Dangerfield go on? Has he suffered an embolism or something on that order?

And then he noticed the crooked grin of triumph on Bruno Bluthgeld's toothless face. At once Stockstill thought, He's taking credit for it, in his own mind. Paranoid delusions of omnipotence; everything that takes place is due to him. Repelled, he turned away, moved his chair so that he could no longer see Bluthgeld.

Now he turned his attention on the young Negro. Yes, he thought, that could well be the Negro television salesman who used to open up the TV store across from my office in Berkeley, years ago. I think I'll go over and ask him.

Rising, he made his way over to Andrew Gill and the Negro. "Pardon me," he said, bending over them. "Did you ever live in Berkeley and sell TV sets on Shattuck Avenue?"

The Negro said, "Doctor Stockstill." He held out his hand and they shook. "It's a small world," the Negro said.

"What's happened to Dangerfield?" Andrew Gill said worriedly. Now June Raub appeared by the radio, fiddling with the knobs; other people began to collect around her, offering advice and murmuring with one another in small, grave clusters. "I think this is the end. What do you say, Doctor?"

"I say," Stockstill said, "that if it is it's a tragedy."

In the rear of the room, Bruno Bluthgeld rose to his feet and said in a loud, husky voice, "The demolition of existence has begun. Everyone present will be spared by special consideration long enough to confess sins and repent if it is sincere."

The room fell silent. The people, one by one, turned in his direction.

"You have a preacher, here?" the Negro said to Stockstill.

To Gill, Stockstill said rapidly, "He's sick, Andy. We've got to get him out of here. Give me a hand."

"Sure," Gill said, following him; they walked toward Bluthgeld, who was still on his feet.

"The high-altitude bombs which I set off in 1972," Bluthgeld was declaring, "find reinforcement in the present act, sanctioned by God Himself in His wisdom for the world. See the Book of Revelations for verification." He watched Stockstill and Gill approach. "Have you cleansed yourself?" he asked them. "Are you prepared for the judgment which is to come?"

All at once, from the speaker of the radio, came a familiar voice; it was shaky and muted, but they all recognized it. "Sorry for the pause, folks," Dangerfield said. "But I sure felt giddy there for a while; I had to lie down and I didn't notice the tape had ended. Anyhow—" He laughed his old, familiar laugh. "I'm back. At least for a while. Now, what was I about to do? Does anybody remember? Wait, I've got a red light on; somebody's calling me from below. Hold on."

The people in the room buzzed with joy and relief; they turned back to the radio, and Bluthgeld was forgotten. Stockstill himself walked toward the radio, and so did Gill and the Negro TV salesman; they joined the circle of smiling people and stood waiting.

"I've got a request for 'Bei Mir Bist Du Schön,'" Dangerfield said. "Can you beat that? Anybody remember the Andrews Sisters? Well, the good old U.S. Government had the kindness to provide me with, believe it or not, a tape of the Andrews Sisters singing this corny but well-loved number . . . I guess they figured I was going to be some sort of time capsule on Mars, there." He chuckled. "So it's 'Bei Mir Bist Du Schön,' for some old codger in the Great Lakes Area. Here we go." The music, tinny and archaic, began, and the people in the room gratefully, joyfully, moved one by one back to their seats.

Standing by his chair rigidly, Bruno Bluthgeld listened to the music and thought, I can't believe it. The man up there is gone; I myself caused him to be destroyed. *This must be a fake of some kind. A deception. I know that it is not real.*

In any case, he realized, I must exert myself more fully; I must begin again and this time with utmost force. No one was paying attention to him—they had all turned their attention back to the radio—so he left his chair and made his way quietly from the Hall, outside into the darkness.

Down the road the tall antenna at Hoppy Harrington's

house glowed and pulsed and hummed; Bruno Bluthgeld, puzzled, noted it as he walked along toward his horse, where he had left the beast tied up. What was the phocomelus doing? Lights blazed behind the windows of the tarpaper house; Hoppy was busy at work.

I must include him, too, Bluthgeld said to himself. He must cease to exist along with the others, for he is as evil as they are. Perhaps more so.

As he passed Hoppy's house he sent a stray, momentary thought of destruction in Hoppy's direction. The lights, however, remained on and the antenna mast continued to hum. It will take more mind-force, Bluthgeld realized, and I don't have the time right now. A little later.

Meditating profoundly, he continued on.

XIII

B ILL KELLER heard the small animal, the snail or slug, near him and at once he got into it. But he had been tricked; it was sightless. He was out but he could not see or hear, he could only move.

"Let me back," he called to his sister in panic. "Look what you did, you put me into something wrong." You did it on purpose, he said to himself as he moved. He moved on and on, searching for her.

If I could reach out, he thought. Reach—upward. But he had nothing to reach with, no limbs of any sort. What am I now that I'm finally out? he asked himself as he tried to reach up. What do they call those things up there that shine? Those lights in the sky . . . can I see them without having eyes? No, he thought, I can't.

He moved on, raising himself now and then as high as possible and then sinking back, once more to crawl, to do the one thing possible for him in his new life, his born, outside life.

In the sky, Walt Dangerfield moved, in his satellite, although he was resting with his head in his hands. The pain inside him grew, changed, absorbed him until, as before, he could imagine nothing else.

And then he thought he saw something. Beyond the window of the satellite—a flash far off, along the rim of the Earth's darker edge. What was that? he asked himself. An explosion, like the ones he had seen and cringed from seven years ago . . . the flares ignited over the surface of the Earth. Were they beginning again?

On his feet he stood peering out, hardly breathing. Seconds passed and there were no further explosions. And the one he had seen; it had been peculiarly vague and shadowy, with a diffuseness that had made it seem somehow unreal, as if it was only imagined.

As if, he thought, it was more a recollection of a fact than the fact itself. It must be some sort of sidereal echo, he concluded. A remnant left over from E Day, still reverberating in space somehow . . . but harmless, now. More so all the time.

And yet it frightened him. Like the pain inside him, it was too odd to be dismissed; it seemed to be dangerous and he could not forget it.

I feel ill, he repeated to himself, resuming his litany based on his great discomfort. Can't they get me down? Do I have to stay up here, creeping across the sky again and again—forever?

For his own needs he put on a tape of the Bach B Minor Mass; the giant choral sound filled the satellite and made him forget. The pain inside, the dull, elderly explosion briefly outlined beyond the window—both began to leave his mind.

"Kyrie eleison," he murmured to himself. Greek words, embedded in the Latin text; strange. Remnants of the past . . . still alive, at least for him. I'll play the B Minor Mass for the New York area, he decided. I think they'll like it; a lot of intellectuals, there. Why should I only play what they request anyhow? I ought to be teaching them, not following. And especially he thought, if I'm not going to be around much longer . . . I better get going and do an especially bang-up job, here at the end.

All at once his vehicle shuddered. Staggering, he caught hold of the wall nearest him; a concussion, series of shock waves, passing through. Objects fell and collided and burst; he looked around amazed.

Meteor? he wondered.

It seemed to him almost as if someone were attacking him.

He shut off the B Minor Mass and stood, listening and waiting. Far off through the window he saw another dull explosion and he thought, they may get me. But why? It won't be long anyhow before I'm finished . . . why not wait? And then the thought came to him, But damn it, I'm alive now, and I better act alive; I'm not utterly dead yet.

He snapped on his transmitter and said into the mike, "Sorry for the pause, folks. But I sure felt giddy there for a while; I had to lie down and I didn't notice the tape had ended. Anyhow—"

Laughing his laugh, he watched through the window of the satellite for more of the strange explosions. There was one, faint and farther off . . . he felt a measure of relief. Maybe they wouldn't get him after all; they seemed to be losing track of the range, as if his location were a mystery to them.

I'll play the corniest record I can think of, he decided, as an act of defiance. "Bei Mir Bist Du Schön"; that ought to do it. Whistling in the dark, as they say, and he laughed again, thinking about it; what an act of defiance it was, by God. It would certainly come as a surprise to whoever was trying to eradicate him—if that was in fact what they wanted to do.

Maybe they're just plain tired of my corny talk and my corny readings, Dangerfield conjectured. Well, if so—this will fix them.

"I'm back," he said into his mike. "At least for a while. Now, what was I about to do? Does anybody remember?"

There were no more concussions. He had a feeling that, for the time being, they had ceased.

"Wait," he said, "I've got a red light on; somebody's calling me from below. Hold on."

From his tape library he selected the proper tape, carried it to the transport and placed it on the spindle.

"I've got a request for 'Bei Mir Bist Du Schön,'" he said, with grim relish, thinking of their dismay down below. "Can you beat that?" No, you can't, he said to himself. And—by the Andrews Sisters. Dangerfield is striking back. Grinning, he started the tape into motion.

Edie Keller, with a delicious shiver of exultation, watched the angle worm crawling slowly across the ground and knew with certitude that her brother was in it.

For inside her, down in her abdomen, the mentality of the worm now resided; she heard its monotonous voice. "Boom, boom, boom," it went, in echo of its nondescript biological processes.

"Get out of me, worm," she said, and giggled. What did the worm think about its new existence? Was it as dumbfounded as Bill probably was? I have to keep my eye on him, she realized, meaning the creature wriggling across the ground. For he might get lost. "Bill," she said, bending over him, "you look funny. You're all red and long; did you know that?" And then she thought, What I should have done was put him in the body of another human being. Why didn't I do that? Then it would be like it ought to be; I would have a real brother, out-side of me, who I could play with.

But, on the other hand, she would have a strange, new per-son inside her. And that did not sound like much fun.

Who would do? she asked herself. One of the kids at school? An adult? I bet Bill would like to be in an adult. Mr. Barnes, maybe. Or Hoppy Harrington, who was afraid of Bill anyhow. Or—she screeched with delight, Mama. It would be so easy; I could snuggle up close to her, lay against her . . . and Bill could switch, and I'd have my own mama inside me—and wouldn't that be wonderful? I could make her do anything I wanted. And she couldn't tell me what to do.

And Edie thought, She couldn't do any more unmention-able things with Mr. Barnes any more, or with anybody else. I'd see to that. I know Bill wouldn't behave that way; he was as shocked as I was.

"Bill," she said, kneeling down and carefully picking up the angleworm; she held it in the palm of her hand. "Wait until you hear my plan—you know what? We're going to fix Mama for the bad things she does." She held the worm against her side, where the hard lump within lay. "Get back inside now. You don't want to be a worm anyhow; it's no fun."

Her brother's voice once more came to her. "You pooh-pooh; I hate you, I'll never forgive you. You put me in a blind thing with no legs or nothing; all I could do was drag myself around!"

"I know," she said, rocking back and forth, cupping the now-useless worm in her hand still. "Listen, did you hear me? You want to do that, Bill, what I said? Shall I get Mama to let me lie against her so you can do you-know-what? You'd have eyes and ears; you'd be a full-grown person."

Nervously, Bill said, "I don't know. I don't think I want to walk around being Mama; it sort of scares me."

"Sissy," Edie said. "You better do it or you may never get out ever again. Well, who do you want to be if not Mama? Tell me and I'll fix it up; I cross my heart and promise to fall down black and hard."

"I'll see," Bill said. "I'll talk to the dead people and see what they say about it. Anyhow I don't know if it'll work; I had trouble getting out into that little thing, that worm."

"You're afraid to try," she laughed; she tossed the worm away, into the bushes at the end of the school grounds. "Sissy! My brother is a big baby sissy!"

There was no answer from Bill; he had turned his thoughts away from her and her world, into the regions which only he could reach. Talking to those old crummy, sticky dead, Edie said to herself. Those empty pooh-pooh dead that never have any fun or nothing.

And then a really stunning idea came to her. I'll fix it so he gets out and into that crazy man Mr. Tree who they're all talking about right now, she decided. Mr. Tree stood up in the Foresters' Hall last night and said those dumb religious things about repenting, and so if Bill acts funny and doesn't know what to do or say, *nobody will pay any attention.*

Yet, that posed the awful problem of her finding herself containing a crazy man. Maybe I could take poison like I'm always saying, she decided. I could swallow a lot of oleander leaves or castor beans or something and get rid of him; he'd be helpless, he couldn't stop me.

Still, it was a problem; she did not relish the idea of having that Mr. Tree—she had seen him often enough not to like him—inside herself. He had a nice dog, and that was about all. . . .

Terry, the dog. That was it. She could lie down against Terry and Bill could get out and into the dog and everything would be fine.

But dogs had a short life. And Terry was already seven years old; according to her mother and father. He had been born the same time almost as she and Bill.

Darn it, she thought. It's hard to decide; it's a real problem, what to do with Bill who wants so bad to get out and see and hear things. And then she thought, Who of all the people I know would I like most to have living inside my stomach? And the answer was: her father.

"You want to walk around as Daddy?" she asked Bill. But Bill did not answer; he was still turned away, conversing with the great majority beneath the ground.

I think, she decided, that Mr. Tree would be the best because he lives out in the country with sheep and doesn't see too many people, and it would be easier on Bill that way because he wouldn't have to know very much about talking. He'd just have Terry out there and all the sheep, and then with Mr. Tree being crazy now it's really perfect. Bill could do a lot better with Mr. Tree's body than Mr. Tree is doing, I bet, and all I have to worry about really is chewing the right number of poisonous oleander leaves—enough to kill him but not me. Maybe two would do. Three at the most, I guess.

Mr. Tree went crazy at the perfect time, she decided. He doesn't know it, though. But wait'll he finds out; won't he be surprised. I might let him live for a while inside me, just so he'd realize what happened; I think that would be fun. I never liked him, even though Mama does, or says she does. He's creepy. Edie shuddered.

Poor, poor Mr. Tree, she thought delightedly. You aren't going to ruin any more meetings at the Foresters' Hall because where you'll be you won't be able to preach to anybody, except maybe to me and I won't listen.

Where can I do it? she asked herself. Today; I'll ask Mama to take us out there after school. And if she won't do it, I'll hike out there by myself.

I can hardly wait, Edie said to herself, shivering with anticipation.

The bell for class rang, and, together with the other children, she started into the building. Mr. Barnes was waiting at the door of the single classroom which served all the children from first grade to sixth; as she passed him, deep in thought, he said to her, "Why so absorbed, Edie? What's on your weighty mind today?"

"Well," she said, halting, "you were for a while. Now it's Mr. Tree instead."

"Oh yes," Mr. Barnes said, nodding. "So you heard about that."

The other children had passed on in, leaving them alone. So Edie said, "Mr. Barnes, don't you think you ought to stop doing what you're doing with my mama? It's wrong; Bill says so and he knows."

The school teacher's face changed color, but he did not speak. Instead he walked away from her, into the room and up to his desk, still darkly flushed. Did I say it wrong? Edie wondered. Is he mad at me now? Maybe he'll make me stay after, for punishment, and maybe he'll tell Mama and she'll spank me.

Feeling discouraged, she seated herself and opened the precious, ragged, fragile, coverless book to the story of *Snow White*; it was their reading assignment for the day.

Lying in the damp rotting leaves beneath the old live oak trees, in the shadows, Bonny Keller clasped Mr. Barnes to her and thought to herself that this was probably the last time; she was tired of it and Hal was scared, and that, she had learned from long experience, was a fatal combination.

"All right," she murmured, "so she knows. But she knows on a small child's level; she has no real understanding."

"She knows it's wrong," Barnes answered.

Bonny sighed.

"Where is she now?" Barnes asked.

"Behind that bay tree over there. Watching."

Hal Barnes sprang to his feet as if stabbed; he whirled around, wide-eyed, then sagged as he comprehended the truth. "You and your malicious wit," he muttered. But he did not return to her; he stayed on his feet, a short distance off, looking glum and uneasy. "Where is she really?"

"She hiked out to Jack Tree's sheep ranch."

"But—" He gestured. "The man's insane! Won't he be— well, isn't it dangerous?"

"She just went out to play with Terry, the verbose canine." Bonny sat up and began picking bits of humus from her hair. "I don't think he's even there. The last time anybody saw Bruno, he—"

"'Bruno,'" Barnes echoed. He regarded her queerly.

"I mean Jack." Her heart labored.

"He said the other night something about having been responsible for the high-altitude devices in 1972." Barnes continued to scrutinize her; she waited, her pulse throbbing in her throat. Well, it was bound to come out sooner or later.

"He's insane," she pointed out. "Right? He believes—"

"He believes," Hal Barnes said, "that he's Bruno Bluthgeld, isn't that right?"

Bonny shrugged. "That, among other things."

"And he is, isn't he? And Stockstill knows it, you know it—that Negro knows it."

"No," she said, "that Negro doesn't know it, and stop saying 'that Negro.' His name is Stuart McConchie; I talked to Andrew about him and he says he's a very fine, intelligent, enthusiastic and alive person."

Barnes said, "So Doctor Bluthgeld didn't die in the Emergency. He came here. He's been here, living among us. The man most responsible for what happened."

"Go murder him," Bonny said.

Barnes grunted.

"I mean it," Bonny said. "I don't care any more. Frankly I wish you would." It would be a good manly act, she said to herself. It would be a distinct change.

"Why have you tried to shield a person like that?"

"I don't know." She did not care to discuss it. "Let's go back to town," she said. His company wearied her and she had begun to think once again about Stuart McConchie. "I'm out of cigarettes," she said. "So you can drop me off at the cigarette factory." She walked toward Barnes' horse, which, tied to a tree, complacently cropped the long grass.

"A darky," Barnes said, with bitterness. "Now you're going to shack up with him. That certainly makes me feel swell."

"Snob," she said. "Anyhow, you're afraid to go on; you want to quit. So the next time you see Edie you can truthfully say, 'I am not doing anything shameful and evil with your mama, scout's honor.' Right?" She mounted the horse, picked up the reins and waited. "Come on, Hal."

An explosion lit up the sky.

The horse bolted, and Bonny leaped from it, throwing herself from its side to roll, sliding, into the shrubbery of the oak forest. Bruno, she thought; can it be him really? She lay clasping her head, sobbing with pain; a branch had laid her scalp open and blood dripped through her fingers and ran down her wrist. Now Barnes bent over her; he tugged her up, turned her over. "Bruno," she said. "God-damn him. Somebody *will* have to kill him; they should have done it long ago—they should have done it in 1970 because he was insane then." She got her handkerchief out and mopped at her scalp. "Oh dear," she said. "I really am hurt. That was a real fall."

"The horse is gone, too," Barnes said.

"It's an evil god," she said, "who gave him that power, whatever it is. I know it's him, Hal. We've seen a lot of strange things over the years, so why not this? The ability to re-create the war, to bring it back, like he said last night. Maybe he's got us snared in time. Could that be it? We're stuck fast; he's—" She broke off as a second white flash broke overhead, traveling at enormous speed; the trees around them lashed and bent and she heard, here and there, the old oaks splinter.

"I wonder where the horse went," Barnes murmured, rising cautiously to his feet and peering around.

"Forget the horse," she said. "We'll have to walk back; that's obvious. Listen, Hal. Maybe Hoppy can do something; he has funny powers, too. I think we ought to go to him and tell him. He doesn't want to be incinerated by a lunatic. Don't you agree? I don't see anything else we can do at this point."

"That's a good idea," Barnes said, but he was still looking for the horse; he did not seem really to be listening.

"Our punishment," Bonny said.

"What?" he murmured.

"You know. For what Edie calls our 'shameful, evil doings.' I thought the other night . . . maybe we should have been killed with the others; maybe it's a good thing this is happening."

"There's the horse," Barnes said, walking swiftly from her. The horse was caught; his reins had become tangled in a bay limb.

The sky, now, had become sooty black. She remembered that color; it had never entirely departed anyhow. It had merely lessened.

Our little fragile world, Bonny thought, that we labored to build up, after the Emergency . . . this puny society with our tattered school books, our "deluxe" cigarettes, our wood-burning trucks—it can't stand much punishment; it can't stand this that Bruno is doing or appears to be doing. One blow again directed at us and we will be gone; the brilliant animals will perish, all the new, odd species will disappear as suddenly as they arrived. Too bad, she thought with grief. It's unfair; Terry, the verbose dog—him, too. Maybe we were too ambitious; maybe we shouldn't have dared to try to rebuild and go on.

I think we did pretty well, she thought, all in all. We've been alive; we've made love and drunk Gill's Five Star, taught our kids in a peculiar-windowed school building, put out *News & Views*, cranked up a car radio and listened daily to W. Somerset Maugham. What more could be asked of us? Christ, she thought. *It isn't fair*, this thing now. It isn't right at all. We have our horses to protect, our crops, our lives. . . .

Another explosion occurred, this time further off. To the south, she realized. Near the site of the old ones. San Francisco.

Wearily, she shut her eyes. And just when this McConchie has shown up, too, she thought. What lousy, stinking luck.

The dog, placing himself across the path, barring her way, groaned in his difficult voice, "Treezzz bizzzzeeeeeee. Stopppppp." He woofed in warning. She was not supposed to continue on to the wooden shack.

Yes, Edie thought, I know he's busy. She had seen the explosions in the sky. "Hey, you know what?" she said to the dog.

"Whuuuuut?" the dog asked, becoming curious; he had a simple mind, as she well knew; he was easily taken in.

"I learned how to throw a stick so far nobody can find it," she said. She bent, picked up a nearby stick. "Want me to prove it?"

Within her Bill said, "Who're you talking to?" He was agitated, now that the time was drawing near. "Is it Mr. Tree?"

"No," she said, "just the dog." She waved the stick. "Bet you a paper ten dollar bill if I throw it you can't find it."

"Surrrrre I cannnnnn," the dog said, and whined in eagerness; this was his favorite sort of sport. "Buuuut I cannnn't bettttt," he added. "I haaaaave no monnnnnneyyyy."

From the wooden shack walked Mr. Tree, all at once; taken by surprise, both she and the dog stopped what they were doing. Mr. Tree paid no attention to them; he continued on up a small hill and then disappeared down the far side, out of sight.

"Mr. Tree!" Edie called. "Maybe he isn't busy now," she said to the dog. "Go ask him, okay? Tell him I want to talk to him a minute."

Within her Bill said restlessly, "He's not far off now, is he? I know he's there. I'm ready; I'm going to try real hard this time. He can do almost anything, can't he? See and walk and hear and smell—isn't that right? It's not like that worm."

"He doesn't have any teeth," Edie said, "but he has everything else that most people have." As the dog obediently loped off in pursuit of Mr. Tree she began walking along the path once more. "It won't be long," she said. "I'll tell him—" She had it all worked out, "I'll say, 'Mr. Tree, you know what? Well, I swallowed one of those duck-callers hunters use, and if you lean close you can hear it.' How's that?"

"I don't know," Bill said desperately. "What's a 'duck-caller'? What's a duck, Edie? Is it alive?" He sounded more and more confused, as if the situation were too much for him.

"You sissy," she hissed. "Be quiet." The dog had reached Tree and now the man had turned; he was starting back toward her, frowning.

"I am very busy, Edie," Mr. Tree called. "Later—I'll talk to you later; I can't be interrupted now." He raised his arms and made a bizarre motion toward her, as if he were keeping time to some music; he scowled and swayed, and she felt like laughing, he looked so foolish.

"I just want to show you something," she called back.

"Later!" He started away, then spoke to the dog.

"Yessirr," the dog growled, and loped back toward the girl. "Nooo," the dog told her. "Stoppppp."

Darn it, Edie thought. We can't do it today; we'll have to come back maybe tomorrow.

"Gooo awayyyy," the dog was saying to her, and it bared its fangs; it had been given the strongest possible instructions.

Edie said, "Listen, Mr. Tree—" And then she stopped, because there was no longer any Mr. Tree there. The dog turned, whined, and within her Bill moaned.

"Edie," Bill cried, "he's gone; I can feel it. Now where'll I go to get out? What'll I do?"

High up in the air, a tiny black speck blew and tumbled; the girl watched it drift as if it were caught in some violent spout of wind. It was Mr. Tree and his arms stuck out as he rolled over and over, dropping and rising like a kite. What's happened to him? she wondered dismally, knowing that Bill was right; their chance, their plan, was gone forever now.

Something had hold of Mr. Tree and it was killing him. It lifted him higher and higher, and then Edie shrieked. Mr. Tree suddenly dropped. He fell like a stone straight at the ground; she shut her eyes and the dog, Terry, let out a howl of stark dismay.

"What is it?" Bill was clamoring in despair. "Who did it to him? They took him away, didn't they?"

"Yes," she said, and opened her eyes.

Mr. Tree lay on the ground, broken and crooked, with his legs and arms sticking up at all angles. He was dead; she knew that and so did the dog. The dog trotted over to him, halted, turned to her with a stricken, numbed look. She said nothing; she stopped, too, a distance away. It was awful, what they—whoever it was—had done to Mr. Tree. It was like the glasses man from Bolinas, she thought; it was a killing.

"Hoppy did it," Bill moaned. "Hoppy killed Mr. Tree from a distance because he was afraid of him; Mr. Tree's down with the dead, now, I can hear him talking. He's saying that; he says Hoppy reached out all the way from his house where he is and grabbed Mr. Tree and picked him up and flung him everywhere!"

"Gee," Edie said. I wonder how come Hoppy did that, she wondered. Because of the explosions Mr. Tree was making in the sky, was that it? Did they bother Hoppy? Make him sore?

She felt fright. That Hoppy, she thought; he can kill from so far off; nobody else can do that. We better be careful. Very careful. Because he could kill all of us; he could fling us all around or squeeze us.

"I guess *News & Views* will put this on the first page," she said, half to herself, half to Bill.

"What's *News & Views*?" Bill protested in anguish. "I don't understand what's going on; can't you explain it to me? *Please*."

Edie said, "We better go back to town now." She started slowly away, leaving the dog sitting there beside the squashed remains of Mr. Tree. I guess, she thought, it's a good thing you didn't switch, because if you had been inside Mr. Tree you would have been killed.

And, she thought, he would be alive inside me. At least until I got the oleander leaves chewed and swallowed. And maybe he would have found a way to stop that. He had funny powers; he could make those explosions, and he might somehow have done that inside me.

"We can try somebody else," Bill said, hopefully. "Can't we? Do you want to try that—what do you call it again? That dog? I think I'd like to be that dog; it can run fast and catch things and see a long way, can't it?"

"Not now," she said, still frightened, wanting to get away. "Some other time. You'd better wait." And she began to run back along the path, in the direction of town.

XIV

O RION STROUD, seated in the center of the Foresters' Hall where he could clearly be heard by everyone, rapped for order and said:

"Mrs. Keller and Doctor Stockstill asked that the West Marin Official Jury and also the West Marin Governing Citizens' Council convene to hear a piece of vital news regarding a killing that just took place today."

Around him, Mrs. Tallman and Cas Stone and Fred Quinn and Mrs. Lully and Andrew Gill and Earl Colvig and Miss Costigan—he glanced from one to the next, satisfied that everyone was present. They all watched with fixed attention, knowing that this was really important. Nothing like this had ever happened in their community before. This was not a killing like that of the glasses man or of Mr. Austurias.

"I understand," Stroud said, "that it was discovered that Mr. Jack Tree who's been living among us—"

From the audience a voice said, "He was Bluthgeld."

"Right," Stroud said, nodding. "But he's dead now so there's nothing to worry about; you have to get that through your heads. And it was Hoppy that done it. Did it, I mean." He glanced at Paul Dietz apologetically. "Have to use proper grammar," he said, "because this is all going to be in *News & Views*—right, Paul?"

"A special edition," Paul said, nodding in agreement.

"Now you understand, we're not here to decide if Hoppy ought to be punished for what he did. There's no problem there because Bluthgeld was a noted war criminal and what's more he was beginning to use his magical powers to restart some of the old war. I guess everybody in this room knows that, because you all saw the explosions. Now—" He glanced toward Gill. "There's a newcomer, here, a Negro named Stuart McConchie, and ordinarily I have to admit we don't welcome darkies to West Marin, but I understand that McConchie was tracking down Bluthgeld, so he's going to be allowed to settle in West Marin if he so desires."

The audience rustled with approval.

417

"Mainly what we're here for," Stroud continued, "is to vote some sort of reward to Hoppy to show our appreciation. We probably would all have been killed, due to Bluthgeld's magical powers. So we owe him a real debt of gratitude. I see he isn't here, because he's busy at work in his house, fixing things; after all, he's our handy and that's a pretty big responsibility, right there. Anyhow, has anybody got an idea of how the people here can express their appreciation for Hoppy's timely killing of Doctor Bluthgeld?" Stroud looked around questioningly.

Rising to his feet, Andrew Gill cleared his throat and said, "I think it's appropriate for me to say a few words. First, I want to thank Mr. Stroud and this community for welcoming my new business associate, Mr. McConchie. And then I want to offer one reward that might be appropriate regarding Hoppy's great service to this community and to the world at large. I'd like to contribute a hundred special deluxe Gold Label cigarettes." He paused, starting to reseat himself, and then added, "And a case of Gill's Five Star."

The audience applauded, whistled, stamped in approval.

"Well," Stroud said, smiling, "that's really something. I guess Mr. Gill is aware of what Hoppy's action spared us all. There's a whole lot of oak trees knocked over along Bear Valley Ranch Road, from the concussion of the blasts Bluthgeld was setting off. Also, as you may know, I understand that he was beginning to turn his attention south toward San Francisco—"

"That's correct," Bonny Keller spoke up.

"So," Stroud said, "Maybe those people down there will want to pitch in and contribute something to Hoppy as a token of appreciation. I guess the best we can do, and it's good but I wish there was more, is turn over Mr. Gill's gift of the hundred special deluxe Gold Label cigarettes and the case of brandy . . . Hoppy will appreciate that, but I was actually thinking of something more in the line of a memorial, like a statue or a park or at least a plaque of some sort. And—I'd be willing to donate the land, and I know Cas Stone would, too."

"Right," Cas Stone declared emphatically.

"Anybody else got an idea?" Stroud asked. "You, Mrs. Tallman; I'd like to hear from you."

Mrs. Tallman said, "It would be fitting to elect Mr. Harrington to an honorary public office, such as President of the West Marin Governing Citizens' Council for instance, or as clerk of the School Trustees Board. That, of course, in addition to the park or memorial and the brandy and cigarettes."

"Good idea," Stroud said. "Well? Anybody else? Because let's be realistic, folks; Hoppy saved our lives. That Bluthgeld had gone out of his mind, as everybody who was at the reading last night knows . . . he would have put us right back where we were seven years ago, and all our hard work in rebuilding would have gone for nothing. Nothing at all."

The audience murmured its agreement.

"When you have magic like he had," Stroud said, "a physicist like Bluthgeld with all that knowledge . . . the world never was in such danger before; am I right? It's just lucky Hoppy can move objects at a distance; it's lucky for us that Hoppy's been practicing that all these years now because nothing else would have reached out like that, over all that distance, and mashed that Bluthgeld like it did."

Fred Quinn spoke up, "I talked to Edie Keller who witnessed it and she tells me that Bluthgeld got flung right up into the air before Hoppy mashed him; tossed all around."

"I know," Stroud said. "I interviewed Edie about it." He looked around the room, at all the people. "If anybody wants details, I'm sure Edie would give them. Right, Mrs. Keller?"

Bonny, seated stiffly, her face pale, nodded.

"You still scared, Bonny?" Stroud asked.

"It was terrible," Bonny said quietly.

"Sure it was," Stroud said, "but Hoppy got him." And then he thought to himself, That makes Hoppy pretty formidable, doesn't it? Maybe that's what Bonny's thinking. Maybe that's why she's so quiet.

"I think the best thing to do," Cas Stone said, "is to go right to Hoppy and say, 'Hoppy, what do you want that we can do for you in token of our appreciation?' We'll put it right to him. Maybe there's something he wants very badly that we don't know about."

Yes, Stroud thought to himself. You have quite a point there, Cas. Maybe he wants many things we don't know about, and maybe one day—not too far off—he'll want to get them. Whether we form a delegation and go inquire after that or not.

"Bonny," he said to Mrs. Keller, "I wish you'd speak up; you're sitting there so quiet."

Bonny Keller murmured, "I'm just tired."

"Did you know Jack Tree was Bluthgeld?"

Silently, she nodded.

"Was it you, then," Stroud asked, "who told Hoppy?"

"No," she said. "I intended to; I was on my way. But it had already happened. He knew."

I wonder how he knew, Stroud asked himself.

"That Hoppy," Mrs. Lully said in a quavering voice, "he seems to be able to do almost anything . . . why, he's even more powerful than that Mr. Bluthgeld, evidently."

"Right," Stroud agreed.

The audience murmured nervously.

"But he's put all his abilities to use for the welfare of our community," Andrew Gill said. "Remember that. Remember he's our handy and he helps bring in Dangerfield when the signal's weak, and he does tricks for us, and imitations when we can't get Dangerfield at all—he does a whole lot of things, including saving our lives from another nuclear holocaust. So I say, God bless Hoppy and his abilities. I think we should thank God that we have a funny here, like him."

"Right," Cas Stone said.

"I agree," Stroud said, with caution. "But I think we ought to sort of put it to Hoppy that maybe from now on—" He hesitated. "Our killings should be like with Austurias, done legally, by our Jury. I mean, Hoppy did right and he had to act quickly and all . . . but the Jury is the legal body that's supposed to decide. And Earl, here should do the actual act. In the future, I mean. That doesn't include Bluthgeld because having all that magic he was different." You can't kill a man with powers like that through the ordinary methods, he realized. Like Hoppy, for instance . . . suppose someone tried to kill him; it would be next to impossible.

He shivered.

"What's the matter, Orion?" Cas Stone asked, acutely.

"Nothing," Orion Stroud said. "Just thinking what we can do to reward Hoppy to show our appreciation; it's a weighty problem because we owe him so much."

The audience murmured, as the individual members discussed with one another how to reward Hoppy.

George Keller, noticing his wife's pale, drawn features, said, "Are you okay?" He put his hand on her shoulder but she leaned away.

"Just tired," she said. "I ran for a mile, I think, when those explosions began. Trying to reach Hoppy's house."

"How did you know Hoppy could do it?" he asked.

"Oh," she said, "we all know that; we all surely know he's the only one of us who has anything remotely resembling that kind of strength. It came into our—" She corrected herself. "My mind right away, as soon as I saw the explosions." She glanced at her husband.

"Who were you with?" he said.

"Barnes. We were hunting chanterelle mushrooms under the oaks along Bear Valley Ranch Road."

George Keller said, "Personally I'm afraid of Hoppy. Look —he isn't even here. He has a sort of contempt for us all. He's always late getting to the Hall; do you know what I mean? Do you sense it? And it gets more true all the time, perhaps as he sharpens his abilities."

"Perhaps," Bonny murmured.

"What do you think will happen to us now?" George asked her. "Now that we've killed Bluthgeld? We're better off, a lot safer. It's a load off everybody's mind. Someone should notify Dangerfield so he can broadcast it from the satellite."

"Hoppy could do that," Bonny said in a remote voice. "He can do anything. Almost anything."

In the speaker's chair, Orion Stroud rapped for order. "Who wants to be in the delegation that goes down to Hoppy's house and confers the reward and notification of honor on him?" He looked all around the room. "Somebody start to volunteer."

"I'll go," Andrew Gill spoke up.

"Me, too," Fred Quinn said.

Bonny said, "I'll go."

To her, George said, "Do you feel well enough to?"

"Sure." She nodded listlessly. "I'm fine, now. Except for the gash on my head." Automatically she touched the bandage.

"How about you, Mrs. Tallman?" Stroud was saying.

"Yes, I'll go," Mrs. Tallman answered, but her voice trembled.

"Afraid?" Stroud asked.

"Yes," she said.

"Why?"

Mrs. Tallman hesitated. "I—don't know, Orion."

"I'll go, too," Orion Stroud announced. "That's five of us, three men and two women; that's just about right. We'll take the brandy and the cigaboos along and announce the rest— about the plaque, and him being President of the Council and clerk and all that."

"Maybe," Bonny said in a low voice, "we ought to send a delegation there that will stone him to death."

George Keller sucked in his breath and said, "For God's sake, Bonny."

"I mean it," she said.

"You're behaving in an incredible way," he said, furious and surprised; he did not understand her. "What's the matter?"

"But of course it wouldn't do any good," she said. "He'd mash us before we got near his house. Maybe he'll mash me now." She smiled. "For saying that."

"Then shut up!" He stared at her in great fear.

"All right," she said. "I'll be quiet. I don't want to be flung up into the air and then dropped all the way to the ground, the way Jack was."

"I should think not." He was trembling.

"You're a coward," she said mildly. "Aren't you? I wonder why I in all this time didn't realize it before. Maybe that's why I feel the way I do about you."

"And what way's that?"

Bonny smiled. And did not answer. It was a hard, hateful and rigidly cold smile and he did not understand it; he glanced away, wondering once again if all the rumors he had heard about his wife, over the years, could be true after all. She was so cold, so independent. George Keller felt miserable.

"Christ," he said, "you call me a coward because I don't want to see my wife mashed flat."

"It's my body and my existence," Bonny said. "I'll do with it what I want. I'm not afraid of Hoppy; actually I am, but I don't intend to act afraid, if you can comprehend the difference. I'll go down there to that tar-paper house of his and face him honestly. I'll thank him but I think I'll tell him that he must be more careful in the future. We insist on it."

He couldn't help admiring her. "Do that," he urged. "It would be a good thing, dear. He should understand that, how we feel."

"Thank you," she said remotely. "Thanks a lot, George, for your encouragement." She turned away, then, listening to Orion Stroud.

George Keller felt more miserable than ever.

First it was necessary to visit Andrew Gill's factory to pick up the special deluxe Gold Label cigarettes and the Five Star brandy; Bonny, along with Orion Stroud and Gill, left the Foresters' Hall and walked up the road together, all of them conscious of the gravity of their task.

"What's this business relationship you're going into with McConchie?" Bonny asked Andrew Gill.

Gill said, "Stuart is going to bring automation to my factory."

Not believing him she said, "And you're going to advertise over the satellite, I suppose. Singing commercials, as they used to be called. How will they go? Can I compose one for you?"

"Sure," he said, "if it'll help business."

"Are you serious, about this automation?" It occurred to her now that perhaps he actually was.

Gill said, "I'll know more when I've visited Stuart's boss in Berkeley. Stuart and I are going to make the trip very shortly. I haven't seen Berkeley in years. Stuart says it's building up again—not as it was before, of course. But even that may eventually come some day."

"I doubt that," Bonny said. "But I don't care anyhow; it wasn't so good as all that. Just so it builds back some."

Glancing about to make sure that Orion could not hear him, Gill said to her, "Bonny, why don't you come along with Stuart and me?"

Astonished, she said, "Why?"

"It would do you good to break with George. And maybe you could manage to make the break with him final. You should, for his sake and yours."

Nodding, she said, "But—" It seemed to her out of the question; it went too far. Appearances would not be maintained. "Then everyone would know," she said. "Don't you think?"

Gill said, "Bon, they know already."

"Oh." Chastened, she nodded meekly. "Well, what a surprise. I've been living under a delusion, evidently."

"Come to Berkeley with us," Gill said, "and start over. In a sense that's what I'm going to be doing; it marks the end of rolling cigarettes by hand, one at a time, on a little cloth and rod machine. It means I'll have a true factory in the old sense, the pre-war sense."

"'The pre-war sense,'" she echoed. "Is that good?"

"Yes," Gill said. "I'm damn sick and tired of rolling them by hand. I've been trying to free myself for years; Stuart has shown me the way. At least, I hope so." He crossed his fingers.

They reached his factory, and there were the men at work in the rear, rolling away. Bonny thought, So this portion of our lives is soon to be over with forever. I must be sentimental because I cling to it. But Andrew is right. This is no way to produce goods; it's too tedious, too slow. And too few cigarettes are made, really, when you get right down to it. With authentic machinery, Andrew can supply the entire country—assuming that the transportation, the means of delivery, is there.

Among the workmen Stuart McConchie crouched by a barrel of Gill's fine ersatz tobacco, inspecting it. Well, Bonny thought, he either has Andrew's special deluxe formula by now or he isn't interested in it. "Hello," she said to him. "Can you sell his cigarettes once they start rolling off the assembly line in quantity? Have you worked that part out?"

"Yes," McConchie said. "'We've set up plans for distribution on a mass basis. My employer, Mr. Hardy—"

"Don't give me a big sales pitch," she interrupted. "I believe you if you say so; I was just curious." She eyed him critically. "Andy wants me to travel to Berkeley with you. What do you say?"

"Sure," he said vaguely.

"I could be your receptionist," Bonny said. "At your central offices. Right in the center of the city. Correct?" She laughed, but neither Stuart McConchie nor Gill joined her. "Is this sacred?" she asked. "Am I treading on holy topics when I joke? I apologize, if I am."

"It's okay," McConchie said. "We're just concerned; there're still a number of details to work out."

"Maybe I will go along," Bonny said. "Maybe it'll solve my problems, finally."

Now it was McConchie's turn to scrutinize her. "What problems do you have? This seems a nice environment here, to bring up your daughter in; and your old man being principal of—"

"Please," she said. "I don't care to hear a summary of my blessings. Spare me." She walked off, to join Gill who was packaging cigarettes in a metal box for presentation to the phocomelus.

The world is so innocent, she thought to herself. Even yet, even after all that's happened to us. Gill wants to cure me of my—restlessness. Stuart McConchie can't imagine what I could wish for that I don't have right here. But maybe they're right and I'm wrong. Maybe I've made my life unduly complicated . . . maybe there's a machine in Berkeley that will save me, too. Perhaps my problems can be automated out of existence.

Off in a corner, Orion Stroud was writing out a speech which he intended to deliver to Hoppy. Bonny smiled, thinking of the solemnity of it all. Would Hoppy be impressed? Would he perhaps be amused or even filled with bitter contempt? No, she thought; he will like it—I have an intuition. It is just the sort of display that he yearns for. Recognition of him; that will please him terribly.

Is Hoppy preparing to receive us? she wondered. Has he washed his face, shaved, put on an especially clean suit . . . is he waiting expectantly for us to arrive? Is this the achievement of his life, the pinnacle?

She tried to imagine the phocomelus at this moment. Hoppy had, a few hours ago, killed a man, and she knew from what Edie said the people all believed he had killed the glasses man. The town rat catcher, she said to herself, and shivered.

Who will be next? And will he get a presentation next time—for each one, from now on?

Maybe we will be returning again and again to make one presentation after another, she thought. And she thought, *I will go to Berkeley; I want to get as far away from here as possible.*

And, she thought, as soon as possible. Today, if I can. Right now. Hands in her coat pockets, she walked quickly back to join Stuart McConchie and Gill; they were conferring, now, and she stood as close to them as she could, listening to their words with complete raptness.

Doubtfully, Doctor Stockstill said to the phocomelus, "Are you sure he can hear me? This definitely transmits all the way to the satellite?" He touched the mike button again, experimentally.

"I can't possibly assure you that he can hear you," Hoppy said with a snigger. "I can only assure you that this is a five hundred watt transmitter; that's not very much by the old standards but it's enough to reach him. I've reached him with it a number of times." He grinned his sharp, alert grin, his intelligent gray eyes alive with splinters of light. "Go ahead. Does he have a couch up there, or can that be skipped?" The phocomelus laughed, then.

Doctor Stockstill said, "The couch can be skipped." He pressed the mike button and said, "Mr. Dangerfield, this is a—doctor, down below here in West Marin. I'm concerned with your condition. Naturally. Everyone down here is. I, um, thought maybe I could help you."

"Tell him the truth," Hoppy said. "Tell him you're an analyst."

Cautiously, Stockstill said into the microphone, "Formerly I was an analyst, a psychiatrist. Of course, now I'm a G.P. Can you hear me?" He listened to the loudspeaker mounted in the corner but heard only static. "He's not picking me up," he said to Hoppy, feeling discouragement.

"It takes time to establish contact," Hoppy said. "Try again." He giggled. "So you think it's just in his mind. Hypochondria. Are you so sure? Well, you might as well assume that because if it's not, there is practically nothing you can do anyhow."

Doctor Stockstill pressed the mike button and said, "Mr. Dangerfield, this is Stockstill, speaking from Marin County, California; I'm a doctor." It seemed to him absolutely hopeless; why go on? But on the other hand—

"Tell him about Bluthgeld," Hoppy said suddenly.

"Okay," Stockstill said. "I will."

"You can tell him my name," Hoppy said. "Tell him I did it; listen, Doctor—this is how he'll sound when he tells it." The phocomelus assumed a peculiar expression and from his mouth, as before, issued the voice of Walt Dangerfield. "Well, friends, I have a bit of good, good news here . . . I think you'll all enjoy this. Seems as if—" The phocomelus broke off, because from the speaker came a faint sound.

". . . hello, Doctor. This is Walt Dangerfield."

Doctor Stockstill said instantly into the microphone, "Good. Dangerfield, what I want to talk to you about is the pains you've been having. Now, do you have a paper bag up there in the satellite? We're going to try a little carbon dioxide therapy, you and I. I want you to take the paper bag and blow into it. You keep blowing into it and inhaling from it, so that you're finally inhaling pure carbon dioxide. Do you understand? It's just a little idea, but it has a sound basis behind it. You see, too much oxygen triggers off certain diencephalic responses which set up a vicious cycle in the autonomic nervous system. One of the systems of a too-active autonomic nervous system is hyperperistalsis, and you may be suffering from that. Fundamentally, it's an anxiety symptom."

The phocomelus shook his head, turned and rolled away.

"I'm sorry . . ." the voice from the speaker came faintly. "I don't understand, Doctor. You say breathe into a paper bag? What about a polyethylene container? Couldn't asphyxiation result?" The voice, querulous and unreasonable, stumbled uncertainly on, "Is there any way I can synthesize phenobarbital out of the constituents available to me up here? I'll give you an inventory list and possibly—" Static interrupted Dangerfield; when he next was audible he was talking about something else. Perhaps, Doctor Stockstill thought, the man's faculties were wandering.

"Isolation in space," Stockstill broke in, "breeds its own disruptive phenomena, similar to what once was termed 'cabin fever.' Specific to this is the feedback of free-floating anxiety so that it assumes a somatic consequence." He felt, as he talked, that he was doing it all wrong; that he had failed already. The phocomelus had retired, too disgusted to listen—he was off somewhere else entirely, puttering. "Mr. Dangerfield," Stockstill said, "what I want to do is interrupt this feedback and the carbon dioxide trick might do just that. Then when tension symptoms have eased, we can begin a form of psychotherapy, including recall of forgotten traumatic material."

The disc jockey said drily, "My traumatic material isn't forgotten, Doctor; I'm experiencing it right now. It's all around me. It's a form of claustrophobia and I have it very, very bad."

"Claustrophobia," Doctor Stockstill said, "is a phobia directly traceable to the diencephalon in that it's a disturbance of the sense of spaciality. It's connected with the panic reaction to the presence or the imagined presence of danger; it's a re-pressed desire to flee."

Dangerfield said, "Well, where can I flee to, Doctor? Let's be realistic. What in Christ's name can psychoanalysis do for me? I'm a sick man; I need an operation, not the crap you're giving me."

"Are you sure?" Stockstill asked, feeling ineffective and fool-ish. "Now, this will admittedly take time, but you and I have at least established basic contact; you know I'm down here trying to help you and I know that you're listening." You are lis-tening, aren't you? he asked silently. "So I think we've accom-plished something already."

He waited. There was only silence.

"Hello, Dangerfield?" he said into the microphone.

Silence.

From behind him the phocomelus said, "He's either cut himself off or the satellite's too far, now. Do you think you're helping him?"

"I don't know," Stockstill said. "But I know it's worth trying."

"If you had started a year ago—"

"But nobody knew." We took Dangerfield for granted, like the sun, Stockstill realized. And now, as Hoppy says, it's a little late.

"Better luck tomorrow afternoon," Hoppy said, with a

faint—almost sneering—smile. And yet Stockstill felt in it a deep sadness. Was Hoppy sorry for him, for his futile efforts? Or for the man in the satellite passing above them? It was difficult to tell.

"I'll keep trying," Stockstill said.

There was a knock at the door.

Hoppy said, "That will be the official delegation." A broad, pleased smile appeared on his pinched features; his face seemed to swell, to fill with warmth. "Excuse me." He wheeled his 'mobile to the door, extended a manual extensor, and flung the door open.

There stood Orion Stroud, Andrew Gill, Cas Stone, Bonny Keller and Mrs. Tallman, all looking nervous and ill-at-ease. "Harrington," Stroud said, "we have something for you, a little gift."

"Fine," Hoppy said, grinning back at Stockstill. "See?" he said to the doctor. "Didn't I tell you? It's their appreciation." To the delegation he said, "Come on in; I've been waiting." He held the door wide and they passed on inside his house.

"What have you been doing?" Bonny asked Doctor Stockstill, seeing him standing by the transmitter and microphone.

Stockstill said, "Trying to reach Dangerfield."

"Therapy?" she said.

"Yes." He nodded.

"No luck, though."

"We'll try again tomorrow," Stockstill said.

Orion Stroud, his presentation momentarily forgotten, said to Doctor Stockstill, "That's right; you used to be a psychiatrist."

Impatiently, Hoppy said, "Well, what did you bring me?" He peered past Stroud, at Gill; he made out the sight of the container of cigarettes and the case of brandy. "Are those mine?"

"Yes," Gill said. "In appreciation."

The container and the case were lifted from his hands; he blinked as they sailed toward the phoce and came to rest on the floor directly in front of the 'mobile. Avidly, Hoppy plucked them open with his extensors.

"Uh," Stroud said, disconcerted, "we have a statement to make. Is it okay to do so now, Hoppy?" He eyed the phocomelus with apprehension.

"Anything else?" Hoppy demanded, the boxes open, now. "What else did you bring me to pay me back?"

To herself as she watched the scene Bonny thought, I had no idea he was so childish. Just a little child . . . we should have brought much more and it should have been wrapped gaily, with ribbons and cards, with as much color as possible. *He must not be disappointed*, she realized. Our lives depend on it, on his being—placated.

"Isn't there more?" Hoppy was saying peevishly.

"Not yet," Stroud said. "But there will be." He shot a swift, flickering glance at the others in the delegation. "Your *real* presents, Hoppy, have to be prepared with care. This is just a beginning."

"I see," the phocomelus said. But he did not sound convinced.

"Honest," Stroud said. "It's the truth, Hoppy."

"I don't smoke," Hoppy said, surveying the cigarettes; he picked up a handful and crushed them, letting the bits drop. "It causes cancer."

"Well," Gill began, "there're two sides to that. Now—"

The phocomelus sniggered. "I think that's all you're going to give me," he said.

"No, there will certainly be more," Stroud said.

The room was silent, except for the static coming from the speaker.

Off in the corner an object, a transmitter tube, rose and sailed through the air, burst loudly against the wall, sprinkling them all with fragments of broken glass.

"'More,'" Hoppy mimicked, in Stroud's deep, portentous voice. "'There will certainly be more.'"

XV

For thirty-six hours Walt Dangerfield had lain on his bunk in a state of semi-consciousness, knowing now that it was not an ulcer; it was cardiac arrest which he was experiencing, and it was probably going to kill him in a very short time. In spite of what Stockstill, the analyst, had said.

The transmitter of the satellite had continued to broadcast a tape of light concert music over and over again; the sound of soothing strings filled his ears in a travesty of unavailing comfort. He did not even have the strength to get up and make his way to the controls to shut it off.

That psychoanalyst, he thought bitterly. Talking about breathing into a paper bag. It had been like a dream . . . the faint voice, so full of self-confidence. So utterly false in its premises.

Messages were arriving from all over the world as the satellite passed through its orbit again and again; his recording equipment caught them and retained them, but that was all. Dangerfield could no longer answer.

I guess I have to tell them, he said to himself. I guess the time—the time we've been expecting, all of us—has finally come at last.

On his hands and knees he crept until he reached the seat by the microphone, the seat in which for seven years he had broadcast to the world below. After he had sat there for a time resting he turned on one of the many tape recorders, picked up the mike, and began dictating a message which, when it had been completed, would play endlessly, replacing the concert music.

"My friends, this is Walt Dangerfield talking and wanting to thank you all for the times we have had together, speaking back and forth, us all keeping in touch. I'm afraid though that this complaint of mine makes it impossible for me to go on any longer. So with great regret I've got to sign off for the last time—" He went on, painfully, picking his words with care, trying to make them, his audience below, as little unhappy as possible. But nevertheless he told them the truth; he told them that it was the end for him and that they would have to find some way to communicate without him, and then he rang off, shut down the microphone, and in a weary reflex, played the tape back.

The tape was blank. There was nothing on it, although he had talked for almost fifteen minutes.

Evidently the equipment had for some reason broken down, but he was too ill to care; he snapped the mike back on, set switches on the control panel, and this time prepared to deliver his message live to the area below. Those people there would just have to pass the word on to the others; there was no other way.

"My friends," he began once more, "this is Walt Dangerfield. I have some bad news to give you but—" And then he realized that he was talking into a dead mike. The loudspeaker above his head had gone silent; nothing was being transmitted. Otherwise he would have heard his own voice from the monitoring system.

As he sat there, trying to discover what was wrong, he noticed something else, something far stranger and more ominous.

Systems on all sides of him were in motion. Had been in motion for some time, by the looks of them. The high-speed recording and playback decks which he had never used—all at once the drums were spinning, for the first time in seven years. Even as he watched he saw relays click on and off; a drum halted, another one began to turn, this time at slow speed.

I don't understand, he said to himself. *What's happening?*

Evidently the systems were receiving at high speed, recording, and now one of them had started to play back, but what had set all this in motion? Not he. Dials showed him that the satellite's transmitter was on the air, and even as he realized that, realized that messages which had been picked up and recorded were now being played over the air, he heard the speaker above his head, return to life.

"Hoode hoode hoo," a voice—his voice—chuckled. "This is your old pal, Walt Dangerfield, once more, and forgive that concert music. Won't be any more of that."

When did I say that? he asked himself as he sat dully lis-

tening. He felt shocked and puzzled. His voice sounded so
vital, so full of good spirits; how could I sound like that now?
he wondered. That's the way I used to sound, years ago, when
I had my health, and when *she* was still alive.

"Well," his voice murmured on, "that bit of indisposition
I've been suffering from . . . evidently mice got into the supply cupboards, and you'll laugh to think of Walt Dangerfield
fending off mice up here in the sky, but 'tis true. Anyhow, part
of my stores deteriorated and I didn't happen to notice . . .
but it sure played havoc with my insides. However—" And he
heard himself give his familiar chuckle. "I'm okay now. I know
you'll be glad to hear that, all you people down there who
were so good as to transmit your get-well messages, and for
that I give you thanks."

Getting up from the seat before the microphone, Walt
Dangerfield made his way unsteadily to his bunk; he lay down,
closing his eyes, and then he thought once more of the pain in
his chest and what it meant. Angina pectoris, he thought, is
supposed to be more like a great fist pressing down; this is
more a burning pain. If I could look at the medical data on the
microfilm again . . . maybe there's some fact I failed to read.
For instance, this is directly under the breastbone, not off to
the left side. Does that mean anything?

Or maybe there's nothing wrong with me, he thought to
himself as he struggled to get up once more. Maybe Stockstill,
that psychiatrist who wanted me to breathe carbon dioxide,
was right; maybe it's just in my mind, from the years of isolation here.

But he did not think so. It felt far too real for that.

There was one other fact about his illness that bewildered
him. For all his efforts, he could not make a thing out of that
fact, and so he had not even bothered to mention it to the several doctors and hospitals below. Now it was too late, because
now he was too sick to operate the controls of the transmitter.

The pain seemed always to get worse when his satellite was
passing over Northern California.

In the middle of the night the din of Bill Keller's agitated
murmurings woke his sister up. "What is it?" Edie said sleepily,

trying to make out what he wanted to tell her. She sat up in her bed, now, rubbing her eyes as the murmurings rose to a crescendo.

"Hoppy Harrington!" he was saying, deep down inside her. "He's taken over the satellite! Hoppy's taken over Dangerfield's satellite!" He chattered on and on excitedly, repeating it again and again.

"How do you know?"

"Because Mr. Bluthgeld says so; he's down below now but he can still see what's going on above. He can't do anything and he's mad. He still knows all about us. He hates Hoppy because Hoppy mashed him."

"What about Dangerfield?" she asked. "Is he dead yet?"

"He's not down below," her brother said, after a long pause. "So I guess not."

"Who should I tell?" Edie said. "About what Hoppy did?"

"Tell Mama," her brother said urgently. "Go right in now."

Climbing from the bed, Edie scampered to the door and up the hall to their parents' bedroom; she flung the door open, calling, "Mama, I have to tell you something—" And then her voice failed her, because her mother was not there. Only one sleeping figure lay in the bed, her father, alone. Her mother—she knew instantly and completely—had gone and she would not be coming back.

"Where is she?" Bill clamored from within her. "I know she's not here; I can't feel her."

Slowly, Edie shut the door of the bedroom. What'll I do? she asked herself. She walked aimlessly, shivering from the night cold. "Be quiet," she said to Bill, and his murmurings sank down a little.

"You have to find her," Bill was saying.

"I can't," she said. She knew it was hopeless. "Let me think what to do instead," she said, going back into her bedroom for her robe and slippers.

To Ella Hardy, Bonny said, "You have a very nice home here. It's strange to be back in Berkeley after so long, though." She felt overwhelmingly tired. "I'm going to have to turn in," she said. It was two in the morning. Glancing at Andrew Gill and Stuart she said, "We made awfully good time getting here, didn't we? Even a year ago it would have taken another three days."

"Yes," Gill said, and yawned. He looked tired, too; he had done most of the driving because it was his horse-car they had taken.

Mr. Hardy said, "Along about this time, Mrs. Keller, we generally tune in a very late pass by the satellite."

"Oh," she said, not actually caring but knowing it was inevitable; they would have to listen at least for a few moments to be polite. "So you get two transmissions a day, down here."

"Yes," Mrs. Hardy said, "and frankly we find it worth staying up for this late one, although in the last few weeks . . ." She gestured. "I suppose you know as well as we do. Dangerfield is such a sick man."

They were all silent, for a moment.

Hardy said, "To face the brutal fact, we haven't been able to pick him up at all the last day or so, except for a program of light opera that he has played over and over again automatically . . . so—" He glanced around at the four of them. "That's why we were pinning so many hopes on this late transmission, tonight."

To herself, Bonny thought, There's so much business to conduct tomorrow, but he's right; we must stay up for this. We must know what is going on in the satellite; it's too important to us all. She felt sad. Walt Dangerfield, she thought, are you dying up there alone? Are you already dead and we don't know yet?

Will the light opera music go on forever? she wondered. At least until the satellite at last falls back to the Earth or drifts off into space and finally is attracted by the sun?

"I'll turn it on," Hardy said, inspecting his watch. He crossed the room to the radio, turned it on carefully. "It takes it a long time to warm up," he apologized. "I think there's a weak tube; we asked the West Berkeley Handyman's Association to inspect it but they're so busy, they're too tied up, they said. I'd look at it myself, but—" He shrugged ruefully. "Last time I tried to fix it, I broke it worse."

Stuart said, "You're going to frighten Mr. Gill away."

"No," Gill said. "I understand. Radios are in the province of the handies. It's the same up in West Marin."

To Bonny, Mrs. Hardy said, "Stuart says you used to live here."

"I worked at the radiation lab for a while," Bonny said. "And then I worked out at Livermore, also for the University. Of course—" She hesitated. "It's so changed. I wouldn't know Berkeley, now. As we came through I saw nothing I recognized except perhaps San Pablo Avenue itself. All the little shops—they look new."

"They are," Dean Hardy said. Now static issued from the radio and he bent attentively, his ear close to it. "Generally we pick up this late transmission at about 640 kc. Excuse me." He turned his back to them, intent on the radio.

"Turn up the fat lamp," Gill said, "so he can see better to tune it."

Bonny did so, marveling that even here in the city they were still dependent on the primitive fat lamp; she had supposed that their electricity had long since been restored, at least on a partial basis. In some ways, she realized, they were actually behind West Marin. And in Bolinas—

"Ah," Mr. Hardy said, breaking into her thoughts. "I think I've got him. And it's not light opera." His face glistened, beamed.

"Oh dear," Ella Hardy said, "I pray to heaven he's better." She clasped her hands together with anxiety.

From the speaker a friendly, informal, familiar voice boomed out loudly, "Hi there, all you night people down below. Who do you suppose this is, saying hello, hello and hello." Dangerfield laughed. "Yes, folks, I'm up and around, on my two feet once more. And just twirling all these little old knobs and controls like crazy . . . yes sir." His voice was warm, and around Bonny the faces in the room relaxed, too, and smiled in company with the pleasure contained in the voice. The faces nodded, agreed.

"You hear him?" Ella Hardy said. "Why, he's better. He is; you can tell. He's not just saying it, you can tell the difference."

"Hoode hoode hoo," Dangerfield said. "Well, now, let us see; what news is there? You heard about that public enemy number one, that one-time physicist we all remember so well. Our good buddy Doctor Bluthgeld, or should I say Doctor

Bloodmoney? Anyhow, I guess you all know by now that dear Doctor Bloodmoney is no longer with us. Yes, that's right."

"I heard a rumor about that," Mr. Hardy said excitedly. "A peddler who hitched a balloon ride out of Marin County—"

"Shhh," Ella Hardy said, listening.

"Yes indeed," Dangerfield was saying. "A certain party up in Northern California took care of Doctor B. For good. And we owe a debt of sheer unadulterated gratitude to that certain little party because—well, just consider this, folks; that party's a bit handicapped. And yet he was able to do what no one else could have done." Now Dangerfield's voice was hard, unbending; it was a new sound which they had not heard from him ever before. They glanced at one another uneasily. "I'm talking about Hoppy Harrington, my friends. You don't know that name? You should, because without Hoppy not one of you would be alive."

Hardy, rubbing his chin and frowning, shot a questioning look at Ella.

"This Hoppy Harrington," Dangerfield continued, "mashed Doctor B. from a good four miles away, and it was easy. Very easy. You think it's impossible for someone to reach out and touch a man four miles off? That's miiiiighty long arms, isn't it, folks? And mighty strong hands. Well, I'll tell you something even more remarkable." The voice became confidential; it dropped to an intimate near-whisper. "Hoppy has no arms and no hands *at all*." And Dangerfield, then, was silent.

Bonny said quietly, "Andrew, it's him, isn't it?"

Twisting around in his chair to face her, Gill said, "Yes, dear. I think so."

"Who?" Stuart McConchie said.

Now the voice from the radio resumed, more calmly this time, but also more bleakly. The voice had become chilly and stark. "There was an attempt made," it stated, "to reward Mr. Harrington. It wasn't much. A few cigarettes and some bad whiskey—if you can call that a 'reward.' And some empty phrases delivered by a cheap local politico. That was all—that was it for the man who saved us all. I guess they figured—"

Ella Hardy said, "That is not Dangerfield."

To Gill and Bonny, Mr. Hardy said, "Who is it? Say."

Bonny said, "It's Hoppy." Gill nodded.

"Is he up there?" Stuart said. "In the satellite?"

"I don't know," Bonny said. But what did it matter? "He's got control of it; that's what's important." And we thought by coming to Berkeley we would get away, she said to herself. That we would have left Hoppy. "I'm not surprised," she said. "He's been preparing a long time; everything else has been practice, for this."

"But enough of that," the voice from the radio declared, in a lighter tone, now. "You'll hear more about the man who saved us all; I'll keep you posted, from time to time . . . old Walt isn't going to forget. Meanwhile, let's have a little music. What about a little authentic five-string banjo music, friends? Genuine authentic U.S. American old-time folk music . . . 'Out on Penny's Farm,' played by Pete Seeger, the greatest of the folk music men."

There was a pause, and then, from the speaker, came the sound of a full symphony orchestra.

Thoughtfully, Bonny said, "Hoppy doesn't have it down quite right. There're a few circuits left he hasn't got control of."

The symphony orchestra abruptly ceased. Silence obtained again, and then something spilled out at the incorrect speed; it squeaked frantically and was chopped off. In spite of herself, Bonny smiled. At last, belatedly, there came the sound of the five-string banjo.

> *Hard times in the country,*
> *Out on Penny's farm.*

It was a folksy tenor voice twanging away, along with the banjo. The people in the room sat listening, obeying out of long habit; the music emanated from the radio and for seven years they had depended on this; they had learned this and it had become a part of their physical bodies, this response. And yet—Bonny felt the shame and despair around her. No one in the room fully understood what had happened; she herself felt only a numbed confusion. They had Dangerfield back and yet they did not; they had the outer form, the appearance, but what was it really, in essence? It was some labored apparition, like a ghost; it was not alive, not viable. It went through the motions but it was empty and dead. It had a peculiar *preserved* quality, as if somehow the cold, the loneliness, had combined to form around the man in the satellite a new shell. A case which fitted over the living substance and snuffed it out.

The killing, the slow destruction of Dangerfield, Bonny thought, was deliberate, and it came—not from space, not from beyond—but from below, from the familiar landscape. Dangerfield had not died from the years of isolation; he had been stricken by careful instruments issuing up from the very world which he struggled to contact. If he could have cut himself off from us, she thought, he would be alive now. At the very moment he listened to us, received us, he was being killed—and did not guess.

He does not guess even now, she decided. It probably baffles him, if he is capable of perception at this point, capable of any form of awareness.

"This is terrible," Gill was saying in a monotone.

"Terrible," Bonny agreed, "but inevitable. He was too vulnerable up there. If Hoppy hadn't done it someone else would have, one day."

"What'll we do?" Mr. Hardy said. "If you folks are so sure of this, we better—"

"Oh," Bonny said, "we're sure. There's no doubt. You think we ought to form a delegation and call on Hoppy again? Ask him to stop? I wonder what he'd say." I wonder, she thought, how near we would get to that familiar little house before we were demolished. Perhaps we are too close even now, right here in this room.

Not for the world, she thought, would I go any nearer. I think in fact I will move farther on; I will get Andrew Gill to go with me and if not him then Stuart, if not Stuart then someone. I will keep going; I will not stay in one place and maybe I will be safe from Hoppy. I don't care about the others at this point, because I am too scared; I only care about myself.

"Andy," she said to Gill, "listen. I want to go."

"Out of Berkeley, you mean?"

"Yes." She nodded. "Down the coast to Los Angeles. I know we could make it; we'd get there and we'd be okay there, I know it."

Gill said, "I can't go, dear. I have to return to West Marin; I have my business—I can't give it up."

Appalled, she said, "You'd go back to West Marin?"

"Yes. Why not? We can't give up just because Hoppy has done this. That's not reasonable to ask of us. Even Hoppy isn't asking that."

"But he will," she said. "He'll ask everything, in time; I know it, I can foresee it."

"Then we'll wait," Gill said. "Until then. Meanwhile, let's do our jobs." To Hardy and Stuart McConchie he said, "I'm going to turn in, because Christ—we have plenty to discuss tomorrow." He rose to his feet. "Things may work themselves out. We mustn't despair." He whacked Stuart on the back. "Right?"

Stuart said, "I hid once in the sidewalk. Do I have to do that again?" He looked around at the rest of them, seeking an answer.

"Yes," Bonny said.

"Then I will," he said. "But I came up out of the sidewalk; I didn't stay there. And I'll come up again." He, too, rose. "Gill, you can stay with me in my place. Bonny, you can stay with the Hardys."

"Yes," Ella Hardy said, stirring. "We have plenty of room for you, Mrs. Keller. Until we can find a more permanent arrangement."

"Good," Bonny said, automatically. "That's swell." She rubbed her eyes. A good night's sleep, she thought. It would help. And then what? We will just have to see.

If, she thought, we are alive tomorrow.

To her, Gill said suddenly, "Bonny, do you find this hard to believe about Hoppy? Or do you find it easy? Do you know him that well? Do you understand him?"

"I think," she said, "it's very ambitious of him. But it's what we should have expected. Now he has reached out farther than any of us; as he says, he's now got long, long arms. He's compensated beautifully. You have to admire him."

"Yes," Gill admitted. "I do. Very much."

"If I only thought this would satisfy him," she said, "I wouldn't be so afraid."

"The man I feel sorry for," Gill said, "is Dangerfield. Having to lie there passively, sick as he is, and just listen."

She nodded, but she refused to imagine it; she could not
bear to.

Hurrying down the path in her robe and slippers, Edie
Keller groped her way toward Hoppy Harrington's house.

"Hurry," Bill said, from within her. "He knows about us,
they're telling me; they say we're in danger. If we can get close
enough to him I can do an imitation of someone dead that'll
scare him, because he's afraid of dead people. Mr. Blaine says
that's because to him the dead are like fathers, lots of fathers,
and—"

"Be quiet," Edie said. "Let me think." In the darkness she
had gotten mixed up. She could not find the path through the
oak forest, now, and she halted, breathing deeply, trying to
orient herself by the dull light of the partial moon overhead.

It's to the right, she thought. Down the hill. I must not fall;
he'd hear the noise, he can hear a long way, almost everything.
Step by step she descended, holding her breath.

"I've got a good imitation ready," Bill was mumbling; he
would not be quiet. "It's like this: when I get near him I
switch with someone dead, and you won't like that because
it's—sort of squishy, but it's just for a few minutes and then
they can talk to him direct, from inside you. Is that okay,
because once he hears—"

"It's okay," she said, "just for a little while."

"Well, then you know what they say? They say 'We have
been taught a terrible lesson for our folly. This is God's way of
making us see.' And you know what that is? That's the minister who used to make sermons when Hoppy was a baby and
got carried on his Dad's back to church. He'll remember that,
even though it was years and years ago. It was the most awful
moment in his life; you know why? Because that minister, he
was making everybody in the church look at Hoppy and that
was wrong, and Hoppy's father never went back after that. But
that's a lot of the reason why Hoppy is like he is today, because
of that minister. So he's really terrified of that minister, and
when he hears his voice again—"

"Shut up," Edie said desperately. They were now above
Hoppy's house; she saw the lights below. "Please, Bill, *please*."

"But I have to explain to you," Bill went on. "When I—"
He stopped. Inside her there was nothing. She was empty.
"Bill," she said.

He had gone.

Before her eyes, in the dull moonlight, something she had never seen before bobbed. It rose, jiggled, its long pale hair streaming behind it like a tail; it rose until it hung directly before her face. It had tiny, dead eyes and a gaping mouth, it was nothing but a little hard round head, like a baseball. From its mouth came a squeak, and then it fluttered upward once more, released. She watched it as it gained more and more height, rising above the trees in a swimming motion, ascending in the unfamiliar atmosphere which it had never known before.

"Bill," she said, "he took you out of me. He put you outside." And you are leaving, she realized; Hoppy is making you go. "Come back," she said, but it didn't matter because he could not live outside of her. She knew that. Doctor Stockstill had said that. He could not be born, and Hoppy had heard him and made him born, knowing that he would die.

You won't get to do your imitation, she realized. I told you to be quiet and you wouldn't. Straining, she saw—or thought she saw—the hard little object with the streamers of hair now above her . . . and then it disappeared, silently.

She was alone.

Why go on now? It was over. She turned, walked back up the hillside, her head lowered, eyes shut, feeling her way. Back to her house, her bed. Inside she felt raw; she felt the tearing loose. If you only could have been quiet, she thought. He would not have heard you. I told you, I told you so.

She plodded on back.

Floating in the atmosphere, Bill Keller saw a little, heard a little, felt the trees and the animals alive and moving among them. He felt the pressure at work on him, lifting him, but he remembered his imitation and he said it. His voice came out tiny in the cold air; then his ears picked it up and he exclaimed.

"We have been taught a terrible lesson for our folly," he squeaked, and his voice echoed in his ears, delighting him.

The pressure on him let go; he bobbed up, swimming happily, and then he dove. Down and down he went and just before he touched the ground he went sideways until, guided by the living presence within, he hung suspended above Hoppy Harrington's antenna and house.

"This is God's way!" he shouted in his thin, tiny voice. "We can see that it is time to call a halt to high-altitude nuclear testing. I want all of you to write letters to President Johnson!" He did not know who President Johnson was. A living person, perhaps. He looked around for him but he did not see him; he saw oak forests of animals, he saw a bird with noiseless wings that drifted, huge-beaked, eyes staring. Bill squeaked in fright as the noiseless, brown-feathered bird glided his way.

The bird made a dreadful sound, of greed and the desire to rend.

"All of you," Bill cried, fleeing through the dark, chill air. "You must write letters in protest!"

The glittering eyes of the bird followed behind him as he and it glided above the trees, in the dim moonlight.

The owl reached him. And crunched him, in a single instant.

XVI

O NCE more he was within. He could no longer see or hear; it had been for a short time and now it was over.

The owl, hooting, flew on.

Bill Keller said to the owl, "Can you hear me?"

Maybe it could, maybe not; it was only an owl, it did not have any sense, as Edie had had. It was not the same. Can I live inside you? he asked it, hidden away in here where no one knows . . . you have your flights that you make, your passes. With him, in the owl, were the bodies of mice and a thing that stirred and scratched, big enough to keep on trying to live.

Lower, he told the owl. He saw, by means of the owl, the oaks; he saw clearly, as if everything were full of light. Millions of individual objects lay immobile and then he spied one that crept—it was alive and the owl turned that way. The creeping thing, suspecting nothing, hearing no sound, wandered on, out into the open.

An instant later it had been swallowed. The owl flew on.

Good, he thought. And, is there more? This goes on all night, again and again, and then there is bathing when it rains, and the long, deep sleeps. Are they the best part? They are.

He said, "Fergesson don't allow his employees to drink; it's against his religion, isn't it?" And then he said "Hoppy, what's the light from? Is it God? You know, like in the Bible. I mean, is it true?"

The owl hooted.

"Hoppy," he said, from within the owl, "you said last time it was all dark. Is that right? No light at all?"

A thousand dead things within him yammered for attention. He listened, repeated, picked among them.

"You dirty little freak," he said. "Now listen. Stay down here; we're below street-level. You moronic jackass, stay where you are, you are, you are. I'll go upstairs and get those. People. Down here you clear. Space. Space for them."

Frightened, the owl flapped; it rose higher, trying to evade him. But he continued, sorting and picking and listening on.

"Stay down here," he repeated. Again the lights of Hoppy's

house came into view; the owl had circled, returned to it, unable to get away. He made it stay where he wanted it. He brought it closer and closer in its passes to Hoppy. "You moronic jackass," he said. "Stay where you are."

The owl flew lower, hooting in its desire to leave. It was caught and it knew it. The owl hated him.

"The president must listen to our pleas," he said, "before it is too late."

With a furious effort the owl performed its regular technique; it coughed him up and he sank in the direction of the ground, trying to catch the currents of air. He crashed among humus and plant-growth; he rolled, giving little squeaks until finally he came to rest in a hollow.

Released, the owl soared off and disappeared.

"Let man's compassion be witness to this," he said as he lay in the hollow; he spoke in the minister's voice from long ago. "It is ourselves who have done this; we see here the results of mankind's own folly."

Lacking the owl eyes he saw only vaguely; the illumination seemed to be gone and all that remained were several nearby shapes. They were trees.

He saw, too, the form of Hoppy's house outlined against the dim night sky. It was not far off.

"Let me in," Bill said, moving his mouth. He rolled about in the hollow; he thrashed until the leaves stirred. "I want to come in."

An animal, hearing him, moved further off, warily.

"In, in, in," Bill said. "I can't stay out here long; I'll die. Edie, where are you?" He did not feel her nearby; he felt only the presence of the phocomelus within the house.

As best he could, he rolled that way.

Early in the morning, Doctor Stockstill arrived at Hoppy Harrington's tar-paper house to make his fourth attempt at treating Walt Dangerfield. The transmitter, he noticed, was on, and so were lights here and there; puzzled, he knocked on the door.

The door opened and there sat Hoppy Harrington in the center of his 'mobile. Hoppy regarded him in an odd, cautious, defensive fashion.

"I want to make another try," Stockstill said, knowing how useless it was but wanting to go ahead anyhow. "Is it okay?"

"Yes sir," Hoppy said. "It's okay."

"Is Dangerfield still alive?"

"Yes sir. I'd know if he was dead." Hoppy wheeled aside to admit him. "He must still be up there."

"What's happened?" Stockstill said. "Have you been up all night?"

"Yes," Hoppy said. "Learning to work things." He wheeled the 'mobile about, frowning. "It's hard," he said, apparently preoccupied.

"I think that idea of carbon dioxide therapy was a mistake, now that I look back on it," Stockstill said as he seated himself at the microphone. "This time I'm going to try some free association with him, if I can get him to."

The phocomelus continued to wheel about; now the 'mobile bumped into the end of a table. "I hit that by mistake," Hoppy said. "I'm sorry; I didn't mean to."

Stockstill said, "You seem different."

"I'm the same; I'm Bill Keller," the phocomelus said. "Not Hoppy Harrington." With his right manual extensor he pointed. "There's Hoppy. That's him, from now on."

In the corner lay a shriveled dough-like object several inches long; its mouth gaped in congealed emptiness. It had a human-like quality to it, and Stockstill went over to pick it up.

"That was me," the phocomelus said. "But I got close enough last night to switch. He fought a lot, but he was afraid, so I won. I kept doing one imitation after another. The minister one got him."

Stockstill, holding the wizened little homunculus, said nothing.

"Do you know how to work the transmitter?" the phocomelus asked, presently. "Because I don't. I tried, but I can't. I got the lights to work; they turn on and off. I practiced that all night." To demonstrate, he rolled his 'mobile to the wall, where with his manual extensor he snapped the light switch up and down.

After a time Stockstill said, looking down at the dead, tiny form he held in his hand, "I knew it wouldn't survive."

"It did for a while," the phocomelus said. "For around an

hour; that's pretty good, isn't it? Part of that time it was in an owl; I don't know if that counts."

"I—better get to work trying to contact Dangerfield," Stockstill said finally. "He may die any time."

"Yes," the phocomelus said, nodding. "Want me to take that?" He held out an extensor and Stockstill handed him the homunculus. "That owl ate me," the phoce said. "I didn't like that, but it sure had good eyes; I liked that part, using its eyes."

"Yes," Stockstill said reflexively. "Owls have tremendously good eyesight; that must have been quite an experience." This, that he had held in his hand—it did not seem at all possible to him. And yet, it was not so strange; the phoce had moved Bill only a matter of a few inches—that had been enough. And what was that in comparison to what he had done to Doctor Bluthgeld? Evidently after that the phoce had lost track because Bill, free from his sister's body, had mingled with first one substance and then another. And at last he had found the phoce and mingled with him, too; had, at the end, supplanted him in his own body.

It had been an unbalanced trade. Hoppy Harrington had gotten the losing end of it, by far; the body which he had received in exchange for his own had lasted only a few minutes, at the most.

"Did you know," Bill Keller said, speaking haltingly as if it was still difficult for him to control the phocomelus' body, "that Hoppy got up in the satellite for a while? Everybody was excited about that; they woke me up in the night to tell me and I woke Edie. That's how I got here," he added, with a strained, earnest expression on his face.

"And what are you going to do now?" Stockstill asked.

The phoce said, "I have to get used to this body; it's heavy. I feel gravity . . . I'm used to just floating about. You know what? I think these extensors are swell. I can do a lot with them already." The extensors whipped about, touched a picture on the wall, flicked in the direction of the transmitter. "I have to go find Edie," the phoce said. "I want to tell her I'm okay; I bet she probably thinks I died."

Turning on the microphone, Stockstill said, "Walter Dangerfield, this is Doctor Stockstill in West Marin. Can you hear me? If you can, give me an answer. I'd like to resume the therapy we were attempting the other day." He paused, then repeated what he had said.

"You'll have to try a lot of times," the phoce said, watching him. "It's going to be hard because he's so weak; he probably can't get up to his feet and he didn't understand what was happening when Hoppy took over."

Nodding, Stockstill pressed the microphone button and tried again.

"Can I go?" Bill Keller asked. "Can I look for Edie now?"

"Yes," Stockstill said, rubbing his forehead; he drew his faculties together and said, "You'll be careful, what you do . . . you may not be able to switch again."

"I don't want to switch again," Bill said. "This is fine because for the first time there's no one in here but me." In explanation, he added, "I mean, I'm alone; I'm not just part of someone else. Of course, I switched before, but it was to that blind thing—Edie tricked me into it and it didn't do at all. This is different." The thin phoce-face broke into a smile.

"Just be careful," Stockstill repeated.

"Yes sir," the phoce said dutifully. "I'll try; I had bad luck with the owl but it wasn't my fault because I didn't want to get swallowed. That was the owl's idea."

Stockstill thought, But this was yours. There is a difference; I can see that. And it is very important. Into the microphone he repeated, "Walt, this is Doctor Stockstill down below; I'm still trying to reach you. I think we can do a lot to help you pull through this, if you'll do as I tell you. I think we'll try some free association, today, in an effort to get at the root causes of your tension. In any case, it won't do any harm; I think you can appreciate that."

From the loudspeaker came only static.

Is it hopeless? Stockstill wondered. Is it worth keeping on?

He pressed the mike button once more, saying, "Walter, who usurped your authority in the satellite—he's dead, now, so you don't have to worry regarding him. When you feel strong enough I'll give you more details. Okay? Do you agree?" He listened. Still only static.

The phoce, rolling about the room on his 'mobile, like a great trapped beetle, said, "Can I go to school now that I'm out?"

"Yes," Stockstill murmured.

"But I know a lot of things already," Bill said, "from listening with Edie when she was in school; I won't have to go back and repeat, I can go ahead, like her. Don't you think so?"

Stockstill nodded.

"I wonder what my mother will say," the phoce said.

Jarred, Stockstill said, "What?" And then he realized who was meant. "She's gone," he said. "Bonny left with Gill and McConchie."

"I know she left," Bill said plaintively. "But won't she be coming back sometime?"

"Possibly not," Stockstill said. "Bonny's an odd woman, very restless. You can't count on it." It might be better if she didn't know, he said to himself. It would be extremely difficult for her; after all, he realized, she never knew about you at all. Only Edie and I knew. And Hoppy. And, he thought, the owl. "I'm going to give up," he said suddenly, "on trying to reach Dangerfield. Maybe some other time."

"I guess I bother you," Bill said.

Stockstill nodded.

"I'm sorry," Bill said. "I was trying to practice and I didn't know you were coming by. I didn't mean to upset you; it happened suddenly in the night—I rolled here and got in under the door before Hoppy understood, and then it was too late because I was close." Seeing the expression on the doctor's face, he ceased.

"It's—just not like anything I ever ran into before," Stockstill said. "I knew you existed. But that was about all."

Bill said, with pride, "You didn't know I was learning to switch."

"No," Stockstill agreed.

"Try talking to Dangerfield again," Bill said. "Don't give up, because I know he's up there. I won't tell you how I know because if I do you'll get more upset."

"Thank you," Stockstill said. "For not telling me."

Once more he pressed the mike button. The phoce opened the door and rolled outside, onto the path; the 'mobile stopped a little way off, and the phoce looked back indecisively.

"Better go find your sister," Stockstill said. "It'll mean a great deal to her, I'm sure."

When next he looked up, the phoce had gone. The 'mobile was nowhere in sight.

"Walt Dangerfield," Stockstill said into the mike, "I'm going to sit here trying to reach you until either you answer or I know you're dead. I'm not saying you don't have a genuine physical ailment, but I am saying that part of the cause lies in your psychological situation, which in many respects is admittedly bad. Don't you agree? And after what you've gone through, seeing your controls taken away from you—"

From the speaker a far-off, laconic voice said, "Okay, Stockstill. I'll make a stab at your free association. If for no other reason than to prove to you by default that I actually am desperately physically ill."

Doctor Stockstill sighed and relaxed. "It's about time. Have you been picking me up all this time?"

"Yes, good friend," Dangerfield said. "I wondered how long you'd ramble on. Evidently forever. You guys are persistent, if nothing else."

Leaning back, Stockstill shakily lit up a special deluxe Gold Label cigarette and said, "Can you lie down and make yourself comfortable?"

"I *am* lying down," Dangerfield said tartly. "I've been lying down for five days, now."

"And you should become thoroughly passive, if possible. Become supine."

"Like a whale," Dangerfield said. "Just lolling in the brine—right? Now, shall I dwell on childhood incest drives? Let's see . . . I think I'm watching my mother and she's combing her hair at her vanity table. She's very pretty. No, sorry, I'm wrong. It's a movie and I'm watching Norma Shearer. It's the late-late show on TV." He laughed faintly.

"Did your mother resemble Norma Shearer?" Stockstill asked; he had pencil and paper out, now, and was making notes.

"More like Betty Grable," Dangerfield said. "If you can remember her. But that probably was before your time. I'm old, you know. Almost a thousand years . . . it ages you, to be up here, alone."

"Just keep talking," Stockstill said. "Whatever comes into your mind. Don't force it, let it direct itself instead."

Dangerfield said, "Instead of reading the great classics to

the world maybe I can free-associate as to childhood toilet traumas, right? I wonder if that would interest mankind as much. Personally, I find it pretty fascinating."

Stockstill, in spite of himself, laughed.

"You're human," Dangerfield said, sounding pleased. "I consider that good. A sign in your favor." He laughed his old, familiar laugh. "We both have something in common; we both consider what we're doing here as being very funny indeed."

Nettled, Stockstill said, "I want to help you."

"Aw, hell," the faint, distant voice answered. "I'm the one who's helping you, Doc. You know that, deep down in your unconscious. You need to feel you're doing something worthwhile again, don't you? When do you first remember ever having had that feeling? Just lie there supine, and I'll do the rest from up here." He chuckled. "You realize, of course, that I'm recording this on tape; I'm going to play our silly conversations every night over New York—they love this intellectual stuff, up that way."

"Please," Stockstill said. "Let's continue."

"Hoode hoode hoo," Dangerfield chortled. "By all means. Can I dwell on the girl I loved in the fifth grade? That was where my incest fantasies really got started." He was silent for a moment and then he said in a reflective voice, "You know, I haven't thought of Myra for years. Not in twenty years."

"Did you take her to a dance or some such thing?"

"In the *fifth grade*?" Dangerfield yelled. "Are you some kind of a nut? Of course not. But I did kiss her." His voice seemed to become more relaxed, more as it had been in former times. "I never forgot that," he murmured.

Static, for a moment, supervened.

". . . and then," Dangerfield was saying when next Stockstill could make his words out, "Arnold Klein rapped me on the noggin and I shoved him over, which is exactly what he deserved. Do you follow? I wonder how many hundreds of my avid listeners are getting this; I see lights lit up—they're trying to contact me on a lot of frequencies. Wait, Doc. I have to answer a few of these calls. Who knows, some of them might be other, better analysts." He added, in parting, "And at lower rates."

There was silence. Then Dangerfield was back.

"Just people telling me I did right to rap Arnold Klein on the noggin," he said cheerfully. "So far the votes are in favor four to one. Shall I continue?"

"Please do," Stockstill said, scratching notes.

"Well," Dangerfield said, "and then there was Jenny Linhart. That was in the low sixth."

The satellite, in its orbit, had come closer; the reception was now loud and clear. Or perhaps it was that Hoppy Harrington's equipment was especially good. Doctor Stockstill leaned back in his chair, smoked his cigarette, and listened, as the voice grew until it boomed and echoed in the room.

How many times, he thought, Hoppy must have sat here receiving the satellite. Building up his plans, preparing for the day. And now it is over. Had the phocomelus—Bill Keller—taken the wizened, dried-up little thing with him? Or was it still somewhere nearby?

Stockstill did not look around; he kept his attention on the voice which came to him so forcefully, now. He did not let himself notice anything else in the room.

In a strange but soft bed in an unfamiliar room, Bonny Keller woke to sleepy confusion. Diffuse light, yellow and undoubtedly the early-morning sun, poured about her, and above her a man whom she knew well bent over her, reaching down his arms. It was Andrew Gill and for a moment she imagined—she deliberately allowed herself to imagine—that it was seven years ago, E Day again.

"Hi," she murmured, clasping him to her. "Stop," she said, then. "You're crushing me and you haven't shaved yet. What's going on?" She sat up, all at once, pushing him away.

Gill said, "Just take it easy." Tossing the covers aside, he picked her up, carried her across the room, toward the door.

"Where are we going?" she asked. "To Los Angeles? This way—with you carrying me in your arms?"

"We're going to listen to somebody." With his shoulder he pushed the door open and carried her down the small, low-ceilinged hall.

"Who?" she demanded. "Hey, I'm not dressed." All she had on was her underwear, which she had slept in.

Ahead, she saw the Hardys' living room, and there, at the

radio, their faces suffused with an eager, youthful joy, stood
Stuart McConchie, the Hardys, and several men whom she realized were employees of Mr. Hardy.

From the speaker came the voice they had heard last night,
or was it that voice? She listened, as Andrew Gill seated himself
with her on his lap. ". . . and then Jenny Linhart said to me,"
the voice was saying, "that I resembled, in her estimation, a
large poodle. It had to do with the way my big sister was cutting my hair, I think. I did look like a large poodle. It was not
an insult. It was merely an observation; it showed she was
aware of me. But that's some improvement over not being noticed at all, isn't it?" Dangerfield was silent, then, as if waiting
for an answer.

"Who's he talking to?" she said, still befuddled by sleep, still
not fully awake. And then she realized what it meant. "He's
alive," she said. And Hoppy was gone. "Goddamn it," she said
loudly, "will somebody tell me what happened?" She squirmed
off Andrew's lap and stood shivering; the morning air was
cold.

Ella Hardy said, "We don't know what happened. He apparently came back on the air sometime during the night. We
hadn't turned the radio off, and so we heard it; this isn't his
regular time to transmit to us."

"He appears to be talking to a doctor," Mr. Hardy said.
"Possibly a psychiatrist who's treating him."

"Dear God," Bonny said, doubling up. "It isn't possible—
he's being psychoanalyzed." But, she thought, *where did
Hoppy go? Did he give up?* Was the strain of reaching out that
far too much for him, was that it? Did he, after all, have limitations, like every other living thing? She returned quickly to her
bedroom, still listening, to get her clothes. No one noticed;
they were all so intent on the radio.

To think, she said to herself as she dressed, that the old witch-
craft could help him. It was incredibly funny; she trembled
with cold and merriment as she buttoned her shirt. Dangerfield, on a couch up in his satellite, gabbling away about his
childhood . . . oh God, she thought, and she hurried back to
the living room to catch it all.

Andrew met her, stopping her in the hall. "It faded out," he
said. "It's gone, now."

"Why?" Her laughter ceased; she was terrified.

"We were lucky to get it at all. He's all right, I think."

"Oh," she said, "I'm so scared. Suppose he isn't?"

Andrew said, "But he is." He put his big hands on her shoulders. "You heard him; you heard the quality of his voice."

"That analyst," she said, "deserves a Hero First Class medal."

"Yes," he said gravely. "Analyst Hero First Class, you're entirely right." He was silent, then, still touching her but standing a little distance from her. "I apologize for barging in on you and dragging you out of bed. But I knew you'd want to hear."

"Yes," she agreed.

"Is it still essential to you that we go further on? All the way to Los Angeles?"

"Well," she said, "you do have business here. We could stay here a while at least. And see if he remains okay." She was still apprehensive, still troubled about Hoppy.

Andrew said, "One can never be really sure, and that's what makes life a problem, don't you agree? Let's face it—he is mortal; someday he has to perish anyhow. Like the rest of us." He gazed down at her.

"But not *now*," she said. "If it only can be later, a few years from now—I could stand it then." She took hold of his hands and then leaned forward and kissed him. Time, she thought. The love we felt for each other in the past; the love we have for Dangerfield right now, and for him in the future. Too bad it is a powerless love; too bad it can't automatically knit him up whole and sound once more, this feeling we have for one another—and for him.

"Remember E Day?" Andrew asked.

"Oh yes, I certainly do," she said.

"Any further thoughts on it?"

Bonny said, "I've decided I love you." She moved quickly away from him, flushing at having said such a thing. "The good news," she murmured. "I'm carried away; please excuse me, I'll recover."

"But you mean it," he said, perceptively.

"Yes." She nodded.

Andrew said, "I'm getting a little old, now."

"We all are," she said. "I creak, when I first get up . . . perhaps you noticed, just now."

"No," he said. "Just so long as your teeth stay in your head, as they are." He looked at her uneasily. "I don't know exactly what to say to you, Bonny. I feel that we're going to achieve a great deal here; I hope so, anyhow. Is it a base, onerous thing, coming here to arrange for new machinery for my factory? Is that—" He gestured. "Crass?"

"It's lovely," she answered.

Coming into the hall, Mrs. Hardy said, "We picked him up again for a just a minute, and he was still talking about his childhood. I would say now that we won't hear again until the regular time at four in the afternoon. What about breakfast? We have three eggs to divide among us; my husband managed to pick them from a peddler last week."

"Eggs," Andrew Gill repeated. "What kind? Chicken?"

"They're large and brown," Mrs. Hardy said. "I'd guess so, but we can't be positive until we open them."

Bonny said, "It sounds marvelous." She was very hungry, now. "I think we should pay for them, though; you've already given us so much—a place to stay and dinner last night." It was virtually unheard of, these days, and certainly it was not what she had expected to find in the city.

"We're in business together," Mrs. Hardy pointed out. "Everything we have is going to be pooled, isn't it?"

"But I have nothing to offer." She felt that keenly, all at once, and she hung her head. I can only take, she thought. Not give.

However, they did not seem to agree. Taking her by the hand, Mrs. Hardy led her toward the kitchen area. "You can help fix," she explained. "We have potatoes, too. You can peel them. We serve our employees breakfast; we always eat together—it's cheaper, and they don't have kitchens, they live in rooms, Stuart and the others. We have to watch out for them."

You're very good people, Bonny thought. So this is the city—this is what we've been hiding from, throughout these years. We heard the awful stories, that it was only ruins, with predators creeping about, derelicts and opportunists and nappers, the dregs of what it had once been . . . and we had fled from that, too, before the war. We had already become too afraid to live here.

As they entered the kitchen she heard Stuart McConchie saying to Dean Hardy, ". . . and besides playing the nose-flute this rat—" He broke off, seeing her. "An anecdote about life here," he apologized. "It might shock you. It has to do with a brilliant animal, and many people find them unpleasant."

"Tell me about it," Bonny said. "Tell me about the rat who plays the nose-flute."

"I may be getting two brilliant animals mixed together," Stuart said as he began heating water for the imitation coffee. He fussed with the pot and then, satisfied, leaned back against the wood-burning stove, his hands in his pockets. "Anyhow, I think the veteran said that it also had worked out a primitive system of bookkeeping. But that doesn't sound right." He frowned.

"It does to me," Bonny said.

"We could use a rat like that working here," Mr. Hardy said. "We'll be needing a good bookkeeper, with our business expanding, as it's going to be."

Outside, along San Pablo Avenue, horse-drawn cars began to move; Bonny heard the sharp sound of the hoofs striking. She heard the stirrings of activity, and she went to the window to peep out. Bicycles, too, and a mammoth old wood-burning truck. And people on foot, many of them.

From beneath a board shack an animal emerged and with caution crossed the open to disappear beneath the porch of a building on the far side of the street. After a moment it reappeared, this time followed by another animal, both of them short-legged and squat, perhaps mutations of bulldogs. The second animal tugged a clumsy sleigh-like platform after it; the platform, loaded with various valuable objects, most of them food, slid and bumped on its runners over the irregular pavement after the two animals hurrying for cover.

At the window, Bonny continued to watch attentively, but the two short-legged animals did not reappear. She was just about to turn away when she caught sight of something else moving into its first activity of the day. A round metal hull, splotched over with muddy colors and bits of leaves and twigs, shot into sight, halted, raised two slender antennae quiveringly into the early morning sun.

What in the world is it? Bonny wondered. And then she realized that she was seeing a Hardy Homeostatic trap in action.

Good luck, she thought.

The trap, after pausing and scouting in all directions, hesitated and then at last doubtfully took off on the trail of the two bulldog-like animals. It disappeared around the side of a nearby house, solemn and dignified, much too slow in its pursuit, and she had to smile.

The business of the day had begun. All around her the city was awakening, back once more into its regular life.

NOW WAIT FOR LAST YEAR

To Nancy Hackett

 . . . A way where you might tread the Sun, and be
  More bright than he.

      Henry Vaughan

One

THE apteryx-shaped building, so familiar to him, gave off its usual smoky gray light as Eric Sweetscent collapsed his wheel and managed to park in the tiny stall allocated him. Eight o'clock in the morning, he thought drearily. And already his employer Mr. Virgil L. Ackerman had opened TF&D Corporation's offices for business. Imagine a man whose mind is most sharp at eight a.m., Dr. Sweetscent mused. It runs against God's clear command. A fine world they're doling out to us; the war excuses any human aberration, even the old man's.

Nonetheless he started toward the in-track—only to be halted by the calling of his name. "Say, Mr. Sweetscent! Just a moment, sir!" The twangy—and highly repellent—voice of a robant; Eric stopped reluctantly, and now the thing coasted up to him, all arms and legs flapping energetically. "Mr. Sweetscent of Tijuana Fur & Dye Corporation?"

The slight got across to him. "Dr. Sweetscent. Please."

"I have a bill, doctor." It whipped a folded white slip from its metal pouch. "Your wife Mrs. Katherine Sweetscent charged this three months ago on her Dreamland Happy Times For All account. Sixty-five dollars plus sixteen per cent charges. And the law, now; you understand. I regret delaying you, but it is, ahem, illegal." It eyed him alertly as he, with massive reluctance, fished out his checkbook.

"What's the purchase?" he asked gloomily as he wrote the check.

"It was a Lucky Strike package, doctor. With the authentic ancient green. Circa 1940, before World War Two when the package changed. 'Lucky Strike green has gone to war,' you know." It giggled.

He couldn't believe it; something was wrong. "But surely," he protested, "that was supposed to be put on the company account."

"No, doctor," the robant declared. "Honest injun. Mrs. Sweetscent made it absolutely clear that this purchase was for her private use." It managed to add, then, an explanation which he knew at once to be spurious. But whether it originated in the robant or with Kathy—that he could not tell, at least not immediately. "Mrs. Sweetscent," the robant stated piously, "is building a Pitts-39."

"The hell she is." He tossed the made-out check at the robant; as it strove to catch the fluttering bit of paper he continued on, toward the in-track.

A Lucky Strike package. Well, he reflected grimly, Kathy is off again. The creative urge, which can only find an outlet in spending. And always above and beyond her own salary—which, he had to admit to himself, was a bit greater than his own, alas. But in any case, why hadn't she told him? A major purchase of that sort . . .

The answer, of course, was obvious. The bill itself pointed out the problem in all its depressing sobriety. He thought, Fifteen years ago I would have said—did say—that the combined incomes of Kathy and me would be enough and certainly *ought* to be enough to maintain any two semireasonable adults at any level of opulence. Even taking into account the wartime inflation.

However, it had not quite worked out that way. And he felt a deep, abiding intuition that it just never quite would.

Within the TF&D Building he dialed the hall leading to his own office, squelching the impulse to drop by Kathy's office upstairs for an immediate confrontation. Later, he decided. After work, perhaps at dinner. Lord, and he had such a full schedule ahead of him; he had no energy—and never had had in the past—for this endless squabbling.

"Morning, doctor."

"Hi," Eric said, nodding to fuzzy Miss Perth, his secretary; this time she had sprayed herself a shiny blue, inlaid with sparkling fragments that reflected the outer office's overhead lighting. "Where's Himmel?" No sign of the final-stage quality-control inspector, and already he perceived reps from subsidiary outfits pulling up at the parking lot.

"Bruce Himmel phoned to say that the San Diego public library is suing him and he may have to go to court and so he'll probably be late." Miss Perth smiled at him engagingly, showing spotless synthetic ebony teeth, a chilling affectation which had migrated with her from Amarillo, Texas, a year ago.

"The library cops broke into his conapt yesterday and found over twenty of their books that he'd stolen—you know Bruce, he has that phobia about checking things out . . . how is it put in Greek?"

He passed on into the inner office which was his alone; Virgil Ackerman had insisted on it as a suitable mark of prestige—in lieu of a raise in salary.

And there, in his office, at his window, smoking a sweet-smelling Mexican cigarette and gazing out at the austere brown hills of Baja California south of the city, stood his wife Kathy. This was the first time he had met up with her this morning; she had risen an hour ahead of him, had dressed and eaten alone and gone on in her own wheel.

"What's up?" Eric said to her tightly.

"Come on in and shut the door." Kathy turned but did not look toward him; the expression on her exquisitely sharp face was meditative.

He closed the door. "Thanks for welcoming me into my own office."

"I knew that damn bill collector would intercept you this morning," Kathy said in a faraway voice.

"Almost eighty greens," he said. "With the fines."

"Did you pay it?" Now for the first time she glanced at him; the flutter of her artificially dark lashes quickened, revealing her concern.

"No," he said sardonically. "I let the robant gun me down where I stood, there in the parking lot." He hung his coat in his closet. "Of course I paid it. It's mandatory, ever since the Mole obliterated the entire class of credit-system purchasing. I realize you're not interested in this, but if you don't pay within—"

"Please," Kathy said. "Don't lecture me. What did it say? That I'm building a Pitts-39? It lied; I got the Lucky Strike green package as a gift. I wouldn't build a babyland without telling you; after all, it would be yours, too."

"Not Pitts-39," Eric said. "I never lived there, in '39 or any other time." He seated himself at his desk and punched the viscombox. "I'm here, Mrs. Sharp," he informed Virgil's secretary. "How are you today, Mrs. Sharp? Get home all right from that war-bond rally last night? No warmongering pickets hit you on the head?" He shut off the box. To Kathy he explained, "Lucile Sharp is an ardent appeaser. I think it's nice for a corporation to permit its employees to engage in political agitation, don't you? And even nicer than that is the fact that it doesn't cost you a cent; political meetings are free."

Kathy said, "But you have to pray and sing. And they do get you to buy those bonds."

"Who was the cigarette package for?"

"Virgil Ackerman, of course." She exhaled cigarette smoke in twin gray trails. "You suppose I want to work elsewhere?"

"Sure, if you could do better."

Kathy said thoughtfully, "It's not the high salary that keeps me here, Eric, despite what you think. I believe we're helping the war effort."

"Here? *How?*"

The office door opened; Miss Perth stood outlined, her luminous, fuzzy, horizontally inclined breasts brushing the frame as she turned toward him and said, "Oh, doctor, sorry to bother you but Mr. Jonas Ackerman is here to see you—Mr. Virgil's great-grandnephew from the Baths."

"How are the Baths, Jonas?" Eric said, holding out his hand; the great-grandnephew of the firm's owner came toward him and they shook in greeting. "Anything bubble out during the night shift?"

"If it did," Jonas said, "it imitated a workman and left by the front gate." He noticed Kathy then. "Morning, Mrs. Sweetscent. Say, I saw that new config you acquired for our Wash-35, that bug-shaped car. What is that, a Volkswagen? Is that what they were called?"

"An air-flow Chrysler," Kathy said. "It was a good car but it had too much unsprung metal in it. An engineering error that ruined it on the market."

"God," Jonas said, with feeling. "To know something really thoroughly; how that must feel. Down with the fliegemer Renaissance—I say specialize in one area until—" He broke off, seeing that both the Sweetscents had a grim, taciturn cast about them. "I interrupted?"

"Company business takes priority," Eric said, "over the creature pleasures." He was glad of the intervention by even this junior member of the organization's convoluted blood hierarchy. "Please scram out of here, Kathy," he said to his wife, and did not trouble himself to make his tone jovial. "We'll talk at dinner. I've got too much to do to spend my time haggling over whether a robant bill collector is mechanically capable of telling lies or not." He escorted his wife to the office door; she moved passively, without resistance. Softly, Eric said, "Like everyone else in the world it's busy deriding you, isn't it? They're all talking." He shut the door after her.

Presently Jonas Ackerman shrugged and said, "Well, that's marriage these days. Legalized hate."

"Why do you say that?"

"Oh, the overtones came through in that exchange; you could feel it in the air like the chill of death. There ought to be an ordinance that a man can't work for the same outfit as his wife; hell, even in the same city." He smiled, his thin, youthful face all at once free of seriousness. "But she really is good, you know; Virgil gradually let go all his other antique collectors after Kathy started here . . . but of course she's mentioned that to you."

"Many times." Almost every day, he reflected caustically.

"Why don't you two get divorced?"

Eric shrugged, a gesture designed to show a deep philosophical nature. He hoped it truly did so.

The gesture evidently fell short, because Jonas said, "Meaning that you like it?"

"I mean," he said resignedly, "that I've been married before and it was no better, and if I divorce Kathy I'll marry again—because as my brainbasher puts it I can't find my identity outside the role of husband and daddy and big butter-and-eggman wage earner—and the next damn one will be the same because that's the kind I select. It's rooted in my temperament." He raised his head and eyed Jonas with as good a show of masochistic defiance as he could manage. "What did you want, Jonas?"

"Trip," Jonas Ackerman said brightly. "To Mars, for all of us, including you. Conference! You and I can nab seats a good long way from old Virgil so we won't have to discuss company business and the war effort and Gino Molinari. And since we're taking the big boat it'll be six hours each way. And for God's sake, let's not find ourselves standing up all the way to Mars and back—let's make sure we do get seats."

"How long will we be there?" He frankly did not look forward to the trip; it would separate him from his work too long.

"We'll undoubtedly be back tomorrow or the day after. Listen; it'll get you out of your wife's path: Kathy's staying here. It's an irony, but I've noticed that when the old fellow's actually at Wash-35 he never likes to have his antique experts around him . . . he likes to slide into the, ahem, magic of the place . . . more so all the time as he gets older. When you're one hundred and thirty you'll begin to understand—so will I, maybe. Meanwhile we have to put up with him." He added, somberly, "You probably know this, Eric, because you are his doctor. He never will die; he'll never make the hard decision—as it's called—no matter what fails and has to be replaced inside him. Sometimes I envy him for being—optimistic. For liking life that much; for thinking it's so important. Now, we puny mortals; at our age—" He eyed Eric. "At a miserable thirty or thirty-three—"

"I've got plenty of vitality," Eric said. "I'm good for a long time. And life isn't going to get the best of me." From his coat pocket he brought forth the bill which the robant collector had presented to him. "Think back. Did a package of Lucky Strike *with the green* show up at Wash-35 about three months ago? A contribution from Kathy?"

After a long pause Jonas Ackerman said, "You poor suspicious stupid creak. That's all you can manage to brood about. Listen, doctor; if you can't get your mind on your job, you're finished; there're twenty artiforg surgeons with applications in our personnel files just waiting to go to work for a man like Virgil, a man of his importance in the economy and war effort. You're really just plain not all that good." His expression was both compassionate and disapproving, a strange mixture which had the effect of waking Eric Sweetscent abruptly. "Personally, if my heart gave out—which it no doubt will do one of these days—I wouldn't particularly care to go to you. You're too tangled in your own personal affairs. You live for yourself, not the planetary cause. My God, don't you remember? We're

fighting a life-and-death war. And we're losing. We're being
pulverized every goddam day!"

True, Eric realized. And we've got a sick, hypochondriacal,
dispirited leader. And Tijuana Fur & Dye Corporation is one
of those vast industrial props that maintain that sick leader,
that manage just barely to keep the Mole in office. Without
such warm, high-placed, personal friendships as that of Virgil
Ackerman, Gino Molinari would be out or dead or in an old
folks' rest home. I know it. And yet—individual life must go
on. After all, he reflected, I didn't choose to get entangled in
my domestic life, my boxer's clinch with Kathy. And if you
think I did or do, it's because you're morbidly young. You've
failed to pass from adolescent freedom into the land which I
inhabit: married to a woman who is economically, intellectually, and even this, too, even erotically my superior.

Before leaving the building Dr. Eric Sweetscent dropped by
the Baths, wondering if Bruce Himmel had shown up. He had;
there he stood, beside the huge reject-basket full of defective
Lazy Brown Dogs.

"Turn them back into groonk," Jonas said to Himmel, who
grinned in his empty, disjointed fashion as the youngest of the
Ackermans tossed him one of the defective spheres which
rolled off TF&D's assembly lines along with those suitable for
wiring into the command guidance structure of interplanetary
spacecraft. "You know," he said to Eric, "if you took a dozen
of these control syndromes—and not the defective ones but
the ones going into shipping cartons for the Army—you'd find
that compared with a year ago or even six months ago their reaction time has slowed by several microseconds."

"By that you mean," Eric said, "our quality standards have
dropped?"

It seemed impossible. TF&D's product was too vital. The
entire network of military operations depended on these head-
sized spheres.

"Exactly." It did not appear to bother Jonas. "Because we
were rejecting too many units. We couldn't show a profit."

Himmel stammered, "S-sometimes I wish we were back in
the Martian bat guano business."

Once the corporation had collected the dung of the Martian flap bat, had made its first returns that way and so had been in position to underwrite the greater economic aspects of another non-terrestrial creature, the Martian print amoeba. This august unicellular organism survived by its ability to mimic other life forms—those of its own size, specifically—and although this ability had amused Terran astronauts and UN officials, no one had seen an industrial usage until Virgil Ackerman of bat guano fame had come upon the scene. Within a matter of hours he had presented a print amoeba with one of his current mistress's expensive furs; the print amoeba had faithfully mimicked it, whereupon, for all intents and purposes, between Virgil and the girl two mink stoles existed. However, the amoeba had at last grown tired of being a fur and had resumed its own form. This conclusion left something to be desired.

The answer, developed over a period of many months, consisted of killing the amoeba during its interval of mimicry and then subjecting the cadaver to a bath of fixing-chemicals which had the capacity to lock the amoeba in that final form; the amoeba did not decay and hence could not later on be distinguished from the original. It was not long before Virgil Ackerman had set up a receiving plant at Tijuana, Mexico, and was accepting shipments of ersatz furs of every variety from his industrial installations on Mars. And almost at once he had broken the natural fur market on Earth.

The war, however, had changed all that.

But, then, what hadn't the war changed? And who had ever thought, when the Pact of Peace was signed with the ally, Lilistar, that things would go so badly? Because according to Lilistar and its Minister Freneksy this was the dominant military power in the galaxy; its enemy, the reegs, was inferior militarily and in every other way and the war would undoubtedly be a short one.

War itself was bad enough, Eric ruminated, but there was nothing quite like a losing war to make one stop and think, to try—futilely—to second-guess one's past decisions—such as the Pact of Peace, to name one example, and an example which currently might have occurred to quite a number of Terrans had they been asked. But these days their opinions were not being solicited by the Mole or by the government of

Lilistar itself. In fact it was universally believed—openly noised about at bars as well as in the privacy of living rooms—that even the Mole's opinion was not being asked.

As soon as hostilities with the reegs had begun, Tijuana Fur & Dye had converted from the luxury trade of ersatz fur production to war work, as, of course, had all other industrial enterprises. Supernaturally accurate duplication of rocketship master syndromes, the ruling monad Lazy Brown Dog, was fatalistically natural for the type of operation which TF&D represented; conversion had been painless and rapid. So here now, meditatively, Eric Sweetscent faced this basket of rejects, wondering—as had everyone at one time or another in the corporation—how these substandard and yet still quite complex units could be put to some economic advantage. He picked up one and handled it; in terms of weight it resembled a baseball, in terms of size a grapefruit. Evidently nothing could be done with these failures which Himmel had rejected, and he turned to toss the sphere into the maw of the hopper, which would return the fixed plastic into its original organic cellular form.

"Wait," Himmel croaked.

Eric and Jonas glanced at him.

"Don't melt it down," Himmel said. His unsightly body twisted with embarrassment; his arms wound themselves about, the long, knobby fingers writhing. Idiotically, his mouth gaped as he mumbled, "I—don't do that any more. Anyhow, in terms of raw material that unit's worth only a quarter of a cent. That whole bin's worth only about a dollar."

"So?" Jonas said. "They still have to go back to—"

Himmel mumbled, "I'll buy it." He dug into his trouser pocket, straining to find his wallet; it was a long and arduous struggle but at last he produced it.

"Buy it for what?" Jonas demanded.

"I have a schedule arranged," Himmel said, after an agonized pause. "I pay a half cent apiece for Lazy Brown Dog rejects, twice what they're worth, so the company's making a profit. So why should anyone object?" His voice rose to a squeak.

Pondering him, Jonas said, "No one's objecting. I'm just curious as to what you want it for." He glanced sideways at Eric as if to ask, What do you say about this?

Himmel said, "Um, I use them." With gloom he turned and shambled toward a nearby door. "But they're all mine because I paid for them in advance out of my salary," he said over his shoulder as he opened the door. Defensively, his face dark with resentment and with the corrosive traces of deeply etched phobic anxiety, he stood aside.

Within the room—a storeroom, evidently—small carts rolled about on silver-dollar-sized wheels; twenty or more of them, astutely avoiding one another in their zealous activity.

On board each cart Eric saw a Lazy Brown Dog, wired in place and controlling the movements of the cart.

Presently Jonas rubbed the side of his nose, grunted, said, "What powers them?" Stooping, he managed to snare a cart as it wheeled by his foot; he lifted it up, its wheels still spinning futilely.

"Just a little cheap ten-year A-battery," Himmel said. "Costs another half cent."

"And *you* built these carts?"

"Yes, Mr. Ackerman." Himmel took the cart from him and set it back on the floor; once more it wheeled industriously off. "These are the ones too new to let go," he explained. "They have to practice."

"And then," Jonas said, "you give them their freedom."

"That's right." Himmel bobbed his large-domed, almost bald head, his horn-rimmed glasses sliding forward on his nose.

"Why?" Eric asked.

Now the crux of the matter had been broached; Himmel turned red, twitched miserably, and yet displayed an obscure, defensive pride. "Because," he blurted, "they deserve it."

Jonas said, "But the protoplasm's not alive; it died when the chemical fixing-spray was applied. You know that. From then on it—all of these—is nothing but an electronic circuit, as dead as—well, as a robant."

With dignity Himmel answered, "But I consider them alive, Mr. Ackerman. And just because they're inferior and incapable of guiding a rocketship in deep space, that doesn't mean they have no right to live out their meager lives. I release them and they wheel around for, I expect, six years or possibly longer; that's enough. That gives them what they're entitled to."

Turning to Eric, Jonas said, "If the old man knew about this—"

"Mr. Virgil Ackerman knows about this," Himmel said at once. "He approves of it." He amended, "Or rather, he lets me do it; he knows I'm reimbursing the company. And I build the carts at night, on my own time; I have an assembly line— naturally very primitive, but effective—in my conapt where I live." He added, "I work till around one o'clock every night."

"What do they do after they're released?" Eric asked. "Just roam the city?"

"God knows," Himmel said. Obviously that part was not his concern; he had done his job by building the carts and wiring the Lazy Brown Dogs in functioning position. And perhaps he was right; he could hardly accompany each cart, defend it against the hazards of the city.

"You're an artist," Eric pointed out, not sure if he was amused or revolted or just what. He was not impressed; that much he was sure of: the entire enterprise had a bizarre, zany quality—it was absurd. Himmel ceaselessly at work both here and at his conapt, seeing to it that the factory rejects got their place in the sun . . . what next? And this, while everyone else sweated out the folly, the greater, collective absurdity, of a bad war.

Against that backdrop Himmel did not look so ludicrous. It was the times. Madness haunted the atmosphere itself, from the Mole on down to this quality-control functionary who was clearly disturbed in the clinical, psychiatric sense.

Walking off down the hall with Jonas Ackerman, Eric said, "He's a pook." That was the most powerful term for aberrance in currency.

"Obviously," Jonas said, with a gesture of dismissal. "But this gives me a new insight into old Virgil, the fact that he'd tolerate this and certainly not because it gives him a profit— that's not it. Frankly I'm glad. I thought Virgil was more hard-boiled; I'd have expected him to bounce this poor nurt right out of here, into a slave-labor gang on its way to Lilistar. God, what a fate that would be. Himmel is lucky."

"How do you think it'll end?" Eric asked. "You think the Mole will sign a separate treaty with the reegs and bail us out of this and leave the 'Starmen to fight it alone—which is what they deserve?"

"He can't," Jonas said flatly. "Freneksy's secret police would swoop down on us here on Terra and make mincemeat out of him. Kick him out of office and replace him overnight with someone more militant. Someone who *likes* the job of prosecuting the war."

"But they can't do that," Eric said. "He's our elected leader, not theirs." He knew, however, that despite these legal considerations Jonas was right. Jonas was merely appraising their ally realistically, facing the facts.

"Our best bet," Jonas said, "is simply to lose. Slowly, inevitably, as we're doing." He lowered his voice to a rasping whisper. "I hate to talk defeatist talk—"

"Feel free."

Jonas said, "Eric, it's the only way out, even if we have to look forward to a century of occupation by the reegs as our punishment for picking the wrong ally in the wrong war at the wrong time. Our very virtuous first venture into interplanetary militarism, and *how* we picked it—how the Mole picked it." He grimaced.

"And we picked the Mole," Eric reminded him. So the responsibility, ultimately, came back to them.

Ahead, a slight, leaflike figure, dry and weightless, drifted all at once toward them, calling in a thin, shrill voice, "Jonas! And you, too, Sweetscent—time to get started for the trip to Wash-35." Virgil Ackerman's tone was faintly peevish, that of a mother bird at her task; in his advanced age Virgil had become almost hermaphroditic, a blend of man and woman into one sexless, juiceless, and yet vital entity.

Two

Opening the ancient, empty Camel cigarettes package, Virgil Ackerman said as he flattened its surfaces, "Hits, cracks, taps, or pops. Which do you take, Sweetscent?"

"Taps," Eric said.

The old man peered at the marking stamped on the inside glued bottom fold of the now two-dimensional package. "It's cracks. I get to cork you on the arm—thirty-two times." He ritualistically tapped Eric on the shoulder, smiling gleefully, his natural-style ivory teeth pale and full of animated luster. "Far be it from me to injure you, doctor; after all, I might need a new liver any moment now . . . I had a bad few hours last night after I went to bed and I think—but check me on this—it was due to toxemia once again. I felt logy."

In the seat beside Virgil Ackerman, Dr. Eric Sweetscent said, "How late were you up and what did you do?"

"Well, doctor, there was this girl." Virgil grinned mischievously at Harvey, Jonas, Ralf and Phyllis Ackerman, those members of the family who sat around him in his thin, tapered interplan ship as it sped from Terra toward Wash-35 on Mars. "Need I say more?"

His great-grandniece, Phyllis, said severely, "Oh Christ, you're too old. Your heart'll give out again right in the middle. And then what'll she—whoever she is—think? It's undignified to die during you know what." She eyed Virgil reprovingly.

Virgil screeched, "Then the dead man's control in my right fist, carried for such emergencies, would summon Dr. Sweetscent here, and he'd dash in and right there on the spot, without removing me, he'd take out that bad, collapsed old heart and stick in a brand new one, and I'd—" He giggled, then patted away the saliva from his lower lip and chin with a folded linen handkerchief from his breast coat pocket, "I'd continue." His paper-thin flesh glowed and beneath it his bones, the outline of his skull, fine and clearly distinguishable, quivered with delight and the joy of tantalizing them; they had no entree into this world of his, the private life which he, because of his privileged position, enjoyed even now during the days of privation which the war had brought on.

"*Mille tre,*'" Harvey said sourly, quoting Da Ponte's libretto. "But with you, you old craknit, it's—however you say a billion and three in Italian. I hope when I'm your age—"

"You won't ever be my age," Virgil chortled, his eyes dancing and flaming up with the vitality of enjoyment. "Forget it, Harv. Forget it and go back to your fiscal records, you walking, droning-on abacus. They won't find you dead in bed with a woman; they'll find you dead with a—" Virgil searched his mind. "With an, ahem, inkwell."

"Please," Phyllis said drily, turning to look out at the stars and the black sky of 'tween space.

Eric said to Virgil, "I'd like to ask you something. About a pack of Lucky Strike green. About three months ago—"

"Your wife loves me," Virgil said. "Yes, it was for me, doctor; a gift without strings. So ease your feverish mind; Kathy's not interested. Anyhow, it would cause trouble. Women, I can get; artiforg surgeons—well . . ." He reflected. "Yes. When you think about it I can get that, too."

"Just as I told Eric earlier today," Jonas said. He winked at Eric, who stoically did not show any response.

"But I like Eric," Virgil continued. "He's a calm type. Look at him right now. Sublimely reasonable, always the cerebral type, cool in every crisis; I've watched him work many times, Jonas; I ought to know. And willing to get up at any hour of the night . . . and that sort you don't see much."

"You pay him," Phyllis said shortly. She was, as always, taciturn and withdrawn; Virgil's attractive great-grandniece, who sat on the corporation's board of directors, had a piercing, raptorlike quality—much like the old man's, but without his sly sense of the peculiar. To Phyllis, everything was business or dross. Eric reflected that had she come onto Himmel there would be no more little carts wheeling about; in Phyllis' world there was no room for the harmless. She reminded him a little of Kathy. And, like Kathy, she was reasonably sexy; she wore her hair in one long braided pigtail dyed a fashionable ultramarine, set off by autonomic rotating earrings and (this he did not especially enjoy) a nose ring, sign of nubility with the higher bourgeois circles.

"What's the purpose of this conference?" Eric asked Virgil Ackerman. "Can we start discussing it now to save time?" He felt irritable.

"A pleasure trip," Virgil said. "Chance to get away from the gloomy biz we're in. We have a guest meeting us at Wash-35; he may already be there . . . he's got a Blank Check: I've opened my babyland to him, the first time I've let anybody but myself experience it freely."

"Who?" Harv demanded. "After all, technically Wash-35 is the property of the corporation, and we're on the board."

Jonas said acidly, "Virgil probably lost all his authentic Horrors of War flipcards to this person. So what else could he do but throw open the gates of the place to him?"

"I never flip with my Horrors of War cards or my FBI cards," Virgil said. "And by the way I have a duplicate of the Sinking of the Panay. Eton Hambro—you know, the fathead who's board chairman of Manfrex Enterprises—gave it to me on my birthday. I thought everyone knew I had a complete file but evidently not Hambro. No wonder Freneksy's boys are running his six factories for him these days."

"Tell us about Shirley Temple in *The Littlest Rebel*," Phyllis said in a bored tone, still looking out at the panorama of stars beyond the ship. "Tell us how she—"

"You've seen that." Virgil sounded testy.

"Yes, but I never get tired of it," Phyllis said. "No matter how hard I try I still can't find it anything but engrossing, right down to the last miserable inch of film." She turned to Harv. "Your lighter."

Rising from his seat, Eric walked to the lounge of the small ship, seated himself at the table, and picked up the drink list. His throat felt dry; the bickering that went on within the Ackerman clan always made him dully thirsty, as if he were in need of some reassuring fluid . . . perhaps, he thought, a substitute for the primordial milk: the *Urmilch* of life. I deserve my own babyland, too, he thought half in jest. But only half.

To everyone but Virgil Ackerman, the Washington, D.C., of 1935 was a waste of time, since only Virgil remembered the authentic city, the authentic time and place, the environment now so long passed away. In every detail, therefore, Wash-35 consisted of a painstakingly elaborate reconstruction of the specific limited universe of childhood which Virgil had known, constantly refined and improved in matters of authenticity by his antique procurer—Kathy Sweetscent—without really ever being in a genuine sense changed: it had coagulated, cleaved to the dead past . . . at least as far as the rest of the clan were concerned. But to Virgil it of course sprouted life. There, he blossomed. He restored his flagging biochemical energy and then returned to the present, to the shared, current world which he eminently understood and manipulated but of which he did not psychologically feel himself a native.

And his vast regressive babyland had caught on: become a fad. On lesser scales other top industrialists and money-boys— to speak in a brutal and frank way, war profiteers—had made life-size models of their childhood worlds, too; Virgil's now had ceased to be unique. None, of course, matched Virgil's in complexity and sheer authenticity; fakes of antique items, not the actual surviving articles, had been strewn about in vulgar approximations of what had been the authentic reality. But in all fairness, it had to be realized, Eric reflected, no one possessed the money and economic know-how to underwrite this admittedly uniquely expensive and beyond all others— imitations all—utterly impractical venture. This—in the midst of the dreadful war.

But still it was, after all, harmless, in its quaint sort of way. A bit, he reflected, like Bruce Himmel's peculiar activity with his many clanky little carts. It slaughtered no one. And this could hardly be said for the national effort . . . the jihad against the creatures from Proxima.

On thinking of this, an unpleasant recollection entered his mind.

On Terra at the UN capital city, Cheyenne, Wyoming, in addition to those in POW camps, there existed a herd of captured, defanged reegs, maintained on public exhibition by the Terran military establishment. Citizens could file past and gawk and ponder at length the meaning of these exoskeletoned beings with six extremities in all, capable of progressing linearly at a great rate on either two or four legs. The reegs had no audible vocal apparatus; they communicated beewise by elaborate, dancelike weavings of their sensory stalks. With Terrans and 'Starmen they employed a mechanical translation box, and through this the gawkers had an opportunity to question their humbled captives.

Questions, until recently, had run to a monotonous, baiting uniformity. But now a new interrogation had begun by subtle stages to put in its very ominous appearance—ominous at least from the standpoint of the Establishment. In view of this inquiry the exhibit had abruptly terminated, and for an indefinite time. *How can we come to a rapprochement?* The reegs, oddly, had an answer. It amounted to: live and let live. Expansion by Terrans into the Proxima System would cease; the reegs would not—and actually had not in the past—invest the Sol System.

But as to Lilistar: The reegs had no answer there because they had developed none for themselves; the 'Starmen had been their enemies for centuries and it was too late for anyone to give or take any advice on this subject. And anyhow 'Star "advisers" had already managed to take up residence on Terra for the performance of security functions . . . as if a four-armed, antlike organism six feet high could pass unnoticed on a New York street.

The presence of 'Star advisers, however, easily passed unnoticed; the 'Starmen were phycomycetous mentally, but morphologically they could not be distinguished from Terrans. There was a good reason for this. In Mousterian times a flotilla from Lilistar's Alpha Centaurus Empire had migrated to the Sol System, had colonized Earth and to some extent Mars. A fracas with deadly overtones had broken out between settlers of the two worlds and a long, degenerating war had followed, the upshot of which had been the decline of both subcultures to acute and dreary barbarism. Due to climatic faults the Mars colony had at last died out entirely; the Terran, however, had groped its way up through historical ages and at last back to civilization. Cut off from Alpha by the Lilistar-reeg conflict, the Terran colony had again become planet-wide, elaborated, bountiful, had advanced to the stage of launching first an orbiting satellite, and then an unmanned ship to Luna, and at last a manned ship . . . and was, as a chef-d'oeuvre, able once more to contact its system of origin. The surprise, of course, had been vast on both sides.

"Cat got your tongue?" Phyllis Ackerman said to Eric,

seating herself beside him in the cramped lounge. She smiled, an effort which transfigured her thin, delicately cut face; she looked, for a moment, appealingly pretty. "Order me a drink, too. So I can face the world of bolo bats and Jean Harlow and Baron von Richtofen and Joe Louis and—what the hell is it?" She searched her memory, eyes squeezed shut. "I've blocked it out of my mind. Oh yes. Tom Mix. And his Ralston Straight-shooters. With the Wrangler. That wretched Wrangler. And that cereal! And those eternal goddam box tops. You know what we're in for, don't you? Another session with Orphan Annie and her li'l decoder badge . . . we'll have to listen to ads for Ovaltine and then those numbers read out for us to take down and decode—to find out what Annie does on Monday. God." She bent to reach for her drink, and he could not resist peering with near-professional interest as the top of her dress gave way to show the natural line of her small, articulated pale breasts.

Put by this spectacle in a reasonably good mood, Eric said playfully but cautiously, "One day we'll jot down the numbers the fake announcer gives over the fake radio, decode them with the Orphan Annie decoder badge, and—" The message will say, he thought glumly, *Make a separate peace with the reegs. At once.*

"I know," Phyllis said, and thereupon finished for him. " 'It's hopeless, Earthmen. Give up now. This is the Monarch of the reegs speaking; looky heah, y'all: I've infiltrated radio station WMAL in Washington, D.C., and I'm going to *des*troy you.' " She somberly drank from her tall stemmed glass. "And in *addition* the Ovaltine you've been drinking—"

"I wasn't going to say precisely that." But she had come awfully darn close. Nettled, Eric said, "Like the rest of your family you've got a gene that requires you to interrupt before a non-blooder—"

"A *what*?"

"That is what we call you," he said grimly. "You Ackermen."

"Go ahead, then, doctor." Her gray eyes lit with amusement. "Say your tiny say."

Eric said, "Never mind. "Who's the guest?"

The great pale eyes of the woman had never seemed so

large, so composed; they dominated and commanded with their utter inner universe of certitude. Of tranquillity created by absolute, unchanging knowledge of all that deserved to be known. "Suppose we wait and see." And then, not yet affecting the changelessness of her eyes, her lips began to dance with a wicked, teasing playfulness; a moment later a new and different spark ignited within her eyes and thereupon the expression of her entire face underwent a total change. "The door," she said wickedly, her eyes gleaming and intense, her mouth twitching in a mirth-ridden giggle almost that of an adolescent girl, "flies open and there stands a silent delegate from Proxima. Ah, what a sight. A bloated greasy enemy reeg. Secretly, and incredibly because of Freneksy's snooping secret police, a reeg here officially to negotiate for a—" She broke off and then at last in a low monotone finished, "—a separate peace between us and them." With a dark and moody expression, her eyes no longer lit by any spark whatsoever, she listlessly finished her drink. "Yes, that'll be the day. How well I can picture it. Old Virgil sits in, beaming and cackling as usual. And sees his war contracts, every fnugging last one of them, slither down the drain. Back to fake mink. Back to the bat crap days . . . when the whole factory stank to high heaven." She laughed shortly, a brisk bark of derision. "Any minute now, doctor. Oh *sure*."

"Freneksy's cops," Eric said, sharing her mood, "as you pointed out yourself, would swoop down on Wash-35 so dalb fast—"

"I know. It's a fantasy, a wish-fulfillment dream. Born out of hopeless longing. So it hardly matters whether Virgil would decide to mastermind—and try to carry off—such an encounter or not, does it? Because it couldn't be done successfully in a million light-years. It could be tried. But not done."

"Too bad," Eric said, half to himself, deep in thought.

"Traitor! You want to be popped into the slave-labor pool?"

Eric, after pondering, said cautiously, "I want—"

"You don't know what you want, Sweetscent; every man involved in an unhappy marriage loses the metabiological capacity to know what he does want—it's been taken away from him. You're a smelly little shell, trying to do the correct thing but never quite making it because your miserable little long-suffering heart isn't in it. Look at you now! You've managed to squirm away from me."

"Have not."

"—So we're no longer touching physically. Especially thigh-wise. Oh, perish thighwise from the universe. But it is hard, is it not, to do it, to squirm away in such close quarters . . . here in the lounge. And yet you've managed to do it, haven't you?"

To change the subject Eric said, "I heard on TV last night that the quatreologist with the funny beard, that Professor Wald, is back from—"

"No. He's not Virgil's guest."

"Marm Hastings, then?"

"That Taoist spellbinding nut and crank and fool? You man-ufacturing a joke, Sweetscent? Is that it? You suppose Virgil would tolerate a marginal fake, that—" She made an obscene upward-jerking gesture with her thumb, at the same time grin-ning in a show of her white, clean, and very impressive clear teeth. "Maybe," she said, "it's Ian Norse."

"Who's he?" He had heard the name; it had a vaguely famil-iar sound to it, and he knew that in asking her he was making a tactical error; still he did it: this, if anything, was his weakness in regard to women. He led where they followed—sometimes. But more than once, especially at critical times in his life, in the major junctions, he followed guilelessly where they led.

Phyllis sighed. "Ian's firm makes all those shiny sterile new very expensive artificial organs you cleverly graft into rich dying people; you mean, doctor, you're not clear as to whom you're indebted?"

"I know," Eric said, irritably, feeling chagrin. "With every-thing else on my mind I forgot momentarily; that's all."

"Maybe it's a composer. As in the days of Kennedy; maybe it's Pablo Casals. God, he *would* be old. Maybe it's Beethoven. Hmm." She pretended to ponder. "By God, I do think he said something about that. Ludwig van *somebody*; is there a Ludwig van Somebody-else other than—"

"Christ," Eric said angrily, weary of being teased. "Stop it."

"Don't pull rank; you're not so great. Keeping one creepy

old man alive century after century." She giggled her low, sweet, and very intimate warm giggle of delighted mirth.

Eric said, with as much dignity as he could manage, "I also maintain TF&D's entire work force of eighty thousand key individuals. And as a matter of fact, I can't do that from Mars, so I resent all this. I resent it very much." You included, he thought bitterly to himself.

"What a ratio," Phyllis said. "One artiforg surgeon to eighty thousand patients—eighty thousand and one. But you have your team of robants to help you . . . perhaps they can make do while you're absent."

"A robant is an it that stinks," he said, paraphrasing T. S. Eliot.

"And an artiforg surgeon," Phyllis said, "is an it that grovels."

He glowered at her; she sipped her drink and showed no contrition. He could not get to her; she simply had too much psychic strength for him.

The omphalos of Wash-35, a five-story brick apartment building where Virgil had lived as a boy, contained a truly modern apartment of their year 2055 with every detail of convenience which Virgil could obtain during these war years. Several blocks away lay Connecticut Avenue, and, along it, stores which Virgil remembered. Here was Gammage's, a shop at which Virgil had bought Tip Top comics and penny candy. Next to it Eric made out the familiar shape of People's Drugstore; the old man during his childhood had bought a cigarette lighter here once and chemicals for his Gilbert Number Five glass-blowing and chemistry set.

"What's the Uptown Theater showing this week?" Harv Ackerman murmured as their ship coasted along Connecticut Avenue so that Virgil could review these treasured sights. He peered.

It was Jean Harlow in *Hell's Angels*, which all of them had seen at least twice. Harv groaned.

"But don't forget that lovely scene," Phyllis reminded him, "where Harlow says, 'I think I'll go slip into something more comfortable,' and then when she returns—"

"I know, I know," Harv said irritably. "Okay, that I like."

The ship taxied from Connecticut Avenue onto McComb Street and soon was parking before 3039 with its black wrought-iron fence and tiny lawn. When the hatch slid back, however, Eric smelled—not the city air of a long-gone Terran capital—but the bitterly thin and cold atmosphere of Mars; he could hardly get his lungs full of it and he stood gasping, feeling disoriented and sick.

"I'll have to goose them about the air machinery," Virgil complained as he descended the ramp to the sidewalk, assisted by Jonas and Harv. It did not seem to bother him, however; he spryly hiked toward the doorway of the apartment building.

Robants in the shape of small boys hopped to their feet and one of them yelled authentically, "Hey Virg! Where you been?"

"Had to do an errand for my mother," Virgil cackled, his face shining with delight. "How are ya, Earl? Hey, I got some good Chinese stamps my dad gave me; he got them at his office. There's duplicates; I'll trade you." He fished in his pocket, halting on the porch of the building.

"Hey, you know what I have?" a second robant child shrilled. "Some dry ice; I let Bob Rougy use my Flexie for it; you can hold it if you want."

"I'll trade you a big-little book for it," Virgil said as he produced his key and unlocked the front door of the building. "How about *Buck Rogers and the Doom Comet*? That's real keen."

As the rest of the party descended from the ship, Phyllis said to Eric, "Offer the children a mint-condition 1952 Marilyn Monroe nude calendar and see what they'll give you for it. At least half a popsicle."

As the apartment house door swung aside, a TF&D guard belatedly appeared. "Oh, Mr. Ackerman; I didn't realize you'd arrived." The guard ushered them into the dark, carpeted hall.

"Is he here yet?" Virgil asked, with sudden apparent tension.

"Yes sir. In the apt resting. He asked not to be disturbed for several hours." The guard, too, seemed nervous.

Halting, Virgil said, "How large is his party?"

"Just himself, an aide, and two Secret Service men."

"Who's for a glass of ice-cold Kool-Aid?" Virgil said reflexively over his shoulder as he led the way.

"Me, me," Phyllis said, mimicking Virgil's enthusiastic tone. "I want imitation fruit raspberry lime; what about you, Eric? How about gin bourbon lime or cherry Scotch vodka? Or didn't they sell those flavors back in 1935?"

To Eric, Harv said, "I'd like a place to lie down and rest, myself. This Martian air makes me weak as a kitten." His face had become mottled and ill-looking. "Why doesn't he build a dome? Keep *real* air in here?"

"Maybe," Eric pointed out, "there's a purpose in this. Prevents him from retiring here for good; makes him leave after a short while."

Coming up to them, Jonas said, "Personally I enjoy coming to this anachronistic place, Harv. It's a fnugging museum." To Eric he said, "In all fairness, your wife does a superb job of providing artifacts for this period. Listen to that—what's it called?—that radio playing in that apt." Dutifully they listened. It was "Betty and Bob," the ancient soap opera, emanating from the long-departed past. And even Eric found himself impressed; the voices seemed alive and totally real. They were here *now*, not mere echoes of themselves. How Kathy had achieved this he didn't know.

Steve, the huge and handsome, masculine Negro janitor of the building—or rather his robant simulacrum—appeared then, smoking his pipe and nodding cordially to them all. "Morning, doctor. Little nip of cold we having these day. Kids be getting they sled out soonly. My own boy, Georgie, he saving for a sled, he say little while ago to me."

"I'll chip in a 1934 dollar," Ralf Ackerman said, reaching for his wallet. In a *sotto voce* aside to Eric he said, "Or does old papa Virgil have it that the colored kid isn't entitled to a sled?"

"That no nevermind, Mr. Ackerman," Steve assured him. "Georgie, he earn he sled; he not want tips but real and troo pay." The dignified dark robant moved off then and was gone.

"Damn convincing," Harv said presently.

"Really is," Jonas agreed. He shivered. "God, to think that the actual man's been dead a century. It's distinctly hard to keep in mind that we're on Mars, not even on Earth in our own time—I don't like it. I like things to appear what they really are."

A thought came to Eric. "Do you object to a stereo tape of a symphony played back in the evening when you're at home in your apt?"

"No," Jonas said. "But that's totally different."

"It's not," Eric disagreed. "The orchestra isn't there, the original sound has departed, the hall in which it was recorded is now silent; all you possess is twelve hundred feet of iron oxide tape that's been magnetized in a specific pattern . . . it's an illusion just like this. Only this is complete." Q.E.D., he thought, and walked on then, toward the stairs. We live with illusion daily, he reflected. When the first bard rattled off the first epic of a sometime battle, illusion entered our lives; the *Iliad* is as much a "fake" as those robant children trading postage stamps on the porch of the building. Humans have always striven to retain the past, to keep it convincing; there's nothing wicked in that. Without it we have no continuity; we have only the moment. And, deprived of the past, the moment —the present—has little meaning, if any.

Maybe, he pondered as he ascended the stairs, that's my problem with Kathy. I can't remember our combined past: can't recall the days when we voluntarily lived with each other . . . Now it's become an involuntary arrangement, derived God knows how from the past.

And neither of us understand it. Neither of us can puzzle out its meaning or its motivating mechanism. With a better memory we could turn it back into something we could fathom.

He thought, Maybe this is the first sign of old age making its dread appearance. And for me at thirty-four!

Phyllis, halting on the stair, waiting for him, said, "Have an affair with me, doctor."

Inwardly he quailed, felt hot, felt terror, felt excitement, felt hope, felt hopelessness, felt guilt, felt eagerness.

He said, "You have the most perfect teeth known to man."

"Answer."

"I—" He tried to think of an answer. Could words respond to this? But this had come in the form of words, had it not? "And be roasted into a cinder by Kathy—who sees everything that goes on?" He felt the woman staring at him, staring and staring with her huge, star-fixed eyes. "Hmm," he said, not too cleverly, and felt miserable and small and exactly precisely right to the last jot and tittle what he ought not to be.

Phyllis said, "But you need it."

"Umm," he said, wilting under this unwanted, undeserved female psychiatric examination of his evil, inner soul; she had it—his soul—and she was turning it over and over on her tongue. Goddam her! She had figured it out; she spoke the truth; he hated her; he longed to go to bed with her. And of course she knew—saw on his face—all this, saw it with her accursed huge eyes, eyes which no mortal woman ought to possess.

"You're going to perish without it," Phyllis said. "Without true, spontaneous, relaxed, physical sheer—"

"One chance," he said hoarsely. "In a billion. Of getting away with it." He managed, then, actually to laugh. "In fact our standing here right now on these damn stairs is folly. But what the —— do you care?" He started on, then, actually passed her, continued on up to the second floor. What do you have to lose? he thought. It's me; I'd be the one. You can handle Kathy just as easily as you can yank me around at the end of that line you keep paying out and reeling back.

The door to Virgil's private, modern apt stood open; Virgil had gone inside. The balance of the party straggled after him, the blood clan first, of course, then the mere titled officers of the firm.

Eric entered—and saw Virgil's guest.

The guest; the man they had come here to see. Reclining, his face empty and slack, lips bulging dark purple and irregular, eyes fixed absently on nothing, was Gino Molinari. Supreme elected leader of Terra's unified planetary culture, and the supreme commander of its armed forces in the war against the reegs.

His fly was unbuttoned.

Three

AT his lunch break Bruce Himmel, technician in charge of the final stage of quality control at Tijuana Fur & Dye Corporation's central installation, left his post and shuffled down the streets of Tijuana toward the café at which he traditionally ate, due to its being cheap plus making the fewest possible social demands on him. The Xanthus, a small yellow wooden building squeezed between two adobe dry-goods shops, attracted a variable trade of workmen and peculiar male types, mostly in their late twenties, who indicated no particular method of earning a living. But they left Himmel alone and that was all he asked. In fact this essentially was all he asked from life itself. And, oddly, life was willing to consummate a deal of this sort with him.

As he sat in the rear, spooning up the amorphous chili and tearing out chunks of the sticky, pale, thick bread which accompanied it, Himinel saw a shape bearing down on him, a tangle-haired Anglo-Saxon wearing a leather jacket, jeans, boots, and gloves, an altogether obsoletely attired individual seemingly from some other era entirely. This was Christian Plout, who drove an ancient turbine-powered taxi in Tijuana; he had hidden out in Lower California for a decade now, being in disagreement with the Los Angeles authorities over an issue involving the sale of capstene, a drug derived from the fly agaric mushroom. Himmel knew him slightly because Plout, like himself, gleeked Taoism.

"*Salve, amicus*," Plout intoned, sliding into the booth to face Himmel.

"Greetings," Himmel mumbled, his mouth full of burdeningly hot chili. "What's new?" Plout always had in his possession the latest. During the course of his day, cruising about Tijuana in his cab, he happened across everyone. If it existed, Chris Plout was on hand to witness it and, if possible, extract some gain. Plout, basically, was a bundle of sidelines.

"Listen," Plout said, leaning toward him, his sand-colored dry face wrinkled in concentration. "See this?" From his clenched fist he rolled across the table a capsule; instantly his palm covered the capsule and it had disappeared once more as suddenly as it had manifested itself.

"I see it," Himmel said, continuing to eat.

Twitching, Plout whispered, "Hey, hee-hoo. This is JJ-180."

"What's that?" Himmel felt sullenly suspicious; he wished Plout would shamble back out of the Xanthus in search of other prospects.

"JJ-180," Plout said in an almost inaudible voice, sitting hunched forward so that his face nearly touched Himmel's, "is the German name for the drug that's about to be marketed in South America as Frohedadrine. A German chemical firm invented it; the pharmaceutical house in Argentina is their cover. They can't get it into the USA; in fact it isn't even easy to get it here in Mexico, if you can believe that." He grinned, showing his irregular, stained teeth. Even his tongue, Himmel noted once again with disgust, had a peculiar tinge, as if corrupted by some unnatural substance. He drew away in aversion.

"I thought everything was available here in Tijuana," Himmel said.

"So did I. That's what interested me in this JJ-180. So I picked up some."

"Have you taken it yet?"

"Tonight," Plout said. "At my place. I got five caps, one of them for you. If you're interested."

"What's it do?" Somehow that seemed pertinent.

Plout, undulating with an internal rhythm, said, "Hallucinogenic. But more than that. Whee, whoo, fic-fic." His eyes glazed over and he retreated into himself, grinning with beatitude. Himmel waited; at last Plout returned. "Varies from person to person. Somehow involved with your sense of what Kant called the 'categories of perception.' Get it?"

"That would be your sense of time and space," Himmel said, having read the *Critique of Pure Reason*, it being his style of prose as well as thought. In his small conapt he kept a paperback copy of it, well marked.

"Right! It alters your perception of time in particular, so it ought to be called a tempogogic drug—correct?" Plout seemed transported by his insight. "The first tempogogic drug . . . or rather maltempogogic, to be precise. Unless you *believe* what you experience."

Himmel said, "I have to get back to TF&D." He started to rise.

Pressing him back down, Plout said, "Fifty bucks. US."

"W-what?"

"For a cap. Creaker, it's *rare*. First I've seen." Once more Plout allowed the capsule to roll briefly across the table. "I hate to give it up but it'll be an experience; we'll find the Tao, the five of us. Isn't it worth fifty US dollars to find the Tao during this nurty war? You may never see JJ-180 again; the Mex coonks are getting ready to crack down on shipments from Argentina or wherever it comes from. And they're good."

"It's really that different from—"

"Oh yes! Listen, Himmel. You know what I almost ran over with my cab just now? One of your little carts. I could have squashed it but I didn't. I see them all the time; I could squash hundreds of them . . . I go by TF&D every few hours. I'll tell you something else: the Tijuana authorities are asking me if I know where those goddam little carts are coming from. I told 'em I don't know . . . but so help me, if we don't all merge with the Tao tonight I might—"

"Okay," Himmel said with a groan. "I'll buy a capsule from you." He dug for his wallet, considering this a shakedown, expecting nothing, really, for his money. Tonight would be a hollow fraud.

He couldn't have been further wrong.

Gino Molinari, supreme leader of Terra in its war against the reegs, wore khaki, as usual, with his sole military decoration on his breast, his Golden Cross First Class, awarded by the UN General Assembly fifteen years before. Molinari, Dr. Eric Sweethscent noted, badly needed a shave; the lower portion of his face was stubbled, stained by a grime and sootlike blackness that had risen massively to the surface from deep within. His shoelaces, after the manner of his fly, were undone.

The appearance of the man, Eric thought, is appalling.

Molinari did not raise his head and his expression remained dull and unfocused as Virgil's party filed one by one into the room, saw him, and gulped in dumfoundment. He was very obviously a sick and worn-out man; the general public impression was, it would seem, quite accurate.

To Eric's surprise he saw that in real life the Mole looked exactly as he had of late on TV, no greater, no sturdier, no more in command. It seemed impossible but it was so, and yet he *was* in command; in every legal sense he had retained his positions of power, yielding to no one—at any rate, no one on Terra. Nor, Eric realized suddenly, did Molinari intend to step down, despite his obviously deteriorated psychophysical condition. Somehow that was clear, made so by the man's utterly slack stance, his willingness to appear this natural way to a collection of rather potent personages. The Mole remained as he was, with no poise, no posture of the militant heroic. Either he was too far gone to care, or—Eric thought, Or there is too much of genuine importance at stake for him to waste his waning strength at merely impressing people, and especially those of his own planet. The Mole had passed beyond that.

For better or worse.

To Eric, Virgil Ackerman said in a low voice, "You're a doctor. You are going to have to ask him if he needs medical attention." He, too, seemed concerned.

Eric looked toward Virgil and thought, I was brought here for this. It all has been arranged for this, for me to meet Molinari. Everything else, all the other people—a cover. To fool the 'Starmen. I see that now; I see what this is and what they want me to do. I see, he realized, whom I must heal; this is the man whom my skills and talents must, from this point on, exist for. The *must*; it is put that way. The must of the situation: this is it.

Bending, he said haltingly, "Mr. Secretary General—" His voice shook. But it was not awe that stopped him—the reclining man certainly did not promote *that* emotion—but ignorance; he simply did not know what to say to a man holding such an office. "I'm a GP," he said finally, and rather emptily, he realized. "As well as an org-trans surgeon." He paused; there came no response, visible or audible. "While you're here at Wash—"

All at once Molinari raised his head; his eyes cleared. He focused on Eric Sweetscent, then abruptly, startlingly, boomed in his familiar low-toned voice, "Hell on that, doctor. I'm okay." He smiled; it was a brief but innately human smile, one of understanding at Eric's clumsy, labored efforts. "Enjoy yourself! Live it up 1935 style! Was that during prohibition? No, I guess that was earlier. Have a Pepsi-Cola."

"I was about to try a raspberry Kool-Aid," Eric said, regaining some of his aplomb; his heart rate returned now to normal.

Molinari said jovially, "Quite a construct old Virgil has, here. I took the opportunity to glim it over. I ought to nationalize the fniggin' thing; too much private capital invested here, should be in the planet's war effort." His half-joking tone was, underneath, starkly serious; obviously this elaborate artifact distressed him. Molinari, as all citizens of Terra knew, lived an ascetic life, yet oddly intersticed with infrequent interludes of priapsistic, little-revealed sybaritic indulgence. Of late, however, the binges were said to have tapered off.

"This individual is Dr. Eric Sweetscent," Virgil said. "The goddam finest nugging org-trans surgeon on Terra, as you well know from the GHQ personnel dossiers; he's put twenty-five —or is it -six?—separate artiforgs in me during the last decade, but I've paid for it; he rakes in a fat haul every month. Not quite so fat a haul, though, as his ever-loving wife." He grinned at Eric, his fleshless, elongated face genial in a fatherly way.

After a pause Eric said to Molinari, "What I'm waiting for is the day when I trans a new brain for Virgil." The irritability in his own voice surprised him; probably it had been the mention of Kathy that had set it off. "I've got several on stand-by. One is a real goozler."

"'Goozler,'" Molinari murmured. "I've missed out on the argot of recent months . . . just plain too busy. Too many official documents to prepare; too much establishment talk. It's a goozlery war, isn't it, doctor?" His great, dark, pain-impregnated eyes fixed on Eric, and Eric saw something he had never come across before; he saw an intensity that was not normal or human. And it was a physiological phenomenon, a swiftness of reflex, due surely to a unique and superior laying-down of the neural pathways during childhood. The Mole's gaze exceeded in its authority and astuteness, its power alone, anything possessed by ordinary persons, and in it Eric saw the difference between them all and the Mole. The primary conduit linking the mind with external reality, the sense of sight, was, in the Mole, so far more developed than one anticipated that by it the man caught and held whatever happened to venture across his path. And, beyond all else, this enormity of visual prowess possessed the aspect of *wariness*. Of recognition of the imminence of *harm*.

By this faculty the Mole remained alive.

Eric realized something then, something that had never occurred to him in all the weary, dreadful years of the war.

The Mole would have been their leader at any time, at any stage in human society. And—anywhere.

"Every war," Eric said with utmost caution and tact, "is a hard war for those involved in it, Secretary." He paused, reflected, and then added, "We all understood this, sir, when we got into it. It's the risk a people, a planet, takes when it voluntarily enters a severe and ancient conflict that's been going on a long time between two other peoples."

There was silence; Molinari scrutinized him wordlessly.

"And the 'Starmen," Eric said, "are of our stock. We are related to them genetically, are we not?"

Against that there was only a silence, a wordless void which no one cared to fill. At last, reflectively, Molinari farted.

"Tell Eric about your stomach pains," Virgil said to Molinari.

"My pains," Molinari said, and grimaced.

"The whole point in bringing you together—" Virgil began.

"Yes," Molinari growled brusquely, nodding his massive head. "I know. And you all know. It was for *exactly* this."

"I'm as certain as I am of taxes and labor unions that Dr. Sweetscent can help you, Secretary," Virgil continued. "The rest of us will go across the hall to the suite of rooms there, so you two can talk in private." With unusual circumspection he moved away, and, one by one, the blood clan and firm officers filed out of the room, leaving Eric Sweetscent alone with the Secretary General.

After a pause Eric said, "All right, sir; tell me about your abdominal complaint, Secretary." In any case a sick man was a sick man; he seated himself in the form-binding armchair across from the UN Secretary General and, in this reflexively assumed professional posture, waited.

Four

THAT evening as Bruce Himmel tromped up the rickety wooden stairs to Chris Plout's conapt in the dismal Mexican section of Tijuana, a female voice said from the darkness behind him, "Hello, Brucie. It looks as if this is an all-TF&D night; Simon Ild is here, too."

On the porch the woman caught up with him. It was sexy, sharp-tongued Katherine Sweetscent; he had run into her at Plout's gatherings a number of times before and so it hardly surprised him to see her now. Mrs. Sweetscent wore a somewhat modified costume from that which she employed on the job; this also failed to surprise him. For tonight's mysterious undertaking Kathy had arrived naked from the waist up, except, of course, for her nipples. They had been—not gilded in the strict sense—but rather treated with a coating of living matter, sentient, a Martian life form, so that each possessed a consciousness. Hence each nipple responded in an alert fashion to everything going on.

The effect on Himmel was immense.

Behind Kathy Sweetscent ascended Simon Ild; in the dim light he had a vacant expression on his sappy, pimply, uneducated face. This was a person whom Himmel could do without; Simon—unfortunately—reminded him of nothing so much as a bad simulacrum of himself. And there was nothing for him quite so unbearable.

The fourth person gathered here in the unheated, low-ceilinged room of Chris Plout's littered, stale-food-smelling conapt was an individual whom Himmel at once recognized—recognized and stared at, because this was a man known to him through pics on the back of book jackets. Pale, with glasses, his long hair carefully combed, wearing expensive, tasteful Io-fabric clothing, seemingly a trifle ill-at-ease, stood the Taoist authority from San Francisco, Marm Hastings, a slight man but extremely handsome, in his mid-forties, and, as Himmel knew, quite well-to-do from his many books on the subject of oriental mysticism. Why was Hastings here? Obviously to sample JJ-180; Hastings had a reputation for essaying

492

an experience with every hallucinogenic drug that came into being, legal or otherwise. To Hastings this was allied with religion.

But as far as Himmel knew, Marm Hastings had never shown up here in Tijuana at Chris Plout's conapt. What did this indicate about JJ-180? He pondered as he stood off in a corner, surveying the goings-on. Hastings was occupied in examining Plout's library on the subject of drugs and religion; he seemed uninterested in the others present, even contemptuous of their existence. Simon Ild, as usual, curled up on the floor, on a pillow, and lit a twisted brown marijuana cigarette; he puffed vacantly, waiting for Chris to appear. And Kathy Sweetscent—she crouched down, stroking reflexively at her hocks, as if grooming herself flywise, putting her slender, muscular body into a state of alertness. Teasing it, he decided, by deliberate, almost yogalike efforts.

Such physicalness disturbed him; he glanced away. It was not in keeping with the spiritual emphasis of the evening. But no one could tell Mrs. Sweetscent anything; she was nearly autistic.

Now Chris Plout, wearing a red bathrobe, his feet bare, entered from the kitchen; through dark glasses he peered to see if it was time to begin. "Marm," he said. "Kathy, Bruce, Simon, and I, Christian; the five of us. An adventure into the unexplored by means of the new substance which has just arrived from Tampico aboard a banana boat . . . I hold it here." He extended his open palm; within lay the five capsules. "One for each of us—Kathy, Bruce, Simon, Marm, and me, Christian; our first journey of the mind together. Will we all return? And will we be translated, as Bottom says?"

Himmel thought, As Peter Quince says to Bottom, actually. Aloud, he said, " 'Bottom, thou art translated.' "

"Pardon?" Chris Plout said, frowning.

"I'm quoting," Himmel explained.

"Come on, Chris," Kathy Sweetscent said crossly. "Give us the jink and let's get started." She snatched—successfully—one of the capsules from Chris's palm. "Here I go," she said. "And without water."

Mildly, Marm Hastings said with his quasi-English accent, "Is it the same, I wonder, taken without water?" Without movement of his eye muscles he clearly succeeded in making a survey of the woman; there was that sudden stricture of his body which gave him away. Himmel felt outraged; wasn't this whole affair designed to raise them all above the flesh?

"It's the same," Kathy informed him. "Everything's the same, when you break through to absolute reality; it's all one vast blur." She then swallowed, coughed. The capsule was gone.

Reaching, Himmel took his. The others followed.

"If the Mole's police caught us," Simon said, to no one in particular, "we'd all be in the Army, serving out at the front."

"Or working in vol-labe camps at Lilistar," Himmel added. They were all tense, waiting for the drug to take effect; it always ran this way, these short seconds before the jink got to them. "For good old Freneksy, as it's translated into English. Bottom, thou are translated as Freneksy." He giggled shakily. Katherine Sweetscent glared at him.

"Miss," Marm Hastings said to her in an unperturbed voice, "I wonder if I haven't met you before; you do seem familiar. Do you spend much time in the Bay area? I have a studio and architect designed home in the hills of West Marin, near the ocean . . . we hold seminars there often; people come and go freely. But I would remember you. Oh yes."

Katherine Sweetscent said, "My damn husband—he wouldn't ever let me. I'm self-supporting—I'm more than economically independent—and yet I have to put up with the rasping little noises and squeaks he makes whenever I try to do something original on my own." She added, "I'm an antique buyer, but old things become boring; I'd love to—"

Marm Hastings interrupted, speaking to Chris Plout, "Where does this JJ-180 originate, Plout? You said Germany, I think. But you see, I have a number of contacts in pharmaceutical research institutes, both public and private, in Germany, and none of them has so much as mentioned anything called JJ-180." He smiled, but it was a sharply formed astute smile, demanding an answer.

Chris shrugged. "That's the poog as I get it, Hastings. Take it or leave it." He was not bothered; he knew, as they all did, that under these circumstances no brief of warranty was incumbent on him.

"Then it's not actually German," Hastings said, with a faint nod. "I see. Could this JJ-180, or Frohedadrine as it's also called . . . *could it possibly originate entirely off Terra?*"

After a pause Chris said, "I dunno, Hastings. I dunno."

To all of them Hastings said in his educated, severe voice, "There have been cases of illegal non-terrestrial drugs before. None of them of any importance. Derived from Martian flora, mostly, and occasionally from Ganymedean lichens. I suppose you've heard; you all *seem* informed on this topic, as you should be. Or at least—" His smile grew, but his eyes, behind his rimless glasses, were codlike. "At the very least you seem satisfied as to the pedigree of this JJ-180 for which you've paid this man fifty US dollars."

"I'm satisfied," Simon Ild said in his stupid way. "Anyhow it's too late; we paid Chris and we've all taken the caps."

"True," Hastings agreed reasonably. He seated himself in one of Chris's tottering easy chairs. "Does anyone feel any change yet? Please speak up as soon as you do." He glanced at Katherine Sweetscent. "Your nipples seem to be watching me, or is that just my imagination? In any case it makes me decidedly uncomfortable."

"As a matter of fact," Chris Plout said in a strained voice, "I feel something, Hastings." He licked his lips, trying to wet them. "Excuse me. I—to be frank, I'm here alone. None of you are with me."

Marm Hastings studied him.

"Yes," Chris went on. "I'm all alone in my conapt. None of you even exist. But the books and chairs, everything else exists. Then who'm I talking to? Have you answered?" He peered about, and it was obvious that he could not see any of them; his gaze passed by them all.

"My nipples are not watching you or anybody else," Kathy Sweetscent said to Hastings.

"I can't hear you," Chris said in panic. "Answer!"

"We're here," Simon Ild said, and sniggered.

"Please," Chris said, and now his voice was pleading. "Say something; it's just shadows. It's—lifeless. Nothing but dead things. And it's only starting—I'm scared of how it's going on; it's still happening."

Marm Hastings laid his hand on Chris Plout's shoulder.

The hand passed through Plout.

"Well, we've gotten our fifty dollars' worth," Kathy Sweet-scent said in a low voice, void of amusement. She walked toward Chris, closer and closer.

"Don't try it," Hastings said to her in a gentle tone.

"I will," she said. And walked through Chris Plout. But she did not reappear on the other side. She had vanished; only Plout remained, still bleating for someone to answer him, still flailing the air in search of companions he could no longer perceive.

Isolation, Bruce Himmel thought to himself. Each of us cut off from all the others. Dreadful. But—it'll wear off. *Won't it?*

As yet he did not know. And for him it had not even started.

"These pains," UN Secretary General Gino Molinari rasped, lying back on the large, red, hand-wrought couch in the living room of Virgil Ackerman's Wash-35 apartment, "generally become most difficult for me at night." He had shut his eyes; his great fleshy face sagged forlornly, the grimy jowls wobbling as he spoke. "I've been examined; Dr. Teagarden is my chief GP. They've made infinite tests, with particular attention directed toward malignancy."

Eric thought, The man's speaking by rote; it's not his natural speech pattern. This has become that ingrained in his mind, this preoccupation; he's gone through this ritual a thousand times, with as many physicians. And—he still suffers.

"There's no malignancy," Molinari added. "That seems to have been authoritatively verified." His words constituted a satire of pompous medical diction, Eric realized suddenly. The Mole had immense hostility toward doctors, since they had failed to help him. "Generally the diagnosis is acute gastritis. Or spasms of the pyloric valve. Or even an hysterical re-enactment of my wife's labor pains, which she experienced three years ago." He finished, half to himself, "Shortly before her death."

"What about your diet?" Eric asked.

The Mole opened his eyes wearily. "My diet. I don't eat, doctor. Nothing at all. The air sustains me; didn't you read that in the homeopapes? I don't need food, like you simple schulps do. I'm different." His tone was urgently, acutely embittered.

"And it interferes with your duties?" Eric asked.

The Mole scrutinized him. "You think it's psychosomatic, that outmoded pseudo science that tried to make people morally responsible for their ailments?" He spat in anger; his face writhed and now the flesh was no longer hanging and loose—it was stretched taut, as if ballooned out from within. "So I can escape my responsibilities? Listen, doctor; I still have my responsibilities—*and* the pain. Can that be called secondary neurotic psychological gain?"

"No," Eric admitted. "But anyhow I'm not qualified to deal with psychosomatic medicine; you'd have to go to—"

"I've seen them," the Mole said. All at once he dragged himself to his feet, stood swaying, facing Eric. "Get Virgil back here; there's no point in your wasting your time interrogating me. And anyhow I don't choose to be interrogated. I don't care for it." He strode unsteadily toward the door, hitching up his sagging khaki trousers as he went.

Eric said, "Secretary, you could have your stomach removed, you realize. At any time. And an artiforg planted in replacement. The operation is simple and almost always successful. Without examining your case records I shouldn't say this, but you may *have* to have your stomach replaced one of these days. Risk or no risk." He was certain that Molinari would survive; the man's fear was palpably phobic.

"No," Molinari said quietly. "I don't have to; it's my choice. I can die instead."

Eric stared at him.

"Sure," Molinari said. "Even though I'm the UN Secretary General. Hasn't it occurred to you that I want to die, that these pains, this developing physical—or psychosomatic—illness is a way out for me? I don't want to go on. Maybe. Who knows? What difference does it make, to anybody? But the hell with it." He tore open the hall door. "'Virgil," he boomed in a surprisingly virile voice. "For chrissake, let's pour and get this party started." Over his shoulder he said to Eric, "Did you know this was a party? I bet the old man told you it was a serious conference for solving Terra's military, political, and economic problems. In one half hour." He grinned, showing his big, white teeth.

"Frankly," Eric said, "I'm glad to hear it's a party." The session with Molinari had been as difficult for him as it had been for the Secretary. And yet—he had an intuition that Virgil Ackerman would not let it end there. Virgil wanted something done for the Mole; he desired to see the man's distress eased, and for a good, practical reason.

The collapse of Gino Molinari would signify an end to Virgil's possession of TF&D. Management of Terra's economic syndromes no doubt held priority for Freneksy's officials; their agenda had probably been drawn up in detail.

Virgil Ackerman was a shrewd businessman.

"How much," Molinari asked suddenly, "does the old fruit pay you?"

"V-very well," Eric said, taken by surprise.

Molinari, eying him, said, "He's talked to me about you. Before this get-together. Sold me on you, how good you are. Because of you he's still alive long after he ought to be dead, all that crap." They both smiled. "What's your choice in liquor, doctor? I like anything. And I like fried chops and Mexican food and spare ribs and fried prawns dipped in horse-radish and mustard. . . . I treat my stomach kind."

"Bourbon," Eric said.

A man entered the room, glanced at Eric. He had a gray, grim expression and Eric realized that this was one of the Mole's Secret Service men.

"This is Tom Johannson," the Mole explained to Eric. "He keeps *me* alive; he's my Dr. Eric Sweetscent. But he does it with his pistol. Show doc your pistol, Tom; show him how you can nam anybody, any time you want, at any distance. Plug Virgil as he comes across the hall, right in the fnigging heart; then doc can paste a new heart in its place. How long does it take, doc? Ten, fifteen minutes?" The Mole laughed loudly. And then he motioned to Johannson. "Shut the door."

His bodyguard did so; the Mole stood facing Eric Sweetscent.

"Listen, doctor. Here's what I want to ask you. Suppose you began to perform an org-trans operation on me, taking out my old stomach and putting in a new one, and something went wrong. It wouldn't hurt, would it? Because I'd be out. Could you do that?" He watched Eric's face. "You understand me, don't you? I see you do." Behind them, at the closed door, the bodyguard stood impassively, keeping everyone else out, preventing them from hearing. This was for Eric alone. In utmost confidence.

"Why?" Eric said, after a time. Why not simply use Johannson's laser-magnum pistol? If this is what you want . . .

"I don't know why, actually," the Mole said. "No one particular reason. The death of my wife, perhaps. Call it the responsibility I have to bear . . . and which I'm not managing to discharge properly, at least according to many people. I don't agree; I think I'm succeeding. But they don't understand all the factors in the situation." He admitted, then, "And I'm tired."

"It—could be done," Eric said truthfully.

"And *you* could do it?" The man's eyes blazed, keen and fixed on him. Sizing him up as each second ticked away.

"Yes, I could do it." He held, personally, an odd view regarding suicide. Despite his code, the ethical understructure of medicine, he believed—and it was based on certain very real experiences in his own life—that if a man wanted to die he had the right to die. He did not possess an elaborated rationalization to justify this belief; he had not even tried to construct one. The proposition, to him, seemed self-evident. There was no body of evidence which proved that life in the first place was a boon. Perhaps it was for some persons; obviously it was not for others. For Gino Molinari it was a nightmare. The man was sick, guilt-ridden, saddled with an enormous, really hopeless task: he did not have the confidence of his own people, the Terran population, and he did not enjoy the respect or trust or admiration of the people of Lilistar. And then, above and beyond all that, lay the personal consideration, the events in his own private life, starting with the sudden, unexpected death of his wife and ending up with the pains in his belly. And then, too, Eric realized with acute comprehension, there was probably more. Factors known only to the Mole. Deciding factors which he did not intend to tell.

" *Would* you do such a thing?" Molinari asked.

After a long, long pause Eric said, "Yes I would. It would be an agreement between the two of us. You'd ask for it and I'd give it to you and it would end there. It would be no one's business but our own."

"Yes." The Mole nodded and on his face relief showed; he seemed now to relax a little, to experience some peace. "I can see why Virgil recommended you."

"I was going to do it to myself, once," Eric said. "Not so long ago."

The Mole's head jerked; he stared at Eric Sweetscent with a look so keen that it cut through his physical self and into that which lay at the deepest, most silent part of him. "Really?" the Mole said then.

"Yes." He nodded. So I can understand, he thought to himself, can empathize with you even without having to know the exact reasons.

"But I," the Mole said, "want to know the reasons." It was so close to a telepathic reading of his mind that Eric felt stunned; he found himself unable to look away from the penetrating eyes and he realized, then, that it had been no parapsychological talent on the Mole's part: it had been swifter and stronger than that.

The Mole extended his hand; reflexively, Eric accepted it. And, once he had done so, he found the grip remaining; the Mole did not release his hand but tightened his grip so that pain flew up Eric's arm. The Mole was trying to see him better, trying, as Phyllis Ackerman had done not so long ago, to discover everything that could be discovered about him. But out of the Mole's mind came no glib, flip theories; the Mole insisted on the truth, and articulated by Eric Sweetscent himself. He had to tell the Mole what it had been; he had no choice.

Actually, in his case it had been a very small matter. Something which if told—and he had never been so foolish as to tell it, even to his professional headbasher—would have proved absurd, would have made him appear, and rightly so, an idiot. Or, even worse, mentally deranged.

It had been an incident between himself and—

"Your wife," the Mole said, staring at him, never taking his eyes from him. And still the steady grip of his hand.

"Yes." Eric nodded. "My Ampex video tapes . . . of the great mid-twentieth century comedian Jonathan Winters."

The pretext for his first invitation of Kathy Lingrom had been his fabulous collection. She had expressed a desire to see them, to drop by his apt—at his invitation—to witness a few choice shots.

The Mole said, "And she read something psychological into your having the tapes. Something 'meaningful' about you."

"Yes." Eric nodded somberly.

After Kathy had sat curled up one night in his living room, as long-legged and smooth as a cat, her bare breasts faintly green from the light coating of polish she had given them (in the latest style), watching the screen fixedly and, of course, laughing—who could fail to?—she had said contemplatively, "You know, what's great about Winters was his talent for role-playing. And, once in a role, he was submerged; he seemed actually to believe in it."

"Is that bad?" Eric had said.

"No. But it tells me why you gravitate to Winters." Kathy fondled the damp, cold glass of her drink, her long lashes lowered in thought. "It's that residual quality in him that could never be submerged in his role. It means you resist life, the role that you play out—being an org-trans surgeon, I suppose. Some childish, unconscious part of you won't enter human society."

"Well, is *that* bad?" He had tried to ask jokingly, wanting—even then—to turn this pseudopsychiatric, ponderous discussion to more convivial areas . . . areas clearly defined in his mind as he surveyed her pure, bare, pale-green breasts flickering with their own luminosity.

"It's deceitful," Kathy said.

Hearing that, then, something in him had groaned, and something in him groaned now. The Mole seemed to hear it, to take note.

"You're cheating other people," Kathy said. "Me, for instance." At that point—mercifully—she changed the topic. For that he felt gratitude. And yet—why did it bother him so?

Later, when they had married, Kathy primly requested that he keep his tape collection in his study and not out in the shared portion of their conapt. The collection vaguely vexed her, she said. But she did not know—or anyhow did not say— why. And when in the evenings he felt the old urge to play a section of tape, Kathy complained.

"Why?" the Mole asked.

He did not know; he had not then and did not now understand it. But it had been an ominous harbinger; he saw her aversion but the significance of it eluded him, and this inability to grasp the meaning of what was taking place in his married life made him deeply uneasy.

Meanwhile, through Kathy's intercession, he had been hired by Virgil Ackerman. His wife had made it possible for him to take a notable leap in the hierarchy of econ and sose— economic and social—life. And of course he felt gratitude toward her; how could he not? His basic ambition has been fulfilled.

The means by which it had been accomplished had not struck him as overpoweringly important: many wives helped their husbands up the long steps in their careers. And vice versa. And yet—

It bothered Kathy. Even though it had been her idea.

"*She* got you your job here?" the Mole demanded, scowling. "And then after that she held it against you? I seem to get the picture, very clear." He plucked at a front tooth, still scowling, his face dark.

"One night in bed—" He stopped, feeling the difficulty of going on. It had been too private. And too awfully unpleasant.

"I want to know," the Mole said, "the rest of it."

He shrugged. "Anyhow—she said something about being 'tired of the sham we're living.' The 'sham,' of course, being my job."

Lying in bed, naked, her soft hair curling about her shoulders —in those days she had worn it longer—Kathy had said, "You married me to get your job. And you're not striving on your own; a man should make his own way." Tears filled her eyes, and she flopped over on her face to cry—or appear, anyhow— to cry.

"'Strive'?" he had said, baffled.

The Mole interrupted, "Rise higher. Get a better job. That's what they mean when they say that."

"But I like my job," he answered.

"So you're content," Kathy said, in a muffled, bitter voice, "to *appear* to be successful. When you really aren't." And then, sniffling and snuffling, she added, "And you're terrible in bed."

He got up and went into the living room of their conapt and sat alone for a time and then, instinctively, he made his way into his study and placed one of his treasured Johnny Winters tapes into the projector. For a while he sat in misery watching Johnny put on one hat after another and become a different person under each. And then—

At the doorway Kathy appeared, smooth and naked and slim, her face contorted. "Have you found it?"

"Found what?" He shut the tape projector off.

"The tape," she stated, "that I destroyed."

He stared at her, unable to take in what he had heard.

"A few days ago." Her tone, defiant, shrilled at him. "I was all alone here in the conapt; I felt blue—you were busy doing some drafk nothing thing for Virgil—and I put on a reel; I put it on exactly right; I followed all the instructions. But *it* did something wrong. So it got erased."

The Mole grunted somberly. "You were supposed to say 'It doesn't matter.'"

He had known that; known it then, knew it now. But in a strangled, thick voice he had said, "Which tape?"

"I don't remember."

His voice rose; it escaped him. "Goddam it, *which tape?*" He ran to the shelf of tapes; grabbed the first box; tore it open; carried it at once to the projector.

"I knew," Kathy said, in a harsh, bleak voice as she watched him with withering contempt, "that your —— tapes meant more to you than I do or ever did."

"Tell me which tape!" he pleaded. "*Please!*"

"No, she wouldn't say," the Mole murmured thoughtfully. "That would be the entire point. You'd have to play every one of them before you could find out. A couple days of playing tapes. Clever dame; damn clever."

"No," Kathy said in a low, embittered, almost frail voice. Now her face was peaked with hatred for him. "I'm *glad* I did it. You know what I'm going to do? I'm going to ruin all of them."

He stared at her. Numbly.

"You deserve it," Kathy said, "for holding back and not giving me all your love. *This* is where you belong, scrabbling like an animal, a panic-ridden animal. Look at you! Contemptible—trembling and about to burst into tears. Because someone ruined one of your INCREDIBLY important tapes."

"But," he said, "it's my hobby. My lifetime hobby."

"Like a kid pulling its pud," Kathy said.

"They—can't be replaced. I have the only copies of some of them. The one from the Jack Paar show—"

"So what? You know something, Eric? Do you know, really know, why you like watching men on tape?"

The Mole grunted; his heavy, fleshy, middle-aged face flinched as he listened.

"Because," Kathy said, "you're a fairy."

"Ouch," the Mole murmured, and blinked.

"You're a repressed homosexual. I sincerely doubt if you're aware of it on a conscious level, but it's there. Look at me; look. Here I am; a perfectly attractive woman, available to you any time you want me."

The Mole said, aside, wryly, "And at no cost."

"And yet you're in here with these tapes and not in the bedroom screwbling with me. I hope—Eric, I hope to *God* I ruined one that—" She turned away from the door then. "Good night. And have fun playing with yourself." Her voice —actually and unbelievably—had become controlled, even placid.

From a crouched position he bolted toward her. Reached for her as she retreated smooth and white and naked down the hall, her back to him. He grabbed her, grabbed firm hold, sank his fingers into her soft arm. Spun her around. Blinking, startled, she faced him.

"I'm going to—" He broke off. *I'm going to kill you*, he had started to say. But already in the unstirred depths of his mind, slumbering beneath the frenzy of his hysterical antics, a cold and rational fraction of him whispered its ice-God voice: Don't say it. Because if you do, then she's got you. She'll never forget. As long as you live she'll make you suffer. This is a woman that one must not hurt because she knows techniques; she knows how to hurt back. A thousandfold. Yes, this is her wisdom, this knowing how to do this. Above all other things.

"Let—go—of—me." Her eyes blazed smokily.

He released her.

After a pause, while she rubbed her arm, Kathy said, "I want that collection of tapes out of this apartment by tomorrow night. Otherwise we're finished, Eric."

"Okay," he said, nodding.

"And then," Kathy said, "I'll tell you what else I want. I want you to start looking for a higher paying job. At another company. So I won't run into you every time I turn around. And then . . . we'll see. Possibly we can stay together. On a new basis, one fairer to me. One in which you make some attempt to pay attention to my needs in addition to your own." Astonishingly, she sounded perfectly rational and in control of herself. Remarkable.

"You got rid of the tapes?" the Mole asked him.

He nodded.

"And you spent the next few years directing your efforts toward controlling your hatred for your wife."

Again he nodded.

"And the hatred for her," the Mole said, "became hatred for yourself. Because you couldn't stand being afraid of one small woman. But a very powerful person—notice I said 'person,' not 'woman.'"

"Those low blows," Eric said. "Like her erasing my tape—"

"The low blow," the Mole interrupted, "was not her erasing the tape. It was her refusing to tell you which one she had erased. And her making it so clear that she enjoyed the situation. If she had been sorry—but a woman, a person, like that; they never become sorry. Never." He was silent for a time. "And you can't leave her."

"We're fused," Eric said. "The damage is done." The mutually inflicted pain delivered at night without the possibility of anyone intervening, overhearing and coming to help. Help, Eric thought. We both need help. Because this will go on, get worse, corrode us further and further until at last, mercifully—

But that might take decades.

So Eric could understand Gino Molinari's yearning for

death. He, like the Mole, could envision it as a release—the only dependable release that existed . . . or appeared to exist, given the ignorance, habit patterns, and foolishness of the participants. Given the timeless human equation.

In fact he felt a considerable bond with Molinari.

"One of us," the Mole said, with perception, "suffering unbearably on the private level, hidden from the public, small and unimportant. The other suffering in the grand Roman public manner, like a speared and dying god. Strange. Completely opposite. The microcosm and the macro."

Eric nodded.

"Anyhow," the Mole said, releasing Eric's hand and slapping him on the shoulder, "I'm making you feel bad. Sorry, Dr. Sweetscent; let's drop the topic." To his bodyguard he said, "Open the door now. We're done."

"Wait," Eric said. But then he did not know how to go on, to say it.

The Mole did it for him. "How would you like to be attached to my staff?" Molinari said abruptly, breaking the silence. "It can be arranged; technically you'd be drafted into military service." He added, "You may take it for granted you'd be my personal physician."

Trying to sound casual, Eric said, "I'm interested."

"You wouldn't be running into her all the time. This might be a beginning. A start toward prying the two of you apart."

"True." He nodded. Very true. And very attractive, when thought of that way. But the irony—this consisted of precisely that which Kathy had goaded him toward all these years. "I'd have to talk it over with my wife," he began, and then flushed. "Virgil, anyhow," he muttered. "In any case. He'd have to approve."

Regarding him with brooding severity, the Mole said in a slow, dark voice, "There is one drawback. You would not see so much of Kathy; true. But by being with me you'd see a great deal of our—" He grimaced. "The ally. How do you suppose you'd enjoy yourself surrounded by 'Starmen? You might find yourself having a few spasms of the gut late at night yourself . . . and perhaps worse—other—psychosomatic disorders, some you may not anticipate, despite your profession."

Eric said, "It's bad enough for me late at night as it is. This way I might have some company."

"Me?" Molinari said. "I wouldn't be company, Sweetscent, for you or anybody else. I'm a creature that's flayed alive at night. I retire at ten o'clock and then I'm back up, usually by eleven; I—" He broke off, meditatively. "No, night is not a good time for me; not at all."

It could clearly be seen in the man's face.

Five

O N the night of his return from Wash-35 Eric Sweetscent encountered his wife at their conapt across the border in San Diego. Kathy had arrived before him. The meeting, of course, was inevitable.

"Back from little red Mars," she observed as he shut the living room door after him. "Two days doing what? Shooting your agate into the ring and beating all the other boys and girls? Or exposing sun pictures of Tom Mix?" Kathy sat in the center of the couch, a drink in one hand, her hair swept back and tied, giving her the look of a teen-ager; she wore a plain black dress and her legs were long and smooth, strikingly tapered at the ankles. Her feet were bare and each toenail bore a shiny decal depicting—he bent to see—a scene in color of the Norman Conquest. The smallest nail on each foot glittered with a picture too obscene for him to contemplate; he went to hang his coat in the closet.

"We pulled out of the war," he said.

"Did we? You and Phyllis Ackerman? Or you and someone else?"

"Everybody was there. Not just Phyllis." He wondered what he could fix for dinner; his stomach was empty and in a state of complaint. As yet, however, there were no pains. Perhaps that came later.

"Any special reason why I wasn't asked along?" Her voice snapped like a lethal whip, making his flesh cringe; the natural biochemical animal in him dreaded the exchange which was in store for him—and also for her. Obviously she, like himself, was compelled to press head-on; she was as much caught up and helpless as he.

"No special reason." He wandered into the kitchen, feeling a little dulled, as if Kathy's opening had flattened his senses. Many such encounters had taught him to shield himself on the somatic level, if at all possible. Only old husbands, tired, experienced husbands, knew to do this. The newcomers . . . they're forced on by diencephalic responses, he reflected. And it's harder on them.

"I want an answer," Kathy said, appearing at the door. "As to why I was deliberately excluded."

God, how physically appealing his wife was; she wore nothing, of course, under the black dress and each curved line of her confronted him with its savory familiarity. But where was the smooth, yielding, familiar mentality to go with this tactile form? The furies had seen to it that the curse—the curse in the house of Sweetscent, as he occasionally thought of it—had arrived full force; he faced a creature which on a physiological level was sexual perfection itself and on the mental level—

Someday the hardness, the inflexibility, would pervade her; the anatomical bounty would calcify. And then what? Already her voice contained it, different now from what he remembered of a few years back, even a few months. Poor Kathy, he thought. Because when the death-dealing powers of ice and cold reach your loins, your breasts and hips and buttocks as well as your heart—it was already deep in her heart, surely—then there will be no more woman. And you won't survive that. No matter what I or any man chooses to do.

"You were excluded," he said carefully, "because you're a pest."

Her eyes flew open wide; for an instant they filled with alarm and simple wonder. She did not understand. Fleetingly, she had been brought back to the level of the merely human; the goading ancestral pressure in her had abated.

"Like you are now," he said. "So leave me alone; I want to fix myself some dinner."

"Get Phyllis Ackerman to fix it for you," Kathy said. The super-personal authority, the derision conjured up from the malformed crypto-wisdom of the ages, had returned. Almost psionically, with a woman's talent, she had intuited his slight romantic brush with Phyllis on the trip to Mars. And on Mars itself, during their overnight stay—

Calmly, he assumed that her heightened faculties could not genuinely ferret out that. Ignoring her, he began, in a methodical manner, to heat a frozen chicken dinner in the infrared oven, his back to his wife.

"Guess what I did," Kathy said. "While you were gone."

"You took on a lover."

"I tried a new hallucinogenic drug. I got it from Chris Plout; we had a jink session at his place and none other than the world-famous Marm Hastings was there. He made a pass at me while we were under the influence of the drug and it was —well, it was a pure vision."

"Did he," Eric said, setting a place for himself at the table.

"How I'd adore to bear his child," Kathy said.

"'Adore to.' Christ, what decadent English." Ensnared, he turned to face her. "Did you and he—"

Kathy smiled. "Well, maybe it was an hallucination. But I don't think so. I'll tell you why. When I got home—"

"Spare me!" He found himself shaking.

In the living room the vidphone chimed.

Eric went to get it and when he lifted the receiver he saw on the small gray screen the features of a man named Captain Otto Dorf, a military adviser to Gino Molinari. Dorf had been at Wash-35, assisting in security measures; he was a thin-faced man with narrow, melancholy eyes, a man utterly dedicated to the protection of the Secretary. "Dr. Sweetscent?"

"Yes," Eric said. "But I haven't—"

"Will an hour be enough? We'd like to send a 'copter to pick you up at eight o'clock your time."

"An hour will do," Eric said. "I'll have my things packed and will be waiting in the lobby of my conapt building."

After he had rung off he returned to the kitchen.

Kathy said, "Oh my God. Oh Eric—can't we talk? Oh dear." She slumped at the table and buried her head in her arms. "I didn't do anything with Marm Hastings; he is handsome and I did take the drug, but—"

"Listen," he said, continuing to prepare his meal. "This was all arranged earlier today at Wash-35. Virgil wants me to do it. We had a long, quiet talk. Molinari's needs are at present greater than Virgil's. And actually I can still serve Virgil in org-trans situations but I'll be stationed at Cheyenne." He added, "I've been drafted; as of tomorrow I'm a medic in the UN military forces, attached to Secretary Molinari's staff. There's nothing I can do to change it; Molinari signed the decree to that effect last night."

"Why?" Terror-stricken, she gazed up at him.

"So I can get out of this. Before one of us—"

"I won't spend any more money."

"There's a war on. Men are being killed. Molinari is sick and he needs medical help. Whether you spend money or not—"

"But you *asked* for this job."

Presently he said, "I begged for it, as a matter of fact. I gave Virgil the greatest line of hot fizz ever strung together at one time in one place."

She had drawn herself together now; she had become poised. "What sort of pay will you receive?"

"Plenty. And I'll continue to draw a salary from TF&D, too."

"Is there a way I can come with you?"

"No." He had seen to that.

"I knew you'd dump me when you finally became a success —you've been trying to extricate yourself ever since we met." Kathy's eyes filled with tears. "Listen, Eric; I'm afraid that that drug I took is addictive. I'm terribly scared. You have no idea what it does; I think it comes from somewhere off Earth, maybe Lilistar. What if I keep taking it? What if because of your leaving—"

Bending, he picked her up in his arms. "You ought to keep away from those people; I've told you so goddam many times—" It was futile talking to her; he could see what lay ahead for both of them. Kathy had a weapon by which she could draw him back to her once more. Without him she would be destroyed by her involvement with Plout, Hastings, and company; leaving her would simply make her situation worse. The sickness that had entered them over the years could not be nullified by the act he had in mind, and only in the Martian babyland could he have imagined otherwise.

He carried her into the bedroom and set her gently on the bed.

"Ah," she said, and shut her eyes. "Oh Eric—" She sighed.

However, he couldn't. This, too. Miserably, he moved from her, sat on the edge of the bed. "I have to leave TF&D," he said presently. "And you have to accept it." He stroked her hair. "Molinari is cracking up; maybe I can't help him but at least I can try. See? That's the real—"

Kathy said, "You're lying."

"When? In what way?" He continued stroking her hair but it had become a mechanical action, without volition or desire.

"You would have made love to me just now, if that was why you were leaving." She rebuttoned her dress. "You don't care about me." Her voice held certitude; he recognized the drab, thin tone. Always this barrier, this impossibility of getting through. This time he did not waste his time trying; he simply went on stroking her, thinking, It'll be on my conscience, whatever happens to her. And she knows it, too. So she's absolved of the burden of responsibility, and that, for her, is the worst thing possible.

Too bad, he thought, I wasn't able to make love to her.

"My dinner's ready," he said, rising.

She sat up. "Eric, I'm going to pay you back for leaving me." She smoothed her dress. "You understand?"

"Yes," he said, and walked into the kitchen.

"I'll devote my life to it," Kathy said, from the bedroom. "Now I have a reason for living. It's wonderful to have a purpose at last; it's thrilling. After all these pointless ugly years with you. God, it's like being born all over again."

"Lots of luck," he said.

"Luck? I don't need luck; I need skill, and I think I have skill. I learned a lot during that episode under the effects of that drug. I wish I could tell you what it is; it's an incredible drug, Eric—it changes your entire perception of the universe and especially of other people. You don't ever view them the same again. You ought to try it. It would help you."

"Nothing," he said, "would help me."

His words, in his ears, sounded like an epitaph.

He had almost finished packing—and had long since eaten —when the doorbell of the conapt rang. It was Otto Dorf, already here with the military 'copter, and Eric soberly went to open the door for him.

Glancing about the conapt, Dorf said, "Did you have an opportunity to say good-by to your wife, doctor?"

"Yes." He added, "She's gone now; I'm alone." He closed his suitcase and carried it and its companion to the door. "I'm ready." Dorf picked up one suitcase and together they walked to the elevator. "She did not take it very well," he remarked to Dorf as they presently descended.

"I'm unmarried, doctor," Dorf said. "I wouldn't know." His manner was correct and formal.

In the parked 'copter another man waited. He held out his hand as Eric ascended the rungs. "Doctor; it's good to meet you." The man, hidden in the shadows, explained, "I'm Harry Teagarden, chief of the Secretary's medical staff. I'm glad you're joining us; the Secretary hadn't informed me in advance but that's no matter—he invariably acts on impulse."

Eric shook hands with him, his mind still on Kathy. "Sweetscent."

"How did Molinari's condition strike you when you met him?"

"He seemed tired."

Teagarden said, "He's dying."

Glancing at him swiftly, Eric said, "From what? In this day and age, with artiforgs available—"

"I am familiar with current surgical techniques; believe me." Teagarden's tone was dry. "You saw how fatalistic he is. He wants to be punished, obviously, for leading us into this war." Teagarden was silent as the 'copter ascended into the night sky and then he continued, "Did it ever occur to you that Molinari *engineered* the losing of this war? That he wants to fail? I don't think even his most rabid political enemies have tried that idea out. The reason I'm saying this to you is that we don't have bales of time. Right at this moment Molinari is in Cheyenne suffering from a massive attack of his acute gastritis—or whatever you care to call it. From your holiday at Wash-35. He's flat on his back."

"Any internal bleeding?"

"Not yet. Or perhaps there has been and Molinari hasn't told us. With him it's possible; he's naturally secretive. Essentially he trusts nobody."

"And you're positive there's no malignancy?"

"We can't find any. But Molinari doesn't allow us to conduct as many tests as we'd like; he bolts. Too busy. Papers to sign, speeches to write, bills to present to the General Assembly. He tries to run everything singlehandedly. He can't seem to delegate authority and then when he does he sets up overlapping organizations that immediately compete—it's his way of protecting himself." Teagarden glanced curiously at Eric. "What did he say to you at Wash-35?"

"Not much." He did not intend to disclose the contents of their discussion. Molinari had beyond doubt meant it for his ears exclusively. In fact, Eric realized, that was the cardinal reason for his being brought to Cheyenne. He had something to offer Molinari that the other medics did not, a strange contribution for a doctor to be making . . . he wondered how Teagarden would react if he were to tell him. Probably—and for good reason—Teagarden would have him put under arrest. And shot.

"I know why you're going to be with us," Teagarden said.

Eric grunted. "You do?" He doubted it.

"Molinari is simply following his instinctive bias, having us double-checked by infusing new blood into our staff. But no one objects; in fact we're grateful—we're all overworked. You know, of course, that the Secretary has a huge family, even larger than that of Virgil Ackerman, your paterfamilias-style former employer."

"I believe I've read it's three uncles, six cousins, an aunt, a sister, an elderly brother who—"

"And they're all in residence at Cheyenne," Teagarden said. "Constantly so. Hanging around him, trying to wangle little favors, better meals, quarters, servants—you get the pic. And—" He paused. "I should add there's a mistress."

That Eric did not know. It had never been mentioned, even in the press hostile to the Secretary.

"Her name is Mary Reineke. He met her before his wife's death. On paper Mary's listed as a personal secretary. I like her. She's done a lot for him, both before and after his wife's death. Without her he probably wouldn't have survived. The 'Starmen loathe her . . . I don't quite know why. Perhaps I've missed out on some fact."

"How old is she?" The Secretary, Eric guessed, was in his late forties or early fifties.

"As young as it's humanly possible to be. Prepare yourself, doctor." Teagarden chuckled. "When he met her she was in high school. Working in the late afternoons as a typist. Perhaps she handed him a document . . . nobody knows for sure, but they did meet over some routine business matter."

"Can his illness be discussed with her?"

"Absolutely. She's the one—the only one—who's been able to get him to take phenobarbital and, when we tried it, pathabamate. Phenobarb made him sleepy, he said, and path made his mouth dry. So of course he dropped them down a waste chute; he quit. Mary made him go back on. She's Italian. As he is. She can bawl him out in a way he remembers from his childhood, from his mama, perhaps . . . or his sister or aunt; they all bawl him out and he tolerates it, but he doesn't listen, except to Mary. She lives in a concealed apt in Cheyenne guarded by lines of Secret Service men—because of the 'Star people. Molinari dreads the day they'll—" Teagarden broke off.

"They'll what?"

"Kill her or maim her. Or weed out half her mental processes, turn her into a debrained vegetable; they've got a spectrum of techniques they can make use of. You didn't know our dealings with the ally were so rough at the top, did you?" Teagarden smiled. "It's a rough war. That's how Lilistar acts toward us, our superior ally beside which we're a flea. So imagine how the enemy, the reegs, would treat us if our defense line cracked and they managed to pour in."

For a time they rode in silence; no one cared to speak.

"What do you think would happen," Eric said finally, "if Molinari passed out of the pic?"

"Well, it would go one of two ways. Either we'd get some-one more pro-Lilistar or we wouldn't. What other choices are there, and why do you ask? Do you believe we're going to lose our patient? If we do, doctor, we also lose our jobs and possi-bly our lives. Your one justification for existence—and mine— is the continual viable presence of one overweight, middle-aged Italian who lives in Cheyenne, Wyoming, with his enormous family and his eighteen-year-old mistress, who has stomach pains and enjoys eating a late-evening snack of batter-fried giant prawns with mustard and horse-radish. I don't care what they told you or what you signed; you're not going to be in-serting any more artiforgs into Virgil Ackerman for a long time; there won't be the opportunity *because keeping Gino Molinari alive is a full-time task.*" Teagarden seemed irritable and upset now; his voice, in the darkness of the 'copter cab, was jerky. "It's too much for me, Sweetscent. You won't have any other life but Molinari; he'll talk your ear off, deliver practice speeches to you on every topic on Earth—ask your opinion about everything from contraception to mushrooms— how to cook them—to God to what would you do *if*, and so forth. For a dictator—and you realize that's what he is, only we don't like to use the name—he's an anomaly. First of all he's probably the greatest political strategist alive; how else do you suppose he rose to be UN Secretary General? It took him twenty years, and fighting all the way; he dislodged every political opponent he met, from every country on Terra. Then he got mixed up with Lilistar. That's called foreign policy. On foreign policy the master strategist failed, because at that point a strange occlusion entered his mind. You know what it's called? Ignorance. Molinari spent all his time learning how to knee people in the groin, and with Freneksy that isn't called for. He could no more deal with Freneksy than you or I could— possibly worse."

"I see," Eric said.

"But Molinari went ahead anyhow. He bluffed. He signed the Pact of Peace which got us into the war. And here's where Molinari differs from all the fat, overblown, strutting dictators in the past. *He took the blame on his own shoulders;* he didn't fire a foreign minister here or shoot a policy adviser from State there. *He* did it and he knows it. And it's killing him, by quarter inches, day in, day out. Starting from the gut. He loves Terra. He loves people, all of them, washed and unwashed; he loves his wretched pack of sponging relatives. He shoots people, arrests people, but he doesn't like it. Molinari is a complex man, doctor. So complex that—"

Dorf interrupted drily, "A mixture of Lincoln and Mussolini."

"He's a different person with everyone he meets," Teagarden continued. "Christ, he's done things so rotten, so goddam wicked that they'd make your hair stand on end. He's had to. Some of them will never be made public, even by his political foes. And he's suffered because of doing them. Did you ever know anyone who *really* accepted responsibility, guilt and blame, before? Do *you*? Does your wife?"

"Probably not," Eric admitted.

"If you or I ever really accepted the moral responsibility for what we've done in our lifetime—we'd drop dead or go mad. Living creatures weren't made to understand what they do. Take the animals we've run over on the road, or the animals we eat. When I was a kid it was my monthly job to go out and poison rats. Did you ever watch a poisoned animal die? And not just one but scores of them, month after month. I don't *feel* it. The blame. The load. Fortunately it doesn't register—it can't, because if it did there'd be no way I could go on. And that's how the entire human race gets by. All but the Mole. As they call him." Teagarden added, "'Lincoln and Mussolini.' I was thinking more of One Other, back about two thousand years."

"This is the first time," Eric said, "I ever heard anyone compare Gino Molinari to Christ. Even in his captive press."

"Perhaps," Teagarden said, "it's because I'm the first person you've ever talked to who's been around the Mole twenty-four hours a day."

"Don't tell Mary Reineke about your comparison," Dorf said. "She'll tell you he's a bastard. A pig in bed and at the table, a lewd middle-aged man with rape in his eye, who ought to be in jail. She tolerates him . . . because she's charitable." Dorf laughed sharply.

"No," Teagarden said, "that's not what Mary would say . . . except when she's sore, which is about a fourth of the time. I don't really know what Mary Reineke would say; maybe she wouldn't even try. She just accepts him as he is; she tries to improve him, but even if he doesn't improve—and he won't—she loves him anyhow. Have you ever known that other kind of woman? Who saw *possibilities* in you? And with the right kind of help from her—"

"Yes," Eric said. He wished to see the subject changed; it made him think about Kathy. And he did not care to.

The 'copter droned on toward Cheyenne.

In bed alone Kathy lay half sleeping as morning sunlight ignited the variegated textures of her bedroom. All the colors so familiar to her in her married life with Eric now became distinguished one from another as the light advanced. Here, where she lived, Kathy had established potent spirits of the past, trapped within the concoctions of other periods: a lamp from early New England, a chest of drawers that was authentic bird's-eye maple, a Hepplewhite cabinet. . . . She lay with her eyes half open, aware of each object and all the connecting strands involved in her acquisition of them. Each was a triumph over a rival; some competing collector had failed, and it did not seem farfetched to regard this collection as a graveyard, with the ghosts of the defeated persisting in the vicinity. She did not mind their activity in her home life; after all, she was tougher than they.

"Eric," she said sleepily, "for chrissake get up and put on the coffee. And help me out of bed. Push or speak." She turned toward him, but no one was there. Instantly she sat up. Then she got from the bed, walked barefoot to the closet for her robe, shivering.

She was putting on a light gray sweater, tugging it with difficulty over her head, when she realized that a man stood watching her. As she had dressed he had lounged in the doorway, making no move to announce his presence; he was enjoying the sight of her dressing, but now he shifted, stood upright and said, "Mrs. Sweetscent?" He was perhaps thirty, with a dark, rough muzzle and eyes which did not encourage her sense of well-being. In addition he wore a drab-gray uniform and she knew what he was: a member of Lilistar's secret police operating on Terra. It was the first time in her life that she had ever run into one of them.

"Yes," she said, almost soundlessly. She continued dressing, sitting on the bed to slip on her shoes, not taking her eyes from him. "I'm Kathy Sweetscent, Dr. Eric Sweetscent's wife, and if you don't—"

"Your husband is in Cheyenne."

"Is he?" She rose to her feet. "I have to fix breakfast; please let me by. And let me see your warrant for coming in here." She held out her hand, waiting.

"My warrant," the Lilistar grayman said, "calls for me to search this conapt for an illegal drug, JJ-180. Frohedadrine. If you have any, hand it over and we'll go directly to the police barracks at Santa Monica." He consulted his notebook. "Last night in Tijuana at 45 Avila Street you used the drug orally in the company of—"

"May I call my attorney?"

"No."

"You mean I have no legal rights at all?"

"This is wartime."

She felt afraid. Nevertheless she managed to speak with reasonable calm. "May I call my employer and tell him I won't be in?"

The gray policeman nodded. So she went to the vidphone and dialed Virgil Ackerman at his home in San Fernando. Presently his birdlike, weathered face appeared, owlishly waking in a fuss of confusion. "Oh, Kathy. Where's the clock?" Virgil peered about.

Kathy said, "Help me, Mr. Ackerman. The Lilistar—" She ceased, because the grayman had broken the connection with a swift movement of his hand. Shrugging, she hung up.

"Mrs. Sweetscent," the grayman said, "I'd like to introduce Mr. Roger Corning to you." He made a motion and into the apartment, from the hall, came a 'Starman dressed in an ordinary business suit, a briefcase under his arm. "Mr. Corning, this is Kathy Sweetscent, Dr. Sweetscent's wife."

"Who are you?" Kathy said.

"Someone who can get you off the hook, dear," Corning said pleasantly. "May we sit down in your living room and discuss this?"

Going into the kitchen, she twisted the knobs for soft-boiled eggs, toast, and coffee without cream. "There's no JJ-180 in this apt. Unless you put it here yourself during the night." The food was ready; she carried it to the table on its throwaway tray and seated herself. The smell of the coffee vanquished the remnants of fear and bewilderment in her; she felt capable again and not so intimidated.

Corning said, "We have a permanent photographic sequence of your evening at 45 Avila Street. From the moment you followed Bruce Himmel up the stairs and inside. Your initial words were, 'Hello, Bruce. It looks as if this is an all-TF&D—'"

"Not quite," Kathy said. "I called him *Brucie*. I always call him Brucie because he's so hebephrenic and dumb." She drank her coffee, her hand steady as it held the throwaway cup. "Does your photographic sequence prove what was in the capsules we took, Mr. Gorning?"

"Corning," he corrected good-naturedly. "No, Katherine, it doesn't. But the testimony of two of the other participants does. Or will when it's entered under oath before a military tribunal." He explained, "This falls outside the jurisdiction of your civilian courts. We ourselves will handle all details of the prosecution."

"Why is that?" she inquired.

"JJ-180 can only be acquired from the enemy. Therefore your use of it—and we can establish this before our tribunal—constitutes intercourse with the enemy. In time of war the tribunal's demand naturally would be death." To the gray-uniformed policeman Corning said, "Do you have Mr. Plout's deposition with you?"

"It's in the 'copter." The grayman started toward the door.

"I thought there was something subhuman about Chris Plout," Kathy said. "Now I'm meditating about the others . . . who else last night had a subhuman quality? Hastings? No. Simon Ild? No, he—"

"All this can be avoided," Corning said.

"But I don't want to avoid it," Kathy said. "Mr. Ackerman heard me on the vidphone; TF&D will send an attorney. Mr. Ackerman is a friend of Secretary Molinari; I don't think—"

"We can kill you, Kathy," Corning said. "By nightfall. The tribunal can meet this morning; it's all arranged."

After a time—she had ceased eating—Kathy said, "Why? I'm that important? What is there in JJ-180? I—" She hesitated. "What I tried last night didn't do so very much." All at once she wished like hell that Eric had not left. This wouldn't have happened with him here, she realized. They would have been afraid.

Soundlessly, she began to cry; she sat hunched over at her plate, tears sliding down her cheeks and dropping to disappear. She did not even try to cover her face; she put her hand to her forehead, rested leaning against her arm, saying nothing. —— it, she thought.

"Your position," Corning said, "is serious but not hopeless;

there's a difference. We can work out something . . . that's why I'm here. Stop crying and sit up straight and listen to me and I'll try to explain." He unzipped his briefcase.

"I know," Kathy said. "You want me to spy on Marm Hastings. You're after him because he advocated signing a separate peace with the reegs that time on TV. Jesus, you've infiltrated this whole planet. Nobody's safe." She got up, groaned with despair, went to the bedroom for a handkerchief, still sniffling.

"Would you watch Hastings for us?" Corning said, when she returned.

"No." She shook her head. Better to be dead, she thought.

"It's not Hastings," the uniformed Lilistar policeman said.

Corning said, "We want your husband. We'd like you to follow him to Cheyenne and take up where you left off. Bed and board, I think the Terran phrase is. As soon as it possibly can be arranged."

She stared at him. "I can't."

"Why can't you?"

"We broke up. He left me." She could not understand why, if they knew everything else, they didn't know that.

"Resolutions of that type in a marriage," Corning said, as if speaking with the weary wisdom of an infinity of ages, "can always be reduced to the status of a temporary misunderstanding. We'll take you to one of our psychologists—we have several excellent ones in residence here on this planet—and he'll brief you on the techniques to use in healing this rift with Eric. Don't worry, Kathy; we know what went on here last night. Actually it works out to our advantage; it gives us an opportunity to talk with you alone."

"No." She shook her head. "We'll never be back together. I don't *want* to be with Eric. No psychologist, even one of yours, can change that. I hate Eric and I hate all this crap you're mixed up in. I hate you 'Starmen, and everyone on Terra feels the same way—I wish you'd get off the planet, I wish we'd never gotten into the war." Impotently, with frenzy, she glared at him.

"Cool off, Kathy." Corning remained unruffled.

"God, I wish Virgil were here; he's not afraid of you—he's one of the few people on Terra—"

"No one on Terra," Corning said absently, "has that status. It's time you faced reality; we could, you know, take you to Lilistar, instead of killing you . . . had you thought about that, Kathy?"

"Oh God." She shuddered. Don't take me to Lilistar, she said to herself, praying in silence. At least let me stay here on Terra with people I know. I'll go back to Eric; I'll *beg* him to take me back. "Listen," she said aloud. "I'm not worrying about Eric. It isn't what you might do to him that frightens me." It's myself, she thought.

"We know that, Kathy," Corning said, nodding. "So this really ought to please you, when you examine it without distracting emotion. By the way . . ." Dipping into the briefcase, Corning brought out a handful of capsules; he laid one on the kitchen table and the capsule rolled off and fell to the floor. "No offense meant, Kathy, but—" He shrugged. "It is addictive. From even one exposure, such as you indulged yourself in at 45 Avila Street last night. And Chris Plout isn't going to get you any more." Picking up the capsule of JJ-180 which had fallen to the kitchen floor, he held it out to Kathy.

"It couldn't be," she said faintly, declining. "After just one try. I've taken dozens of drugs before and never—" She regarded him then. "You bastards," she said. "I don't believe it and anyhow, even if it is true, I can get unaddicted—there're clinics."

"Not for JJ-180." Returning the capsule to his briefcase, Corning added casually, "*We* can free you of your addiction, not here but at a clinic in our own system . . . perhaps later we can arrange this. Or you can stay on it and we can supply you the rest of your life. Which won't be long."

"Even to break a drug habit," Kathy said, "I wouldn't go to Lilistar. I'll go to the reegs; it's their drug—you said so. They must know more about it than you do if they invented it." Turning her back to Corning, she walked to the living room closet and got her coat. "I'm going to work. Good-by." She opened the door to the hall. Neither 'Starman made a move to halt her.

It must be true, then, she thought. JJ-180 must be as addictive as they say. I haven't got a goddam chance; they know it and I know it. I have to co-operate with them or try to escape all the way across to the reeg lines, where it originates, and even then I'd still be addicted; I wouldn't have gained anything. And the reegs would probably kill me.

Corning said, "Take my card, Kathy." He walked to her, extending the small white square. "When you find yourself requiring the drug, must at any cost have it—" He dropped the card into the breast pocket of her coat. "Come and see me. We'll be expecting you, dear; we'll see you're supplied." He added, as an afterthought, "Of course it's addictive, Kathy; that's why we put you on it." He smiled at her.

Shutting the door after her, Kathy made her way blindly to the elevator, numbed now to the point where she felt nothing, not even fear. Only a vague emptiness inside her, the vacuum left by the extinction of hope, of the ability even to conceive a possibility of escape.

But Virgil Ackerman could help me, she said to herself as she entered the elevator and touched the button. I'll go to him; he'll know exactly what I should do. I'll never work with the 'Starmen, addiction or not; I won't co-operate with them about Eric.

But she knew, before long, that she would.

Six

IT was during the early afternoon, as she sat in her office at TF&D arranging for the purchase of a 1935 artifact, a reasonably unworn Decca record of the Andrews Sisters singing "Bei Mir Bist Du Schön," that Kathy Sweetscent felt the first withdrawal symptoms.

Her hands became oddly heavy.

With extreme care she put the delicate record down. And there was a physiognomic alteration in the objects around her. While at 45 Avila Street, under the influence of JJ-180, she had experienced the world as consisting of airy, penetrable, and benign entities, like so many bubbles; she had found herself able—at least in hallucination—to pass through them at will. Now, in the familiar environment of her office, she experienced a transformation of reality along the lines of an ominous progression: ordinary things, whichever way she looked, seemed to be gaining density. They were no longer susceptible to being moved or changed, affected in any way, by her.

And, from another viewpoint, she simultaneously experienced the oppressive change as taking place within her own body. From either standpoint the ratio between herself, her physical powers, and the outside world had altered for the worst; she experienced herself as growing progressively more and more helpless in the literal physical sense—there was, with each passing moment, less which she could do. The ten-inch Decca record, for instance. It lay within touch of her fingers, but suppose she reached out for it? The record would evade her. Her hand, clumsy with unnatural weight, hobbled by the internal gathering of density, would crush or break the record; the concept of performing intricate, skillful actions in reference to the record seemed out of the question. Refinements of motion were no longer a property belonging to her; only gross, sinking mass remained.

Wisely, she realized that this told her something about JJ-180; it lay in the class of thalamic stimulants. And now, in this withdrawal period, she was suffering a deprivation of thalamic energy; these changes, experienced as taking place in the outside world and in her body, were in actuality minute alterations of the metabolism of her brain. But—

This knowledge did not help her. For these changes in herself and her world were not beliefs; they were authentic experiences, reported by the normal sensory channels, imposed on her consciousness against her will. As stimuli they could not be avoided. And—the alteration of the world's physiognomy continued; the end was not in sight. In panic she thought, How far will this go? How much worse can it get? Certainly not much worse . . . the impenetrability of even the smallest objects around her now seemed almost infinite; she sat rigidly, unable to move, incapable of thrusting her great body into any new relationship with the crushingly heavy objects that surrounded her and seemed to be pressing nearer and nearer.

And, even as the objects in her office settled massively against her, they became, on another level, remote; they receded in a meaningful, terrifying fashion. They were losing, she realized, their animation, their—so to speak—working souls. The animae which inhabited them were departing as her powers of psychological projection deteriorated. The objects had lost their heritage of the familiar; by degrees they became cold, remote, and—hostile. Into the vacuum left by the decline in her relatedness to them the things surrounding her achieved their original isolation from the taming forces which normally emanated from the human mind; they became raw, abrupt, with jagged edges capable of cutting, gashing, inflicting fatal wounds. She did not dare stir. Death, in potentiality, lay inherent in every object; even the hand-wrought brass ash tray on her desk had become irregular, and in its lack of symmetry it obtained projecting planes, shot out surfaces which, like spines, could tear her open if she was stupid enough to come near.

The combox on her desk buzzed. Lucile Sharp, Virgil Ackerman's secretary, said, "Mrs. Sweetscent, Mr. Ackerman would like to see you in his office. I'd suggest you bring along the new 'Bei Mir Bist Du Schön' record you purchased today; he expressed interest in it."

"Yes," Kathy said, and the effort almost buried her; she ceased breathing and sat with her rib-cage inert, the basic physiological processes slowing under the pressure, dying by degrees. And then, somehow, she breathed one breath; she filled her lungs and then exhaled raggedly, noisily. For the moment she had escaped. But it was all worsening. What next? She rose to her feet, stood. So this is how it feels to be hooked on JJ-180, she thought. She managed to pick up the Decca record. Its dark edges were like knife blades sawing into her hands as she carried it across the office to the door. Its hostility toward her, its inanimate and yet ferocious desire to inflict destruction on her, became overwhelming; she cringed from the disc's touch.

And dropped it.

The record lay on the thick carpet, apparently unbroken. But how to pick it up once more? How to drag it loose from the nap, the backdrop, surrounding it? Because the record no longer seemed separate; it had fused. With the carpet, the floor, the walls, and now everything in the office, it presented a single indivisible, unchangeable surface, without rupture. No one could come or go within this cubelike spaciality; every place was already filled, complete—nothing could change because everything was present already.

My God, Kathy thought as she stood gazing down at the record by her feet. I can't free myself; I'm going to remain here, and they'll find me like this and know something's terribly wrong. This is catalepsy!

She was still standing there when the office door opened and Jonas Ackerman, briskly, with a jovial expression on his smooth, youthful face, entered, strode up to her, saw the record, bent unhinderedly down and gently lifted it up and placed it in her outstretched hands.

"Jonas," she said in a slow, thickened voice, "I—need medical help. I'm sick."

"Sick how?" He stared at her with concern, his face twisted up, wriggling, she thought, like nests of snakes. His emotion overpowered her; it was a sickening, fetid force. "My God," Jonas said, "what a time you picked—Eric's not here today, he's in Cheyenne, and we haven't got the new man that's replacing him yet. But I could drive you to the Tijuana Government Clinic. What is it?" He gripped her arm, pinching her flesh. "I think you're just blue because Eric's gone."

"Take me upstairs," she managed to say. "To Virgil."

"Boy, you *do* sound awful," Jonas said. "Yes, I'll be glad to get you upstairs to the old man; maybe he'll know what to do." He guided her toward the office door. "Maybe I better take that record; you look like you're about to drop it again."

It could not have taken more than two minutes to reach Virgil Ackerman's office and yet to her the ordeal consumed a vast interval. When she found herself facing Virgil at last she was exhausted; she panted for breath, unable to speak. It was just too goddam much for her.

Eying her curiously, and then with alarm, Virgil said in his thin, penetrating voice, "Kathy, you better go home today; fix yourself up with an armful of woman type magazines and a drink, propped up in bed—"

"Leave me alone," she heard herself say. "Christ," she said, then, in despair. "*Don't* leave me alone, Mr. Ackerman; please!"

"Well, make up your mind," Virgil said, still scrutinizing her. "I can see that Eric's leaving here and going to Cheyenne to—"

"No," she said. "I'm okay." Now it had worn off a little; she felt as if she had imbibed some strength from him, perhaps because he had so much. "Here's a fine item for Wash-35." She turned to Jonas for the record. "It was one of the most popular tunes of the times. This and 'The Music Goes Round and Round.'" Taking the record, she placed it before him on his big desk. I'm not going to die, she thought; I'm going to get through this and recover my health. "I'll tell you what else I have a line on, Mr. Ackerman." She seated herself in a chair by the desk, wanting to conserve what energy she had. "A private recording which someone made, at the time, of Alexander Woollcott on his program, 'The Town Crier.' So the next time we're up at Wash-35 we'll be able to listen to Woollcott's actual voice. And not an imitation. As we're doing."

"'The Town Crier'!" Virgil exclaimed in childish joy. "My favorite program!"

"I'm reasonably sure I can get it," Kathy said. "Of course, until I actually pay over the money there could still be a hitch. I have to fly out to Boston to make the final arrangements; the recording is there, in the possession of a rather shrewd

spinster-lady named Edith B. Scruggs. It was made on a
Packard-Bell Phon-o-cord, she tells me in her correspondence."

"Kathy," Virgil Ackerman said, "if you can actually turn up
an authentic recording of the voice of Alexander Woollcott—
I'm going to raise your salary, so help me God. Mrs. Sweetscent, sweetheart, I'm in love with you because of what you do
for me. Was Woollcott's radio program over WMAL or WJSV?
Research that for me, will you? Go through those '35 copies of
the *Washington Post*—and by the way, that reminds me. That
American Weekly with the article on the Sargasso Sea. I think
we'll finally decide to exclude that from Wash-35 because when
I was a boy my parents didn't take the Hearst papers; I only
saw it when I—"

"Just a moment, Mr. Ackerman," Kathy said, raising her
hand.

He cocked his head expectantly. "Yes, Kathy?"

"What if I went to Cheyenne and joined Eric?"

"But—" Virgil bleated, gesturing. "I need you!"

"For a while," she said. Maybe that will be enough, she
thought. They might not demand any more. "You let *him* go,"
she said, "and he keeps you alive; he's a lot more vital than
I am."

"But Molinari needs him. And he doesn't need you; he has
no babyland he's building; he's not a bit interested in the
past—he's full of gas about the future, like an adolescent."
Virgil looked stricken. "I can't spare you, Kathy; losing Eric
was bad enough but the deal in his case is that I can send for
him any time I get into difficulty. I *had* to let him go; it was
the patriotic thing, in wartime—I didn't want to; in fact I'm
scared as hell without him. But not you." His tone became
plaintive. "No, that's too much. Eric swore to me when we
were at Wash-35 that you wouldn't want to go with him." He
shot a mute, appealing glance at Jonas. "Make her stay, Jonas."

Rubbing his chin thoughtfully, Jonas said to her, "You don't
love Eric, Kathy. I've talked to you and to him; you both tell
me your domestic woes. You're as far apart from each other as
it's possible to be and not commit an outright crime . . . I
don't get this."

"I believed that," she said, "while he was here. But I kidded myself. Now I know better, and I'm sure he feels the same way."

"Are you sure?" Jonas said acutely. "Call him." He indicated the vidphone on Virgil's desk. "See what he says. Frankly I think you're better off separated, and I have no doubt Eric knows it."

Kathy said, "May I be excused to go? I want to get back down to my office." She felt sick at her stomach and achingly frightened. Her damaged, drug-addicted body yearned for relief and in its thrashings it directed her actions; it was compelling her to follow Eric to Cheyenne. Despite what the Ackermans said. She could not stop, and even now in her confusion she could read the future; she could not escape the drug JJ-180—the 'Starmen had been correct. She would have to go back to them, follow up on the card that Corning had given her. God, she thought, if I only could tell Virgil. I have to tell someone.

And then she thought, I'll tell Eric. He's a doctor; he'll be able to help me. I'll go to Cheyenne for that, *not for them.*

"Will you do me one favor?" Jonas Ackerman was saying to her. "For heaven's sake, Kathy; listen." Again he squeezed her arm.

"I'm listening," she said with irritation. "And let go." She tugged her arm away, stepped back from him, feeling rage. "Don't treat me like this; I can't stand it." She glared at him.

Carefully, in a deliberately calm voice, Jonas said to her, "We'll let you follow your husband to Cheyenne, Kathy, *if* you promise to wait twenty-four hours before you go."

"Why?" She could not understand.

"So that this initial period of shock at the separation has a chance to wear off," Jonas said. "I'm hoping that in twenty-four hours you'll see your way clear to changing your mind. And meanwhile—" He glanced at Virgil; the old man nodded in agreement. "I'll stay with you," Jonas said to her. "All day and all night, if necessary."

Appalled, she said, "Like hell you will. I won't—"

"I know there's something wrong with you," Jonas said quietly. "It's obvious. I don't think you should be left alone. I'm making it my responsibility to see that nothing happens to you." He added in a low voice, "You're too valuable to us to do something terminal." Again, and this time with harsh firmness, he took hold of her arm. "Come on; let's go downstairs to your office—it'll do you good to get wrapped up in your work, and I'll just sit quietly, not interfering. After work tonight I'll fly you up to L.A. to Spingler's for dinner; I know you like sea food." He guided her toward the door of the office.

She thought, *I'll get away*. You're not that smart, Jonas; sometime today, perhaps tonight, I'll lose you and go to Cheyenne. Or rather, she thought with nausea and an upsurge of her former terror, I'll lose you, dump you, slip away from you in the labyrinth that's the night city of Tijuana, where all kinds of things, some of them terrible, some of them wonderful and full of beauty, happen. Tijuana will be too much for you. It's almost too much for me. And I know it fairly well; I've spent so much of my time, my life, in Tijuana at night.

And look how it's worked out, she thought bitterly. I wanted to find something pure and mystical in life and instead I wound up spliced to people who hate us, who dominate our race. Our ally, she thought. We ought to be fighting them; it's clear to me now. If I ever get to see Molinari alone at Cheyenne—and maybe I will—I'll tell him that, tell him we have the wrong ally and the wrong enemy.

"Mr. Ackerman," she said, turning urgently to Virgil. "I have to go to Cheyenne to tell the Secretary something. It affects all of us; it has to do with the war effort."

Virgil Ackerman said drily, "Tell me and I'll tell him. There's a better chance that way; you'll never get in to see him . . . not unless you're one of his bambinos or cousins."

"That's it," she said. "I'm his child." It made perfect sense to her; all of them on Terra were children of the UN Secretary. And they had been expecting their father to lead them to safety. But somehow he had failed.

Unresistingly, she followed Jonas Ackerman. "I know what you're doing," she said to him. "You're using this opportunity, with Eric away and me in this terrible state, to take sexual advantage of me."

Jonas laughed. "Well, we'll see." His laugh, to her, did not sound guilty; it sounded sleekly confident.

"Yes," she agreed, thinking of the 'Star policeman Corning.

"We'll see how lucky you are in making out with me. Personally I wouldn't bet on it." She did not bother to remove his big, determined hand from her shoulder; it would only reappear.

"You know," Jonas said, "if I didn't know better, I'd say from the way you've been acting that you're on a substance which we call JJ-180." He added, "But you couldn't be because there's no way you could get hold of it."

Staring at him Kathy said, "What—" She couldn't go on.

"It's a drug," Jonas said. "Developed by one of our subsidiaries."

"It wasn't developed by the reegs?"

"Frohedadrine, or JJ-180, was developed in Detroit, last year, by a firm which TF&D controls called Hazeltine Corporation. It's a major weapon in the war—or will be when it's in production, which will be later this year."

"Because," she said numbly, "it's so addictive?"

"Hell no. Many drugs are addictive, starting with the opium derivatives. Because of the nature of the hallucinations it causes its users." He explained, "It's hallucinogenic, as LSD was."

Kathy said, "Tell me about the hallucinations."

"I can't; that's classified military information."

Laughing sharply, she said, "Oh God—so the only way I could find out would be to take it."

"How can you take it? It's not available, and even when it's in production we wouldn't conceivably under any circumstances allow our own population to use it—the stuff's toxic!" He glared at her. "Don't even talk about using it; every test animal to which it was administered died. Forget I even mentioned it; I thought Eric had probably told you about it—I shouldn't have brought it up, but you have been acting strangely; it made me think of JJ-180 because I'm so scared—we all are—that someone, some way, will get hold of it on the domestic market, one of our own people."

Kathy said, "Let's hope that never happens." She felt like laughing, still; the whole thing was insane. The 'Starmen had obtained the drug on Terra but pretended to have gotten it from the reegs. Poor Terra, she thought. We can't even get credit for this, for this noxious, destructive chemical which destroys the mind—as Jonas says, a potent weapon of war. And who's using it? Our ally. And on whom? On us. The irony is complete; it forms a circle. Certainly cosmic justice that a Terran should be one of the first to become addicted to it.

Frowning, Jonas said, "You asked if JJ-180 hadn't been developed by the enemy; that suggests you have heard of it. So Eric did mention it to you. It's all right; only knowledge of its properties is classified, not its existence. The reegs know we've been experimenting with drug warfare for decades, back into the twentieth century. It's one of Terra's specialties." He chuckled.

"Maybe we'll win after all," Kathy said. "That ought to cheer up Gino Molinari. Perhaps he'll be able to stay in office with the assistance of a few new miracle weapons. Is he counting on this? Does he know?"

"Of course Molinari knows; Hazeltine has kept him informed at every stage of development. But for chrissake don't go and—"

"I won't get you in trouble," Kathy said. I think I'll get you addicted to JJ-180, she said to herself. That's what you deserve; everyone who helped develop it, who knows about it. Stay with me night and day during the next twenty-four hours, she thought. Eat with me, go to bed with me, and by the time it's over you'll be earmarked for death just as I am. And then, she thought, maybe I can get Eric on it. Him most of all.

I'll carry it with me to Cheyenne, Kathy decided. Infect everyone there, the Mole and his entourage. And for a good reason.

They'll be forced to discover a method of breaking the addiction. Their own lives will depend on it, not just mine. And for me alone it wouldn't be worth seeking; even Eric wouldn't have tried, and certainly Corning and his people don't care— no one cares about me, when you get right down to it.

This was probably not at all what Corning and those above him had in mind in sending her to Cheyenne. But that was just too bad; this was what she intended to do.

"It'll go in their water supply," Jonas was explaining. "The reegs—they maintain huge central water sources, as Mars did once. JJ-180 will be introduced there, carried throughout their

planet. I admit it sounds desperate on our part, a—you know.
A tour de force. But actually it's very rational and reasonable."

"I'm not criticizing it at all," Kathy said. "In fact I think the
idea sounds brilliant."

The elevator arrived; they entered and descended.

"Look what the ordinary citizen of Terra doesn't know,"
Kathy said. "He goes merrily on about his daily life . . . it
would never occur to him that his government has developed
a drug that in one exposure turns you into a—how would you
put it, Jonas? Something less than a robant? Certainly less than
human. I wonder where you would place it on the evolutionary ladder."

"I never told you that one exposure to JJ-180 meant addiction," Jonas said. "Eric must have told you that."

"With the lizards of the Jurassic Period," Kathy decided.
"Things with tiny brains and immense tails. Creatures with
almost no mentalities; just reflex machines acting out the externals of living, going through the motions but not actually
there. Right?"

"Well," Jonas said, "it's reegs that'll be receiving the drug; I
wouldn't waste any tears on reegs."

"I'd waste a tear on anything," Kathy said, "that got hooked
by JJ-180. I hate it; I wish—" She broke off. "Don't mind me;
I'm just upset by Eric's leaving. I'll be okay." To herself she
wondered when she would have an opportunity to look for
Corning. And get more capsules of the drug. It was clear now
that she had become an addict. By now she had to face it.

She felt only resignation.

At noon, in the neat, modern, but excessively small conapt
provided him by the mystifying workings of the higher governmental authorities at Cheyenne, Dr. Eric Sweetscent finished reading the medical charts on his new patient—referred
to throughout the enormous body of writings merely as "Mr.
Brown." Mr. Brown, he reflected as he locked the folio back in
its unbreakable plastic box, is a sick man, but his sickness simply could not be diagnosed, at least in the customary way.
Because—and this was the odd thing, for which Teagarden
had not prepared him—the patient had shown, over the years,

symptoms of major organic diseases, symptoms not associated with psychosomatic disorders. There had been at one time a malignancy in the liver which had metastasized—and yet Mr. Brown had not died. And the malignancy had gone away. Anyhow it was not there now; tests during the last two years proved that. An exploratory operation had even been performed, finally, and Mr. Brown's liver had not even shown the degeneracy anticipated in a man of his age.

It was the liver of a youth of nineteen or twenty.

And this oddity had been observed in other organs subjected to acute examination. But Mr. Brown was failing in his over-all powers; palpably, he was in the process of declining— he looked considerably older than his chronological age, and the aura around him was one of ill health. It was as if his body on a purely physiological level were growing younger while his essence, his total psychobiological *Gestalt*, aged naturally—in fact failed conspicuously.

Whatever physiological force it was that maintained him organically, Mr. Brown was not receiving any benefit therefrom, except of course that he had not died of the malignant tumor in his liver or the earlier one detected in his spleen, or the surely fatal cancer of the prostate gland which had gone undetected during his third decade.

Mr. Brown was alive—but just barely so. Throughout, his body was overworked and in a state of deterioration; take his circulatory system, for instance. Brown's blood pressure was 220—despite vasodilators administered orally; already his eyesight had been materially affected. And yet, Eric reflected, Brown would undoubtedly surmount this as he had every other ailment; one day it would simply go away, even though he refused to stay on the prescribed diet and did not respond to reserpine.

The outstanding fact was simply that Mr. Brown had had at one time or another almost every serious disease known, from infarcts in his lungs to hepatitis. He was a perambulating symposium of illness, never well, never functioning properly; at any given time some vital portion of his body was affected. And then—

In some fashion he had cured himself. And without the use of artiforgs. It was as if Brown practiced some folk-style, homeopathic medicine, some idiotic herbal remedy which he had never disclosed to his attending physicians. And probably never would.

Brown needed to be sick. His hypochondriasis was real; he did not merely have hysterical symptoms—he had true diseases which usually turned the patient into a terminal case. If this was hysteria, a variety of a purely psychological complaint, Eric had never run across it before. And yet, despite this, Eric had the intuition that all these illnesses had existed for a reason; they were engendered from the complexity, the undisclosed depths, of Mr. Brown's psyche.

Three times in his life Mr. Brown had given himself cancer. But how? And—why?

Perhaps it arose from his death wish. And each time, Mr. Brown halted at the brink, pulled himself back. He needed to be sick—but not to die. The suicide wish, then, was spurious.

This was important to know. If it was so, Mr. Brown would fight to survive—would fight against the very thing he had hired Eric to bring about.

Therefore Mr. Brown would be an exceedingly difficult patient. To say the least. And all this—beyond doubt—functioned at an unconscious level; Mr. Brown was certainly unaware of his twin, opposing drives.

The door chimes of the conapt sounded. He went to answer —and found himself facing an official-looking individual in a natty business suit. Producing identification, the man explained, "Secret Service, Dr. Sweetscent. Secretary Molinari needs you; he's in a good deal of pain so we'd better hurry."

"Of course." Eric dashed to the closet for his coat; a moment later he and the Secret Service man were hiking toward the parked wheel. "More abdominal pains?" Eric asked.

"Now the pains seem to have shifted over to his left side," the Secret Service man said as he piloted the wheel out into traffic. "In the region of his heart."

"He didn't describe them as feeling as if a great hand was pressing down on him, did he?"

"No, he's just lying there groaning. And asking for you." The Secret Service man seemed to take it matter-of-factly; evidently for him this was old and familiar. The Secretary, after all, was always sick.

Presently they had reached the UN White House and Eric was descending by in-track. If only I could install an artiforg, he reflected. It would end all this—

But it was clear to him, now that he had read the file, why Molinari refused artiforg transplant on principle. If he accepted a transplant he would recover; the ambiguity of his existence—hovering between illness and health—would cease. His twin drives would be resolved in favor of health. Hence the delicate psychic dynamism would be upset and Molinari would be delivered over to one of the two forces striving for mastery within him. And this he could not afford to do.

"This way, doctor." The Secret Service man led him down a corridor, to a door at which several uniformed police stood. They stepped aside and Eric entered.

In the center of the room, in a vast rumpled bed, lay Gino Molinari, on his back, watching a television set fixed to the ceiling. "I'm dying, doctor," Molinari said, turning his head. "I think these pains are coming from my heart now. It probably was my heart all the time." His face, enlarged and florid, shone with sweat.

Eric said, "We'll run an EKG on you."

"No, I had that, about ten minutes ago; it showed nothing. My illness is too goddam subtle for your instruments to detect. That doesn't mean it's not there. I've heard of people who've had massive coronaries and have taken EKGs and nothing showed up; isn't that a fact? Listen, doctor. I know something that you don't. You wonder why I have these pains. Our ally— our partner in this war. They've got a master plan which includes seizing Tijuana Fur & Dye; they showed me the document—they're that confident. They've got an agent planted in your firm already. But I'm telling you in case I die suddenly from this ailment; I could go any minute, you know that."

"Did you tell Virgil Ackerman?" Eric asked.

"I started to but—Christ, how can you tell an old man something like that? He doesn't understand what sort of things go on in an all-out war; this is nothing, this seizing of Terra's major industries. This is probably only the beginning."

"Now that I know," Eric said, "I feel I should tell Virgil."

"Okay, tell him," Molinari grated. "Maybe you can find a

way. I was going to when we were at Wash-35 but—" He rolled in pain. "Do something for me, doctor; this is killing me!"

Eric gave him an intravenous injection of morprocaine and the UN Secretary quieted.

"You just don't know," Molinari mumbled in a lulled, relaxed voice, "what I'm up against with these 'Starmen. I did my best to keep them off us, doctor." He added, "I don't feel the pain now; what you did seems to have taken care of it."

Eric asked, "When are they going ahead with seizing TF&D? Soon?"

"A few days. Week. Elastic schedule. It makes a drug they're interested in . . . you probably don't know. Neither do I. In fact I don't know anything, doctor; that's the whole secret of my situation. Nobody tells me a thing. Even you; what's wrong with me, for instance—you won't tell me that, I bet."

To one of the watching Secret Service men Eric said, "Where can I find a vidphone booth?"

"Don't go off," Molinari said, from his bed, half rising. "The pain would come back right away; I can tell. What I want you to do is get Mary Reineke here; I need to talk to her, now that I'm feeling better. See, doctor, I haven't told her about it, about how sick I am. And don't you, either; she needs to hold an idealized image of me. Women are like that; to love a man they have to look up to him, glorify him. See?"

"But when she sees you lying in bed doesn't she think—"

"Oh, she knows I'm sick; she just doesn't know that it's fatal. You see?"

Eric said, "I promise I won't tell her it's fatal."

"Is it?" Molinari's eyes flew open in alarm.

"Not to my knowledge," Eric said. Cautiously he added, "Anyhow, I learn from your file that you've survived several customarily fatal illnesses, including cancer of—"

"I don't want to talk about it. I get depressed when I'm reminded how many times I've had cancer."

"I should think—"

"That it would elate me that I recovered? No, *because maybe the next time I'm not going to recover*. I mean, sooner or later it'll get me, and before my job is done. And what'll happen to Terra then? You figure it out; you make an educated guess."

"I'll go and contact Miss Reineke for you," Eric said, and

started toward the door of the room. A Secret Service man detached himself to lead the way to the vidphone.

Outside in the corridor the Secret Service man said in a low voice, "Doctor, there's an illness on level three, one of the White House cooks passed out about an hour ago; Dr. Teagarden's with him and wants you for a confab."

"Certainly," Eric said. "I'll look in on him before I make my phone call." He followed the Secret Service man to the elevator.

In the White House dispensary he found Dr. Teagarden. "I needed you," Teagarden said at once, "because you're an artiforg man; this is a clear case of angina pectoris and we're going to need an org-trans right away. I assume you brought at least one heart with you."

"Yes," Eric murmured. "Had there been a history of heart trouble with this patient?"

"Not until two weeks ago," Teagarden said. "When he had a mild attack. Then of course dorminyl was administered, twice daily. And he seemed to recover. But now—"

"What's the relationship between this man's angina and the Secretary's pains?"

" 'Relationship'? Is there one?"

"Doesn't it seem strange? Both men develop severe abdominal pains at about the same time—"

"But in the case of McNeil, here," Teagarden said, leading Eric to the bed, "the diagnosis is unmistakable. Whereas with Secretary Molinari no such diagnosis as angina can be made; the symptoms are not there. So I don't see the relationship." Teagarden added, "Anyhow this is a very tense place, doctor; people get sick here regularly."

"It still seems—"

"In any case," Teagarden said, "the problem is simply a technical one; transplant the fresh heart and that's that."

"Too bad we can't do the same upstairs." Eric bent over the cot on which the patient McNeil lay. So this was the man who had the ailment which Molinari imagined *he* had. Which came first? Eric wondered. McNeil or Gino Molinari? Which is cause and which effect—assuming that such a relationship exists, and that is a mighty tenuous assumption at best. As Teagarden points out.

But it would be interesting to know, for instance, if anyone in the vicinity had cancer of the prostate gland when Gino had it . . . and the other cancers, infarcts, hepatitis, and whatever else as well.

It might be worth checking the medical records of the entire White House staff, he conjectured.

"Need me to assist in the org-trans?" Teagarden asked. "If not I'll go upstairs to the Secretary. There's a White House nurse who can help you; she was here a minute ago."

"I don't need you. What I'd like is a list of all the current complaints among members of the local entourage; everyone who's in physical contact with Molinari from day to day, whether these people are staff members or frequent official visitors—whatever their posts are. Can that be done?"

"With the staff, yes," Teagarden said. "But not with visitors; we have no medical files on them. Obviously." He eyed Eric.

"I have a feeling," Eric said, "that the moment a fresh heart is transplanted to McNeil here the Secretary's pains will go away. And later records will show that as of this date the Secretary recovered from severe angina pectoris."

Teagarden's expression fused over, became opaque. "Well," he said, and shrugged. "Metaphysics, along with surgery. We've obtained a rare combination in you, doctor."

"Would you say that Molinari is empathic enough to develop every ailment suffered by every person around him? And I don't mean just hysterically; I mean he genuinely experiences it. *Gets* it."

"No such empathic faculty," Teagarden said, "if you can bring yourself to dignify it by calling it a faculty, is known to exist."

"But you've seen the file," Eric pointed out quietly. He opened his instrument case and began to assemble the robant, self-guiding tools which he would need for the transplant of the artificial heart.

Seven

A FTER the operation—it required only half an hour's labor on his part—Eric Sweetscent, accompanied by two Secret Service men, set off for the apartment of Mary Reineke.

"She's dumb," the man to his left said, gratuitously.

The other Secret Service man, older and grayer, said, "'Dumb'? She knows what makes the Mole work; nobody else has been able to dope that out."

"There's nothing to dope out," the first—youthful—Secret Service man said. "It's just the meeting of two vacuums and that's the same as one big vacuum."

"Yeah, some vacuum. He rises to the UN Secretaryship; you think you or anybody else you know could do that? Here's her conapt." The older Secret Service man halted and indicated a door. "Don't act surprised when you see her," he told Eric. "I mean, when you see she's just a kid."

"I was told," Eric said. And rang the bell. "I know all about it."

"'You know all about it,'" the Secret Service man to his left mocked. "Good for you—without even seeing her. Maybe you'll be the next UN Secretary after the Mole finally succumbs."

The door opened. An astonishingly small, dark, pretty girl wearing a man's red silk shirt with the tails out and tapered, tight slacks stood facing them. She held a pair of cuticle scissors; evidently she had been trimming and improving her nails, which Eric saw were long and luminous.

"I'm Dr. Sweetscent. I've joined Gino Molinari's staff." He almost said *your father's* staff; he caught the words barely in time.

"I know," Mary Reineke said. "And he wants me; he's feeling lousy. Just a minute." She turned to look for a coat, disappearing momentarily.

"A high school girl," the Secret Service man on Eric's left said. He shook his head. "For any ordinary guy it'd be a felony."

"Shut up," his companion snapped, as Mary Reineke returned wearing a heavy, blue-black, large-button, navy-style jacket.

"Couple of smart guys," Mary said to the Secret Service men. "You two take off; I want to talk to Dr. Sweetscent without you sticking your big fat ears into it."

"Okay, Mary." Grinning, the Secret Service men departed. Eric was alone in the corridor with the girl in the heavy jacket, pants and slippers.

They walked in silence and then Mary said, "How is he?"

Cautiously, Eric said, "In many ways exceptionally healthy. Almost unbelievably so. But—"

"But he's dying. All the time. Sick, but it just goes on and on—I wish it would end; I wish he'd—" She paused thoughtfully. "No, I don't wish that. If Gino died I'd be booted out. Along with all the cousins and uncles and bambinos. There'd be a general housecleaning of all the debris that clutters up this place." Her tone was amazingly bitter and fierce; Eric glanced sharply at her, taken aback. "Are you here to cure him?" Mary asked.

"Well, I can try. I can at least—"

"Or are you here to administer the—what do they call it? The final blow. You know. Coup something."

"Coup de grace," Eric said.

"Yes." Mary Reineke nodded. "Well? Which did you come for? Or don't you know? Are you as confused as he is, is that it?"

"I'm not confused," Eric said, after a pause.

"Then you know your duty. You're the artiforg man, aren't you? The top org-trans surgeon . . . I read about you in *Time*, I think. Don't you think *Time* is a highly informative magazine in all fields? I read it from cover to cover every week, especially the medical and scientific sections."

Eric said, "Do—you go to school?"

"I graduated. High school, not college; I've got no interest in what they call 'higher learning.'"

"What did you want to be?"

"What do you mean?" She eyed him suspiciously.

"I mean what career did you intend to enter?"

"I don't need a career."

"But you didn't know that; you had no way of telling you'd wind up—" He gestured. "Be here at the White House."

"Sure I did. I always knew, all my life. Since I was three."

"How?"

"I was—I am—one of those precogs. I could tell the future." Her tone was calm.

"Can you still do it?"

"Sure."

"Then you don't need to ask me why I'm here; you can look ahead and see what I do."

"What you do," Mary said, "isn't that important; it doesn't register." She smiled then, showing beautiful, regular, white teeth.

"I can't believe that," he said, nettled.

"Then be your own precog; don't ask me what I know if you're not interested in the results. Or not able to accept them. This is a cutthroat environment, here at the White House; a hundred people are clamoring to get Gino's attention all the time, twenty-four hours a day. You have to fight your way through the throngs. That's why Gino gets sick—or rather pretends to be sick."

" 'Pretends,' " Eric said.

"He's an hysteric; you know, where they think they have illnesses but really don't. It's his way of keeping people off his back; he's just too sick to deal with them." She laughed merrily. "You know that—you've examined him. He doesn't actually have anything."

"Have you read the file?"

"Sure."

"Then you know that Gino Molinari has had cancer at three separate occasions."

"So what?" She gestured. "Hysterical cancer."

"In the medical profession no such—"

"Which are you going to believe, your textbooks or what you see with your own eyes?" She studied him intently. "If you expect to survive here you better become a realist; you better learn to detect facts when you meet up with them. You think Teagarden is glad you're here? You're a menace to his status; he's already begun trying to find ways to discredit you—or haven't you noticed?"

"No," he said. "I haven't noticed."

"Then you haven't got a chance. Teagarden will have you out of here so fast—" She broke off. Ahead lay the sick man's door and the two rows of Secret Service men. "You know why Gino has those pains actually? So he can be pampered. So people will wait on him as if he's a baby; he wants to be a baby again so he won't have grownup responsibilities. See?"

"Theories like that," Eric said, "sound so perfect, they're so glib, so easy to say—"

"But true," Mary said. "In this case." She pushed past the Secret Service men, opened the door, and entered. Going up to Gino's bed, she gazed down at him and said, "Get on your feet, you big lazy bastard."

Opening his eyes, Gino stirred leadenly. "Oh. It's you. Sorry, but I—"

"Sorry nothing," Mary said in a sharp voice. "You're not sick. Get up! I'm ashamed of you; everybody's ashamed of you. You're just scared and acting like a baby—how do you expect me to respect you when you act like this?"

After a time Gino said, "Maybe I don't expect you to." He seemed depressed more than anything else by the girl's tirade. Now he made out Eric. "You hear her, doctor?" he said gloomily. "Nobody can stop her; she comes in here when I'm dying and talks to me like that—maybe that's the reason I'm dying." He rubbed his stomach gingerly. "I don't feel them right now. I think that shot you gave me did it; what was in that?"

Not the shot, Eric thought, but the surgery downstairs on McNeil. Your complaint is gone because an assistant cook on the White House staff now has an artiforg heart. I was right.

"If you're okay—" Mary began.

"Okay," Molinari sighed. "I'll get up; just leave me alone, will you, for chrissake?" He stirred about, struggling to get from the bed. "Okay—I'll get up; will that satisfy you?" His voice rose to a shout of anger.

Turning to Eric, Mary Reineke said, "You see? I can get him out of bed; I can put him back on his feet like a man."

"Congratulations," Gino murmured sourly as he shakily rose to a standing position. "I don't need a medical staff; all I need is you. But I notice it was Dr. Sweetscent here who got rid of my pains, not you. What did you ever do but bawl me out? If I'm back up it's because of him." He passed by her, to the closet for his robe.

"He resents me," Mary said to Eric. "But underneath he knows I'm right." She seemed perfectly placid and sure of herself; she stood with her arms folded, watching the Secretary as he tied the sash of his blue robe and got on his deerskin slippers.

"Big-time," Molinari muttered to Eric, jerking his head at Mary. "She runs things—according to her."

"Do you have to do what she says?" Eric inquired.

Molinari laughed. "Sure. Don't I?"

"What happens if you don't? Does she make the heavens fall?"

"Yes, she pulls down everything." Molinari nodded. "It's a psionic talent she has . . . it's called *being a woman*. Like your wife Kathy. I'm glad to have her around; I like her. I don't care if she bawls me out—after all, I did get out of bed and it didn't hurt me; she was right."

"I always know when you're malingering," Mary said.

"Come with me, doctor," Molinari said to Eric. "There's something they've set up for me to watch; I want you to see it too."

Trailed by Secret Service men, they crossed the corridor and entered a guarded, locked room which Eric realized was a projection chamber; the far wall consisted of a permanent vidscreen installation on a grand scale.

"Me making a speech," Molinari explained to Eric as they seated themselves. He signaled and a video tape began to roll, projected on the large screen. "It'll be delivered tomorrow night, over all the TV networks. I want your opinion on it in advance, in case there's anything I should change." He glanced slyly at Eric, as if there was more he was not saying.

Why would he want my opinion? Eric wondered as he watched the image of the UN Secretary fill the screen. The Mole in full military regalia as C-in-C of Terra's armed forces: medals and arm bands and ribbons and, above all, the stiff marshal's hat with its visor partly shielding the round, heavy-jowled face so that only the lower part, the grimy chin, was visible with its disconcertingly harsh scowl.

And the jowls, unaccountably, were not flabby; they had become, for no reason which Eric could conjure up, firm and determined. It was a rocklike, severe face which showed on the screen, stern and strengthened by an inner authority that Eric had not seen before in the Mole . . . or had he?

Yes, he thought. But it had been years ago, when the Mole had first taken office, when he had been younger and there had not been the crushing responsibility. And now, on the screen, the Mole spoke. And his voice—*it was the old original voice from past times*; it was exactly as it had all been, a decade ago, before this terrible, losing war.

Chuckling, Molinari said from the deep, foam-rubber chair in which he lounged beside Eric, "I look pretty good, don't I?"

"You do." The speech rolled on, sonorous, even containing, now and then, a trace of the awesome, the majestic. And it was precisely this which Molinari had lost: he had become pitiable. On the screen the mature, dignified man in military garb expressed himself clearly in a voice that snapped out its sentences without hesitancy; the UN Secretary, in the video tape, demanded and informed, did not beg, did not turn to the electorate of Terra for help . . . he *told* them what to do in this period of crisis. And that was as it should be. But how had it been done? How did the pleading, hypochondriacal invalid, suffering from his eternal half-killing complaints, rise up and do this? Eric was mystified.

Beside him Molinari said, "It's a fake. That's not me." He grinned with delight as Eric stared first at him and then again at the screen.

"Then who is it?"

"It's nobody. It's a robant. General Robant Servant Enterprises made it up for me—this speech is its first appearance. Pretty good, like my old self; makes me feel young again just to watch it." And, Eric saw, the UN Secretary did seem more his old self; he had genuinely perked up as he sat watching the simulacrum on the screen. The Mole, above and beyond everyone else, was taken in by the ersatz spectacle; he was its first convert. "Want to see the thing? It's top secret, of course —only three or four people know about it, besides Dawson Cutter of GRS Enterprises, of course. But they'll keep it confidential; they're used to handling classified material in the process of war-contract letting." He thumped Eric on the back. "You're getting let in on one of the secrets of state—how does that feel? This is the way the modern state is run; there're things the electorate doesn't know, shouldn't know for their own good. All governments have functioned this way, not just mine. You imagine it's just mine? If you do you've got a lot to learn. I'm using a robant to make my speeches for me because at this point I don't—" He gestured "—present quite the proper visual image, despite the make-up technicians who work me over. It's just an impossible job." Now he had become dour, no longer joking. "So I gave up. I'm being realistic." He settled back in his chair, moodily.

"Who wrote the speech?"

"I did. I can still put together a political manifesto, depicting the situation, telling them how we stand and where we're going and what we've got to do. My mind is still there." The Mole tapped his big bulging forehead. "However, I naturally had help."

"'Help,'" Eric echoed.

"A man I want you to meet—a brilliant new young lawyer who acts as confidential adviser to me, without pay. Don Festenburg, a whiz; you'll be as impressed as I was. He has a knack for remolding, condensing, extracting the substance and presenting it in a few distilled sentences . . . I always had a tendency to run on at excessive length; everybody knows that. But not any more, not with Festenburg around. He programmed this simulacrum—he's really saved my life."

On the screen his synthetic image was saying commandingly, "—and gathering up the collective éclat of our several national societies, we as Terrans present a formidable association, more than just a planet but admittedly less, at the moment, than an interplanetary empire on the order of Lilistar . . . although perhaps—"

"I—would prefer not to have a look at the simulacrum," Eric decided.

Molinari shrugged. "It's an opportunity, but if you're not interested or if it distresses you—" He eyed Eric. "You'd rather retain your idealistic image of me; rather imagine that the thing talking up there on the screen is real." He laughed. "I thought a doctor, like a lawyer and a priest, could withstand the shock of seeing life as it is; I thought truth was your daily bread." He leaned toward Eric earnestly; under him his chair squeaked in protest, giving under his excessive weight. "I'm too old. I can't talk brilliantly any more. God knows I'd like to. But this is a solution; would it be better just to give up?"

"No," Eric admitted. That wouldn't solve their problems.

"So I use a robant substitute, speaking lines that Don Festenburg programmed. The point is: we'll go on. And that's what matters. So learn to live with it, doctor; grow up." His face was cold now, unyielding.

"Okay," Eric said after a moment.

Molinari tapped him on the shoulder and said in a low voice, "The 'Starmen don't know about this simulacrum and Don Festenburg's work; I don't want them to find out, doctor, because I'd like to impress them, too. You understand? In fact I'm sending a print of this video tape to Lilistar; it's already on the way. You want to know the truth, doctor? Frankly I'm more interested in impressing them than I am our own population. How does that strike you? Tell me honestly."

"It strikes me," Eric said, "as an acute commentary on our plight."

The Mole regarded him somberly. "Perhaps so. But what you don't realize is that this is nothing; if you had any idea of—"

"Don't tell me any more. Not right now."

On the screen the imitation of Gino Molinari boomed and expostulated, gesticulated to the unseen TV audience.

"Sure, sure," Molinari agreed, mollified. "Sorry to have bothered you with my troubles in the first place." Downcast, his face more lined and weary than before, he turned his attention back to the screen, to the healthy, vigorous, completely synthetic image of his earlier self.

In the kitchen of her conapt Kathy Sweetscent lifted a small paring knife with difficulty, attempted to cut a purple onion but found to her incredulity that she had somehow slashed her finger; she stood mutely holding the knife, watching the crimson drops slide from her finger to merge with the water sprinkled across her wrist. She could no longer handle even the most commonplace object. The damn drug! she thought with embittered fury. Every minute it's making me more powerless. Now everything defeats me. So how the hell am I going to fix dinner?

Standing behind her, Jonas Ackerman said with concern, "Something has to be done for you, Kathy." He watched her as she went to the bathroom for a Band-Aid. "Now you're spilling the Band-Aids everywhere; you can't even handle that." He complained, "If you'd tell me what it is, what—"

"Put the Band-Aid on for me, will you?" She stood silently as Jonas wrapped her cut finger. "It is JJ-180," she blurted suddenly, without premeditation. "I'm on it, Jonas. The 'Starmen did it. Please help me, get me off it. Okay?"

Shaken, Jonas said, "I—don't know exactly what I can do, because it's such a new drug. Of course we'll get in touch with our subsidiary right away. And the whole company will back you up, including Virgil."

"Go talk to Virgil right now."

"*Now?* Your time sense, Kathy; you feel this urgency because of the drug. I can see him tomorrow."

"Damn it, I'm not going to die because of this drug. So you better see him tonight, Jonas; do you understand?"

After a pause Jonas said, "I'll call him."

"The vidlines are tapped. By the 'Starmen."

"That's a paranoid idea. From the drug."

"I'm afraid of them." She was trembling. "They can do anything. You go and see Virgil face to face, Jonas; calling isn't enough. Or don't you care what happens to me?"

"Of course I care! Okay, I'll go and see the old man. But will you be all right alone?"

"Yes," Kathy said. "I'll just sit in the living room and do nothing. I'll just wait for you to come back with some kind of help. What could happen to me if I don't try to do anything, if I just sit there?"

"You might get yourself into a state of morbid agitation. You might be swamped by panic . . . start to run. If it's true you're on JJ-180—"

"It's true!" she said loudly. "Do you think I'm kidding?"

"Okay," Jonas said, giving in. He led her to the couch in the living room, sat her down. "God, I hope you'll be all right—I hope I'm not making a mistake." He was sweating and pale, his face wizened with worry. "See you in about half an hour, Kathy. Christ, if something goes wrong, Eric'll never forgive me and I won't blame him." The apartment door shut after him. He did not even say good-by.

She was alone.

At once she went to the vidphone and dialed. "A cab." She gave her address and hung up.

A moment later, her coat over her shoulders, she hurried from the building and out onto the nocturnal sidewalk.

When the autonomic cab had picked her up she instructed it by means of the card which Corning had given her.

If I can get more of the drug, she thought, my mind will clear and I can reason out what I have to do; as I am now I can't think. Anything I decide now, in this state, would be spurious. I owe it to myself to restore the normal functioning—or rather the desired functioning—of my faculties; without that I can't plan or survive and I'm doomed. I know, she thought fiercely, that the only way out for me would be suicide; it's just a matter of a few hours at the most. And Jonas couldn't help me in that short a time.

The only way I could have gotten rid of him, she realized, is the way I chose: by telling him of my addiction. Otherwise he would have hung around me forever and I never would have had a chance to get to Corning for more. I gained the opportunity I need, but now the Ackermans understand what's wrong with me and they'll try even harder to keep me from going to Cheyenne and joining Eric. Maybe I should go there tonight, not even return to my apartment. Just take off as soon as I have the capsules. Leave everything I own behind, abandoned.

How demented can you get? she asked herself. And it required only one exposure to JJ-180 to do this; what'll I be like when I've taken it repeatedly . . . or even just *twice?*

The future, to her, was mercifully obscure. She frankly did not know.

"Your destination, miss." The cab settled onto the rooftop landing field of a building. "That will be one dollar and twenty cents US plus a twenty-five-cent tip."

"Screw you and the tip," Kathy said, opening her purse; her hands shook and she could barely get out the money.

"Yes, miss," the autonomic cab said obediently.

She paid and then stepped out. A dull guide-light showed her the descent. What a rundown building for 'Starmen to inhabit, she thought. It surely isn't good enough for them; they must be pretending to be Terrans. The only consolation was a bitter one: the 'Starmen, like Terra, were losing the war, would ultimately be defeated. Relishing that thought, she increased her pace, felt more confidence; she did not simply hate the 'Starmen: she could, for a moment, despise them.

In this fortified frame of mind she reached the conapt held by the 'Starmen, rang the bell, and waited.

It was Corning himself who answered; she saw, behind him, other 'Starmen, evidently in conference. *In camera*, she said to herself; I'm disturbing them. Too bad; he said to come.

"Mrs. Sweetscent." Corning turned to the people behind him. "Isn't that a superb name? Come in, Kathy." He held the door wide.

"Give it to me out here." She remained in the hall. "I'm on my way to Cheyenne; you'll be glad to hear that. So don't waste my time." She held out her hand.

An expression of pity—incredibly—passed over Corning's face; he masterfully suppressed it. But she had seen it, and this, more than anything else that had happened, even the addiction itself or her suffering when the drug had worn off—nothing shocked her so much as Corning's pity. If it could move a 'Starman . . . she cringed. Oh God, she thought; I really am in trouble. I must be on my way to death.

"Look," she said reasonably. "My addiction may not last forever. I've found out that you lied; the drug comes from Terra, not from the enemy, and sooner or later our subsidiary will be able to free me. So I'm not afraid." She waited while Corning went to get the drug; at least she presumed that this was what he had gone for. He certainly had vanished somewhere.

One of the other 'Starmen, observing her leisurely, said, "You could float that drug around Lilistar for a decade and never find anyone unstable enough to succumb."

"Right," Kathy agreed. "That's the difference between you and us; we look alike but inside you're tough and we're weak. Gosh, I envy you. How long is it going to take Mr. Corning?"

"He'll be back in a moment," the 'Starman said. To a companion he said, "She's pretty."

"Yes, pretty as an animal," the other 'Starman answered. "So you like pretty animals? Is that why you were assigned to this?"

Corning returned. "Kathy, I'm giving you three caps. Don't take more than one at a time. Otherwise its toxicity would probably be fatal to your heart action."

"Okay." She accepted the capsules. "Do you have a cup or a glass of water so I can take one right now?"

He brought her a glass, stood watching sympathetically as she swallowed the capsule. "I'm doing this," she explained, "to clear my mind so I can plan what to do. I've got friends helping me. But I will go to Cheyenne because a deal is a deal, even with you. Can you give me the name of someone there— you know, who can give me further supplies when I need them? *If* I need them, I mean."

"We have no one in Cheyenne who can help you. I'm very much afraid you'll have to travel back here when your three caps are gone."

"Your infiltration of Cheyenne doesn't consist of much, then."

"I guess not." Corning did not appear perturbed, however.

"Good-by," Kathy said, starting away from the door. "Look at you," she said, addressing the group of 'Starmen within the apartment. "God but you're detestable. So confident. What kind of victory is it to—" She broke off; what was the use? "Virgil Ackerman knows about me. I'll bet he can do something; he's not afraid of you, he's too big a man."

"All right," Corning said, nodding. "You cherish that comforting delusion, Kathy. Meanwhile be sure you don't tell anyone else, because if you do, then no more caps. You shouldn't have told the Ackermans but I'll let that pass; after all, you were dazed when the drug wore off—we expected that. You did it in a state of panic. Good luck, Kathy. And we'll hear from you shortly."

"Can't you give her further instructions now?" a 'Starman said from behind Corning, sleepy-eyed and toadlike, drawling his question.

"She wouldn't be able to retain anything more," Corning

said. "It's asking a lot of her already; can't you see how over-taxed she is?"

"Kiss her good-by," the 'Starman behind him suggested. He strolled forward. "Or if that doesn't cheer her up—"

The apartment door shut in Kathy's face.

She stood a moment and then started back down the hall, toward the ascent ramp. Dizzy, she thought; I'm beginning to become disoriented—I hope I can make it to a cab. Once I'm in the cab I'll be okay. Jesus, she thought, they treated me badly; I should care but I really don't. Not as long as I have these two remaining capsules of JJ-180. And can get more.

The capsules were like a contracted form of life itself and yet at the same time everything they contained was fabricated from absolute delusion. What a mess, she thought drably as she emerged on the roof field and glanced about for the red, winking light of an autonomic cab. A——mess.

She had found a cab, was seated in it and on her way to Cheyenne, when she experienced the drug beginning to take effect.

Its initial manifestation was baffling. She wondered if per-haps a clue to its true action could be inferred from this; it seemed to her terribly important and she tried with every bit of mental energy she had to comprehend it. So simple and yet so meaningful.

The cut on her finger had disappeared.

She sat examining the spot, touching the smooth, perfect skin. No break. No scar. Her finger, exactly as before . . . as if time had been rolled back. The Band-Aid, too, was gone, and that seemed to clinch it, make it thoroughly comprehensi-ble, even to her swiftly deteriorating faculties.

"Look at my hand," she instructed the cab, holding her hand up. "Do you see any sign of an injury? Would you believe that I slashed myself badly, just half an hour ago?"

"No, miss," the cab said as it passed out over the flat desert of Arizona, heading north toward Utah. "You appear un-injured."

Now I understand what the drug does, she thought. Why it causes objects and people to become insubstantial. It's not so magical, and it's not merely hallucinogenic; my cut is really gone—*this is no illusion.* Will I remember this later on? Maybe, because of the drug, I'll forget; there never will have been a cut, after a little while longer, as the action of the drug spreads out, engulfs more and more of me.

"Do you have a pencil?" she asked the cab.

"Here, miss." From a slot in the seat-back ahead of her a tablet of paper with attached writing stylus appeared.

Carefully Kathy wrote: *JJ-180 took me back to before I had severe cut on finger.* "What day is this?" she asked the cab.

"May 18, miss."

She tried to recall if that was correct, but now she felt muddled; was it already slipping away from her? Good thing she had written the note. Or had she written the note? On her lap the tablet lay with its stylus.

The note read: *JJ-180 took me*

And that was all; the remainder dwindled into mere labored convolutions without meaning.

And yet she knew that she had completed the sentence, whatever it had been; now she could not recall it. As if by reflex she examined her hand. But how was her hand involved? "Cab," she said hurriedly, as she felt the balance of her personality ebbing away, "what did I ask you just a moment ago?"

"The date."

"Before that."

"You requested a writing implement and paper, miss."

"Anything before that?"

The cab seemed to hesitate. But perhaps that was her imagination. "No, miss; nothing before that."

"Nothing about *my hand?*"

Now there was no doubt of it; the circuits of the cab did stall. At last it said creakily, "No, miss."

"Thank you," Kathy said, and sat back against the seat, rubbing her forehead and thinking, So it's confused, too. Then this is not merely subjective; there's been a genuine snarl in time, involving both me and my surroundings.

The cab said, as if in apology for its inability to assist her, "Since the trip will be several hours, miss, would you enjoy to watch TV? It, the screen, is placed directly before you; only touch the pedal."

Reflexively she lit the screen with the tip of her toe; it came to life at once and Kathy found herself facing a familiar image, that of their leader, Gino Molinari, in the middle of a speech.

"Is that channel satisfactory?" the cab asked, still apologetic.

"Oh sure," she said. "Anyhow when he gets up and rants it's on all channels." That was the law.

And yet here, too, in this familiar spectacle, something strange absorbed her; peering at the screen, she thought, He looks younger. The way I remember him when I was a child. Ebullient, full of animation and shouting excitement, his eyes alive with that old intensity: his original self that no one has forgotten, although long since gone. However, obviously it was *not* long since gone; she witnessed it now with her own eyes, and was more bewildered than ever.

Is JJ-180 doing this to me? she asked herself, and got no answer.

"You enjoy to watch Mr. Molinari?" the cab inquired.

"Yes," Kathy said, "I enjoy to watch."

"May I hazard," the cab said, "that he will obtain the office for which he is running, that of UN Secretary?"

"You stupid autonomic robant machine," Kathy said witheringly. "He's been in office years now." Running? she thought. Yes, the Mole had looked like this during his campaign, decades ago . . . perhaps that was what had confused the circuits of the cab. "I apologize," she said. "But where the hell have you been? Parked in an autofac repair garage for twenty-two years?"

"No, miss. In active service. Your own wits, if I may say so, seem scrambled. Do you request medical assistance? We are at this moment over desert land but soon we will pass St. George, Utah."

She felt violently irritable. "Of course I don't need medical assistance; I'm healthy." But the cab was right. The influence of the drug was upon her full force now. She felt sick and she shut her eyes, pressing her fingers against her forehead as if to push back the expanding zone of her psychological reality, her private, subjective self. I'm scared, she realized. I feel as if my womb is about to fall out; this time it's hitting me much harder than before, it's not the same, maybe because I'm alone instead of with a group. But I'll just have to endure it. If I can.

"Miss," the cab said suddenly, "would you repeat my destination? I have forgotten it." Its circuits clicked in rapid succession as if it were in mechanical distress. "Assist me, please."

"I don't know where you're going," she said. "That's your business; you figure it out. Just fly around, if you can't remember." What did she care where it went? What did it have to do with her?

"It began with a *C*," the cab said hopefully.

"Chicago."

"I feel otherwise. However, if you're sure—" Its mechanism throbbed as it altered course.

You and I are both in this, Kathy realized. This drug-induced fugue. You made a mistake, Mr. Corning, to give me the drug without supervision. Corning? Who was Corning?

"I know where we were going," she said aloud. "To Corning."

"There is no such place," the cab said flatly.

"There must be." She felt panic. "Check your data again."

"Honestly, there isn't!"

"Then we're lost," Kathy said, and felt resigned. "God, this is awful. I have to be in Corning tonight, and there's no such place; what'll I do? Suggest something. I depend on you; please don't leave me to flounder like this—I feel as if I'm losing my mind."

"I'll request administrative assistance," the cab said. "From top-level dispatching service at New York. Just a moment." It was silent for a time. "Miss, there *is* no top-level dispatching service at New York, or if there is, I can't raise them."

"Is there anything at New York?"

"Radio stations, lots of them. But no TV transmissions or anything on the FM band or ultra-high frequency; nothing on the band we use. Currently I am picking up a radio station which is broadcasting something entitled 'Mary Marlin.' A piano piece by Debussy is being played as theme."

She knew her history; after all she was an antique collector and it was her job. "Put it on your audio system so I can hear it," she instructed.

A moment later she heard a female voice, retailing a wretched tale of suffering to some other female, a dreary account at best. And yet it filled Kathy with frantic excitement.

They're wrong, she thought, her mind working at its peak pitch. This won't destroy me. They forgot this era is my specialty—I know it as well as the present. There's nothing threatening or disintegrative about this experience for me; in fact it's an opportunity.

"Leave the radio on," she told the cab. "And just keep flying." Attentively, she listened to the soap opera as the cab continued on.

Eight

IT had—against nature and reason—become daytime. And the autonomic cab knew the impossibility of this; its voice was screechy with pain as it exclaimed to Kathy, "On the highway below, miss! An ancient car, that can't possibly exist!" It sank lower. "See for yourself! *Look!*"

Gazing down, Kathy agreed, "Yes. A 1932 Model A Ford. And I agree with you; there haven't been any Model A Fords for generations." Rapidly and with precision she reflected, then said, "I want you to land."

"Where?" Decidedly, the autonomic cab did not like the idea.

"That village ahead. Land on a rooftop there." She felt calm. But in her mind one realization dominated: it was the drug. And only the drug. This would last only so long as the drug operated within her cycle of brain metabolism; JJ-180 had brought her here without warning and JJ-180 would, eventually, return her to her own time—also without warning. "I am going to find a bank," Kathy said aloud. "And set up a savings account. By doing so—" And then she realized that she possessed no currency of this period; hence there existed no way by which she could transact business. So what could she do? Nothing? Call President Roosevelt and caution him about Pearl Harbor, she decided caustically. Change history. Suggest that years from now they not develop the atom bomb.

She felt impotent—and yet overwhelmed with her potential power; she experienced both sensations at once, finding the mixture radically unpleasant. Bring some artifact back to the present for Wash-35? Or check on some research quibble, settle some historical dispute? Snare the actual authentic Babe Ruth, bring him back to inhabit our Martian enterprise? It would certainly impart verisimilitude.

"Virgil Ackerman," she said slowly, "is alive in this period as a small boy. Does that suggest anything?"

"No," the cab said.

"It gives me enormous power over him." She opened her purse. "I'll give him something. The coins I have, bills."

Whisper to him the date the United States enters the war, she thought. He can use that knowledge later on, somehow . . . he'll find a way; he's always been smart, much smarter than I. God, she thought, if only I could put my finger on it! Tell him to invest in what? General Dynamics? Bet on Joe Louis in every fight? Buy real estate in Los Angeles? What do you tell an eight- or nine-year-old boy when you have exact and complete knowledge of the next hundred and twenty years?

"Miss," the cab said plaintively, "we've been in the air so long that I'm running short of fuel."

Chilled, she said, "But you ought to be good for fifteen hours."

"I was low." It admitted this reluctantly. "It's my fault; I'm sorry. I was on my way to a service station when you contacted me."

"You damn fool mechanism," she said with fury. But that was that; they couldn't reach Washington, D.C.; they were at least a thousand miles from it. And this period, of course, lacked the high-grade super-refined protonex which the cab required. And then all at once she knew what she had to do. The cab had given her the idea, unintentionally. Protonex was the finest fuel ever developed—and it was derived from sea water. All she had to do was mail a container of protonex to Virgil Ackerman's father, instruct him to procure an analysis of it and then a patent on it.

But there was no way she could mail anything, not without money to buy stamps. In her purse she had a small wad of dog-eared postage stamps, but of course all from her own era, from 2055. ——, she said furiously to herself, overwhelmed. Here I have it right before me, the solution as to what I should do—and I *can't* do it.

"How," she asked the cab, "can I send a letter in this time period with no contemporary stamps? Tell me that."

"Send the letter unstamped, with no return address, miss. The post office will deliver it with a postage due stamp attached."

"Yes," she said, "of course." But she could not get protonex into a first-class envelope; it would have to go parcel post, and in that class, lacking franking power, it would not be delivered.

"Listen," she said. "Do you have any transistors in your circuits?"

"A few. But transistors became obsolete when—"

"Give me one. I don't care what it does to you; yank it out and let me have it, and the smaller it is the better."

Presently, from the slot in the back of the seat before her, a transistor rolled; she caught it as it fell.

"That puts my radio transmitter out of service," the cab complained. "I'll have to bill you for it; it'll be expensive because of—"

"Shut up," Kathy said. "And land in that town; get down as soon as you can." She wrote hurriedly on the tablet of paper: "This is a radio part from the future, Virgil Ackerman. Show it to no one but save it until the early 1940s. Then take it to Westinghouse Corp. or to General Electric or any electronics (radio) firm. It will make you rich. I am Katherine Sweetscent. Remember me for this, later on."

The cab landed gingerly on the roof of an office building in the center of the small town. Below on the sidewalk the rustic, archaic-looking passers-by gaped.

"Land on the street," Kathy reinstructed the cab. "I have to put this in the mail." She found an envelope in her purse, hurriedly wrote out Virgil's address in Wash-35, put the transistor and note into the envelope and sealed it. Below them the street with its obsolete old cars rose slowly.

A moment later she was racing to a mailbox; she deposited the letter and then stood gasping for breath.

She had done it. Insured Virgil's economic future and therefore her own. This would make his career and hers forever.

The hell with you, Eric Sweetscent, she said to herself. I don't ever have to marry you now; I've left you behind.

And then she realized with dismay, I've still got to marry you in order to acquire the name. So that Virgil can identify me, later on in the future, in our own time. What she had done, then, came to exactly nothing.

Slowly, she returned to the parked cab.

"Miss," the cab said, "can you help me find fuel, please?"

"You won't find any fuel here," Kathy said. Its obstinate refusal—or inability—to grasp the situation maddened her.

"Unless you can run on sixty octane gasoline, which I very much doubt."

A passer-by, a middle-aged man wearing a straw hat, frozen in his tracks by the sight of the autonomic cab, called to her, "Hey lady, what's that, anyhow? A US Marine Corps secret weapon for war games?"

"Yes," Kathy answered. "And in addition later on it'll stop the Nazis." As she boarded the cab she said to the group of people who had cautiously formed around the cab at a safe distance, "Keep the date December 7, 1941, in mind; it'll be a day to remember." She closed the cab door. "Let's go. I could tell those people so much . . . but it seems hardly worth it. A bunch of Middle Western hicks." This town, she decided, lay either in Kansas or Missouri, from the looks of it. Frankly, it repelled her.

The cab dutifully ascended.

The 'Starmen should see Kansas in 1935, she said to herself. If they did they might not care to take over Terra; it might not seem worth it.

To the cab she said, "Land in a pasture. We'll sit it out until we're back in our own time period." It probably would not be long, now; she had an impression of a devouring insubstantiality here in this era—the reality outside the cab had gained a gaseous quality which she recognized from her previous encounter with the drug.

"Are you joking?" the cab said. "Is it actually possible that we—"

"The problem," she said tartly, "is not in returning to our own time; the problem is finding a way to stay under the drug's influence until something of worth can be accomplished." The time was just not long enough.

"What drug, miss?"

"None of your goddam business," Kathy said. "You nosy autonomic nonentity with your big prying circuits all opened up and flapping." She lit a cigarette and leaned back against the seat, feeling weary. It had been a tough day and she knew, with acuity, that more lay ahead.

The sallow-faced young man, who oddly enough already possessed a conspicuous paunch, as if physically yielding to the more lush pleasures at this, the planet's financial and political capital, shook Eric Sweetscent's hand damply and said, "I'm Don Festenburg, doctor. It's good to hear you're joining us. How about an old-fashioned?"

"No thanks," Eric said. There was something about Festenburg which he did not care for, but he could not put his finger on it. Despite his obesity and bad complexion Festenburg seemed friendly enough, and certainly he was competent; the latter alone counted, after all. But—Eric pondered as he watched Festenburg mix himself his drink. Perhaps it's because I don't think anyone should speak for the Secretary, he decided. I'd resent anyone who holds the job Festenburg does.

"Since we're alone," Festenburg said, glancing around the room, "I'd like to suggest something that may make me more palatable to you." He grinned knowingly. "I can tell what your feelings are; I'm sensitive, doctor, even if I'm the pyknic body-type. Suppose I suggested that an elaborate ruse has been carried off successfully, convincing even you. The flabby, aging, utterly discouraged and hypochondriacal Gino Molinari whom you've met and accepted as the authentic UN Secretary—" Festenburg lazily stirred his drink, eying Eric. "*That's the robant simulacrum.* And the robust, energetic figure you witnessed on video tape a short while ago is the living man. And this ruse must necessarily be maintained, of course, to sidetrack no one else but our beloved ally, the 'Starmen."

"*What?*" Startled, he gaped. "Why would—"

"The 'Starmen consider us harmless, unworthy of their military attention, only so long as our leader is palpably feeble. Quite visibly unable to discharge his responsibilities—in other words, in no sense a rival to them, a threat."

After a pause Eric said, "I don't believe this."

"Well," Festenburg said, shrugging, "it's an interesting idea from the ivory tower, intellectual standpoint. Don't you agree?" He walked toward Eric, swirling the contents of his glass. Standing very close to him, Festenburg breathed his noxious breath into Eric's face and said, "It *could* be. And until you actually subject Gino to an intensive physical examination you won't know, because everything in that file you read—it could all be faked. Designed to validate a gross, well-worked-out swindle." His eyes twinkled with merciless amusement. "You think I'm out of my mind? I'm just playing, like a schizoid, with ideas for the fun of it, without regard to their actual consequences? Maybe so. But you can't prove what I just now told you is untrue, and as long as this remains the case—" He took a massive swallow of his drink, then made a face. "Don't deplore what you saw on that Ampex video tape. Okay?"

"But as you say," Eric said, "I'll know as soon as I have a chance to examine him." And, he thought, that will come soon. "So if you'll excuse me I'd like to end this conversation. I haven't yet had time to set up my conapt here satisfactorily."

"Your wife—what's her name? Kathy?—isn't coming, is she?" Don Festenburg winked. "You can enjoy yourself. I'm in a position to give you a hand. That's my department, the land of the illicit, the feral, and the—let's just call it the peculiar. Instead of the unnatural. But you come from Tijuana; I probably can't teach you a thing."

Eric said, "You can teach me to deplore not only what I saw on the video tape but—" He broke off. Festenburg's personal life was, after all, his own business.

"But its creator as well," Festenburg finished for him. "Doctor, did you know that in the Middle Ages the ruling courts had people who lived in bottles, spent their entire lives . . . all shrunken, of course, put in while babies, allowed to grow— to some extent, anyhow—within the bottle. We don't have that now. However—Cheyenne is the contemporary ranking seat of kings; there are a few sights that could be shown you, if you're interested. Perhaps from the purely medical standpoint—a sort of professional, disinterested—"

"I think whatever it is you want to show me would only make me less pleased with my decision to come to Cheyenne," Eric said. "So frankly I don't see what profit it would serve."

"Wait," Festenburg said, holding up his hand. "One item. Just this particular exhibit, all properly sealed hermetically, bathed in a solution that maintains the thing ad infinitum, or, as you probably will prefer, ad nauseam. May I take you there? It's in what we at the White House call room 3-C." Festenburg walked to the door, held it open for Eric.

After a pause Eric followed.

Hands in the pockets of his rumpled, unpressed trousers,

Festenburg led the way down one corridor after another until at last they stood on a subsurface level, facing two high-ranking Secret Service men stationed at a metal reinforced door marked TOP SECRET. NO UNAUTHORIZED PERSONNEL PERMITTED.

"I'm authorized," Festenburg said genially. "Gino's given me the run of the warren; he has great trust in me, and because of this you're going to see a state secret which you normally would never in a thousand years be allowed to view." As he passed by the uniformed Secret Service men and pushed open the door he added, "However, there will be one disappointing aspect of this; I'm going to show it to you but not explain it. I'd *like* to explain it but—very simply I can't."

In the center of the murky, cold room Eric saw a casket. As Festenburg had said, it was hermetically sealed; a pump throbbed dully, at its task of maintaining at extreme low temperatures whatever lay within the casket.

"Look at it," Festenburg said sharply.

Deliberately pausing, Eric lit a cigarette, then walked over.

In the casket, supine, lay Gino Molinari, his face locked in agony. He was dead. Blood could be seen, dried drops on his neck. His uniform was torn, stained with mud. Both hands were lifted, the fingers writhing, as if trying even now to fight back at whatever—whoever—it was that had murdered him. Yes, Eric thought. I'm seeing the results of an assassination; this is the leader's corpse, flailed with bullets emanating from a weapon with notably high muzzle velocity; the man's body had been twisted, almost torn apart. It had been a savage assault. And—successful.

"Well," Festenburg said, after a time, taking in a deep rush of breath, "there are several ways this item—which I like to think of as Exhibit One of the Cheyenne Freak Show—can be explained. Let's assume it's a robant. Waiting here in the wings for the moment that Gino needs it. Built by GRS Enterprises, the inventive Dawson Cutter, whom you must meet someday."

"Why would Molinari need this?"

Festenburg, scratching his nose, said, "Several reasons. In case of an attempted assassination—one which failed—this could be exhibited, taking the heat off Gino while he hid out. Or—it could be for the benefit of our sanguine ally; Gino may have it in the back of his mind that some incredibly complex, baroque plan will be necessary, something involving his retirement from office under the pressure they're exerting on him."

"You're sure this is a robant?" To Eric the thing in the casket looked real.

"I don't even *think* it is, let alone know." Festenburg jerked his head and Eric saw that the two Secret Service men had entered the room; obviously it would not be possible to inspect the corpse.

"How long has it been here?"

"Only Gino knows and he won't say; he just smiles slyly. 'You wait, Don,' he says in his secretive fashion. 'I got a big use for it.'"

"And if it's not a robant—"

"Then it's Gino Molinari lying there ripped apart by machine-gun slugs. A primitive, outmoded weapon but it certainly can kill its victim beyond the possibility of even org-trans repair; you can see that the brain case has been punctured—the brain is destroyed. If it is Gino, *then where's it from?* The future? There is a theory, having to do with your firm, TF&D. A subsidiary has developed a drug which permits its user to move freely in time. You know about that?" He studied Eric intently.

"No," Eric admitted. The rumor was more or less new to him.

"Anyhow, here's this corpse," Festenburg said. "Lying here day after day, driving me nuts. Perhaps it's from an alternate present in which Gino has been assassinated, driven out of office the hard way by a splinter political group of Terrans backed by Lilistar. But there's a further ramification of this theory, one which really haunts me." Festenburg's tone now was somber; he was no longer in a joking mood. "That would imply something about the virile, strutting Gino Molinari who made that video tape; that's not a robant either and GRS Enterprises did not manufacture it because it too is an authentic Gino Molinari from an alternate present. One in which war didn't come about, one perhaps in which Terra didn't even get mixed up with Lilistar. Gino Molinari has gone into a more reassuring world and plucked his healthy counterpart over here to assist him. What do you think, doctor? Could that be it?"

Baffled, Eric said, "If I knew something about that drug—"

"I assumed you would. I'm disappointed; that was my reason for bringing you here. Anyhow—there's one other possibility . . . logically. Suggested by this assassinated corpse, here." Festenburg hesitated. "I hate to mention it because it's so bizarre that it makes my other conjectures look tainted by association."

"Go ahead," Eric said tightly.

"There is no Gino Molinari."

Eric grunted. Good grief, he thought.

"*All* of them are robants. The healthy one who's on the video tape, the tired, sick one you've met, this dead one here in the casket—that somebody, possibly GRS Enterprises, engineered this to keep the 'Starmen from taking over our planet. So far they've made use of the ill one." Festenburg gestured. "And now they've hauled out the healthy one, made the first tape of him. *And there may be more.* Logically why not? I've even tried to imagine what other alternatives might be like. You tell me. In addition to the three we know, *what's left?*"

Eric said, "Obviously it leaves the possibility of building one with powers above the norm. Beyond the merely healthy." He thought, then, of Molinari's recovery from one terminal illness after another. "But maybe we have that already. Have you read the medical file?"

"Yes." Festenburg nodded. "And there's one very interesting quality about it. None of the tests were conducted by any persons now on his medical staff. Teagarden didn't authorize any of them; the tests predate him, and as far as I know, Teagarden, like yourself, has never managed to subject Gino to even a cursory physical exam. Nor do I think he ever will. Nor do I think *you* ever will, doctor. Even if you're kept around here for years."

"Your mind," Eric said, "is certainly hyperactive."

"Am I a glandular case?"

"That has no bearing on the matter. But you certainly have spun a lot of ad hoc ideas out of your own head."

"Based on facts," Festenburg pointed out. "I want to know what Gino is up to. I think he's one hell of a smart man. I think he can outthink the 'Starmen any day of the week, and if he had the economic resources and the population behind him that they have, he'd be in the driver's seat, no contest. As it is, he's in charge of one dinky planet and they have a system-wide empire of twelve planets and eight moons. It's frankly a wonder he's been able to accomplish all he has. You know, doctor, you're here to find out what's making Gino sick. I say that's not the issue. It's obvious what's making him sick: the whole darn situation. The real question is: *What's keeping him alive?* That's the real mystery. The miracle."

"I guess you're right." Grudgingly, he had to admit that despite his repellent qualities Festenburg was intelligent and original; he had managed to see the problem properly. No wonder Molinari had hired him.

"You've met the schoolgirl shrew?"

"Mary Reineke?" Eric nodded.

"Christ, here's this tragic, complicated mess, this sick man barely making it through the day with the weight of the world, of Terra itself, on his back, knowing he's losing the war, knowing the reegs are going to get us if by some miracle Lilistar doesn't—and in addition he's got Mary on his back. And the final blistering irony is that Mary, by being a shrew and simple-minded, selfish, demanding, and anything else you want to articulate as a basic character defect—she does have him on his feet; you've seen her get him out of bed and back into uniform, functioning again. Do you know anything about Zen, doctor? This is a Zen paradox, because from a logical standpoint Mary ought to have been the final straw that utterly destroyed Gino. It makes you rethink the entire role of adversity in human life. To tell you the truth, I detest her. She detests me, too, naturally. Our only working connection is through Gino; we both want him to make it."

"Has she been shown the video tape of the healthy Molinari?"

Festenburg glanced up swiftly. "A wise thought. Has Mary seen the tape? Yes, maybe or no—check one. Not to my knowledge. But if you suppose my alternate-present theory, and that it's *not* a robant on that tape, if it's a human being, that magnetic, fire-eating, striving demigod, and if Mary catches sight of it—you can assume the following: the other Molinaris will disappear. Because what you saw on that tape is exactly what Mary Reineke wants—insists—that Gino be."

It was an extraordinary thought. Eric wondered if Gino was aware of this aspect of the situation; if so, it might explain why he had waited so long to employ this tactic.

"I wonder," he said to Festenburg, "how the sick Gino whom we know could be a robant, in view of Mary Reineke's existence."

"How so? Why not?"

"To put it in delicate terms . . . wouldn't Mary be somewhat peeved by being the mistress of a product of GRS Enterprises?"

"I'm getting tired, doctor," Festenburg said. "Let's write finis to this discussion—you go and fix up your swinkly new conapt which they've donated to you for your loyal services here at Cheyenne." He moved toward the door; the two top-position Secret Service men stepped aside.

Eric said, "I'll give you one opinion of my own. Having met Gino Molinari I refuse to believe GRS could construct something so human and—"

"But you haven't met the one they filmed," Festenburg said quietly. "It's interesting, doctor. By drawing on himself from the alternates contained in the mishmash of time Gino may have collected an ensemble capable of facing the ally. Three or four Gino Molinaris, forming a committee, would be rather formidable . . . don't you agree? Think of the combined ingenuity; think of the harebrained, clever, wild schemes they could hatch up working collectively." As he opened the door he added, "You've met the sick one and glimpsed the well one—weren't *you* impressed?"

"Yes," Eric admitted.

"Would you now vote with those who want to see him sacked? And yet when you try to pin down what he's actually done that's so impressive—it isn't there. If we were winning the war, or forcing back Lilistar's investment of our planet . . . but we're not. So what is it specifically, doctor, that Gino's done that so impresses you? Tell me." He waited.

"I—guess I can't say specifically. But—"

A White House employee, a uniformed robant, appeared and confronted Eric Sweetscent. "Secretary Molinari has been looking for you, doctor. He's waiting to see you in his office; I'll lead the way."

"Oops," Festenburg said, chagrined and all at once quite nervous. "Evidently I kept you too long."

Without a further exchange Eric followed the robant up the corridor to the elevator. This was probably important; he had that intuition.

In his office Molinari sat in a wheel chair, a blanket over his lap, his face gray and sunken. "Where were you?" he said, as Eric came into sight. "Well, it doesn't matter; listen, doctor—the 'Starmen have called a conference and I want you to be with me while I attend. I want you to be on hand constantly, just in case. I'm not feeling well and I wish this damn get-together could be avoided or at least postponed for a few weeks. But they insist." He began to wheel himself from the office. "Come on. It's going to start any time."

"I met Don Festenburg."

"Brilliant rat, isn't he? I put complete faith in our eventual success in him. What did he show you?"

It seemed unreasonable to tell Molinari that he had been viewing his corpse, especially in view of the fact that the man had just now said he did not feel well. So Eric merely said, "He took me around the building."

"Festenburg has the run of the place—because of the trust I put in him." At a bend in the corridor a gang of stenographers, translators, State Department officials, and armed guards met Molinari; his wheel chair disappeared into the corporate body and did not reappear. Eric, however, could still hear him talking away, explaining what lay ahead. "Freneksy is here. So this is going to be rough. I have an idea what they want, but we'll have to wait and see. Better not to anticipate; that way you do their work for them, you sort of turn on yourself and do yourself in."

Freneksy, Eric thought with a sensation of dread. Lilistar's Prime Minister, here personally on Terra.

No wonder Molinari felt sick.

Nine

THE members of Terra's delegation to the hastily called conference occupied seats on one side of the long oak table, and now, on the far side, the personages from Lilistar began to emerge from side corridors and find chairs. As a whole they did not look sinister; they looked, in fact, overworked and harried, caught up, as was Terra, by the strain of conducting the war. Obviously they had no time to spare. They were clearly mortal.

"Translation," a 'Starman said in English, "will be done by human agency not by machine, as any machine might make a permanent record, which is contrary to our desires here."

Molinari grunted, nodded.

Now Freneksy appeared; the 'Star delegation and several members of the Terran rose in a show of respect; the 'Starmen clapped their hands as the bald, lean, oddly round-skulled man took a chair at the center of the delegation and began without preliminaries to open a briefcase of documents.

But his eyes. Eric noticed that, as Freneksy glanced briefly up at Molinari and smiled in greeting. Freneksy had what Eric thought of—and recognized in his practice as—paranoid eyes. Once he had learned to spot this, future identification generally came easy. This was not the glittering, restless stare of ordinary suspicion; this was a motionless gaze, a gathering of the totality of faculties within to comprise a single undisturbed psychomotor concentration. Freneksy did not decide to do this; in fact he was helpless, compelled to confront his compatriots and adversaries alike in this fashion, with this unending ensnaring fixity. It was an attentiveness which made empathic understanding impossible; the eyes did not reflect any inner reality; they gave back to the viewer exactly what he himself was. The eyes stopped communication dead; they were a barrier that could not be penetrated this side of the tomb.

Freneksy was not a bureaucrat and he did not—could not even if he tried—subordinate himself to his office. Freneksy remained a man—in the bad sense; he retained, in the midst of the busy activity of official conduct, the essence of the purely personal, as if to him everything was deliberate and intentional—a contest between people, not one between abstract or ideal issues.

What Minister Freneksy does, Eric realized, is to deprive all the others of the sanctity of their office. Of the security-producing reality of their titled position. Facing Freneksy, they became as they were born: isolated and individual, unsupported by the institutions which they were supposed to represent.

Take Molinari. Customarily, the Mole was the UN Secretary; he as an individual had—and properly so—dissolved into his function. But facing Minister Freneksy, the naked, hapless, lonely man re-emerged—and was required to stand up to the Minister in this unhappy infinitude. The normal *relativeness* of existence, lived with others in a fluctuating state of more or less adequate security, had vanished.

Poor Gino Molinari, Eric thought. Because facing Freneksy the Mole might as well not have become UN Secretary. And meanwhile Minister Freneksy became even more cold, more lifeless; he did not burn with the desire to destroy or dominate: he merely took away what his antagonist possessed—and left him nothing and nowhere, literally.

It was perfectly clear to Eric, at this point, why Molinari's procession of lethal illnesses had not proved fatal. The illnesses were not merely a symptom of the stress under which he lay; *they were simultaneously a solution to that stress.*

He could not as yet make out quite precisely how the illnesses behaved in order to function as a response to Freneksy. But he had the deep and acute intuition that he would very soon; the confrontation between Freneksy and Molinari lay only moments away, and everything which the Mole had would have to be trotted out, if the Mole wished to survive.

Beside Eric a minor State Department official muttered, "Oppressive in here, isn't it? Wish they'd open a window or turn on the vent system."

Eric thought, No mechanical vent system will clear this air. Because the oppression emanates from those seated across from us and it will not depart until they depart—and perhaps not even then.

Leaning toward Eric, Molinari said, "Sit here beside me."

He drew the chair back. "Listen, doctor, do you have your bag of instruments with you?"

"It's in my conapt."

Molinari at once dispatched a robant runner. "I want you to have the bag at all times." He cleared his throat, then turned toward those seated on the far side of the table. "Minister Freneksy, I have a, uh, statement. I'd like to read it; the statement summarizes Earth's present position as regards—"

"Secretary," Freneksy said suddenly in English, "before you read any statement I would like to describe the status of the war effort on Front A." Freneksy rose; an aide at once unrolled a map projection which took effect on the far wall. The room sank into shadow.

Grunting, Molinari placed his written statement back inside the jacket of his uniform; he would not get his opportunity to read it. In an obvious manner he had been pre-empted. And, for a political strategist, this was a grave defeat. The initiative, if it had ever been his, was now gone.

"Our combined armies," Freneksy stated, "are shortening their lines for strategic purposes. The reegs are expending inordinate amounts of men and material in this area." He indicated a sector on the map; it lay halfway between two planets of the Alpha System. "They will not be able to continue this long; I predict a bankruptcy of their strength no later than a month—Terran count—from now. The reegs do not understand yet that this is to be a long war. Victory, for them, must come soon or not at all. We, however—" Freneksy indicated the entire map with a sweep of the pointer. "We are maturely aware of the over-all strategic meaning of this struggle, and how long it must remain with us in terms of time as well as space. Also, the reegs are spread too thinly. If a major battle were to break out here—" Freneksy indicated the spot "—they could not support their forces already committed. Further, we will have twenty more first-line divisions in action by the end of the Terran year; this is a promise, Secretary. We have yet to call up several classes here on Terra, whereas the reegs have scraped the barrel." He paused.

Molinari murmured, "Is your bag here yet, doctor?"

"Not yet," Eric said, looking for the robant runner; it had not returned.

Leaning close to Eric, the Mole whispered, "Listen. You know what I've been experiencing lately? Head noises. Rushing sounds—you know, in my ears. Swoop, zwoop. Does that sound like anything?"

Minister Freneksy had continued. "We have new weapons, also, emanating from Planet Four of the Empire; you will be astonished, Secretary, when you see video clips of them in tactical operation. They are devastating in their accuracy. I will not attempt to describe them in detail now; I prefer to wait until the tapes are available. I personally supervised their engineering and construction."

His head almost touching Eric's, Molinari whispered, "And when I turn my head from side to side I get a distinct cracking sound from the base of my neck. Can you hear it?" He turned his head from side to side, nodding in a slow, stiff manner. "What is that? It resounds unpleasantly as hell in my ears."

Eric said nothing; he was watching Freneksy, barely paying attention to the whispering from the man beside him.

"Secretary," Freneksy said, pausing, "consider this aspect of our joint effort; the reegs' space-drive output has been severely restricted due to the successes by our W-bombs. Those which have come off their assembly lines recently—we are informed by MCI—are unreliable, and a number of highly destructive contaminations have occurred in deep space aboard their line ships."

The robant runner entered the room now, with Eric's instrument case.

Ignoring this, Freneksy continued, his voice harsh and insistent. "I also point out, Secretary, that on Front Blue the Terran brigades have not performed well, no doubt due to a lack of proper equipment. Victory is of course inevitable for us— eventually. But right now we must see to it that our troops who hold the line against the reegs are not put in the position of facing the enemy deprived of adequate material. It is criminal to allow men to fight under those circumstances; don't you agree, Secretary?" Without pausing, Freneksy continued, "Therefore you can see the urgency of increasing Terra's output of strategic war goods and weapons of all sort."

Molinari saw Eric's instrument case and nodded with relief.

"You have it," he said. "Good. Keep it ready, just in case. You know what I think these head noises are from? Hypertension."

Cautiously, Eric said, "Could be."

Now Minister Freneksy had ceased; his expressionless face seemed to become more severe, more withdrawn into the vacuum of his own intensity, the nonBeing which seemed to be his major quality. Irritated by Molinari's lack of attention, Freneksy was drawing from this well of his own antiexistence, Eric decided. Casting his principle over the conference room and the people in it, as if forcing everyone away from each other step by step.

"Secretary," Freneksy said, "this now is most crucial. My generals in the field tell me that the new reeg offensive weapon, their—"

"Wait," Molinari croaked. "I wish to confer with my colleague, here beside me." Bending so close to Eric that his soft, perspiration-dampened cheek pressed against his neck, Molinari whispered to him, "And you know what else? I seem to be having trouble with my eyes. As if I'm going completely blind. Here's what I want you to do, doctor; give me a pressure reading right now. Just to be sure it's not dangerously high. I feel it is, frankly."

Eric opened his instrument case.

At the wall map Minister Freneksy said, "Secretary, we must attend to this decisive detail before we can continue. Terran troops do not stand up well against the reegs' new homeostatic bomb, hence I would like to relieve a million and a half of my own factory workers and put them into uniform, replacing them in Empire factories with Terrans. This is an advantage for you, Secretary, in that Terrans will not be fighting and dying in the lines but will be safe inside Empire factories. However, this must be done soon or not at all." He added, "This explains my desire for an immediate conference at a superior level."

Eric read, from the testing disc, a pressure of 290 for Molinari, an elevation unnaturally high and ominous.

"Bad, isn't it?" Molinari said, resting his head on his arms. "Get Teagarden in here," he instructed a robant. "I want him to confer with Dr. Sweetscent; tell him to be prepared to make a diagnosis on the spot."

"Secretary," Freneksy said, "we cannot continue unless you turn your attention to what I'm saying. My request for a million and a half Terran males and females for work in Empire factories—did you hear that? This crucial requisition must be honored at once; transport of these entities must begin no later than the end of this week, your time."

"Um," Molinari murmured. "Yes, Minister, I heard; I'm pondering this request."

"There is nothing to ponder," Freneksy said. "It must be achieved if we are to hold the line on Front C, where reeg pressure is now greatest. A breakthrough is imminent, and Terran brigades have not—"

"I'll have to consult with my Labor Secretary," Molinari said, after a long pause. "Get his approval."

"We *must* have the one and a half million of your people!"

Reaching into his jacket, Molinari fished out his folded sheets of paper. "Minister, this statement which I—"

"Do I have your promise?" Freneksy demanded. "So that we can go on to other matters, now?"

"I'm sick," Molinari said.

There was silence.

At last Freneksy said thoughtfully, "I am aware, Secretary, that your health has not been good for years now. Therefore I took the liberty of bringing an Empire physician with me to this conference. This is Dr. Gornel." On the far side of the table a lank-faced 'Starman nodded curtly to the Mole. "I would like him to examine you, with a view toward making a permanent correction of your physical problems."

"Thank you, Minister," Molinari said. "Your kindness in bringing Dr. Gornel is deeply appreciated. However, I have my own staff physician here, Dr. Sweetscent. He and Dr. Teagarden are about to perform an exploratory examination to determine the cause of my hypertension."

"*Now?*" Freneksy said, and showed, for the first time, a trace of genuine emotion. Amazed anger.

"My blood pressure is dangerously high," Molinari explained. "If it continues I'll lose my eyesight. In fact already I'm suffering impaired vision." In a low voice he said to Eric, "Doctor, everything around me has become dim; I think I'm already blind. Where the hell's Teagarden?"

Eric said, "I can seek for the source of the hypertension, Secretary; I have the necessary diagnostic instruments with me." He reached into his case once more. "Initially I'll give you an injection of radioactive salts which will carry through your bloodstream—"

"I know," Molinari said. "And collect at the source of the vasoconstriction. Go ahead." He rolled up his sleeve and held out his furry arm; Eric pressed the self-cleansing head of the injecting tube against a vein near the elbow and pressed the tab.

Severely, Minister Freneksy said, "What is taking place, Secretary? Can't we continue with the conference?"

"Yes, go ahead," Molinari said, nodding. "Dr. Sweetscent is merely making an exploration to—"

"Medical matters bore me," Freneksy interrupted. "Secretary, there is a further proposal I wish to make to you now. First, I would like to have my physician, Dr. Gornel, placed permanently on your staff to supervise your medical care. Secondly, I have been informed by the Empire counterintelligence agency operating here on Terra that a group of malcontents, desiring an end to Terra's participation in the war, are planning your assassination; hence I wish, for your safety, to provide you with a perpetual armed guard of 'Starmen commando troops who will, by their extreme courage and determination and efficiency, protect your person at all times. They number twenty-five, an adequate number, given their unique quality."

"What?" Molinari said. He shuddered. "What do you find, doctor?" He seemed confused now, unable to keep his attention fixed on both Eric and the progress of the conference. "Wait, Minister." To Eric he murmured, "What the hell do you find, doctor? Or did you just tell me? Sorry." He rubbed his forehead. "I'm blind!" His voice was filled with panic. "Do something, doctor!"

Eric, examining the sighting graph which traced the movement of the radioactive salts in Molinari's circulatory system, said, "There appears to be a stricture of the renal artery which passes through your right kidney. A ring which—"

"I know," Molinari said, nodding. "I knew the stricture was in my right kidney; I've had it before. You'll have to operate, doctor, and cut the ring or it'll kill me." He seemed too weak now to raise his head; he sat slumped over, face in his hands. "God, I feel terrible," he mumbled. Then he raised his head and said to Freneksy, "Minister, I must undergo an immediate corrective operation to relieve this arterial stricture. We'll have to postpone this discussion." He rose to his feet, swayed, and then fell noisily back; Eric and the man from State caught him, helped him back into his chair. The Mole seemed incredibly heavy and inert; Eric could hardly support him, even with assistance.

Freneksy declared, "The conference must continue."

"All right," Molinari gasped. "I'll have the operation while you talk?" He nodded weakly to Eric. "Don't wait for Tea-garden; get started."

"*Here?*" Eric said.

"It'll have to be," Molinari whimpered. "Cut the ring, doc-tor, or I'm dead. I'm dying—I know it." He slumped, then, against the table. And this time he did not draw himself back up to a sitting position; he remained as he was. Like some great discarded, tossed sack.

At the far end of the table UN Vice Secretary Rick Prindle said to Eric, "Begin, doctor. As he said, it's urgent; you know that." Obviously he—and the others present—had been through this before.

Freneksy said, "Secretary, will you empower Mr. Prindle to take your official place in Terra-Lilistar negotiations?"

There was no answer from Molinari; he had passed into un-consciousness.

From his case Eric lifted a small surgical homeostatic unit; it would suffice—he hoped—for the delicate operation. Drilling its own path, and closing the passage behind it, the tool would penetrate the dermal layer and then the omentum until it reached the renal stricture, whereupon, if it was behaving properly, it would begin construction of a plastic bypass for the arterial section; this would be safer, at the moment, than at-tempting to remove the ring.

The door opened and Dr. Teagarden entered; he hurried up to Eric, saw Molinari lying unconscious with his head on the table, said, "Are you prepared to operate?"

"I have the equipment; yes, I'm ready."

"No artiforg, of course?"

"It isn't necessary."

Teagarden took hold of Molinari by the wrist, measured his pulse; then he whipped out a stethoscope, unbuttoned the Secretary's jacket and shirt, listened to his heart. "Weak and irregular. We'd better cool him off."

"Yes," Eric agreed, and brought a cold-pak assembly from his case.

Freneksy, coming over to see, said, "You're going to lower his body temperature during the operation?"

"Yes, we'll put him out," Eric said. "The metabolic processes—"

"I don't care to hear," Freneksy said. "Biological matters do not interest me; all I am concerned with is the evident fact that the Secretary is unable to continue at present with this discussion. A discussion for which we have traveled a number of light-years." His face displayed a dull, baffled anger which he could not suppress.

Eric said, "We have no choice, Minister. Molinari is dying."

"I realize that," Freneksy said, and walked away, his fists clenched.

"He's technically dead," Teagarden said, still listening to Molinari's heart action. "Put the freeze into effect at once, doctor."

Eric swiftly attached the cold-pak to Molinari's neck, started its self-contained compression-circuit up. The cold radiated out from it; he let go and turned his attention to the surgical tool.

Minister Freneksy conferred, speaking in his own tongue, with the Empire doctor; he lifted his head all at once and said crisply, "I would like Dr. Gornel to assist in this operation."

Vice Secretary Prindle spoke up. "It can't be permitted. Molinari has given strict orders that only his own staff doctors, chosen by himself personally, are to touch his person." He nodded to Tom Johannson and his corps of Secret Service men; they moved closer to Molinari.

"Why?" Freneksy asked.

"They're familiar with his case history," Pnindle said woodenly.

Freneksy shrugged, walked away; he seemed even more

baffled now, even bewildered. "It's inconceivable to me," he said aloud, his back to the table, "that this could be permitted to happen, that Secretary Molinari could let his physical condition deteriorate to such a point."

To Teagarden, Eric said, "Has this happened before?"

"You mean has Molinari died during a conference with the 'Starmen?" Teagarden smiled reflexively. "Four times. Right here in this room, even in the same chair. You may start your borer, now."

Placing the homeostatic surgical tool against Molinari's lower right side, Eric activated it; the device, the size of a shot glass, at once flung itself into activity, delivering first a strong local anesthetic and then beginning its task of cutting its way to the renal artery and the kidney.

The only sound in the room now was the whirring caused by the action of the tool; everyone, including Minister Freneksy, watched it disappear from sight, burrowing into Molinari's heavy, motionless, slumped body.

"Teagarden," Eric said, "I suggest that we keep—" He stood back and lit a cigarette. "Watch for a case of hypertension occurring somewhere here in the White House, another partially blocked renal artery or—"

"It's come up already. A maid on the third floor. Hereditary malformation, as it has to be of course. But coming to a crisis in this woman during the last twenty-four hours because of an overdose of amphetamines; she began to lose her sight and we decided to go ahead and operate—that's where I was when I was summoned here. I was just finishing up."

"Then you know," Eric said.

"Know what?" Teagarden's voice was low, concealed from those across the table. "We'll discuss it later. But I can assure you that I know nothing. *Nor do you.*"

Coming over to them, Minister Freneksy said, "How soon will Molinari be capable of resuming this discussion?"

Eric and Teagarden glanced at each other. Caught each other's eye.

"Hard to say," Teagarden said presently.

"Hours? Days? *Weeks?* Last time it was ten days." Freneksy's face writhed with impotence. "I am simply unable to remain here on Terra that long; the conference will have to be re-scheduled for later in the year if it's to be a wait of more than seventy-two hours." Behind him his consulting staff, his military and industrial and protocol advisers, were already putting their notes away in their briefcases, closing up shop.

Eric said, "Probably he won't be strong enough within the two-day period generally allowed in cases like this; his over-all condition is too—"

Turning to Prindle, Minister Freneksy said, "And you decline any authority as Vice Secretary to speak in his place? What an abominable situation! It's obvious why Terra—" He broke off. "Secretary Molinari is a personal friend of mine," he said, then. "I'm keenly concerned as to his welfare. But why must Lilistar bear the major burden in this war? Why can Terra go on dragging her feet indefinitely?"

Neither Prindle nor the two doctors answered.

In his own language Freneksy spoke to his delegation; they rose en masse, obviously prepared to depart.

The conference, because of Molinari's sudden near-fatal illness, had been called off. At least for now. Eric felt overwhelming relief.

Through his illness Molinari had escaped. But only temporarily.

Nevertheless, that was something. *That was enough.* The million and a half Terrans, demanded by Lilistar for its factories, would not be rounded up . . . Eric glanced at Teagarden, exchanged a brief flash of agreement and comprehension. Meanwhile, the borer went about its task, unaided, whining on.

A psychosomatic, hypochrondriacal illness had protected the lives of a great many people and it made Eric rethink, already, the value of medicine, the effect of bringing about a "cure" for Molinari's condition.

It seemed to him as he listened to the borer at work that he was now beginning to understand the situation—and what was really required of him by the ailing UN Secretary who lay against the conference table, neither seeing nor hearing, in a state where the problems of the discussion with Minister Freneksy did not exist.

*

Later, in his well-guarded bedroom, Gino Molinari sat propped up on pillows, weakly contemplating the homeopape the *New York Times*, which had been placed at his disposal.

"It's okay to read, isn't it, doctor?" he murmured faintly.

"I think so," Eric said. The operation had been totally successful; the elevated blood pressure had been restored to a normal plateau, commensurate with the patient's age and general condition.

"Look at what the damn papes are able to get wind of." Molinari passed the first section to Eric.

POLICY MEET CALLED OFF ABRUPTLY DUE TO
SECRETARY'S ILLNESS. 'STAR DELEGATION
HEADED BY FRENEKSY IN SECLUSION.

"How do they find those things out?" Molinari complained peevishly. "God, it makes me look bad; makes it obvious I finked out at a crucial time." He glared at Eric. "If I had any guts I'd have stood up to Freneksy on that labor-force conscription demand." He shut his eyes wearily. "I knew the demand was coming. Knew it last week, even."

"Don't blame yourself," Eric said. How much of the physiological fugal dynamism was comprehensible to Molinari? None of it, evidently; Molinari not only did not grasp the purpose of his illness—he did not even approve of it. And so it continued to function at an unconscious level.

But how long can this go on? Eric wondered. With such a powerful dichotomy between conscious aspiration and unconscious will to escape . . . perhaps, finally, an illness would be produced from which the Secretary would never emerge; it would not only be fatal, *it would be final.*

The door to the room opened; there stood Mary Reineke.

Taking her by the arm, Eric led her back out into the hall, shutting the door after them. "Can't I see him?" she demanded indignantly.

"In a minute." He studied her, still unable to determine just how well she understood the situation. "I want to ask you something. Has Molinari undergone any psychiatric therapy or analysis that you know of?" No mention existed in the file but he had a hunch.

"Why should he?" Mary toyed with the zipper of her skirt. "He's not crazy."

That certainly was true; he nodded. "But his physical—"

"Gino has bad luck. That's why he's always getting sick. You know no psychiatrist is going to change his luck." Mary Reineke added with reluctance, "Yes, he did consult an analyst once, last year, a few times. But that's a top secret; if the homeopapes got hold of it—"

"Give me the analyst's name."

"The hell I will." Her black eyes snapped with hostile triumph; she glared at him unwinkingly. "I won't even tell Dr. Teagarden, and him I like."

"After watching Gino's illness in action I feel I—"

"The analyst," Mary broke in, "is dead. Gino had him killed."

Eric stared at her.

"Guess why." She smiled with the random malice of a teen-age girl, the purposeless, delicious cruelty which took him back in a flash to his own boyhood. To the agonies such girls had caused him before. "It was something the analyst said. About Gino's illness. I don't know what it was but I assume he was on the right track . . . as you think you are. So do you really want to be so clever?"

"You remind me," he said, "of Minister Freneksy."

She pushed by him, toward Gino's door. "I want to go on in; good-by."

"Did you know that Gino died there in that conference room today?"

"Yes, he had to. Just for a few moments, of course; not long enough to muddle his brain cells. And of course you and Teagarden cooled him right down; I know about that, too. Why do I remind you of Freneksy, *that* crulp!" She came back toward him, studying him intently. "I'm not like him at all. You're just trying to make me sore so I'll tell you something."

Eric said, "What do you think I want you to tell me?"

"About Gino's suicide impulses." She spoke matter-of-factly. "He has them; everybody knows that. That's why I was brought here by his relatives, to make sure somebody spent every night with him, snuggled right up against him in bed every hour or watching him while he paces around when he can't sleep. He can't be alone at night; he's got to have me to talk to. And I can talk sense to him—you know, restore his perspective at four o'clock in the morning. That's hard to do, but I do it." She smiled. "See? Do you have somebody to do that for *you*, doctor? At your four a.m. moments?"

Presently he shook his head no.

"A shame. You need it. Too bad I can't do it for you, too, but one's enough. Anyhow you're not my type. But good luck —maybe someday you'll find someone like me." Opening the door, she disappeared. He stood alone in the corridor, feeling futile. And, all at once, extremely lonely.

I wonder what became of the analyst's files? he thought mechanically, turning his mind back to his job. No doubt Gino had them destroyed, so as not to fall into 'Star hands.

That's right, he thought. It is about four a.m. when it hits the hardest. But there's no one else like you, he thought. So that's that.

"Dr. Sweetscent?"

He glanced up. A Secret Service man had approached him. "Yes."

"Doctor, there's a woman outside who says she's your wife; she wants to be admitted to the building."

"It can't be," Eric said, with fear.

"You want to come with me and see if you can identify her, please?"

Automatically he fell in beside the Secret Service man. "Tell her to go away," he said. No, he thought, that won't do; you don't handle your problems like that, like a child waving a wand. "I have no doubt it's Kathy," he said. "Followed me here after all. In the name of God—what dreadful luck. Did you ever feel this way?" he asked the Secret Service man. "Did you ever find yourself unable to live with someone you had to live with?"

"Nope," the Secret Service man said unfeelingly, leading the way.

Ten

His wife stood in a corner of the outside compound which was the White House receiving room, reading a homeopape, the *New York Times*; she wore a dark coat and a good deal of make-up. Her skin, however, looked pale and her eyes seemed enormous, filled with anguish.

As he entered the compound she glanced up and said, "I'm reading about you; it seems you operated on Molinari and saved his life. Congratulations." She smiled at him but it was a bleak, trembling smile. "Take me somewhere and buy me a cup of coffee; I have a lot to tell you."

"You've got nothing to tell me," he said, unable to keep his stunned dismay out of his voice.

"I had a major insight after you left," Kathy said.

"So did I. It was that we'd done the right thing by splitting up."

"That's strange, because my insight was just the opposite," she said.

"I see that. Obviously. You're here. Listen: by law I don't have to live with you. All I'm required to do—"

"You ought to listen to what I have to say," Kathy said steadily. "It wouldn't be morally right for you just to walk off; that's too easy."

He sighed. Useful philosophy by which to achieve one's goals. But nevertheless he was snared. "Okay," he agreed. "I can't do that, just as I couldn't honestly deny you're my wife. So let's have the coffee." He felt fatalistic. Perhaps it was an attenuated form of his self-destructive instinct. In any case he had given in; taking her arm, he guided her along the passage, past the White House guards, toward the nearest cafeteria. "You look bad," he said. "Your color. And you're so tense."

"I've had a bad time," she admitted, "since you left. I guess I'm really dependent on you."

"Symbiosis," he said. "Unhealthy."

"It's not that!"

"Sure it is. This proves it. No, I'm not going to go back with you on the old basis." He felt—at least for the moment—

determined; he was prepared to fight it out, here and now. Eying her, he said, "Kathy, you look quite sick."

"That's because you've been hanging around the Mole; you're getting used to a sick environment. I'm perfectly well, just a little tired."

But she looked—smaller. As if something in her had dwindled away, as if she had dried up. It was almost—age. Yet not quite. Could their separation have done this much damage? He doubted it. His wife, since he had seen her last, had become frail, and he did not like this; despite his animosity he felt concern.

"You better get a multiphasic," he said. "A complete check-up."

"Christ," Kathy said, "I'm okay. I mean, I'll be okay, if you and I can iron out our misunderstanding and—"

"The termination of a relationship," he said, "is not a misunderstanding. It's a reorganization of life." He got his coffee cup and hers, filled both from the dispenser, paid the robant cashier.

When they had seated themselves at a table, Kathy lit a cigarette and said, "All right, suppose I admit it; without you I'm completely falling apart. Do you care?"

"I care, but that doesn't mean—"

"You'd just let me fade away and perish."

"I have one sick man who occupies all my time and attention. I can't heal you too." Especially, he thought, when I don't genuinely want to.

"But all you have to do is—" She sighed, sipped her coffee glumly; her hand trembled, he noticed, in an almost pseudo Parkinsonism. "Nothing. Just accept me back. Then I'll be well."

"No," he said. "I frankly don't believe it. You're sicker than that; there's some other cause." I'm not in the medical profession by mistake, he thought. I can spot a thoroughgoing illness pattern when I see it. But he could not diagnose it beyond that. "I think you know what ails you," he said bluntly. "You could tell me if you cared to. This makes me more wary than ever; you're not telling me all that you should, you're not being honest or responsible, and that's a hell of a basis on which to—"

"Okay!" She stared at him. "I'm sick; I admit it! But let's just say it's my business; you don't have to worry."

"I'd say," he said, "that there's been neurological damage."

Her head jerked; what color she had now drained from her face.

"I think," he said suddenly, "that I'm going to do something I genuinely think may be premature and overly drastic, but I'll try it and see what comes of it. I'm going to have you arrested."

"Good God *why?*" Panic-stricken, she gazed at him, now speechless; her hands lifted in defense, then fell back.

He rose, walked over to a cafeteria employee. "Miss," he said, "would you have a Secret Service man come to my table?" He pointed to his table.

"Yes sir," the woman said, blinking but unperturbed. She turned to a busboy, who, without further discussion, scampered off into the kitchen.

Eric returned to his table, reseated himself opposite Kathy. He resumed sipping his coffee, trying to keep himself calm and at the same time bracing himself for the scene that lay ahead. "My rationale," he said, "is that it's for your own good. Of course I don't know yet. But I think it'll turn out that way. And I think you know it."

Blanched, wizened with fright, Kathy implored, "I'll leave, Eric; I'll go back to San Diego—okay?"

"No," he said. "You got yourself into this by coming here; you made it my business. So you'll have to suffer the consequences. As they say." He felt completely rational and in control; it was a bad situation but he sensed the possibilities of something imminent which was far worse.

Kathy said huskily, "Okay, Eric. I'll tell you what it is. I've got myself addicted to JJ-180. That's the drug I told you about, the drug we all, including Marm Hastings, took. Now you know. I have nothing more to say; that covers it. And I've taken it once since. And just one exposure is addicting. As you no doubt realize; after all, you are a doctor."

"Who else knows?"

"Jonas Ackerman."

"You got it through Tijuana Fur & Dye? From our subsidiary?"

"Y-yes." She did not meet his gaze. Presently she added, "That's why Jonas knows; he got it for me—but don't tell anybody that. Please."

Eric said, "I won't." His mind had begun to function properly again, thank God. Was this the drug which Don Festenburg had obliquely referred to? The term JJ-180 roused dormant memories; he tried to straighten them out. "You made a hell of a mistake," he said, "from what I remember hearing about Frohedadrine, as it's also called. Yes, Hazeltine makes it."

At the table a Secret Service man appeared. "Yes, doctor?"

"I just wanted to inform you that this woman is my wife, as she says. And I'd like to have her cleared to remain here with me."

"All right, doctor. We'll run a routine security probe on her. But I'm certain it's okay." The Secret Service man nodded and departed.

"Thanks," Kathy said presently.

"I consider addiction to such a toxic drug a major illness," Eric said. "In this day and age worse than cancer or a massive cardiac arrest. It's obvious I can't dump you. You'll probably have to enter a hospital; you're probably aware of that already. I'll contact Hazeltine, find out all they know . . . but you understand it may be hopeless."

"Yes." She ducked her head in a spasmodic nod.

"Anyhow, you seem to have a great deal of courage." He reached out, took hold of her hand; it was dry and cold. Lifeless. He let it go. "That has always been one thing I've admired in you—you're not a coward. Of course that's how you got yourself into this in the first place, by having the guts to try some new substance. Well, so now we're back together." Glued fast to each other by your possibly fatal drug habit, he thought with morose despair. What a reason to resume our marriage. It was just a little too much for him.

"You're a good egg, too," Kathy said.

"Do you have any more of the stuff?"

She hesitated. "N-no."

"You're lying."

"I won't give it up. I'd rather leave you and try to make it on my own." Her fear had become, momentarily, obstinate defiance. "Look, if I'm hooked on JJ-180 I *can't* give you the supply I possess—that's what it means to be hooked! I don't want to take any more; I have to take it. Anyhow, there's not much." She shuddered. "It makes me wish I were dead; that goes without saying. God, I don't know how I got myself into this."

"What's the experience like? I understand it involves time."

"Yes, you lose your fixed point of reference; you pass easily back and forth. What I'd like to do is put myself at the service of someone or something, find a use for the period that I'm in the hands of. Could the Secretary use me? Eric, maybe I could get us out of the war; I could warn Molinari before he signs the Pact of Peace." Her eyes glowed with hope. "Isn't it worth trying?"

"Maybe so." However, he recalled Festenburg's statements on the subject; perhaps Molinari had use of JJ-180 already. But the Mole clearly had not tried—or been able—to find a route back to pre-pact days. Perhaps the drug affected each person uniquely. Many stimulant, hallucinogenic drugs did.

"Can I get access to him through you?" Kathy asked.

"I—suppose so." But something sprang to life inside him and made him wary. "It would take time. Right now he's recovering from the kidney operation, as you seem to know."

She shook her head then, nodding with pain. "Jesus, I feel awful, Eric. Like I'm not going to survive. You know . . . impending disaster. Give me a bunch of tranquilizers; it might help a little." She held out her hand and again he saw how badly it shook. Even worse, it seemed, than before.

"I'll put you in the building's infirmary," he decided, rising to his feet. "For the time being. While I figure out what to do. I'd prefer not to give you any medication, though; it might further potentiate the drug. With a new substance you never—"

Kathy broke in, "Want to know what I did, Eric, while you were off getting the Secret Service? I dropped a cap of JJ-180 into your coffee cup. Don't laugh; I'm serious. It's true, and you've drunk it. So you're addicted now. The effects should begin any time; you'd better get out of this cafeteria and to your own conapt because they're enormous." Her voice was flat and drab. "I did it because I thought you were going to have me arrested; you said you were and I believed you. So it's your own fault. I'm sorry . . . I wish I hadn't, but anyhow now you have a motive for curing me; you've *got* to find a solution. I just couldn't depend on your sheer goodwill; we've had too much trouble between us. Isn't that so?"

He managed to say, "I've heard that about addicts in general; they like to hook other people."

"Do you forgive me?" Kathy asked, also rising.

"No," he said. He felt wrathful and dizzy. Not only do I not forgive you, he thought, but I'll do everything I can to deny you a cure; nothing means anything to me now except getting back at you. Even my own cure. He felt pure, absolute hate for her. Yes, this was what she would do; this was his wife. This was precisely why he had tried to get away.

"We're in this together," Kathy said.

As steadily as possible he walked toward the exit of the cafeteria, step by step, past the tables, people. Leaving her

He almost made it. He almost

Everything returned. But totally different. New. Changed.

Across from him Don Festenburg leaned back, said, "You're lucky. But I'd better explain this. Here. The calendar." He pushed a brass object; across the desk Eric saw. "You've moved slightly over one year ahead." Eric stared. Sightlessly. Ornate inscriptions. "This is June 17, 2056. You're one of the happy few the drug affects this way. Most of them wander off into the past and get bogged down in manufacturing alternate universes; you know, playing God until at last the nerve destruction is too great and they degenerate to random twitches."

Eric tried to think of something useful to say. Could not.

"Save yourself the effort," Festenburg said, seeing him struggle. "I can do the talking; you'll only be here a few minutes so let me get it said. A year ago, when you were given JJ-180 in the building cafeteria, I was fortunate enough to get in on the flurry; your wife became hysterical and you of course —disappeared. She was taken in tow by the Secret Service and she admitted her addiction and what she had done."

"Oh." The room dropped and rose as he reflexively nodded.

"So that—you're feeling better? So anyhow, but now Kathy is cured, but we won't go into that; it hardly matters."

"What about—"

"Yes, your problem. Your addiction. There was no cure then, a year ago. However, you'll be gratified to hear that there is now. It came into being a couple of months ago, and I've been waiting for you to show up—so much more is known about JJ-180 now that I was privileged to compute almost to the minute when and where you'd appear." Reaching into his rumpled coat pocket, Festenburg brought out a small glass bottle. "This is the antidote which TF&D's subsidiary now manufactures. Would you like it? If you took it now, twenty milligrams, you'd be free of your addiction even after you return to your own time." He smiled, his sallow face wrinkling unnaturally. "But—there are problems."

Eric said, "How is the war going?"

Deprecatingly, Festenburg said, "What do you care? Good God, Sweetscent; your life depends on this bottle—you don't know what addiction to that stuff is like!"

"Is Molinari still alive?"

Festenburg shook his head. "Minutes he's got and he wants to know about the Mole's state of health. Listen." He leaned toward Eric, his mouth turned down poutingly, his face puffy with agitation. "*I want to make a deal, doctor.* I'm asking astonishingly little in return for these medication tablets. *Please* do business with me; the next time you take the drug—if you're not cured—you'll go ten years into the future and that'll be too late, too far."

Eric said, "Too late for you, but not for me. The cure will still exist."

"You won't even ask what I want in return?"

"No."

"Why not?"

Eric shrugged. "I don't feel comfortable; I'm being subjected to pressure and I don't care for that—I'll take my chances with the drug without you." It was sufficient merely to know that a cure existed. Such knowledge obliterated his anxiety and left him free to do as he liked. "Obviously, my best bet is to use the drug as often as physiologically possible, two or three times, going farther into the future each time, and then when its destructive effects become too great—"

"Even one use," Festenburg said between his clenched

teeth, "causes irreversible, brain damage. You damn fool—
you've already used it too much. You saw your wife; you want
that damage for yourself?"

After a moment, considering deeply, Eric said, "For what I'll
get out of it, yes. By the time I've used it twice I'll know the
outcome of the war and if the outcome is unfavorable possibly
I'll be in a position to advise Molinari how it could be avoided.
What's my health compared to that?" He was silent then; it
seemed perfectly clear to him. There was nothing to discuss;
he sat waiting for the effects of the drug to wear off. He waited
to return to his own time.

Opening the glass bottle, Festenburg poured out the white
tablets; he dropped them to the floor and ground them to dust
under his heel.

"Did it occur to you," Festenburg said, "that within the
next ten years Terra may be so destroyed in the war that
TF&D's subsidiary may no longer be in a position to supply
this antidote?"

It had not occurred to him; although jolted, he managed
not to show it. "We'll see," he murmured.

"Frankly I have no knowledge of the future. However, I
have knowledge of the past—of *your* future, this last year." He
produced a homeopape, which he turned toward Eric and
spread out on the desk. "Six months following your experience in the White House cafeteria. It'll interest you."

Eric scanned the lead article and its headline.

SWEETSCENT IMPLICATED AS PRIME MOVER IN
DOCTORS' PLOT AGAINST ACTING UN SECRETARY
DONALD FESTENBURG, HELD BY SECRET SERVICE

Abruptly Festenburg whipped the newspaper away, crumpling it and tossing it behind him. "I'm not saying what
became of Molinari—find that out for yourself, since you're
uninterested in reaching a rational agreement with me."

After a pause Eric said, "You've had a year to print up a fake
of the *Times*. I seem to recall that such has been done before in
political history . . . Joseph Stalin did it to Lenin during
Lenin's last year. Had a completely phony edition of *Pravda*
printed, given to Lenin, who—"

"My uniform," Festenburg said wildly, his face dark red and quivering as if it were about to burst. "Look at my shoulder patches!"

"Why couldn't that be faked, too? I'm not saying it is, or that the homeopape was faked." After all, he was not in a position to know one way or another. "I'm merely saying it could be, and that's enough to cause me to suspend my judgment."

With enormous effort Festenburg managed to gain partial control of himself. "All right; you're playing it cautious. This entire experience is disorienting to you—I understand. But doctor, be realistic for a moment; you've seen the pape, you know that in a way which I'm not specifying I succeeded Molinari as UN Secretary. Plus the fact that six months from your own time period you were caught red-handed conspiring against me. And—"

"Acting UN Secretary," Eric amended.

"What?" Festenburg stared at him.

"A pro tem situation is implied. Transitional. And I wasn't —or won't be—caught 'red-handed.' The pape merely relates an accusation; there's been no trial, no conviction. I could be innocent. I could be about to be framed, and by you. Again, recall Stalin during his last year, the so-called—"

"Don't lecture me in my own field! Yes, I know of the situation you related; I know how completely Stalin fooled the dying Lenin. And I know about the doctors' plot, paranoiacally engineered by Stalin during his final illness. Okay—" Festenburg's voice was steady. "I admit it. That homeopape which I showed you just now—it was faked."

Eric smiled.

"And I'm not Acting UN Secretary," Festenburg continued. "But as to what actually has happened—*I'll leave it to you to guess*. And you're not going to be able to; you're going to return to your own time a few moments from now knowing nothing, not a damn thing, about the world of the future— whereas if you had made a few deals with me you could know everything." He glowered at Eric.

"I guess," Eric said, "I'm a fool."

"More than that: polymorphic perverse. You could be going back armed with incredible weapons—in the figurative sense, of course—to save yourself, your wife, Molinari. And for one year you'll stew . . . assuming that you survive your drug addiction that long. We'll see."

For the first time Eric felt a wavering doubt. Was he making an error? After all, he had not even heard what he would need to pony up in order to consummate the deal. But now the antidote had been destroyed; it was too late. This was just talk.

Rising, Eric took a quick look out of the window at the city of Cheyenne.

The city was in ruins.

While he stood staring at that he felt the reality of the room, the substantiality of what he saw, ebb; it eased away from him and he clutched at it, trying to retain it.

"Much luck, doctor," Festenburg said hollowly, and then he, too, became a streak of foglike wispiness that eddied gray and indistinct around him, blending with the disintegrated remnants of the desk, the walls of the room, the objects that a moment before had been utterly stable.

He lurched—and struggled to catch himself. Losing his balance, he pitched into the sickening experience of no weight . . . and then, with pain banging at his head, he looked up, saw around him the tables and people of the White House cafeteria.

A group had formed around him. Concerned but hesitant. Unwilling to actually touch him; they remained spectators.

"Thanks for the help," he grated, and got unsteadily to his feet.

The spectators melted guiltily off to their tables, leaving him alone. Alone—except for Kathy.

"You were out about three minutes," she said.

He said nothing; he had no desire to speak to her, to have anything to do with her. He felt nauseated and his legs shook under him; his head felt splintered and broken and he thought, This must be how it feels to experience carbon monoxide poisoning. As described in the old textbooks. A sense of having imbibed of death itself.

"Can I help you?" Kathy asked. "I remember how I felt the first time."

Eric said, "I'll take you to the infirmary now." He grabbed her by the arm; her purse bobbed against him. "You must have your supply in your purse," he said, and yanked it away from her.

A moment later he held two elongated spansules in his hand. Dropping them into his pocket, he returned her purse to her.

"Thanks," she said with massive irony.

"Thank you, too, dear. We've each got a lot of love for one another. In this new phase of our marital relationship." He led her from the cafeteria then; she accompanied him without resistance.

I'm glad I didn't make a deal with Festenburg, he thought. But Festenburg would be after him again; this was not the end. However, he possessed an advantage over Festenburg, one which the sallow-faced speech writer did not—at this date—know of.

From his encounter a year hence he knew that Festenburg had political ambitions. That in some fashion he would attempt a coup and would try to buy support. The UN Secretary uniform had turned out to be ersatz, but Festenburg's aspirations had not.

And it was entirely possible that Festenburg had not yet begun this phase of his career.

Festenburg, in this time period, could not take Eric Sweetscent by surprise because one year in the future, unknown to his present self, he had tipped his hand. And, in doing so, had not grasped the implications of what he had done.

It was a major political error and one which could not be retrieved. Especially in view of the fact that other political strategists, some with immense capabilities, were on the scene.

One of these was Gino Molinari.

After he had gotten his wife admitted to the White House infirmary, he placed a vidphone call to Jonas Ackerman at TF&D in Tijuana.

"So you know about Kathy," Jonas said. He did not look happy.

"I'm not going to ask you why you did it," Eric said. "I'm calling in order to—"

"Did what?" Jonas' face convulsed. "She told you I put her on the stuff, did she? Not true, Eric. Why should I do that? Ask yourself."

"We won't discuss that now." There was no time. "I want to find out, first, if Virgil knows anything about JJ-180."

"Yes, but no more than I do. There's not much—"

"Let me talk to Virgil."

Reluctantly, Jonas switched the call to Virgil's office. Eric after a moment faced the old man, who leered with guileless abandon when he saw who was calling. "Eric! I read in the pape—you've already saved his life once. I knew you'd make out. Now, if you can do that every day—" Virgil chuckled delightedly.

"Kathy is addicted to JJ-180. I need help; I have to get her off it."

The pleased emotions left Virgil's face. "That's horrible! But what can I do, Eric? I'd like to, of course. We all love Kathy around here. You're a doctor, Eric; you ought to be able to do something for her." He tried to babble on but Eric interrupted.

"Tell me who to contact at the subsidiary. Where JJ-180 is made."

"Oh yes. Hazeltine Corporation, in Detroit. Let's see . . . who should you talk to there. Maybe Bert Hazeltine himself. Just a minute; Jonas is up here in my office. He's saying something."

Jonas appeared on the vidscreen. "I was trying to tell you, Eric. When I found out about Kathy's situation I contacted Hazeltine Corporation immediately. They've already sent someone out; he's on his way to Cheyenne; I figured Kathy would show up there after she disappeared. Keep Virgil and me posted as to what progress he can make. Good luck." He disappeared from the screen, evidently relieved to have contributed his share.

Thanking Virgil, Eric rang off. Rising, he at once went to the White House receiving room to see if the representative of Hazeltine Corporation had shown up yet.

"Oh yes, Dr. Sweetscent," the girl said, checking her book. "Two persons arrived just a moment ago; you're being paged in the halls and in the cafeterias." She read the names from the book. "A Mr. Bert Hazeltine and a woman, Miss Bachis . . . I'm trying to read her writing; I think that's it. They were sent upstairs to your conapt."

When he reached his conapt he found the door ajar; in the small living room sat two individuals, a middle-aged man, well dressed, in a long overcoat, and a blonde-haired woman, in her late thirties; she wore glasses and her features were heavy and professionally competent.

"Mr. Hazeltine?" Eric said, entering with his hand out.

Both the man and woman rose. "Hello, Dr. Sweetscent." Bert Hazeltine shook hands with him. "This is Hilda Bachis; she's with the UN Narcotics Control Bureau. They had to be informed of your wife's situation, doctor; it's the law. However—"

Miss Bachis spoke up crisply, "We're not interested in arresting or punishing your wife, doctor; we want to help her, as you do. We've already arranged to see her but we thought we'd talk with you first and then go down to the infirmary."

In a quiet voice Hazeltine said, "Your wife has how large a supply of the drug with her?"

"None," Eric said.

"Let me explain to you, then," Hazeltine said, "the difference between habituation and addiction. In addiction—"

"I'm a doctor," Eric reminded him. "You don't have to spell it out for me." He seated himself, still feeling the effects of his bout with the drug; his head still ached and his chest hurt when he breathed.

"Then you realize that the drug has entered her liver metabolism and now is required for that metabolism to continue. If she's denied the drug she'll die in—" Hazeltine calculated. "How much has she taken?"

"Two or three capsules."

"Without it she'll die very possibly within twenty-four hours."

"And with it?"

"She'll live roughly four months. By that time, doctor, we may have an antidote; don't think we're not trying. We've even tried artiforg transplant, removing the liver and substituting—"

"Then she's got to have more of the drug," Eric said, and he thought about himself. His own situation. "Suppose she had only taken it once. Would that—"

"Doctor," Hazeltine said, "don't you understand? JJ-180 was not designed as a medicine; *it's a weapon of war.* It was *intended* to be capable of creating an absolute addiction by a single dose; it was *intended* to bring about extensive nerve and brain damage. It's odorless and tasteless; you can't tell when it's being administered to you in, say, food or drink. From the start we faced the problem of our own people becoming accidentally addicted; we were waiting until we had the cure and then we would use JJ-180 against the enemy. But—" He eyed Eric. "Your wife was not accidentally addicted, doctor. It was done with deliberate intent. We know where she got it." He glanced at Miss Bachis.

"Your wife couldn't have obtained it from Tijuana Fur & Dye," Miss Bachis said, "because no quantity of the drug whatsoever has been released by Hazeltine to its parent company."

"Our ally," Bert Hazeltine said. "It was a protocol of the Pact of Peace; we had to deliver to them a sample of every new weapon of war produced on Terra. The UN compelled me to ship a quantity of JJ-180 to Lilistar." His face had become slack with what for him was now a stale, flat resentment.

Miss Bachis said, "The quantity of JJ-180, for security purposes, was shipped to Lilistar in five separate containers on five separate transports. Four reached Lilistar. One did not; the reegs destroyed it with an automine. And, since then, we've heard persistent rumors through our intelligence service operating within the Empire that 'Star agents have carried the drug back here to Terra, to use against our people."

Eric nodded. "All right; she didn't get it at Tijuana Fur & Dye." But what did it matter where Kathy had gotten it?

"So your wife," Miss Bachis said, "has been approached by 'Star intelligence agents and therefore can't be kept here in Cheyenne; we've already talked to the Secret Service and she's to be transferred back to Tijuana or San Diego. There's no alternative; she hasn't admitted it, of course, but she's being supplied in exchange for acting as a 'Star recruit. That could be why she followed you here."

"But," Eric said, "if you cut off her supply of the drug—"

"We don't intend that," Hazeltine said. "In fact just the opposite; the most thoroughgoing method of detaching her from the 'Star agents is to supply her directly from our stock. That's policy in cases such as this . . . and your wife is not the first, doctor; we've seen this before and take my word for it, we know what to do. That is, within the limited number of possibilities open to us. First, she needs the drug merely to stay alive; that alone makes it essential to keep her supplied. But there's one more fact you should know. The shipment that was sent to Lilistar but was destroyed by a reeg mine . . . we understand now that the reegs were able to salvage portions of that ship. They obtained a minute but nonetheless real quantity of JJ-180." He paused. "They're working on a cure, too."

The room was silent.

"*We* don't have a cure anywhere on Terra," Hazeltine continued, after a pause. "Lilistar, of course, isn't even trying, despite what they may have told your wife; they're simply cranking out their own supply of the drug, no doubt to use against us as well as the enemy. That's a fact of life. But—a cure may already exist among the reegs; it would be unfair and morally wrong not to tell you this. I'm not suggesting that you defect to the enemy; I'm not suggesting anything—I'm just being honest with you. In four months we may have it or we may not; I have no way of knowing the future."

"The drug," Eric said, "permits some of its users to pass into the future."

Hazeltine and Miss Bachis exchanged glances.

"True," Hazeltine said, nodding. "That's highly classified information, as you no doubt know. I suppose you learned that from your wife. Is that the direction she moves when she's under the influence of the drug? It's relatively rare; withdrawal into the past seems to be the rule."

Guardedly Eric said, "Kathy and I have talked about it."

"Well," Hazeltine said, "it's a possibility, logically at least. To go into the future, obtain the cure—perhaps not a quantity of it but anyhow the formula; memorize it and then return to the present, turn the formula over to our chemists at H. Corporation. And that would be that. It seems almost *too* easy, doesn't it? The drug's effects contain the method for procuring the nullifying agent, the source of a new, unknown molecule to enter the liver metabolism in place of JJ-180. . . . The first objection that occurs to me is that there may never be such an antidote, in which case going into the future is useless. After all, there is not yet any sure cure for addiction to opium derivatives; heroin is still illegal and dangerous, as much so as a century ago. But another objection, a deeper one, occurs to me. Frankly—and I've supervised all phases of testing JJ-180—I feel that the time period entered by the subject under its influence is phony. I don't believe it's the real future or the real past."

"Then what is it?" Eric asked.

"What we at Hazeltine Corporation have maintained from the start; we claim that JJ-180 is an hallucinogenic drug and we mean just that. Just because the hallucinations seem real, that's no criterion to go by; *most* hallucinations seem real whatever the cause, whether from a drug, a psychosis, brain damage, or electrical stimulation given directly to specific areas of the brain. You must know that, doctor; a person experiencing hallucinosis doesn't merely think he sees, say, a tree of oranges—he really does see it. For him it's an authentic experience, as much so as our presence here in your living room. No one who's taken JJ-180 and gone into the past has returned with any artifact; he doesn't disappear or—"

Miss Bachis interrupted, "I disagree, Mr. Hazeltine. I've talked to a number of JJ-180 addicts and they've given details about the past which I'm positive they wouldn't know except by having gone there. I can't prove it but I do believe it. Excuse me for interrupting."

"Buried memories," Hazeltine said irritably. "Or Christ, possibly past lives; maybe there is reincarnation."

Eric said, "If JJ-180 did induce authentic time travel it might not constitute a good weapon to use against the reegs. It might give them more than it took. So you must believe it's hallucinosis, Mr. Hazeltine. As long as you have plans of selling it to the government."

"An *ad hominem* argument," Hazeltine said. "Attack my motives, not my argument; I'm surprised, doctor." He looked glum. "But maybe you're right. How do I know? I've never taken it, and we've given it to no one once we discovered its addictive properties; we're limited to animal experiments, our first—and unfortunate—human subjects, and more recent ones such as your wife whom the 'Starmen have made into addicts. And—" He hesitated, then shrugged and continued. "And, obviously, we've given it to captured reegs in POW camps; otherwise we would have no way of determining its effects on them."

"How have they responded?" Eric asked.

"More or less as our own people. Complete addiction, neurological decay, hallucinations of an overpowering order which made them apathetic to their actual situation." He added, half to himself, "The things you have to do in wartime. And they talk about the Nazis."

Miss Bachis said, "We must win the war, Mr. Hazeltine."

"Yes," Hazeltine said lifelessly. "Oh, you're so goddam right, Miss Bachis; how truly right you are." He stared sightlessly down at the floor.

"Give Dr. Sweetscent the supply of the drug," Miss Bachis said.

Nodding, Hazeltine reached into his coat. "Here." He held out a flat metal tin. "JJ-180. Legally we can't give it to your wife; we can't supply a known addict. So you take it—this is a formality, obviously—and what you do with it is your own business. Anyhow, there's enough in that tin to keep her alive for as long as she'll live." He did not meet Eric's gaze; he continued to stare at the floor.

Eric, as he accepted the tin, said, "You're not very happy about this invention of your company's."

"Happy?" Hazeltine echoed. "Oh sure; can't you see? Doesn't it show? You know, oddly enough, the worst has been watching the reeg POWs after they've taken it. They just plain fold up, wilt; there's no remission at all for them . . . they live JJ-180, once they've touched it. They're *glad* to be on it; the hallucinations are that—what should I say?—entertaining for them . . . no, not entertaining. Engrossing? I don't know, but they act as if they've looked into the ultimate. But it's one which clinically speaking, physiologically speaking, constitutes an insidious hell."

"Life is short," Eric pointed out.

"And brutish and nasty," Hazeltine added, vaguely quoting, as if responding unconsciously. "I can't be fatalistic, doctor. Maybe you're lucky or smart, some such thing."

"No," Eric said. "Hardly that." To be a depressive was certainly not desirable; fatalism was not a talent but a protracted illness. "How soon after taking JJ-180 do the withdrawal symptoms appear? In other words must—"

"You can go from twelve to twenty-four hours between dosages," Miss Bachis said. "Then the physiological requirements, the collapse of adequate liver metabolism, sets in. It's— unpleasant. So to speak."

Hazeltine said hoarsely, "Unpleasant—God in heaven, be realistic; it's unendurable. It's a death agony, literally. And the person knows it. *Feels* it without being able to label it. After all, how many of us have gone into our death agonies?"

"Gino Molinari has," Eric said. "But he's unique." Placing the tin of JJ-180 in his coat pocket, he thought, So I have up to twenty-four hours before I'll be forced to take my second dose of the drug. But it could come as soon as this evening.

So the reegs may have a cure, he thought. Would I go over to them to save my life? Kathy's life? I wonder. He did not really know.

Perhaps, he thought, I'll know after I undergo my first bout with the withdrawal symptoms. And, if not that, after I detect the first signs of neurological deterioration in my body.

It still dazed him that his wife had, just like that, addicted him. What hatred that showed. What enormous contempt for the value of life. But didn't he feel the same way? He remembered his initial discussion with Gino Molinari; his sentiments had emerged then and he had faced them. In the final analysis he felt as Kathy did. This was one great effect of war; the survival of one individual seemed trivial. So perhaps he could blame it on the war. That would make it easier.

But he knew better.

Eleven

On his way to the infirmary to turn over to Kathy her supply of the drug, he found himself facing, unbelievably, the slumped, ill figure of Gino Molinari. In his wheel chair the UN Secretary sat with his heavy wool rug over his knees, his eyes writhing like separate living things, pinning Eric into immobility.

"Your conapt was bugged," Molinari said. "Your conversation with Hazeltine and Bachis was picked up, recorded, and delivered in transcript form to me."

"So quickly?" Eric managed to say. Thank God he had made no reference to his own addiction.

"Get her out of here," Molinari moaned. "She's a 'Star fink; she'll do anything—I know. This has happened before." He was shaking. "As a matter of fact she's already out of here; my Secret Service men grabbed her and took her to the field, to a 'copter. So I don't know why I'm getting myself upset like this . . . intellectually I know the situation's in hand."

"If you have a transcript you know that Miss Bachis already arranged for Kathy to—"

"I know! All right." Molinari panted for breath, his face unhealthy and raw; his skin hung in folds, dark wrinkled wattles of loose flesh. "See how Lilistar operates? Using our own drug against us; it's just like the bastards, something they'd get a kick out of. We ought to drop it in their reservoirs. I let you in here and then you let your wife in; to obtain that crap, that miserable drug, she'd be willing to do anything—assassinate me if they asked her to. I know everything there is to know about Frohedadrine; I'm the one who thought up the name. From the German *Froh*, meaning joy, and the Latin *heda-*, the root for pleasure. *Drine*, of course—" He broke off, his swollen lips twitching. "I'm too sick to get agitated like this; I'm supposed to be recovering from that operation. *Are you tying to heal me or kill me, doctor? Or do you know?*"

Eric said, "I don't know." He felt confused, numbed; this was just too much.

"You look bad. This is tough on you, even though

601

according to your security file and your own statements you detest your wife—and her you. I guess you figure if you'd stayed with her she wouldn't have become an addict. Listen: everyone has to live his own life; she has to take the responsibility. You didn't make her do it. She *decided* to do it. Does that help you? Feel any better?" He scanned Eric's face for his reaction.

"I'll—be okay," Eric said briefly.

"In a pig's ass. You look as bad as she does; I went down there to have a look at her, I couldn't resist. The poor goddam dame; you already can make out the destruction caused by that stuff. And giving her a new liver and all new blood won't help; that's been tried before, as they told you."

"Did you talk to Kathy at all?"

"Me? Talk to a 'Star fink?" Molinari glared at him. "Yes, I talked to her a little. While they were wheeling her out. I was curious to see what sort of woman you'd get mixed up with; you've got a masochistic streak eight yards wide and she proves it; she's a harpy, Sweetscent, a monster. Like you told me. You know what she said?" He grinned. "She told me *you're* an addict. Anything to cause trouble, right?"

"Right," Eric said stiffly.

"Why are you looking at me that way?" Molinari regarded him, his black, fat eyes showing his regained control. "It upsets you to hear that, doesn't it? To know she'd do everything possible to destroy your career here. Eric, if I thought you'd dabbled with that stuff I wouldn't have you kicked out of here; *I'd have you killed.* During wartime I kill people; it's my job. Just as you know and I know, because we discussed it, there may come a time not far from now when it'll be necessary for you to—" He hesitated. "What we said. Kill even me. Right, doctor?"

Eric said, "I have to give her the drug supply. May I go, Secretary? Before they take off."

"No," Molinari said. "You can't go because there's something I want to ask you. Minister Freneksy is here still; you're aware of that. With his party, in the East Wing, in seclusion." He held out his hand. "I want one capsule of JJ-180, doctor. Give it to me and then forget we had this talk."

To himself Eric thought, I know what you're going to do.

Or rather try to do. But you don't have a chance; this isn't the Renaissance.

"I'm going to hand it to him personally," Molinari said. "To see that it actually gets there and isn't drunk by some pimp along the way."

"No," Eric said. "I absolutely refuse."

"Why?" Molinari cocked his head on one side.

"It's suicidal. For everyone on Terra."

"You know how the Russians got rid of Beria? Beria carried a pistol into the Kremlin, which was against the law; he had it in his briefcase and they stole his briefcase and shot him with his own pistol. You think matters at the top have to be complex? There're simple solutions average people always overlook; that's the main defect of the mass man—" Molinari broke off, put his hand suddenly to his chest. "My heart. I think it stopped. It's going now, but for a second there, nothing." He had blanched and his voice now ebbed to a whisper.

"I'll wheel you to your room." Eric stepped behind Molinari's wheel chair and began to push it; the Mole did not protest but sat slumped forward, massaging his fleshy chest, exploring and touching himself, with the tentativeness of disintegrating, overwhelming fear. Everything else was forgotten; he perceived nothing more than his sick, failing body. It had become his universe.

With the assistance of two nurses he managed to get Molinari back into bed.

"Listen, Sweetscent," Molinari whispered as he lay back against the pillow. "I don't have to get that stuff through you; I can put pressure on Hazeltine and he'll deliver it right to me. Virgil Ackerman is a friend of mine; Virgil will see to it that Hazeltine complies. And don't try to tell me my job; you do yours and I'll do mine." He shut his eyes and groaned. "God, I know an artery near my heart just burst; I can feel the blood leaking out. Get Teagarden in here." Again he groaned and then turned his face to the wall. "What a day. But I'll get that Freneksy yet." All at once he opened his eyes and said, "I knew it was a stupid idea. But that's the kind of ideas I've been having lately, dumb ideas like that. And what else can I do but that? Can you think of something else?" He waited. "No.

Because there isn't anything else, that's why." Again he shut
his eyes. "I feel terrible. I think I really am dying this time and
you won't be able to save me."

"I'll get Dr. Teagarden," Eric said, and started toward the
door.

Molinari said, "I know you're an addict, doctor." He drew
himself up slightly. "I can almost invariably tell when someone
is lying, and your wife wasn't. As soon as I saw you I spotted it;
you don't know how much you've changed."

After a pause Eric said, "What are you going to do?"

"We'll see, doctor," Molinari said, and again turned his face
to the wall.

As soon as he had completed the task of delivering the supply of JJ-180 to Kathy he boarded an express ship for Detroit.

Forty-five minutes later he had reached the Detroit field and
was on his way to Hazeltine Corporation by taxi. Gino Molinari, not the drug, had forced him to move this swiftly; he
could not even wait until evening.

"Here we are, sir," the autonomic circuit of the cab said respectfully. It slid open its door so that he could emerge. "That
gray one-story building with the hedge of rose-colored calyx
with the whorl of green bracts at the base . . . that is Hazeltine Corporation." Looking out, Eric saw the building, the
lawn and heather hedge. It wasn't a large structure as industrial installations went. So this was the point at which JJ-180
had entered the world.

"Wait," he instructed the cab. "Do you have a glass of
water?"

"Certainly." From the slot facing Eric a paper cup of water
slid forward, teetered on the lip of the slot, and then halted.

Seated in the cab Eric swallowed the capsule of JJ-180 which
he had brought with him. Purloined from Kathy's stock.

Several minutes passed.

"Why aren't you getting out, sir?" the cab inquired. "Have
I done something wrong?"

Eric waited. When he felt the drug begin to reach him he
paid the cab, got out and walked slowly up the redwood-
round path toward the office of Hazeltine Corporation.

The building flashed as if caught by a whip of lightning.

And, overhead, the sky twisted laterally. He saw, gazing up, the clear blue of day dawdle as if attempting to remain and then collapse; he shut his eyes because the dizziness was too great, the reference point of outside objects had become too tenuous, and he walked, step by step, feeling his way ahead, bent down, for some reason motivated to continue in motion, however slow.

It hurt. This, unlike the initial exposure, was a major readjustment of the reality structure impinging on him. His steps made no sound, he noticed; he had strayed onto the lawn, but he still kept his eyes shut. Hallucination, he thought, of another world. Is Hazeltine right? By a paradox perhaps I can answer that within the hallucination itself . . . if that is what it is. He did not think so; Hazeltine was wrong.

When a heather branch brushed his arm he let his eyes open. One of his feet had penetrated the soft black soil of a flower bed; he rested on a half-crushed tuberous begonia. Past the heather hedge the gray side of Hazeltine Corporation rose, exactly as before, and above it the sky was a washed-out blue with irregular clouds sweeping toward the north, the same sky, as nearly as he could tell. What had changed? He returned to the redwood-round path. Shall I go in? he asked himself. He looked back toward the street. The cab had gone. Detroit, the buildings and ramps of the city, seemed somehow elaborate. But he did not know this area.

When he reached the porch the door flew open automatically for him and he looked in on a neat office, with relaxing, leather-covered chairs, magazines, a deep-pile carpet whose design changed continuously . . . he saw, through an open doorway, a business area: accounting machines and a computer of some ordinary kind, and at the same time he heard the buzz of activity beyond that, from the labs themselves.

As he started to sit down, a four-armed reeg walked into the office, its blue, chitinous face inexpressive, its embryonic wings pressed tightly to its sloping, bullet-shiny back. It whistled a greeting to him—he had not heard that about them—and passed on out through the doorway. Another reeg, manipulating its extensive network of double-jointed arms vigorously, made its appearance, traveled up to Eric Sweetscent, halted, and produced a small square box.

Scudding across the side of the box, words in English took shape and departed; he woke to the fact that he had to pay attention to them. The reeg was communicating with him.

WELCOME TO HAZELTINE CORPORATION

He read the words but did not know what to do with them. This was a receptionist; he saw that the reeg was a female. How did he reply? The reeg waited, buzzing; its structure was so convoluted that it seemed unable to remain entirely still; its multilensed eyes shrank and grew as they were partially absorbed back into the skull, then pushed out like flattened corks. If he hadn't known better he would have said it was blind. And then he realized that these were its false eyes; the genuine ones, compound, were at its top-arm elbows.

He said, "May I speak to one of your chemists?" And he thought, So we did lose the war. To these things. And now Terra is occupied. And its industries are run by these. But, he thought, human beings still exist, because this reeg was not dumfounded to see me; it has accepted my presence as natural. So we can't be mere slaves, either.

REGARDING WHAT MATTER?

Hesitating, he said, "A drug. Produced here in the past. Called either Frohedadrine or JJ-180; both names refer to the same product."

JUST A MOMENT PLEASE

The female reeg scuttled through the inner doorway to the business office, then disappeared entirely. He stood waiting, thinking to himself that if this was an hallucination it certainly was not a voluntary one.

A larger reeg, a male, appeared; its joints seemed stiff and Eric realized that it was old. They had a short life span, measured in terms of months, not years. This one had almost come to the end of his.

Utilizing the translating box, the elderly male reeg said:

WHAT IS YOUR INQUIRY ABOUT JJ-180?
PLEASE BE BRIEF

Eric bent, picked up a magazine that lay on a table nearby. It was not in English; the cover bore a picture of two reegs and the writing consisted of the crabbed, pictorial reegian script. Startled, he stared at it. The magazine was *Life*. Somehow it shocked him more than the actual sight of the enemy itself.

PLEASE

The elderly reeg rattled with impatience.

Eric said, "I want to purchase an antidote to the addictive drug JJ-180. In order to break my addiction."

YOU DID NOT NEED ME FOR THAT; THE
RECEPTIONIST COULD HAVE TAKEN CARE OF YOU

Turning, the elderly reeg scrabbled haltingly off, eager to return to his work. Eric was left alone.

The receptionist returned with a small brown paper bag; she held it out to him, not with a jointed arm but with a mandible. Eric accepted it, opened it, and looked inside. A bottle of pills. This was it; there was nothing more to be done.

THAT WILL BE FOUR THIRTY-FIVE SIR

The receptionist watched as he got out his wallet; he took a five-dollar-bill from it and passed it to her.

I AM SORRY SIR; THIS IS OUTDATED WARTIME
CURRENCY NO LONGER IN USE

"You can't take it?" he said.

WE HAVE A RULE FORBIDDING US TO

"I see," he said numbly, and wondered what to do. He could gulp down the contents of the bottle before she could stop him. But then he would probably be arrested, and the rest he could visualize in an instant: once their police had examined his identification they would know that he came from the past. And they would be aware that he might carry back information affecting the outcome—which had obviously been favorable for them—of the war. And they couldn't afford that. They would have to murder him. Even if the two races now lived in concert.

"My watch," he said. He unfastened it from his wrist, passed it to the female reeg. "Seventeen jewel, seventy-year battery."

On inspiration he added, "An antique, perfectly preserved. From prewar days."

JUST A MOMENT SIR

Accepting the watch, the receptionist made her way on her long yielding legs to the business office, conferred with someone invisible to Eric; he waited, making no attempt to devour the pills—he felt trapped in a membrane of crushing density, unable to act or escape from action, caught in a halfway land between.

From the business office something emerged. He looked up.

It was a human. A man, young, with close-cropped hair, wearing a work smock that was stained and rumpled. "What's the trouble, buddy?" the man asked. Behind him the reeg receptionist followed, her joints clacking.

Eric said, "Sorry to bother you. Could you and I talk in private?"

The man shrugged. "Sure." He led Eric from the room and into what appeared to be a storage chamber; shutting the door, the man turned to him placidly and said, "That watch is worth three hundred dollars; she doesn't know what to do with it—she's only got a 600-type brain; you know how the D-class is." He lit a cigarette, offered the pack—Camels—to Eric.

"I'm a time traveler," Eric said as he took a cigarette.

"Sure you are." The man laughed. He extended his match to Eric.

"Don't you know the action of JJ-180? It was made right here."

After a thoughtful pause the man said, "But not for years. Because of its addictive qualities and its toxicity. In fact there hasn't been any since the war."

"They won the war?"

"'They'? Who's that?"

"The reegs," Eric said.

"The reegs," the man said, "is us. Not they. *They* was Lilistar. If you're a time traveler you ought to know that even better than I."

"The Pact of Peace—"

"There was no 'Pact of Peace.' Listen, buddy, I minored in world history in college; I was going to teach. I know all about the last war; it was my specialty. Gino Molinari—he was UN Secretary then, just before hostilities broke out—signed the Era of Common Understanding Protocols with the reegs and then the reegs and the 'Starmen started fighting and Molinari brought us in, on the reeg side, because of the protocols, and we won." He smiled. "And this stuff you say you're hooked on, it was a weapon that Hazeltine Corp. developed in 2055, during the war, for use against Lilistar, and it didn't work out because the Freneksytes were advanced even over us in pharmacology and quickly worked out an antidote—which antidote you're attempting to buy. God, they *had* to develop it; we got the snunk into their drinking water; that was the Mole's idea himself." He explained, "That was Molinari's nickname."

"All right," Eric said. "Let's just leave it at this. I want to buy the antidote. I want to trade that watch. Is it satisfactory?" He still held the brown paper bag; reaching into it, he lifted out the bottle. "Get me some water and let me take it and then let me get out of here; I don't know how long it'll be before I go back to my own time. Is there any objection to that?" He had difficulty controlling his voice; it tried to rise and escape. And he was shaking, but he did not know with what. Anger, possibly fear—more likely bewilderment. At this point he did not even know if he were bewildered.

"Calm down." Cigarette jutting from his lips, the man walked off, evidently in search of water. "Can you take them with a Coke?"

"Yes," Eric said.

The man returned with a half-empty bottle of Coca-Cola and watched as Eric struggled to get the pills down one after another.

At the door the female reeg receptionist appeared.

IS HE ALL RIGHT?

"Yes," the man said, as Eric managed to wash down the last pill.

WILL YOU TAKE CHARGE OF THE WATCH?

Accepting it from her, the man said, "Of course it's company property; that goes without saying." He started out of the storeroom.

"Was there ever a UN Secretary near the end of the war named Donald Festenburg?" Eric asked.

"No," the man said.

HE SHOULD RECEIVE SOME CASH SETTLEMENT
FOR THE WATCH IN ADDITION TO THE MEDICATION

The flashing box, declaring its message, was extended by the female reeg toward the man; he halted, frowning, then shrugged. "One hundred in cash," he said to Eric. "Take it or leave it; it's all the same to me."

"I'll take it," Eric said, and followed him to the business office. As the man counted out the money—in odd, unfamiliar bills which Eric had never seen the like of—he thought of another question. "How did Gino Molinari end his term in office?"

The man glanced up. "Assassinated."

"Shot?"

"Yes, by old-fashioned lead slugs. A fanatic got him. Because of his lenient immigration policy, his letting the reegs settle here on Terra. There was a racist faction, scared about polluting the blood . . . as if reegs and humans could inter-breed." He laughed.

This, then, Eric thought, may be the world from which Molinari got that bullet-riddled corpse which Festenburg showed me. The dead Gino Molinari lying mangled and blood-spattered in his helium-filled casket.

From behind him a dry, matter-of-fact voice said, "Are you not going to make the attempt, Dr. Sweetscent, to take the an-tidote for JJ-180 back to your wife?"

It was an organism without eyes entirely, and he thought, seeing it, of fruit he had come onto as a child, overripe pears lying in the weedy grass, covered by a crawling layer of yellow jackets attracted by the sweet odor of rot. The creature was vaguely spherical. It had fitted itself into a harness, however, which had squeezed its soft body tortuously; no doubt it needed this in order to get around in the Terran environment. But he wondered why it was worth it to the thing.

"Is he really a time traveler?" the man at the cash register asked, jerking his head at Eric.

The spherical organism, wedged within its plastic harness,

said by means of its mechanical audio system, "Yes, Mr. Taub-man, he is." It floated toward Eric, then halted, a foot above the ground, making an indistinct sucking noise, as if pulling fluids through its artificial tubes.

"This guy," Taubman said to Eric, indicating the spherical organism, "is from Betelgeuse. His name is Willy K. He's one of our best chemists." He shut the register. "He's a telepath; they all are. They get a kick out of prying into our minds and the reegs' but they're harmless. We like them." He walked over to Willy K, bent toward him, and said, "Listen, if he's a time traveler—I mean, we can't let him just walk out of here; isn't he dangerous or worth something? Shouldn't we at least call in the city police? I thought he was nuts or kidding me."

Willy K floated a little closer to Eric, then withdrew. "There is no way we can keep him here, Mr. Taubman. When the drug wears off he will go back to his own period. However, I would like to interrogate him to a certain extent while he's here." To Eric he said, "Unless you object, sir."

"I don't know," Eric said, rubbing his forehead. It had been too much of the unexpected, hearing Willy K ask about Kathy; it had disoriented him entirely and all he wanted to do now was leave—he had no curiosity, no interest in the situation.

"I sympathize with your situation," Willy K said. "In any case to question you formally is sham; I am getting everything I want from you as it is. What I had hoped to do was answer, if I could, some of your questions by the way I phrased mine. Your wife, for example. You have great conflicting emotions about her, fear for the most part, then hatred, and also a good deal of undistorted love."

Taubman said, "God, how the Betels love to be psycholo-gists. It must come natural to telepaths; I don't think they can even help it." He loitered nearby, evidently interested in Willy K's probing.

"*Can* I take the antidote back to Kathy?"

"No, but you can memorize the formula," Willy K said. "So that Hazeltine Corporation, in your time, can reproduce it. But I don't think you want to. I'm not going to urge you to . . . and I can't force you to."

"You mean his wife's hooked on JJ-180, too," Taubman said, "and he isn't going to try to help her?"

"You're not married," Willy K said. "In marriage the greatest hatred that is possible between human beings can be generated, perhaps because of the constant proximity, perhaps because once there was love. The intimacy is still there, even though the love element has disappeared. So a will to power, a struggle for domination, comes into being." To Taubman he explained, "It was his wife Kathy who addicted him in the first place, so it is easy to understand his sentiments."

"I hope I never get in a fix like that," Taubman said. "Hating someone I once loved."

The female reeg had clacked up to listen, watching the conversation as it was reproduced on the surface of her translating box. Now she added her own comment.

HATE AND LOVE ARE CLOSELY LINKED, MUCH
MORE SO THAN MOST TERRANS REALIZE

"Do you have another cigarette?" Eric asked Taubman.

"Sure." Taubman passed him the pack.

"What I find most interesting of all," Willy K said, "is that Dr. Sweetscent comes from a universe in which a pact exists between Terra and Lilistar. And that in his year, 2055, a war is being fought in which they are slowly but steadily losing. Clearly this is not our past but another past entirely. And, in his mind, I find the excruciatingly interesting thought that Terra's quondam warlord, Gino Molinari, has already discovered this rank of parallel universes and has made use of it for his immediate political advantage." Willy K was silent a moment and then declared, "No, Dr. Sweetscent, after having visualized your memory of the Molinari corpse I am fairly certain that it was not obtained from our world; true, Molinari died by assassination, but I recall pics of his corpse and there is a small but crucial difference. In our world the Secretary was hit repeatedly in the facial area; his features were destroyed. The corpse you saw was not so damaged and I would assume it comes from *another* world in which he was assassinated, similar to ours but not identical."

"This must be why so few time travelers have shown up here," Taubman said. "They're scattered through all the different possible futures."

"As to the virile Molinari," Willy K said thoughtfully. "I

suppose that, too, is an alternate configuration. You realize of course, doctor, that all this indicates that your Secretary *has taken JJ-180 himself*; there is therefore an element of cruel hypocrisy in his threatening you with death if you became addicted. But I would guess, by several clues in your mind, that he also possesses the 'Star-manufactured antidote which you just now took. So he has no fears and can move freely about among the worlds."

The Mole, Eric realized, could have given me and Kathy the antidote any time.

It was hard for him to accept that about Gino Molinari; he had seemed more humane than this. He was just playing with us, Eric realized. As Willy K said, with an element of cruel hypocrisy.

"But wait," Willy K cautioned. "We don't know what he intended to do; he had just found out about your addiction, and he was as usual suffering from a spasm of his chronic illness pattern. He might have given it to you in time. Before it ceased to matter."

COULD YOU EXPLAIN THIS DISCUSSION?

The reeg receptionist, and also Taubman, had lost the thread of the discourse.

"Would you care to begin the laborious process of memorizing the formula?" Willy K said to Eric. "It will take all the time you have left."

"All right," Eric said, and listened intently.

WAIT

Willy K ceased, rotated his supporting mechanism inquiringly.

THE DOCTOR HAS LEARNED SOMETHING MORE
IMPORTANT THAN ANY CHEMICAL FORMULA

"What is it?" Eric asked her.

IN YOUR UNIVERSE WE ARE YOUR ENEMY BUT HERE YOU
HAVE SEEN TERRANS AND OURSELVES LIVE TOGETHER. YOU
KNOW THAT WAR AGAINST US IS UNNECESSARY. AND WHAT IS
MORE IMPORTANT, SO DOES YOUR LEADER.

That was so. No wonder Molinari had no heart for the war; it was not merely a suspicion on his part that this was the wrong war with the wrong enemy and the wrong ally; it was a fact which he had experienced for himself, perhaps many times. And all due to JJ-180.

But not only that. There was something more, something so ominous that he wondered why the inhibition barriers of his mind had permitted the thought to rise from his unconscious. JJ-180 had reached Lilistar—and in quantity. 'Starmen had certainly been experimenting with it. So they, too, knew the alternate possibility, knew that Terra's better hope lay in co-operation with the reegs. Had witnessed it for themselves.

In both branches of possibility Lilistar had lost the war. With or without Terra on her side. Or—

Was there a third alternative, one in which Lilistar and the reegs joined against Terra?

"A pact between Lilistar and the reegs is unlikely," Willy K said. "They have been antagonists for too many years. I feel that it is only your planet, on which we now stand, that hangs in the balance; Lilistar will be defeated by the reeg power in any eventuality."

"But that means," Eric said, "that the 'Starmen have nothing to lose; if they know they can't win—" He could imagine Freneksy's reaction to this information. The nihilism, the destructive violence of the 'Starmen, would be inconceivable.

"True," Willy K agreed. "So your Secretary is wise to walk softly. Now perhaps you can comprehend why his illness pattern must be so vast, why he must push himself actually over the brink, into repeated death, to serve his people. And why he would hesitate to provide you with the antidote to JJ-180; if 'Star intelligence agents—and your wife may be one—learned that he possessed it, they might—" Willy K was silent. "It is hard, as you yourself might observe, to predict the behavior of psychotics. But this much is clear: they would not ignore the situation."

"They'd find a way to get it away from him," Eric said.

"You've missed the point. Their attitude would be punitive; they would know that Molinari possesses too much power, that by having unhindered use of JJ-180, without the possibility of addiction, of neural deterioration, *he can't be controlled by them*. This is why, on a deep, psychosomatic basis, Molinari can defy Minister Freneksy. He is not entirely helpless."

"This is all over my head," Taubman said. "Excuse me." He walked off.

The reeg receptionist remained.

URGE YOUR SECRETARY TO CONTACT THE REEG
AUTHORITY. WE WOULD ASSIST IN PROTECTING
TERRA FROM STAR VENGEANCE, I AM SURE.

It was, Eric thought, a rather wistful message which the multiarmed creature had flashed at him with her translation box. The reegs might *want* to assist, but 'Starmen were already on Terra, holding key positions. At the first hint that Terra was negotiating with the reegs the 'Starmen would move in prearranged order; they would seize the planet overnight.

A tiny Terran-controlled state might function for a limited time in the Cheyenne vicinity, shelled and bombed day and night by the 'Starmen. But then it, too, would capitulate. Its shield of Jupiter-obtained rexeroid compounds would not protect it forever—and Molinari knew that. Terra would become a conquered state, supplying war material and slave labor to Lilistar. And the war would go on.

And the irony was this: as a slave planet Terra would be able to contribute more to the war effort than she did now as a quasi-independent entity. And no one recognized this more than did the Mole. Hence his entire foreign policy; this explained everything that he did.

"By the way," Willy K said, and there was a trace of amusement in his voice. "Your former employer, Mr. Virgil Ackerman, is still alive; he still governs Tijuana Fur & Dye. He is two hundred and thirty years old and retains twenty org-trans surgeons within call. I believe I have read that he has gone through four matched sets of kidneys, five livers, spleens, and undetermined numbers of hearts—"

"I feel sick," Eric said, and rocked back and forth.

"The drug is wearing off." Willy K floated toward a chair. "Miss Ceeg, assist him, please!"

"I'm okay," Eric said thickly. His head ached and nausea staggered him. All the lines, the surfaces around him, had become astigmatic; under him the chair felt unreal and then, abruptly, he fell, lay on his side.

"The transition is difficult," Willy K said. "Apparently we can't help him, Miss Ceeg. Good luck to your Secretary, doctor. I can appreciate what a great service he performed for your people. Perhaps I will write a letter to the *New York Times*, conveying this knowledge."

A prism of primal colors tapped at Eric like an illuminated wind; it was, he thought, the wind of life blowing over him, sweeping him where it desired without regard for his small wishes. And then the winds became black; they were no longer the winds of life but the opaque smoke of death.

He saw, projected as a pseudo environment around him, a travesty of his injured nervous system; the multitudes of conduits were visibly corrupted, had turned inky as the drug's damage spread throughout him and established its grim self. A voiceless bird, some carrion eater of the storm, sat on his chest, croaking in the silence left behind as the winds receded from him. The bird remained and he felt its dunglike claws penetrate his lungs, his chest cavity, and then his abdominal cavity. Nothing within him remained untouched; it had all been disfigured and even the antidote had not stopped this. As long as he lived he would never regain the purity of the original organism.

This was the price exacted from him by the deciding forces.

Dragging himself to a crouched position, he saw that he inhabited an empty waiting room. No one had seen him and he was free to get up and go. He rose to his feet, steadied himself by means of a chrome and leather chair.

The magazines, in the nearby rack, were in English. And on their covers, laughing Terrans. Not reegs.

"Did you want something?" A male voice, lisping slightly. A Hazeltine employee wearing florid, fashionable robes.

"No," Eric said. This was his own time; he recognized the trappings of 2055. "Thanks just the same."

A moment later he had made his way painfully outdoors in the direction of the sidewalk, down the path of redwood rounds.

What he wanted was a cab, a place to sit down and rest. As he made his trip back to Cheyenne. He had gotten what he wanted; presumably he was no longer an addict and if he cared to he could also free his wife. And in addition he had viewed a world over which the shadow of Lilistar did not obtain.

"Ferry you somewhere, sir?" An autonomic cab drifted toward him.

"Yes," he said, and walked toward it.

Suppose an entire planet took the drug, he thought as he boarded. A mass fugue away from our dismal, ever-narrowing world of reality. Suppose Tijuana Fur & Dye gave the order to produce it in enormous quantity, distributed it, through the government's help, to everyone. Would that be a moral solution? Are we entitled to that?

Anyhow it couldn't be done. The 'Starmen would move in first.

"Where to, sir?" the cab's circuit inquired.

He decided to use it for the entire trip; it would take only a few minutes longer. "To Cheyenne."

"I can't, sir. Not *there*." It sounded nervous. "Request another—"

"Why not?" He came awake instantly.

"Because as is well known all Cheyenne belongs to *them*. To the enemy." It added, "And traffic into enemy areas is illegal, as you know."

"What enemy?"

"The traitor Gino Molinari," the cab answered. "Who sought to betray the war effort; you know, sir. The former UN Secretary who conspired with reeg agents to—"

"What is the date?" Eric demanded.

"June 15, 2056."

He had—possibly through the action of the antidote—failed to make it to his own time; it was one year later and there was nothing he could do about it. And he had saved out no more of the drug; the rest had been given to Kathy at the airfield, and so he was stuck here in what obviously was 'Star-dominated territory. Like most of Terra.

And yet Gino Molinari was alive! He still hung on; Cheyenne had not fallen in a day or a week—perhaps the reegs had been able to bring in reinforcements to assist the Secret Service.

He could find out from the cab. As they flew along.

And Don Festenburg could have told me this, he realized, because this is precisely the time period at which I encountered him there in his office with the phony homeopape and mock-up UN Secretary uniform.

"Just head west," he told the cab. I've got to get back to Cheyenne, he realized. Somehow, by some route.

"Yes sir," the cab said. "And by the way, sir, you failed to show me your travel permit. May I see it now? Just a formality, of course."

"What travel permit?" But he knew; it would be an issue of the governing 'Star occupation agency, and without their permission Terrans could not come and go. This was a conquered planet and very much still at war.

"Please, sir," the cab said. It had begun to descend once more. "Otherwise I am required to carry you to the nearest 'Star military police barracks; that is one mile east. A short trip from here."

"I'll bet it is," Eric agreed. "From any point, not just from here. I'll bet they're all over."

The cab dropped lower and lower. "Right you are, sir. They're very convenient." It clicked off its engine and coasted.

Twelve

I'LL tell you what," Eric said as the cab's wheels touched the ground; it slid to a gradual halt at the curb and he saw, just ahead, an ominous structure with armed guards at the entrance. The guards wore the gray of Lilistar. "I'll make a deal with you."

"What deal?" the cab said, with suspicion.

"My travel permit is back at Hazeltine Corporation—remember, where you picked me up? Along with my wallet. All my money's there, too. If you turn me over to the 'Star military police my money won't be worth anything to me; you know what they'll do."

"Yes sir," the cab agreed. "You'll be put to death. It's the new law, passed by decree on the tenth of May. Unauthorized travel by—"

"So why not give my money to you? As a tip. You take me back to Hazeltine Corporation, I'll pick up my wallet, I'll show you my travel permit so you won't have to bring me here again. And you can have the money. You can see how I'd benefit by the deal and how you would, too."

"We'd both gain," the cab agreed. Its autonomic circuit clicked rapidly as it calculated. "How much money do you have, sir?"

"I'm a courier for Hazeltine. In my wallet there's about twenty-five thousand dollars."

"I see! In occupation scrip or in pre-occupation UN banknotes?"

"The latter of course."

"I'll comply!" the cab decided eagerly. And took off once more. "In the strict sense you can't be said to have traveled, inasmuch as the destination you gave me is enemy territory and hence I did not turn even for a moment in that direction. No law has been broken." It turned in the direction of Detroit, greedy for its loot.

When it set down at the parking lot of Hazeltine Corporation Eric got out hurriedly. "I'll be right back." He loped across the pavement toward a doorway of the building; a moment later he was inside. An immense testing lab lay extended before him.

When he found a Hazeltine employee he said, "My name is Eric Sweetscent; I'm on the personal staff of Virgil Ackerman and there's been an accident. Will you get in touch with Mr. Ackerman at TF&D for me, please?"

The employee, a male clerk, hesitated. "I understood—" He lowered his voice fearfully. "Isn't Mr. Virgil Ackerman at Wash-35 on Mars? Mr. Jonas Ackerman is in charge at Tijuana Fur & Dye now and I know Mr. Virgil Ackerman is listed in the Weekly Security Bulletins as a war criminal because he fled when the occupation began."

"Can you contact Wash-35 for me?"

"*Enemy territory?*"

"Get me Jonas on the vidphone, then." There was not much else he could do. He followed the clerk into the business office, feeling futile.

Presently the call had been put through. Jonas' features formed on the screen; when he saw Eric he blinked and stammered, "But—they got *you*, too?" He blurted, "Why'd you leave Wash-35? My God, you were safe there with Virgil. I'm ringing off; this is some kind of a trap—the MPs will—" The screen died. Jonas had hurriedly cut the circuit.

So his other self, his normally phased, one-year-later self, had made it to Wash-35 with Virgil; that was terribly reassuring—almost unthinkably so. No doubt the reegs had managed to—

His one-year-later self.

That meant that somehow he had gotten back to 2055. Otherwise there couldn't be a self of 2056 to have fled with Virgil. And the only way he could reach 2055 would be by means of JJ-180.

And the only source of the drug was here. He was standing in the one right spot on the entire planet, by accident, due to the trick he had managed to pull off at the expense of the idiotic autonomic cab.

Relocating the clerk, Eric said, "I'm supposed to requisition a supply of the drug Frohedadrine. One hundred milligrams. And I'm in a hurry. You want to see my identification? I can prove I work for TF&D." And then it came to him. "Call Bert

Hazeltine; he'll identify me." Undoubtedly Hazeltine would remember him from the encounter at Cheyenne.

The clerk muttered, "But they shot Mr. Hazeltine. You must remember that; how come you don't? When they took over this place in January."

The expression on Eric's face must have conveyed his shock. Because all at once the clerk's manner changed.

"You were a friend of his, I guess," the clerk said.

"Yes." Eric nodded; that could be said.

"Bert was a good man to work for. Nothing like these 'Star bastards." The clerk made up his mind. "I don't know why you're here or what's wrong with you but I'll get the hundred milligrams of JJ-180; I know where it's kept."

"Thanks."

The clerk hurried off. Time passed. Eric wondered about the cab; was it still waiting outside on the lot? Would it, if pressed too hard, attempt to come into the building after him? An absurd and yet nerve-wracking thought, the autonomic cab forcing its way into Hazeltine, bursting—or trying to burst—through the cement wall.

The clerk returned and held out a handful of capsules to Eric.

From a nearby water cooler Eric got a cup, filled it, mouthed a capsule, and raised the Dixie cup.

"That's the recently altered JJ-180 formula," the clerk said, watching him keenly. "I better tell you, now that I see it's for yourself." He was all at once pale.

Lowering the cup of water, Eric said, "Altered how?"

"Retains the addictive and liver-toxic properties but the time-freeing hallucinations are gone." The clerk explained, "When the 'Starmen came in here they ordered our chemists to reconstruct the drug; it was their idea, not ours."

"*Why?*" In the name of God, what good was a drug consisting of nothing but addictive and toxic properties?

"For a weapon of war against the reegs. And—" The clerk hesitated. "Also it's used to addict rebel Terrans who've gone over to the enemy." He did not look very happy about that part of it.

Tossing the capsules of JJ-180 onto a nearby lab bench, Eric said, "I give up." And then he had one more—meager—idea.

"If I can get approval from Jonas will you supply me a company ship? I'll call him again; Jonas is an old friend of mine." He walked toward the vidphone, the clerk trailing after him. If he could get Jonas to listen—

Two Lilistar MPs entered the lab; behind them, in the parking lot, Eric saw a 'Star patrol ship parked beside his autonomic cab.

"You're under arrest," one of the MPs said to him, pointing an oddly shaped stick in Eric's direction. "For travel without authorization and felony fraud. Your cab got tired of waiting and called in a complaint."

"What fraud?" Eric said. The clerk, now, had wisely vanished. "I'm a staff member of Tijuana Fur & Dye; I'm here on business."

The oddly shaped stick glowed and Eric felt as if his brain had been touched; without hesitation he moved toward the lab door, his right hand pawing in a ticlike, useless gesture at his forehead. Okay, he thought. I'm coming. He had lost any idea of resisting the Lilistar MPs now, or even of arguing with them; he was glad to get into their patrol ship.

A moment later they had taken off; the ship glided above the rooftops of Detroit, heading toward the barracks two miles away.

"Kill him now," one of the MPs said to his companion. "And drop his body out; why take him to the barracks?"

"Hell, we can just push him out," the other MP said. "The fall will kill him." He touched a button at the control panel of the ship and a vertical hatch slipped open; Eric saw the buildings below, the streets and conapts of the city. "Think happy thoughts," the MP said to Eric, "on the way down." Grabbing Eric by the arm, he slung him into a helpless, crippled posture and shoved him toward the hatch. It was all expert and entirely professional; he found himself teetering at the lip of the hatch and then the MP released him in order to escape falling himself.

From beneath the patrol ship a second ship, larger, pitted and scarred, an interplan military vessel with cannon bristling as spines, floated on its back as it ascended like some raptorial water creature. With care it fired a microbolt into the open hatch, picking off the MP who stood by Eric and then one of its larger cannon opened up and the front portion of the MP patrol ship burst and flew outward, spattering Eric and the remaining MP with molten debris.

The MP patrol ship dropped like a stone toward the city below.

Awakening from his stricken trance, the remaining MP ran to the wall of the ship and threw on the emergency manually-operated guidance system. The ship ceased to fall; it glided, wind-swept, in a spiral pattern until at last it crashed and bumped and skidded along a street, missing wheels and cabs, nosed into the curb, lifted its tail into the air and came to rest.

The remaining MP staggered up, grabbed his pistol, and somehow got to the hatch; he crouched sideways and began firing. After the third shot he snapped backward; his pistol dropped from his hand and skidded against the hull of the ship and he tumbled into a ball that rolled helplessly like an animal that had been run over until at last it collided with a portion of the hull. There it stopped, gradually unwinding into man shape once more.

The pitted, grimy military ship had parked on the street close by and now its forward side-hatch opened and a man hopped out. As Eric stepped from the MP patrol ship the man sprinted up to him.

"Hey," the man panted. "It's me."

"Who are you?" Eric said; the man who had tackled the MP ship with his own was certainly familiar—Eric confronted a face which he had seen many times and yet it was distorted now, witnessed from a weird angle, as if inside out, pulled through infinity. The man's hair was parted on the wrong side so that his head seemed lopsided, wrong in all its lines. What amazed him was the physical unattractiveness of the man. He was too fat and a little too old. Unpleasantly gray. It was a shock to see himself like this, without preparation; do I really look like that? he asked himself morosely. What had become of the clean-cut youth whose image he still, evidently, superimposed onto his shaving mirror each morning . . . who had substituted this man bordering on middle age?

"So I've gotten fat; so what?" his self of 2056 said. "Christ, I saved your life; they were going to pitch you out."

"I know that," Eric said irritably. He hurried along beside

the man who was himself; they entered the interplan ship and his 2056 self at once slammed the hatch shut and sent the ship hurtling into the sky, out of reach of any possibility of containment by the Lilistar military police. This was obviously an advanced ship of the line; this was no barge.

"Without intending to insult your intelligence," his 2056 self said, "which I personally consider very high, I'd like to review for your benefit a few of the moronic aspects of what you had in mind. First, if you had been able to obtain the original type of JJ-180 it would have carried you to the future, not back to 2055, and you would have been readdicted. What you need—and you seemed for a time to have worked this out—is not more JJ-180 but something to balance the effects of the antidote." His 2056 self nodded his head. "Over there in my coat." His coat hung by magnetic spot on the wall of the ship. "Hazeltine has had a year to develop it. In exchange for your bringing them the formula for the antidote—you couldn't give them the formula if you couldn't get back to 2055. And you know you do. Or will, rather."

"Whose ship is this?" It impressed him. It could pass freely through Lilistar lines, penetrate Terra's defenses with ease.

"It's reeg. Made available to Virgil at Wash-35. In case something goes wrong. We're going to bring Molinari to Wash-35 when Cheyenne falls, which it eventually will, probably in another month."

"How's his health?"

"Much better. He's doing what he wants now, what he knows he should be doing. And there's more . . . but you'll find out. Go get the antidote to Lilistar's antidote."

Eric fumbled in the pockets of the coat, found the tablets, took them without benefit of water. "Listen," he said, "what's the story on Kathy? We ought to confer." It was good having someone he could talk to about his most wasting, obsessive problem, even if it was only himself; at least the illusion of collaboration was achieved.

"Well, you got—will get—her off JJ-180. But not before she's suffered major physical damage. She'll never be pretty again, even with reconstructive surgery, which she'll try several times before she gives up. There's more but I'd rather not tell you; it'll just make your difficulties worse. I'll say only this. Have you ever heard of Korsakow's syndrome?"

"No," Eric said. But of course he had. It was his job.

"Traditionally it's a psychosis occurring in alcoholics; it consists of actual pathological destruction of cortical brain tissue due to long periods of intoxication. But it also can occur from the steady use of narcotic drugs."

"Are you saying that Kathy has it?"

"Remember those periods when she wouldn't eat for three days at a time? And her violent, destructive rages—and ideas of reference, that everyone was being mean to her. Korsakow's syndrome, and not from JJ-180, but from all the drugs she took prior to that. The doctors at Cheyenne, while getting her ready to be returned to San Diego, ran an EEG on her and picked it up. They'll tell you very soon after you return to 2055. So prepare yourself." He added, "It's irreversible. Needless to say. Removal of the toxic agents is not enough."

Both of them were silent then.

"It's rough," his 2056 self said finally, "to be married to a woman with psychotic traits. As well as showing her physical deterioration. She's still my wife. Our wife. Under phenothiazine sedation she's quiet, anyhow. You know, it's interesting that I—we—didn't pick it up, weren't able to diagnose a case we're living with day in, day out. A commentary on the blinding aspects of subjectivity and overfamiliarity. It unfolded slowly, of course; that tended to conceal its identity. I think eventually she'll have to be institutionalized, but I'm putting that off. Possibly until after the war's won. Which it will be."

"You have proof? Through JJ-180?"

"Nobody's using JJ-180 any more except for Lilistar, and that as you know is only for the toxic and addictive properties. So many alternate futures have been disclosed that the task of relating them to our world had to be put aside for after the war. It takes literally years to test out a new drug thoroughly; we both know that. But of course we'll win the war; the reegs have invested half of Lilistar's Empire. Now listen to me. I have instructions for you and you must fulfill them; otherwise another alternate future will split off and it may cancel my stand with you against the 'Star MPs."

"I understand," Eric said.

"In Arizona, at POW Camp 29, there's a reeg major from the reegian intelligence service. Deg Dal Il is his code name; you can contact him through that, since it's Terra's code, not theirs. The camp authorities have got him studying insurance claims filed against the government in order to detect frauds, if you can believe that. So he's still busy at work piping data back to his superiors, even though our POW. It's he who'll be the link between Molinari and the reegs."

"What do I do with him? Take him to Cheyenne?"

"To Tijuana. To TF&D's central offices. You buy him from the camp authorities; it's slave labor. You didn't know that, did you, that large Terran industrial constellations could acquire free labor from the POW camps. Well, when you show up at Camp 29 and tell them you're from TF&D and you want a clever reeg, they'll understand."

"You learn something new every day of the week," Eric said.

"But your main problem lies with Molinari. It's up to you to persuade him to visit Tijuana to confer with Deg Dal Il and hence establish the first link in the chain of circumstances that's going to get Terra pried loose from Lilistar and over to the reegs without everyone being killed in the process. I'll tell you why it'll be difficult. Molinari has a scheme. He's been involved in a personal struggle, man to man, against Freneksy; it's his masculinity that he feels is at stake. For him it's not abstract, it's immediate and physical. And you saw the virile Molinari strutting on the video tape. That's his secret weapon, his V-2. He's starting to throw in the healthy duplicates of himself from the rank of parallel worlds, and as he knows he's got quite a supply of them to draw on. *His whole psychology, his point of orientation, is to dabble with death and yet somehow surmount it.* Now's the time for him to demonstrate his way. In the confrontation with Minister Freneksy—whom he fears—he can die a thousand times and still spring back. The deteriorating process, the encroachment of his psychosomatic illness process, will cease as soon as he throws the first healthy Molinari in. And when you get back to Cheyenne you'll just be in time to witness it; the video tapes go on all the TV networks that night. At prime viewing time."

Eric said musingly, "So he's as sick right now as it will be necessary for him ever to be."

"And that's exceedingly sick, doctor."

"Yes, doctor." Eric eyed his 2056 self. "We agree in our diagnoses."

"Late tonight, by your time, not mine, Minister Freneksy will demand—and get—another face-to-face conference with Molinari. And the healthy, virile substitute will be the one there in that room . . . while the sick one, our one, recovers in his upstairs private quarters, guarded by his Secret Service, watching the video tapes on TV and thinking grand thoughts to himself as to how easily he has found a way of evading Minister Freneksy and his burgeoning, excessive demands."

"I assume the virile Molinari from the other Terra has involved himself willingly."

"Delighted to. All of them are. All of them see the penultimate in life as a successful grudge-battle waged above and below the belt against Freneksy. Molinari is a politician and he lives for this—lives for it while at the same time it kills him. The healthy one, after his conference with Freneksy, will suffer his first attack of pyloric spasms; the attrition will start to eat away at him, too. And so on down the rank, until at last Freneksy is dead, as someday he has to be, and hopefully before Molinari."

"Beating Molinari to it will take some doing," Eric said.

"But this isn't morbid; this is straight out of the Middle Ages, the clash of armed knights. Molinari is Arthur with the spear wound in his side; guess who Freneksy is. And the interesting thing, to me, is that since Lilistar has no period of chivalry, Freneksy has no comprehension of this. He simply sees it in terms of a struggle for economic domination; who runs whose factories and can sequester whose labor force."

"No romance," Eric said. "How about the reegs? Will they understand the Mole? Have they a period of knighthood in their past?"

"With four arms and a chitinous shell," his 2056 counterpart said, "it would have been something to see one of them in action. I don't know, because neither you nor I nor any other Terran that I ever met bothered to learn as much about reeg civilization as we should have. You have the name of the reeg intelligence major?"

"Deg something."

"Deg. Dal. Il. Think to yourself: the dog dallied and it made him ill."

"Christ," Eric said.

"I nauseate you, don't I? Well, you nauseate me, too; you strike me as flabby and blubbery and your posture is terrible. No wonder you're stuck with a wife like Kathy; you got what you deserved. During the next year why don't you show some guts? Why don't you pull yourself together and go find another woman so by the time it gets to me, in 2056, things aren't quite so goddam fouled up? You owe it to me; I saved your life, got you away from Lilistar's police." His 2056 self glowered at him.

"What woman do you suggest?" Eric said guardedly.

"Mary Reineke."

"You're out of your mind."

"Listen; Mary and Molinari have a quarrel about a month from now, your time. You could exploit it. I didn't but that can be changed; you can set up a slightly different future, everything the same except for the marital situation. Divorce Kathy and marry Mary Reineke or *someone*—anyone." There was desperation, all at once, in his counterpart's voice. "My God, I see this ahead, this having to institutionalize her, and for the rest of her life—*I don't want to do that; I want out.*"

"With or without us—"

"I know. She'll wind up there anyhow. But do I have to be the one? Together you and I ought to be able to reinforce ourselves. It'll be hard; Kathy'll fight a divorce action like a crazed thing. But bring the action in Tijuana; Mexican divorce law is looser than in the States. Get a good lawyer. I've picked one; he's in Ensenada. Jesus Guadarala. Can you remember that? I couldn't quite make it there to start litigation through him, but dammit, you can." He eyed Eric hopefully.

"I'll try," Eric said presently.

"Now I have to let you out. The medication you took will start to work on you in a few minutes and I don't care to have you drop five miles to the surface of the planet." The ship began to descend. "I'll let you off in Salt Lake City; it's a big place, you won't be noticed. And when you're back in 2055 you can catch a cab to Arizona."

"I don't have any 2055 money," Eric remembered. "Or do I?" He was confused; too much had happened. He groped for his wallet. "I got into a panic after that attempt on my part to buy the antidote from Hazeltine with wartime—"

"Don't ruminate over the details. I know them already."

They completed the flight to Earth's surface in silence, each inhibited by his gloomy contempt for the other. It was, Eric decided, a graphic demonstration of the necessity for having respect for one's own self. And this gave him for the first time an insight into his fatalistic quasi-suicidal inclinations . . . they were undoubtedly based on this same flaw. To survive he would have to learn to view himself and his accomplishments differently.

"You're wasting your time," his counterpart said after the ship had landed in an irrigated pasture outside Salt Lake City. "You're not going to change."

As he stepped from the ship onto the spongy, moist alfalfa Eric said, "According to you, anyhow. But we'll see."

Without a further word his 2056 self slammed the hatch and took off; the ship shot up into the sky and disappeared.

Eric trudged toward the nearby paved road.

In Salt Lake City proper he snared a cab. It did not ask for his travel permit and he realized that imperceptibly, probably as he was walking toward town along the road, he had slipped a year back and was now in his own time. Nevertheless he decided to make sure.

"Give me the date," he instructed the cab.

"June 15, sir," the cab said as it buzzed south over green mountains and valleys.

"What year?"

The cab said, "Are you a Mr. Rip Van Winkle or something, sir? It's 2055. And I hope it satisfies you." The cab was old and somewhat seedy, needing repairs; its irritability showed in the activity of its autonomic circuitry.

"It does," Eric said.

By use of the cab's vidphone he learned from the information center at Phoenix the location of the prisoner of war camp; this was not classified information. Presently the cab flew above flat desert lands and monotonous hills of rock and empty basins which in former times had been lakes. And then, in the midst of this barren, unexploited wilderness, the cab set him down; he had arrived at POW Camp 29, and it was just where he had expected it to be: in the most uninhabitable spot conceivable. To him the great desert lands of Nevada and Arizona were like a dismal alien planet, not Earth at all; frankly he preferred the parts of Mars which he had seen near Wash-35.

"Lots of luck, sir," the cab said. He paid it and it zoomed noisily off, its plate shuddering.

"Thanks," Eric said. He walked to the guardhouse at the entrance of the camp; to the soldier within he explained that he had been sent by Tijuana Fur & Dye to buy a POW for clerical work that had to be processed with absolute accuracy.

"Just one?" the soldier asked him as he led the way to his superior's office. "We can give you fifty reegs. Two hundred. We're overrun with them right now. From that last battle where we nailed six of their transports."

In the colonel's office he filled out forms, signed for TF&D. Payment, he explained, would be forwarded through normal channels at the end of the month in response to presentation of a formal statement.

"Take your pick," the colonel, bored to death, told him. "Look all around; you can have any one of them—they're all alike, though."

Eric said, "I see a reeg filing forms there in the next room. He—or it—looks efficient."

"That's old Deg," the colonel said. "Deg's a fixture around here; captured in the first week of the war. Even built himself one of those translating boxes so he could be of more use to us. I wish all of them were as co-operative as Deg."

"I'll take him," Eric said.

"We'll have to affix a considerable additional fee," the colonel said slyly. "Because of the amount of training he's received here from us." He made a note of that. "And a service charge for the translating box."

"You said he built it."

"We supplied the materials."

At last they agreed on a price and then Eric walked into the next room and up to the reeg, busy with his four multijointed arms at the insurance claim files. "You belong to TF&D now," Eric informed him. "So come along." To the colonel he said, "Will he try to escape or fight me?"

"They never do," the colonel said, lighting a cigar and leaning against the wall of his office with dreary ennui. "They don't have the mentality for it; they're just bugs. Huge, shiny bugs."

Presently he was back outside in the hot sun, waiting for a cab from nearby Phoenix. If I had known it would take such a short time, he said to himself, I would have held onto the cranky, elderly cab. He felt uncomfortable, standing with the silent reeg; this was, after all, their formal enemy. Reegs battled with and killed Terrans, and this one had been and still was a commissioned officer.

Like a fly the reeg cleaned himself, combing his wings, his sensory antennae, then his lower set of extremities. He carried his translating box under one brittle arm, never letting go of it.

"Are you glad to get out of that POW camp?" Eric asked.

Words, pale in the strong desert sun, appeared on the box.

NOT PARTICULARLY

The cab arrived and Eric, along with Deg Dal Il, entered it. Soon they were in the air, turning in the direction of Tijuana.

Eric said, "I know you're an officer in reeg intelligence. That's why I bought you."

The box remained blank. But the reeg trembled. His opaque, compound eyes became even more filmed-over and the false ones gaped emptily.

"I'll take the risk of telling you this right now," Eric said. "I'm an intermediary acting to bring you together with someone high in UN circles. It's in your interest, yours and your people's, to co-operate with me. You will be dropped off at my firm—"

The box came to life.

RETURN ME TO THE CAMP

"All right," Eric said. "I know you have to act out the pose you've maintained for so long now. Even though it's no longer necessary. I'm aware that you're still in contact with your government. That's why you can be useful to the personage you're to meet in Tijuana. Through you he can establish relations with your government—" He hesitated, then plunged in. "Without the 'Starmen knowing." That was saying a lot; he had mightily presumed on what, for his part, was a very small role.

After a pause the box relit.

I HAVE ALWAYS CO-OPERATED

"But this is different." And he dropped the subject then and there. For the remainder of the trip he did not try to communicate with Deg Dal Il; it was obviously the wrong thing to do. Deg Dal Il knew it and he knew it. The rest was up to someone else, not him.

When they reached Tijuana Eric rented a room at the Caesar Hotel on the main street of town; the desk clerk, a Mexican, stared at the reeg but asked no questions. This was Tijuana, Eric reflected as he and Deg ascended to their floor. Everyone minded his own business; it had always been like this here, and even now, in wartime, Tijuana remained unchanged. You could obtain anything, do anything, you wanted. As long as it was not done blatantly on the public street. And most especially if it was consummated at night. Because at night Tijuana became a transformed city in which everything, even unimaginable things, was possible. Once it had been abortions, narcotics, women, and gambling. Now it was concourse with the enemy.

In the hotel room he handed over a copy of the ownership papers to Deg Dal Il; in case trouble arose during his absence the papers would prove that the reeg had not escaped from a POW camp, nor was he a spy. In addition Eric provided him with money. And instructed him to contact TF&D if any difficulty—especially the appearance of 'Star intelligence agents—supervened. The reeg was to remain in the hotel room at all times, eating his meals there, watching the TV if he wished, admitting no one if he could avoid it, and if somehow 'Star agents got through to him, he was to reveal nothing. Even if this brought about his death.

"I think it's my place to tell you that," Eric said, "not

because I lack respect for reeg life or because I believe Terrans ought to tell a reeg when to die and when not to but simply because I know the situation and you do not. You'll just have to accept my word that it's that important." He waited for the box to light up but it did not. "No comment?" he asked, disappointed in a vague way. There had been so little real contact between him and the reeg; it seemed a bad omen, somehow.

At last the box, reluctantly, lit.

GOOD-BY

"You have nothing else to say?" Eric said, incredulous.

WHAT IS YOUR NAME?

"It's on the forms I gave you," Eric said, and left the hotel room, shutting the door loudly after him.

Outdoors on the sidewalk he hailed an old-fashioned surface cab and told its human driver to take him to TF&D.

Fifteen minutes later he once more entered the attractive apteryx-shaped, gray-lit building and made his way down the familiar corridor to his own office. Or what had until recently been his office.

Miss Perth, his secretary, blinked in amazement. "Why, Dr. Sweetscent—I thought you were in Cheyenne!"

"Is Jack Blair around?" He glanced toward the parts bins but did not see his departmental assistant. Bruce Himmel, however, lurked in the dim last row, an inventory chart and clipboard in one hand. "How'd you make out with the San Diego Public Library?" Eric asked him.

Startled, Himmel rose to a standing position. "I'm appealing, doctor. I'll never give up. How come you're back here in Tijuana?"

Til Perth said, "Jack is upstairs conferring with Mr. Virgil Ackerman, doctor. You look tired. It's a lot of work there in Cheyenne, isn't it? Such a big responsibility." Her long-lashed blue eyes showed sympathy and her large breasts seemed to swell a trifle in a motherly, mobile, nourishing way. "Can I fix you a cup of coffee?"

"Sure. Thanks." He seated himself at his desk and rested for a moment, thinking back over the day. Strange that all these things had happened in a sequence which had returned him to this spot, to his own chair at last. Was this in some sense the end? Had he played out his little—or not so little—part in a brawl involving three races of the galaxy? Four, if the rotten-pear-shaped creatures from Betelgeuse were included . . . and out of sentiment he did. Perhaps the load was off him. A vidcall to Cheyenne, to Molinari; that would do it and once more he would be Virgil Ackerman's physician, replacing organ after organ as they gave out. But there was still Kathy. Was she here at TF&D's infirmary? Or in a San Diego hospital? Perhaps she was trying to resume her life, despite the addiction, doing her job for Virgil. She was not a coward; she would keep pushing until the end.

"Is Kathy here in the building?" he asked Til Perth.

"I'll check for you, doctor." She jiggled the button of her deskcom. "There's your coffee, beside your elbow."

"Thanks." He sipped the coffee with gratitude. It was almost like old times; his office had always been for him an oasis where things were rational, safe from the fury of his botched-up domestic life. Here he could pretend that people were nice to one another, that relationships between people could be merely friendly, merely casual. And yet—that was not enough. There had to be intimacy, too. Even with its threat of becoming a destroying force.

Taking paper and pen, he wrote out from memory the formula for the antidote to JJ-180.

"She's in the infirmary on the fourth floor," Miss Perth informed him. "I didn't know she was sick; is it serious?"

Eric handed her the paper, folded. "Take this to Jonas. He'll know what it is and what to do with it." He wondered if he should go up to Kathy, tell her that the antidote would soon be in existence. Beyond the shadow of a doubt he was obliged to, by the most fundamental structure of decency. "Okay," he said, rising. "I'll go see her."

"Give her my best," Til Perth called after him as he plodded out of the office into the hall.

"Sure," he murmured.

When he reached the fourth floor infirmary he found Kathy, wearing a white cotton gown, seated in a reclining chair, her legs crossed, feet bare. She was reading a magazine. She looked old and shrunken, and obviously under heavy sedation.

"Best wishes," he said to her, "from Til."

Slowly, with conspicuous difficulty, Kathy glanced up, focused her gaze on him. "Any—news for me?"

"The antidote's in town. Or soon will be. All Hazeltine Corp. has to do is whip up a batch and express it here. Another six hours." He made an attempt to smile encouragingly; it failed. "How do you feel?"

"Fine now. Since you brought me the news." She was surprisingly matter-of-fact, even for her with her schiziod ways. The sedation no doubt accounted for it. "You did it, didn't you? Found it for me."

Then, at last remembering, she added, "Oh yes. And for yourself, too. But you could have kept it, not told me. Thanks, dear."

"'Dear.'" It hurt to hear her use such a word to him.

"I can see," Kathy said carefully, "that underneath you really are fond of me still, despite what I've done to you. Otherwise you wouldn't—"

"Sure I would; you think I'm a moral monster? The cure should be a matter of public record, available for anyone who's on the damn stuff. Even 'Starmen. As far as I'm concerned deliberately addictive, toxic drugs are an abomination, a crime against life." He was silent then, thinking to himself, And someone who addicts another is a criminal and ought to be hanged or shot. "I'm leaving," he said. "Going back to Cheyenne. I'll see you. Good luck on your therapy." He added, trying not to make it sound deliberately unkind, "You know, it won't restore the physical damage already done; you understand that, Kathy."

"How old," she asked, "do I look?"

"You look what you are, about thirty-five."

"No." She shook her head. "I've seen in the mirror."

Eric said, "See to it, will you, that everyone who took the drug that night with you, that first time, gets some of the antidote; I'll trust you to do that. Okay?"

"Of course. They're my friends." She toyed with a corner of her magazine. "Eric, I can't expect you to stay with me now, with the way I am physically. All withered and—" She broke off and became silent.

Was this his chance? He said, "You want a divorce, Kathy? If you do I'll give it to you. But personally—" He hesitated. How far could hypocrisy go? What was really required of him now? His future self, his compatriot from 2056, had pleaded with him to break loose from her. Didn't all aspects of reason dictate that he do so and if possible right now?

In a low voice Kathy said, "I still love you. I don't want to separate. I'll try to treat you better; honestly I will. I *promise*."

"Shall I be honest?"

"Yes," she said. "You should always be honest."

"Let me go."

She looked up at him. Some of the old spirit, the venom that had etched away the fiber of their relationship, glowed in her eyes. But it was vitiated now. Her addiction, plus the sedation, had weakened her; the power which she had formerly exerted over him, trapping him and hugging him to her, had gone. Shrugging, she murmured, "Well, I asked you to be honest and I got just that. I guess I should be glad."

"Will you agree, then? You'll commence litigation?"

Kathy said carefully, "On one condition. If there's no other woman."

"There isn't." He thought of Phyllis Ackerman; that surely didn't count. Even in Kathy's suspicion-haunted world.

"If I find out there is," she stated, "I'll fight a divorce; I won't cooperate. You'll never get free from me; that's a promise, too."

"Then it's agreed." He felt a great weight slide into the abyss of infinity, leaving him with a merely earthly load, one which an ordinary human being could bear. "Thanks," he said.

Kathy said, "Thank you, Eric, for the antidote. So look what my drug addiction, my years of using drugs, has meant, finally. It's made it possible for you to escape. It did accomplish some good after all."

For the life of him he could not determine if she meant that sardonically. He decided to inquire about something else. "When you feel better are you going to resume your job here at TF&D?"

"Eric, I may have something stirring for me. When I was under the drug's influence, back in the past—" She halted, then painfully continued; talking was difficult for her now. "I mailed an electronic part to Virgil. Back in the mid 1930s. With a note telling him what to do about it and also who I was. So he'd remember me later on. About now, in fact."

Eric said, "But—" He broke off.

"Yes?" She managed to fix her attention on him, what he was saying. "Did I do something wrong? Alter the past and disturb things?"

It was almost impossible, he discovered, to tell her. But she would find out anyhow, as soon as she made inquiries. Virgil would have received no part, because as soon as she left the past the part left, too; Virgil, as a child, had received an empty envelope or nothing at all. He found this mournfully sad.

"What is it?" she was asking laboriously. "I can tell by your expression—I know you so well—that I did something bad."

Eric said, "I'm just surprised. By your ingenuity. Listen." He crouched down beside her, put his hand on her shoulder. "Don't count on it making much difference; your job here with Virgil can't basically be improved on and anyhow Virgil is hardly the grateful type."

"But it was worth a try, don't you think?"

"Yes," he said, straightening up. He was glad at that point to let it drop.

He said good-by to her, patted her—futilely—once more, and then he made his way to the elevator and from it to Virgil Ackerman's office.

Virgil, glancing up as he entered, cackled, "I *heard* you were back, Eric. Sit down and tell me how it is; Kathy looks bad, doesn't she? Hazeltine wasn't—"

"Listen," Eric said, shutting the door. The two of them were alone. "Virgil, can you get Molinari here to TF&D?"

"Why?" Birdlike, Virgil regarded him alertly.

Eric told him.

When he had heard, Virgil said, "I'll call Gino. I can hint and because we know each other he'll understand on an intuitive level. He'll come. Probably right away; when he acts he goes fast."

"I'll stay here, then," Eric decided. "I won't return to Cheyenne. In fact maybe I'd better go back to the Caesar Hotel and stay with Deg."

"And take a gun with you," Virgil said. He picked up the

vidphone receiver and said, "Get me the White House in Cheyenne." To Eric he said, "If they've got this line tapped it won't help them; they won't be able to tell what we're talking about." Into the receiver he said, "I want to talk to Secretary Molinari; this is Virgil Ackerman calling personally."

Eric sat back and listened. It was going well now, finally. He could take this moment to rest. Become simply a spectator.

From the vidphone a voice, that of the White House switchboard operator, squalled in frantic hysteria, "Mr. Ackerman, is Dr. Sweetscent there? We can't locate him and Molinari, Mr. Molinari, I mean, is dead and can't be revived."

Virgil raised his eyes and confronted Eric.

"I'm on my way," Eric said. He felt only numb. Nothing more.

"Too late," Virgil said. "I'll bet you."

The operator shrilled, "Mr. Ackerman, he's been dead two hours now; Dr. Teagarden can't do anything with him, and—"

"Ask what organ gave out," Eric said.

The operator heard him. "His heart. Is that you, Dr. Sweetscent? Dr. Teagarden said the aortic artery ruptured—"

"I'll take an artiforg heart with me," Eric said to Virgil. To the operator at the White House he said, "Tell Teagarden to keep the body temp as low as he can; I'm sure he's doing that anyhow."

"There's one good high-speed ship on the roof field," Virgil said. "It's the ship we flew to Wash-35 in; it's undoubtedly the best anywhere near here."

"I'll pick out the heart myself," Eric decided. "So I'll go back to my office; why don't you get the ship readied for me?" He was calm at this point. It was either too late or it wasn't. He got there in time or he didn't. Haste, right now, had remote value.

Virgil, as he tapped the vidphone switch for TF&D's switchboard, said, "The 2056 you were in is *not* the one connected to our world."

"Evidently not," Eric agreed. And started on the run for the elevator.

Thirteen

AT the White House roof field Don Festenburg met him, pale and stammering with tension. "W-where were you, doctor? You didn't notify anybody you were leaving Cheyenne; we thought you were somewhere nearby." He strode ahead of Eric, toward the field's nearest in-track.

Carrying the boxed artiforg, Eric followed.

At the door of the Secretary's bedroom Teagarden appeared, his face constricted with fatigue. "Just for the hell of it, where were you, doctor?"

I was trying to end the war, Eric thought. He said merely, "How cool is he?"

"No appreciable metabolism; don't you think I know how to conduct that aspect of restoration? I've got written instructions here which automatically become operative the moment he's unconscious or dead and can't be revived." He handed Eric the sheets.

At a glance Eric saw the vital paragraph. No artiforg. Under any circumstance. Even if it were the only chance for Molinari's survival.

"Is this binding?" Eric asked.

"We've consulted the Attorney General," Dr. Teagarden said. "It is. You ought to know; any artiforg, in anybody, can only be inserted with written permission in advance."

"Why does he want it this way?" Eric asked.

"I don't know," Teagarden said. "Will you make an attempt to revive him without use of the artiforg heart which I see you brought? That's all we're left with." His tone drooped with bitterness and defeat. "With nothing. He complained about his heart before you left; he told you—I heard him—that he thought an artery had ruptured. And you walked out of here." He stared at Eric.

Eric said, "That's the problem with hypochondria. You never know."

"Well," Teagarden said with a ragged sigh, "okay—I didn't realize it either."

Turning to Don Festenburg, Eric said, "What about Freneksy? Does he know?"

With a faint, quivering smirk of nervousness Festenburg said, "Of course."

"Any reaction from him?"

"Concern."

"You're not letting any further 'Star ships in here, I assume."

Festenburg said, "Doctor, your job is to heal the patient, not to dictate policy."

"It would help me heal the patient if I knew that—"

"Cheyenne is sealed off," Festenburg conceded at last. "No ship except yours has been permitted to land since this occurred."

Eric walked to the bed and gazed down at Gino Molinari lost in the tangle of machinery that maintained his temperature and measured a thousand conditions extant deep within his body. The plump, short figure could hardly be seen; the face was completely obscured by a new item, scarcely ever employed up to now, for catching extremely delicate alterations in the brain. It was the brain, at all costs, that had to be protected. Everything could go but that.

Everything could go—except that Molinari had forbidden the use of an artiforg heart. So that was that. Medically speaking the clock had been set back a century by this neurotic, self-destructive injunction.

Already, without examining the now-open chest of the man, Eric knew that he was helpless. Outside of the field of org-trans he was probably no more competent a surgeon than Teagarden. Everything in his own career had hung on the possibility of replacing the failing organ.

"Let's see that document again." He took the paper back from Teagarden, studied it more thoroughly. Surely as wily and resourceful a man as Molinari had imagined some viable alternative to org-trans. It couldn't end here.

"Prindle has been notified, of course," Festenburg said. "He's standing by, ready to speak over TV when and if it's certain we can't revive Molinari." His voice was flat, unnaturally so; Eric glanced at him, wondering how he truly felt about this.

"What about this paragraph?" Eric said, showing the document to Dr. Teagarden. "About the activation of the GRS Enterprises robant simulacrum, the one of Molinari used in the video tape. To be put on TV tonight."

"What about it?" Teagarden said, rereading the paragraph. "The airing of the tape will be scratched, of course. As far as the robant itself goes I know nothing about it. Maybe Festenburg does." He turned questioningly to Don Festenburg.

"That paragraph," Festenburg said, "is senseless. Literally. For instance, what's a robant doing in cold-pak? We can't make out Molinari's reasoning and anyhow we've got our hands full. There're forty-three paragraphs to this damn document; we can't carry them all out simultaneously, can we?"

Eric said, "But you know where—"

"Yes," Festenburg said, "I know where the simulacrum is."

"Get it out of the cold-pak," Eric said. "Activate it as per the instructions in this document. Which you already know to be legally binding."

"Activate it and then what?"

"It'll tell you itself," Eric said, "from then on." And for years to come, he said to himself. Because that's the whole point of the document. There will be no public announcement that Gino Molinari has died because as soon as that so-called robant is activated *it will not be so.*

And, he thought, I think you know it, Festenburg.

They looked at each other silently.

To a Secret Service man Eric said, "I want four of you to accompany him while he does it. Just a suggestion, but I hope you take me up on it."

The man nodded, beckoned to a group of his co-workers; they fell in behind Festenburg, who looked confused and frightened now and in no way self-possessed. He left on his reluctant errand, the group of Secret Service men close behind.

"What about a further attempt to repair the ruptured aortic artery?" Dr. Teagarden demanded. "Aren't you going to try? A plastic section can still be—"

"The Molinari in this time sequence," Eric said, "has been battered enough. Don't you agree? This is the moment to retire it; that's what he wants." We're going to have to face a fact, he realized, that perhaps none of us wants to face because it means we're in for a kind of government—have had a kind of government already—hardly in accord with our theoretical ideas.

Molinari had founded a dynasty consisting of himself.

"That simulacrum can't rule in Gino's place," Teagarden protested. "It's a construct and the law forbids—"

"That's why Gino refused the use of an artificial organ. He can't do what Virgil has done, replace each in turn, because by doing so he'd be open to legal challenge. But that's not important." Not now, anyhow. He thought, Prindle isn't the Mole's heir and neither is Don Festenburg, however much he'd like to be. I doubt if the dynasty is endless but at least it'll survive this blow. And that's quite a lot.

After a pause Teagarden said, "That's why it's in cold-pak. I see."

"And it'll stand up to any test you care to give it." You, Minister Freneksy, anyone, including Don Festenburg who probably figured it out before I did, he realized, but couldn't do anything about it. "That's what distinguishes this solution; even if you know what's going on you can't stop it." This rather enlarged the concept of political maneuvering. Was he horrified by this? Or impressed? To be honest, as yet he did not know. It was too novel a solution, this collusion of Gino Molinari with himself, behind the scenes. His tinkering with the colossal entity of rebirth in his own inimitable, faster-than-the-eye way.

"But," Teagarden protested, "that leaves another time continuum without a UN Secretary. So what's gained if—"

"The one which Don Festenburg has gone to activate," Eric said, "undoubtedly comes from a world in which the Mole was not elected." In which he went down to political defeat and someone else became UN Secretary. There no doubt were a number of such worlds, considering the closeness of the original vote in this world.

In that other world the absence of the Mole would have no meaning, because he was simply one more defeated political figure, perhaps even in retirement. And—in a position to be thoroughly rested up and fresh. Ready to tackle Minister Freneksy.

"It's admirable," Eric decided. "I think, anyhow." The Mole had known that sooner or later this battered body would die beyond the possibility of reconstruction except by artiforg means. And what good was a political strategist who couldn't look ahead to his own death? Without that he would have been merely another Hitler, who didn't *want* his country to survive him.

Once more Eric glanced over the document which Molinari had presented them. It indeed was airtight. Legally the next Molinari absolutely had to be activated.

And that one, in turn, would see to it that he provided himself with a replacement. Like any good tag-team of wrestlers it could theoretically go on forever.

Could it?

All the Molinaris, in all the time-continua, were aging at the same rate. It could only go on for thirty or forty more years. At the most.

But that would carry Terra through and out of the war.

And that was all the Mole cared about.

He was not trying to be immortal, a god. He was simply interested in serving out his term of office. What had happened to Franklin D. Roosevelt in a previous major war was not going to happen to him. Molinari had learned from the mistakes of the past. And had acted accordingly, in typical Piedmontese style. He had found a bizarre and colorfully idiosyncratic solution to his political problem.

This explained why the UN Secretary's uniform and homeopape shown to Eric a year hence by Don Festenburg were counterfeit.

Without this, they might conceivably have been real.

That alone justified what Molinari had done.

An hour later Gino Molinari summoned him to his private office.

Flushed, glowing with good humor, the Mole in a spanking new uniform leaned back in his chair and expansively, at leisure, surveyed Eric. "So the nurts weren't going to start me up," he boomed out. Then abruptly he laughed. "I knew you'd put pressure on them, Sweetscent; I had it all worked out. Nothing by accident. You believe me? Or you think there was a loophole, they might have gotten away with it, especially that Festenburg—he's plenty smart, you know. I admire the hell out of him." He belched. "Listen to me. Well, so much for Don."

"I think they almost got by," Eric said.

"Yes, they did," Molinari agreed, somber now. "It was very close. But everything in politics is close; that's what makes it worth the effort. Who wants a sure thing? Not me. By the way: those video tapes are going on the air as planned; I sent poor Prindle back to the vault or wherever it is he hangs out." Again Molinari laughed loudly.

"Am I right," Eric said, "that in your world—"

"This is my world," Molinari interrupted; putting his hands behind his head he rocked back and forth, eying Eric brightly.

Eric said, "In the parallel world you came from—"

"Garbage!"

"—you were defeated in your attempt to become UN Secretary; is that right? I'm just curious. I don't intend to discuss it with anyone."

"If you do," Molinari said, "I'll have the Secret Service glunk you and sink you in the Atlantic. Or drop you in deep space." He was silent a moment. "I got elected, Sweetscent, but the drats knocked me right out of office in a no-confidence recall thing they cooked up. Having to do with the Pact of Peace. They were right, of course; I shouldn't have gotten involved in it. But who *wants* to make a deal with four-armed shiny bugs who can't even talk, who have to go around carrying a translation box like an indoor potty?"

"You know now," Eric said guardedly, "that you have to. Reach an understanding with the reegs."

"Sure. But it's easy to see that now." The Mole's eyes were dark and intense, fighting this out with vast, native intelligence. "What do you have in mind, doctor? Let's have a look. What did they used to say in the last century? Let's kick it up on the roof and see if it—some damn thing."

"A contact is ready for you in Tijuana."

"Hell, I'm not going to Tijuana; that's a dirty town—that's where you go for a broad, age thirteen. Even younger than Mary."

"You know about Mary, then?" Had she been his mistress in the alternate world?

"*He* introduced us," Molinari said blandly. "My best friend;

he fixed me up. The one they're burying or whatever it is they're doing with the corpse. It couldn't interest me less, just so they get rid of it. I've already got one, that bullet-riddled one in the casket. Which you saw. One is enough; they make me nervous."

"What were you going to do with the assassinated one?"

Molinari showed his teeth in a great grin. "You don't get it, do you. *That was the previous one.* That came before the one that just died. I'm not the second; I'm the third." He cupped his ear, then. "Okay, let's hear what you've got; I'm waiting."

Eric said, "Um, you'll go to TF&D to visit Virgil Ackerman. That won't arouse suspicion. It's my job to get the contact into the factory so he can confer with you. I think I can do it. Unless—"

"Unless Corning, the top 'Star agent in Tijuana, gets to your reeg first. Listen, I'll give the Secret Service orders to round him up; that'll keep the 'Stars busy for a while, get them off our knabs. We can cite their activity regarding your wife, their getting her addicted; that'll be the covering story. You agree? Yes? No?"

"It'll do." Once more he felt weary, even more so than before. It was a day, he decided, that would never terminate; the huge former burden had returned to weigh him into submission.

"I don't impress you very much," Molinari said.

"On the contrary. I'm just exhausted." And he still had to go back to Tijuana to bring Deg Dal Il into the factory from his room at the Caesar Hotel; it was not over yet.

"Someone else," Molinari said acutely, "can pick up your reeg and bring it to TF&D. Give me the location and I'll see that it's done right. You don't have to do any more; go get drunk or find some fresh new girl. Or take some more JJ-180, visit another time period. Anyhow enjoy yourself. How's your addiction coming? Broken it yet, like I told you to?"

"Yes."

Molinari raised his thick eyebrows. "I'll be darned. Amazing; I didn't think it could be done. Get it from your reeg contact?"

"No. From the future."

"How's the war come out? I don't move ahead, like you do; I move sideways only, into the parallel presents."

"It's going to be tough," Eric said.

"Occupation?"

"For most of Terra."

"How about me?"

"Apparently you manage to get away to Wash-35. After holding out long enough for the reegs to come in with strength."

"I don't care for it," Molinari decided. "But I guess I've got to do it. How's your wife Katherine?"

"The antidote—"

"I mean your relationship."

"We're separating. It's decided."

"Okay." Molinari nodded briskly. "You write out the address you have for me and in exchange I'll write out a name and address for you." He took pen and paper, wrote rapidly. "A relative of Mary's. A cousin. Bit player in TV dramatic series, lives in Pasadena. Nineteen. Too young?"

"Illegal."

"I'll get you off." He tossed Eric the paper. Eric did not pick it up. "What's the matter?" Molinari shouted at him. "Has using that time-travel drug scrambled your wits, you don't know you've got only one tiny life and that lies ahead of you, not sideways or back? Are you waiting for last year to come by again or something?"

Reaching out, Eric took the paper. "That's exactly right. I've been waiting a long time for last year. But I guess it's just not coming again."

"Don't forget to say I sent you," Molinari said, and beamed broadly as Eric put the paper in his wallet.

It was night and Eric walked the dark side street, hands in his pockets, wondering if he was going in the right direction. He had not been in Pasadena, California, for years.

Ahead a major conapt building rose squarely against the sky, more dense than the atmosphere behind it, windows lit like the eyes of some great block-shaped synthetic pumpkin. Eyes, Eric thought, are the window of the soul, but a conapt is a conapt. What lies inside there? A bossy—or perhaps not so bossy—black-haired girl whose ambition it is to appear in one-minute beer and cigarette commercials on TV or whatever it is

Molinari said. Someone to goad you to your feet when you're sick, travesty of the marital vows, of mutual help, protection.

He thought about Phyllis Ackerman, their conversation at Wash-35, not so long ago. If I really want to repeat the pattern stamped on the matrix of my life, he thought, I need only look her up; Phyllis is just enough like Kathy to attract me. As both of us understand. And enough different from her so that it would seem—I say seem—like something new in my life. But then all at once he thought, This girl here in Pasadena; I didn't pick her out. Gino Molinari did. So perhaps the matrix breaks here. And can be discarded. And I can go on in something that does not merely seem new but is new.

Locating the front entrance of the conapt building, he got out the slip of paper, again memorized the name, then found the proper button among the host of identical rows in the big brass plate and gave it a vigorous, Gino Molinari inspired push.

A ghostly voice presently issued from the speaker and a microscopic image formed on the monitoring screen set in the wall above the buttons. "Yes? Who is it?" In such absurd miniature the girl's image could not be deciphered; he could not tell a thing about her. The voice, however, sounded rich and throaty and although nervous with the typical caution of the unattached girl living alone it had its warmth.

"Gino Molinari asked me to look you up," Eric said, supporting his burden on the rock they all depended on in this, their collective journey.

"Oh!" She sounded flustered. "To look *me* up? Are you sure you have the right person? I only met him once and that was casually."

Eric said, "May I come in for a minute, Miss Garabaldi?"

"Garabaldi is my old name," the girl said. "My name, the name I work under when I do TV shows, is Garry. Patricia Garry."

"Just let me come in," Eric said, and waited. "Please."

The door buzzed; he pushed it open and entered the foyer. A moment later by elevator he had ascended to the fifteenth floor and was at her door, ready to knock but finding it ajar in expectation of him.

Wearing a flowered apron, her long dark hair hanging in

twin braids down her back, Patricia Garry met him, smiling; she had a sharp face, tapering to a flawless chin, and lips so dark as to appear black. Every feature had been cut cleanly and with such delicate precision as to suggest a new order of perfection in human symmetry and balance. He could see why she had gone into TV; features like that, when ignited even by the ersatz enthusiasm of a mock-up beer-bust on a California ocean beach, could impale any viewer. She was not just pretty; she was strikingly, lavishly unique and he had a precognition as he looked at her of a long and vital career ahead, if the war did not catch her up in tragedy.

"Hi," she said gaily. "Who are you?"

"Eric Sweetscent. I'm on the Secretary's medical staff." Or was, he thought. Up to a little earlier today. "Could I have a cup of coffee with you and talk? It would mean a lot to me."

"What a strange come-on," Patricia Garry said. "But why not?" She whirled about, her long Mexican skirt spinning out, and bobbed her way down the hall of her conapt, with him following, to the kitchen. "I have a pot on, in fact. Why did Mr. Molinari tell you to look me up? For any special reason?"

Could a girl look like this and not be conscious of what an overriding special reason she constituted? "Well," he said, "I live out here in California, in San Diego." And, he thought, I guess I work in Tijuana. Again. "I'm an org-trans surgeon, Miss Garry. Or Pat. Okay to call you Pat?" He found a seat at the bench table, clasped his hands before him, resting his elbows against the hard, irregular redwood.

"If you're an org-trans surgeon," Patricia Garry said as she got cups from the cupboard over the sink, "why aren't you at the military satellites or at the front hospitals?"

He felt his world sink from beneath him. "I don't know," he said.

"There is a war on, you realize." Her back to him, she said, "The boy I was going with, he was mangled when a reeg bomb got his cruiser. He's still in a base hospital."

"What can I say," he said, "except that maybe you've put your finger on the great central weak link of my life. Why it hasn't got the meaning it should have."

"Well, who do you blame for that? Everyone else?"

"It seemed to me," he said, "at the time anyhow, that keeping Gino Molinari alive somehow contributed to the war effort." But, after all, he had only done that for a short time and had gotten into it not by his own efforts but by Virgil Ackerman's.

"I'm just curious," Patricia said. "I just would have thought that a good org-trans surgeon would *want* to be at the front where the real work is." She poured coffee into two plastic cups.

"Yes, you'd think so," he said, and felt futile. She was nineteen years old, roughly half his age, and already she had a better grasp on what was right, what one ought to do. With such directness of vision she had certainly patterned her own career out to the last stitch. "Do you want me to leave?" he asked her. "Just say so if you do."

"You just got here; of course I don't want you to go. Mr. Molinari wouldn't have sent you here if there hadn't been a good reason." She eyed him critically as she seated herself across from him. "I'm Mary Reineke's cousin, did you know that?"

"Yes." He nodded. And she's quite tough, too, he thought. "Pat," he said, "take my word for it that I have accomplished something today that affects us all, even if it isn't connected with my medical tasks. Can you accept that? If so then we can go on from there."

"Whatever you say," she said with nineteen-year-old nonchalance.

"Have you been watching Molinari's TV cast tonight?"

"I had it on a little while earlier. It was interesting; he looked so much bigger."

"'Bigger.'" Yes, he thought; that described it.

"It's good to see him back in his old form. But I have to admit—all that political spouting, you know how he does, sort of lectures in that feverish way, with his eyes flashing; it's too long-winded for me. I put on the record player instead." She rested her chin in her open palm. "You know what? It bores the hell out of me."

The vidphone in the living room rang.

"Excuse me." Pat Garry rose and skipped from the kitchen.

He sat silently, no particular thoughts in his mind, only a little of the old weariness weighing on him, and then suddenly she was back. "For you. Dr. Eric Sweetscent, that's you, isn't it?"

"Who is it?" He labored to get up, his heart strangely leaden.

"The White House in Cheyenne."

He made his way to the vidphone. "Hello. This is Sweetscent."

"Just a moment, please." The screen blanked out. The next image which formed was that of Gino Molinari.

"Well, doctor," Molinari said, "they got your reeg."

"Jesus," he said.

"When we got there all we found was a banged-up big dead bug. Somebody, one of them, must have seen you go in. Too bad you didn't take it directly to TF&D. Instead of that hotel."

"I see that now."

"Listen," Molinari said briskly. "I called to tell you because I knew you would want to know. But don't knock yourself; those 'Starmen are professionals. It could have happened to anyone." He leaned closer to the screen, speaking with emphasis. "*It's not that important;* there're other ways to contact the reegs, three or four—we're looking into how best to exploit it right now."

"Should this be said on the vidphone?"

Molinari said, "Freneksy and his party just now took off for Lilistar, shot out of here as fast as they could. Take my word for it, Sweetscent, *they know*. So our problem is that we have to work fast. We expect to raise a reeg government station within two hours; if necessary we'll do our negotiating on an open broadcast with Lilistar listening in." He glanced at his wrist watch. "I have to ring off; I'll keep you posted." The screen, then, became dark. Busy, in hectic haste, Molinari had gone on to the next task. He could not sit gossiping. And then, all at once, the screen relit; again Molinari faced him. "Remember, doctor, you did your job; you forced them to honor that will I left, that ten-page document they were passing back and forth when you arrived. I wouldn't be here now except for you; I already told you that and I don't want you to forget it—I haven't got time to keep repeating it again and again." He grinned briefly and then once more the image faded. This time the screen stayed dark.

But to fail is to fail, Eric said to himself. He walked back into Pat Garry's kitchen and reseated himself at his cup of coffee. Neither of them spoke. Because I messed it up, he realized, the 'Starmen will have just that much more time to close in on us, come rushing here to Terra with everything they have. Millions of human lives, perhaps years of occupation—that's the price we'll collectively pay. Because it seemed, earlier today, a good idea to put Deg Dal Il in a room at the Caesar Hotel instead of bringing him directly to TF&D. But then he thought, They have at least one agent at TF&D too; they might even have gotten him there.

Now what? he asked himself.

"Maybe you're right, Pat," he said. "Maybe I ought to become a military surgeon and go to a base hospital near the front."

"Yes, why not?" she said.

"But in a little while," he said, "and you don't know this, the front will be on Terra."

She blanched, tried to smile. "Why is that?"

"Politics. The tides of war. Unreliability of alliances. The ally of today is the enemy of tomorrow. And the other way around." He finished his coffee and rose. "Good luck, Pat, in your television career and in every other aspect of your glowing, just beginning life. I hope the war doesn't touch you too deeply." The war I helped bring here, he said to himself. "So long."

At the kitchen table she remained seated, drinking her coffee and saying nothing, as he walked down the hall to the door, opened it, and then shut it behind him. She did not even nod good-by; she was too frightened, too stunned by what he had told her.

Thanks anyhow, Gino, he said to himself as he descended to the ground floor. It was a good idea; not your fault nothing came of it. Nothing but a greater awareness on my part of how little good I've done and how much harm—by commission or omission—I'm responsible for in my time.

He walked the dark Pasadena street until he located a cab;

he hailed and boarded it, then wondered where he was supposed to go.

"You mean you don't know where you live, sir?" the cab asked.

"Take me to Tijuana," he told it, suddenly.

"Yes sir," the cab said and turned south at great speed.

Fourteen

NIGHTTIME in Tijuana.

He walked aimlessly, scuffing the pavement, passing one after another the neon signs of the narrow boothlike shops, listening to the clamor of the Mexican hucksters and enjoying as he always did the steady motion and ceaseless, nervous honking of wheels and autonomic cabs and old-time turbine surface cars made in the USA, which somehow, in their last decrepitude, had been brought across the border.

"Girl, mister?" A boy no older than eleven seized Eric by the sleeve and hung on, dragging him to a stop. "My sister, only seven, and never lay with a man in her life; I guarantee before God, you be assuredly first."

"How much?" Eric asked.

"Ten dollars plus the cost of the room; there must be in name of God a room. The sidewalk makes love into something sordid; you cannot do it here and respect yourself after."

"There's wisdom in that," Eric agreed. But he continued on anyhow.

At night the robant peddlers and their enormous, useless, machine-made rugs and baskets, their carts of tamales, customarily vanished; the daytime people of Tijuana disappeared along with the middle-aged American tourists to make way for the night people. Men, hurrying, pushed past him; a girl wearing a crushingly tight skirt and sweater squeezed past him, pressing momentarily against him . . . as if, he thought, we had some durable relationship penetrating our two lives and this sudden heat exchange through body contact expressed the deepest possible understanding between the two of us. The girl went on, disappeared. Small tough Mexicans, youths wearing open-throated fur shirts, strode directly at him, their mouths agape as if they were strangling. He carefully stepped from their path.

In a town where everything is legal, he thought, and nothing achieves worth, you are wrenched back into childhood. Placed among your blocks and toys, with all your universe within grasp. The price for license is high: it consists of a forfeit of adulthood. And yet he loved it here. The noise and stirrings represented authentic life. Some people found all this evil; he did not. People who thought that were wrong. The restless, roving bands of males who sought God knew what— they themselves didn't know: their striving was the genuine primal under-urge of protoplasmic material itself. This irritable ceaseless motion had once carried life right out of the sea and onto land; creatures of the land now, they still roamed on, up one street and down another. And he went along with them.

Ahead, a tattoo parlor, modern and efficient, lit by a wall of glowing energy, the proprietor inside with his electric needle that did not touch the skin, only brushed near it as it wove a cat's cradle of design. How about that? Eric asked himself. What could I have etched on me, what motto or picture which would give me comfort in these unusual times of duress? In times when we wait for the 'Starmen to appear and take over. Helpless and frightened, all of us become essentially unmanly.

Entering the tattoo parlor, he seated himself and said, "Can you write on my chest something like—" He pondered. The proprietor continued with his previous customer, a beefy UN soldier who stared sightlessly ahead. "I want a picture," Eric decided.

"Look through the book." Huge sample-caselike ledger passed to him; he opened at random. Woman with four breasts; each spoke a complete sentence. Not quite it; he turned the page. Rocketship with puffs belching from its tail. No. Re-minded him of his 2056 self whom he had failed. *I am for the reegs*, he decided. Tattoo that on me so the 'Star MPs can find it. And I won't have to make further decisions.

Self-pity, he thought. Or is there such a thing as self-compassion? Not much mentioned, anyhow.

"Made up your mind, buddy?" the proprietor asked him, now finished.

Eric said, "I want you to write on my chest, 'Kathy is dead.' Okay? How much will that cost?"

" 'Kathy is dead,' " the proprietor said. "Dead of what?"

"Korsakow's syndrome."

"You want me to put that too? Kathy is dead from—how you spell it?" The proprietor got pen and paper. "I want it to be right."

"Where around here," Eric said, "can I find drugs? You know, real drugs?"

"Across the street at the pharmacy. Their specialty, creaker."

He left the tattoo parlor, crossed against the seething, mass-like organism of traffic. The pharmacy looked old-fashioned, with displays of foot-ailment models and hernia belts and bottles of cologne. Eric opened the door, manually operated, and walked to the counter in the back.

"Yes sir." A gray-haired respectable professional-looking man in a white smock, waiting on him.

"JJ-180," Eric said. He laid a fifty-dollar US bill on the counter. "Three or four caps."

"One hundred US." This was business. With no sentiment.

He added two twenties and two fives. The pharmacist disappeared. When he returned he had a glass vial which he placed close to Eric; he took the bills and rang them up on his antique register. "Thanks," Eric said. Carrying the vial, he left the pharmacy.

He walked until more or less by chance he located the Caesar Hotel. Entering, he approached the desk clerk. It appeared to be the same man who had taken care of him and Deg Dal Il earlier in the day. A day, Eric thought, made out of years.

"You remember the reeg I came here with?" he asked the clerk.

The clerk eyed him silently.

"Is he still here?" Eric said. "Was he really cut to bits by Corning, the 'Star hatchet man in this area? Show me the room. I want the same room."

"Pay in advance, sir."

He paid, received the key, took the elevator to the proper floor; he walked down the dark carpeted empty hall to the door of the room, unlocked it, and stepped in, feeling for the light switch.

The room lit up and he saw that there was no sign of anything; the room was simply empty. As if the reeg had gone. Stepped out, perhaps. He was right, Eric decided, when he asked me to take him back to the POW camp; he was on the right track all the time. Knew how it would end.

Standing there, he realized that the room horrified him.

He opened the glass vial, got out one capsule of JJ-180, laid it on the vanity table, and with a dime cut the capsule into three parts. There was water in a pitcher nearby; he swallowed one third of the capsule and then walked to the window to look out and wait.

Night became day. He was still in the room at the Caesar Hotel but it was later; he could not tell how much. Months? Years? The room looked the same but probably it always would; it was eternal and static. He left the room, descended to the lobby, asked for a homeopape at the newsstand next to the reservations desk. The vendor, a plump old Mexican woman, handed him a Los Angeles daily; he examined it and saw that he had gone ahead ten years. The date was June 1, 2065.

So he had been correct as to the amount of JJ-180 needed.

Seating himself in a pay vidphone booth, he inserted a coin and dialed Tijuana Fur & Dye. The time appeared to be about noon.

"Let me speak to Mr. Virgil Ackerman."

"Who is calling, please?"

"Dr. Eric Sweetscent."

"Yes of course, Dr. Sweetscent. Just a moment." The screen became fused over and then Virgil's face, as dry and weathered as ever, basically unchanged, appeared.

"Well I'll be darned! Eric Sweetscent! How the hell are you, kid? Gosh, it's been—what has it been? Three years? Four? How is it at—"

"Tell me about Kathy," he said.

"Pardon?"

Eric said, "*I want to know about my wife.* What's her medical condition by now? Where is she?"

"Your ex-wife."

"All right," he said reasonably. "My ex-wife."

"How would I know, Eric? I haven't seen her since she quit her job here and that was at least—well, you remember—six years ago. Right after we rebuilt. Right after the war."

"Tell me anything that would help me find out about her."

Virgil pondered. "Well Christ, Eric; you remember how sick she became. Those psychopathic rages."

"I don't remember."

Raising his eyebrows, Virgil said, "You were the one who signed the commitment papers."

"You think she's institutionalized now? Still?"

"As you explained it to me it's irreversible brain damage. From those toxic drugs she was taking. So I presume she is. Possibly in San Diego. I think Simon Ild told me that one day, not long ago; you want me to check with him? He said he met somebody who had a friend in a psychiatric hospital north of San Diego and—"

"Check with him." He waited while the screen showed nothing, while Virgil conferred on the interdepartmental circuit with Simon.

At last the elongated, doleful face of his former inventory control clerk appeared. "You want to know about Kathy," Simon said. "I'll tell you what this fellow told me. He met her in Edmund G. Brown Neuropsychiatric Hospital; he had a nervous breakdown, as you call it."

"I don't call anything that," Eric said, "but go ahead."

Simon said, "She couldn't control herself; her rages, those destructive binges where she'd break everything, they were coming every day, sometimes four times a day. They kept her on phenothiazine and it had helped—she told him that herself—but finally no matter how much phenothiazine they gave her it didn't help. Damage to the frontal lobe, I guess. And she had difficulty remembering things properly. And ideas of reference; she thought everyone was against her, trying to hurt her . . . not grandiose paranoia, of course, but just the never-ending irritability, accusing people as if they were cheating her, holding out on her—she blamed everyone." He added, "She still talked about you."

"Saying what?"

"Blaming you and that psychiatrist—what was his name?— for making her go into the hospital and then not letting her out."

"Does she have any idea why we did it?" Why we had to do it, he thought.

"She said she loved *you*, but you wanted to get rid of her so you could marry someone else. And you had sworn, at the time of the divorce, that there wasn't anyone else."

"Okay," Eric said. "Thanks, Simon." He cut the connection

and then called Edmund G. Brown Neuropsychiatric Hospital in San Diego.

"Edmund G. Brown Neuropsychiatric Hospital." A rapid, overworked middle-aged female at the hospital switchboard.

"I wish to ask about Mrs. Katherine Sweetscent's condition," Eric said.

"Just a moment, sir." The woman consulted her records, then switched his call to one of the wards; he found himself facing a younger woman, not in white uniform but in an ordinary flowered cotton dress.

"This is Dr. Eric Sweetscent. What can you tell me about Katherine Sweetscent's condition? Is she making any progress?"

"There hasn't been any change since you called last, doctor, two weeks ago. I'll get her file, however." The woman disappeared from the screen.

Good Lord, Eric thought. I'm still watching over her ten years from now; am I caught in this one way or another the rest of my life?

The ward technician returned. "You know that Dr. Bramelman is trying the new Gloser-Little unit with Mrs. Sweetscent. In order to induce the brain tissue to start repair of itself. But so far—" She leafed through the pages. "Results have been meager. I would suggest you contact us again in another month or possibly two. There won't be any change before that."

"But it could work," he said. "This new unit you spoke about." He had never heard of it; obviously it was a construct of the future. "I mean, there's still hope."

"Oh yes, doctor. There's definitely hope." She said it in such a way as to convey to him that this was merely a philosophical answer; there was hope in every case, as far as she was concerned. So it meant nothing.

"Thank you." And then he said, "Check your files, please, and see what it says as to my place of business. I've changed jobs recently so it may be wrong."

After a pause the ward technician said, "You're listed as Chief Org-trans Surgeon at Kaiser Foundation in Oakland."

"That's correct," Eric said. And rang off.

He obtained the number from information and dialed Kaiser Foundation in Oakland.

"Let me talk to Dr. Sweetscent."

"Who is calling, please?"

That stopped him momentarily. "Tell him it's his younger brother."

"Yes sir. Just a moment, please."

His face, his older, grayer face, appeared on the screen. "Hi."

"Hello," Eric said. He was not sure what to say. "Am I bothering you when you're busy?" He did not look bad, ten years from now. Dignified.

"No, go ahead. I've been expecting the call; I remember the approximate date. You just called Edmund G. Brown Neuropsychiatric Hospital and learned about the Gloser-Little unit. I'll tell you something the ward technician didn't. The Gloser-Little unit constitutes the only brain artiforg they've managed to come up with. It replaces portions of the frontal lobe; once it's installed it stays as long as the person lives. *If* it helps. To be truthful with you, it should have worked right away."

"So you don't think it's going to."

"No," the older Eric Sweetscent said.

"Do you think if we hadn't divorced her—"

"It would have made no difference. Tests we give now—believe me."

Then even that wouldn't help, Eric realized. Staying with her, even for the rest of my life. "I appreciate your help," he said. "And I find it interesting—I guess that's the word—that you're still keeping tabs on her."

"Conscience is conscience. In some respects the divorce put more of a responsibility on us to see about her welfare. Because she got so much worse immediately after."

"Is there *any* way out?" Eric asked.

The older Eric Sweetscent, of the year 2065, shook his head.

"Okay," Eric said. "Thanks for being honest with me."

"Like you yourself say, you should always be honest with yourself." He added, "Good luck on the commitment proceedings; they're going to be rough. But that won't come for a while."

"How about the rest of the war, in particular the take-over of Terra by the 'Starmen?"

The older Eric Sweetscent grinned. "Hell, you're too

bogged down in your own personal troubles to notice. War?
What war?"

"So long," Eric said, and rang off.

He left the vidphone booth. He's got a point, he admitted
to himself. If I were rational—but I'm not. The 'Starmen are
probably assembling an emergency plan right now, getting
ready for the jump-off; I know this and yet I don't feel it, I
feel—

The need for death, he thought.

Why not? Gino Molinari made his death into an instrument
of political strategy; he outwitted his opponents through it
and he'll probably do so again. Of course, he realized, that's
not what I had in mind. I'm outwitting nobody. Many people
will die in this invasion; why not one more? Who loses by it?
Who am I close to? He thought, Those future Eric Sweetscents are going to be sore as hell about it but that's just too
bad. I don't particularly give a damn about them anyhow.
And, except that their existences depend on mine, they feel the
same about me. Perhaps, he decided, that's the problem. Not
my relationship with Kathy but my relationship with myself.

Passing through the lobby of the Caesar Hotel, he emerged
on the daytime, busy Tijuana street of ten years hence.

Sunlight blinded him; he stood blinking and adjusting. The
surface vehicles, even here, had changed. Sleeker, more attractive. The street, now, was adequately paved. There came the
tamale vendors and the rug vendors except that now they were
not robants; they were, he saw with a start, reegs. Evidently
they had entered Terran society at the bottom rung, would
have to work their way to the equality he had witnessed a century from his own time, ninety years from now. It did not
seem fair to him, but there it was.

Hands in his pockets, he walked with the surging crowd that
inhabited the sidewalks of Tijuana throughout all the ages,
until he arrived at the pharmacy at which he had bought the
capsules of JJ-180. As always it was open for business. It, too,
had not altered in a decade, except that now the hernia belt
display had gone. In its place he saw a contrivance unfamiliar
to him. Halting, he examined the Spanish sign propped behind
it. The thing evidently increased one's sexual potency, he decided. Permitted—as he translated the Spanish—an infinitude

of orgasms, one immediately following the other. Amused, he continued on inside the pharmacy, to the counter in the rear.

A different pharmacist, this one a black-haired elderly female, greeted him. "*Sí?*" she leered, showing cheap chromium teeth.

Eric said, "You have a West German product, g-Totex blau?"

"I look. You wait, okay?" The woman trudged off and disappeared among the pharmaceuticals. Eric wandered around the displays sightlessly. "G-Totex blau a terrible poison," the old woman called to him. "You have to sign the book for it; *sí?*"

"*Sí,*" Eric said.

The product, in its black carton, was laid on the counter before him. "Two dollars fifty US," the old woman said. She lugged the control book out, put it where he could reach it with the chained pen. As he signed she wrapped the black carton. "You going to kill yourself, *señor?*" she asked acutely. "Yes, I can tell. This will not hurt with this product; I have seen it. No pain, just no heart all of a sudden."

"Yes," he agreed. "It's a good product."

"From A. G. Chemie. Reliable." She beamed in what seemed approval.

He paid the money—his ten-year-old bills were accepted without comment—and left the pharmacy with his package. Weird, he thought. In Tijuana it's still as it was. Always will be. Nobody even cares if you destroy yourself; it's a wonder they don't have booths at night where it's done for you, at ten pesos. Perhaps there is, by now.

It shook him a little, the woman's evident approval—and she did not know anything about him, even who he was. The war did it, he said to himself. I don't know why I let it surprise me.

When he returned to the Caesar Hotel and started upstairs to his room, the desk clerk—unfamiliar to him—halted him. "Sir, you are not a resident here." The clerk had moved swiftly from behind the counter to bar his way. "Did you want a room?"

"I have one," Eric said, and then remembered it had been ten years in the past; his occupancy had lapsed long ago.

"Nine US dollars each night in advance," the desk clerk said. "Since you do not have luggage."

Eric got out his wallet, passed over a ten-dollar bill. The clerk, however, inspected the bill with professional disavowal and mounting suspicion.

"These were called in," the clerk informed him. "Hard to exchange now because no more legal." He raised his head and scrutinized Eric with defiance. "Twenty. Two tens. And maybe even then I not accept them." He waited, devoid of enthusiasm; he clearly resented being paid in currency of this kind. It probably reminded him of the old days, the bad times of the war.

He had only one more bill in his wallet and that was a five. And, incredibly, through some freakish foul-up, perhaps because he had traded his watch for them, the useless currency from ninety years in the future; he spread them on the counter, their intricate, multicolored scrollwork shimmering. So perhaps, he thought, Kathy's electronic part had reached Virgil Ackerman back in the mid thirties after all; at least it had a chance. That cheered him.

The clerk picked up one of the 2155 bills. "What is this?" He held it to the light. "I never see before. You make it yourself?"

"No," Eric said.

"I can't use," the clerk decided. "Go before I call the police; you make it yourself, I know." He tossed the bill back with the others in a gesture of repugnance. "Funny money. Go away."

Leaving the 2155 bills on the counter but retrieving the five, Eric turned and walked out the door of the hotel, his package of g-Totex blau under his arm.

There were many malformed little alleys in Tijuana, even now after the war; he found a narrow, dark passage between brick buildings, littered with debris and the overflow from two immense ash-cans that had once been oil drums. In the alley he seated himself on the wooden step by a boarded-up entrance, lit a cigarette, sat smoking and pondering. He could not be seen from the street; the people rushing by on the sidewalk paid no attention to him and he focused his attention by watching them, in particular the girls. This, too, was as he knew it in the previous decade. A girl during daylight hours on the streets of Tijuana dressed with incomprehensible smartness: high heels, angora sweater, shiny purse, gloves, coat over her shoulders, preceded, as she hurried, by high, sharp-as-tacks breasts, the smartness carrying even to the detail of her modern bra. What did these girls do for a living? Where had they learned to dress so well, not to mention the problem of financing such a wardrobe? He had wondered this in his own time and he wondered it now.

The answer, he speculated, would be to stop one of these daytime Tijuana girls in flight, ask her where she lived and if she bought her clothes here or across the border. He wondered if these girls had ever been across to the United States, if they had boy friends in Los Angeles, if they were as good in bed as they looked to be. Something, some force not visible, made their lives possible. He hoped that at the same time it did not make them frigid; what a travesty on life, on the potency of natural creatures, that would be.

The trouble with such girls, he thought, is that they get old so fast. What you hear is true; by thirty they're worn out, fat, the bra and the coat and purse and gloves are gone; all that remains is the black, burning eyes peering out from beneath the shaggy brows, the original slender creature still imprisoned somewhere within but unable to speak any longer, play or make love or run. The click of heels against the pavement, the rushing forward into life; that's gone and only a slopping, dragging sound is left behind. The most horrid sound in the world, that of the *once-was*: alive in the past, perishing in the present, a corpse made of dust in the future. Nothing changes in Tijuana and yet nothing lives out its normal span. Time moves too fast here and also not at all. Look at my situation, for instance, he thought. I'm committing suicide ten years in the future, or rather I'll wipe out a life ten years ago. If I do this, what becomes of the Eric Sweetscent now working for Kaiser in Oakland? And the ten years he's spent watching over Kathy—what does that do to her?

Maybe this is my weak way of hurting her. A further punishment because she's sick.

Underneath my rationality my warped view, he thought. You can't quite manage to punish the sick enough. Is that it? Christ, he thought. No wonder I feel hatred for myself.

Holding the package of g-Totex blau in the palm of his

hand, he weighed it, experienced its mass. Felt the Earth's attraction for it. Yes, he thought, the Earth likes even this. She accepts everything.

Something ran across his shoe.

He saw, skittering away into the safety of the shadows and heaps of debris, a small wheeled cart.

The cart was pursued by another of its kind. They met, in the tangle of newspapers and bottles, and then the debris trembled and bits flew everywhere as the carts fought it out, ramming each other head-on, trying for the cephalic unit mounted in each other's center. Trying to knock out the Lazy Brown Dog.

Still alive? he thought in disbelief. Ten years later? But possibly Bruce Himmel still manufactured them. By now Tijuana must be overrun by them, if that was so. It was hard to know how to take such a sight. He continued to watch the two carts as they battled it out to the end; now one had knocked its antagonist's Lazy Brown Dog loose, seemed to be triumphing. It withdrew and, like a goat, maneuvered to locate itself for the coup de grace.

While it was positioning itself the damaged one, in a last burst of native wit, popped into the sanctuary of a discarded galvanized zinc bucket and was out of the fray. Protected, it became inert, prepared to wait things out, forever if necessary.

Getting to his feet, Eric stooped and grabbed up the stronger cart; its wheels spun futilely and then somehow it managed to twist out of his grasp. It bounced clatteringly to the pavement, backed, maneuvered, and then hurled itself against his foot. Surprised, he retreated. The cart made another menacing move toward him and he retreated again. Satisfied, the cart wheeled in a circle and then rattled off, out of sight.

In the bucket the loser could still be seen. Still waiting.

"I won't hurt you," Eric said to it, crouching down in order to get a better glimpse of it. The damaged thing, however, remained where it was. "Okay," he said and straightened up. "I get the idea." It knew what it wanted. There was no point in molesting it.

Even these things, he decided, are determined to live. Bruce was right. They deserve their opportunity, their minuscule place under the sun and sky. That's all they're asking for and it isn't much. He thought, And I can't even do what they do, make my stand, use my wits to survive in a debris-littered alley in Tijuana; that thing that's taken refuge there in that zinc bucket, without a wife, a career, a conapt or money or the possibility of encountering any of these, still persists. For reasons unknown to me its stake in existence is greater than mine.

The g-Totex blau no longer seemed attractive to him.

Even if I'm going to do this, he thought, *why does it have to be now?* Like everything else it can be put off—ought, in this case, to be put off. And anyhow he did not feel well; he felt dizzy and he shut his eyes, although by doing so he was inviting another attack by the fearsome Lazy Brown Dog cart which Bruce Himmel had made.

The slight weight in his hand disappeared entirely. He opened his eyes, saw that the paper bag with its black carton inside, the box of g-Totex blau, had disappeared. And the litter heaped here and there in the alley did not appear quite as extensive. From the long shadows cast by the sun he knew that it had become late in the day and this meant that the JJ-180 had worn off and he had gone back in time to—roughly—his own period. But he had taken the piece of capsule at night, in the dark, and this seemed more like five p.m. So, as before, the return was not exact and he wondered just how far off it was in this instance. After all, the 'Starmen were on their way.

In fact, he saw, they had already arrived.

Overhead a vast, dark, ugly mass hung in the sky, like something that had descended into this world from a lightless land of iron and surprise and frightened, purposeful silence. It was huge enough, he thought, to feed forever; even from the spot where he stood, at the very least a mile from it, he could see that it consisted of a limitless, appetitive self which would begin any time now to gulp down everything in sight. It made no sound. Its engines were off. This ship had come a long way, from the lines deep in intersystem space. It was a seasoned, informed, world-weary apparition, brought out by strange needs from its normal place of residence.

I wonder how easy it's going to be, Eric wondered. For

them simply to drop to the surface and enter key buildings and take everything over. Probably easier than I think, than anyone here on Terra thinks.

He walked from the alley to the street, thinking to himself, I wish I had a gun.

Strange, he thought, that in the center of the greatest abomination of our times, this war, I should find something meaningful. A desire animating me equal to that possessed by the Lazy Brown Dog cart hiding in the zinc pail ten years from now. Maybe I'm its compatriot at last. Able to take my place in the world beside it, do as it does, fight as it fights: whenever it's necessary and then some, for the pleasure of it. For the joy. As was intended from the start anterior to any time or condition I could comprehend or call my own or enter into.

Traffic had slowed to a near stop along the street. Everyone, in the vehicles and on foot, watched the 'Star ship.

"Taxi!" Walking out into the street he hailed an autonomic cab capable of non-surface flight. "Take me to Tijuana Fur & Dye," he ordered it. "Make it as fast as you can and don't pay any attention to that ship up there, including any instructions it might broadcast."

The cab shuddered, rose slightly from the asphalt, and hung stationary. "We've been forbidden to take off, sir. The Lilistar Army Command for this area sent out orders that—"

"I'm in supreme charge of this situation," Eric told the cab. "I outrank the Lilistar Army Command; they're dirt compared with me. I have to be at Tijuana Fur & Dye immediately—the war effort hangs on my being there."

"Yes sir," the cab said, and soared up into the sky. "And it's an honor, sir; believe me, a rare honor to convey you."

"My presence there," Eric said, "is of incomparable strategic importance." At the factory I'll make my stand, he said to himself. With the people I know. And, when Virgil Ackerman escapes to Wash-35, I'll go along with him; it's beginning to unfold as I witnessed it a year from now.

And, at Tijuana Fur & Dye, he realized, I'll undoubtedly run into Kathy.

To the cab he said suddenly, "If your wife were sick—"

"I have no wife, sir," the cab said. "Autonomic mechanisms never marry; everyone knows that."

"All right," Eric agreed. "If you were me, and your wife were sick, desperately so, with no hope of recovery, would you leave her? Or would you stay with her, even if you had traveled ten years into the future and knew for an absolute certainty that the damage to her brain could never be reversed? And staying with her would mean—"

"I can see what it would mean, sir," the cab broke in. "It would mean no other life for you beyond caring for her."

"That's right," Eric said.

"I'd stay with her," the cab decided.

"Why?"

"Because," the cab said, "life is composed of reality configurations so constituted. To abandon her would be to say, I can't endure reality as such. I have to have uniquely special easier conditions."

"I think I agree," Eric said after a time. "I think I will stay with her."

"God bless you, sir," the cab said. "I can see that you're a good man."

"Thank you," Eric said.

The cab soared on toward Tijuana Fur & Dye Corporation.

FLOW MY TEARS,
THE POLICEMAN SAID

The love in this novel is for Tessa,
and the love in me is for her, too.
She is my little song.

Part One

ONE

ON Tuesday, October 11, 1988, the *Jason Taverner Show* ran thirty seconds short. A technician, watching through the plastic bubble of the control dome, froze the final credit on the video section, then pointed to Jason Taverner, who had started to leave the stage. The technician tapped his wrist, pointed to his mouth.

Into the boom mike Jason said smoothly, "Keep all those cards and V-letters coming in, folks. And stay tuned now for *The Adventures of Scotty, Dog Extraordinary.*"

The technician smiled; Jason smiled back, and then both the audio and the video clicked off. Their hour-long music and variety program, which held the second highest rating among the year's best TV shows, had come to an end. And it had all gone well.

"Where'd we lose half a minute?" Jason said to his special guest star of the evening, Heather Hart. It puzzled him. He liked to time his own shows.

Heather Hart said, "Baby bunting, it's all right." She put her cool hand across his slightly moist forehead, rubbed the perimeter of his sand-colored hair affectionately.

"Do you realize what power you have?" Al Bliss, their business agent, said to Jason, coming up close—too close as always —to him. "Thirty million people saw you zip up your fly tonight. That's a record of sorts."

"I zip up my fly every week," Jason said. "It's my trademark. Or don't you catch the show?"

"But thirty million," Bliss said, his round, florid face spotted with drops of perspiration. "Think of it. And then there's the residuals."

Jason said crisply, "I'll be dead before the residuals on this show pay off. Thank God."

"You'll probably be dead tonight," Heather said, "with all those fans of yours packed in outside there. Just waiting to rip you into little tiny squares like so many postage stamps."

"Some of them are your fans, Miss Hart," Al Bliss said, in his doglike panting voice.

"God damn them," Heather said harshly. "Why don't they go away? Aren't they breaking some law, loitering or something?"

Jason took hold of her hand and squeezed it forcefully, attracting her frowning attention. He had never understood her dislike for fans; to him they were the lifeblood of his public existence. And to him his public existence, his role as worldwide entertainer, was existence itself, period. "You shouldn't be an entertainer," he said to Heather, "feeling the way you do. Get out of the business. Become a social worker in a forced labor camp."

"There're people there, too," Heather said grimly.

Two special police guards shouldered their way up to Jason Taverner and Heather. "We've got the corridor as clear as we're going to get it," the fatter of the two cops wheezed. "Let's go now, Mr. Taverner. Before the studio audience can trickle around to the side exits." He signaled to three other special police guards, who at once advanced toward the hot, packed passageway that led, eventually, to the nocturnal street. And out there the parked Rolls flyship in all its costly splendor, its tail rocket idling throbbingly. Like, Jason thought, a mechanical heart. A heart that beat for him alone, for him the star. Well, by extension, it throbbed in response to the needs of Heather, too.

She deserved it: she had sung well, tonight. Almost as well as—Jason grinned inwardly, to himself. Hell, let's face it, he thought. They don't turn on all those 3-D color TV sets to see the special guest star. There are a thousand special guest stars scattered over the surface of earth, and a few in the Martian colonies.

They turn on, he thought, to see *me*. And I am always there. Jason Taverner has never and will never disappoint his fans. However Heather may feel about hers.

"You don't like them," Jason said as they squirmed and pushed and ducked their way down the steaming, sweat-smelling corridor, "because you don't like yourself. You secretly think they have bad taste."

"They're dumb," Heather grunted, and cursed quietly as her flat, large hat flopped from her head and disappeared forever within the whale's belly of close-pressing fans.

"They're ordinaries," Jason said, his lips at her ear, partly lost as it was in her great tangle of shiny red hair. The famous cascade of hair so widely and expertly copied in beauty salons throughout Terra.

Heather grated, "Don't say that word."

"They're ordinaries," Jason said, "and they're morons. Because"—he nipped the lobe of her ear—"because that's what it means to be an ordinary. Right?"

She sighed. "Oh, God, to be in the flyship cruising through the void. That's what I long for: an infinite void. With no human voices, no human smells, no human jaws masticating plastic chewing gum in nine iridescent colors."

"You really do hate them," he said.

"Yes." She nodded briskly. "And so do you." She halted briefly, turning her head to confront him. "You know your goddamn voice is gone; you know you're coasting on your glory days, which you'll never see again." She smiled at him, then. Warmly. "Are we growing old?" she said, above the mumbles and squeaks of the fans. "Together? Like man and wife?"

Jason said, "Sixes don't grow old."

"Oh yes," Heather said. "Oh yes they do." Reaching upward, she touched his wavy brown hair. "How long have you been tinting it, dearheart? A year? Three?"

"Get in the flyship," he said brusquely, maneuvering her ahead of him, out of the building and onto the pavement of Hollywood Boulevard.

"I'll get in," Heather said, "if you'll sing me a high B natural. Remember when you—"

He thrust her bodily into the flyship, squeezed in after her, turned to help Al Bliss close the door, and then they were up and into the rain-clouded nighttime sky. The great gleaming sky of Los Angeles, as bright as if it were high noon. And that's what it is for you and for me, he thought. For the two of us, in all times to come. It will always be as it is now, because we are sixes. Both of us. Whether *they* know it or not.

And it's not, he thought grimly, enjoying the bleak humor of it. The knowledge which they together had, the knowledge unshared. Because that was the way it was meant to be. And always had . . . even now after it had all turned out so badly. Badly, at least, in the designers' eyes. The great pundits who had guessed and guessed wrong. Forty-five beautiful years ago, when the world was young and droplets of rain still clung to the now-gone Japanese cherry trees in Washington, D.C. And the smell of spring that had hovered over the noble experiment. For a short while, anyhow.

"Let's go to Zürich," he said aloud.

"I'm too tired," Heather said. "Anyhow, that place bores me."

"The house?" He was incredulous. Heather had picked it out for the two of them, and for years there they had gotten away—away especially from the fans that Heather hated so much.

Heather sighed and said, "The house. The Swiss watches. The bread. The cobblestones. The snow on the hills."

"Mountains," he said, feeling aggrieved still. "Well, hell," he said. "I'll go without you."

"And pick up someone else?"

He simply could not understand. "Do you *want* me to take someone else with me?" he demanded.

"You and your magnetism. Your charm. You could get any girl in the world into that big brass bed with you. Not that you're so much once you get there."

"God," he said with disgust. "That again. Always the same old gripes. And the ones that're fantasy—they're the ones you really hang on to."

Turning to face him, Heather said earnestly, "You know how you look, even now at the age you are. You're beautiful. Thirty million people ogle you an hour a week. It's not your singing they're interested in . . . it's your incurable physical beauty."

"The same can be said for you," he said caustically. He felt tired and he yearned for the privacy and seclusion that lay there on the outskirts of Zürich, silently waiting for the two of them to come back once more. And it was as if the house wanted them to stay, not for a night or a week of nights, but forever.

"I don't show my age," Heather said.

He glanced at her, then studied her. Volumes of red hair, pale skin with a few freckles, a strong roman nose. Deep-set huge violet eyes. She was right; she didn't show her age. Of course she never tapped into the phone-grid transex network, as he did. But in point of fact he did so very little. So he was not hooked, and there had not been, in his case, brain damage or premature aging.

"You're a goddamn beautiful-looking person," he said grudgingly.

"And you?" Heather said.

He could not be shaken by this. He knew that he still had his charisma, the force they had inscribed on the chromosomes forty-two years ago. True, his hair had become mostly gray and he did tint it. And a few wrinkles had appeared here and there. But—

"As long as I have my voice," he said, "I'll be okay. I'll have what I want. You're wrong about me—it's your six aloofness, your cherished so-called individuality. Okay, if you don't want to fly over to the house in Zürich, where *do* you want to go? Your place? My place?"

"I want to be married to you," Heather said. "So then it won't be my place versus your place but it'll be our place. And I'll give up singing and have three children, all of them looking like you."

"Even the girls?"

Heather said, "They'll all be boys."

Leaning over he kissed her on the nose. She smiled, took his hand, patted it warmly. "We can go anywhere tonight," he said to her in a low, firm, controlled, and highly projected voice, almost a father voice; it generally worked well with Heather, whereas nothing else did. Unless, he thought, I walk off.

She feared that. Sometimes in their quarrels, especially at the house in Zürich, where no one could hear them or interfere, he had seen the fear on her face. The idea of being alone appalled her; he knew it; she knew it; the fear was part of the reality of their joint life. Not their public life; for them, as genuinely professional entertainers, there they had complete, rational control: however angry and estranged they became they would function together in the big worshiping world of viewers, letter writers, noisy fans. Even outright hatred could not change that.

But there could be no hate between them anyhow. They had too much in common. They got so damn much from each other. Even mere physical contact, such as this, sitting together in the Rolls skyfly, made them happy. For as long, anyhow, as it lasted.

Reaching into the inner pocket of his custom-tailored genuine silk suit—one of perhaps ten in the whole world—he brought out a wad of government-certified bills. A great number of them, compressed into a fat little bundle.

"You shouldn't carry so much cash on you," Heather said naggingly, in the tone he disliked so much: the opinionated-mother tone.

Jason said, "With this"—he displayed the package of bills— "we can buy our way into any—"

"If some unregistered student who has sneaked across from a campus burrow just last night doesn't chop your hand off at the wrist and run away with it, both your hand and your flashy money. You always have been flashy. Flashy and loud. Look at your tie. Look at it!" She had risen her voice, now; she seemed genuinely angry.

"Life is short," Jason said. "And prosperity even shorter." But he placed the package of bills back in his inside coat pocket, smoothed away at the lump it created in his otherwise perfect suit. "I wanted to buy you something with it," he said. Actually the idea had just come to him now; what he had planned to do with the money was something a little different: he intended to take it to Las Vegas, to the blackjack tables. As a six he could—and did—always win at blackjack; he had the edge over everyone, even the dealer. Even, he thought sleekly, the pit boss.

"You're lying," Heather said. "You didn't intend to get me anything; you never do, you're so selfish and always thinking about yourself. That's screwing money; you're going to buy some big-chested blonde and go to bed together with her.

Probably at our place in Zürich, which, you realize, I haven't seen for four months now. I might as well be pregnant."

It struck him as odd that she would say that, out of all the possible retorts that might flow up into her conscious, talking mind. But there was a good deal about Heather that he did not understand; with him, as with her fans, she kept many things about her private.

But, over the years, he had learned a lot about her. He knew, for example, that in 1982 she had had an abortion, a well-kept secret, too. He knew that at one time she had been illegally married to a student commune leader, and that for one year she had lived in the rabbit warrens of Columbia University, along with all the smelly, bearded students kept subsurface life-long by the pols and the nats. The police and the national guard, who ringed every campus, keeping the students from creeping across to society like so many black rats swarming out of a leaky ship.

And he knew that one year ago she had been busted for possession of drugs. Only her wealthy and powerful family had been able to buy her out of *that* one: her money and her charisma and fame hadn't worked when confrontation time with the police came.

Heather had been scarred a little by all that had overtaken her, but, he knew, she was all right now. Like all sixes she had enormous recuperative ability. It had been carefully built into each of them. Among much, much else. Things which even he, at forty-two years, didn't know them all. And a lot had happened to him, too. Mostly in the form of dead bodies, the remains of other entertainers he had trampled on his long climb to the top.

"These 'flashy' ties—" he began, but then the skyfly's phone rang. He took it, said hello. Probably it was Al Bliss with the ratings on tonight's show.

But it was not. A girl's voice came to him, penetrating sharply, stridently into his ear. "Jason?" the girl said loudly.

"Yeah," he said. Cupping the mouthpiece of the phone he said to Heather, "It's Marilyn Mason. Why the hell did I give her my skyfly number?"

"Who the hell is Marilyn Mason?" Heather asked.

"I'll tell you later." He uncupped the phone. "Yes, dear; this is Jason for real, in the true reincarnated flesh. What is it? You sound terrible. Are they evicting you again?" He winked at Heather and grinned wryly.

"Get rid of her," Heather said.

Again cupping the mouthpiece of the phone he said to her, "I will; I'm trying to; can't you see?" Into the phone he said, "Okay, Marilyn. Spill your guts out to me; that's what I'm for."

For two years Marilyn Mason had been his protégée, so to speak. Anyhow, she wanted to be a singer—be famous, rich, loved—like him. One day she had come wandering into the studio, during rehearsal, and he had taken notice of her. Tight little worried face, short legs, skirt far too short—he had, as was his practice, taken it all in at first glance. And, a week later, he had arranged for an audition for her with Columbia Records, their artists and repertoire chief.

A lot had gone on in that week, but it hadn't had anything to do with singing.

Marilyn said shrilly into his ear, "I have to see you. Otherwise I'll kill myself and the guilt will be on you. For the rest of your life. And I'll tell that Heather Hart woman about us sleeping together all the time."

Inwardly he sighed. Hell, he was tired already, worn out by his hour-long show during which it was smile, smile, smile. "I'm on my way to Switzerland for the rest of tonight," he said firmly, as if speaking to a hysterical child. Usually, when Marilyn was in one of her accusatory, quasi-paranoid moods it worked. But not this time, naturally.

"It'll take you five minutes to get over here in that million-dollar Rolls skyfly of yours," Marilyn dinned in his ear. "I just want to talk to you for five seconds. I have something very important to tell you."

She's probably pregnant, Jason said to himself. Somewhere along the line she intentionally—or maybe unintentionally—forgot to take her pill.

"What can you tell me in five seconds that I don't already know?" he said sharply. "Tell me now."

"I want you here with me," Marilyn said, with her customary total lack of consideration. "You must come. I haven't seen you in six months and during that time I've done a lot of thinking about us. And in particular about that last audition."

"Okay," he said, feeling bitter and resentful. This was what he got for trying to manufacture for her—a no-talent—a career. He hung up the phone noisily, turned to Heather and said, "I'm glad you never ran into her; she's really a—"

"Bullshit," Heather said. "I didn't 'run into her' because you made damn sure you saw to that."

"Anyhow," he said, as he made a right turn for the skyfly, "I got her not one but two auditions, and she snurfled them both. And to keep her self-respect she's got to blame it on me. I somehow herded her into failing. You see the picture."

"Does she have nice boobs?" Heather said.

"Actually, yes." He grinned and Heather laughed. "You know my weakness. But I did my part of the bargain; I got her an audition—*two* auditions. The last one was six months ago and I know goddamn well she's still smoldering and brooding over it. I wonder what she wants to tell me."

He punched the control module to set up an automatic course for Marilyn's apartment building with its small but adequate roof field.

"She's probably in love with you," Heather said, as he parked the skyfly on its tail, releasing then the descent stairs.

"Like forty million others," Jason said genially.

Heather, making herself comfortable in the bucket seat of the skyfly said, "Don't be gone very long or so help me I'm taking off without you."

"Leaving me stuck with Marilyn?" he said. They both laughed. "I'll be right back." He crossed the field to the elevator, pressed the button.

When he entered Marilyn's apartment he saw, at once, that she was out of her mind. Her entire face had pinched and constricted; her body so retracted that it looked as if she were trying to ingest herself. And her eyes. Very few things around or about women made him uneasy, but this did. Her eyes, completely round, with huge pupils, bored at him as she stood silently facing him, her arms folded, everything about her unyielding and iron rigid.

"Start talking," Jason said, feeling around for the handle of the advantage. Usually—in fact virtually always—he could control a situation that involved a woman; it was, in point of fact, his specialty. But this . . . he felt uncomfortable. And still she said nothing. Her face, under layers of makeup, had become completely bloodless, as if she were an animated corpse. "You want another audition?" Jason asked. "Is that it?"

Marilyn shook her head no.

"Okay; tell me what it is," he said wearily but uneasily. He kept the unease out of his voice, however; he was far too shrewd, far too experienced, to let her hear his uncertainty. In a confrontation with a woman it ran nearly ninety per cent bluff, on both sides. It all lay in *how* you did it, not what you did.

"I have something for you." Marilyn turned, walked off out of sight into the kitchen. He strolled after her.

"You still blame me for the lack of success of both—" he began.

"Here you are," Marilyn said. She lifted up a plastic bag from the drainboard, stood holding it a moment, her face still bloodless and stark, her eyes jutting and unblinking, and then she yanked the bag open, swung it, moved swiftly up to him.

It happened too fast. He backed away out of instinct, but too slowly and too late. The gelatinlike Callisto cuddle sponge with its fifty feeding tubes clung to him, anchored itself to his chest. Already he felt the feeding tubes dig into him, into his chest.

He leaped to the overhead kitchen cabinets, grabbed out a half-filled bottle of scotch, unscrewed the lid with flying fingers, and poured the scotch onto the gelatinlike creature. His thoughts had become lucid, even brilliant; he did not panic, but stood there pouring the scotch onto the thing.

For a moment nothing happened. He still managed to hold himself together and not flee into panic. And then the thing bubbled, shriveled, fell from his chest onto the floor. It had died.

Feeling weak, he seated himself at the kitchen table. Now he found himself fighting off unconsciousness; some of the feeding tubes remained inside him, and they were still alive. "Not bad," he managed to say. "You almost got me, you fucking little tramp."

"Not almost," Marilyn Mason said flatly, emotionlessly.

"Some of the feeding tubes are still in you and you know it; I can see it on your face. And a bottle of scotch isn't going to get them out. *Nothing* is going to get them out."

At that point he fainted. Dimly, he saw the green-and-gray floor rise to take him and then there was emptiness. A void without even himself in it.

Pain. He opened his eyes, reflexively touched his chest. His hand-tailored silk suit had vanished; he wore a cotton hospital robe and he was lying flat on a gurney. "God," he said thickly as the two staff men wheeled the gurney rapidly up the hospital corridor.

Heather Hart, hovering over him, anxious and in shock, but, like him, she retained full possession of her senses. "I knew something was wrong," she said rapidly as the staff men wheeled him into a room. "I didn't wait for you in the skyfly; I came down after you."

"You probably thought we were in bed together," he said weakly.

"The doctor said," Heather said, "that in another fifteen seconds you would have succumbed to the somatic violation, as he calls it. The entrance of that *thing* into you."

"I got the thing," he said. "But I didn't get all the feeding tubes. It was too late."

"I know," Heather said. "The doctor told me. They're planning surgery for as soon as possible; they may be able to do something if the tubes haven't penetrated too far."

"I was good in the crisis," Jason grated; he shut his eyes and endured the pain. "But not quite good enough. Just not quite." Opening his eyes, he saw that Heather was crying. "Is it that bad?" he asked her; reaching up he took hold of her hand. He felt the pressure of her love as she squeezed his fingers, and then there was nothing. Except the pain. But nothing else, no Heather, no hospital, no staff men, no light. And no sound. It was an eternal moment and it absorbed him completely.

TWO

Light filtered back, filling his closed eyes with a membrane of illuminated redness. He opened his eyes, lifted his head to look around him. To search out Heather or the doctor.

He lay alone in the room. No one else. A bureau with a cracked vanity mirror, ugly old light fixtures jutting from the grease-saturated walls. And from somewhere nearby the blare of a TV set.

He was not in a hospital.

And Heather was not with him; he experienced her absence, the total emptiness of everything, because of her.

God, he thought. *What's happened?*

The pain in his chest had vanished, along with so much else. Shakily, he pushed back the soiled wool blanket, sat up, rubbed his forehead reflexively, gathered together his vitality.

This is a hotel room, he realized. A lousy, bug-infested cheap wino hotel. No curtains, no bathroom. Like he had lived in years ago, at the start of his career. Back when he had been unknown and had no money. The dark days he always shut out of his memory as best he could.

Money. He groped at his clothes, discovered that he no longer wore the hospital gown but had back, in wrinkled condition, his hand-tailored silk suit. And, in the inner coat pocket, the wad of high-denomination bills, the money he had intended to take to Vegas.

At least he had that.

Swiftly, he looked around for a phone. No, of course not. But there'd be one in the lobby. But whom to call? Heather? Al Bliss, his agent? Mory Mann, the producer of his TV show? His attorney, Bill Wolfer? Or all of them, as soon as possible, perhaps.

Unsteadily, he managed to get to his feet; he stood swaying, cursing for reasons he did not understand. An animal instinct held him; he readied himself, his strong six body, to fight. But he could not discern the antagonist, and that frightened him. For the first time in as long as he could remember he felt panic.

Has a lot of time passed? he asked himself. He could not tell; he had no sense of it either way. Daytime. Quibbles zooming and bleating in the skies outside the dirty glass of his window. He looked at his watch; it read ten-thirty. So what? It could be a thousand years off, for all he knew. His watch couldn't help him.

But the phone would. He made his way out into the dust-saturated corridor, found the stairs, descended step by step, holding on to the rail until at last he stood in the depressing, empty lobby with its ratty old overstuffed chairs.

Fortunately he had change. He dropped a one-dollar gold piece into the slot, dialed Al Bliss's number.

"Bliss Talent Agency," Al's voice came presently.

"Listen," Jason said. "I don't know where I am. In the name of Christ come and get me; get me out of here; get me someplace else. You understand, Al? Do you?"

Silence from the phone. And then in a distant, detached voice Al Bliss said, "Who am I talking to?"

He snarled his answer.

"I don't know you, Mr. Jason Taverner," Al Bliss said, again in his most neutral, uninvolved voice. "Are you sure you have the right number? Who did you want to talk to?"

"To you. Al. Al Bliss, my agent. What happened in the hospital? How'd I get out of there into here? Don't you know?" His panic ebbed as he forced control on himself; he made his words come out reasonably. "Can you get hold of Heather for me?"

"Miss Hart?" Al said, and chuckled. And did not answer.

"You," Jason said savagely, "are through as my agent. Period. No matter what the situation is. You are out."

In his ear Al Bliss chuckled again and then, with a click, the line became dead. Al Bliss had hung up.

I'll kill the son of a bitch, Jason said to himself. I'll tear that fat balding little bastard into inch-square pieces.

What was he trying to do to me? I don't understand. What all of a sudden does he have against me? What the hell did I do to him, for chrissakes? He's been my friend and agent nineteen years. And nothing like this has ever happened before.

I'll try Bill Wolfer, he decided. He's always in his office or on call; I'll be able to get hold of him and find out what this is all about. He dropped a second gold dollar into the phone's slot and, from memory, once more dialed.

"Wolfer and Blaine, Attorneys-at-law," a female receptionist's voice sounded in his ear.

"Let me talk to Bill," Jason said. "This is Jason Taverner. You know who I am."

The receptionist said, "Mr. Wolfer is in court today. Would you care to speak to Mr. Blaine instead, or shall I have Mr. Wolfer call you back when he returns to the office later on this afternoon?"

"Do you know who I am?" Jason said. "Do you know who Jason Taverner is? Do you watch TV?" His voice almost got away from him at that point; he heard it break and rise. With great effort he regained control over it, but he could not stop his hands from shaking; his whole body, in fact, shook.

"I'm sorry, Mr. Taverner," the receptionist said. "I really can't talk for Mr. Wolfer or—"

"Do you watch TV?" he said.

"Yes."

"And you haven't heard of me? The *Jason Taverner Show*, at nine on Tuesday nights?"

"I'm sorry, Mr. Taverner. You really must talk directly to Mr. Wolfer. Give me the number of the phone you're calling from and I'll see to it that he calls you back sometime today."

He hung up.

I'm insane, he thought. Or she's insane. She and Al Bliss, that son of a bitch. God. He moved shakily away from the phone, seated himself in one of the faded overstuffed chairs. It felt good to sit; he shut his eyes and breathed slowly and deeply. And pondered.

I have five thousand dollars in government high-denomination bills, he told himself. So I'm not completely helpless. And that thing is gone from my chest, including its feeding tubes. They must have been able to get at them surgically in the hospital. So at least I'm alive; I can rejoice over that. Has there been a time lapse? he asked himself. Where's a newspaper?

He found an L.A. *Times* on a nearby couch, read the date. October 12, 1988. No time lapse. This was the day after his show and the day Marilyn had sent him, dying, to the hospital.

An idea came to him. He searched through the sections of newspaper until he found the entertainment column. Currently he was appearing nightly at the Persian Room of the Hollywood Hilton—had been in fact for three weeks, but of course less Tuesdays because of his show.

The ad for him which the hotel people had been running during the past three weeks did not seem to be on the page anywhere. He thought groggily, maybe it's been moved to another page. He thereupon combed that section of the paper thoroughly. Ad after ad for entertainers but no mention of him. And his face had been on the entertainment page of some newspaper or another for ten years. Without an ellipsis.

I'll make one more try, he decided. I'll try Mory Mann.

Fishing out his wallet, he searched for the slip on which he had written Mory's number.

His wallet was very thin.

All his identification cards were gone. Cards that made it possible for him to stay alive. Cards that got him through pol and nat barricades without being shot or thrown into a forced-labor camp.

I can't live two hours without my ID, he said to himself. I don't even dare walk out of the lobby of this rundown hotel and onto the public sidewalk. They'll assume I'm a student or teacher escaped from one of the campuses. I'll spend the rest of my life as a slave doing heavy manual labor. I am what they call an *unperson*.

So my first job, he thought, is to stay alive. The hell with Jason Taverner as a public entertainer; I can worry about that later.

He could feel within his brain the powerful six-determined constituents moving already into focus. I am not like other men, he told himself. I will get out of this, whatever it is. Somehow.

For example, he realized, with all this money I have on me I can get myself down to Watts and buy phony ID cards. A whole walletful of them. There must be a hundred little operators scratching away at that, from what I've heard. But I never thought I'd be using one of them. Not Jason Taverner. Not a public entertainer with an audience of thirty million.

Among all those thirty million people, he asked himself, isn't there one who remembers me? If "remember" is the right word. I'm talking as if a lot of time has passed, that I'm an old man now, a has-been, feeding off former glories. And that's not what's going on.

Returning to the phone, he looked up the number of the birth-registration control center in Iowa; with several gold coins he managed to reach them at last, after much delay.

"My name is Jason Taverner," he told the clerk. "I was born in Chicago at Memorial Hospital on December 16, 1946. Would you please confirm and release a copy of my certificate of birth? I need it for a job I'm applying for."

"Yes, sir." The clerk put the line on hold; Jason waited.

The clerk clicked back on. "Mr. Jason Taverner, born in Cook County on December 16, 1946."

"Yes," Jason said.

"We have no birth registration form for such a person at that time and place. Are you absolutely sure of the facts, sir?"

"You mean do I know my name and when and where I was born?" His voice again managed to escape his control, but this time he let it; panic flooded him. "Thanks," he said and hung up, shaking violently, now. Shaking in his body and in his mind.

I don't exist, he said to himself. There is no Jason Taverner. There never was and there never will be. The hell with my career; I just want to live. If someone or something wants to eradicate my career, okay; do it. But aren't I going to be allowed to exist at all? Wasn't I even born?

Something stirred in his chest. With terror he thought, They didn't get the feed tubes out entirely; some of them are still growing and feeding inside of me. That god-damn tramp of a no-talent girl. I hope she winds up walking the streets for two bits a try.

After what I did for her: getting her those two auditions for A and R people. But hell—I did get to lay her a lot. I suppose it comes out even.

Returning to his hotel room, he took a good long look at himself in the flyspecked vanity mirror. His appearance hadn't changed, except that he needed a shave. No older. No more lines, no gray hair visible. The good shoulders and biceps. The fat-free waist that let him wear the current form-fitting men's clothing.

And that's important to your image, he said to himself. What kind of suits you can wear, especially those tucked-in-waist numbers. I must have fifty of them, he thought. Or did have. Where are they now? he asked himself. The bird is gone, and in what meadow does it now sing? Or however that goes. Something from the past, out of his days at school. Forgotten until this moment. Strange, he thought, what drifts up into your mind when you're in an unfamiliar and ominous situation. Sometimes the most trivial stuff imaginable.

If wishes were horses then beggars might fly. Stuff like that. It's enough to drive you crazy.

He wondered how many pol and nat check stations there were between this miserable hotel and the closest ID forger in Watts? Ten? Thirteen? Two? For me, he thought, all it takes is one. One random check by a mobile vehicle and crew of three. With their damn radio gear connecting them to pol-nat data central in Kansas City. Where they keep the dossiers.

He rolled back his sleeve and examined his forearm. Yes, there it was: his tattooed ident number. His somatic license plate, to be carried by him throughout his life, buried at last with him in his longed-for grave.

Well, the pols and nats at the mobile check station would read off the ident number to Kansas City and then—what then? Was his dossier still there or was it gone, too, like his birth certificate? And if it wasn't there, what would the pol-nat bureaucrats think it meant?

A clerical error. Somebody misfiled the microfilm packet that made up the dossier. It'll turn up. Someday, when it doesn't matter, when I've spent ten years of my life in a quarry on Luna using a manual pickax. If the dossier isn't there, he mused, they'll assume I'm an escaped student, because it's only students who don't have pol-nat dossiers, and even some of them, the important ones, the leaders—they're in there, too.

I am at the bottom of life, he realized. And I can't even climb my way up to mere physical existence. Me, a man who yesterday had an audience of thirty million. Someday, somehow, I will grope my way back to them. But not now. There are other things that come first. The bare bones of existence that every man is born with: I don't even have that. But I will get it; a six is not an ordinary. No ordinary could have physically or psychologically survived what's happened to me —especially the uncertainty—as I have.

A six, no matter what the external circumstances, will always prevail. Because that's the way they genetically defined us.

He left his hotel room once more, walked downstairs and up to the desk. A middle-aged man with a thin mustache was reading a copy of *Box* magazine; he did not look up but said, "Yes, sir."

Jason brought out his packet of government bills, laid a five-hundred-dollar note on the counter before the clerk. The clerk glanced at it, glanced again, this time with wide-opened eyes. Then he cautiously looked up into Jason's face, questioningly.

"My ident cards were stolen," Jason said. "That five-hundred-dollar bill is yours if you can get me to someone who can replace them. If you're going to do it, do it right now; I'm not going to wait." Wait to be picked up by a pol or a nat, he thought. Caught here in this rundown dingy hotel.

"Or caught on the sidewalk in front of the entrance," the clerk said. "I'm a telepath of sorts. I know this hotel isn't much, but we have no bugs. Once we had Martian sand fleas, but no more." He picked up the five-hundred-dollar bill. "I'll get you to someone who can help you," he said. Studying Jason's face intently, he paused, then said, "You think you're world-famous. Well, we get all kinds."

"Let's go," Jason said harshly. "Now."

"Right now," the clerk said, and reached for his shiny plastic coat.

THREE

As the clerk drove his old-time quibble slowly and noisily down the street he said casually to Jason, seated beside him, "I'm picking up a lot of odd material in your mind."

"Get out of my mind," Jason said brusquely, with aversion. He had always disliked the prying, curiosity-driven telepaths, and this time was no exception. "Get out of my mind," he said, "and get me to the person who's going to help me. And don't run into any pol-nat barricades. If you expect to live through this."

The clerk said mildly, "You don't have to tell me that; I

know what would happen to you if we got stopped. I've done this before, many times. For students. But you're not a student. You're a famous man and you're rich. But at the same time you aren't. At the same time you're a nobody. You don't even exist, legally speaking." He laughed a thin, effete laugh, his eyes fixed on the traffic ahead of him. He drove like an old woman, Jason noted. Both hands fixedly hanging on to the steering wheel.

Now they had entered the slums of Watts proper. Tiny dark stores on each side of the cluttered street, overflowing ashcans, the pavement littered with pieces of broken bottles, drab painted signs that advertised Coca-Cola in big letters and the name of the store in small. At an intersection an elderly black man haltingly crossed, feeling his way along as if blind with age. Seeing him, Jason felt an odd emotion. There was so few blacks alive, now, because of Tidman's notorious sterilization bill passed by Congress back in the terrible days of the Insurrection. The clerk carefully slowed his rattly quibble to a stop so as not to harass the elderly black man in his rumpled, seam-torn brown suit. Obviously he felt it, too.

"Do you realize," the clerk said to Jason, "that if I hit him with my car it would mean the death penalty for me?"

"It should," Jason said.

"They're like the last flock of whooping cranes," the clerk said, starting forward now that the old black had reached the far side. "Protected by a thousand laws. You can't jeer at them; you can't get into a fistfight with one without risking a felony rap—ten years in prison. Yet we're making them die out— that's what Tidman wanted and I guess what the majority of Silencers wanted, but"—he gestured, for the first time taking a hand off the wheel—"I miss the kids. I remember when I was ten and I had a black boy to play with . . . not far from here as a matter of fact. He's undoubtedly sterilized by now."

"But then he's had one child," Jason pointed out. "His wife had to surrender their birth coupon when their first and only child came . . . but they've got that child. The law lets them have it. And there're a million statutes protecting their safety."

"Two adults, one child," the clerk said. "So the black population is halved every generation. Ingenious. You have to hand it to Tidman; he solved the race problem, all right."

"Something had to be done," Jason said; he sat rigidly in his seat, studying the street ahead, searching for a sign of a pol-nat checkpoint or barricade. He saw neither, but how long were they going to have to continue driving?

"We're almost there," the clerk said calmly. He turned his head momentarily to face Jason. "I don't like your racist views," he said. "Even if you are paying me five hundred dollars."

"There're enough blacks alive to suit me," Jason said.

"And when the last one dies?"

Jason said, "You can read my mind; I don't have to tell you."

"Christ," the clerk said, and returned his attention to the street traffic ahead.

They made a sharp right turn, down a narrow alley, at both sides of which closed, locked wooden doors could be seen. No signs here. Just shut-up silence. And piles of ancient debris.

"What's behind those doors?" Jason asked.

"People like you. People who can't come out into the open. But they're different from you in one way: they don't have five hundred dollars . . . and a lot more besides, if I read you correctly."

"It's going to cost me plenty," Jason said acidly, "to get my ID cards. Probably all I've got."

"She won't overcharge you," the clerk said as he brought his quibble to a halt half on the sidewalk of the alley. Jason peered out, saw an abandoned restaurant, boarded up, with broken windows. Entirely dark inside. It repelled him, but apparently this was the place. He'd have to go along with it, his need being what it was: he could not be choosy.

And—they had avoided every checkpoint and barricade along the way; the clerk had picked a good route. So he had damn little to complain about, all things considered.

Together, he and the clerk approached the open-hanging broken front door of the restaurant. Neither spoke; they concentrated on avoiding the rusted nails protruding from the sheets of plywood hammered into place, presumably to protect the windows.

"Hang on to my hand," the clerk said, extending it in the shadowy dimness that surrounded them. "I know the way and it's dark. The electricity was turned off on this block three years ago. To try to get the people to vacate the buildings here so that they could be burned down." He added, "But most of them stayed on."

The moist, cold hand of the hotel clerk led him past what appeared to be chairs and tables, heaped up into irregular tumbles of legs and surfaces, interwoven with cobwebs and grainy patterns of dirt. They bumped at last against a black, unmoving wall; there the clerk stopped, retrieved his hand, fiddled with something in the gloom.

"I can't open it," he said as he fiddled. "It can only be opened from the other side, *her* side. What I'm doing is signaling that we're here."

A section of the wall groaningly slid aside. Jason, peering, saw into nothing more than additional darkness. And abandonment.

"Step on through," the clerk said, and maneuvered him forward. The wall, after a pause, slid shut again behind them.

Lights winked on. Momentarily blinded, Jason shielded his eyes and then took a good look at her workshop.

It was small. But he saw a number of what appeared to be complex and highly specialized machines. On the far side a workbench. Tools by the hundreds, all neatly mounted in place on the walls of the room. Below the workbench large cartons, probably containing a variety of papers. And a small generator-driven printing press.

And the girl. She sat on a high stool, hand-arranging a line of type. He made out pale hair, very long but thin, dribbling down the back of her neck onto her cotton work shirt. She wore jeans, and her feet, quite small, were bare. She appeared to him to be, at a guess, fifteen or sixteen. No breasts to speak of, but good long legs; he liked that. She wore no makeup whatsoever, giving her features a white, slightly pastel tint.

"Hi," she said.

The clerk said, "I'm going. I'll try not to spend the five hundred dollars in one place." Touching a button, he caused the section of wall to slide aside; as it did so the lights in the workroom clicked out, leaving them once again in absolute darkness.

From her stool the girl said, "I'm Kathy."

"I'm Jason," he said. The wall had slid shut, now, and the

lights had come on again. She's really very pretty, he thought. Except that she had a passive, almost listless quality about her. As if nothing to her, he thought, is worth a damn. Apathy? No, he decided. She was shy; that was the explanation.

"You gave him five hundred dollars to bring you here?" Kathy said wonderingly; she surveyed him critically, as if seeking to make some kind of value judgment about him, based on his appearance.

"My suit isn't usually this rumpled," Jason said.

"It's a nice suit. Silk?"

"Yes." He nodded.

"Are you a student?" Kathy asked, still scrutinizing him. "No, you're not; you don't have that pulpy pasty color they have, from living subsurface. Well, that leaves only one other possibility."

"That I'm a criminal," Jason said. "Trying to change my identity before pols and nats get me."

"Are you?" she said, with no sign of uneasiness. It was a simple, flat question.

"No." He did not amplify, not at that moment. Perhaps later.

Kathy said, "Do you think a lot of those nats are robots and not real people? They always have those gas masks on so you can't really tell."

"I'm content just to dislike them," Jason said. "Without looking into it any further."

"What ID do you need? Driver's license? Police-file ident card? Proof of employment at a legal job?"

He said, "Everything. Including membership tab in the Musicians Union Local Twelve."

"Oh, you're a musician." She regarded him with more interest, now.

"I'm a vocalist," he said. "I host an hour-long TV variety show Tuesday night at nine. Maybe you've seen it. The *Jason Taverner Show*."

"I don't own a TV set any more," the girl said. "So I guess I wouldn't recognize you. Is it fun to do?"

"Sometimes. You meet a lot of show-biz people and that's fine if that's what you like. I've found them mostly to be people like anybody else. They have their fears. They're not perfect. Some of them are very funny, both on and off camera."

"My husband always used to tell me I have no sense of humor," the girl said. "He thought everything was funny. He even thought it was funny when he was drafted into the nats."

"Did he still laugh by the time he got out?" Jason asked.

"He never did. He was killed in a surprise attack by students. But it wasn't their fault; he was shot by a fellow nat."

Jason said, "How much is it going to cost me to get my full set of ID? You better tell me now before you start on them."

"I charge people what they can afford," Kathy said, once more setting up her line of type. "I'm going to charge you a lot because I can tell you're rich, by the way you gave Eddy five hundred dollars to get you here, and by your suit. Okay?" Briefly she glanced in his direction. "Or am I wrong? Tell me."

"I have five thousand dollars on me," Jason said. "Or, rather, less five hundred. I'm a world-famous entertainer; I work a month every year at the Sands in addition to my show. In fact, I appear at a number of first-class clubs, when I can squeeze them into my tight schedule."

"Gee," Kathy said. "I wish I had heard of you; then I could be impressed."

He laughed.

"Did I say something stupid?" Kathy asked timidly.

"No," Jason said. "Kathy, how old are you?"

"I'm nineteen. My birthday is in December, so I'm almost twenty. How old did you think I am by looking at me?"

"About sixteen," he said.

Her mouth turned down in a childlike pout. "That's what everybody says," she said in a low voice. "It's because I don't have any bosom. If I had a bosom I'd look twenty-one. How old are you?" She stopped fiddling with her type and eyed him intently. "I'd guess about fifty."

Fury flowed through him. And misery.

"You look like your feelings are hurt," Kathy said.

"I'm forty-two," Jason said tightly.

"Well, what's the difference? I mean, they're both—"

"Let's get down to business," Jason broke in. "Give me a pen and paper and I'll write down what I want and what I want each card to say about me. I want this done exactly right. You better be good."

"I made you mad," Kathy said. "By saying you look fifty. I guess on closer examination you really don't. You look about thirty." She handed him pen and paper, smiling shyly. And apologetically.

Jason said, "Forget it." He patted her on the back.

"I'd rather people didn't touch me," Kathy said; she slid away.

Like a fawn in the woods, he thought. Strange; she's afraid to be touched even a little and yet she's not afraid to forge documents, a felony that could get her twenty years in prison. Maybe nobody bothered to tell her it's against the law. Maybe she doesn't know.

Something bright and colorful on the far wall caught his attention; he walked over to inspect it. A medieval illuminated manuscript, he realized. Or, rather, a page from it. He had read about them but up until now he had never set eyes on one.

"Is this valuable?" he asked.

"If it was the real thing it might be worth a hundred dollars," Kathy said. "But it's not; I made it years ago, when I was in junior high school at North American Aviation. I copied it, the original, ten times before I had it right. I love good calligraphy; even when I was a kid I did. Maybe it's because my father designed book covers; you know, the dust jackets."

He said, "Would this fool a museum?"

For a moment Kathy gazed intently at him. And then she nodded yes.

"Wouldn't they know by the paper?"

"It's parchment and it's from that period. That's the same way you fake old stamps; you get an old stamp that's worthless, eradicate the imprint, then—" She paused. "You're anxious for me to get to work on your ID," she said.

"Yes," Jason said. He handed her the piece of paper on which he had written the information. Most of it called for pol-nat standard postcurfew tags, with thumbprints and photographs and holographic signatures, and everything with short expiration dates. He'd have to get a whole new set forged within three months.

"Two thousand dollars," Kathy said, studying the list.

He felt like saying, For that do I get to go to bed with you, too? But aloud he said, "How long will it take? Hours? Days? And if it's days, where am I—"

"Hours," Kathy said.

He experienced a vast wave of relief.

"Sit down and keep me company," Kathy said, pointing to a three-legged stool pushed off to one side. "You can tell me about your career as a successful TV personality. It must be fascinating, all the bodies you have to walk over to get to the top. Or did you get to the top?"

"Yes," he said shortly. "But there's no bodies. That's a myth. You make it on talent and talent alone, not what you do or say to other people either above or below you. And it's work; you don't breeze in and do a soft-shoe shuffle and then sign your contract with NBC or CBS. They're tough, experienced businessmen. Especially the A and R people. Artists and Repertoire. They decide who to sign. I'm talking about records now. That's where you have to start to be on a national level; of course you can work club dates all over everywhere until—"

"Here's your quibble driver's license," Kathy said. She carefully passed him a small black card. "Now I'll get started on your military service-status chit. That's a little harder because of the full-face and profile photos, but I can handle that over there." She pointed at a white screen, in front of which stood a tripod with camera, a flash gun mounted at its side.

"You have all the equipment," Jason said as he fixed himself rigidly against the white screen; so many photos had been taken of him during his long career that he always knew exactly where to stand and what expression to reveal.

But apparently he had done something wrong this time. Kathy, a severe expression on her face, surveying him.

"You're all lit up," she said, half to herself. "You're glowing in some sort of phony way."

"Publicity stills," Jason said. "Eight-by-ten glossy—"

"These aren't. These are to keep you out of a forced-labor camp for the rest of your life. Don't smile."

He didn't.

"Good," Kathy said. She ripped the photos from the camera,

carried them cautiously to her workbench, waving them to dry them. "These damn 3-D animateds they want on the military service papers—that camera cost me a thousand dollars and I need it only for this and nothing else . . . but I have to have it." She eyed him. "It's going to cost you."

"Yes," he said, stonily. He felt aware of that already.

For a time Kathy puttered, and then, turning abruptly toward him, she said, "Who are you *really*? You're used to posing; I saw you, I saw you freeze with that glad smile in place and those lit-up eyes."

"I told you. I'm Jason Taverner. The TV personality guest host. I'm on every Tuesday night."

"No," Kathy said; she shook her head. "But it's none of my business—sorry—I shouldn't have asked." But she continued to eye him, as if with exasperation. "You're doing it all wrong. You really are a celebrity—it was reflexive, the way you posed for your picture. But you're not a celebrity. There's no one named Jason Taverner who matters, who is anything. So what are you, then? A man who has his picture taken all the time that no one's ever seen or heard of."

Jason said, "I'm going about it the way any celebrity who no one has ever heard of would go about it."

For a moment she stared at him and then she laughed. "I see. Well, that's cool; that's really cool. I'll have to remember that." She turned her attention back to the documents she was forging. "In this business," she said, absorbed in what she was doing, "I don't want to get to know people I'm making cards for. But"—she glanced up—"I'd sort of like to know you. You're strange. I've seen a lot of types—hundreds, maybe— but none like you. Do you know what I think?"

"You think I'm insane," Jason said.

"Yes." Kathy nodded. "Clinically, legally, whatever. You're psychotic; you have a split personality. Mr. No One and Mr. Everyone. How have you survived up until now?"

He said nothing. It could not be explained.

"Okay," Kathy said. One by one, expertly and efficiently, she forged the necessary documents.

Eddy, the hotel clerk, lurked in the background, smoking a fake Havana cigar; he had nothing to say or do, but for some obscure reason he hung around. I wish he'd fuck off, Jason thought to himself. I'd like to talk to her more . . .

"Come with me," Kathy said, suddenly; she slid from her work stool and beckoned him toward a wooden door at the right of her bench. "I want your signature five times, each a little different from the others so they can't be superimposed. That's where so many documenters"—she smiled as she opened the door—"that's what we call ourselves—that's where so many of us fuck it up. They take one signature and transfer it to all the documents. See?"

"Yes," he said, entering the musty little closetlike room after her.

Kathy shut the door, paused a moment, then said, "Eddy is a police fink."

Staring at her he said, "Why?"

" 'Why?' Why what? Why is he a police fink? For money. For the same reason I am."

Jason said, "God damn you." He grabbed her by the right wrist, tugged her toward him; she grimaced as his fingers tightened. "And he's already—"

"Eddy hasn't done anything yet," she grated, trying to free her wrist. "That hurts, Look; calm down and I'll show you. Okay?"

Reluctantly, his heart hammering in fear, he let her go. Kathy turned on a bright, small light, laid three forged documents in the circle of its glare. "A purple dot on the margin of each," she said, indicating the almost invisible circle of color. "A microtransmitter, so you'll emit a bleep every five seconds as you move around. They're after conspiracies; they want the people you're with."

Jason said harshly, "I'm not with anyone."

"But they don't know that." She massaged her wrist, frowning in a girlish, sullen way. "You TV celebrities no one's ever heard of sure have quick reactions," she murmured.

"Why did you tell me?" Jason asked. "After doing all the forging, all the—"

"I want you to get away," she said, simply.

"Why?" He still did not understand.

"Because hell, you've got some sort of magnetic quality

about you; I noticed it as soon as you came into the room. You're"—she groped for the word—"sexy. Even at your age."

"My presence," he said.

"Yes." Kathy nodded. "I've seen it before in public people, from a distance, but never up close like this. I can see why you imagine you're a TV personality; you really seem like you are."

He said, "How do I get away? Are you going to tell me that? Or does that cost a little more?"

"God, you're so cynical."

He laughed, and again took hold of her by the wrist.

"I guess I don't blame you," Kathy said, shaking her head and making a masklike face. "Well, first of all, you can buy Eddy off. Another five hundred should do it. Me you don't have to buy off—*if*, and only if, and I mean it, if you stay with me awhile. You have . . . allure, like a good perfume. I respond to you and I just never do that with men."

"With women, then?" he said tartly.

It passed her without registering. "Will you?" she said.

"Hell," he said, "I'll just leave." Reaching, he opened the door behind her, shoved past her and out into her workroom. She followed, rapidly.

Among the dim, empty shadows of the abandoned restaurant she caught up with him; she confronted him in the gloom. Panting, she said, "You've already got a transmitter planted on you."

"I doubt it," he answered.

"It's true. Eddy planted it on you."

"Bullshit," he said, and moved away from her toward the light of the restaurant's sagging, broken front door.

Pursuing him like a deft-footed herbivore, Kathy gasped, "But suppose it's true. It could be." At the half-available doorway she interposed herself between him and freedom; standing there, her hands lifted as if to ward off a physical blow, she said swiftly, "Stay with me one night. Go to bed with me. Okay? That's enough. I promise. Will you do it, for just one night?"

He thought, Something of my abilities, my alleged and well-known properties, have come with me, to this strange place I now live in. This place where I do not exist except on forged cards manufactured by a pol fink. Eerie, he thought, and he shuddered. Cards with microtransmitters built into them, to betray me and everyone with me to the pols. I haven't done very well here. Except that, as she says, I've got allure. Jesus, he thought. And that's all that stands between me and a forced-labor camp.

"Okay," he said, then. It seemed the wiser choice—by far.

"Go pay Eddy," she said. "Get that over with and him out of here."

"I wondered why he's still hanging around," Jason said. "Did he scent more money?"

"I guess so," Kathy said.

"You do this all the time," Jason said as he got out his money. SOP: standard operating procedure. And he had tumbled for it.

Kathy said blithely, "Eddy is psionic."

FOUR

Two city blocks away, upstairs in an unpainted but once white wooden building, Kathy had a single room with a hot-compart in which to fix one-person meals.

He looked around him. A girl's room: the cotlike bed had a handmade spread covering it, tiny green balls of textile fibers in row after row. Like a graveyard for soldiers, he thought morbidly as he moved about, feeling compressed by the smallness of the room.

On a wicker table a copy of Proust's *Remembrance of Things Past*.

"How far'd you get into it?" he asked her.

"To *Within a Budding Grove*." Kathy double-locked the door after them and set into operation some kind of electronic gadget; he did not recognize it.

"That's not very far," Jason said.

Taking off her plastic coat, Kathy asked, "How far did you get into it?" She hung her coat in a tiny closet, taking his, too.

"I never read it," Jason said. "But on my program we did a dramatic rendering of a scene . . . I don't know which. We got a lot of good mail about it, but we never tried it again. Those out things, you have to be careful and not dole out too much. If you do it kills it dead for everybody, all networks, for the rest of the year." He prowled, crampedly, about the room, examining a book here, a cassette tape, a micromag. She even had a talking toy. Like a kid, he thought; she's not really an adult.

With curiosity, he turned on the talking toy.

"Hi!" it declared. "I'm Cheerful Charley and I'm definitely tuned in on your wavelength."

"Nobody named Cheerful Charley is tuned in on my wavelength," Jason said. He started to shut it off, but it protested. "Sorry," Jason told it, "but I'm tuning you out, you creepy little bugger."

"But I love you!" Cheerful Charley complained tinnily.

He paused, thumb on off button. "Prove it," he said. On his show he had done commercials for junk like this. He hated it and them. Equally. "Give me some money," he told it.

"I know how you can get back your name, fame, and game," Cheerful Charley informed him. "Will that do for openers?"

"Sure," he said.

Cheerful Charley bleated, "Go look up your girlfriend."

"Who do you mean?" he said guardedly.

"Heather Hart," Cheerful Charley bleeped.

"Hard by," Jason said, pressing his tongue against his upper incisors. He nodded. "Any more advice?"

"I've heard of Heather Hart," Kathy said as she brought a bottle of orange juice out of the cold-cupboard of the room's wall. The bottle had already become three-fourths empty; she shook it up, poured foamy instant ersatz orange juice into two jelly glasses. "She's beautiful. She has all that long red hair. Is she really your girl friend? Is Charley right?"

"Everybody knows," he said, "that Cheerful Charley is always right."

"Yes, I guess that's true." Kathy poured bad gin (Mountbatten's Privy Seal Finest) into the orange juice. "Screwdrivers," she said, proudly.

"No, thanks," he said. "Not at this hour of the day." Not even B&L scotch bottled in Scotland, he thought. This damn little room . . . isn't she making anything out of pol-finking and card-forging, whichever it is she does? Is she really a police informer, as she says? he wondered. Strange. Maybe she's both. Maybe neither.

"Ask me!" Cheerful Charley piped. "I can see you have

something on your mind, mister. You good-looking bastard, you."

He let that pass. "This girl," he began, but instantly Kathy grabbed Cheerful Charley away from him, stood holding it, her nostrils flaring, her eyes filled with indignation.

"The hell you're going to ask my Cheerful Charley about me," she said, one eyebrow raised. Like a wild bird, he thought, going through elaborate motions to protect her nest. He laughed. "What's funny?" Kathy demanded.

"These talking toys," he said, "are more nuisance than utilitarian. They ought to be abolished." He walked away from her, then to a clutter of mail on a TV-stand table. Aimlessly, he sorted among the envelopes, noticing vaguely that none of the bills had been opened.

"Those are mine," Kathy said defensively, watching him.

"You get a lot of bills," he said, "for a girl living in a one-room schmalch. You buy your clothes—or what else?—at Metter's? Interesting."

"I—take an odd size."

He said, "And Sax and Crombie shoes."

"In my work—" she began, but he cut her off with a convulsive swipe of his hand.

"Don't give me that," he grated.

"Look in my closet. You won't see much there. Nothing out of the ordinary, except that what I do have is good. I'd rather have a little amount of something good . . ." Her words trailed off. "You know," she said vaguely, "than a lot of junk."

Jason said, "You have another apartment."

It registered; her eyes flickered as she looked into herself for an answer. That, for him, constituted plenty.

"Let's go there," he said. He had seen enough of this cramped little room.

"I can't take you there," Kathy said, "because I share it with two other girls and the way we've divided up the use, this time is—"

"Evidently you weren't trying to impress me." It amused him. But also it irritated him; he felt downgraded, nebulously.

"I would have taken you there if today were my day," Kathy said. "That's why I have to keep this little place going; I've got to have *someplace* to go when it's not my day. My day, my next one, is Friday. From noon on." Her tone had become earnest. As if she wished very much to convince him. Probably, he mused, it was true. But the whole thing irked him. Her and her whole life. He felt, now, as if he had been snared by something dragging him down into depths he had never known about before, even in the early, bad days. And he did not like it.

He yearned all at once to be out of here. The animal at bay was himself.

"Don't look at me like that," Kathy said, sipping her screwdriver.

To himself, but aloud, he said, "You have bumped the door of life open with your big, dense head. And now it can't be closed."

"What's that from?" Kathy asked.

"From my life."

"But it's like poetry."

"If you watched my show," he said, "you'd know I come up with sparklers like that every so often."

Appraising him calmly, Kathy said, "I'm going to look in the TV log and see if you're listed." She set down her screwdriver, fished among discarded newspapers piled at the base of the wicker table.

"I wasn't even born," he said. "I checked on that."

"And your show isn't listed," Kathy said, folding the newsprint page back and studying the log.

"That's right," he said. "So now you have all the answers about me." He tapped his vest pocket of forged ID cards. "Including these. With their microtransmitters, if that much is true."

"Give them back to me," Kathy said, "and I'll erad the microtransmitters. It'll only take a second." She held out her hand.

He returned them to her.

"Don't you care if I take them off?" Kathy inquired.

Candidly, he answered, "No, I really don't. I've lost the ability to tell what's good or bad, true or not true, any more. If you want to take the dots off, do it. If it pleases you."

A moment later she returned the cards, smiling her sixteen-year-old hazy smile.

Observing her youth, her automatic radiance, he said, "'I feel as old as yonder elm.'"

"From *Finnegans Wake*," Kathy said happily. "When the old washerwomen at dusk are merging into trees and rocks."

"You've read *Finnegans Wake*?" he asked, surprised.

"I saw the film. Four times. I like Hazeltine; I think he's the best director alive."

"I had him on my show," Jason said. "Do you want to know what he's like in real life?"

"No," Kathy said.

"Maybe you ought to know."

"No," she repeated, shaking her head; her voice had risen. "And don't try to tell me—okay? I'll believe what I want to believe, and you believe what you believe. All right?"

"Sure," he said. He felt sympathetic. The truth, he had often reflected, was overrated as a virtue. In most cases a sympathetic lie did better and more mercifully. Especially between men and women; in fact, whenever a woman was involved.

This, of course, was not, properly speaking, a woman, but a girl. And therefore, he decided, the kind lie was even more of a necessity.

"He's a scholar and an artist," he said.

"Really?" She regarded him hopefully.

"Yes."

At that she sighed in relief.

"Then you believe," he said, pouncing, "that I have met Michael Hazeltine, the finest living film director, as you said yourself. So you do believe that I am a six—" He broke off; that had not been what he intended to say.

"'A six,'" Kathy echoed, her brow furrowing, as if she were trying to remember. "I read about them in *Time*. Aren't they all dead now? Didn't the government have them all rounded up and shot, after that one, their leader—what was his name? —Teagarden; yes, that's his name. Willard Teagarden. He tried to—how do you say it?—pull off a coup against the federal nats? He tried to get them disbanded as an illegal pari-mutuel—"

"Paramilitary," Jason said.

"You don't give a damn about what I'm saying."

Sincerely, he said, "I sure do." He waited. The girl did not continue. "Christ," he spat out. "Finish what you were saying!"

"I think," Kathy said at last, "that the *sevens* made the coup not come off."

He thought, Sevens. Never in his life had he heard of sevens. Nothing could have shocked him more. Good, he thought, that I let out that lapsus linguae. I have genuinely learned something, now. At last. In this maze of confusion and the half real.

A small section of wall creaked meagerly open and a cat, black and white and very young, entered the room. At once Kathy gathered him up, her face shining.

"Dinman's philosophy," Jason said. "The mandatory cat." He was familiar with the viewpoint; he had in fact introduced Dinman to the TV audience on one of his fall specials.

"No, I just love him," Kathy said, eyes bright as she carried the cat over to him for his inspection.

"But you do believe," he said, as he patted the cat's little head, "that owning an animal increases a person's empathic—"

"Screw that," Kathy said, clutching the cat to her throat as if she were a five-year-old with its first animal. Its school project: the communal guinea pig. "This is Domenico," she said.

"Named after Domenico Scarlatti?" he asked.

"No, after Domenico's Market, down the street; we passed it on our way here. When I'm at the Minor Apartment—this room—I shop there. Is Domenico Scarlatti a musician? I think I've heard of him."

Jason said, "Abraham Lincoln's high school English teacher."

"Oh." She nodded absently, now rocking the cat back and forth.

"I'm kidding you," he said, "and it's mean. I'm sorry."

Kathy gazed up at him earnestly as she clutched her small cat. "I never know the difference," she murmured.

"That's why it's mean," Jason said.

"Why?" she asked. "If I don't even know. I mean, that means I'm just dumb. Doesn't it?"

"You're not dumb," Jason said. "Just inexperienced." He calculated, roughly, their age difference. "I've lived over twice as long as you," he pointed out. "And I've been in the position, in the last ten years, to rub elbows with some of the most famous people on earth. And—"

"And," Kathy said, "you're a six."

She had not forgotten his slip. Of course not. He could tell her a million things, and all would be forgotten ten minutes later, except the one real slip. Well, such was the way of the world. He had become used to it in his time; that was part of being his age and not hers.

"What does Domenico mean to you?" Jason said, changing the subject. Crudely, he realized, but he went ahead. "What do you get from him that you don't get from human beings?"

She frowned, looked thoughtful. "He's always busy. He always has some project going. Like following a bug. He's very good with flies; he's learned how to eat them without their flying away." She smiled engagingly. "And I don't have to ask myself about him, Should I turn him in to Mr. McNulty? Mr. McNulty is my pol contact. I give him the analog receivers for the microtransmitters, the dots I showed you—"

"And he pays you."

She nodded.

"And yet you live like this."

"I—" she struggled to answer—"I don't get many customers."

"Nonsense. You're good; I watched you work. You're experienced."

"A talent."

"But a trained talent."

"Okay; it all goes into the apartment uptown. My Major Apartment." She gritted her teeth, not enjoying being badgered.

"No." He didn't believe it.

Kathy said, after a pause, "My husband's alive. He's in a forced-labor camp in Alaska. I'm trying to buy his way out by giving information to Mr. McNulty. In another year"—she shrugged, her expression moody now, introverted—"he *says* Jack can come out. And come back here."

So you send other people into the camps, he thought, to get your husband out. It sounds like a typical police deal. It's probably the truth.

"It's a terrific deal for the police," he said. "They lose one man and get—how many would you say you've bugged for them? Scores? Hundreds?"

Pondering, she said at last, "Maybe a hundred and fifty."

"It's evil," he said.

"Is it?" She glanced at him nervously, clutching Domenico to her flat chest. Then, by degrees, she became angry; it showed on her face and in the way she crushed the cat against her rib cage. "The hell it is," she said fiercely, shaking her head no. "I love Jack and he loves me. He writes to me all the time."

Cruelly, he said, "Forged. By some pol employee."

Tears spilled from her eyes in an amazing quantity; they dimmed her gaze. "You think so? Sometimes I think they are, too. Do you want to look at them? Could you tell?"

"They're probably not forged. It's cheaper and simpler to keep him alive and let him write his own letters." He hoped that would make her feel better, and evidently it did; the tears stopped coming.

"I hadn't thought of that," she said, nodding, but still not smiling; she gazed off into the distance, reflexively still rocking the small black and white cat.

"If your husband's alive," he said, cautiously this time, "do you believe it to be all right for you to go to bed with other men, such as me?"

"Oh, sure. Jack never objected to that. Even before they got him. And I'm sure he doesn't object now. As a matter of fact, he wrote me about that. Let's see; it was maybe six months ago. I think I could find the letter; I have them all on micro-film. Over in the shop."

"Why?"

Kathy said, "I sometimes lens-screen them for customers. So that later on they'll understand why I do what I did."

At this point he frankly did not know what emotion he felt toward her, nor what he ought to feel. She had become, by de-grees, over the years, involved in a situation from which she could not now extricate herself. And he saw no way out for her now; it had gone on too long. The formula had become fixed. The seeds of evil had been allowed to grow.

"There's no turning back for you," he said, knowing it, knowing that she knew it. "Listen," he said to her in a gentle voice. He put his hand on her shoulder, but as before she at

once shrank away. "Tell them you want him out right now, and
you're not turning in any more people."

"Would they release him, then, if I said that?"

"Try it." Certainly it wouldn't do any harm. But—he could
imagine Mr. McNulty and how he looked to the girl. She
could never confront him; the McNultys of the world did not
get confronted by anyone. Except when something went
strangely wrong.

"Do you know what you are?" Kathy said. "You're a very
good person. Do you understand that?"

He shrugged. Like most truths it was a matter of opinion.
Perhaps he was. In this situation, anyhow. Not so in others.
But Kathy didn't know about that.

"Sit down," he said, "pet your cat, drink your screwdriver.
Don't think about anything; just be. Can you do that? Empty
your mind for a little while? Try it." He brought her a chair;
she dutifully seated herself on it.

"I do it all the time," she said emptily, dully.

Jason said, "But not negatively. Do it positively."

"How? What do you mean?"

"Do it for a real purpose, not just to avoid facing unfortunate verities. Do it because you love your husband and you
want him back. You want everything to be as it was before."

"Yes," she agreed. "But now I've met you."

"Meaning what?" He proceeded cautiously; her response
puzzled him.

Kathy said, "You're more magnetic than Jack. He's magnetic, but you're so much, much more. Maybe after meeting
you I couldn't really love him again. Or do you think a person
can love two people equally, but in different ways? My therapy
group says no, that I have to choose. They say that's one of the
basic aspects of life. See, this has come up before; I've met several men more magnetic than Jack . . . but none of them as
magnetic as you. Now I really don't know what to do. It's very
difficult to decide such things because there's no one you can
talk to: no one understands. You have to go through it alone,
and sometimes you choose wrong. Like, what if I choose you
over Jack and then he comes back and I don't give a shit about
him; what then? How is he going to feel? That's important,
but it's also important how I feel. If I like you or someone like

you better than him, then I have to act it out, as our therapy group puts it. Did you know I was in a psychiatric hospital for eight weeks? Morningside Mental Hygiene Relations in Atherton. My folks paid for it. It cost a fortune because for some reason we weren't eligible for community or federal aid. Anyhow, I learned a lot about myself and I made a whole lot of friends, there. Most of the people I truly know I met at Morningside. Of course, when I originally met them back then I had the delusion that they were famous people like Mickey Quinn and Arlene Howe. You know—celebrities. Like you."

He said, "I know both Quinn and Howe, and you haven't missed anything."

Scrutinizing him, she said, "Maybe you're not a celebrity; maybe I've reverted back to my delusional period. They said I probably would, sometime. Sooner or later. Maybe it's later now."

"That," he pointed out, "would make me a hallucination of yours. Try harder; I don't feel completely real."

She laughed. But her mood remained somber. "Wouldn't that be strange if I made you up, like you just said? That if I fully recovered you'd disappear?"

"I wouldn't disappear. But I'd cease to be a celebrity."

"You already have." She raised her head, confronted him steadily. "Maybe that's it. Why you're a celebrity that no one's ever heard of. I made you up, you're a product of my delusional mind, and now I'm becoming sane again."

"A solipsistic view of the universe—"

"Don't do that. You know I haven't any idea what words like that mean. What kind of person do you think I am? I'm not famous and powerful like you; I'm just a person doing a terrible, awful job that puts people in prison, because I love Jack more than all the rest of humanity. Listen." Her tone became firm and crisp. "The only thing that got me back to sanity was that I loved Jack more than Mickey Quinn. See, I thought this boy named David was really Mickey Quinn, and it was a big secret that Mickey Quinn had lost his mind and he had gone to this mental hospital to get himself back in shape, and no one was supposed to know about it because it would ruin his image. So he pretended his name was David. But I knew. Or rather, I thought I knew. And Dr. Scott said I had to choose between Jack and David, or Jack and Mickey Quinn, which I thought it was. And I chose Jack. So I came out of it. Maybe"—she wavered, her chin trembling—"maybe now you can see why I have to believe Jack is more important than anything or anybody, or a lot of anybodys, else. See?"

He saw. He nodded.

"Even men like you," Kathy said, "who're more magnetic than him, even you can't take me away from Jack."

"I don't want to." It seemed a good idea to make that point.

"Yes you do. On some level you do. It's a competition."

Jason said, "To me you're just one small girl in one small room in one small building. For me the whole world is mine, and everybody in it."

"Not if you're in a forced-labor camp."

He had to nod in agreement to that, too. Kathy had an annoying habit of spiking the guns of rhetoric.

"You understand a little now," she said, "don't you? About me and Jack, and why I can go to bed with you without wronging Jack? I went to bed with David when we were at Morningside, but Jack understood; he knew I had to do it. Would you have understood?"

"If you were psychotic—"

"No, not because of that. Because it was my destiny to go to bed with Mickey Quinn. It had to be done; I was fulfilling my cosmic role. Do you see?"

"Okay," he said, gently.

"I think I'm drunk." Kathy examined her screwdriver. "You're right; it's too early to drink one of these." She set the half-empty glass down. "Jack saw. Or anyhow he said he saw. Would he lie? So as not to lose me? Because if I had had to choose between him and Mickey Quinn"—she paused—"but I chose Jack. I always would. But still I had to go to bed with David. With Mickey Quinn, I mean."

I have gotten myself mixed up with a complicated, peculiar, malfunctioning creature, Jason Taverner said to himself. As bad as—worse than—Heather Hart. As bad as I've yet encountered in forty-two years. But how do I get away from her without Mr. McNulty hearing all about it? Christ, he thought dismally. Maybe I don't. Maybe she plays with me until she's bored, and then she calls in the pols. And that's it for me.

"Wouldn't you think," he said aloud, "that in four decades plus, I could have learned the answer to this?"

"To me?" she said. Acutely.

He nodded.

"You think after you go to bed with me I'll turn you in."

At this point he had not boiled it down to precisely that. But the general idea was there. So, carefully, he said, "I think you've learned in your artless, innocent, nineteen-year-old way, to use people. Which I think is very bad. And once you begin you can't stop. You don't even know you're doing it."

"I would never turn you in. I love you."

"You've known me perhaps five hours. Not even that."

"But I can always tell." Her tone, her expression, both were firm. And deeply solemn.

"You're not even sure who I am!"

Kathy said, "I'm never sure who *anybody* is."

That, evidently, had to be granted. He tried, therefore, another tack. "Look. You're an odd combination of the innocent romantic, and a"—he paused; the word "treacherous" had come to mind, but he discarded it swiftly—"and a calculating, subtle manipulator." You are, he thought, a prostitute of the mind. And it's your mind that is prostituting itself, before and beyond anyone else's. Although you yourself would never recognize it. And, if you did, you'd say you were forced into it. Yes; forced into it, but by whom? By Jack? By David? By yourself, he thought. By wanting two men at the same time—and getting to have both.

Poor Jack, he thought. You poor goddamn bastard. Shoveling shit at the forced-labor camp in Alaska, waiting for this elaborately convoluted waif to save you. Don't hold your breath.

That evening, without conviction, he had dinner with Kathy at an Italian-type restaurant a block from her room. She seemed to know the owner and the waiters, in some dim fashion; anyhow, they greeted her and she responded absentmindedly, as if only half hearing them. Or, he thought, only half aware of where she was.

Little girl, he thought, where is the rest of your mind?

"The lasagna is very good," Kathy said, without looking at the menu; she seemed a great distance away now. Receding further and further. With each passing moment. He sensed an approaching crisis. But he did not know her well enough; he had no idea what form it would take. And he did not like that.

"When you blep away," he said abruptly, trying to catch her offguard, "how do you do it?"

"Oh," she said tonelessly, "I throw myself down on the floor and scream. Or else I kick. Anyone who tries to stop me. Who interferes with my freedom."

"Do you feel like doing that now?"

She glanced up. "Yes." Her face, he saw, had become a mask, both twisted and agonized. But her eyes remained totally dry. This time no tears would be involved. "I haven't been taking my medication. I'm supposed to take twenty milligrams of Actozine per diem."

"Why don't you take it?" They never did; he had run across that anomaly several times.

"It dulls my mind," she answered, touching her nose with her forefinger, as if involved in a complex ritual that had to be done absolutely correctly.

"But if it—"

Kathy said sharply, "They can't fuck with my mind. I'm not letting any MFs get to me. Do you know what a MF is?"

"You just said." He spoke quietly and slowly, keeping his attention firmly fixed on her . . . as if trying to hold her there, to keep her mind together.

The food came. It was terrible.

"Isn't this wonderfully authentically Italian?" Kathy said, deftly winding spaghetti on her fork.

"Yes," he agreed, aimlessly.

"You think I'm going to blep away. And you don't want to be involved with it."

Jason said, "That's right."

"Then leave."

"I"—he hesitated—"I like you. I want to make sure you're

all right." A benign lie, of the kind he approved. It seemed better than saying, Because if I walk out of here you will be on the phone to Mr. McNulty in twenty seconds. Which, in fact, was the way he saw it.

"I'll be all right. They'll take me home." She vaguely indicated the restaurant around them, the customers, waiters, cashier. Cook steaming away in the overheated, underventilated kitchen. Drunk at the bar, fiddling with his glass of Olympia beer.

He said, calculating carefully, fairly, reasonably sure that he was doing the right thing, "You're not taking responsibility."

"For who? I'm not taking responsibility for your life, if that's what you mean. That's your job. Don't burden me with it."

"Responsibility," he said, "for the consequences to others of your acts. You're morally, ethically drifting. Hitting out here and there, then submerging again. As if nothing happened. Leaving it to everyone else to pick up the sweltering moons."

Raising her head she confronted him and said, "Have I hurt you? I saved you from the pols; that's what I did for you. Was that the wrong thing to do? Was it?" Her voice increased in volume; she stared at him pitilessly, unblinkingly, still holding her forkful of spaghetti.

He sighed. It was hopeless. "No," he said, "it wasn't the wrong thing to do. Thanks. I appreciate it." And, as he said it, he felt unwavering hatred toward her. For enmeshing him this way. One puny nineteen-year-old ordinary, netting a full-grown six like this—it was so improbable that it seemed absurd; he felt on one level like laughing. But on the other levels he did not.

"Are you responding to my warmth?" she inquired.

"Yes."

"You do feel my love reaching out to you, don't you? Listen. You can almost hear it." She listened intently. "My love is growing, and it's a tender vine."

Jason signaled the waiter. "What have you got here?" he asked the waiter brusquely. "Just beer and wine?"

"And pot, sir. The best-grade Acapulco Gold. And hash, grade A."

"But no hard liquor."

"No, sir."

Gesturing, he dismissed the waiter.

"You treated him like a servant," Kathy said.

"Yeah," he said, and groaned aloud. He shut his eyes and massaged the bridge of his nose. Might as well go the whole way now; he had managed, after all, to inflame her ire. "He's a lousy waiter," he said, "and this is a lousy restaurant. Let's get out of here."

Kathy said bitterly, "So that's what it means to be a celebrity. I understand." She quietly put down her fork.

"What do you think you understand?" he said, letting it all hang out; his conciliatory role was gone for good now. Never to be gotten back. He rose to his feet, reached for his coat. "I'm leaving," he told her. And put on his coat.

"Oh, God," Kathy said, shutting her eyes; her mouth, bent out of shape, hung open. "Oh, God. No. What have you done? Do you know what you've done? Do you understand fully? Do you grasp it at all?" And then, eyes shut, fists clenched, she ducked her head and began to scream. He had never heard screams like it before, and he stood paralyzed as the sound—and the sight of her constricted, broken face— dinned at him, numbing him. These are psychotic screams, he said to himself. From the racial unconscious. Not from a person but from a deeper level; from a collective entity.

Knowing that did not help.

The owner and two waiters hustled over, still clutching menus; Jason saw and marked details, oddly; it seemed as if everything, at her screams, had frozen over. Become fixed. Customers raising forks, lowering spoons, chewing . . . everything stopped and there remained only the terrible, ugly noise.

And she was saying words. Crude words, as if read off some back fence. Short, destructive words that tore at everyone in the restaurant, including himself. Especially himself.

The owner, his mustache twitching, nodded to the two waiters, and they lifted Kathy bodily from her chair; they raised her by her shoulders, held her, then, at the owner's curt nod, dragged her from the booth, across the restaurant and out onto the street.

He paid the bill, hurried after them.

At the entrance, however, the owner stopped him. Holding out his hand. "Three hundred dollars," the owner said.

"For what?" he demanded. "For dragging her outside?"

The owner said, "For not calling the pols."

Grimly, he paid.

The waiters had set her down on the pavement, at the curb's edge. She sat silent now, fingers pressed to her eyes, rocking back and forth, her mouth making soundless images. The waiters surveyed her, apparently essaying whether or not she would make any more trouble, and then, their joint decision made, they hurried back into the restaurant. Leaving him and Kathy there on the sidewalk, under the red-and-white neon sign, together.

Kneeling by her, he put his hand on her shoulder. This time she did not try to pull away. "I'm sorry," he said. And he meant it. "For pushing you." I called your bluff, he said to himself, and it was not a bluff. Okay; you won. I give up. From now on it's whatever you want. Name it. He thought, Just make it brief, for God's sake. Let me out of this as quickly as you possibly can.

He had an intuition that it would not be soon.

FIVE

Together, hand in hand, they strolled along the evening side-walk, past the competing, flashing, winking, flooding pools of color created by the rotating, pulsating, jiggling, lit-up signs. This kind of neighborhood did not please him; he had seen it a million times, duplicated throughout the face of earth. It had been from such as this that he had fled, early in his life, to use his sixness as a method of getting out. And now he had come back.

He did not object to the people: he saw them as trapped here, the ordinaries, who through no fault of their own had to remain. They had not invented it; they did not like it; they endured it, as he had not had to. In fact, he felt guilty, seeing their grim faces, their turned-down mouths. Jagged, unhappy mouths.

"Yes," Kathy said at last, "I think I really am falling in love with you. But it's your fault; it's your powerful magnetic field that you radiate. Did you know I can see it?"

"Gee," he said mechanically.

"It's dark velvet purple," Kathy said, grasping his hand tightly with her surprisingly strong fingers. "Very intense. Can you see mine? My magnetic aura?"

"No," he said.

"I'm surprised. I would have thought you could." She seemed calm, now; the explosive screaming episode had left, trailing after it, relative stability. An almost pseudo-epileptoid personality structure, he conjectured. That works up day after day to—

"My aura," she broke into his thoughts, "is bright red. The color of passion."

"I'm glad for you," Jason said.

Halting, she turned to peer into his face. To decipher his expression. He hoped it was appropriately opaque. "Are you mad because I lost my temper?" she inquired.

"No," he said.

"You *sound* mad. I think you are mad. Well, I guess only Jack understands. And Mickey."

"Mickey Quinn," he said reflexively.

"Isn't he a remarkable person?" Kathy said.

"Very." He could have told her a lot, but it was pointless. She did not really want to know; she believed she understood already.

What else do you believe, little girl? he wondered. For example, what do you believe you know about me? As little as you know about Mickey Quinn and Arlene Howe and all the rest of them who, for you, do not in reality exist? Think what I could tell you if, for a moment, you were able to listen. But you can't listen. It would frighten you, what you might hear. And anyhow, you know everything already.

"How does it feel," he asked, "to have slept with so many famous people?"

At that she stopped short. "Do you think I slept with them because they were famous? Do you think I'm a CF, a celebrity fucker? Is that your real opinion about me?"

Like flypaper, he thought. She enmeshed him by every word he said. He could not win.

"I think," he said, "you've led an interesting life. You're an interesting person."

"And important," Kathy added.

"Yes," he said. "Important, too. In some ways the most important person I've ever encountered. It's a thrilling experience."

"Do you mean that?"

"Yes," he said emphatically. And in a peculiar, ass-backward way, it was true. No one, not even Heather, had ever tied him up so completely as this. He could not endure what he found himself going through, and he could not get away. It seemed to him as if he sat behind the tiller of his custom-made unique quibble, facing a red light, green light, amber light all at once; no rational response was possible. Her irrationality made it so. The terrible power, he thought, of illogic. Of the archetypes. Operating out of the drear depths of the collective unconscious which joined him and her—and everyone else—together. In a knot which never could be undone, as long as they lived.

No wonder, he thought, some people, many people, long for death.

"You want to go watch a captain kirk?" Kathy asked.

"Whatever," he said, briefly.

"There's a good one on at Cinema Twelve. It's set on a planet in the Betelgeuse System, a lot like Tarberg's Planet— you know, in the Proxima System. Only in the captain kirk it's inhabited by minions of an invisible—"

"I saw it," he said. As a matter of fact, a year ago they had had Jeff Pomeroy, who played the captain kirk in the picture, on his show; they had even run a short scene: the usual flick-plugging, you-visit-us deal with Pomeroy's studio. He had not liked it then and he doubted if he would like it now. And he detested Jeff Pomeroy, both on and off the screen. And that, as far as he was concerned, was that.

"It really wasn't any good?" Kathy asked trustingly.

"Jeff Pomeroy," he said, "as far as I'm concerned, is the itchy asshole of the world. He and those like him. His imitators."

Kathy said, "He was at Morningside for a while. I didn't get to know him, but he was there."

"I can believe it," he said, half believing it.

"Do you know what he said to me once?"

"Knowing him," Jason began, "I'd say—"

"He said I was the tamest person he ever knew. Isn't that interesting? And he saw me go into one of my mystic states—you know; when I lie down and scream—and still he said that. I think he's a very perceptive person; I really do. Don't you?"

"Yes," he said.

"Shall we go back to my room, then?" Kathy asked. "And screw like minks?"

He grunted in disbelief. Had she really said that? Turning, he tried to make out her face, but they had come to a patch between signs; all was dark for the moment. Jesus, he said to himself. *I've got to get myself out of this.* I've got to find my way back to my own world!

"Does my honesty bother you?" she asked.

"No," he said grimly. "Honesty never bothers me. To be a celebrity you have to be able to take it." Even that, he thought. "All kinds of honesty," he said. "Your kind most of all."

"What kind is mine?" Kathy asked.

"Honest honesty," he said.

"Then you do understand me," she said.

"Yes," he said, nodding. "I really do."

"And you don't look down on me? As a little worthless person who ought to be dead?"

"No," he said, "you're a very important person. And very honest, too. One of the most honest and straight-forward individuals I've ever met. I mean that; I swear to God I do."

She patted him friendlily on the arm. "Don't get all worked up over it. Let it come naturally."

"It comes naturally," he assured her. "It really does."

"Good," Kathy said. Happily. He had, evidently, eased her worries; she felt sure of him. And on that his life depended . . . or did it really? Wasn't he capitulating to her pathological reasoning? At the moment he did not really know.

"Listen," he said, haltingly. "I'm going to tell you something and I want you to listen carefully. You belong in a prison for the criminally insane."

Eerily, frighteningly, she did not react; she said nothing.

"And," he said, "I'm getting as far away from you as I can." He yanked his hand loose from hers, turned, made his way off in the opposite direction. Ignoring her. Losing himself among the ordinaries who milled in both directions along the cheap, neon-lit sidewalks of this unpleasant part of town.

I've lost her, he thought, and in doing so I have probably lost my goddamn life.

Now what? He halted, looked around him. Am I carrying a microtransmitter, as she says? he asked himself. Am I giving myself away with every step I take?

Cheerful Charley, he thought, told me to look up Heather Hart. And as everybody in TV-land knows, Cheerful Charley is never wrong.

But will I live long enough, he asked himself, to reach Heather Hart? And if I do reach her and I'm bugged, won't I simply be carrying my death onto her? Like a mindless plague? And, he thought, if Al Bliss didn't know me and Bill Wolfer didn't know me, why should Heather know me? But Heather, he thought, is a six, like myself. The only other six I know. Maybe that will be the difference. If there is any difference.

He found a public phone booth, entered, shut the door against the noise of traffic, and dropped a gold quinque into the slot.

Heather Hart had several unlisted numbers. Some for business, some for personal friends, one for—to put it bluntly—lovers. He, of course, knew that number, having been to Heather what he had, and still was, he hoped.

The viewscreen lit up. He made out the changing shapes as indicating that she was taking the call on her carphone.

"Hi," Jason said.

Shading her eyes to make him out, Heather said, "Who the hell are you?" Her green eyes flashed. Her red hair dazzled.

"Jason."

"I don't know anybody named Jason. How'd you get this number?" Her tone was troubled but also harsh. "Get the hell off my goddamn phone!" she scowled at him from the viewscreen and said, "Who gave you this number? I want his name."

Jason said, "You told me the number six months ago. When you first had it installed. Your private of the private lines; right? Isn't that what you called it?"

"Who told you that?"

"You did. We were in Madrid. You were on location and I had me a six-day vacation half a mile from your hotel. You used to drive over in your Rolls quibble about three each afternoon. Right?"

Heather said in a chattering, staccato tone, "Are you from a magazine?"

"No," Jason said. "I'm your number one paramour."

"My *what*?"

"Lover."

"Are you a fan? You're a fan, a goddamn twerp fan. I'll kill you if you don't get off my phone." The sound and image died; Heather had hung up.

He inserted another quinque into the slot, redialed.

"The twerp fan again," Heather said, answering. She seemed more poised, now. Or was it resigned?

"You have one imitation tooth," Jason said. "When you're with one of your lovers you glue it into place in your mouth with a special epoxy cement that you buy at Harney's. But with me you sometimes take it out, put it in a glass with Dr. Sloom's denture foam. That's the denture cleanser you prefer. Because, you always say, it reminds you of the days when Bromo Seltzer was legal and not just black market made in somebody's basement lab, using all three bromides that Bromo Seltzer discontinued years ago when—"

"How," Heather interrupted, "did you get hold of this information?" Her face was stiff, her words brisk and direct. Her tone . . . he had heard it before. Heather used it with people she detested.

"Don't use that 'I don't give a fuck' tone with me," he said angrily. "Your false tooth is a molar. You call it Andy. Right?"

"A twerp fan knows all this about me. God. My worst nightmare confirmed. What's the name of your club and how many fans are there in it and where are you from and how, God damn it, did you get hold of personal details from my private life that you have no right to know in the first place? I mean, what you're doing is illegal; it's an invasion of privacy. I'll have the pols after you if you call me once more." She reached to hang up her receiver.

"I'm a six," Jason said.

"A what? A six what? You have six legs; is that it? Or more likely six heads."

Jason said, "You're a six, too. That's what's kept us together all this time."

"I'm going to die," Heather said, ashen, now; even in the dim light of her quibble he could make out the change of color in her features. "What'll it cost me to have you leave me alone? I always knew that some twerp fan would eventually—"

"Stop calling me a twerp fan," Jason said bitingly; it infuriated him absolutely. It struck him as the ultimate in something or other; maybe a bird down, as the expression went now.

Heather said, "What do you want?"

"To meet you at Altrocci's."

"Yes, you'd know about that, too. The one place I can go without being ejaculated on by nerds who want me to sign menus that don't even belong to them." She sighed wretchedly. "Well, now that's over. I won't meet you at Altrocci's or anywhere. Keep out of my life or I'll have my prive-pols deball you and—"

"You have *one* private pol," Jason interrupted. "He's sixty-two years old and his name is Fred. Originally he was a sharpshooter with the Orange County Minutemen; used to pick off student jeters at Cal State Fullerton. He was good then, but he's nothing to worry about now."

"Is that so," Heather said.

"Okay, let me tell you something else that how do you think I would know. Remember Constance Ellar?"

"Yes," Heather said. "That nonentity starlet that looked like a Barbie Doll except that her head was too small and her body looked as if someone had inflated her with a CO_2 cartridge, overinflated her." Her lip curled. "She was utterly damn dumb."

"Right," he agreed. "Utterly damn dumb. That's the exact word. Remember what we did to her on my show? Her first planetwide exposure, because I had to take her in a tie-in deal. Do you remember that, what we did, you and I?"

Silence.

Jason said, "As a sop to us for having her on the show, her

agent agreed to let her do a commercial for one of our quarter-time sponsors. We got curious as to what the product was, so before Miss Ellar showed up we opened the paper bag and discovered it was a cream for removing leg hair. God, Heather, you must—"

"I'm listening," Heather said.

Jason said, "We took the spray can of leg-hair cream out and put a spray can of FDS back in with the same ad copy, which simply read, 'Demonstrate use of product with expression of contentment and satisfaction,' and then we got the hell out of there and waited."

"Did we."

"Miss Ellar finally showed up, went into her dressing room, opened the paper bag, and then—and this is the part that still makes me break up—she came up to me, perfectly seriously, and said, 'Mr. Taverner, I'm sorry to bother you about this, but to demonstrate the Feminine Hygiene Deodorant Spray I'll have to take off my skirt and underpants. Right there before the TV camera.' 'So?' I said. 'So what's the problem?' And Miss Ellar said, 'I'll need a little table on which I can put my clothes. I can't just drop them on the floor; that wouldn't look right. I mean, I'll be spraying that stuff into my vagina in front of sixty million people, and when you're doing that you can't just leave your clothes lying all around you on the floor; that isn't elegant.' She really would have done it, too, right on the air, if Al Bliss hadn't—"

"It's a tasteless story."

"All the same, you thought it was pretty funny. That utterly dumb girl with her first big break ready to do that. 'Demonstrate use of product with expression of contentment and—'"

Heather hung up.

How do I make her understand? he asked himself savagely, grinding his teeth together, nearly biting off a silver filling. He hated that sensation: grinding off a piece of filling. Destroying his own body, impotently. Can't she see that my knowledge of everything about her means something important? he asked himself. Who would know these things? Obviously only someone who had been very close physically with her for some time. There could be no other explanation, and yet she had conjured up such an elaborate other reason that he couldn't penetrate through to her. And it hung directly in front of her eyes. Her six's eyes.

Once more he dropped in a coin, dialed.

"Hi again," he said, when Heather at last picked up the phone in her car. "I know that about you, too," he said. "You can't let a phone ring; that's why you have ten private numbers, each for a different purpose of your very special own."

"I have three," Heather said. "So you don't know everything."

Jason said, "I merely meant—"

"How much?"

"I've had enough of that today," he said sincerely. "You can't buy me off because that's not what I want. I want—listen to me, Heather—I want to find out why nobody knows me. You most of all. And since you're a six I thought you might be able to explain it. Do you have *any* memory of me? Look at me on the picture screen. Look!"

She peered, one eyebrow cocked. "You're young but not too young. You're good-looking. Your voice is commanding and you have no reluctance about brigging me like this. You're exactly what a twerp fan would look like, sound like, act like. Okay; are you satisfied?"

"I'm in trouble," he said. It was blatantly irrational for him to tell her this, since she had no recollection of any sort of him. But over the years he had become accustomed to laying his troubles before her—and listening to hers—and the habit had not died. The habit ignored what he saw the reality situation to be: it cruised on under its own power.

"That's a shame," Heather said.

Jason said, "Nobody remembers me. And I have no birth certificate; I was never born, never even born! So naturally I have no ID cards except a forged set I bought from a pol fink for two thousand dollars plus one thousand for my contact. I'm carrying them around, but, God: they may have micro-transmitters built into them. Even knowing that I have to keep them on me; you know why—even you up at the top, even you know how this society works. Yesterday I had thirty million viewers who would have shrieked their aggrieved heads

off if a pol or a nat so much as touched me. Now I'm looking
into the eyes of an FLC."

"What's an FLC?"

"Forced-labor camp." He snarled the words at her, trying to
pin her down and finally nail her. "The vicious little bitch who
forged my papers made me take her out to some God-forsaken
broken-down wop restaurant, and while we were there, just
talking, she threw herself down on the floor screaming. Psychotic screaming; she's an escapee from Morningside, by her
own admission. That cost me another three hundred dollars
and by now who knows? She's probably sicced the pols and
nats *both* on me." Pushing his self-pity gingerly a little further,
he said, "They're probably monitoring this phone line right
now."

"Oh, Christ, no!" Heather shrieked and again hung up.

He had no more gold quinques. So, at this point, he gave
up. That was a stupid thing to say, he realized, that about the
phone lines. That would make anybody hang up. I strangled
myself in my own word web, right down the old freeber.
Straight down the middle. Beautifully flat at both ends, too.
Like a great artificial anus.

He shoved the door of the phone booth aside and stepped
out onto the busy nocturnal sidewalk . . . down here, he
thought acidly, in Slumsville. Down where the pol finks hang
out. Jolly good show, as that classic TV muffin ad went that we
studied in school, he said to himself.

It would be funny, he thought, if it were happening to
someone else. But it's happening to me. No, it's not funny
either way. Because there is real suffering and real death passing
the time of day in the wings. Ready to come on any minute.

I wish I could have taped the phone call, plus everything
Kathy said to me and me to her. In 3-D color, on videotape it
would be a nice bit on my show, somewhere near the end
where we run out of material occasionally. Occasionally, hell:
generally. Always. For the rest of my life.

He could hear his intro now. "What can happen to a man, a
good man without a pol record, a man who suddenly one day
loses his ID cards and finds himself facing . . ." And so forth.
It would hold them, all thirty million of them. Because that

was what each of them feared. "An invisible man," his intro would go, "yet a man all too conspicuous. Invisible legally; conspicuous illegally. What becomes of such a man, if he cannot replace . . ." Blah blah. On and on. The hell with it. Not everything that he did or said or had happen to him got onto the show; so it went with this. Another loser, among many. Many are called, he said to himself, but few are chosen. That's what it means to be a pro. That's how I manage things, public and private. Cut your losses and run when you have to, he told himself, quoting himself from back in the good days when his first full worldwide show got piped onto the satellite grid.

I'll find another forger, he decided, one that isn't a pol informer, and get a full new set of ID cards, ones without microtransmitters. And then, evidently, I need a gun.

I should have thought of that about the time I woke up in that hotel room, he said to himself. Once, years ago, when the Reynolds syndicate had tried to buy into his show, he had learned to use—and had carried—a gun: a Barber's Hoop with a range of two miles with no loss of peak trajectory until the final thousand feet.

Kathy's "mystical trance," her screaming fit. The audio portion would carry a mature male voice saying against her screams as BG, "This is what it is to be psychotic. To be psychotic is to suffer, suffer beyond . . ." And so forth. Blah blah. He inhaled a great, deep lungful of cold night air, shuddered, joined the passengers on the sea of sidewalk, his hands thrust deep into his trouser pockets.

And found himself facing a queue lined up ten deep before a pol random checkpoint. One gray-clad policeman stood at the end of the line, loitering there to make sure no one doubled back in the opposite direction.

"Can't you pass it, friend?" the pol said to him as he involuntarily started to leave.

"Sure," Jason said.

"That's good," the pol said good-humoredly. "Because we've been checking here since eight this morning and we still don't have our work quota."

SIX

Two husky gray pols, confronting the man ahead of Jason, said in unison, "These were forged an hour ago; they're still damp. See? See the ink run under the heat? Okay." They nodded, and the man, gripped by four thungly pols, disappeared into a parked van-quibble, ominously gray and black: police colors.

"Okay," one of the husky pols said genially to Jason, "let's see when yours were printed."

Jason said, "I've been carrying these for years." He handed his wallet, with the seven ID cards, to the pols.

"Graph his signatures," the senior pol told his companion. "See if they superimpose."

Kathy had been right.

"Nope," the junior pol said, putting away his official camera. "They don't super. But it looks like this one, the military service chit, had a trans dot on it that's been scraped off. Very expertly, too, if so. You have to view it through the glass." He swung the portable magnifying lens and light over, illuminating Jason's forged cards in stark white detail. "See?"

"When you left the service," the senior pol said to Jason, "did this record have an electronic dot on it? Do you remember?" Both of them scrutinized Jason as they awaited his response.

What the hell to say? he asked himself. "I don't know," he said. "I don't even know what a"—he started to say, "Microtransmitter dot," but quickly corrected himself—soon enough, he hoped—"what an electronic dot looks like."

"It's a dot, mister," the junior pol informed him. "Aren't you listening? Are you on drugs? Look; on his drug-status card there isn't an entry for the last year."

One of the thungly pols spoke up. "Proves they're not faked, though, because who would fake a felony onto an ID card? They'd have to be out of their minds."

"Yes," Jason said.

"Well, it's not part of our area," the senior pol said. He handed Jason's ID cards back to him. "He'll have to take it up with his drug inspector. Move on." With his nightstick the pol shoved Jason out of the way, reaching meanwhile for the ID cards of the man behind him.

"That's it?" Jason said to the thungly pols. He could not believe it. Don't let it show, he said to himself. Just *move on!*

He did so.

From the shadows beneath a broken streetlight, Kathy reached out, touched him; he froze at the touch, feeling himself turn to ice, starting with his heart. "What do you think of me now?" Kathy said. "My work, what I did for you."

"They did it," he said shortly.

"I'm not going to turn you in," Kathy said, "even though you insulted and abandoned me. But you have to stay with me tonight like you promised. You understand?"

He had to admire her. By lurking around the random checkpoint she had obtained firsthand proof that her forged documents had been well enough done to get him past the pols. So all at once the situation between them had altered: he was now in her debt. He no longer held the status of aggrieved victim.

Now she owned a moral share of him. First the stick: the threat of turning him in to the pols. Then the carrot: the adequately forged ID cards. The girl had him, really. He had to admit it, to her and to himself.

"I could have gotten you through anyhow," Kathy said. She held up her right arm, pointing to a section of her sleeve. "I've got a gray pol-ident tab, there; it shows up under their macrolens. So I don't get picked up by mistake. I would have said—"

"Let it lie there," he broke in harshly. "I don't want to hear about it." He walked away from her; the girl skimmed after him, like a skillful bird.

"Want to go back to my Minor Apartment?" Kathy asked.

"That goddamn shabby room." I have a floating house in Malibu, he thought, with eight bedrooms, six rotating baths and a four-dimensional living room with an infinity ceiling. And, because of something I don't understand and can't control, I have to spend my time like this. Visiting run-down marginal places. Crappy eateries, crappier workshops, crappiest one-room lodgings. Am I being paid back for something I did? he asked himself. Something I don't know about or remember? But nobody pays back, he reflected. I learned that a long time ago: you're not paid back for the bad you do nor the good you do. It all comes out uneven at the end. Haven't I learned that by now, if I've learned anything?

"Guess what's at the top of my shopping list for tomorrow," Kathy was saying. "Dead flies. Do you know why?"

"They're high in protein."

"Yes, but that's not why; I'm not getting them for myself. I buy a bag of them every week for Bill, my turtle."

"I didn't see any turtle."

"At my major apartment. You didn't really think I'd buy dead flies for myself, did you?'

"*De gustibus non disputandum est*," he quoted.

"Let's see. In matters of taste there's no dispute. Right?"

"Right," he said. "Meaning that if you want to eat dead flies go ahead and eat them."

"Bill does; he likes them. He's just one of those little green turtles . . . not a land tortoise or anything. Have you ever watched the way they snap at food, at a fly floating on their water? It's very small but it's awful. One second the fly's there and then the next, glunk. It's inside the turtle." She laughed. "Being digested. There's a lesson to be learned there."

"What lesson?" He anticipated it then. "That when you bite," he said, "you either get all of it or none of it, but never part."

"That's how I feel."

"Which do you have?" he asked her. "All or none?"

"I—don't know. Good question. Well, I don't have Jack. But maybe I don't want him any more. It's been so fucking long. I guess I still need him. But I need you more."

Jason said, "I thought you were the one who could love two men equally."

"Did I say that?" She pondered as they walked. "What I meant was is that's ideal, but in real life you can only approximate it . . . do you see? Can you follow my line of thought?"

"I can follow it," he said, "and I can see where it's leading. It's leading to a temporary abandonment of Jack while I'm around and then a psychological returning to him when I'm gone. Do you do it every time?"

"I never abandon him," Kathy said sharply. They then continued on in silence until they reached her great old apartment building with its forest of no-longer-used TV masts jutting from every part of the roof. Kathy fumbled in her purse, found her key, unlocked the door to her room.

The lights had been turned on. And, seated on the moldering sofa facing them, a middle-aged man with gray hair and a gray suit. A heavy-set but immaculate man, with perfectly shaved jowls: no nicks, no red spots, no errors. He was perfectly attired and groomed; each hair on his head stood individually in place.

Kathy said falteringly, "Mr. McNulty."

Rising to his feet, the heavy-set man extended his right hand toward Jason. Automatically, Jason reached out to shake it.

"No," the heavy-set man said. "I'm not shaking hands with you; I want to see your ID cards, the ones she made for you. Let me have them."

Wordlessly—there was nothing to say—Jason passed him his wallet.

"You didn't do these," McNulty said, after a short inspection. "Unless you're getting a hell of a lot better."

Jason said, "I've had some of those cards for years."

"Have you," McNulty murmured. He returned the wallet and cards to Jason. "Who planted the microtrans on him? You?" He addressed Kathy. "Ed?"

"Ed," Kathy said.

"What do we have here?" McNulty said, scrutinizing Jason as if measuring him for a coffin. "A man in his forties, well dressed, modern clothing style. Expensive shoes . . . made of actual authentic leather. Isn't that right, Mr. Taverner?"

"They're cowhide," Jason said.

"Your papers identify you as a musician," McNulty said. "You play an instrument?"

"I sing."

McNulty said, "Sing something for us now."

"Go to hell," Jason said, and managed to control his breathing; his words came out exactly as he wanted them to. No more, no less.

To Kathy, McNulty said, "He's not exactly cowering. Does he know who I am?"

"Yes," Kathy said. "I—told him. Part of it."

"You told him about Jack," McNulty said. To Jason he said, "There is no Jack. She thinks so but it's a psychotic delusion.

Her husband died three years ago in a quibble accident; he was
never in a forced-labor camp."

"Jack is still alive," Kathy said.

"You see?" McNulty said to Jason. "She's made a pretty fair
adjustment to the outside world except for this one fixed idea.
It will never go away; she'll have it for the balance of her life."
He shrugged. "It's a harmless idea and it keeps her going. So
we've made no attempt to deal with it psychiatrically."

Kathy, quietly, had begun to cry. Large tears slid down her
cheeks and dropped, bloblike, onto her blouse. Tear stains, in
the form of dark circles, appeared here and there.

"I'll be talking to Ed Pracim in the next couple of days,"
McNulty said. "I'll ask him why he put the microtrans on you.
He has hunches; it must have been a hunch." He reflected.
"Bear in mind, the ID cards in your wallet are reproductions
of actual documents on file at various central data banks
throughout earth. Your reproductions are satisfactory, but I
may want to check on the originals. Let's hope they're in as
good order as the repros you carry."

Kathy said feebly, "But that's a rare procedure. Statisti-
cally—"

"In this case," McNulty said, "I think it's worth trying."

"Why?" Kathy said.

"Because we don't think you're turning everyone over to
us. Half an hour ago this man Taverner passed successfully
through a random checkpoint. We followed him using the microtrans. And his papers look fine to me. But Ed says—"

"Ed drinks," Kathy said.

"But we can count on him." McNulty smiled, a professional
beam of sunshine in the shabby room. "And we can't, not
quite, on you."

Bringing forth his military-service chit, Jason rubbed the
small profile 4-D picture of himself. And it said tinnily, "How
now, brown cow?"

"How can that be faked?" Jason said. "That's the tone of
voice I had back ten years ago when I was an involnat."

"I doubt that," McNulty said. He examined his wristwatch.
"Do we owe you anything, Miss Nelson? Or are we clear for
this week?"

"Clear," she said, with an effort. Then, in a low, unsteady

voice, she half-whispered, "After Jack gets out you won't be able to count on me at all."

"For you," McNulty said genially, "Jack will never get out." He winked at Jason. Jason winked back. Twice. He understood McNulty. The man preyed on the weaknesses of others; the kind of manipulation that Kathy employed had probably been learned from him. And from his quaint, genial companions.

He could understand now how she had become what she had become. Betrayal was an everyday event; a refusal to betray, as in his case, was miraculous. He could only wonder at it and thank it dimly.

We have a betrayal state, he realized. When I was a celebrity I was exempt. Now I'm like everyone else: I now have to face what they've always faced. And—what I faced in the old days, faced and then later on repressed from my memory. Because it was too distressing to believe . . . once I had a choice, and could choose not to believe.

McNulty put his fleshy, red-speckled hand on Jason's shoulder and said, "Come along with me."

"Where to?" Jason demanded, moving away from McNulty exactly, he realized, the way Kathy had moved away from *him*. She had learned this, too, from the McNultys of the world.

"You don't have anything to charge him with!" Kathy said hoarsely, clenching her fists.

Easily, McNulty said, "We're not going to charge him with anything; I just want a fingerprint, voiceprint, footprint, EEG wave pattern from him. Okay, Mr. Tavern?"

Jason started to say, "I hate to correct a police officer—" and then broke off at the warning look on Kathy's face— "who's doing his duty," he finished, "so I'll go along." Maybe Kathy had a point; maybe it was worth something for the pol officer to get Jason Taverner's name wrong. Who knew? Time would tell.

"'Mr. Tavern,'" McNulty said lazily, propelled him toward the door of the room. "Suggests beer and warmth and coziness, doesn't it?" He looked back at Kathy and said in a sharp voice, "Doesn't it?"

"Mr. Tavern is a warm man," Kathy said, her teeth locked together. The door shut after them, and McNulty steered him down the hallway to the stairs, breathing, meanwhile, the odor of onion and hot sauce in every direction.

At the 469th Precinct station, Jason Taverner found himself lost in a multitude of men and women who moved aimlessly, waiting to get in, waiting to get out, waiting for information, waiting to be told what to do. McNulty had pinned a colored tag on his lapel; God and the police alone knew what it meant.

Obviously it did mean something. A uniformed officer behind a desk which ran from wall to wall beckoned to him.

"Okay," the cop said. "Inspector McNulty filled out part of your J-2 form. Jason Tavern. Address: 2048 Vine Street."

Where had McNulty come up with that? Jason wondered. Vine Street. And then he realized that it was Kathy's address. McNulty had assumed they were living together; overworked, as was true of all the pols, he had written down the information that took the least effort. A law of nature: an object—or living creature—takes the shortest route between two points. He filled out the balance of the form.

"Put your hand into that slot," the officer said, indicating a fingerprinting machine. Jason did so. "Now," the officer said, "remove one shoe, either left or right. And that sock. You may sit down here." He slid a section of desk aside, revealing an entrance and a chair.

"Thanks," Jason said, seating himself.

After the recording of the footprint he spoke the sentence, "Down goes the right hut and ate a put object beside his horse." That took care of the voiceprint. After that, again seated, he allowed terminals to be placed here and there on his head; the machine cranked out three feet of scribbled-on paper, and that was that. That was the electrocardiogram. It ended the tests.

Looking cheerful, McNulty appeared at the desk. In the harsh white overhead light his five-o'clock shadow could be seen over all his jaw, his upper lip, the higher part of his neck. "How's it going with Mr. Tavern?" he asked.

The officer said, "We're ready to do a nomenclature file-pull."

"Fine," McNulty said. "I'll stick around and see what comes up."

The uniformed officer dropped the form Jason had filled out into a slot, pressed lettered buttons, all of which were green. For some reason Jason noticed that. And the letters capitals.

From a mouthlike aperture on the very long desk a Xeroxed document slid out, dropped into a metal basket.

"Jason Tavern," the uniformed officer said, examining the document. "Of Kememmer, Wyoming. Age: thirty-nine. A diesel engine mechanic." He glanced at the photo. "Pic taken fifteen years ago."

"Any police record?" McNulty asked.

"No trouble of any kind," the uniformed officer said.

"There are no other Jason Taverns on record at Pol-Dat?" McNulty asked. The officer pressed a yellow button, shook his head. "Okay," McNulty said. "That's him." He surveyed Jason. "You don't look like a diesel engine mechanic."

"I don't do that any more," Jason said. "I'm now in sales. For farm equipment. Do you want my card?" A bluff; he reached toward the upper right-hand pocket of his suit. McNulty shook his head no. So that was that; they had, in their usual bureaucratic fashion, pulled the wrong file on him. And, in their rush, they had let it stand.

He thought, Thank God for the weaknesses built into a vast, complicated, convoluted, planetwide apparatus. Too many people; too many machines. This error began with a pol inspec and worked its way to Pol-Dat, their pool of data at Memphis, Tennessee. Even with my fingerprint, footprint, voiceprint and EEG print they probably won't be able to straighten it out. Not now; not with my form on file.

"Shall I book him?" the uniformed officer asked McNulty.

"For what?" McNulty said. "For being a diesel mechanic?" He slapped Jason convivially on the back. "You can go home, Mr. Tavern. Back to your child-faced sweetheart. Your little virgin." Grinning, he moved off into the throng of anxious and bewildered human men and women.

"You may go, sir," the uniformed officer told Jason.

Nodding, Jason made his way out of the 469th Precinct

police station, onto the nighttime street, to mix with the free and self-determined people who resided there.

But they will get me finally, he thought. They'll match up the prints. And yet—if it's been fifteen years since the photo was taken, maybe it's been fifteen years since they took an EEG and a voiceprint.

But that still left the finger- and footprints. They did not change.

He thought, Maybe they'll just toss the Xerox copy of the file into a shredding bin, and that will be that. And transmit the data they got out of me to Memphis, there to be incorporated in my—or rather "my"—permanent file. In Jason Tavern's file, specifically.

Thank God Jason Tavern, diesel mechanic, had never broken a law, had never tangled with the pols or nats. Good for him.

A police flipflap wobbled overhead, its red searchlight glimmering, and from its PA speakers it said, "Mr. Jason Tavern, return to 469th Precinct Police Station at once. This is a police order. Mr. Jason Tavern—" It raved on and on as Jason stood stunned. They had figured it out already. In a matter not of hours, days, or weeks, but minutes.

He returned to the police station, climbed the styraplex stairs, passed through the light-activated doors, through the milling throng of the unfortunate, back to the uniformed officer who had handled his case—and there stood McNulty, too. The two of them were in the process of frowningly conferring.

"Well," McNulty said, glancing up, "here's our Mr. Tavern again. What are you doing back here, Mr. Tavern?"

"The police flipflap—" he began, but McNulty cut him off.

"That was unauthorized. We merely put out an APB and some figtail hoisted it to flipflap level. But as long as you're here"—McNulty turned the document so that Jason could see the photo—"is that how you looked fifteen years ago?"

"I guess so," Jason said. The photo showed a sallow-faced individual with protruding Adam's apple, bad teeth and eyes, sternly staring into nothing. His hair, frizzy and corn-colored, hung over two near-jug ears.

"You've had plastic S," McNulty said.

Jason said, "Yes."

"Why?"

Jason said, "Who would want to look like that?"

"So no wonder you're so handsome and dignified," McNulty said. "So stately. So"—he groped for the word— "commanding. It's really hard to believe that they could do to *that*"—he put his index finger on the fifteen-year-old photo— "something to make it look like *that*." He tapped Jason friendlily on the arm. "But where'd you get the money?"

While McNulty talked, Jason had begun swiftly reading the data printed on the document. Jason Tavern had been born in Cicero, Illinois, his father had been a turret lathe operator, his grandfather had owned a chain of retail farm-equipment stores —a lucky break, considering what he had told McNulty about his current career.

"From Windslow," Jason said. "I'm sorry; I always think of him like that, and I forget that others can't." His professional training had helped him: he had read and assimilated most of the page while McNulty was talking to him. "My grandfather. He had a good deal of money, and I was his favorite. I was the only grandson, you see."

McNulty studied the document, nodded.

"I looked like a rural hick," Jason said. "I looked like what I was: a hayseed. The best job I could get involved repairing diesel engines, and I wanted more. So I took the money that Windslow left me and headed for Chicago—"

"Okay," McNulty said, still nodding. "It fits together. We are aware that such radical plastic surgery can be accomplished, and at not too large a cost. But generally it's done by unpersons or labor-camp inmates who've escaped. We monitor all graft-shops, as we call them."

"But look how ugly I was," Jason said.

McNulty laughed a deep, throaty laugh. "You sure were, Mr. Tavern. Okay; sorry to trouble you. Go on." He gestured, and Jason began to part the throng of people before him. "Oh!" McNulty called, gesturing to him. "One more—" His voice, drowned out by the noise of the milling, did not reach Jason. So, his heart frozen in ice, he walked back.

Once they notice you, Jason realized, *they never completely close the file.* You can never get back your anonymity. It is vital not to be noticed in the first place. But I have been.

"What is it?" he asked McNulty, feeling despair. They were playing games with him, breaking him down; he could feel, inside him, his heart, his blood, all his vital parts, stagger in their processes. Even the superb physiology of a six tumbled at this.

McNulty held out his hand. "Your ID cards. I want some lab work on them. If they're okay you'll get them back the day after tomorrow."

Jason said, protestingly, "But if a random pol-check—"

"We'll give you a police pass," McNulty said. He nodded to a great-bellied older officer to his right. "Get a 4-D photo of him and set up a blanket pass."

"Yes, Inspector," the tub of guts said, reaching out an over-stuffed paw to turn on the camera equipment.

Ten minutes later, Jason Taverner found himself out once more on the now almost deserted early evening sidewalk, and this time with a bona fide pol-pass—better than anything Kathy could have manufactured for him . . . except that the pass was valid only for one week. But still . . .

He had one week during which he could afford not to worry. And then, after that . . .

He had done the impossible: he had traded a walletful of bogus ID cards for a genuine pol-pass. Examining the pass under the streetlights, he saw that the expiration notice was holographic . . . and there was room for the insertion of an additional number. It read *seven*. He could get Kathy to alter that to seventy-five or ninety-seven, or whatever was easiest.

And then it occurred to him that as soon as the pol lab made out that his ID cards were spurious the number of his pass, his name, his photo, would be transmitted to every police check-point on the planet.

But until that happened he was safe.

Part Two

Down, vain lights, shine you no more!
No nights are black enough for those
That in despair their lost fortunes deplore.
Light doth but shame disclose.

SEVEN

EARLY in the gray of evening, before the cement sidewalks bloomed with nighttime activity, Police General Felix Buckman landed his opulent official quibble on the roof of the Los Angeles Police Academy building. He sat for a time, reading page-one articles on the sole evening newspaper, then, folding the paper up carefully, he placed it on the back seat of the quibble, opened the locked door, and stepped out.

No activity below him. One shift had begun to trail off; the next had not quite begun to arrive.

He liked this time: the great building, in these moments, seemed to belong to him. "And leaves the world to darkness and to me," he thought, recalling a line from Thomas Gray's *Elegy*. A longcherished favorite of his, in fact from boyhood.

With his rank key he opened the building's express descent sphincter, dropped rapidly by chute to his own level, fourteen. Where he had worked most of his adult life.

Desks without people, rows of them. Except that at the far end of the major room one officer still sat painstakingly writing a report. And, at the coffee machine, a female officer drinking from a Dixie cup.

"Good evening," Buckman said to her. He did not know her, but it did not matter: she—and everyone else in the building—knew *him*.

"Good evening, Mr. Buckman." She drew herself upright, as if at attention.

"Be tired," Buckman said.

"Pardon, sir?"

"Go home." He walked away from her, passed by the posterior row of desks, the rank of square gray metal shapes upon

736

which the business of this branch of earth's police agency was conducted.

Most of the desks were clean: the officers had finished their work neatly before leaving. But, on desk 37, several papers. Officer Someone worked late, Buckman decided. He bent to see the nameplate.

Inspector McNulty, of course. The ninety-day wonder of the academy. Busily dreaming up plots and remnants of treason . . . Buckman smiled, seated himself on the swivel chair, picked up the papers.

TAVERNER, JASON. CODE BLUE.

A Xeroxed file from police vaults. Summoned out of the void by the overly eager—and overweight—Inspector McNulty. A small note in pencil: "Taverner does not exist."

Strange, he thought. And began to leaf through the papers.

"Good evening, Mr. Buckman." His assistant, Herbert Maime, young and sharp, nattily dressed in a civilian suit: he rated that privilege, as did Buckman.

"McNulty seems to be working on the file of someone who does not exist," Buckman said.

"In which precinct doesn't he exist?" Maime said, and both of them laughed. They did not particularly like McNulty, but the gray police required his sort. Everything would be fine unless the McNultys of the academy rose to policy-making levels. Fortunately that rarely happened. Not, anyhow, if *he* could help it.

Subject gave false name Jason Tavern. Wrong file pulled of Jason Tavern of Kememmer, Wyoming, diesel motor repairman. Subject claimed to be Tavern, with plastic S. ID cards identify him as Taverner, Jason, but no file.

Interesting, Buckman thought as he read McNulty's notes. Absolutely no file on the man. He finished the notes:

Well-dressed, suggest has money, perhaps influence to get his file pulled out of data bank. Look into relationship with Katharine Nelson, pol contact in area. Does she know who he is? Tried not to turn him in, but pol contact 1659BD planted microtrans on him. Subject now in cab. Sector N8823B, moving east in the direction of Las Vegas.

Due 11/4 10:00 P.M. academy time. Next report due at 2:40 P.M. academy time.

Katharine Nelson. Buckman had met her once, at a pol-contact orientation course. She was the girl who only turned in individuals whom she did not like. In an odd, elliptical way he admired her; after all, had he not intervened, she would have been shipped on 4/8/82 to a forced-labor camp in British Columbia.

To Herb Maime, Buckman said, "Get me McNulty on the phone. I think I'd better talk to him about this."

A moment later, Maime handed him the instrument. On the small gray screen McNulty's face appeared, looking rumpled. As did his living room. Small and untidy, both of them.

"Yes, Mr. Buckman," McNulty said, focusing on him and coming to a stiff attention, tired as he was. Despite fatigue and a little hype of something, McNulty knew exactly how to comport himself in relation to his superiors.

Buckman said, "Give me the story, briefly, on this Jason Taverner. I can't piece it together from your notes."

"Subject rented hotel room at 453 Eye Street. Approached pol contact 1659BD, known as Ed, asked to be taken to ID forger. Ed planted microtrans on him, took him to pol contact 1980CC, Kathy."

"Katharine Nelson," Buckman said.

"Yes, sir. Evidently she did an unusually expert job on the ID cards; I've put them through prelim lab tests and they work out *almost* okay. She must have wanted him to get away."

"You contacted Katharine Nelson?"

"I met both of them at her room. Neither cooperated with me. I examined subject's ID cards, but—"

"They seemed genuine," Buckman interrupted.

"Yes, sir."

"You still think you can do it by eye."

"Yes, Mr. Buckman. But it got him through a random pol checkpoint; the stuff was that good."

"How nice for him."

McNulty bumbled on, "I took his ID cards and issued him a seven-day pass, subject to recall. Then I took him to the 469th Precinct station, where I have my aux office, and had his file pulled . . . the Jason Tavern file, it turned out. Subject went into a long song and dance about plastic S; it sounded plausible, so we let him go. No, wait a minute; I didn't issue him the pass until—"

"Well," Buckman interrupted, "what's he up to? Who is he?"

"Were following him, via the microtrans. We're trying to come up with data-bank material on him. But as you read in my notes, I think subject has managed to get his file out of every central data bank. It's just not there, and it has to be because we have a file on everyone, as every school kid knows; it's the law, we've got to."

"But we don't," Buckman said.

"I know, Mr. Buckman. But when a file isn't there, there has to be a reason. It didn't just *happen* not to be there: someone filched it out of there."

" 'Filched,' " Buckman said, amused.

"Stole, purloined." McNulty looked discomfited. "I've just begun to go into it, Mr. Buckman; I'll know more in twenty-four hours. Hell, we can pick him up any time we want. I don't think this is important. He's just some well-heeled guy with enough influence to get his file out—"

"All right," Buckman said. "Go to bed." He rang off, stood for a moment, then walked in the direction of his inner offices. Pondering.

In his main office, asleep on the couch, lay his sister Alys. Wearing, Felix Buckman saw with acute displeasure, skin-tight black trousers, a man's leather shirt, hoop earrings, and a chain belt with a wrought-iron buckle. Obviously she had been drugging. And had, as so often before, gotten hold of one of his keys.

"God damn you," he said to her, closing the office door before Herb Maime could catch a glimpse of her.

In her sleep Alys stirred. Her catlike face screwed up into an irritable frown and, with her right hand, she groped to put out the overhead fluorescent light, which he had now turned on.

Grabbing her by the shoulders—and experiencing without pleasure her taut muscles—he dragged her to a sitting position. "What was it this time?" he demanded. "Termaline?"

"No." Her speech, of course, came out slurred. "Hexophenophrine hydrosulphate. Uncut. Subcutaneous." She opened her great pale eyes, stared at him with rebellious displeasure.

Buckman said, "Why in hell do you always come here?" Whenever she had been heavily fetishing and/or drugging she crashed here in his main office. He did not know why, and she had never said. The closest she had come, once, was a mumbled declaration about the "eye of the hurricane," suggesting that she felt safe from arrest here at the core offices of the Police Academy. Because, of course, of his position.

"Fetishist," he snapped at her, with fury. "We process a hundred of you a day, you and your leather and chain mail and dildoes. God." He stood breathing noisily, feeling himself shake.

Yawning, Alys slid from the couch, stood straight upright and stretched her long, slender arms. "I'm glad it's evening," she said airily, her eyes squeezed shut. "Now I can go home and go to bed."

"How do you plan to get out of here?" he demanded. But he knew. Every time the same ritual unfolded. The ascent tube for "secluded" political prisoners got brought into use: it led from his extreme north office to the roof, hence to the quibble field. Alys came and went that way, his key breezily in hand. "Someday," he said to her darkly, "an officer will be using the tube for a legitimate purpose, and he'll run into you."

"And what would he do?" She massaged his short-cropped gray hair. "Tell me, please, sir. Muff-dive me into panting contrition?"

"One look at you with that sated expression on your face—"

"They know I'm your sister."

Buckman said harshly, "They know because you're always coming in here for one reason or another or no damn reason at all."

Perching knees up on the edge of a nearby desk, Alys eyed him seriously. "It really bothers you."

"Yes, it really bothers me."

"That I come here and make your job unsafe."

"You can't make my job unsafe," Buckman said. "I've got only five men over me, excluding the national director, and all of them know about you and they can't do anything. So you can do what you want." Thereupon he stormed out of the north office, down the dull corridor to the larger suite where he did most of his work. He tried to avoid looking at her.

"But you carefully closed the door," Alys said, sauntering after him, "so that that Herbert Blame or Mame or Maine or whatever it is wouldn't see me."

"You," Buckman said, "are repellent to a natural man."

"Is Maime natural? How do you know? Have you screwed him?"

"If you don't get out of here," he said quietly, facing her across two desks, "I'll have you shot. So help me God."

She shrugged her muscular shoulders. And smiled.

"Nothing scares you," he said, accusingly. "Since your brain operation. You systematically, deliberately, had all your human centers removed. You're now a"—he struggled to find the words; Alys always hamstrung him like this, even managed to abolish his ability to use words—"you," he said chokingly, "are a reflex machine that diddles itself endlessly like a rat in an experiment. You're wired into the pleasure nodule of your brain and you push the switch five thousand times an hour every day of your life when you're not sleeping. It's a mystery to me why you bother to sleep; why not diddle yourself a full twenty-four hours a day?"

He waited, but Alys said nothing.

"Someday," he said, "one of us will die."

"Oh?" she said, raising a thin green eyebrow.

"One of us," Buckman said, "will outlive the other. And that one will rejoice."

The pol-line phone on the larger desk buzzed. Reflexively, Buckman picked it up. On the screen McNulty's rumpled hyped-up features appeared. "Sorry to bother you, General Buckman, but I just got a call from one of my staff. There's no record in Omaha of a birth certificate ever being issued for a Jason Taverner."

Patiently, Buckman said, "Then it's an alias."

"We took fingerprints, voiceprints, footprints, EEG prints. We sent them to One Central, to the overall data bank in Detroit. No match-up. Such fingerprints, footprints, voiceprints, EEG prints, don't exist in any data banks on earth." McNulty tugged himself upright and wheezed apologetically, "Jason Taverner doesn't exist."

EIGHT

Jason Taverner did not, at the moment, wish to return to Kathy. Nor, he decided, did he want to try Heather Hart once again. He tapped his coat pocket; he still had his money, and, because of the police pass, he could feel free to travel anywhere. A pol-pass was a passport to the entire planet; until they APB-ed on him he could travel as far as he wanted, including unimproved areas such as specific, acceptable jungle-infested islands in the South Pacific. There they might not find him for months, not with what his money would buy in an open-area spot such as that.

I've got three things going for me, he realized. I've got money, good looks, and personality. Four things: I also have forty-two years of experience as a six.

An apartment.

But, he thought, if I rent an apartment, the rotive manager will be required by law to take my fingerprints; they'll be routinely mailed to Pol-Dat Central . . . and when the police have discovered that my ID cards are fakes, they'll find they have a direct line to me. So there goes that.

What I need, he said to himself, *is to find someone who already has an apartment. In their name, with their prints.*

And that means another girl.

Where do I find such a one? he asked himself, and had the answer already on his tongue: at a first-rate cocktail lounge. The kind many women go to, with a three-man combo playing fob jazzy, preferably blacks. Well dressed.

Am I well enough dressed, though? he wondered, and took a good look at his silk suit under the steady white-and-red light of a huge AAMCO sign. Not his best but nearly so . . . but wrinkled. Well, in the gloom of a cocktail lounge it wouldn't show.

He hailed a cab, and presently found himself quibbling toward the more acceptable part of the city to which he was accustomed—accustomed, at least, during the most recent years of his life, his career. When he had reached the very top.

A club, he thought, where I've appeared. A club I really know. Know the maître d', the hatcheck girl, the flower girl . . . unless they, like me, are somehow now changed.

But as yet it appeared that nothing but himself had changed. *His* circumstances. Not theirs.

The Blue Fox Room of the Hayette Hotel in Reno. He had played there a number of times; he knew the layout and the staff backward and forward.

To the cab he said, "Reno."

Beautifully, the cab peeled off in a great swooping right-hand motion; he felt himself going with it, and enjoyed it. The cab picked up speed: they had entered a virtually unused air corridor, and the upper velocity limit was perhaps as high as twelve hundred m.p.h.

"I'd like to use the phone," Jason said.

The left wall of the cab opened and a picphone slid out, cord twisted in a baroque loop.

He knew the number of the Blue Fox Room by heart; he dialed it, waited, heard a click and then a mature male voice saying, "Blue Fox Room, where Freddy Hydrocephalic is appearing in two shows nightly, at eight and at twelve; only thirty dollars' cover charge and girls provided while you watch. May I help you?"

"Is this good old Jumpy Mike?" Jason said. "Good old Jumpy Mike himself?"

"Yes, this certainly is." The formality of the voice ebbed. "Who am I speaking to, may I ask?" A warm chuckle.

Taking a deep breath, Jason said, "This is Jason Taverner."

"I'm sorry, Mr. Taverner." Jumpy Mike sounded puzzled. "Right now at the moment I can't quite—"

"It's been a long time," Jason interrupted. "Can you give me a table toward the front of the room—"

"The Blue Fox Room is completely sold out, Mr. Taverner," Jumpy Mike rumbled in his fat way. "I'm very sorry."

"No table at all?" Jason said. "At any price?"

"Sorry, Mr. Taverner, none." The voice faded in the direction of remoteness. "Try us in two weeks." Good old Jumpy Mike hung up.

Silence.

Jesus shit Christ, Jason said to himself. "God," he said aloud. "God damn it." His teeth ground against one another, sending sheets of pain through his trigeminal nerve.

"New instructions, big fellow?" the cab asked tonelessly.

"Make it Las Vegas," Jason grated. I'll try the Nellie Melba Room of the Drake's Arms, he decided. Not too long ago he had had good luck there, at a time when Heather Hart had been fulfilling an engagement in Sweden. A reasonable number of reasonably high class chicks hung out there, gambling, drinking, listening to the entertainment, getting it on. It was worth a try, if the Blue Fox Room—and the others like it— were closed to him. After all, what could he lose?

Half an hour later the cab deposited him on the roof field of the Drake's Arms. Shivering in the chill night air, Jason made his way to the royal descent carpet; a moment later he had stepped from it into the warmth-color-light-movement of the Nellie Melba Room.

The time: seven-thirty. The first show would begin soon. He glanced at the notice; Freddy Hydrocephalic was appearing here, too, but doing a lesser tape at lower prices. Maybe he'll remember me, Jason thought. Probably not. And then, as he thought more deeply on it, he thought, No chance at all.

If Heather Hart didn't remember him no one would.

He seated himself at the crowded bar—on the only stool left—and, when the bartender at last noticed him, ordered scotch and honey, mulled. A pat of butter floated in it.

"That'll be three dollars," the bartender said.

"Put it on my—" Jason began and then gave up. He brought out a five.

And then he noticed her.

Seated several seats down. She had been his mistress years ago; he had not seen her in a hell of a while. But she still has a good figure, he observed, even though she's gotten a lot older. Ruth Rae. Of all people.

One thing about Ruth Rae: she was smart enough not to let her skin become too tanned. Nothing aged a woman's skin faster than tanning, and few women seemed to know it. For a woman Ruth's age—he guessed she was now thirty-eight or -nine—tanning would have turned her skin into wrinkled leather.

And, too, she dressed well. She showed off her excellent figure. If only time had avoided its constant series of appointments with her face . . . anyhow, Ruth still had beautiful black hair, all coiled in an upsweep at the back of her head. Featherplastic eyelashes, brilliant purple streaks across her cheek, as if she had been seared by psychedelic tiger claws.

Dressed in a colorful sari, barefoot—as usual she had kicked off her high-heeled shoes somewhere—and not wearing her glasses, she did not strike him as bad-looking. Ruth Rae, he mused. Sews her own clothes. Bifocals which she never wears when anyone's around . . . excluding me. Does she still read the Book-of-the-Month selection? Does she still get off reading those endless dull novels about sexual misdeeds in weird, small, but apparently normal Midwestern towns?

That was one factor about Ruth Rae: her obsession with sex. One year that he recalled she had laid sixty men, not including him: he had entered and left earlier, when the stats were not so high.

And she had always liked his music. Ruth Rae liked sexy vocalists, pop ballads and sweet—sickeningly sweet—strings. In her New York apartment at one time she had set up a huge quad system and more or less lived inside it, eating dietetic sandwiches and drinking fake frosty slime drinks made out of nothing. Listening forty-eight hours at a stretch to disc after disc by the Purple People Strings, which he abominated.

Because her general taste appalled him, it annoyed him that he himself constituted one of her favorites. It was an anomaly which he had never been able to take apart.

What else did he remember about her? Tablespoons of oily yellow fluid every morning: vitamin E. Strangely enough it did not seem to be a shuck in her case: her erotic stamina increased with each spoonful. Lust virtually leaked out of her.

And as he recalled she hated animals. This made him think about Kathy and her cat Domenico. Ruth and Kathy would never groove, he said to himself. But that doesn't matter; they'll never meet.

Sliding from his stool he carried his drink down the bar until he stood before Ruth Rae. He did not expect her to know him, but, at one time, she had found him unable to avoid . . . why wouldn't that be true now? No one was a better judge of sexual opportunity than Ruth.

"Hi," he said.

Foggily—because she did not have on her glasses—Ruth

Rae lifted her head, scrutinized him. "Hi," she rasped in her bourbon-bounded voice. "Who are you?"

Jason said, "We met a few years ago in New York. I was doing a walk-on in an episode of *The Phantom Baller* . . . as I recall it, you had charge of costumes."

"The episode," Ruth Rae rasped, "where the Phantom Baller was set upon by pirate queers from another time-period." She laughed, smiled up at him. "What's your name?" she inquired, jiggling her wire-supported exposed boobs.

"Jason Taverner," he said.

"Do you remember my name?"

"Oh yes," he said. "Ruth Rae."

"It's Ruth Gomen now," she rasped. "Sit down." She glanced around her, saw no vacant stools. "Table over there." She stepped supercarefully from her stool and careened in the direction of a vacant table; he took her arm, guided her along. Presently, after a moment of difficult navigation, he had her seated, with himself close beside her.

"You look every bit as beautiful—" he began, but she cut him off brusquely.

"I'm old," she rasped. "I'm thirty-nine."

"That's not old," Jason said. "I'm forty-two."

"It's all right for a man. Not for a woman." Blearily she stared into her half-raised martini. "Do you know what Bob does? Bob Gomen? He raises dogs. Big, loud, pushy dogs with long hair. It gets into the refrigerator." She sipped moodily at her martini; then, all at once, her face glowed with animation; she turned toward him and said, "You don't look forty-two. You look all *right!* Do you know what I think? You ought to be in TV or the movies."

Jason said cautiously, "I have been in TV. A little."

"Oh, like the *Phantom Baller Show.*" She nodded. "Well, let's face it; neither of us made it."

"I'll drink to that," he said, ironically amused; he sipped at his mulled scotch and honey. The pat of butter had melted.

"I believe I do remember you," Ruth Rae said. "Didn't you have some blueprints for a house out on the Pacific, a thousand miles away from Australia? Was that you?"

"That was me," he said, lying.

"And you drove a Rolls-Royce flyship."

"Yes," he said. That part was true.

Ruth Rae said, smiling, "Do you know what I'm doing here? Do you have any idea? I'm trying to get to see, to meet, Freddy Hydrocephalic. I'm in love with him." She laughed the throaty laugh he remembered from the old days. "I keep sending him notes reading 'I love you,' and he writes *typed* notes back saying 'I don't want to get involved; I have personal problems.'" She laughed again, and finished her drink.

"Another?" Jason said, rising.

"No." Ruth Rae shook her head. "I don't drink any more. There was a period"—she paused, her face troubled —"I wonder if anything like that has ever happened to you. I wouldn't think so, to look at you."

"What happened?"

Ruth Rae said, fooling with her empty glass, "I drank *all* the time. Starting at nine o'clock in the morning. And you know what it did for me? It made me look older. I looked fifty. Goddamn booze. Whatever you fear will happen to you, booze will make it happen. In my opinion booze is the great enemy of life. Do you agree?"

"I'm not sure," Jason said. "I think life has worse enemies than booze."

"I guess so. Like the forced-labor camps. Do you know they tried to send me to one last year? I really had a terrible time; I had no money—I hadn't met Bob Gomen yet—and I worked for a savings-and-loan company. One day a deposit *in cash* came in . . . fifty-dollar-bill stuff, three or four of them." She introspected for a time. "Anyhow, I took them and put the deposit slip and envelope into the shredder. But they caught me. Entrapment—a setup."

"Oh," he said.

"But—see, I had a thing going with my boss. The pols wanted to drag me off to a forced-labor camp—one in Georgia —where I'd be gangbanged to death by rednecks, but he protected me. I still don't know how he did it, but they let me go. I owe that man a lot, and I never see him any more. You never see the ones who really love you and help you; you're always involved with strangers."

"Do you consider me a stranger?" Jason asked. He thought to himself, I remember one more thing about you, Ruth Rae.

She always maintained an impressively expensive apartment. No matter who she happened to be married to: she always lived well.

Ruth Rae eyed him questioningly. "No. I consider you a friend."

"Thanks." Reaching, he took hold of her dry hand and held it a second, letting go at exactly the right time.

NINE

Ruth Rae's apartment appalled Jason Taverner with its luxury. It must cost her, he reasoned, at least four hundred dollars a day. Bob Gomen must be in good financial shape, he decided. Or anyhow was.

"You didn't have to buy that fifth of Vat 69," Ruth said as she took his coat, carrying it and her own to a self-opening closet. "I have Cutty Sark and Hiram Walker's bourbon—"

She had learned a great deal since he had last slept with her: it was true. Emptied, he lay naked on the blankets of the waterbed, rubbing a broken-out spot at the rim of his nose. Ruth Rae, or rather Mrs. Ruth Gomen now, sat on the carpeted floor, smoking a Pall Mall. Neither of them had spoken for some time; the room had become quiet. And, he thought, as drained as I am. Isn't there some principle of thermodynamics, he thought, that says heat can't be destroyed, it can only be transferred? But there's also entropy.

I feel the weight of entropy on me now, he decided. I have discharged myself into a vacuum, and I will never get back what I have given out. It goes only one way. Yes, he thought, I'm sure that is one of the fundamental laws of thermodynamics.

"Do you have an encyclopedia machine?" he asked the woman.

"Hell, no." Worry appeared on her prunelike face. Prunelike—he withdrew the image; it did not seem fair. Her weathered face, he decided. That was more like it.

"What are you thinking?" he asked her.

"No, you tell me what you're thinking," Ruth said. "What's

on that big alpha-consciousness-type supersecret brain of yours?"

"Do you remember a girl named Monica Buff?" Jason asked.

"'Remember' her! Monica Buff was my sister-in-law for six years. In all that time she never washed her hair once. Tangled, messy, dark-brown ooze of dog fur hanging around her pasty face and dirty short neck."

"I didn't realize you disliked her."

"Jason, she used to *steal*. If you left your purse around she'd rip you off; not just the paper scrip but all the coins as well. She had the brain of a magpie and the voice of a crow, when she talked, which thank God wasn't often. Do you know that that chick used to go six or seven—sometimes, one time in particular—eight days without saying a word? Just huddled up in a corner like a fractured spider strumming on that five-dollar guitar she owned and never learned the chords for. Okay, she did look pretty in an unkempt messy sort of way. I'll concede that. If you like gross tail."

"How'd she stay alive?" Jason asked. He had known Monica Buff only briefly, and by way of Ruth. But during that time he and she had had a short, mind-blowing affair.

"Shoplifting," Ruth Rae said. "She had that big wicker bag she got in Baja California . . . she used to stuff stuff into that and then go cruising out of the store big as life."

"Why didn't she get caught?"

"She did. They fined her and her brother came up with the bread, so there she was again, out on the street, strolling along barefoot—I mean it!—down Shrewsbury Avenue in Boston, tweaking all the peaches in the grocery-store produce sections. She used to spend ten hours a day in what she called shopping." Glaring at him, Ruth said, "You know what she did that she never got caught at?" Ruth lowered her voice. "She used to feed escaped students."

"And they never busted her for that?" Feeding or sheltering an escaped student meant two years in an FLC—the first time. The second time the sentence was five years.

"No, they never busted her. If she thought a pol team was about to run a spot check she'd quickly phone pol center and say a man was trying to break into her house. And then she'd maneuver the student outside and then lock him out, and the pols would come and there he'd be, beating on the door exactly as she said. So they'd cart him off and leave her free." Ruth chuckled. "I heard her make one of those phone calls to pol central once. The way she told it, the man—"

Jason said, "Monica was my old lady for three weeks. Five years ago, roughly."

"Did you ever see her wash her hair during that time?"

"No," he admitted.

"And she didn't wear underpants," Ruth said. "Why would a good-looking man like you want to have an affair with a dirty, stringy, mangy freak like Monica Buff? You couldn't have been able to take her anywhere; she smelled. She never bathed."

"Hebephrenia," Jason said.

"Yes." Ruth nodded. "That was the diagnosis. I don't know if you know this but finally she just wandered off, during one of her shopping trips, and never came back; we never saw her again. By now she's probably dead. Still clutching that wicker shopping bag she got in Baja. That was the big moment in her life, that trip to Mexico. She *bathed* for the occasion, and I fixed up her hair—after I washed it half a dozen times. What did you ever see in her? How could you stand her?"

Jason said, "I liked her sense of humor."

It's unfair, he thought, comparing Ruth with a nineteen-year-old girl. Or even with Monica Buff. But—the comparison remained there, in his mind. Making it impossible for him to feel attraction toward Ruth Rae. As good—as experienced, anyhow—as she was in bed.

I am using her, he thought. As Kathy used me. As McNulty used Kathy.

McNulty. Isn't there a microtrans on me somewhere?

Rapidly, Jason Taverner grabbed up his clothing, swiftly carried it to the bathroom. There, seated on the edge of the tub, he began to inspect each article.

It took him half an hour. But he did, at last, locate it. Small as it was. He flushed it down the toilet; shaken, he made his way back into the bedroom. So they know where I am after all, he realized. I can't stay here after all.

And I've jeopardized Ruth Rae's life for nothing.

*

"Wait," he said aloud.

"Yes?" Ruth said, leaning wearily against the wall of the bathroom, arms folded under her breasts.

"Microtransmitters," Jason said slowly, "only give approximate locations. Unless something actually tracks back to them locked on their signal." Until then—

He could not be sure. After all, McNulty had been waiting in Kathy's apartment. But had McNulty come there in response to the microtransmitter, or because he knew that Kathy lived there? Befuddled by too much anxiety, sex, and scotch, he could not remember; he sat on the tub edge rubbing his forehead, straining to think, to recall exactly what had been said when he and Kathy entered her room to find McNulty waiting for them.

Ed, he thought. They said that Ed planted the microtrans on me. So it did locate me. But—

Still, maybe it only told them the general area. And they assumed, correctly, that it would be Kathy's pad.

To Ruth Rae he said, his voice breaking, "God damn it, I hope I haven't got the pols oinking their asses after you; that would be too much, too goddamn much." He shook his head, trying to clear it. "Do you have any coffee that's super-hot?"

"I'll go punch the stove-console." Ruth Rae skittered barefoot, wearing only a box bangle, from the bathroom into the kitchen. A moment later she returned with a big plastic mug of coffee, marked KEEP ON TRUCKIN'. He accepted it, drank down the steaming coffee.

"I can't stay," he said, "any longer. And anyhow, you're too old."

She stared at him, ludicrously, like a warped, stomped doll. And then she ran off into the kitchen. Why did I say that? he asked himself. The pressure; my fears. He started after her.

In the kitchen doorway Ruth appeared, holding up a stoneware platter marked SOUVENIR OF KNOTTS BERRY FARM. She ran blindly at him and brought it down on his head, her mouth twisting like newborn things just now alive. At that last instant he managed to lift his left elbow and take the blow there; the stoneware platter broke into three jagged pieces, and, down his elbow, blood spurted. He gazed at the blood, the shattered pieces of platter on the carpet, then at her.

"I'm sorry," she said, whispering it faintly. Barely forming the words. The newborn snakes twisted continually, in apology.

Jason said, "I'm sorry."

"I'll put a Band-Aid on it." She started for the bathroom.

"No," he said, "I'm leaving. It's a clean cut; it won't get infected."

"Why did you say that to me?" Ruth said hoarsely.

"Because," he said, "of my own fears of age. Because they're wearing me down, what's left of me. I virtually have no energy left. Even for an orgasm."

"You did really well."

"But it was the last," he said. He made his way into the bathroom; there he washed the blood from his arm, kept cold water flowing on the gash until coagulation began. Five minutes, fifty; he could not tell. He merely stood there, holding his elbow under the faucet. Ruth Rae had gone God knew where. Probably to nark to the pols, he said wearily to himself; he was too exhausted to care.

Hell, he thought. After what I said to her I wouldn't blame her.

TEN

"No," Police General Felix Buckman said, shaking his head rigidly. "Jason Taverner does exist. He's somehow managed to get the data out of all the matrix banks." The police general pondered. "You're sure you can lay your hands on him if you have to?"

"A downer about that, Mr. Buckman," McNulty said. "He's found the microtrans and snuffed it. So we don't know if he's still in Vegas. If he has any sense he's hustled on. Which he almost certainly has."

Buckman said, "You had better come back here. If he can lift data, prime source material like that, out of our banks, he's involved in effective activity that's probably major. How precise is your fix on him?"

"He is—was—located in one apartment of eighty-five in one wing of a complex of six hundred units, all expensive and fashionable in the West Fireflash District, a place called Copperfield II."

"Better ask Vegas to go through the eighty-five units until they find him. And when you get him, have him airmailed directly to me. But I still want you at your desk. Take a couple of uppers, forget your hyped-out nap, and get down here."

"Yes, Mr. Buckman," McNulty said, with just a trace of pain. He grimaced.

"You don't think we're going to find him in Vegas," Buckman said.

"No, sir."

"Maybe we will. By snuffing the microtrans he may rationalize that he's safe, now."

"I beg to differ," McNulty said. "By finding it he'd know we had bugged him to there in West Fireflash. He'd split. Fast."

Buckman said, "He would if people acted rationally. But they don't. Or haven't you noticed that, McNulty? Mostly they function in a chaotic fashion." Which, he meditated, probably serves them in good stead . . . it makes them less predictable.

"I've noticed that—"

"Be at your desk in half an hour," Buckman said, and broke the connection. McNulty's pedantic foppery, and the fogged-up lethargy of a hype after dark, irritated him always.

Alys, observing everything, said, "A man who's unexisted himself. Has that ever happened before?"

"No," Buckman said. "And it hasn't happened this time. Somewhere, some obscure place, he's overlooked a micro-document of a minor nature. We'll keep searching until we find it. Sooner or later we'll match up a voiceprint or an EEG print and then we'll know who he really is."

"Maybe he's exactly who he says he is." Alys had been examining McNulty's grotesque notes. "Subject belongs to musicians' union. Says he's a singer. Maybe a voiceprint would be your—"

"Get out of my office," Buckman said to her.

"I'm just speculating. Maybe he recorded that new porno-chord hit, 'Go Down, Moses' that—"

"I'll tell you what," Buckman said. "Go home and look in

the study, in a glassine envelope in the center drawer of my maple desk. You'll find a lightly canceled perfectly centered copy of the one-dollar black U.S. Trans-Mississippi issue. I got it for my own collection but you can have it for yours; I'll get another. *Just go.* Go and get the damn stamp and put it away in your album in your safe forever. Don't ever even look at it again; just have it. And leave me alone at work. Is that a deal?"

"Jesus," Alys said, her eyes alive with light. "Where'd you get it?"

"From a political prisoner on his way to a forced-labor camp. He traded it for his freedom. I thought it was an equitable arrangement. Don't you?"

Alys said, "The most beautifully engraved stamp ever issued. At any time. By any country."

"Do you want it?" he said.

"Yes." She moved from the office, out into the corridor. "I'll see you tomorrow. But you don't have to give me something like that to make me go; I want to go home and take a shower and change my clothes and go to bed for a few hours. On the other hand, if you want to—"

"I want to," Buckman said, and to himself he added, Because I'm so goddamn afraid of you, so basically, ontologically scared of everything about you, even your willingness to leave. I'm even afraid of that!

Why? he asked himself as he watched her head for the secluded prison ascent tube at the far end of his suite of offices. I've known her as a child and I feared her then. Because, I think, in some fundamental way that I don't comprehend, she doesn't play by the rules. We all have rules; they differ, but we all play by them. For example, he conjectured, we don't murder a man who has just done us a favor. Even in this, a police state—even *we* observe *that* rule. And we don't deliberately destroy objects precious to us. But Alys is capable of going home, finding the one-dollar black, and setting fire to it with her cigarette. I know that and yet I gave it to her; I'm still praying that underneath or eventually or whatever she'll come back and shoot marbles the way the rest of us do.

But she never will.

He thought, And the reason I offered her the one-dollar black was because, simply, I hoped to beguile her, tempt her, into returning to rules that we can understand. Rules the rest of us can apply. I'm bribing her, and it's a waste of time—if not much much more—and I know it and she knows it. Yes, he thought. She probably will set fire to the one-dollar black, the finest stamp ever issued, a philatelic item I have never seen for sale during my lifetime. Even at auctions. And when I get home tonight she'll show me the ashes. Maybe she'll leave a corner of it unburned, to prove she really did it.

And I'll believe it. And I'll be even more afraid.

Moodily, General Buckman opened the third drawer of the large desk and placed a tape-reel in the small transport he kept there. Dowland aires for four voices . . . he stood listening to one which he enjoyed very much, among all the songs in Dowland's lute books.

> . . . For now left and forlorn
> I sit, I sigh, I weep, I faint, I die
> In deadly pain and endless misery.

The first man, Buckman mused, to write a piece of abstract music. He removed the tape, put in the lute one, and stood listening to the "Lachrimae Antiquae Pavan." From this, he said to himself, came, at last, the Beethoven final quartets. And everything else. Except for Wagner.

He detested Wagner. Wagner and those like him, such as Berlioz, had set music back three centuries. Until Karlheinz Stockhausen in his "Gesang der Jünglinge" had once more brought music up to date.

Standing by the desk, he gazed down for a moment at the recent 4-D photo of Jason Taverner—the photograph taken by Katharine Nelson. What a damn good-looking man, he thought. Almost professionally good-looking. Well, he's a singer; it fits. He's in show business.

Touching the 4-D photo, he listened to it say, "How now, brown cow?" And smiled. And, listening once more to the "Lachrimae Antiquae Pavan," thought:

> Flow, my tears . . .

Do I really have pol-karma? he asked himself. Loving words and music like this? Yes, he thought. I make a superb pol because I *don't think like a pol.* I don't, for example, think like McNulty, who will always be—what did they used to say?—a pig all his life. I think, not like the people we're trying to apprehend, but like the *important* people we're trying to apprehend. Like this man, he thought, this Jason Taverner. I have a hunch, an irrational but beautifully functional intuition, that he's still in Vegas. We will trap him *there*, and not where McNulty, thinks: rationally and logically somewhere farther on.

I am like Byron, he thought, fighting for freedom, giving up his life to fight for Greece. Except that I am not fighting for freedom; I am fighting for a coherent society.

Is that actually true? he asked himself. Is that why I do what I do? To create order, structure, harmony? Rules. Yes, he thought; rules are goddamn important to me, and that is why Alys threatens me; that's why I can cope with so much else but not with her.

Thank God they're not all like her, he said to himself. Thank God, in fact, that she's one of a kind.

Pressing a button on his desk intercom he said, "Herb, will you come in here, please?"

Herbert Maime entered the office, a stack of computer cards in his hands; he looked harried.

"You want to buy a bet, Herb?" Buckman said. "That Jason Taverner is in Las Vegas?"

"Why are you concerning yourself with such a funky little chickenshit matter?" Herb said. "It's on McNulty's level, not yours."

Seating himself, Buckman began an idle colortone game with the picphone; he flashed the flags of various extinct nations. "Look at what this man has done. Somehow he's managed to get all data pertaining to him out of every data bank on the planet *and* the lunar *and* Martian colonies . . . McNulty even tried there. Think for a minute what it would take to do that. Money? Huge sums. Bribes. Astronomical. If Taverner has used that kind of heavy bread he's playing for big stakes. Influence? Same conclusion: he's got a lot of power and we must consider him a major figure. It's who he represents that concerns me most; I think some group, somewhere on earth, is backing him, but I have no idea what for or why. All right; so they expunge all data concerning him; Jason Taverner is the man who doesn't exist. But, having done that, what have they achieved?"

Herb pondered.

"I can't make it out," Buckman said. "It has no sense to it. But, if they're interested in doing it, it must signify something. Otherwise they wouldn't expend so much"—he gestured—"whatever they've expended. Money, time, influence, whatever. Maybe all three. Plus large slabs of effort."

"I see," Herb said, nodding.

Buckman said, "Sometimes you catch big fish by hooking one small fish. That's what you never know: will the next small fish you catch be the link with something giant or"—he shrugged—"just more small fry to be tossed into the labor pool. Which, perhaps, is all Jason Taverner is. I may be completely wrong. But I'm interested."

"Which," Herb said, "is too bad for Taverner."

"Yes." Buckman nodded. "Now consider this." He paused a moment to quietly fart, then continued, "Taverner made his way to an ID forger, a run-of-the-mill forger operating behind an abandoned restaurant. He had no contacts; he worked through, for God's sake, the desk clerk at the hotel he was staying at. So he must have been desperate for ident cards. All right, where were his powerful backers then? Why couldn't they supply him with excellent forged ID cards, if they could do all this else? Good Christ; they sent him out into the street, into the urban cesspool jungle, right to a pol informant. They jeopardized everything!"

"Yes," Herb said, nodding. "Something screwed up."

"Right. *Something went wrong.* All of a sudden there he was, in the middle of the city, with no ID. Everything he had on him Kathy Nelson forged. How did that come to happen? How did they manage to fuck up and send him groping desperately for forged ID cards, so he could walk three blocks on the street? You see my point."

"But that's how we get them."

"Pardon?" Buckman said. He turned down the lute music on the tape player.

Herb said, "If they didn't make mistakes like that we wouldn't have a chance. They'd remain a metaphysical entity to us, never glimpsed or suspected. Mistakes like that are what we live on. I don't see that it's important *why* they made such a mistake; all that matters is that they did. And we should be damn glad of it."

I am, Buckman thought to himself. Leaning, he dialed McNulty's extension. No answer. McNulty wasn't back in the building yet. Buckman consulted his watch. Another fifteen or so minutes.

He dialed central clearing Blue. "What's the story on the Las Vegas operation in the Fireflash District?" he asked the chick operators who sat perched on high stools at the map board pushing little plastic representations with long cue sticks. "The netpull of the individual calling himself Jason Taverner."

A whirr and click of computers as the operator deftly punched buttons. "I'll tie you in with the captain in charge of that detail." On Buckman's pic a uniformed type appeared, looking idiotically placid. "Yes, General Buckman?"

"Have you got Taverner?"

"Not yet, sir. We've hit roughly thirty of the rental units in—"

"When you have him," Buckman said, "call me direct." He gave the nerdish pol type his extension code and rang off, feeling vaguely defeated.

"It takes time," Herb said.

"Like good beer," Buckman murmured, staring emptily ahead, his mind working. But working without results.

"You and your intuitions in the Jungian sense," Herb said. "That's what you are in the Jungian typology: an intuitive, thinking personality, with intuition your main function-mode and thinking—"

"Balls." He wadded up a page of McNulty's coarse notations and tossed it into the shredder.

"Haven't you read Jung?"

"Sure. When I got my master's at Berkeley—the whole poli sci department had to read Jung. I learned everything you learned and a lot more." He heard the irritability in his voice and disliked it. "They're probably conducting their hits like garbage collectors. Banging and clanking . . . Taverner will hear them long before they reach the apartment he's in."

"Do you think you'll net anyone with Taverner? Someone who's his higher-up in the—"

"He wouldn't be with anyone crucial. Not with his ID cards in the local precinct stationhouse. Not with us as close to him as he knows we are. I expect nothing. Nothing but Taverner himself."

Herb said, "I'll make you a bet."

"Okay."

"I'll bet you five quinques, gold ones, that when you get him you get nothing."

Startled, Buckman sat bolt upright. It sounded like his own style of intuition: no facts, no data to base it on, just pure hunch.

"Want to make the bet?" Herb said.

"I'll tell you what I'll do," Buckman said. He got out his wallet, counted the money in it. "I'll bet you one thousand paper dollars that when we net Taverner we enter one of the most important areas we've ever gotten involved with."

Herb said, "I won't bet that kind of money."

"Do you think I'm right?"

The phone buzzed; Buckman picked up the receiver. On the screen the features of the nerdish Las Vegas functionary captain formed. "Our thermo-radex shows a male of Taverner's weight and height and general body structure in one of the as yet unapproached remaining apartments. We're moving in very cautiously, getting everyone else out of the other nearby units."

"Don't kill him," Buckman said.

"Absolutely not, Mr. Buckman."

"Keep your line to me open," Buckman said. "I want to sit in on this from here on in."

"Yes, sir."

Buckman said to Herb Maime, "They've really already got him." He smiled, chuckling with delight.

ELEVEN

When Jason Taverner went to get his clothes he found Ruth Rae seated in the semi-darkness of the bedroom on the

rumpled, still-warm bed, fully dressed and smoking her customary tobacco cigarette. Gray nocturnal light filtered in
through the windows. The coal of the cigarette glowed its high,
nervous temperature.

"Those things will kill you," he said. "There's a reason why
they're rationed out one pack to a person a week."

"Fuck off," Ruth Rae said, and smoked on.

"But you get them on the black market," he said. Once he
had gone with her to buy a full carton. Even on his income the
price had appalled him. But she had not seemed to mind. Obviously she expected it; she knew the cost of her habit.

"I get them." She stubbed out the far-too-long cigarette in
a lung-shaped ceramic ashtray.

"You're wasting it."

"Did you love Monica Buff?" Ruth asked.

"Sure."

"I don't see how you could."

Jason said, "There are different kinds of love."

"Like Emily Fusselman's rabbit." She glanced up at him. "A
woman I knew, married, with three kids; she had two kittens
and then she got one of those big gray Belgian rabbits that go
lipperty lipperty lipperty on those huge hind legs. For the first
month the rabbit was afraid to come out of his cage. It was a
he, we think, as best we could tell. Then after a month he
would come out of his cage and hop around the living room.
After two months he learned to climb the stairs and scratch on
Emily's bedroom door to wake her up in the morning. He
started playing with the cats, and there the trouble began
because he wasn't as smart as a cat."

"Rabbits have smaller brains," Jason said.

Ruth Rae said, "Hard by. Anyhow, he adored the cats and
tried to do everything they did. He even learned to use the
catbox most of the time. Using tufts of hair he pulled from his
chest, he made a nest behind the couch and wanted the kittens
to get into it. But they never would. The end of it all—nearly
—came when he tried to play Gotcha with a German shepherd
that some lady brought over. You see, the rabbit learned to
play this game with the cats and with Emily Fusselman and the
children where he'd hide behind the couch and then come
running out, running very fast in circles, and everyone tried to

catch him, but they usually couldn't and then he'd run back to safety behind the couch, where no one was supposed to follow. But the dog didn't know the rules of the game and when the rabbit ran back behind the couch the dog went after him and snapped its jaws around the rabbit's rear end. Emily managed to pry the dog's jaws open and she got the dog outside, but the rabbit was badly hurt. He recovered, but after that he was terrified of dogs and ran away if he saw one even through the window. And the part of him the dog bit, he kept that part hidden behind the drapes because he had no hair there and was ashamed. But what was so touching about him was his pushing against the limits of his—what would you say?—physiology? His limitations as a rabbit, trying to become a more evolved life form, like the cats. Wanting all the time to be with them and play with them as an equal. That's all there is to it, really. The kittens wouldn't stay in the nest he built for them, and the dog didn't know the rules and got him. He lived several years. But who would have thought that a rabbit could develop such a complex personality? And when you were sitting on the couch and he wanted you to get off, so he could lie down, he'd nudge you and then if you didn't move he'd bite you. But look at the aspirations of that rabbit and look at his failing. A little life trying. And all the time it was hopeless. But the rabbit didn't know that. Or maybe he did know and kept trying anyhow. But I think he didn't understand. He just wanted to do it so badly. It was his whole life, because he loved the cats."

"I thought you didn't like animals," Jason said.

"Not any more. Not after so many defeats and wipeouts. Like the rabbit; he eventually, of course, died. Emily Fusselman cried for days. A week. I could see what it had done to her and I didn't want to get involved."

"But stopping loving animals entirely so that you—"

"Their lives are so short. Just so fucking goddamn short. Okay, some people lose a creature they love and then go on and transfer that love to another one. But it hurt; it hurts."

"Then why is love so good?" He had brooded about that, in and out of his own relationships, all his long adult life. He brooded about it acutely now. Through what had recently happened to him, up to Emily Fusselman's rabbit. This moment of painfulness. "You love someone and they leave. They come home one day and start packing their things and you say, 'What's happening?' and they say, 'I got a better offer someplace else,' and there they go, out of your life forever, and after that until you're dead you're carrying around this huge hunk of love with no one to give it to. And if you do find someone to give it to, the same thing happens all over. Or you call them up on the phone one day and say, 'This is Jason,' and they say, 'Who?' and then you know you've had it. They don't know who the hell you are. So I guess they never did know; you never had them in the first place."

Ruth said, "Love isn't just wanting another person the way you want to own an object you see in a store. That's just desire. You want to have it around, take it home and set it up somewhere in the apartment like a lamp. Love is"—she paused, reflecting—"like a father saving his children from a burning house, getting them out and dying himself. When you love you cease to live for yourself; you live for another person."

"And that's good?" It did not sound so good to him.

"It overcomes instinct. Instincts push us into fighting for survival. Like the pols ringing all the campuses. Survival of ourselves at the expense of others; each of us claws his way up. I can give you a good example. My twenty-first husband, Frank. We were married six months. During that time he stopped loving me and became horribly unhappy. *I* still loved him; I wanted to remain with him, but it was hurting him. So I let him go. You see? It was better for him, and because I loved him that's what counted. See?"

Jason said, "But why is it good to go against the instinct for self-survival?"

"You don't think I can say."

"No," he said.

"Because the instinct for survival loses in the end. With every living creature, mole, bat, human, frog. Even frogs who smoke cigars and play chess. You can never accomplish what your survival instinct sets out to do, so ultimately your striving ends in failure and you succumb to death, and that ends it. But if you love you can fade out and watch—"

"I'm not ready to fade out," Jason said.

"—you can fade out and watch with happiness, and with

cool, mellow, alpha contentment, the highest form of contentment, the living on of one of those you love."

"But they die, too."

"True." Ruth Rae chewed on her lip.

"It's better not to love so that never happens to you. Even a
pet, a dog or a cat. As you pointed out—you love them and
they perish. If the death of a rabbit is bad—" He had, then, a
glimpse of horror: the crushed bones and hair of a girl, held
and leaking blood, in the jaws of a dimly-seen enemy out-
looming any dog.

"But you can grieve," Ruth said, anxiously studying his face.
"Jason! Grief is the most powerful emotion a man or child or
animal can feel. It's a *good* feeling."

"In what fucking way?" he said harshly.

"Grief causes you to leave yourself. You step outside your
narrow little pelt. And you can't feel grief unless you've had
love before it—grief is the final outcome of love, because it's
love lost. You do understand; I know you do. But you just
don't want to think about it. It's the cycle of love completed:
to love, to lose, to feel grief, to leave, and then to love again.
Jason, grief is awareness that you will have to be alone, and
there is nothing beyond that because being alone is the ultimate final destiny of each individual living creature. That's
what death is, the great loneliness. I remember once when I
first smoked pot from a waterpipe rather than a joint. It, the
smoke, was cool, and I didn't realize how much I had inhaled.
All of a sudden I died. For a little instant, but several seconds
long. The world, every sensation, including even the awareness of my own body, of even having a body, faded out. And it
didn't like leave me in isolation in the usual sense because
when you're alone in the usual sense you still have sense data
coming in even if it's only from your own body. But even the
darkness went away. Everything just ceased. Silence. Nothing.
Alone."

"They must have soaked it in one of those toxic shit things.
That used to burn out so many people back then."

"Yes, I'm lucky I ever got my head back. A freak thing—I
had smoked pot a lot of times before and that never happened.
That's why I do tobacco, now, after that. Anyhow, it wasn't
like fainting; I didn't feel I was going to fall, because I had

nothing to fall with, no body . . . and there was no down to fall toward. Everything, including myself, just"—she gestured —"expired. Like the last drop out of a bottle. And then, presently, they rolled the film again. The big feature we call reality." She paused, puffing on her tobacco cigarette. "I never told anyone about it before."

"Were you frightened by it?"

She nodded. "Consciousness of unconsciousness, if you dig what I mean. When we do die we won't feel it because that's what dying is, the loss of all that. So, for example, I'm not at all scared of dying any more, not after that pot bad trip. But to grieve; it's to die and be alive at the same time. The most absolute, overpowering experience you can feel, therefore. Sometimes I swear we weren't constructed to go through such a thing; it's too much—your body damn near self-destructs with all that heaving and surging. But I *want* to feel grief. To have tears."

"Why?" He couldn't grasp it; to him it was something to be avoided. When you felt that you got the hell out fast.

Ruth said, "Grief reunites you with what you've lost. It's a merging; you go with the loved thing or person that's going away. In some fashion you split with yourself and accompany it, go part of the way with it on its journey. You follow it as far as you can go. I remember one time when I had this dog I loved. I was roughly seventeen or eighteen—just around the age of consent, that's how I remember. The dog got sick and we took him to the vet's. They said he had eaten rat poison and was nothing more than a sack of blood inside and the next twenty-four hours would determine if he'd survive. I went home and waited and then around eleven P.M. I crashed. The vet was going to phone me in the morning when he got there to tell me if Hank had lived through the night. I got up at eight-thirty and tried to get it all together in my head, waiting for the call. I went into the bathroom—I wanted to brush my teeth—and I saw Hank, at the bottom left part of the room; he was slowly in a very measured dignified fashion climbing invisible stairs. I watched him go upward diagonally as he trudged and then at the top right margin of the bathroom he disappeared, still climbing. He didn't look back once. I knew he had died. And then the phone rang and the vet told me that

Hank was dead. But I saw him going upward. And of course I felt terrible overwhelming grief, and as I did so, I lost myself and followed along with him, up the fucking stairs."

Both of them stayed silent for a time.

"But finally," Ruth said, clearing her throat, "the grief goes away and you phase back into this world. Without him."

"And you can accept that."

"What the hell choice is there? You cry, you continue to cry, because you don't ever completely come back from where you went with him—a fragment broken off your pulsing, pumping heart is there still. A nick out of it. A cut that never heals. And if, when it happens to you over and over again in life, too much of your heart does finally go away, then you can't feel grief any more. And then you yourself are ready to die. You'll walk up the inclined ladder and someone else will remain behind grieving for you."

"There are no cuts in my heart," Jason said.

"If you split now," Ruth said huskily, but with composure unusual for her, "that's the way it'll be for me right then and there."

"I'll stay until tomorrow," he said. It would take at least until then for the pol lab to discern the spuriousness of his ID cards.

Did Kathy save me? he wondered. Or destroy me? He really did not know. Kathy, he thought, who used me, who at nineteen knows more than you and I put together. More than we will find out in the totality of our lives, all the way to the graveyard.

Like a good encounter-group leader she had torn him down —for what? To rebuild him again, stronger than before? He doubted it. But it remained a possibility. It should not be forgotten. He felt toward Kathy a certain strange cynical trust, both absolute and unconvincing; one half of his brain saw her as reliable beyond the power of the telling of it, and the other half saw her as debased, for sale, and fucking up right and left. He could not put it together into one view. The two images of Kathy remained superimposed in his head.

Maybe I can resolve my parallel conceptions of Kathy before I leave here, he thought. Before morning. But maybe he could stay even one day after that . . . it would be stretching it, however. How good really are the police? he asked himself.

They managed to get my name wrong; they pulled the wrong file on me. Isn't it possible they'll fuck up all down the line? Maybe. But maybe not.

He had mutually opposing conceptions of the police, too. And could not resolve those either. And so, like a rabbit, like Emily Fusselman's rabbit, froze where he was. Hoping as he did so that everyone understood the rules: you do not destroy a creature that does not know what to do.

TWELVE

The four gray-wrapped pols clustered in the light of the candlelike outdoor fixture made of black iron and cone of perpetual fake flame flickering in the night dark.

"Just two left," the corporal said almost soundlessly; he let his fingers speak for him as he drew them across the rental lists. "A Mrs. Ruth Gomen in two eleven and an Allen Mufi in two twelve. Which'll we hit first?"

"The Mufi man's," one of the uniformed officers said; he smacked his plastic and shot nightstick against his fingers, eager in the dim light to finish it up, now that the end had at last come into sight.

"Two twelve it is," the corporal said, and reached to stroke the door chimes. But then it occurred to him to try the doorknob.

Good. One chance out of several, a minor possibility but suddenly, usefully true. The door was unlocked. He signaled silence, grinned briefly, then pushed the door open.

They saw into a dark living room with empty and nearly empty drink glasses placed here and there, some on the floor. And a great variety of ashtrays overfilled with crushed cigarette packages and ground-out butts.

A cigarette party, the corporal decided. Broken up, now. Everyone went home. With the exception perhaps of Mr. Mufi.

He entered, shone his light here and there, shone it at last toward the far door leading deeper into the overpriced apartment. No sound. No motion. Except the dim, distant, muted chatter of a radio talk show at minimal volume.

He trod across the wall-to-wall carpet, which depicted in gold Richard M. Nixon's final ascent into heaven amid joyous singing above and wails of misery below. At the far door he trod on God, who was smiling a lot as He received his Second Only Begotten Son back into His bosom, and pushed open the bedroom door.

In the big double bed, pulpy-soft, a man asleep, shoulders and arms bare. His clothes heaped on a handy chair. Mr. Allen Mufi, of course. Safe and home in his own private double bed. But—Mr. Mufi was not alone in his very own private bed. Involved with the pastel sheets and blankets a second indistinct shape lay curled up, asleep. Mrs. Mufi, the corporal thought, and shone his light toward her, with mannish curiosity.

All at once Allen Mufi—assuming it was he—stirred. He opened his eyes. And instantly sat bolt upright, staring fixedly at the pols. At the light of the flashlight.

"What?" he said, and he rasped with fear, a deep, convulsive release of shaking breath. "No," Mufi said, and then snatched for some object on the table beside his bed; he dove into the darkness, white and hairy and naked, for something invisible but precious to him. Desperately. He sat back up then, panting, clutching it. A pair of scissors.

"What's that for?" the corporal asked, shining the light into the metal of the scissors.

"I'll kill myself," Mufi said. "If you don't go away and— leave us alone." He stuck the closed blades of the scissors against his hair-darkened chest, near his heart.

"Then it isn't Mrs. Mufi," the corporal said. He returned the circle of light to the other, huddled up, sheet-covered shape. "A wham-bam-thank-you-ma'am one-time gangbang? Turning your foxy apartment into a motel room?" The corporal walked to the bed, took hold of the top sheet and blankets, then yanked them back.

In the bed beside Mr. Mufi lay a boy, slender, young, naked, with long golden hair.

"I'll be darned," the corporal said.

One of his men said, "I've got the scissors." He tossed them onto the floor by the corporal's right foot.

To Mr. Mufi, who sat trembling and panting, his eyes startled with terror, the corporal said, "How old is this boy?"

The boy had awakened now; he gazed fixedly up but did not stir. No expression appeared on his soft, vaguely formed face.

"Thirteen," Mr. Mufi said croakingly, almost pleadingly. "Legal age of consent."

To the boy the corporal said, "Can you prove it?" He felt intense revulsion now. Acute physical revulsion, making him want to barf. The bed was stained and damp with half-dried sweat and genital secretions.

"ID," Mufi panted. "In his wallet. In his pants on the chair."

One of the team of pols said to the corporal, "You mean if this juve's thirteen there's no crime involved?"

"Hell," another pol said indignantly. "It's obviously a crime, a perverted crime. Let's run them both in."

"Wait a minute. Okay?" The corporal found the boy's pants, rummaged, found the wallet, got it out, inspected the identification. Sure enough. Thirteen years old. He shut the wallet and put it back in the pocket. "No," he said, still half enjoying the situation, amused by Mufi's naked shame but becoming each moment more and more revolted by the man's cowardly horror at being disclosed. "The new revision of the Penal Code, 640.3, has it that twelve is the age of consent for a minor to engage in a sexual act either with another child of either sex or an adult also of either sex but with only one at a time."

"But it's goddamn sick," one of his pols protested.

"That's your opinion," Mufi said, more bravely now.

"Why isn't it a bust, a hell of a big bust?" the pols standing beside him persisted.

"They're systematically taking all victimless crimes off the books," the corporal said. "That's been the process for ten years."

"*This? This* is victimless?"

To Mufi, the corporal said, "What do you find about young boys that you like? Let me in on it; I've always wondered about scans like you."

"'Scans,'" Mufi echoed, his mouth twisting with discomfort. "So that's what I am."

"It's a category," the corporal said. "Those who prey on minors for homosexual purposes. Legal but still abhorred. What do you do during the day?"

"I'm a used-quibble salesman."

"And if they, your employers, knew you were a scan they wouldn't want you handling their quibbles. Not after what

those hairy white hands have been handling outside the workday. Right, Mr. Mufi? Even a used-quibble salesman can't get
away morally with being a scan. Even if it's no longer on the
books."

Mufi said, "It was my mother's fault. She dominated my
father, who was a weak man."

"How many little boys have you induced to go down on
you during the last twelve months?" the corporal inquired.
"I'm serious. Are these all one-night stands, is that it?"

"I love Ben," Mufi said, staring fixedly ahead, his mouth
barely moving. "Later on, when I'm better off financially and
can provide, I intend to marry him."

To the boy Ben, the corporal said, "Do you want us to take
you out of here? Return you to your parents?"

"He lives here," Mufi said, grinning a little.

"Yeah, I'll stay here," the boy said sullenly. He shivered.
"Cripes, could you give me the covers back?" He reached irritably for the top blanket.

"Just keep the noise level down in here," the corporal said,
moving away wearily. "Christ. And they took it off the books."

"Probably," Mufi said, with confidence now that the pols
were beginning to depart from his bedroom, "because some
of those big overweight old police marshals are screwing kids
themselves and don't want to get sent up. They couldn't stand
the scandal." His grin grew into an insinuating leer.

"I hope," the corporal said, "that someday you do commit a
statute violation of some kind, and they haul you in, and I'm
on duty the day it happens. So I can book you personally." He
hawked, then spat on Mr. Mufi. Spat into his hairy, empty face.

Silently, the team of pols made their way through the living
room of cigarette butts, ashes, twisted-up packs, half-filled
drink glasses, to the corridor and porchway outside. The corporal yanked the door shut, shivered, stood for a moment,
feeling the bleakness of his mind, its withdrawal, for a moment, from the environment around him. He then said, "Two
eleven. Mrs. Ruth Gomen. Where the Taverner suspect has to
be, if he's anywhere around here at all, it being the last one."
Finally, he thought.

He knocked on the front door of 211. And stood waiting
with his plastic and shot nightstick gripped at ready, terribly

and completely all at once not caring shit about his job. "We've seen Mufi," he said, half to himself. "Now let's see what Mrs. Gomen is like. You think she'll be any better? Let's hope so. I can't take much more of that tonight."

"Anything would be better," one of the pols beside him said somberly. They all nodded and shuffled about, preparing themselves for slow footsteps beyond the door.

THIRTEEN

In the living room of Ruth Rae's lavish, lovely, newly built apartment in the Fireflash District of Las Vegas, Jason Taverner said, "I'm reasonably sure I can count on forty-eight hours on the outside and twenty-four on the inside. So I feel fairly certain that I don't have to get out of here immediately." And if our revolutionary new principle is correct, he thought, then this assumption will modify the situation to my advantage. I will be safe. THE THEORY CHANGES—

"I'm glad," Ruth said wanly, "that you're able to remain here with me in a civilized way so we can rap a little longer. You want anything more to drink? Scotch and Coke, maybe?"

THE THEORY CHANGES THE REALITY IT DESCRIBES. "No," he said, and prowled about the living room, listening . . . to what he did not know. Perhaps the *absence* of sounds. No TV sets muttering, no thump of feet against the floor above their heads. Not even a pornochord somewhere, blasting out from a quad. "Are the walls fairly thick in these apartments?" he asked Ruth sharply.

"I never hear anything."

"Does anything seem strange to you? Out of the ordinary?"

"No." Ruth shook her head.

"You damn dumb floogle," he said savagely. She gaped at him in injured perplexity. "I know," he grated, "that they have me. *Now. Here.* In this room."

The doorbell bonged.

"Let's ignore it," Ruth said rapidly, stammering and afraid. "I just want to sit and rap with you, about the mellow things in life you've seen and what you want to achieve that you haven't achieved already . . ." Her voice died into silence as he went to the door. "It's probably the man from upstairs. He borrows things. Weird things. Like two fifths of an onion."

Jason opened the door. Three pols in gray uniforms filled the doorway, with weapon tubes and nightsticks aimed at him. "Mr. Taverner?" the pol with the stripes said.

"Yes."

"You are being taken into protective custody for your own protection and welfare, effective immediately, so please come with us and do not turn back or in any way remove yourself physically from contact with us. Your possessions if any will be picked up for you later and transferred to wherever you will be at the time."

"Okay," he said, and felt very little.

Behind him, Ruth Rae emitted a muffled shriek.

"You also, miss," the pol with the stripes said, motioning toward her with his nightstick.

"Can I get my coat?" she asked timidly.

"Come on." The pol stepped briskly past Jason, grabbed Ruth Rae by the arm, and dragged her out the apartment door onto the walkway.

"Do what he says," Jason said harshly to her.

Ruth sniveled, "They're going to put me in a forced-labor camp."

"No," Jason said. "They'll probably kill you."

"You're really a nice guy," one of the pols—without stripes —commented as he and his companions herded Jason and Ruth Rae down the wrought-iron staircase to the ground floor. Parked in one of the slots was a police van, with several pols standing idly around it, weapons held loosely. They looked inert and bored.

"Show me your ID," the pol with stripes said to Jason; he extended his hand, waiting.

"I've got a seven-day police pass," Jason said. His hands shaking, he fished it out, gave it to the pol officer.

Scrutinizing the pass the officer said, "You admit freely of your own volition that you are Jason Taverner?"

"Yes," he said.

Two of the pols expertly searched him for arms. He complied silently, still feeling very little. Only a half-assed hopeless wish that he had done what he knew he should have done: moved on. Left Vegas. Headed anywhere.

"Mr. Taverner," the pol officer said, "the Los Angeles Police Bureau has asked us to take you into protective custody for your own protection and welfare and to transport you safely and with due care to the Police Academy in downtown L.A., which we will now do. Do you have any complaints as to the manner in which you have been treated?"

"No," he said. "Not yet."

"Enter the rear section of the quibble van," the officer said, pointing at the open doors.

Jason did so.

Ruth Rae, stuffed in beside him, whimpered to herself in the darkness as the doors slammed shut and locked. He put his arm around her, kissed her on the forehead. "What did you do?" she whimpered raspingly in her bourbon voice, "that they're going to kill us for?"

A pol, getting into the rear of the van with them from the front cab, said, "We aren't going to snuff you, miss. We're transporting you both back to L.A. That's all. Calm down."

"I don't like Los Angeles," Ruth Rae whimpered. "I haven't been there in years. I *hate* L.A." She peered wildly around.

"So do I," the pol said as he locked the rear compartment off from the cab and dropped the key through a slot to the pols outside. "But we must learn to live with it; it's there."

"They're probably going all through my apartment," Ruth Rae whimpered. "Picking through everything, breaking everything."

"Absolutely," Jason said tonelessly. His head ached, now, and he felt nauseated. And tired. "Who are we going to be taken to?" he asked the pol. "To Inspector McNulty?"

"Most likely no," the pol said conversationally as the quibble van rose noisily into the sky. "The drinkers of intoxicating liquor have made you the subject of their songs and those sitting in the gate are concerning themselves about you, and according to them Police General Felix Buckman wants to interrogate you." He explained, "That was from Psalm Sixty-nine. I sit here by you as a Witness to Jehovah Reborn, who is in this very hour creating new heavens and a new earth, and the former things will not be called to mind, neither will they come up into the heart. Isaiah 65:13, 17."

"A police general?" Jason said, numbed.

"So they say," the obliging young Jesus-freak pol answered. "I don't know what you folks did, but you sure did it right."

Ruth Rae sobbed to herself in the darkness.

"All flesh is like grass," the Jesus-freak pol intoned. "Like low-grade roachweed most likely. Unto us a child is born, unto us a hit is given. The crooked shall be made straight and the straight loaded."

"Do you have a joint?" Jason asked him.

"No, I've run out." The Jesus-freak pol rapped on the forward metal wall. "Hey, Ralf, can you lay a joint on this brother?"

"Here." A crushed pack of Goldies appeared by way of a gray-sleeved hand and arm.

"Thanks," Jason said as he lit up. "You want one?" he asked Ruth Rae.

"I want Bob," she whimpered. "I want my husband."

Silently, Jason sat hunched over, smoking and meditating.

"Don't give up," the Jesus-freak pol crammed in beside him said, in the darkness.

"Why not?" Jason said.

"The forced-labor camps aren't that bad. In Basic Orientation they took us through one; there're showers, and beds with mattresses, and recreation such as volleyball, and arts and hobbies; you know—crafts, like making candles. By hand. And your family can send you packages and once a month they or your friends can visit you." He added, "And you get to worship at the church of your choice."

Jason said sardonically, "The church of my choice is the free, open world."

After that there was silence, except for the noisy clatter of the quibble's engine, and Ruth Rae's whimpering.

FOURTEEN

Twenty minutes later the police quibble van landed on the roof of the Los Angeles Police Academy building.

Stiffly, Jason Taverner stepped out, looked warily around, smelled smog-saturated foul air, saw above him once again the yellowness of the largest city in North America . . . he turned to help Ruth Rae out, but the friendly young Jesus-freak pol had done that already.

Around them a group of Los Angeles pols gathered, interested. They seemed relaxed, curious, and cheerful. Jason saw no malice in any of them and he thought, When they have you they are kind. It is only in netting you that they are venomous and cruel. Because then there is the possibility that you might get away. And here, now, there is no such possibility.

"Did he make any suicide tries?" a L.A. sergeant asked the Jesus-freak pol.

"No, sir."

So that was why he had ridden there.

It hadn't even occurred to Jason, and probably not to Ruth Rae either . . . except perhaps as a heavy, shucky gesture, thought of but never really considered.

"Okay," the L.A. sergeant said to the Las Vegas pol team. "From here on in we'll formally take over custody of the two suspects."

The Las Vegas pols hopped back into their van and it zoomed off into the sky, back to Nevada.

"This way," the sergeant said, with a sharp motion of his hand in the direction of the descent sphincter tube. The L.A. pols seemed to Jason a little grosser, a little tougher and older, than the Las Vegas ones. Or perhaps it was his imagination; perhaps it meant only an increase in his own fear.

What do you say to a police general? Jason wondered. Especially when all your theories and explanations about yourself have worn out, when you know nothing, believe nothing, and the rest is obscure. Aw, the hell with it, he decided wearily, and allowed himself to drop virtually weightlessly down the tube, along with the pols and Ruth Rae.

At the fourteenth floor they exited from the tube.

A man stood facing them, well dressed, with rimless glasses, a topcoat over his arm, pointed leather Oxfords, and, Jason noted, two gold-capped teeth. A man, he guessed, in his mid-fifties. A tall, gray-haired, upright man, with an expression of authentic warmth on his excellently proportioned aristocratic face. He did not look like a pol.

"You are Jason Taverner?" the man inquired. He extended his hand; reflexively, Jason accepted it and shook. To Ruth, the police general said, "You may go downstairs. I'll interview you later. Right now it's Mr. Taverner I want to talk to."

The pols led Ruth off; he could hear her complaining her way out of sight. He now found himself facing the police general and no one else. No one armed.

"I'm Felix Buckman," the police general said. He indicated the open door and hallway behind him. "Come into the office." Turning, he ushered Jason ahead of him, into a vast pastel blue-and-gray suite; Jason blinked: he had never seen this aspect of a police agency before. He had never imagined that quality like this existed.

With incredulity, Jason a moment later found himself seated in a leather-covered chair, leaning back into the softness of styroflex. Buckman, however, did not sit down behind his top-heavy, almost clumsily bulky oak desk; instead he busied himself at a closet, putting away his topcoat.

"I intended to meet you on the roof," he explained. "But the Santana wind blows like hell up there this time of night. It affects my sinus passages." He turned, then, to face Jason. "I see something about you that didn't show up in your 4-D photo. It never does. It's always a complete surprise, at least to me. You're a six, aren't you?"

Waking to full alertness, Jason half rose, said, "You're also a six, General?"

Smiling, showing his gold-capped teeth—an expensive anachronism—Felix Buckman held up seven fingers.

FIFTEEN

In his career as a police official, Felix Buckman had used this shuck each time he had come up against a six. He relied on it especially when, as with this, the encounter was sudden. There had been four of them. All, eventually, had believed him. This he found amusing. The sixes, eugenic experiments themselves, and secret ones, seemed unusually gullible when confronted with the assertion that there existed an additional project as classified as their own.

Without this shuck he would be, to a six, merely an "ordinary." He could not properly handle a six under such a disadvantage. Hence the ploy. Through it his relationship to a six inverted itself. And, under such recreated conditions, he could deal successfully with an otherwise unmanageable human being.

The actual psychological superiority over him which a six possessed was abolished by an unreal fact. He liked this very much.

Once, in an off moment, he had said to Alys, "I can outthink a six for roughly ten to fifteen minutes. But if it goes on any longer—" He had made a gesture, crumpling up a blackmarket cigarette package. With two cigarettes in it. "After that their overamped field wins out. What I need is a pry bar by which I can jack open their haughty damn minds." And, at last, he had found it.

"Why a 'seven'?" Alys had said. "As long as you're shucking them why not say eight or thirty-eight?"

"The sin of vainglory. Reaching too far." He had not wanted to make that legendary mistake. "I will tell them," he had told her grimly, "what I think they'll believe." And, in the end, he had proved out right.

"They won't believe you," Alys had said.

"Oh, hell, will they!" he had retorted. "It's their secret fear, their bête noire. They're the sixth in a line of DNA reconstruction systems and they know that if it could be done to them it could be done to others in a more advanced degree."

Alys, uninterested, had said faintly, "You should be an announcer on TV selling soap." And that constituted the totality of her reaction. If Alys did not give a damn about something, that something, for her, ceased to exist. Probably she should not have gotten away with it for as long as she had . . . but sometime, he had often thought, the retribution will come: *reality denied comes back to haunt*. To overtake the person without warning and make him insane.

And Alys, he had a number of times thought, was in some odd sense, in some unusual clinical way, pathological.

He sensed it but could not pin it down. However, many of his hunches were like that. It did not bother him, as much as he loved her. He knew he was right.

Now, facing Jason Taverner, a six, he developed his shuck ploy.

"There were very few of us," Buckman said, now seating himself at his oversize oak desk. "Only four in all. One is already dead, so that leaves three. I don't have the slightest idea where they are; we retain even less contact among ourselves than do you sixes. Which is little enough."

"Who was your muter?" Jason asked.

"Dill-Temko. Same as yours. He controlled groups five through seven and then he retired. As you certainly know he's dead now."

"Yes," Jason said. "It shocked us all."

"Us, too," Buckman said, in his most somber voice. "Dill-Temko was our parent. Our *only* parent. Did you know that at the time of his death he had begun to prepare schema on an eighth group?"

"What would they have been like?"

"Only Dill-Temko knew," Buckman said, and felt his superiority over the six facing him grow. And yet—how fragile his psychological edge. One wrong statement, one statement too much, and it would vanish. Once lost, he would never regain it.

It was the risk he took. But he enjoyed it; he had always liked betting against the odds, gambling in the dark. He had in him, at times like this, a great sense of his own ability. And he did not consider it imagined . . . despite what a six that knew him to be an ordinary would say. That did not bother him one bit.

Touching a button, he said, "Peggy, bring us a pot of coffee, cream and the rest. Thanks." He then leaned back with studied leisure. And surveyed Jason Taverner.

Anyone who had met a six would recognize Taverner. The strong torso, the massive conformation of his arms and back. His powerful, ramlike head. But most ordinaries had never knowingly come up against a six. They did not have his experience. Nor his carefully synthesized knowledge of them.

To Alys he had once said, "They will never take over and run *my* world."

"You don't have a world. You have an office."

At that point he terminated the discussion.

"Mr. Taverner," he said bluntly, "how have you managed to get documents, cards, microfilm, even complete files out of data banks all over the planet? I've tried to imagine how it could be done, but I come up with a blank." He fixed his attention on the handsome—but aging—face of the six and waited.

SIXTEEN

What can I tell him? Jason Taverner asked himself as he sat mutely facing the police general. The total reality as I know it? That is hard to do, he realized, because I really do not comprehend it myself.

But perhaps a seven could—well, God knew what it could do. I'll opt, he decided, on a complete explanation.

But when he started to answer, something blocked his speech. *I don't want to tell him anything*, he realized. There is no theoretical limit to what he can do to me; he has his generalship, his authority, and if he's a seven . . . for him, the sky may be the limit. At least for my self-preservation if for nothing else I ought to operate on that assumption.

"Your being a six," Buckman said, after an interval of silence, "makes me see this in a different light. It's other sixes that you're working with, is it?" He kept his eyes rigidly fixed on Jason's face; Jason found it uncomfortable and disconcerting. "I think what we have here," Buckman said, "is the first concrete evidence that sixes are—"

"No," Jason said.

"'No'?" Buckman continued to stare fixedly at him. "You're not involved with other sixes in this?"

Jason said, "I know one other six. Heather Hart. And she considers me a twerp fan." He ground out the words bitterly.

That interested Buckman; he had not been aware that the well-known singer Heather Hart was a six. But, thinking about it, it seemed reasonable. He had never, however, come up against a female six in his career; his contacts with them were just not that frequent.

"If Miss Hart is a six," Buckman said aloud, "maybe we

should ask her to come in too and consult with us." A police euphemism that rolled easily off his tongue.

"Do that," Jason said. "Put her through the wringer." His tone had become savage. "Bust her. Put her in a forced-labor camp."

You sixes, Buckman said to himself, have little loyalty to one another. He had discovered this already, but it always surprised him. An elite group, bred out of aristocratic prior circles to set and maintain the mores of the world, who had in practice drizzled off into nothingness because they could not stand one another. To himself he laughed, letting his face show, at least, a smile.

"You're amused?" Jason said. "Don't you believe me?"

"It doesn't matter." Buckman brought a box of Cuesta Rey cigars from a drawer of his desk, used his little knife to cut off the end of one. The little steel knife made for that purpose alone.

Across from him Jason Taverner watched with fascination.

"A cigar?" Buckman inquired. He held the box toward Jason.

"I have never smoked a good cigar," Jason said. "If it got out that I—" He broke off.

"'Got out'?" Buckman asked, his mental ears pricking up. "Got out to whom? The police?"

Jason said nothing. But he had clenched his fist and his breathing had become labored.

"Are there strata in which you're well known?" Buckman said. "For example, among intellectuals in forced-labor camps. You know—the ones who circulate mimeographed manuscripts."

"No," Jason said.

"Musical strata, then?"

Jason said tightly, "Not any more."

"Have you ever made phonograph records?"

"Not here."

Buckman continued to scrutinize him unblinkingly; over long years he had mastered the ability. "Then where?" he asked, in a voice barely over the threshold of audibility. A voice deliberately sought for: its tone lulled, interfered with identification of the words' meaning.

But Jason Taverner let it slide by; he failed to respond. These damn bastard sixes, Buckman thought, angered—mostly at himself. *I can't play funky games with a six.* It just plain does not work. And, at any minute, he could cancel my statement out of his mind, my claim to superior genetic heritage.

He pressed a stud on his intercom. "Have a Miss Katharine Nelson brought in here," he instructed Herb Maime. "A police informant down in the Watts District, that ex-black area. I think I should talk to her."

"Half hour."

"Thanks."

Jason Taverner said hoarsely, "Why bring her into this?"

"She forged your papers."

"All she knows about me is what I had her put on the ID cards."

"And that was spurious?"

After a pause Jason shook his head no.

"So you do exist."

"Not—here."

"Where?"

"I don't know."

"Tell me how you got those data deleted from all the banks."

"I never did that."

Hearing that, Buckman felt an enormous hunch overwhelm him; it gripped him with paws of iron. "You haven't been taking material out of the data banks; you've been trying to put material in. *There were no data there in the first place.*"

Finally, Jason Taverner nodded.

"Okay," Buckman said; he felt the glow of discovery lurking inside him, now, revealing itself in a cluster of comprehensions. "You took nothing out. But there's some reason why the data weren't there in the first place. Why not? Do you know?"

"I know," Jason Taverner said, staring down at the table; his face had twisted into a gross mirror-thing. "I don't exist."

"But you once did."

"Yes," Taverner said, nodding unwillingly. Painfully.

"Where?"

"I don't know!"

It always comes back to that, Buckman said to himself. I

don't know. Well, Buckman thought, maybe he doesn't. But he did make his way from L.A. to Vegas; he did shack up with that skinny, wrinkled broad the Vegas pols loaded into the van with him. Maybe, he thought, I can get something from her. But his hunch registered a no.

"Have you had dinner?" Buckman inquired.

"Yes," Jason Taverner said.

"But you'll join me in the munchies. I'll have them bring something in to us." Once more he made use of the intercom. "Peggy—it's so late now . . . get us two breakfasts at that new place down the street. Not the one we used to go to, but the new one with the sign showing the dog with the girl's head. Barfy's."

"Yes, Mr. Buckman," Peggy said and rang off.

"Why don't they call you 'General'?" Jason Taverner asked.

Buckman said, "When they call me 'General' I feel I ought to have written a book on how to invade France while staying out of a two-front war."

"So you're just plain 'Mister.'"

"That's right."

"And they let you do it?"

"For me," Buckman said, "there is no 'they.' Except for five police marshals here and there in the world, and they call themselves 'Mister,' too." And how they would like to demote me further, he thought. Because of all that I did.

"But there's the Director."

Buckman said, "The Director has never seen me. He never will. Nor will he see you either, Mr. Taverner. But nobody can see you, because, as you pointed out, you don't exist."

Presently a gray uniformed pol woman entered the office, carrying a tray of food. "What you usually order this time of night," she said as she set the tray down on Buckman's desk. "One short stack of hots with a side order of ham; one short stack of hots with a side order of sausage."

"Which would you like?" Buckman asked Jason Taverner.

"Is the sausage well cooked?" Jason Taverner asked, peering to see. "I guess it is. I'll take it."

"That's ten dollars and one gold quinque," the pol woman said. "Which of you is going to pay for it?"

Buckman dug into his pockets, fished out the bills and

change. "Thanks." The woman departed. "Do you have any children?" he asked Taverner.

"No."

"I have a child," General Buckman said. "I'll show you a little 3-D pic of him that I received." He reached into his desk, brought out a palpitating square of three-dimensional but nonmoving colors. Accepting the picture, Jason held it properly in the light, saw outlined statically a young boy in shorts and sweater, barefoot, running across a field, tugging on the string of a kite. Like the police general, the boy had light short hair and a strong and impressive wide jaw. Already.

"Nice," Jason said. He returned the pic.

Buckman said, "He never got the kite off the ground. Too young, perhaps. Or afraid. Our little boy has a lot of anxiety. I think because he sees so little of me and his mother; he's at a school in Florida and we're here, which is not a good thing. You say you have no children?"

"Not that I know of," Jason said.

"'Not that you know of'?" Buckman raised an eyebrow. "Does that mean you don't go into the matter? You've never tried to find out? By law, you know, you as the father are required to support your children in or out of wedlock."

Jason nodded.

"Well," General Buckman said, as he put the pic away in his desk, "everyone to his own. But consider what you've left out of your life. Haven't you ever loved a child? It hurts your heart, the innermost part of you, where you can easily die."

"I didn't know that," Jason said.

"Oh, yes. My wife says you can forget any kind of love except what you've felt toward children. That only goes one way; it never reverts. And if something comes between you and a child—such as death or a terrible calamity such as a divorce—you never recover."

"Well, hell, then"—Jason gestured with a forkful of sausage —"then it would be better not to feel that kind of love."

"I don't agree," Buckman said. "You should always love, and especially a child, because that's the strongest form of love."

"I see," Jason said.

"No, you don't see. Sixes never see; they don't understand.

It's not worth discussing." He shuffled a pile of papers on his desk, scowling, puzzled, and nettled. But gradually he calmed down, became his cool assured self once more. But he could not understand Jason Taverner's attitude. But he, his child, was all-important; it, plus his love of course for the boy's mother—this was the pivot of his life.

They ate for a time without speaking, with, suddenly, no bridge connecting them one to the other.

"There's a cafeteria in the building," Buckman said at last, as he drank down a glass of imitation Tang. "But the food there is poisoned. All the help must have relatives in forced-labor camps. They're getting back at us." He laughed. Jason Taverner did not. "Mr. Taverner," Buckman said, dabbing at his mouth with his napkin, "I am going to let you go. I'm not holding you."

Staring at him, Jason said, "Why?"

"Because you haven't done anything."

Jason said hoarsely, "Getting forged ID cards. A felony."

"I have the authority to cancel any felony charge I wish," Buckman said. "I consider that you were forced into doing that by some situation you found yourself in, a situation which you refuse to tell me about, but of which I have gotten a slight glimpse."

After a pause Jason said, "Thanks."

"But," Buckman said, "you will be electronically monitored wherever you go. You will never be alone except for your own thoughts in your own mind and perhaps not even there. Everyone you contact or reach or see will be brought in for questioning eventually . . . just as we're bringing in the Nelson girl right now." He leaned toward Jason Taverner, speaking slowly and intently so that Taverner would listen and understand. "I believe you took no data from any data banks, public or private. I believe you don't understand your own sit-uation. But"—he let his voice rise perceptibly—"sooner or later you will understand your situation and when that hap-pens we want to be in on it. So—we will always be with you. Fair enough?"

Jason Taverner rose to his feet. "Do all you sevens think this way?"

"What way?"

"Making strong, vital, instant decisions. The way you do. The way you ask questions, listen—God, how you listen!—and then make up your mind absolutely."

Truthfully, Buckman said, "I don't know because I have so little contact with other sevens."

"Thanks," Jason said. He held out his hand; they shook. "Thanks for the meal." He seemed calm now. In control of himself. And very much relieved. "Do I just wander out of here? How do I get onto the street?"

"We'll have to hold you until morning," Buckman said. "It's a fixed policy; suspects are never released at night. Too much goes on in the streets after dark. We'll provide you a cot and a room; you'll have to sleep in your clothes . . . and at eight o'clock tomorrow morning I'll have Peggy escort you to the main entrance of the academy." Pressing the stud on his intercom, Buckman said, "Peg, take Mr. Taverner to detention for now; take him out again at eight A.M. sharp. Understood?"

"Yes, Mr. Buckman."

Spreading his hands, smiling, General Buckman said, "So that's it. There is no more."

SEVENTEEN

"Mr. Taverner," Peggy was saying insistently. "Come along with me; put your clothes on and follow me to the outside office. I'll meet you there. Just go through the blue-and-white doors."

Standing off to one side, General Buckman listened to the girl's voice; pretty and fresh, it sounded good to him, and he guessed that it sounded that way to Taverner, too.

"One more thing," Buckman said, stopping the sloppily dressed, sleepy Taverner as he started to make his way toward the blue-and-white doors. "I can't renew your police pass if someone down the line voids it. Do you understand? What you've got to do is apply to us, exactly following legal lines, for a total set of ID cards. It'll mean intensive interrogation, but"—he thumped Jason Taverner on the arm—"a six can take it."

"Okay," Jason Taverner said. He left the office, closing the blue-and-white doors behind him.

Into his intercom Buckman said, "Herb, make sure they put both a microtrans and a heterostatic class eighty warhead on him. So we can follow him and if it's necessary at any time we can destroy him."

"You want a voice tap, too?" Herb said.

"Yes, if you can get it onto his throat without him noticing."

"I'll have Peg do it," Herb said, and signed off.

Could a Mutt and Jeff, say, between me and McNulty, have brought any more information out? he asked himself. No, he decided. Because the man himself simply doesn't know. What we must do is wait for him to figure it out . . . and be there with him, either physically or electronically, when it happens. As in fact I pointed out to him.

But it still strikes me, he realized, that we very well may have blundered onto something the sixes are doing as a group—despite their usual mutual animosity.

Again pressing the button of his intercom he said, "Herb, have a twenty-four-hour surveillance put on that pop singer Heather Hart or whatever she calls herself. And get from Data Central the files of all what they call 'sixes.' You understand?"

"Are the cards punched for that?" Herb said.

"Probably not," Buckman said drearily. "Probably nobody thought to do it ten years ago when Dill-Temko was alive, thinking up more and weirder life forms to shamble about." Like us sevens, he thought wryly. "And they certainly wouldn't think of it these days, now that the sixes have failed politically. Do you agree?"

"I agree," Herb said, "but I'll try for it anyhow."

Buckman said, "If the cards *are* punched for that, I want a twenty-four-hour surveillance on all sixes. And even if we can't roust them all out we can at least put tails on the ones we know."

"Will do, Mr. Buckman." Herb clicked off.

EIGHTEEN

"Goodbye and good luck, Mr. Taverner," the pol chick named Peg said to him at the wide entrance to the great gray academy building.

"Thanks," Jason said. He inhaled a deep sum of morning

air, smog-infested as it was. I got out, he said to himself. They could have hung a thousand busts on me but they didn't.

A female voice, very throaty, said from close by, "How now, little man?"

Never in his life had he been called "little man"; he stood over six feet tall. Turning, he started to say something in answer, then made out the creature who had addressed him.

She too stood a full six feet in height; they matched in that department. But in contrast to him she wore tight black pants, a leather shirt, red, with tassel fringes, gold hooped earrings, and a belt made of chain. And spike heeled shoes. Jesus Christ, he thought, appalled. Where's her whip?

"Were you talking to me?" he said.

"Yes." She smiled, showing teeth ornamented with gold signs of the zodiac. "They put three items on you before you got out of there; I thought you ought to know."

"I know," Jason said, wondering who or what she was.

"One of them," the girl said, "is a miniaturized H-bomb. It can be detonated by a radio signal emitted from this building. Did you know about that?"

Presently he said, "No. I didn't."

"It's the way he works things," the girl said. "My brother . . . he raps mellow and nice to you, civilizedly, and then he has one of his staff—he has a huge staff—plant that garbage on you before you can walk out the door of the building."

"Your brother," Jason said. "General Buckman." He could see, now, the resemblance between them. The thin, elongated nose, the high cheekbones, the neck, like a Modigliani, tapered beautifully. Very patrician, he thought. They, both of them, impressed him.

So she must be a seven, too, he said to himself. He felt himself become wary, again; the hackles on his neck burned as he confronted her.

"I'll get them off you," she said, still smiling, like General Buckman, a gold-toothed smile.

"Good enough," Jason said.

"Come over to my quibble." She started off lithely; he loped clumsily after her.

A moment later they sat together in the front bucket seats of her quibble.

"Alys is my name," she said.

He said, "I'm Jason Taverner, the singer and TV personality."

"Oh, really? I haven't watched a TV program since I was nine."

"You haven't missed much," he said. He did not know if he meant it ironically; frankly, he thought, I'm too tired to care.

"This little bomb is the size of a seed," Alys said. "And it's embedded, like a tick, in your skin. Normally, even if you knew it was there someplace on you, you still could never find it. But I borrowed this from the academy." She held up a tubelike light. "This glows when you get it near a seed bomb." She began at once, efficiently and nearly professionally, to move the light across his body.

At his left wrist the light glowed.

"I also have the kit they use to remove a seed bomb," Alys said. From her mailpouch purse she brought a shallow tin, which she at once opened. "The sooner it's cut out of you the better," she said, as she lifted a cutting tool from the kit.

For two minutes she cut expertly, meanwhile spraying an analgesic compound on the wound. And then—it lay in her hand. As she had said, the size of a seed.

"Thanks," he said. "For removing the thorn from my paw."

Alys laughed gaily; she replaced the cutting tool in the kit, shut the lid, returned it to her huge purse. "You see," she said, "he never does it himself; it's always one of his staff. So he can remain ethical and aloof, as if it has nothing to do with him. I think I hate that the most about him." She pondered. "I really hate him."

"Is there anything else you can cut or tear off me?" Jason inquired.

"They tried—Peg, who is a police technician expert at it, tried—to stick a voice tap on your gullet. But I don't think she got it to stick." Cautiously, she explored his neck. "No, it didn't catch; it fell off. Fine. That takes care of that. You do have a microtrans on you somewhere; we'll need a strobe light to pick up its flux." She fished in the glove compartment of the quibble and came up with a battery-operated strobe disc. "I think I can find it," she said, setting the strobe light into activity.

The microtrans turned out to be in residence in the cuff of his left sleeve. Alys pushed a pin through it, and that was that.

"Is there anything else?" Jason asked her.

"Possibly a minicam. A very small camera transmitting a TV image back to academy monitors. But I didn't see them wind one into you; I think we can take a chance and forget that." She turned, then, to scrutinize him. "Who are you?" she asked. "By the way."

Jason said, "An unperson."

"Meaning what?"

"Meaning that I don't exist."

"Physically?"

"I don't know," he said, truthfully. Maybe, he thought, if I had been more open with her brother the police general . . . maybe he could have worked it out. After all, Felix Buckman was a seven. Whatever that meant.

But still—Buckman had probed in the right direction; he had brought out a good deal. And in a very short time—a period punctuated by a late-night breakfast and a cigar.

The girl said, "So you're Jason Taverner. The man McNulty was trying to pin down and couldn't. The man with no data on him anywhere in the world. No birth certificate; no school records; no—"

"How is it you know all this?" Jason said.

"I looked over McNulty's report." Her tone was blithe. "In Felix's office. It interested me."

"Then why did you ask me who I am?"

Alys said, "I wondered if you knew. I had heard from McNulty; this time I wanted your side of it. The antipol side, as they call it."

"I can't add anything to what McNulty knows," Jason said.

"That's not true." She had begun to interrogate him now, precisely in the manner her brother had a short time ago. A low, informal tone of voice, as if something merely casual were being discussed, then the intense focus on his face, the graceful motions of her arms and hands, as if, while talking to him, she danced a little. With herself. Beauty dancing on beauty, he thought; he found her physically, sexually exciting. And he had had enough of sex, God knew, for the next several days.

"Okay," he conceded. "I know more."

"More than you told Felix?"

He hesitated. And, in doing so, answered.

"Yes," Alys said.

He shrugged. It had become obvious.

"Tell you what," Alys said briskly. "Would you like to see how a police general lives? His home? His billion-dollar castle?"

"You'd let me in there?" he said, incredulous. "If he found out—" He paused. Where is this woman leading me? he asked himself. Into terrible danger; everything in him sensed it, became at once wary and alert. He felt his own cunning course through him, infusing every part of his somatic being. His body knew that here, more than at any other time, he had to be careful. "You have legal access to his home?" he said, calming himself; he made his voice natural, devoid of any unusual tension.

"Hell," Alys said, "I live with him. We're twins; we're very close. Incestuously close."

Jason said, "I don't want to walk into a setup hammered out between you and General Buckman."

"A setup between Felix and me?" She laughed sharply. "Felix and I couldn't collaborate in painting Easter eggs. Come on; let's shoot over to the house. Between us we have a good deal of interesting objects. Medieval wooden chess sets, old bone-china cups from England. Some beautiful early U.S. stamps printed by the National Banknote Company. Do stamps interest you?"

"No," he said.

"Guns?"

He hesitated. "To some extent." He remembered his own gun; this was the second time in twenty-four hours that he had had reason to remember it.

Eying him, Alys said, "You know, for a small man you're not bad-looking. And you're older than I like . . . but not much so. You're a six, aren't you?"

He nodded.

"Well?" Alys said. "Do you want to see a police general's castle?"

Jason said, "Okay." They would find him wherever he went, whenever they wanted him. With or without a microtrans pinned on his cuff.

*

Turning on the engine of her quibble, Alys Buckman spun the wheel, pressed down on the pedal; the quibble shot up at a ninety-degree angle to the street. A police engine, he realized. Twice the horsepower of domestic models.

"There is one thing," Alys said as she steered through traffic, "that I want you to get clear in your mind." She glanced over at him to be sure he was listening. "Don't make any sexual advances toward me. If you do I'll kill you." She tapped her belt and he saw, tucked within it, a police-model weapon tube; it glinted blue and black in the morning sun.

"Noticed and attended to," he said, and felt uneasy. He already did not like the leather and iron costume she wore; fetishistic qualities were profoundly involved, and he had never cared for them. And now this ultimatum. Where was her head sexually? With other lesbians? Was that it?

In answer to his unspoken question, Alys said calmly, "All my libido, my sexuality, is tied up with Felix."

"Your *brother*?" He felt cold, frightened incredulity. "How?"

"We've lived an incestuous relationship for five years," Alys said, adroitly maneuvering her quibble in the heavy morning Los Angeles traffic. "We have a child, three years old. He's kept by a housekeeper and nurse down in Key West, Florida. Barney is his name."

"And you're telling me this?" he said, amazed beyond belief. "Someone you don't even know?"

"Oh, I know you very well, Jason Taverner," Alys said; she lifted the quibble up into a higher lane, increased velocity. The traffic, now, had thinned; they were leaving greater L.A. "I've been a fan of yours, of your Tuesday night TV show, for years. And I have records of yours, and once I heard you sing live at the Orchid Room at the Hotel St. Francis in San Francisco." She smiled briefly at him. "Felix and I, we're both collectors . . . and one of the things I collect is Jason Taverner records." Her darting, frenetic smile increased. "Over the years I've collected all nine."

Jason said huskily, his voice shaking, "Ten. I've put out ten LPs. The last few with light-show projection tracks."

"Then I missed one," Alys said, agreeably. "Here. Turn around and look in the back seat."

Twisting about, he saw in the rear seat his earliest album:

Taverner and the Blue, Blue Blues. "Yes," he said, seizing it and bringing it forward onto his lap.

"There's another one there," Alys said. "My favorite out of all of them."

He saw, then, a dog-eared copy of *There'll Be a Good Time with Taverner Tonight.* "Yes," he said. "That's the best one I ever did."

"You see?" Alys said. The quibble dipped now, spiraling down in a helical pattern toward a cluster of large estates, tree- and grass-surrounded, below. "Here's the house."

NINETEEN

Its blades vertical now, the quibble sank to an asphalt spot in the center of the great lawn of the house. Jason barely noticed the house: three story, Spanish style with black iron railings on the balconies, red-tile roof, adobe or stucco walls; he could not tell. A large house, with beautiful oak trees surrounding it; the house had been built into the landscape without destroying it. The house blended and seemed a part of the trees and grass, an extension into the realm of the man-made.

Alys shut off the quibble, kicked open a balky door. "Leave the records in the car and come along," she said to him as she slid from the quibble and upright, onto the lawn.

Reluctantly, he placed the record albums back on the seat and followed her, hurrying to catch up with her; the girl's long black-sheathed legs carried her rapidly toward the huge front gate of the house.

"We even have pieces of broken glass bottles embedded in the top of the walls. To repel bandits . . . in this day and age. The house once belonged to the great Ernie Till, the Western actor." She pressed a button mounted on the front gate before the house and there appeared a brown-uniformed private pol, who scrutinized her, nodded, released the power surge that slid the gate aside.

To Alys, Jason said, "What do you know? You know I'm—"

"You're fabulous," Alys said matter-of-factly. "I've known it for years."

"But you've been where I was. Where I always am. Not here."

Taking his arm, Alys guided him down an adobe-and-slate corridor and then down a flight of five brick steps, into a sunken living room, an ancient place in this day, but beautiful.

He did not, however, give a damn; he wanted to talk to her, to find out what and how she knew. And what it signified.

"Do you remember this place?" Alys said.

"No," he said.

"You should. You've been here before."

"I haven't," he said, guardedly; she had thoroughly trapped his credulity by producing the two records. *I've got to have them,* he said to himself. To show to—yes, he thought; to whom? To General Buckman? And if I do show him, what will it get me?

"A cap of mescaline?" Alys said, going to a drug case, a large hand-oiled walnut cabinet at the end of the leather and brass bar on the far side of the living room.

"A little," he said. But then his response surprised him; he blinked. "I want to keep my head clear," he amended.

She brought him a tiny enameled drug tray on which rested a crystal tumbler of water and a white capsule. "Very good stuff. Harvey's Yellow Number One, imported from Switzerland in bulk, capsuled on Bond Street." She added, "And not strong at all. Color stuff."

"Thanks." He accepted the glass and the white capsule; he drank the mescaline down, placed the glass back on the tray. "Aren't you having any?" he asked her, feeling—belatedly—wary.

"I'm already spaced," Alys said genially, smiling her gold baroque tooth smile. "Can't you tell? I guess not; you've never seen me any other way."

"Did you know I'd be brought to the L.A. Police Academy?" he asked. You must have, he thought, *because you had the two records of mine with you.* Had you not known, the chances of your having them alone are zero out of a billion, virtually.

"I monitored some of their transmissions," Alys said; turning, she roamed restlessly off, tapping on the small enameled tray with one long fingernail. "I happened to pick up the official traffic between Vegas and Felix. I like to listen to him now and then during the time he's on duty. Not always, but"—she pointed toward a room beyond an open corridor at the near side—"I want to look at something; I'll show it to you, if it's as good as Felix said."

He followed, the buzz of questions in his mind dinning at him as he walked. If she can get across, he thought, go back and forth, as she seems to have done—

"He said the center drawer of his maple desk," Alys said reflectively as she stood in the center of the house's library; leather-bound books rose up in cases mounted to the high ceiling of the chamber. Several desks, a glass case of tiny cups, various early chess sets, two ancient Tarot card decks . . . Alys wandered over to a New England desk, opened a drawer, peered within. "Ah," she said, and brought out a glassine envelope.

"Alys—" Jason began, but she cut him off with a brusque snap of her fingers.

"Be quiet while I look at this." From the surface of the desk she took a large magnifying glass; she scrutinized the envelope. "A stamp," she explained, then, glancing up. "I'll take it out so you can look at it." Finding a pair of philatelic tongs she carefully drew the stamp from its envelope and set it down on the felt pad at the front edge of the desk.

Obediently, Jason peeped through the magnifying lens at the stamp. It seemed to him a stamp like any other stamp, except that unlike modern stamps it had been printed in only one color.

"Look at the engraving on the animals," Alys said. "The herd of steer. It's absolutely perfect; every line is exact. This stamp has never been—" She stopped his hand as he started to touch the stamp. "Oh no," she said. "Don't ever touch a stamp with your fingers; always use tongs."

"Is it valuable?" he asked.

"Not really. But they're almost never sold. I'll explain it to you someday. This is a present to me from Felix, because he loves me. Because, he says, I'm good in bed."

"It's a nice stamp," Jason said, disconcerted. He handed the magnifying glass back to her.

"Felix told me the truth; it's a good copy. Perfectly centered, light cancellation that doesn't mar the center picture, and—" Deftly, with the tongs, she flipped the stamp over on its back, allowed it to lie on the felt pad face down. All at once her expression changed; her face glowed hotly and she said, "That motherfucker."

"What's the matter?" he said.

"A thin spot." She touched a corner of the stamp's back side with the tongs. "Well, you can't tell from the front. But that's Felix. Hell, it's probably counterfeit anyhow. Except that Felix always somehow manages not to buy counterfeits, Okay, Felix; that's one for you." Thoughtfully, she said, "I wonder if he's got another one in his own collection. I could switch them." Going to a wall safe, she twiddled for a time with the dials, opened the safe at last, and brought out a huge and heavy album, which she lugged to the desk. "Felix," she said, "does not know I know the combination to that safe. So don't tell him." She cautiously turned heavy-gauge pages, came to one on which four stamps rested. "No one-dollar black," she said. "But he may have hidden it elsewhere. He may even have it down at the academy." Closing the album, she restored it to the wall safe.

"The mescaline," Jason said, "is beginning to affect me." His legs ached: for him that was always a sign that mescaline was beginning to act in his system. "I'll sit down," he said, and managed to locate a leather-covered easy chair before his legs gave way. Or *seemed* to give way; actually they never did: it was a drug-instigated illusion. But all the same it felt real.

"Would you like to see a collection of chaste and ornate snuffboxes?" Alys inquired. "Felix has a terribly fine collection. All antiques, in gold, silver, alloys, with cameo engravings, hunting scenes—no?" She seated herself opposite him, crossed her long, black-sheathed legs; her high-heeled shoe dangled as she swung it back and forth. "One time Felix bought an old snuffbox at an auction, paid a lot for it, brought it home. He cleaned the old snuff out of it and found a spring-operated lever mounted at the bottom of the box, or what seemed to be the bottom. The lever operated when you screwed down a tiny screw. It took him all day to find a tool small enough to rotate the screw. But at least he got it." She laughed.

"What happened?" Jason said.

"The bottom of the box—a false bottom with a tin plate concealed in it. He got the plate out." She laughed again, her gold tooth ornamentation sparkling. "It turned out to be a two-hundred-year-old dirty picture. Of a chick copulating with a Shetland pony. Tinted, too, in eight colors. Worth, oh, say, five thousand dollars—not much, but it genuinely delighted us. The dealer, of course, didn't know it was there."

"I see," Jason said.

"You don't have any interest in snuffboxes," Alys said, still smiling.

"I'd like—to see it," he said. And then he said, "Alys, you know about me; you know who I am. *Why doesn't anybody else know?*"

"Because they've never been there."

"*Where?*"

Alys massaged her temples, twisted her tongue, stared blankly ahead, as if lost in thought. As if barely hearing him. "You know," she said, sounding bored and a little irritable. "Christ, man, you lived there forty-two years. What can I tell you about that place that you don't already know?" She glanced up, then, her heavy lips curling mischievously; she grinned at him.

"How did I get here?" he said.

"You—" She hesitated. "I'm not sure I should tell you."

Loudly, he said, "*Why not?*"

"Let it come in time." She made a damping motion with her hand. "In time, in time. Look, man; you've already been hit by a lot; you almost got shipped to a labor camp, and you know what kind, today. Thanks to that asshole McNulty and my dear brother. My brother the police general." Her face had become ugly with revulsion, but then she smiled her provocative smile once again. Her lazy, gold-toothed, inviting smile.

Jason said, "I want to know where I am."

"You're in my study in my house. You're perfectly safe; we got all the insects off you. And no one's going to break in here. Do you know what?" She sprang from her chair, bounding to her feet like a superlithe animal; involuntarily he drew back. "Have you ever made it by phone?" she demanded, bright-eyed and eager.

"Made what?"

"The grid," Alys said. "Don't you know about the phone grid?"

"No," he admitted. But he had heard of it.

"Your—everybody's—sexual aspects are linked electronically, and amplified, to as much as you can endure. It's addictive, because it's electronically enhanced. People, some of them, get so deep into it they can't pull out; their whole lives revolve around the weekly—or, hell, even daily!—setting up of the network of phone lines. It's regular picturephones, which you activate by credit card, so it's free at the time you do it; the sponsors bill you once a month and if you don't pay they cut your phone out of the grid."

"How many people," he asked, "are involved in this?"

"Thousands."

"At one time?"

Alys nodded. "Most of them have been doing it two, three years. And they've deteriorated physically—and mentally—from it. Because the part of the brain where the orgasm is experienced is gradually burned out. But don't put down the people; some of the finest and most sensitive minds on earth are involved. For them it's a sacred, holy communion. Except you can spot a gridder when you see one; they look debauched, old, fat, listless—the latter always *between* the phone-line orgies, of course."

"And you do this?" She did not look debauched, old, fat or listless to him.

"Now and then. But I never get hooked; I cut myself out of the grid just in time. Do you want to try it?"

"No," he said.

"Okay," Alys said reasonably, undaunted. "What would you like to do? We have a good collection of Rilke and Brecht in interlinear translation discs. The other day Felix came home with a quad-and-light set of all seven Sibelius symphonies; it's very good. For dinner Emma is preparing frog's legs . . . Felix loves both frog's legs and escargot. He eats out in good French and Basque restaurants most of the time but tonight—"

"I want to know," Jason interrupted, "where I am."

"Can't you simply be happy?"

He rose to his feet—with difficulty—and confronted her. Silently.

TWENTY

The mescaline had furiously begun to affect him; the room grew lit up with colors, and the perspective factor altered so that the ceiling seemed a million miles high. And, gazing at Alys, he saw her hair come alive . . . like Medusa's, he thought, and felt fear.

Ignoring him, Alys continued, "Felix especially likes Basque cuisine, but they cook with so much butter that it gives him pyloric spasms. He also has a good collection of *Weird Tales*, and he loves baseball. And—let's see." She wandered off, a finger tapping against her lips as she reflected. "He's interested in the occult. Do you—"

"I feel something," Jason said.

"What do you feel?"

Jason said, "I can't get away."

"It's the mes. Take it easy."

"I—" He pondered; a giant weight lay on his brain, but all throughout the weight streaks of light, of satori-like insight, shot here and there.

"What I collect," Alys said, "is in the next room, what we call the library. This is the study. In the library Felix has all his law books . . . did you know he's a lawyer, as well as a police general? And he has done some good things; I have to admit it. Do you know what he did once?"

He could not answer; he could only stand. Inert, hearing the sounds but not the meaning. Of it.

"For a year Felix was legally in charge of one fourth of Terra's forced-labor camps. He discovered that by virtue of an obscure law passed years ago when the forced-labor camps were more like death camps—with a lot of blacks in them— anyhow, he discovered that this statute permitted the camps to operate only during the Second Civil War. And he had the power to close any and all camps at any time he felt it to be in the public interest. And those blacks and the students who'd been working in the camps are damn tough and strong, from years of heavy manual labor. They're not like the effete, pale, clammy students living beneath the campus areas. And then he researched and discovered another obscure statute. Any camp that isn't operating at a profit *has* to be—or rather had to be—closed. So Felix changed the amount of money—very little, of course—paid to the detainees. So all he had to do was jack up their pay, show red ink in the books, and bam; he could shut down the camps." She laughed.

He tried to speak but couldn't. Inside him his mind churned like a tattered rubber ball, sinking and rising, slowing down, speeding up, fading and then flaring brilliantly; the shafts of light scampered all through him, piercing every part of his body.

"But the big thing Felix did," Alys said, "had to do with the student kibbutzim under the burned-out campuses. A lot of them are desperate for food and water; you know how it is: the students try to make it into town, foraging for supplies, ripping off and looting. Well, the police maintain a lot of agents among the students agitating for a final shootout with the police . . . which the police and nats are hopefully waiting for. Do you see?"

"I see," he said, "a hat."

"But Felix tried to keep off any sort of shootout. But to do it he had to get supplies to the students; do you see?"

"The hat is red," Jason said. "Like your ears."

"Because of his position as marshal in the pol hierarchy, Felix had access to informant reports as to the condition of each student kibbutz. He knew which ones were failing and which were making it. It was his job to boil out of the horde of abstracts the ultimately important facts: which kibbutzim were going under and which were not. Once he had listed those in trouble, other high police officers met with him to decide how to apply pressure which would hasten the end. Defeatist agitation by police finks, sabotage of food and water supplies. Desperate—actually hopeless—forays out of the campus area in search of help—for instance, at Columbia one time they had a plan of getting to the Harry S Truman Labor Camp and liberating the detainees and arming them, but at that even Felix had to say 'Intervene!' But anyhow it was Felix's job to determine the tactic for each kibbutz under scrutiny. Many, many times he advised no action at all. For this, of course, the hardhats criticized him, demanded his removal from his position." Alys paused. "He was a full police marshal, then, you have to realize."

"Your red," Jason said, "is fantidulous."

"I know." Alys's lips turned down. "Can't you hold your hit, man? I'm trying to tell you something. Felix got *demoted*, from police marshal to police general, because he saw to it, when he could, that in the kibbutzim the students were bathed, fed, their medical supplies looked after, cots provided. Like he did for the forced-labor camps under his jurisdiction. So now he's just a general. But they leave him alone. They've done all they can to him for now and he still holds a high office."

"But your incest," Jason said. "What if?" He paused; he could not remember the rest of his sentence. "If," he said, and that seemed to be it; he felt a furious glow, arising from the fact that he had managed to convey his message to her. "If," he said again, and the inner glow became wild with happy fury. He exclaimed aloud.

"You mean what if the marshals knew that Felix and I have a son? What would they do?"

"They would do," Jason said. "Can we hear some music? Or give me—" His words ceased; none more entered his brain. "Gee," he said. "My mother wouldn't be here. Death."

Alys inhaled deeply, sighed. "Okay, Jason," she said. "I'll give up trying to rap with you. Until your head is back."

"Talk," he said.

"Would you like to see my bondage cartoons?"

"What," he said, "that's?"

"Drawings, very stylized, of chicks tied up, and men—"

"Can I lie down?" he said. "My legs won't work. I think my right leg extends to the moon. In other words"—he considered—"I broke it standing up."

"Come here." She led him, step by step, from the study and back into the living room. "Lie down on the couch," she told him. With agonizing difficulty he did so. "I'll go get you some Thorazine; it'll counteract the mes."

"This is a mess," he said.

"Let's see . . . where the hell did I put that? I rarely if ever have to use it, but I keep it in case something like this . . . God damn it, can't you drop a single cap of mes and *be* something? I take five at once."

"But you're vast," Jason said.

"I'll be back; I'm going upstairs." Alys strode off, toward a door located several distances away; for a long, long time he watched her dwindle—how did she accomplish it? It seemed incredible that she could shrink down to almost nothing—and then she vanished. He felt, at that, terrible fear. He knew that he had become alone, without help. Who will help me? he asked himself. I have to get away from these stamps and cups and snuffboxes and bondage cartoons and phone grids and frog's legs I've got to get to that quibble I've got to fly away and back to where I know back in town maybe with Ruth Rae if they've let her go or even back to Kathy Nelson this woman is too much for me so is her brother them and their incest child in Florida named what?

He rose unsteadily, groped his way across a rug that sprang a million leaks of pure pigment as he trod on it, crushing it with his ponderous shoes, and then, at last, he stumbled against the front door of the unsteady room.

Sunlight. He had gotten outside.

The quibble.

He hobbled to it.

Inside he sat at the controls, bewildered by legions of knobs, levers, wheels, pedals, dials. "Why doesn't it go?" he said aloud. "Get going!" he told it, rocking back and forth in the driver's seat. "Won't she let me go?" he asked the quibble.

The keys. Of course he couldn't fly it no keys.

Her coat in the back seat; he had witnessed it. And also her large mailpouch purse. There, the keys in her purse. There.

The two record albums. *Taverner and the Blue, Blue Blues.* And the best of them all: *There'll Be a Good Time.* He groped, managed somehow to lift *both* record albums up, conveyed them to the empty seat beside him. I have the proof here, he realized. It's here in these records and it's here in the house. With her. I've got to find it here if I'm going to. Find it. Nowhere else. Even General Mr. Felix What-Is-He-Named? he won't find it. He doesn't know. As much as me.

Carrying the enormous record albums he ran back to the house—around him the landscape flowed, with whip, tall, tree-like organisms gulping in air out of the sweet blue sky, organisms which absorbed water and light, ate the hue into the sky . . . he reached the gate, pushed against it. The gate did not budge. Button.

He found no.

Step by step. Feel each inch with fingers. Like in the dark. Yes, he thought, I'm in darkness. He set down the much-too-big record albums, stood against the wall beside the gate, slowly massaged the rubberlike surface of the wall. Nothing. Nothing.

The button.

He pressed it, grabbed up the record albums, stood in front of the gate as it incredibly slowly creaked its noisy protesting way open.

A brown-uniformed man carrying a gun appeared. Jason said, "I had to go back to the quibble for something."

"Perfectly all right, sir," the man in the brown uniform said. "I saw you leave and I knew you'd be back."

"Is she insane?" Jason asked him.

"I'm not in a position to know, sir," the man in the brown uniform said, and he backed away, touching his visored cap.

The front door of the house hung open as he had left it. He scrambled through, descended brick steps, found himself once more in the radically irregular living room with its million-mile-high ceiling. "Alys!" he said. Was she in the room? He carefully looked in all directions; as he had done when searching for the button he phased his way through every visible inch of the room. The bar at the far end with the handsome walnut drug cabinet . . . couch, chairs. Pictures on the walls. A face in one of the pictures jeered at him but he did not care; it could not leave the wall. The quad phonograph. . . .

His records. Play them.

He lifted at the lid of the phonograph but it wouldn't open. Why? he asked. Locked? No, it slid out. He slid it out, with a terrible noise, as if he had destroyed it. Tone arm. Spindle. He got one of his records out of its sleeve and placed it on the spindle. I can work these things, he said, and turned on the amplifiers, setting the mode to *phono*. Switch that activated the changer. He twisted it. The tone arm lifted; the turntable began to spin, agonizingly slowly. What was the matter with it? Wrong speed? No; he checked. Thirty-three and a third. The mechanism of the spindle heaved and the record dropped.

Loud noise of the needle hitting the lead-in groove. Crackles of dust, clicks. Typical of old quad records. Easily misused and damaged; all you had to do was breathe on them.

Background hiss. More crackles.

No music.

Lifting the tone arm, he set it farther in. Great roaring crash as the stylus struck the surface; he winced, sought the volume control to turn it down. Still no music. No sound of himself singing.

The strength the mescaline had over him began now to waver; he felt coldly, keenly sober. The other record. Swiftly he got it from its jacket and sleeve, placed it on the spindle, rejected the first record.

Sound of the needle touching plastic surface. Background hiss and the inevitable crackles and clicks. Still no music.

The records were blank.

Part Three

Never may my woes be relieved,
Since pity is fled;
And tears and sighs and groans my weary days
Of all joys have deprived.

TWENTY-ONE

"ALYS!" Jason Taverner called loudly. No answer. Is it the mescaline? he asked himself. He made his way clumsily from the phonograph toward the door through which Alys had gone. A long hallway, deep-pile wool carpet. At the far end stairs with a black iron railing, leading up to the second floor.

He strode as quickly as possible up the hall, to the stairs, and then, step by step, up the stairs.

The second floor. A foyer, with an antique Hepplewhite table off to one side, piled high with *Box* magazines. That, weirdly, caught his attention; who, Felix or Alys, or both, read a low-class mass-circulation pornographic magazine like *Box*? He passed on then, still—because of the mescaline, certainly—seeing small details. The bathroom; that was where he would find her.

"Alys," he said grimly; perspiration trickled from his forehead down his nose and cheeks; his armpits had become steamy and damp with the emotions cascading through his body. "God damn it," he said, speaking to her although he could not see her. "There's no music on those records, no me. They're fakes. Aren't they?" Or is it the mescaline? he asked himself. "I've got to know!" he said. "Make them play if they're okay. Is the phonograph broken, is that it? Needle point or stylus or whatever you call them broken off?" It happens, he thought. Maybe it's riding on the tops of the grooves.

A half-open door; he pushed it wide. A bedroom, with the bed unmade. And on the floor a mattress with a sleeping bag thrown onto it. A little pile of men's supplies: shaving cream, deodorant, razor, aftershave, comb . . . a guest, he thought, here before but now gone.

"Is anybody here?" he yelled.

Silence.

Ahead he saw the bathroom; past the partially opened door he caught sight of an amazingly old tub on painted lion's legs. An antique, he thought, even down to their bathtub. He loped haltingly down the hall, past other doors, to the bathroom; reaching it, he pushed the door aside.

And saw, on the floor, a skeleton.

It wore black shiny pants, leather shirt, chain belt with wrought-iron buckle. The foot bones had cast aside the high-heeled shoes. A few tufts of hair clung to the skull, but outside of that, there remained nothing: the eyes had gone, all the flesh had gone. And the skeleton itself had become yellow.

"God," Jason said, swaying; he felt his vision fail and his sense of gravity shift: his middle ear fluctuated in its pressures so that the room caromed around him, silently in perpetual ball motion. Like a pourout of Ferris wheel at a child's circus.

He shut his eyes, hung on to the wall, then, finally, looked again.

She has died, he thought. But when? A hundred thousand years ago? A few minutes ago?

Why has she died? he asked himself.

Is it the mescaline? That I took? *Is this real?*

It's real.

Bending, he touched the leather fringed shirt. The leather felt soft and smooth; it hadn't decayed. Time hadn't touched her clothing; that meant something but he did not comprehend what. Just her, he thought. Everything else in this house is the same as it was. So it can't be the mescaline affecting me. But I can't be sure, he thought.

Downstairs. Get out of here.

He loped erratically back down the hall, still in the process of scrambling to his feet, so that he ran bent over like an ape of some unusual kind. He seized the black iron railing, descended two, three steps at once, stumbled and fell, caught himself and hauled himself back up to a standing position. In his chest his heart labored, and his lungs, overtaxed, inflated and emptied like a bellows.

In an instant he had sped across the living room to the front door—then, for reasons obscure to him but somehow important, he snatched up the two records from the phonograph, stuffed them into their jackets, carried them with him through the front door of the house, out into the bright warm sun of midday.

"Leaving, sir?" the brown-uniformed private cop asked, noticing him standing there, his chest heaving.

"I'm sick," Jason said.

"Sorry to hear that, sir. Can I get you anything?"

"The keys to the quibble."

"Miss Buckman usually leaves the keys in the ignition," the cop said.

"I looked," Jason said, panting.

The cop said, "I'll go ask Miss Buckman for you."

"No," Jason said, and then thought, But if it's the mescaline it's okay. Isn't it?

"'No'?" the cop said, and all at once his expression changed. "Stay where you are," he said. "Don't head toward that quibble." Spinning, he dashed into the house.

Jason sprinted across the grass, to the asphalt square and the parked quibble. The keys; were they in the ignition? No. Her purse. He seized it and dumped everything out on the seats. A thousand objects, but no keys. And then, crushing him, a hoarse scream.

At the front gate of the house the cop appeared, his face distorted. He stood sideways, reflexively, lifted his gun, held it with both hands, and fired at Jason. But the gun wavered; the cop was trembling too badly.

Crawling out of the far side of the quibble, Jason lurched across the thick moist lawn, toward the nearby oak trees.

Again the cop fired. Again he missed. Jason heard him curse; the cop started to run toward him, trying to get closer to him; then all at once the cop spun and sped back into the house.

Jason reached the trees. He crashed through dry underbrush, limbs of bushes snapping as he forced his way through. A high adobe wall . . . and what had Alys said? Broken bottles cemented on top? He crawled along the base of the wall, fighting the thick underbrush, then abruptly found himself facing a broken wooden door; it hung partially open, and beyond it he saw other houses and a street.

It was not the mescaline, he realized. The cop saw it, too.

Her lying there. The ancient skeleton. As if dead all these years.

On the far side of the street a woman, with an armload of packages, was unlocking the door of her flipflap.

Jason made his way across the street, forcing his mind to work, forcing the dregs of the mescaline away. "Miss," he said, gasping.

Startled, the woman looked up. Young, heavy-set, but with beautiful auburn hair. "Yes?" she said nervously, surveying him.

"I've been given a toxic dose of some drug," Jason said, trying to keep his voice steady. "Will you drive me to a hospital?"

Silence. She continued to stare at him wide-eyed; he said nothing—he merely stood panting, waiting. Yes or no; it had to be one or the other.

The heavy-set girl with the auburn hair said, "I—I'm not a very good driver. I just got my license last week."

"I'll drive," Jason said.

"But I won't come along." She backed away, clutching her armload of badly-wrapped brown-paper parcels. Probably she had been on her way to the post office.

"Can I have the keys?" he said; he extended his hand. Waited.

"But you might pass out and then my flipflap—"

"Come with me then," he said.

She handed him the keys and crept into the rear seat of the flipflap. Jason, his heart pulsing with relief, got in behind the wheel, stuck the key into the ignition, turned the motor on, and, in a moment, sent the flipflap flipflapping up into the sky, at its maximum speed of forty knots an hour. It was, he noted for some odd reason, a very inexpensive model flipflap: a Ford Greyhound. An economy flipflap. And not new.

"Are you in great pain?" the girl asked anxiously; her face, in his rear-view mirror, still showed nervousness, even panic. The situation was too much for her.

"No," he said.

"What was the drug?"

"They didn't say." The mescaline had virtually worn off,

now; thank God his six physiology had the strength to combat it: he did not relish the idea of piloting a slow-moving flipflap through the midday Los Angeles traffic while on a hit of mescaline. And, he thought savagely, a big hit. Despite what she said.

She. Alys. Why are the records blank? he asked silently. The records—where were they? He peered about, stricken. Oh. On the seat beside him; automatically he had thrust them in as he himself got into the flipflap. So they're okay. I can try to play them again on another phonograph.

"The nearest hospital," the heavy-set girl said, "is St. Martin's at Thirty-fifth and Webster. It's small, but I went there to have a wart removed from my hand, and they seemed very conscientious and kind."

"We'll go there," Jason said.

"Are you feeling worse or better?"

"Better," he said.

"Did you come from the Buckmans' house?"

"Yes." He nodded.

The girl said, "Is it true that they're brother and sister, Mr. and Mrs. Buckman? I mean—"

"Twins," he said.

"I understand that," the girl said. "But you know, it's strange; when you see them together it's as if they're husband and wife. They kiss and hold hands, and he's very deferential to her and then sometimes they have terrible fights." The girl remained silent a moment and then leaning forward said, "My name is Mary Anne Dominic. What is your name?"

"Jason Taverner," he informed her. Not that it meant anything. After all. After what had seemed for a moment—but then the girl's voice broke into his thoughts.

"I'm a potter," she said shyly. "These are pots I'm taking to the post office to mail to stores in northern California, especially to Gump's in San Francisco and Frazer's in Berkeley."

"Do you do good work?" he asked; almost all of his mind, his faculties, remained fixed in time, fixed at the instant he had opened the bathroom door and seen her—it—on the floor. He barely heard Miss Dominic's voice.

"I try to. But you never know. Anyhow, they sell."

"You have strong hands," he said, for want of anything better to say; his words still emerged semireflexively, as if he were uttering them with only a fragment of his mind.

"Thank you," Mary Anne Dominic said.

Silence.

"You passed the hospital," Mary Anne Dominic said. "It's back a little way and to the left." Her original anxiety had now crawled back into her voice. "Are you really going there or is this some—"

"Don't be scared," he said, and this time he paid attention to what he said; he used all his ability to make his tone kind and reassuring. "I'm not an escaped student. Nor am I an escapee from a forced-labor camp." He turned his head and looked directly into her face. "But I am in trouble."

"Then you didn't take a toxic drug." Her voice wavered. It was as if that which she had most feared throughout her whole life had finally overtaken her.

"I'll land us," he said. "To make you feel safer. This is far enough for me. Please don't freak; I won't hurt you." But the girl sat rigid and stricken, waiting for—well, neither of them knew.

At an intersection, a busy one, he landed at the curb, quickly opened the door. But then, on impulse, he remained within the flipflap for a moment, turned still in the girl's direction.

"Please get out," she quavered. "I don't mean to be impolite, but I'm really scared. You hear about hunger-crazed students who somehow get through the barricades around the campuses—"

"Listen to me," he said sharply, breaking into her flow of speech.

"Okay." She composed herself, hands on her lapful of packages, dutifully—and fearfully—waiting.

Jason said, "You shouldn't be frightened so easily. Or life is going to be too much for you."

"I see." She nodded humbly, listening, paying attention as if she were at a college classroom lecture.

"Are you always afraid of strangers?" he asked her.

"I guess so." Again she nodded; this time she hung her head as if he had admonished her. And in a fashion he had.

"Fear," Jason said, "can make you do more wrong than hate

or jealousy. If you're afraid you don't commit yourself to life completely; fear makes you always, always hold something back."

"I think I know what you mean," Mary Anne Dominic said. "One day about a year ago there was this dreadful pounding on my door, and I ran into the bathroom and locked myself in and pretended I wasn't there, because I thought somebody was trying to break in . . . and then later I found out that the woman upstairs had got her hand caught in the drain of her sink—she has one of those Disposall things—and a knife had gotten down into it and she reached her hand down to get it and got caught. And it was her little boy at the door—"

"So you do understand what I mean," Jason interrupted.

"Yes. I wish I wasn't that way. I really do. But I still am."

Jason said, "How old are you?"

"Thirty-two."

That surprised him; she seemed much younger. Evidently she had not ever really grown up. He felt sympathy for her; how hard it must have been for her to let him take over her flipflap. And her fears had been correct in one respect: he had not been asking for help for the reason he claimed.

He said to her, "You're a very nice person."

"Thank you," she said dutifully. Humbly.

"See that coffee shop over there?" he said, pointing to a modern, well-patronized cafe. "Let's go over there. I want to talk to you." I have to talk to someone, anyone, he thought, or six or not I am going to lose my mind.

"But," she protested anxiously, "I have to get my packages into the post office before two so they'll get the midafternoon pickup for the Bay Area."

"We'll do that first, then," he said. Reaching for the ignition switch, he pulled out the key, handed it back to Mary Anne Dominic. "You drive. As slowly as you want."

"Mr.—Taverner," she said. "I just want to be let alone."

"No," he said. "You shouldn't be alone. It's killing you; it's undermining you. All the time, every day, you should be somewhere with people."

Silence. And then Mary Anne said, "The post office is at Forty-ninth and Fulton. Could you drive? I'm sort of nervous."

It seemed to him a great moral victory; he felt pleased. He

took back the key, and, shortly, they were on their way to Forty-ninth and Fulton.

TWENTY-TWO

Later, they sat in a booth at a coffee shop, a clean and attractive place with young waitresses and a reasonably loose patronage. The jukebox drummed out Louis Panda's "Memory of Your Nose." Jason ordered coffee only; Miss Dominic had a fruit salad and iced tea.

"What are those two records you're carrying?" she asked.

He handed them to her.

"Why, they're by you. If you're Jason Taverner. Are you?"

"Yes." He was certain of that, at least.

"I don't think I've ever heard you sing," Mary Anne Dominic said. "I'd love to, but I don't usually like pop music; I like those great old-time folk singers out of the past, like Buffy St. Marie. There's nobody now who could sing like Buffy."

"I agree," he said somberly, his mind still returning to the house, the bathroom, the escape from the frantic brown-uniformed private cop. *It wasn't the mescaline*, he told himself once again. Because the cop saw it, too.

Or saw *something*.

"Maybe he didn't see what I saw," he said aloud. "Maybe he just saw her lying there. Maybe she fell. Maybe—" He thought, Maybe I should go back.

"Who didn't see what?" Mary Anne Dominic asked, and then flushed bright scarlet. "I didn't mean to poke into your life; you said you're in trouble and I can see you have something weighty and heavy on your mind that's obsessing you."

"I have to be sure," he said, "what actually happened. Everything is there in that house." And on these records, he thought.

Alys Buckman knew about my TV program. She knew about my records. She knew which one was the big hit; she owned it. But—

There had been no music on the records. Broken stylus, hell—some kind of sound, distorted perhaps, should have come out. He had handled records too long and phonographs too long not to know that.

"You're a moody person," Mary Anne Dominic said. From her small cloth purse she had brought a pair of glasses; she now laboriously read the bio material on the back of the record jackets.

"What's happened to me," Jason said briefly, "has made me moody."

"It says here that you have a TV program."

"Right." He nodded. "At nine on Tuesday night. On NBC."

"Then you're really famous. I'm sitting here talking to a famous person that I ought to know about. How does it make you feel—I mean, my not recognizing who you are when you told me your name?"

He shrugged. And felt ironically amused.

"Would the jukebox have any songs by you?" She pointed to the multicolored Babylonian Gothic structure in the far corner.

"Maybe," he said. It was a good question.

"I'll go look." Miss Dominic fished a half quinque from her pocket, slid from the booth, and crossed the coffee shop to stare down at the titles and artists of the jukebox's listing.

When she gets back she is going to be less impressed by me, Jason mused. He knew the effect of one ellipsis: unless he manifested himself everywhere, from every radio and phonograph, jukebox and sheet-music shop, TV screen, in the universe, the magic spell collapsed.

She returned smiling. "'Nowhere Nuthin' Fuck-up,'" she said, reseating herself. He saw then that the half quinque was gone. "It should play next."

Instantly he was on his feet and across the coffee shop to the jukebox.

She was right. Selection B4. His most recent hit, "Nowhere Nuthin' Fuck-up," a sentimental number. And already the mechanism of the jukebox had begun to process the disc.

A moment later his voice, mellowed by quad sound points and echo chambers, filled the coffee shop.

Dazed, he returned to the booth.

"You sound superwonderful," Mary Anne said, politely, perhaps, given her taste, when the disc had ended.

"Thanks." It had been him, all right. The grooves on *that* record hadn't been blank.

"You're really far out," Mary Anne said enthusiastically, all smiles and twinkly glasses.

Jason said simply, "I've been at it a long time." She had sounded as if she meant it.

"Do you feel bad that I hadn't heard of you?"

"No." He shook his head, still dazed. Certainly she was not alone in that, as the events of the past two days—two days? had it only been that?—had shown.

"Can—I order something more?" Mary Anne asked. She hesitated. "I spent all my money on stamps; I—"

"I'm picking up the tab," Jason said.

"How do you think the strawberry cheesecake would be?"

"Outstanding," he said, momentarily amused by her. The woman's earnestness, her anxieties . . . does she have any boy friends of any kind? he wondered. Probably not . . . she lived in a world of pots, clay, brown wrapping paper, troubles with her little old Ford Greyhound, and, in the background, the stereo-only voices of the old-time greats: Judy Collins and Joan Baez.

"Ever listened to Heather Hart?" he asked. Gently.

Her forehead wrinkled. "I—don't recall for sure. Is she a folk singer or—" Her voice trailed off; she looked sad. As if she sensed that she was failing to be what she ought to be, failing to know what every reasonable person knew. He felt sympathy for her.

"Ballads," Jason said. "Like what I do."

"Could we hear your record again?"

He obligingly returned to the jukebox, scheduled it for replay.

This time Mary Anne did not seem to enjoy it.

"What's the matter?" he asked.

"Oh," she said, "I always tell myself I'm creative; I make pots and like that. But I don't know if they're actually any good. I don't know how to tell. People say to me—"

"People tell you everything. From that you're worthless to priceless. The worst and the best. You're always reaching somebody here"—he tapped the salt shaker—"and not reaching somebody there." He tapped her fruit-salad bowl.

"But there has to be some way—"

"There are experts. You can listen to them, to their theories.

They always have theories. They write long articles and discuss your stuff back to the first record you cut nineteen years ago. They compare recordings you don't even remember having cut. And the TV critics—"

"But to be noticed." Again, briefly, her eyes shone.

"I'm sorry," he said, rising to his feet once more. He could wait no longer. "I have to make a phone call. Hopefully I'll be right back. If I'm not"—he put his hand on her shoulder, on her knitted white sweater, which she had probably made herself—"it's been nice meeting you."

Puzzled, she watched him in her wan, obedient way as he elbowed a path to the back of the crowded coffee shop, to the phone booth.

Shut up inside the phone booth, he read off the number of the Los Angeles Police Academy from the emergency listings and, after dropping in his coin, dialed.

"I'd like to speak to Police General Felix Buckman," he said, and, without surprise, heard his voice shake. Psychologically I've had it, he realized. Everything that's happened . . . up to the record on the jukebox—it's too goddamn much for me. I am just plain scared. And disoriented. So maybe, he thought, the mescaline has not worn completely off after all. But I did drive the little flipflap okay; that indicates something. Fucking dope, he thought. You can always tell when it hits you but never when it unhits, if it ever does. It impairs you forever or you think so; you can't be sure. Maybe it never leaves. And they say, Hey, man, your brain's burned out, and you say, Maybe so. You can't be sure and you can't not be sure. And all because you dropped a cap or one cap too many that somebody said, Hey this'll get you off.

"This is Miss Beason," a female voice sounded in his ear. "Mr. Buckman's assistant. May I help you?"

"Peggy Beason," he said. He took a deep, unsteady breath and said, "This is Jason Taverner."

"Oh yes, Mr. Taverner. What did you want? Did you leave anything behind?"

Jason said, "I want to talk to General Buckman."

"I'm afraid Mr. Buckman—"

"It has to do with Alys," Jason said.

Silence. And then: "Just a moment please, Mr. Taverner,"

Peggy Beason said. "I'll ring Mr. Buckman and see if he can free himself a moment."

Clicks. Pause. More silence. Then a line opened.

"Mr. Taverner?" It was not General Buckman. "This is Herbert Maime, Mr. Buckman's chief of staff. I understand you told Miss Beason that it has to do with Mr. Buckman's sister, Miss Alys Buckman. Frankly I'd like to ask just what are the circumstances under which you happen to know Miss—"

Jason hung up the phone. And walked sightlessly back to the booth, where Mary Anne Dominic sat eating her strawberry cheesecake.

"You did come back after all," she said cheerfully.

"How," he said, "is the cheesecake?"

"A little too rich." She added, "But good."

He grimly reseated himself. Well, he had done his best to get through to Felix Buckman. To tell him about Alys. But—what would he have been able to say, after all? The futility of everything, the perpetual impotence of his efforts and intentions . . . weakened even more, he thought, by what she gave me, that cap of mescaline.

If it had been mescaline.

That presented a new possibility. He had no proof, no evidence, that Alys had actually given him mescaline. It could have been anything. What, for example, was mescaline doing coming from Switzerland? That made no sense; that sounded synthetic, not organic: a product of a lab. Maybe a new multi-ingredient cultish drug. Or something stolen from police labs.

The record of "Nowhere Nuthin' Fuck-up." Suppose the drug had made him hear it. And see the listing on the jukebox. But Mary Anne Dominic had heard it, too; in fact she had discovered it.

But the two blank records. What about them?

As he sat pondering, an adolescent boy in a T-shirt and jeans bent over him and mumbled, "Hey, you're Jason Taverner, aren't you?" He extended a ballpoint pen and piece of paper. "Could I have your autograph, sir?"

Behind him a pretty little red-haired teenybopper, braless, in white shorts, smiled excitedly and said, "We always catch you on Tuesday night. You're fantastic. And you look in real life, you look just like on the screen, except that in real life you're more, you know, tanned." Her friendly nipples jiggled.

Numbly, by habit, he signed his name. "Thanks, guys," he said to them; there were four of them in all now.

Chattering to themselves, the four kids departed. Now people in nearby booths were watching Jason and muttering interestedly to one another. As always, he said to himself. This is how it's been up to the other day. *My reality is leaking back.* He felt uncontrollably, wildly elated. This was what he knew; this was his life-style. He had lost it for a short time but now— finally, he thought, I'm starting to get it back!

Heather Hart. He thought, I can call her now. And get through to her. She won't think I'm a twerp fan.

Maybe I only exist so long as I take the drug. That drug, whatever it is, that Alys gave me.

Then my career, he thought, the whole twenty years, is nothing but a retroactive hallucination created by the drug.

What happened, Jason Taverner thought, *is that the drug wore off.* She—somebody—stopped giving it to me and I woke up to reality, there in that shabby, broken-down hotel room with the cracked mirror and the bug-infested mattress. And I stayed that way until now, until Alys gave me another dose.

He thought, No wonder she knew about me, about my Tuesday-night TV show. Through her drug she created it. And those two record albums—props which she kept to reinforce the hallucination.

Jesus Christ, he thought, is that it?

But, he thought, the money I woke up with in the hotel room, this whole wad of it. Reflexively he tapped his chest, felt its thick existence, still there. If in real life I doled out my days in fleabag hotels in the Watts area, where did I get that money?

And I would have been listed in the police files, and in all the other data banks throughout the world. I wouldn't be listed as a famous entertainer, but I'd be there as a shabby bum who never amounted to anything, whose only highs came from a pill bottle. For God knows how long. I may have been taking the drug for years.

Alys, he remembered, said I had been to the house before.

And apparently, he decided, it's true. I had. To get my doses of the drug.

Maybe I am only one of a great number of people leading synthetic lives of popularity, money, power, by means of a capsule. While living actually, meanwhile, in bug-infested, ratty old hotel rooms. On skid row. Derelicts, nobodies. Amounting to zero. But, meanwhile, dreaming.

"You certainly are deep in a brown study," Mary Anne said. She had finished her cheesecake; she looked satiated, now. And happy.

"Listen," he said hoarsely. "Is my record really in that jukebox?"

Her eyes widened as she tried to understand. "How do you mean? We listened to it. And the little thingy, where it tells the selections, that's there. Jukeboxes never make mistakes."

He fished out a coin. "Go play it again. Set it up for three plays."

Obediently, she surged from her seat, into the aisle, and bustled over to the jukebox, her lovely long hair bouncing against her ample shoulders. Presently he heard it, heard his big hit song. And the people in the booths and at the counter were nodding and smiling at him in recognition; they knew it was he who was singing. His audience.

When the song ended there was a smattering of applause from the patrons of the coffee shop. Grinning reflexively, professionally in return he acknowledged their recognition and approval.

"It's there," he said, as the song replayed. Savagely, he clenched his fist, struck the plastic table separating him from Mary Anne Dominic. "God damn it, *it's there*."

With some odd twist of deep, intuitive, female desire to help him Mary Anne said, "And I'm here, too."

"I'm not in a run-down hotel room, lying on a cot dreaming," he said huskily.

"No, you're not." Her tone was tender, anxious. She clearly felt concern for him. For his alarm.

"Again I'm real," he said. "But if it could happen once, for two days—" To come and go like this, to fade in and out—

"Maybe we should leave," Mary Anne said apprehensively.

That cleared his mind. "Sorry," he said, wanting to reassure her.

"I just mean that people are listening."

"It won't hurt them," he said. "Let them listen; let them see how you carry your worries and troubles with you even when you're a world-famous star." He rose to his feet, however. "Where do you want to go?" he asked her. "To your apartment?" It meant doubling back, but he felt optimistic enough to take the risk.

"'My apartment'?" she faltered.

"Do you think I'd hurt you?" he said.

For an interval she sat nervously pondering. "N-no," she said at last.

"Do you have a phonograph?" he asked. "At your apartment?"

"Yes, but not a very good one; it's just stereo. But it works."

"Okay," he said, herding her up the aisle toward the cash register. "Let's go."

TWENTY-THREE

Mary Anne Dominic had decorated the walls and ceiling of her apartment herself. Beautiful, strong, rich colors; he gazed about, impressed. And the few art objects in the living room had a powerful beauty about them. Ceramic pieces. He picked up one lovely blue-glaze vase, studied it.

"I made that," Mary Anne said.

"This vase," he said, "will be featured on my show."

Mary Anne gazed at him in wonder.

"I'm going to have this vase with me very soon. In fact"—he could visualize it—"a big production number in which I emerge from the vase singing, like the magic spirit of the vase." He held the blue vase up high, in one hand, revolving it. "'Nowhere Nuthin' Fuck-up,'" he said. "And your career is launched."

"Maybe you should hold it with both hands," Mary Anne said uneasily.

"'Nowhere Nuthin' Fuck-up,' the song that brought us more recognition—" The vase slid from between his fingers and dropped to the floor. Mary Anne leaped forward, but too late.

The vase broke into three pieces and lay there beside Jason's shoe, rough unglazed edges pale and irregular and without artistic merit.

A long silence passed.

"I think I can fix it," Mary Anne said.

He could think of nothing to say.

"The most embarrassing thing that ever happened to me," Mary Anne said, "was one time with my mother. You see, my mother had a progressive kidney ailment called Bright's disease; she was always going to the hospital for it when I was a kid growing up and she was forever working it into the conversation that she was going to die from it and wouldn't I be sorry then—as if it was my fault—and I really believed her, that she would die one day. But then I grew up and moved away from home and she still didn't die. And I sort of forgot about her; I had my own life and things to do. So naturally I forgot about her damn kidney condition. And then one day she came to visit, not here but at the apartment I had before this, and she really bugged me, sitting around narrating all her aches and complaints on and on . . . I finally said, 'I've got to go shopping for dinner,' and I split for the store. My mother limped along with me and on the way she laid the news on me that now both her kidneys were so far gone that they would have to be removed and she would be going in for that and so forth and they'd try to install an artificial kidney but it probably wouldn't work. So she was telling me this, how it really had come now; she really was going to die finally, like she'd always said . . . and all of a sudden I looked up and realized I was in the supermarket, at the meat counter, and this real nice clerk that I liked was coming over to say hello, and he said, 'What would you like today, miss?' and I said, 'I'd like a kidney pie for dinner.' It was embarrassing. 'A great big kidney pie,' I said, 'all flaky and tender and steaming and full of nice juices.' 'To serve how many?' he asked. My mother sort of kept staring at me with this creepy look. I really didn't know how to get out of it once I was in it. Finally I did buy a kidney pie, but I had to go to the delicatessen section; it was in a sealed can, from England. I paid I think four dollars for it. It tasted very good."

"I'll pay for the vase," Jason said. "How much do you want for it?"

Hesitating, she said, "Well, there's the wholesale price I get when I sell to stores. But I'd have to charge you retail prices because you don't have a wholesale number, so—"

He got out his money. "Retail," he said.

"Twenty dollars."

"I can work you in another way," he said. "All we need is an angle. How about this—we can show the audience a priceless vase from antiquity, say from fifth-century China, and a museum expert will step out, in uniform, and certify its authenticity. And then you'll have your wheel there—you'll make a vase before the audience's very eyes, and we'll show them that your vase is better."

"It wouldn't be. Early Chinese pottery is—"

"We'll show them; we'll make them believe. I know my audience. Those thirty million people take their clue from my reaction; there'll be a pan up on my face, showing my response."

In a low voice Mary Anne said, "I can't go up there on stage with those TV cameras looking at me; I'm so—overweight. People would laugh."

"The exposure you'll get. The sales. Museums and stores will know your name, your stuff, buyers will be coming out of the woodwork."

Mary Anne said quietly, "Leave me alone, please. I'm very happy. I know I'm a good potter; I know that the stores, the good ones, like what I do. Does everything have to be on a great scale with a cast of thousands? Can't I lead my little life the way I want to?" She glared at him, her voice almost inaudible. "I don't see what all your exposure and fame have done for you—back at the coffee shop you said to me, 'Is my record really on that jukebox?' You were afraid it wasn't; you were a lot more insecure than I'll ever be."

"Speaking of that," Jason said, "I'd like to play these two records on your phonograph. Before I go."

"You'd better let me put them on," Mary Anne said. "My set is tricky." She took the two albums, and the twenty dollars; Jason stood where he was, by the broken pieces of vase.

As he waited there he heard familiar music. His biggest-selling album. The grooves of the record were no longer blank.

"You can keep the records," he said. "I'll be going." Now,

he thought, I have no further need for them; I'll probably be able to buy them in any record shop.

"It's not the sort of music I like . . . I don't think I'd really be playing them all that much."

"I'll leave them anyhow," he said.

Mary Anne said, "For your twenty dollars I'm giving you another vase. Just a moment." She hurried off; he heard the noises of paper and labored activity. Presently the girl reappeared, holding another blue-glaze vase. This one had more to it; the intuition came to him that she considered it one of her best.

"Thank you," he said.

"I'll wrap it and box it, so it won't get broken like the other." She did so, working with feverish intensity mixed with care. "I found it very thrilling," she said as she presented him with the tied-up box, "to have had lunch with a famous man. I'm extremely glad I met you and I'll remember it a long time. And I hope your troubles work out; I mean, I hope what's worrying you turns out okay."

Jason Taverner reached into his inside coat pocket, brought forth his little initialed leather card case. From it he extracted one of his embossed multicolored business cards and passed it to Mary Anne. "Call me at the studio any time. If you change your mind and want to appear on the program. I'm sure we can fit you in. By the way—this has my private number."

"Goodbye," she said, opening the front door for him.

"Goodbye." He paused, wanting to say more. But there remained nothing to say. "We failed," he said, then. "We absolutely failed. Both of us."

She blinked. "How do you mean?"

"Take care of yourself," he said, and walked out of the apartment, onto the midafternoon sidewalk. Into the hot sun of full day.

TWENTY-FOUR

Kneeling over Alys Buckman's body, the police coroner said, "I can only tell you at this point that she died from an overdose of a toxic or semitoxic drug. It'll be twenty-four hours before we can tell what specifically the drug was."

Felix Buckman said, "It had to happen. Eventually." He did not, surprisingly, feel very much. In fact, in a way, on some level, he experienced deep relief to have learned from Tim Chancer, their guard, that Alys had been found dead in their second-floor bathroom.

"I thought that guy Taverner did something to her," Chancer repeated, over and over again, trying to get Buckman's attention. "He was acting funny; I knew something was wrong. I took a couple of shots at him but he got away. I guess maybe it's a good thing I didn't get him, if he wasn't responsible. Or maybe he felt guilty because he got her to take the drug; could that be?"

"No one had to make Alys take a drug," Buckman said bitingly. He walked from the bathroom, out into the hall. Two gray-clad pols stood at attention, waiting to be told what to do. "She didn't need Taverner or anyone else to administer it to her." He felt, now, physically sick. God, he thought. What will the effect be on Barney? That was the bad part. For reasons obscure to him, their child adored his mother. Well, Buckman thought, there's no accounting for other people's tastes.

And yet he, himself—he loved her. She had a powerful quality, he reflected. I'll miss it. She filled up a good deal of space.

And a good part of his life. For better or worse.

White-faced, Herb Maime climbed the stairs two steps at a time, peering up at Buckman. "I got here as quickly as I could," Herb said, holding out his hand to Buckman. They shook. "What was it?" Herb said. He lowered his voice. "An overdose of something?"

"Apparently," Buckman said.

"I got a call earlier today from Taverner," Herb said. "He wanted to talk to you; he said it had something to do with Alys."

Buckman said, "He wanted to tell me about Alys's death. He was here at the time."

"Why? How did he know her?"

"I don't know," Buckman said. But at the moment it did not seem to matter to him much. He saw no reason to blame Taverner . . . given Alys's temperament and habits, she had probably instigated his coming here. Perhaps when Taverner left the academy building she had nailed him, carted him off in her souped-up quibble. To the house. After all, Taverner was a six. And Alys liked sixes. Male and female both.

Especially female.

"They may have been having an orgy," Buckman said.

"Just the two of them? Or do you mean other people were here?"

"Nobody else was here. Chancer would have known. They may have had a phone orgy; that's what I meant. She's come so damn close so many times to burning out her brain with those goddamn phone orgies—I wish we could track down the new sponsors, the ones that took over when we shot Bill and Carol and Fred and Jill. Those degenerates." His hand shaking, he lit a cigarette, smoking rapidly. "That reminds me of something Alys said one time, unintentionally funny. She was talking about having an orgy and she wondered if she should send out formal invitations. 'I'd better,' she said, 'or everyone won't come at the same time.'" He laughed.

"You've told me that before," Herb said.

"She's really dead. Cold, stiff dead." Buckman stubbed out his cigarette in a nearby ashtray. "My wife," he said to Herb Maime. "She was my wife."

Herb, with a shake of his head, indicated the two gray-wrapped pols standing at attention.

"So what?" Buckman said. "Haven't they read the libretto of *Die Walküre*?" Tremblingly, he lit another cigarette. "Sigmund and Sieglinde. 'Schwester und Braut.' Sister and bride. And the hell with Hunding." He dropped the cigarette to the carpet; standing there, he watched it smolder, starting the wool on fire. And then, with his boot heel, he ground it out.

"You should sit down," Herb said. "Or lie down. You look terrible."

"It's a terrible thing," Buckman said. "It genuinely is. I disliked a lot about her, but, Christ—how vital she was. She always tried anything new. That's what killed her, probably some new drug she and her fellow witch friends brewed up in their miserable basement labs. Something with film developer in it or Drano or a lot worse."

"I think we should talk to Taverner," Herb said.

"Okay. Pull him in. He's got that microtrans on him, doesn't he?"

"Evidently not. All the insects we placed on him as he was leaving the academy building ceased to function. Except, perhaps, for the seed warhead. But we have no reason to activate it."

Buckman said, "Taverner is a smart bastard. Or else he got help. From someone or ones he's working with. Don't bother to try to detonate the seed warhead; it's undoubtedly been cut out of his pelt by some obliging colleague." Or by Alys, he conjectured. My helpful sister. Assisting the police at every turn. Nice.

"You'd better leave the house for a while," Herb said. "While the coroner's staff does its procedural action."

"Drive me back to the academy," Buckman said. "I don't think I can drive; I'm shaking too bad." He felt something on his face; putting up his hand, he found that his chin was wet. "What's this on me?" he said, amazed.

"You're crying," Herb said.

"Drive me back to the academy and I'll wind up what I have to do there before I can turn it over to you," Buckman said. "And then I want to come back here." Maybe Taverner did give her something, he said to himself. But Taverner is nothing. She did it. And yet . . .

"Come on," Herb said, taking him by the arm and leading him to the staircase.

Buckman, as he descended, said, "Would you ever in Christ's world have thought you'd see me cry?"

"No," Herb said. "But it's understandable. You and she were very close."

"You could say that," Buckman said, with sudden savage anger. "God damn her," he said. "I told her she'd eventually do it. Some of her friends brewed it up for her and made her the guinea pig."

"Don't try to do much at the office," Herb said as they passed through the living room and outside, where their two quibbles sat parked. "Just wind it up enough for me to take over."

"That's what I said," Buckman said. "Nobody listens to me, God damn it."

Herb thumped him on the back and said nothing; the two men walked across the lawn in silence.

On the ride back to the academy building, Herb, at the wheel of the quibble, said, "There're cigarettes in my coat." It was the first thing either of them had said since boarding the quibble.

"Thanks," Buckman said. He had smoked up his own week's ration.

"I want to discuss one matter with you," Herb said. "I wish it could wait but it can't."

"Not even until we get to the office?"

Herb said, "There may be other policy-level personnel there when we get back. Or just plain other people—my staff, for instance."

"Nothing I have to say is—"

"Listen," Herb said. "About Alys. About your marriage to her. Your sister."

"My incest," Buckman said harshly.

"Some of the marshals may know about it. Alys told too many people. You know how she was about it."

"Proud of it," Buckman said, lighting a cigarette with difficulty. He still could not get over the fact that he had found himself crying. I really must have loved her, he said to himself. And all I seemed to feel was fear and dislike. And the sexual drive. How many times, he thought, we discussed it before we did it. All the years. "I never told anybody but you," he said to Herb.

"But Alys."

"Okay. Well, then possibly some of the marshals know, and if he cares, the Director."

"The marshals who are opposed to you," Herb said, "and who know about the"—he hesitated—"the incest—will say that she committed suicide. Out of shame. You can expect that. And they will leak it to the media."

"You think so?" Buckman said. Yes, he thought, it would make quite a story. Police general's marriage to his sister, blessed with a secret child hidden away in Florida. The general and his sister posing as husband and wife in Florida, while they're with the boy. And the boy: product of what must be a deranged genetic heritage.

"What I want you to see," Herb said, "and I'm afraid you're going to have to take a look at it now, which isn't an ideal time with Alys just recently dead and—"

"It's our coroner," Buckman said. "We own him, there at the academy." He did not understand what Herb was getting at. "He'll say it was an overdose of a semitoxic drug, as he already told us."

"But taken deliberately," Herb said. "A suicidal dose."

"What do you want me to do?"

Herb said, "Compel him—order him—to find an inquest verdict of murder."

He saw, then. Later, when he had overcome some of his grief, he would have thought of it himself. But Herb Maime was right: it had to be faced now. Even before they got back to the academy building and their staffs.

"So we can say," Herb said, "that—"

"That elements within the police hierarchy hostile to my campus and labor-camp policies took revenge by murdering my sister," Buckman said tightly. It froze his blood to find himself thinking of such matters already. But—

"Something like that," Herb said. "No one named specifically. No marshals, I mean. Just suggest that *they* hired someone to do it. Or ordered some junior officer eager to rise in the ranks to do it. Don't you agree I'm right? And we must act rapidly; it's got to be declared immediately. As soon as we get back to the academy you should send a memo to all the marshals and the Director, stating that."

I must turn a terrible personal tragedy into an advantage, Buckman realized. Capitalize on the accidental death of my own sister. If it *was* accidental.

"Maybe it's true," he said. Possibly Marshal Holbein, for example, who hated him enormously, had arranged it.

"No," Herb said. "It's not true. But start an inquiry. And you must find someone to pin it on; there must be a trial."

"Yes," he agreed dully. With all the trimmings. Ending in an execution, with many dark hints in media releases that "higher authorities" were involved, but who, because of their positions, could not be touched. And the Director, hopefully, would officially express his sympathy concerning the tragedy, and his hope that the guilty party would be found and punished.

"I'm sorry that I have to bring this up so soon," Herb said. "But they got you down from marshal to general; if the incest story is publicly believed they might be able to force you to retire. Of course, even if we take the initiative, they may air the incest story. Let's hope you're reasonably well covered."

"I did everything possible," Buckman said.

"Whom should we pin it on?" Herb asked.

"Marshal Holbein and Marshal Ackers." His hatred for them was as great as theirs for him: they had, five years ago, slaughtered over ten thousand students at the Stanford Campus, a final bloody—and needless—atrocity of that atrocity of atrocities, the Second Civil War.

Herb said, "I don't mean who planned it. That's obvious; as you say, Holbein and Ackers and the others. I mean who actually injected her with the drug."

"The small fry," Buckman said. "Some political prisoner in one of the forced-labor camps." It didn't really matter. Any one of a million camp inmates, or any student from a dying kibbutz, would do.

"I would say pin it on somebody higher up," Herb said.

"Why?" Buckman did not follow his thinking. "It's always done that way; the apparatus always picks an unknown, unimportant—"

"Make it one of her friends. Somebody who *could have* been her equal. In fact, make it somebody well known. In fact, make it somebody in the acting field here in this area; she was a celebrity-fucker."

"Why somebody important?"

"To tie Holbein and Ackers in with those gunjy, degenerate phone-orgy bastards she hung out with." Herb sounded genuinely angry, now; Buckman, startled, glanced at him. "The ones who really killed her. Her cult friends. Pick someone as high as you can. And then you'll really have something to pin on the marshals. Think of the scandal that'll make. Holbein part of the phone grid."

Buckman put out his cigarette and lit another. Meanwhile thinking. What I have to do, he realized, is outscandal them. My story has to be more lurid than theirs.

It would take some story.

TWENTY-FIVE

In his suite of offices at the Los Angeles Police Academy building, Felix Buckman sorted among the memos, letters, and documents on his desk, mechanically selecting the ones that needed Herb Maime's attention and discarding those that could wait. He worked rapidly, with no real interest. As he inspected the various papers, Herb, in his own office, began typing out the first informal statement which Buckman would make public concerning the death of his sister.

Both men finished after a brief interval and met in Buckman's main office, where he kept his crucial activities. At his oversize oak desk.

Seated behind the desk he read over Herb's first draft. "Do we have to do this?" he said, when he had finished reading it.

"Yes," Herb said. "If you weren't so dazed by grief you'd be the first to recognize it. Your being able to see matters of this sort clearly has kept you at policy level; if you hadn't had that faculty they'd have reduced you to training-school major five years ago."

"Then release it," Buckman said. "Wait." He motioned for Herb to come back. "You quote the coroner. Won't the media know that the coroner's investigation couldn't be completed this soon?"

"I'm backdating the time of death. I'm stipulating that it took place yesterday. For that reason."

"Is that necessary?"

Herb said simply, "Our statement has to come first. Before theirs. And they won't wait for the coroner's inquest to be completed."

"All right," Buckman said. "Release it."

Peggy Beason entered his office, carrying several classified police memoranda and a yellow file. "Mr. Buckman," she said, "at a time like this I don't want to bother you, but these—"

"I'll look at them," Buckman said. But that's all, he said to himself. Then I'm going home.

Peggy said, "I knew you were looking for this particular file. So was Inspector McNulty. It just arrived, about ten minutes ago, from Data Central." She placed the file before him on the blotter of his desk. "The Jason Taverner file."

Astonished, Buckman said, "But there is no Jason Taverner file."

"Apparently someone else had it out," Peggy said. "Anyhow they just now put it on the wire, so they must have just now gotten it back. There's no note of explanation; Data Central merely—"

"Go away and let me look at it," Buckman said.

Quietly, Peggy Beason left his office, closing the door behind her.

"I shouldn't have talked to her like that," Buckman said to Herb Maime.

"It's understandable."

Opening the Jason Taverner file, Buckman uncovered a glossy eight-by-five publicity still. Clipped to it a memo read: *Courtesy of the Jason Taverner Show, nine o'clock Tuesday nights on NBC.*

"Jesus God," Buckman said. The gods, he thought, are playing with us. Pulling off our wings.

Leaning over, Herb looked to see, too. Together, they gazed down at the publicity still, wordlessly, until finally Herb said, "Let's see what else there is."

Buckman tossed the eight-by-five photo aside with its memo, read the first page of the file.

"How many viewers?" Herb said.

"Thirty million," Buckman said. Reaching, he picked up his phone. "Peggy," he said, "get the NBC-TV outlet here in L.A. KNBC or whatever it is. Put me through to one of the network executives, the higher the better. Tell them it's us."

"Yes, Mr. Buckman."

A moment later a responsible-looking face appeared on the phone screen and in Buckman's ear a voice said, "Yes, sir. What can we do for you, General?"

"Do you carry the *Jason Taverner Show*?" Buckman said.

"Every Tuesday night for three years. At nine o'clock sharp."

"You've aired it for *three years*?"

"Yes, General."

Buckman hung up the phone.

"Then what was Taverner doing in Watts," Herb Maime said, "buying forged ID cards?"

Buckman said, "We couldn't even get a birth record on him. We worked every data bank that exists, every newspaper file. Have you ever heard of the *Jason Taverner Show* on NBC at nine o'clock Tuesday night?"

"No," Herb said cautiously, hesitating.

"You're not sure?"

"We've talked so much about Taverner—"

"I never heard of it," Buckman said. "And I watch two hours of TV every night. Between eight and ten." He turned to the next page of the file, hurling the first page away; it fell to the floor and Herb retrieved it.

On the second page: a list of the recordings that Jason Taverner had made over the years, giving title, stock number, and date. He stared sightlessly at the list; it went back nineteen years.

Herb said, "He did tell us he's a singer. And one of his ID cards put him in the musicians' union. So that part is true."

"It's all true," Buckman said harshly. He flipped to page three. It disclosed Jason Taverner's financial worth, the sources and amounts of his income. "A lot more than I make," Buckman said, "as a police general. More than you and I make together."

"He had plenty of money when we had him in here. And he gave Kathy Nelson a hell of a lot of money. Remember?"

"Yes, Kathy told McNulty that; I remember it from Mc-Nulty's report." Buckman pondered, meanwhile mindlessly dog-earing the edge of the Xerox page. And then ceased. Abruptly.

"What is it?" Herb said.

"This is a Xerox copy. The file at Data Central is never pulled; only copies are sent out."

Herb said, "But it has to be pulled to be Xeroxed."

"A period of five seconds," Buckman said.

"I don't know," Herb said. "Don't ask me to explain it. I don't know how long it takes."

"Sure you do. We all do. We've watched it done a million times. It goes on all day."

"Then the computer erred."

Buckman said, "Okay. He has never had any political affiliations; he's entirely clean. Good for him." He leafed further into the file. "Mixed up with the Syndicate for a while. Carried a gun but had a permit for it. Was sued two years ago by a viewer who said a blackout skit was a take-off on him. Someone named Artemus Franks living in Des Moines. Taverner's attorneys won." He read here and there, not searching for anything in particular, just marveling. "His forty-five record, 'Nowhere Nuthin' Fuck-up,' which is his latest, has sold over two million copies. Ever heard of it?"

"I don't know," Herb said.

Buckman gazed up at him for a time. "I never heard of it. That's the difference between you and me, Maime. You're not sure. I am."

"You're right," Herb said. "But I really don't know, at this point. I find this very confusing, and we have other business; we have to think about Alys and the coroner's report. We should talk to him as soon as possible. He's probably still at the house; I'll call him and you can—"

"Taverner," Buckman said, "was with her when she died."

"Yes, we know that. Chancer said so. You decided it wasn't important. But I do think just for the record we should haul him in and talk to him. See what he has to say."

"Could Alys have known him before today?" Buckman said. He thought, Yes, she always liked sixes, especially the ones in the entertainment field. Such as Heather Hart. She and the Hart woman had a three-month romance the year before last . . . a relationship which I almost failed to hear about: they did a good job of hushing it up. That was one time Alys kept her mouth shut.

He saw, then, in Jason Taverner's file a mention of Heather Hart; his eyes fixed on it as he thought about her. Heather Hart had been Taverner's mistress for roughly a year.

"After all," Buckman said, "both of them are sixes."

"Taverner and who?"

"Heather Hart. The singer. This file is up to date; it says Heather Hart appeared on Jason Taverner's show this week. His special guest." He tossed the file away from him, rummaged in his coat pocket for his cigarettes.

"Here." Herb extended his own pack.

Buckman rubbed his chin, then said, "Let's have the Hart woman brought in, too. Along with Taverner."

"Okay." Nodding, Herb made a note of that on his customary vest-pocket pad.

"It was Jason Taverner," Buckman said quietly, as if to himself, "who killed Alys. Jealous over Heather Hart. He found out about their relationship."

Herb Maime blinked.

"Isn't that right?" Buckman gazed up at Herb Maime, steadily.

"Okay," Herb Maime said after a time.

"Motive. Opportunity. A witness: Chancer, who can testify that Taverner came running out apprehensively and tried to get hold of the keys to Alys's quibble. And then when Chancer went in the house to investigate, his suspicions aroused, Taverner ran off and escaped. With Chancer shooting over his head, telling him to stop."

Herb nodded. Silently.

"That's it," Buckman said.

"Want him picked up right away?"

"As soon as possible."

"We'll notify all the checkpoints. Put out an APB. If he's still in Los Angeles we may be able to catch him with an EEG-gram projection from a copter. A match of patterns, as they're beginning to do now in New York. In fact we can have a New York police copter brought in just for this."

Buckman said, "Fine."

"Will we say that Taverner was involved in her orgies?"

"There were no orgies," Buckman said.

"Holbein and those with him will—"

"Let them prove it," Buckman said. "Here in a court in California. Where we have jurisdiction."

Herb said, "Why Taverner?"

"It has to be somebody," Buckman said, half to himself; he intertwined his fingers before him on the surface of his great antique oak desk. With his fingers he pressed convulsively, straining with all the force he possessed, one finger against another. "It always, always," he said, "has to be somebody. And Taverner is somebody important. Just what she liked. In fact that's why he was there; that's the celebrity type she preferred. And"—he glanced up—"why not? He'll do just fine." Yes, why not? he thought, and continued grimly to press his fingers tighter and tighter together on the desk before him.

TWENTY-SIX

Walking down the sidewalk, away from Mary Anne's apartment, Jason Taverner said to himself, My luck has turned. It's all come back, everything I lost. Thank God!

I'm the happiest man in the whole fucking world, he said to himself. This is the greatest day of my life. He thought, You never appreciate until you lose it, until all of a sudden you don't have it any more. Well, for two days I lost it and now it's back and now I appreciate it.

Clutching the box containing the pot Mary Anne had made, he hurried out into the street to flag down a passing cab.

"Where to, mister?" the cab asked as it slid open its door.

Panting with fatigue, he climbed inside, shut the door manually. "803 Norden Lane," he said, "in Beverly Hills." Heather Hart's address. He was going back to her at last. And as he really was, not as she had imagined him during the awful last two days.

The cab zoomed up into the sky and he leaned gratefully back, feeling even more weary than he had at Mary Anne's apartment. So much had happened. What about Alys Buckman? he wondered. Should I try to get in touch with General Buckman again? But by now he probably knows. And I should keep out of it. A TV and recording star should not get mixed up in lurid matters, he realized. The gutter press, he reflected, is always ready to play it up for all it's worth.

But I owed her something, he thought. She cut off those electronic devices the pols fastened onto me before I could get out of the Police Academy building.

But they won't be looking for me now. I have my ID back; I'm known to the entire planet. Thirty million viewers can testify to my physical and legal existence.

I will never have to fear a random checkpoint again, he said to himself, and shut his eyes in dozing sleep.

"Here we are, sir," the cab said suddenly. His eyes flew open and he sat upright. Already? Glancing out he saw the apartment complex in which Heather had her West Coast hideaway.

"Oh, yeah," he said, digging into his coat for his roll of paper money. "Thanks." He paid the cab and it opened its door to let him out. Feeling in a good mood again, he said, "If I didn't have the fare wouldn't you open the door?"

The cab did not answer. It had not been programed for that question. But what the hell did he care? He had the money.

He strode up onto the sidewalk, then along the redwood rounds path to the main lobby of the choice ten-story structure that floated, on compressed air jets, a few feet from the ground. The flotation gave its inhabitants a ceaseless sensation of being gently lulled, as if on a giant mother's bosom. He had always enjoyed that. Back East it had not caught on, but out here on the Coast it enjoyed an expensive vogue.

Pressing the stud for her apartment, he stood holding the cardboard box with its vase on the tips of the upraised fingers of his right hand. I better not, he decided; I might drop it like I did before, with the other one. But I'm not going to drop it; my hands are steady now.

I'll give the damn vase to Heather, he decided. A present I picked up for her because I understand her consummate taste.

The viewscreen for Heather's unit lit up and a female face appeared, peering at him. Susie, Heather's maid.

"Oh, Mr. Taverner," Susie said, and at once released the latch of the door, operated from within regions of vast security. "Come on in. Heather's gone out but she—"

"I'll wait," he said. He skipped across the foyer to the elevator, punched the *up* button, waited.

A moment later Susie stood holding the door of Heather's unit open for him. Dark-skinned, pretty and small, she greeted him as she always had: with warmth. And—familiarity.

"Hi," Jason said, and entered.

"As I was telling you," Susie said, "Heather's out shopping but she should be back by eight o'clock. Today she has a lot of free time and she told me she wanted to make the best use of it because there's a big recording session with RCA scheduled for the latter part of the week."

"I'm not in a hurry," he said candidly. Going into the living room, he placed the cardboard box on the coffee table, dead

center, where Heather would be certain to see it. "I'll listen to
the quad and crash," he said. "If it's all right."

"Don't you always?" Susie said. "I've got to go out, too; I
have a dentist's appointment at four-fifteen and it's all the way
on the other side of Hollywood."

He put his arm around her and gripped her firm right boob.

"We're horny today," Susie said, pleased.

"Let's get it on," he said.

"You're too tall for me," Susie said, and moved off to resume whatever she had been doing when he rang.

At the phonograph he sorted through a stack of recently
played albums. None of them appealed to him, so he bent
down and examined the spines of her full collection. From
them he took several of her albums and a couple of his own.
These he stacked up on the changer and set it into motion. The
tone arm descended, and the sound of *The Heart of Hart* disc,
a favorite of his, edged out and echoed through the large
living room, with all its drapes beautifully augmenting the natural quad acoust-tones, spotted artfully here and there.

He lay down on the couch, removed his shoes, made himself comfortable. She did a damn good job when she taped
this, he said to himself, half out loud. I'm as exhausted as I've
ever been in my life, he realized. Mescaline does that to me.
I could sleep for a week. Maybe I will. To the sound of
Heather's voice and mine. Why haven't we ever done an
album together? he asked himself. A good idea. Would sell.
Well. He shut his eyes. Twice the sales, and Al could get us
promotion from RCA. But I'm under contract to Reprise.
Well, it can be worked out. There's work in. Everything. But,
he thought, it's worth it.

Eyes shut, he said, "And now the sound of Jason Taverner."
The changer dropped the next disc. Already? he asked himself.
He sat up, examined his watch. He had dozed through *The
Heart of Hart*, had barely heard it. Lying back again he once
more shut his eyes. Sleep, he thought, to the sound of me. His
voice, enhanced by a two-track overlay of guitars and strings,
resonated about him.

Darkness. Eyes open, he sat up, knowing that a great deal of
time had passed.

Silence. The changer had played the entire stack, hours' worth. What time was it?

Groping, he found a lamp familiar to him, located the switch, turned it on.

His watch read ten-thirty. Cold and hungry. Where's Heather? he wondered, fumbling with his shoes. My feet cold and damp and my stomach is empty. Maybe I can—

The front door flew open. There stood Heather, in her cheruba coat, holding a copy of the L.A. *Times*. Her face, stark and gray, confronted him like a death mask.

"What is it?" he said, terrified.

Coming toward him, Heather held out the paper. Silently. Silently, he took it. Read it.

TV PERSONALITY SOUGHT IN
CONNECTION WITH DEATH OF
POL GENERAL'S SISTER

"Did you kill Alys Buckman?" Heather rasped.

"No," he said, reading the article.

> Popular television personality Jason Taverner, star of his own hour-long evening variety show, is believed by the Los Angeles Pol Dept to have been deeply involved in what pol experts say is a carefully planned vengeance murder, the Police Academy announced today. Taverner, 42, is sought by both

He ceased reading, crumpled the newspaper savagely. "Shit," he said, then. Sucking in his breath he shuddered. Violently.

"It gives her age as thirty-two," Heather said. "I know for a fact that she's—was—thirty-four."

"I saw it," Jason said. "I was in the house."

Heather said, "I didn't know you knew her."

"I just met her. Today."

"Today? Just today? I doubt that."

"It's true. General Buckman interrogated me at the academy building and she stopped me as I was leaving. They had planted a bunch of electronic tracking devices on me, including—"

"They only do that to students," Heather said.

He finished, "And Alys cut them off. And then she invited me to their house."

"And she died."

"Yes." He nodded. "I saw her body as a withered yellow skeleton and it frightened me; you're damn right it frightened me. I got out of there as quickly as I could. Wouldn't you have?"

"Why did you see her as a skeleton? Had you two taken some sort of dope? She always did, so I suppose you did, too."

"Mescaline," Jason said. "That's what she told me, but I don't think it was." I wish I knew what it was, he said to himself, his fear still freezing his heart. Is this a hallucination brought on by it, as was the sight of her skeleton? Am I living this or am I in that fleabag hotel room? He thought, Good God, *what do I do now?*

"You better turn yourself in," Heather said.

"They can't pin it on me," he said. But he knew better. In the last two days he had learned a great deal about the police who ruled their society. Legacy of the Second Civil War, he thought. From pigs to pols. In one easy jump.

"If you didn't do it they won't charge you. The pols are fair. It's not as if the nats are after you."

He uncrumpled the newspaper, read a little more.

> believed to be an overdose of a toxic compound admin-
> istered by Taverner while Miss Buckman was either
> sleeping or in a state

"They give the time of the murder as yesterday," Heather said. "Where were you yesterday? I called your apartment and didn't get any answer. And you just now said—"

"It wasn't yesterday. It was earlier today." Everything had become uncanny; he felt weightless, as if floating along with the apartment into a bottomless sky of oblivion. "They back-dated it. I had a pol lab expert on my show once and after the show he told me how they—"

"Shut up," Heather said sharply.

He ceased talking. And stood. Helplessly. Waiting.

"There's something about me in the article," Heather said, between clenched teeth. "Look on the back page."

Obediently, he turned to the back page, the continuation of the article.

as a hypothesis pol officials offered the theory that the relationship between Heather Hart, herself also a popular TV and recording personality, and Miss Buckman triggered Taverner's vengeful spree in which

Jason said, "What kind of relationship did you have with Alys? Knowing her—"

"You said you didn't know her. You said you just met her today."

"She was weird. Frankly I think she was a lesbian. Did you and she have a sexual relationship?" He heard his voice rise; he could not control it. "That's what the article hints at. Isn't that right?"

The force of her blow stung his face; he retreated involuntarily, holding his hands up defensively. He had never been slapped like that before, he realized. It hurt like hell. His ears rang.

"Okay," Heather breathed. "Hit me back."

He drew his arm back, made a fist, then let his arm fall, his fingers relaxing. "I can't," he said. "I wish I could. You're lucky."

"I guess I am. If you killed her you could certainly kill me. What do you have to lose? They'll gas you anyhow."

Jason said, "You don't believe me. That I didn't do it."

"That doesn't matter. They think you did it. Even if you get off it means the end of your goddamn career, and mine, for that matter. We're finished; do you understand? Do you realize what you've done?" She was screaming at him, now; frightened, he moved toward her, then, as the volume of her voice increased, away again. In confusion.

"If I could talk to General Buckman," he said, "I might be able to—"

"Her *brother*? You're going to appeal to him?" Heather strode at him, her fingers writhing clawlike. "He's head of the commission investigating the murder. As soon as the coroner reported that it was homicide, General Buckman announced he personally was taking charge of the incident—can't you manage to read the whole article? I read it ten times on the way back here; I picked it up in Bel Aire after I got my new fall, the one they ordered for me from Belgium. It finally arrived. And now look. What does it matter?"

Reaching, he tried to put his arms about her. Stiffly, she pulled away.

"I'm not going to turn myself in," he said.

"Do whatever you want." Her voice had sunk to a blunted whisper. "I don't care. Just go away. I don't want to have anything more to do with you. I wish you were both dead, you and her. That skinny bitch—all she ever meant to me was trouble. Finally I had to throw her bodily out; she clung to me like a leech."

"Was she good in bed?" he said, and drew back as Heather's hand rose swiftly, fingers groping for his eyes.

For an interval neither of them spoke. They stood close together. Jason could hear her breathing and his own. Rapid, noisy fluctuations of air. In and out, in and out. He shut his eyes.

"You do what you want," Heather said presently. "I'm going to turn myself in at the academy."

"They want you, too?" he said.

"Can't you read the whole article? Can't you just do *that*? They want my testimony. As to how you felt about my relationship with Alys. It was public knowledge that you and I were sleeping together then, for Christ's sake."

"I didn't know about your relationship."

"I'll tell them that. When"—she hesitated, then went on— "when did you find out?"

"From this newspaper," he said. "Just now."

"You didn't know about it yesterday when she was killed?"

At that he gave up; hopeless, he said to himself. Like living in a world made of rubber. Everything bounced. Changed shape as soon as it was touched or even looked at.

"Today, then," Heather said. "If that's what you believe. You would know, if anyone would."

"Goodbye," he said. Sitting down, he fished his shoes out from beneath the couch, put them on, tied the laces, stood up. Then, reaching, he lifted the cardboard box from the coffee table. "For you," he said, and tossed it to her. Heather clutched at it; the box struck her on the chest and then fell to the floor.

"What is it?" she asked.

"By now," he said, "I've forgotten."

Kneeling, Heather picked up the box, opened it, brought forth newspapers and the blue-glazed vase. It had not broken. "Oh," she said softly. Standing up she inspected it; she held it close to the light. "It's incredibly beautiful," she said. "Thank you."

Jason said, "I didn't kill that woman."

Wandering away from him, Heather placed the vase on a high shelf of knickknacks. She said nothing.

"What can I do," he said, "but go?" He waited but still she said nothing. "Can't you speak?" he demanded.

"Call them," Heather said. "And tell them you're here."

He picked up the phone, dialed the operator. "I want to put through a call to the Los Angeles Police Academy," he told the operator. "To General Felix Buckman. Tell him it's Jason Taverner calling." The operator was silent. "Hello?" he said.

"You can dial that direct, sir."

"I want you to do it," Jason said.

"But, sir—"

"Please," he said.

TWENTY-SEVEN

Phil Westerburg, the Los Angeles Police Agency chief deputy coroner, said to General Felix Buckman, his superior, "I can explain the drug best this way. You haven't heard of it because it isn't in use yet; she must have ripped it off from the academy's special-activities lab." He sketched on a piece of paper. "Time-binding is a function of the brain. It's a structuralization of perception and orientation."

"Why did it kill her?" Buckman asked. It was late and his head hurt. He wished the day would end; he wished everyone and everything would go away. "An overdose?" he demanded.

"We have no way of determining as yet what would constitute an overdose with KR-3. It's currently being tested on detainee volunteers at the San Bernardino forced-labor camp, but so far"—Westerburg continued to sketch—"anyhow, as I was explaining. Time-binding is a function of the brain and goes on as long as the brain is receiving input. Now, we know that the brain can't function if it can't bind space as well . . . but as to why, we don't know yet. Probably it has to do with the instinct to stabilize reality in such a fashion that sequences can be ordered in terms of before-and-after—that would be time—and, more importantly, space-occupying, as with a three-dimensional object as compared to, say, a drawing of that object."

He showed Buckman his sketch. It meant nothing to Buckman; he stared at it blankly and wondered where, this late at night, he could get some Darvon for his headache. Had Alys had any? She had squirreled so many pills.

Westerburg continued, "Now, one aspect of space is that any given unit of space excludes all other given units; if a thing is there it can't be here. Just as in time if an event comes before, it can't also come after."

Buckman said, "Couldn't this wait until tomorrow? You originally said it would take twenty-four hours to develop a report on the exact toxin involved. Twenty-four hours is satisfactory to me."

"But you requested that we speed up the analysis," Westerburg said. "You wanted the autopsy to begin immediately. At two-ten this afternoon, when I was first officially called in."

"Did I?" Buckman said. Yes, he thought, I did. Before the marshals can get their story together. "Just don't draw pictures," he said. "My eyes hurt. Just tell me."

"The exclusiveness of space, we've learned, is only a function of the brain as it handles perception. It regulates data in terms of mutually restrictive space units. Millions of them. Trillions, theoretically, in fact. But in itself, space is not exclusive. In fact, in itself, space does not exist at all."

"Meaning?"

Westerburg, refraining from sketching, said, "A drug such as KR-3 breaks down the brain's ability to exclude one unit of space out of another. So here versus there is lost as the brain tries to handle perception. It can't tell if an object has gone away or if it's still there. When this occurs the brain can no longer exclude alternative spatial vectors. It opens up the entire range of spatial variation. The brain can no longer tell which objects exist and which are only latent, unspatial possibilities. So as a result, competing spatial corridors are opened, into which the garbled percept system enters, and a whole new universe appears to the brain to be in the process of creation."

"I see," Buckman said. But actually he did not either see or care. I only want to go home, he thought. And forget this.

"That's very important," Westerburg said earnestly. "KR-3 is a major breakthrough. Anyone affected by it is forced to perceive irreal universes, whether they want to or not. As I said, trillions of possibilities are theoretically all of a sudden real; chance enters and the person's percept system chooses one possibility out of all those presented to it. It *has* to choose, because if it didn't, competing universes would overlap, and the concept of space itself would vanish. Do you follow me?"

Seated a short way off, at his own desk, Herb Maime said, "He means that the brain seizes on the spatial universe nearest at hand."

"Yes," Westerburg said. "You've read the classified lab report on KR-3, have you, Mr. Maime?"

"I read it a little over an hour ago," Herb Maime said. "Most of it was too technical for me to grasp. But I did notice that its effects are transitory. The brain finally reestablishes contact with the actual space-time objects that it formerly perceived."

"Right," Westerburg said, nodding. "But during the interval in which the drug is active the subject exists, or thinks he exists—"

"There's no difference," Herb said, "between the two. That's the way the drug works; it abolishes that distinction."

"Technically," Westerburg said. "But to the subject an actualized environment envelopes him, one which is alien to the former one that he always experienced, and he operates as if he had entered a new world. A world with changed aspects . . . the amount of change being determined by how great the so-to-speak distance is between the space-time world he formerly perceived and the new one he's forced to function in."

"I'm going home," Buckman said. "I can't stand any more of this." He rose to his feet. "Thanks, Westerburg," he said, automatically extending his hand to the chief deputy coroner. They shook. "Put together an abstract for me," he said to Herb Maime, "and I'll look it over in the morning." He started off, his gray topcoat over his arm. As he always carried it.

"Do you now see what happened to Taverner?" Herb said.

Halting, Buckman said, "No."

"He passed over to a universe in which he didn't exist. And we passed over with him because we're objects of his percept-system. And then when the drug wore off he passed back again. What actually locked him back here was nothing he took or didn't take but her death. So then of course his file came to us from Data Central."

"Good night," Buckman said. He left the office, passed through the great, silent room of spotless metal desks, all alike, all cleared at the end of the day, including McNulty's, and then at last found himself in the ascent tube, rising to the roof.

The night air, cold and clear, made his head ache terribly; he shut his eyes and gritted his teeth. And then he thought, I could get an analgesic from Phil Westerburg. There's probably fifty kinds in the academy's pharmacy, and Westerburg has the keys.

Taking the descent tube he rearrived on the fourteenth floor, returned to his suite of offices, where Westerburg and Herb Maime still sat conferring.

To Buckman, Herb said, "I want to explain one thing I said. About us being objects of his percept system."

"We're not," Buckman said.

Herb said, "We are and we aren't. Taverner wasn't the one who took the KR-3. It was Alys. Taverner, like the rest of us, became a datum in your sister's percept system and got dragged across when she passed into an alternate construct of coordinates. She was very involved with Taverner as a wish-fulfillment performer, evidently, and had run a fantasy number in her head for some time about knowing him as an actual person. But although she did manage to accomplish this by taking the drug, he and we at the same time remained in our own universe. We occupied two space corridors at the same time, one real, one irreal. One is an actuality; one is a latent possibility among many, spatialized temporarily by the KR-3. But just temporarily. For about two days."

"That's long enough," Westerburg said, "to do enormous physical harm to the brain involved. Your sister's brain, Mr. Buckman, was probably not so much destroyed by toxicity but by a high and sustained overload. We may find that the ultimate cause of death was irreversible injury to cortical tissue, a speed-up of normal neurological decay . . . her brain so to speak died of old age over an interval of two days."

"Can I get some Darvon from you?" Buckman said to Westerburg.

"The pharmacy is locked up," Westerburg said.

"But you have the key."

Westerburg said, "I'm not supposed to use it when the pharmacist isn't on duty."

"Make an exception," Herb said sharply. "This time."

Westerburg moved off, sorting among his keys.

"If the pharmacist was there," Buckman said, after a time, "he wouldn't need the key."

"This whole planet," Herb said, "is run by bureaucrats." He eyed Buckman. "You're too sick to take any more. After he gets you the Darvon, go home."

"I'm not sick," Buckman said. "I just don't feel well."

"But don't stick around here. I'll finish up. You start to leave and then you come back."

"I'm like an animal," Buckman said. "Like a laboratory rat."

The phone on his big oak desk buzzed.

"Is there any chance it's one of the marshals?" Buckman said. "I can't talk to them tonight; it'll have to wait."

Herb picked up the phone. Listened. Then, cupping his hand over the receiver, he said, "It's Taverner. Jason Taverner."

"I'll talk to him." Buckman took the phone from Herb Maime, said into it, "Hello, Taverner. It's late."

In his ear, Taverner said tinnily, "I want to give myself up. I'm at the apartment of Heather Hart. We're waiting here together."

To Herb Maime, Buckman said, "He wants to give himself up."

"Tell him to come down here," Herb said.

"Come down here," Buckman said into the phone. "Why do you want to give up?" he said. "We'll kill you in the end, you miserable murdering motherfucker; you know that. Why don't you run?"

"Where?" Taverner squeaked.

"To one of the campuses. Go to Columbia. They're stabilized; they have food and water for a while."

Taverner said, "I don't want to be hunted any more."

"To live is to be hunted," Buckman rasped. "Okay, Taverner," he said. "Come down here and we'll book you. Bring the Hart woman with you so we can record her testimony." You goddamn fool, he thought. Giving yourself up. "Cut your testicles off while you're at it. You stupid bastard." His voice shook.

"I want to clear myself," Taverner's voice echoed thinly in Buckman's ear.

"When you show up here," Buckman said, "I'll kill you with my own gun. Resisting arrest, you degenerate. Or whatever we want to call it. We'll call it what we feel like. Anything." He hung up the phone. "He's coming down here to be killed," he said to Herb Maime.

"You picked him. You can unpick him if you want. Clear him. Send him back to his phonograph records and his silly TV show."

"No." Buckman shook his head.

Westerburg appeared with two pink capsules and a paper cup of water. "Darvon compound," he said, presenting them to Buckman.

"Thank you." Buckman swallowed the pills, drank the water, crushed the paper cup and dropped it into his shredder. Quietly, the teeth of the shredder spun, then ceased. Silence.

"Go home," Herb said to him. "Or, better yet, go to a motel, a good downtown motel for the night. Sleep late tomorrow; I'll handle the marshals when they call."

"I have to meet Taverner."

"No you don't. I'll book him. Or a desk sergeant can book him. Like any other criminal."

"Herb," Buckman said, "I intend to kill the guy, as I said on the phone." Going to his desk he unlocked the bottom drawer, got out a cedar box, set it on the desk. He opened the box and from it brought forth a single-shot Derringer twenty-two pistol. He loaded it with a hollow-nosed shell, half cocked it, held it with its muzzle pointed at the ceiling. For safety's sake. Habit.

"Let's see that," Herb said.

Buckman handed it to him. "Made by Colt," he said. "Colt acquired the dies and patents. I forget when."

"This is a nice gun," Herb said, weighing it, balancing it in his hand. "A fine handgun." He gave it back. "But a twenty-two slug is too small. You'd have to get him exactly between the eyes. He'd have to be standing directly in front of you." He placed his hand on Buckman's shoulder. "Use a thirty-eight special or a forty-five," he said. "Okay? Will you do that?"

"You know who owns this gun?" Buckman said. "Alys. She kept it here because she said if she kept it at home she might use it on me sometime during an argument, or late at night when she gets—got—depressed. But it's not a woman's gun. Derringer made women's guns, but this isn't one of them."

"Did you get it for her?"

"No," Buckman said. "She found it in a pawnshop down in the Watts area. Twenty-five bucks she paid for it. Not a bad price, considering its condition." He glanced up, into Herb's face. "We really have to kill him. The marshals will crucify me if we don't hang it on him. And I've got to stay at policy level."

"I'll take care of it," Herb said.

"Okay." Buckman nodded. "I'll go home." He placed the pistol back in its box, back on its red-velvet cushion, closed the box, then opened it once more and dumped the twenty-two bullet from the barrel. Herb Maime and Phil Westerburg watched. "The barrel breaks to the side in this model," Buckman said. "It's unusual."

"You better get a black-and-gray to take you home," Herb said. "The way you feel and with what's happened you shouldn't be driving."

"I can drive," Buckman said. "I can always drive. What I can't do properly is kill a man with a twenty-two slug who's standing directly in front of me. Somebody has to do it for me."

"Good night," Herb said quietly.

"Good night." Buckman left them, made his way through the various offices, the deserted suites and chambers of the academy, once more to the ascent tube. The Darvon had already begun to lessen the pain in his head; he felt grateful for that. Now I can breathe the night air, he thought. Without suffering.

The door of the ascent tube slid open. There stood Jason Taverner. And, with him, an attractive woman. Both of them looked frightened and pale. Two tall, handsome, nervous people. Obviously sixes. Defeated sixes.

"You are under police arrest," Buckman said. "Here are your rights. Anything you say may be held against you. You have a right to counsel and if you cannot afford an attorney one will be appointed for you. You have a right to be tried by a jury, or you can waive that right and be tried by a judge appointed by the Police Academy of Los Angeles City and County. Do you understand what I have just said?"

"I came here to clear myself," Jason Taverner said.

"My staff will take your depositions," Buckman said. "Go into the blue-colored offices over there where you were taken before." He pointed. "Do you see him in there? The man in the single-breasted suit with the yellow tie?"

"Can I clear myself?" Jason Taverner said. "I admit to being in the house when she died, but I didn't have anything to do with it. I went upstairs and found her in the bathroom. She was getting some Thorazine for me. To counteract the mescaline she gave me."

"He saw her as a skeleton," the woman—evidently Heather Hart—said. "Because of the mescaline. Can't he get off on the grounds that he was under the influence of a powerful hallucinogenic chemical? Doesn't that legally clear him? He had no control over what he did, and I didn't have anything to do with it at all. I didn't even know she was dead until I read tonight's paper."

"In some states it might," Buckman said.

"But not here," the woman said wanly. Comprehendingly.

Emerging from his office, Herb Maime sized up the situation and declared, "I'll book him and take their statements, Mr. Buckman. You go ahead on home as we agreed."

"Thank you," Buckman said. "Where's my topcoat?" He glanced around for it. "God, it's cold," he said. "They turn the heat off at night," he explained to Taverner and the Hart woman. "I'm sorry."

"Good night," Herb said to him.

Buckman entered the ascent tube and pressed the button that closed the door. He still did not have his topcoat. Maybe I should take a black-and-gray, he said to himself. Get some junior-grade eager cadet type to drive me home, or, like Herb said, go to one of the good downtown motels. Or one of the new soundproof hotels by the airport. But then my quibble would be here and I wouldn't have it to drive to work tomorrow morning.

The cold air and the darkness of the roof made him wince. Even the Darvon can't help me, he thought. Not completely. I can still feel it.

He unlocked the door of his quibble, got inside and slammed the door after him. Colder in here than out there, he thought. Jesus. He started up the engine and turned on the heater. Frigid wind blew up at him from the floor vents. He began to shake. I'll feel better when I can get home, he thought. Looking at his wristwatch, he saw that it was two-thirty. No wonder it's so cold, he thought.

Why did I pick Taverner? he asked himself. Out of a planet of six billion people . . . this one specific man who never harmed anyone, never did anything except let his file come to the attention of the authorities. That's it right there, he realized. Jason Taverner let himself come to our attention, and, as they say, once come to the authorities' attention, never completely forgotten.

But I can unpick him, he thought, as Herb pointed out.

No. Again it had to be no. The die was cast from the beginning. Before any of us even laid hands on it. Taverner, he thought, you were doomed from the start. From your first act upward.

We play roles, Buckman thought. We occupy positions, some small, some large. Some ordinary, some strange. Some outlandish and bizarre. Some visible, some dim or not visible at all. Jason Taverner's role was large and visible at the end, and it was at the end that the decision had to be made. If he could have stayed as he started out: one small man without proper ID cards, living in a ratty, broken-down, slum hotel—if he could have remained that he might have gotten away . . . or at the very worst wound up in a forced-labor camp. But Taverner did not elect to do that.

Some irrational will within him made him want to appear, to be visible, to be *known*. All right, Jason Taverner, Buckman thought, you are known, again, as you were once before, but better known now, known in a new way. In a way that serves higher ends—ends you know nothing about, but must accept without understanding. As you go to your grave your mouth will be still open, asking the question, "What did I do?" You will be buried that way: with your mouth still open.

And I could never explain it to you, Buckman thought. Except to say: don't come to the attention of the authorities. Don't ever interest us. Don't make us want to know more about you.

Someday your story, the ritual and shape of your downfall, may be made public, at a remote future time when it no longer matters. When there are no more forced-labor camps and no more campuses surrounded by rings of police carrying rapid-fire submachine guns and wearing gas masks that make them look like great-snouted, huge-eyed root-eaters, some kind of noxious lower animal. Someday there may be a post mortem inquiry and it will be learned that you in fact did no harm—did nothing, actually, but become noticed.

The real, ultimate truth is that despite your fame and your great public following you are expendable, he thought. And I am not. That is the difference between the two of us. Therefore you must go and I remain.

His ship floated on, up into the band of nighttime stars. And to himself he sang quietly, seeking to look ahead, to see forward into time, to the world of his home, of music and thought and love, to books, ornate snuffboxes and rare stamps. To the blotting out, for a moment, of the wind that rushed about him as he drove on, a speck nearly lost in the night.

There is beauty which will never be lost, he declared to himself; I will preserve it; I am one of those who cherishes it. And I abide. And that, in the final analysis, is all that matters.

Tunelessly, he hummed to himself. And felt at last some

meager heat as, finally, the standard police model quibble heater mounted below his feet began to function.

Something dripped from his nose onto the fabric of his coat. My God, he thought in horror. I'm crying again. He put up his hand and wiped the greaselike wetness from his eyes. Who for? he asked himself. Alys? For Taverner? The Hart woman? Or for all of them?

No, he thought. It's a reflex. From fatigue and worry. It doesn't mean anything. Why does a man cry? he wondered. Not like a woman; not for that. Not for sentiment. A man cries over the loss of something, something alive. A man can cry over a sick animal that he knows won't make it. The death of a child: a man can cry for that. But not because things are sad.

A man, he thought, cries not for the future or the past but for the present. And what is the present, now? They are booking Jason Taverner back at the Police Academy building and he is telling them his story. Like everyone else, he has an account to give, an offering which makes clear his lack of guilt. Jason Taverner, as I fly this craft, is doing that right now.

Turning the steering wheel, he sent his quibble in a long trajectory that brought it at last into an Immelmann; he made the craft fly back the way it had come, at no increase in speed, nor at any loss. He merely flew in the opposite direction. Back toward the academy.

And yet still he cried. His tears became each moment denser and faster and deeper. I'm going the wrong way, he thought. Herb is right; I have to get away from there. All I can do there now is witness something I can no longer control. I am painted on, like a fresco. Dwelling in only two dimensions. I and Jason Taverner are figures in an old child's drawing. Lost in dust.

He pressed his foot down on the accelerator and pulled back on the steering wheel of the quibble; it spluttered up, its engine missing and misfiring. The automatic choke is still closed, he said to himself. I should have revved it up for a while. It's still cold. Once more he changed direction.

Aching, and with fatigue, he at last dropped his home route card into the control turret of the quibble's guiding section and snapped on the automatic pilot. I should rest, he said to himself. Reaching, he activated the sleep circuit above his head; the mechanism hummed and he shut his eyes.

Sleep, artificially induced, came as always at once. He felt himself spiraling down into it and was glad. But then, almost at once, beyond the control of the sleep circuit, a dream came. Very clearly he did not want the dream. But he could not stop it.

The countryside, brown and dry, in summer, where he had lived as a child. He rode a horse, and approaching him on his left a squad of horses nearing slowly. On the horses rode men in shining robes, each a different color; each wore a pointed helmet that sparkled in the sunlight. The slow, solemn knights passed him and as they traveled by he made out the face of one: an ancient marble face, a terribly old man with rippling cascades of white beard. What a strong nose he had. What noble features. So tired, so serious, so far beyond ordinary men. Evidently he was a king.

Felix Buckman let them pass; he did not speak to them and they said nothing to him. Together, they all moved toward the house from which he had come. A man had sealed himself up inside the house, a man alone, Jason Taverner, in the silence and darkness, without windows, by himself from now on into eternity. Sitting, merely existing, inert. Felix Buckman continued on, out into the open countryside. And then he heard from behind him one dreadful single shriek. They had killed Taverner, and seeing them enter, sensing them in the shadows around him, knowing what they intended to do with him, Taverner had shrieked.

Within himself Felix Buckman felt absolute and utter desolate grief. But in the dream he did not go back nor look back. There was nothing that could be done. No one could have stopped the posse of varicolored men in robes; they could not have been said no to. Anyhow, it was over. Taverner was dead.

His heaving, disordered brain managed to spike a relay signal via minute electrodes to the sleep circuit. A voltage breaker clicked open, and a solid, disturbing tone awakened Buckman from his sleep and from his dream.

God, he thought, and shivered. How cold it had become. How empty and alone he felt himself to be.

The great, weeping grief within him, left from the dream,

meandered in his breast, still disturbing him. I've got to land, he said to himself. See some person. Talk to someone. I can't stay alone. Just for a second if I could—

Shutting off the automatic pilot he steered the quibble toward a square of fluorescent light below: an all-night gas station.

A moment later he bumpily landed before the gas pumps of the station, rolling to a stop near another quibble, parked and empty, abandoned. No one in it.

Glare lit up the shape of a middle-aged black man in a top-coat, neat, colorful tie, his face aristocratic, each feature starkly outlined. The black man paced about across the oil-streaked cement, his arms folded, an absent expression on his face. Evidently he waited for the robotrix attendant to finish fueling up his ship. The black man was neither impatient nor resigned; he merely existed, in remoteness and isolation and splendor, strong in his body, standing high, seeing nothing because there was nothing he cared to see.

Parking his quibble, Felix Buckman shut off the motor, activated the door latch and lock, stepped stiffly out into the cold of night. He made his way toward the black man.

The black man did not look at him. He kept his distance. He moved about, calmly, distantly. He did not speak.

Into his coat pocket Felix Buckman reached with cold-shakened fingers; he found his ballpoint pen, plucked it out, groped in his pockets for a square of paper, any paper, a sheet from a memo pad. Finding it, he placed it on the hood of the black man's quibble. In the white, stark light of the service station Buckman drew on the paper a heart pierced by an arrow. Trembling with cold he turned toward the black man pacing and extended the piece of drawn-on paper to him.

His eyes igniting briefly, in surprise, the black man grunted, accepted the piece of paper, held it by the light, examining it. Buckman waited. The black man turned the paper over, saw nothing on the back, once again scrutinized the heart with the arrow piercing it. He frowned, shrugged, then handed the paper back to Buckman and wandered on, his arms once again folded, his large back to the police general. The slip of paper fluttered away, lost.

Silently, Felix Buckman returned to his own quibble, lifted

open the door, squeezed inside behind the wheel. He turned on the motor, slammed the door, and flew up into the night sky, his ascent warning bulbs winking red before him and behind. They shut automatically off, then, and he droned along the line of the horizon, thinking nothing.

The tears came once again.

All of a sudden he spun the steering wheel; the quibble popped violently, bucked, leveled out laterally on a descending trajectory; moments later he once again glided to a stop in the hard glare beside the parked, empty quibble, the pacing black man, the fuel pumps. Buckman braked to a stop, shut off his engine, stepped creakingly out.

The black man was looking at him.

Buckman walked toward the black man. The black man did not retreat; he stood where he was. Buckman reached him, held out his arms and seized the black man, enfolded him in them, and hugged him. The black man grunted in surprise. And dismay. Neither man said anything. They stood for an instant and then Buckman let the black man go, turned, walked shakingly back to his quibble.

"Wait," the black man said.

Buckman revolved to face him.

Hesitating, the black man stood shivering and then said, "Do you know how to get to Ventura? Up on air route thirty?" He waited. Buckman said nothing. "It's fifty or so miles north of here," the black man said. Still Buckman said nothing. "Do you have a map of this area?" the black man asked.

"No," Buckman said. "I'm sorry."

"I'll ask the gas station," the black man said, and smiled a little. Sheepishly. "It was—nice meeting you. What's your name?" The black man waited a long moment. "Do you want to tell me?"

"I have no name," Buckman said. "Not right now." He could not really bear to think of it, at this time.

"Are you an official of some kind? Like a greeter? Or from the L.A. Chamber of Commerce? I've had dealings with them and they're all right."

"No," Buckman said. "I'm an individual. Like you."

"Well, I have a name," the black man said. He deftly

reached into his inner coat pocket, brought out a small stiff card, which he passed to Buckman. "Montgomery L. Hopkins is the handle. Look at the card. Isn't that a good printing job? I like the letters raised like that. Fifty dollars a thousand it cost me; I got a special price because of an introductory offer not to be repeated." The card had beautiful great embossed black letters on it. "I manufacture inexpensive biofeedback headphones of the analog type. They sell retail for under a hundred dollars."

"Come and visit me," Buckman said.

"Call me," the black man said. Slowly and firmly, but also a little loudly, he said, "These places, these coin-operated robot gas stations, are downers late at night. Sometime later on we can talk more. Where it's friendly. I can sympathize and understand how you're feeling, when it happens that places like this get you on a bummer. A lot of times I get gas on my way home from the factory so I won't have to stop late. I go out on a lot of night calls for several reasons. Yes, I can tell you're feeling down at the mouth—you know, depressed. That's why you handed me that note which I'm afraid I didn't flash on at the time but do now, and then you wanted to put your arms around me, you know, like you did, like a child would, for a second. I've had that sort of inspiration, or rather call it impulse, from time to time during my life. I'm forty-seven now. I understand. You want to not be by yourself late at night, especially when it's unseasonably chilly like it is right now. Yes, I agree completely, and now you don't exactly know what to say because you did something suddenly out of irrational impulse without thinking through to the final consequences. But it's okay; I can dig it. Don't worry about it one damn bit. You must drop over. You'll like my house. It's very mellow. You can meet my wife and our kids. Three in all."

"I will," Buckman said. "I'll keep your card." He got out his wallet, pushed the card into it. "Thank you."

"I see that my quibble's ready," the black man said. "I was low on oil, too." He hesitated, started to move away, then returned and held out his hand. Buckman shook it briefly. "Goodbye," the black man said.

Buckman watched him go; the black man paid the gas station, got into his slightly battered quibble, started it up, and lifted off into the darkness. As he passed above Buckman the black man raised his right hand from the steering wheel and waved in salutation.

Good night, Buckman thought as he silently waved back with cold-bitten fingers. Then he reentered his own quibble, hesitated, feeling numb, waited, then, seeing nothing, slammed his door abruptly and started up his engine. A moment later he had reached the sky.

Flow, my tears, he thought. The first piece of abstract music ever written. John Dowland in his Second Lute Book in 1600. I'll play it on that big new quad phonograph of mine when I get home. Where it can remind me of Alys and all the rest of them. Where there will be a symphony and a fire and it will all be warm.

I will go get my little boy. Early tomorrow I'll fly down to Florida and pick up Barney. Have him with me from now on. The two of us together. No matter what the consequences. But now there won't be any consequences; it's all over. It's safe. Forever.

His quibble crept across the night sky. Like some wounded, half-dissolved insect. Carrying him home.

Part Four

Hark! you shadows that in darkness dwell,
Learn to contemn light.
Happy, happy they that in hell
Feel not the world's despite.

EPILOG

THE trial of Jason Taverner for the first-degree murder of
Alys Buckman mysteriously backfired, ending with a verdict of not guilty, due in part to the excellent legal help NBC
and Bill Wolfer provided, but due also to the fact that Taverner
had committed no crime. There had in fact been no crime, and
the original coroner's finding was reversed—accompanied by
the retirement of the coroner and his replacement by a younger
man. Jason Taverner's TV ratings, which had dropped to a low
point during the trial, rose with the verdict, and Taverner
found himself with an audience of thirty-five million, rather
than thirty.

The house which Felix Buckman and his sister Alys had
owned and occupied drifted along in a nebulous legal status
for several years; Alys had willed her part of the equity to a lesbian organization called the Sons of Caribron with headquarters in Lee's Summit, Missouri, and the society wished to
make the house into a retreat for their several saints. In March
of 2003 Buckman sold his share of the equity to the Sons of
Caribron, and, with the money derived, moved himself and all
the items of his many collections to Borneo, where living was
cheap and the police amiable.

Experiments with the multiple-space-inclusion drug KR-3
were abandoned late in 1992, due to its toxic qualities. However, for several years the police covertly experimented with it
on inmates in forced-labor camps. But ultimately, due to the
general widespread hazards involved, the Director ordered the
project abandoned.

Kathy Nelson learned—and accepted—a year later that her
husband Jack had been long dead, as McNulty had told her.
The recognition of this precipitated a blatant psychotic break

in her, and she again became hospitalized, this time for good at a far less stylish psychiatric hospital than Morningside.

For the fifty-first and final time in her life Ruth Rae married, in this terminal instance to an elderly, wealthy, potbellied importer of firearms located in lower New Jersey, barely operating within the limit of the law. In the spring of 1994 she died of an overdose of alcohol taken with a new tranquilizer, Phrenozine, which acts as a central nervous system depressant, as well as suppressing the vagus nerve. At the time of her death she weighed ninety-two pounds, the result of difficult—and chronic—psychological problems. It never became possible to certify with any clarity the death as either an accident or a deliberate suicide; after all, the medication was relatively new. Her husband, Jake Mongo, at the time of her death had become heavily in debt and outlasted her barely a year. Jason Taverner attended her funeral and, at the later graveside ceremony, met a girl friend of Ruth's named Fay Krankheit, with whom he presently formed a working relationship that lasted two years. From her Jason learned that Ruth Rae had periodically attached herself to the phone-grid sex network; learning this, he understood better why she had become as she had when he met her in Vegas.

Cynical and aging, Heather Hart gradually abandoned her singing career and dropped out of sight. After a few tries to locate her, Jason Taverner gave up and wrote it off as one of the better successes of his life, despite its dreary ending.

He heard, too, that Mary Anne Dominic had won a major international prize for her ceramic kitchenware, but he never bothered to trace her down. Monica Buff, however, showed up in his life toward the end of 1998, as unkempt as ever but still attractive in her grubby way. Jason dated her a few times and then dumped her. For months she wrote him odd, long letters with cryptic signs drawn over the words, but that, too, stopped at last, and for this he was glad.

In the warrens under the ruins of the great universities the student populations gradually gave up their futile attempts to maintain life as they understood it, and voluntarily—for the most part—entered forced-labor camps. So the dregs of the Second Civil War gradually ebbed away, and in 2004, as a pilot model, Columbia University was rebuilt and a safe, sane student body allowed to attend its police-sanctioned courses.

Toward the end of his life retired Police General Felix Buckman, living in Borneo on his pension, wrote an autobiographical exposé of the planetwide police apparatus, the book soon being circulated illegally throughout the major cities of earth. For this, in the summer of 2017, General Buckman was shot by an assassin, never identified, and no arrests were ever made. His book, *The Law-and-order Mentality,* continued to clandestinely circulate for a number of years after his death, but even that, too, eventually became forgotten. The forced-labor camps dwindled away and at last ceased to exist. The police apparatus became by degrees, over the decades, too cumbersome to threaten anyone, and in 2136 the rank of police marshal was abandoned.

Some of the bondage cartoons that Alys Buckman had collected during her aborted life found their way into museums displaying artifacts of faded-out popular cultures, and ultimately she became officially identified by the *Librarian's Journal Quarterly* as the foremost authority of the late twentieth century in the matter of S-M art. The one-dollar black Trans-Mississippi postage stamp which Felix Buckman had laid on her was bought at auction in 1999 by a dealer from Warsaw, Poland. It disappeared thereupon into the hazy world of philately, never to surface again.

Barney Buckman, the son of Felix and Alys Buckman, grew eventually into difficult manhood, joined the New York police, and during his second year as a beat cop fell from a substandard fire escape while responding to a report of burglary in a tenement where wealthy blacks had once lived. Paralyzed from the waist down at twenty-three, he began to interest himself in old television commercials, and, before long, owned an impressive library of the most ancient and sought-after items of this sort, which he bought and sold and traded shrewdly. He lived a long life, with only a feeble memory of his father and no memory at all of Alys. By and large Barney Buckman complained little, and continued in particular to absorb himself in old-time Alka-Seltzer plugs, his specialty out of all the rest of such golden trivia.

Someone at the Los Angeles Police Academy stole the twenty-two Derringer pistol which Felix Buckman had kept in his desk, and with this the gun vanished forever. Lead slug weapons had by that time become generally extinct except as collector's pieces, and the inventory clerk at the academy whose job it was to keep track of the Derringer assumed wisely that it had become a prop in the bachelors' quarters of some minor police official, and let the investigation drop there.

In 2047 Jason Taverner, long since retired from the entertainment field, died in an exclusive nursing home of acolic fibrosis, an ailment acquired by Terrans at various Martian colonies privately maintained for dubious enthallment of the weary rich. His estate consisted of a five-bedroom house in Des Moines, filled mostly with memorabilia, and many shares of stock in a corporation which had tried—and failed—to finance a commercial shuttle service to Proxima Centaurus. His passing was not generally noticed, although small obit squibs appeared in most metropolitan newspapers, ignored by the TV news people but not by Mary Anne Dominic, who, even in her eighties, still considered Jason Taverner a celebrity, and her meeting him an important milestone in her long and successful life.

The blue vase made by Mary Anne Dominic and purchased by Jason Taverner as a gift for Heather Hart wound up in a private collection of modern pottery. It remains there to this day, and is much treasured. And, in fact, by a number of people who know ceramics, openly and genuinely cherished. And loved.

A SCANNER DARKLY

Chapter One

ONCE a guy stood all day shaking bugs from his hair. The doctor told him there were no bugs in his hair. After he had taken a shower for eight hours, standing under hot water hour after hour suffering the pain of the bugs, he got out and dried himself, and he still had bugs in his hair; in fact, he had bugs all over him. A month later he had bugs in his lungs.

Having nothing else to do or think about, he began to work out theoretically the life cycle of the bugs, and, with the aid of the *Britannica*, try to determine specifically which bugs they were. They now filled his house. He read about many different kinds and finally noticed bugs outdoors, so he concluded they were aphids. After that decision came to his mind it never changed, no matter what other people told him . . . like "Aphids don't bite people."

They said that to him because the endless biting of the bugs kept him in torment. At the 7-11 grocery store, part of a chain spread out over most of California, he bought spray cans of Raid and Black Flag and Yard Guard. First he sprayed the house, then himself. The Yard Guard seemed to work the best.

As to the theoretical side, he perceived three stages in the cycle of the bugs. First, they were carried to him to contaminate him by what he called Carrier-people, which were people who didn't understand their role in distributing the bugs. During that stage the bugs had no jaws or mandibles (he learned that word during his weeks of scholarly research, an unusually bookish occupation for a guy who worked at the Handy Brake and Tire place relining people's brake drums). The Carrier-people therefore felt nothing. He used to sit in the far corner of his living room watching different Carrier-people enter—most of them people he'd known for a while, but some new to him—covered with the aphids in this particular nonbiting stage. He'd sort of smile to himself, because he knew that the person was being used by the bugs and wasn't hip to it.

"What are you grinning about, Jerry?" they'd say.

He'd just smile.

In the next stage the bugs grew wings or something, but they really weren't precisely wings; anyhow, they were append- ages of a functional sort permitting them to swarm, which was how they migrated and spread—especially to him. At that point the air was full of them; it made his living room, his whole house, cloudy. During this stage he tried not to inhale them.

Most of all he felt sorry for his dog, because he could see the bugs landing on and settling all over him, and probably get- ting into the dog's lungs, as they were in his own. Probably— at least so his empathic ability told him—the dog was suffering as much as he was. Should he give the dog away for the dog's own comfort? No, he decided: the dog was now, inadvertently, infected, and would carry the bugs with him everywhere.

Sometimes he stood in the shower with the dog, trying to wash the dog clean too. He had no more success with him than he did with himself. It hurt to feel the dog suffer; he never stopped trying to help him. In some respects this was the worst part, the sufferings of the animal, who could not complain.

"What the fuck are you doing there all day in the shower with the goddamn dog?" his buddy Charles Freck asked one time, coming in during this.

Jerry said, "I got to get the aphids off him." He brought Max, the dog, out of the shower and began drying him. Charles Freck watched, mystified, as Jerry rubbed baby oil and talc into the dog's fur. All over the house, cans of insect spray, bottles of talc and baby oil and skin conditioners were piled and tossed, most of them empty; he used many cans a day now.

"I don't see any aphids," Charles said. "What's an aphid?"

"It eventually kills you," Jerry said. "That's what an aphid is. They're in my hair and my skin and my lungs, and the god- damn pain is unbearable—I'm going to have to go to the hospital."

"How come I can't see them?"

Jerry put down the dog, which was wrapped in a towel, and knelt over the shag rug. "I'll show you one," he said. The rug was covered with aphids; they hopped up everywhere, up and down, some higher than others. He searched for an especially large one, because of the difficulty people had seeing them.

"Bring me a bottle or jar," he said, "from under the sink. We'll cap it or put a lid on it and then I can take it with me when I go to the doctor and he can analyze it."

Charles Freck brought him an empty mayonnaise jar. Jerry went on searching, and at last came across an aphid leaping up at least four feet in the air. The aphid was over an inch long. He caught it, carried it to the jar, carefully dropped it in, and screwed on the lid. Then he held it up triumphantly. "See?" he said.

"Yeahhhhh," Charles Freck said, his eyes wide as he scrutinized the contents of the jar. "What a big one! Wow!"

"Help me find more for the doctor to see," Jerry said, again squatting down on the rug, the jar beside him.

"Sure," Charles Freck said, and did so.

Within half an hour they had three jars full of the bugs. Charles, although new at it, found some of the largest.

It was midday, in June of 1994. In California, in a tract area of cheap but durable plastic houses, long ago vacated by the straights. Jerry had at an earlier date sprayed metal paint over all the windows, though, to keep out the light; the illumination for the room came from a pole lamp into which he had screwed nothing but spot lamps, which shone day and night, so as to abolish time for him and his friends. He liked that; he liked to get rid of time. By doing that he could concentrate on important things without interruption. Like this: two men kneeling down on the shag rug, finding bug after bug and putting them into jar after jar.

"What do we get for these," Charles Freck said, later on in the day. "I mean, does the doctor pay a bounty or something? A prize? Any bread?"

"I get to help perfect a cure for them this way," Jerry said. The pain, constant as it was, had become unbearable; he had never gotten used to it, and he knew he never would. The urge, the longing, to take another shower was overwhelming him. "Hey, man," he gasped, straightening up, "you go on putting them in the jars while I take a leak and like that." He started toward the bathroom.

"Okay," Charles said, his long legs wobbling as he swung toward a jar, both hands cupped. An ex-veteran, he still had good muscular control, though; he made it to the jar. But then he said suddenly, "Jerry, hey—these bugs sort of scare me. I don't like it here by myself." He stood up.

"Chickenshit bastard," Jerry said, panting with pain as he halted momentarily at the bathroom.

"Couldn't you—"

"I got to take a leak!" He slammed the door and spun the knobs of the shower. Water poured down.

"I'm afraid out here." Charles Freck's voice came dimly, even though he was evidently yelling loud.

"Then go fuck yourself!" Jerry yelled back, and stepped into the shower. What fucking good are friends? he asked himself bitterly. No good, no good! No fucking good!

"Do these fuckers sting?" Charles yelled, right at the door.

"Yeah, they sting," Jerry said as he rubbed shampoo into his hair.

"That's what I thought." A pause. "Can I wash my hands and get them off and wait for you?"

Chickenshit, Jerry thought with bitter fury. He said nothing; he merely kept on washing. The bastard wasn't worth answering . . . He paid no attention to Charles Freck, only to himself. To his own vital, demanding, terrible, urgent needs. Everything else would have to wait. There was no time, no time; these things could not be postponed. Everything else was secondary. Except the dog; he wondered about Max, the dog.

Charles Freck phoned up somebody who he hoped was holding. "Can you lay about ten deaths on me?"

"Christ, I'm entirely out—I'm looking to score myself. Let me know when you find some, I could use some."

"What's wrong with the supply?"

"Some busts, I guess."

Charles Freck hung up and then ran a fantasy number in his head as he slumped dismally back from the pay phone booth— you never used your home phone for a buy call—to his parked Chevy. In his fantasy number he was driving past the Thrifty Drugstore and they had a huge window display: bottles of slow death, cans of slow death, jars and bathtubs and vats and bowls of slow death, millions of caps and tabs and hits of slow death, slow death mixed with speed and junk and barbiturates and psychedelics, everything—and a giant sign: YOUR CREDIT IS GOOD HERE. Not to mention: LOW LOW PRICES, LOWEST IN TOWN.

But in actuality the Thrifty usually had a display of nothing: combs, bottles of mineral oil, spray cans of deodorant, always crap like that. But I bet the pharmacy in the back has slow death under lock and key in an unstepped-on, pure, unadulterated, uncut form, he thought as he drove from the parking lot onto Harbor Boulevard, into the afternoon traffic. About a fifty-pound bag.

He wondered when and how they unloaded the fifty-pound bag of Substance D at the Thrifty Pharmacy every morning, from wherever it came from—God knew, maybe from Switzerland or maybe from another planet where some wise race lived. They'd deliver probably real early, and with armed guards— the Man standing there with Laser rifles looking mean, the way the Man always did. Anybody rip off my slow death, he thought through the Man's head, I'll snuff them.

Probably Substance D is an ingredient in every legal medication that's worth anything, he thought. A little pinch here and there according to the secret exclusive formula at the issuing house in Germany or Switzerland that invented it. But in actuality he knew better; the authorities snuffed or sent up everybody selling or transporting or using, so in that case the Thrifty Drugstore—all the millions of Thrifty Drugstores— would get shot or bombed out of business or anyhow fined. More likely just fined. The Thrifty had pull. Anyhow, how do you shoot a chain of big drugstores? Or put them away?

They just got ordinary stuff, he thought as he cruised along. He felt lousy because he had only three hundred tabs of slow death left in his stash. Buried in his back yard under his camellia, the hybrid one with the cool big blossoms that didn't burn brown in the spring. I only got a week's supply, he thought. What then when I'm out? Shit.

Suppose everybody in California and parts of Oregon runs out the same day, he thought. Wow.

This was the all-time winning horror-fantasy that he ran in his head, that every doper ran. The whole western part of the United States simultaneously running out and everybody crashing on the same day, probably about 6 A.M. Sunday morning, while the straights were getting dressed up to go fucking pray.

Scene: The First Episcopal Church of Pasadena, at 8:30 A.M. on Crash Sunday.

"Holy parishioners, let us call on God now at this time to request His intervention in the agonies of those who are thrashing about on their beds withdrawing."

"Yeah, yeah." The congregation agreeing with the priest.

"But before He intervenes with a fresh supply of—"

A black-and-white evidently had noticed something in Charles Freck's driving he hadn't noticed; it had taken off from its parking spot and was moving along behind him in traffic, so far without lights or siren, but . . .

Maybe I'm weaving or something, he thought. Fucking goddamn fuzzmobile saw me fucking up. I wonder what.

COP: "All right, what's your name?"

"My *name*?" (CAN'T THINK OF NAME.)

"You don't know your own name?" Cop signals to other cop in prowl car. "This guy is really spaced."

"Don't shoot me here." Charles Freck in his horror-fantasy number induced by the sight of the black-and-white pacing him. "At least take me to the station house and shoot me there, out of sight."

To survive in this fascist police state, he thought, you gotta always be able to come up with a name, your name. At all times. That's the first sign they look for that you're wired, not being able to figure out who the hell you are.

What I'll do, he decided, is I'll pull off soon as I see a parking slot, pull off voluntarily before he flashes his light, or does anything, and then when he glides up beside me I'll say I got a loose wheel or something mechanical.

They always think that's great, he thought. When you give up like that and can't go on. Like throwing yourself on the ground the way an animal does, exposing your soft unprotected defenseless underbelly. I'll do that, he thought.

He did so, peeling off to the right and bumping the front wheels of his car against the curb. The cop car went on by.

Pulled off for nothing, he thought. Now it'll be hard to back out again, traffic's so heavy. He shut off his engine. Maybe I'll just sit here parked for a while, he decided, and alpha meditate or go into various different altered states of consciousness. Possibly by watching the chicks going along on foot. I wonder if they manufacture a bioscope for horny. Rather than alpha. Horny waves, first very short, then longer, larger, larger, finally right off the scale.

This is getting me nowhere, he realized. I should be out trying to locate someone holding. I've got to get my supply or pretty soon I'll be freaking, and then I won't be able to do anything. Even sit at the curb like I am. I not only won't know who I am, I won't even know where I am, or what's happening.

What is happening? he asked himself. What day is this? If I knew what day I'd know everything else; it'd seep back bit by bit.

Wednesday, in downtown L.A., the Westwood section. Ahead, one of those giant shopping malls surrounded by a wall that you bounced off like a rubber ball—unless you had a credit card on you and passed in through the electronic hoop. Owning no credit card for any of the malls, he could depend only on verbal report as to what the shops were like inside. A whole bunch, evidently, selling good products to the straights, especially to the straight wives. He watched the uniformed armed guards at the mall gate checking out each person. Seeing that the man or woman matched his or her credit card and that it hadn't been ripped off, sold, bought, used fraudulently. Lots of people moved on in through the gate, but he figured many were no doubt window-shopping. Not all that many people can have the bread or the urge to buy this time of day, he reflected. It's early, just past two. At night; that was when. The shops all lit up. He could—all the brothers and sisters could—see the lights from without, like showers of sparks, like a fun park for grown-up kids.

Stores this side of the mall, requiring no credit card, with no armed guards, didn't amount to much. Utility stores: a shoe and a TV shop, a bakery, small-appliance repair, a laundromat. He watched a girl who wore a short plastic jacket and stretch pants wander along from store to store; she had nice hair, but he couldn't see her face, see if she was foxy. Not a bad figure, he thought. The girl stopped for a time at a window where leather goods were displayed. She was checking out a purse with tassels; he could see her peering, worrying, scheming on the purse. Bet she goes on in and requests to see it, he thought.

The girl bopped on into the store, as he had figured.

Another girl, amid the sidewalk traffic, came along, this one in a frilly blouse, high heels, with silver hair and too much make-up. Trying to look older than she is, he thought. Probably not out of high school. After her came nothing worth mentioning, so he removed the string that held the glove compartment shut and got out a pack of cigarettes. He lit up and turned on the car radio, to a rock station. Once he had owned a tape-cartridge stereo, but finally, while loaded one day, he had neglected to bring it indoors with him when he locked up the car; naturally, when he returned the whole stereo tape system had been stolen. That's what carelessness gets you, he had thought, and so now he had only the crummy radio. Someday they'd take that too. But he knew where he could get another for almost nothing, used. Anyhow, the car stood to be wrecked any day; its oil rings were shot and compression had dropped way down. Evidently, he had burned a valve on the freeway coming home one night with a whole bunch of good stuff; sometimes when he had really scored heavy he got paranoid—not about the cops so much as about some other heads ripping him off. Some head desperate from withdrawing and dingey as a motherfucker.

A girl walked along now that made him take notice. Black hair, pretty, cruising slow; she wore an open midriff blouse and denim white pants washed a lot. Hey, I know her, he thought. That's Bob Arctor's girl. That's Donna.

He pushed open the car door and stepped out. The girl eyed him and continued on. He followed.

Thinks I'm fixing to grab-ass, he thought as he snaked among the people. How easily she gained speed; he could barely see her now as she glanced back. A firm, calm face . . . He saw large eyes that appraised him. Calculated his speed and would he catch up. Not at this rate, he thought. She can really move.

At the corner people had halted for the sign to say WALK instead of DON'T WALK; cars were making wild left turns. But the girl continued on, fast but with dignity, threading her path among the nut-o cars. The drivers glared at her with indignation. She didn't appear to notice.

"Donna!" When the sign flashed WALK he hurried across after her and caught up with her. She declined to run but merely walked rapidly. "Aren't you Bob's old lady?" he said. He managed to get in front of her to examine her face.

"No," she said. "No." She came toward him, directly at him; he retreated backward, because she held a short knife pointed at his stomach. "Get lost," she said, continuing to move forward without slowing or hesitating.

"Sure you are," he said. "I met you at his place." He could hardly see the knife, only a tiny section of blade metal, but he knew it was there. She would stab him and walk on. He continued to retreat backward, protesting. The girl held the knife so well concealed that probably no one else, the others walking along, could notice. But he did; it was going right at him as she approached without hesitation. He stepped aside, then, and the girl traveled on, in silence.

"*Jeez!*" he said to the back of her. I know it's Donna, he thought. She just doesn't flash on who I am, that she knows me. Scared, I guess; scared I'm going to hustle her. You got to be careful, he thought, when you come to a strange chick on the street; they're all prepared now. Too much has happened to them.

Funky little knife, he thought. Chicks shouldn't carry those; any guy could turn her wrist and the blade back on her any time he wanted. I could have. If I really wanted to git her. He stood there, feeling angry. I know that was Donna, he thought.

As he started to go back toward his parked car, he realized that the girl had halted, out of the movement of passers-by, and now stood silently gazing at him.

He walked cautiously toward her. "One night," he said, "me and Bob and another chick had some old Simon and Garfunkel tapes, and you were sitting there—" She had been filling capsules with high-grade death, one by one, painstakingly. For over an hour. El Primo. Numero Uno: Death. After she had finished she had laid a cap on each of them and they had dropped them, all of them together. Except her. I just sell them, she had said. If I start dropping them I eat up all my profits.

The girl said, "I thought you were going to knock me down and bang me."

"No," he said. "I just wondered if you . . ." He hesitated. "Like, wanted a ride. On the sidewalk?" he said, startled. "In broad daylight?"

"Maybe in a doorway. Or pull me into a car."

"I *know* you," he protested. "And Arctor would snuff me if I did that."

"Well, I didn't recognize you." She came toward him three steps. "I'm sorta nearsighted."

"You ought to wear contacts." She had, he thought, lovely large dark warm eyes. Which meant she wasn't on junk.

"I did have. But one fell out into a punch bowl. Acid punch, at a party. It sank to the bottom, and I guess someone dipped it up and drank it. I hope it tasted good; it cost me thirty-five dollars, originally."

"You want a ride where you're going?"

"You'll bang me in the car."

"No," he said, "I can't get it on right now, these last couple of weeks. It must be something they're adulterating all the stuff with. Some chemical."

"That's a neat-o line, but I've heard it before. Everybody bangs me." She amended that. "Tries to, anyhow. That's what it's like to be a chick. I'm suing one guy in court right now, for molestation and assault. We're asking punitive damages in excess of forty thousand."

"How far'd he get?"

Donna said, "Got his hand around my boob."

"That isn't worth forty thousand."

Together, they walked back toward his car.

"You got anything to sell?" he asked. "I'm really hurting. I'm virtually out, in fact, hell, I am out, come to think of it. Even a few, if you could spare a few."

"I can get you some."

"Tabs," he said. "I don't shoot up."

"Yes." She nodded intently, head down. "But, see, they're real scarce right now—the supply's temporarily dried up. You probably discovered that already. I can't get you very many, but—"

"When?" he broke in. They had reached his car; he halted,

opened the door, got in. On the far side Donna got in. They sat side by side.

"Day after tomorrow," Donna said. "If I can git ahold of this guy. I think I can."

Shit, he thought. Day after tomorrow. "No sooner? Not like, say, tonight?"

"Tomorrow at the earliest."

"How much?"

"Sixty dollars a hundred."

"Oh, Jeez," he said. "That's a burn."

"They're super good. I've got them from him before; they're really not what you usually buy into. Take my word for it—they're worth it. Actually, I prefer to get them from him rather than from anybody else—when I can. He doesn't always have them. See, he just took a trip down south, I guess. He just got back. He picked them up himself, so I know they're good for sure. And you don't have to pay me in advance. When I get them. Okay? I trust you."

"I never front," he said.

"Sometimes you have to."

"Okay," he said. "Then can you get me at least a hundred?" He tried to figure, rapidly, how many he could get; in two days he probably could raise one hundred twenty dollars and get two hundred tabs from her. And if he ran across a better deal in the meantime, from other people who were holding, he could forget her deal and buy from them. That was the advantage of never fronting, that plus never being burned.

"It's lucky for you that you ran into me," Donna said as he started up his car and backed out into traffic. "I'm supposed to see this one dude in about an hour, and he'd probably take all I could get . . . you'd have been out of luck. This was your day." She smiled, and he did too.

"I wish you could get them sooner," he said.

"If I do . . ." Opening her purse, she got out a little note pad and a pen that had SPARKS BATTERY TUNE-UP stamped on it. "How do I get hold of you, and I forget your name."

"Charles B. Freck," he said. He told her his phone number—not his, really, but the one he made use of at a straight friend's house, for messages like this—and laboriously she wrote it down. What difficulty she had writing, he thought.

Peering and slowly scrawling . . . They don't teach the
chicks jack shit in school any more, he thought. Flat-out illit-
erate. But foxy. So she can't hardly read or write; so what?
What matters with a fox is nice tits.

"I think I remember you," Donna said. "Sort of. It's all
hazy, that night; I was really out of it. All I definitely remember was getting the powder into those little caps—Librium
caps—we dumped the original contents. I must have dropped
half. I mean, on the floor." She gazed at him meditatively as he
drove. "You seem like a mellow dude," she said. "And you'll
be in the market later on? After a while you'll want more?"

"Sure," he said, wondering to himself if he could beat her
price by the time he saw her again; he felt he could, most
likely. Either way he won. That is, either way he scored.

Happiness, he thought, is knowing you got some pills.

The day outside the car, and all the busy people, the sunlight and activity, streamed past unnoticed; he was happy.

Look what he had found by chance—because, in fact, a
black-and-white had accidentally paced him. An unexpected
new supply of Substance D. What more could he ask out of
life? He could probably now count on two weeks lying ahead
of him, nearly *half a month*, before he croaked or nearly
croaked—withdrawing from Substance D made the two the
same. Two weeks! His heart soared, and he smelled, for a moment, coming in from the open windows of the car, the brief
excitement of spring.

"Want to go with me to see Jerry Fabin?" he asked the girl.
"I'm taking a load of his things over to him at the Number
Three Federal Clinic, where they took him last night. I'm just
carting over a little at a time, because there's a chance he might
get back out and I don't want to have to drag it all back."

"I'd better not see him," Donna said.

"You know him? Jerry Fabin?"

"Jerry Fabin thinks I contaminated him orginally with those
bugs."

"Aphids."

"Well, *then* he didn't know what they were. I better stay
away. Last time I saw him he got really hostile. It's his receptor
sites, in his brain, at least I think so. It seems like it, from what
the government pamphlets say now."

"That can't be restored, can it?" he said.

"No," Donna said. "That's irreversible."

"The clinic people said they'd let me see him, and they said they believed he could work some, you know—" He gestured. "Not be—" Again he gestured; it was hard to find words for that, what he was trying to say about his friend.

Glancing at him, Donna said, "You don't have speech-center damage, do you? In your—what is it called?—occipital lobe."

"No," he said. Vigorously.

"Do you have any kind of damage?" She tapped her head.

"No, it's just . . . you know. I have trouble saying it about those fucking clinics; I hate the Neural-Aphasia Clinics. One time I was there visiting a guy, he was trying to wax a floor—they said he couldn't wax the floor, I mean he couldn't figure out how to do it . . . What got me was he kept trying. I mean not just for like an hour; he was still trying a month later when I came back. Just like he had been, over and over again, when I first saw him there, when I first went to visit him. He couldn't figure out why he couldn't get it right. I remember the look on his face. He was sure he'd get it right if he kept trying to flash on what he was doing wrong. 'What am I doing wrong?' he kept asking them. There was no way to tell him. I mean, they told him—hell, I told him—but he still couldn't figure it out."

"The receptor sites in his brain are what I've read usually goes first," Donna said placidly. "Someone's brain where he's gotten a bad hit or like that, like too heavy." She was watching the cars ahead. "Look, there's one of those new Porsches with two engines." She pointed excitedly. "Wow."

"I knew a guy who hot-wired one of those new Porsches," he said, "and got it out on the Riverside Freeway and pushed it up to one seventy-five—wipe-out." He gestured. "Right into the ass of a semi. Never saw it, I guess." In his head he ran a fantasy number: himself at the wheel of a Porsche, but noticing the semi, all the semis. And everyone on the freeway—the Hollywood Freeway at rush hour—noticing him. Noticing him for sure, the lanky big-shouldered good-looking dude in the new Porsche going two hundred miles an hour, and all the cops' faces hanging open helplessly.

"You're shaking," Donna said. She reached over and put her hand on his arm. A quiet hand that he at once responded to. "Slow down."

"I'm tired," he said. "I was up two nights and two days counting bugs. Counting them and putting them in bottles. And finally when we crashed and got up and got ready the next morning to put the bottles in the car, to take to the doctor to show him, there was nothing in the bottles. Empty." He could feel the shaking now himself, and see it in his hands, on the wheel, the shaking hands on the steering wheel, at twenty miles an hour. "Every fucking one," he said. "Nothing. No bugs. And then I realized, I fucking realized. It came to me, about his brain, Jerry's brain."

The air no longer smelled of spring and he thought, abruptly, that he urgently needed a hit of Substance D; it was later in the day than he had realized, or else he had taken less than he thought. Fortunately, he had his portable supply with him, in the glove compartment, way back. He began searching for a vacant parking slot, to pull over.

"Your mind plays tricks," Donna said remotely; she seemed to have withdrawn into herself, gone far away. He wondered if his erratic driving was bumming her. Probably so.

Another fantasy film rolled suddenly into his head, without his consent: He saw, first, a big parked Pontiac with a bumper jack on the back of it that was slipping and a kid around thirteen with long thatched hair struggling to hold the car from rolling, meanwhile yelling for assistance. He saw himself and Jerry Fabin running out of the house together, Jerry's house, down the beer-can-littered driveway to the car. Himself, he grabbed at the car door on the driver's side to open it, to stomp the brake pedal. But Jerry Fabin, wearing only his pants, without even shoes, his hair all disarranged and streaming—he had been sleeping—Jerry ran past the car to the back and knocked, with his bare pale shoulder that never saw the light of day, the boy entirely away from the car. The jack bent and fell, the rear of the car crashed down, the tire and wheel rolled away, and the boy was okay.

"Too late for the brake," Jerry panted, trying to get his ugly greasy hair from his eyes and blinking. "No time."

"'S he okay?" Charles Freck yelled. His heart still pounded.

"Yeah." Jerry stood by the boy, gasping. "Shit!" he yelled at the boy in fury. "Didn't I tell you to wait until we were doing it with you? And when a bumper jack slips—shit, man, you can't hold back five thousand pounds!" His face writhed. The boy, little Ratass, looked miserable and twitched guiltily. "I repeatedly and repeatedly told you!"

"I went for the brake," Charles Freck explained, knowing his idiocy, his own equal fuckup, great as the boy's and equally lethal. His failure as a full-grown man to respond right. But he wanted to justify it anyhow, as the boy did, in words. "But now I realize—" he yammered on, and then the fantasy number broke off; it was a documentary rerun, actually, because he remembered the day when this had happened, back when they were all living together. Jerry's good instinct—otherwise Ratass would have been under the back of the Pontiac, his spine smashed.

The three of them plodded gloomily back toward the house, not even chasing the tire and wheel, which was still rolling off.

"I was asleep," Jerry muttered as they entered the dark interior of the house. "It's the first time in a couple weeks the bugs let up enough so I could. I haven't got any sleep at all for five days—I been runnin' and runnin'. I thought they were maybe gone; they've *been* gone. I thought they finally gave up and went somewhere else, like next door and out of the house entirely. Now I can feel them again. That tenth No Pest Strip I got, or maybe it's the eleventh—they cheated me again, like they did with all the others." But his voice was subdued now, not angry, just low and perplexed. He put his hand on Ratass's head and gave him a sharp smack. "You dumb kid—when a bumper jack slips get the hell out of there. Forget the car. Don't ever get behind it and try to push back against all that mass and block it with your body."

"But, Jerry, I was afraid the axle—"

"Fuck the axle. Fuck the car. It's your life." They passed on through the dark living room, the three of them, and the rerun of a now gone moment winked out and died forever.

Chapter Two

"GENTLEMEN of the Anaheim Lions Club," the man at the microphone said, "we have a wonderful opportunity this afternoon, for, you see, the County of Orange has provided us with the chance to hear from—and then put questions to and of—an undercover narcotics agent from the Orange County Sheriff's Department." He beamed, this man wearing his pink waffle-fiber suit and wide plastic yellow tie and blue shirt and fake leather shoes; he was an overweight man, overaged as well, overhappy even when there was little or nothing to be happy about.

Watching him, the undercover narcotics agent felt nausea.

"Now, you will notice," the Lions Club host said, "that you can barely see this individual, who is seated directly to my right, because he is wearing what is called a scramble suit, which is the exact same suit he wears—and in fact must wear—during certain parts, in fact most, of his daily activities of law enforcement. Later he will explain why."

The audience, which mirrored the qualities of the host in every possible way, regarded the individual in his scramble suit.

"This man," the host declared, "whom we will call Fred, because this is the code name under which he reports the information he gathers, once within the scramble suit, cannot be identified by voice, or by even technological voiceprint, or by appearance. He looks, does he not, like a vague blur and nothing more? Am I right?" He let loose a great smile. His audience, appreciating that this was indeed funny, did a little smiling on their own.

The scramble suit was an invention of the Bell Laboratories, conjured up by accident by an employee named S. A. Powers. He had, a few years ago, been experimenting with disinhibiting substances affecting neural tissue, and one night, having administered to himself an IV injection considered safe and mildly euphoric, had experienced a disastrous drop in the GABA fluid of his brain. Subjectively, he had then witnessed lurid phosphene activity projected on the far wall of his bedroom, a frantically progressing montage of what, at the time, he imagined to be modern-day abstract paintings.

For about six hours, entranced, S. A. Powers had watched thousands of Picasso paintings replace one another at flash-cut speed, and then he had been treated to Paul Klees, more than the painter had painted during his entire lifetime. S. A. Powers, now viewing Modigliani paintings replace themselves at furious velocity, had conjectured (one needs a theory for everything) that the Rosicrucians were telepathically beaming pictures at him, probably boosted by microrelay systems of an advanced order; but then, when Kandinsky paintings began to harass him, he recalled that the main art museum at Leningrad specialized in just such nonobjective moderns, and he decided that the Soviets were attempting telepathically to contact him.

In the morning he remembered that a drastic drop in the GABA fluid of the brain normally produced such phosphene activity; nobody was trying telepathically, with or without microwave boosting, to contact him. But it did give him the idea for the scramble suit. Basically, his design consisted of a multifaced quartz lens hooked to a miniaturized computer whose memory banks held up to a million and a half physiognomic fraction-representations of various people: men and women, children, with every variant encoded and then projected outward in all directions equally onto a superthin shroud-like membrane large enough to fit around an average human.

As the computer looped through its banks, it projected every conceivable eye color, hair color, shape and type of nose, formation of teeth, configuration of facial bone structure—the entire shroudlike membrane took on whatever physical characteristics were projected at any nanosecond, and then switched to the next. Just to make his scramble suit more effective, S. A. Powers programmed the computer to randomize the sequence of characteristics within each set. And to bring the cost down (the federal people always liked that), he found the source for the material of the membrane in a by-product of a large industrial firm already doing business with Washington.

In any case, the wearer of a scramble suit was Everyman and in every combination (up to combinations of a million and a half sub-bits) during the course of each hour. Hence, any description of him—or her—was meaningless. Needless to say, S. A. Powers had fed his own personal physiognomic characteristics into the computer units, so that, buried in the frantic permutation of qualities, his own surfaced and combined . . . on an average, he had calculated, of once each fifty years per suit, served up and reassembled, given enough time per suit. It was his closest claim to immortality.

"Let's hear it for the vague blur!" the host said loudly, and there was mass clapping.

In his scramble suit, Fred, who was also Robert Arctor, groaned and thought: This is terrible.

Once a month an undercover narcotics agent of the county was assigned at random to speak before bubblehead gatherings such as this. Today was his turn. Looking at his audience, he realized how much he detested straights. They thought this was all great. They were smiling. They were being entertained.

Maybe at this moment the virtually countless components of his scramble suit had served up S. A. Powers.

"But to be serious for just a moment," the host said, "this man here . . ." He paused, trying to remember.

"Fred," Bob Arctor said. S. A. Fred.

"Fred, yes." The host, invigorated, resumed, booming in the direction of his audience, "You see, Fred's voice is like one of those robot computer voices down in San Diego at the bank when you drive in, perfectly toneless and artificial. It leaves in our minds no characteristics, exactly as when he reports to his superiors in the Orange County Drug Abuse, ah, Program." He paused meaningfully. "You see, there is a dire risk for these police officers because the forces of dope, as we know, have penetrated with amazing skill into the various law-enforcement apparatuses throughout our nation, or may well have, according to most informed experts. So for the protection of these dedicated men, this scramble suit is necessary."

Slight applause for the scramble suit. And then expectant gazes at Fred, lurking within its membrane.

"But in his line of work in the field," the host added finally, as he moved away from the microphone to make room for Fred, "he, of course, does not wear this. He dresses like you or I, although, of course, in the hippie garb of those of the various subculture groups within which he bores in tireless fashion."

He motioned to Fred to rise and approach the microphone. Fred, Robert Arctor, had done this six times before, and he knew what to say and what was in store for him: the assorted degrees and kinds of asshole questions and opaque stupidity. The waste of time for him out of this, plus anger on his part, and a sense of futility each time, and always more so.

"If you saw me on the street," he said into the microphone, after the applause had died out, "you'd say, 'There goes a weirdo freak doper.' And you'd feel aversion and walk away."

Silence.

"I don't look like you," he said. "I can't afford to. My life depends on it." Actually, he did not look that different from them. And anyhow, he would have worn what he wore daily anyhow, job or not, life or not. He liked what he wore. But what he was saying had, by and large, been written by others and put before him to memorize. He could depart some, but they all had a standard format they used. Introduced a couple of years ago by a gung-ho division chief, it had by now become writ.

He waited while that sank in.

"I am not going to tell you first," he said, "what I am attempting to do as an undercover officer engaged in tracking down dealers and most of all the source of their illegal drugs in the streets of our cities and corridors of our schools, here in Orange County. I am going to tell you"—he paused, as they had trained him to do in PR class at the academy—"what I am afraid of," he finished.

That gaffed them; they had become all eyes.

"What I fear," he said, "night and day, is that our children, your children and my children . . ." Again he paused. "I have two," he said. Then, extra quietly, "Little ones, very little." And then he raised his voice emphatically. "But not too little to be addicted, calculatedly addicted, for profit, by those who would destroy this society." Another pause. "We do not know as yet," he continued presently, more calmly, "specifically who these men—or rather animals—are who prey on our young, as if in a wild jungle abroad, as in some foreign country, not ours.

The identity of the purveyors of the poisons concocted of brain-destructive filth shot daily, orally taken daily, smoked daily by several million men and women—or rather, that were once men and women—is gradually being unraveled. But finally we will, before God, know for sure."

A voice from the audience: "Sock it to 'em!"

Another voice, equally enthusiastic: "Get the commies!"

Applause and reprise severally.

Robert Arctor halted. Stared at them, at the straights in their fat suits, their fat ties, their fat shoes, and he thought, Substance D can't destroy their brains; they have none.

"Tell it like it is," a slightly less emphatic voice called up, a woman's voice. Searching, Arctor made out a middle-aged lady, not so fat, her hands clasped anxiously.

"Each day," Fred, Robert Arctor, whatever, said, "this disease takes its toll of us. By the end of each passing day the flow of profits—and where they go we—" He broke off. For the life of him he could not dredge up the rest of the sentence, even though he had repeated it a million times, both in class and at previous lectures.

All in the large room had fallen silent.

"Well," he said, "it isn't the profits anyhow. It's something else. What you see happen."

They didn't notice any difference, he noticed, even though he had dropped the prepared speech and was wandering on, by himself, without help from the PR boys back at the Orange County Civic Center. What difference anyhow? he thought. So what? What, really, do they know or care? The straights, he thought, live in their fortified huge apartment complexes guarded by their guards, ready to open fire on any and every doper who scales the wall with an empty pillowcase to rip off their piano and electric clock and razor and stereo that they haven't paid for anyhow, so he can get his fix, get the shit that if he doesn't he maybe dies, outright flat-out dies, of the pain and shock of withdrawal. But, he thought, when you're living inside looking safely out, and your wall is electrified and your guard is armed, why think about that?

"If you were a diabetic," he said, "and you didn't have money for a hit of insulin, would you steal to get the money? Or just die?"

Silence.

In the headphone of his scramble suit a tinny voice said, "I think you'd better go back to the prepared text, Fred. I really do advise it."

Into his throat mike, Fred, Robert Arctor, whatever, said, "I forget it." Only his superior at Orange County GHQ, which was not Mr. F., that is to say, Hank, could hear this. This was an anonymous superior, assigned to him only for this occasion.

"Riiiight," the official tinny prompter said in his earphone. "I'll read it to you. Repeat it after me, but try to get it to sound casual." Slight hesitation, riffling of pages. "Let's see . . . 'Each day the profits flow—where they go we—' That's about where you stopped."

"I've got a block against this stuff," Arctor said.

" '—will soon determine,' " his official prompter said, unheeding, " 'and then retribution will swiftly follow. And at that moment I would not for the life of me be in their shoes.' "

"Do you know why I've got a block against this stuff?" Arctor said. "Because this is what gets people on dope." He thought, This is why you lurch off and become a doper, this sort of stuff. This is why you give up and leave. In disgust.

But then he looked once more out at his audience and realized that for them this was not so. This was the only way they could be reached. He was talking to nitwits. Mental simps. It had to be put in the same way it had been put in first grade: *A* is for Apple and the Apple is Round.

"*D*," he said aloud to his audience, "is for Substance D. Which is for Dumbness and Despair and Desertion, the desertion of your friends from you, you from them, everyone from everyone, isolation and loneliness and hating and suspecting each other. *D*," he said then, "is finally Death. Slow Death, we—" He halted. "We, the dopers," he said, "call it." His voice rasped and faltered. "As you probably know. Slow Death. From the head on down. Well, that's it." He walked back to his chair and reseated himself. In silence.

"You blew it," his superior the prompter said. "See me in my office when you get back. Room 430."

"Yes," Arctor said. "I blew it."

They were looking at him as if he had pissed on the stage before their eyes. Although he was not sure just why.

Striding to the mike, the Lions Club host said, "Fred asked me in advance of this lecture to make it primarily a question-and-answer forum, with only a short introductory statement by him. I forgot to mention that. All right"—he raised his right hand—"who first, people?"

Arctor suddenly got to his feet again, clumsily.

"It would appear that Fred has something more to add," the host said, beckoning to him.

Going slowly back over to the microphone, Arctor said, his head down, speaking with precision, "Just this. Don't kick their asses after they're on it. The users, the addicts. Half of them, most of them, especially the girls, didn't know what they were getting on or even that they were getting on anything at all. Just try to keep them, the people, any of us, from getting on it." He looked up briefly. "See, they dissolve some reds in a glass of wine, the pushers, I mean—they give the booze to a chick, an underage little chick, with eight to ten reds in it, and she passes out, and then they inject her with a mex hit, which is half heroin and half Substance D—" He broke off. "Thank you," he said.

A man called up, "How do we stop them, sir?"

"Kill the pushers," Arctor said, and walked back to his chair.

He did not feel like returning right away to the Orange County Civic Center and Room 430, so he wandered down one of the commercial streets of Anaheim, inspecting the McDonaldburger stands and car washes and gas stations and Pizza Huts and other marvels.

Roaming aimlessly along like this on the public street with all kinds of people, he always had a strange feeling as to who he was. As he had said to the Lions types there in the hall, he looked like a doper when out of his scramble suit; he conversed like a doper; those around him now no doubt took him to be a doper and reacted accordingly. Other dopers—See there, he thought; "other," for instance—gave him a "peace, brother" look, and the straights didn't.

You put on a bishop's robe and miter, he pondered, and walk around in that, and people bow and genuflect and like that, and try to kiss your ring, if not your ass, and pretty soon you're a bishop. So to speak. What is identity? he asked himself. Where does the act end? Nobody knows.

What really fouled up his sense of who and what he was came when the Man hassled him. When harness bulls, beat cops, or cops in general, any and all, for example, came cruising up slowly to the curb near him in an intimidating manner as he walked, scrutinized him at length with an intense, keen, metallic, blank state, and then, often as not, evidently on whim, parked and beckoned him over.

"Okay, let's see your I.D.," the cop would say, reaching out; and then, as Arctor-Fred-Whatever-Godknew fumbled in his wallet pocket, the cop would yell at him, "Ever been ARRESTED?" Or, as a variant on that, adding, "BEFORE?" As if he were about to go into the bucket right then.

"What's the beef?" he usually said, if he said anything at all. A crowd naturally gathered. Most of them assumed he'd been nailed dealing on the corner. They grinned uneasily and waited to see what happened, although some of them, usually Chicanos or blacks or obvious heads, looked angry. And those that looked angry began after a short interval to be aware that they looked angry, and they changed that swiftly to impassive. Because everybody knew that anyone looking angry or uneasy—it didn't matter which—around cops must have something to hide. The cops especially knew that, legend had it, and they hassled such persons automatically.

This time, however, no one bothered him. Many heads were in evidence; he was only one of many.

What am I actually? he asked himself. He wished, momentarily, for his scramble suit. Then, he thought, I could go on being a vague blur and passers-by, street people in general, would applaud. Let's hear it for the vague blur, he thought, doing a short rerun. What a way to get recognition. How, for instance, could they be sure it wasn't some other vague blur and not the right one? It could be somebody other than Fred inside, or another Fred, and they'd never know, not even when Fred opened his mouth and talked. They wouldn't really know then. They'd never know. It could be Al pretending to be Fred, for example. It could be anyone in there, it could even be empty. Down at Orange County GHQ they could be piping a voice to the scramble suit, animating it from the sheriff's office. Fred could in that case be anybody who happened to be at his desk that day and happened to pick up the script and the mike, or a composite of all sorts of guys at their desks.

But I guess what I said at the end, he thought, finishes off that. That wasn't anybody back in the office. The guys back in the office want to talk to me about that, as a matter of fact.

He didn't look forward to that, so he continued to loiter and delay, going nowhere, going everywhere. In Southern California it didn't make any difference anyhow where you went; there was always the same McDonaldburger place over and over, like a circular strip that turned past you as you pretended to go somewhere. And when finally you got hungry and went to the McDonaldburger place and bought a McDonald's hamburger, it was the one they sold you last time and the time before that and so forth, back to before you were born, and in addition bad people—liars—said it was made out of turkey gizzards anyhow.

They had by now, according to their sign, sold the same original burger fifty billion times. He wondered if it was to the same person. Life in Anaheim, California, was a commercial for itself, endlessly replayed. Nothing changed; it just spread out farther and farther in the form of neon ooze. What there was always more of had been congealed into permanence long ago, as if the automatic factory that cranked out these objects had jammed in the *on* position. How the land became plastic, he thought, remembering the fairy tale "How the Sea Became Salt." Someday, he thought, it'll be mandatory that we all sell the McDonald's hamburger as well as buy it; we'll sell it back and forth to each other forever from our living rooms. That way we won't even have to go outside.

He looked at his watch. Two-thirty: time to make a buy call. According to Donna, he could score, through her, on perhaps a thousand tabs of Substance D cut with meth.

Naturally, once he got it, he would turn it over to County Drug Abuse to be analyzed and then destroyed, or whatever they did with it. Dropped it themselves, maybe, or so another legend went. Or sold it. But his purchase from her was not to bust her for dealing; he had bought many times from her and had never arrested her. That was not what it was all about, busting a small-time local dealer, a chick who considered it cool and far-out to deal dope. Half the narcotics agents in Orange County were aware that Donna dealt, and recognized her on sight. Donna even dealt sometimes in the parking lot of the 7-11 store, in front of the automatic holo-scanner the police kept going there, and got away with it. In a sense, Donna could never be busted no matter what she did and in front of whom.

What his transaction with Donna, like all those before, added up to was an attempt to thread a path upward via Donna to the supplier she bought from. So his purchases from her gradually grew in quantity. Originally he had coaxed her—if that was the word—into laying ten tabs on him, as a favor: friend-to-friend stuff. Then, later on, he had wangled a bag of a hundred for recompense, then three bags. Now, if he lucked out, he could score a thousand, which was ten bags. Eventually, he would be buying in a quantity which would be beyond her economic capacity; she could not front enough bread to her supplier to secure the stuff at her end. Therefore, she would lose instead of getting a big profit. They would haggle; she would insist that he front at least part of it; he would refuse; she couldn't front it herself to her source; time would run out—even in a deal that small a certain amount of tension would grow; everyone would be getting impatient; her supplier, whoever he was, would be holding and mad because she hadn't shown. So eventually, if it worked out right, she would give up and say to him and to her supplier, "Look, you better deal direct with each other. I know you both; you're both cool. I'll vouch for both of you. I'll set a place and a time and you two can meet. So from now on, Bob, you can start buying direct, if you're going to buy in this quantity." Because in that quantity he was for all intents and purposes a dealer; these were approaching dealer's quantities. Donna would assume he was reselling at a profit per hundred, since he was buying a thousand at a time at least. This way he could travel up the ladder and come to the next person in line, become a dealer like her, and then later on maybe get another step up and another as the quantities he bought grew.

Eventually—this was the name of the project—he would meet someone high enough to be worth busting. That meant someone who knew something, which meant someone either in contact with those who manufactured or someone who ran it in from the supplier who himself knew the source.

Unlike other drugs, Substance D had—apparently—only one source. It was synthetic, not organic; therefore, it came from a lab. It could be synthesized, and already had been in federal experiments. But the constituents were themselves derived from complex substances almost equally difficult to synthesize. Theoretically it could be manufactured by anyone who had, first, the formula and, second, the technological capacity to set up a factory. But in practice the cost was out of reach. Also, those who had invented it and were making it available sold it too cheaply for effective competition. And the wide distribution suggested that even though a sole source existed, it had a diversified layout, probably a series of labs in several key areas, perhaps one near each major urban drug-using spot in North America and Europe. Why none of these had been found was a mystery; but the implication was, both publicly and no doubt under official wraps, that the S. D. Agency—as the authorities arbitrarily termed it—had penetrated so far up into law-enforcement groups, both local and national, that those who found out anything usable about its operations soon either didn't care or didn't exist.

He had, naturally, several other leads at present besides Donna. Other dealers he pressured progressively for larger quantities. But because she was his chick—or anyhow he had hopes in that direction—she was for him the easiest. Visiting her, talking to her on the phone, taking her out or having her over—that was a personal pleasure as well. It was, in a sense, the line of least resistance. If you had to spy on and report about someone, it might as well be people you'd see anyhow; that was less suspicious and less of a drag. And if you did not see them frequently before you began surveillance, you would have to eventually anyhow; it worked out the same in the end.

Entering the phone booth, he did a phone thing.

Ring-ring-ring.

"Hello," Donna said.

Every pay phone in the world was tapped. Or if it wasn't, some crew somewhere just hadn't gotten around to it. The taps fed electronically onto storage reels at a central point, and about once every second day a print-out was obtained by an officer who listened to many phones without having to leave his office. He merely rang up the storage drums and, on signal, they played back, skipping all dead tape. Most calls were harmless. The officer could identify ones that weren't fairly readily. That was his skill. That was what he got paid for. Some officers were better at it than others.

As he and Donna talked, therefore, no one was listening. The playback would come maybe the next day at the earliest. If they discussed anything strikingly illegal, and the monitoring officer caught it, then voiceprints would be made. But all he and she had to do was keep it mild. The dialogue could still be recognizable as a dope deal. A certain governmental economy came into play here—it wasn't worth going through the hassle of voiceprints and track-down for routine illegal transactions. There were too many each day of the week, over too many phones. Both Donna and he knew this.

"How you doin'?" he asked.

"Okay." Pause in her warm, husky voice.

"How's your head today?"

"Sort of in a bad space. Sort of down." Pause. "I was bumtripped this A.M. by my boss at the shop." Donna worked behind the counter of a little perfume shop in Gateside Mall in Costa Mesa, to which she drove every morning in her MG. "You know what he said? He said this customer, this old guy, gray hair, who bilked us out of ten bucks—he said it was my fault and I've got to make it good. It's coming out of my paycheck. So I'm out ten bucks through no fucking—excuse me—fault of my own."

Arctor said, "Hey, can I get anything from you?"

She sounded sullen now. As if she didn't want to. Which was a shuck. "How—much do you want? I don't know."

"Ten of them," he said. The way they had it set up, one was a hundred; this was a request for a thousand, then.

Among fronts, if transactions had to take place over public communications, a fairly good try consisted of masking a large one by an apparently small one. They could deal and deal forever, in fact, in these quantities, without the authorities taking any interest; otherwise, the narcotics teams would be raiding apartments and houses up and down each street each hour of the day, and achieving little.

"'Ten,'" Donna muttered, irritably.

"I'm really hurting," he said, like a user. Rather than a dealer. "I'll pay you back later, when I've scored."

"No," she said woodenly. "I'll lay them on you gratis. Ten." Now, undoubtedly, she was speculating whether he was dealing. Probably he was. "Ten. Why not? Say, three days from now?"

"No sooner?"

"These are—"

"Okay," he said.

"I'll drop over."

"What time?"

She calculated. "Say around eight in the P.M. Hey, I want to show you a book I got, somebody left it at the shop. It's cool. It has to do with wolves. You know what wolves do? The male wolf? When he defeats his foe, he doesn't snuff him—he pees on him. Really! He stands there and pees on his defeated foe and then he splits. That's it. Territory is what they mostly fight over. And the right to screw. You know."

Arctor said, "I peed on some people a little while ago."

"No kidding? How come?"

"Metaphorically," he said.

"Not the usual way?"

"I mean," he said, "I told them—" He broke off. Talking too much; a fuckup. Jesus, he thought. "These dudes," he said, "like biker types, you dig? Around the Foster's Freeze? I was cruising by and they said something raunchy. So I turned around and said something like—" He couldn't think of anything for a moment.

"You can tell me," Donna said, "even if it's super gross. You gotta be super gross with biker types or they won't understand."

Arctor said, "I told them I'd rather ride a pig than a hog. Any time."

"I don't get it."

"Well, a pig is a chick that—"

"Oh yeah. Okay, well I get it. Barf."

"I'll see you at my place like you said," he said. "Good-by." He started to hang up.

"Can I bring the wolf book and show you? It's by Konrad Lorenz. The back cover, where they tell, says he was the foremost authority on wolves on earth. Oh yeah, one more thing. Your roommates both came into the shop today, Ernie what's-his-name and that Barris. Looking for you, if you might have—"

"What about?" Arctor said.

"Your cephalochromoscope that cost you nine hundred dollars, that you always turn on and play when you get home— Ernie and Barris were babbling away about it. They tried to use it today and it wouldn't work. No colors and no ceph patterns, neither one. So they got Barris's tool kit and unscrewed the bottom plate."

"The hell you say!" he said, indignant.

"And they say it's been fucked over. Sabotaged. Cut wires, and like sort of weird stuff—you know, freaky things. Shorts and broken parts. Barris said he'd try to—"

"I'm going right home," Arctor said, and hung up. My primo possession, he thought bitterly. And that fool Barris tinkering with it. But I can't go home right now, he realized. I've got to go over to New-Path to check on what they're up to.

It was his assignment: mandatory.

Chapter Three

CHARLES FRECK, too, had been thinking about visiting New-Path. The freakout of Jerry Fabin had gotten to him that much.

Seated with Jim Barris in the Fiddler's Three coffee shop in Santa Ana, he fooled around with his sugar-glazed doughnut morosely. "It's a heavy decision," he said. "That's cold turkey they do. They just keep with you night and day so you don't snuff yourself or bite off your arm, but they never give you anything. Like, a doctor will prescribe. Valium, for instance."

Chuckling, Barris inspected his patty melt, which was melted imitation cheese and fake ground beef on special organic bread. "What kind of bread is this?" he asked.

"Look on the menu," Charles Freck said. "It explains."

"If you go in," Barris said, "you'll experience symptoms that emanate up from the basic fluids of the body, specifically those located in the brain. By that I refer to the catecholamines, such as noradrenalin and seratonin. You see, it functions this way: Substance D, in fact all addictive dope, but Substance D most of all, interacts with the catecholamines in such a fashion that involvement is locked in place at a subcellular level. Biological counter-adaptation has occurred, and in a sense forever." He ate a huge bite of the right half of his patty melt. "They used to believe this occurred only with the alkaloid narcotics, such as heroin."

"I never shot smack. It's a downer."

The waitress, foxy and nice in her yellow uniform, with pert boobs and blond hair, came over to their table. "Hi," she said. "Is everything all right?"

Charles Freck gazed up in fear.

"Is your name Patty?" Barris asked her, signaling to Charles Freck that it was cool.

"No." She pointed to the name badge on her right boob. "It's Beth."

I wonder what the left one's called, Charles Freck thought.

"The waitress we had last time was named Patty," Barris said, eying the waitress grossly. "Same as the sandwich."

"That must have been a different Patty from the sandwich. I think she spells it with an *i*."

"Everything is super good," Barris said. Over his head Charles Freck could see a thought balloon in which Beth was stripping off her clothes and moaning to be banged.

"Not with me," Charles Freck said. "I got a lot of problems nobody else has."

In a somber voice, Barris said, "More people than you'd think. And more each day. This is a world of illness, and getting progressively worse." Above his head, the thought balloon got worse too.

"Would you like to order dessert?" Beth asked, smiling down at them.

"What like?" Charles Freck said with suspicion.

"We have fresh strawberry pie and fresh peach pie," Beth said smiling, "that we make here ourselves."

"No, we don't want any dessert," Charles Freck said. The waitress left. "That's for old ladies," he said to Barris, "those fruit pies."

"The idea of turning yourself over for rehabilitation," Barris said, "certainly makes you apprehensive. That's a manifestation of purposeful negative symptoms, your fear. It's the drug talking, to keep you out of New-Path and keep you from getting off it. You see, all symptoms are purposeful, whether they are positive or negative."

"No shit," Charles Freck muttered.

"The negative ones show up as the cravings, which are deliberately generated by the total body to force its owner— which in this case is you—to search frantically—"

"The first thing they do to you when you go into New-Path," Charles Freck said, "is they cut off your pecker. As an object lesson. And then they fan out in all directions from there."

"Your spleen next," Barris said.

"They what, they cut— What does that do, a spleen?"

"Helps you digest your food."

"How?"

"By removing the cellulose from it."

"Then I guess after that—"

"Just noncellulose foods. No leaves or alfalfa."

"How long can you live that way?"

Barris said, "It depends on your attitude."

"How many spleens does the average person have?" He knew there usually were two kidneys.

"Depends on his weight and age."

"Why?" Charles Freck felt keen suspicion.

"A person grows more spleens over the years. By the time he's eighty"—

"You're shitting me."

Barris laughed. Always he had been a strange laugher, Charles Freck thought. An unreal laugh, like something breaking. "Why your decision," Barris said presently, "to turn yourself in for residence therapy at a drug rehab center?"

"Jerry Fabin," he said.

With a gesture of easy dismissal, Barris said, "Jerry was a special case. I once watched Jerry Fabin staggering around and falling down, shitting all over himself, not knowing where he was, trying to get me to look up and research what poison he'd got hold of, thallium sulfate most likely . . . it's used in insecticides and to snuff rats. It was a burn, somebody paying him back. I could think of ten different toxins and poisons that might"—

"There's another reason," Charles Freck said. "I'm running low again in my supply, and I can't stand it, this always running low and not knowing if I'm fucking ever going to see any more."

"Well, we can't even be sure we'll see another sunrise."

"But shit—I'm down so low now that it's like a matter of days. And also . . . I think I'm being ripped off. I can't be taking them that fast; somebody must be pilfering from my fucking stash."

"How many tabs do you drop a day?"

"That's very difficult to determine. But not that many."

"A tolerance builds up, you know."

"Sure, right, but not like that. I can't stand running out and like that. On the other hand . . ." He reflected. "I think I got a new source. That chick, Donna. Donna something."

"Oh, Bob's girl."

"His old lady," Charles Freck said, nodding.

"No, he never got into her pants. He tries to."

"Is she reliable?"

"Which way? As a lay or—" Barris gestured: hand to mouth and swallowing.

"What kind of sex is that?" Then he flashed on it. "Oh, yeah, the latter."

"Fairly reliable. Scatterbrained, somewhat. Like you'd expect with a chick, especially the darker ones. Has her brain between her legs, like most of them. Probably keeps her stash there too." He chuckled. "Her whole dealer's stash."

Charles Freck leaned toward him. "Arctor never balled Donna? He talks about her like he did."

Barris said, "That's Bob Arctor. Talks like he did many things. Not the same, not at all."

"Well, how come he never laid her? Can't he get it on?"

Barris reflected wisely, still fiddling with his patty melt; he had now torn it into little bits. "Donna has problems. Possibly she's on junk. Her aversion to bodily contact in general—junkies lose interest in sex, you realize, due to their organs swelling up from vasoconstriction. And Donna, I've observed, shows an inordinate failure of sexual arousal, to an unnatural degree. Not just toward Arctor but toward . . ." He paused grumpily. "Other males as well."

"Shit, you just mean she won't come across."

"She would," Barris said, "if she were handled right. For instance . . ." He glanced up in a mysterious fashion. "I can show you how to lay her for ninety-eight cents."

"I don't want to lay her. I just want to buy from her." He felt uneasy. There was perpetually something about Barris that made his stomach uncomfortable. "Why ninety-eight cents?" he said. "She wouldn't take money; she's not turning tricks. Anyhow, she's Bob's chick."

"The money wouldn't be paid directly to her," Barris said in his precise, educated way. He leaned toward Charley Freck, pleasure and guile quivering amid his hairy nostrils. And not only that, the green tint of his shades had steamed up. "Donna does coke. Anybody who would give her a gram of coke she'd undoubtedly spread her legs for, especially if certain rare chemicals were added in strictly scientific fashion that I've done painstaking original research on."

"I wish you wouldn't talk that way," Charles Freck said.

"About her. Anyhow, a gram of coke's selling now for over a hundred dollars. Who's got that?"

Half sneezing, Barris declared, "I can derive a gram of pure cocaine at a total cost to me, for the ingredients from which I get it, not including my labor, of less than a dollar."

"Bullshit."

"I'll give you a demonstration."

"Where do these ingredients come from?"

"The 7-11 store," Barris said, and stumbled to his feet, discarding bits of patty melt in his excitement. "Get the check," he said, "and I'll show you. I've got a temporary lab set up at the house, until I can create a better one. You can watch me extract a gram of cocaine from common legal materials purchased openly at the 7-11 food store for under a dollar total cost." He started down the aisle. "Come on." His voice was urgent.

"Sure," Charles Freck said, picking up the check and following. The mother's dingey, he thought. Or maybe he isn't. With all those chemistry experiments he does, and reading and reading at the county library . . . maybe there's something to it. Think of the profit, he thought. Think what we could clear!

He hurried after Barris, who was getting out the keys to his Karmann Ghia as he strode, in his surplus flier's jump suit, past the cashier.

They parked in the lot of the 7-11, got out and walked inside. As usual, a huge dumb cop stood pretending to read a stroke-book magazine at the front counter; in actuality, Charles Freck knew, he was checking out everyone who entered, to see if they were intending to hit the place.

"What do we pick up here?" he asked Barris, who was casually strolling about the aisles of stacks of food.

"A spray can," Barris said. "Of Solarcaine."

"Sunburn spray?" Charles Freck did not really believe this was happening, but on the other hand, who knew? Who could be sure? He followed Barris to the counter; this time Barris paid.

They purchased the can of Solarcaine and then made it past the cop and back to their car. Barris drove rapidly from the lot, down the street, on and on at high speed, ignoring posted speed-limit signs, until finally he rolled to a halt before Bob Arctor's house, with all the old unopened newspapers in the tall grass of the front yard.

Stepping out, Barris lifted some items with wires dangling from the back seat to carry indoors. Voltmeter, Charles Freck saw. And other electronic testing gear, and a soldering gun. "What's that for?" he asked.

"I've got a long and arduous job to do," Barris said, carrying the various items, plus the Solarcaine, up the walk to the front door. He handed Charles Freck the door key. "And I'm probably not getting paid. As is customary."

Charles Freck unlocked the door, and they entered the house. Two cats and a dog rattled at them, making hopeful noises; he and Barris carefully edged them aside with their boots.

At the rear of the dinette Barris had, over the weeks, laid out a funky lab of sorts, bottles and bits of trash here and there, worthless-looking objects he had filched from different sources. Barris, Charles Freck knew, from having to hear about it, believed not so much in thrift as in ingenuity. You should be able to use the first thing that came to hand to achieve your objective, Barris preached. A thumbtack, a paper clip, part of an assembly the other part of which was broken or lost . . . It looked to Charles Freck as if a rat had set up shop here, was performing experiments with what a rat prized.

The first move in Barris's scheme was to get a plastic bag from the roll by the sink and squirt the contents of the spray can into it, on and on until the can or at least the gas was exhausted.

"This is unreal," Charles Freck said. "Super unreal."

"What they have deliberately done," Barris said cheerfully as he labored, "is mix the cocaine with oil so it can't be extracted. But my knowledge of chemistry is such that I know precisely how to separate the coke from the oil." He had begun vigorously shaking salt into the gummy slime in the bag. Now he poured it all into a glass jar. "I'm freezing it," he announced, grinning, "which causes the cocaine crystals to rise to the top, since they are lighter than air. Than the oil, I mean. And then the terminal step, of course, I keep to myself, but it involves an intricate methodological process of filtering." He opened the freezer above the refrigerator and carefully placed the jar inside.

"How long will it be in there?" Charles Freck asked.

"Half an hour." Barris got out one of his hand-rolled cigarettes, lit it, then strolled over to the heap of electronic testing equipment. He stood there meditating, rubbing his bearded chin.

"Yeah," Charles Freck said, "but I mean, so even if you get a whole gram of pure coke out of this, I can't use it on Donna to . . . you know, get into her pants in exchange. It's like buying her; that's what it amounts to."

"Exchange," Barris corrected. "You give her a gift, she gives you one. The most precious gift a woman has."

"She'd know she was being bought." He had seen enough of Donna to flash on that; Donna would make out the shuck right off.

"Cocaine is an aphrodisiac," Barris muttered, half to himself; he was setting up the testing equipment beside Bob Arctor's cephalochromoscope, which was Bob's most expensive possession. "After she's snorted a good part of it she'll be happy to uncork herself."

"Shit, man," Charles Freck protested. "You're talking about Bob Arctor's girl. He's my friend, and the guy you and Luckman live with."

Barris momentarily raised his shaggy head; he scrutinized Charles Freck for a time. "There's a great deal about Bob Arctor you're not aware of," he said. "That none of us are. Your view is simplistic and naïve, and you believe about him what he wants you to."

"He's an all-right guy."

"Certainly," Barris said, nodding and grinning. "Beyond a doubt. One of the world's best. But I have come—we have come, those of us who have observed Arctor acutely and perceptively—to distinguish in him certain contradictions. Both in terms of personality structure and in behavior. In his total relatedness to life. In, so to speak, his innate style."

"You have anything specific?"

Barris's eyes, behind his green shades, danced.

"Your eyes dancing don't mean nothing to me," Charles Freck said. "What's wrong with the cephscope that you're working on it?" He moved in closer to look for himself.

Tilting the central chassis on end, Barris said, "Tell me what you observe there with the wiring underneath."

"I see cut wires," Charles Freck said. "And a bunch of what look like deliberate shorts. Who did it?"

Still Barris's merry knowing eyes danced with special delight.

"This crummy significant crud doesn't go down with me worth shit," Charles Freck said. "Who damaged this cephscope? When did it happen? You just find out recently? Arctor didn't say anything the last time I saw him, which was the day before yesterday."

Barris said, "Perhaps he wasn't prepared to talk about it yet."

"Well," Charles Freck said, "as far as I'm concerned, you're talking in spaced-out riddles. I think I'll go over to one of the New-Path residences and turn myself in and go through withdrawal cold turkey and get therapy, the destruct game they play, and be with those guys day and night, and not have to be around mysterious nuts like yourself that don't make sense and I can't understand. I can see this cephscope has been fucked over, but you're not telling me anything. Are you trying to allege that Bob Arctor did it, to his own expensive equipment, or are you not? What are you saying? I wish I was living over at New-Path, where I wouldn't have to go through this meaningful shit I don't dig day after day, if not with you then with some burned-out freak like you, equally spaced." He glared.

"I did not damage this transmitting unit," Barris said speculatively, his whiskers twitching, "and doubt seriously that Ernie Luckman did."

"I doubt seriously if Ernie Luckman ever damaged anything in his life, except that time he flipped out on bad acid and threw the living-room coffee table and everything else besides out through the window of that apartment they had, him and that Joan chick, onto the parking area. That's different. Normally Ernie's got it all together more than the rest of us. No, Ernie wouldn't sabotage somebody else's cephscope. And Bob

Arctor—it's his, isn't it? What'd he do, get up secretly in the middle of the night without his knowledge and do this, burn himself like this? This was done by somebody out to burn him. That's what this was." You probably did it, you gunjy mother-fucker, he thought. You got the technical know-how and your mind's weird. "The person that did this," he said, "ought to be either in a federal Neural-Aphasia Clinic or the marble orchard. Preferably, in my opinion, the latter. Bob always really got off on this Altec cephscope; I musta seen him put it on, put it on, every time as soon as he gets home from work at night, soon as he steps in the door. Every guy has one thing he treasures. This was his. So I say, this is shit to do to him, man, shit."

"That's what I mean."

"What's what you mean?"

"'As soon as he gets home from work at night,'" Barris repeated. "I have been for some time conjecturing as to who Bob Arctor is really employed by, what specific actual organization it is that he can't tell us."

"It's the fucking Blue Chip Redemption Stamp Center in Placentia," Charles Freck said. "He told me once."

"I wonder what he does there."

Charles Freck sighed. "Colors the stamps blue." He did not like Barris, really. Freck wished he were elsewhere, maybe scoring from the first person he ran into or called. Maybe I should split, he said to himself, but then he recalled the jar of oil and cocaine cooling in the freezer, one hundred dollars' worth for ninety-eight cents. "Listen," he said, "when will that stuff be ready? I think you're shucking me. How could the Solarcaine people sell it for that little if it has a gram of pure coke in it? How could they make a profit?"

"They buy," Barris declared, "in large quantities."

In his head, Charles Freck rolled an instant fantasy: dump trucks full of cocaine backing up to the Solarcaine factory, wherever it was, Cleveland maybe, dumping tons and tons of pure, unstepped-on, uncut, high-grade cocaine into one end of the factory, where it was mixed with oil and inert gas and other garbage and then stuck in little bright-colored spray cans to be stacked up by the thousands in 7-11 stores and drugstores and supermarkets. What we ought to do, he ruminated, is knock over one of those dump trucks; take the whole load, maybe seven or eight hundred pounds—hell, lots more. What does a dump truck hold?

Barris brought him the now empty Solarcaine spray can for his inspection; he showed him the label, on which were listed all the contents. "See? Benzocaine. Which only certain gifted people know is a trade name for cocaine. If they said cocaine on the label people would flash on it and they'd eventually do what I do. People just don't have the education to realize. The scientific training, such as I went through."

"What are you going to do with this knowledge?" Charles Freck asked. "Besides making Donna Hawthorne horny?"

"I plan to write a best-seller eventually," Barris said. "A text for the average person about how to manufacture safe dope in his kitchen without breaking the law. You see, this does not break the law. Benzocaine is legal. I phoned a pharmacy and asked them. It's in a lot of things."

"Gee," Charles Freck said, impressed. He examined his wristwatch, to see how much longer they had to wait.

Bob Arctor had been told by Hank, who was Mr. F., to check out the local New-Path residence centers in order to locate a major dealer, whom he had been watching, but who had abruptly dropped from sight.

Now and then a dealer, realizing he was about to be busted, took refuge in one of the drug-rehabilitation places, like Synanon and Center Point and X-Kalay and New-Path, posing as an addict seeking help. Once inside, his wallet, his name, everything that identified him, was stripped away in preparation for building up a new personality not drug-oriented. In this stripping-away process, much that the law-enforcement people needed in order to locate their suspect disappeared. Then, later on, when the pressure was off, the dealer emerged and resumed his usual activity outside.

How often this happened nobody knew. The drug-rehab outfits tried to discern when they were being so used, but not always successfully. A dealer in fear of forty years' imprisonment had motivation to spin a good story to the rehab staff that had the power to admit or refuse him. His agony at that point was mainly real.

Driving slowly up Katella Boulevard, Bob Arctor searched

for the New-Path sign and the wooden building, formerly a
private dwelling, that the energetic rehab people operated in
this area. He did not enjoy shucking his way into a rehab place
posing as a prospective resident in need of help, but this was
the only way to do it. If he identified himself as a narcotics
agent in search of somebody, the rehab people—most of them
usually, anyhow—would begin evasive action as a matter of
course. They did not want their family hassled by the Man,
and he could get his head into that space, appreciate the valid-
ity of that. These ex-addicts were supposed to be safe at last;
in fact, the rehab staff customarily officially guaranteed their
safety on entering. On the other hand, the dealer he sought
was a mother of the first water, and to use the rehab places this
way ran contrary to every good interest for everyone. He saw
no other choice for himself, or for Mr. F., who had originally
put him onto Spade Weeks. Weeks had been Arctor's main
subject for an interminable time, without result. And now, for
ten whole days, he had been unfindable.

He made out the bold sign, parked in their little lot, which
this particular branch of New-Path shared with a bakery, and
walked in an uneven manner up the path to the front door,
hands stuffed in his pockets, doing his loaded-and-miserable
number.

At least the department didn't hold it against him for losing
Spade Weeks. In their estimation, officially, it just proved how
slick Weeks was. Technically Weeks was a runner rather than a
dealer: he brought shipments of hard dope up from Mexico
at irregular intervals, to somewhere short of L.A., where the
buyers met and split it up. Weeks's method of sneaking the
shipment across the border was a neat one: He taped it on
the underside of the car of some straight type ahead of him at
the crossing, then tracked the dude down on the U.S. side and
shot him at the first convenient opportunity. If the U.S. border
patrol discovered the dope taped on the underside of the
straight's vehicle, then the straight got sent up, not Weeks.
Possession was prima facie in California. Too bad for the
straight, his wife and kids.

Better than anyone else in Orange County undercover work,
he recognized Weeks on sight: fat black dude, in his thirties,
with a unique slow and elegant speech pattern, as if memo-

rized at some phony English school. Actually, Weeks came from the slums of L.A. He'd learned his diction, most likely, from edutapes loaned by some college library.

Weeks liked to dress in a subdued but classy way, as if he were a doctor or a lawyer. Often he carried an expensive alligator-hide attaché case and wore horn-rimmed glasses. Also, he usually was armed, with a shotgun for which he had commissioned a custom-made pistol grip from Italy, very posh and stylish. But at New-Path his assorted shucks would have been stripped away; they would have dressed him like every-one else, in random, donated clothes, and stuck his attaché case in the closet.

Opening the solid wood door, Arctor entered.

Gloomy hall, lounge to his left, with guys reading. A ping-pong table at the far end, then a kitchen. Slogans on the walls, some hand-done and some printed: THE ONLY REAL FAILURE IS TO FAIL OTHERS and so forth. Little noise, little activity. New-Path maintained assorted retail industries; probably most of the residents, guys and chicks alike, were at work, at their hair shops and gas stations and ballpoint-pen works. He stood there, waiting in a weary way.

"Yes?" A girl appeared, pretty, wearing an extremely short blue cotton skirt and T-shirt with NEW-PATH dyed across it from nipple to nipple.

He said, in a thick, croaking, humiliated voice, "I'm—in a bad space. Can't get it together any more. Can I sit down?"

"Sure." The girl waved, and two guys, mediocre in appear-ance, showed up, looking impassive. "Take him where he can sit down and get him some coffee."

What a drag, Arctor thought as he let the two guys co-erce him to a seedy-looking overstuffed couch. Dismal walls, he noticed. Dismal low-quality donated paint. They sub-sisted, though, on contributions; difficulty in getting funded. "Thanks," he grated shakily, as if it was an overwhelming relief to be there and sit. "Wow," he said, attempting to smooth his hair; he made it seem that he couldn't, and gave up.

The girl, directly before him, said firmly, "You look like hell, mister."

"Yeah," both guys agreed, in a surprisingly snappy tone. "Like real shit. What you been doing, lying in your own crap?"

Arctor blinked.

"Who are you?" one guy demanded.

"You can see what he is," the other said. "Some scum from the fucking garbage pail. Look." He pointed at Arctor's hair. "Lice. That's why you itch, Jack."

The girl, calm and above it, but not in any way friendly, said, "Why did you come in here, mister?"

To himself Arctor thought, Because you have a big-time runner in here somewhere. And I'm the Man. And you're stupid, all of you. But instead he muttered cringingly, which was evidently what was expected, "Did you say—"

"Yes, mister, you can have some coffee." The girl jerked her head, and one of the guys obediently strode off to the kitchen.

A pause. Then the girl bent down and touched his knee. "You feel pretty bad, don't you?" she said softly.

He could only nod.

"Shame and a sense of disgust at the thing you are," she said.

"Yeah," he agreed.

"At the pollution you've made of yourself. A cesspool. Sticking that spike up your ass day after day, injecting your body with—"

"I couldn't go on any more," Arctor said. "This place is the only hope I could think of. I had a friend come in here, I think, he said he was going to. A black dude, in his thirties, educated, very polite and—"

"You'll meet the family later," the girl said. "If you qualify. You have to pass our requirements, you realize. And the first one is sincere need."

"I have that," Arctor said. "Sincere need."

"You've got to be bad off to be let in here."

"I am," he said.

"How strung out are you? What's your habit up to?"

"Ounce a day," Arctor said.

"Pure?"

"Yeah." He nodded. "I keep a sugar bowl of it on the table."

"It's going to be super rough. You'll gnaw your pillow into feathers all night; there'll be feathers everywhere when you wake up. And you'll have seizures and foam at the mouth. And dirty yourself the way sick animals do. Are you ready for that? You realize we don't give you anything here."

"There isn't anything," he said. This was a drag, and he felt restless and irritable. "My buddy," he said, "the black guy. Did he make it here? I sure hope he didn't get picked up by the pigs on the way—he was so out of it, man, he could hardly navigate. He thought—"

"There are no one-to-one relationships at New-Path," the girl said. "You'll learn that."

"Yeah, but did he make it here?" Arctor said. He could see he was wasting his time. Jesus, he thought; this is worse than we do downtown, this hassling. And she won't tell me jack shit. Policy, he realized. Like an iron wall. Once you go into one of these places you're dead to the world. Spade Weeks could be sitting beyond the partition, listening and laughing his ass off, or not be here at all, or anything in between. Even with a warrant—that never worked. The rehab outfits knew how to drag their feet, stall around until anyone living there sought by the police had zipped out a side door or bolted himself inside the furnace. After all, the staff here were all ex-addicts themselves. And no law-enforcement agency liked the idea of rousting a rehab place: the yells from the public never ceased.

Time to give up on Spade Weeks, he decided, and extricate myself. No wonder they never sent me around here before; these guys are not nice. And then he thought, So as far as I'm concerned, I've indefinitely lost my main assignment; Spade Weeks no longer exists.

I'll report back to Mr. F., he said to himself, and await reassignment. The hell with it. He rose to his feet stiffly and said, "I'm splitting." The two guys had now returned, one of them with a mug of coffee, the other with literature, apparently of an instructional kind.

"You're chickening out?" the girl said, haughtily, with contempt. "You don't have it at gut level to stick with a decision? To get off the filth? You're going to crawl back out of here on your belly?" All three of them glared at him with anger.

"Later," Arctor said, and moved toward the front door, the way out.

"Fucking doper," the girl said from behind him. "No guts, brain fried, nothing. Creep out, creep; it's your decision."

"I'll be back," Arctor said, nettled. The mood here oppressed him, and it had intensified now that he was leaving.

"We may not want you back, gutless," one of the guys said.

"You'll have to plead," the other said. "You may have to do a lot of heavy pleading. And even then we may not want you."

"In fact, we don't want you now," the girl said.

At the door Arctor paused and turned to face his accusers. He wanted to say something, but for the life of him he couldn't think of anything. They had blanked out his mind.

His brain would not function. No thoughts, no response, no answer to them, even a lousy and feeble one, came to him at all.

Strange, he thought, and was perplexed.

And passed on out of the building to his parked car.

As far as I'm concerned, he thought, Spade Weeks has disappeared forever. I ain't going back inside one of those places.

Time, he decided queasily, to ask to be reassigned. To go after somebody else.

They're tougher than we are.

Chapter Four

F ROM within his scramble suit the nebulous blur who signed in as Fred faced another nebulous blur representing himself as Hank.

"So much for Donna, for Charley Freck, and—let's see . . ." Hank's metallic monotone clicked off for a second. "All right, you've covered Jim Barris." Hank made an annotation on the pad before him. "Doug Weeks, you think, is probably dead or out of this area."

"Or hiding and inactive," Fred said.

"Have you heard anyone mention this name: Earl or Art De Winter?"

"No."

"How about a woman named Molly? Large woman."

"No."

"How about a pair of spades, brothers, about twenty, named something like Hatfield? Possibly dealing in pound bags of heroin."

"Pounds? *Pound* bags of heroin?"

"That's right."

"No," Fred said. "I'd remember that."

"A Swedish person, tall, Swedish name. Male. Served time, wry sense of humor. Big man but thin, carrying a great deal of cash, probably from the split of a shipment earlier this month."

"I'll watch for him," Fred said. "Pounds." He shook his head, or rather the nebulous blur wobbled.

Hank sorted among his holographic notes. "Well, this one is in jail." He held up a picture briefly, then read the reverse. "No, this one's dead; they've got the body downstairs." He sorted on. Time passed. "Do you think the Jora girl is turning tricks?"

"I doubt it." Jora Kajas was only fifteen. Strung out on injectable Substance D already, she lived in a slum room in Brea, upstairs, the only heat radiating from a water heater, her source of income a State of California tuition scholarship she had won. She had not attended classes, so far as he knew, in six months.

"When she does, let me know. Then we can go after the parents."

"Okay." Fred nodded.

"Boy, the bubblegummers go downhill fast. We had one in here the other day—she looked fifty. Wispy gray hair, missing teeth, eyes sunk in, arms like pipe cleaners . . . We asked her what her age was and she said, 'Nineteen.' We double-checked. 'You know how old you look?' this one matron said to her. 'Look in the mirror.' So she looked in the mirror. She started to cry. I asked her how long she'd been shooting up."

"A year," Fred said.

"Four months."

"The street stuff is bad right now," Fred said, not trying to imagine the girl, nineteen, with her hair falling out. "Cut with worse garbage than usual."

"You know how she got strung out? Her brothers, both of them, who were dealing, went in her bedroom one night, held her down and shot her up, then balled her. Both of them. To break her in to her new life, I guess. She'd been on the corner several months when we hauled her in here."

"Where are they now?" He thought he might run into them.

"Serving a six-month sentence for possession. The girl's also got the clap, now, and didn't realize it. So it's gone up deep inside her, the way it does. Her brothers thought that was funny."

"Nice guys," Fred said.

"I'll tell you one that'll get you for sure. You're aware of the three babies over at Fairfield Hospital that they have to give hits of smack to every day, that are too young to withdraw yet? A nurse tried to—"

"It gets me," Fred said in his mechanical monotone. "I heard enough, thanks."

Hank continued, "When you think of newborn babies being heroin addicts because—"

"Thanks," the nebulous blur called Fred repeated.

"What do you figure the bust should be for a mother that gives a newborn baby a joypop of heroin to pacify it, to keep it from crying? Overnight in the county farm?"

"Something like that," Fred said tonelessly. "Maybe a weekend, like they do the drunks. Sometimes I wish I knew how to go crazy. I forget how."

"It's a lost art," Hank said. "Maybe there's an instruction manual on it."

"There was this flick back around 1970," Fred said, "called *The French Connection*, about a two-man team of heroin narks, and when they made their hit one of them went totally bananas and started shooting everyone in sight, including his superiors. It made no difference."

"It's maybe better you don't know who I am, then," Hank said. "You could only get me by accident."

"Somebody," Fred said, "will get us all anyhow eventually."

"It'll be a relief. A distinct relief." Going farther into his pile of notes, Hank said, "Jerry Fabin. Well, we'll write him off. N.A.C. The boys down the hall say Fabin told the responding officers on the way to the clinic that a little contract man three feet high, legless, on a cart, had been rolling after him day and night. But he never told anybody because if he did they'd freak and get the hell out and then he'd have no friends, nobody to talk to."

"Yeah," Fred said stoically. "Fabin has had it. I read the EEG analysis from the clinic. We can forget about him."

Whenever he sat facing Hank and did his reporting thing, he experienced a certain deep change in himself. Afterward was when he usually noticed it, although at the time he sensed that for a reason he assumed a measured and uninvolved attitude. Whatever came up and whoever it was about possessed no emotional significance to him during these sessions.

At first he had believed it to be the scramble suits that both of them wore; they could not physically sense each other. Later on he conjectured that the suits made no actual difference; it was the situation itself. Hank, for professional reasons, purposefully played down the usual warmth, the usual arousal in all directions; no anger, no love, no strong emotions of any sort would help either of them. How could intense natural involvement be of use when they were discussing crimes, serious crimes, committed by persons close to Fred and even, as in the case of Luckman and Donna, dear to him? He had to neutralize himself; they both did, him more so than Hank. They became neutral; they spoke in a neutral fashion; they looked neutral. Gradually it became easy to do so, without prearrangement.

And then afterward all his feelings seeped back.

Indignation at many of the events he had seen, even horror, in retrospect: shock. Great overpowering runs for which there had been no previews. With the audio always up too loud inside his head.

But while he sat across the table from Hank he felt none of these. Theoretically, he could describe anything he had witnessed in an impassive way. Or hear anything from Hank.

For example, he could offhandedly say "Donna is dying of hep and using her needle to wipe out as many of her friends as she can. Best thing here would be to pistol-whip her until she knocks it off." His own chick . . . *if* he had observed that or knew it for a fact. Or "Donna suffered a massive vasoconstriction from a mickey-mouse LSD analogue the other day and half the blood vessels in her brain shut down." Or "Donna is dead." And Hank would note that down and maybe say "Who sold her the stuff and where's it made?" or "Where's the funeral, and we should get license numbers and names," and he'd discuss that without feeling.

This was Fred. But then later on Fred evolved into Bob Arctor, somewhere along the sidewalk between the Pizza Hut and the Arco gas station (regular now a dollar two cents a gallon), and the terrible colors seeped back into him whether he liked it or not.

This change in him as Fred was an economy of the passions. Firemen and doctors and morticians did the same trip in their work. None of them could leap up and exclaim each few moments; they would first wear themselves out and be worthless and then wear out everyone else, both as technicians on the job and as humans off. An individual had just so much energy.

Hank did not force this dispassion on him; he *allowed* him to be like this. For his own sake. Fred appreciated it.

"What about Arctor?" Hank asked.

In addition to everyone else, Fred in his scramble suit naturally reported on himself. If he did not, his superior—and through him the whole law-enforcement apparatus—would become aware of who Fred was, suit or not. The agency plants would report back, and very soon he as Bob Arctor, sitting in his living room smoking dope and dropping dope with the other dopers, would find he had a little three-foot-high contract man on a cart coasting after him, too. And he would not be hallucinating, as had been Jerry Fabin.

"Arctor's not doing anything much," Fred said, as he always did. "Works at his nowhere Blue Chip Stamp job, drops a few tabs of death cut with meth during the day—"

"I'm not sure." Hank fiddled with one particular sheet of paper. "We have a tip here from an informant whose tips generally pan out that Arctor has funds above and beyond what the Blue Chip Redemption Center pays him. We called them and asked what his take-home pay is. It's not much. And then we inquired into that, why that is, and we found he isn't employed there full time throughout the week."

"No shit," Fred said dismally, realizing that the "above-and-beyond" funds were of course those provided him for his narking. Every week small-denomination bills were dispensed to him by a machine masquerading as a Dr. Pepper source at a Mexican bar and restaurant in Placentia. This was in essence payoffs on information he gave that resulted in convictions. Sometimes this sum became exceptionally great, as when a major heroin seizure occurred.

Hank read on reflectively, "And according to this informant, Arctor comes and goes mysteriously, especially around sunset. After he arrives home he eats, then on what may be pretexts takes off again. Sometimes very fast. But he's never gone for long." He glanced up—the scramble suit glanced up—at Fred. "Have you observed any of this? Can you verify? Does it amount to anything?"

"Most likely his chick, Donna," Fred said.

"Well, 'most likely.' You're supposed to know."

"It's Donna. He's over there banging her night and day." He felt acutely uncomfortable. "But I'll check into it and let you know. Who's this informant? Might be a burn toward Arctor."

"Hell, we don't know. On the phone. No print—he used some sort of rinky-dink electronic grid." Hank chuckled; it sounded odd, coming out metallically as it did. "But it worked. Enough."

"Christ," Fred protested, "it's that burned-out acid head

Jim Barris doing a schizy grudge number on Arctor's head! Barris took endless electronic-repair courses in the Service, plus heavy-machinery maintenance. I wouldn't give him the time of day as an informant."

Hank said, "We don't know it's Barris, and anyhow there may be more to Barris than 'burned-out acid head.' We've got several people looking into it. Nothing I feel would be of use to you, at least so far."

"Anyhow, it's one of Arctor's friends," Fred said.

"Yes, it's undoubtedly a vengeance burn trip. These dopers —phoning in on each other every time they get sore. As a matter of fact, he did seem to know Arctor from a close standpoint."

"Nice guy," Fred said bitterly.

"Well, that's how we find out," Hank said. "What's the difference between that and what you're doing?"

"I'm not doing it for a grudge," Fred said.

"Why are you doing it, actually?"

Fred, after an interval said, "Damned if I know."

"You're off Weeks. I think for the time being I'll assign you primarily to observe Bob Arctor. Does he have a middle name? He uses the initial—"

Fred made a strangled, robotlike noise. "Why Arctor?"

"Covertly funded, covertly engaged, making enemies by his activities. What's Arctor's middle name?" Hank's pen poised patiently. He waited to hear.

"Postlethwaite."

"How do you spell that?"

"I don't know, I don't fucking know," Fred said.

"Postlethwaite," Hank said, writing a few letters. "What nationality is that?"

"Welsh," Fred said curtly. He could barely hear; his ears had blurred out, and one by one his other senses as well.

"Are those the people who sing about the men of Harlech? What is 'Harlech'? A town somewhere?"

"Harlech is where the heroic defense against the Yorkists in 1468—" Fred broke off. Shit, he thought. This is terrible.

"Wait, I want to get this down," Hank was saying, writing away with his pen.

Fred said, "Does this mean you'll be bugging Arctor's house and car?"

"Yes, with the new holographic system; it's better, and we currently have a number of them unrequisitioned. You'll want storage and printout on everything, I would assume." Hank noted that too.

"I'll take what I can get," Fred said. He felt totally spaced from all this; he wished the debriefing session would end and he thought: If only I could drop a couple tabs—

Across from him the other formless blur wrote and wrote, filling in all the inventory ident numbers for all the technological gadgetry that would, if approval came through, soon be available to him, by which to set up a constant monitoring system of the latest design, on his own house, on himself.

For over an hour Barris had been attempting to perfect a silencer made from ordinary household materials costing no more than eleven cents. He had almost done so, with aluminum foil and a piece of foam rubber.

In the night darkness of Bob Arctor's back yard, among the heaps of weeds and rubbish, he was preparing to fire his pistol with the homemade silencer on it.

"The neighbors will hear," Charles Freck said uneasily. He could see lit windows all over, many people probably watching TV or rolling joints.

Luckman, lounging out of sight but able to watch, said, "They only call in murders in this neighborhood."

"Why do you need a silencer?" Charles Freck asked Barris. "I mean, they're illegal."

Barris said moodily, "In this day and age, with the kind of degenerate society we live in and the depravity of the individual, every person of worth needs a gun at all times. To protect himself." He half shut his eyes, and fired his pistol with its homemade silencer. An enormous report sounded, temporarily deafening the three of them. Dogs in far-off yards barked.

Smiling, Barris began unwrapping the aluminum foil from the foam rubber. He appeared to be amused.

"That's sure some silencer," Charles Freck said, wondering when the police would appear. A whole bunch of cars.

"What it did," Barris explained, showing him and Luckman black-seared passages burned through the foam rubber, "is augment the sound rather than dampen it. But I almost have it right. I have it in principle, anyhow."

"How much is that gun worth?" Charles Freck asked. He had never owned a gun. Several times he had owned a knife, but somebody always stole it from him. One time a chick had done that, while he was in the bathroom.

"Not much," Barris said. "About thirty dollars used, which this is." He held it out to Freck, who backed away apprehensively. "I'll sell it to you," Barris said. "You really ought to have one, to guard yourself against those who would harm you."

"There's a lot of those," Luckman said in his ironic way, with a grin. "I saw in the L. A. *Times* the other day, they're giving away a free transistor radio to those who would harm Freck most successfully."

"I'll trade you a Borg-Warner tach for it," Freck said.

"That you stole from the guy's garage across the street," Luckman said.

"Well, probably the gun's stolen, too," Charles Freck said. Most everything that was worth something was originally ripped off anyhow; it indicated the piece had value. "As a matter of fact," he said, "the guy across the street ripped the tach off in the first place. It's probably changed hands like fifteen times. I mean, it's a really cool tach."

"How do you know he ripped it off?" Luckman asked him.

"Hell, man, he's got eight tachs there in his garage, all dangling cut wires. What else would he be doing with them, that many, I mean? Who goes out and buys eight tachs?"

To Barris, Luckman said, "I thought you were busy working on the cephscope. You finished already?"

"I cannot continually work on that night and day, because it is so extensive," Barris said. "I've got to knock off." He cut, with a complicated pocketknife, another section of foam rubber. "This one will be totally soundless."

"Bob thinks you're at work on the cephscope," Luckman said. "He's lying there in his bed in his room imagining that, while you're out here firing off your pistol. Didn't you agree with Bob that the back rent you owe would be compensated by your—"

"Like good beer," Barris said, "an intricate, painstaking reconstruction of a damaged electronic assembly—"

"Just fire off the great eleven-cent silencer of our times," Luckman said, and belched.

I've had it, Robert Arctor thought.

He lay alone in the dim light of his bedroom, on his back, staring grimly at nothing. Under his pillow he had his .32 police-special revolver; at the sound of Barris's .22 being fired in the back yard he had reflexively gotten his own gun from beneath the bed and placed it within easier reach. A safety move, against any and all dangers; he hadn't even thought it out consciously.

But his .32 under his pillow wouldn't be much good against anything so indirect as sabotage of his most precious and expensive possession. As soon as he had gotten home from the debriefing with Hank he had checked out all the other appliances, and found them okay—especially the car—always the car first, in a situation like this. Whatever was going on, whoever it was by, it was going to be chickenshit and devious: some freak without integrity or guts lurking on the periphery of his life, taking indirect potshots at him from a position of concealed safety. Not a person but more a sort of walking, hiding symptom of their way of life.

There had been a time, once, when he had not lived like this, a .32 under his pillow, a lunatic in the back yard firing off a pistol for God knew what purpose, some other nut or perhaps the same one imposing a brain-print of his own shorted-out upstairs on an incredibly expensive and valued cephscope that everyone in the house, plus all their friends, loved and enjoyed. In former days Bob Arctor had run his affairs differently: there had been a wife much like other wives, two small daughters, a stable household that got swept and cleaned and emptied out daily, the dead newspapers not even opened carried from the front walk to the garbage pail, or even, sometimes, read. But then one day, while lifting out an electric corn popper from under the sink, Arctor had hit his head on the corner of a kitchen cabinet directly above him. The pain, the cut in his scalp, so unexpected and undeserved, had for some reason cleared away the cobwebs. It flashed on him instantly that he didn't hate the kitchen cabinet: he hated his wife, his two daughters, his whole house, the back yard with its power mower, the garage, the radiant heating system, the front yard, the fence, the whole fucking place and everyone in it. He wanted a divorce; he wanted to split. And so he had, very soon. And entered, by degrees, a new and somber life, lacking all of that.

Probably he should have regretted his decision. He had not. That life had been one without excitement, with no adventure. It had been too safe. All the elements that made it up were right there before his eyes, and nothing new could ever be expected. It was like, he had once thought, a little plastic boat that would sail on forever, without incident, until it finally sank, which would be a secret relief to all.

But in this dark world where he now dwelt, ugly things and surprising things and once in a long while a tiny wonderous thing spilled out at him constantly; he could count on nothing. Like the deliberate, evil damage to his Altec cephalo-chromoscope, around which he had built the pleasure part of his schedule, the segment of the day in which they all relaxed and got mellow. For someone to damage that made no sense, viewed rationally. But not much among these long dark evening shadows here was truly rational, at least in the strict sense. The enigmatic act could have been done by anyone for almost any reason. By any person he knew or had ever encountered. Any one of eight dozen weird heads, assorted freaks, burned-out dopers, psychotic paranoids with hallucinatory grudges acted out in reality, not fantasy. Somebody, in fact, he'd *never* met, who'd picked him at random from the phonebook.

Or his closest friend.

Maybe Jerry Fabin, he thought, before they carted him off. There was a burned-out, poisoned husk. Him and his billions of aphids. Blaming Donna—blaming all chicks, in fact—for "contaminating" him. The queer. But, he thought, if Jerry had gone out to get anybody it'd have been Donna, not me. He thought, And I doubt if Jerry could figure out how to remove the bottom plate from the unit; he might try, but he'd still be there now, screwing and unscrewing the same screw. Or he'd try to get the plate off with a hammer. Anyhow, if Jerry

Fabin had done it, the unit would be full of bug eggs that dropped off him. Inside his head Bob Arctor grinned wryly.

Poor fucker, he thought, and his inner grin departed. Poor nowhere mother: once the trace amounts of complex heavy metals got carried to his brain—well, that was it. One more in a long line, a dreary entity among many others like him, an almost endless number of brain-damaged retards. Biological life goes on, he thought. But the soul, the mind—everything else is dead. A reflex machine. Like some insect. Repeating doomed patterns, a single pattern, over and over now. Appropriate or not.

Wonder what he used to be like, he mused. He had not known Jerry that long. Charles Freck claimed that once Jerry had functioned fairly well. I'd have to see that, Arctor thought, to believe it.

Maybe I should tell Hank about the sabotage of my cephscope, he thought. They'd know immediately what it implies. But what can they do for me anyhow? This is the risk you run when you do this kind of work.

It isn't worth it, this work, he thought. There isn't that much money on the fucking planet. But it wasn't the money anyhow. "How come you do this stuff?" Hank had asked him. What did any man, doing any kind of work, know about his actual motives? Boredom, maybe; the desire for a little action. Secret hostility toward every person around him, all his friends, even toward chicks. Or a horrible positive reason: to have watched a human being you loved deeply, that you had gotten real close to, held and slept with and kissed and worried about and befriended and most of all *admired*—to see that warm living person burn out from the inside, burn from the heart outward. Until it clicked and clacked like an insect, repeating one sentence again and again. A *recording*. A closed loop of tape.

". . . I know if I just had another hit . . ."

I'd be okay, he thought. And still saying that, like Jerry Fabin, when three quarters of the brain was mush.

". . . I know, if I just had another hit, that my brain would repair itself."

He had a flash then: Jerry Fabin's brain as the fucked-over wiring of the cephalochromoscope: wires cut, shorts, wires twisted, parts overloaded and no good, line surges, smoke, and a bad smell. And somebody sitting there with a voltmeter, tracing the circuit and muttering, "My, my, a lot of resistors and condensers need to be replaced," and so forth. And then finally from Jerry Fabin would come only a sixty-cycle hum. And they'd give up.

And in Bob Arctor's living room his thousand-dollar custom-quality cephscope crafted by Altec would, after supposedly being repaired, cast onto the wall in dull gray on one small spot:

I KNOW IF I JUST HAD ANOTHER HIT . . .

After that they'd throw the cephscope, damaged beyond repair, and Jerry Fabin, damaged beyond repair, into the same ash can.

Oh well, he thought. Who needs Jerry Fabin? Except maybe Jerry Fabin, who had once envisioned designing and building a nine-foot-long quad-and-TV console system as a present for a friend, and when asked how he would get it from his garage to the friend's house, it being so huge when built and weighing so much, had replied, "No problem, man, I'll just fold it up—I've got the hinges bought already—fold it up, see, fold the whole thing up and put it in an envelope and mail it to him."

Anyhow, Bob Arctor thought, we won't have to keep sweeping aphids out of the house after Jerry's been by to visit. He felt like laughing, thinking about it; they had, once, invented a routine—mostly Luckman had, because he was good at that, funny and clever—about a psychiatric explanation for Jerry's aphid trip. It had to do, naturally, with Jerry Fabin as a small child. Jerry Fabin, see, comes home from first grade one day, with his little books under his arm, whistling merrily, and there, sitting in the dining room beside his mother, is this great aphid, about four feet high. His mother is gazing at it fondly.

"What's happening?" little Jerry Fabin inquires.

"This here is your older brother," his mother says, "who you've never met before. He's come to live with us. I like him better than you. He can do a lot of things you can't."

And from then on, Jerry Fabin's mother and father continually compare him unfavorably with his older brother, who is an aphid. As the two of them grow up, Jerry progressively gets more and more of an inferiority complex—naturally. After high school his brother receives a scholarship to college, while Jerry goes to work in a gas station. After that this brother the aphid becomes a famous doctor or scientist; he wins the Nobel Prize; Jerry's still rotating tires at the gas station, earning a dollar-fifty an hour. His mother and father never cease reminding him of this. They keep saying,

"If only you could have turned out like your brother."

Finally Jerry runs away from home. But he still subconsciously believes aphids to be superior to him. At first he imagines he is safe, but then he starts seeing aphids everywhere, in his hair and around the house, because his inferiority complex has turned into some kind of sexual guilt, and the aphids are a punishment he inflicts on himself, etc.

It did not seem funny now. Now that Jerry had been lugged off in the middle of the night at the request of his own friends. They themselves, all of them present with Jerry that night, had decided to do it; it couldn't be either postponed or avoided. Jerry, that night, had piled every goddamn object in his house against the front door, like maybe nine hundred pounds of assorted crap, including couches and chairs and the refrigerator and TV set, and then told everybody that a giant super-intelligent aphid from another planet was out there preparing to break in and git him. And more would be landing later on, even if he got this one. These extraterrestrial aphids were smarter by far than any humans, and would come directly through the walls if necessary, revealing their actual secret powers in such ways. To save himself as long as possible, he had to flood the house with cyanide gas, which he was prepared to do. How was he prepared to do this? He had already taped all the windows and doors airtight. He then proposed to turn on the water faucets in the kitchen and bathroom, flooding the house, saying that the hot-water tank in the garage was filled with cyanide, not water. He had known this for a long time and was saving it for last, as a final defense. They would all die themselves, but at least it would keep the super-intelligent aphids out.

His friends phoned the police, and the police broke down

the front door and dragged Jerry off to the N.A. Clinic. The last thing Jerry said to them all was "Bring my things later on—bring my new jacket with the beads on the back." He had just bought it. He liked it a lot. It was about all he liked any more; he considered everything else he owned contaminated.

No, Bob Arctor thought, it doesn't seem funny now, and he wondered why it ever had. Maybe it had stemmed from fear, the dreadful fear they had all felt during the last weeks being around Jerry. Sometimes in the night, Jerry had told them, he prowled his house with a shotgun, sensing the presence of an enemy. Preparing to shoot first, before being shot. That is, both of them.

And now, Bob Arctor thought, I've got an enemy. Or anyhow I've come onto his trail: signs of him. Another slushed creep in his final stages, like Jerry. And when the final stages of that shit hits, he thought, it really does hit. Better than any special Ford or GM ever sponsored on prime-time TV.

A knock at his bedroom door.

Touching the gun beneath his pillow, he said, "Yeah?"

Mubble-mubble. Barris's voice.

"Come in," Arctor said. He reached to snap on a bedside lamp.

Barris entered, eyes twinkling. "Still awake?"

"A dream woke me," Arctor said. "A religious dream. In it there was this huge clap of thunder, and all of a sudden the heavens rolled aside and God appeared and His voice rumbled at me—what the hell did He say?—oh yeah. 'I am vexed with you, my son,' He said. He was scowling. I was shaking, in the dream, and looking up, and I said, 'What'd I do now, Lord?' And He said, 'You left the cap off the toothpaste tube again.' And then I realized it was my ex-wife."

Seating himself, Barris placed a hand on each of his leather-covered knees, smoothed himself, shook his head, and confronted Arctor. He seemed in an extremely good mood. "Well," he said briskly, "I've got an initial theoretical view as to who might have systematically damaged with malice your cephscope and may do it again."

"If you're going to say it was Luckman—"

"Listen," Barris said, rocking back and forth in agitation. "W-w-what if I told you I've anticipated for weeks a serious malfunction in one of the household appliances, especially an expensive one difficult to repair? My theory *called* for this to happen! This is a confirmation of my over-all theory!"

Arctor eyed him.

Slowly sinking back down, Barris resumed his calm and bright smiling. "You," he said, pointing.

"You think I did it," Arctor said. "Screwed up my own ceph-scope, with no insurance." Disgust and rage swelled through him. And it was late at night; he needed his sleep.

"No, no," Barris said rapidly, looking distressed. "You are *looking* at the person who did it. Buggered your cephscope. That was my complete intended statement, which I was not allowed to utter."

"You did it?" Mystified, he stared at Barris, whose eyes were murky with a sort of dim triumph. "Why?"

"I mean, it's my theory that I did it," Barris said. "Under posthypnotic suggestion, evidently. With an amnesia block so I wouldn't remember." He began to laugh.

"Later," Arctor said, and snapped off his bedside lamp. "Much later."

Barris rose, dithering. "Hey, but don't you see—I've got the advanced specialized electronic technical skills, and I have access to it—I live here. What I can't figure out, though, is my motive."

"You did it because you're nuts," Arctor said.

"Maybe I was hired by secret forces," Barris muttered in perplexity. "But what would their motives be? Possibly to start suspicion and trouble among us, to cause dissension to break out, causing us to be pitted against one another, all of us, un-certain of whom we can trust, who is our enemy, and like that."

"Then they've succeeded," Arctor said.

"But why would they want to do that?" Barris was saying as he moved toward the door; his hands flapped urgently. "So much trouble—removing that plate on the bottom, getting a passkey to the front door—"

I'll be glad, Bob Arctor thought, when we get in the holo-scanners and have them set up all over this house. He touched his gun, felt reassured, then wondered if he should make cer-tain it was still full of shells. But then, he realized, I'll wonder if the firing pin is gone or if the powder has been removed from the shells and so forth, on and on, obsessively, like a little boy counting cracks in the sidewalk to reduce his fear. Little Bobby Arctor, coming home from the first grade with his little schoolbooks, frightened at the unknown lying ahead.

Reaching down, he fumbled at the bed frame, along and along until his fingers touched Scotch tape. Pulling it loose, he tore from it, with Barris still in the room and watching, two tabs of Substance D mixed with quaak. Lifting them to his mouth, he tossed them down his throat, without water, and then lay back, sighing.

"Get lost," he said to Barris.

And slept.

Chapter Five

I T was necessary for Bob Arctor to be out of his house for a period of time in order that it be properly (which meant unerringly) bugged, phone included, even though the phone line was tapped elsewhere. Usually the practice consisted of observing the house involved until everyone was seen to leave it in such a fashion as to suggest they were not going to return soon. The authorities sometimes had to wait for days or even several weeks. Finally, if nothing else worked, a pretext was arranged: the residents were informed that a fumigator or some such shuck personality was going to be coming in for a whole afternoon and everybody had to get lost until, say, six P.M.

But in this case the suspect Robert Arctor obligingly left his house, taking his two roommates with him, to go check out a cephalochromoscope they could use on loan until Barris had his working again. The three of them were seen to drive off in Arctor's car, looking serious and determined. Then later on, at a convenient point, which was a pay phone at a gas station, using the audio grid of his scramble suit, Fred called in to report that definitely nobody would be home the rest of that day. He'd overheard the three men deciding to cruise down all the way to San Diego in search of a cheap, ripped-off cephscope that some dude had for sale for around fifty bucks. A smack-freak price. At that price it was worth the long drive and all that time.

Also, this gave the authorities the opportunity to do a little illegal searching above and beyond what their undercover people did when no one was looking. They got to pull out bureau drawers to see what was taped to the backs. They got to pull apart pole lamps to see if hundreds of tabs sprang out. They got to look down inside toilet bowls to see what sort of little packets in toilet paper were lodged out of sight where the running water would automatically flush them. They got to look in the freezer compartment of the refrigerator to see if any of the packages of frozen peas and beans actually contained frozen dope, slyly mismarked. Meanwhile, the complicated holo-scanners were mounted, with officers seating

themselves in various places to test the scanners out. The same
with the audio ones. But the video part was more important
and took more time. And of course the scanners should never
be visible. It took skill to so mount them. A number of locations had to be tried. The technicians who did this got paid
well, because if they screwed up and a holo-scanner got detected later on by an occupant of the premises, then the occu-
pants, all of them, would know they had been penetrated and
were under scrutiny, and cool their activities. And in addition
they would sometimes tear off the whole scanning system and
sell it.

It had proven difficult in the courts, Bob Arctor reflected as
he drove along the San Diego Freeway south, to get convictions on theft and sale of electronic detection devices illegally
installed in someone's residence. The police could only tack
the bust on somewhere else, under another statute violation.
However, the pushers, in an analogous situation, reacted
directly. He recalled a case in which a heroin dealer, out to
burn a chick, had planted two packets of heroin in the handle
of her iron, then phoned in an anonymous tip on her to
WE TIP. Before the tip could be acted on, the chick found
the heroin, but instead of flushing it she had sold it. The police
came, found nothing, then made a voiceprint on the phone
tip, and arrested the pusher for giving false information to
the authorities. While out on bail, the pusher visited the chick
late one night and beat her almost to death. When caught and
asked why he'd put out one of her eyes and broken both her
arms and several ribs, he explained that the chick had come
across two packets of high-grade heroin belonging to him,
sold them for a good profit, and not cut him in. Such, Arctor
reflected, went the pusher mentality.

He dumped off Luckman and Barris to do a scrounging
number for the cephscope; this not only stranded both men
and kept them from getting back to the house while the bugging installation was going on, but permitted him to check up
on an individual he hadn't seen for over a month. He seldom
got down this way, and the chick seemed to be doing nothing
more than shooting meth two or three times a day and turning
tricks to pay for it. She lived with her dealer, who was therefore
also her old man. Usually Dan Mancher was gone during the

day, which was good. The dealer was an addict, too, but Arctor had not been able to figure out to what. Evidently a variety of drugs. Anyhow, whatever it was, Dan had become weird and vicious, unpredictable and violent. It was a wonder the local police hadn't picked him up long ago on local disturbance-of-the-peace infractions. Maybe they were paid off. Or, most likely, they just didn't care; these people lived in a slum-housing area among senior citizens and the other poor. Only for major crimes did the police enter the Cromwell Village series of buildings and related garbage dump, parking lots, and rubbled roads.

There seemed to be nothing that contributed more to squalor than a bunch of basalt-block structures designed to lift people out of squalor. He parked, found the right urine-smelling stairs, ascended into darkness, found the door of Building 4 marked *G*. A full can of Drāno lay before the door, and he picked it up automatically, wondering how many kids played here and remembering, for a moment, his own kids and the protective moves he had made on their behalf over the years. This was one now, picking up this can. He rapped against the door with it.

Presently the door lock rattled and the door opened, chained inside; the girl, Kimberly Hawkins, peered out. "Yes?"

"Hey, man," he said. "It's me, Bob."

"What do you have there?"

"Can of Drāno," he said.

"No kidding." She unchained the door in a listless way; her voice, too, was listless. Kimberly was down, he could see: very down. Also, the girl had a black eye and a split lip. And as he looked around he saw that the windows of the small, untidy apartment were broken. Shards of glass lay on the floor, along with overturned ashtrays and Coke bottles.

"Are you alone?" he asked.

"Yeah. Dan and I had a fight and he split." The girl, half Chicano, small and not too pretty, with the sallow complexion of a crystal freak, gazed down sightlessly, and he realized that her voice rasped when she spoke. Some drugs did that. Also, so did strep throat. The apartment probably couldn't be heated, not with the broken windows.

"He beat you up." Arctor set the can of Drāno down on a

high shelf, over some paperback porn novels, most of them out of date.

"Well, he didn't have his knife, thank God. His Case knife that he carries on his belt in a sheath now." Kimberly seated herself in an overstuffed chair out of which springs stuck. "What do you want, Bob? I'm bummed, I really am."

"You want him back?"

"Well—" She shrugged a little. "Who knows?"

Arctor walked to the window and looked out. Dan Mancher would no doubt be showing up sooner or later: the girl was a source of money, and Dan knew she'd need her regular hits once her supply had run out. "How long can you go?" he asked.

"Another day."

"Can you get it anywhere else?"

"Yeah, but not so cheap."

"What's wrong with your throat?"

"A cold," she said. "From the wind coming in."

"You should—"

"If I go to a doctor," she said, "then he'll see I'm on crystal. I can't go."

"A doctor wouldn't care."

"Sure he would." She listened then: the sound of car pipes, irregular and loud. "Is that Dan's car? Red Ford 'seventy-nine Torino?"

At the window Arctor looked out onto the rubbishy lot, saw a battered red Torino stopping, its twin exhausts exhaling dark smoke, the driver's door opening. "Yes."

Kimberly locked the door: two extra locks. "He probably has his knife."

"You have a phone?"

"No," she said.

"You should get a phone."

The girl shrugged.

"He'll kill you," Arctor said.

"Not now. You're here."

"But later, after I'm gone."

Kimberly reseated herself and shrugged again.

After a few moments they could hear steps outside, and then a knock on the door. Then Dan yelling for her to open the door. She yelled back no and that someone was with her. "Okay," Dan yelled, in a high-pitched voice, "I'll slash your tires." He ran downstairs, and Arctor and the girl watched through the broken window together as Dan Mancher, a skinny, short-haired, homosexual-looking dude waving a knife, approached her car, still yelling up at her, his words audible to everyone else in the housing area. "I'll slash your tires, your fucking tires! And then I'll fucking kill you!" He bent down and slashed first one tire and then another on the girl's old Dodge.

Kimberly suddenly aroused, sprang to the door of the apartment and frantically began unlocking the various locks. "I got to stop him! He's slashing all my tires! I don't have insurance!"

Arctor stopped her. "My car's there too." He did not have his gun with him, of course, and Dan had the Case knife and was out of control. "Tires aren't—"

"My *tires!*" Shrieking, the girl struggled to open the door.

"That's what he wants you to do," Arctor said.

"Downstairs," Kimberly panted. "We can phone the police —they have a phone. Let me *go!*" She fought him off with tremendous strength and managed to get the door open. "I'm going to call the police. My tires! One of them is new!"

"I'll go with you." He grabbed her by the shoulder; she tumbled ahead of him down the steps, and he barely managed to catch up. Already she had reached the next apartment and was pounding on its door. "Open, please?" she called. "Please, I want to call the police! Please let me call the police!"

Arctor got up beside her and knocked. "We need to use your phone," he said. "It's an emergency."

An elderly man, wearing a gray sweater and creased formal slacks and a tie, opened the door.

"Thanks," Arctor said.

Kimberly pushed inside, ran to the phone, and dialed the operator. Arctor stood facing the door, waiting for Dan to show up. There was no sound now, except for Kimberly babbling at the operator: a garbled account, something about a quarrel about a pair of boots worth seven dollars. "He said they were his because I got them for him for Christmas," she was babbling, "but they were mine because I paid for them, and then he started to take them and I ripped the backs of them with a can opener, so he—" She paused; then, nodding: "All right, thank you. Yes, I'll hold on."

The elderly man gazed at Arctor, who gazed back. In the next room an elderly lady in a print dress watched silently, her face stiff with fear.

"This must be bad on you," Arctor said to the two elderly people.

"It goes on all the time," the elderly man said. "We hear them all night, night after night, fighting, and him saying all the time he'll kill her."

"We should have gone back to Denver," the elderly lady said. "I told you that, we should have moved back."

"These terrible fights," the elderly man said. "And smashing things, and the noise." He gazed at Arctor, stricken, appealing for help maybe, or maybe understanding. "On and on, it never does stop, and then, what is worse, do you know that every time—"

"Yes, tell him that," the elderly lady urged.

"What is worse," the elderly man said with dignity, "is that every time we go outdoors, we go outside to shop or mail a letter, we step in . . . you know, what the dogs leave."

"Dog do," the elderly lady said, with indignation.

The local police car showed up. Arctor gave him deposition as a witness without identifying himself as a law-enforcement officer. The cop took down his statement and tried to take one from Kimberly, as the complaining party, but what she said made no sense: she rambled on and on about the pair of boots and why she had gotten them, how much they meant to her. The cop, sitting with his clipboard and sheet, glanced up once at Arctor and regarded him with a cold expression that Arctor could not read but did not like anyhow. The cop finally advised Kimberly to get a phone and to call if the suspect returned and made any more trouble.

"Did you note the slashed tires?" Arctor said as the cop started to leave. "Did you examine her vehicle out there on the lot and note personally the number of tires slashed, casing slashes with a sharp instrument, recently made—there is still some air leaking out?"

The cop glanced at him again with the same expression and left with no further comment.

"You better not stay here," Arctor said to Kimberly. "He should have advised you to clear out. Asked if there was some other place you could stay."

Kimberly sat on her seedy couch in her debris-littered living room, her eyes lusterless again now that she had ceased the futile effort of trying to explain her situation to the investigating officer. She shrugged.

"I'll drive you somewhere," Arctor said. "Do you know some friend you could—"

"Get the fuck out!" Kimberly said abruptly, with venom, in a voice much like Dan Mancher's but more raspy. "Get the fuck out of here, Bob Arctor—get lost, get lost, goddammit. Will you get lost?" Her voice rose shrilly and then broke in despair.

He left and walked slowly back down the stairs, step by step. When he reached the bottom step something banged and rolled down after him: it was the can of Drāno. He heard her door lock, one bolt after another. Futile locks, he thought. Futile everything. The investigating officer advises her to call if the suspect returns. How can she, without going out of her apartment? And there Dan Mancher will stab her like he did the tires. And—remembering the complaint of the old folks downstairs—she will probably first step on and then fall dead into dog shit. He felt like laughing hysterically at the old folks' priorities: not only did a burned-out freak upstairs night after night beat up and threaten to kill and probably would soon kill a young girl addict turning tricks who no doubt had strep throat if not much else besides, but *in addition to that—*

As he drove Luckman and Barris back north, he chuckled aloud. "Dog shit," he said. "Dog shit." Humor in dog shit, he thought, if you can flash on it. Funny dog shit.

"Better change lanes and pass that Safeway truck," Luckman said. "The humper's hardly moving."

He moved into the lane to the left and picked up speed. But then, when he took his foot off the throttle, the pedal all at once fell to the floor mat, and at the same time the engine roared all the way up furiously and the car shot forward at enormous, wild speed.

"Slow down!" both Luckman and Barris said together.

By now the car had reached almost one hundred; ahead, a VW van loomed. His gas pedal was dead: it did not return and it did nothing. Both Luckman, who sat next to him, and Barris, beyond him, threw up their arms instinctively. Arctor twisted the wheel and shot by the VW van, to its left, where a limited space remained before a fast-moving 'Vet filled it up. The Corvette honked, and they heard its brakes screech. Now Luckman and Barris were yelling; Luckman suddenly reached and shut off the ignition; meanwhile, Arctor shifted out of gear into neutral. The car slowed, and he braked it down, moved into the right-hand lane and then, with the engine finally dead and the transmission out of gear, rolled off onto the emergency strip and came by degrees to a stop.

The Corvette, long gone down the freeway, still honked its indignation. And now the giant Safeway truck rolled by them and for a deafening moment sounded its own warning air horn.

"What the hell happened?" Barris said.

Arctor, his hands and voice and the rest of him shaking, said, "The return spring on the throttle cable—the gas. Must have caught or broken." He pointed down. They all peered at the pedal, which lay still flat against the floor. The engine had revved up to its entire maximum rpm, which for his car was considerable. He had not clocked their final highest road speed, probably well over one hundred. And, he realized, though he had been reflexively pushing down on the power brakes, the car had only slowed.

Silently the three of them got out onto the emergency pavement and raised the hood. White smoke drifted up from the oil caps and from underneath as well. And near-boiling water fizzled from the overflow spout of the radiator.

Luckman reached over the hot engine and pointed. "Not the spring," he said. "It's the linkage from the pedal to the carb. See? It fell apart." The long rod lay aimlessly against the block, hanging impotently and uselessly down with its locking ring still in place. "So the gas pedal didn't push back up when you took your foot off. But—" He inspected the carb for a time, his face wrinkled.

"There's a safety override on the carb," Barris said, grinning and showing his syntheticlike teeth. "This system when the linkage parts—"

"Why'd it part?" Arctor broke in. "Shouldn't this locking ring hold the nut in place?" He stroked along the rod. "How could it just fall off like that?"

As if not hearing him, Barris continued, "If for any reason the linkage gives, then the engine should drop down to idle. As a safety factor. But it revved up all the way instead." He bent his body around to get a better look at the carb. "This screw has been turned all the way out," he said. "The idle screw. So that when the linkage parted the override went the other way, up instead of down."

"How could that happen?" Luckman said loudly. "Could it screw itself all the way out like that accidentally?"

Without answering, Barris got out his pocketknife, opened the small blade, and began slowly screwing the idle-adjustment screw back in. He counted aloud. Twenty turns of the screw to get it in. "To loosen the lock ring and nut assembly that holds the accelerator-linkage rods together," he said, "a special tool would be needed. A couple, in fact. I'd estimate it'll take about half an hour to get this back together. I have the tools, though, in my toolbox."

"Your toolbox is back at the house," Luckman said.

"Yes." Barris nodded. "Then we'll have to get to a gas station and either borrow theirs or get their tow truck out here. I suggest we get them out here to look it over before we drive it again."

"Hey, man," Luckman said loudly, "did this happen by accident or was this done deliberately? Like the cephscope?"

Barris pondered, still smiling his wily, rueful smile. "I couldn't say for sure about this. Normally, sabotage on a car, malicious damage to cause an accident . . ." He glanced at Arctor, his eyes invisible behind his green shades. "We almost piled up. If that 'Vet had been coming any faster . . . There was almost no ditch to head for. You should have cut the ignition as soon as you realized what happened."

"I got it out of gear," Arctor said. "When I realized. For a second I couldn't figure it out." He thought, If it had been the brakes, if the brake pedal had gone to the floor, I'd have flashed on it sooner, known better what to do. This was so— weird.

"Someone deliberately did it," Luckman said loudly. He spun around in a circle of fury, lashing out with both fists. "MOTHER-FUCKER! We almost bought it! They fucking almost got us!"

Barris, standing visible by the side of the freeway with all its heavy traffic whizzing by, got out a little horn snuffbox of death tabs and took several. He passed the snuffbox to Luckman, who took a few, then passed it to Arctor.

"Maybe that's what's fucking us up," Arctor said, declining irritably. "Messing up our brains."

"Dope can't screw up an accelerator linkage and carb-idle adjustment," Barris said, still holding the snuffbox out to Arctor. "You'd better drop at least three of these—they're Primo, but mild. Cut with a little meth."

"Put the damn snuffbox away," Arctor said. He felt, in his head, loud voices singing: terrible music, as if the reality around him had gone sour. Everything now—the fast-moving cars, the two men, his own car with its hood up, the smell of smog, the bright, hot light of midday—it all had a rancid quality, as if, throughout, his world had putrefied, rather than anything else. Not so much become all at once, because of this, dangerous, not frightening, but more as if rotting away, stinking in sight and sound and odor. It made him sick, and he shut his eyes and shuddered.

"What do you smell?" Luckman asked. "A clue, man? Some engine smell that—"

"Dog shit," Arctor said. He could smell it, from within the engine area. Bending, he sniffed, smelled it distinctly and more strongly. Weird, he thought. Freaky and fucking weird. "Do you smell dog shit?" he asked Barris and Luckman.

"No," Luckman said, eying him. To Barris he said, "Were there any psychedelics in that dope?"

Barris, smiling, shook his head.

As he bent over the hot engine, smelling dog shit, Arctor knew to himself that it was an illusion; there was no dog-shit smell. But still he smelled it. And now he saw, smeared across the motor block, especially down low by the plugs, dark-brown stains, an ugly substance. Oil, he thought. Spilled oil, thrown oil: I may have a leaky head gasket. But he needed to reach down and touch to be sure, to fortify his rational conviction. His fingers met the sticky brown smears, and his fingers leaped back. He had run his fingers into dog shit. There was a coating of dog shit all over the block, on the wires. Then he realized it was on the fire wall as well. Looking up, he saw it on the soundproofing underneath the hood. The stink overpowered him, and he shut his eyes, shuddering.

"Hey, man," Luckman said acutely, taking hold of Arctor by the shoulder. "You're getting a flashback, aren't you?"

"Free theater tickets," Barris agreed, and chuckled.

"You better sit down," Luckman said; he guided Arctor back to the driver's seat and got him seated there. "Man, you're really freaked. Just sit there. Take it easy. Nobody got killed, and now we're warned." He shut the car door beside Arctor. "We're okay now, dig?"

Barris appeared at the window and said, "Want a lump of dog shit, Bob? To chew on?"

Opening his eyes, chilled, Arctor stared at him. Barris's dead green-glass eyes gave nothing back, no clue. Did he really say that? Arctor wondered. Or did my head make that up? "What, Jim?" he said.

Barris began to laugh. And laugh and laugh.

"Leave him alone, man," Luckman said, punching Barris on the back. "Fuck off, Barris!"

Arctor said to Luckman, "What did he say just now? What the hell exactly did he say to me?"

"I don't know," Luckman said. "I can't figure out half the things Barris lays on people."

Barris still smiled, but had become silent.

"You goddamn Barris," Arctor said to him. "I know you did it, screwed over the cephscope and now the car. You fucking did it, you kinky freak mother bastard." His voice was hardly audible to him, but as he yelled that out at smiling Barris, the dreadful stench of dog shit grew. He gave up trying to speak and sat there at the useless wheel of his car trying not to throw up. Thank God Luckman came along, he thought. Or it'd be all over for me this day. It'd all fucking be over, at the hands of this burned-out fucking creep, this mother living right in the same house with me.

"Take it easy, Bob," Luckman's voice filtered to him through the waves of nausea.

"I know it's him," Arctor said.

"Hell, why?" Luckman seemed to be saying, or trying to say. "He'd of snuffed himself too this way. Why, man? Why?"

The smell of Barris still smiling overpowered Bob Arctor, and he heaved onto the dashboard of his own car. A thousand little voices tinkled up, shining at him, and the smell receded finally. A thousand little voices crying out their strangeness; he did not understand them, but at least he could see, and the smell was going away. He trembled, and reached for his handkerchief from his pocket.

"What was in those tabs you gave us?" Luckman demanded at smiling Barris.

"Hell, I dropped some too," Barris said, "and so did you. And it didn't give us a bad trip. So it wasn't the dope. And it was too soon. How could it have been the dope? The stomach can't absorb—"

"You poisoned me," Arctor said savagely, his vision almost clear, his mind clearing, except for the fear. Now fear had begun, a rational response instead of insanity. Fear about what had almost happened, what it signified, fear fear terrible fear of smiling Barris and his fucking snuffbox and his explanations and his creepy sayings and ways and habits and customs and comings and goings. And his anonymous phoned-in tip to the police about Robert Arctor, his mickey-mouse grid to conceal his real voice that had pretty well worked. Except that it had to have been Barris.

Bob Arctor thought, *The fucker is on to me.*

"I never saw anybody space out as fast," Barris was saying, "but then—"

"You okay now, Bob?" Luckman said. "We'll clean up the barf, no trouble. Better get in the back seat." Both he and Barris opened the car door; Arctor slid dizzily out. To Barris, Luckman said, "You sure you didn't slip him anything?"

Barris waved his hands up high, protesting.

Chapter Six

ITEM. What an undercover narcotics agent fears most is not that he will be shot or beaten up but that he will be slipped a great hit of some psychedelic that will roll an endless horror feature film in his head for the remainder of his life, or that he will be shot up with a mex hit, half heroin and half Substance D, or both of the above plus a poison such as strychnine, which will nearly kill him but not completely, so that the above can occur: lifelong addiction, lifelong horror film. He will sink into a needle-and-a-spoon existence, or bounce off the walls in a psychiatric hospital or, worst of all, a federal clinic. He will try to shake the aphids off him day and night or puzzle forever over why he cannot any longer wax a floor. And all this will occur deliberately. Someone figured out what he was doing and then got him. And they got him this way. The worst way of all: with the stuff they sell that he was after them for selling.

Which, Bob Arctor considered as he cautiously drove home, meant that both the dealers and the narks knew what the street drugs did to people. On that they agreed.

A Union station near where they had parked had driven out and gone over the car and finally fixed it up at a cost of thirty dollars. Nothing else seemed wrong, except that the mechanic had examined the left front suspension for quite a while.

"Anything wrong there?" Arctor had asked.

"Seems like you should be experiencing trouble when you corner sharply," the mechanic had said. "Does it yaw at all?"

The car didn't yaw, not that Arctor had noticed. But the mechanic refused to say more; he just kept poking at the coil spring and ball joint and oil-filled shock. Arctor paid him, and the tow truck drove off. He then got back into his own car, along with Luckman and Barris—both of whom now rode in back—and started north toward Orange County.

As he drove, Arctor ruminated about other ironic agreements in the minds of narcotics agents and dealers. Several narcotics agents that he had known had posed as dealers in their undercover work and wound up selling like hash and then, sometimes, even smack. This was a good cover, but it also brought the nark a gradually increasing profit over and above his official salary plus what he made when he helped bust and seize a good-sized shipment. Also, the agents got deeper and deeper into using their own stuff, the whole way of life, as a matter of course; they became rich dealer addicts as well as narks, and after a time some of them began to phase out their law-enforcement activities in favor of full-time dealing. But then, too, certain dealers, to burn their enemies or when expecting imminent busts, began narking and went that route, winding up as sort of unofficial undercover narks. It all got murky. The drug world was a murky world for everyone anyhow. For Bob Arctor, for example, it had become murky now: during this afternoon along the San Diego Freeway, while he and his two buddies had been within foot-seconds of being wiped out, the authorities, on his behalf, had been—he hoped —properly bugging their house, and if this had been done, then possibly he would be safe from now on from the kind of thing that had happened today. It was a piece of luck that ultimately might mean the difference between him winding up poisoned or shot or addicted or dead compared to nailing his enemy, nailing whoever was after him and who today had in fact almost gotten him. Once the holo-scanners were mounted in place, he ruminated, there would be very little sabotage or attacks against him. Or anyhow successful sabotage or successful attacks.

This was about the only thought that reassured him. The guilty, he reflected as he drove amid the heavy late-afternoon traffic as carefully as possible, may flee when no one pursues— he had heard that, and maybe that was true. What for a certainty was true, however, was that the guilty fled, fled like hell and took plenty of swift precautions, when someone did pursue: someone real and expert and at the same time hidden. And very close by. As close, he thought, as the back seat of this car. Where, if he has his funky .22 single-action German-made nowhere pistol with him and his equally funky rinky-dink laughable alleged silencer on it, and Luckman has gone to sleep as usual, he can put a hollow-nose bullet through the back of my skull and I will be as dead as Bobby Kennedy, who died from gunshot wounds of the same caliber—a bore that small.

And not only today but every day. And every night.

Except that in the house, when I check the storage drums of the holo-scanners, I'll pretty well know pretty soon what everyone in my house is doing and when they do it and probably even why, myself included. I will watch my own self, he thought, get up in the night to pee. I will watch all the rooms on a twenty-four-hour basis . . . although there will be a lag. It won't help me much if the holo-scanners pick up me being given a hotshot of some disorientation drug ripped off by the Hell's Angels from a military arsenal and dumped in my coffee; someone else from the academy who goes over the storage drums will have to watch my thrashing around, unable to see or know where or what I am any more. It will be a hindsight I won't even get to have. Somebody else will have to have it for me.

Luckman said, "I wonder what's been going on back at the house while we've been gone all day. You know, this proves you got somebody out to burn you real bad, Bob. I hope when we get back the house is still there."

"Yeah," Arctor said. "I didn't think of that. And we didn't get a loan cephscope anyhow." He made his voice sound leaden with resignation.

Barris said, in a surprisingly cheerful voice, "I wouldn't worry too much."

With anger, Luckman said, "You wouldn't? Christ, they may have broken in and ripped off all we got. All Bob's got, anyhow. And killed or stomped the animals. Or—"

"I left a little surprise," Barris said, "for anybody entering the house while we're gone today. I perfected it early this morning . . . I worked until I got it. An electronic surprise."

Sharply, concealing his concern, Arctor said, "What kind of electronic surprise? It's my house, Jim, you can't start rigging up—"

"Easy, easy," Barris said. "As our German friends would say, *leise*. Which means be cool."

"What is it?"

"If the front door is opened," Barris said, "during our absence, my cassette tape recorder starts recording. It's under the couch. It has a two-hour tape. I placed three omnidirectional Sony mikes at three different—"

"You should have told me," Arctor said.

"What if they come in through the windows?" Luckman said. "Or the back door?"

"To increase the chances of their making their entry via the front door," Barris continued, "rather than in other less usual ways, I providentially left the front door unlocked."

After a pause, Luckman began to snigger.

"Suppose they don't know it's unlocked?" Arctor said.

"I put a note on it," Barris said.

"You're jiving me!"

"Yes," Barris said, presently.

"Are you fucking jiving us or not?" Luckman said. "I can't tell with you. Is he jiving, Bob?"

"We'll see when we get back," Arctor said. "If there's a note on the door and it's unlocked we'll know he isn't jiving us."

"They probably would take the note down," Luckman said, "after ripping off and vandalizing the house, and then lock the door. So we won't know. We'll never know. For sure. It's that gray area again."

"Of course I'm kidding!" Barris said, with vigor. "Only a psychotic would do that, leave the front door of his house unlocked and a note on the door."

Turning, Arctor said to him, "What did you write on the note, Jim?"

"Who's the note to?" Luckman chimed in. "I didn't even know you knew how to write."

With condescension, Barris said, "I wrote: 'Donna, come on inside; door's unlocked. We—'" Barris broke off. "It's to Donna," he finished, but not smoothly.

"He did do that," Luckman said. "He really did. All of it."

"That way," Barris said, smoothly again, "we'll know who had been doing this, Bob. And that's of prime importance."

"Unless they rip off the tape recorder when they rip off the couch and everything else," Arctor said. He was thinking rapidly as to how much of a problem this really was, this additional example of Barris's messed-up electronic nowhere genius of a kindergarten sort. Hell, he concluded, they'll find the mikes in the first ten minutes and trace them back to the recorder. They'll know exactly what to do. They'll erase the tape, rewind it, leave it as it was, leave the door unlocked and the note on it. In fact, maybe the unlocked door will make their job easier. Fucking Barris, he thought. Great genius plans which will work out so as to screw up the universe. He probably forgot to plug the recorder into the wall outlet anyhow. Of course, if he finds it unplugged—

He'll reason that proves someone was there, he realized. He'll flash on that and rap at us for days. Somebody got in who was hip to his device and cleverly unplugged it. So, he decided, if they find it unplugged I hope they think to plug it in, and not only that, make it run right. In fact, what they really should do is test out his whole detection system, run it through its cycle as thoroughly as they do their own, be absolutely certain it functions perfectly, and then wind it back to a blank state, a tablet on which nothing is inscribed but on which something would for sure be had anyone—themselves, for example—entered the house. Otherwise, Barris's suspicions will be aroused forever.

As he drove, he continued his theoretical analysis of his situation by means of a second well-established example. They had brought it up and drilled it into his own memory banks during his police training at the academy. Or else he had read it in the newspapers.

Item. One of the most effective forms of industrial or military sabotage limits itself to damage that can never be thoroughly proven—or even proven at all—to be anything deliberate. It is like an invisible political movement; perhaps it isn't there at all. If a bomb is wired to a car's ignition, then obviously there is an enemy; if a public building or a political headquarters is blown up, then there is a political enemy. But if an accident, or a series of accidents, occurs, if equipment merely fails to function, if it appears faulty, especially in a slow fashion, over a period of natural time, with numerous small failures and misfirings—then the victim, whether a person or a party or a country, can never marshal itself to defend itself.

In fact, Arctor speculated as he drove along the freeway very slowly, the person begins to assume he's paranoid and has no enemy; he doubts himself. His car broke down normally; his luck has just become bad. And his friends agree. It's in his head. And this wipes him out more thoroughly than anything that can be traced. However, it takes longer. The person or persons doing him in must tinker and putter and make use of chance over a long interval. Meanwhile, if the victim can figure out who they are, he has a better chance of getting them—certainly better than if, say, they shoot him with a scope-sight rifle. That is *his* advantage.

Every nation in the world, he knew, trains and sends out a mass of agents to loosen bolts here, strip threads there, break wires and start little fires, lose documents—little misadventures. A wad of gum inside a Xerox copying machine in a government office can destroy an irreplaceable—and vital—document: instead of a copy coming out, the original is wiped out. Too much soap and toilet paper, as the Yippies of the sixties knew, can screw up the entire sewage of an office building and force all the employees out for a week. A mothball in a car's gas tank wears out the engine two weeks later, when it's in another town, and leaves no fuel contaminants to be analyzed. Any radio or TV station can be put off the air by a pile driver accidentally cutting a microwave cable or a power cable. And so forth.

Many of the previous aristocratic social class knew about maids and gardeners and other serf-type help: a broken vase here, a dropped priceless heirloom that slips out of a sullen hand . . .

"Why'd you do that, Rastus Brown?"

"Oh, Ah jes' fogot ta—" and there was no recourse, or very little. By a rich homeowner, by a political writer unpopular with the regime, a small new nation shaking its fist at the U.S. or at the U.S.S.R.—

Once, an American ambassador to Guatemala had had a wife who had publicly boasted that her "pistol-packin'" husband had overthrown that little nation's left-wing government. After its abrupt fall, the ambassador, his job done, had been transferred to a small Asian nation, and while driving his sports car he had suddenly discovered a slow-moving hay truck pulling out of a side road directly ahead of him. A moment later nothing remained of the ambassador except a bunch of splatted bits. Packing a pistol, and having at his call an entire CIA raised private army, had done him no good. His wife wrote no proud poetry about that.

"Uh, do what?" the owner of the hay truck had probably said to the local authorities. "Do what, massah? Ah jes'—"

Or like his own ex-wife, Arctor remembered. At that time he had worked for an insurance firm as an investigator ("Do your neighbors across the hall drink a lot?"), and she had objected to his filling out his reports late at night instead of thrilling at the very sight of her. Toward the end of their marriage she had learned to do such things during his late-night work period as burn her hand while lighting a cigarette, get something in her eye, dust his office, or search forever throughout or around his typewriter for some little object. At first he had resentfully stopped work and succumbed to thrilling at the very sight of her; but then he had hit his head in the kitchen while getting out the corn popper and had found a better solution.

"If they kill our animals," Luckman was saying, "I'll fire bomb them. I'll get all of them. I'll hire a professional down from L.A., like a bunch of Panthers."

"They won't," Barris said. "There's nothing to be gained by injuring animals. The animals haven't done anything."

"Have I?" Arctor said.

"Evidently they think so," Barris said.

Luckman said, "*If I had known it was harmless I would have killed it myself.* Remember?"

"But she was a straight," Barris said. "That girl never turned on, and she had heavy bread. Remember her apartment? The rich never understand the value of life. That's something else. Remember Thelma Kornford, Bob? The short girl with the huge breasts—she never wore a bra and we used to just sit and look at her nipples? She came over to our place to get us to kill that mosquito hawk for her? And when we explained—"

At the wheel of his slow car, Bob Arctor forgot theoretical matters and did a rerun of a moment that had impressed them all: the dainty and elegant straight girl in her turtleneck sweater and bell-bottoms and trippy boobs who wanted them to murder a great harmless bug that in fact did good by wiping out mosquitoes—and in a year in which an outbreak of encephalitis had been anticipated in Orange County—and when they saw what it was and explained, she had said words that

became for them their parody evil-wall-motto, to be feared
and despised:

IF I HAD KNOWN IT WAS HARMLESS
I WOULD HAVE KILLED IT MYSELF.

That had summed up to them (and still did) what they distrusted in their straight foes, assuming they had foes; anyhow,
a person like well-educated-with-all-the-financial-advantages
Thelma Kornford became at once a foe by uttering that, from
which they had run that day, pouring out of her apartment and
back to their own littered pad, to her perplexity. The gulf
between their world and hers had manifested itself, however
much they'd meditated on how to ball her, and remained. Her
heart, Bob Arctor reflected, was an empty kitchen: floor tile
and water pipes and a drainboard with pale scrubbed surfaces,
and one abandoned glass on the edge of the sink that nobody
cared about.

One time before he got solely into undercover work he had
taken a deposition from a pair of upper-class well-off straights
whose furniture had been ripped off during their absence, evidently by junkies; in those days such people still lived in areas
where roving rip-off bands stole what they could, leaving little.
Professional bands, with walkie-talkies in the hands of spotters
who watched a couple miles down the street for the marks' return. He remembered the man and his wife saying, "People
who would burglarize your house and take your color TV are
the same kind of criminals who slaughter animals or vandalize
priceless works of art." No, Bob Arctor had explained, pausing
in writing down their deposition, what makes you believe that?
Addicts, in his experience anyhow, rarely hurt animals. He had
witnessed junkies feeding and caring for injured animals over
long periods of time, where straights probably would have had
the animals "put to sleep," a straight-type term if there ever
was one—and also an old Syndicate term as well, for murder.
Once he had assisted two totally spaced-out heads in the sad
ordeal of unscrewing a cat which had impaled herself within a
broken window. The heads, hardly able to see or understand
anything any more, had over almost an entire hour deftly and
patiently worked the cat loose until she was free, bleeding a

little, all of them, heads and cat alike, with the cat calm in their hands, one dude inside the house with Arctor, the other outdoors, where the ass and tail were. The cat had come free at last with no real injury, and then they had fed her. They did not know whose cat she was; evidently she had been hungry and smelled food through their broken window and finally, unable to rouse them, had tried to leap in. They hadn't noticed her until her shriek, and then they had forgotten their various trips and dreams for a while in her behalf.

As to "priceless works of art" he wasn't too sure, because he didn't exactly understand what that meant. At My Lai during the Viet Nam War, four hundred and fifty priceless works of art had been vandalized to death at the orders of the CIA— priceless works of art plus oxen and chickens and other animals not listed. When he thought about that he always got a little dingey and was hard to reason with about paintings in museums and like that.

"Do you think," he said aloud as he painstakingly drove, "that when we die and appear before God on Judgment Day, that our sins will be listed in chronological order or in order of severity, which could be ascending or descending, or alphabetically? Because I don't want to have God boom out at me when I die at the age of eighty-six, 'So you're the little boy who stole the three Coke bottles off the Coca-Cola truck when it was parked in the 7-11 lot back in 1962, and you've got a lot of fast talking to do.'"

"I think they're cross-referenced," Luckman said. "And they just hand you a computer printout that's the total of a long column that's been added up already."

"Sin," Barris said, chuckling, "is a Jewish-Christian myth that is outdated."

Arctor said, "Maybe they've got all your sins in one big pickle barrel"—he turned to glare at Barris the anti-Semite— "a kosher pickle barrel, and they just hoist it up and throw the whole contents all at once in your face, and you just stand there dripping sins. Your own sins, plus maybe a few of somebody else's that got in by mistake."

"Somebody else by the same name," Luckman said. "Another Robert Arctor. How many Robert Arctors do you think there are, Barris?" He nudged Barris. "Could the Cal Tech computers tell us that? And cross-file all the Jim Barrises too while they're doing it?"

To himself, Bob Arctor thought, *How many Bob Arctors are there?* A weird and fucked-up thought. Two that I can think of, he thought. The one called Fred, who will be watching the other one, called Bob. The same person. Or is it? Is Fred actually the same as Bob? Does anybody know? I would know, if anyone did, because I'm the only person in the world that knows that Fred is Bob Arctor. *But,* he thought, *who am I? Which of them is me?*

When they rolled to a stop in the driveway, parked, and walked warily toward the front door, they found Barris's note and the door unlocked, but when they cautiously opened the door everything appeared as it had been when they left.

Barris's suspicions surfaced instantly. "Ah," he murmured, entering. He swiftly reached to the top of the bookshelf by the door and brought down his .22 pistol, which he gripped as the other men moved about. The animals approached them as usual, clamoring to be fed.

"Well, Barris," Luckman said, "I can see you're right. There definitely was someone here, because you see—you see, too, don't you, Bob?—the scrupulous covering-over of all the signs they would have otherwise left testifies to their—" He farted then, in disgust, and wandered into the kitchen to look in the refrigerator for a can of beer. "Barris," he said, "you're fucked."

Still moving about alertly with his gun, Barris ignored him as he sought to discover telltale traces. Arctor, watching, thought, Maybe he will. They may have left some. And he thought, Strange how paranoia can link up with reality now and then, briefly. Under very specialized conditions, such as today. Next thing, Barris will be reasoning that I lured everyone out of the house deliberately to permit secret intruders to accomplish their thing here. And later on he will discern why and who and everything else, and in fact maybe he already has. Had a while ago, in fact; long-enough ago to initiate sabotage and destruct actions on the cephscope, car, and God knows what else. Maybe when I turn on the garage light the house will burn down. But the main things is, did the bugging crew arrive and get all the monitors in and finish up? He would not know until he talked to Hank and Hank gave him a proof-positive layout of the monitors and where their storage drums could be serviced. And whatever additional information the bugging crew's boss, plus other experts involved in this operation, wanted to dump on him. In their concerted play against Bob Arctor, the suspect.

"Look at this!" Barris said. He bent over an ashtray on the coffee table. "Come here!" he called sharply to both of them, and both men responded.

Reaching down, Arctor felt heat rising from the ashtray.

"A still-hot cigarette butt," Luckman said, marveling. "It sure is."

Jesus, Arctor thought. They did screw up. One of the crew smoked and then reflexively put the butt here. So they must just have gone. The ashtray, as always, overflowed; the crewman probably assumed no one would notice the addition, and in another few moments it would have cooled.

"Wait a second," Luckman said, examining the ashtray. He fished out, from among the tobacco butts, a roach. "This is what's hot, this roach. They lit up a joint while they were here. But what did they do? What the hell did they do?" He scowled and peered about, angry and baffled. "Bob, fuck it—Barris was right. *There was somebody here!* This roach is still hot, and you can smell it if you hold it—" He held it under Arctor's nose. "Yeah, it's still burning a little down inside. Probably a seed. They didn't manicure it too good before they rolled it."

"That roach," Barris said, equally grim, "may not have been left here by accident. This evidence may not be a slip-up."

"What now?" Arctor said, wondering what kind of police bugging crew would have a member who smoked a joint in front of the others while on the job.

"Maybe they were here specifically to plant dope in this house," Barris said. "Setting us up, then phone in a tip later . . . Maybe there's dope hidden like this in the phone, for example, and the wall outlets. We're going to have to go through the whole house and get it absolutely clean before they phone the tip in. And we've probably got only hours."

"You check the wall sockets," Luckman said. "I'll take the phone apart."

"Wait," Barris said, holding up his hand. "If they see us scrambling around just before the raid—"

"What raid?" Arctor said.

"If we're running frantically around flushing dope," Barris said, "then we can't allege, even though it's true, that we didn't know the dope was there. They'll catch us actually holding it. And maybe that, too, is part of their plan."

"Aw shit," Luckman said in disgust. He threw himself down on the couch. "Shit shit shit. We can't do anything. There's probably dope hidden in a thousand places we'll never find. We've had it." He glared up at Arctor in baffled fury. *"We've had it!"*

Arctor said to Barris, "What about your electronic cassette thing rigged to the front door?" He had forgotten about it. So had Barris, evidently. Luckman, too.

"Yes, this should be extremely informational at this point," Barris said. He knelt down by the couch, reached underneath, grunted, then hauled forth a small plastic cassette tape recorder. "This should tell us a great deal," he began, and then his face sank. "Well, it probably wouldn't ultimately have proven that important." He pulled out the power plug from the back and set the cassette down on the coffee table. "We know the main fact—that they did enter during our absence. That was its main task."

Silence.

"I'll bet I can guess," Arctor said.

Barris said, "The first thing they did when they entered was switch it to the *off* position. I left it set to *on*, but look—now it's turned to *off*. So although I—"

"It didn't record?" Luckman said, disappointed.

"They made their move swiftly," Barris said. "Before so much as an inch of tape passed through the recording head. This, by the way, is a neat little job, a Sony. It has a separate head for playback, erase and record, and the Dolby noise-reduction system. I got it cheap. At a swap meet. And it's never given me any trouble."

Arctor said, "Mandatory soul time."

"Absolutely," Barris agreed as he seated himself in a chair and leaned back, removing his shades. "At this point we have no other recourse in view of theft evasive tactics. You know,

Bob, there is one thing you could do, although it would take time."

"Sell the house and move out," Arctor said.

Barris nodded.

"But hell," Luckman protested. "This is our *home*."

"What are houses like this in this area worth now?" Barris asked, hands behind his head. "On the market? I wonder, too, what interest rates are up to. Maybe you could make a considerable profit, Bob. On the other hand, you might have to take a loss on a quick sale. But, Bob, my God, you're up against professionals."

"Do you know a good realtor?" Luckman asked both of them.

Arctor said, "What reason should we give for selling? They always ask."

"Yeah, we can't tell the realtor the truth," Luckman agreed. "We could say . . ." He pondered as he moodily drank his beer. "I can't think of a reason. Barris, what's a reason, a shuck we could give?"

Arctor said, "We'll just say flat-out there's narcotics planted all over the house and since we don't know where it is we decided to move out and let the new owner get busted instead of us."

"No," Barris disagreed, "I don't think we can afford to be up front like that. I'd suggest you say, Bob, you say that you got a job transfer."

"Where to?" Luckman said.

"Cleveland," Barris said.

"I think we should tell them the truth," Arctor said. "In fact, we could put an ad in the L.A. *Times*: 'Modern three-bedroom tract house with two bathrooms for easy and fast flushing, high-grade dope stashed throughout all rooms; dope included in sale price.'"

"But they'd be calling asking what kind of dope," Luckman said. "And we don't know; it could be anything."

"And how much there is," Barris murmured. "Prospective buyers might inquire about the quantity."

"Like," Luckman said, "it could be an ounce of roachweed, just shit like that, or it could be pounds of heroin."

"What I suggest," Barris said, "is that we phone county

drug abuse and inform them of the situation and ask them to come in and remove the dope. Search the house, find it, dispose of it. Because, to be realistic, there really isn't time to sell the house. I researched the legal situation once for this type of bind, and most lawbooks agree—"

"You're crazy," Luckman said, staring at him as if he were one of Jerry's aphids. "Phone *drug abuse*? There'll be narks in here within less time than—"

"That's the best hope," Barris continued smoothly, "and we can all take lie-detector tests to prove we didn't know where it was or what it was or even put it there. It is there without our knowledge or permission. If you tell them that, Bob, they'll exonerate you." After a pause he admitted, "Eventually. When all the facts are known in open court."

"But on the other hand," Luckman said, "we've got our own stashes. We *do* know where they are and like that. Does this mean we've got to flush all our stashes? And suppose we miss some? Even one? Christ, this is awful!"

"There is no way out," Arctor said. "They appear to have us."

From one of the bedrooms Donna Hawthorne appeared, wearing a funny little knee-pants outfit, hair tumbled in disarray, her face puffy with sleep.

"I came on in," she said, "like the note said. And I sat around for a while and then crashed. The note didn't say when you'd be back. Why were you yelling? God, you're uptight. You woke me."

"You smoked a joint just now?" Arctor asked her. "Before you crashed?"

"Sure," she said. "Otherwise I can't ever sleep."

"It's Donna's roach," Luckman said. "Give it to her."

My God, Bob Arctor thought. I was into that trip as much as they were. We all got into it together that deep. He shook himself, shuddered, and blinked. Knowing what I know, I still stepped across into that freaked-out paranoid space with them, viewed it as they viewed it—muddled, he thought. Murky again; the same murk that covers them covers me; the murk of this dreary dream world we float around in.

"You got us out of it," he said to Donna.

"Out of what?" Donna said, puzzled and sleepy.

Not what I am, he thought, or what I know was supposed

to take place here today, but this chick—*she* put my head back together, got all three of us out. A little black-haired chick wearing a funky outfit who I report on and am shucking and hopefully will be fucking . . . another shuck-and-fuck reality world, he thought, with this foxy girl the center of it: a rational point that unwired us abruptly. Otherwise where would our heads finally have gone? We, all three of us, had gotten out of it entirely.

But not for the first time, he thought. Not even today.

"You shouldn't leave your place unlocked like that," Donna said. "You could get ripped off and it'd be your own fault. Even the giant capitalist insurance companies say that if you leave a door or window unlocked they won't pay. That's the main reason I came in when I saw the note. Somebody ought to be here if it's unlocked like that."

"How long have you been here?" Arctor asked her. Maybe she had aborted the bugging; maybe not. Probably not.

Donna consulted her twenty-dollar electric Timex wristwatch, which he had given her. "About thirty-eight minutes. Hey." Her face brightened. "Bob, I got the wolf book with me—you want to look at it now? It's got a lot of heavy shit in it, if you can dig it."

"Life," Barris said, as if to himself, "is only heavy and none else; there is only the one trip, all heavy. Heavy that leads to the grave. For everyone and everything."

"Did I hear you say you're going to sell your house?" Donna asked him. "Or was that—you know, me dreaming? I couldn't tell; what I heard sounded spaced out and weird."

"We're all dreaming," Arctor said. If the last to know he's an addict is the addict, then maybe the last to know when a man means what he says is the man himself, he reflected. He wondered how much of the garbage that Donna had overheard he had seriously meant. He wondered how much of the insanity of the day—his insanity—had been real, or just induced as a contact lunacy, by the situation. Donna, always, was a pivot point of reality for him; for her this was the basic, natural question. He wished he could answer.

Chapter Seven

Tᴴᴱ, next day Fred showed up in his scramble suit to hear about the bugging installation.

"The six holo-scanners now operating within the premises —six should be sufficient for now, we feel—transmit to a safe apartment down the street in the same block as Arctor's house," Hank explained, laying out a floor plan of Bob Arctor's house on the metal table between them. It chilled Fred to see this, but not overly much. He picked the sheet up and studied the locations of the various scanners, in the various rooms, here and there so that everything fell under constant video scrutiny, as well as audio.

"So I do the playback at that apartment," Fred said.

"We use it as a playback-monitor spot for about eight—or perhaps it's nine, now—houses or apartments under scrutiny in that particular neighborhood. So you'll be bumping into other undercover people doing their playbacks. *Always have your suit on then.*"

"I'll be seen going into the apartment. It's too close."

"Guess so, but it's an enormous complex, hundreds of units, and it's the only one we've found electronically feasible. It'll have to do, at least until we get legal eviction on another unit elsewhere. We're working on it . . . two blocks farther away, where you'll be less conspicuous. Week or so, I'd guess. If holo-scans could be transmitted with acceptable resolution along micro-relay cables and ITT lines like the older—"

"I'll just use the shuck that I'm balling some broad in that complex, if Arctor or Luckman or any of those heads see me entering." It really didn't complicate matters that much; in fact, it would cut down his in-transit unpaid time, which was an important factor. He could easily truck on over to the safe apartment, do the scanning replay, determine what was relevant to his reports and what could be discarded, and then return very soon to—

To my own house, he thought. Arctor's house. Up the street at the house I am Bob Arctor, the heavy doper suspect being

948

scanned without his knowledge, and then every couple of days I find a pretext to slip down the street and into the apartment where I am Fred replaying miles and miles of tape to see what I did, and this whole business, he thought, depresses me. Except for the protection—and valuable personal information— it will give me.

Probably whoever's hunting me will be caught by the holo-scanners within the first week.

Realizing that, he felt mellow.

"Fine," he said to Hank.

"So you see where the holos are placed. If they need servicing, you probably can do it yourself while you're in Arctor's house and no one else is around. You do get into his house, normally, don't you?"

Well shit, Fred thought. If I do that, then I will be on the holo-replays. So when I turn them over to Hank I have to be, obviously, one of the individuals visible on them, and that cuts it down.

Up to now he had never actually laid it on Hank as to how he knew what he knew about his suspects; he himself as Fred the effective screening device carried the information. But now: audio- and holo-scanners, which did not automatically edit out as did his verbal report all identifying mention of himself. There would be Robert Arctor tinkering with the holos when they malfunctioned, his face mushrooming up to fill the screen. But on the other hand *he* would be the first to replay the storage tapes; he could still edit. Except that it would take time and care.

But edit out *what*? Edit out Arctor—entirely? Arctor was the suspect. Just Arctor when he went to fiddle with the holos.

"I'll edit myself out," he said. "So you won't see me. As a matter of conventional protection."

"Of course. You haven't done this before?" Hank reached to show him a couple of pictures. "You use a bulk erasing device that wipes out any section where you as the informant appear. That's the holos, of course; for audio, there's no set policy followed. You won't have any real trouble, though. We take it for granted that you're one of the individuals in Arctor's circle of friends who frequent that house—you are either

Jim Barris or Ernie Luckman or Charles Freck or Donna Hawthorne—"

"Donna?" He laughed. The suit laughed, actually. In its way.

"Or Bob Arctor," Hank continued, studying his list of suspects.

"I report on myself all the time," Fred said.

"So you will have to include yourself from time to time in the holo-tapes you turn over to us, because if you systematically edit yourself out then we can deduce who you are by a process of elimination, whether we want to or not. What you must do, really, is edit yourself out in—what should I call it?— an inventive, artistic . . . Hell, the word is, *creative* way . . . as for instance during the brief intervals when you're in the house alone and doing research, going through papers and drawers, or servicing a scanner within view of another scanner, or—"

"You should just send someone to the house once a month in a uniform," Fred said. "And have him say, 'Good morning! I'm here to service the monitoring devices covertly installed on your premises, in your phone, and in your car.' Maybe Arctor would pick up the bill."

"Arctor would probably off him and then disappear."

The scramble suit Fred said, "If Arctor is hiding that much. That's not been proved."

"Arctor may be hiding a great deal. We've got more recent information on him gathered and analyzed. There is no substantial doubt of it: he is a ringer, a three-dollar bill. He is *phony*. So keep on him until he drops, until we have enough to arrest him and make it stick."

"You want stuff planted?"

"We'll discuss that later."

"You think he's up high in the, you know, the S. D. Agency?"

"What we *think* isn't of any importance in your work," Hank said. "We evaluate; *you* report with your own limited conclusions. This is not a put-down of you, but we have information, lots of it, not available to you. The broad picture. The computerized picture."

"Arctor is doomed," Fred said. "If he's up to anything. And I have a hunch from what you say that he is."

"We should have a case on him this way soon," Hank said. "And then we can close the book on him, which will please us all."

Fred stoically memorized the address and number of the apartment and suddenly recalled that he had seen a young head-type couple who had recently abruptly disappeared now and then entering and leaving the building. Busted, and their apartment taken over for this. He had liked them. The girl had long flaxen hair, wore no bra. One time he had driven past as she was lugging groceries and offered her a lift; they had talked. She was an organic type, into megavitamins and kelp and sunlight, nice, shy, but she'd declined. Now he could see why. Evidently the two of them had been holding. Or, more likely, dealing. On the other hand, if the apartment was needed, a possession rap would do, and you could always get that.

What, he wondered, would Bob Arctor's littered but large house be used for by the authorities when Arctor had been hauled off? An even vaster intelligence-processing center, most likely.

"You'd like Arctor's house," he said aloud. "It's run-down and typically doper dirty, but it's big. Nice yard. Lots of shrubs."

"That's what the installation crew reported back. Some excellent possibilities."

"They *what*? They reported it had 'plenty of possibilities,' did they?" The scramble suit voice clacked out maddeningly without tone or resonance, which made him even angrier. "Like what?"

"Well, one obvious possibility: its living room gives a view of an intersection, so passing vehicles could be graphed and their license plates . . ." Hank studied his many, many papers. "But Burt What's-his-face, who headed the crew, felt the house had been allowed to deteriorate so badly that it wouldn't be worth our taking over. As an investment."

"In what way? In what fashion deteriorated?"

"The roof."

"The roof's perfect."

"The interior and exterior paint. The condition of the floors. The kitchen cabinets—"

"Bullshit," Fred said, or anyhow the suit droned. "Arctor may have let dishes pile up and the garbage and not dusted, but after all, three dudes living there with no chicks? His wife left him; women are supposed to do all that. If Donna Hawthorne had moved in like Arctor wanted her to, begged her to, she would have kept it up. Anyhow, any professional janitorial service could put the whole house in top shape as far as cleaning goes in a half a day. Regarding the roof, that really makes me mad, because—"

"Then you recommend we acquire it after Arctor's been arrested and loses title."

Fred, the suit, stared at him.

"Well?" Hank said impassively, ballpoint pen ready.

"I have no opinion. One way or another." Fred rose from his chair to leave.

"You're not splitting yet," Hank said, motioning him to reseat himself. He fished among the papers on his desk. "I have a memo here—"

"You always have memos," Fred said. "For everybody."

"This memo," Hank said, "instructs me to send you over to Room 203 before you leave today."

"If it's about that anti-drug speech I gave at the Lion's Club, I've already had my ass chewed about it."

"No, this isn't that." Hank tossed him the fluttery note. "This is something different. I'm finished with you, so why don't you head right over there now and get it done with."

He found himself confronting an all-white room with steel fixtures and steel chairs and steel desk, all bolted down, a hospital-like room, purified and sterile and cold, with the light too bright. In fact, to the right stood a weighing scale with a sign HAVE TECHNICIAN ONLY ADJUST. Two deputies regarded him, both in full uniform of the Orange County Sheriff's Office, but with medical stripes.

"You are Officer Fred?" one of them, with a handle-bar mustache, said.

"Yes, sir," Fred said. He felt scared.

"All right, Fred, first let me state that, as you undoubtedly are aware, your briefings and debriefings are monitored and later played back for study, in case anything was missed at the original sessions. This is SOP, of course, and applies to all officers reporting in orally, not you alone."

The other medical deputy said, "Plus all other contacts you maintain with the department, such as phone contacts, and additional activities, such as your recent public speech in Anaheim to the Rotary Club boys."

"Lions," Fred said.

"Do you take Substance D?" the left-hand medical deputy said.

"That question," the other said, "is moot because it's taken for granted that in your work you're compelled to. So don't answer. Not that it would be incriminating, but it's simply moot." He indicated a table on which a bunch of blocks and other riff-raff colorful plastic objects lay, plus peculiar items that Officer Fred could not identify. "Step over here and be seated, Officer Fred. We are going to administer, briefly, several easy tests. This won't consume much of your time, and there will be no physical discomfort involved."

"About that speech I gave—" Fred said.

"What this is about," the left-hand medical deputy said, as he seated himself and produced a pen and some forms, "stems from a recent departmental survey showing that several undercover agents working in this area have been admitted to Neural Aphasia Clinics during the past month."

"You're conscious of the high factor of addictiveness of Substance D?" the other deputy said to Fred.

"Sure," Fred said. "Of course I am."

"We're going to give you these tests now," the seated deputy said, "in this order, starting with what we call the BG or—"

"You think I'm an addict?" Fred said.

"Whether you are an addict or not isn't a prime issue, since a blocking agent is expected from the Army Chemical Warfare Division sometime within the next five years."

"These tests do not pertain to the addictive properties of Substance D but to— Well, let me give you this Set-Ground Test first, which determines your ability readily to distinguish set from ground. See this geometric diagram?" He laid a drawn-on card before Fred, on the table. "Within the apparently meaningless lines is a familiar object that we would all recognize. You are to tell me what the . . ."

Item. In July 1969, Joseph E. Bogen published his revolutionary article "The Other Side of the Brain: An Appositional Mind." In this article he quoted an obscure Dr. A. L. Wigan, who in 1844 wrote:

> The mind is essentially dual, like the organs by which it is exercised. This idea has presented itself to me, and I have dwelt on it for more than a quarter of a century, without being able to find a single valid or even plausible objection. I believe myself then able to prove—(1) That each cerebrum is a distinct and perfect whole as an organ of thought. (2) That a separate and distinct process of thinking or ratiocination may be carried on in each cerebrum simultaneously.

In his article, Bogen concluded: "I believe [with Wigan] that each of us has two minds in one person. There is a host of detail to be marshaled in this case. But we must eventually confront directly the principal resistance to the Wigan view: that is, the subjective feeling possessed by each of us that we are One. This inner conviction of Oneness is a most cherished opinion of Western Man. . . ."

". . . object is and point to it in the total field."

I'm being Mutt-and-Jeffed, Fred thought. "What is all this?" he said, gazing at the deputy and not the diagram. "I'll bet it's the Lion Club speech," he said. He was positive.

The seated deputy said, "In many of those taking Substance D, a split between the right hemisphere and the left hemisphere of the brain occurs. There is a loss of proper gestalting, which is a defect within both the percept and cognitive systems, although *apparently* the cognitive system continues to function normally. But what is now received from the percept system is contaminated by being split, so it too, therefore, fails gradually to function, progressively deteriorating. Have you located the familiar object in this line drawing? Can you find it for me?"

Fred said, "You're not talking about heavy metals trace deposits in the neuroreceptor sites, are you? Irreversible—"

"No," the standing deputy said. "This is not brain damage

but a form of toxicity, brain toxicity. It's a toxic brain psychosis affecting the percept system by splitting it. What you have before you, this BG test, measures the accuracy of your percept system to act as a unified whole. Can you see the form here? It should jump right out at you."

"I see a Coke bottle," Fred said.

"A soda pop bottle is correct," the seated deputy said, and whipped the drawing away, replacing it with another.

"Have you noticed anything," Fred said, "in studying my briefings and like that? Anything slushed?" It's the speech, he thought. "What about the speech I gave?" he said. "Did I show bilateral dysfunction there? Is that why I've been hauled in here for these tests?" He had read about these split-brain tests, given by the department from time to time.

"No, this is routine," the seated deputy said. "We realize, Officer Fred, that undercover agents must of necessity take drugs in the line of duty; those who've had to go into federal—"

"Permanently?" Fred asked.

"Not many permanently. Again, this is percept contamination that could in the course of time rectify itself as—"

"Murky," Fred said. "It murks over everything."

"Are you getting any cross-chatter?" one of the deputies asked him suddenly.

"What?" he said uncertainly.

"Between hemispheres. If there's damage to the left hemisphere, where the linguistic skills are normally located, then sometimes the right hemisphere will fill in to the best of its ability."

"I don't know," he said. "Not that I'm aware of."

"Thoughts not your own. As if another person or mind were thinking. But different from the way you would think. Even foreign words that you don't know. That it's learned from peripheral perception sometime during your lifetime."

"Nothing like that. I'd notice that."

"You probably would. From people with left-hemisphere damage who've reported it, evidently it's a pretty shattering experience."

"Well, I guess I'd notice that."

"It used to be believed the right hemisphere had no linguistic faculties at all, but that was before so many people had screwed up their left hemispheres with drugs and gave it—the right—a chance to come on. To fill the vacuum."

"I'll certainly keep my eyes open for that," Fred said, and heard the mere mechanical quality of his voice, like that of a dutiful child in school. Agreeing to obey whatever dull order was imposed on him by those in authority. Those taller than he was, and in a position to impose their strength and will on him, whether it was reasonable or not.

Just agree, he thought. And do what you're told.

"What do you see in this second picture?"

"A sheep," Fred said.

"Show me the sheep." The seated deputy leaned forward and rotated the picture. "An impairment in set-background discrimination gets you into a heap of trouble—instead of perceiving no forms you perceive faulty forms."

Like dog shit, Fred thought. Dog shit certainly would be considered a faulty form. By any standard. He . . .

> The data indicate that the mute, minor hemisphere is specialized for Gestalt perception, being primarily a synthesist in dealing with information input. The speaking, major hemisphere, in contrast, seems to operate in a more logical, analytic, computerlike fashion and the findings suggest that a possible reason for cerebral lateralization in man is basic incompatibility of language functions on the one hand and synthetic perceptual functions on the other.

. . . felt ill and depressed, almost as much as he had during his Lions Club speech. "There's no sheep there, is there?" he said. "But was I close?"

"This is not a Rorschach test," the seated deputy said, "where a muddled blot can be interpreted many ways by many subjects. In this, one specific object, as such, has been delineated and one only. In this case it's a dog."

"A what?" Fred said.

"A dog."

"How can you tell it's a dog?" He saw no dog. "Show me." The deputy . . .

This conclusion finds its experimental proof in the split-brain animal whose two hemispheres can be trained to perceive, consider, and act independently. In the human, where propositional thought is typically lateralized in one hemisphere, the other hemisphere evidently specializes in a different mode of thought, which may be called *appositional*. The rules or methods by which propositional thought is elaborated on "this" side of the brain (the side which speaks, reads, and writes) have been subjected to analyses of syntax, semantics, mathematical logic, etc. for many years. The rules by which appositional thought is elaborated on the other side of the brain will need study for many years to come.

. . . turned the card over; on the back the formal stark simple outline of A DOG had been inscribed, and now Fred recognized it as the shape drawn within the lines on the front side. In fact it was a specific type of dog: a greyhound, with drawn-in gut.

"What's that mean," he said, "that I saw a sheep instead?"

"Probably just a psychological block," the standing deputy said, shifting his weight about. "Only when the whole set of cards is run, and then we have the several other tests—"

"Why this is a superior test to the Rorschach," the seated deputy interrupted, producing the next drawing, "is that it is not interpretive; there are as many wrongs as you can think up, *but only one right*. The right object that the U. S. Department of Psych-Graphics drew into it and certified for it, for each card; that's what's right, because it is handed down from Washington. You either get it or you don't, and if you show a *run* of not getting it, then we have a fix on a functional impairment in perception and we dry you out for a while, until you test okay later on."

"A federal clinic?" Fred said.

"Yes. Now, what do you see in this drawing, among these particular black and white lines?"

Death City, Fred thought as he studied the drawing. That is what I see: death in pluriform, not in just the one correct form but throughout. Little three-foot-high contract men on carts.

"Just tell me," Fred said, "was it the Lions Club speech that alerted you?"

The two medical deputies exchanged glances.

"No," the standing one said finally. "It had to do with an exchange that was—actually—off the cuff, in fact just bull-shitting between you and Hank. About two weeks ago . . . you realize, there's a technological lag in processing all this garbage, all this raw information that flows in. They haven't gotten to your speech yet. They won't in fact for another couple of days."

"What was this bullshitting?"

"Something about a stolen bicycle," the other deputy said. "A so-called seven-speed bicycle. You'd been trying to figure out where the missing three speeds had gone, was that it?" Again they glanced at each other, the two medical deputies. "You felt they had been left on the floor of the garage it was stolen from?"

"Hell," Fred protested. "That was Charles Freck's fault, not mine; he got everybody's ass in an uproar talking about it. I just thought it was funny."

BARRIS: (*Standing in the middle of the living room with a great big new shiny bike, very pleased*) Look what I got for twenty dollars.

FRECK: What is it?

BARRIS: A bike, a ten-speed racing bike, virtually brand new. I saw it in the neighbor's yard and asked about it and they had four of them so I made an offer of twenty dollars cash and they sold it to me. Colored people. They even hoisted it over the fence for me.

LUCKMAN: I didn't know you could get a ten-speed nearly new for twenty dollars. It's amazing what you can get for twenty dollars.

DONNA: It resembles the one the chick across the street from me had that got ripped off about a month ago. They probably ripped it off, those black guys.

ARCTOR: Sure they did, if they've got four. And selling it that cheap.

DONNA: You ought to give it back to the chick across the

street from me, if it's hers. Anyhow you should let her look at it to see if it's hers.

BARRIS: It's a man's bike. So it can't be.

FRECK: Why do you say it's ten speeds when it's only got seven gears?

BARRIS: (*Astonished*) What?

FRECK: (*Going over to bike and pointing*) Look, five gears here, two gears here at the other end of the chain. Five and two . . .

> When the optic chiasm of a cat or a monkey is divided sagittally, the input into the right eye goes only into the right hemisphere and similarly the left eye informs only the left hemisphere. If an animal with this operation is trained to choose between two symbols while using only one eye, later tests show that it can make the proper choice with the other eye. But if the commissures, especially the corpus callosum, have been severed before training, the initially covered eye and its ipsilateral hemisphere must be trained from the beginning. That is, the training does not transfer from one hemisphere to the other if the commissures have been cut. This is the fundamental split-brain experiment of Myers and Sperry (1953; Sperry, 1961; Myers, 1965; Sperry, 1967).

. . . makes seven. So it's only a seven-speed bike.

LUCKMAN: Yeah, but even a seven-speed racing bike is worth twenty dollars. He still got a good buy.

BARRIS: (*Nettled*) Those colored people told me it was ten speeds. It's a rip-off.

(*Everyone gathers to examine bike. They count the gears again and again.*)

FRECK: Now I count eight. Six in front, two in back. That makes eight.

ARCTOR: (*Logically*) But it should be ten. There are no seven- or eight-speed bikes. Not that I ever heard of. What do you suppose happened to the missing gears?

BARRIS: Those colored guys must have been working on it, taking it apart with improper tools and no technical knowledge, and when they reassembled it they left three gears lying on the floor of their garage. They're probably still lying there.

LUCKMAN: Then we should go ask for the missing gears back.

BARRIS: (*Pondering angrily*) But that's where the rip-off is: they'll probably offer to sell them to me, not give them to me as they should. I wonder what else they've damaged. (*Inspects entire bike*)

LUCKMAN: If we all go together they'll give them to us; you can bet on it, man. We'll all go, right? (*Looks around for agreement*)

DONNA: Are you positive there're only seven gears?

FRECK: Eight.

DONNA: Seven, eight. Anyhow, I mean, before you go over there, ask somebody. I mean, it doesn't look to me like they've done anything to it like taking it apart. Before you go over there and lay heavy shit on them, find out. Can you dig it?

ARCTOR: She's right.

LUCKMAN: Who should we ask? Who do we know that's an authority on racing bikes?

FRECK: Let's ask the first person we see. Let's wheel it out the door and when some freak comes along we'll ask him. That way we'll get a disheartened viewpoint.

(*They collectively wheel bike out front, right off encounter young black man parking his car. They point to the seven—eight? —gears questioningly and ask how many there are, although they can see—except for Charles Freck—that there are only seven: five at one end of the chain, two at the other. Five and two add up to seven. They can ascertain it with their own eyes. What's going on?*)

YOUNG BLACK MAN: (*Calmly*) What you have to do is multiply the number of gears in front by the number in the rear. It is not an adding but a multiplying, because, you see, the chain leaps across from gear to gear, and in terms of gear ratios you obtain five (*He indicates the five gears.*) times one of the two in front (*He points to that.*), which gives you one times five, which is five, and then when you shift with this lever on the handle-bar (*He demonstrates.*) the chain jumps to the other one of the two in front and interacts with the same five in the back all over again, which is an additional five. The addition involved is five plus five, which is ten. Do you see how that works? You see, gear ratios are always derived by—

(*They thank him and silently wheel the bike back inside the house. The young black man, whom they have never seen before and who is no more than seventeen and driving an incredibly beat-up old transportation-type car, goes on locking up, and they close the front door of the house and just stand there.*)

LUCKMAN: Anybody got any dope? "Where there's dope there's hope." (*No-one . . .*

> All the evidence indicates that separation of the hemispheres creates two independent spheres of consciousness within a single cranium, that is to say, within a single organism. This conclusion is disturbing to some people who view consciousness as an indivisible property of the human brain. It seems premature to others, who insist that the capacities revealed thus far for the right hemisphere are at the level of an automaton. There is, to be sure, hemispheric inequality in the present cases, but it may well be a characteristic of the individuals we have studied. It is entirely possible that if a human brain were divided in a very young person, both hemispheres could as a result separately and independently develop mental functions of a high order at the level attained only in the left hemisphere of normal individuals.

. . . laughs.)

"We know you were one of the people in that group," the seated medical deputy said. "It doesn't matter which one. None of you could look at the bike and perceive the simple mathematical operation involved in determining the number of its very small system of gear ratios." In the deputy's voice Fred heard a certain compassion, a measure of being kind. "An operation like that constitutes a junior high school aptitude test. Were you all stoned?"

"No," Fred said.

"They give aptitude tests like that to children," the other medical deputy said.

"So what was wrong, Fred?" the first deputy asked.

"I forget," Fred said. He shut up now. And then he said, "It sounds to me like a cognitive fuckup, rather than perceptive. Isn't abstract thinking involved in a thing like that? Not—"

"You might imagine so," the seated deputy said. "But tests show that the cognitive system fails because it isn't receiving accurate data. In other words, the inputs are distorting in such a fashion that when you go to reason about what you see you reason wrongly because you don't—" The deputy gestured, trying to find a way to express it.

"But a ten-speed bike *has* seven gears," Fred said. "What we saw was accurate. Two in front, five in back."

"But you didn't perceive, any of you, how they interact: five in back with *each* of the two in front, as the black told you. Was he a highly educated man?"

"Probably not," Fred said.

"What the black saw," the standing deputy said, "was different from what all of you saw. He saw two separate connecting lines between the rear gear system and the front, two simultaneous different lines perceptible to him between the gears in front running to each of the five back ones in turn. . . . What you saw was *one* connective to all back ones."

"But that would make six gears, then," Fred said. "Two front gears but one connective."

"Which is inaccurate perception. Nobody taught that black boy that; what they taught him to do, if anyone taught him at all, was to figure out, cognitively, what the meaning of those two connectives were. You missed one of them entirely, all of you. What you did was that although you counted two front gears, you *perceived* them as a homogeneity."

"I'll do better next time," Fred said.

"Next time what? When you buy a ripped-off ten-speed bike? Or abstracting all daily percept input?"

Fred remained silent.

"Let's continue the test," the seated deputy said. "What do you see in this one, Fred?"

"Plastic dog shit," Fred said. "Like they sell here in the Los Angeles area. Can I go now?" It was the Lions Club speech all over again.

Both deputies, however, laughed.

"You know, Fred," the seated one said, "if you can keep your sense of humor like you do you'll perhaps make it."

"Make it?" Fred echoed. "Make what? The team? The chick? Make good? Make do? Make out? Make sense? Make money? Make time? Define your terms. The Latin for 'make' is *facere*,

which always reminds me of *fuckere*, which is Latin for 'to fuck,' and I haven't . . .

> The brain of the higher animals, including man, is a double organ, consisting of right and left hemispheres connected by an isthmus of nerve tissue called the corpus callosum. Some 15 years ago Ronald E. Myers and R. W. Sperry, then at the University of Chicago, made a surprising discovery: when this connection between the two halves of the cerebrum was cut, each hemisphere functioned independently as if it were a complete brain.

. . . been getting it on worth jack shit lately, plastic shit or otherwise, any kind of shit. If you boys are psychologist types and you've been listening to my endless debriefings with Hank, what the hell is Donna's handle? How do I get next to her? I mean, how is it done? With that kind of sweet, unique, stubborn little chick?"

"Each girl is different," the seated deputy said.

"I mean approach her ethically," Fred said. "Not cram her with reds and booze and then stick it into her while she's lying on the living-room floor."

"Buy her flowers," the standing deputy said.

"What?" Fred said, his suit-filtered eyes opening wide.

"This time of year you can get little spring flowers. At the nursery departments of, say, Penney's or K Mart. Or an azalea."

"Flowers," Fred murmured. "You mean plastic flowers or real flowers? Real ones, I guess."

"The plastic ones are no good," the seated deputy said. "They look like they're . . . well, fake. Somehow fake."

"Can I leave now?" Fred asked.

After an exchange of glances, both deputies nodded. "We'll evaluate you some other time, Fred," the standing one said. "It's not that urgent. Hank will notify you of a later appointment time."

For some obscure reason Fred felt like shaking hands with them before he left, but he did not; he just left, saying nothing, a little down and a little bewildered, because, probably, of the way it had shot out of left field at him, so suddenly. They've been going over and over my material, he thought, trying to find signs of my being burned out, and they did find some. Enough, anyhow, to want to run these tests.

Spring flowers, he thought as he reached the elevator. Little ones; they probably grow close to the ground and a lot of people step on them. Do they grow wild? Or in special commercial vats or in huge enclosed farms? I wonder what the country is like. The fields and like that, the strange smells. And, he wondered, where do you find that? Where do you go and how do you get there and stay there? What kind of trip is that, and what kind of ticket does it take? And who do you buy the ticket from?

And, he thought, I would like to take someone with me when I go there, maybe Donna. But how do you ask that, ask a chick that, when you don't even know how to get next to her? When you've been scheming on her and achieving nothing—not even step one. We should hurry, he thought, because later on all the spring flowers like they told me about will be dead.

Chapter Eight

O N HIS way over to Bob Arctor's house, where a bunch of heads could usually be found for a mellow turned-on time, Charles Freck worked out a gag to put ol' Barris on, to pay him back for the spleen jive at the Fiddler's Three restaurant that day. In his head, as he skillfully avoided the radar traps that the police kept everywhere (the police radar vans checking out drivers usually took the disguise of old raunchy VW vans, painted dull brown, driven by bearded freaks; when he saw such vans he slowed), he ran a preview fantasy number of his put-on:

FRECK: (*Casually*) I bought a methedrine plant today.

BARRIS: (*With a snotty expression on his face*) Methedrine is a benny, like speed; it's crank, it's crystal, it's amphetamine, it's made synthetically in a lab. So it isn't organic, like pot. There's no such thing as a methedrine plant like there is a pot plant.

FRECK: (*Springing the punch line on him*) I mean I inherited forty thousand from an old uncle and purchased a plant hidden in this dude's garage where he makes methedrine. I mean, he's got a factory there where he manufactures meth. Plant in the sense of—

He couldn't get it phrased exactly right as he drove, because part of his mind stayed on the vehicles around him and the lights; but he knew when he got to Bob's house he'd lay it on Barris super good. And, especially if a bunch of people were there, Barris would rise to the bait and be visible to everyone flat-out as a clear and evident asshole. And that would super pay him back, because Barris worse than anybody else couldn't stand to be made fun of.

When he pulled up he found Barris outdoors working on Bob Arctor's car. The hood was up, and both Barris and Arctor stood together with a pile of car tools.

"Hey, man," Freck said, slamming his door and sauntering casually over. "Barris," he said right off in a cool way, putting his hand on Barris's shoulder to attract his attention.

"Later," Barris growled. He had his repair clothes on; grease and like that covered the already dirty fabric.

Freck said, "I bought a methedrine plant today."

With an impatient scowl, Barris said, "How big?"

"What do you mean?"

"How big a plant?"

"Well," Freck said, wondering how to go on.

"How much'd you pay for it?" Arctor said, also greasy from the car repair. They had the carb off, Freck saw, air filter, hoses, and all.

Freck said, "About ten bucks."

"Jim could have gotten it for you cheaper," Arctor said, resuming his labors. "Couldn't you, Jim?"

"They're practically giving meth plants away," Barris said.

"This is a whole fucking garage!" Freck protested. "A factory! It turns out a million tabs a day—the pill-rolling machinery and everything. *Everything!*"

"All that cost ten dollars?" Barris said, grinning widely.

"Where's it located?" Arctor said.

"Not around here," Freck said uneasily. "Hey, fuck it, you guys."

Pausing in his work—Barris did a lot of pausing in his work, whether anyone was talking to him or not—Barris said, "You know, Freck, if you drop or shoot too much meth you start talking like Donald Duck."

"So?" Freck said.

"Then nobody can understand you," Barris said.

Arctor said, "What'd you say, Barris? I couldn't understand you."

His face dancing with merriment, Barris made his voice sound like Donald Duck's. Freck and Arctor grinned and enjoyed it. Barris went on and on, gesturing finally at the carburetor.

"What about the carburetor?" Arctor said, not smiling now.

Barris, in his regular voice, but still grinning widely, said, "You've got a bent choke shaft. The whole carb should be rebuilt. Otherwise the choke's going to shut on you while you're driving along the freeway and then you'll find your motor is flooded and dead and some asshole will rear-end you. And possibly in addition that raw gas washing down the cylinder walls—if it goes on long enough—will wash the lubrication away, so your cylinders will be scored and permanently damaged. And then you'll need them rebored."

"Why is the choke rod bent?" Arctor asked.

Shrugging, Barris resumed taking apart the carb, he did not answer. He left that up to Arctor and to Charles Freck, who knew nothing about engines, especially complex repairs like this.

Coming out of the house, Luckman, wearing a snazzy shirt and tight high-style Levi jeans, carrying a book and wearing shades, said, "I phoned and they're checking to see what a re-built carb will set you back for this car. They'll phone in a while, so I left the front door open."

Barris said, "You could put a four-barrel on instead of this two, while you're at it. But you'd have to put on a new manifold. We could pick up a used one for not very much."

"It would idle too high," Luckman said, "with like a Rochester four-barrel—is that what you mean? And it wouldn't shift properly. It wouldn't upshift."

"The idling jets could be replaced with smaller jets," Barris said, "that would compensate. And with a tach he could watch his rpms so it didn't over-rev. He'd know by the tach when it wasn't upshifting. Usually just backing off on the gas pedal causes it to upshift if the automatic linkage to the transmission doesn't do it. I know where we can get a tach, too. In fact, I have one."

"Yeah," Luckman said, "well, if he tromped down heavy on the step-down passing gear to get a lot of torque suddenly in an emergency on the freeway, it'd downshift and rev up so high it'd blow the head gasket or worse, a lot worse. Blow up the whole engine."

Barris, patiently, said, "He'd see the tach needle jump and he'd back right off."

"While passing?" Luckman said. "Halfway past a fucking big semi? Shit, he'd have to keep barreling on, high revs or not; he'd have to blow up the engine rather than back off, because if he backed off he'd never get around what he was trying to pass."

"Momentum," Barris said. "In a car this heavy, momentum would carry him on by even if he backed off."

"What about uphill?" Luckman said. "Momentum doesn't carry you very far uphill when you're passing."

To Arctor, Barris said, "What does this car . . ." He bent to see what make it was. "This . . ." His lips moved. "Olds."

"It weighs about a thousand pounds," Arctor said. Charles Freck saw him wink toward Luckman.

"You're right, then," Barris agreed. "There wouldn't be much inertia mass at that light weight. Or would there?" He groped for a pen and something to write on. "A thousand pounds traveling at eighty miles an hour builds up force equal to—"

"That's a thousand pounds," Arctor put in, "with the passengers in it and with a full tank of gas and a big carton of bricks in the trunk."

"How many passengers?" Luckman said, deadpan.

"Twelve."

"Is that six in back," Luckman said, "and six in—"

"No," Arctor said, "that's eleven in back and the driver sitting alone in front. So, you see, so there will be more weight on the rear wheels for more traction. So it won't fishtail."

Barris glanced alertly up. "This car fishtails?"

"Unless you get eleven people riding in the back," Arctor said.

"Be better, then, to load the trunk with sacks of sand," Barris said. "Three two-hundred-pound sacks of sand. Then the passengers could be distributed more evenly and they would be more comfortable."

"What about one six-hundred-pound box of gold in the trunk?" Luckman asked him. "Instead of three two-hundred—"

"Will you lay off?" Barris said. "I'm trying to calculate the inertial force of this car traveling at eighty miles an hour."

"It won't go eighty," Arctor said. "It's got a dead cyclinder. I meant to tell you. It threw a rod last night, on my way home from the 7-11."

"Then why are we pulling the carb?" Barris demanded. "We have to pull the whole head for that. In fact, much more. In fact, you may have a cracked block. Well, that's why it won't start."

"Won't your car start?" Freck asked Bob Arctor.

"It won't start," Luckman said, "because we pulled the carb off."

Puzzled, Barris said, "Why'd we pull the carb? I forget."

"To get all the springs and little dinky parts replaced," Arctor said. "So it won't fuck up again and nearly kill us. The Union station mechanic advised us to."

"If you bastards wouldn't rappity-rap on," Barris said, "like a lot of speed freaks, I could complete my computations and tell you how this particular car with its weight would handle with a four-barrel Rochester carb, modified naturally with smaller idling jets." He was genuinely sore now. "So SHUT UP!"

Luckman opened the book he was carrying. He puffed up, then, to much larger than usual; his great chest swelled, and so did his biceps. "Barris, I'm going to read to you." He began to read from the book, in a particularly fluent way. " 'He to whom it is given to see Christ *more real* than any other reality . . .' "

"What?" Barris said.

Luckman continued reading. " '. . . than any other reality in the World, Christ everywhere present and everywhere growing more great, Christ the final determination and plasmatic Principle of the Universe—' "

"What is that?" Arctor said.

"Chardin. Teilhard de Chardin."

"Jeez, Luckman," Arctor said.

" '. . . that man indeed lives in a zone where no multiplicity can distress him and which is nevertheless the most active workshop of universal fulfilment.' " Luckman shut the book.

With a high degree of apprehension, Charles Freck moved in between Barris and Luckman. "Cool it, you guys."

"Get out of the way, Freck," Luckman said, bringing back his right arm, low, for a vast sweeping haymaker at Barris. "Come on, Barris, I'm going to coldcock you into tomorrow, for talking to your betters like that."

With a bleat of wild, appealing terror, Barris dropped his felt pen and pad of paper and scuttled off erratically toward the open front door of the house, yelling back as he ran, "I hear the phone about the rebuilt carb."

They watched him go.

"I was just kidding him," Luckman said, rubbing his lower lip.

"What if he gets his gun and silencer?" Freck said, his nervousness off the scale entirely. He moved by degrees in the direction of his own parked car, to drop swiftly behind it if Barris reappeared firing.

"Come on," Arctor said to Luckman; they fell back together into their car work, while Freck loitered apprehensively by his own vehicle, wondering why he had decided to bop over here today. It had no mellow quality today, here, none at all, as it usually did. He had sensed the bad vibes under the kidding right from the start. What's the motherfuck wrong? he wondered, and got back somberly into his own car, to start it up.

Are things going to get heavy and bad here too, he wondered, like they did at Jerry Fabin's house during the last few weeks with him? It used to be mellow here, he thought, everybody kicking back and turning on, grooving to acid rock, especially the Stones. Donna sitting there in her leather jacket and boots, filling caps, Luckman rolling joints and telling about the seminar he planned to give at UCLA in dope-smoking and joint-rolling, and how someday he'd suddenly roll the perfect joint and it would be placed under glass and helium back at Constitution Hall, as part of American history with those other items of similar importance. When I look back, he thought, even to when Jim Barris and I were sitting at the Fiddler's, the other day . . . it was better even then. Jerry began it, he thought; that's what's coming down here, that there which carried off Jerry. How can days and happenings and moments so good become so quickly ugly, and for no reason, for no real reason? Just—change. With nothing causing it.

"I'm splitting," he said to Luckman and Arctor, who were watching him rev up.

"No, stay, hey, man," Luckman said with a warm smile. "We need you. You're a brother."

"Naw, I'm cutting out."

From the house Barris appeared cautiously. He carried a hammer. "It was a wrong number," he shouted, advancing with great caution, halting and peering like a crab-thing in a drive-in movie.

"What's the hammer for?" Luckman said.

Arctor said, "To fix the engine."

"Thought I would bring it with me," Barris explained as he returned gingerly to the Olds, "since I was indoors and noticed it."

"The most dangerous kind of person," Arctor said, "is one who is afraid of his own shadow." That was the last Freck heard as he drove away; he pondered over what Arctor meant, if he meant him, Charles Freck. He felt shame. But shit, he thought, why stick around when it's such a super bummer? Where's the chicken in that? Don't never participate in no bad scenes, he reminded himself; that was his motto in life. So he drove away now, without looking back. Let them snuff each other, he thought. Who needs them? But he felt bad, really bad, to leave them and to have witnessed the darkening change, and he wondered again why, and what it signified, but then it occurred to him that maybe things would go the other way again and get better, and that cheered him. In fact, it caused him to roll a short fantasy number in his head as he drove along avoiding invisible police cars:

THERE THEY ALL SAT AS BEFORE.

Even people who were either dead or burned out, like Jerry Fabin. They all sat here and there in a sort of clear white light, which wasn't daylight but better light than that, a kind of sea which lay beneath them and above them as well.

Donna and a couple other chicks looked so foxy—they had on halters and hot pants, or tank tops with no bras. He could hear music although he could not quite distinguish what track it was from what LP. Maybe Hendrix! he thought. Yeah, an old Hendrix track, or now all at once it was J.J. All of them: Jim Croce, and J.J., but especially Hendrix. "Before I die," Hendrix was murmuring, "let me live my life as I want to," and then immediately the fantasy number blew up because he had forgotten both that Hendrix was dead and how Hendrix and also Joplin had died, not to mention Croce. Hendrix and J.J. OD'ing on smack, both of them, two neat cool fine people like that, two outrageous humans, and he remembered how he'd heard that Janis's manager had only allowed her a couple hundred bucks now and then; she couldn't have the rest, all that she earned, because of her junk habit. And then he heard in his head her song "All Is Loneliness," and he began to cry. And in that condition drove on toward home.

In his living room, sitting with his friends and attempting to determine whether he needed a new carb, a rebuilt carb, or a modification carb-and-manifold, Robert Arctor sensed the silent constant scrutiny, the electronic presence, of the holo-scanners. And felt good about it.

"You look mellow," Luckman said. "Putting out a hundred bucks wouldn't make me mellow."

"I decided to cruise along the street until I come across an Olds like mine," Arctor explained, "and then unbolt their carb and pay nothing. Like everyone else we know."

"Especially Donna," Barris said in agreement. "I wish she hadn't been in here the other day while we were gone. Donna steals everything she can carry, and if she can't carry it she phones up her rip-off gang buddies and they show up and carry it off for her."

"I'll tell you a story I heard about Donna," Luckman said. "One time, see, Donna put a quarter into one of those auto-matic stamp machines that operate off a coil of stamps, and the machine was dingey and just kept cranking out stamps. Finally she had a market-basket full. It *still* kept cranking them out. Ultimately she had like—she and her rip-off friends counted them—over eighteen thousand U.S. fifteen-cent stamps. Well, that was cool, except what was Donna Hawthorne going to do with them? She never wrote a letter in her life, except to her lawyer to sue some guy who burned her in a dope deal."

"Donna does *that*?" Arctor said. "She has an attorney to use in a default on an illegal transaction? How can she do that?"

"She just probably says the dude owes her bread."

"Imagine getting an angry pay-up-or-go-to-court letter from an attorney about a dope deal," Arctor said, marveling at Donna, as he frequently did.

"Anyhow," Luckman continued, "there she was with a market-basket full of at least eighteen thousand U.S. fifteen-cent stamps, and what the hell to do with them? You can't sell them back to the Post Office. Anyhow, when the P.O. came to service the machine they'd know it went dingey, and anyone who showed up at a window with all those fifteen-cent stamps, especially a coil of them—shit, they'd flash on it; in fact, they'd be waiting for Donna, right? So she thought about it—after of course she'd loaded the coil of stamps into her MG and drove off—and then she phoned up more of those rip-off freaks she works with and had them drive over with a jack-hammer of some kind, water-cooled and water-silenced, a real kinky special one which, Christ, they ripped off, too, and they dug the stamp machine loose from the concrete in the middle of the night and carried it to her place in the back of a Ford Ranchero. Which they also probably ripped off. For the stamps."

"You mean she sold the stamps?" Arctor said, marveling. "From a vending machine? One by one?"

"They remounted—this is what I heard, anyhow—they relocated the U.S. stamp machine at a busy intersection where a lot of people pass by, but back out of sight where no mail truck would spot it, and they put it back in operation."

"They would have been wiser just to knock over the coin box," Barris said.

"So they were selling stamps, then," Luckman said, "for like a few weeks until the machine ran out, like it naturally had to eventually. And what the fuck next? I can imagine Donna's brain working on that during those weeks, that peasant-thrift brain . . . her family is peasant stock from some European country. Anyhow, by the time it ran out of its coil, Donna had decided to convert it over to soft drinks, which are from the P.O.—they're really guarded. And you go into the bucket forever for that."

"Is this true?" Barris said.

"Is what true?" Luckman said.

Barris said, "That girl is disturbed. She should be forcibly commited. Do you realize that all our taxes were raised by her stealing those stamps?" He sounded angry again.

"Write the government and tell them," Luckman said, his face cold with distaste for Barris. "Ask Donna for a stamp to mail it; she'll sell you one."

"At full price," Barris said, equally mad.

The holos, Arctor thought, will have miles and miles of this on their expensive tapes. Not miles and miles of dead tape but miles and miles of tripped out tape.

It was not what went on while Robert Arctor sat before a holo-scanner that mattered so much, he considered; it was what took place—at least for him . . . for whom? . . . for Fred—while Bob Arctor was elsewhere or asleep and others were within scanning range. So I should split, he thought, as I planned it out, leaving these guys, and sending other people I know over here. I should make my house superaccessible from now on.

And then a dreadful, ugly thought rose inside him. Suppose when I play the tapes back I see Donna when she's in here—opening a window with a spoon or knife blade—and slipping in and destroying my possessions and stealing. *Another* Donna: the chick as she really is, or anyhow as she is when I can't see her. The philosophical "when a tree falls in the forest" number. What is Donna like when no one is around to watch her?

Does, he wondered, the gentle lovely shrewd and very kind, super-kind girl transform herself instantly into something sly? Will I see a change which will blow my mind? Donna or Luckman, anyone I care about. Like your pet cat or dog when you're out of the house . . . the cat empties a pillowcase and starts stuffing your valuables in it: electric clock and bedside radio, shaver, all it can stuff in before you get back; another cat entirely while you're gone, ripping you off and pawning it all, or lighting up your joints, or walking on the ceiling, or phoning people long distance . . . God knows. A nightmare, a weird other world beyond the mirror, a terror city reverse thing, with unrecognizable entities creeping about; Donna crawling on all fours, eating from the animals' dishes . . . any kind of psychedelic wild trip, unfathomable and horrid.

Hell, he thought; for that matter, maybe Bob Arctor rises up in the night from deep sleep and does trips like that. Has sexual relations with the wall. Or mysterious freaks show up who he's never seen before, a whole bunch of them, with special heads that swivel all the way around, like owls'. And the audio-scanners will pick up the far-out demented conspiracies hatched out by him and them to blow up the men's room at the Standard station by filling the toilet with plastic explosives for God knows what brain-charred purpose. Maybe this sort of stuff goes on every night while he just imagines he's asleep—and is gone by day.

Bob Arctor, he speculated, may learn more new information about himself than he is ready for, more than he will about Donna in her little leather jacket, and Luckman in his fancy duds, and even Barris—maybe when nobody's around Jim Barris merely goes to sleep. And sleeps until they reappear.

But he doubted it. More likely Barris whipped out a hidden transmitter from the mess and chaos of his room—which, like all the other rooms in the house, had now for the first time come under twenty-four-hour scanning—and sent a cryptic signal to the other bunch of cryptic motherfuckers with whom he currently conspired for whatever people like him or them conspired for. Another branch, Bob Arctor reflected, of the authorities.

On the other hand, Hank and those guys downtown would not be too happy if Bob Arctor left his house, now that the monitors had been expensively and elaborately installed, and was never seen again: never showed up on any of the tape. He could not therefore take off in order to fulfill his personal surveillance plans at the expense of theirs. After all, it was their money.

In the script being filmed, he would at all times have to be the star actor. Actor, Arctor, he thought. Bob the Actor who is being hunted; he who is the El Primo huntee.

They say you never recognize your own voice when you first hear it played back on tape. And when you see yourself on video tape, or like this, in a 3-D hologram, you don't recognize yourself visually either. You imagined you were a tall fat man with black hair, and instead you're a tiny thin woman with no hair at all . . . is that it? I'm sure I'll recognize Bob Arctor, he thought, if by nothing else than by the clothes he wears or by a process of elimination. What isn't Barris or Luckman and lives here must be Bob Arctor. Unless it's one of the dogs or cats. I'll try to keep my professional eye trained on something which walks upright.

"Barris," he said, "I'm going out to see if I can score some beans." Then he pretended to remember he had no car; he got that sort of expression. "Luckman," he said, "is your Falcon running?"

"No," Luckman said thoughtfully, after consideration, "I don't think so."

"Can I borrow your car, Jim?" Arctor asked Barris.

"I wonder . . . if you can handle my car," Barris said.

This always arose as a defense when anyone tried to borrow Barris's car, because Barris had had secret unspecified modifications done on it, in its

(a) suspension

(b) engine

(c) transmission

(d) rear end

(e) drive train

(f) electrical system

(g) front end and steering

(h) as well as clock, cigar lighter, ashtray, glove compartment. In particular the glove compartment. Barris kept it locked always. The radio, too, had been cunningly *changed* (never explained how or why). If you tuned one station you got only one-minute-apart blips. All the push-buttons brought in a single transmission that made no sense, and, oddly, there was never any rock played over it. Sometimes when they were accompanying Barris on a buy and Barris parked and got out of the car, leaving them, he turned the particular station on in a special fashion very loud. If they changed it while he was gone he became incoherent and refused to speak on the trip back or ever to explain. He had not explained yet. Probably when set to that frequency his radio transmitted

(a) to the authorities.

(b) to a private paramilitary political organization.

(c) to the Syndicate.

(d) to extraterrestrials of higher intelligence.

"By that I mean," Barris said, "it will cruise at—"

"Aw fuck!" Luckman broke in harshly. "It's an ordinary six-cylinder motor, you humper. When we park it in downtown L.A. the parking-lot jockey drives it. So why can't Bob? You asshole."

Now, Bob Arctor had a few devices too, a few covert modifications built into his own car radio. But he didn't talk about them. Actually, it was Fred who had. Or anyhow somebody had, and they did a few things a little like what Barris claimed his several electronic assists did, and then on the other hand they did not.

For example, every law-enforcement vehicle emits a particular full-spectrum interference which sounds on ordinary car radios like a failure in the spark-suppressors of that vehicle. As if the police car's ignition is faulty. However, Bob Arctor, as a peace officer, had been allocated a gadget which, when he had mounted it within his car radio, told him a great deal, whereas the noises told other people—most other people—no information at all. These other people did not even recognize the static as information-bearing. First of all, the different sub-sounds told Bob Arctor how close the law-enforcement vehicle was to his own and, next, what variety of department it represented: city or county, Highway Patrol, or federal, whatever. He, too, picked up the one-minute-apart blips which acted as a time check for a parked vehicle; those in the parked vehicle could determine how many minutes they had waited without any obvious arm gestures. This was useful, for instance, when they had agreed to hit a house in exactly three minutes. The *zt zt zt* on their car radio told them precisely when three minutes had passed.

He knew, too, about the AM station that played the top-ten-type tunes on and on plus an enormous amount of DJ chatter in between, which sometimes was not chatter, in a sense. If that station had been tuned to, and the racket of it filled your car, anyone casually overhearing it would hear a conventional pop music station and typical boring DJ talk, and either not hang around at all or flash on in any way to the fact that the so-called DJ suddenly, in exactly the same muted chatty style of voice in which he said, "Now here's a number for Phil and Jane, a new Cat Stevens tune called—" occasionally said something more like "Vehicle blue will proceed a mile north to Bastanchury and the other units will—" and so on. He had never—with all the many dudes and chicks who rode with him, even when he had been obliged to keep tuned to police info-instruct, such as when a major bust was going down or any big action was in progress which might involve him—had anyone notice. Or if they noticed, they probably thought they were personally spaced and paranoid and forgot it.

And also he knew about the many unmarked police vehicles like old Chevys jacked up in the back with loud (illegal) pipes and racing stripes, with wild-looking hip types driving them erratically at high speed—he knew from what his radio emitted in the way of the special information-carrying static at all frequencies when one buzzed him or shot past. He knew to ignore.

Also, when he pushed the bar that supposedly switched from AM to FM on his car radio, a station on a particular frequency groaned out indefinite Muzak-type music, but this noise being transmitted to his car was filtered out, unscrambled, by the microphone-transmitter within his radio, so that whatever was said by those in his car at the time was picked up by his equipment and broadcast to the authorities; but this one funky station playing away, no matter how loud, was not received by them and did not interfere at all; the grid eliminated it.

What Barris *claimed* to have did bear a certain resemblance to what he, Bob Arctor, as an undercover law-enforcement officer did have in his own car radio; but beyond that, in regard to other modifications such as suspension, engine, transmission, etc., there had been no alterations whatsoever. That would be uncool and obvious. And secondly, millions of car freaks could make equally hairy modifications in their cars, so he simply had gotten allocation for a fairly potent mill for his wheels and let it go at that. Any highpowered vehicle can overtake and leave behind any other. Barris was full of shit about that; a Ferrari has suspension and handling and steering that no "special secret modifications" can match, so the hell with it. And cops can't drive sports cars, even cheap ones. Let alone Ferraris. Ultimately it is the driver's skill that decides it all.

He did have one other law-enforcement allocation, though. Very unusual tires. They had more than steel bands inside, like Michelin had introduced years ago in their X types. These were all metal and wore out fast, but they had advantages in speed and acceleration. Their disadvantage was their cost, but he got them free, from his allocation service, which was not a Dr. Pepper machine like the money one. This worked fine, but he could get allocations only when absolutely necessary. The tires he put on himself, when no one was watching. As he had put in the radio alterations.

The only fear about the radio was not detection by someone

snooping, such as Barris, but simple theft. Its added devices made it expensive to replace if it got ripped off; he would have to talk fast.

Naturally, too, he carried a gun hidden in his car. Barris in all his lurid acid-trip, spaced-out fantasies would never have designed its hiding place, where it actually was. Barris would have directed there to be an exotic spot of concealment for it, like in the steering column, in a hollow chamber. Or inside the gas tank, hanging down on a wire like the shipment of coke in the classic flick *Easy Rider*, that place as a stash place, incidentally, being about the worst spot on a hog. Every law-enforcement officer who had caught the film had flashed right away on what clever psychiatrist types had elaborately figured out: that the two bikers wanted to get caught and if possible killed. His gun, in his car, was in the glove compartment.

The pseudo-clever stuff that Barris continually alluded to about his own vehicle probably bore some resemblance to reality, the reality of Arctor's own modified car, because many of the radio gimmicks which Arctor carried were SOP and had been demonstrated on late-night TV, on network talk shows, by electronic experts who had helped design them, or read about them in trade journals, or seen them, or gotten fired from police labs and harbored a grudge. So the average citizen (or, as Barris always said in his quasi-educated lofty way, the *typical* average citizen) knew by now that no black-and-white ran the risk of pulling over a fast-moving souped-up, racing-striped '57 Chevy with what appeared to be a wild teen-ager spaced out behind the wheel on Coors beer—and then finding he'd halted an undercover nark vehicle in hot pursuit of its quarry. So the typical average citizen these days knew how and why all those nark vehicles as they roared along, scaring old ladies and straights into indignation and letter-writing, continually signaled their identity back and forth to one another and their peers . . . what difference did it make? But what *would* make a difference—a dreadful one—would be if the punks, the hot-rodders, the bikers, and especially the dealers and runners and pushers, managed to build and incorporate into their own similar cars such sophisticated devices.

They could then whiz right on by. With impunity.

"I'll walk, then," Arctor said, which was what he had

wanted to do anyhow; he had set up both Barris and Luck-man. He *had* to walk.

"Where you going?" Luckman said.

"Donna's." Getting to her place on foot was almost impossible; saying this ensured neither man accompanying him. He put on his coat and set off toward the front door. "See you guys later."

"My car—" Barris continued by way of more cop-out.

"If I tried to drive your car," Arctor said, "I'd press the wrong button and it'd float up over the Greater L.A. downtown area like the Goodyear blimp, and they'd have me dumping borate on oil-well fires."

"I'm glad you can appreciate my position," Barris was muttering as Arctor shut the door.

Seated before the hologram cube of Monitor Two, Fred in his scramble suit watched impassively as the hologram changed continually before his eyes. In the safe apartment other watchers watched other holograms from other source points, mostly playbacks. Fred, however, watched a live hologram unfolding; it recorded, but he had by-passed the stored tape to pick up the transmission at the instant it emanated from Bob Arctor's allegedly run-down house.

Within the hologram, in broad-band color, with high resolution, sat Barris and Luckman. In the best chair in the living room, Barris sat bent over a hash pipe he had been putting together for days. His face had become a mask of concentration as he wound white string around and around the bowl of the pipe. At the coffee table Luckman hunched over a Swanson's chicken TV dinner, eating in big clumsy mouthfuls while he watched a western on TV. Four beer cans—empties—lay squashed by his mighty fist on the table; now he reached for a fifth half-full can, knocked it over, spilled it, grabbed it, and cursed. At the curse, Barris peered up, regarded him like Mime in *Siegfried*, then resumed work.

Fred continued to watch.

"Fucking late-night TV," Luckman gargled, his mouth full of food, and then suddenly he dropped his spoon and leaped staggering to his feet, tottered, spun toward Barris, both hands raised, gesturing, saying nothing, his mouth open and half-chewed food spilling from it onto his clothes, onto the floor. The cats ran forward eagerly.

Barris halted in his hash-pipe making, gazed up at hapless Luckman. In a frenzy, now gargling horrid noises, Luckman with one hand swept the coffee table bare of beer cans and food; everything clattered down. The cats sped off, terrified. Still, Barris sat gazing fixedly at him. Luckman lurched a few steps toward the kitchen; the scanner there, on its cube before Fred's horrified eyes, picked up Luckman as he groped blindly in the kitchen semidarkness for a glass, tried to turn on the faucet and fill it with water. At the monitor, Fred jumped up; transfixed, on Monitor Two he saw Barris, still seated, return to painstakingly winding string around and around the bowl of his hash pipe. Barris did not look up again; Monitor Two showed him again intently at work.

The aud tapes clashed out great breaking, tearing sounds of agony: human strangling and the furious din of objects hitting the floor as Luckman hurled pots and pans and dishes and flat-ware about in an attempt to attract Barris's attention. Barris, amid the noise, continued methodically at his hash pipe and did not look up again.

In the kitchen, on Monitor One, Luckman fell to the floor all at once, not slowly, onto his knees, but completely, with a sodden thump, and lay spread-eagled. Barris continued winding the string of his hash pipe, and now a small snide smile appeared on his face, at the corners of his mouth.

On his feet, Fred stared in shock, galvanized and paralyzed simultaneously. He reached for the police phone beside the monitor, halted, still watched.

For several minutes Luckman lay on the kitchen floor with-out moving as Barris wound and wound the string, Barris bent over like an intent old lady knitting, smiling to himself, smiling on and on, and rocking a trifle; then abruptly Barris tossed the hash pipe away, stood up, gazed acutely at Luckman's form on the kitchen floor, the broken water glass beside him, all the de-bris and pans and broken plates, and then Barris's face sud-denly reacted with mock dismay. Barris tore off his shades, his eyes widened grotesquely, he flapped his arms in helpless fright, he ran about a little here and there, then scuttled toward Luck-man, paused a few feet from him, ran back, panting now.

He's building up his act, Fred realized. He's getting his panic-and-discovery act together. Like he just came onto the scene. Barris, on the cube of Monitor Two, twisted about, gasped in grief, his face dark red, and then he hobbled to the phone, yanked it up, dropped it, picked it up with trembling fingers . . . he has just discovered that Luckman, alone in the kitchen, has choked to death on a piece of food, Fred realized; with no one there to hear him or help him. And now Barris is frantically trying to summon help. Too late.

Into the phone, Barris was saying in a weird, high-pitched slow voice, "Operator, is it called the inhalator squad or the resuscitation squad?"

"Sir," the phone tab squawked from its speaker by Fred, "is there someone unable to breathe? Do you wish—"

"It, I believe, is a cardiac arrest," Barris was saying now in his low, urgent, professional-type, calm voice into the phone, a voice deadly with awareness of peril and gravity and the running out of time. "Either that or involuntary aspiration of a bolus within the—"

"What is the address, sir?" the operator broke in.

"The address," Barris said, "let's see, the address is—"

Fred, aloud, standing, said, "Christ."

Suddenly Luckman, lying stretched out on the floor, heaved convulsively. He shuddered and then barfed up the material obstructing his throat, thrashed about, and opened his eyes, which stared in swollen confusion.

"Uh, he appears to be all right now," Barris said smoothly into the phone. "Thank you; no assistance is needed after all." He rapidly hung the phone up.

"Jeez," Luckman muttered thickly as he sat up. "Fuck." He wheezed noisily, coughing and struggling for air.

"You okay?" Barris asked, in tones of concern.

"I must have gagged. Did I pass out?"

"Not exactly. You did go into an altered state of consciousness, though. For a few seconds. Probably an alpha state."

"God! I soiled myself!" Unsteadily, swaying with weakness, Luckman managed to get himself to his feet and stood rocking back and forth dizzily, holding on to the wall for support. "I'm really getting degenerate," he muttered in disgust. "Like an old wino." He headed toward the sink to wash himself, his steps uncertain.

Watching all this, Fred felt the fear drain from him. The man would be okay. But Barris! What sort of person was he? Luckman had recovered despite him. What a freak, he thought. What a kinky freak. Where's his head at, just to stand idle like that?

"A guy could cash in that way," Luckman said as he splashed water on himself at the sink.

Barris smiled.

"I got a really strong physical constitution," Luckman said, gulping water from a cup. "What were you doing while I was lying there? Jacking off?"

"You saw me on the phone," Barris said. "Summoning the paramedics. I moved into action at—"

"Balls," Luckman said sourly, and went on gulping down fresh clean water. "I know what you'd do if I dropped dead— you'd rip off my stash. You'd even go through my pockets."

"It's amazing," Barris said, "the limitation of the human anatomy, the fact that food and air must share a common passage. So that the risk of—"

Silently, Luckman gave him the finger.

A screech of brakes. A horn. Bob Arctor looked swiftly up at the night traffic. A sports car, engine running, by the curb; inside it, a girl waving at him.

Donna.

"Christ," he said again. He strode toward the curb.

Opening the door of her MG, Donna said, "Did I scare you? I passed you on my way to your place and then I flashed on it that it was you truckin' along, so I made a U-turn and came back. Get in."

Silently he got in and shut the car door.

"Why are you out roaming around?" Donna said. "Because of your car? It's still not fixed?"

"I just did a freaky number," Bob Arctor said. "Not like a fantasy trip. Just . . ." He shuddered.

Donna said, "I have your stuff."

"What?" he said.

"A thousand tabs of death."

"*Death?*" he echoed.

"Yeah, high-grade death. I better drive." She shifted into low, took off and out onto the street; almost at once she was driving along too fast. Donna always drove too fast, and tailgated, but expertly.

"That fucking Barris!" he said. "You know how he works? He doesn't kill anybody he wants dead; he just hangs around until a situation arises where they die. And he just sits there while they die. In fact, he sets them up to die while he stays out of it. But I'm not sure how. Anyhow, he arranges to allow them to fucking die." He lapsed into silence then, brooding to himself. "Like," he said, "Barris wouldn't wire plastic explosives into the ignition system of your car. What he'd do—"

"Do you have the money?" Donna said. "For the stuff? It's really Primo, and I need the money right now. I have to have it tonight because I have to pick up some other things."

"Sure." He had it in his wallet.

"I don't like Barris," Donna said as she drove, "and I don't trust him. You know, he's crazy. And when you're around him you're crazy too. And then when you're not around him you're okay. You're crazy right now."

"I am?" he said, startled.

"Yes," Donna said calmly.

"Well," he said. "Jesus." He did not know what to say to that. Especially since Donna was never wrong.

"Hey," Donna said with enthusiasm, "could you take me to a rock concert? At the Anaheim Stadium next week? Could you?"

"Right on," he said mechanically. And then it flashed on him what Donna had said—asking him to take her out. "*Alll riiiight!*" he said, pleased; life flowed back into him. Once again, the little dark-haired chick whom he loved so much had restored him to caring. "Which night?"

"It's Sunday afternoon. I'm going to bring some of that oily dark hash and get really loaded. They won't know the difference; there'll be thousands of heads there." She glanced at him, critically. "But you've got to wear something neat, not those funky clothes you sometimes put on. I mean—" Her voice softened. "I want you to look foxy because you are foxy."

"Okay," he said, charmed.

"I'm taking us to my place," Donna said as she shot along through the night in her little car, "and you do have the money and you will give it to me, and then we'll drop a few of the tabs and kick back and get really mellow, and maybe you'd like to go buy us a fifth of Southern Comfort and we can get bombed as well."

"Oh wow," he said, with sincerity.

"What I really genuinely want to do tonight," Donna said as she shifted down and swiveled the car onto her own street and into her driveway, "is go to a drive-in movie. I bought a paper and read what's on, but I couldn't find anything good except at the Torrance Drive-in, but it's already started. It started at five-thirty. Bummer."

He examined his watch. "Then we've missed—"

"No, we could still see most of it." She shot him a warm smile as she stopped her car and shut off the engine. "It's all the *Planet of the Apes* pictures, all eleven of them; they run from 7:30 P.M. all the way through to 8 A.M. tomorrow morning. I'll go to work directly from the drive-in, so I'll have to change now. We'll sit there at the movie loaded and drinking Southern Comfort all night. Wow, can you dig it?" She peered at him hopefully.

"All night," he echoed.

"Yeah yeah yeah." Donna hopped out and came around to help him open his little door. "When did you last see all the *Planet of the Apes* pictures? I saw most of them earlier this year, but then I got sick toward the last ones and had to split. It was a ham sandwich they vended me there at the drive-in. That really made me mad; I missed the last picture, where they reveal that all the famous people in history like Lincoln and Nero were secretly apes and running all human history from the start. That's why I want to go back now so bad." She lowered her voice as they walked toward her front door. "They burned me by vending that ham sandwich, so what I did—don't rat on me—the next time we went to the drive-in, the one in La Habra, I stuck a bent coin in the slot and a couple more in other vending machines for good measure. Me and Larry Talling—you remember Larry, I was going with him?—bent a whole bunch of quarters and fifty-cent pieces using his vise and a big wrench. I made sure all the vending machines were owned by the same firm, of course. And then we fucked up a bunch of them, practically all of them, if the truth were known." She unlocked her front door with her key, slowly and gravely, in the dim light.

"It is not good policy to burn you, Donna," he said as they entered her small neat place.

"Don't step on the shag carpet," Donna said.

"Where'll I step, then?"

"Stand still, or on the newspapers."

"Donna—"

"Now don't give me a lot of heavy shit about having to walk on the newspapers. Do you know how much it cost me to get my carpet shampooed?" She stood unbuttoning her jacket.

"Thrift," he said, taking off his own coat. "French peasant thrift. Do you ever throw anything away? Do you keep pieces of string too short for any—"

"Someday," Donna said, shaking her long black hair back as she slid out of her leather jacket, "I'm going to get married and I'll need all that, that I've put away. When you get married you need everything there is. Like, we saw this big mirror in the yard next door; it took three of us over an hour to get it over the fence. Someday—"

"How much of what you've got put away did you buy," he asked, "and how much did you steal?"

"*Buy?*" She studied his face uncertainly. "What do you mean by *buy?*"

"Like when you buy dope," he said. "A dope deal. Like now." He got out his wallet. "I give you money, right?"

Donna nodded, watching him obediently (actually, more out of politeness) but with dignity. With a certain reserve.

"And then you hand me a bunch of dope for it," he said, holding out the bills. "What I mean by *buy* is an extension into the greater world of human business transactions of what we have present now, with us, as dope deals."

"I think I see," she said, her large dark eyes placid but alert. She was willing to learn.

"How many—like when you ripped off that Coca-Cola truck you were tailgating that day—how many bottles of Coke did you rip off? How many crates?"

"A month's worth," Donna said. "For me and my friends."

He glared at her reprovingly.

"It's a form of barter," she said.

"What do—" He started to laugh. "What do you give back?"

"I give of myself."

Now he laughed out loud. "To who? To the driver of the truck, who probably had to make good—"

"The Coca-Cola Company is a capitalist monopoly. No one else can make Coke but them, like the phone company does when you want to phone someone. They're all capitalist monopolies. Do you know"—her dark eyes flashed—"that the formula for Coca-Cola is a carefully guarded secret handed down through the ages, known only to a few persons all in the same family, and when the last of them dies that's memorized the formula, there will be no more Coke? So there's a backup written formula in a safe somewhere," she added meditatively. "I wonder where," she ruminated to herself, her eyes flickering.

"You and your rip-off friends will never find the Coca-Cola formula, not in a million years."

"WHO THE FUCK WANTS TO MANUFACTURE COKE ANYHOW WHEN YOU CAN RIP IT OFF THEIR TRUCKS? They've got a lot of trucks. You see them driving constantly, real slow. I tailgate them every chance I get; it makes them mad." She smiled a secret, cunning, lovely little impish smile at him, as if trying to beguile him into her strange reality, where she tailgated and tailgated a slow truck and got madder and madder and more impatient and then, when it pulled off, instead of shooting on by like other drivers would, she pulled off too, and stole everything the truck had on it. Not so much because she was a thief or even for revenge but because by the time it finally pulled off she had looked at the crates of Coke so long that she had figured out what she could do with all of them. *Her impatience had turned to ingenuity.* She had loaded her car—not the MG but the larger Camaro she had been driving then, before she had totaled it—with crates and crates of Coke, and then for a month she and all her jerk friends had drunk all the free Coke they wanted to, and then after that—

She had turned the empties back in at different stores for the deposits.

"What'd you do with the bottle caps?" he once asked her. "Wrap them in muslin and store them away in your cedar chest?"

"I threw them away," Donna said glumly. "There's nothing you can do with Coke bottle caps. There's no contests or anything any more." Now she disappeared into the other room, returned presently with several polyethylene bags. "You wanta count these?" she inquired. "There's a thousand *for sure*. I weighed them on my gram scale before I paid for them."

"It's okay," he said. He accepted the bags and she accepted the money and he thought, Donna, once more I could send you up, but I probably never will no matter what you do even if you do it to me, because there is something wonderful and full of life about you and sweet and I would never destroy it. I don't understand it, but there it is.

"Could I have ten?" she asked.

"Ten? Ten tabs back? Sure." He opened one of the bags—it was hard to untie, but he had the skill—and counted her out precisely ten. And then ten for himself. And retied the bag. And then carried all the bags to his coat in the closet.

"You know what they do in cassette-tape stores now?" Donna said energetically when he returned. The ten tabs were nowhere in sight; she had already stashed them. "Regarding tapes?"

"They arrest you," he said, "if you steal them."

"They always did that. Now what they do—you know when you carry an LP or a tape to the counter and the clerk removes the little price tag that's gummed on? Well, guess what. Guess what I found out almost the hard way." She threw herself down in a chair, grinned in anticipation, and brought forth a foil-wrapped tiny cube, which he identified as a fragment of hash even before she unwrapped it. "That isn't only a gummed-on price sticker. There's also a tiny fragment of some kind of alloy in it, and if that sticker isn't removed by the clerk at the counter, and you try to go out through the door with it, then an alarm goes off."

"How did you find out almost the hard way?"

"Some teenybopper tried to walk out with one under her coat ahead of me and the alarm went off and they grabbed her and the pigs came."

"How many did *you* have under your coat?"

"Three."

"Did you also have dope in your car?" he said. "Because once they got you for the tape rip-off, they'd impound your car, because you'd be downtown looking out, and the car would be routinely towed away and then they'd find the dope and send you up for that, too. I'll bet that wasn't locally, either; I'll bet you did that where—" He had started to say, Where you don't know anybody in law enforcement who would intervene. But he could not say that, because he meant himself; were Donna ever busted, at least where he had any pull, he would work his ass off to help her. But he could do nothing, say, up in L.A. County. And if it ever happened, which eventually it would, there it would happen: too far off for him to hear or help. He had a scenario start rolling in his head then, a horror fantasy: Donna, much like Luckman, dying with no one hearing or caring or doing anything; they might hear, but they, like Barris, would remain impassive and inert until for her it was all over. She would not literally die, as Luckman had—had? He meant *might*. But she, being an addict to Substance D, would not only be in jail but she would have to withdraw, cold turkey. And since she was dealing, not just using—and there was a rap for theft as well—she would be in for a while, and a lot of other things, dreadful things, would happen to her. So when she came back out she would be a different Donna. The soft, careful expression that he dug so much, the warmth—that would be altered into God knew what, anyhow something empty and too much used. Donna translated into a thing; and so it went, for all of them someday, but for Donna, he hoped, far and away beyond his own lifetime. And not where he couldn't help.

"Spunky," he said to her now, unhappily, "without Spooky."

"What's that?" After a moment she understood. "Oh, that TA therapy. But when I do hash . . ." She had gotten out her very own little round ceramic hash pipe, like a sand dollar, which she had made herself, and was lighting it. "Then I'm Sleepy." Gazing up at him, bright-eyed and happy, she laughed and extended to him the precious hash pipe. "I'll supercharge you," she declared. "Sit down."

As he seated himself, she rose to her feet, stood puffing the hash pipe into lively activity, then waddled at him, bent, and as he opened his mouth—like a baby bird, he thought, as he always thought when she did this—she exhaled great gray forceful jets of hash smoke into him, filling him with her own hot and bold and incorrigible energy, which was at the same time a pacifying agent that relaxed and mellowed them both out together: she who supercharged and Bob Arctor who received.

"I love you, Donna," he said. This supercharging, this was the substitute for sexual relations with her that he got, and maybe it was better; it was worth so much; it was so intimate, and very strange viewed that way, because first she could put something inside him, and then, if she wanted, he put something into her. An even exchange, back and forth, until the hash ran out.

"Yeah, I can dig it, your being in love with me," she said, chuckled, sat down beside him, grinning, to take a hit from the hash pipe now, for herself.

Chapter Nine

"H ey, Donna, man," he said. "Do you like cats?"

She blinked, red-eyed. "Drippy little things. Moving along about a foot above the ground."

"Above, no, *on* the ground."

"Drippy. Behind furniture."

"Little spring flowers, then," he said.

"Yes," she said. "I can dig it—little spring flowers, with yellow in them. That first come up."

"Before," he said. "Before anyone."

"Yes." She nodded, eyes shut, off in her trip. "Before anyone stomps them, and they're—gone."

"You know me," he said. "You can read me."

She lay back, setting down the hash pipe. It had gone out. "No more," she said, and her smile slowly dwindled away.

"What's wrong?" he said.

"Nothing." She shook her head and that was all.

"Can I put my arms around you?" he said. "I want to hold you. Okay? Hug you, like. Okay?"

Her dark, enlarged, unfocused weary eyes opened. "No," she said. "No, you're too ugly."

"What?" he said.

"No!" she said, sharply now. "I snort a lot of coke; I have to be super careful because I snort a lot of coke."

"*Ugly?*" he echoed, furious at her. "Fuck you, Donna."

"Just leave my body alone," she said, staring at him.

"Sure," he said. "Sure." He got to his feet and backed away. "You better believe it." He felt like going out to his car, getting his pistol from the glove compartment, and shooting her face off, bursting her skull and eyes to bits. And then that passed, that hash hate and fury. "Fuck it," he said dismally.

"I don't like people to grope my body," Donna said. "I have to watch out for that because I do so much coke. Someday I have it planned I'm going over the Canadian border with four pounds of coke in it, in my snatch. I'll say I'm a Catholic and a virgin. Where are you going?" Alarm had her now; she half rose.

"I'm taking off," he said.

"Your car is at your place. I drove you." The girl struggled up, tousled and confused and half asleep, wandered toward the closet to get her leather jacket. "I'll drive you back. But you can see why I have to protect my snatch. Four pounds of coke is worth—"

"No fucking way," he said. "You're too stoned to drive ten feet, and you never fucking let anybody else drive that little roller skate of yours."

Facing him, she yelled wildly, "That's because nobody else can fucking drive my car! Nobody else ever gets it right, no man especially! Driving or anything else! You had your hands down into my—"

And then he was somewhere outside in the darkness, roaming, without his coat, in a strange part of town. Nobody with him. Fucking alone, he thought, and then he heard Donna hurrying along after him, trying to catch up with him, panting for breath, because she did so much pot and hash these days that her lungs were half silted up with resins. He halted, stood without turning, waiting, feeling really down.

Approaching him, Donna slowed, panted, "I am dreadfully sorry I've hurt your feelings. By what I said. I was out of it."

"Yeah," he said. "*Too ugly!*"

"Sometimes when I've worked all day and I'm super super tired, the first hit I take just spaces me. You wanta come back? Or what? You wanta go to the drive-in? What about the Southern Comfort? I can't buy it . . . they won't sell it to me," she said, and paused. "I'm underage, right?"

"Okay," he said. Together they walked back.

"That sure is good hash, isn't it?" Donna said.

Bob Arctor said, "It's black sticky hash, which means it's saturated in opium alkaloids. What you're smoking is opium, not hash—do you know that? That's why it costs so much—do you know that?" He heard his voice rise; he stopped walking. "You aren't doing hash, sweetie. You're doing opium, and that means a lifetime habit at a cost of . . . what's 'hash' selling for now a pound? And you'll be smoking and nodding off and nodding off and not being able to get your car in gear and rear-ending trucks and needing it every day before you go to work—"

"I need to now," Donna said. "Take a hit before I go to work. And at noon and as soon as I get home. That's why I deal, to buy my hash. Hash is mellow. Hash is where it's at."

"Opium," he repeated. "What's *hash* sell for now?"

"About ten thousand dollars a pound," Donna said. "The good kind."

"Christ! As much as smack."

"I would never use a needle. I never have and I never will. You last about six months when you start shooting, whatever you shoot. Even tap water. You get a habit—"

"You *have* a habit."

Donna said, "We all do. You take Substance D. So what? What's the difference now? I'm happy; aren't you happy? I get to come home and smoke high-grade hash every night . . . it's my trip. Don't try to change me. Don't ever try to change me. Me or my morals. I am what I am. And I get off on hash. It's my life."

"You ever seen pictures of an old opium smoker? Like in China in the old days? Or a hash smoker in India now, what they look like later on in life?"

Donna said, "I don't expect to live long. So what? I don't *want* to be around long. Do you? Why? What's in this world? And have you ever seen— Shit, what about Jerry Fabin; look at someone too far into Substance D. What's there really in this world, Bob? It's a stopping place to the next where they punish us here because we were born evil—"

"You *are* a Catholic."

"We're being punished here, so if we can get off on a trip now and then, fuck it, *do it*. The other day I almost cashed in driving my MG to work. I had the eight-track stereo on and I was smoking my hash pipe and I didn't see this old dude in an 'eighty-four Ford Imperator—"

"You are dumb," he said. "Super dumb."

"I am, you know, going to die early. Anyhow. Whatever I do. Probably on the freeway. I got hardly any brakes on my MG, you realize that? And I've picked up four speeding tickets this year already. Now I got to go to traffic school. It's a bummer. For six whole months."

"So someday," he said, "I will all of a sudden never lay eyes on you again. Right? Never again."

"Because of traffic school? No, after the six months—"

"In the marble orchard," he explained. "Wiped out before you're allowed under California law, fucking goddamn California law, to purchase a can of beer or a bottle of booze."

"Yeah!" Donna exclaimed, alerted. "The Southern Comfort! Right on! Are we going to do a fifth of Southern Comfort and take in the *Ape* flicks? Are we? There's still like eight left, including the one—"

"Listen to me," Bob Arctor said, taking hold of her by the shoulder; she instinctively pulled away.

"No," she said.

He said, "You know what they ought to let you do one time? Maybe just one time? Let you go in legally, just once, and buy a can of beer."

"Why?" she said wonderingly.

"A present to you because you are good," he said.

"They served me once!" Donna exclaimed in delight. "At a bar! The cocktail waitress—I was dressed up and like with some people—asked me what I wanted and I said, 'I'll have a vodka collins,' and she served me. It was at the La Paz, too, which is a really neat place. Wow, can you believe it? I memorized that, the vodka collins, from an ad. So if I ever got asked at a bar, like that, I'd sound cool. Right?" She suddenly put her arm through his, and hugged him as they walked, something she almost never did. "It was the most all-time super trip of my life."

"Then I guess," he said, "you have your present. Your one present."

"I can dig it," Donna said. "I can dig it! Of course they told me later—these people I was with—I should have ordered a Mexican drink like a tequila sunrise, because, see, it's a Mexican kind of bar, there with the La Paz Restaurant. Next time I'll know that; I've got that taped in my memory banks, if I go there again. You know what I'm going to do someday, Bob? I'm going to move north to Oregon and live in the snow. I'm going to shovel snow off the front walk every morning. And have a little house and garden with vegetables."

He said, "You have to save up for that. Save all your money. It costs."

Glancing at him, suddenly shy, Donna said, "He'll get me that. What's-his-name."

"Who?"

"You know." Her voice was soft, sharing her secret. Imparting it to him because he, Bob Arctor, was her friend and she could trust him. "Mister Right. I know what he'll be like—he'll drive an Aston-Martin and he'll take me north in it. And that's where the little old-fashioned house will be in the snow, north from here." After a pause she said, "Snow is supposed to be nice, isn't it?"

He said, "Don't you know?"

"I never have been in the snow except once in San Berdoo up in those mountains and then it was half sleet and muddy and I fucking fell. I don't mean snow like that; I mean *real* snow."

Bob Arctor, his heart heavy in a certain way, said, "You feel positive about all this? It'll really happen?"

"It'll happen!" She nodded. "It's in the cards for me."

They walked on then, in silence. Back to her place, to get her MG. Donna, wrapped up in her own dreams and plans; and he—he recalled Barris and he recalled Luckman and Hank and the safe apartment, and he recalled Fred.

"Hey, man," he said, "can I go with you to Oregon? When you do take off finally?"

She smiled at him, gently and with acute tenderness, with the answer no.

And he understood, from knowing her, that she meant it. And it would not change. He shivered.

"Are you cold?" she asked.

"Yeah," he said. "Very cold."

"I got that good MG heater in my car," she said, "for when we're at the drive-in . . . you'll warm up there." She took his hand, squeezed it, held it, and then, all at once, she let it drop.

But the actual touch of her lingered, inside his heart. That remained. In all the years of his life ahead, the long years without her, with never seeing her or hearing from her or knowing anything about her, if she was alive or happy or dead or what, that touch stayed locked within him, sealed in himself, and never went away. That one touch of her hand.

*

He brought a cute little needle-freak named Connie home with him that night, to ball her in exchange for him giving her a bag of ten mex hits.

Skinny and lank-haired, the girl sat on the edge of his bed, combing her odd hair; this was the first time she had ever come along with him—he had met her at a head party—and he knew very little about her, although he'd carried her phone number for weeks. Being a needle-freak, she was naturally frigid, but this wasn't a downer; it made her indifferent to sex in terms of her own enjoyment, but on the other hand, she didn't mind what sort of sex it was.

This was obvious just watching her. Connie sat half-dressed, her shoes off, a bobby pin in her mouth, gazing off listlessly, evidently doing a private trip in her head. Her face, elongated and bony, had a strength to it; probably, he decided, because the bones, especially the jaw lines, were pronounced. On her right cheek was a zit. Undoubtedly she neither cared about nor noticed that, either; like sex, zits meant little to her.

Maybe she couldn't tell the difference. Maybe, to her, a longtime needle-freak, sex and zits had similar or even identical qualities. What a thought, he thought, this glimpse into a hype's head for a moment.

"Do you have a toothbrush I can use?" Connie said; she had begun to nod a little, and to mumble, as hypes tended to do this time of night. "Aw screw it—teeth are teeth. I'll brush them . . ." Her voice had sunk so low he couldn't hear her, although he knew from the movement of her lips that she was droning on.

"Do you know where the bathroom is?" he asked her.

"What bathroom?"

"In this house."

Rousing herself, she resumed reflexively combing. "Who are those guys out there this late? Rolling joints and rattling on and on? They live here with you, I guess. Sure they do. Guys like that must."

"Two of them do." Arctor said.

Her dead-codfish eyes turned to fix their gaze on him. "You're queer?" Connie asked.

"I try not to be. That's why you're here tonight."

"Are you putting up a pretty good battle against it?"

"You better believe it."

Connie nodded. "Yes, I suppose I'm about to find out. If you're a latent gay you probably want me to take the initiative. Lie down and I'll do you. Want me to undress you? Okay, you just lie there and I'll do it all." She reached for his zipper.

Later, in the semidarkness he drowsed, from—so to speak— his own fix. Connie snored on beside him, lying on her back with her arms at her sides outside the covers. He could see her dimly. They sleep like Count Dracula, he thought, junkies do. Staring straight up until all of a sudden they sit up, like a machine cranked from position A to position B. "It—must—be— day," the junkie says, or anyhow the tape in his head says. Plays him his instructions, the mind of a junkie being like the music you hear on a clock radio . . . it sometimes sounds pretty, but it is only there to make you do something. The music from the clock radio is to wake you up; the music from the junkie is to get you to become a means for him to obtain more junk, in whatever way you can serve. He, a machine, will turn you into *his* machine.

Every junkie, he thought, is a recording.

Again he dozed, meditating about these bad things. And eventually the junkie, if it's a chick, has nothing to sell but her body. Like Connie, he thought; Connie right here.

Opening his eyes, he turned toward the girl beside him and saw Donna Hawthorne.

Instantly he sat up. Donna! he thought. He could make out her face clearly. No doubt. Christ! he thought, and reached for the bedside light. His fingers touched it; the lamp tumbled and fell. The girl, however, slept on. He still stared at her, and then by degrees he saw Connie again, hatchet-faced, bleak-jawed, sunken, the gaunt face of the out-of-it junkie, Connie and not Donna; one girl, not the other.

He lay back and, miserable, slept somewhat again, wondering what it meant and so forth and on and on, into darkness.

"I don't care if he stunk," the girl beside him muttered later on, dreamily, in her sleep. "I still loved him."

He wondered who she meant. A boy friend? Her father? A tomcat? A childhood precious stuffed toy? Maybe all of them,

he thought. But the words were "I loved," not "I still love."
Evidently he, whatever or whoever he had been, was gone
now. Maybe, Arctor reflected, they (whoever they were) had
made her throw him out, because he stank so bad.

Probably so. He wondered how old she had been then, the
remembering worn-out junkie girl who dozed beside him.

Chapter Ten

IN his scramble suit, Fred sat before a battery of whirling holo-playbacks, watching Jim Barris in Bob Arctor's living room reading a book on mushrooms. Why mushrooms? Fred wondered, and sped the tapes at high-speed forward to an hour later. There sat Barris yet, reading with great concentration and making notes.

Presently Barris set the book down and left the house, passing out of scanning range. When he returned he carried a little brown-paper bag which he set on the coffee table and opened. From it he removed dried mushrooms, which he then began to compare one by one with the color photos in the book. With excessive deliberation, unusual for him, he compared each. At last he pushed one miserable-looking mushroom aside and restored the others to the bag; from his pocket he brought a handful of empty capsules and then with equally great precision began crumbling bits of the one particular mushroom into the caps and sealing each of them in turn.

After that, Barris started phoning. The phone tap automatically recorded the numbers called.

"Hello, this is Jim."

"So?"

"Say, have I scored."

"No shit."

"*Psilocybe mexicana.*"

"What's that?"

"A rare hallucinogenic mushroom used in South American mystery cults thousands of years ago. You fly, you become invisible, understand the speech of animals—"

"No thanks." Click.

Redialing. "Hello, this is Jim."

"Jim? Jim who?"

"With the beard . . . green shades, leather pants. I met you at a happening over at Wanda—"

"Oh yeah. Jim. Yeah."

"You interested in scoring on some organic psychedelics?"

"Well, I don't know . . ." Unease. "You sure this is Jim? You don't sound like him."

"I've got something unbelievable, a rare organic mushroom from South America, used in Indian mystery cults thousands of years ago. You fly, become invisible, your car disappears, you are able to understand the speech of animals—"

"My car disappears all the time. When I leave it in a tow-away zone. Ha-ha."

"I can lay perhaps six caps of this *Psilocybe* on you."

"How much?"

"Five dollars a cap."

"Outrageous! No kidding? Hey, I'll meet you somewhere." Then suspicion. "You know, I believe I remember you—you burned me once. Where'd you get these mushrooms hits? How do I know they're not weak acid?"

"They were brought to the U.S. inside a clay idol," Barris said. "As part of a carefully guarded art shipment to a museum, with this one idol marked. The customs pigs never suspected." Barris added, "If they don't get you off I'll refund your money."

"Well, that's meaningless if my head's been eaten and I'm swinging through the trees."

"I dropped one two days ago myself," Barris said. "To test it out. The best trip I ever had—lots of colors. Better than mescaline, for sure. I don't want my customers burned. I always test my stuff myself. It's guaranteed."

Behind Fred another scramble suit was watching the holo-monitor now too. "What's he peddling? Mescaline, he says?"

"He's been capping mushrooms," Fred said, "that either he picked or someone else picked, locally."

"Some mushrooms are toxic in the extreme," the scramble suit behind Fred said.

A third scramble suit knocked off its own holo scrutiny for a moment and stood with them now. "Certain *Amanita* mushrooms contain four toxins that are red-blood-cell cracking agents. It takes two weeks to die and there's no antidote. It's incalculably painful. Only an expert can tell what mushroom he's picking for sure when they're wild."

"I know," Fred said, and marked the ident numbers of this tape section for department use.

Barris again was dialing.

"What's the statute violation cited on this?" Fred said.

"Misrepresentation in advertising," one of the other scramble suits said, and both laughed and returned to their own screens. Fred continued watching.

On Holo Monitor Four the front door of the house opened and Bob Arctor entered, looking dejected. "Hi."

"Howdy," Barris said, gathering his caps together and thrusting them deep into his pocket. "How'd you make out with Donna?" He chuckled. "In several ways, maybe, eh?"

"Okay, fuck off," Arctor said, and passed from Holo Monitor Four, to be picked up in his bedroom a moment later by scanner five. There, with the door kicked shut, Arctor brought forth a number of plastic bags filled with white tabs; he stood a moment uncertainly and then he stuffed them down under the covers of his bed, out of sight. And took off his coat. He appeared weary and unhappy; his face was drawn.

For a moment Bob Arctor sat on the edge of his unmade bed, all by himself. He at last shook his head, rose, stood uncertain . . . them he smoothed his hair and left the room, to be picked up by the central living-room scanner as he approached Barris. During this time scanner two had witnessed Barris hiding the brown bag of mushrooms under the couch cushions and placing the mushroom textbook back on the bookshelf where it was not noticeable.

"What you been doing?" Arctor asked him.

Barris declared, "Research."

"Into what?"

"The properties of certain mycological entities of a delicate nature." Barris chuckled. "It didn't go too well with little miss big-tits, did it?"

Arctor regarded him and then went into the kitchen to plug in the coffeepot.

"Bob," Barris said, following him leisurely, "I'm sorry if I said anything that offended you." He hung around as Arctor waited for the coffee to heat, drumming and humming aimlessly.

"Where's Luckman?"

"I suppose out somewhere trying to rip off a pay phone. He took your hydraulic axle jack with him; that usually means he's out to knock over a pay phone, doesn't it?"

"My axle jack," Arctor echoed.

"You know," Barris said, "I could assist you professionally in your attempts to hustle little miss—"

Fred shot the tape ahead at high-speed wind. The meter at last read a two-hour passage.

"—pay up your goddamn back rent or goddamn get to work on the cephscope," Arctor was saying hotly to Barris.

"I've already ordered resistors which—"

Again Fred sent the tape forward. Two more hours passed.

Now Holo Monitor Five showed Arctor in his bedroom, in bed, a clock FM radio on to KNX, playing folk rock dimly. Monitor Two in the living room showed Barris alone, again reading about mushrooms. Neither man did much for a long period. Once, Arctor stirred and reached out to increase the radio's volume as a song, evidently one he liked, came on. In the living room Barris read on and on, hardly moving. Arctor again at last lay back in bed unmoving.

The phone rang. Barris reached out and lifted it to his ear. "Hello?"

On the phone tap the caller, a male, said, "Mr. Arctor?"

"Yes, this is," Barris said.

I'll be fucked for a nanny goat, Fred said to himself. He reached to turn up the phone-tap volume level.

"Mr. Arctor," the unidentified caller said in a slow, low voice, "I'm sorry to bother you so late, but that check of yours that did not clear—"

"Oh yes," Barris said. "I've been intending to call you about that. The situation is this, sir. I have had a severe bout of intestinal flu, with loss of body heat, pyloric spasms, cramps . . . I just can't get it all together right now to make that little twenty-dollar check good, and frankly I don't intend to make it good."

"What?" the man said, not startled but hoarsely. Ominously.

"Yes, sir," Barris said, nodding. "You heard me correctly, sir."

"Mr. Arctor," the caller said, "that check has been returned by the bank twice now, and these flu symptoms that you describe—"

"I think somebody slipped me something bad," Barris said, with a stark grin on his face.

"*I* think," the man said, "that you're one of those—" He groped for the word.

"Think what you want," Barris said, still grinning.

"Mr. Arctor," the man said, breathing audibly into the phone, "I am going to the D.A.'s office with that check, and while I'm on the phone I have a couple of things to tell you about what I feel about—"

"Turn on, tune out, and good-by," Barris said, and hung up.

The phone-tap unit had automatically recorded the digits of the caller's own phone, picking them up electronically from an inaudible signal generated as soon as the circuit was in place. Fred read off the number now visible on a meter, then shut off the tape-transport for all his holo-scanners, lifted his own police phone, and called in for a print-out on the number.

"Englesohn Locksmith, 1343 Harbor in Anaheim," the police info operator informed him. "Lover boy."

"Locksmith," Fred said. "Okay." He had that written down and now hung up. A locksmith . . . twenty dollars, a round sum: that suggested a job outside the shop—probably driving out and making a duplicate key. When the "owner's" key had gotten lost.

Theory. Barris had posed as Arctor, phoned Englesohn Locksmith to have a "duplicate" key made illicitly, for either the house or the car or even both. Telling Englesohn he'd lost his whole key ring . . . but then the locksmith, doing a security check, had sprung on Barris a request for a check as I.D. Barris had gone back in the house and ripped off an unfilled-out checkbook of Arctor's and written a check out on it to the locksmith. The check hadn't cleared. But why not? Arctor kept a high balance in his account; a check that small would clear. But if it cleared Arctor would come across it in his statement and recognize it as not his, as Jim Barris's. So Barris had rooted about in Arctor's closets and located—probably at some previous time—an old checkbook from a now abandoned account and used that. The account being closed, the check hadn't cleared. Now Barris was in hot water.

But why didn't Barris just go in and pay off the check in cash? This way the creditor was already mad and phoning, and eventually would take it to the D.A. Arctor would find out. A skyful of shit would land on Barris. But the way Barris had talked on the phone to the already outraged creditor . . . he had slyly goaded him into even further hostility, out of which the locksmith might do anything. And worse—Barris's description of his "flu" was a description of coming off heroin, and anybody would know who knew anything. And Barris had signed off the phone call with a flat-out insinuation that he was a heavy doper and so what about it? Signed all this off as Bob Arctor.

The locksmith at this point knew he had a junkie debtor who'd written him a rubber check and didn't care shit and had no intention of making good. And the junkie had this attitude because obviously he was so wired and spaced and mind-blown on his dope it didn't matter to him. And this was an insult to America. Deliberate and nasty.

In fact, Barris's sign-off was a direct quote of Tim Leary's original funky ultimatum to the establishment and all the straights. And this was Orange County. Full of Birchers and Minutemen. With guns. Looking for just this kind of uppity sass from bearded dopers.

Barris had set Bob Arctor up for a fire-bombing. A bust on the bad check at the least, a fire-bombing or other massive retaliatory strike at worst, without Arctor having any notion what was coming down.

Why? Fred wondered. He noted on his scratch pad the ident code on this tape sequence, plus the phone-tap code as well. What was Barris getting Arctor back for? What the hell had Arctor been up to? Arctor must have burned him pretty bad, Fred thought, for this. This is sheer malice. Little, vile, and evil.

This Barris guy, he thought, is a motherfucker. He's going to get somebody killed.

One of the scramble suits in the safe apartment with him roused him from his introspection. "Do you actually know these guys?" The suit gestured at the now blank holo-monitors Fred had before him. "You in there among them on cover assignment?"

"Yep," Fred said.

"It wouldn't be a bad idea to warn them in some way about this mushroom toxicity he's exposing them to, that clown with the green shades who's peddling. Can you pass it on to them without faulting your cover?"

The other nearly scramble suit called from his swivel chair, "Any time one of them gets violently nauseous—that's sometimes a tip-off on mushroom poisoning."

"Resembling strychnine?" Fred said. A cold insight grappled with his head then, a rerun of the Kimberly Hawkins dogshit day and his illness in his car after what—

His.

"I'll tell Arctor," he said. "I can lay it on him. Without him flashing on me. He's docile."

"Ugly-looking, too," one of the scramble suits said. "He the individual came in the door stoop-shouldered and hung over?"

"Aw," Fred said, and swiveled back to his holos. Oh goddamn, he thought, that day Barris gave us the tabs at the roadside—his mind went into spins and double trips and then split in half, directly down the middle. The next thing he knew, he was in the safe apartment's bathroom with a Dixie cup of water, rinsing out his mouth, by himself, where he could think. When you get down to it, I'm Arctor, he thought. I'm the man on the scanners, the suspect Barris was fucking over with his weird phone call with the locksmith, and I was asking, What's Arctor been up to to get Barris on him like that? I'm slushed; my brain is slushed. This is not real. I'm not believing this, watching what is me, is Fred—that was Fred down there without his scramble suit; that's how Fred appears without the suit!

And Fred the other day possibly almost got it with toxic mushroom fragments, he realized. He almost didn't make it here to this safe apartment to get these holos going. But now he has.

Now Fred has a chance. But only barely.

Crazy goddamn job they gave me, he thought. But if I wasn't doing it someone else would be, and they might get it wrong. They'd set him up—set Arctor up. They'd turn him in for the reward; they'd plant dope on him and collect. If anyone, he thought, has to be watching that house, it better ought to be me by far, despite the disadvantages; just protecting everybody against kinky fucking Barris in itself justifies it right there.

And if any other officer monitoring Barris's actions sees what I probably will see, they'll conclude Arctor is the biggest drug runner in the western U.S. and recommend a—Christ!—covert snuff. By our unidentified forces. The ones in black we borrow from back East that tiptoe a lot and carry the scope-site Winchester 803's. The new infrared sniper-scope sights synched with the EE-tropic shells. Those guys who don't get paid at all, even from a Dr. Pepper machine; they just get to draw straws to see which of them gets to be the next U.S. President. My God, he thought, those fuckers can shoot down a passing plane. And make it look like one engine inhaled a flock of birds. Those EE-tropic shells—why fuck me, man, he thought; they'd leave traces of feathers in the ruins of the engines; they'd prime them for that.

This is awful, he thought, thinking about this. Not Arctor as suspect but Arctor as . . . whatever. Target. I'll keep on watching him; Fred will keep on doing his Fred-thing; it'll be a lot better; I can edit and interpret and do a great deal of "Let's wait until he actually" and so on, and, realizing this, he tossed the Dixie cup away and emerged from the safe apartment's bathroom.

"You look done in," one of the scramble suits said to him.

"Well," Fred said, "funny thing happened to me on the way to the grave." He saw in his mind a picture of the supersonic tight-beam projector which had caused a forty-nine-year-old district attorney to have a fatal cardiac arrest, just as he was about to reopen the case of a dreadful and famous political assassination here in California. "I almost got there," he said aloud.

"Almost is almost," the scramble suit said. "It's not there."

"Oh," Fred said. "Yeah. Right."

"Sit down," a scramble suit said, "and get back to work, or for you no Friday, just public assistance."

"Can you imagine listing this job as a job skill on the—" Fred began, but the two other scramble suits were not amused and in fact weren't even listening. So he reseated himself and lit a cigarette. And started up the battery of holos once more.

What I ought to do, he decided, is walk back up the street to the house, right now, while I'm thinking about it, before I get side-tracked, and walk in on Barris real fast and shoot him.

In the line of duty.

I'll say, "Hey, man, I'm hurtin'—can you lay a joint on me? I'll pay you a buck." And he will, and then I'll arrest him, drag him to my car, throw him inside, drive onto the freeway, and then pistol-whip him out of the car in front of a truck. And I can say he fought loose and tried to jump. Happens all the time.

Because if I don't I can never eat or drink any open food or beverage in the house, and neither can Luckman or Donna or Freck or we'll all croak from toxic mushroom fragments, after which Barris will explain about how we were all out in the woods picking them at random and eating them and he tried to dissuade us but we wouldn't listen because we didn't go to college.

Even if the court psychiatrists find him totally burned out and nuts and toss him in forever, somebody'll be dead. He thought, Maybe Donna, for instance. Maybe she'll wander in, spaced on hash, looking for me and the spring flowers I promised her, and Barris will offer her a bowl of Jell-O he made himself special, and ten days later she'll be thrashing in agony in an intensive-care ward and it won't do any good then.

If that happens, he thought, I'll boil him in Drāno, in the bathtub, in hot Drāno, until only bones remain, and then mail the bones to his mother or kids, whichever he has, and if he hasn't either then just toss the bones out at passing dogs. But the deed will be done to that little girl anyhow.

Excuse me, he rolled in his head in fantasy to the other two scramble suits. Where can I get a hundred-pound can of Drāno this time of night?

I've had it, he thought, and turned on the holos so as not to attract any more static from the other suits in the safe room.

On Monitor Two, Barris was talking to Luckman, who apparently had rolled in the front door dead drunk, no doubt on Ripple. "There are more people addicted to alcohol in the

U.S.," Barris was telling Luckman, who was trying to find the door to his bedroom, to go pass out, and having a terrible time, "than there are addicts of all other forms of drugs. And brain damage and liver damage from the alcohol plus impurities—"

Luckman disappeared without ever having noticed Barris was there. I wish him luck, Fred thought. It's not a workable policy, though, not for long. Because the fucker is there.

But now Fred is here, too. But all Fred's got is hindsight. Unless, he thought, unless maybe if I run the holo-tapes backward. Then I'd be there first, before Barris. What I do would precede what Barris does. If with me first he gets to do anything at all.

And then the other side of his head opened up and spoke to him more calmly, like another self with a simpler message flashed to him as to how to handle it.

"The way to cool the locksmith check," it told him, "is to go down there to Harbor tomorrow first thing very early and redeem the check and get it back. Do that first, before you do anything else. Do that right away. Defuse that, at that end. And after that, do the other more serious things, once that's finished. Right?" Right, he thought. That will remove me from the disadvantage list. That's where to start.

He put the tape on fast forward, on and on until he figured from the meters that it would show a night scene with everyone asleep. For a pretext to sign off his workday, here.

It now showed lights off, the scanners on infra. Luckman in his bed in his room; Barris in his; and in his room, Arctor beside a chick, both of them asleep.

Let's see, Fred thought. Connie something. We have her in the computer files as strung out on hard stuff and also turning tricks and dealing. A true loser.

"At least you didn't have to watch your subject have sexual intercourse," one of the other scramble suits said, watching from behind him and then passing on by.

"That's a relief," Fred said, stoically viewing the two sleeping figures in the bed; his mind was on the locksmith and what he had to do there. "I always hate to—"

"A nice thing to do," the scramble suit agreed, "but not too nice to watch."

Arctor asleep, Fred thought. With his trick. Well, I can wind up soon; they'll undoubtedly ball on arising but that's about it for them.

He continued watching, however. The sight of Bob Arctor sleeping . . . on and on, Fred thought, hour after hour. And then he noticed something he had not noticed. *That doesn't look like anybody else but Donna Hawthorne!* he thought. There in bed, in the sack with Arctor.

It doesn't compute, he thought, and reached to snap off the scanners. He ran the tape back, then forward again. Bob Arctor and a chick, but not Donna! It was the junkie chick Connie! He had been right. The two individuals lay there side by side, both asleep.

And then, as Fred watched, Connie's hard features melted and faded into softness, and into Donna Hawthorne's face.

He snapped off the tape again. Sat puzzled. I don't get it, he thought. It's—what they call that? Like a goddamn dissolve! A film technique. Fuck, what is this? Pre-editing for TV viewing? By a director, using special visual effects?

Again he ran the tape back, then forward; when he first came to the alteration in Connie's features he then stopped the transport, leaving the hologram filled with one freeze-frame.

He rotated the enlarger. All the other cubes cut out; one huge cube formed from the previous eight. A single nocturnal scene: Bob Arctor, unmoving, in his bed, the girl unmoving, beside him.

Standing, Fred walked into the holo-cube, into the three-dimensional projection, and stood close to the bed to scrutinize the girl's face.

Halfway between, he decided. Still half Connie; already half Donna. I better turn this over to the lab, he thought; it's been tampered with by an expert. I've been fed fake tape.

Who by? he wondered. He emerged from the holo-cube, collapsed it, and restored the small eight ones. Still sat there, pondering.

Somebody faked in Donna. Superimposed over Connie. Forged evidence that Arctor was laying the Hawthorne girl. Why? As a good technician can do with either audio or video tape and now—as witness—with holo-tapes. Hard to do, but . . .

If this was a click-on, click-off, interval scan, he thought, we'd have a sequence showing Arctor in bed with a girl he probably never did get into bed and never will, but there it is on the tape.

Or maybe it's a visual interruption or breakdown electronically, he pondered. What they call *printing*. Holo-printing: from one section of the tape storage to another. If the tape sits too long, if the recording gain was too high initially, it prints across. Jeez, he thought. It printed Donna across from a previous or later scene, maybe from the living room.

I wish I knew more about the technical side of this, he reflected. I'd better acquire more background on this before jumping the gun. Like another AM station filtering in, interfering—

Crosstalk, he decided. Like that: accidental.

Like ghosts on a TV screen. Functional, a malfunction. A transducer opened up briefly.

Again he rolled the tape. Connie again, and Connie it stayed. And then . . . again Fred saw Donna's face melt back in, and this time the sleeping man beside her in the bed, Bob Arctor, woke up after a moment and sat up abruptly, then fumbled for the light beside him; the light fell to the floor and Arctor sat staring on and on at the sleeping girl, at sleeping Donna.

When Connie's face seeped back, Arctor relaxed, and at last he sank back and again slept. But restlessly.

Well, that shoots down the "technical interference" theory, Fred thought. Printing or crosstalk. *Arctor saw it too.* Woke up, saw it, stared, then gave up.

Christ, Fred thought, and shut off the equipment before him entirely. "I guess that's enough for me for now," he declared, and rose shakily to his feet. "I've had it."

"Saw some kinky sex, did you?" a scramble suit asked. "You'll get used to this job."

"I never will get used to this job," Fred said. "You can make book on that."

Chapter Eleven

THE next morning, by Yellow Cab, since now not only was his cephscope laid up for repairs but so was his car, he appeared at the door of Englesohn Locksmith with forty bucks in cash and a good deal of worry inside his heart.

The store had an old wooden quality, with a more modern sign but many little brass doodads in the windows of a lock type: funky ornate mailboxes, trippy doorknobs made to resemble human heads, great fake black iron keys. He entered, into semigloom. Like a doper's place, he thought, appreciating the irony.

At a counter where two huge key-grinding machines loomed up, plus thousands of key blanks dangling from racks, a plump elderly lady greeted him. "Yes, sir? Good morning."

Arctor said, "I'm here . . .

> *Ihr Instrumente freilich spottet mein,*
> *Mit Rad and Kämmen, Walz' und Bügel:*
> *Ich stand am Tor, ihr solltet Schlüssel sein;*
> *Zwar euer Bart ist kraus, doch hebt ihr nicht die Riegel.*

. . . to pay for a check of mine which the bank returned. It's for twenty dollars, I believe."

"Oh." The lady amiably lifted out a locked metal file, searched for the key to it, then discovered the file wasn't locked. She opened it and found the check right away, with a note attached. "Mr. Arctor?"

"Yes," he said, his money already out.

"Yes, twenty dollars." Detaching the note from the check, she began laboriously writing on the note, indicating that he had shown up and purchased the check back.

"I'm sorry about this," he told her, "but by mistake I wrote the check on a now closed account rather than my active one."

"Umm," the lady said, smiling as she wrote.

"Also," he said, "I'd appreciate it if you'd tell your husband, who called the other day—"

"My brother Carl," the lady said, "actually." She glanced over her shoulder. "If Carl spoke to you . . ." She gestured, smiling. "He gets overwrought sometimes about checks . . . I apologize if he spoke . . . you know."

"Tell him," Arctor said, his speech memorized, "that when he called I was distraught myself, and I apologize for that, too."

"I believe he did say something about that, yes." She laid out his check; he gave her twenty dollars.

"Any extra charge?" Arctor said.

"No extra charge."

"I was distraught," he said, glancing briefly at the check and then putting it away in his pocket, "because a friend of mine had just passed on unexpectedly."

"Oh dear," the lady said.

Arctor, lingering, said, "He choked to death alone, in his room, on a piece of meat. No one heard him."

"Do you know, Mr. Arctor, that more deaths from that happen than people realize? I read that when you are dining with a friend, and he or she does not speak for a period of time but just sits there, you should lean forward and ask him if he can talk? Because he may not be able to; he may be strangling and can't tell you."

"Yes," Arctor said. "Thanks. That's true. And thanks about the check."

"I'm sorry about your friend," the lady said.

"Yes," he said. "He was about the best friend I had."

"That is so dreadful," the lady said. "How old was he, Mr. Arctor?"

"In his early thirties," Arctor said, which was true: Luckman was thirty-two.

"Oh, how terrible. I'll tell Carl. And thank you for coming all the way down here."

"Thank you," Arctor said. "And thank Mr. Englesohn too, for me. Thank you both so much." He departed, finding himself back out on the warm morning sidewalk, blinking in the bright light and foul air.

He phoned for a cab, and on the journey back to his house sat advising himself as to how well he had gotten out of this net of Barris's with no real overly bad scene. Could have been a lot worse, he pointed out to himself. The check was still there. And I didn't have to confront the dude himself.

He got out the check to see how closely Barris had been

able to approximate his handwriting. Yes, it was a dead account; he recognized the color of the check right away, an entirely closed one, and the bank had stamped it ACCOUNT CLOSED. No wonder the locksmith had gone bananas. And then, studying the check as he rode along, Arctor saw that the handwriting was his.

Not anything like Barris's. A perfect forgery. He would never have known it wasn't his, except that he remembered not having written it.

My God, he thought, how many of these has Barris done by now? Maybe he's embezzled me out of half I've got.

Barris, he thought, is a genius. On the other hand, it's probably a tracing reproduction or anyhow mechanically done. But I never made a check out to Englesohn Locksmith, so how could it be a transfer forgery? This is a unique check. I'll turn it over to the department graphologists, he decided, and let them figure out how it was done. Maybe just practice, practice, practice.

As to the mushroom jazz— He thought, I'll just walk up to him and say people told me he's been trying to sell them mushroom hits. And to knock it off. I got feedback from somebody worried, as they should be.

But, he thought, these items are only random indications of what he's up to, discovered on the first replay. *They only represent samples of what I'm up against.* Christ knows what else he's done: he's got all the time in the world to loaf around and read reference books and dream up plots and intrigues and conspiracies and so forth . . . Maybe, he thought abruptly, I better have a trace run on my phone right away to see if it's tapped. Barris has a box of electronic hardware, and even Sony, for example, makes and sells an induction coil that can be used as a phone-tapping device. The phone probably is. It probably has been for quite a while.

I mean, he thought, in addition to my own recent— necessary—phone tap.

Again he studied the check as the cab jiggled along, and all at once he thought, What if I made it out myself? What if Arctor wrote this? I think I did, he thought; I think the motherfucking dingey Arctor himself wrote this check, very fast—the letters slanted—because for some reason he was in a hurry; he dashed it off, got the wrong blank check, and afterward forgot all about it, forgot the incident entirely.

Forgot, he thought, the time Arctor . . .

Was grinsest du mir, hohler Schädel, her?
Als dass dein Hirn, wie meines, einst verwirret
Den leichten Tag gesucht und in der Dämmrung schwer,
Mit Lust nach Wahrheit, jämmerlich geirret.

. . . oozed out of that huge dope happening in Santa Ana, where he met that little blond chick with odd teeth, long blond hair, and a big ass, but so energetic and friendly . . . he couldn't get his car started; he was wired up to his nose. He kept having trouble—there was so much dope dropped and shot and snorted that night, it went on almost until dawn. So much Substance D, and very Primo. Very very Primo. His stuff.

Leaning forward, he said, "Pull over at that Shell station. I'll get out there."

He got out, paid the cab driver, then entered the pay phone, looked up the locksmith's number, phoned him.

The old lady answered. "Englesohn Locksmith, good—"

"This is Mr. Arctor again, I'm sorry to bother you. What address do you have for the call, the service call for which my check was made out?"

"Well, let me see. Just a moment, Mr. Arctor." Bumping of the phone as she set it down.

Distant muffled man's voice: "Who is it? That Arctor?"

"Yes, Carl, but don't say anything, please. He came in just now—"

"Let me talk to him."

Pause. Then the old lady again. "Well, I have this address, Mr. Arctor." She read off his home address.

"That's where your brother was called out to? To make the key?"

"Wait a moment. Carl? Do you remember where you went in the truck to make the key for Mr. Arctor?"

Distant man's rumble: "On Katella."

"Not his home?"

"On Katella!"

"Somewhere on Katella, Mr. Arctor. In Anaheim. No, wait —Carl says it was in Santa Ana, on Main. Does that—"

"Thanks," he said and hung up. Santa Ana. Main. That's where the fucking dope party was, and I must have turned in thirty names and as many license plates that night; that was not your standard party. A big shipment had arrived from Mexico; the buyers were splitting and, as usual with buyers, sampling as they split. Half of them now probably have been busted by buy agents sent out . . . Wow, he thought: I still remember—or never will correctly remember—that night.

But that still doesn't excuse Barris from impersonating Arctor with malice aforethought on that phone call coming in. Except that, by the evidence, Barris had made it up on the spot —improvised. Shit, maybe Barris was wired the other night and did what a lot of dudes do when they're wired: just sort of groove with what's happening. Arctor wrote the check for a certainty; Barris just happened to pick up the phone. Thought, in his charred head, that it was a cool gag. Being irresponsible only, nothing more.

And, he reflected as he dialed Yellow Cab again, Arctor has not been very responsible in making good on that check over this prolonged period. Whose fault is that? Getting it out once more, he examined the date on the check. A month and a half. Jesus, talk about irresponsibility! Arctor could wind up inside looking out, for that; it's God's mercy that nutty Carl didn't go to the D.A. already. Probably his sweet old sister restrained him.

Arctor, he decided, better get his ass in gear; he's done a few dingey things himself I didn't know about until now. Barris isn't the only one or perhaps even the primary one. For one thing, there is still to be explained the cause of Barris's intense, concerted malice toward Arctor; a man doesn't set out over a long period of time to burn somebody for no reason. And Barris isn't trying to burn anybody else, not, say, Luckman or Charles Freck or Donna Hawthorne; he helped get Jerry Fabin to the federal clinic more than anyone else, and he's kind to all the animals in the house.

One time Arctor had been going to send one of the dogs— what the hell was the little black one's name, Popo or something?—to the pound to be destroyed, she couldn't be trained, and Barris had spent hours, in fact days, with Popo, gently training her and talking with her until she calmed down and could be trained and so didn't have to go be snuffed. If Barris had general malice toward all, he wouldn't do numbers, good numbers, like that.

"Yellow Cab," the phone said.

He gave the address of the Shell station.

And if Carl the locksmith had pegged Arctor as a heavy doper, he pondered as he lounged around moodily waiting for the cab, it isn't Barris's fault; when Carl must've pulled up in his truck at 5 A.M. to make a key for Arctor's Olds, Arctor probably was walking on Jell-O sidewalks and up walls and batting off fisheyes and every other kind of good dope-trip thing. Carl drew his conclusions then. As Carl ground the new key, Arctor probably floated around upside down or bounced about on his head, talking sideways. No wonder Carl had not been amused.

In fact, he speculated, maybe Barris is trying to cover up for Arctor's increasing fuckups. Arctor is no longer keeping his vehicle in safe condition, as he once did, he's been hanging paper, not deliberately but because his goddamn brain is slushed from dope. But, if anything, that's worse. Barris is doing what he can; that's a possibility. Only, *his* brain, too, is slushed. *All* their brains are . . .

> *Dem Wurme gleich' ich, der den Staub durchwühlt,*
> *Den, wie er sich im Staube nährend lebt,*
> *Des Wandrers Tritt vernichtet und begräbt.*

. . . slushed and mutually interacting in a slushed way. It's the slushed leading the slushed. And right into doom.

Maybe, he conjectured, Arctor cut the wires and bent the wires and created all the shorts in his cephscope. In the middle of the night. But for what reason?

That would be a difficult one: *why?* But with slushed brains anything was possible, any variety of twisted—like the wires themselves—motives. He'd seen it, during his undercover law-enforcement work, many, many times. This tragedy was not new to him; this would be, in their computer files, just one more case. This was the phase ahead of the journey to the federal clinic, as with Jerry Fabin.

All these guys walked one game board, stood now in different squares various distances from the goal, and would reach it at several times. But all, eventually, would reach it: the federal clinics.

It was inscribed in their neural tissue. Or what remained of it. Nothing could halt it or turn it back now.

And, he had begun to believe, for Bob Arctor most of all. It was his intuition, just beginning, not dependent on anything Barris was doing. A new, professional insight.

And also, his superiors at the Orange County Sheriff's Office had decided to focus on Bob Arctor; they no doubt had reasons which he knew nothing about. Perhaps these facts confirmed one another: their growing interest in Arctor—after all, it had cost the department a bundle to install the holo-scanners in Arctor's house, and to pay him to analyze the print-outs, as well as others higher up to pass judgment on what he periodically turned over—this fitted in with Barris's unusual attention toward Arctor, both having selected Arctor as a Primo target. But what had he seen himself in Arctor's conduct that struck him as unusual? Firsthand, not dependent on these two interests?

As the taxi drove along, he reflected that he would have to watch awhile to come across anything, more than likely; it would not disclose itself to the monitors in a day. He would have to be patient; he would have to resign himself to long-term scrutiny and to put himself in a space where he was willing to wait.

Once he saw something on the holo-scanners, however, some enigmatic or suspicious behavior on Arctor's part, then a three-point fix would exist on him, a third verification of the others' interests. Certainly this would be a confirm. It would justify the expense and time of everyone's interest.

I wonder what Barris knows that we don't know, he wondered. Maybe we should haul him in and ask him. But—better to obtain material developed independently from Barris; otherwise it would be a duplication of what Barris, whoever he was or represented, had.

And then he thought, What the hell am I talking about? I must be nuts. I know Bob Arctor; he's a good person. He's up to nothing. At least nothing unsavory. In fact, he thought, he works for the Orange County Sheriff's Office, covertly. Which is probably . . .

> *Zwei Seelen wohnen, ach! in meiner Brust,*
> *Die eine will sich von der andern trennen:*
> *Die eine hält, in derber Liebeslust,*
> *Sich an die Welt mit klammernden Organen;*
> *Die andre hebt gewaltsam sich vom Dust*
> *Zu den Gefilden hoher Ahnen.*

. . . why Barris is after him.

But, he thought, that wouldn't explain why the Orange County Sheriff's Office is after him—especially to the extent of installing all those holos and assigning a full-time agent to watch and report on him. That wouldn't account for that.

It does not compute, he thought. More, a lot more, is going down in that house, that run-down rubble-filled house with its weed-patch backyard and catbox that never gets emptied and animals walking on the kitchen table and garbage spilling over that no one ever takes out.

What a waste, he thought, of a truly good house. So much could be done with it. A family, children and a woman, could live there. It was designed for that: three bedrooms. Such a waste; such a fucking waste! They ought to take it away from him, he thought; enter the situation and foreclose. Maybe they will. And put it to better use; that house yearns for that. That house has seen so much better days, long ago. Those days could return. If another kind of person had it and kept it up.

The yard especially, he thought, as the cab pulled into the newspaper-splattered driveway.

He paid the driver, got out his door key, and entered the house.

Immediately he felt something watching: the holo-scanners on him. As soon as he crossed his own threshold. Alone—no one but him in the house. Untrue! Him and the scanners, insidious and invisible, that watched him and recorded. Everything he did. Everything he uttered.

Like the scrawls on the wall when you're peeing in a public urinal, he thought. SMILE! YOU'RE ON CANDID CAMERA! I am, he thought, as soon as I enter this house. It's eerie. He did not like it. He felt self-conscious; the sensation had grown since the first day, when they'd arrived home—the "dog-shit day," as he thought of it, couldn't keep from thinking of it. Each day the experience of the scanners had grown.

"Nobody home, I guess," he stated aloud as usual, and was aware that the scanners had picked that up. But he had to take care always: he wasn't supposed to know they were there. Like an actor before a movie camera, he decided, you act like the camera doesn't exist or else you blow it. It's all over.

And for this shit there are no take-two's.

What you get instead is wipeout. I mean, what *I* get. Not the people behind the scanners but me.

What I ought to do, he thought, to get out of this, is sell the house; it's run down anyway. But . . . I love this house. No way!

It's my house.

Nobody can drive me out.

For whatever reasons they would or do want to.

Assuming there's a "they" at all.

Which may just be my imagination, the "they" watching me. Paranoia. Or rather the "it." The depersonalized *it.*

Whatever it is that's watching, it is not a human.

Not by my standards, anyhow. Not what I'd recognize.

As silly as this is, he thought, it's frightening. Something is being done to me and by a mere thing, here in my own house. Before my very eyes.

Within *something's* very eyes; within the sight of some *thing.* Which, unlike little dark-eyed Donna, does not ever blink. What does a scanner see? he asked himself. I mean, really see? Into the head? Down into the heart? Does a passive infrared scanner like they used to use or a cube-type holo scanner like they use these days, the latest thing, see into me—into us— clearly or darkly? I hope it does, he thought, see clearly, because I can't any longer these days see into myself. I see only murk. Murk outside; murk inside. I hope, for everyone's sake, the scanners do better. Because, he thought, if the scanner sees only darkly, the way I myself do, then we are cursed, cursed again and like we have been continually, and we'll wind up dead this way, knowing very little and getting that little frag- ment wrong too.

From the living-room bookcase he took down a volume at

random; it turned out to be, he discovered, *The Picture Book of Sexual Love.* Opening at random, he perceived a page—which showed a man nibbling happily at a chick's right tit, and the chick sighing—and said aloud, as if reading to himself from the book, as if quoting from some famous old-time double-dome philosopher, which he was not:

"Any given man sees only a tiny portion of the total truth, and very often, in fact almost . . .

> *Weh! steck' ich in dem Kerker noch?*
> *Verfluchtes dumpfes Mauerloch,*
> *Wo selbst das liebe Himmelslicht*
> *Trüb durch gemalte Scheiben bricht!*
> *Beschränkt mit diesem Bücherhauf,*
> *Den Würme nagen, Staub bedeckt,*
> *Den bis ans hohe.*

 . . . perpetually, he deliberately deceives himself about that little precious fragment as well. A portion of him turns against him and acts like another person, defeating him from inside. A man inside a man. Which is no man at all."

Nodding, as if moved by the wisdom of the nonexisting written words on that page, he closed the large red-bound, gold-stamped *Picture Book of Sexual Love* and restored it to the shelf. I hope the scanners don't zoom in on the cover of this book, he thought, and blow my shuck.

Charles Freck, becoming progressively more and more depressed by what was happening to everybody he knew, decided finally to off himself. There was no problem, in the circles where he hung out, in putting an end to yourself: you just bought into a large quantity of reds and took them with some cheap wine, late at night, with the phone off the hook so no one would interrupt you.

The planning part had to do with the artifacts you wanted found on you by later archeologists. So they'd know from which stratum you came. And also could piece together where your head had been at the time you did it.

He spent several days deciding on the artifacts. Much longer than he had spent deciding to kill himself, and approximately the same time required to get that many reds. He would be found lying on his back, on his bed, with a copy of Ayn Rand's *The Fountainhead* (which would prove he had been a misunderstood superman rejected by the masses and so, in a sense, murdered by their scorn) and an unfinished letter to Exxon protesting the cancellation of his gas credit card. That way he would indict the system and achieve something by his death, over and above what the death itself achieved.

Actually, he was not as sure in his mind what the death achieved as what the two artifacts achieved; but anyhow it all added up, and he began to make ready, like an animal sensing its time has come and acting out its instinctive programming, laid down by nature, when its inevitable end was near.

At the last moment (as end-time closed in on him) he changed his mind on a decisive issue and decided to drink the reds down with a connoisseur wine instead of Ripple or Thunderbird, so he set off on one last drive, over to Trader Joe's, which specialized in fine wines, and bought a bottle of 1971 Mondavi Cabernet Sauvignon, which set him back almost thirty dollars—all he had.

Back home again, he uncorked the wine, let it breathe, drank a few glasses of it, spent a few minutes contemplating his favorite page of *The Illustrated Picture Book of Sex*, which showed the girl on top, then placed the plastic bag of reds beside his bed, lay down with the Ayn Rand book and unfinished protest letter to Exxon, tried to think of something meaningful but could not, although he kept remembering the girl being on top, and then, with a glass of the Cabernet Sauvignon, gulped down all the reds at once. After that, the deed being done, he lay back, the Ayn Rand book and letter on his chest, and waited.

However, he had been burned. The capsules were not barbiturates, as represented. They were some kind of kinky psychedelics, of a type he had never dropped before, probably a mixture, and new on the market. Instead of quietly suffocating, Charles Freck began to hallucinate. Well, he thought philosophically, this is the story of my life. Always ripped off. He had to face the fact—considering how many of the capsules he had swallowed—that he was in for some trip.

The next thing he knew, a creature from between dimensions was standing beside his bed looking down at him disapprovingly.

The creature had many eyes, all over it, ultra-modern expensive-looking clothing, and rose up eight feet high. Also, it carried an enormous scroll.

"You're going to read me my sins," Charles Freck said.

The creature nodded and unsealed the scroll.

Freck said, lying helpless on his bed, "And it's going to take a hundred thousand hours."

Fixing its many compound eyes on him, the creature from between dimensions said, "We are no longer in the mundane universe. Lower-plane categories of material existence such as 'space' and 'time' no longer apply to you. You have been elevated to the transcendent realm. Your sins will be read to you ceaselessly, in shifts, throughout eternity. The list will never end."

Know your dealer, Charles Freck thought, and wished he could take back the last half-hour of his life.

A thousand years later he was still lying there on his bed with the Ayn Rand book and the letter to Exxon on his chest, listening to them read his sins to him. They had gotten up to the first grade, when he was six years old.

Ten thousand years later they had reached the sixth grade.

The year he had discovered masturbation.

He shut his eyes, but he could still see the multi-eyed, eight-foot-high being with its endless scroll reading on and on.

"And next—" it was saying.

Charles Freck thought, At least I got a good wine.

Chapter Twelve

Two days later Fred, puzzled, watched Holo-Scanner Three as his subject Robert Arctor pulled a book, evidently at random, from his bookshelf in the living room of his house. Dope stashed behind it? Fred wondered, and zoomed the scanner lens in. Or a phone number or address written in it? He could see that Arctor hadn't pulled the book to read; Arctor had just entered the house and still wore his coat. He had a peculiar air about him: tense and bummed out both at once, a sort of dulled urgency.

The zoomar lens of the scanner showed the page had a color photo of a man gnawing on a woman's right nipple, with both individuals nude. The woman was evidently having an orgasm; her eyes had half shut and her mouth hung open in a soundless moan. Maybe Arctor's using it to get off on, Fred thought as he watched. But Arctor paid no attention to the picture; instead, he creakingly recited something mystifying, partly in German obviously to puzzle anyone overhearing him. Maybe he imagined his roommates were somewhere in the house and wanted to bait them into appearing. Fred speculated.

No one appeared. Luckman, Fred knew from having been at the scanners a long while, had dropped a bunch of reds mixed with Substance D and passed out fully dressed in his bedroom, a couple of steps short of his bed. Barris had left entirely.

What is Arctor doing? Fred wondered, and noted the ident code for these sections. He's becoming more and more strange. I can see now what that informant who phoned in about him meant.

Or, he conjectured, those sentences Arctor spoke aloud could be a voice command to some electronic hardware he's installed in the house. Turn on or turn off. Maybe even create an interference field against scanning . . . such as this. But he doubted it. Doubted if it was in any way rational or purposeful or meaningful, except to Arctor.

The guy is nuts, he thought. He really is. From the day he found his cephscope sabotaged—certainly the day he arrived home with his car all fucked up, fucked up in such a way as to almost kill him—he's been dingey ever since. And to some extent before that, Fred thought. Anyhow, ever since the "dog-shit day," as he knew Arctor called it.

Actually, he could not blame him. That, Fred reflected as he watched Arctor peel off his coat wearily, would blow anyone's mind. But most people would phase back in. He hasn't. He's getting worse. Reading aloud to no one messages that don't exist and in foreign tongues.

Unless he's shucking me, Fred thought with uneasiness. In some fashion figured out he's being monitored and is . . . covering up what he's actually doing? Or just playing head games with us? Time, he decided, will tell.

I say he's shucking us, Fred decided. Some people can tell when they're being watched. A sixth sense. Not paranoia, but a primitive instinct: what a mouse has, any hunted thing. Knows it's being stalked. *Feels* it. He's doing shit for our benefit, stringing us along. But—you can't be sure. There are shucks on top of shucks. Layers and layers.

The sound of Arctor reading obscurely had awakened Luckman according to the scanner covering his bedroom. Luckman sat up groggily and listened. He then heard the noise of Arctor dropping a coat hanger while hanging up his coat. Luckman slid his long muscular legs under him and in one motion picked up a hand ax which he kept on the table by his bed; he stood erect and moved animal-smoothly toward the door of his bedroom.

In the living room, Arctor picked up the mail from the coffee table and started through it. He tossed a large junk-mail piece toward the wastebasket. It missed.

In his bedroom Luckman heard that. He stiffened and raised his head as if to sniff the air.

Arctor, reading the mail, suddenly scowled and said, "I'll be dipped."

In his bedroom Luckman relaxed, set the ax down with a clank, smoothed his hair, opened the door, and stepped out. "Hi. What's happening?"

Arctor said, "I drove by the Maylar Microdot Corporation Building."

"You're shitting me."

"And," Arctor said, "they were taking an inventory. But one

of the employees evidently had tracked the inventory outdoors on the heel of his shoe. So they were all outside there in the Maylar Microdot Corporation parking lot with a pair of tweezers and lots and lots of little magnifying glasses. And a little paper bag."

"Any reward?" Luckman said, yawning and beating with his palms on his flat, hard gut.

"They had a reward they were offering," Arctor said. "But they lost that, too. It was a little tiny penny."

Luckman said, "You see very many events of this nature as you're driving along?"

"Only in Orange County," Arctor said.

"How large is the Maylar Microdot Corporation building?"

"About an inch high," Arctor said.

"How much would you estimate it weighs?"

"Including the employees?"

Fred sent the tape spinning ahead at fast wind. When an hour had passed, according to the meter, he halted it momentarily.

"—about ten pounds," Arctor was saying.

"Well, how can you tell, then, when you pass by it, if it's only an inch high and only weighs ten pounds?"

Arctor, now sitting on the couch with his feet up, said, "They have a big sign."

Jesus! Fred thought, and again sent the tape ahead. He halted it at only ten minutes elapsed real time, on a hunch.

"—what's the sign look like?" Luckman was saying. He sat on the floor, cleaning a boxful of grass. "Neon and like that? Colors? I wonder if I've seen it. Is it conspicuous?"

"Here, I'll show it to you," Arctor said, reaching into his shirt pocket. "I brought it home with me."

Again Fred sent the tape at fast forward.

"—you know how you could smuggle microdots into a country without them knowing?" Luckman was saying.

"Just about any way you wanted," Arctor said, leaning back, smoking a joint. The air was cloudy.

"No, I mean a way they'd never flash on," Luckman said. "It was Barris who suggested this to me one day, confidentially; I wasn't supposed to tell anyone, because he's putting it in his book."

"What book? *Common Household Dope and*—"

"No. *Simple Ways to Smuggle Objects into the U.S. and out, Depending, on Which Way You're Going.* You smuggle it in with a shipment of dope. Like with heroin. The microdots are down inside the packets. Nobody'd notice, they're so small. They won't—"

"But then some junkie'd shoot up a hit of half smack and half microdots."

"Well, then, he'd be the fuckingest educated junkie you ever did see."

"Depending on what was on the microdots."

"Barris had this other way to smuggle dope across the border. You know how the customs guys, they ask you to declare what you have? And you can't say dope because—"

"Okay, how?"

"Well, see, you take a huge block of hash and carve it in the shape of a man. Then you hollow out a section and put a wind-up motor like a clockworks in it, and a little cassette tape, and you stand in line with it, and then just before it goes through customs you wind up the key and it walks up to the customs man, who says to it, 'Do you have anything to declare?' and the block of hash says, 'No, I don't,' and keeps on walking. Until it runs down on the other side of the border."

"You could put a solar-type battery in it instead of a spring and it could keep walking for years. Forever."

"What's the use of that? It'd finally reach either the Pacific or the Atlantic. In fact, it'd walk off the edge of the Earth, like—"

"Imagine an Eskimo village, and a six-foot-high block of hash worth about—how much would that be worth?"

"About a billion dollars."

"More. Two billion."

"These Eskimos are chewing hides and carving bone spears, and this block of hash worth two billion dollars comes walking through the snow saying over and over, 'No, I don't.'"

"They'd wonder what it meant by that."

"They'd be puzzled forever. There'd be legends."

"Can you imagine telling your grandkids, 'I saw with my own eyes the six-foot-high block of hash appear out of the blinding fog and walk past, that way, worth two billion dollars, saying, "No, I don't."' His grandchildren would have him committed."

"No, see, legends build. After a few centuries they'd be saying, 'In my forefathers' time one day a ninety-foot-high block of extremely good quality Afghanistan hash worth eight trillion dollars came at us dripping fire and screaming, "Die, Eskimo dogs!" and we fought and fought with it, using our spears, and finally killed it.' "

"The kids wouldn't believe that either."

"Kids never believe anything any more."

"It's a downer to tell anything to a kid. I once had a kid ask me, 'What was it like to see the first automobile?' Shit, man, I was born in 1962."

"Christ," Arctor said, "I once had a guy I knew burned out on acid ask me that. He was twenty-seven years old. I was only three years older than him. He didn't know anything any more. Later on he dropped some more hits of acid—or what he was sold as acid—and after that he peed on the floor and crapped on the floor, and when you said something to him, like 'How are you, Don?', he just repeated it after you, like a bird. 'How are you, Don?' "

Silence, then. Between the two joint-smoking men in the cloudy living room. A long, somber silence.

"Bob, you know something . . ." Luckman said at last. "I used to be the same age as everyone else."

"I think so was I," Arctor said.

"I don't know what did it."

"Sure, Luckman," Arctor said, "you know what did it to all of us."

"Well, let's not talk about it." He continued inhaling noisily, his long face sallow in the dim midday light.

One of the phones in the safe apartment rang. A scramble suit answered it, then extended it toward Fred. "Fred."

He shut off the holos and took the phone.

"Remember when you were downtown last week?" a voice said. "Being administered the BG test?"

After an interval of silence Fred said, "Yes."

"You were supposed to come back." A pause at that end,

too. "We've processed more recent material on you . . . I have taken it upon myself to schedule you for the full standard battery of percept tests plus other testing. Your time for this is tomorrow, three o'clock in the afternoon, the same room. It will take about four hours in all. Do you remember the room number?"

"No," Fred said.

"How are you feeling?"

"Okay," Fred said stoically.

"Any problems? In your work or outside your work?"

"I had a fight with my girl."

"Any confusion? Are you experiencing any difficulty identifying persons or objects? Does anything you see appear inverted or reversed? And while I'm asking, any space-time or language disorientation?"

"No," he said glumly. "No to all of the above."

"We'll see you tomorrow at Room 203," the psychologist deputy said.

"What material of mine did you find to be—"

"We'll take that up tomorrow. Be there. All right? And, Fred, don't get discouraged." *Click.*

Well, click to you too, he thought, and hung up.

With irritation, sensing that they were leaning on him, making him do something he resented doing, he snapped the holos into print-out once more; the cubes lit up with color and the three-dimensional scenes within animated. From the aud tap more purposeless, frustrating—to Fred—babble emerged:

"This chick," Luckman droned on, "had gotten knocked up, and she applied for an abortion because she'd missed like four periods and she was conspicuously swelling up. She did nothing but gripe about the cost of the abortion; she couldn't get on public assistance for some reason. One day I was over at her place, and this girl friend of hers was there telling her she only had a hysterical pregnancy. 'You just *want* to believe you're pregnant,' the chick was nattering at her. 'It's a guilt trip. And the abortion, and the heavy bread it's going to cost you, that's a penance trip.' So the chick—I really dug her—she looked up calmly and she said, 'Okay, then if it's a hysterical pregnancy I'll get a hysterical abortion and pay for it with hysterical money.'"

Arctor said, "I wonder whose face is on the hysterical five-dollar bill."

"Well, who was our most hysterical President?"

"Bill Falkes. He only *thought* he was President."

"When did he think he served?"

"He imagined he served two terms back around 1882. Later on after a lot of therapy he came to imagine he served only one term—"

With great fury Fred slammed the holos ahead two and a half hours. How long does this garbage go on? he asked himself. All day? Forever?

"—so you take your child to the doctor, to the psychologist, and you tell him how your child screams all the time and has tantrums." Luckman had two lids of grass before him on the coffee table plus a can of beer; he was inspecting the grass. "And lies; the kid lies. Makes up exaggerated stories. And the psychologist examines the kid and his diagnosis is 'Madam, your child is hysterical. You have a hysterical child. But I don't know why.' And then you, the mother, there's your chance and you lay it on him, 'I know why, doctor. It's because I had a hysterical pregnancy.'" Both Luckman and Arctor laughed, and so did Jim Barris; he had returned sometime during the two hours and was with them, working on his funky hash pipe, winding white string.

Again Fred spun the tape forward a full hour.

"—this guy," Luckman was saying, manicuring a box full of grass, hunched over it as Arctor sat across from him, more or less watching, "appeared on TV claiming to be a world-famous impostor. He had posed at one time or another, he told the interviewer, as a great surgeon at Johns Hopkins Medical College, a theoretical submolecular high-velocity particle-research physicist on a federal grant at Harvard, as a Finnish novelist who'd won the Nobel Prize in literature, as a deposed president of Argentina married to—"

"And he got away with all that?" Arctor asked. "He never got caught?"

"The guy never posed as any of those. He never posed as anything but a world-famous impostor. That came out later in the L.A. *Times*—they checked up. The guy pushed a broom at Disneyland, or had until he read this autobiography about this world-famous impostor—there really was one—and he said, 'Hell, I can pose as all those exotic dudes and get away with it like he did,' and then he decided, 'Hell, why do that; I'll just pose as another impostor.' He made a lot of bread that way, the *Times* said. Almost as much as the real world-famous impostor. And he said it was a lot easier."

Barris, off to himself in a corner winding string, said, "We see impostors now and then. In our lives. But not posing as subatomic physicists."

"Narks, you mean," Luckman said. "Yeah, narks. I wonder how many narks we know. What's a nark look like?"

"It's like asking, What's an impostor look like?" Arctor said. "I talked one time to a big hash dealer who'd been busted with ten pounds of hash in his possession. I asked him what the nark who busted him looked like. You know, the—what do they call them?—buying agent that came out and posed as a friend of a friend and got him to sell him some hash."

"Looked," Barris said, winding string, "just like us."

"*More* so," Arctor said. "The hash-dealer dude—he'd already been sentenced and was going in the following day— he told me, 'They have longer hair than we do.' So I guess the moral of that is, Stay away from guys looking the same as us."

"There are female narks," Barris said.

"I'd like to meet a nark," Arctor said. "I mean knowingly. Where I could be positive."

"Well," Barris said, "you could be positive when he claps the cuffs on you, when that day comes."

Arctor said, "I mean, do narks have friends? What sort of social life do they have? Do their wives know?"

"Narks don't have wives," Luckman said. "They live in caves and peep out from under parked cars as you pass. Like trolls."

"What do they eat?" Arctor said.

"People," Barris said.

"How could a guy do that?" Arctor said. "Pose as a nark?"

"*What?*" both Barris and Luckman said together.

"Shit, I'm spaced," Arctor said, grinning. "'Pose as a nark' —wow." He shook his head, grimacing now.

Staring at him, Luckman said, "POSE AS A NARK? *POSE AS A NARK?*"

"My brains are scrambled today," Arctor said. "I better go crash."

At the holos, Fred cut the tape's forward motion; all the cubes froze, and the sound ceased.

"Taking a break, Fred?" one of the other scramble suits called over to him.

"Yeah," Fred said. "I'm tired. This crap gets to you after a while." He rose and got out his cigarettes. "I can't figure out half what they're saying, I'm so tired. Tired," he added, "of listening to them."

"When you're actually down there with them," a scramble suit said, "it's not so bad; you know? Like I guess you were—on the scene itself up until now, with a cover. Right?"

"I would never hang around with creeps like that," Fred said. "Saying the same things over and over, like old cons. Why do they do what they do, sitting there shooting the bull?"

"Why do we do what we do? This is pretty damn monotonous, when you get down to it."

"But we have to; this is our job. We have no choice."

"Like the cons," a scramble suit pointed out. "We have no choice."

Posing as a nark, Fred thought. What does that mean? Nobody knows . . .

Posing, he reflected, as an impostor. One who lives under parked cars and eats dirt. Not a world-famous surgeon or novelist or politician; nothing that anyone would care to hear about on TV. No life that anyone in their right mind . . .

> I resemble that worm which crawls through dust,
> Lives in the dust, eats dust
> Until a passerby's foot crushes it.

Yes, that expresses it, he thought. That poetry. Luckman must have read it to me, or maybe I read it in school. Funny what the mind pops up. Remembers.

Arctor's freaky words still stuck in his mind, even though he had shut off the tape. I wish I could forget it, he thought. I wish I could, for a while, forget *him*.

"I get the feeling," Fred said, "that sometimes I know what they're going to say before they say it. Their exact words."

"It's called *déjà vu*," one of the scramble suits agreed. "Let me give you a few pointers. Run the tape ahead over longer break-intervals, not an hour but, say, six hours. Then run it back if there's nothing until you hit something. Back, you see, rather than forward. That way you don't get into the rhythm of their flow. Six or even eight ahead, then big jumps back . . . You'll get the hang of it pretty soon, you'll get so you can sense when you've got miles and miles of nothing or when somewhere you've got something useful."

"And you won't really listen at all," the other scramble suit said, "until you do actually hit something. Like a mother when she's asleep—nothing wakes her, even a truck going by, until she hears her baby cry. That wakes her—that alerts her. No matter how faint that cry is. The unconscious is selective, when it learns what to listen for."

"I know," Fred said. "I've got two kids."

"Boys?"

"Girls," he said. "Two little girls."

"That's allll riiight," one of the scramble suits said. "I have one girl, a year old."

"No names please," the other scramble suit said, and they all laughed. A little.

Anyhow, there is an item, Fred said to himself, to extract from the total tape and pass along. That cryptic statement about "posing as a nark." The other men in the house with Arctor—it surprised them, too. When I go in tomorrow at three, he thought, I'll take a print of that—aud alone would do—and discuss it with Hank, along with what else I obtain between now and then.

But even if that's all I've got to show Hank, he thought, it's a beginning. Shows, he thought, that this around-the-clock scanning of Arctor is not a waste.

It shows, he thought, that I was right.

That remark was a slip. Arctor blew it.

But what it meant he did not yet know.

But we will, he said to himself, find out. We will keep on Bob Arctor until he drops. Unpleasant as it is to have to watch and listen to him and his pals all the time. Those pals of his, he thought, are as bad as he is. How'd I ever sit around in that house with them all that time? What a way to live a life; what, as the other officer said just now, an endless nothing.

Down there, he thought, in the murk, the murk of the mind and the murk outside as well; murk everywhere. Thanks to what they are: that kind of individual.

Carrying his cigarette, he walked back to the bathroom, shut and locked the door, then, from inside the cigarette package, he got out ten tabs of death. Filling a Dixie cup with water, he dropped all ten tabs. He wished he had brought more tabs with him. Well, he thought, I can drop a few more when I get through work, when I get back home. Looking at his watch, he tried to compute how long that would be. His mind felt fuzzy; how the hell long will it be? he asked himself, wondering what had become of his time sense. Watching the holos has fucked it up, he realized. I can't tell what time it is at all any more.

I feel like I've dropped acid and then gone through a car wash, he thought. Lots of titanic whirling soapy brushes coming at me; dragged along by a chain into tunnels of black foam. What a way to make a living, he thought, and unlocked the bathroom door to go back—reluctantly—to work.

When he turned on the tape-transport once more, Arctor was saying, "—as near as I can figure out, God is dead."

Luckman answered, "I didn't know He was sick."

"Now that my Olds is laid up indefinitely," Arctor said, "I've decided I should sell it and buy a Henway."

"What's a Henway?" Barris said.

To himself Fred said, About three pounds.

"About three pounds," Arctor said.

The following afternoon at three o'clock two medical officers—not the same two—administered several tests to Fred, who was feeling even worse than he had the day before.

"In rapid succession you will see a number of objects with which you should be familiar pass in sequence before—first—your left eye and then your right. At the same time, on the illuminated panel directly before you, outline reproductions will appear simultaneously of several such familiar objects, and you are to match, by means of the punch pencil, what you consider to be the correct outline reproduction of the actual object visible at that instant. Now, these objects will move by you very rapidly, so do not hesitate too long. You will be time-scored as well as scored for accuracy. Okay?"

"Okay," Fred said, punch pencil ready.

A whole flock of familiar objects jogged past him then, and he punched away at the illuminated photos below. This took place for his left eye, and then it all happened again for his right.

"Next, with your left eye covered, a picture of a familiar object will be flashed to your right eye. You are to reach with your left hand, repeat, left hand, into a group of objects and find the one whose picture you saw."

"Okay," Fred said. A picture of a single die was flashed; with his left hand he groped around among small objects placed before him until he found a die.

"In the next test, several letters which spell out a word will be available to your left hand, unseen. You will feel them and then, with your right hand, write out the word the letters spell."

He did that. They spelled HOT.

"Now name the word spelled."

So he said, "Hot."

"Next, you will reach into this absolutely dark box with both eyes covered, and with your left hand touch an object in order to identify it. Then tell us what the object is, without having seen it visually. After that you will be shown three objects somewhat resembling one another, and you will tell us which of the three that you see most resembles the object you manually touched."

"Okay," Fred said, and he did that then, and other tests, for almost an hour. Grope, tell, look at with one eye, select. Grope, tell, look at with the other eye, select. Write down, draw.

"In this following test you will, with your eyes again covered, reach out and feel an object with each hand. You are to tell us if the object presented to your left hand is identical to the object presented to your right."

He did that.

"Here in rapid succession are pictures of triangles in various positions. You are to tell us if it is the same triangle or—"

After two hours they had him fit complicated blocks into

complicated holes and timed him doing this. He felt as if he was in first grade again, and screwing up. Doing worse than he had then. Miss Frinkel, he thought; old Miss Frinkel. She used to stand there and watch me do this shit back then, flashing me "Die!" messages, like they say in transactional analysis. Die. Do not be. Witch messages. A whole bunch of them, until I did finally fuck up. Probably Miss Frinkel was dead by now. Probably somebody had managed to flash her a "Die!" message back, and it had caught. He hoped so. Maybe it had been one of his. As with the psych testers now, he flashed such messages right back.

It didn't seem to be doing much good now. The test continued.

"What is wrong with this picture? One object among the others does not belong. You are to mark—"

He did that. And then it was actual objects, one of which did not belong; he was supposed to reach out and manually remove the offending object, and then, when the test was over, pick up all the offending objects from a variety of "sets," as they were called, and say what characteristic, if any, all the offending objects had in common: if *they* constituted a "set."

He was still trying to do that when they called time and ended the battery of testing and told him to go have a cup of coffee and wait outside until called.

After an interval—which seemed damn long to him—a tester appeared and said, "One more thing, Fred—we want a sample of your blood." He gave him a slip of paper: a lab requisition. "Go down the hall to the room marked 'Pathology Lab' and give them this and then after they have taken a blood sample come back here again and wait."

"Sure," he said glumly, and shuffled off with the requisition.

Traces in the blood, he realized. They're testing for that.

When he had gotten back to Room 203 from the pathology lab he rounded up one of the testers and said, "Would it be all right if I went upstairs to confer with my superior while I'm waiting for your results? He'll be taking off for the day soon."

"Affirmative," the psych tester said. "Since we decided to have a blood sample taken, it will be longer before we can make our evaluation; yes, go ahead. We'll phone upstairs when we're ready for you back here. Hank, is it?"

"Yes," Fred said. "I'll be upstairs with Hank."

The psych tester said, "You certainly seem much more depressed today than you did when we first saw you."

"Pardon?" Fred said.

"The first time you were in. Last week. You were kidding and laughing. Although very tense."

Gazing at him, Fred realized that this was one of the two medical deputies he had originally encountered. But he said nothing; he merely grunted and then left their office, made his way to the elevator. What a downer, he thought. This whole thing. I wonder which of the two medical deputies it is, he wondered. The one with the handle-bar mustache or the other . . . I guess the other. This one has no mustache.

"You will manually feel this object with your left hand," he said to himself, "and at the same time you will look at it with your right. And then in your own words you will tell us—" He could not think out any more nonsense. Not without their help.

When he entered Hank's office he found another man, not in a scramble suit, seated in the far corner, facing Hank.

Hank said, "This is the informant who phoned in about Bob Arctor using the grid—I mentioned him."

"Yes," Fred said, standing there unmoving.

"This man again phoned in, with more information about Bob Arctor; we told him he'd have to step forth and identify himself. We challenged him to appear down here and he did. Do you know him?"

"Sure I do," Fred said, staring at Jim Barris, who sat grinning and fiddling with a pair of scissors. Barris appeared ill at ease and ugly. Super ugly, Fred thought, with revulsion. "You're James Barris, aren't you?" he said. "Have you ever been arrested?"

"His I.D. shows him to be James R. Barris," Hank said, "and that is who he claims to be." He added, "He has no arrest record."

"What does he want?" To Barris, Fred said, "What's your information?"

"I have evidence," Barris said in a low voice, "that Mr. Arctor is part of a large secret covert organization, well funded, with arsenals of weapons at their disposal, using code words, probably dedicated to the overthrow of—"

"That part is speculation," Hank interrupted. "What you suppose it's up to? What's your evidence? Now don't give us anything that is not firsthand."

"Have you ever been sent to a mental hospital?" Fred said to Barris.

"No," Barris said.

"Will you sign a sworn, notarized statement at the D.A.'s office," Fred continued, "regarding your evidence and information? Will you be willing to appear in court *under oath* and—"

"He has already indicated he would," Hank interrupted.

"My evidence," Barris said, "which I mostly don't have with me today, but which I can produce, consists of tape recordings I have made of Robert Arctor's phone conversations. I mean, conversations when he didn't know I was listening."

"What is this organization?" Fred said.

"I believe it to be—" Barris began, but Hank waved him off. "It is political," Barris said, perspiring and trembling a little, but looking pleased, "and against the country. From outside. An enemy against the U.S."

Fred said, "What is Arctor's relationship with the source of Substance D?"

Blinking, then licking his lip and grimacing, Barris said, "It is in my—" He broke off. "When you examine all my information you will—that is, my evidence—you will undoubtedly conclude that Substance D is produced by a foreign nation determined to overthrow the U.S. and that Mr. Arctor has his hands deep within the machinery of this—"

"Can you tell us specific names of anyone else in this organization?" Hank said. "Persons Arctor has met with? You understand that giving false information to the legal authorities is a crime and if you do so you can and probably will be cited."

"I understand that," Barris said.

"Who has Arctor conferred with?" Hank said.

"A Miss Donna Hawthorne," Barris said. "On various pretexts he goes over to her place and colludes with her regularly."

Fred laughed. "*Colludes*. What do you mean?"

"I have followed him," Barris said, speaking slowly and distinctly, "in my own car. Without his knowledge."

"He goes there often?" Hank said.

"Yes, sir," Barris said. "Very often. As often as—"

"She's his girl," Fred said.

Barris said, "Mr. Arctor also—"

Turning to Fred, Hank said, "You think there's any substance in this?"

"We should definitely look at his evidence," Fred said.

"Bring in your evidence," Hank instructed Barris. "All of it. Names we want most of all—names, license-plate numbers, phone numbers. Have you ever seen Arctor deeply involved in large amounts of drugs? More than a user's?"

"Certainly," Barris said.

"What types?"

"Several kinds. I have samples. I carefully took samples . . . for you to analyze. I can bring them in too. Quite a bit, and varied."

Hank and Fred glanced at each other.

Barris, sightlessly gazing straight ahead, smiled.

"Is there anything else you want to say at this time?" Hank said to Barris. To Fred he said, "Maybe we should send an officer with him to get his evidence." Meaning, To make sure he doesn't panic and split, doesn't try to change his mind and pull out.

"There is one thing I would like to say," Barris said. "Mr. Arctor is an addict, addicted to Substance D, and his mind is deranged now. It has slowly become deranged over a period of time, and he is dangerous."

"*Dangerous*," Fred echoed.

"Yes," Barris declared. "He is already having episodes such as occur with brain damage from Substance D. The optic chiasm must be deteriorated, since a weak ipsilateral component . . . But also—" Barris cleared his throat. "Deterioration, as well, in the corpus callosum."

"This kind of unsupported speculation," Hank said, "as I already informed you, warned you, is worthless. Anyhow, we will send an officer with you to get your evidence. All right?"

Grinning, Barris nodded. "But naturally—"

"We'll arrange for an officer out of uniform."

"I might—" Barris gestured. "Be murdered. Mr. Arctor, as I say—"

Hank nodded. "All right, Mr. Barris, we appreciate this, and your extreme risk, and if it works out, if your information is of significant value in obtaining a conviction in court, then naturally—"

"I'm not here for that reason," Barris said. "The man is sick. Brain-damaged. From Substance D. The reason I am here—"

"We don't care why you're here," Hank said. "We only care whether your evidence and material amount to anything. The rest is your problem."

"Thank you, sir," Barris said, and grinned and grinned.

Chapter Thirteen

BACK at Room 203, the police psychology testing lab, Fred listened without interest as his test results were explained to him by both the psychologists.

"You show what we regard more as a competition phenomenon than impairment. Sit down."

"Okay," Fred said stoically, sitting down.

"Competition," the other psychologist said, "between the left and right hemispheres of your brain. It's not so much a single signal, defective or contaminated; it's more like two signals that interfere with each other by carrying conflicting information."

"Normally," the other psychologist explained, "a person uses the left hemisphere. The self-system or ego, or consciousness, is located there. It is dominant, because it's in the left hemisphere always that the speech center is located; more precisely, bilateralization involves a verbal ability or valency in the left, with spatial abilities in the right. The left can be compared to a digital computer; the right to an analogic. So bilateral function is not mere duplication; both percept systems monitor and process incoming data differently. But for you, neither hemisphere is dominant and they do *not* act in a compensatory fashion, each to the other. One tells you one thing, the other another."

"It's as if you have two fuel gauges on your car," the other man said, "and one says your tank is full and the other registers empty. They can't both be right. They conflict. But it's—in your case—not one functioning and one malfunctioning; it's . . . Here's what I mean. Both gauges study exactly the same amount of fuel: the same fuel, the same tank. Actually they test the same thing. You as the driver have only an indirect relationship to the fuel tank, via the gauge or, in your case, gauges. In fact, the tank could fall off entirely and you wouldn't know until some dashboard indicator told you or finally the engine stopped. There should never be two gauges reporting conflicting information, because as soon as that happens you have no knowledge of the condition being reported on *at all*. This is not the same as a gauge and a backup gauge, where the backup one cuts in when the regular one fouls up."

Fred said, "So what does this mean?"

"I'm sure you know already," the psychologist to the left said. "You've been experiencing it, without knowing why or what it is."

"The two hemispheres of my brain are competing?" Fred said.

"Yes."

"Why?"

"Substance D. It often causes that, functionally. This is what we expected; this is what the tests confirm. Damage having taken place in the normally dominant left hemisphere, the right hemisphere is attempting to compensate for the impairment. But the twin functions do not fuse, because this is an abnormal condition the body isn't prepared for. It should never happen. *Cross-cuing*, we call it. Related to split-brain phenomena. We could perform a right hemispherectomy, but—"

"Will this go away," Fred interrupted, "when I get off Substance D?"

"Probably," the psychologist on the left said, nodding. "It's a functional impairment."

The other man said, "It may be organic damage. It may be permanent. Time'll tell, and only after you are off Substance D for a long while. And off entirely."

"What?" Fred said. He did not understand the answer—was it yes or no? Was he damaged forever or not? Which had they said?

"Even if it's brain-tissue damage," one of the psychologists said, "there are experiments going on now in the removal of small sections from each hemisphere, to abort competing gestalt-processing. They believe eventually this may cause the original hemisphere to regain dominance."

"However, the problem there is that then the individual may only receive *partial* impressions—incoming sense data—for the rest of his life. Instead of two signals, he gets half a signal. Which is equally impairing, in my opinion."

"Yes, but partial noncompeting function is better than no function, since twin competing cross-cuing amounts to zero recept form."

"You see, Fred," the other man said, "you no longer have—"

"I will never drop any Substance D again," Fred said. "For the rest of my life."

"How much are you dropping now?"

"Not much." After an interval he said, "More, recently. Because of job stress."

"They undoubtedly should relieve you of your assignments," one psychologist said. "Take you off everything. You *are* impaired, Fred. And will be a while longer. At the very least. After that, no one can be sure. You may make a full comeback; you may not."

"How come," Fred grated, "that even if both hemispheres of my brain are dominant they don't receive the same stimuli? Why can't their two whatevers be synchronized, like stereo sound is?"

Silence.

"I mean," he said, gesturing, "the left hand and the right hand when they grip an object, the same object, should—"

"Left-handedness versus right-handedness, as for example what is meant by those terms with, say, a mirror image—in which the left hand 'becomes' the right hand . . ." The psychologist leaned down over Fred, who did not look up. "How would you define a left-hand glove compared to a right-hand glove so a person who had no knowledge of those terms could tell you which you meant? And not get the other? The mirror opposite?"

"A left-hand glove . . ." Fred said, and then stopped.

"It is as if one hemisphere of your brain is perceiving the world as reflected in a mirror. Through a mirror. See? So left becomes right, and all that that implies. And we don't know yet what that does imply, to see the world reversed like that. Topologically speaking, a left-hand glove is a right-hand glove *pulled through infinity."*

"Through a mirror," Fred said. A darkened mirror, he thought; a darkened scanner. And St. Paul meant, by a mirror, not a glass mirror—they didn't have those then—but a reflection of himself when he looked at the polished bottom of a metal pan. Luckman, in his theological readings, had told him that. Not through a telescope or lens system, which does not reverse, not through anything but seeing his own face reflected back up at him, reversed—pulled through infinity. Like they're telling me. It is not *through* a glass but as reflected *back* by a glass. And that reflection that returns to you: it is you, it is your face, but it isn't. And they didn't have cameras in those old days, and so that's the only way a person saw himself: backward.

I have seen myself backward.

I have in a sense begun to see the entire universe backward. With the other side of my brain!

"Topology," one psychologist was saying. "A little-understood science or math, whichever. As with the black holes in space, how—"

"Fred is seeing the world from inside out," the other man was declaring at the same moment. "From in front and from behind both, I guess. It's hard for us to say how it appears to him. Topology is the branch of math that investigates the properties of a geometric or other configuration that are unaltered if the thing is subjected to a one-to-one, *any* one-to-one, continuous transformation. But applied to psychology . . ."

"And when that occurs to objects, who knows what they're going to look like then? They'd be unrecognizable. As when a primitive sees a photograph of himself the first time, he doesn't recognize it as himself. Even though he's seen his reflection many times, in streams, from metal objects. Because his reflection is reversed and the photograph of himself isn't. So he doesn't know it's the identical person."

"He's accustomed only to the reversed reflected image and thinks he looks like that."

"Often a person hearing his own voice played back—"

"That's different. That has to do with the resonance in the sinus—"

"Maybe it's you fuckers," Fred said, "who're seeing the universe backward, like in a mirror. Maybe I see it right."

"You see it *both ways.*"

"Which is the—"

A psychologist said, "They used to talk about seeing only 'reflections' of reality. Not reality itself. The main thing wrong with a reflection is not that it isn't real, *but that it's reversed.* I wonder." He had an odd expression. "Parity. The scientific principle of parity. Universe and reflected image, the latter we take for the former, for some reason . . . because we lack bilateral parity."

"Whereas a photograph can compensate for the lack of bilateral hemispheric parity; it's not the object but it's not reversed, so that objection would make photographic images not images at all but the true form. Reverse of a reverse."

"But a photo can get accidentally reversed, too, if the negative is flipped—printed backward; you usually can tell only if there's writing. But not with a man's face. You could have two contact prints of a given man, one reversed, one not. A person who'd never met him couldn't tell which was correct, but he could see they were different and couldn't be superimposed."

"There, Fred, does that show you how complex the problem of formulating the distinction between a left-hand glove and—"

"Then shall it come to pass the saying that is written," a voice said. "Death is swallowed up. In victory." Perhaps only Fred heard it. "Because," the voice said, "as soon as the writing appears backward, then you know which is illusion and which is not. The confusion ends, and death, the last enemy, Substance Death, is swallowed not down into the body but up—in victory. Behold, I tell you the sacred secret now: *we shall not all sleep in death.*"

The mystery, he thought, the explanation, he means. Of a secret. A sacred secret. We shall not die.

The reflections shall leave
And it will happen fast.

We shall all be changed, and by that he means reversed back, suddenly. In the
twinkling of an eye!

Because, he thought glumly as he watched the police psychologists writing out their conclusions and signing them, we are fucking backward right now, I guess, every one of us; everyone and every damn thing, and distance, and even time. But how long, he thought, when a print is being made, a contact print, when the photographer discovers he's got the negative reversed, how long does it take to flip it? To reverse it again so it's like it's supposed to be?

A fraction of a second.

I understand, he thought, what that passage in the Bible means, Through a glass darkly. But my percept system is as fucked up as ever. Like they say. I understand but am helpless to help myself.

Maybe, he thought, since I see both ways at once, correctly and reversed, I'm the first person in human history to have it flipped and not-flipped simultaneously, and so get a glimpse of what it'll be when it's right. Although I've got the other as well, the regular. And which is which?

Which is reversed and which is not?

When do I see a photograph, when a reflection?

And how much allotment for sick pay or retirement or disability do I get while I dry out? he asked himself, feeling horror already, deep dread and coldness everywhere. *Wie kalt ist es in diesem unterirdischen Gewölbe! Das ist natürlich, es ist ja tief.* And I have to withdraw from the shit. I've seen people go through that. Jesus Christ, he thought, and shut his eyes.

"This may sound like metaphysics," one of them was saying, "but the math people say we may be on the verge of a new cosmology so much—"

The other said excitedly, "The infinity of time, which is expressed as eternity, as a loop! Like a loop of cassette tape!"

He had an hour to kill before he was supposed to be back in Hank's office, to listen to and inspect Jim Barris's evidence.

The building's cafeteria attracted him, so he walked that way, among those in uniform and those in scramble suits and those in slacks and ties.

Meanwhile, the psychologists' findings presumably were being taken up to Hank. They would be there when he arrived.

This will give me time to think, he reflected as he wandered into the cafeteria and lined up. Time. Suppose, he thought, time is round, like the Earth. You sail west to reach India. They laugh at you, but finally there's India in front, not behind. In time—maybe the Crucifixion lies ahead of us as we all sail along, thinking it's back east.

Ahead of him a secretary. Tight blue sweater, no bra, almost no skirt. It felt nice, checking her out; he gazed on and on, and finally she noticed him and edged off with her tray.

The First and Second Coming of Christ the same event, he thought; time a cassette loop. No wonder they were sure it'd happen, He'd be back.

He watched the secretary's behind, but then he realized that she could not possibly be noticing him back as he noticed her because in his suit he had no face and no ass. But she senses my scheming on her, he decided. Any chick with legs like that would sense it a lot, from every man.

You know, he thought, in this scramble suit I could hit her over the head and bang her forever and who'd know who did it? How could she identify me?

The crimes one could commit in these suits, he pondered. Also lesser trips, short of actual crimes, which you never did; always wanted to but never did.

"Miss," he said to the girl in the tight blue sweater, "you certainly have nice legs. But I suppose you recognize that or you wouldn't be wearing a microskirt like that."

The girl gasped. "Eh," she said. "Oh, now I know who you are."

"You do?" he said, surprised.

"Pete Wickam," the girl said.

"What?" he said.

"Aren't you Pete Wickam? You always are sitting across from me—aren't you, Pete?"

"Am I the guy," he said, "who's always sitting there and studying your legs and scheming a lot about you know what?"

She nodded.

"Do I have a chance?" he said.

"Well, it depends."

"Can I take you out to dinner some night?"

"I guess so."

"Can I have your phone number? So I can call you?"

The girl murmured, "You give me yours."

"I'll give it to you," he said, "if you'll sit with me right now, here, and have whatever you're having with me while I'm having my sandwich and coffee."

"No, I've got a girl friend over there—she's waiting."

"I could sit with you anyhow, both of you."

"We're going to discuss something private."

"Okay," he said.

"Well, then I'll see you, Pete." She moved off down the line with her tray and flatware and napkin.

He obtained his coffee and sandwich and found an empty table and sat by himself, dropping little bits of sandwich into the coffee and staring down at it.

They're fucking going to pull me off Arctor, he decided. I'll be in Synanon or New-Path or some place like that withdrawing and they'll station someone else to watch him and evaluate him. Some asshole who doesn't know jack shit about Arctor—they'll have to start all over from the beginning.

At least they can let me evaluate Barris's evidence, he thought. Not put me on temsuspens until after we go over that stuff, whatever it is.

If I did bang her and she got pregnant, he ruminated, the babies—no faces. Just blurs. He shivered.

I know I've got to be taken off. But why necessarily right away? If I could do a few more things . . . process Barris's info, participate in the decision. Or even just sit there and see what he's got. Find out for my own satisfaction finally what Arctor is up to. Is he anything? Is he not? They owe it to me to allow me to stay on long enough to find that out.

If I could just listen and watch, not say anything.

He sat there on and on, and later he noticed the girl in the tight blue sweater and her girl friend, who had short black hair, get up from their table and start to leave. The girl friend, who wasn't too foxy, hesitated and then approached Fred where he sat hunched over his coffee and sandwich fragments.

"Pete?" the short-haired girl said.

He glanced up.

"Um, Pete," she said nervously. "I just have a sec. Um, Ellen wanted to tell you this, but she chickened out. Pete, she would have gone out with you a long time ago, like maybe a month ago, like back in March even. If—"

"If what?" he said.

"Well, she wanted me to tell you that for some time she's wanted to clue you into the fact that you'd do a whole lot better if you used like, say, Scope."

"I wish I had known," he said, without enthusiasm.

"Okay, Pete," the girl said, relieved now and departing. "Catch you later." She hurried off, grinning.

Poor fucking Pete, he thought to himself. Was that for real? Or just a mind-blowing put-down of Pete by a pair of malice-head types who cooked it up seeing him—me—sitting here alone. Just a nasty little dig to— Aw, the hell with it, he thought.

Or it could be true, he decided as he wiped his mouth, crumpled up his napkin, and got heavily to his feet. I wonder if St. Paul had bad breath. He wandered from the cafeteria, his hands again shoved down in his pockets. Scramble suit pockets first and then inside that real suit pockets. Maybe that's why Paul was always in jail the latter part of his life. They threw him in for that.

Mindfucking trips like this always get laid on you at a time like this, he thought as he left the cafeteria. She dumped that on me on top of all the other bummers today—the big one out of the composite wisdom of the ages of psychological-testing pontification. That and then this. Shit, he thought. He felt even worse now than he had before; he could hardly walk, hardly think; his mind buzzed with confusion. Confusion and despair. Anyhow, he thought, Scope isn't any good; Lavoris is better. Except when you spit it out it looks like you're spitting blood. Maybe Micrin, he thought. That might be best.

If there was a drugstore in this building, he thought, I could get a bottle and use it before I go upstairs to face Hank. That way—maybe I'd feel more confident. Maybe I'd have a better chance.

I could use, he reflected, anything that'd help, anything at all. Any hint, like from that girl, any suggestion. He felt dismal and afraid. *Shit*, he thought, *what am I going to do?*

If I'm off everything, he thought, then I'll never see any of them again, any of my friends, the people I watched and knew. I'll be out of it; I'll be maybe retired the rest of my life—anyhow, I've seen the last of Arctor and Luckman and Jerry Fabin and Charles Freck and most of all Donna Hawthorne. I'll never see any of my friends again, for the rest of eternity. It's over.

Donna. He remembered a song his great-uncle used to sing years ago, in German. *"Ich seh', wie ein Engel im rosigen Duft / Sich tröstend zur Seite mir stellet,"* which his great-uncle had explained to him meant "I see, dressed like an angel, standing by my side to give me comfort," the woman he loved, the woman who saved him (in the song). In the song, not in real life. His great-uncle was dead, and it was a long time ago he'd heard those words. His great-uncle, German-born, singing in the house, or reading aloud.

> *Gott! Welch Dunkel hier! O grauenvolle Stille!*
> *Oed' ist es um mich her. Nichts lebet ausser mir . . .*

> God, how dark it is here, and totally silent.
> Nothing but me lives in this vacuum . . .

Even if my brain's not burned out, he realized, by the time I'm back on duty somebody else will have been assigned to them. Or they'll be dead or in the bucket or in federal clinics or just scattered, scattered, scattered. Burned out and destroyed, like me, unable to figure out what the fuck is happening. It has reached an end in any case, anyhow, for me. I've without knowing it already said good-by.

All I could ever do sometime, he thought, is play the holo-tapes back, to remember.

"I ought to go to the safe apartment . . ." He glanced around and became silent. I ought to go to the safe apartment and rip them off now, he thought. While I can. Later, they might be erased, and later I would not have access. Fuck the department, he thought; they can bill me against my back salary. By every ethical consideration those tapes of that house and the people in it belong to me.

And now those tapes, they're all I've got left out of all this; that's all I can hope to carry away.

But also, he thought rapidly, to play the tapes back I need the entire holo transport cube-projection resolution system there in the safe apartment. I'll need to disassemble it and cart it out of there piece by piece. The scanners and recording assemblies I won't need: just transport, playback components, and especially all the cube-projection gear. I can do it bit by bit; I have a key to that apartment. They'll require me to turn in the key, but I can get a dupe made right here before I turn it in; it's a conventional Schlag lock key. Then I can do it! He felt better, realizing this; he felt grim and moral and a little angry. At everyone. Pleasure at how he would make matters okay.

On the other hand, he thought, if I ripped off the scanners and recording heads and like that, I could go on monitoring. On my own. Keep surveillance alive, as I've been doing. For a while at least. But I mean, everything in life is just for a while —as witness this.

The surveillance, he thought, essentially should be maintained. And, if possible, by me. I should always be watching, watching and figuring out, even if I never do anything about what I see; even if I just sit there and observe silently, not seen: that is important, that I as a watcher of all that happens should be at my place.

Not for their sake. For mine.

Yeah, he amended, for theirs too. In case something happens, like when Luckman choked. If someone is watching—if I am watching—I can notice and get help. Phone for help. Bring assistance to them right away, the right kind.

Otherwise, he thought, they could die and no one would be the wiser. Know or even fucking care.

In wretched little lives like that, someone must intervene. Or at least mark their sad comings and goings. Mark and if possible permanently record, so they'll be remembered. For a better day, later on, when people will understand.

In Hank's office he sat with Hank and a uniformed officer and the sweating, grinning informant Jim Barris, while one of Barris's cassette tapes played on the table in front of them. Beside it, a second cassette recorded what it was playing, for a department duplicate.

". . . Oh, hi. Look, I can't talk."

"When, then?"

"Call you back."

"This can't wait."

"Well, what is it?"

"We intend to—"

Hank reached out, signaling to Barris to halt the tape. "Would you identify the voices for us, Mr. Barris?" Hank said.

"Yes," Barris eagerly agreed. "The female's voice is Donna Hawthorne, the male's is Robert Arctor."

"All right," Hank said nodding, then glancing at Fred. He

had Fred's medical report before him and was glancing at it. "Go ahead with your tape."

". . . half of Southern California tomorrow night," the male's voice, identified by the informant as Bob Arctor's, continued. "The Air Force Arsenal at Vandenberg AFB will be hit for automatic and semiautomatic weapons—"

Hank stopped reading the medical report and listened, cocking his scramble-suit-blurred head.

To himself and now to all in the room, Barris grinned; his fingers fiddled with paper clips taken from the table, fiddled and fiddled, as if knitting with metal webs of wire, knitting and fiddling and sweating and knitting.

The female, identified as Donna Hawthorne, said, "What about that disorientation drug the bikers nipped off for us? When do we carry that crud up to the watershed area to—"

"The organization needs the weapons first," the male's voice explained. "That's step B."

"Okay, but now I gotta go; I got a customer."

Click. Click.

Barris aloud, shifting in his chair, said, "I can identify the biker gang mentioned. It is mentioned on another—"

"You have more material of this sort?" Hank said. "To build up background? Or is this tape substantially it?"

"Much more."

"But it's this same sort of thing."

"It refers, yes, to the same conspiratorial organization and its plans, yes. This particular plot."

"Who are these people?" Hank said. "What organization?"

"They are a world-wide—"

"Their names. You're speculating."

"Robert Arctor, Donna Hawthorne, primarily. I have coded notes here, too . . ." Barris fumbled with a grubby notebook, half dropping it as he tried to open it.

Hank said, "I'm impounding all this stuff here, Mr. Barris, tapes and what you've got. Temporarily they're our property. We'll go over them ourselves."

"My handwriting, and the enciphered material which I—"

"You'll be on hand to explain it to us when we get to that point or feel we want anything explained." Hank signaled the uniformed cop, not Barris, to shut off the cassette. Barris reached toward it. At once the cop stopped him and pushed him back. Barris, blinking, gazed around, still fixedly smiling. "Mr. Barris," Hank said, "you will not be released, pending our study of this material. You're being charged, as a formality to keep you available, with giving false information to the authorities knowingly. This is, of course, only a pretext for your own safety, and we all realize that, but the formal charge will be lodged anyhow. It will be passed on to the D.A. but marked for hold. Is that satisfactory?" He did not wait for an answer; instead, he signaled the uniformed cop to take Barris out, leaving the evidence and shit and what-not on the table.

The cop led grinning Barris out. Hank and Fred sat facing each other across the littered table. Hank said nothing; he was reading the psychologists' findings.

After an interval he picked up his phone and dialed an in-building number. "I've got some unevaluated material here—I want you to go over it and determine how much of it is fake. Let me know about that, and then I'll tell you what to do with it next. It's about twelve pounds; you'll need one cardboard box, size three. Okay, thanks." He hung up. "The electronics and crypto lab," he informed Fred, and resumed reading.

Two heavily armed uniformed lab technicians appeared, bringing with them a lock-type steel container.

"We could only find this," one of them apologized as they carefully filled it with the items on the table.

"Who's down there?"

"Hurley."

"Have Hurley go over this sometime today for sure, and report when he's got a spurious index-factor for me. It must be today; tell him that."

The lab technicians locked the metal box and lugged it out of the office.

Tossing the medical-findings report on the table, Hank leaned back and said, "What do you— Okay, what's your response to Barris's evidence so far?"

Fred said, "That is my medical report you have there, isn't it?" He reached to pick it up, then changed his mind. "I think what he played, the little he played, it sounded genuine to me."

"It's a fake," Hank said. "Worthless."

"You may be right," Fred said, "but I don't agree."

"The arsenal they're talking about at Vandenberg is probably the OSI Arsenal." Hank reached for the phone. To himself, aloud, he said, "Let's see—who's the guy at OSI I talked to that time . . . he was in on Wednesday with some pictures . . ." Hank shook his head and turned away from the phone to confront Fred. "I'll wait. It can wait for the prelim spurious report. Fred?"

"What does my medical—"

"They say you're completely cuckoo."

Fred (as best he could) shrugged. "Completely?"

Wie kalt ist es in diesem unterirdischen Gewölbe!

"Possibly two brain cells still light up. But that's about all. Mostly short circuits and sparks."

Das ist natürlich, es ist ja tief.

"Two, you say," Fred said. "Out of how many?"

"I don't know. Brains have a lot of cells, I understand—trillions."

"More possible connections between them," Fred said, "than there are stars in the universe."

"If that's so, then you're not batting too good an average right now. About two cells out of—maybe sixty-five trillion?"

"More like sixty-five trillion trillion," Fred said.

"That's worse than the old Philadelphia Phillies under Connie Mack. They used to end the season with a percentage—"

"What do I get," Fred said, "for saying it happened on duty?"

"You get to sit in a waiting room and read a lot of *Saturday Evening Posts* and *Cosmopolitans* free."

"Where's that?"

"Where would you like?"

Fred said, "Let me think it over."

"I'll tell you what I'd do," Hank said. "I wouldn't go into a Federal clinic; I'd get about six bottles of good bourbon, I. W. Harper, and go up into the hills, up into the San Bernadino Mountains near one of the lakes, by myself, and just stay there all alone until it's over. Where no one can find me."

"But it may never be over," Fred said.

"Then never come back. Do you know anyone who has a cabin up there?"

"No," Fred said.

"Can you drive okay?"

"My—" He hesitated, and a dreamlike strength fell over him, relaxing him and mellowing him out. All the spatial relationships in the room shifted; the alteration affected even his awareness of time. "It's in the . . ." He yawned.

"You don't remember."

"I remember it's not functioning."

"We can have somebody drive you up. That would be safer, anyhow."

Drive me up where? he wondered. Up to what? Up roads, trails, paths, hiking and striding through Jell-O, like a tomcat on a leash who only wants to get back indoors, or get free.

He thought, *Ein Engel, der Gattin, so gleich, der führt mich zur Freiheit ins himmlische Reich.* "Sure," he said, and smiled. Relief. Pulling forward against the leash, trying and striving to get free, and then to lie down. "What do you think about me now," he said, "now that I've proved out like this—burned out, temporarily, anyhow. Maybe permanently."

Hank said, "I think you're a very good person."

"Thank you," Fred said.

"Take your gun with you."

"What?" he said.

"When you go off to the San Bernadino Mountains with the fifths of I. W. Harper. Take your gun."

"You mean for if I don't come out of it?"

Hank said, "Either way. Coming down off the amount they say you're on . . . Have it there with you."

"Okay."

"When you get back," Hank said, "call me. Let me know."

"Hell, I won't have my suit."

"Call me anyhow. With or without your suit."

Again he said, "Okay." Evidently it didn't matter. Evidently that was over.

"When you go pick up your next payment, there'll be a different amount. A considerable change this one time."

Fred said, "I get some sort of bonus for this, for what happened to me?"

"No. Read your penal code. An officer who willingly becomes an addict and does not promptly report it is subject on a misdemeanor charge—a fine of three thousand dollars and/or six months. You'll probably just be fined."

"*Willingly?*" he said, marveling.

"Noboby held a gun to your head and shot you up. Nobody dropped something in your soup. You knowingly and willingly took an addictive drug, brain-destructive and disorienting."

"I had to!"

Hank said, "You could have pretended to. Most officers manage to cope with it. And from the quantity they say you were dropping, you had to have been—"

"You're treating me like a crook. I am not a crook."

Picking up a clipboard and pen, Hank began to figure. "How much are you at, paywise? I can calculate it now if—"

"Could I pay the fine later on? Maybe in a series of monthly installments over like two years?"

Hank said, "Come on, Fred."

"Okay," he said.

"How much per hour?"

He couldn't remember.

"Well, then, how many logged hours?"

That, neither.

Hank tossed his clipboard back down. "Want a cigarette?" He offered Fred his pack.

"I'm getting off that, too," Fred said. "Everything. Including peanuts and . . ." He couldn't think. They both sat there, the two of them, in their scramble suits, both silent.

"Like I tell my kids," Hank began.

"I've got two kids," Fred said. "Two girls."

"I don't believe you do; you're not supposed to."

"Maybe not." He had begun to try to figure out when withdrawal would begin, and then he began to try to figure how many tabs of Substance D he had hidden here and there. And how much money he would have, when he got paid, for scoring.

"Maybe you want me to continue figuring what your payoff amount will consist of," Hank said.

"Okay," he said, and nodded vigorously. "Do that." He sat waiting, tensely, drumming on the table, like Barris.

"How much per hour?" Hank repeated, and then presently reached for his phone. "I'll call payroll."

Fred said nothing. Staring down, he waited. He thought, Maybe Donna can help me. Donna, he thought, please help me now.

"I don't think you're going to make it to the mountains," Hank said. "Even if somebody drives you."

"No."

"Where do you want to go?"

"Let me sit and think."

"Federal clinic?"

They sat.

He wondered what *not supposed to* meant.

"What about over to Donna Hawthorne's?" Hank said. "From all the information you've brought in and everyone else has, I know you're close."

"Yes." He nodded. "We are." And then he looked up and said, "How do you know that?"

Hank said, "By a process of elimination. I know who you *aren't* and there aren't an infinite number of suspects in this group—in fact, they're a very small group. We thought they'd lead us up higher, and maybe Barris will. You and I have spent a lot of time rapping together. I pieced it together a long time ago. That you're Arctor."

"I'm *who*?" he said, staring at Hank the scramble suit facing him. "I'm Bob Arctor?" He could not believe it. It made no sense to him. It did not fit anything he had done or thought; it was grotesque.

"Never mind," Hank said. "What's Donna's phone number?"

"She's probably at work." His voice trembled. "The perfume store. The number is—" He couldn't keep his voice steady, and he couldn't remember the number. The hell I am, he said to himself. I'm not Bob Arctor. But who am I? Maybe I'm—

"Get me Donna Hawthorne's number at work," Hank was saying rapidly into the phone. "Here," he said, holding the phone toward Fred. "I'll put you on the line. No, maybe I better not. I'll tell her to pick you up—where? We'll drive you there and drop you off; can't meet her here. What's a good place? Where do you usually meet her?"

"Take me to her place," he said. "I know how to get in."

"I'll tell her you're there and that you're withdrawing. I'll just say I know you and you asked me to call."

"Far out," Fred said. "I can dig it. Thanks, man."

Hank nodded and began to redial, an outside number. It seemed to Fred that he dialed each digit more and more slowly and it went on forever, and he shut his eyes, breathing to himself and thinking, Wow. I'm really out of it.

You really are, he agreed. Spaced, wired, burned out and strung-out and fucked. Completely fucked. He felt like laughing.

"We'll get you over there to her—" Hank began, and then shifted his attention to the phone, saying, "Hey, Donna, this is a buddy of Bob's, you know? Hey, man, he's in a bad way, I'm not jiving you. Hey, he—"

I can dig it, two voices thought inside his mind in unison as he heard his buddy laying it on Donna. And don't forget to tell her to bring me something; I'm really hurting. Can she score for me or something? Maybe supercharge me, like she does? He reached out to touch Hank but could not; his hand fell short.

"I'll do the same for you sometime," he promised Hank as Hank hung up.

"Just sit there until the car's outside. I'll put through the call now." Again Hank phoned, this time saying, "Motor pool? I want an unmarked car and officer out of uniform. What do you have available?"

They, inside the scramble suit, the nebulous blur, shut their eyes to wait.

"It might be I should get you taken to the hospital," Hank said. "You're very bad off; maybe Jim Barris poisoned you. We really are interested in Barris, not you; the scanning of the house was primarily to keep on Barris. We hoped to draw him in here . . . and we did." Hank was silent. "So that's why I knew pretty well that his tapes and the other items were faked. The lab will confirm. But Barris is into something heavy. Heavy and sick, and it has to do with guns."

"I'm a what, then?" he said suddenly, very loud.

"We had to get to Jim Barris and set him up."

"You fuckers," he said.

"The way we arranged it, Barris—if that's who he is—got progressively more and more suspicious that you were an undercover police agent, about to nail him or use him to get higher. So he—"

The phone rang.

"All right," Hank said later. "Just sit, Bob. Bob, Fred, whatever. Take comfort—we did get the bugger and he's a—well, what you just now called us. You know it's worth it. Isn't it? To entrap him? A thing like that, whatever it is he's doing?"

"Sure, worth it." He could hardly speak; he grated mechanically.

Together they sat.

On the drive to New-Path, Donna pulled off the road where they could see the lights below, on all sides. But the pain had started for him now; she could see that, and there wasn't much time left. She had wanted to be with him one more time. Well, she had waited too long. Tears ran down his cheeks, and he had started to heave and vomit.

"We'll sit for a few minutes," she told him, guiding him through the bushes and weeds, across the sandy soil, among the discarded beer cans and debris. "I—"

"Do you have your hash pipe?" he managed to say.

"Yes," she said. They had to be far enough from the road not to be noticed by the police. Or at least far enough so they could ditch the hash pipe if an officer came along. She would see the police car park, its lights off, covertly, a way off, and the officer approach on foot. There would be time.

She thought, Time enough for that. Time enough to be safe from the law. But no time any more for Bob Arctor. His time —at least if measured in human standards—had run out. It was another kind of time which he had entered now. Like, she thought, the time a rat has: to run back and forth, to be futile. To move without planning, back and forth, back and forth. But at least he can still see the lights below us. Although maybe for him it doesn't matter.

They found a sheltered place, and she got out the foil-wrapped fragment of hash and lit the hash pipe. Bob Arctor, beside her, did not seem to notice. He had dirtied himself, but she knew he could not help it. In fact, he probably didn't even know it. They all got this way during withdrawal.

"Here." She bent toward him, to supercharge him. But he did not notice her either. He just sat doubled up, enduring the stomach cramps, vomiting and soiling himself, shivering, and crazily moaning to himself, a kind of song.

She thought then of a guy she had known once, who had seen God. He had acted much like this, moaning and crying, although he had not soiled himself. He had seen God in a flashback after an acid trip; he had been experimenting with water-soluble vitamins, huge doses of them. The orthomolecular formula that was supposed to improve neural firing in the brain, speed it up and synchronize it. With that guy, though, instead of merely becoming smarter, he had seen God. It had been a complete surprise to him.

"I guess," she said, "we never know what's in store for us."

Beside her, Bob Arctor moaned and did not answer.

"Did you know a dude named Tony Amsterdam?"

There was no response.

Donna inhaled from the hash pipe and contemplated the lights spread out below them; she smelled the air and listened. "After he saw God he felt really good, for around a year. And then he felt really bad. Worse than he ever had before in his life. Because one day it came over him, he began to realize, that he was never going to see God again; he was going to live out his whole remaining life, decades, maybe fifty years, and see nothing but what he had always seen. What we see. He was worse off than if he hadn't seen God. He told me one day he got really mad; he just freaked out and started cursing and smashing things in his apartment. He even smashed his stereo. He realized he was going to have to live on and on like he was, seeing nothing. Without any purpose. Just a lump of flesh grinding along, eating, drinking, sleeping, working, crapping."

"Like the rest of us." It was the first thing Bob Arctor had managed to say; each word came with retching difficulty.

Donna said, "That's what I told him. I pointed that out. We were all in the same boat and it didn't freak the rest of us. And he said, 'You don't know what I saw. You don't know.'"

A spasm passed through Bob Arctor, convulsing him, and then he choked out, "Did . . . he say what it was like?"

"Sparks. Showers of colored sparks, like when something goes wrong with your TV set. Sparks going up the wall, sparks in the air. And the whole world was a living creature, wherever he looked. And there were no accidents: everything fitted together and happened on purpose, to achieve something— some goal in the future. And then he saw a doorway. For about a week he saw it wherever he looked—inside his apartment, outdoors when he was walking to the store or driving. And it was always the same proportions, very narrow. He said it was very—pleasing. That's the word he used. He never tried to go through it; he just looked at it, because it was so pleasing. Outlined in vivid red and gold light, he said. As if the sparks had collected into lines, like in geometry. And then after that he never saw it again his whole life, and that's what finally made him so fucked up."

After a time Bob Arctor said, "What was on the other side?"

Donna said, "He said there was another world on the other side. He could see it."

"He . . . never went through it?"

"That's why he kicked the shit out of everything in his apartment; he never thought of going through it, he just admired the doorway and then later he couldn't see it at all and it was too late. It opened for him a few days and then it was closed and gone forever. Again and again he took a whole lot of LSD and those water-soluble vitamins, but he never saw it again; he never found the combination."

Bob Arctor said, "What was on the other side?"

"He said it was always nighttime."

"Nighttime!"

"There was moonlight and water, always the same. Nothing moved or changed. Black water, like ink, and a shore, a beach of an island. He was sure it was Greece, ancient Greece. He figured out the doorway was a weak place in time, and he was seeing back into the past. And then later on, when he couldn't see it any more, he'd be on the freeway driving along, with all the trucks, and he'd get madder than hell. He said he couldn't stand all the motion and noise, everything going this way and that, all the clanking and banging. Anyhow, he never could figure out why they showed him what they showed him. He really believed it was God, and it was the doorway to the next world, but in the final analysis all it did was mess up his head. He couldn't hold on to it so he couldn't cope with it. Every time he met anybody, after a while he'd tell them he'd lost everything."

Bob Arctor said, "That's how I am."

"There was a woman on the island. Not exactly—more a statue. He said it was of the Cyrenaican Aphrodite. Standing there in the moonlight, pale and cold and made out of marble."

"He should have gone through the doorway when he had the chance."

Donna said, "He didn't have the chance. It was a promise. Something to come. Something better a long time in the future. Maybe after he—" She paused. "When he died."

"He missed out," Bob Arctor said. "You get one chance and that's it." He shut his eyes against the pain and the sweat streaking his face. "Anyhow what's a burned-out acid head know? What do any of us know? I can't talk. Forget it." He turned away from her, into the darkness, convulsing and shuddering.

"They show us trailers now," Donna said. She put her arms around him and held on to him as tightly as she could, rocking him back and forth. "So we'll hold out."

"That's what you're trying to do. With me now."

"You're a good man. You've been dealt a bad deal. But life isn't over for you. I care for you a lot. I wish . . ." She continued to hold him, silently, in the darkness that was swallowing him up from inside. Taking over even as she held on to him. "You are a good and kind person," she said. "And this is unfair but it has to be this way. Try to wait for the end. Sometime, a long time from now, you'll see the way you saw before. It'll come back to you." Restored, she thought. On the day when everything taken away unjustly from people will be restored to them. It may take a thousand years, or longer than that, but that day will come, and all the balances will be set right. Maybe, like Tony Amsterdam, you have seen a vision of God that is gone only temporarily; withdrawn, she thought, rather than ended. Maybe inside the terribly burned and burning circuits of your head that char more and more, even as I hold you, a spark of color and light in some disguised form manifested itself, unrecognized, to lead you, by its memory, through the years to come, the dreadful years ahead. A word not fully understood, some small thing seen but not understood; some fragment of a star mixed with the trash of this world, to guide you by reflex until the day . . . but it was so remote. She could not herself truly imagine it. Mingled with the commonplace, something from another world perhaps had appeared to Bob Arctor before it was over. All she could do now was hold him and hope.

But when he found it once again, if they were lucky, pattern-recognition would take place. Correct comparison in the right hemisphere. Even at the subcortical level available to him. And the journey, so awful for him, so costly, so evidently without point, would be finished.

A light shone in her eyes. Standing in front of her, a cop with nightstick and flashlight. "Would you two please stand up?" the officer said. "And show me your identification? You first, miss."

She let go of Bob Arctor, who slid sideways until he lay against the ground; he was unaware of the cop, who had approached them up the hill, stealthily, from a service road below. Getting her wallet out of her purse, Donna motioned the officer away, where Bob Arctor could not hear. For several minutes the officer studied her identification by the muted light of his flashlight, and then he said,

"You're undercover for the federal people."

"Keep your voice down," Donna said.

"I'm sorry." The officer handed the wallet back to her.

"Just fucking take off," Donna said.

The officer shone his light in her face briefly, and then turned away; he departed as he had approached, noiselessly.

When she returned to Bob Arctor, it was obvious that he had never been aware of the cop. He was aware of almost nothing, now. Scarcely of her, let alone anyone or anything else.

Far off, echoing, Donna could hear the police car moving down the rutted, invisible service road. A few bugs, perhaps a lizard, made their way through the dry weeds around them. In the distance the 91 Freeway glowed in a pattern of lights, but no sound reached them; it was too remote.

"Bob," she said softly. "Can you hear me?"

No answer.

All the circuits are welded shut, she thought. Melted and fused. And no one is going to get them open, no matter how hard they try. And they are going to try.

"Come on," she said, tugging at him, attempting to get him to his feet. "We've got to get started."

Bob Arctor said, "I can't make love. My thing's disappeared."

"They're expecting us," Donna said firmly. "I have to sign you in."

"But what'll I do if my thing's disappeared? Will they still take me in?"

Donna said, "They'll take you."

It requires the greatest kind of wisdom, she thought, to know when to apply injustice. How can justice fall victim, ever, to what is right? How can this happen? She thought, Because there is a curse on this world, and all this proves it; this is the proof right here. Somewhere, at the deepest level possible, the mechanism, the construction of things, fell apart, and up from what remained swam the need to do all the various sort of unclear wrongs the wisest choice has made us act out. It must have started thousands of years ago. By now it's infiltrated into the nature of everything. And, she thought, into every one of us. We can't turn around or open our mouth and speak, decide at all, without doing it. I don't even care how it got started, when or why. She thought, I just hope it'll end some time. Like with Tony Amsterdam; I just hope one day the shower of brightly colored sparks will return, and this time we'll all see it. The narrow doorway where there's peace on the far side. A statue, the sea, and what looks like moonlight. And nothing stirring, nothing to break the calm.

A long, long time ago, she thought. Before the curse, and everything and everyone became this way. The Golden Age, she thought, when wisdom and justice were the same. Before it all shattered into cutting fragments. Into broken bits that don't fit, that can't be put back together, hard as we try.

Below her, in the darkness and distribution of urban lights, a police siren sounded. A police car in hot pursuit. It sounded like a deranged animal, greedy to kill. And knowing that it soon would. She shivered; the night air had become cold. It was time to go.

It isn't the Golden Age now, she thought, with noises like that in the darkness. Do I emit that kind of greedy noise? she asked herself. Am I that thing? Closing in, or having closed in?

Having caught?

Beside her, the man stirred and moaned as she helped him up. Helped him to his feet and back to her car, step by step, helped him, helped him, helped him continue on. Below them, the noise of the police car had abruptly ceased; it had stopped its quarry. Its job was done. Holding Bob Arctor against her, she thought, Mine is done, too.

The two New-Path staff members stood surveying the thing on their floor that lay puking and shivering and fouling itself, its arms hugging itself, embracing its own body as if to stop itself, against the cold that made it tremble so violently.

"What is it?" one staff member said.

Donna said, "A person."

"Substance D?"

She nodded.

"It ate his head. Another loser."

She said to the two of them, "It's easy to win. Anybody can win." Bending down over Robert Arctor she said, silently,

Good-by.

They were putting an old army blanket over him as she left. She did not look back.

Getting into her car, she drove at once onto the closest freeway, into the thickest traffic possible. From the box of tapes on the floor of the car she took the Carole King *Tapestry* tape, her favorite of all she had, and pushed it into the tape deck; at the same time, she tugged loose the Ruger pistol magnetically mounted out of sight beneath the dashboard. In top gear she tailgated a truck carrying wooden cases of quart bottles of Coca-Cola, and as Carole King sang in stereo she emptied the clip of the Ruger at the Coke bottles a few feet ahead of her.

While Carole King sang soothingly about people sitting down and turning into toads, Donna managed to get four bottles before the gun's clip was empty. Bits of glass and smears of Coke splattered the windshield of her car. She felt better.

Justice and honesty and loyalty are not properties of this

world, she thought; and then, by God, she rammed her old enemy, her ancient foe, the Coca-Cola truck, which went right on going without noticing. The impact spun her small car around; her headlights dimmed out, horrible noises of fender against tire shrieked, and then she was off the freeway onto the emergency strip, facing the other direction, water pouring from her radiator, with motorists slowing down to gape.

Come back, you motherfucker, she said to herself, but the Coca-Cola truck was long gone, probably undented. Maybe a scratch. Well, it was bound to happen sooner or later, her war, her taking on a symbol and a reality that outweighed her. Now my insurance rates will go up, she realized as she climbed from her car. In this world you pay for tilting with evil in cold, hard cash.

A late-model Mustang slowed and the driver, a man, called to her, "You want a ride, miss?"

She did not answer. She just kept on going. A small figure on foot facing an infinity of oncoming lights.

Chapter Fourteen

MAGAZINE clipping thumbtacked to the wall of the lounge at Samarkand House, New-Path's residence building in Santa Ana, California:

> When the senile patient awakens in the morning and asks
> for his mother, remind him that she is long since dead,
> that he is over eighty years old and living in a convales-
> cent home, and that this is 1992 and not 1913 and that he
> must face reality and the fact that

A resident had torn down the rest of the item; it ended there. Evidently it had been clipped from a professional nursing magazine; it was on slick paper.

"What you'll be doing here first," George, the staff member, told him, leading him down the hall, "is the bathrooms. The floors, the basins, especially the toilets. There're three bathrooms in this structure, one on each floor."

"Okay," he said.

"Here's a mop. And a pail. You feel you know how to do this? Clean a bathroom? Start, and I'll watch you and give you pointers."

He carried the pail to the tub on the back porch and he poured soap into it and then ran the hot water. All he could see was the foam of water directly before him; foam and the roar.

But he could hear George's voice, out of sight. "Not too full, because you won't be able to lift it."

"Okay."

"You have a little trouble telling where you are," George said, after a time.

"I'm at New-Path." He set the pail down on the floor and it slopped; he stood staring down at it.

"New-Path where?"

"In Santa Ana."

George lifted the pail up for him, showing him how to grip the wire handle and swing it along as he walked. "Later on I think we'll transfer you to the island or one of the farms. First you have to go through the dishpan."

"I can do that," he said. "Dishpans."

"Do you like animals?"

"Sure."

"Or farming?"

"Animals."

"We'll see. We'll wait until we're acquainted with you better. Anyhow, that'll be a while; everyone is in the dishpan for a month. Everyone who comes in the door."

"I'd sort of like to live in the country," he said.

"We maintain several types of facilities. We'll determine what's best suited. You know, you can smoke here, but it isn't encouraged. This isn't Synanon; they don't let you smoke."

He said, "I don't have any more cigarettes."

"We give each resident one pack a day."

"Money?" He didn't have any.

"It's without cost. There's never any cost. You paid your cost." George took the mop, pushed it down into the pail, showed him how to mop.

"How come I don't have any money?"

"The same reason you don't have any wallet or any last name. It'll be given back to you, all given back. That's what we want to do: give you back what's been taken away from you."

He said, "These shoes don't fit."

"We depend on donations, but new ones only, from stores. Later on maybe we can measure you. Did you try all the shoes in the carton?"

"Yes," he said.

"All right, this is the bathroom here on the basement floor; do it first. Then when that's done, really done well, really perfect, then go upstairs—bring the mop and bucket—and I'll show you the bathroom up there, and then after that the bathroom on the third floor. But you got to get permission to go up there to the third floor, because that's where the chicks live, so ask one of the staff first; never go up there without permission." He slapped him on the back. "All right, Bruce? Understand?"

"Okay," Bruce said, mopping.

George said, "You'll be doing this kind of work, cleaning these bathrooms, until you get so you can do a good job. It doesn't matter what a person does; it's that he gets so he can do it right and be proud of it."

"Will I ever be like I was again?" Bruce asked.

"What you were brought you here. If you become what you were again then sooner or later it'd bring you here again. Next time you might not make it here, even. Isn't that right? You're lucky you got here; you almost didn't get here."

"Somebody else drove me here."

"You're fortunate. The next time they might not. They might dump you on the side of the freeway somewhere and say the hell with it."

He continued mopping.

"The best way is to do the bowls first, then the tub, then the toilets, and the floor last."

"Okay," he said, and put the mop away.

"There's a certain knack to it. You'll master it."

Concentrating, he saw before him cracks in the enamel of the basin; he dribbled cleanser down into the cracks and ran hot water. The steam rose, and he stood within it, unmoving, as the steam grew. He liked the smell.

After lunch he sat in the lounge drinking coffee. No one spoke to him, because they understood he was withdrawing. Sitting drinking from his cup, he could hear their conversation. They all knew one another.

"If you could see out from inside a dead person you could still see, but you couldn't operate the eye muscles, so you couldn't focus. You couldn't turn your head or your eyeballs. All you could do would be wait until some object passed by. You'd be frozen. Just wait and wait. It'd be a terrible scene."

He gazed down at the steam of his coffee, only that. The steam rose; he liked the smell.

"Hey."

A hand touched him. From a woman.

"Hey."

He looked sideways a little.

"How you doing?"

"Okay," he said.

"Feel any better?"

"I feel okay," he said.

He watched his coffee and the steam and did not look at her

or any of them; he looked down and down at the coffee. He liked the warmth of the smell.

"You could see somebody when they passed by directly in front of you, and only then. Or whichever way you were looking, no other. If a leaf or something floated over your eye, that would be it, forever. Only the leaf. Nothing more; you couldn't turn."

"Okay," he said, holding the coffee, the cup with both his hands.

"Imagine being sentient but not alive. Seeing and even knowing, but not alive. Just looking out. Recognizing but not being alive. A person can die and still go on. Sometimes what looks out at you from a person's eyes maybe died back in childhood. What's dead in there still looks out. It's not just the body looking at you with nothing in it; there's still something in there but it died and just keeps on looking and looking; it can't stop looking."

Another person said, "That's what it means to die, to not be able to stop looking at whatever's in front of you. Some darn thing placed directly there, with nothing you can do about it such as selecting anything or changing anything. You can only accept what's put there as it is."

"How'd you like to gaze at a beer can throughout eternity? It might not be so bad. There'd be nothing to fear."

Before dinner, which was served to them in the dining room, they had Concept time. Several Concepts were put on the blackboard by different staff members and discussed.

He sat with his hands folded in his lap, watching the floor and listening to the big coffee urn heating up; it went *whoop-whoop,* and the sound frightened him.

"Living and unliving things are exchanging properties."

Seated here and there on folding chairs, everyone discussed that. They seemed familiar with the Concept. Evidently these were parts of New-Path's way of thought, perhaps even memorized and then thought about again and again. *Whoop-whoop.*

"The drive of unliving things is stronger than the drive of living things."

They talked about that. *Whoop-whoop.* The noise of the

coffee urn got louder and louder and scared him more, but he did not move or look; he sat where he was, listening. It was hard to hear what they were saying, because of the urn.

"We are incorporating too much unliving drive within us. And exchanging— Will somebody go look at that damn coffeepot to see why it's doing that?"

There was a break while someone examined the coffee urn. He sat staring down, waiting.

"I'll write this again. *'We are exchanging too much passive life for the reality outside us.'*"

They discussed that. The coffee urn became silent, and they trooped over to get coffee.

"Don't you want some coffee?" A voice behind him, touching him. "Ned? Bruce? What's his name—Bruce?"

"Okay." He got up and followed them to the coffee urn. He waited his turn. They watched as he put cream and sugar into his cup. They watched him return to his chair, the same one; he made certain he found it again, to reseat himself and go on listening. The warm coffee, its steam, made him feel good.

"Activity does not necessarily mean life. Quasars are active. And a monk meditating is not inanimate."

He sat looking at the empty cup; it was a china mug. Turning it over, he discovered printing on the bottom, and cracked glaze. The mug looked old, but it had been made in Detroit.

"Motion that is circular is the deadest form of the universe."

Another voice said, "Time."

He knew the answer to that. Time is round.

"Yes, we've got to break now, but does anyone have a fast final comment?"

"Well, following the line of least resistance, that's the rule of survival. Following, not leading."

Another voice, older, said, "Yes, the followers survive the leader. Like with Christ. Not vice versa."

"We better eat, because Rick stops serving exactly at five-fifty now."

"Talk about that in the Game, not now."

Chairs screaked, creaked. He rose too, carried the old mug to the tray of others, and joined them in line out. He could smell cold clothes around him, good smells but cold.

It sounds like they're saying passive life is good, he thought. But there is no such thing as passive life. That's a contradiction.

He wondered what life was, what it meant; maybe he did not understand.

A huge bunch of donated flashy clothes had arrived. Several people stood with armfuls, and some had put shirts on, trying them out and getting approval.

"Hey, Mike. You're a sharp dude."

In the middle of the lounge stood a short stocky man, with curly hair and pug face; he shifted his belt, frowning. "How do you work this here? I don't see how you get it to stay. Why doesn't it loosen?" He had a three-inch buckleless belt with metal rings and he did not know how to cinch the rings. Glancing around, eyes twinkling, he said, "I think they gave me one nobody else could work."

Bruce went over behind him, reached around him, and cinched the belt looped back through the rings.

"Thanks," Mike said. He sorted through several dress shirts, lips pursed. To Bruce he said, "When I get married I'm going to wear one of these."

"Nice," he said.

Mike strolled toward two women at the far end of the lounge; they smiled. Holding a burgundy floral shirt up against himself, Mike said, "I'm going out on the town."

"All right, go in and get dinner!" the house director yelled briskly, in his powerful voice. He winked at Bruce. "How you doing, fella?"

"Fine," Bruce said.

"Sound like you got a cold."

"Yes," he agreed, "it's from coming off. Could I have any Dristan or—"

"No chemicals," the house director said. "Nothing. Hurry on in and eat. How's your appetite?"

"Better," he said, following. They smiled at him, from tables.

After dinner he sat halfway up the wide stairs to the second floor. No one spoke to him; a conference was taking place. He sat there until it finished. Everyone emerged, filling the hall.

He felt them seeing him, and maybe some spoke to him. He

sat on the stairs, hunched over, his arms wrapped around him, seeing and seeing. The dark carpet before his eyes.

Presently no more voices.

"Bruce?"

He did not stir.

"Bruce?" A hand touched him.

He said nothing.

"Bruce, come on into the lounge. You're supposed to be in your room in bed, but, see, I want to talk to you." Mike led him by waving him to follow. He accompanied Mike down the stairs and into the lounge, which was empty. When they were in the lounge Mike shut the door.

Seating himself in a deep chair, Mike indicated for him to sit down facing him. Mike appeared tired; his small eyes were ringed, and he rubbed his forehead.

"I been up since five-thirty this morning," Mike said.

A knock; the door started to open.

Very loudly, Mike yelled, "I want nobody to come in here; we're talking. Hear?"

Mumbles. The door shut.

"Y'know, you better change your shirt a couple times a day," Mike said. "You're sweating something fierce."

He nodded.

"What part of the state are you from?"

He said nothing.

"You come to me from now on when you feel this bad. I went through the same thing, about a year and a half ago. They used to drive me around in cars. Different staff members. You met Eddie? The tall thin drink-a-water that puts down everybody? He drove me for eight days around and around. Never left me alone." Mike yelled suddenly, "Will you get out of here? We're in here talking. Go watch the TV." His voice sank, and he eyed Bruce. "Sometimes you got to do that. Never leave someone alone."

"I see," Bruce said.

"Bruce, be careful you don't take your own life."

"Yes, sir," Bruce said, staring down.

"Don't call me sir!"

He nodded.

"Were you in the Service, Bruce? Is that what it was? You got on the stuff in the Service?"

"No."

"You shoot it or drop it?"

He made no sound.

" 'Sir,' " Mike said. "I've served, myself, ten years in prison. One time I saw eight guys in our row of cells cut their throats in one day. We slept with our feet in the toilet, our cells were that small. That's what prison is, you sleep with your feet in the toilet. You never been in prison, have you?"

"No," he said.

"But on the other hand, I saw prisoners eighty years old still happy to be alive and wanting to stay alive. I remember when I was on dope, and I shot it; I started shooting when I was in my teens. I never did anything else. I shot up and then I went in for ten years. I shot up so much—heroin and D together— that I never did anything else; I never saw anything else. Now I'm off it and I'm out of prison and I'm here. You know what I notice the most? You know what the big difference is I notice? Now I can walk down the street outside and see something. I can hear water when we visit the forest—you'll see our other facilities later on, farms and so forth. I can walk down the street, the ordinary street, and see the little dogs and cats. I never saw them before. All I saw was dope." He examined his wristwatch. "So," he added, "I understand how you feel."

"It's hard," Bruce said, "getting off."

"Everybody here got off. Of course, some go back on. If you left here you'd go back on. You know that."

He nodded.

"No person in this place has had an easy life. I'm not saying your life's been easy. Eddie would. He'd tell you that your troubles are mickey mouse. Nobody's troubles are mickey mouse. I see how bad you feel, but I felt that way once. Now I feel a lot better. Who's your roommate?"

"John."

"Oh yeah. John. Then you must be down in the basement."

"I like it," he said.

"Yeah, it's warm there. You probably get cold a lot. Most of us do, and I remember I did; I shook all the time, and crapped in my pants. Well, I tell you, you won't have to go through this again, if you stay here at New-Path."

"How long?" he said.

"The rest of your life."

Bruce raised his head.

"*I* can't leave," Mike said. "I'd get back on dope if I went out there. I've got too many buddies outside. I'd be back on the corner again, dealing and shooting, and then back in the prison for twenty years. You know—hey—I'm thirty-five years old and I'm getting married for the first time. Have you met Laura? My fiancée?"

He wasn't sure.

"Pretty girl, plump. Nice figure?"

He nodded.

"She's afraid to go out the door. Someone has to go with her. We're going to the zoo . . . we're taking the Executive Director's little boy to the San Diego Zoo next week, and Laura's scared to death. More scared than I am."

Silence.

"You heard me say that?" Mike said. "That I'm scared to go to the zoo?"

"Yes."

"I never have been to a zoo that I can recall," Mike said. "What do you do at a zoo? Maybe you know."

"Look into different cages and open confined areas."

"What kind of animals do they have?"

"All kinds."

"Wild ones, I guess. Normally wild. And exotical ones."

"At the San Diego Zoo they have almost every wild animal," Bruce said.

"They have one of those . . . what are they? Koala bears."

"Yes."

"I saw a commercial on TV," Mike said. "With a koala bear in it. They hop. They resemble a stuffed toy."

Bruce said, "The old Teddy bear, that kids have, that was created based on the koala bear, back in the twenties."

"Is that right. I guess you'd have to go to Australia to see a koala bear. Or are they extinct now?"

"There're plenty in Australia," Bruce said, "but export is banned. Live or the hides. They almost got extinct."

"I never been anywhere," Mike said, "except when I ran stuff from Mexico up to Vancouver, British Columbia. I always took the same route, so I never saw anything. I just drove very fast to get it over with. I drive one of the Foundation cars. If you feel like it, if you feel very bad, I'll drive you around. I'll drive and we can talk. I don't mind. Eddie and some others not here now did it for me. I don't mind."

"Thank you."

"Now we both ought to hit the sack. Have they got you on kitchen stuff in the morning yet? Setting tables and serving?"

"No."

"Then you get to sleep to the same time I do. I'll see you at breakfast. You sit at the table with me and I'll introduce you to Laura."

"When are you getting married?"

"A month and a half. We'd be pleased if you were there. Of course, it'll be here at the building, so everyone will attend."

"Thank you," he said.

He sat in the Game and they screamed at him. Faces, all over, screaming; he gazed down.

"Y'know what he is? A kissy-facy!" One shriller voice made him peer up. Among the awful screaming distortions one Chinese girl, howling. "You're a kissy-facy, that's what you are!"

"Can you fuck yourself? Can you fuck yourself?" the others chanted at him, curled up in a circle on the floor.

The Executive Director, in red bell-bottoms and pink slippers, smiled. Glittery little broken eyes, like a spook's. Rocking back and forth, his spindly legs tucked under him, without a pillow.

"Let's see you fuck yourself!"

The Executive Director seemed to enjoy it when his eyes saw something break; his eyes glinted and filled with mirth. Like a dramatic stage queer, from some old court, draped in flair, colorful, he peeped around and enjoyed. And then from time to time his voice warbled out, grating and monotonous, like a metal noise. A scraping mechanical hinge.

"The kissy-facy!" the Chinese girl howled at him; beside her another girl flapped her arms and bulged her cheeks, plop-plop.

"Here!" the Chinese girl howled, swiveled around to jut her rump at him, pointing to it and howling at him, "Kiss my ass, then, kissy-facy! He wants to kiss people, kiss this, kissy-facy!"

"Let's see you fuck yourself!" the family chanted. "Jack yourself off, kissy-facy!"

He shut his eyes, but his ears still heard.

"You pimp," the Executive Director said slowly to him. Monotonously. "You fuck. You dong. You shit. You turd prick. You—" On and on.

His ears still brought in sounds, but they blended. He glanced up once when he made out Mike's voice, audible during a lull. Mike sat gazing at him impassively, a little reddened, his neck swollen in the too-tight collar of his dress shirt.

"Bruce," Mike said, "what's the matter? What brought you here? What do you want to tell us? Can you tell us anything about yourself at all?"

"Pimp!" George screamed, bouncing up and down like a rubber ball. "What were you, pimp?"

The Chinese girl leaped up, shrieking, "Tell us, you cocksucking fairy whore pimp, you ass-kisser, you fuck!"

He said, "I am an eye."

"You turd prick," the Executive Director said. "You weakling. You puke. You suck-off. You snatch."

He heard nothing now. And forgot the meaning of the words, and, finally, the words themselves.

Only, he sensed Mike watching him, watching and listening, hearing nothing; he did not know, he did not recall, he felt little, he felt bad, he wanted to leave.

The Vacuum in him grew. And he was actually a little glad.

It was late in the day.

"Look in here," a woman said, "where we keep the freaks."

He felt frightened as she opened the door. The door fell aside and noise spilled out of the room, the size surprising him; but he saw many little children playing.

That evening he watched two older men feed the children milk and little foods, sitting in a separate small alcove near the kitchen. Rick, the cook, gave the two older men the children's food first while everyone waited in the dining room.

Smiling at him, a Chinese girl, carrying plates to the dining room, said, "You like kids?"

"Yes," he said.

"You can sit with the kids and eat there with them."

"Oh," he said.

"You can feed them later on like in a month or two." She hesitated. "When we're positive you won't hit them. We have a rule: the children can't never be hit for anything they do."

"Okay," he said. He felt warmed into life, watching the children eat; he seated himself, and one of the smaller children crept up on his lap. He began spooning food to the child. Both he and the child felt, he thought, equally warm. The Chinese girl smiled at him and then passed on with the plates to the dining room.

For a long time he sat among the children, holding first one and then another. The two older men quarreled with the children and criticized each other's way of feeding. Bits and hunks and smudges of food covered the table and floor; startled, he realized that the children had been fed and were going off into their big playroom to watch cartoons on TV. Awkwardly, he bent down to clean up spilled food.

"No, that's not your job!" one of the elderly men said sharply. "I'm supposed to do that."

"Okay," he agreed, rising, bumping his head on the edge of the table. He held spilled food in his hand and he gazed at it, wonderingly.

"Go help clear the dining room!" the other older man said to him. He had a slight speech impediment.

One of the kitchen help, someone from the dishpan, said to him in passing, "You need permission to sit with the kids."

He nodded, standing there, puzzled.

"That's for the old folk," the dishpan person said. "Baby-sitting." He laughed. "That can't do nothing else." He continued by.

One child remained. She studied him, large-eyed, and said to him, "What's your name?"

He answered nothing.

"I said, what's your name?"

Reaching cautiously, he touched a bit of beef on the table. It had cooled now. But, aware of the child beside him, he still felt warm; he touched her on the head, briefly.

"My name is Thelma," the child said. "Did you forget your name?" She patted him. "If you forget your name, you can write it on your hand. Want me to show you how?" She patted him again.

"Won't it wash off?" he asked her. "If you write it on your hand, the first time you do anything or take a bath it'll wash off."

"Oh, I see." She nodded. "Well, you could write it on the wall, over your head. In your room where you sleep. Up high where it won't wash off. And then when you want to know your name better you can—"

"Thelma," he murmured.

"No, that's *my* name. You have to have a different name. And that's a girl's name."

"Let's see," he said, meditating.

"If I see you again I'll give you a name," Thelma said. "I'll make one up for you. 'Kay?"

"Don't you live here?" he said.

"Yes, but my mommy might leave. She's thinking about taking us, me and my brother, and leaving."

He nodded. Some of the warmth left him.

All of a sudden, for no reason he could see, the child ran off.

I should work out my own name, anyhow, he decided; it's my responsibility. He examined his hand and wondered why he was doing that; there was nothing to see. Bruce, he thought; that's my name. But there ought to be better names than that, he thought. The warmth that remained gradually departed, as had the child.

He felt alone and strange and lost again. And not very happy.

One day Mike Westaway managed to get sent out to pick up a load of semirotten produce donated by a local supermarket to New-Path. However, after making sure no staff member had tailed him, he made a phone call and then met Donna Hawthorne at a McDonald's fast-food stand.

They sat together outside, with Cokes and hamburgers between them on the wooden table.

"Have we really been able to duke him?" Donna asked.

"Yes," Westaway said. But he thought, The guy's so burned out. I wonder if it matters. I wonder if we accomplished anything. And yet it had to be like this.

"They're not paranoid about him."

"No," Mike Westaway said.

Donna said, "Are you personally convinced they're growing the stuff?"

"Not me. It's not what I believe. It's them." Those who pay us, he thought.

"What's the name mean?"

"*Mors ontologica*. Death of the spirit. The identity. The essential nature."

"Will he be able to act?"

Westaway watched the cars and people passing; he watched moodily as he fooled with his food.

"You really don't know."

"Never can know until it happens. A memory. A few charred brain cells flicker on. Like a reflex. React, not act. We can just hope. Remember what Paul says in the Bible: faith, hope, and giving away your money." He studied the pretty, dark-haired young girl across from him and could perceive, in her intelligent face, why Bob Arctor— No, he thought; I always have to think of him as Bruce. Otherwise I cop out to knowing too much: things I shouldn't, couldn't, know. Why Bruce thought so much of her. Thought when he was capable of thought.

"He was very well drilled," Donna said, in what seemed to him an extraordinarily forlorn voice. And at the same time an expression of sorrow crossed her face, straining and warping its lines. "Such a cost to pay," she said then, half to herself, and drank from her Coke.

He thought, But there is no other way. To get in there. *I* can't get in. That's established by now; think how long I've been trying. They'd only let a burned-out husk like Bruce in. Harmless. He would have to be . . . the way he is. Or they wouldn't take the risk. It's their policy.

"The government asks an awful lot," Donna said.

"Life asks an awful lot."

Raising her eyes, she confronted him, darkly angry. "In this case the federal government. Specifically. From you, me. From—" She broke off. "From what was my friend."

"He's still your friend."

Fiercely Donna said, "What's left of him."

What's left of him, Mike Westaway thought, is still searching for you. After its fashion. He too felt sad. But the day was nice, the people and cars cheered him, the air smelled good. And there was the prospect of success; that cheered him the most. They had come this far. They could go the rest of the way.

Donna said, "I think, really, there is nothing more terrible than the sacrifice of someone or something, a living thing, without its ever knowing. If it *knew*. If it understood and volunteered. But—" She gestured. "He doesn't know; he never did know. He didn't volunteer—"

"Sure he did. It was his job."

"He had no idea, and he hasn't any idea now, because now he hasn't any ideas. You know that as well as I do. And he will never again in his life, as long as he lives, have any ideas. Only reflexes. And this didn't happen accidentally; it was supposed to happen. So we have this . . . bad karma on us. I feel it on my back. Like a corpse. I'm carrying a corpse—Bob Arctor's corpse. Even while he's technically alive." Her voice had risen; Mike Westaway gestured, and, with visible effort, she calmed herself. People at other wooden tables, enjoying their burgers and shakes, had glanced inquiringly.

After a pause Westaway said, "Well, look at it this way. They can't interrogate something, someone, who doesn't have a mind."

"I've got to get back to work," Donna said. She examined her wristwatch. "I'll tell them everything seems okay, according to what you told me. In your opinion."

"Wait for winter," Westaway said.

"Winter?"

"It'll take until then. Never mind why, but that's how it is; it will work in winter or it won't work at all. We'll get it then or not at all." Directly at the solstice, he thought.

"An appropriate time. When everything's dead and under the snow."

He laughed. "In California?"

"The winter of the spirit. *Mors ontologica*. When the spirit is dead."

"Only asleep," Westaway said. He rose. "I have to split, too. I have to pick up a load of vegetables."

Donna gazed at him with sad, mute, afflicted dismay.

"For the kitchen," Westaway said gently. "Carrots and lettuce. That kind. Donated by McCoy's Market, for us poor at New-Path. I'm sorry I said that. It wasn't meant to be a joke. It wasn't meant to be anything." He patted her on the shoulder of her leather jacket. And as he did so it came to him that probably Bob Arctor, in better, happier days, had gotten this jacket for her as a gift.

"We have worked together on this a long time," Donna said in a moderate, steady voice. "I don't want to be on this much longer. I want it to end. Sometimes at night, when I can't sleep, I think, shit, we are colder than they are. The adversary."

"I don't see a cold person when I look at you," Westaway said. "Although I guess I really don't know you all that well. What I do see, and see clearly, is one of the warmest persons I ever knew."

"I am warm on the outside, what people see. Warm eyes, warm face, warm fucking fake smile, but inside I am cold all the time, and full of lies. I am not what I seem to be; I am awful." The girl's voice remained steady, and as she spoke she smiled. Her pupils were large and mellow and without guile. "But, then, there's no other way. Is there? I figured that out a long time ago and made myself like this. But it really isn't so bad. You get what you want this way. And everybody is this way to a degree. What I am that's actually so bad—I am a liar. I lied to my friend, I lied to Bob Arctor all the time. I even told him one time not to believe anything I said, and of course he just believed I was kidding; he didn't listen. But if I told him, then it's his responsibility not to listen, not to believe me any more, after I said that. I warned him. But he forgot as soon as I said it and went right on. Kept right on truckin'."

"You did what you had to. You did more than you had to."

The girl started away from the table. "Okay, then there really isn't anything for me to report, so far. Except your confidence. Just that he's duked in and they accept him. They didn't get anything out of him in those—" She shuddered. "Those gross games."

"Right."

"I'll see you later." She paused. "The federal people aren't going to want to wait until winter."

"But winter it is," Westaway said. "The winter solstice."

"The what?"

"Just wait," he said. "And pray."

"That's bullshit," Donna said. "Prayer, I mean. I prayed a long time ago, a lot, but not any more. We wouldn't have to do this, what we're doing, if prayer worked. It's another shuck."

"Most things are." He followed after the girl a few steps as she departed, drawn to her, liking her. "I don't feel you destroyed your friend. It seems to me you've been as much destroyed, as much the victim. Only on you it doesn't show. Anyhow, there was no choice."

"I'm going to hell," Donna said. She smiled suddenly, a broad, boyish grin. "My Catholic upbringing."

"In hell they sell you nickel bags and when you get home there's M-and-M's in them."

"M-and-M's made out of turkey turds," Donna said, and then all at once she was gone. Vanished away into the hither-and-thither-going people; he blinked. Is this how Bob Arctor felt? he asked himself. Must have. There she was, stable and as if forever; then—nothing. Vanished like fire or air, an element of the earth back into the earth. To mix with the everyone-else people that never cease to be. Poured out among them. The evaporated girl, he thought. Of transformation. That comes and goes as she will. And no one, nothing, can hold on to her.

I seek to net the wind, he thought. And so had Arctor. Vain, he thought, to try to place your hands firmly on one of the federal drug-abuse agents. They are furtive. Shadows which melt away when their job dictates. As if they were never really there in the first place. Arctor, he thought, was in love with a phantom of authority, a kind of hologram, through which a normal man could walk, and emerge on the far side, alone. Without ever having gotten a good grip on it—on the girl itself.

God's M.O., he reflected, is to transmute evil into good. If He is active here, He is doing that now, although our eyes can't perceive it; the process lies hidden beneath the surface of reality, and emerges only later. To, perhaps, our waiting heirs. Paltry people who will not know the dreadful war we've gone through, and the losses we took, unless in some footnote in a minor history book they catch a notion. Some brief mention. With no list of the fallen.

There should be a monument somewhere, he thought, listing those who died in this. And, worse, those who didn't die. Who had to live on, past death. Like Bob Arctor. The saddest of all.

I get the idea Donna is a mercenary, he thought. Not on salary. And they are the most wraithlike. They disappear forever. New names, new locations. You ask yourself, where is she now? And the answer is—

Nowhere. Because she was not there in the first place.

Reseating himself at the wooden table, Mike Westaway finished eating his burger and drinking his Coke. Since it was better than what they were served at New-Path. Even if the burger had been made from ground-up cows' anuses.

To call Donna back, to seek to find her or possess her . . . I seek what Bob Arctor sought, so maybe he is better off now, this way. The tragedy in his life already existed. To love an atmospheric spirit. That was the real sorrow. Hopelessness itself. Nowhere on the printed page, nowhere in the annals of man, would her name appear: no local habitation, no name. There are girls like that, he thought, and those you love the most, the ones where there is no hope because it has eluded you at the very moment you close your hands around it.

So maybe we saved him from something worse, Westaway concluded. And, while accomplishing that, put what remained of him to use. To good and valuable use.

If we turn out lucky.

"Do you know any stories?" Thelma asked one day.

"I know the story about the wolf," Bruce said.

"The wolf and the grandmother?"

"No," he said. "The black-and-white wolf. It was up in a tree, and again and again it dropped down on the farmer's animals. Finally one time the farmer got all his sons and all his sons' friends and they stood around waiting for the black-and-white wolf in the tree to drop down. At last the wolf dropped down on a mangy-looking brown animal, and there in his black-and-white coat he was shot by all of them."

"Oh," Thelma said. "That's too bad."

"But they saved the hide," he continued. "They skinned the great black-and-white wolf that dropped from the tree and preserved his beautiful hide, so that those to follow, those who came later on, could see what he had been like and could marvel at him, at his strength and size. And future generations talked about him and related many stories of his prowess and majesty, and wept for his passing."

"Why did they shoot him?"

"They had to," he said. "You must do that with wolves like that."

"Do you know any other stories? Better ones?"

"No," he said, "that's the only story I know." He sat remembering how the wolf had enjoyed his great springing ability, his leaping down again and again in his fine body, but now that body was gone, shot down. And for meager animals to be slaughtered and eaten anyhow. Animals with no strength that never sprang, that took no pride in their bodies. But anyhow, on the good side, those animals trudged on. And the black-and-white wolf had never complained; he had said nothing even when they shot him. His claws had still been deep in his prey. For nothing. Except that that was his fashion and he liked to do it. It was his only way. His only style by which to live. All he knew. And they got him.

"Here's the wolf!" Thelma exclaimed, leaping about clumsily. "Voob, voob!" She grabbed at things and missed, and he saw with dismay that something was wrong with her. He saw for the first time, distressed and wondering how it could happen, that she was impaired.

He said, "You are not the wolf."

But even so, as she groped and hobbled, she stumbled; even so, he realized, the impairment continued. He wondered how it could be that . . .

> *Ich unglücksel'ger Atlas! Eine Welt,*
> *Die ganze Welt der Schmerzen muss ich tragen,*

Ich trage Unerträgliches, und brechen
Will mir das Herz im Leibe.

. . . such sadness could exist. He walked away.

Behind him she still played. She tripped and fell. How must that feel? he wondered.

He roamed along the corridor, searching for the vacuum cleaner. They had informed him that he must carefully vacuum the big playroom where the children spent most of the day.

"Down the hall to the right." A person pointed. Earl.

"Thanks, Earl," he said.

When he arrived at a closed door he started to knock, and then instead he opened it.

Inside the room an old woman stood holding three rubber balls, which she juggled. She turned toward him, her gray stringy hair falling on her shoulders, grinning at him with virtually no teeth. She wore white bobby socks and tennis shoes. Sunken eyes, he saw; sunken eyes, grinning, empty mouth.

"Can you do this?" she wheezed, and threw all three balls up into the air. They fell back, hitting her, bouncing down to the floor. She stooped over, spitting and laughing.

"I can't do that," he said, standing there dismayed.

"I can." The thin old creature, her arms cracking as she moved, raised the balls, squinted, tried to get it right.

Another person appeared at the door beside Bruce and stood with him, also watching.

"How long has she been practicing?" Bruce said.

"Quite a while." The person called, "Try again. You're getting close!"

The old woman cackled as she bent to fumble to pick the balls up once again.

"One's over there," the person beside Bruce said. "Under your night table."

"Ohhhh!" she wheezed.

They watched the old woman try again and again, dropping the balls, picking them back up, aiming carefully, balancing herself, throwing them high into the air, and then hunching as they rained down on her, sometimes hitting her head.

The person beside Bruce sniffed and said, "Donna, you better go clean yourself. You're not clean."

Bruce, stricken, said, "That isn't Donna. Is that Donna?" He raised his head to peer at the old woman and he felt great terror; tears of a sort stood in the old woman's eyes as she gazed back at him, but she was laughing, laughing as she threw the three balls at him, hoping to hit him. He ducked.

"No, Donna, don't do that," the person beside Bruce said to her. "Don't hit people. Just keep trying to do what you saw on TV, you know, catch them again yourself and throw them right back up. But go clean yourself now; you stink."

"Okay," the old woman agreed, and hurried off, hunched and little. She left the three rubber balls still rolling on the floor.

The person beside Bruce shut the door, and they walked along the hall. "How long has Donna been here?" Bruce said.

"A long time. Since before I came, which was six months ago. She started trying to juggle about a week ago."

"Then it isn't Donna," he said. "If she's been here that long. Because I just got here a week ago." And, he thought, Donna drove me here in her MG. I remember that, because we had to stop while she got the radiator filled back up. And she looked fine then. Sad-eyed, dark, quiet and composed in her little leather jacket, her boots, with her purse that has the rabbit's foot dangling. Like she always is.

He continued on then, searching for the vacuum cleaner. He felt a great deal better. But he didn't understand why.

Chapter Fifteen

BRUCE said, "Could I work with animals?"

"No," Mike said, "I think I'm going to put you on one of our farms. I want to try you with plants for a while, a few months. Out in the open, where you can touch the ground. With all these rocket-ship space probes there's been too much trying to reach the sky. I want you to make the attempt to reach—"

"I want to be with something living."

Mike explained, "The ground is living. The Earth is still alive. You can get the most help there. Do you have any agricultural background? Seeds and cultivation and harvesting?"

"I worked in an office."

"You'll be outside from now on. If your mind comes back it'll have to come back naturally. You can't make yourself think again. You can only keep working, such as sowing crops or tilling on our vegetable plantations—as we call them—or killing insects. We do a lot of that, driving insects out of existence with the right kind of sprays. We're very careful, though, with sprays. They can do more harm than good. They can poison not only the crops and the ground but the person using them. Eat his head." He added, "Like yours has been eaten."

"Okay," Bruce said.

You have been sprayed, Mike thought as he glanced at the man, so that now you've become a bug. Spray a bug with a toxin and it dies; spray a man, spray his brain, and he becomes an insect that clacks and vibrates about in a closed circle forever. A reflex machine, like an ant. Repeating his last instruction.

Nothing new will ever enter his brain, Mike thought, because that brain is gone.

And with it, that person who once gazed out. That I never knew.

But maybe, if he is placed in the right spot, in the right stance, he can still see down, and see the ground. And recognize that it is there. And place something which is alive, something different from himself, in it. To grow.

1087

Since that is what he or it can't do any longer: this creature beside me has died, and so can never again grow. It can only decay gradually until what remains, too, is dead. And then we cart that off.

There is little future, Mike thought, for someone who is dead. There is, usually, only the past. And for Arctor-Fred-Bruce there is not even the past; there is only this.

Beside him, as he drove the staff car, the slumped figure jiggled. Animated by the car.

I wonder, he thought, if it was New-Path that did this to him. Sent a substance out to get him like this, to make him this way *so they would ultimately receive him back?*

To build, he thought, their civilization within the chaos. If "civilization" it really is.

He did not know. He had not been at New-Path long enough; their goals, the Executive Director had informed him once, would be revealed to him only after he had been a staff member another two years.

Those goals, the Executive Director had said, had nothing to do with drug rehabilitation.

No one but Donald, the Executive Director, knew where the funding for New-Path originated. Money was always there. Well, Mike thought, there is a lot of money in manufacturing Substance D. Out in various remote rural farms, in small shops, in several facilities labeled "schools." Money in manufacturing it, distributing it, and finally selling it. At least enough to keep New-Path solvent and growing—and more. Sufficient for a variety of ultimate goals.

Depending on what New-Path intended to do.

He knew something—U. S. Drug Restriction knew something—that most of the public, even the police, did not know.

Substance D, like heroin, was organic. Not the product of a lab.

So he meant quite a bit when he thought, as he frequently did, that all those profits could well keep New-Path solvent—*and growing.*

The living, he thought, should never be used to serve the purposes of the dead. But the dead—he glanced at Bruce, the empty shape beside him—should, if possible, serve the purposes of the living.

That, he reasoned, is the law of life.

And the dead, if they could feel, might feel better doing so.

The dead, Mike thought, who can still see, even if they can't understand: they are our camera.

Chapter Sixteen

U NDER the sink in the kitchen he found a small bone fragment, down with the boxes of soap and brushes and
buckets. It looked human, and he wondered if it was Jerry
Fabin.

This made him remember an event from a long way back in
his life. Once he had lived with two other guys and sometimes
they had kidded about owning a rat named Fred that lived
under their sink. And when they got really broke one time,
they told people, they had to eat poor old Fred.

Maybe this was one of his bone fragments, the rat who had
lived under their sink, who they had made up to keep them
company.

Hearing them talking in the lounge.

"This guy was more burned out than he showed. I felt so.
He drove up to Ventura one day, cruising all over to find an
old friend back inland toward Ojai. Recognized the house
on sight without the number, stopped, and asked the people if
he could see Leo. 'Leo died. Sorry you didn't know.' So this
guy said then, 'Okay, I'll come back again on Thursday.' And
he drove off, he drove back down the coast, and I guess he went
back up on Thursday again looking for Leo. How about that?"

He listened to their talk, drinking his coffee.

"—works out, the phone book has only one number in it;
you call that number for whoever you want. Listed on page
after page . . . I'm talking about a totally burned-out society.
And in your wallet you have that number, *the* number, scrib-
bled down on different slips and cards, for different people.
And if you forget the number, you couldn't call *anybody*."

"You could dial Information."

"It's the same number."

He still listened; it was interesting, this place they were de-
scribing. When you called it, the phone number was out of
order, or if it wasn't they said, "Sorry, you have the wrong
number." So you called it again, the same number, and got the
person you wanted.

When a person went to the doctor—there was only one, and he specialized in everything—there was only one medicine. After he had diagnosed you he prescribed the medicine. You took the slip to the pharmacy to have it filled, but the pharmacist never could read what the doctor had written, so he gave you the only pill he had, which was aspirin. And it cured whatever you had.

If you broke the law, there was only the one law, which everybody broke again and again. The cop laboriously wrote it all up, which law, which infraction each time, the same one. And there was always the same penalty for any breaking of the law, from jaywalking to treason: the penalty was the death penalty, and there was agitation to have the death penalty removed, but it could not be because then, for like jaywalking, there would be no penalty at all. So it stayed on the books and finally the community burned out entirely and died. No, not burned out—they had been that already. They faded out, one by one, as they broke the law, and sort of died.

He thought, I guess when people heard that the last one of them had died they said, I wonder what those people were like. Let's see—well, we'll come back on Thursday. Although he was not sure, he laughed, and when he said that aloud, so did everyone else in the lounge.

"Very good, Bruce," they said.

That got to be a sort of tag line then; when somebody there at Samarkand House didn't understand anything or couldn't find what he was sent to get, like a roll of toilet paper, they said, "Well, I guess I'll come back on Thursday." Generally, it was credited to him. His saying. Like with comics on TV who said the same tag-line thing again and again each week. It caught on at Samarkand House and meant something to them all.

Later, at the Game one night, when they gave credit in turn to each person for what he had brought to New-Path, such as Concepts, they credited him with bringing humor there. He had brought with him an ability to see things as funny no matter how bad he felt. Everybody in the circle clapped, and, glancing up, startled, he saw the ring of smiles, everybody's eyes warm with approval, and the noise of their applause remained with him for quite a period, inside his heart.

Chapter Seventeen

IN late August of that year, two months after he entered New-Path, he was transferred to a farm facility in the Napa Valley, which is located inland in Northern California. It is the wine country, where many fine California vineyards exist.

Donald Abrahams, the Executive Director of New-Path Foundation, signed the transfer order. On the suggestion of Michael Westaway, a member of his staff who had become especially interested in seeing what could be done with Bruce. Particularly since the Game had failed to help him. It had, in fact, made him more deteriorated.

"Your name is Bruce," the manager of the farm said, as Bruce stepped clumsily from the car, lugging his suitcase.

"My name is Bruce," he said.

"We're going to try you on farming for a period, Bruce."

"Okay."

"I think you'll like it better here, Bruce."

"I think I'll like it," he said. "Better here."

The farm manager scrutinized him. "They gave you a haircut recently."

"Yes, they gave me a haircut." Bruce reached up to touch his shaved head.

"What for?"

"They gave me a haircut because they found me in the women's quarters."

"That the first you've had?"

"That is the *second* one I've had." After a pause Bruce said, "One time I got violent." He stood, still holding the suitcase; the manager gestured for him to set it down on the ground. "I broke the violence rule."

"What'd you do?"

"I threw a pillow."

"Okay, Bruce," the manager said. "Come with me and I'll show you where you'll be sleeping. We don't have a central building residence here; each six persons have a little cabin. They sleep and fix their meals there and live there when they're not working. There's no Game sessions, here, just the work. No more Games for you, Bruce."

Bruce seemed pleased; a smile appeared on his face.

"You like mountains?" The farm manager indicated to their right. "Look up. Mountains. No snow, but mountains. Santa Rosa is to the left; they grow really great grapes on those mountain slopes. We don't grow any grapes. Various other farm products, but no grapes."

"I like mountains," Bruce said.

"Look at them." The manager again pointed. Bruce did not look. "We'll round up a hat for you," the manager said. "You can't work out in the fields with your head shaved without a hat. Don't go out to work until we get you a hat. Right?"

"I won't go to work until I have a hat," Bruce said.

"The air is good here," the manager said.

"I like air," Bruce said.

"Yeah," the manager said, indicating for Bruce to pick up his suitcase and follow him. He felt awkward, glancing at Bruce: he didn't know what to say. A common experience for him, when people like this arrived. "We all like air, Bruce. We really all do. We do have that in common." He thought, We do still have that.

"Will I be seeing my friends?" Bruce asked.

"You mean from back where you were? At the Santa Ana facility?"

"Mike and Laura and George and Eddie and Donna and—"

"People from the residence facilities don't come out to the farms," the manager explained. "These are closed operations. But you'll probably be going back once or twice a year. We have gatherings at Christmas and also at—"

Bruce had halted.

"The next one," the manager said, again motioning for him to continue walking, "is at Thanksgiving. We'll be sending workers back to their residences-of-origin for that, for two days. Then back here again until Christmas. So you'll see them again. If they haven't been transferred to other facilities. That's three months. But you're not supposed to make any one-to-one relationships here at New-Path—didn't they tell you that? You're supposed to relate only to the family as a whole."

"I understand that," Bruce said. "They had us memorize that as part of the New-Path Creed." He peered around and said, "Can I have a drink of water?"

"We'll show you the water source here. You've got one in your cabin, but there's a public one for the whole family here." He led Bruce toward one of the prefab cabins. "These farm facilities are closed, because we've got experimental and hybrid crops and we want to keep insect infestation out. People come in here, even staff, track in pests on their clothes, shoes, and hair." He selected a cabin at random. "Yours is 4-G," he decided. "Can you remember it?"

"They look alike," Bruce said.

"You can nail up some object by which to recognize it, this cabin. That you can easily remember. Something with color in it." He pushed open the cabin door; hot stinking air blew out at them. "I think we'll put you in with the artichokes first," he ruminated. "You'll have to wear gloves—they've got stickers."

"Artichokes," Bruce said.

"Hell, we've got mushrooms here too. Experimental mushroom farms, sealed in, of course—all domestic mushroom growers need to seal in their yield—to keep pathogenic spores from drifting in and contaminating the beds. Fungus spores, of course, are airborne. That's a hazard to all mushroom growers."

"Mushrooms," Bruce said, entering the dark, hot cabin. The manager watched him enter.

"Yes, Bruce," he said.

"Yes, Bruce," Bruce said.

"Bruce," the manager said. "Wake up."

He nodded, standing in the stale gloom of the cabin, still holding his suitcase. "Okay," he said.

They nod off as soon as it's dark, the manager said to himself. Like chickens.

A vegetable among vegetables, he thought. Fungus among fungus. Take your pick.

He yanked on the overhead electric light of the cabin, and then began to show Bruce how to operate it. Bruce did not appear to care; he had caught a glimpse of the mountains now, and stood gazing at them fixedly, aware of them for the first time.

"Mountains, Bruce, mountains," the manager said.

"Mountains, Bruce, mountains," Bruce said, and gazed.

"Echolalia, Bruce, echolalia," the manager said.

"Echolalia, Bruce—"

"Okay, Bruce," the manager said, and shut the cabin door behind him, thinking, I believe I'll put him among the carrots. Or beets. Something simple. Something that won't puzzle him.

And another vegetable in the other cot, there. To keep him company. They can nod their lives away together, in unison. Rows of them. Whole acres.

They faced him toward the field, and he saw the corn, like ragged projections. He thought, Garbage growing. They run a garbage farm.

He bent down and saw growing near the ground a small flower, blue. Many of them in short tinkly tinky stalks. Like stubble. Chaff.

A lot of them, he saw now that he could get his face close enough to make them out. Fiends, within the taller rows of corn. Here concealed within, as many farmers planted: one crop inside another, like concentric rings. As, he remembered, the farmers in Mexico plant their marijuana plantations: circled—ringed—by tall plants, so the *federales* won't spot them by jeep. But then they're spotted from the air.

And the *federales,* when they locate such a pot plantation down there—they machine-gun the farmer, his wife, their children, even the animals. And then drive off. And their copter search continues, backed by the jeeps.

Such lovely little blue flowers.

"You're seeing the flower of the future," Donald, the Executive Director of New-Path, said. "But not for you."

"Why not for me?" Bruce asked.

"You've had too much of a good thing already," the Executive Director said. He chuckled. "So get up and stop worshiping—this isn't your god any more, your idol, although it was once. A transcendent vision, is that what you see growing here? You look as if it is." He tapped Bruce firmly on the shoulder, and then, reaching down his hand, he cut the sight off from the frozen eyes.

"Gone," Bruce said. "Flowers of spring gone."

"No, you simply can't see them. That's a philosophical problem you wouldn't comprehend. Epistemology—the theory of knowledge."

Bruce saw only the flat of Donald's hand barring the light, and he stared at it a thousand years. It locked; it had locked; it will lock for him, lock forever for dead eyes outside time, eyes that could not look away and a hand that would not move away. Time ceased as the eyes gazed and the universe jelled along with him, at least for him, froze over with him and his understanding, as its inertness became complete. There was nothing he did not know; there was nothing left to happen.

"Back to work, Bruce," Donald, the Executive Director, said.

"I saw," Bruce said. He thought, I knew. That was it: I saw Substance D growing. I saw death rising from the earth, from the ground itself, in one blue field, in stubbled color.

The farm-facility manager and Donald Abrahams glanced at each other and then down at the kneeling figure, the kneeling man and the *Mors ontologica* planted everywhere, within the concealing corn.

"Back to work, Bruce," the kneeling man said then, and rose to his feet.

Donald and the farm-facility manager strolled off toward their parked Lincoln. Talking together; he watched—without turning, without being able to turn—them depart.

Stooping down, Bruce picked one of the stubbled blue plants, then placed it in his right shoe, slipping it down out of sight. A present for my friends, he thought, and looked forward inside his mind, where no one could see, to Thanksgiving.

Author's Note

This has been a novel about some people who were punished entirely too much for what they did. They wanted to have a good time, but they were like children playing in the street; they could see one after another of them being killed—run over, maimed, destroyed—but they continued to play anyhow. We really all were very happy for a while, sitting around not toiling but just bullshitting and playing, but it was for such a terribly brief time, and then the punishment was beyond belief: even when we could see it, we could not believe it. For example, while I was writing this I learned that the person on whom the character Jerry Fabin is based killed himself. My friend on whom I based the character Ernie Luckman died before I began the novel. For a while I myself was one of these children playing in the street; I was, like the rest of them, trying to play instead of being grown up, and I was punished. I am on the list below, which is a list of those to whom this novel is dedicated, and what became of each.

Drug misuse is not a disease, it is a decision, like the decision to step out in front of a moving car. You would call that not a disease but an error in judgment. When a bunch of people begin to do it, it is a social error, a life-style. In this particular life-style the motto is "Be happy now because tomorrow you are dying," but the dying begins almost at once, and the happiness is a memory. It is, then, only a speeding up, an intensifying, of the ordinary human existence. It is not different from your life-style, it is only faster. It all takes place in days or weeks or months instead of years. "Take the cash and let the credit go," as Villon said in 1460. But that is a mistake if the cash is a penny and the credit a whole lifetime.

There is no moral in this novel; it is not bourgeois; it does not say they were wrong to play when they should have toiled; it just tells what the consequences were. In Greek drama they were beginning, as a society, to discover science, which means causal law. Here in this novel there is Nemesis: not fate, because any one of us could have chosen to stop playing in the street, but, as I narrate from the deepest part of my life and heart, a dreadful Nemesis for those who kept on playing. I myself, I am not a character in this novel; I am the novel. So, though, was our entire nation at this time. This novel is about more people than I knew personally. Some we all read about in the newspapers. It was, this sitting around with our buddies and bullshitting while making tape recordings, the bad decision of the decade, the sixties, both in and out of the establishment. And nature cracked down on us. We were forced to stop by things dreadful.

If there was any "sin," it was that these people wanted to keep on having a good time forever, and were punished for that, but, as I say, I feel that, if so, the punishment was far too great, and I prefer to think of it only in a Greek or morally neutral way, as mere science, as deterministic impartial cause-and-effect. I loved them all. Here is the list, to whom I dedicate my love:

To Gaylene	deceased
To Ray	deceased
To Francy	permanent psychosis
To Kathy	permanent brain damage
To Jim	deceased
To Val	massive permanent brain damage
To Nancy	permanent psychosis
To Joanne	permanent brain damage
To Maren	deceased
To Nick	deceased
To Terry	deceased
To Dennis	deceased
To Phil	permanent pancreatic damage
To Sue	permanent vascular damage
To Jerri	permanent psychosis and vascular damage

. . . and so forth.

In Memoriam. These were comrades whom I had; there are no better. They remain in my mind, and the enemy will never be forgiven. The "enemy" was their mistake in playing. Let them all play again, in some other way, and let them be happy.

CHRONOLOGY

NOTE ON THE TEXTS

NOTES

Chronology

1928   Born Philip Kindred Dick on December 16 at home in
        Chicago, Illinois—six weeks premature, with twin sister
        Jane Charlotte Dick—to Dorothy Kindred Dick, an edi-
        torial secretary and Joseph Edgar Dick, a World War I
        veteran working at the Department of Agriculture.
        Mother, suffering from chronic kidney disease, finds
        nourishing twins difficult and receives poor support from
        doctor; neither child thrives.

1929   On January 26, both babies, severely dehydrated and
        undernourished, rushed to hospital; sister dies en route.
        Philip is nursed to health in incubator until reaching the
        weight of five pounds. (Haunted by his twin's death, later
        writes: "She fights for her life & I for hers, eternally. . . .
        My sister is *everything* to me. I am damned always to be
        separated from her/& with her, in an oscillation.") Father
        is granted a transfer from Department of Agriculture to
        posting in San Francisco. Family travels to Fort Morgan,
        Colorado, for vacation, and Dorothy and Philip remain,
        staying with relatives while awaiting father's transfer. Sis-
        ter is buried in Fort Morgan cemetery. Family moves to
        the Bay Area in California, first to Sausalito, then the
        peninsula, at last to Alameda.

1930   Father promoted to director, Western Division National
        Recovery Act posting in Reno, Nevada. Family settles in
        Berkeley; father commutes, remaining in Reno during
        work week.

1931   Attends the University of California Institute of Child
        Welfare experimental nursery school, where he tests high
        in memory, language, and manual coordination. Praised
        for his musical ability.

1933–34 Mother asks father for divorce and parents separate.
        Mother and son live with maternal grandparents and Aunt
        Marion. Dorothy begins to work full time, leaving Philip
        in the care of his warmly loving grandmother, "Meemaw."
        Attends kindergarten at Bruce Tatlock School, a pro-
        gressive nursery. Develops loving relationship with Aunt

Marion, despite her psychological difficulties including occasional institutionalization.

1935–37   After parents' divorce is final, mother moves with Philip to Washington, D.C. Father remarries. Begins to experience asthma and tachycardia. Doctor recommends Philip be sent away to boarding school. Attends Country Day School for children with behavior difficulties. There he first experiences fear of vomiting; cannot swallow and is unable to eat in public. Sent home after six months and sees first therapist. Attends Friends Quaker day school, then attends public school through second grade. Philip experiences isolation; struggles in school begin pattern of absenteeism. ("There then followed a long period in which I did nothing in particular except go to school— which I loathed—and fiddle with my stamp collection . . . plus other boyhood activities such as marbles, flipcards, bolo bats, and the new invented comic books. . . .") Experiences a spontaneous vision of peace and empathy he will later refer to in interviews as a childhood "Satori" experience. First attempts at writing encouraged by mother.

1938   With mother, returns to Berkeley. After three year separation, visits father. Introduces himself at new public school as "Jim Dick," but soon reverts to Phil. Creates a personal newspaper, "The Daily Dick," with local news items and comic strips.

1940–43   Discovers passion for classical music and opera, a lifelong pursuit. Reads *The Little Prince*, *The Hobbit*, *Winnie the Pooh*, and the *Oz* books. Discovers and begins avidly collecting science-fiction magazines (*Astounding, Amazing, Unknown*), which he begins to emulate by both drawing and writing. Teaches himself to type. Follows World War II through radio broadcasts, frequently discussing war progress with his friends. Begins second self-published newspaper, "The Truth," featuring a comic-strip hero "Future-Human": "Using his super-science for the welfare of humanity, he pits his strength against the underworld of the future." Completes first novel, *Return to Lilliput*, now lost. Regularly publishes stories and poems in the *Berkeley Gazette*. Attends Garfield Junior High public school and California Prep boarding school in Ojai. Continued difficulties overcoming emotional illnesses. Demonstrates intimate knowledge of psychiatry and psychiatric testing to classmates. (In 1974 he writes to his daughter Laura, "In a sense, the better you adapt to school the less your chances are of later adapting to the actual world. So I figure, the worse you adapt to school, the better you will be able to handle reality when you finally manage to get loose at last from school, if that ever happens. But I guess I have what in the military they call a 'poor attitude,' which means 'shape up or ship out.' I always elected to ship out.") Agoraphobia and panic attacks increase.

1944–47   Begins high school at Berkeley High. Studies German. Begins reading Jung. Bouts of dizziness leave him intermittently bedridden. Attends weekly psychotherapy at Langley Porter Clinic in San Francisco, where he is treated by a Jungian analyst, for whom he eventually develops a thoroughgoing intellectual contempt. Begins working as a sales clerk at University Radio, then later at Art Music, two music shops selling records, sheet music, and electronics, as well as offering repairs. Herb Hollis, the charismatic and demanding owner of the shops, becomes a mentor and father figure (and will become a model for many warmly tyrannical "boss" figures in his fiction). Dick's anxiety recedes while he is employed by Hollis, but so cripples him at school that he is forced to complete his senior year working at home with a tutor. The following autumn, leaves home and moves to a group apartment in a converted warehouse with writers and poets Robert Duncan, Jack Spicer, and Philip Lamantia, among others. The bohemian, writerly—and largely homosexual—contingent of roommates becomes another source of Dick's autodidactical intellectual growth. Briefly attends UC Berkeley, where he majors in philosophy; dislikes mandatory ROTC training, experiences further agoraphobic attacks, and by November withdraws permanently. Maintains later that he was expelled from university for refusing to re-assemble his rifle in ROTC.

1948–49   Knowing of Dick's lack of experience with women, the manager of Art Music arranges a sexual liaison with a young woman in the finished basement of the store. Meets and quickly marries Jeanette Marlin and moves into a Berkeley apartment, where they live in clumsy distress for six months, and divorce before the year's end. Reconnects with his father. Begins fragmentary novel *The Earthshaker* (lost).

1950   Marries second wife, Kleo Apostolides, in June. Buys a small house on Francisco Street in Berkeley. Sees father for last time. Enters the orbit of Anthony Boucher (Anthony White), an editor, reviewer, and writing teacher in the fields of crime and SF (science fiction). Under Boucher's influence begins to write a spate of SF stories. (Dick later recalled, "I discovered that a person could be not only mature, but matured and educated, and still enjoy SF.") Lives in a condition of extreme poverty (as later described in his 1980 introduction to *The Golden Man*: "The horse-meat they sell at Lucky Dog Pet Store is only for animal consumption. But Kleo and I are eating it ourselves. . . . It's called poverty . . .").

1951–52   Sells first story, "Roog," to *The Magazine of Fantasy and Science Fiction*. Loses job at Art Music over a breach of loyalty to Hollis. First published story, "Beyond Lies the Wub," appears in *Planet Stories*. Is represented by the Scott Meredith Literary Agency. Writes first realist novels *Voices From the Street* (published 2007) and *Mary and the Giant* (published 1987), but agency fails to sell them during his lifetime. (Later writes, "I made my first sale in November of 1951, and my first stories were published in 1952. At the time I graduated from high school I was writing regularly, one novel after another. None of which, of course, sold. I was living in Berkeley, and all the milieu-reinforcement there was for the literary stuff. I knew all kinds of people who were doing literary-type novels. And I knew some of the very fine avant-garde poets in the Bay area. They all encouraged me to write, but there was no encouragement to sell anything. But I wanted to sell, and I also wanted to do science fiction. My ultimate dream was to be able to do both literary stuff *and* science fiction.")

1953–54   Sells first SF novels *Solar Lottery* (published 1955), *The World Jones Made* (published 1956), and fantasy novel *The Cosmic Puppets* (published 1957), along with realist novel *Gather Yourselves Together* (published 1994). Briefly works for Tupper and Reed, another music store, where he again experiences panic attacks, agoraphobia, and claustrophobia. Begins taking amphetamines prescribed for phobias and depression. Writes many dozens of stories and places the majority of them, becoming one of the most prolific writers in science fiction (30 of his stories appear in pulp magazines in 1953 alone). Visited and gently interrogated by a pair of FBI investigators, inspiring the lifelong sense that he was under surveillance. Despite both ambivalence about assuming the identity of an SF writer and agoraphobic tendencies, visits an SF convention for the first time and meets A. E. Van Vogt, whose fiction is highly influential on Dick's early SF novels. With proceeds from sale of short stories and the help of his wife's salary from a variety of part-time jobs, pays off his mortgage and enjoys brief period of financial stability. Aunt Marion dies. Mother marries Marion's widower, Joe Hudner, and adopts eight-year-old twins.

1955   First published novel, *Solar Lottery*, is published in U.S. by Ace Books, as a paperback original. First published short-story collection, *A Handful of Darkness*, is brought out in England by Rich & Cowan. Dick writes novels *The Man Who Japed* (published 1956) and *Eye in the Sky* (published 1957).

1956–57   In renewed effort at literary respectability, writes realist novels *A Time for George Stavros* (lost), *Pilgrim on the Hill* (lost), *The Broken Bubble of Thisbe Holt* (published 1988), and *Puttering About in a Small Land* (published 1985). With Kleo, takes two road trips, touring the country as far east as Arkansas. *The Variable Man and Other Stories*, an expanded version of *A Handful of Darkness*, is published by Ace as a paperback original. Briefly breaks with Scott Meredith Agency, but returns.

1958   Dick applies his realist motifs to a science-fiction novel for the first time; the result, *Time Out of Joint*, is accepted for publication by Lippincott (1959). It is his first hardcover in the U.S., marketed not as SF but as a "Novel of Menace." Writes realist novels *In Milton Lumky Territory* (published 1985) and *Nicholas and the Higs* (lost). Learns that short story "Foster, You're Dead" has been published without permission in a magazine in USSR. Corresponds with Soviet scientist Alexander Topchiev on the subject of Einstein's theory of relativity, CIA reads this correspondence (as Dick learns after submitting a Freedom of Information Act request in 1970s). Moves with Kleo in September to Point Reyes Station, in Marin County. Meets Anne Rubenstein, a widow, in October, and begins a tumultuous romance. In December, asks Kleo for a divorce.

1959   Divorces Kleo, who leaves Point Reyes Station to return
            to Berkeley. Moves in with Anne and her three daughters
            (Hatte, Jayne, and Tandy), assuming the role of stepfather;
            they raise fowl and sheep, and live primarily on Anne's
            child-support settlement from her deceased husband's
            family in St. Louis. Begins to see Anne's psychiatrist, with
            whom he will consult intermittently until 1971. Marries
            Anne on April Fool's Day, in Ensenada, Mexico. Seeking
            income, reworks two earlier novellas into SF novels, each
            to be published in 1960 as half of an Ace "double": *Dr.
            Futurity* and *Vulcan's Hammer*. Writes realist novel *Con-
            fessions of a Crap Artist*, based largely on his fresh divorce
            from Kleo and romance with Anne, and which is nearly
            accepted for publication by both Knopf and Harcourt.
            On the strength of the near-miss, is offered advance from
            Harcourt for his next realist novel. Anne is pregnant. Con-
            tinues taking prescription amphetamine, Semoxydrine.

1960   First child, a daughter, Laura Archer Dick, is born on
            February 25. The Harcourt prospect goes unrealized, as
            the publisher during a merger fumbles two realist novels
            in turn when the editor goes on leave, *The Man Whose
            Teeth Were All Exactly Alike* and *Humpty Dumpty in Oak-
            land*, a rewrite of *A Time for George Stavros*. In autumn
            Anne becomes pregnant again. Fearing financial hardship
            she has an abortion, over Dick's initial objections.

1961   Works briefly in Anne's handcrafted jewelry business. Dis-
            covers the *I Ching*, the Chinese *Book of Changes*, the
            oracular advice of which he will consult for the next two
            decades. Retreats to what he calls "the hovel," a cabin he
            equips with his typewriter, stereo, and books. There be-
            gins writing *The Man in the High Castle*, plotted partly
            with the assistance of the *I Ching*.

1962   *The Man in the High Castle* is published by Putnam as a
            thriller, to positive reviews but few sales. Putnam sells the
            rights to the Science Fiction Book Club. Dick writes *We
            Can Build You*, which is serialized as "A. Lincoln, Simu-
            lacrum" in 1969–70 in *Amazing*, and *Martian Time-Slip*,
            which is serialized the following year in *Worlds of Tomor-
            row* as "All We Marsmen." (Dick later recalls: "With *High
            Castle* and *Martian Time-Slip*, I thought I had bridged
            the gap between the experimental mainstream novel and
            science fiction. Suddenly I'd found a way to do every-
            thing I wanted to do as a writer.")

1963   In July, Meredith Agency returns 10 or more manuscripts of the realist novels as unsaleable. Financially strapped, considers mortgaging Anne's house to finance a record store. In September, *The Man in the High Castle* wins the Hugo Award for best novel, SF's highest honor. Marriage degenerates; Dick claims to friends that his wife is trying to kill him. During a protracted marital fight, arranges to have Anne committed to Ross Psychiatric Hospital, where she consents to two weeks of observation at Langley Porter Clinic. In an attempt to save marriage they begin attending Episcopal church services, where Dick is baptized. Maren Hackett, a fan, arranges to meet Dick through a friend. She and her stepdaughters are Episcopalian. Fueled by amphetamines, writes *Dr. Bloodmoney, or How We Got Along After the Bomb*, *The Game-Players of Titan* (published by Ace that year), *The Simulacra*, *Now Wait for Last Year*, and begins *Clans of the Alphane Moon* and *The Crack in Space*. While walking to his writing shack, experiences devastating vision of a cruelly masked human face in the sky, which he will later incorporate into *The Three Stigmata of Palmer Eldritch*.

1964   Visits to Berkeley become frequent. Writes *The Three Stigmata of Palmer Eldritch*, which he delivers to his agent in March. On March 9, files for divorce, and briefly moves in with his mother. Enters the lively Bay Area SF social scene, spending time with writers Poul Anderson, Marion Zimmer Bradley, Ron Goulart, and Ray Nelson. Begins and abandons a sequel to *The Man in the High Castle*. Writes *The Crack in Space*, *The Zap Gun* (serialized that year as "Project Plowshare"), and *The Penultimate Truth* (published that year), and begins *The Unteleported Man*. Begins epistolary romance with Grania Davidson (later to publish fiction as Grania Davis), the separated wife of SF writer Avram Davidson. In July, Dick flips his car, resulting in serious injuries. Suffers major depression and loss of writing impetus. Attends the 1964 World Science Fiction convention, held in Oakland, which is marked by a proliferation of drug use. Friends Jack and Margo Newkom move into the Oakland house. In December, begins courting the 21-year-old Nancy Hackett, stepdaughter of Maren Hackett: "I want you to move in here for my sake, because otherwise I will go clean out of my balmy wits, take more and more pills . . . and do no real writing. . . . I need you as a sort of incentive and muse."

1965   In March, Hackett moves in. Domesticity, agoraphobia, and writing resume. Dick takes LSD twice, leading to uncomfortable visions. ("I perceived Him as a pulsing, furious, throbbing mass of vengeance-seeking authority, demanding an audit [like a sort of metaphysical IRS agent].") In "Drugs, Hallucinations, and the Quest for Reality," essay for fanzine *Lighthouse*, writes: "One doesn't have to depend on hallucinations. One can unhinge oneself by many other roads." Completes *The Unteleported Man*. Gains rewarding friendship with James Pike, the Episcopal bishop of California, who had taken Maren Hackett, Nancy's stepmother, as his secret lover while she was employed as his secretary. In conversation with Pike becomes increasingly involved in theological speculation and research into the early origins of Christianity. Moves with Nancy to San Rafael. Works on *The Ganymede Takeover* with Ray Nelson. Writes *Counter-Clock World*.

1966   Completes *The Ganymede Takeover*, and writes *Do Androids Dream of Electric Sheep?*, *Ubik*, and *The Glimmung of Plowman's Planet*, a children's story (published in 1988 in the United Kingdom as *Nick and the Glimmung*). In July, marries Nancy. Despite skepticism, participates with Bishop Pike, Maren Hackett, and Nancy in a séance conducted by a medium, with the intention of making contact with Pike's son Jim, who had committed suicide. *Now Wait for Last Year*, *The Unteleported Man*, and *The Crack in Space* published.

1967   Second daughter, Isolde (Isa) Freya Dick, born March 15. Writes treatment for television show *The Invaders*, which goes unsold. *Counter-Clock World*, *The Zap Gun*, and *The Ganymede Takeover* published as paperback originals. In June, Maren Hackett commits suicide. IRS demands payment of overdue back taxes, penalty and interest, devastating already fragile household finances. Short story "Faith of Our Fathers" is published in Harlan Ellison's *Dangerous Visions* anthology; Dick falsely leads Ellison to believe and claim in his introduction that the story was written under the influence of LSD.

1968   Signs "Writers and Editors War Tax Protest" petition published in February issue of *Ramparts* magazine, aggravating his conflict with the IRS. With Nancy, attends the 1968 SF Baycon, a science-fiction convention known anecdotally as "Drug Con." Meets Roger Zelazny, with whom he will begin collaborative novel *Deus Irae*. *Do Androids Dream of Electric Sheep?* published as hardcover original. Sells first film option, for *Androids*. Writes *Galactic Pot-Healer* and *A Maze of Death*. Anthony Boucher, Dick's longtime mentor, dies. Writes unpublished biographical statement: ". . . Married, has two daughters and young, pretty, nervous wife . . . Spends most of his time listening to first Scarlatti and then the Jefferson Airplane, then 'Gotterdammerung,' in an attempt to fit them all together. Has many phobias . . . Owes creditors a fortune, which he does not have. Warning: don't lend him any money. In addition he will steal your pills."

1969   Writes *Our Friends from Frolix 8*. The paperback original *Galactic Pot-Healer* and hardcover *Ubik* are published. Receives phone call from Timothy Leary who is attending John Lennon and Yoko Ono's "bed-in" in a Montreal hotel. Leary puts Lennon and Ono on phone; they discuss their admiration for his novel *The Three Stigmata of Palmer Eldritch* and their desire to adapt it to film. Visited by journalist Paul Williams. Marriage increasingly strained by escalating prescription drug use, particularly Ritalin. Hospitalized in an emergency intervention for pancreatitis and near-kidney failure, the result of compulsive amphetamine abuse. In September, Bishop Pike dies in the Judean desert, searching for proof of the historical Jesus.

1970   Begins *Flow My Tears, the Policeman Said*, and, contrary to his usual method, rewrites it several times between March and August. Nancy's brother, Michael Hackett, in the midst of a divorce, moves in. Dick takes mescaline and experiences a vision of radiant love, which he incorporates into *Flow My Tears*. Applies for food stamps in July. *The Preserving Machine*, a story collection, is published. *Our Friends from Frolix 8* is published as a paperback original and *A Maze of Death* in hardcover. In September, Nancy leaves with Isa, beginning a period for Dick of communal living characterized by extensive drug use (adding illegal street drugs to the mix), late-night amphetamine-fueled conversation, paranoia, and bohemian squalor. Dick does little writing, working intermittently on *Flow My Tears, the Policeman Said*. In October Tom

Schmidt moves in. (In a November letter, Dick writes: "We all take speed and we are all going to die, but we will have a few more years . . . and while we live we will live it as we are: stupid, blind, loving, talking, being together, kidding, propping one another up.")

1971   Places unfinished manuscript of *Flow My Tears, the Policeman Said* into the care of his attorney for protection from the chaos of his home life. Mike Hackett leaves house as a stream of young hippies, bikers, and addicts pass through. In May, Dick is committed by a friend to the psychiatric ward of Stanford University Hospital. In August, he is admitted to both Marin General Psychiatric Hospital and Ross Psychiatric Clinic. Asserts belief that he is probably under surveillance by the FBI or CIA. Purchases gun. In November, the house is violently broken into, leaving file cabinets apparently blown up, windows and doors smashed, and personal and financial papers stolen. (Theories as to responsibility for the break-in preoccupy Dick for years to come; suspects include government agents, religious fanatics, Black Panthers, himself.) Dick abandons the house.

1972   Visits Vancouver, Canada, SF Con in February, as guest of honor. Delivers well-received convention speech ("The Android and the Human"), and declares intention to remain in Canada. Rapidly becomes disenchanted with Vancouver and seeks another destination; writes to Ursula K. Le Guin in Portland, asking for permission to visit, and to Cal State Fullerton professor Willis McNelly, asking if Fullerton would be a good place to relocate. (Letter-writing increases dramatically at this point and continues until his death. In addition to Le Guin, he regularly corresponds with other writers including James Tiptree, Stanislaw Lem, John Brunner, Norman Spinrad, Thomas Disch, Bryan Aldiss, Robert Silverberg, Theodore Sturgeon, and Philip José Farmer.) In March, makes his first suicide attempt. Enters X-Kalay rehabilitation center, a facility primarily for heroin addicts, where he participates in confrontational group therapy. Ends decades-long abuse of prescription amphetamines. Professor McNelly and his students write to invite him to Orange County. Dick settles in Fullerton, living with a series of roommates, and surrounds himself with young friends, including aspiring writer Tim Powers. McNelly arranges paid guest lecturer position and houses bulk of Dick's papers at the California State University at Fullerton's library. Assembles personal letters and dream notes, creating *The Dark-Haired Girl* (expanded and published 1988). Assists in the selection of stories for collection *The Best of Philip K. Dick*, published that year. In July, meets 18-year-old Leslie (Tessa) Busby, and they soon move in together. In September, Dick attends Los Angeles SF Worldcon. In October, travels with Tessa to Marin County to finalize divorce from Nancy Hackett, who is awarded full custody of Isa. Corresponds with Stanislaw Lem, who arranges for Polish translation of *Ubik*. Completes work on *Flow My Tears, the Policeman Said*, and writes "A Little Something for Us Tempunauts."

1973   Resumes full-time writing. From February to April, writes *A Scanner Darkly*. Is interviewed by BBC and French documentarians. In April, marries Tessa. Son Christopher Kenneth Dick born on July 25. Visited by Jean-Pierre Gorin, then a doctoral student, who tells Dick commentators on French television have proposed him for Nobel Prize. Is interviewed by the London *Daily Telegraph*. Money and health worries continue. United Artists reacquires film option on *Do Androids Dream of Electric Sheep?*

1974   *Flow My Tears, the Policeman Said*, published in hardcover in February, is his best-received novel since *The Man in the High Castle*, gaining nominations for the Hugo and Nebula awards, and winning, in 1975, the John W. Campbell Memorial Award. Dick dreads upcoming April tax period, fearing retribution for signing the *Ramparts* petition. In February, after oral surgery for an impacted wisdom tooth, during which he is given sodium pentothal, experiences the first of a sequence of overwhelming visions that will last through and intensify during March, then taper intermittently throughout the year. Interpretation of these revelations, which are variously ascribed to benign and malign influences both religious and political (including but not limited to God, Gnostic Christians, the Roman Empire, Bishop Pike, and the KGB), will preoccupy Dick for much of his remaining life. "It hasn't spoken a word to me since I wrote *The Divine Invasion*. The voice is identified as Ruah, which is the Old Testament word for the Spirit of God. It speaks in a feminine voice and tends to express statements regarding the messianic expectation. It guided me for a while. It has spoken to me sporadically since I was in high school. I expect that if a crisis arises it will say something again. . . ." He begins writing speculative commentary on what he comes to call "2-3-74"; these writings are eventually assembled into a disordered manuscript of approximately 8,000 mostly handwritten pages, and which Dick will call the *Exegesis* (excerpts from which are published posthumously, though the whole remains unpublished and largely unread). Fires and within the week rehires the Meredith Agency after they agree to move contract for *Flow My Tears, the Policeman Said* from Doubleday to DAW. Is hospitalized for five days for extremely high blood pressure and possibly a minor stroke. Dick is visited again by French film director Jean-Pierre Gorin, who negotiates an out-of-pocket film option for *Ubik*, with Dick to write the screenplay. Writes *Ubik* screenplay in one month (never produced, but published in 1985). Is visited by two different screenwriters who have worked on adapting *Do Androids Dream of Electric Sheep?* (filmed as *Blade Runner*). Is interviewed by Paul Williams for *Rolling Stone*, a conversation dominated by a recounting and analysis of the 1971 break-in.

1975   Injures shoulder, and following surgery, dictates notes on novel-in-progress *Valisystem A* (the material eventually to bifurcate into *Radio Free Albemuth*, published posthumously, and *Valis*, published in 1981) into a portable tape recorder but resumes typing within two weeks. *The New Yorker* publishes a two-part interview in successive issues in January and February in the "Talk of the Town" section, calling Dick "our favorite science fiction writer." Last flares of visionary experience occur in January and February. Works nightly on the *Exegesis*, fueled by readings on Gnosticism, Zoroastrianism, and Buddhism. *Confessions of a Crap Artist* published, the only one of the early realist novels to be published during his lifetime. Receives visit from cartoonist Art Spiegelman. Dick becomes increasingly enamored of an earlier friend and a trainee for Episcopal priesthood, Doris Sauter. In May, Sauter is diagnosed with cancer. Has a falling-out with Harlan Ellison. *Deus Irae* is completed, with collaborator Roger Zelazny. Dick earns somewhat better income for the year, largely due to foreign royalties. During a brief flush period, thanks to the release of foreign royalties, purchases a used sports car and an *Encyclopedia Britannica*, but within months is reduced to borrowing funds from idol and mentor Robert Heinlein. Finishes revisions on *A Scanner Darkly*. In November, *Rolling Stone* magazine publishes Paul Williams's long profile, billing Dick as "The Most Brilliant SF Mind on Any Planet."

1976   Dick asks Doris Sauter to marry him; she refuses, not wanting to interfere with his family. In February, Christopher is hospitalized for hernia. Later that month Dick and Tessa separate. Within hours Dick attempts suicide by simultaneous multiple methods. He is hospitalized at Orange County Medical Center, where he is soon transferred to the psychiatric ward, and stays for 14 days, under observation. Afterward, Tessa briefly returns, but Dick ends the relationship and moves in with Sauter, in a Santa Ana apartment where he will live for the remainder of his life. (The relationship remains platonic.) In May, Bantam acquires three novels for reprint—*Palmer Eldritch*, *Ubik*, and *A Maze of Death*—and offers an advance for the 2-3-74–based novel-in-progress, still called *Valisystem A*. In September Sauter decides to move into the apartment next door. Depressed again and fearful of suicidal impulses, Dick checks into the mental ward of St. Joseph's Hospital in October. Near the year's end, editor at Bantam requests minor revisions to *Valisystem A*, which triggers a re-drafting of the book so different that it becomes another novel, *Valis*. (*Valisystem A*, in the form submitted in 1976, will be published in 1985 as *Radio Free Albemuth*.) *Deus Irae* is published.

1977   Dick adjusts to living alone for the first time. Tessa and Christopher become regular visitors. In February, divorce from Tessa becomes final. *A Scanner Darkly* is published. Friendship with Tim Powers is at its height, and evenings with Powers, K. W. Jeter, and James Blaylock, all destined for SF writing careers, become a regular occasion. Powers and Jeter, with whom he recounts and debates the 2-3-74 visions, will become models for characters in the still-gestating, highly autobiographical *Valis* manuscript. Novels *Ubik*, *The Three Stigmata of Palmer Eldritch,* and *A Maze of Death* republished by Bantam, with blurb from *Rolling Stone* article and endorsements from contemporaries acknowledging Dick as a major American writer. In

April, meets Joan Simpson, a 32-year-old social worker. After three weeks together in Orange County, Dick follows Simpson to Sonoma, where he spends part of the summer. Dick is plagued by bouts of fierce depression. Travels to France for the Metz Festival, where he is guest of honor. The overseas travel represents a personal triumph over phobia. His speech, "If You Find This World Bad, You Should See Some of the Others," is received with bewilderment due to heavy religious content and difficulties with simultaneous translation. On return, suffers a split with Simpson over his unwillingness to permanently relocate to Northern California. Continues to work on *Exegesis*. Short story "We Can Remember It For You Wholesale" optioned for film adaptation (later released as *Total Recall*).

1978   With new version of *Valis* overdue at Bantam, continues work on *Exegesis* instead. Mother dies in August. Is thrilled when daughters Laura and Isa finally meet. In September, struggling to find appropriate fictional form for 2-3-74 experiences, writes in *Exegesis*: "My books (& stories) are intellectual (conceptual) mazes. & I am in an intellectual maze in trying to figure out our situation . . . because the *situation* is a maze, leading back to itself. . . ." New Meredith Agency contact Russell Galen provides encouragement by aggressively marketing titles for reprint, and by proposing a book of nonfiction, a suggestion that at last triggers an effective approach to the *Valis* material. Writes *Valis* in two weeks in November, dedicating the book to Galen.

1979   Daughters Laura and Isa each visit several times. *A Scanner Darkly* wins the Grand Prix du Festival at Metz, France. Works with tremendous devotion on the *Exegesis*, which he remarks may be his most significant work. Russell Galen places new short stories in high-paying markets: *Playboy* and *Omni*. Dick and Galen finally meet in person when he visits Orange County, but Galen finds the resultant all-night talk marathon exhausting. When his building is converted to condominiums, Dick purchases his apartment. Doris Sauter, unable to afford purchasing her own, is forced to move. The separation causes great distress. Fictionalizes his attachment to Sauter in the short story "Chains of Air, Webs of Aether." Short story "Second Variety" optioned (premieres in 1995 as *Screamers*).

1980   Incorporating "Chains of Air, Webs of Aether," completes *The Divine Invasion*, conceived as a sequel to *Valis*, by late March. Continues efforts on *Exegesis*, but does little other writing for remainder of year. Outlines several novels that remain unwritten. Increasingly anxious about the cessation of visionary inspiration, experiences flash of revelation in late November, from which he infers that he should stop working on the *Exegesis*. After writing a five-page concluding parable, on December 2 types the words "End" and creates a title page (*THE DIALECTIC: God against Satan, & God's Final Victory foretold & shown/ Philip K. Dick/AN EXEGESIS/Apologia Pro Mia Vita*). Ten days later, resumes compulsive writing of *Exegesis*.

1981   In February, *Valis* is published. Falls out painfully from friendship with Ursula K. Le Guin but quickly reconciles. Concerned by loss of energy, takes up dieting and quickly loses weight. Director Ridley Scott begins work on *Blade Runner*, a film adaptation of *Do Androids Dream of Electric Sheep?*, written by Hampton Fancher and David Peoples. Dick's reaction to the production is alternately jubilant and disdainful. The film's financiers seek a novelization of the screenplay, but Russell Galen insists that *Androids* should be released in conjunction with the film instead (*Androids* is reissued under the film's title in 1982). Accepts offer from Simon & Schuster editor David Hartwell for a realist novel and an SF novel. In April and May writes *The Transmigration of Timothy Archer*, a fictionalization of the events surrounding Bishop James Pike's death, and the first non-SF work he has written since the final rejection of his realist novels by the Meredith Agency in 1963. Dick tells Galen, in a June letter, that exclusion from non-genre publication "has been the tragedy—and a very long-term tragedy—of my creative life." Two months later, contemplating *The Owl in Daylight*, his proposed next SF novel, writes: "Yes, I think I will continue to write SF novels. It's in my blood. . . ." Finds himself depleted and unable to begin writing. On September 17, receives a nighttime vision of a savior named "Tagore," who he is convinced is alive and living in Ceylon, and from whom he begins to feel he is receiving instruction. Drawn by the possibility of family life, considers remarriage with Tessa. In November is invited to Hollywood to a screening of a reel of special effects from the early cut of *Blade Runner*. Invited to return to Metz Festival, he begins to make plans to travel. Begins series of interviews with Gregg Rickman; invites Rickman to be his official biographer. Writes two (wholly different) outline proposals for "Owl in Daylight."

1982   In January, becomes enthusiastic about the prophecies of a British mystic, Benjamin Creme, who predicts the coming of a future Buddha called Maitreya. Continues interviews with Rickman, to whom Dick confesses uncertainty and weariness with spiritual matters. In what was likely his final interview, Dick is interviewed by Doris Sauter's friend Gwen Lee for a college paper. He reveals details about "Owl in Daylight," which he does not live to write. On February 18, Dick suffers a stroke alone in his apartment, where he is found unconscious by neighbors. In hospital recovers consciousness but not speech, and remains paralyzed on left side. Dies in hospital of further strokes and heart failure on March 2. Buried in a twin grave beside sister Jane in Fort Morgan, Colorado. *The Transmigration of Timothy Archer* is published after his death. Dedicated to Dick's memory, the film *Blade Runner* premieres in May. Philip K. Dick Award, awarded annually for distinguished science fiction published in paperback original form in the United States, is established.

Note on the Texts

This volume contains five novels by Philip K. Dick: *Martian Time-Slip* (1963); *Dr. Bloodmoney* (1965); *Now Wait for Last Year* (1966); *Flow My Tears, the Policeman Said* (1974); and *A Scanner Darkly* (1977).

Using the working title "Goodmember Arnie Kott of Mars," Dick wrote *Martian Time-Slip* in 1962. In shortened form, it was serialized the following year as "All We Marsmen" in *Worlds of Tomorrow* magazine. After being rejected by Ace Books, it was accepted by Ballantine, which published *Martian Time-Slip* as a paperback original in 1964. This volume prints the text of the 1964 Ballantine Books edition.

Dick once remarked that an early version of *Dr. Bloodmoney, or How We Got Along After the Bomb* was an unspecified "long ago straight novel"; Paul Williams, author of *Only Apparently Real: The World of Philip K. Dick* (1986), speculates that this precursor work of fiction might be the unfinished novel *The Earthshaker* (1948–50), and Dick's biographer Lawrence Sutin writes that it could also be the lost *Pilgrim on the Hill*, which Dick worked on in the mid-1950s. *Dr. Bloodmoney* was written in 1963 and published by Ace Books in 1965. Dick suggested the titles *In Earth's Diurnal Course* and *A Terran Odyssey*, but Ace editor Donald Wollheim, making an obvious reference to Stanley Kubrick's recent film *Dr. Strangelove or: How I Learned to Stop Worrying and Love the Bomb* (1964), proposed the final title. The text in the present volume is taken from the 1965 Ace Books paperback edition of *Dr. Bloodmoney*.

Like *Dr. Bloodmoney* and several other novels, Dick wrote *Now Wait for Last Year* in 1963. It was revised in or around 1965 and published by Doubleday in hardcover in 1966; the 1966 Doubleday edition contains the text printed here.

The genesis of *Flow My Tears, the Policeman Said* lies in a May 1970 mescaline trip (probably his only experience with the drug), in which Dick, as he described the experience in a letter four months later, was "overwhelmed by terribly powerful feelings—emotions, I guess. I felt an overpowering love for other people, and this is what I put into the novel: it studies different kinds of love which I had never known of. I am saying, 'In answer to the question, "What is real?" the answer is: this kind of overpowering love.'" He wrote most of the novel quickly—at one point completing 140 pages in 48 hours —but could not quite finish it; setting it aside in August 1970, he did not begin work on it again until 1972. This volume prints the text of the first edition of *Flow My Tears, the Policeman Said*, published in hardcover by Doubleday in 1974.

Dick began writing *A Scanner Darkly* early in 1973 and finished a draft in April of that year; two years later, with input from editor Judy-Lynn Del Rey ("she went over that novel page by page and showed me how to create a character," Dick later recalled), he made extensive revisions to the novel, which was published in hardcover by Doubleday in 1977. The text printed in this volume is taken from the 1977 Doubleday edition of *A Scanner Darkly*.

This volume presents the texts of the original printings chosen for inclusion here, but it does not attempt to reproduce nontextual features of their typographic design. The texts are presented without change, except for the correction of typographical errors. Spelling, punctuation, and capitalization are not altered, even when inconsistent or irregular. The following is a list of typographical errors corrected, cited by page and line number: 3.16, nodded turned; 8.35, bactria; 12.10, praire-like; 32.4, physical; 34.34, authristic; 35.34, Oh, she; 36.37, Ann; 50.28, right, Silvia; 53.37, opeartors; 56.3, settlers,; 58.39, Merely; 65.34, natural,; 65.35, horrible,; 67.5, said.; 71.27, that that; 73.16, Dad, he; 74.29, opague; 75.29, you're; 83.8, Stenier; 94.23, mater; 98.9, it's; 99.7, said; 101.11, gone. Including; 107.23, I; 108.6, interesting David; 108.37, Below,; 111.2, you; 113.18, miligram; 120.5, had; 120.11, weekened; 120.27, It'll; 122.9, if; 122.12, hunderd; 124.38, form; 126.29, Bubbish; 127.21, be; 132.7, bleared; 133.14, did; 133.20, said; 133.20, kids's; 135.9, gubble.; 135.13, more."; 136.2, we're; 137.15, you; 137.34, repeat:,; 140.11, It's; 140.20, day; 143.27, there's; 144.2, anixiety; 144.14, your; 144.25, it; 148.13, beyone; 149.1, imbided; 149.38, exeperience; 151.31, busines; 154.6, She; 156.31, bacame; 160.38, belive; 163.6, á; 165.23, "what?"; 165.24, meant..; 167.10, doorchimes; 167.18, he; 172.26, retarded,; 172.29, pill; 172.32, ago,; 179.28, approched; 185.3–4, an an; 190.38, you.; 194.8, decide; 200.18, emereged; 201.24, I'll; 202.8, me? he; 204.33, more.; 211.36, realized,; 211.37, it's; 215.1, Arnie; 215.9, Mountain; 215.13, Year; 215.19, belive; 216.6, appear,; 218.16–17, real-/alized; 226.22, is wasn't; 230.6, said.; 230.19, coveerd; 237.10, see; 238.29, There're; 238.29, Thery're; 240.20, realize; 242.28, Fergessson; 243.1, Ater; 249.36, "Well; 252.6, like; 252.14, Forces'; 253.7, laughted; 262.32, clowly; 263.9, ¶ "It's; 264.28, him; 269.10, Orio; 270.16, it it; 282.28, above."; 287.5, them"; 294.37, 38, momento; 298.31, hands.; 300.1, Where; 301.17, it against it against; 303.26, littler; 304.23, symbold; 315.17, ¶ "In; 316.25, 30, 33, Walzing; 316.33, branch; 316.33, Sctoch; 320.29, Happy; 325.14, who it; 326.29, swapped; 331.31, words; 334.25, told hold; 336.19, if; 336.23, be; 337.27, nodding; 338.12, terrific.; 345.27, thought; 347.21, cassal; 348.11, a entire; 352.35, of; 360.21, Blane; 362.25, Rab; 364.2, sure,";

367.29, though; 370.33, chance,"; 371.32, if; 375.1, here won't; 376.29, What; 382.16, with; 382.32, Labe; 391.28, dow.; 392.24, Bill he; 400.39, pretened; 403.10, of Hoppy's; 404.3, he been; 406.26, new; 410.17, by tree; 411.4, Negro."; 411.25, truthgully; 412.32, out; 413.3, "I; 414.14, to; 417.24, right Paul; 418.25, attmtion; 418.28, poeple; 419.4, Board,; 422.1, enought; 433.15, from from; 433.38, it? Edie; 435.19, them; 440.34, him"; 442.23, hair hair; 448.19, careful"; 448.34, the who; 452.37, she on; 456.1, to afraid; 473.14, loggy; 526.14, nape; 534.30, through; 540.25, cutical; 665.1, miniscule; 671.19, show; 751.24, bathroon; 776.38, hin; 777.35, confirmation; 779.3, though; 830.37, singer,; 856.1, become; 873.12, its; 898.8, Prefera-/ably; 944.22, casette; 945.33, price."; 948.34, to—"; 954.2, the . . . ; 970.16, Fabian's; 988.21, cassett-tape; 1006.16, EE-trophic; 1022.9, and; 1026.34, over.; 1029.32, Finish; 1030.7, we; 1033.18, titantic; 1042.27, lefthand; 1049.7, Od; 1049.7, *auszer*; 1080.5, him Mike.

Notes

In the notes below, the reference numbers denote page and line of this volume (the line count includes chapter headings). No note is made for material included in the eleventh edition of *Merriam-Webster's Collegiate Dictionary*. Biblical quotations are keyed to the King James Version. Quotations from Shakespeare are keyed to *The Riverside Shakespeare*, ed. G. Blakemore Evans (Boston: Houghton Mifflin, 1974). For further background, see: Lawrence Sutin, *Divine Invasions: A Life of Philip K. Dick* (New York: Harmony Books, 1989); *The Shifting Realities of Philip K. Dick: Selected Literary and Philosophical Writings*, edited by Lawrence Sutin (New York: Pantheon Books, 1995); Gregg Rickman, *To the High Castle, Philip K. Dick: A Life, 1928–1982* (Long Beach, CA: Fragments West/The Valentine Press, 1989).

The editor of the present volume wishes to thank Laura Leslie and Isa Hackett for their assistance in researching the Chronology.

MARTIAN TIME-SLIP

1.1   MARTIAN TIME-SLIP] In the second printing, October 1976, Dick added a dedication: "To Mark and Jodie."

4.20   "Bitte, mein herr,"] Please, sir.

6.8   Bunchewood] Named for Ralph Bunche (1904–1971), American diplomat who held several high-ranking posts at the United Nations from 1947 until 1971. He was the first African-American to be awarded the Nobel Peace Prize, which he received in 1950 for his role in mediating the cease-fire agreements that ended the 1948–49 Arab-Israeli war.

11.13   Alger Hiss] Alger Hiss (1904–1996) held several positions in the administration of Franklin D. Roosevelt and began working for the State Department in 1936. In 1945 Hiss served as secretary general of the San Francisco Conference that founded the United Nations. He was accused in 1948 by Whittaker Chambers, a former Communist, of having been a Communist spy. Hiss sued Chambers for slander, and in grand jury testimony denied Chambers' charges that he had transmitted secret documents to the Soviet Union; he was then indicted and convicted of perjury, serving 44 months of a five-year sentence.

19.10   Samuel Gompers] American union leader (1850–1924), founder of the American Federation of Labor (AFL).

19.39   Bernard Baruch] American financier and philanthropist (1870–1965), adviser to several presidents including Franklin D. Roosevelt.

32.20   Weizmann] Chaim Weizmann (1874–1952), first president (1949–52) of Israel.

36.27   Ben-Gurion] David Ben-Gurion (1886–1973), Zionist leader and Israeli statesman, prime minister of Israel, 1948–53 and 1955–63.

41.14–15   babies with seal flippers . . . German drug] Thalidomide, a drug developed by the West German pharmaceutical company Chemie Grünewald, was widely prescribed as a sedative and anti-emetic in the late 1950s and early 1960s, particularly to pregnant women. It caused thousands of children to be born with deformities, most prominently phocomelia, in which the limbs are abnormally short and resemble amphibian flippers.

77.23   Heliogabalus] The Bleekman's name is that of the third-century Roman emperor Varius Avitus Bassianus, who assumed the name of the Syrian sun god.

123.2   Henry Wallace] American politician (1888–1965), vice-president (1941–45) in the Roosevelt administration. He was the Progressive candidate for president in 1948.

130.10   G mol.] G-minor.

DR. BLOODMONEY

235.10–11   running over . . . Bible] Cf. Psalm 23:5: "Thou preparest a table before me in the presence of mine enemies: thou anointest my head with oil; my cup runneth over."

235.11–12   Buddy Greco] Singer (b. 1926) who was a vocalist with Benny Goodman in the late 1940s and whose later hits included "I Ran All the Way Home" (1951) and "The Lady Is a Tramp" (1960).

237.18–19   Iris Tree, Max Beerbohm] The actress Iris Tree (1897–1968) and the writer Max Beerbohm (1872–1956) were the daughter and the half-brother of the actor and theatrical manager Sir Herbert Beerbohm Tree.

239.19   Gestalt] German: shape, configuration. The term was popularized in the early 20th century by theorists of "Gestalt psychology" such as Max Wertheimer and Wolfgang Köhler.

241.13   Livermore] Lawrence Livermore National Laboratory, research institute run by the U.S. Department of Energy; established in 1952, it was active in developing the American nuclear arsenal.

250.8   *The Decline of the West*] *Der Untergang des Abendlandes* (1918–22), historical study by Oswald Spengler.

252.38   Herb Caen's] Newspaper columnist (1916–1997), chiefly for the *San Francisco Chronicle*.

254.2   Will Rogers]   Humorist, vaudeville performer, and screen actor (1879–1935) known for folksy, gently satirical humor; his films included *David Harum* (1934) and *Steamboat 'Round the Bend* (1935).

254.37   John L. Lewis]   Labor organizer (1880–1969), long-time president of the United Mine Workers of America and a founder of the Congress of Industrial Organizations.

272.4–5   *Of Human Bondage*]   Novel (1915) by W. Somerset Maugham.

274.40   Mildred]   Café waitress in *Of Human Bondage*, with whom the protagonist Philip Carey falls in love and who exercises a destructive influence on his life.

286.26   conalrad]   Emergency broadcasting system, established during the Truman administration and designed to warn of nuclear attack.

311.31   Pascal's *Provincial Letters*]   Series of 18 polemical letters (1656–57) by Blaise Pascal (1623–1662) in defense of Jansenist conceptions of divine grace and sharply critical of Jesuit ethics.

316.25–26   'Waltzing . . . Song.']   "Waltzing Matilda" (1895), Australian song with lyrics by the poet Banjo Peterson; "The Woodpecker Song" (1940), a hit for Glenn Miller, based on the Italian song "Reginella Campagnola."

316.32   baritone Peter Dawson]   Popular Australian concert singer (1882–1961).

320.1–2   'Thy Tiny Hand is Frozen' from *La Boheme*]   "Che gelida mannina," tenor aria from Act I of Puccini's 1896 opera.

324.29   Carl Jung's *Psychological Types*]   Study published in 1921, known for its distinction between extroverted and introverted personalities.

343.6   "Good Rockin' Tonight,"]   Blues song recorded by Roy Brown (1947) and Wynonie Harris (1948), and subsequently revived on Sun Records by Elvis Presley (1954).

343.22–26   the tune . . . voice]   "Mack the Knife," an American version of the "Moritat" from Kurt Weill and Bertolt Brecht's *The Threepenny Opera*, was a hit for Louis Armstrong.

349.22   Luther Burbank]   American horticulturist (1849–1926), known for developing improved varieties of many plants and foodstuffs.

355.40   The grasshopper who fiddled]   In Aesop's fable, the grasshopper who fiddles and is left starving when winter comes is contrasted with the ant who has stockpiled food during the summer months.

402.19–21   'Bei Mir . . . Sisters]   "You Are Beautiful to Me": Yiddish song written by Jacob Jacobs (1890–1977) and Sholem Secunda (1894–1974) for the 1932 musical *If I Could I Would*. An English adaptation by Sammy

Cahn and Saul Chaplin was recorded by the Andrews Sisters in 1937 and was their first hit.

438.15   'Out on Penny's Farm,' . . . Seeger]   The song, originally sung by the Bently Boys in 1929, is a protest against the exploitation of sharecroppers: "It's hard times in the country / Out on Penny's farm." Pete Seeger recorded it in 1950 as "Down on Penny's Farm."

450.30   Norma Shearer]   Movie actress (1900–1983), known for roles in such M-G-M productions as *The Barretts of Wimpole Street* (1934), *Romeo and Juliet* (1936), and *Marie Antoinette* (1938).

450.34   Betty Grable]   Movie actress (1916–1973) known for roles in 20th Century–Fox musicals such as *Moon Over Miami* (1941), *Pin-Up Girl* (1944), and *My Blue Heaven* (1950).

NOW WAIT FOR LAST YEAR

461.29   'Lucky Strike . . . war,']   The American Tobacco Company's ubiquitous advertising slogan, introduced in 1942, was based on the claim that the war effort required copper, which had been used in its phased-out green packages of Lucky Strike cigarettes. In fact, the green dye was chromium-based; the company had been looking for an excuse to change the package because their research suggested that women didn't like the design.

474.3–4   "'*Mille* . . . libretto]   *Mille tre*, Italian for "one thousand three." In Mozart's *Don Giovanni* (1787), with libretto by Lorenzo da Ponte (1749–1838), Don Giovanni boasts that he seduced 1,003 women in Spain.

475.16   Sinking of the Panay]   The American naval gunboat *Panay* was sunk in the Yangtze River near Nanking by Japanese aircraft on December 12, 1937. The Japanese government accepted responsibility for the attack, which killed three men, and paid an indemnity in 1938. Dick's fictional "Horrors of War" trading cards were first presented in *The Man In the High Castle*.

477.22   phycomycetous]   Fungal.

478.7–9   Tom Mix . . . tops]   Tom Mix (1880–1940), a movie actor in westerns (mostly from the silent era), endorsed Ralston, a hot cereal product, in 1933. On his popular radio show, listeners were encouraged to save Ralston box-tops to exchange for secret decoder rings, invisible-ink pens, and other toys. His sidekick on the show, played by Percy Hemus, was called the "Old Wrangler."

478.10–13   Orphan Annie . . . decode]   "Little Orphan Annie," a radio serial based on Harold Gray's comic strip, ran from 1930 to 1942. The show gave out prizes in exchange for seals found under the lids of cans of Ovaltine, which sponsored the program. A decoder pin, which could decipher secret messages broadcast at the end of each show, was a popular prize.

480.34   Pablo Casals]   Spanish cellist and composer (1876–1973).

481.12–13   paraphrasing T. S. Eliot]   The paraphrase is not of an Eliot quotation but of "a salesman is an it that stinks," the opening of an E. E. Cummings' poem published in *1x1* (1944).

482.22   big-little book]   Popular in the 1930s and early 1940s, Big Little Books were thick, compact children's books in which a page with a captioned illustration was paired with an opposing page of text. The books featured adventure tales and stories with popular characters drawn from children's novels, radio shows, and comic strips such as Dick Tracy and Little Orphan Annie.

483.17   "Betty and Bob,"]   An early radio soap opera, *Betty and Bob* ran from 1932 to 1940.

486.27   "*Salve, amicus,*"]   Latin: hello, friend.

487.35–36   *Critique* . . . prose]   The prose style of Kant's *Critique of Pure Reason* (1781) is notoriously difficult to understand.

493.30–32   will we . . . translated.'"]   See Shakespeare, *A Midsummer Night's Dream*, III.i.118–19: "Bless thee, Bottom, bless thee! Thou art translated." The line is indeed spoken by Peter Quince.

504.11   Jack Paar show—]   Television and variety show hosted by Jack Paar (1918–2004), renamed *The Tonight Show* when Paar was replaced by Johnny Carson in 1962.

518.6   Hepplewhite]   Eighteenth-century English furniture maker George Hepplewhite.

524.5   "Bei . . . Schön,"]   See note 402.19–21.

527.30–31   Alexander Woollcott . . . Crier.']   Alexander Woollcott (1887–1943), critic and member of the Algonquin Round Table of wits. His radio program *The Town Crier* ran on CBS from 1933 to 1938.

555.33–34   'Mary Marlin . . . Debussy]   A popular radio soap opera that ran from 1934 to 1945; its theme song was Debussy's "Claire de Lune."

561.16–17   pyknic body-type]   Classification of a short, thick body type coined by the German psychiatrist Ernst Kretschmer (1888–1964) in his now-discredited study of criminality and body types, *Körperbau und Charakter* (*Physique and Character*, 1921).

591.25–26   the doctors' plot . . . by Stalin]   On January 13, 1953, an article in the Communist party newspaper *Pravda* accused nine leading Soviet physicians, six of them Jewish, of conspiring with Anglo-American intelligence services and with an "international bourgeois Jewish-Zionist organization" to murder Soviet leaders by medical mistreatment. The doctors had been arrested in late 1952 and were beaten on Stalin's orders to extract their confessions. Stalin died on March 5, 1953, and on April 4 *Pravda* announced that the accused doctors had been exonerated.

599.34–35   "Life . . . quoting]   Cf. *Leviathan* (1651) by Thomas Hobbes (1588–1679): "the life of man, solitary, poor, nasty, brutish, and short."

603.9   Russians get rid of Beria?]   Lavrenti Beria (1899–1953) was the head of Soviet state security, 1938–46 and March–June 1953, deputy prime minister of the Soviet Union, 1941–53, and a full member of the Communist party Politburo, 1946–53. As the result of a power struggle following Stalin's death, Beria was arrested in the Kremlin during a meeting of the party leadership on June 26, 1953, and shot on December 23, 1953, following a secret trial. Although he was unarmed at the time of his arrest, rumors circulated in the western press that Beria had been carrying a pistol and that he had been immediately executed.

657.16   Edmund G. Brown]   American politician (1905–1996), governor of California from 1959 to 1967.

FLOW MY TEARS, THE POLICEMAN SAID

671.2–5   *Flow my tears . . . forlorn.*]   First stanza of "Lacrime" ("Tears"), one of John Dowland's madrigals included in his *Second Book of Songs or Ayres* (1600).

687.4–5   bird . . . sing?]   Cf. Henry Vaughan, "They Are All Gone into the World of Light" (1655), stanza 5: "He that hath found some fledged bird's nest may know, / At first sight, if the bird be flown; / But what fair well or grove he sings in now, / That is to him unknown."

704.7   lapsus linguae]   Latin: a slip of the tongue.

736.2–5   *Down, vain lights . . . disclose.*]   The second stanza of Dowland's madrigal (see note 671.2–5).

736.19   *Elegy*]   "Elegy Written In a Country Church-Yard" (1750), by English poet Thomas Gray (1716–1771).

756.9–10   like Byron . . . Greece]   Byron traveled to Greece to fight alongside the Greeks in their struggle for independence from the Ottoman Empire; he died of a fever while there.

772.33–38   "The drinkers . . . Sixty-nine.]   Cf. Psalm 69: "They that sit in the gate speak against me; and I was the song of the drunkards."

797.9   *Weird Tales*]   An American pulp magazine featuring tales of horror and fantasy, first published in 1923 and lasting, in its first incarnation, until 1954.

803.2–5   *Never . . . deprived.*]   The third stanza of Dowland's madrigal (see note 671.2–5).

810.15–16   Buffy St. Marie]   Buffy Sainte-Marie (b. 1941) Canadian-born Cree Indian singer and composer.

855.2–5   *Hark! . . . despite*] The fifth and final stanza of Dowland's madrigal (see note 671.2–5). Dick's epigraphs omit only the fourth stanza: "From the highest spire of contentment / My fortune is thrown; / And fear and grief and pain for my deserts /Are my hopes, since hope is gone."

A SCANNER DARKLY

877.9   Rosicrucians] A secretive organization dedicated to alchemy, mysticism, and occult reputed to have been founded in Germany in the 15th century.

884.27–28   the fairy tale "How the Sea Became Salt."] A folktale told in the Icelandic *Prose Edda* by 13th-century poet Snorri Sturlson. A mill with two magical millstones could grind anything its miller asked. King Frode ordered two strong maidservants, Fenja and Menja, to use the millstones to grind him gold, peace, and happiness, but "he gave them no longer time to rest or sleep than while the cuckoo was silent or while they sang a song." They ground instead an army to attack Frode, who was slain when the sea-king Mysing joined the assault. He took the mill with him on a ship and demanded that Fenja and Menja grind salt. The ship then sank, and a maelstrom was formed in the sea. The *Prose Edda*'s account of the tale ends: "Thus the sea became salt."

889.3–4   Konrad Lorenz] Austrian zoologist (1903–1989) who wrote about the behavior of wolves in books such as *King Solomon's Ring* (1949), *Man Meets Dog* (1949), and *On Aggression* (1963).

910.34–37   sing about the men of Harlech . . . Yorkists in 1468—] The popular war song "March of the Men of Harlech" celebrates Welsh military glory; Harlech Castle was the site of a long siege during the Wars of the Roses, in which Yorkists laid siege to the fortress for several years before its defenders capitulated because of starvation.

912.17   tach] Tachometer.

938.12–13   the Yippies of the sixties] Members of the Youth International Party (YIP), a group of activist provocateurs, led by Abbie Hoffman and Jerry Rubin, who staged disruptive anti-establishment stunts.

938.30–39   her "pistol-packin'" husband . . . proud poetry about that] John Peurifoy (1907–1955) was American ambassador to Guatemala during the CIA-backed overthrow of the leftist government of Jacobo Arenz in 1953. Two year later, he died in a car accident while serving as ambassador to Thailand. Peurifoy's wife had written a poem celebrating Arenz's downfall, quoted in *Time* in 1954: "Sing a song of quetzals, pockets full of peace! / The junta's in the palace, they've taken out a lease. / The Commies are in hiding, just across the street; / To the embassy of Mexico they beat a quick retreat. / And pistol-packing Peurifoy looks mighty optimistic / For the land of Guatemala is no longer Communistic."

941.11   My Lai]   Central Vietnamese village in which American soldiers massacred between 200 and 500 unarmed civilians in March 1968.

969.25   Teilhard de Chardin]   French Jesuit theologian Pierre Teilhard de Chardin (1881–1955), author of *The Divine Milieu* and *The Phenomenon of Man*, published posthumously in 1957 and 1959, respectively.

971.35   died . . . Croce]   Thirty-year-old singer-songwriter Jim Croce died in a plane crash in 1973.

980.34   *Siegfried*]   Wagner's 1876 opera, part of the *Ring* cycle.

989.34   TA therapy]   Transactional analysis, a form of psychotherapy developed by Canadian psychiatrist Eric Berne (1910–1970), author of the best-selling book *Games People Play* (1964).

1004.19–20   direct quote . . . funky ultimatum]   "Turn on, tune in, drop out."

1004.21   Birchers]   Members of the John Birch Society, an extreme right-wing political organization founded in Indiana in 1958 by candy manufacturer Robert Welch (1899–1985) and named after John Birch (1918–1945), an American intelligence officer killed by the Chinese Communists at the end of World War II.

1004.22   Minutemen]   Paramilitary right-wing movement, led by Robert DePugh, that was organized into small armed cells in preparation to fight what they regarded as an imminent Communist takeover of the United States.

1006.29–30   forty-nine-year-old district attorney]   Most likely Robert L. Meyer, who was forced to resign his post as U.S. Attorney in Los Angeles on January 1, 1972, because of disputes with his superiors about civil-rights and police-misconduct cases. Less than a year later, the 49-year-old Meyer died of a heart attack while driving.

1011.16–19   *Ihr Instrumente . . . Riegel.*]   From Goethe's *Faust*, Part I: "You instruments, I know you are mocking me / With cog and crank and cylinder. / I stood at the door, you were to be the key; / A key with intricate wards—but the bolt declines to stir." (This quotation and those cited below from *Faust* are from Louis MacNiece's translation.)

1014.4–7   *Was grinsest . . . geirret.*]   Lines from Goethe's *Faust*, Part I, just preceding those quoted at 1011.16–19: "Why do you grin at me, you hollow skull? / To point out that your brain was once, like mine, confused / And looked for the easy day but in the difficult dusk, / Lusting for truth was led astray and abused?"

1016.23–25   *Dem Wurme . . . begräbt.*]   From *Faust*, Part I: "I am like the worm that burrows through the dust / Which, as it keeps itself alive in the dust, / Is annulled and buried by some casual heel." These lines are translated slightly differently at 1031.28–30.

1018.1–6   *Zwei Seelen . . . Ahnen*]   From *Faust*, Part I: "Two souls, alas, cohabit in my breast, / A contract one of them desires to sever. / The one like a rough lover clings / To the world with the tentacles of its senses; / The other lifts itself to Elysian Fields / Out of the mist on powerful wings."

1018.35 SMILE! . . . CAMERA!] The catchphrase used on the popular television program *Candid Camera* when an unsuspecting person was told that he or she had been filmed by a hidden camera.

1020.9–15 *Weh! . . . hohe.*] From *Faust*, Part I: "Oh! Am I still stuck in this jail? / This God-damned dreary hole in the wall / Where even the lovely light of heaven / Breaks wanly though the painted panes! / Cooped up among these heaps of books / Gnawed by worms, coated with dust, / Round which to the top [of the Gothic vault / A smoke-stained paper forms a crust.]"

1031.28–30 I resemble . . . crushes it.] Translation of lines from Goethe's *Faust* that were quoted in German at 1016.23–25.

1035.5 transactional analysis] See note 989.34.

1042.35 And St. Paul meant, by a mirror] See 1 Corinthians 13:12: "For now we see through a glass, darkly."

1044.16–30 "Then shall . . . eye!] See 1 Corinthians 15:51–54: "Behold, I shew you a mystery. We shall not all sleep, but we shall all be changed, in a moment, in the twinkling of an eye, at the last trump: for the trumpet shall sound, and the dead shall be raised incorruptible, and we shall be changed. For this corruptible must put on incorruption, and this mortal *must* put on immortality. So when this corruptible shall have put on incorruption, and this mortal shall have put on immortality, then shall be brought to pass the saying that is written, Death is swallowed up in victory."

1045.14–15 *Wie . . . tief.*] "How cold it is in this underground vault! That is only natural, it's so deep." From Beethoven's opera Fidelio (1814), Act 2.

1048.37–39 a song . . . *stellet,"*] From *Fidelio*, Act 2, as are the lines at 1049.6–7.

1064.34–35 Carole King . . . toads] See the title song of King's *Tapestry* (1971): "He sat down on a river rock / And turned into a toad. / It seemed that he had fallen / Into someone's wicked spell, / And I wept to see him suffer, / Though I didn't know him well."

1084.37–1085.2 *Ich . . . Leibe.*] "Unhappy Atlas that I am! a world, / The entire world of sorrows I must bear. / I bear the unbearable, and / In my body, my heart wants to break." From poem 24 of the sequence "The Homecoming" (1823–24) by Heinrich Heine. It was set to music by Franz Schubert in his *Schwanengesang.*

1097.28–29 "Take . . . Villon] The line is not from French poet François Villon but from *The Rubáiyát of Omar Khayyám*, in English poet Edward FitzGerald's adaptation.

THE LIBRARY OF AMERICA SERIES

The Library of America fosters appreciation and pride in America's literary heritage by publishing, and keeping permanently in print, authoritative editions of America's best and most significant writing. An independent nonprofit organization, it was founded in 1979 with seed money from the National Endowment for the Humanities and the Ford Foundation.

This book is set in 10 point Linotron Galliard,
a face designed for photocomposition by Matthew Carter
and based on the sixteenth-century face Granjon. The paper
is acid-free lightweight opaque and meets the requirements
for permanence of the American National Standards Institute.
The binding material is Brillianta, a woven rayon cloth made
by Van Heek-Scholco Textielfabrieken, Holland. Compo-
sition by Dedicated Business Services. Printing by
Malloy Incorporated. Binding by Dekker Book-
binding. Designed by Bruce Campbell.

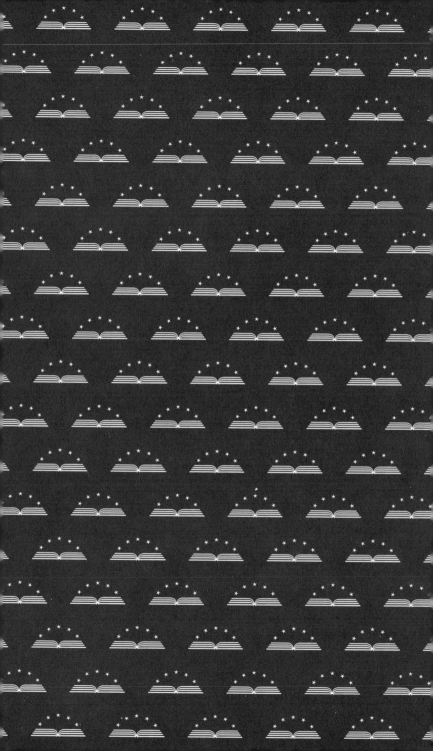